LEON URIS

LEON URIS

EXODUS

MILA 18

QB VII

Octopus/Heinemann

Exodus was first published in the United States by Doubleday & Company, Inc in 1958;
in Great Britain by Alan Wingate in 1959
Mila 18 was first published in the United States by Doubleday & Company, Inc in 1961
in Great Britain by William Heinemann Limited in 1961
QB VII was first published in the United States by Doubleday & Company, Inc in 197
in Great Britain by William Kimber & Co. Ltd in 1971

This edition first published in the United States of America by arrangement with
Doubleday & Company, Inc in 1981 jointly by

William Heinemann Inc

and

Octopus Books Inc
747 Third Avenue
New York, NY 10017

ISBN 0 905712 62 5

Printed in the United States of America
by R. R. Donnelley and Sons Company

CONTENTS

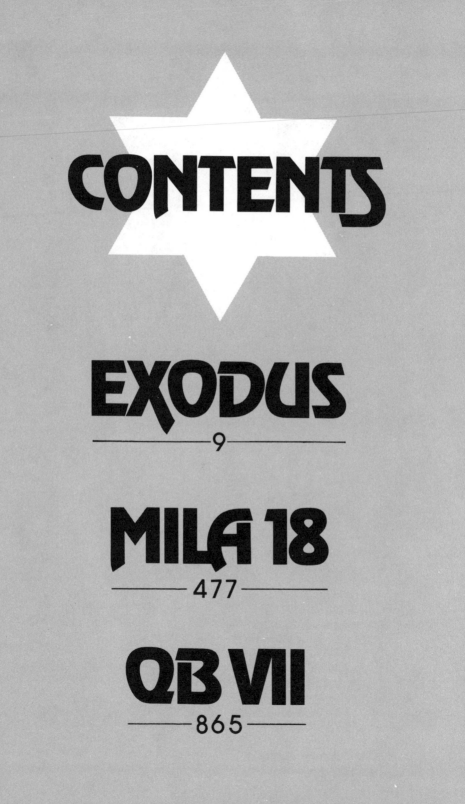

EXODUS

Exodus

This book is dedicated to my daughter,
KAREN
and my sons
MARK and MICHAEL
– and their mother

Most of the events in *Exodus* are a matter of history and public record. Many of the scenes were created around historical incidents for the purpose of fiction.

There may be persons alive who took part in events similar to those described in this book. It is possible, therefore, that some of them may be mistaken for characters in this book.

Let me emphasize that all characters in *Exodus* are the complete creation of the author, and entirely fictional.

The exceptions, of course, are those public figures mentioned by name, such as Churchill, Truman, Pearson, and the rest who were related to this particular period.

A NOTE OF THANKS

The space covered in my gathering of material for *Exodus* was nearly fifty thousand miles. The yards of recording tape used, the number of interviews, the tons of research books, and the number of film exposures and vanished greenbacks make equally impressive figures.

During the course of two years, tens of dozens of people gave me their time, energy, and confidence. I was twice blessed every foot of the way with uncommon co-operation and faith.

It is unfortunate, but the sheer weight of numbers precludes my thanking everyone here. Such listing would fill a volume in itself.

I would be less than grateful if I did not acknowledge the efforts of those two men who were truly instrumental in making *Exodus* a reality.

I hope I am not setting a dangerous precedent by publicly thanking my agent. *Exodus* evolved out of a conversation at lunch and became a tangible project because of the dogged persistence of Malcolm Stuart. He refused to give up the idea despite a dozen setbacks.

I most humbly thank Ilan Hartuv of Jerusalem. He made my arrangements, and traveled with me over every foot of Israel by train, plane, Vauxhall, and Austin, jeep and by foot. At times it was a pretty rough go. Mainly, I thank Ilan for sharing with me his vast knowledge of the subject.

BOOK ONE

Beyond Jordan

Until the Lord have given rest unto your brethren, as well as unto you, and until they also possess the land which the Lord your God hath given them beyond Jordan: and then shall ye return every man unto his possession, which I have given you.

THE WORD OF GOD AS GIVEN TO
MOSES IN DEUTERONOMY

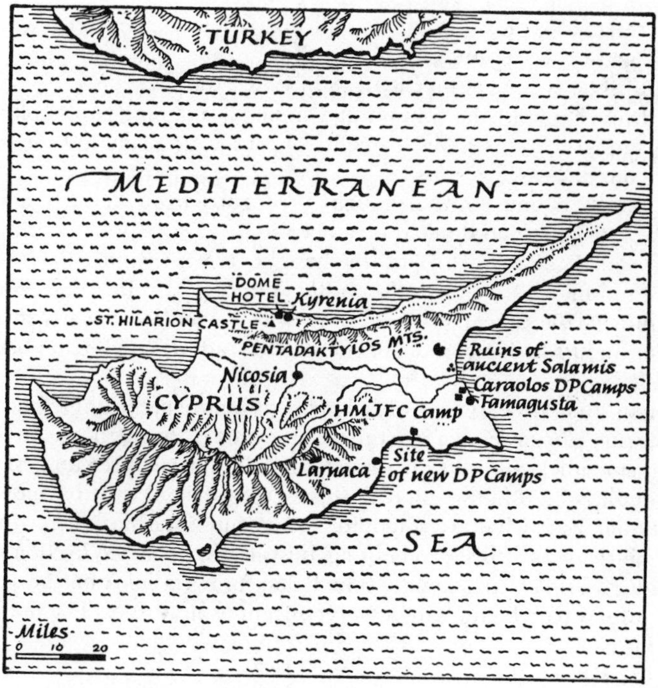

Chapter One

NOVEMBER 1946

WELCOME TO CYPRUS

WILLIAM SHAKESPEARE

The airplane plip-plopped down the runway to a halt before the big sign: WELCOME TO CYPRUS. Mark Parker looked out of the window and in the distance he could see the jagged wonder of the Peak of Five Fingers of the northern coastal range. In an hour or so he would be driving through the pass to Kyrenia. He stepped into the aisle, straightened out his necktie, rolled down his sleeves, and slipped into his jacket. 'Welcome to Cyprus, welcome to Cyprus ...' It ran through his head. It was from *Othello*, he thought, but the full quotation slipped his mind.

'Anything to declare?' the customs inspector said.

'Two pounds of uncut heroin and a manual of pornographic art,' Mark answered, looking about for Kitty.

All Americans are comedians, the inspector thought, as he passed Parker through. A government tourist hostess approached him. 'Are you Mr Mark Parker?'

'Guilty.'

'Mrs Kitty Fremont phoned to say she is unable to meet you at the airport and for you to come straight to Kyrenia to the Dome Hotel. She has a room there for you.'

'Thanks, angel. Where can I get a taxi to Kyrenia?'

'I'll arrange a car for you, sir. It will take a few moments.'

'Can I get a transfusion around here?'

'Yes, sir. The coffee counter is straight down the hall.'

Mark leaned against the counter and sipped a steaming cup of black coffee ... 'Welcome to Cyprus ... welcome to Cyprus' ... he couldn't for the life of him remember.

'Say!' a voice boomed out. 'I thought I recognized you on the plane. You're Mark Parker! I bet you don't remember me.'

Fill in one of the following, Mark thought. It was: Rome, Paris, London, Madrid (and match carefully); Jose's Bar, James's Pub, Jacques's Hideaway, Joe's Joint. At the time I was covering: war, revolution, insurrection. That particular night I had a: blonde, brunette, redhead (or maybe that broad with two heads).

The man stood nose to nose with Mark, gushing on all eight cylinders now. 'I was the guy who ordered a martini and they didn't have orange bitters. Now do you remember me?' Mark sighed, sipped some coffee, and braced for another onslaught. 'I know you hear this all the time but I really enjoy reading your columns. Say, what are you doing in Cyprus?' The man then winked and jabbed Mark in the ribs. 'Something hush-hush, I bet. Why don't we get together for a drink? I'm staying at the Palace in Nicosia.' A business card was slapped into Mark's hand. 'Got a few connections here, too.' The man winked again.

'Oh, Mr Parker. Your car is ready.'

Mark put the cup down on the counter. 'Nice seeing you again,' he said, and walked out quickly. As he departed he dropped the business card into a trash basket.

The taxi headed out from the airport. Mark rested back and closed his eyes for a moment. He was glad that Kitty couldn't get to the airport to meet him. So much time had passed and there was so much to say and so much to remember. He felt a surge of excitement pass through him at the thought of seeing her again. Kitty, beautiful, beautiful, Kitty. As the taxi passed through the outer gates Mark was already lost in thought.

... Katherine Fremont. She was one of those great American traditions like Mom's apple pie, hot dogs, and the Brooklyn Dodgers. For Kitty Fremont was the proverbial 'girl next door.' She was the cliché of pigtails, freckles, tomboys, and braces on the teeth; and true to the cliché the braces came off one day, the lipstick went on and the sweater popped out and the ugly duckling had turned into a graceful swan. Mark smiled to himself – she was so beautiful in those days, so fresh and clean.

... and Tom Fremont. He was another American tradition. Tom was the crew-cut kid with the boyish grin who could run the hundred in ten flat, sink a basket from thirty feet out, cut a rug, and put a Model A together blindfolded. Tom Fremont had been Mark's best pal as long as he could remember for as far back as he could remember. We must have been weaned together, Mark thought.

... Tom and Kitty ... apple pie and ice cream ... hot dogs and mustard. The all-American boy, the all-American girl, and the all-American Midwest of Indiana. Yes, Tom and Kitty fitted together like the rain and springtime.

Kitty had always been a quiet girl, very deep, very thoughtful. There was a tinge of sadness in her eyes. Perhaps it was only Mark who detected that sadness, for she was joy itself to everyone around her. Kitty had been one of those wonderful towers of strength. She always had both hands on the rudder, always had the right words to say, always decent and thoughtful. But that sadness was there ... Mark knew it if no one else did.

Mark often wondered what made her so desirable. Maybe it was because she seemed so unreachable to him. The iced champagne – the look and the word that could tear a man to pieces. Anyhow, Kitty had always been Tom's girl and the most he could do was envy Tom.

Tom and Mark were roommates at State University. That first year Tom was absolutely miserable being away from Kitty. Mark remembered the hours on end he would have to listen to Tom's mournful laments and console him. Summer came, Kitty went off to Wisconsin with her parents. She was still a high-school girl and her folks wanted to dampen the fervor of the affair with a separation. Tom and Mark hitchhiked to Oklahoma to work in the oil fields.

By the time school started again Tom had cooled down considerably. To remain in Mark's company one had to sample the field. The times between Tom and Kitty's letters lengthened and the times between Tom's dates on the campus shortened. It began to look like a strike-out for the college hero and the girl back home.

By their senior year Tom had all but forgotten Kitty. He had become the Beau Brummell of State, a role befitting the ace forward on the basketball team. As for Mark, he was content to bask in Tom's glory and generally make a name for himself as one of the worst journalism students in the university's history.

Kitty came to State as a freshman.

Lightning struck!

Mark could see Kitty a thousand times and it was always as exciting as the first. This time Tom saw her the same way. They eloped a month before Tom's graduation. Tom and Kitty, Mark and Ellen, a Model A Ford and four dollars and ten cents crossed the state line and sought out a justice of the peace. Their honeymoon was in the back seat of the Model A, bogged down in the mud of a back road and leaking like a sieve in a downpour. It was an auspicious beginning for the all-American couple.

Tom and Kitty kept their marriage a secret until a full year after his graduation. Kitty stayed on at State to finish her pre-nursing training. Nursing and Kitty seemed to go together, too, Mark always thought.

Tom worshiped Kitty. He had always been a bit wild and too independent, but he settled down to very much the devoted husband. He started out as a very little executive in a very big public relations firm. They moved to Chicago. Kitty nursed in Children's Hospital. They inched their way up, typical American style. First an apartment and then a small home. A new car, monthly bills, big hopes. Kitty became pregnant with Sandra.

Mark's thoughts snapped as the taxi slowed through the outskirts of Nicosia, the capital city that sat on the flat brown plain between the northern and southern mountain ranges. 'Driver, speak English?' Mark asked.

'Yes, sir?'

'They've got a sign at the airport, Welcome to Cyprus. What is the full quotation?'

'As far as I know,' the driver answered, 'they're just trying to be polite to tourists.'

They entered Nicosia proper. The flatness, the yellow stone houses with their red tiled roofs, the sea of date palms all reminded Mark of Damascus. The road ran alongside the ancient Venetian wall which was built in a perfect circle and surrounded the old city. Mark could see the twin minarets that spiraled over the skyline from the Turkish section of the old city. The minarets that belonged to St Sophia's, that magnificent crusader cathedral turned into a Moslem mosque. As they drove along the wall they passed the enormous ramparts shaped like arrowheads. Mark remembered from his last visit to Cyprus that there was the odd number of eleven of these arrowheads jutting from the wall. He was about to ask the driver why eleven but decided not to.

In a matter of moments they were out of Nicosia and moving north on the plain. They passed one village after another, monotonously similar, made of gray mud-brick cottages. Each village had one water fountain which bore an inscription that it was built through the generosity of His Majesty, the King of England. In the colorless fields the peasants labored with the potato crop, working behind those magnificent beasts, the Cyprus mules.

The taxi picked up speed again and Mark sank back to his reveries.

. . . Mark and Ellen had gotten married a little after Tom and Kitty. It was a mistake from the first day. Two nice people not made for each other. Kitty Fremont's quiet and gentle wisdom held Mark and Ellen together. They both could come to her and pour their hearts out. Kitty kept the marriage intact long after time had run out. Then it broke wide open and they were divorced. Mark was thankful there had been no children.

After the divorce Mark moved East and began banging around from job to job, having matriculated from the world's worst journalism student to the world's worst newspaperman. He became one of those drifters who inhabit the newspaper world. It was not stupidity nor lack of talent, but complete inability to find his niche in life. Mark was a creative man and the business or routine reporting cut that creativity. Yet he had no desire to attempt the life of a creative writer. He knew that his personality would not take the demands on a novelist. So Mark hung in limbo, being neither fish nor fowl.

Each week there was a letter from Tom, and it would be filled with enthusiasm and the vigor of his climb to the top. The letters were also filled with Tom's love for Kitty and their baby girl Sandra.

Mark remembered Kitty's letters. A calm appraisal of Tom's effervescence. Kitty always kept Mark posted on Ellen's whereabouts until Ellen remarried.

In 1938 the world opened up for Mark Parker. There was a post to be filled in Berlin with American News Syndicate, and Mark was suddenly transformed from a 'newspaper bum' into the respectability of a 'foreign correspondent.'

In this capacity Mark proved to be a talented journeyman. He was able to fill part of his desire for creativity by developing a style that labeled him as an individual – as Mark Parker and no one else. Mark was by no means a world-beater but he did have that one great instinct of a crack foreign correspondent: an ability to smell out a story in the making.

The world was a lark. He covered Europe, Asia, and Africa from one end to the other. He had a title, he was doing work he liked, his credit was good at Jose's Bar, James's Pub, Joe's and Jacques's Hideaway, and he had an inexhaustible list of candidates for his blonde-, brunette-, or redhead-of-the-month club.

When the war broke out Mark chased all over Europe. It was good to settle back in London for a few days where a stack of mail from Tom and Kitty would be waiting.

Early in 1942 Tom Fremont enlisted in the Marine Corps. He was killed at Guadalcanal.

Two months after Tom's death, their baby, Sandra, died of polio.

Mark took emergency leave to return home, but by the time he arrived Kitty Fremont had disappeared. He searched for her without success until he had to return to Europe. To all intents she had disappeared from the face of the earth. It was strange to Mark, but that sadness that he always saw in Kitty's eyes seemed like a fulfilled prophecy.

The moment the war was over he returned to look for her again, but the trail had grown cold.

In November of 1945, American News Syndicate recalled him to Europe to cover the war-crimes trials in Nuremberg. By now Mark was an established craftsman and bore the title 'distinguished' foreign correspondent. He stayed on, turning in a brilliant series, until the top Nazis were hanged, only a few months back.

ANS granted Mark a much-needed leave of absence before transferring him to Palestine, where it appeared local war was brewing. To spend his leave in the accepted Mark Parker fashion, he chased down a passionate French UN girl he had met earlier, who had been transferred to the United Nations Relief in Athens.

It all happened from a clear blue sky. He was sitting in the American Bar, passing the time of day with a group of fellow newsmen, when the conversation somehow drifted to a particular American nurse in Salonika doing fabulous work with Greek orphans. One of the correspondents had just returned from there with a story on her orphanage.

The nurse was Kitty Fremont.

Mark inquired immediately and discovered that she was on vacation in Cyprus.

The taxi began to move upwards, out of the plain, on a twisting little road that led through the pass in the Pentadaktylos Mountains. It was turning dusk. They reached the peak and Mark ordered the car to pull over to the side.

He stepped out and looked down at the magnificent jewel-like little town of Kyrenia nestled against the sea at the foot of the mountain. To the left and above him stood the ruins of St Hilarion Castle, haunted with the memory of Richard the Lion-Hearted and his beautiful Berengaria. He made a mental note to come back again with Kitty.

It was nearing dark as they reached Kyrenia. The little town was all white plaster and red tiled roofs, with the castle above it and the sea beside it. Kyrenia was picturesque and remote and quaint to a point where it could not have been more picturesque or remote or quaint. They passed the miniature harbor, filled with fishing smacks and small yachts, set inside two arms of a sea wall. On one arm was the quay. On the other arm stood an ancient fortress rampart, the Virgin Castle.

Kyrenia had long been a retreat for artists and retired British Army officers. It was, indeed, one of the most peaceful places on earth.

A block away from the harbor stood the Dome Hotel. Physically the big building seemed outsized and out of place for the rest of the sleepy little town. The Dome, however, had become a crossroads of the British Empire. It was known in every corner of the world that flew a Union Jack as a place where Englishmen met. It was a maze of public rooms and terraces and verandas sitting over the sea. A long pier of a hundred yards or more connected the hotel to a tiny island offshore used by swimmers and sun bathers.

The taxi pulled to a stop. The bellboy gathered in Mark's luggage. Mark paid off his driver and looked about. It was November but it was warmish yet and it was serene. What a wonderful place for a reunion with Kitty Fremont!

The desk clerk handed Mark a message.

MARK DARLING:

I AM STUCK IN FAMAGUSTA UNTIL NINE O'CLOCK. WILL YOU EVER FORGIVE ME??? DYING WITH ANXIETY. LOVE.

KITTY

'I want some flowers, a bottle of scotch, and a bucket of ice,' Mark said.

'Mrs Fremont has taken care of everything,' the room clerk said, handing a key to the bellboy. 'You have adjoining rooms overlooking the sea.'

Mark detected a smirk on the clerk's face. It was the same kind of dirty look he had seen in a hundred hotels with a hundred women. He was about to set the record straight but decided to let the clerk think anything he damned well pleased.

He gathered in the view of the sea as it turned dark, then he unpacked and mixed himself a scotch and water and drank it while he soaked in a steaming tub.

Seven o'clock ... still two hours to wait.

He opened the door of Kitty's room. It smelled good. Her bathing suit and some freshly washed hosiery hung over the bathtub. Her shoes were lined up beside the bed and her make-up on the vanity. Mark smiled. Even with Kitty gone the empty room was full of the character of an unusual person.

He went back and stretched out on his bed. What had the years done to her? What had the tragedy done? Kitty, beautiful Kitty ... please be all right. It was now November of 1946, Mark figured; when was the last time he saw her? Nineteen thirty-eight ... just before he went to Berlin for ANS. Eight years ago. Kitty would be twenty-eight years old now.

The excitement and tension caught up with Mark. He was tired and he began to doze.

The tinkle of ice cubes, a sweet sound to Mark Parker, brought him out of a deep sleep. He rubbed his eyes and groped around for a cigarette.

'You sleep as though you were drugged,' a very British accent said. 'I knocked for five minutes. The bellboy let me in. Hope you don't mind me helping myself to the whisky.'

The voice belonged to Major Fred Caldwell of the British Army. Mark yawned, stretched himself into wakefulness, and checked his watch. It was eight-fifteen. 'What the hell are you doing on Cyprus?' Mark asked.

'I believe that is my question.'

Mark lit a cigarette and looked at Caldwell. He didn't like the major nor did he hate him. 'Despise' was the suitable word. They had met before twice. Caldwell had been the aide of Colonel, later Brigadier, Bruce Sutherland, quite a good field officer in the British Army. Their first meeting had been in the lowlands near Holland during the war. In one of his reports Mark had pointed out a British tactical blunder that had caused a regiment of men to get cut to pieces. The second meeting had been at the Nuremberg war crimes trials which Mark was covering for ANS.

Toward the end of the war Bruce Sutherland's troops were the first to enter the Bergen-Belsen concentration camp in Germany. Both Sutherland and Caldwell had come to Nuremberg to give testimony.

Mark walked to the bathroom, washed his face with icy water, and fished around for a towel. 'What can I do for you, Freddie?'

'CID phoned over to our headquarters this afternoon and told us you landed. You haven't been issued credentials.'

'Christ, you're a suspicious bunch of bastards. Sorry to disappoint you, Freddie. I'm here on vacation en route to Palestine.'

'This isn't an official call, Parker,' Caldwell said; 'just say we are a bit touchy over past relationships.'

'You have long memories,' Mark said, and began dressing. Caldwell mixed Mark a drink. Mark studied the British officer and wondered why Caldwell always managed to rub him the wrong way. There was that arrogance about him that stamped him as a member of that quaint breed, the Colonizer. Caldwell was a stuffy and narrow-minded bore. A gentleman's game of tennis, in whites ... a bashing gin and tonic and damn the natives. It was Freddie Caldwell's conscience or the utter lack of it that bothered Mark. The meaning of right and wrong came to Caldwell through an army manual or an order. 'You boys covering up some dirty work on Cyprus?'

'Don't be a bore, Parker. We own this island and we want to know what you want here.'

'You know ... that's what I like about you British. A Dutchman would tell me to get the hell out. You fellows always say, "please go to hell." I said I was on vacation. A reunion with an old friend.'

'Who?'

'A girl named Kitty Fremont.'

'Kitty, the nurse. Yes, smashing woman, smashing. We met at the governor's a few days back.' Freddie Caldwell's eyebrows raised questioningly as he looked at the connecting door to Kitty's room, which stood ajar.

'Go give your filthy mind a bath,' Mark said. 'I've known her for twenty-five years.'

'Then, as you Americans say – everything's on the up and up.'

'That's right and from this point on your visit becomes social, so get out.'

Freddie Caldwell smiled and set down his glass and tucked the swagger stick under his arm.

'Freddie Caldwell,' Mark said. 'I want to see you when that smile is wiped off your face.'

'What in the devil are you talking about?'

'This is 1946, Major. A lot of people read the campaign slogans in the last war and believed them. You're a dollar short and an hour late. You're going to lose the whole shooting match . . . first it's going to be India, then Africa, then the Middle East. I'll be there to watch you lose the Palestine mandate. They're going to boot you out of even Suez and Trans-Jordan. The sun is setting on the empire, Freddie . . . what is your wife going to do without forty little black boys to whip?'

'I read your coverage of the Nuremberg trials, Parker. You have that terrible American tendency toward being overdramatic. Corny is the word, I think. Besides, old boy, I don't have a wife.'

'You boys are polite.'

'Remember, Parker, you are on vacation. I'll give Brigadier Sutherland your regards. Cheerio.'

Mark smiled and shrugged. Then it came back to him. The sign at the airport . . . WELCOME TO CYPRUS: WILLIAM SHAKESPEARE. The full quote was – 'Welcome to Cyprus, goats and monkeys.'

Chapter Two

During the hours in which Mark Parker awaited his long-delayed reunion with Kitty Fremont, two other men awaited a reunion of a far different sort in a different part of Cyprus. Forty miles away from Kyrenia, north of the port city of Famagusta, they waited in a forest.

It was cloudy, socked-in with no light from the sky. The two men stood in utter silence and squinted through the dark toward the bay a half mile down the hill.

They were in an abandoned white house on the hill in the midst of a forest of pines and eucalyptus and acacias. It was still and black except for a wisp of wind and the muffled unsteady breathing of the two men.

One of the men was a Greek Cypriot, a forest service ranger, and he was nervous.

The other man appeared as calm as a statue, never moving his eyes from the direction of the water. His name was David Ben Ami. His name meant David, Son of My People.

The clouds began to break. Light fell over the still waters of the bay and on the forest and the white house. David Ben Ami stood in the window and the light played on his face. He was a man of slight build in his early twenties. Even in the poor light his thin face and his deep eyes showed the sensitivity of a scholar.

As the clouds swept away, the light crept over fields of broken marble columns and statuary that littered the ground about the white house.

Broken stone. The mortal remains of the once-great city of Salamis which stood mighty in the time of Christ. What history lay beneath this ground and throughout the fields of marble! Salamis, founded in times barely recorded by men, by the warrior Teucer on his return from the Trojan Wars. It fell by earthquake and it rose again and it fell once more to the Arab sword under the banner of Islam, never to arise again. The light danced over the acres and acres of thousands of broken columns where a great Greek forum once stood.

The clouds closed and it was dark again.

'He is long overdue,' the Greek Cypriot forest ranger whispered nervously.

'Listen,' David Ben Ami said.

A faint sound of a boat's motor was heard from far out on the water. David Ben Ami lifted his field glasses, hoping for a break in the clouds. The sound of the motor grew louder.

A flash of light streaked out from the water toward the white house on the hill. Another flash. Another.

David Ben Ami and the forest ranger raced from the white house, down the hill, and through the rubble and the woods till they reached the shore line. Ben Ami returned the signal with his own flashlight.

The sound of the motor stopped.

A shadowy figure of a man slipped over the side of the boat and began to swim toward the shore. David Ben Ami cocked his Sten gun and looked up and down the beach for signs of a British patrol. The figure emerged from the deep water and waded in. 'David!' a voice called from the water.

'Ari,' he answered back, 'this way, quickly.'

On the beach the three men ran past the white house and onto a dirt road. A taxi waited, hidden in the brush. Ben Ami thanked the Cypriot forest ranger, and he and the man from the boat sped off in the direction of Famagusta.

'My cigarettes are soaked,' Ari said.

David Ben Ami passed him a pack. A brief flame glowed over the face of the man who was called Ari. He was large and husky, in complete contrast to the small Ben Ami. His face was handsome but there was a set hardness in his eyes.

He was Ari Ben Canaan and he was the crack agent of the Mossad Aliyah Bet – the illegal organization.

Chapter Three

There was a knock on Mark Parker's door. He opened it. Katherine Fremont stood before him. She was even more beautiful than he remembered. They stared at each other silently for a long time. He studied her face and her eyes. She was a woman now, soft and compassionate in the way one gets only through terrible suffering.

'I ought to break your damned neck for not answering my letters,' Mark said.

'Hello, Mark,' she whispered.

They fell into each other's arms and clung to each other. Then for the first hour they spoke little but contented themselves with looking at each other, with quick smiles, occasional pressing of hands, and affectionate kisses on the cheek.

At dinner they made small talk, mostly of Mark's adventures as a foreign correspondent. Then Mark became aware that Kitty was steering all the conversation away from any talk of herself.

The final dish of cheeses came. Mark poured the last of his Keo beer and another of the many awkward silent periods followed. Now Kitty was obviously growing uncomfortable under his questioning stare.

'Come on,' he said, 'let's take a walk to the harbor.'

'I'll get my stole,' she said.

They walked silently along the quay lined with white buildings and onto the sea wall and out to the lighthouse which stood at the narrow opening of the harbor. It was cloudy and they could see but dim outlines of the little boats resting at anchor. They watched the lighthouse blink out to sea, guiding a trawler toward the shelter of the harbor. A soft wind blew through Kitty's golden hair. She tightened the stole over her shoulders. Mark lit a cigarette and sat on the wall. It was deathly still.

'I've made you very unhappy by coming here,' he said, 'I'll leave tomorrow.'

'I don't want you to go,' she said. She looked away out to the sea. 'I don't know how I felt when I received your cable. It opened the door on a lot of memories that I have tried awfully hard to bury. Yet I knew that one day this minute would come . . . in a way I've dreaded it . . . in a way, I'm glad it's here.'

'It's been four years since Tom got killed. Aren't you ever going to shake this?'

'Women lose husbands in war,' she whispered. 'I cried for Tom. We were very much in love, but I knew I would go on living. I don't even know how he died.'

'There wasn't much to it,' Mark said. 'Tom was a marine and he went in to take a beach with ten thousand other marines. A bullet hit him and he died. No hero, no medals . . . no time to say, "tell Kitty I love her." Just got hit by a bullet and died . . . that's it.'

The blood drained from her face. Mark lit a cigarette and handed it to her. 'Why did Sandra die? Why did my baby have to die too?'

'I'm not God. I can't answer that.'

She sat beside Mark on the sea wall and rested her head on his shoulder and sighed unevenly. 'I guess there is no place left for me to run,' she said.

'Why don't you tell me about it.'

'I can't . . .'

'I think it's about time that you did.'

A half dozen times Kitty tried to speak, but her voice held only short disconnected whispers. The years of terror were locked deep in her. She threw the cigarette into the water and looked at Mark. He was right and he was the only one in the world she could confide in.

'It was pretty terrible,' she said, 'when I got the telegram about Tom, I loved him so. Just . . . just two months after that Sandra died of polio. I . . . I don't remember too much. My parents took me away to Vermont and put me in a home.'

'Asylum?'

'No . . . that's the name they give it for poor people . . . they called mine a rest home for a breakdown. I don't know how many months passed there. I couldn't remember everything. I was in a complete fog day and night. Melancholia, they call it.'

Suddenly Kitty's voice became steady. The door had opened and the torment was finding its way out. 'One day the veil over my mind lifted and I remembered that Tom and Sandra were dead. A pain clung to me. Everything every minute of the day reminded me of them. Every time I heard a song, every time I heard laughter . . . every time I saw a child. Every breath I took hurt me. I prayed . . . I prayed, Mark, that the fog would fall on me again. Yes, I prayed I'd go insane so I couldn't remember.'

She stood up tall and straight and the tears streamed down her cheeks. 'I ran away to New York. Tried to bury myself in the throngs. I had four walls, a chair, a table, a swinging light bulb.' She let out a short ironic laugh. 'There was even a flickering neon sign outside my window. Corny, wasn't it? I'd walk aimlessly for hours on the streets till all the faces were a blur, or I'd sit and look out of the window for days at a time. Tom, Sandra, Tom, Sandra . . . it never left me for a moment.'

Kitty felt Mark behind her. His hands gripped her shoulders. Out in the water the trawler was nearing the opening between the arms of the sea wall. She brushed her cheek against Mark's hand.

'One night I drank too much. You know me . . . I'm a terrible drinker. I saw a boy in a green uniform like Tom's. He was lonely and crew-cut and tall . . . like Tom. We drank together . . . I woke up in a cheap, dirty hotel room . . . God knows where. I was still half drunk. I staggered to the mirror and I looked at myself. I was naked. The boy was naked too . . . sprawled out on the bed.'

'Kitty, for God's sake . . .'

'It's all right, Mark . . . let me finish. I stood there looking in that mirror . . . I don't know how long. I had reached the bottom of my life. There was no place lower for me. That moment . . . that second I was done. The boy was unconscious . . . strange . . . I don't even remember his name. I saw his razor blades in the bathroom and the gas pipe from the ceiling and for a minute or an hour . . . I don't know how long I stood looking down ten stories over the sidewalk. The end of my life had come but I did not have the strength to take it. Then a strange thing happened, Mark. I knew that I was going to go on living without Tom and Sandra and suddenly the pain was gone.'

'Kitty, darling. I wanted so much to find you and help you.'

'I know. But it was something I had to fight out myself, I suppose. I went back to nursing, plunged into it like crazy. The minute it was over in Europe I took on this Greek orphanage . . . it was a twenty-four-hour-a-day job. That's what I needed of course, to work myself to the limit. Mark . . . I . . . I've started a hundred letters to you. Somehow I've been too terrified of this minute. I'm glad now, I'm glad it's over.'

'I'm glad I found you,' Mark said.

She spun around and faced him. '. . . so that is the story of what has become of Kitty Fremont.'

Mark took her hand and they began walking back along the sea wall to the quay. From the Dome Hotel they could hear the sound of music.

Chapter Four

Brigadier Bruce Sutherland sat behind a big desk as military commander of Cyprus in his house on Hippocrates Street in Famagusta, some forty miles from Kyrenia. Except for small telltale traces – a slight roll around his middle and a whitening of the hair about his temples – Sutherland's appearance belied his fifty-five years. His ramrod posture clearly identified a military man. A sharp knock sounded on the door and his aide, Major Fred Caldwell, entered.

'Good evening, Caldwell. Back from Kyrenia already? Have a chair.' Sutherland shoved the papers aside, stretched, and put his glasses on the desk. He selected a GBD pipe from the rack and dipped it into a humidor of Dunhill mix. Caldwell thanked the brigadier for a cigar and the two men soon clouded the room in smoke. The Greek houseboy appeared in answer to a buzz.

'Gin and tonic twice.'

Sutherland arose and walked into the full light. He was wearing a deep red velvet smoking jacket. He settled into a leather chair before the high shelves of books. 'Did you see Mark Parker?'

'Yes, sir.'

'What do you think?'

Caldwell shrugged. 'On the face of it we certainly can't accuse him of anything. He is on the way to Palestine ... here to see that American nurse, Katherine Fremont.'

'Fremont? Oh yes, that lovely woman we met at the governor's.'

'So I say, sir, it all appears quite innocent ... yet, Parker is a reporter and I can't forget that trouble he caused us in Holland.'

'Oh, come now,' Sutherland retorted, 'we all made blunders in the war. He just happened to catch one of ours. Fortunately our side won, and I don't think there are ten people who remember.'

The gin and tonics arrived. 'Cheers.'

Sutherland set his glass down and patted his white walrus mustache. Fred Caldwell wasn't satisfied.

'Sir,' he persisted, 'in case Parker does become curious and does decide to snoop around, don't you think it would be wise to have a couple of CID men watching him?'

'See here, you leave him alone. Just tell a newspaperman "no" and you're apt to stir up a hornet's nest. Refugee stories are out of style these days and I don't believe he would be interested in their camps here. None the less we are not going to run the risk of arousing his curiosity by forbidding him to do anything. If you ask me I think it was a mistake for you to see him today.'

'But, Brigadier ... after that trouble in Holland ...'

'Bring the chess table, Freddie!'

There was something absolutely final about the way Sutherland said 'Freddie.' Caldwell grumbled under his breath as they set up the chessmen. They made their opening moves but Sutherland could see that his aide was unhappy. He set down his pipe and leaned back.

'Caldwell, I have tried to explain to you that we are not running concentration camps here. The refugees at Caraolos are merely being detained on Cyprus until those blockheads in Whitehall decide what they are going to do with the Palestine mandate.'

'But those Jews are so unruly,' Caldwell said, 'I'm certainly in favor of some good old-fashioned discipline.'

'No, Freddie, not this time. These people are not criminals and they've got world sympathy on their side. It is your job and mine to see that there are no riots, no outbreaks, and nothing that can be used as propaganda against us. Do you understand that?'

Caldwell didn't understand. He damned well thought that the brigadier should be much tougher with the refugees. But no one wins an argument with a general unless he happens to be a bigger general and it was all so deep – so Caldwell moved a pawn forward.

'Your move, sir,' he said.

Caldwell looked up from the board. Sutherland seemed completely withdrawn and oblivious of him. It was happening more and more lately.

'Your move, sir,' Caldwell repeated.

Sutherland's face was troubled. Poor chap, Caldwell thought. The brigadier had been married to Neddie Sutherland for almost thirty years, and suddenly she had left him and run off to Paris with a lover ten years her junior. It was a scandal that rocked army circles for months, and Sutherland must still be taking it hard. Terrible blow for the brigadier. He had always been such a decent sort of chap. The white face of Sutherland was lined with wrinkles, and little red veins on his nose turned bright. At this moment he looked all of his fifty-five years and more.

Bruce Sutherland was not thinking about Neddie, as Caldwell believed. His mind was on the refugee camps at Caraolos.

'Your move, sir.'

'*So shall your enemies perish, Israel . . .*' Sutherland mumbled.

'What did you say, sir?'

Chapter Five

Mark led Kitty back to the table, both of them breathless. 'Do you know the last time I danced a samba?' she said.

'You're not so bad for an old broad.'

Mark looked around the room filled with British officers in their army khakis and navy whites and their high and low English accents. Mark loved places like this. The waiter brought a new round of drinks and they clicked glasses.

'To Kitty . . . wherever she may be,' Mark said. 'Well ma'am, where do you go from here?'

Kitty shrugged, 'Golly, I don't know, Mark. My work is finished at Salonika and I am getting restless. I've got a dozen offers I can take around Europe with the United Nations.'

'It was a lovely war,' Mark said. 'Lots of orphans.'

'Matter of fact,' Kitty said, 'I got a real good offer to stay right here on Cyprus just yesterday.'

'On Cyprus?'

'They have some refugee camps around Famagusta. Anyhow, some American woman contacted me. Seems that the camps are overcrowded and they're opening new ones on the Larnaca road. She wanted me to take charge.'

Mark frowned.

'That's one of the reasons I couldn't meet you at the airport. I went to Famagusta to see her today.'

'And what did you tell her?'

'I told her no. They were Jews. I suppose Jewish children are pretty much like any others but I'd just rather not get mixed up with them. It seems that there's an awful lot of politics connected with those camps and they're not under UN auspices.'

Mark was silent in thought. Kitty winked mischievously and waggled a finger under his nose. 'Don't be so serious ... you want to know the other reason I didn't meet you at the airport?'

'You're acting tipsy.'

'I'm starting to feel that way. Well, Mr Parker, I was in Famagusta seeing my boy friend off. You know me ... one lover leaves by ship while another lands by airplane.'

'As long as you brought it up ... who was this guy you came to Cyprus with?'

'Wouldn't you like to know?'

'Uh-huh.'

'Colonel Howard Hillings of the British Army.'

'Anything dirty between you two?'

'Dammit, no. He was so proper it was disgusting.'

'Where did you meet this guy?'

'Salonika. He was in charge of the British mission in the area. When I took over the orphanage we were short of everything ... beds, medicine, food, blankets ... everything. Anyhow, I went to him and he cut wads of red tape for me and we became friends for ever and ever and ever. He really is a dear man.'

'Go on. It's getting interesting.'

'He got notice a few weeks ago that he was being transferred to Palestine and he had leave coming and wanted me to spend it with him here. You know, I'd been working so hard I'd completely forgotten I haven't had a day off in eighteen months. Anyhow, they cut his leave short and he had to report to Famagusta to sail to Palestine today.'

'Future prospects as Mrs Hillings?'

Kitty shook her head. 'I like him very much. He brought me all the way to Cyprus to find the right setting to ask me to marry him ...'

'And?'

'I loved Tom. I'll never feel that way again.'

'You're twenty-eight years old, Kitty. It's a good age to retire.'

'I'm not complaining. I've found something that keeps me content. Mark, you're going to Palestine too. There are a lot of officers here leaving for Palestine.'

'There's going to be a war, Kitty.'

'Why . . . ? I don't understand.'

'Oh, lots of reasons. Lot of people around the world have decided they want to run their own lives. Colonies are going out of vogue this century. These boys here are riding a dead horse. This is the soldier of the new empire,' Mark said, taking a dollar bill from his pocket; 'we've got millions of these green soldiers moving into every corner of the world. Greatest occupying force you've ever seen. A bloodless conquest . . . but Palestine . . . that's different again. Kitty, there's almost something frightening about it. Some people are out to resurrect a nation that has been dead for two thousand years. Nothing like that has ever happened before. What's more, I think they're going to do it. It's these same Jews you don't like.'

'I didn't say I didn't like Jews,' Kitty insisted.

'I won't debate with you now. Think real hard, honey . . . since you've been on Cyprus. Have you heard anything or seen anything that might be, well, unusual?'

Kitty bit her lip in thought and sighed. 'Only the refugee camps. I hear they are overcrowded and in deplorable condition. Why do you ask?'

'I don't know. Just say I've got an intuition that something very big is happening on Cyprus.'

'Why don't you just say you're naturally nosey by profession?'

'It's more than that. Do you know a Major Fred Caldwell? He's aide to Brigadier Sutherland.'

'Terrible bore. I met him at the governor's.'

'He met me in my room before you got in. Why would a general's aide be sitting on my lap ten minutes after I landed on a matter that is seemingly trivial? Kitty, I tell you the British are nervous about something here. I . . . I can't put my finger on it, but five will get you ten it's tied up with those refugee camps. Look . . . would you go to work in those camps for me for a few weeks?'

'Certainly, Mark. If you want me to.'

'Oh, the hell with it,' Mark said, setting down his drink, 'us two kids are on vacation. You're right . . . I'm nosey and suspicious by profession. Forget it, let's dance.'

Chapter Six

On Arsinos Street in Famagusta, facing the wall of the old city, sat a large and luxurious house belonging to a Greek Cypriot named Mandria, who was owner of the Cyprus-Mediterranean Shipping Company as well as owner of a great number of the island's taxicabs. Mandria and David Ben Ami waited anxiously as Ari Ben Canaan cleaned up and changed into dry clothing after his swim ashore.

They both knew that the appearance of Ari Ben Canaan on Cyprus meant a top-level mission for Mossad Aliyah Bet. British policy for many years had been to exclude or extremely limit the Jewish immigration to Palestine. They had the Royal Navy to execute this policy. The Mossad Aliyah Bet was an organization of Palestinian Jews whose business it was to help smuggle other Jews into Palestine. However, as fast as the British Navy caught the Mossad boats trying to run the blockade the refugees would be transferred to detention camps on Cyprus.

Ari Ben Canaan, in a fresh change of clothing, entered the room and nodded to Mandria and David Ben Ami. The Palestinian was a big man, well over six feet and well built. He and Ben Ami had long been intimate friends but they played a role of formality in front of Mandria, the Cypriot, who was not a member of their organization but merely a sympathizer.

Ari lit a cigarette and got right to the point. 'Headquarters has sent me here to stage a mass escape from the detention camps. The reasons are obvious to all of us. What is your opinion, David?'

The thin young man from Jerusalem paced the room thoughtfully. He had been sent to Cyprus months before by the secret army of the Jews in Palestine called the Palmach. He and dozens of other Palmachniks smuggled themselves into the compounds of refugees without the knowledge of the British and set up schools, hospitals, and synagogues, built sanitation facilities, and organized light industry. The refugees who had been turned back from Palestine to Cyprus were hopeless people. The appearance of young Palestinians of the Jews' army infused new hope and morale. David Ben Ami and the other Palmachniks gave military training to several thousand men and women among the refugees, using sticks as rifles and rocks as grenades. Although he was but twenty-two years of age David was the Palmach commander in Cyprus. If the British had gotten wind that there were Palestinians inside the camps they kept quiet about it, for they did their guarding from the outside – having no desire to go into the hate-riddled compounds.

'How many people do you want to escape?' David asked.

'Three hundred, more or less.'

David shook his head. 'We have a few tunnels dug but those lead to the sea. As you know by coming in here tonight, the tides are treacherous and only strong swimmers can make it. Second, we move in and out through the garbage dumps. They are loosely guarded, but we could never get that many people through. Third, British uniforms and false papers . . . again, we can only get a few in and out at a time. Last, we crate some of our members up in boxes and send them to the docks. Mr Mandria here owns the shipping company and his dock hands are on the alert for these crates. At this moment, Ari, I see no way to pull a mass escape.'

'We will find a way,' Ben Canaan said matter of factly, 'but we only have a few weeks to complete this job.'

Mandria, the Greek, arose, sighed, and shook his head. 'Mr Ben Canaan, you have swum ashore tonight and asked us to do the impossible . . . in two weeks, yet. In my heart,' Mandria said, touching his heart, 'I say that it will be done, but! . . . in my head' – and Mandria tapped his skull with his forefinger – 'it cannot be done.' The Cypriot clasped his hands behind him and paced the dining room. 'Believe me, Mr Ben Canaan' – he swung around and made a bravado sweep of the arm – 'you Palmach and Mossad people can count on the Greeks of Cyprus to back you to the last drop of blood. We are for you! We are with you! We are behind you! Nevertheless . . . ! Cyprus is an island and it is surrounded by water on all sides and the British are not stupid or asleep. I,

Mandria, will do everything for you, but still you are not getting three hundred people out of Caraolos. There are ten-foot walls of barbed wire around those compounds and the guards carry rifes . . . with bullets in them.'

Ari Ben Canaan arose and towered over the other two men. He had ignored much of Mandria's dramatics. 'I will need a British uniform, papers, and a driver by morning. You can start looking for a boat, Mr Mandria. Something between a hundred and two hundred tons. David, we will need an expert forger.'

'We have a boy out in the children's compound who is supposed to be a real artist but he won't work. The rest of the stuff is primitive.'

'I'll go out to Caraolos tomorrow and talk to him. I want to look over the camp, anyhow.'

Mandria was elated. What a man of action Ari Ben Canaan was! Find a ship! Find a forger! Get me a uniform and a driver! Life was so exciting since the Mossad and Palmach had come to Cyprus, and he so loved being a part of the cat-and-mouse game with the British. He stood up and pumped Ari Ben Canaan's hand. 'We Cypriots are with you. Your battle is our battle!'

Ben Canaan looked at Mandria disgustedly. 'Mr Mandria,' he said, 'you are being well paid for your time and efforts.'

A stunned silence fell on the room. Mandria turned as white as a sheet. 'Do you believe . . . do you dare believe, sir, that I, I, Mandria, would do this for money? Do you think I risk ten years in prison and exile from my home? It has cost me over five thousand pounds since I began working with your Palmach.'

David stepped in quickly. 'I think you had better apologize to Mr Mandria. He and his taxi drivers and his dock hands take all sorts of risks. Without the help of the Greek people our work would be nearly impossible.'

Mandria slumped into a chair deeply wounded. 'Yes, Mr Ben Canaan, we admire you. We feel that if you can throw the British out of Palestine then maybe we can do the same on Cyprus someday.'

'My apologies, Mr Mandria,' Ari said. 'I must be overtense.' He recited the words completely without meaning.

A shrill sound of sirens outside brought the conversation to a stop. Mandria opened the french doors to the balcony and walked outside with David. Ari Ben Canaan stood behind them. They saw an armored car with machine guns leading a convoy of lorries up the street from the docks. There were twenty-five lorries, in all, surrounded by machine guns mounted on jeeps.

The lorries were packed with refugees from the illegal ship, *Door of Hope*, which had tried to run the British blockade from Italy to Palestine. The *Door of Hope* had been rammed by a British destroyer, towed to Haifa, and the refugees transferred immediately to Cyprus.

The sirens shrieked louder as the convoy swept close to the balcony of Mandria's home. The lorries passed one by one. The three men could see the jam of tattered, ragged misery. They were beaten people – at the end of the line – dazed, withered, exhausted. The sirens shrieked and the convoy turned at the Land Gate of the old wall and onto the road to Salamis, in the direction of the British detention camps at Caraolos. The convoy faded from sight but the shrieks of the sirens lingered on and on.

David Ben Ami's hands were tight fists and his teeth were clenched in a face livid with helpless rage. Mandria wept openly. Only Ari Ben Canaan showed no emotion. They walked in from the balcony.

'I know you two have much to talk over,' Mandria said between sobs. 'I hope you find your room comfortable, Mr Ben Canaan. We will have your uniform, papers, and a taxi by morning. Good night.'

The instant David and Ari were alone they threw their arms about each other. The big man picked the little man up and set him down as though he were a child. They looked each other over and congratulated each other on looking well and went into another bear hug.

'Jordana!' David said anxiously. 'Did you see her before you left? Did she give you a message?'

Ari scratched his jaw teasingly. 'Now let me see ...'

'Please, Ari ... it has been months since I have received a letter ...'

Ari sighed and withdrew an envelope which David snatched from his hands. 'I put it in a rubber pouch. The only thing I could think of tonight when I was swimming in was that you would break my neck if I got your damned letter wet.'

David was not listening. He squinted in the half light and slowly read the words of a woman who missed and longed for her lover. He folded the letter tenderly and carefully placed it in his breast pocket to be read again and again, for it might be months before she could send another. 'How is she?' David asked.

'I don't see what my sister sees in you, Jordana? Jordana is Jordana. She is wild and beautiful and she loves you very much.'

'My parents ... my brothers ... how is our Palmach gang ... what ...'

'Wait a minute, wait a minute. I'll be here for a while – one question at a time.'

David pulled out the letter and read it again, and the two men were silent. They stared out of the french doors at the ancient wall across the road. 'How are things at home?' David whispered.

'Things at home? The same as always. Bombings, shootings. Exactly as it has been every day since we were children. It never changes. Every year we come to a crisis which is sure to wipe us out – then we go on to another crisis worse than the last. Home is home,' Ari said, 'only this time there is going to be a war.' He put his arm on the shoulder of his smaller friend. 'We are all damned proud of the work you have done in Caraolos with these refugees.'

'I have done as well as can be expected, trying to train soldiers with broomsticks. Palestine is a million miles away to these people. They have no hope left. Ari ... I don't want you antagonizing Mandria any more. He is a wonderful friend.'

'I can't stand people patronizing us, David.'

'And we can't do the job here without him and the Greek people.'

'Don't be fooled by the Mandrias all over the world. They weep crocodile tears and they pay lip service to our millions of slaughtered, but when the final battle comes we will stand alone. Mandria will sell us out like all the others. We will be betrayed and double-crossed as it has always been. We have no friends except our own people, remember that.'

'And you are wrong,' David snapped back.

'David, David, David. I have been with the Mossad and the Palmach for more years than I care to remember. You are young yet. This is your first big assignment. Don't let emotion cloud your logic.'

'I *want* emotion to cloud my logic,' David answered. 'I burn inside every time I see something like that convoy. Our people locked up in cages like animals.'

'We try all sorts of schemes,' Ari said; 'we must keep a clear head. Sometimes we are successful, sometimes we fail. Work with a clear mind, always.'

Even now they could still hear the sound of sirens over the breeze. The young man from Jerusalem lit a cigarette and stood for a moment in thought. 'I must never stop believing,' he said solemnly, 'that I am carrying on a new chapter of a story started four thousand years ago.' He spun around and looked up at the big man excitedly. 'Look, Ari. Take the place you landed tonight. Once the city of Salamis stood there. It was in Salamis that the Bar Kochba revolution began in the first century. He drove the Romans from our country and re-established the Kingdom of Judah. There is a bridge near the detention camps – they call it the Jews' Bridge. It has been called that for two thousand years. I can't forget these things. Right in the same place we fought the Roman Empire we now fight the British Empire two thousand years later.'

Ari Ben Canaan stood a head taller than David Ben Ami. He smiled down at the younger man as a father might smile at an overenthusiastic son. 'Finish the story. After the Bar Kochba revolution the legions of Rome returned and massacred our people in city after city. In the final battle at Beitar the blood of murdered women and children made a crimson river which flowed for a full mile. Akiva, one of the leaders, was skinned alive – and Bar Kochba was carried off to Rome in chains to die in the lions' den. Or was it Bar Giora who died in the lions' den in another revolution? I can get these revolutions mixed up. Oh yes, the Bible and our history are filled with wonderful tales and convenient miracles. But this is real today. We have no Joshua to make the sun stand still or the walls to come tumbling down. The British tanks will not get stuck in the mud like Canaanite chariots, and the sea has not closed in on the British Navy as it did on Pharaoh's army. The age of miracles is gone, David.'

'It is not gone! Our very existence is a miracle. We outlived the Romans and the Greeks and even Hitler. We have outlived very oppressor and we will outlive the British Empire. That is a miracle, Ari.'

'Well, David – one thing I can say about the Jews. We certainly know how to argue. Let's get some sleep.'

Chapter Seven

'Your move, sir,' Fred Caldwell repeated.

'Yes, yes, forgive me.' Brigadier Sutherland studied the chessboard and moved his pawn forward. Caldwell brought out a knight and Sutherland countered with his own. 'Dash it!' the brigadier mumbled as his pipe went out. He relit it.

The two men glanced up as they heard the dim but steady shrill screams of sirens. Sutherland looked at the wall clock. That would be the refugees from the illegal ship, *Door of Hope.*

'*Door of Hope, Gates of Zion, Promised Land, Star of David,*' Caldwell said with a snicker. 'I will say one thing. They do give those blockade runners colorful names.'

Sutherland's brow furrowed. He tried to study out his next move on the board, but the sirens would not leave his ears. He stared at the ivory chessmen, but he was visualizing the convoy of lorries packed with agonized faces, machine guns, armored cars. 'If you don't mind, Caldwell, I think I'll turn in.'

'Anything wrong, sir?'

'No. Good night.' The brigadier walked from the room quickly and closed the door of his bedroom and loosened his smoking jacket. The sirens seemed to screech unbearably loudly. He slammed the window shut to drown the noise but still he could hear it.

Bruce Sutherland stood before the mirror and wondered what was going wrong with him. Sutherland from Sutherland Heights. Another distinguished career in a line of distinguished careers that went on, the same as England itself.

But these past weeks on Cyprus something was happening. Something tearing him to pieces. He stood there before the mirror and looked into his own watery eyes and wondered where it had all begun.

Sutherland: Good fellow to have on your team, said the yearbook at Eton. *Right sort of chap, that Sutherland. Proper family, proper schooling, proper career.*

The army? Good choice, Bruce old man. We Sutherlands have served in the army for centuries . . .

Proper marriage. Neddie Ashton. The daughter of Colonel Ashton was a clever catch. Fine stock, Neddie Ashton. Fine hostess, that woman. She always has the ear of the right person. She'll be a big help to your career. Spendid match! The Ashtons and the Sutherlands.

Where the failure, Sutherland wondered? Neddie had given him two lovely children. Albert was a real Sutherland. A captain in his father's old regiment already, and Martha had made herself a splendid marriage.

Bruce Sutherland opened the closet and put on his pajamas. He touched the roll of fat about his waist. Not too bad for a man of fifty-five. He still had plenty of punch left.

Sutherland had come up fast in World War II by comparison to the slow tedious advancements in the peacetime service. There had been India, Hong Kong, Singapore, and the Middle East. But it took a war to show what he was made of. He proved to be an exceptional infantry commander. V-E Day found him a brigadier.

He put on his bedroom slippers and sank slowly into a deep chair and dimmed the lamp and he was filled with remembering.

Neddie had always been a good wife. She was a good mother, a tremendous hostess, and a woman cut out for colonial service in the army. He had been very fortunate. When had the break come between them? Yes, he remembered. It was in Singapore so many years ago.

He was a major when he met Marina, the olive-skinned Eurasian woman. Marina – born and made for love. Each man has a Marina hidden deep in his inner thoughts, but he had his in the flesh and she was real. Laughter and fire and tears and passion. Being with Marina was like being in a bubbling volcano ready to erupt. He was insane for her – he desired her wildly, madly. He threw jealous tantrums before her only to half sob, begging forgiveness. Marina . . . Marina . . . Marina . . . the black eyes and the raven hair. She could torment him. She could delight him. She could spiral him to heights he never knew existed on this earth. Those precious, magnificent moments of their trysts ...

His hands had clutched her hair and pulled her head back and he had looked at her deep red sensuous lips ... 'I love you, you bitch ... I love you.'

'I love you, Bruce,' Marina had whispered.

... Bruce Sutherland remembered the stunned hurt look on Neddie's face as she confronted him with evidence of his affair.

'I won't say this hasn't hurt me deeply,' Neddie said, too proud for tears, 'but I am willing to forgive and forget. There are the children to think of. There is your career ... and our families. I'll try to make a go of it with you, Bruce, but you must swear you'll never see that woman again and that you'll put in an immediate request for transfer from Singapore.'

That woman – that woman, you call her, Bruce thought – is my love. She has given me something that you or a thousand Neddies never could or never will. She has given me something no man has a right to expect on this earth.

'I want your answer now, Bruce.'

Answer? What could the answer be? A man can have a woman like Marina for a night, for a touch, but she is not real. There is only one Marina to a man ... one to a lifetime. Answer? Throw away his career for a Eurasian girl? Bring scandal on the name of Sutherland?

'I will never see her again, Neddie,' Bruce Sutherland promised.

Bruce Sutherland never saw her again but he never stopped thinking of her. Perhaps that is where it all started.

The sounds of the sirens were very faint now. The convoy must be quite near Caraolos, Sutherland thought. Soon the sirens would stop and he could sleep. He began thinking of the retirement that would be coming in another four or five years. The family house at Sutherland Heights would be far too big. A cottage, perhaps in the country. Soon it would be time to think about a pair of good hunting setters and gathering rose catalogues and building up his library. Time to start thinking about a decent club to join in London. Albert, Martha, and his grandchildren would indeed be a comfort in retirement. Perhaps ... perhaps he would take a mistress, too.

It seemed strange that after nearly thirty years of marriage he would be going into retirement without Neddie. She had been so quiet, reserved, and distinguished all those years. She had been so sporting about his affair with Marina. Suddenly, after a lifetime of complete propriety Neddie burst out frantically to salvage her few years left as a woman. She ran off to Paris with a Bohemian chap ten years her junior. Everyone sympathized with Bruce, but it really didn't matter to him much. There had been no contact and little feeling for Neddie for many years. She could have her fling. They were quite civilized about it. Perhaps he would take her back later ... perhaps a mistress would be better.

At last the sirens from the convoy stopped. There was complete silence in the room except for the muffled shushing of the surf breaking on the shore. Bruce Sutherland opened the window and breathed in the cool crisp November air. He went to the bathroom and washed and placed the bridge of four teeth in a glass of solution. Damned shame, he thought, losing those four teeth. He had said the same thing for thirty years. It was the result of a rugby game. He examined the other teeth to satisfy himself they were still in good shape.

He opened the medicine chest and studied the row of bottles. He took down a tin of sleeping powders and mixed a double dose. It was difficult to sleep these days.

His heart began racing as he drank down the solution. He knew it was going to be another one of those horrible nights. He tried desperately to lock out or stifle the thoughts creeping into his brain. He covered himself in bed and hoped sleep would come quickly, but it was already beginning to whirl around and around and around in his mind ...

... Bergen-Belsen ... Bergen-Belsen ... Bergen-Belsen ... NUREMBERG ... NUREMBERG! NUREMBERG! NUREMBERG!

'Take the stand and give your name.'

'Bruce Sutherland, Brigadier General, Commander of...'

'Describe, in your own words...'

'My troops entered Bergen-Belsen at twenty minutes past five in the evening of April 15.'

'Describe in your own words...'

'Camp Number One was an enclosure of four hundred yards wide by a mile long. That area held eighty thousand people. Mostly Hungarian and Polish Jews.'

'Describe in your own words...'

'The ration for Camp Number One was ten thousand loaves of bread a week.'

'Identify...'

'Yes, those are testicle crushers and thumbscrews used in torture...'

'Describe...'

'Our census showed thirty thousand dead in Camp Number One, including nearly fifteen thousand corpses just littered around. There were twenty-eight thousand women and twelve thousand men still alive.'

'DESCRIBE...!'

'We made desperate efforts but the survivors were so emasculated and diseased that thirteen thousand more died within a few days after our arrival.'

'DESCRIBE...!'

'Conditions were so wretched when we entered the camp that the living were eating the flesh of the corpses.'

The moment Bruce Sutherland had completed his testimony at the Nuremberg war crimes trials he received an urgent message to return to London at once. The message came from an old and dear friend in the War Office, General Sir Clarence Tevor-Browne. Sutherland sensed it was something out of the ordinary.

He flew to London the next day and reported at once to that huge, ungainly monstrosity of a building on the corner of Whitehall and Great Scotland Yard which housed the British War Office.

'Bruce, Bruce, Bruce! Come in, come in, man! Good to see you. I followed your testimony at the Nuremberg trials. Nasty bit of business.'

'I am glad it is over,' Sutherland said.

'Sorry to hear about you and Neddie. If there is anything at all I can do...'

Sutherland shook his head.

At last Tevor-Browne led up to the reason for asking him to come to London. 'Bruce,' he said, 'I called you here because a rather delicate assignment has come up. I must give a recommendation and I want to put your name up. I wanted to talk it over with you first.'

'Go on, Sir Clarence.'

'Bruce, these Jews escaping from Europe have posed quite a problem. They are simply flooding Palestine. Frankly, the Arabs are getting quite upset about the numbers getting into the mandate. We here have decided to set up detention camps on Cyprus to contain these people – at least as a temporary measure until Whitehall decides what we are going to do with the Palestine mandate.'

'I see,' Sutherland said softly.

Tevor-Browne continued. 'This entire thing is touchy and must be handled with great tact. Now, no one wants to ride herd on a bunch of downtrodden refugees, and the fact is ... well, they have a great deal of sympathy on their side in high quarters – especially in France and America. Things must be kept very quiet on Cyprus. We want nothing to happen to create unfavorable opinion.'

Sutherland walked to the window and looked out to the Thames River and watched the big double-deck buses drive over the Waterloo Bridge. 'I think the whole idea is wretched,' he said.

'It is not for you and me to decide, Bruce. Whitehall gives the orders. We merely carry them out.'

Sutherland continued looking out of the window. 'I saw those people at Bergen-Belsen. Must be the same ones who are trying to get into Palestine now.' He returned to his chair. 'We have broken one promise after another to those people in Palestine for thirty years.'

'See here, Bruce,' Tevor-Browne said, 'you and I see eye to eye on this, but we are in a minority. We both served together in the Middle East. Let me tell you something, man. I sat here at this desk during the war as one report after another of Arab sellouts came in. The Egyptian Chief of Staff selling secrets to the Germans; Cairo all decked out to welcome Rommel as their liberator; the Iraqis going to the Germans; the Syrians going to the Germans; the Mufti of Jerusalem a Nazi agent. I could go on for hours. You must look at Whitehall's side of this, Bruce. We can't risk losing our prestige and our hold on the entire Middle East over a few thousand Jews.'

Sutherland sighed. 'And this is our most tragic mistake of all, Sir Clarence. We are going to lose the Middle East despite it.'

'You are all wound up, Bruce.'

'There is a right and a wrong, you know.'

General Sir Clarence Tevor-Browne smiled slightly and shook his head sadly. 'I have learned very little in my years, Bruce, but one thing I have learned. Foreign policies of this, or any other, country are not based on right and wrong. Right and wrong? It is not for you and me to argue the right or the wrong of this question. The only kingdom that runs on righteousness is the kingdom of heaven. The kingdoms of the earth run on oil. The Arabs have oil.'

Bruce Sutherland was silent. Then he nodded. 'Only the kingdom of heaven runs on righteousness,' he repeated. 'The kingdoms of the earth run on oil. You have learned something, Sir Clarence. It seems that all of life itself is wrapped up in those lines. All of us ... people ... nations ... live by need and not by truth.'

Tevor-Browne leaned forward. 'Somewhere in God's scheme of things he gave us the burden of an empire to rule ...'

'Ours not to reason why,' Sutherland whispered. 'But I can't seem to forget the Arab slave markets in Saudi Arabia and the first time I was invited to watch a man have his hands amputated as punishment for stealing, and somehow I can't forget those Jews at Bergen-Belsen.'

'It is not too good to be a soldier and have a conscience. I won't force you to take this post on Cyprus.'

'I'll go. Of course I'll go. But tell me. Why did you choose me?'

'Most of our chaps are pro-Arab for no other reason than our tradition has been pro-Arab and soldiers are not in a position to do much other than follow policy. I don't want to send someone to Cyprus who will antagonize these refugees. It is a problem that calls for understanding and compassion.'

Sutherland arose. 'I sometimes think,' he said, 'that it is almost as much a curse being born an Englishman as it is being born a Jew.'

Sutherland accepted the assignment on Cyprus, but his heart was filled with fear. He wondered if Tevor-Browne had known he was half Jewish.

That decision, that horrible decision he had made so long ago was coming back to haunt him now.

He remembered that afterward he began to find solace in the Bible. There were those empty years with Neddie, the painful loss of the Eurasian girl he loved, and it all seemed to plunge him deeper and deeper into a longing to find peace of mind. How wonderful for a soldier like him to read of the great campaigns of Joshua and Gideon and Joab. And those magnificent women – Ruth and Esther and Sarah . . . and . . . and Deborah. Deborah, the Joan of Arc, the liberator of her people.

He remembered the chill as he read the words: *Awake, awake, Deborah; awake, awake.*

Deborah! That was his mother's name.

Deborah Davis was a rare and beautiful woman. It was small wonder that Harold Sutherland was smitten with her. The Sutherland family was tolerant when Harold sat through fifteen performances of *The Taming of the Shrew* to watch the beautiful actress, Deborah Davis, and they smiled benevolently as he went over his allowance on flowers and gifts. It was a boyish fling, they thought, and he'd get over it.

Harold could not get over Deborah Davis, and the family stopped being tolerant. She defied an edict they issued for her to appear at Sutherland Heights. It was then that Harold's father, Sir Edgar, traveled to London to see this amazing young woman who refused to travel to Sutherland Heights. Deborah was as clever and witty as she was beautiful. She dazzled Sir Edgar and completely won him.

Sir Edgar decided then and there that his son had been damned lucky. After all, the Sutherlands were known to have a tradition of inclining toward actresses and some of them had become the grandest dames in the family's long history.

There was, of course, the touchy business of Deborah Davis being a Jewess, but the matter was closed when she agreed to take instructions in the Church of England.

Harold and Deborah had three children. There was Mary, their only girl, and there was moody, irresponsible Adam. And there was Bruce. Bruce was the oldest and Deborah's favorite. The boy adored his mother. But as close as they were she never spoke of her own childhood, or of her parents. He knew only that she had been very poor and run away to the stage.

The years passed. Bruce took up his army career and married Neddie Ashton. The children, Albert and Martha, came. Harold Sutherland died, and Deborah moved along in age.

Bruce remembered so well the day that it happened. He was coming to Sutherland Heights for a long visit and bringing Neddie and the children. Deborah would always be in the rose garden or the conservatory or floating about gaily on her duties – smiling, happy, gracious. But this day as he drove up to Sutherland Heights she was not there to greet him nor was she anywhere about to be found. At last he discovered her sitting in darkness in her drawing room. This was so unlike Mother that it startled him. She was sitting like a statue, looking at the wall, oblivious to her surroundings.

Bruce kissed her on the cheek softly and knelt beside her. 'Is something wrong, Mother?'

She turned slowly and whispered, 'Today is Yom Kippur – the Day of Atonement.'

Her words chilled Bruce to the bone.

Bruce talked it over with Neddie and his sister, Mary. They decided that since Father had died she had been alone too much. Furthermore, Sutherland Heights was too big for her. She should move into an apartment in London where she could be closer to Mary. Then, too, Deborah was getting old. It was hard for them to realize, because she seemed to them as beautiful as when they were children.

Bruce and Neddie went off for his tour of service in the Middle East. Mary wrote happy letters that Mother was getting along fine, and the letters from Deborah told of her happiness to be in London near Mary's family.

But when Bruce returned to England it was a different story. Mary was beside herself. Mother was seventy years old now and acting more and more strangely. A creeping on of senility. She could not remember something that had happened a day ago, but she would utter disconnected things about events that took place fifty years ago. It was frightening to Mary because Deborah had never spoken of her past to her children. Mary was most alarmed of her mother's strange disappearances.

Mary was glad that Bruce had returned. He was the oldest and Mother's favorite and he was so steady. Bruce followed his mother one day on one of her mysterious walks. It led to a synagogue in Whitechapel.

He thought it all over carefully and decided to leave her alone. She was old; he did not feel it proper to confront her with things that had happened over fifty years before. It was best to let it pass quietly.

At the age of seventy-five Deborah Sutherland lay on her deathbed. Bruce got back to England just in time.

The old woman smiled as she saw her son sitting on the edge of the bed. 'You are a Lieutenant Colonel now . . . you look fine . . . Bruce, my son . . . I haven't too many hours left . . .'

'Hush now, Mother. You'll be up and about in no time.'

'No, I must tell you something. I wanted to be your father's wife so badly. I wanted so much . . . so very very much to be the mistress of Sutherland Heights. I did a terrible thing Bruce. I denied my people. I denied them in life. I want to be with them now. Bruce . . . Bruce, promise that I shall be buried near my father and my mother . . .'

'I promise, Mother.'

'My father . . . your grandfather . . . you never knew him. When . . . when I was a little girl he would hold me on his lap and he would say to me ... "awake, awake, Deborah; awake, awake..."'

Those were the last words Deborah Sutherland spoke.

Bruce Sutherland sat in numb grief for a long hour beside the lifeless body of his mother. Then the numbness began to thaw under the nagging burn of a doubt that would not be kept out of his mind. Must he be bound by a promise he had made a dying woman? A promise he was forced to make? Would it be breaking the code of honor by which he had always lived? Wasn't it true that Deborah Sutherland's mind had been going on her bit by bit over the past years? She had never been a Jewess in life, why should she be one in death? Deborah had been a Sutherland and nothing else.

What a terrible scandal would be created if he were to bury her in a shabby run-down Jewish cemetery on the poverty side of London. Mother was dead. The living – Neddie, Albert and Martha and Mary's family and Adam would be hurt deeply. The living had to be served.

As he kissed his mother farewell and walked from her room he had made his decision.

Deborah was put to rest in the family vault at Sutherland Heights.

The sirens!

The sirens from the convoy of refugees!

The sirens shrieked louder and louder and louder until they tore through his eardrums. *Bergen-Belsen ... Marina ... Neddie ... caged trucks ... the camps at Caraolos ... I promise, Mother ... I promise, Mother...*

A burst of thunder rocked the house to its very foundation, and the sea outside became wild and waves smashed up the shore and raced nearly to the house. Sutherland threw off the covers and staggered about the room as though drunk. He froze at the window. Lightning! Thunder! The raging water grew higher and higher!

'*God ... God ... God ... God...!*'

'Brigadier Sutherland! Brigadier Sutherland! Wake up, sir! Wake up, sir!'

The Greek houseboy shook him hard.

Sutherland's eyes opened and he looked about wildly. The sweat poured from his body and his heart pounded painfully. He gasped for breath. The houseboy quickly brought him a brandy.

He looked outside to the sea. The night was calm and the water was as smooth as glass and lapped gently against the shore.

'I'll be all right,' he said. 'I'll be all right...'

'Are you sure, sir?'

'Yes.'

The door closed.

Bruce Sutherland slumped into a chair and buried his face in his hands and wept and whispered over and over, '... my mother in heaven ... my mother in heaven...'

Chapter Eight

Brigadier Bruce Sutherland slept the sleep of the tormented and the damned.

Mandria, the Cypriot, twisted and turned in a nervous but exhilarated sleep.

Mark Parker slept the sleep of a man who had accomplished a mission.

Kitty Fremont slept with a peace of mind she had not known in years.

David Ben Ami slept only after reading Jordana's letter so many times he knew it by memory.

Ari Ben Canaan did not sleep. There would be other times for that luxury, but not now. There was much to learn and little time to learn it in. All during the night he pored over maps and documents and papers, absorbing every fact about Cyprus, the British operation, and his own people there. He waded through the stacks of data with a cigarette or a coffee cup continuously at hand. There was a calm ease, a sureness about him.

The British had said many times that the Palestinian Jews were a match for anyone on matters of intelligence. The Jews had the advantage that every Jew in every country in the world was a potential source of information and protection for a Mossad Aliyah Bet agent.

At daybreak Ari awakened David, and after a quick breakfast they rode in one of Mandria's taxis out to the detention camp at Caraolos.

The compounds themselves stretched for many miles in an area that hugged the bay, midway between Famagusta and the ruins of Salamis. The garbage dumps were a contact point between the refugees and the Cypriots. The British guarded them loosely because the garbage detail was made up of 'trusties.' The garbage dumps became trading centers where leather goods and art work made in the camp were exchanged for bread and clothing. David led Ari through the dumps where the early morning bartering between Greeks and Jews was already going on. From here they entered their first compound.

Ari stood and looked at the mile after mile of barbed wire. Although it was November it was chokingly hot under a constant swirl of blowing dust. Compound after compound of tents were stretched along the bay, all set in an area, of low hanging acacia trees. Each compound was closed in by ten- to twelve-foot walls of barbed wire. On the corners there were searchlight towers manned by British guards armed with machine guns. A skinny dog began following them. The word 'BEVIN' was painted on the dog's sides – a bow to the British Foreign Minister.

It was the same scene in each compound they visited: packed with miserable and angry people. Almost everyone was dressed in crudely sewn purple shorts and shirts made from cloth that had been torn from the inner linings of the tents. Ari studied the faces filled with suspicion, hatred, defeat.

In each new compound Ari would suddenly be embraced by a boy or girl in the late teens or early twenties who had been smuggled in by the Palestine Palmach to work with the refugees. They would throw their arms about him and begin to ask questions about home. Each time Ari begged off, promising to hold a Palmach meeting for the whole group in a few days. Each Palmach head showed Ari around the particular compound he or she was in charge of, and occasionally Ari would ask a question.

For the most part, he was very quiet. His eyes were searching the miles of barbed wire for some key that would help him get three hundred people out.

Many of the compounds were grouped together by nationalities. There were compounds of Poles and of French and of Czechs. There were compounds of Orthodox Jews and there were compounds of those who banded together with similar political beliefs. Most compounds, however, were merely survivals of the war, with no identity other than that they were Jews who wanted to go to Palestine. They all had a similarity in their uniform misery.

David led Ari to a wooden bridge that connected two main portions of the camp by crossing over the top of the barbed wire walls. There was a sign on the bridge that read: WELCOME TO BERGEN-BEVIN. 'It is rather bitter irony, Ari, this bridge. There was one exactly like it in the Lodz ghetto in Poland.'

By now David was seething. He berated the British for the subhuman conditions of the camp, for the fact that German prisoners of war on Cyprus had a greater degree of freedom, for the lack of food and medical care, and just for the general gross injustice. Ari was not listening to David's ranting. He was too intent on studying the structure and arrangement of the place. He asked David to show him the tunnels.

Ari was led to a compound of Orthodox Jews close to the bay. There was a row of outside toilets near the barbed wire wall. On the first toilet shack was a sign that read: BEVINGRAD. Ari was shown that the fifth and sixth toilets in the line of sheds were fakes. The holes under the seats led under the barbed wire and through tunnels to the bay. Ari shook his head – it was all right for a few people at a time but not suited for a mass escape.

Several hours had passed. They had nearly completed the inspection. Ari had hardly spoken a word for two hours. At last, bursting with anxiety, David asked, 'Well, what do you think?'

'I think,' Ari answered, 'that Bevin isn't very popular around here. What else is there to see?'

'I saved the children's compound for last. We have Palmach headquarters there.'

As they entered the children's compound Ari was once again pounced upon by a Palmachnik. But this time he returned the embrace with vigor and a smile on his face, for it was an old and dear friend, Joab Yarkoni. He whirled Yarkoni around, set him down, and hugged him again. Joab Yarkoni was a dark-skinned Moroccan Jew who had emigrated to Palestine as a youngster. His black eyes sparkled and a huge brush of a mustache seemed to take up half of his face. Joab and Ari had shared many adventures together, for although Joab was still in his early twenties he was one of the crack agents in the Mossad Aliyah Bet, with an intimate knowledge of the Arab countries.

From the beginning Yarkoni had been one of the wiliest and most daring operators in Mossad. His greatest feat was one which started the Jews of Palestine in the date-palm industry. The Iraqi Arabs guarded their date palms jealously, but Yarkoni had managed to smuggle a hundred saplings into Palestine from Iraq.

David Ben Ami had given Joab Yarkoni command of the children's compound, for it was, indeed, the most important place in the Caraolos camp.

Joab showed Ari around the compound, which was filled with orphans from infancy to seventeen years of age. Most of them had been inmates of concentration camps during the war, and many of them had never known a life outside of barbed wire. Unlike the other compounds, the children's section had several permanent structures erected. There was a school, a dining hall, a hospital, smaller units, and a large playground. There was a great deal of activity here in contrast to the lethargy in the other areas. Nurses, doctors, teachers, and welfare people from the outside, sponsored by money from American Jews, worked in the compound.

Because of the flow of outsiders, the children's compound was the most loosely guarded in Caraolos. David and Joab were quick to capitalize on this fact by establishing Palmach headquarters in the compound.

At night the playground was transformed into a military training camp for refugees. The classrooms were turned from standard schools into indoctrination centers in Arab psychology, Palestine geography, tactics, weapons identification, and a hundred other phases of warfare instruction.

Each refugee receiving military training by the Palmach had to stand trial by a kangaroo court. The pretense was that the refugee had got to Palestine and had been picked up by the British. The Palmach instructor would then put him through an interrogation to try to establish that the refugee was not in the country legally. The refugee had to answer a thousand questions about the geography and history of Palestine to 'prove' he had been there many years.

When a 'candidate' successfully completed the course, the Palmach arranged an escape, generally through the children's compound or the tunnels, to the white house on the hill at Salamis, whence he would be smuggled into Palestine. Several hundred refugees had been sent to Palestine that way, in groups of twos and threes.

British CID was not unaware of the fact that irregular things took place inside the children's compound. Time and again they planted spies among the outside teachers and welfare workers, but the ghetto and the concentration camps had bred a tight-lipped generation of children and the intruders were always discovered within a day or two.

Ari ended the inspection of the children's compound in the schoolhouse. One of the schoolrooms was, in fact, Palmach headquarters. Inside the teacher's desk was a secret radio and transmitter which maintained contact with Palestine. Under the floor boards weapons were hidden for the military training courses. In this room papers and passes were forged.

Ari looked over the forgery plant and shook his head. 'This counterfeit work is terrible,' he said. 'Joab, you are very sloppy.'

Yarkoni merely shrugged.

'In the next few weeks,' Ari continued, 'we are going to need an expert. David, you said there is one right here.'

'That's right. He is a Polish boy named Dov Landau, but he refuses to work.'

'We have tried for weeks,' Joab added.

'Let me speak to him.'

Ari told the two men to wait outside as he stepped into Dov Landau's tent. He looked over at a blond boy, undersized and tense and suspicious at the sudden intrusion. Ari knew the look – the eyes filled with hate. He studied the turned-down mouth and the snarling lips of the youngster: the expression of viciousness that stamped so many of the concentration-camp people.

'Your name is Dov Landau,' Ari said, looking directly into his eyes. 'You are seventeen years old and Polish. You have a concentration camp background and you are an expert forger, counterfeiter, and duplicator. My name is Ari Ben Canaan. I'm a Palestinian from Mossad Aliyah Bet.'

The boy spat on the ground.

'Look, Dov, I'm not going to plead and I'm not going to threaten. I've got a plain out-and-out business proposition . . . let's call it a mutual assistance pact.'

Dov Landau snarled, 'I want to tell you something, Mr Ben Canaan. You guys aren't any better than the Germans or the British. The only reason you want us over there so bad is to save your necks from the Arabs. Let me tell you – I'm getting to Palestine all right and when I do I'm joining an outfit that's going to let me kill!'

Ari did not change expression at the outburst of venom that erupted from the boy. 'Good. We understand each other perfectly. You don't like my motives for wanting you in Palestine and I don't like yours for wanting to get there. We do agree on one thing: you belong in Palestine and not here.'

The boy's eyes narrowed with suspicion. This Ben Canaan was not like the others.

'Let's take it a step further,' Ari said. 'You're not going to get to Palestine by sitting here on your arse and doing nothing. You help me and I'll help you. What happens after you get there is your business.'

Dov Landau blinked with surprise.

'Here's the point,' Ari said. 'I need forged papers. I need piles of them in the next few weeks and these boys here can't forge their own names. I want you to work for me.'

The boy had been thrown completely off guard by Ari's rapid and direct tactics. He wanted time to look for a hidden trick. 'I'll think it over,' he said.

'Sure, think it over. You've got thirty seconds.'

'And what will you do if I refuse? You going to try to beat it out of me?'

'Dov, I said we need each other. Let me make myself clear. If you don't go along with this I'm going to personally see to it that you're the last person out of the Caraolos detention camp. With thirty-five thousand people ahead of you, you'll be too old and feeble to lift one of those bombs by the time you get to Palestine. Your thirty seconds are up.'

'How do I know I can trust you?'

'Because I said you could.'

A faint smile crossed the boy's face, and he nodded that he would go to work.

'All right. You get your orders from either David Ben Ami or Joab Yarkoni. I don't want you giving anyone a bad time. If you have any problems, you ask for me. I want you to report to Palmach headquarters in a half hour and look over their plant and let David know what special materials you'll need.'

Ari turned and walked out of the tent to where David and Joab waited. 'He'll report to work in a half hour,' Ari said.

David gaped and Joab's mouth fell open in awe.

'How did you do it?'

'Child psychology. I'm going back to Famagusta,' Ari said. 'I want to see you two boys at Mandria's house tonight. Bring Zev Gilboa with you. Don't bother to show me out. I know the way.'

David and Joab stared in fascination as their friend, the remarkable Ari Ben Canaan, crossed the playground in the direction of the garbage dumps.

That night in his living room Mandria, the Cypriot, waited, along with David, Joab, and a newcomer, Zev Gilboa, for the appearance of Ari Ben Canaan.

Zev Gilboa, also a Palestinian Palmachnik, was a broadbacked farmer from the Galilee. Like Yarkoni, he, too, wore a large brushlike mustache and was in his early twenties. Zev Gilboa was the best of the soldiers among the Palmach Palestinians working inside Caraolos. David had given Zev the task of heading military training for the refugees. With zest, with improvised weapons, and by using the children's playground at night he had taught his trainees nearly everything that could be taught without actual arms. Broomsticks were rifles, rocks were grenades, bedsprings were bayonets. He set up courses in hand-to-hand fighting and stick fighting. Mostly he instilled tremendous spirit into the spiritless refugees.

The hour grew very late. Mandria began pacing nervously. 'All I know,' he said, 'I gave him a taxi and a driver this afternoon.'

'Relax, Mr Mandria,' David said. 'Ari may not be back for three days. He has strange ways of working. We are used to it.'

Midnight passed and the four men began to sprawl out and make themselves comfortable. In a half hour they began to doze, and in an hour they were all asleep.

At five o'clock in the morning Ari Ben Canaan entered the room. His eyes were bleary from a night of traveling around the island. He had slept only in brief naps since he had landed on Cyprus. He and Zev Gilboa hugged each other in the traditional Palmach manner, then he set right to work without offering excuse or apology for being eight hours late.

'Mr Mandria. Have you got us our boat yet?'

Mandria was aghast. He slapped his forehead in amazement. 'Mr Ben Canaan! You landed on Cyprus less than thirty hours ago and asked me for a boat. I am not a shipbuilder, sir. My company, Cyprus-Mediterranean Shipping, has offices in Famagusta, Larnaca, Kyrenia, Limassol, and Paphos. There are no other ports in Cyprus. All my offices are looking for a boat for you. If there is a boat on Cyprus you will know it, sir.'

Ari ignored Mandria's sarcasm and turned to the others.

'Zev, I suppose David has told you what we're going to do.'

The Galilee farmer nodded.

'From now on you three boys are working for me. Find replacements for your jobs at Caraolos. Joab, how many healthy children are there in that compound between the ages of ten and seventeen?'

'Oh ... probably around six or seven hundred.'

'Zev. Pick out three hundred of the strongest. Get them in the peak of physical condition.'

Zev nodded.

Ari arose. 'It will be light in another half hour. I'll need a taxi to start out again, Mr Mandria. I think that man I had yesterday is a little tired.'

'I will drive you around, myself,' Mandria said.

'Good. We'll leave just as soon as it turns light. Excuse me. I want to look over some papers in my room.'

He left as suddenly as he had entered. Everyone began talking at once.

'Then the escape is going to be made by three hundred children,' Zev said.

'It certainly appears so,' Mandria said. 'He is such a strange man. He expects miracles ... he doesn't tell anything.'

'On the contrary,' David said, 'he does not believe in miracles. That is why he works so hard. It seems to me that there is more to this than Ari is telling us.

I have a feeling that the escape of three hundred children is only part of what is in his mind.'

Joab Yarkoni smiled. 'We all have known Ari Ben Canaan long enough not to try to second guess him. We also have known him long enough to know that he knows his business. We will learn, in due time, just what Ari is up to.'

The next day Mandria drove Ari around Cyprus in what seemed to be an aimless chase. They drove from the sweeping Eastern Bay past Salamis and Famagusta clear to Cape Greco. In Famagusta he walked along the old wall and studied the harbor area. Ari barely spoke to Mandria the entire day, except to ask a pertinent question now and then. It seemed to the Cypriot that the big Palestinian was the coldest human being he had ever met. He felt a certain hostility, but he could not help admiring Ari for his absolute concentration and seemingly superhuman stamina. He must, Mandria thought, be a tremendously dedicated man – but that was puzzling because Ben Caanan seemed to show no traces of human emotion.

From Cape Greco they drove along the Southern Bay on the underbelly of Cyprus and then into the high jagged mountains where the resorts prepared for the winter season of skiing and ice sports. If Ben Canaan had found anything of interest he certainly was not showing it. Mandria was exhausted when they arrived back in Famagusta after midnight, but there was another meeting held with Zev, David, and Joab. Then Ari went into another all-night session of study.

On the morning of the fourth day after Ari Ben Canaan had swum ashore onto Cyprus, Mandria received a call from his Larnaca office to the effect that a ship had just come in from Turkey that fitted his specifications and could be purchased. Mandria drove Ari to Caraolos to pick up David and Joab, and the four of them drove off for Larnaca.

Zev Gilboa was left behind, as he was already at work selecting the three hundred children and setting up special training courses for them.

Mandria was feeling quite proud of himself as they drove along the Famagusta-Larnaca road. At a halfway point Ari was suddenly attracted by some activity taking place in a large field off to the left of the road. He asked Mandria to stop the car and stepped outside for a look. There was feverish building going on in what appeared to be a military barracks.

'The British are building new detention compounds,' David said; 'they've reached the saturation point at Caraolos.'

'Why wasn't I told about this?' Ari snapped.

'You didn't ask,' Joab Yarkoni answered.

'The best we can figure,' David said, 'is that they'll begin transferring the overload from Caraolos in two or three weeks.'

Ari returned to the car and they drove on. Joab Yarkoni, who declined to try to second guess his friend, could nevertheless see that Ari was definitely intrigued by the new compounds. Joab could almost hear the wheels grinding in Ari's brain.

The car entered the narrow bending streets of Larnaca and moved onto the waterfront road, lined with its neat two-storied white houses. They stopped before the Four Lanterns Tavern where the Turkish owner of the ship, a man named Armatau, awaited them. Ari insisted they forego the round of drinks, the fencing for price, and general bartering that was so much a part of the normal business transactions. He wanted to see the ship immediately.

Armatau led them over the street to the long pier that jutted more than a half mile into the water. As they walked past a dozen or more trawlers, launches, and sailboats Armatau kept up a constant stream of talk over his shoulder. He assured them that the ship they were about to inspect was, indeed, a queen of the sea. They came to a halt near the end of the pier before an ancient wooden-hulled salvage tug that bore the faded name on her bow: *Aphrodite*.

'Isn't she a beauty?' Armatau said, glowing. Then he held his breath apprehensively as four pairs of cold eyes surveyed the old scow from stem to stern. 'Of course,' the Turk continued, 'she is no racing cruiser.'

Ari's practiced eye estimated the *Aphrodite* at a hundred and fifty feet in length and displacing around two hundred tons. By her general build and appearance she was in the neighborhood of forty-five years of age.

'Now just who was Aphrodite?' Joab Yarkoni asked.

'Aphrodite was the goddess of Love. She was washed up in the surf just a few miles from here – five thousand years ago,' David answered.

'Well, this old girl has sure had her change of life,' Joab said.

The Turk swallowed and tried to smile at the jibes. Ben Canaan spun around and faced him. 'Armatau, I'm interested in one thing. It's two hundred miles to Palestine. She's got to make one run. Yes or no?'

Armatau threw up both arms. 'On my mother's honor,' he said, 'I have made three hundred runs between Cyprus and Turkey. Mr Mandria owns the shipping company. He knows.'

'It is true,' Mandria said. 'She is old but reliable.'

'Mr Armatau, take my two friends aboard and show them the engines.'

When the other three had gone below decks Mandria turned to Ari. 'Armatau may be a Turk but he can be trusted.'

'What kind of speed can we get out of this thing?' Ari asked.

'Probably five knots – with a gale in her back. The *Aphrodite* is in no hurry.'

They went on deck and looked over the topside. She was half rotted away and long past the time it would have paid to repair her. Yet, despite the obvious qualifications there was something very sound about her. A solid feeling that she knew the tricks of the sea and had won many battles against it.

In a half hour David and Joab completed their inspection.

'This ship is an absolute abortion,' David said, 'but I am positive she'll make it.'

'Can we get three hundred aboard?' Ari asked.

David rubbed his jaw. 'Well ... maybe, with a shoehorn.'

Ari turned to Mandria. 'We will have a lot of refitting to do. Of course it is necessary that we don't attract any attention.'

Mandria smiled. He was in his glory now. 'I have, as you may well know, very good connections. It is merely a matter of greasing the right palms and you can be sure that nothing can be seen, heard, or reported.'

'David. Send a radio message to Palestine tonight. Tell them we need a captain and a two-man crew.'

'Is a crew of three going to be enough?'

'I might as well tell you. You two boys and Zev are coming back to Palestine with me on this mud scow. We'll fill out the crew. Joab! You've always had a tendency toward mature women. Well, you've got one now. You're in charge of getting this thing refitted and stocked up.' At last he turned to Armatau, who was still bewildered by Ari's rapid fire questions and commands. 'O.K., Armatau, you can breathe easy, you've sold us this monstrosity – but not at your price. Let's go into the Four Lanterns and lock this up.'

Ari jumped off the deck onto the pier and gave Mandria a hand. 'David, you and Joab find your own way back to Famagusta. Mr Mandria is driving me to Kyrenia after we finish our business.'

'Kyrenia?' Mandria said, startled. 'Doesn't that man ever get tired? Kyrenia is on the other side of the island,' he protested.

'Is something wrong with your automobile?' Ari asked.

'No ... no ... we shall drive for Kyrenia.'

Ari started off down the pier with Mandria and the Turk.

'Ari!' David called, 'what shall we name the old woman?'

'You're the poet,' Ari called back. 'You name her.'

Joab and David watched the three men disappear at the end of the pier. Suddenly they broke out in smiles and threw their arms about each other. 'That son of a gun Ari! He picks a fine way to tell us we are going home.'

'You know Ari. The scorner of sentiment and emotion,' David said.

They sighed happily, and for a moment both thought about Palestine. Then they looked about the *Aphrodite*. She certainly was a sorry old girl.

They walked around the deck examining the ancient hulk. 'I've got a good name for her,' Joab said, 'why don't we call her the *Bevin*?'

'I've got a better name,' David Ben Ami said. 'From now on she will be known as the *Exodus*.'

Chapter Nine

Mark pulled the rented car off the road and parked it. He had driven high up in the mountains directly over Kyrenia. An enormous jagged rock several hundred feet high rose to a peak before them. On the peak were the ruins of St Hilarion Castle. It was a fairy castle, suggesting even in semicollapse the might and splendor of Gothic power.

Mark took Kitty's hand and led her over the field toward the peak, and they climbed the battlements until they stood on the lower wall and looked into the castle yards.

They picked their way through royal apartments and great halls and stables and the monastery and fortifications. It was deathly silent, but the grounds seemed to be alive and breathing, with ghosts of the past whispering of another day filled with love and hate and war and intrigue.

For almost an hour Mark and Kitty climbed slowly up the peak toward the summit. Then at last they stood on the very top, perspiring and breathless, dazzled at the breathtaking panorama below them. Below was a sheer cliff that fell nearly three thousand feet to Kyrenia. On the horizon they saw the coast line of Turkey, and to the left and right the lush green forests and terraced vineyards and houses hanging on cliff edges. Below, the olive orchards' leaves turned to a shimmering silver as zephyrs played through them.

Mark watched Kitty standing silhouetted against the sky as a cloud passed behind her. How very lovely she is, Mark thought. Kitty Fremont was the one woman in his world who was different. He had no desire to make love to her. Mark Parker honored little in the world. He wanted to honor Kitty. Moreover, she was the only woman he was absolutely comfortable with, for between them there was no pretense, no impression to make, no games to play.

They sat down on a huge boulder and continued to stare at the splendor all about them. The castle, the sea, the sky, the mountains.

'I think,' Mark said at last, 'this is the most beautiful vista in the world.'

She nodded.

They had been wonderful days for both of them. Kitty seemed renewed since Mark's arrival. She had enjoyed the wonderful therapy of confession.

'I am thinking something terrible,' Kitty said. 'I am thinking of how glad I am that Colonel Howard Hillings was sent off to Palestine and I have you all to myself. How long can you stay, Mark?'

'Few weeks. As long as you want me.'

'I never want us to become far away from each other again.'

'You know,' he said, 'everyone at the Dome is certain we're shacked up.'

'Good!' Kitty said. 'I'll put a sign on my door tonight in big red letters to read, "I love Mark Parker madly."'

They sat for another hour, then reluctantly began working their way down from the summit to descend before it turned dark.

After Mark and Kitty had returned to the hotel, Mandria drove his car into Kyrenia to the harbor and stopped on the quay. He stepped outside with Ari and they walked to the docks. Ari looked across the harbor to the tower of the Virgin Castle which stood on the sea's edge. They crossed over and climbed up inside the tower and from this vantage point could see the entire area perfectly. Ari studied in his usual silence.

The harbor had two sea walls. One ran out from the Virgin Castle and the tower where he now stood. Opposite him were the houses on the quay, and from that side the wall ran out to the sea so that the right and left arms of the sea wall formed a new circle, almost touching each other. There was a small break which was the entrance to the harbor. The inside of the harbor was tiny, not more than a few hundred yards in diameter. It was filled with small boats.

'Do you think we can get the *Aphrodite* inside the harbor here?' Ari asked.

'Getting it in won't be a problem,' Mandria answered, 'but turning it around and getting it out again will be.'

Ari was silent in thought as the two men walked back toward the car. His eye was on the little harbor. It was beginning to turn dark as they reached the car.

'You might as well drive on back to Famagusta by yourself. I have to see someone at the Dome Hotel,' Ari said, 'and I don't know how long it's going to take. I'll find my own way back to Famagusta.'

Mandria would have resented being dismissed like a taxi driver, but he was getting used to taking orders from Ben Canaan. He turned the ignition key and pressed the starter.

'Mandria. You have been a big help. Thanks.'

Mandria beamed as Ari walked away. These were the first words of kindness he had heard from Ben Canaan. He was surprised and touched.

The dining room of the Dome Hotel was filled with the strains of a Strauss waltz playing softly over the drone of British voices, the clink of glasses, and the whisper of the sea outside. Mark sipped his coffee, wiped his lips with his napkin, and then stared over Kitty's shoulder intently at the figure who had entered the doorway. A tall man was whispering into the ear of the head-waiter, and the waiter pointed to Mark's table. Mark's eyes widened as he recognized Ari Ben Canaan.

'Mark, you look as though you've seen a ghost,' Kitty said.

'I have and he's just about here. We are going to have a very interesting evening.'

Kitty turned around to see Ari Ben Canaan towering over their table. 'I see that you remember me, Parker,' he said, taking a seat without invitation and turning to Kitty. 'You must be Mrs Katherine Fremont.'

Ari's and Kitty's eyes met and held. Several awkward seconds of silence followed, then Ari looked around for a waiter and called him over. He ordered sandwiches.

'This is Ari Ben Canaan,' Mark was saying, 'he is a very old acquaintance of mine. I see that you seem to know Mrs Fremont.'

'Ari Ben Canaan,' Kitty said. 'What an odd name.'

'It is Hebrew, Mrs Fremont. It means "Lion, Son of Canaan."'

'That's quite confusing.'

'On the contrary, Hebrew is a very logical language.'

'Funny, it didn't strike me that way,' Kitty said, with an edge of sarcasm.

Mark looked from one to the other. They had only met, and yet they were already engaged in the verbal fencing and maneuvering he himself so often played. Obviously Ben Canaan had struck either a sweet or a sour chord in Kitty, Mark thought, because she had her claws bared.

'Strange that it wouldn't strike you as logical,' Ari was answering. 'God thought Hebrew was so logical He had the Bible written in that language.'

Kitty smiled and nodded. The orchestra changed to a fox trot. 'Dance, Mrs Fremont?'

Mark leaned back and watched Ben Canaan walk Kitty onto the floor, hold her, and lead her about with smooth gliding grace. For the moment Mark didn't like the spark that had obviously struck the second they met: it was hard to think of Kitty as a mere mortal playing mortals' games. They danced close to his table. There seemed to be a dazed look on Kitty's face and it was unnatural.

Then Mark began thinking of himself. He had had the feeling that something was brewing on Cyprus from the moment he landed. Now it was confirmed by Ben Canaan's appearance. He knew enough of the Palestinian to realize he was one of the top Mossad Aliyah Bet agents. He also knew that he was going to be approached for something, because Ben Canaan had sought him out. What about Kitty? Did he know of her only because she was with him or was there another reason?

Kitty was a tall girl but she felt lost in Ari Ben Canaan's arms. A strange sensation swept over her. The appearance of this strapping, handsome man had thrown her off guard. Now, in his arms only a moment after their meeting, she felt – unraveled. The sensation was attractive – it had been many, many years. But she felt rather foolish at the same time.

The music stopped and they returned to the table.

'I didn't think you Palestinians danced anything but a *hora*,' Mark said.

'I've been exposed to too much of your culture,' Ari answered.

His sandwiches arrived and he ate hungrily. Mark waited patiently for him to reveal the nature of his visit. He looked at Kitty carefully. She seemed to be regaining her composure, although she glanced at Ari from the corner of her eye as though she were wary and ready to strike.

At last Ari finished eating and said casually, 'I have something I want to talk over with both of you.'

'Here, in the middle of the British Army?'

Ari smiled. He turned to Kitty. 'Parker didn't have a chance to tell you, Mrs Fremont, that my employment is considered *sub rosa* in some quarters. Every so often the British even glorify us by calling us "underground." One of the first things I try to impress a new member of our organization with is the danger of making secret midnight rendezvous. I'd say there isn't a better place in the world to discuss this.'

'Let's move the party up to my room,' Mark said.

As soon as they had closed the door behind them Ari got right to the point. 'Parker, you and I are in a position to do each other a good turn.'

'Go on.'

'Are you familiar with the detention camps at Caraolos?'

Both Mark and Kitty nodded.

'I have just completed plans for three hundred children to make an escape. We are going to bring them over here and load them aboard a ship in the Kyrenia harbor.'

'You boys have been smuggling refugees into Palestine for years. That isn't news any more, Ben Canaan.'

'It will be news if you help make it news. You remember the commotion over our illegal ship, the *Promised Land*?'

'Sure.'

'The British looked pretty bad then. We feel that if we can create another incident as important as the *Promised Land* we stand a chance of breaking their immigration policy on Palestine.'

'You just lost me,' Mark said. 'If you can pull a mass escape from Caraolos how are you going to get them to Palestine? If they do escape then where is the story?'

'That's the point,' Ari said. 'They aren't going any farther than boarding ship in Kyrenia. I have no intention of making a run for Palestine.'

Mark leaned forward. He was interested, and there was obviously more to Ben Canaan's plan than first appeared.

'Let's say,' Ari said, 'that I get three hundred orphans out of Caraolos and on a ship in Kyrenia. Let's say the British find out and stop the ship from sailing. Now – let's say you have already written a story and it is sitting in Paris or New York. The minute those children board ship your story hits the headlines.'

Mark whistled under his breath. Like most American correspondents he had sympathy for the refugee's plight. Mark would get the story, Ben Canaan would get the propaganda value. Was the story going to be big enough for him to become involved? There was no way he could seek instructions or talk it over. He alone had to evaluate and make the decision. Ari had thrown him just enough to whet his appetite. To question the Palestinian further could open the door to involvement. Mark looked at Kitty. She seemed completely puzzled by the whole thing.

'How are you going to get three hundred children from Caraolos to Kyrenia?'

'Do I take that to understand you are coming in?'

'Take it to understand I want to know. It doesn't commit me to a thing. If I decide against it you have my word that anything said will not leave this room.'

'Good enough,' Ari said. He balanced himself on the edge of the dresser and explained his escape plan step by step. Mark frowned. It was daring, audacious, even fantastic. Yet – there was an admirable simplicity about it. For his part, Mark had to write a report and smuggle it out of Cyprus to the ANS Paris or London bureau. By some prearranged signal the report would be published at the exact moment the escape was taking place. Ari finished and Mark digested the plan for many moments.

He lit a cigarette, paced the room, and fired a dozen questions at Ari. Ari seemed to have considered all the angles. Yes, there was a possibility of a sensational series of stories. Now Mark tried to weigh the odds of Ari's wild scheme. There was no better than a fifty-fifty chance of success. Mark took into account the fact that Ari was an extremely clever man and he knew the British thinking on Cyprus. He also knew that Ari had the kind of people working with him who would be most likely to pull such a thing off.

'Count me in,' Mark said.

'Good,' Ari said, 'I thought you'd see the possibilities.' He turned to Kitty. 'Mrs Fremont, about a week ago you were offered a job working in the children's compound. Have you considered it?'

'I decided not to take it.'

'Would you reconsider it now ... say, to help Parker?'

'Just what do you have in mind for Kitty?' Mark asked.

'All of the teachers, nurses, and welfare people coming in from the outside are Jews,' Ari said, 'and we must go under the assumption they are suspect by the British.'

'Suspect of what?'

'Co-operation with the Mossad. You are a Christian, Mrs Fremont. We feel that someone of your background and religion could move about more freely.'

'In other words, you want to use Kitty as a courier.'

'More or less. We manufacture quite a few papers inside the camp that are needed outside.'

Mark said, 'I think I'd better tell you that I'm not too popular with the British. Sutherland's aide was sitting on my lap the minute I landed. I don't think this will affect me, but if Kitty goes to work at Caraolos it would be a cinch they'd suspect her of working with me.'

'On the contrary. They would be dead certain you would not send her to work at Caraolos.'

'Maybe you're right.'

'Of course I'm right,' Ari said. 'Let us assume that the worst happens. Let us say Mrs Fremont gets caught with forged papers. Absolutely nothing will happen to her except some embarrassment, an escort, and a free ticket away from Cyprus.'

'Just a moment,' Kitty said. 'I've listened to you two divide me up. I am very sorry that I had to hear any of what went on here tonight. I am not going to work at Caraolos, Mr Ben Canaan, and I am not getting mixed up in this scheme of yours.'

Ari looked quickly to Mark, who merely shrugged. 'She's a big girl.'

'I thought you were a friend of Parker's.'

'I am,' Kitty said, 'and I understand his interest.'

'I don't understand your lack of it, Mrs Fremont. This is the end of 1946. In a few months the war in Europe will have been over for two years. We have people behind barbed wire under the most terrible conditions. There are children in Caraolos who have no idea there is a world outside barbed wire. If we don't break this British policy they can well be behind barbed wire the rest of their lives.'

'That is just the point,' Kitty fired back; 'everything connected with Caraolos is neck deep in politics. I am certain that the British have their reasons. I don't wish to take sides.'

'Mrs Fremont. I was a captain in the British Army and I hold a Military Cross for valor. To coin an old cliché – some of my best friends are British. The fact is that we have dozens of British officers and soldiers who can't stomach what is happening in Palestine and who work with us twenty-four hours a day. This is not a case of politics but of humanity.'

'I doubt your sincerity. Why would you risk the lives of three hundred children?'

'Most human beings have a purpose for living,' Ari said; 'there is no purpose in Caraolos. Fighting for your freedom is a purpose. We have a quarter of a million people in Europe who want to get into Palestine. Any one of them would board that ship in Kyrenia if given the choice.'

'You are a very clever man, Mr Ben Canaan. I cannot argue with you. I don't have your stock list of answers.'

'I thought you were a nurse,' he said sarcastically.

'The world is filled with suffering. I can give my services a thousand places just as needful as Caraolos, without the strings attached.'

'Why don't you visit Caraolos and tell me that afterwards?'

'You're not going to trick me and you're not going to issue me challenges. I worked the night shift in a Cook County hospital, and more nights than not I've blotted up bodies off the receiving-room floor. You can't show me anything at Caraolos that I haven't seen before.'

The room became quiet. Ari Ben Canaan blew a long breath and threw up his hands in defeat. 'I am sorry,' he said. 'I'll be in touch with you in a few days, Parker.' He turned for the door.

'Mr Ben Canaan,' Kitty said, 'are you quite certain that I won't go telling this story to our mutual friends?'

Ari walked back and looked down into her eyes. She knew that instant she had said the wrong thing. A cruel little smile crossed his face. 'I think you are just trying to be a woman and have the last word. I don't misjudge people very often. I can't afford to. I like Americans. Americans have consciences. As soon as yours begins to get the best of you, you can reach me at Mr Mandria's and I'll be glad to show you around Caraolos.'

'You are quite sure of yourself, aren't you?'

'Let us say,' Ari answered, 'that right this minute I am surer of myself than you are.' Ari walked from the room.

It took a long time after Ari left for the impact of this visit to subside.

Kitty kicked off her shoes, at last, and sat back on the bed. 'Well! You did say we were in for an interesting evening.'

'I think you made a wise choice by staying out of this thing.'

'And you?'

'It's a day's work. It could turn into something very big.'

'Suppose you had refused him?'

'Oh, they'd get another correspondent somewhere in Europe to come over to Cyprus. They are very resourceful people. I just happened to be conveniently here.'

'Mark,' Kitty said thoughtfully, 'did I make a fool of myself?'

'I don't suppose you made yourself any more foolish than a hundred other women have.' Mark said it deliberately to let Kitty know she had been obvious about her attraction to Ari.

'He is a gorgeous man. When did you meet him?'

'The first time was in Berlin in the early part of 1939. That was my first ANS post. He had been sent over by Mossad Aliyah Bet to get as many Jews out of Germany as he could before the war started. He was in his early twenties then. I saw him again in Palestine. He was in the British Army . . . this was during the war. There was some kind of undercover assignment. I don't know exactly what it was. Since the war he has been heard of showing up all over Europe, buying arms, smuggling refugees into Palestine.'

'Do you really think he can get away with this utterly fantastic plan of his?'

'He's a clever man.'

'Well . . . I'll say one thing. This Ben Canaan doesn't act like any Jew I've ever met. You know what I mean. You don't particularly think of them in a capacity like his . . . or fighters . . . things of that sort.'

'How do you think of them, Kitty? The good old Indiana version. The little Jew boy named Maury who's going to marry a little Jew girl named Sadie . . .'

'Oh, stop it, Mark! I've worked with enough Jewish doctors to know they are arrogant and aggressive people. They look down on us.'

'With what? An inferiority complex?'

'I'd buy that if you were talking about Germany.'

'What are you trying to say, Kitty – that we're pure?'

'I'm saying no American Jew would trade places with a Negro or a Mexican or an Indian for that matter.'

'And I'm saying you don't have to lynch a man to rip his insides out. Oh sure, the American Jews have it good, but just enough of your thinking and enough of two thousand years of being a scapegoat has rubbed off on them. Why don't you argue it with Ben Canaan? He seems to know how to handle you.'

Kitty shot off the bed angrily. Then both she and Mark began to laugh. They were Mark and Kitty and they could not really be angry.

'Exactly what is this Mossad Aliyah Bet?'

'The word *aliyah* means to arise, go up, ascend. When a Jew goes to Palestine it is always referred to as an *aliyah* . . . always going higher than he was. *Aleph* or the letter *a* was used to designate the legal immigration. *Bet* or the letter *b* for the illegal. Therefore Mossad Aliyah Bet means Organization for Illegal Immigration.'

Kitty smiled. 'My goodness,' she said, 'Hebrew is such a logical language.'

For the next two days after Ari Ben Canaan's visit Kitty was perturbed and restless. She would not admit to herself that she wanted to see the big Palestinian again. Mark knew Kitty well and sensed her irritation, but he pretended to carry on as though Ben Canaan had never entered the scene.

She did not exactly know what was disturbing her, except that Ben Canaan's visit had left a strong impression. Was it that American conscience that Ben Canaan knew so well, or was she sorry about her anti-Jewish outburst?

Almost but not quite casually Kitty inquired when Mark expected to see Ari. Another time she made an unsubtle suggestion that it would be nice to go sight-seeing in Famagusta. Then again she would grow angry with herself and resolve to wipe out any thought of Ari.

On the third night Mark could hear Kitty's footsteps through the connecting door as she paced back and forth in her room.

She sat in the darkness in an overstuffed chair and puffed on a cigarette and decided that she would reason out the whole matter.

She did not like being drawn against her will into Ben Canaan's strange world. Her entire approach to life had been sane, even calculating. 'Kitty is such a sensible girl,' they always said of her.

When she fell in love with Tom Fremont and set out to win him it had all been a well-thought-out move. She ran a sensible home and served sensible meals on a sensible budget. She planned to give birth to Sandra in the springtime and that had been sensible too. She stifled spur-of-the-moment impulses in favor of planned decisions.

These past two days seemed to make no sense to her at all. A strange man appeared from nowhere and told her an even stranger story. She saw that hard handsome face of Ari Ben Canaan with his penetrating eyes that seemed to read her mind mockingly. She remembered the sensation in his arms, dancing with him.

There was no logic to this at all. For one thing Kitty always felt uncomfortable around Jewish people; she had admitted as much to Mark. Then why did this thing continue to grow?

Finally she knew that she would continue to be disturbed until she saw Ari again and saw the camp at Caraolos. She decided that the way to beat this whole idea was to see him again and assure herself she was not mystically involved but had merely been jolted by a sudden and brief infatuation. She would beat Ari Ben Canaan at his own game on his own ground.

At breakfast the next morning Mark was not surprised when Kitty asked him to make an appointment with Ben Canaan for her to visit Caraolos.

'Honey, I was happy with the decision you made the other night. I wish you'd stick to it.'

'I don't quite understand this myself,' she said.

'Ben Canaan called the shot. He knew you'd come around. Don't be a damned fool. If you go to Caraolos, you're in. Look ... I'll pull out, myself. We'll leave Cyprus right away ...'

Kitty shook her head.

'You're letting your curiosity throw you. You've always been smart. What's happening?'

'This sounds funny coming from me, doesn't it, Mark, but it almost feels as if some force were pushing me. Believe me, I'm going to Caraolos to end all this ... and not to start something.'

Mark told himself that she was hooked even though she was pretending she wasn't. He hoped that whatever lay ahead would treat her kindly.

Chapter Ten

Kitty handed her passes to the British sentry at the gate and entered Caraolos at Compound 57, which was closest to the children's compound.

'Are you Mrs Fremont?'

She turned, nodded, and looked into the face of a young man who smiled and offered his hand. She thought that he was certainly a much friendlier-appearing person than his compatriot.

'I am David Ben Ami,' he said. 'Ari asked me to meet you. He will be along in a few moments.'

'Now what does Ben Ami mean? I've taken a recent interest in Hebrew names.'

'It means Son of My People,' he answered. 'We hope that you will help us in "Operation Gideon."'

'Operation Gideon?'

'Yes, that's what I call Ari's plan. Do you remember your Bible, Judges? Gideon had to select a group of soldiers to go against the Midianites. He picked three hundred. We have also picked three hundred to go against the British. I guess I may be stretching a point for the parallel and Ari does accuse me of being too sentimental.'

Kitty had braced herself for a difficult evening. Now she was disarmed by this mild-appearing young man. The day was closing and a cool breeze whipped up a swirl of dust. Kitty slipped into her topcoat. On the other side of the compound she could make out the unmistakable towering figure of Ari Ben Canaan crossing over to meet her. She drew a deep breath and steadied herself to fight off the same electric sensation she had felt the first time she saw him.

He stopped before her and they nodded silently. Kitty's eyes were cold. She was letting him know, without a word, that she had come to accept a challenge and she had no intention of losing.

Compound 57 consisted mostly of the aged and very religious. They passed slowly between two rows of tents filled with dirty and unkempt people. The water shortage, Ben Ami explained, made bathing virtually impossible. There was also insufficient diet. The inmates appeared weak, some angry, some dazed, and all haunted by ghosts of the dead.

They stopped for a moment at an opened tent where a wrinkled old specimen worked on a wood carving. He held it up for her to see. It was a pair of hands, clasped in prayer and bound by barbed wire. Ari watched her closely for a sign of weakening.

It was squalid, filthy, and wretched here, but Kitty had prepared herself to accept even worse. She was beginning to be convinced that Ari Ben Canaan held no mysterious power over her.

They stopped once more to look into a large tent used as a synagogue. Over the entrance was a crudely made symbol of the Menorah, the ritual candelabra. She stared at the strange sight of old men swaying back and forth and reciting weird prayers. To Kitty it seemed another world. Her gaze became fixed on one particularly dirty, bearded old individual who wept and cried aloud in anguish.

She felt David's hand lead her away. 'He is just an old man,' David said. 'He is telling God that he has lived a life of faith ... he has kept God's laws, cherished the Holy Torah, and kept the covenants in face of unbelievable hardships. He asks God to kindly deliver him for being a good man.'

'The old men in there,' Ari said, 'don't quite realize that the only Messiah that will deliver them is a bayonet on the end of a rifle.'

Kitty looked at Ari. There was something deadly about this man.

Ari felt Kitty's disdain. His hands grabbed her arms. 'Do you know what a *Sonderkommando* is?'

'Ari, please...' David said.

'A *Sonderkommando* is one who was forced by the Germans to work inside of their crematoriums. I'd like to show you another old man here. He took the bones of his grandchildren out of a crematorium in Buchenwald and carted them off in a wheelbarrow. Tell me, Mrs Fremont, did you see one better than that at the Cook County Hospital?'

Kitty felt her stomach turn over. Then resentment took over and she fired back, eyes watering with anger. 'You'll stop at nothing.'

'I'll stop at nothing to show you how desperate we are.'

They glared at each other wordlessly. 'Do you wish to see the children's compound or not?' he said at last.

'Let's get it over with,' Kitty answered.

The three crossed the bridge over the barbed-wire wall into the children's compound and looked upon war's merciless harvest. She went through the hospital building past the long row of tuberculars and into the other wards of bones bent with rickets and skins yellow of jaundice and festering sores of poisoned blood. She went through a locked ward filled with youngsters who had the hollow blank stares of the insane.

They walked along the tents of the graduation class of 1940–45. The matriculants of the ghettos, the concentration camp students, scholars of rubble. Motherless, fatherless, homeless. Shaved heads of the deloused, ragged clothing. Terror-filled faces, bed wetters, night shriekers. Howling infants, and scowling juveniles who had stayed alive only through cunning.

They finished the inspection.

'You have an excellent staff of medical people,' Kitty said, 'and this children's compound is getting the best of the supplies.'

'The British have given us none of it,' Ari snapped. 'It has come as gifts from our own people.'

'You made the point right there,' Kitty said. 'I don't care if your facilities are manna from heaven. I came at the request of my American conscience. It has been satisfied. I'd like to go.'

'Mrs Fremont...' David Ben Ami said.

'David! Don't argue. Some people find just the sight of us repulsive. Show Mrs Fremont out.'

David and Kitty walked along a tent street. She turned slightly and saw Ari staring at her back. She wanted to get out as quickly as possible. She wanted to return to Mark and forget the whole wretched business.

A sound of uninhibited laughter burst from a large tent near her. It was the laughter of happy children and it sounded out of place at Caraolos. Kitty stopped in curiosity before the tent and listened. A girl was reading a story. She had a beautiful voice.

'That is an exceptional girl,' David said. 'She does fantastic work with these children.'

Again laughter erupted from the children.

Kitty stepped to the tent flap and drew it open. The girl had her back to Kitty. She sat on a wooden box, bent close to a kerosene lamp. Circling her sat twenty wide-eyed children. They looked up as Kitty and David entered.

The girl stopped reading and turned around and arose to greet the newcomers. The lamp flickered from a gust of air that swept in from the open flap and cast a dancing shadow of children's silhouettes.

Kitty and the girl stood face to face. Kitty's eyes opened wide, registering shock.

She walked out of the tent quickly, then stopped and turned and stared through the flap at the astonished girl. Several times she started to speak and lapsed into bewildered silence.

'I want to see that girl ... alone,' she finally said in a hushed voice.

Ari had come up to them. He nodded to David. 'Bring the child to the school building. We will wait there.'

Ari lit the lantern in the schoolroom and closed the door behind them. Kitty had remained wordless and her face was pale.

'That girl reminds you of someone,' Ari said abruptly. She did not answer. He looked through the window and saw the shadows of David and the girl crossing the compound. He glanced at Kitty again and walked from the room.

As he left, Kitty shook her head. It was mad. Why did she come? *Why did she come?* She fought to get herself under command – to brace herself to look at that girl again.

The door opened and Kitty tensed. The girl stepped slowly into the room. She studied the girl's face, fighting off the urge to clutch the child in her arms.

The girl looked at her curiously, but she seemed to understand something and her gaze conveyed pity.

'My name ... is Katherine Fremont,' Kitty said unevenly. 'Do you speak English?'

'Yes.'

What a lovely child she was! Her eyes sparkled and she smiled now and held out her hand to Kitty.

Kitty touched the girl's cheek – then she dropped her hand.

'I ... I am a nurse. I wanted to meet you. What is your name?'

'My name is Karen,' the girl said, 'Karen Hansen Clement.'

Kitty sat on the cot and asked the girl to sit down, too.

'How old are you?'

'I'm sixteen now, Mrs Fremont.'

'Please call me Kitty.'

'All right, Kitty.'

'I hear that ... you work with the children.'

The girl nodded.

'That's wonderful. You see ... I ... I may be coming to work here and ... and, well ... I'd like to know all about you. Would you mind telling me?'

Karen smiled. Already she liked Kitty and she knew instinctively that Kitty wanted – needed – to be liked.

'Originally,' Karen said, 'I came from Germany . . . Cologne, Germany. But that was a long time ago . . .'

Chapter Eleven

COLOGNE, GERMANY, 1938

Life is quite wonderful if you are a young lady of seven and your daddy is the famous Professor Johann Clement and it is carnival time in Cologne. Many things are extra special around carnival time, but something that is always extra special is taking a walk with Daddy. You can walk under the linden trees along the banks of the Rhine or you can walk through the zoo that has the most magnificent monkey cages in the entire world or you can walk past the big cathedral and stare up at those twin towers over five hundred feet high that seem to push right through the sky. Best of all is walking through the municipal forest very early in the morning with Daddy and Maximilian. Maximilian is the most remarkable dog in Cologne, even though he looks kind of funny. Of course, Maximilian isn't allowed in the zoo.

Sometimes you take Hans along on your walks, too, but little brothers can be a nuisance.

If you are such a little girl you love your mommy, too, and wish she would come along with you and Daddy and Hans and Maximilian, but she is pregnant again and feeling rather grumpy these days. It would be nice if the new baby is a sister because one brother is just about as much as a girl can bear.

On Sunday everyone, except poor Maximilian, who has to watch the house, gets into the auto and Daddy drives along the Rhine River to Grandma's house in Bonn. Many of the aunts and uncles and bratty cousins gather every Sunday and Grandma has baked a hundred cookies, or maybe even more.

Soon, when summer comes, there will be a wonderful trip along the coast up north and through the Black Forest or to Brenner's Park Hotel at the springs at Baden-Baden. What a funny name – Baden-Baden.

Professor Johann Clement is a terribly important man. Everyone at the university doffs his cap and smiles and bows and says, 'Good morning, Herr Doctor.' At night there are other professors and their wives and sometimes fifteen or twenty students pack into Daddy's study. They sing and argue and drink beer all night along. Before Mommy's stomach started showing she used to like to joke and dance with them.

There are so many wonderful tastes and smells and feelings and sounds for a happy seven-year-old girl.

The best times of all were those nights when there would be no visitors and Daddy didn't have to work in his study or give a lecture. The whole family would sit before the fireplace. It was wonderful to sit on Daddy's lap and watch the flames and smell his pipe and hear his soft deep voice as he read a fairy tale.

In those years of 1937 and 1938 many strange things were happening you could not quite understand. People seem frightened of something and spoke in whispers ... especially at a place like the university. But ... these things seem quite unimportant when it comes carnival time.

Professor Johann Clement had very much to think about. With so much utter insanity all about, a man had to keep a clear head. Clement reckoned a scientist could actually chart the course of human events as one would chart the tides and waves of the sea. There were waves of emotion and hate and waves of complete unreason. They'd reach a peak and fall to nothingness. All mankind lived in this sea except for a few who perched on islands so high and dry they remained always out of the reach of the mainstream of life. A university, Johann Clement reasoned, was such an island, such a sanctuary.

Once, during the Middle Ages, there had been a wave of hatred and ignorance as the Crusaders killed off Jews. But the day had passed when Jews were blamed for the Black Death and for poisoning the wells of Christians. During the enlightenment that followed the French Revolution the Christians themselves had torn down the gates of the ghettos. In this new era the Jews and the greatness of Germany had been inseparable. Jews subordinated their own problems to the greater problems of mankind; they assimilated to the larger society. And what great men came from this! Heine and Rothschild and Karl Marx and Mendelssohn and Freud. The list was endless. These men, like Johann Clement himself, were Germans first, last, and always.

Anti-Semitism was synonymous with the history of man, Johann Clement reasoned. It was a part of living – almost a scientific truth. Only the degree and the content varied. Certainly, he felt, he was far better off than the Jews of eastern Europe or those in semibarbaric condition in Africa. The 'humiliation oaths' and the Frankfurt massacre belonged to another age.

Germany might be riding a new wave but he was not going to turn around and run. Nor would he stop believing that the German people, with their great cultural heritage, would ultimately dispose of the abnormal elements which had temporarily got control of the country.

Johann Clement watched the blows fall. First there had been wild talk and then printed accusations and insinuations. Then came a boycott of Jewish business and professional people, then the public humiliations: beatings and beard pullings. Then came the night terror of the Brown Shirts. Then came the concentration camps.

Gestapo, SS, SD, KRIPO, RSHA. Soon every family in Germany was under Nazi scrutiny, and the grip of tyranny tightened until the last croak of defiance strangled and died.

Still Professor Johann Clement, like most of the Jews in Germany, continued to believe he was immune to the new menace. His grandfather had established a tradition at the university. It was Johann Clement's island and his sanctuary. He identified himself completely as a German.

There was one particular Sunday that you would never forget. Everyone had assembled at Grandma's house in Bonn. Even Uncle Ingo had come all the way from Berlin. All of the children were sent outside to play and the door to the living room had been locked.

On the way home to Cologne neither Mommy nor Daddy spoke a single word. Grownups act like children sometimes. As soon as you reached home you and your brother Hans were bundled right off to bed. But more and more of these secret talks had been taking place, and if you stood by the door and opened it just a crack you could hear everything. Mommy was terribly upset. Daddy was as calm as ever.

'Johann, darling, we must think about making a move. This time it is not going to pass us by. It's getting so I'm afraid to go out into the street with the children.'

'Perhaps it is only your pregnancy that makes you think things are worse.'

'For five years you have been saying it is going to get better. It is not going to get better.'

'As long as we stay at the university ... we are safe.'

'For God's sake, Johann. Stop living in a fool's paradise! We have no friends left. The students never come any more. Everyone we know is too terrified to speak to us.'

Johann Clement lit his pipe and sighed. Miriam cuddled at his feet and lay her head on his lap and he stroked her hair. Nearby, Maximilian stretched and groaned before the fire.

'I want so much to be as brave and as understanding as you are,' Miriam said.

'My father and my grandfather taught here. I was born in this house. My life, the only things I've ever wanted, the only things I've ever loved are in these rooms. My only ambition is that Hans will come to love it so after me. Sometimes I wonder if I have been fair to you and the children ... but something inside of me will not let me run. Just a little longer, Miriam ... it will pass ... it will pass ...'

NOVEMBER 19, 1938

200 synagogues gutted!
200 Jewish apartment houses torn apart!
8000 Jewish shops looted and smashed!
50 Jews murdered!
3000 Jews seriously beaten!
20,000 Jews arrested!

FROM THIS DAY ON NO JEW MAY BELONG TO A CRAFT OR TRADE!

FROM THIS DAY ON NO JEWISH CHILD MAY ENTER A PUBLIC SCHOOL!

FROM THIS DAY ON NO JEWISH CHILD MAY ENTER A PUBLIC PARK OR RECREATION GROUND!

A SPECIAL FINE OF ONE HUNDRED AND FIFTY MILLION DOLLARS IS HEREBY LEVIED ON ALL THE JEWS OF GERMANY!

FROM THIS DAY ON ALL JEWS MUST WEAR A YELLOW ARM BAND WITH THE STAR OF DAVID!

It was hard to believe that things could get worse. But the tide ran higher and higher, and the waves finally crashed onto Johann Clement's island when one day little Karen ran into the house, her face covered with blood and the words, 'Jew! Jew! Jew!' ringing in her ears.

When a man has roots so deep and faith so strong the destruction of his faith is an awesome catastrophe. Not only had Johann Clement been a fool, but he had endangered the life of his family as well. He searched for some way out, and his path led to the Gestapo in Berlin. When he returned from Berlin, he locked himself in his study for two days and two nights, remaining there hunched over his desk, staring at the document that lay before him. It was a magic paper the Gestapo had presented him with. His signature on the paper would free him and his family from any further harm. It was a life-giving document. He read it over and over again until he knew every word on its pages.

... I, Johann Clement, after the above detailed search and the undeniable facts contained herein, am of the absolute conviction that the facts concerning my birth have been falsified. I am not now or never have been of the Jewish religion I am an Aryan and ...

Sign it! Sign it! A thousand times he picked up the pen to write his name on the paper. This was no time for noble stands! He had never been a Jew ... Why not sign? ... it made no difference. Why not sign?

The Gestapo made it absolutely clear that Johann Clement had but one alternative. If he did not sign the paper and continue his work in research his family could leave Germany only if he remained as a political hostage.

On the third morning he walked from the study, haggard, and looked into Miriam's anxious eyes. He went to the fireplace and threw the document into the flames. 'I cannot do it,' he whispered. 'You must plan to leave Germany with the children immediately.'

A terrible fear overtook him now for every moment that his family remained. Every knock on the door, every ring of the phone, every footstep brought a new terror he had never known.

He made his plans. First, the family would go to live with some colleagues in France. Miriam was nearly due and she could not travel far. After the baby came and her strength had returned they would continue on to England or America.

It was not all hopeless. Once the family was safe he could worry about himself. There were a few secret societies working in Germany which specialized in smuggling out German scientists. He had been tipped off to one working in Berlin – a group of Palestinian Jews who called themselves Mossad Aliyah Bet.

The trunks were all packed, the house closed down. The man and his wife sat that last night in silence, desperately hoping for some sudden miracle to give them a reprieve.

But that night – the day before departure – Miriam Clement began having her labor pains. She was not permitted into a hospital so she gave birth in her own bedroom. Another son was born. It had been a difficult and complicated delivery and she needed several weeks to convalesce.

Panic seized Johann Clement! He had visions of his family being trapped and never able to escape the approaching holocaust.

He frantically rushed to Berlin to Number 10 Meinekestrasse, the building which housed the Mossad Aliyah Bet. The place was a bedlam of people trying desperately to get out of Germany.

At two o'clock in the morning he was led into an office where a very young and very exhausted man met him. The man was named Ari Ben Canaan and he was a Palestinian in charge of the escape of the German Jews.

Ben Canaan looked at him through bloodshot eyes. He sighed. 'We will arrange your escape, Dr Clement. Go home, you will be contacted. I have to get a passport, a visa ... I have to pay the right people off. It will take a few days.'

'It is not for me. I cannot go, nor can my wife. I have three children. You must get them out.'

'I must get them out,' Ben Canaan mimicked. 'Doctor, you are an important man. I may be able to help you. I cannot help your children.'

'You must! You must!' he shrieked.

Ari Ben Canaan slammed his fist on his desk and jumped up. 'Did you see that mob out there! They all want to get out of Germany!' He leaned over the desk an inch from Johann Clement. 'For five years we have pleaded, we have begged you to leave Germany. Now even if you can get out the British won't let you into Palestine. "We are Germans . . . we are Germans . . . they won't hurt us," you said. What in God's name can I do!'

Ari swallowed and slumped down into his chair. His eyes closed a moment, his face masked in weariness. He picked up a sheaf of papers from his desk and thumbed through them. 'I have obtained visas for four hundred children to leave Germany. Some families in Denmark have agreed to take them. We have a train organized. I will put one of your children on.'

'I . . . I . . . have three children . . .'

'And I have ten thousand children. I have no visas. I have nothing to fight the British Navy with. I suggest you send your oldest who will be better able to take care of itself. The train leaves tomorrow night from Berlin from the Potsdam Station.'

Karen clung drowsily to her favorite rag doll. Daddy knelt before her. In her half sleep she could smell that wonderful smell of his pipe.

'It is going to be a wonderful trip, Karen. Just like going to Baden-Baden.'

'But I don't want to, Daddy.'

'Well, now . . . look at all these nice boys and girls going along with you.'

'But I don't want them. I want you and Mommy and Hans and Maximilian. And I want to see my new baby brother.'

'See here, Karen Clement. My girl doesn't cry.'

'I won't . . . I promise I won't . . . Daddy . . . Daddy . . . will I see you soon?'

'We'll . . . all try very hard . . .'

A woman stepped behind Johann Clement and tapped him on the shoulder. 'I am sorry,' she said. 'It is time for departure.'

'I'll take her on.'

'No . . . I am sorry. No parents on the train.'

He nodded and hugged Karen quickly and stood back biting his pipe so hard his teeth hurt. Karen took the woman's hand, then stopped and turned around. She handed her father her rag doll. 'Daddy . . . you take my dolly. She'll look after you.'

Scores of anguished parents pressed close to the sides of the train, and the departing children pressed against the windows, shouting, blowing kisses, waving, straining desperately for a last glimpse.

He looked but could not see her.

The steel train grumbled into motion. The parents ran alongside, screaming final farewells.

Johann Clement stood motionless on the fringe of the crowd. As the last car passed he looked up and saw Karen standing calmly on the rear platform. She put her hand to her lips and blew him a kiss as though she knew she would never see him again.

He watched her tiny figure grow smaller and smaller and smaller. And then she was gone. He looked at the little rag doll in his hand. 'Good by, my life,' he whispered.

Chapter Twelve

Aage and Meta Hansen had a lovely home in the suburbs of Aalborg; it was just right for a little girl, for they had no children of their own. The Hansens were quite a bit older than the Clements; Aage was graying and Meta was nowhere as beautiful as Miriam but none the less Karen felt warm and protected from the moment they carried her drowsy little body into their car.

The train ride into Denmark had been bewildering. All she could remember was the stifled sobs of children all around her. The rest was a blur – standing in lines, being tagged, strange faces, strange language. Then waiting rooms, buses, more tags.

At last she was led alone into the room where Meta and Aage Hansen stood waiting anxiously. Aage knelt down and lifted her and carried her to the car, and Meta held her in her lap and fussed and petted her all the way to Aalborg, and Karen knew she was safe.

Aage and Meta stood back expectantly in the doorway as Karen tiptoed cautiously into the room they had prepared for her. It was filled with dolls and toys and books and dresses and records and just about everything one little girl could ever want. Then Karen saw the floppy little puppy on her bed. She knelt beside him and stroked him and he licked her face and she felt a wet nose against her cheek. She turned and smiled at the Hansens and they smiled back.

Those first few nights without her daddy and mommy were awful. It was surprising how much she missed her brother Hans. She nibbled at her food and just sat alone quietly in her room with the little dog she had named Maximilian. Meta Hansen understood. At night she lay beside Karen and held her and soothed her until her soft little sobs subsided into sleep.

During the next week a steady stream of visitors came with presents and made a great fuss over Karen and babbled in a language she still could not understand. The Hansens were very proud and she did her best to be nice to everyone. In a few more days she ventured out of the house.

Karen was terribly fond of Aage Hansen. He smoked a pipe like her daddy and he liked to take walks. Aalborg was an interesting place. Like Cologne, it had a river, called the Limfjorden. Mr Hansen was a lawyer and very important and almost everyone seemed to know him. Of course, he wasn't as important as her daddy ... but few people were.

'Well now, Karen. You have been with us for nearly three weeks,' Aage said one night, 'and we would like to have a very important talk with you.'

He clasped his hands behind him and paced back and forth and talked to her in a very wonderful way so that she understood. He told her that there was much unhappiness in Germany and her mommy and daddy thought it would be better if she remained with them for the time being. Aage Hansen went on to say that they knew they could never replace her own parents but because God had not let them have children of their own they were very happy to have her and wanted her to be happy too.

Yes, Karen understood it all and told Aage and Meta she didn't mind staying with them for the time being.

'And Karen, darling. Because we are borrowing you for a little while and because we love you so much, we wonder ... would you mind borrowing our name?'

Karen thought about that. It seemed to her that Aage had other reasons. His question had that grown-up sound ... like the sound of her mommy and daddy talking behind closed doors. She nodded and said that it would be fine with her too.

'Good! Karen Hansen it is, then.'

They took her hands as they did every night and led her to her room and put on the low lamp. Aage played with her and tickled her, and Maximilian got mixed up in the fracas. She laughed until she couldn't stand any more. Then she got under the covers and said her prayers.

'... God bless Mommy and Daddy and Hans and my new baby brother and all my aunts and uncles and cousins ... and God bless the Hansens who are so nice ... and God bless both Maximilians.'

'I will be back in a few minutes to sit with you,' Meta said.

'That's all right. You don't have to stay with me any more. Maximilian will take care of me.'

'Good night, Karen.'

'Aage?'

'Yes?'

'Do the Danish people hate the Jews too?'

My dear Dr and Mrs Clement,

Has it already been six weeks since Karen came to us? What an exceptional child she is. Her teacher tells us she is doing extremely well in school. It is amazing how quickly she is picking up Danish. I suppose that is because she is with children of her own age. She has already gathered a large number of girl friends.

The dentist advised us to have one tooth pulled to make room for another. It was a small matter. We want to start her on some sort of music lessons soon and will write more about that.

Every night in her prayers ...

And there was a letter from Karen in big block print:

DEAR MOMMY, DADDY, HANS, MAXIMILIAN, AND MY NEW BABY BROTHER: I MISS YOU MORE THAN I CAN TELL YOU ...

Wintertime is a time for ice skating on the frozen banks of the Limfjorden and for building snow castles and for sledding and for sitting before a blazing fire and having Aage rub your icy feet.

But winter passed and the Limfjorden flowed again and the countryside burst into wild bloom. And summertime came and they all went away to the beach at Blokhus on the North Sea and she and Meta and Aage took a sailboat a hundred miles out.

Life was full and rich with the Hansens. She had a flock of 'best' girl friends, and she loved to shop with Meta at the smelly fish market or stand beside her in the kitchen learning to bake. And Meta was so good in so many things like sewing or with studies, and she was a wonderful comfort at Karen's bedside if there was a sudden fever or sore throat.

Aage always had a smile and open arms and seemed nearly as wise and gentle as her own daddy. Aage could be mighty stern, too, when the occasion demanded.

One day, Aage told Meta to come into the office when Karen was at her dancing lesson. He was pale and excited.

'I have just heard from the Red Cross,' he said to his wife. 'They have all disappeared. Completely, no trace. The entire family. I cannot get any information from Germany. I've tried everything ...'

'What do you think, Aage?'

'What is there to think? They've all been put into a concentration camp ... or worse.'

'Oh, dear God.'

They could not bring themselves to tell Karen that her entire family had disappeared. Karen was suspicious when the letters stopped coming from Germany, but she was too frightened to ask questions. She loved the Hansens and trusted them implicitly. Instinct told her that if they did not mention her family there was a reason for it.

Then, too, a strange thing was happening. Karen missed her family a great deal, but somehow the images of her mother and father seemed to grow dimmer and dimmer. When a child of eight has been removed from her parents for such a long time, it gets harder and harder to remember. Karen felt bad sometimes that she could not remember more vividly.

At the end of a year she could hardly remember when she was not Karen Hansen and a Dane.

CHRISTMAS 1939

There was a war in Europe and a year had passed since Karen arrived at the Hansen house. Her bell-like voice carried a sweet hymn as Meta played the piano. After the hymns Karen went to the closet in her room where she had hidden the Christmas present she had made at school. She handed them the package proudly. It bore a label printed in her hand that read: TO MOMMY AND DADDY FROM YOUR DAUGHTER, KAREN.

APRIL 8, 1940

The night was filled with treachery. A misty dawn brought the chilling sound of marching boots to the frontiers of Denmark. Dawn brought barge after barge of gray-helmeted soldiers creeping through fog-filled inlets and canals. The German Army moved in silently with robot-like efficiency and dispersed over the length and breadth of Denmark.

April 9, 1940!

Karen and her classmates rushed to the window and looked up at a sky black with thundering airplanes, which one by one descended on the Aalborg airdrome.

April 9, 1940!

People rushed into the streets in confusion.

'This is the Danish State Radio. Today at 4:15 the German Army crossed our frontier at Saed and Krussa!'

Completely shocked by the lightning stroke and its masterful execution, the Danes clung desperately to their radios to await word from King Christian.

Then the proclamation came. Denmark capitulated without firing a shot in her own defense. The crushing of Poland had taught them that resistance was futile.

Meta Hansen pulled Karen out of school and packed to flee to Bornholm or some other remote island. Aage calmed her and persuaded her to sit and wait it out. It would be weeks, even months, before the Germans got the government functioning.

The sight of the swastika and German soldiers opened a flood of memories for Karen, and with them came fear. Everyone was confused these first weeks, but Aage remained calm.

The German administration and occupation forces made glowing promises. The Danes, they said, were Aryans like themselves. They were, indeed brothers, and the main reason for the occupation was to protect the Danes from Bolsheviks. Denmark, they said, would be allowed to continue to rule her own internal affairs. She would become a model protectorate. Thus, after the initial shock had subsided, a semblance of normalcy returned.

The venerable King Christian resumed his daily horseback rides from the Amalienborg Palace in Copenhagen. He rode proudly alone through the streets, and his people followed his lead. Passive resistance was the order of the day.

Aage had been right. Karen returned to school and to her dancing lessons, and life resumed in Aalborg almost as though nothing had happened.

The year of 1941 came. Eight months of German occupation. It was becoming more obvious each day that tension was growing between the Germans and the people of their 'model protectorate.' King Christian continued to irritate the conquerors by snubbing them. The people, too, ignored the Germans as much as they could, or, worse, poked fun at their struttings and laughed at the proclamations. The more the Danes laughed the angrier the Germans became.

Any illusions the Danes had had at the beginning of the German occupation were soon dispelled. There was a place for Danish machinery and Danish food and Danish geography in the German master plan; Denmark was to become another cog in the German war machine. So with the example of their fellow Scandinavians in Norway before them, the Danes, by the middle of 1941, had established a small but determined little underground.

Dr Werner Best, the German governor of Denmark, favored a policy of moderation for the 'model protectorate,' so long as the Danes co-operated peaceably. The measures against the Danes were mild by comparison to those of other occupied countries. None the less, the underground movement mushroomed. Although the members of the resistance could not hope to take on German troops in combat or to plan for a general uprising, they found a way to unleash their hatred for the Germans – *sabotage.*

Dr Werner Best did not panic. He calmly went about organizing Nazi sympathizers among the Danes to combat this new threat. The German-sponsored HIPO Corps became a Danish terrorist gang for punitive action against their own people. Each act of sabotage was answered by an action by the HIPOS.

As the months and years of German occupation rolled by, Karen Hansen passed her eleventh and twelfth birthdays in faraway Aalborg, where life seemed quite normal. The reports of sabotage and the occasional sound of gunfire or an explosion were only momentary causes for excitement.

Karen began to blossom into womanhood. She felt the first thrills and despairs that come with caring deeply for someone other than parents or a girl friend. Young Mogens Sorensen, the best soccer player in the school, was Karen's beau, and she was the envy of every other girl.

Her dancing ability led her teacher to urge Meta and Aage to let her try out for the Royal Ballet in Copenhagen. She was a gifted child, the teacher said, and seemed to express through dance a sensitivity far beyond her years.

At the turn of 1943 the Hansens became more and more uneasy. The Danish underground was in communication with Allied Headquarters and was getting out vital information with regard to the location of essential war manufacturing plants and supply depots inside Denmark. They co-operated further by spotting these targets for the British RAF Mosquito bombers.

The HIPOS and the other German-sponsored terrorists stepped up reprisals. As the activity heightened, Aage began to ponder. Everyone in Aalborg knew of Karen's origin. Although no move had as yet been made against the Danish Jews, a sudden break could come. He could be fairly certain, too, that the facts concerning Karen had been relayed to the Germans by the HIPOS. At last Meta and Aage decided to sell their home in Aalborg and move to Copenhagen on the pretext that there was a better position for Aage there and that Karen could receive better instruction in ballet.

In the summer of 1943 Aage became affiliated with a law firm in Copenhagen, where they hoped they could become completely anonymous among its million inhabitants. A birth certificate and papers were forged for Karen to prove she was their natural child. Karen said her goodbys to Mogens Sorensen, and suffered the pain of a badly broken heart.

The Hansens found a lovely apartment situated on the Sortedams Dosseringen. It was a tree-lined street looking out on the artificial lake and crossed by numerous bridges which led into the old town.

Once the strangeness of resettlement had worn off, Karen loved Copenhagen. It was a fairyland on earth. Karen, Aage, and Maximilian would walk for hours and hours to see the wonders of the town. There were so many wonderful places – around the port past the statue of the Little Mermaid, along the Langelinie or through the bursting gardens of the Citadel or the gardens at the Christiansborg Palace; there were the waterways and the narrow little alleys crammed with ancient five-story brick houses. There were the never-ending streams of bicycles and that wonderful fish market at Gammel Strand, so vast and noisome it put the one in Aalborg to shame.

The crown jewel in that fairyland known as Copenhagen was the Tivoli – a maze of whirling lights and rides and theaters and restaurants and miles of flower beds – the children's band and the Wivex Restaurant and the fireworks and the laughter. Karen soon wondered how on earth she had ever managed to lived away from Copenhagen.

One day Karen ran down her street, up the stairs, and threw open the apartment door. She flung her arms about Aage, who was trying to read his newspaper.

'Daddy! Daddy! Daddy!'

She pulled him from his seat and began to waltz around the room. Then she left him standing dazed in the center of the floor and began dancing over the furniture and back to him and threw her arms around him again. Meta appeared in the doorway and smiled.

'Your daughter is trying to tell you that she has been accepted by the Royal Ballet.'

'Well now,' Aage said, 'that is pretty good.'

That night, after Karen was asleep, Meta could at last pour out her pride to Aage. 'They said she is one in a thousand. With five or six years of intensive training she can go right to the top.'

'That is good ... that is good,' Aage said, trying not to show how very proud he was.

But not everything was fairylands and happiness in Copenhagen. Each night the earth was rocked by explosions caused by the underground, explosions that lit the skies, and dancing flames and the sounds of cracking rifles and stuttering machine guns filled the air.

Sabotage!

Reprisal!

The HIPOS began methodically to destroy places and things that were sources of pleasure for the Danes. The German-sponsored Danish terrorists blew up theaters and breweries and entertainment palaces. The Danish underground lashed back at places where the German war machine was being fed. Soon both the days and the nights were racked by the thunder of destruction and flying debris.

The streets were empty during German parades. Danes turned their backs on German ceremony. The streets were mobbed by silent mourners on every Danish national holiday. The daily horseback rides of the old King became a signal for hundreds upon hundreds of Danes to rally behind him shouting and cheering.

The situation seethed and seethed – and finally erupted! The morning of August 29, 1943, was ushered in with a blast heard across Zealand. The Danish fleet had scuttled itself in an effort to block the shipping channels!

The enraged Germans moved their forces on the government buildings and royal palace at Amalienborg. The King's guard fought them off. A furious pitched battle broke out, but it was all over rather quickly. German soldiers replaced the King's guard at Amalienborg. A score of German field generals, SS and Gestapo officials descended on Denmark to whip the Danes into line. The Danish Parliament was suspended and a dozen angry decrees invoked. The model protectorate was no longer a 'model,' if indeed it ever had been.

The Danes answered the Germans by stepping up their acts of sabotage. Arsenals, factories, ammunition dumps, bridges were blown to bits. The Germans were getting jittery. Danish sabotage was beginning to hurt badly.

From German occupation headquarters at the Hotel D'Angleterre came the decree: ALL JEWS MUST WEAR A YELLOW ARM BAND WITH A STAR OF DAVID.

That night the underground radio transmitted a message to all Danes. 'From Amalienborg Palace King Christian has given the following answer to the German command that Jews must wear a Star of David. The King has said that one Dane is exactly the same as the next Dane. He himself will wear the first Star of David and he expects that every loyal Dane will do they same.'

The next day in Copenhagen almost the entire population wore arm bands showing a Star of David.

The following day the Germans rescinded the order.

Although Aage was not active in the underground the partners of his law firm were leading members, and from time to time he received information of their activities. At the end of the summer of 1943 he became terribly worried and decided that he and Meta must reach a decision concerning Karen.

'It is true,' Aage told his wife. 'In a matter of months the Germans will round up all the Jews. We just don't know the exact time the Gestapo will strike.'

Meta Hansen walked to the window and stared blankly down at the lake and the bridge to the old town. It was evening and soon Karen would be coming home from ballet school. Meta's mind had been filled with many things she had been planning for Karen's thirteenth birthday party. It was going to be quite a wonderful affair – forty children – at the Tivoli Gardens.

Aage lit his pipe and stared at the picture of Karen on his desk. He sighed.

'I am not giving her up,' Meta said.

'We have no right . . .'

'It is different. She is not a Danish Jew. We have records to show she is our child.'

Aage put his hand on his wife's shoulder. 'Someone in Aalborg may inform the Germans.'

'They won't go to that trouble for one child.'

'Don't you know these people by now?'

Meta turned around. 'We will have her baptized and adopt her legally.'

Aage shook his head slowly. His wife slumped into a chair and bit her lip. She clutched the arms of the chair so tightly her hand turned white. 'What will happen, Aage?'

'They are organizing to get all the Jewish people up to the Zealand beaches near the straits. We are purchasing as many boats as we can to make runs over to Sweden. The Swedes have sent word that they will accept everyone and provide for them.'

'How many nights I have lain awake and thought of this. I have tried to tell myself that she is in greater danger if she must flee. I tell myself over and over that she is safer here with us.'

'Think of what you are saying, Meta.'

The woman looked at her husband with an expression of anguish and determination he had never seen from her before. 'I will never give her up, Aage. I cannot live without her.'

Every Dane who was called upon co-operated in a gigantic effort. The entire Jewish population of Denmark was whisked secretly north to Zealand and smuggled to the safety of Sweden.

Later that month the Germans made a sweep of Denmark to catch the Jews. There were none to be caught.

Although Karen remained unharmed in Copenhagen with the Hansens the responsibility of the decision weighed heavily on Meta. From that second on the German occupation became a prolonged nightmare. A dozen new rumors would send her into a panic. Three or four times she fled from Copenhagen with Karen to relatives on Jutland.

Aage became more and more active in the underground. He was gone three or four nights a week now. These nights were long and horrible for Meta.

The Danish underground, now directed and co-ordinated, turned its energies against German transportation. Every half hour a rail line was bombed. Soon the entire rail network of the country was littered with the wreckage of blasted trains.

The HIPOS took their revenge by blowing up the beloved Tivoli Gardens.

The Danes called a general strike against the Germans. They poured into the streets and set up barricades all over Copenhagen flying Danish, American, British, and Russian flags.

The Germans declared Copenhagen in a state of siege!

From German headquarters at the Hotel D'Angleterre, Dr Werner Best shrieked in fury, 'The rabble of Copenhagen shall taste the whip!'

The general strike was beaten down, but the underground kept up its acts of destruction.

SEPTEMBER 19, 1944

The Germans interned the entire Danish police force for failing to control the people and for overt sympathy with their actions against the occupation forces. The underground, in a daring raid, destroyed the Nazi record offices.

The underground manufactured small arms and smuggled fighters into Sweden to join Danish Free Forces. It turned its wrath on the HIPOS, dispensing quick justice to some of its members and to Danish traitors.

The HIPOS and the Gestapo went berserk in an aimless wave of reprisal murders.

Then German refugees began pouring over the border into Denmark. These were people bombed out by the Allies. They swarmed all over the country, taking food and shelter without asking; stealing and preying on the Danes. The Danes turned their backs on these refugees with utter contempt.

In April 1945 there were all sorts of rumors.

MAY 4, 1945

'Mommy! Daddy! The war is over! The war is over!'

Chapter Thirteen

The victors entered Denmark – the Yanks and the British and the Danish Free Forces. It was a great week – a week of retribution to the HIPOS and the Danish traitors, to Dr Werner Best and the Gestapo. A week of din and delirious joy, climaxed by the appearance of creaking old King Christian to reopen the Danish Parliament. He spoke in a proud but tired voice which broke with emotion.

For Meta and Aage Hansen the week of the liberation was a time of sorrow. Seven years before they had rescued a child from grave danger and they had raised her into a blossoming young woman. What a lovely girl she was! Karen was grace and beauty and laughter. Her voice was pure and sweet and she danced with magic wings on her feet. Now: the Day of Judgment.

Once in a fit of anguish Meta Hansen had sworn she would never give Karen up. Now Meta Hansen was becoming a victim of her own decency. There were no Germans left to fight now, only her own Christian goodness. And Aage would fall victim, as he had to, to his Danish sense of honor. Liberation brought upon them a fear of the haunted nights and the life of emptiness that lay ahead of them without Karen. The Hansens had aged badly during the last seven years. It was apparent the moment they were allowed to relax from the tension of war. No matter how trying things had been there had always been room for laughter, but now while Denmark laughed there was no laughter for them. The Hansens wanted only to look at Karen, hear her voice, spend the hours in her room in a desperate attempt to gather for themselves a lifetime of memories.

Karen knew it was coming. She loved the Hansens. Aage had always done what was right. She had to wait for him to speak first. For two weeks after the liberation the gloom thickened. At last, one evening after another wordless meal Aage rose from the table and put down his napkin. His kindly face was wrinkled and his voice a listless monotone. 'We must try to find your parents, Karen. It is the thing to do.' He walked from the room quickly. Karen looked to the empty doorway and then to Meta across the table.

'I love you,' Karen said, and ran to her room and threw herself on the bed and sobbed, hating herself for bringing this sorrow on them. And now she was hating herself for another reason. She wanted to learn about her past. In a few more days they sought out the International Refugee Organization.

'This is my foster daughter,' Aage said.

The case worker had been on her job only the few weeks since the liberation, but already she was becoming sick at the sight of couples like the Hansens and Karen. Day after day the woman was being forced to become a party to tragedy. In Denmark and Holland, in Sweden and Belgium and France, couples like the Hansens who had hidden and sheltered and raised children were now stepping forward to receive their bitter reward.

'You must be prepared for a long and difficult task. There are millions of displaced people in Europe. We have absolutely no idea how long it is going to take to reunite families.'

They left with her all the known facts, a list of all the known relatives, and the letters. Karen had a large family and her father had been a prominent man. The woman gave them a little hope.

A week passed, and two, and then three. June – July. Months of torture for Aage and Meta. They would stand in the doorway of Karen's room more and more often. It was frilly and soft and it smelled good. There were her ice skates and her ballet slippers and pictures of classmates and prima ballerinas. There was a picture of her beau, the Petersen boy.

At last they were called to the Refugee Organization.

'We are faced with the fact,' the woman said, 'that all our initial inquiries have turned up nothing. This is not to be taken as conclusive. It means a long hard task. Were it my own decision I would absolutely forbid Karen to travel to Germany alone or even with Mr Hansen. There is utter chaos inside Germany and you won't find a thing that we can't do from here.' The woman looked squarely at the three of them. 'I must warn you about one thing. We have been receiving more and more reports each day that something pretty hideous has happened. Many Jews have been put to death. It is beginning to look as though the numbers may run into the millions.'

It was another reprieve for the Hansens, but what a ghastly thought! Were they to keep this girl only because over fifty members of her immediate family had been put to death? The Hansens were being pulled in two directions. The solution came from Karen herself.

Despite the love she had given and received from the Hansens, there had always been a strange, invisible barrier between them. Early in the German occupation when she was but eight years old Aage had told her she must never speak about being Jewish because it could endanger her life. Karen followed this order as she did all of Aage's decisions because she loved him and trusted him. But even though she obeyed it she could not keep from wondering why she was different from other people and exactly what this difference was that endangered her very life. It was a question she could never ask and therefore it was never answered. Furthermore, Karen had been completely isolated from any contact with Jews. She felt herself to be like other people and she looked like other people. Yet the invisible barrier was there.

Her question might well have died, but Aage and Meta kept it alive inadvertently. The Hansens were faithful to the traditions of the Danish Lutheran Church and were very devout. Each Sunday the three of them went to church together, and each night before bedtime Aage read from the Book of Psalms. Karen treasured the little white leather Bible the Hansens gave her on her tenth birthday and she loved the magnificent fairylike stories, especially those in Judges and Samuel and Kings, which were filled with all the wonderment of great loves and wars and passions. Reading the Bible was like reading Hans Christian Andersen himself!

But reading the Bible only led to confusion for Karen. So many times she wanted to talk it all over with Aage. Jesus was born one of these Jews, and his mother and all his disciples were Jews. The first part of the Bible, the most fascinating to Karen's mind, was all about Jews. Didn't it say over and over again that the Jews were people chosen by God Himself to carry out His laws?

If this was all true then why was it so dangerous to be Jewish and why were the Jews hated so? Karen probed deeper as she grew older. She read that God often punished the Jews when they were bad. Had they been very bad?

Karen was a naturally curious girl, and so long as these questions arose she became more and more perplexed by them. The Bible became her secret obsession. In the quiet of her room she studied its passages in the hope of finding some answers to the great riddle.

The more she read, the older she became, the more puzzled she was. By the time she was fourteen she was able to reason out many of the passages and their meanings. Almost everything that Jesus taught, all His ideas, had been set down before in the Old Testament. Then came the largest riddle of all. If Jesus were to return to the earth she was certain He would go to a synagogue rather than a church. Why could people worship Jesus and hate His people?

Another thing happened on her fourteenth birthday. At that age Danish girls are confirmed in the church with a great deal of ceremony and celebration. Karen had lived as a Dane and a Christian, yet the Hansens hesitated in the matter of her confirmation. They talked it over and felt that they could not take upon themselves a matter that had been decided by God. They told Karen the confirmation would be set aside because of the war and the uncertainty of the times. But Karen knew the real reason.

When she had first come to the Hansens she had needed love and shelter. Now her needs had expanded into a longing for identification. The mystery of her family and her past ran parallel with this mystery of being Jewish. In order to take her place forever as a Dane she had to close the door on these burning questions. She was unable to do so. Her life was based on something temporary, an invisible wall – her past and her religion – always stood between her and the Hansens.

As the war drew to a close Karen knew that she would be torn from them. Wisely she conditioned herself to the shock of the inevitable parting. Being Karen Hansen was merely playing a game. She made the need of becoming Karen Clement urgent. She tried to reconstruct threads of her past life; to remember her father, her mother, and her brothers. Pieces and snatches came back to her in dim and disconnected hazes. She pretended over and over again how the reunion with them would be. She made her longing constant.

By the time the war was over, Karen had conditioned herself completely. One night a few months after the end of the war she told the Hansens that she was going away to find her parents. She told them she had seen the woman at the Refugee Organization and her chances of finding her family would be better if she moved to a displaced persons' camp in Sweden. Actually the chances were the same if she stayed, but she could not bear to prolong the Hansens' agony.

Karen cried for Aage and Meta far more than for herself. With promises to write and with the slim hope of another reunion with them, Karen Hansen Clement, aged fourteen, cast herself adrift in the stream of roamers of the backwash of war.

Chapter Fourteen

The dream was ruthless to the reality. The first month away from Denmark was a nightmare. She was frightened, for she had always been sheltered, but a dogged determination carried her on.

First to a camp in Sweden and then to a château in Belgium where there were armies of homeless, penniless drifters; inmates of concentration camps; those who fled and those who hid and were hidden and those who fought in the hills and forests as partisans and those legions of forced labor. Each day was riddled with rumors and new stories of horror. Each day brought a succession of new shocks to Karen. Twenty-five million people lay dead in the wake of war.

The trail led to the displaced persons' camp, La Ciotat, on the Gulf of Lions in southern France a few miles from Marseilles. La Ciotat seemed a morbid place packed with lusterless concrete-block barracks which seemed to slosh in a never-ending sea of mud. The numbers of refugees multiplied daily. It was overcrowded, short of everything, and the specter of death seemed to haunt the inmates. To them, all Europe had become a coffin.

Genocide! A dance of death with six million dancers! Karen heard the names of Frank and Mueller and Himmler and Rosenberg and Streicher and Kaltenbrunner and Heydrich. She heard the names of thousands of lesser ones: Ilsa Koch, who won infamy by making lampshades out of human tattooed skins, and of Dieter Wisliczeny, who played the role of stockyard goat leading the sheep to slaughter, or Kramer, who sported in horsewhipping naked women and some of whose handiwork she saw. The name of the greatest killer of them all came up over and over again: Eichmann, the German Palestinian who spoke fluent Hebrew and was the master of genocide.

Karen rued the day she had opened that secret door marked *Jew*, for behind it lay death. One by one the death of an aunt or uncle or cousin was confirmed.

Genocide – carried out with the precision and finality of a machine. At first the efforts of the Germans had been clumsy. They killed by rifle. It was too slow. They organized their transport and their scientists for the great effort. Steel-covered trucks were designed to lock in and gas to death prisoners en route to burial grounds. But even the gas vans proved slow. Next came the crematoriums and the gas chambers capable of killing two thousand people in a half hour – ten thousand on a good day in a major camp. The organization and planning proved itself and genocide proceeded on an assembly-line basis.

And Karen heard of thousands of prisoners who threw themselves on the quick mercy of electrified barbed wire to cheat the gas chambers.

And Karen heard of hundreds of thousands who fell to disease and hunger, stacked-up emaciated corpses thrown into unmarked ditches, with logs placed between them and gasoline poured over them.

And Karen heard of the game of deception that was played to tear children away from their mothers under the guise of resettlement, and of trains packed with the old and feeble. Karen heard of the delousing chambers where prisoners were given bars of soap. The chambers were gas and the soap was made of stone.

Karen heard of mothers who hid children in their clothing, which was hung up on pegs before going into the chambers. But the Germans knew the ruse and always found the little ones.

Karen heard of thousands who knelt naked beside graves they had dug. Fathers holding their hands over the eyes of their sons as German pistols went off in the backs of their heads.

She heard of SS *Haupsturmfuehrer* Fritz Gebauer, who specialized in strangling women and children barehanded and who liked watching infants die in barrels of freezing water.

She heard of Heinen, who perfected a method of killing several people in a row with one bullet, always trying to beat his previous record.

She heard of Frank Warzok, who liked to bet on how long a human could live hanging by the feet.

She heard of *Obersturbannfuehrer* Rokita, who ripped bodies apart.

She heard of Steiner, who bored holes into prisoners' heads and stomachs and pulled fingernails and gouged eyes and liked to swing naked women from poles by their hair.

She heard of General Franz Jaeckeln who conducted the massacre of Babi Yar. Babi Yar was a suburb of Kiev and in two days thirty-three thousand Jews were rounded up and shot – to the approval of many cheering Ukrainians.

She heard of Professor Hirts' Anatomical Institute at Strasbourg and of his scientists, and she saw evidences of the deformed women who had been subjects of their experiments.

Dachau was the biggest of the 'scientific' centers. She learned that Dr Heisskever injected children with t.b. germs and observed their death. Dr Schutz was interested in blood poisoning. Dr Rascher wanted to save the lives of German air crews and in his experiments high-altitude conditions were simulated and human guinea pigs frozen to death while they were carefully observed through special windows. There were other experiments in what the Germans referred to as 'truth in science' which reached a peak, perhaps, in the attempted implantation of animal sperm in human females.

Karen heard of Wilhaus, the commander of the camp at Janowska, who commissioned the composer Mund to write the 'Death Tango.' The notes of this song were the last sounds heard by two hundred thousand Jews who were liquidated at Janowska. She heard other things about Wilhaus at Janowska. She heard his hobby was throwing infants into the air and seeing how many bullets he could fire into the body before it reached the ground. His wife, Otile, was also an excellent shot.

Karen heard about the Lithuanian guards of the Germans who merely clubbed and kicked people to death and of the Croátian Ustashis and their violent killings of hundreds of thousands of prisoners too.

Karen wept and she was dazed and she was haunted. Her nights were sleepless and the names of the land tore through her brain. Had her father and mother and brothers been sent to Buchenwald or had they met death in the horror of Dachau? Maybe it was Chelmno with a million dead or Maidanek with seven hundred and fifty thousand. Or Belzec or Treblinka with its lines of vans or Sobibor or Trawniki or Poniatow or Krivoj Rog. Had they been shot in the pits of Krasnik or burned at the stake at Klooga or torn apart by dogs at Diedzyn or tortured to death at Stutthof?

The lash! The ice bath! The electric shock! The soldering iron! Genocide!

Was it the camp at Choisel or Dora or Neuengamme or was it at Gross-Rosen or did they hear Wilhaus' 'Death Tango' at Janowska?

Was her family among the bodies which were melted to fat in the manufacture of soap at Danzig?

Death lingered on and on at the displaced persons' camp at La Ciotat near Marseilles, France.

. . . and Karen heard more names of the land. Danagien, Eivari, Goldpilz, Vievara, Portkunde.

She could not eat and she could not sleep – Kivioli, Varva, Magdeburg, Plaszow, Szebnie, Mauthausen, Sachsenhausen, Oranienburg, Landsberg, Bergen-Belsen, Reinsdorf, Bliziny.

Genocide!

Fossenberg! Ravensbrück! Natzweiler!

But all these names were small beside the greatest of them all – *Auschwitz!*

Auschwitz with its three million dead!

Auschwitz with its warehouses crammed with eyeglasses

Auschwitz with its warehouses crammed with boots and clothing and pitiful rag dolls.

Auschwitz with its warehouse of human hair for the manufacture of mattresses!

Auschwitz, where the gold teeth of the dead were methodically pulled and melted down for shipment to Himmler's Science Institute. Auschwitz, where an especially finely shaped skull would be preserved as a paperweight!

Auschwitz, where the bones of the cremated were broken up with sledge hammers and pulverized so that there would never be a trace of death.

Auschwitz which had the sign over the main entrance: LABOR LIBERATES.

Karen Hansen Clement sank deep in melancholy. She heard till she could hear no more. She saw until she could see no more. She was exhausted and confused, and the will to go on was being drained from her blood. Then, as so often happens when one reaches the end of the line, there was a turning upward and she emerged into the light.

It began when she smiled and patted the head of an orphan and the child sensed great compassion in her. Karen was able to give children what they craved the most, tenderness. They flocked to her. She seemed to know instinctively how to dry a runny nose, kiss a wounded finger, or soothe a tear, and she could tell stories and sing at the piano in many languages.

She plunged into her work with the younger children with a fevor that helped her forget a little of the pain within her. She never seemed to run out of patience nor of time for giving.

Her fifteenth birthday came and went at La Ciotat. Aside from the fact that she was just plain stubborn, Karen clung to two great hopes. Her father had been a prominent man, and the Germans had kept one 'prestige' camp where prisoners were neither tortured nor killed. It was the camp at Theresienstadt in Czechoslovakia. If he had been sent there, as well he might, he could still be alive. The second hope, a slimmer one, was that many German scientists had been smuggled out of the country even after being sent to concentration camps. Against these hopes she had the confirmed deaths of over half of her family.

One day several dozen new people entered the camp and the place seemed to transform overnight. The new people were Palestinians from the Mossad Aliyah Bet and the Palmach who had come to take over the interior organization.

A few days after they arrived, Karen danced for her youngsters – the first time she had danced since the summer. From that moment on she was in constant demand and one of the most popular figures in La Ciotat. Her renown spread even as far as Marseilles where she was invited to dance in an annual Christmas presentation of the *Nutcracker Suite*.

CHRISTMAS 1945

The pangs of loneliness of her first Christmas away from the Hansens were terrible. Half the children in La Ciotat had come to Marseilles to watch her dance in a special performance. Karen danced that night as she had never danced before.

When the performance was over a Palestinian Palmach girl named Galil, who was the section head at La Ciotat, asked Karen to wait until everyone had left. Tears streamed down Galil's cheeks. 'Karen. We have just received positive confirmation that your mother and your two brothers were exterminated at Dachau.'

Karen tumbled into a sorrow even deeper than before. The undaunted spirit which had kept her going vanished. She felt the curse of being born a Jewess had led her to the madness of leaving Denmark.

Every child in La Ciotat had one thing in common. Every one of them believed their parents were alive. All of them waited for the miracle which never came. What a fool she had been to believe!

When she was able to come to her senses several days later she talked it all over with Galil. She did not feel she had the strength to sit and wait until she heard that her father was dead also.

Galil, the Palestine girl, was her only confidante and felt that Karen, like all Jews, should go to Palestine. It was the only place a Jew could live with dignity, Galil argued. But, with her faith destroyed, Karen was about ready to close the door on Judaism, for it had brought her only misery and left her as Karen Hansen, a Dane.

At night Karen asked herself the same question that every Jew had asked of himself since the Temple in Jerusalem had been destroyed and the Jews were dispersed to the four corners of the earth as eternal drifters two thousand years before. Karen asked herself, 'Why me?'

Each day brought her closer to that moment when she would write the Hansens and ask to return to them forever.

Then one morning Galil rushed into Karen's barrack and half dragged her to the administration building, where she was introduced to a Dr Brenner, a new refugee at La Ciotat.

'Oh, God!' Karen cried as she heard the news. 'Are you certain?'

'Yes,' Brenner answered, 'I am absolutely positive. You see, I knew your father in the old days. I was a teacher in Berlin. We often exchanged correspondence and met at conventions. Yes, my dear, we were in Theresienstadt together and I saw him last only a few weeks before the war ended.'

Chapter Fifteen

A week later Karen received a letter from the Hansens stating that there had been inquiries from the Refugee Organization as to her whereabouts, as well as questions as to whether the Hansens had any information about her mother or brothers.

It was assumed that the inquiries came from Johann Clement or from someone on his behalf. Karen surmised from this that her father and mother had been separated and he was unaware of her death and the death of the brothers. The next letter from the Hansens stated that they had replied but the Refugee Organization had lost contact with Clement.

But he was alive! Every horrible moment of the months in the camps in Sweden, Belgium, and La Ciotat was worth it now! Once again she found the courage to search for her past.

Karen wondered why La Ciotat was being supported by money from Jews in America. After all, there was everything in the camp but Americans. She asked Galil, who shrugged. 'Zionism is a first person asking money from a second person to give to a third person to send a fourth person to Palestine.'

'It is good,' Karen said, 'that we have friends who stick together.'

'We also have enemies who stick together,' Galil answered.

The people at La Ciotat certainly looked and acted much like any other people, Karen thought. Most of them seemed just as confused by being Jewish as she was.

When she had learned enough Hebrew to handle herself she ventured into the religious compound to observe the weird rituals, the dress and prayer of those people who were truly different. The vastness of the sea of Judaism can drown a girl of fifteen. The religion was based on a complex set of laws. Some were written and some were oral. They covered the most minute of subjects, such as how to pray on a camel. The holiest of the holy were the five books of Moses, the Torah.

Once again Karen turned to her Bible. This time what she read seemed to throw new light and have new meaning for her and she would think for hours about lines like the cry of the prophet Isaiah: '*We grope for the wall like the blind, and we grope as if we had no eyes: we stumble at noon day as in the night; we are in desolate places as dead men. We roar like bears, and mourn sore like doves . . . we look for salvation, but it is far off from us.*'

These words seemed to fit the situation at La Ciotat. Her Bible was filled with stories of bondage and freedom, and she tried to apply these things to herself and her family.

'*Look from heaven and see how we have become a scorn and a derision among the nations; we are accounted as sheep and brought to the slaughter to be slain and destroyed or to be smitten and reproached. Yet, despite all this, we have not forgotten thy Name; we beseech thee, forget us not . . .*'

And again the path would end in confusion. Why would God let six million of His people be killed? Karen concluded that only the experiences of life would bring her the answer, someday.

The inmates of La Ciotat seethed with a terrible desire to leave Europe behind them and get to Palestine. The only force that kept them from turning into a wild mob was the presence of the Palmachniks from Palestine.

They cared little about the war of intrigue that raged about them between the British and the Mossad Aliyah Bet. They did not care about British desperation to hold onto the Middle East or oil or canals or traditional co-operation with the Arabs.

For a brief instant a year earlier everyone's hopes had soared as the Labour party swept into power and with it promises to turn Palestine into a model mandate with open immigration. Talk was even revived of making Palestine a member of the British Commonwealth.

The promises exploded as the Labour Government listened to the voice of black gold that bubbled beneath Arab sand. The decisions were delayed for more study, more commissions, more talk, as it had been for twenty-five years.

But nothing could curb the craving of the Jews in La Ciotat to get to Palestine. Mossad Aliyah Bet agents poured all over Europe looking for Jewish survivors and leading them through friendly borders with bribes, forgery, stealing, or any other means short of force.

A gigantic game was played as the scene shifted from one country to another. From the very beginning France and Italy allied themselves with the refugees in open co-operation with the Mossad. They kept their borders open to receive refugees and to establish camps. Italy, occupied by British troops, was severely hampered, so France became the major refugee center.

Soon places like La Ciotat were bulging. The Mossad answered with illegal immigration. Every seaport of Europe was covered by Mossad agents who used the money sent them by American Jews to purchase and refit boats to run the British blockade into Palestine. The British not only used their navy but their embassies and consulates as counter-spying centers against the Mossad.

Leaky little boats of the Mossad Aliyah Bet, overloaded with desperate people, set out for Palestine, only to be caught by the British as soon as they entered the three-mile zone. The refugees would be interned in yet another camp, this one in Atlit in Palestine.

After Karen learned her father was alive she, too, became swept up in the desire to get to Palestine. It seemed natural to her that her father would come to Palestine also.

Although she was only fifteen she was drawn into the Palmach group, whose members held nightly campfires and told wonderful stories of the Land of Milk and Honey and sang wonderful oriental songs right out of the Bible. They joked and spun tall yarns all night long and they would call, 'Dance, Karen, dance!'

She was made a section chief to take care of a hundred children and prepare them for the moment a Mossad boat would take them to run the blockade into Palestine.

The British quota for Palestine was only fifteen hundred a month, and they always took old people or those too young to fight. Men grew beards and grayed their hair to look old, but such ruses usually didn't work.

In April of 1946, nine months after Karen had left Denmark, Galil gave her the great news one day.

'An Aliyah Bet ship is coming in a few days and you and your section are going on it.'

Karen's heart nearly tore through her dress.

'What is the name of it?'

'The *Star of David*,' Galil answered.

Chapter Sixteen

British CID had a running acquaintance with the Aegean tramp steamer, *Karpathos*. They knew the instant the *Karpathos* was purchased in Salonika by the Mossad Aliyah Bet. They followed the movements of the eight-hundred-ton, forty-five-year-old tramp to Piraeus, the port of Athens where an American Aliyah Bet crew boarded her and sailed her to Genoa, Italy. They observed as the *Karpathos* was refitted into an immigrant runner and they knew the exact instant she left and sailed toward the Gulf of Lions.

The entire southern coast of France was alive with CID men. A twenty-four-hour watch was thrown around La Ciotat for signs of a large-scale movement. A dozen major and minor French officials were bribed. Pressure came from Whitehall to Paris to prevent the *Karpathos* from getting inside French territorial waters. But British pressure and bribes had no effect. French co-operation with Aliyah Bet remained solid. The *Karpathos* moved inside the three-mile zone.

The next stage of the game was set. A half-dozen trial runs were made from La Ciotat to trick and divert the British. Trucks were donated by the French teamsters and driven by French drivers. When the British were thoroughly confused, the real break was made. Sixteen hundred refugees, Karen's section included, were sped out from La Ciotat to a secret rendezvous point along the coast. The entire area was blocked off from outside traffic by the French Army.

The trucks unloaded the refugees on a quiet beach and they were transferred by rubber boats to the ancient *Karpathos*, which waited offshore.

The line of rubber boats moved back and forth all night. The strong hands of the American crew lifted the anxious escapees aboard. Palmach teams on board quickly moved each boatload to a predesignated section. A knapsack, a bottle of water, and an obsession to leave Europe was all the refugees had.

Karen's children, the youngest, were boarded first and given a special position in the hold. They were placed below deck near the ladder which ran to the deck. She worked quickly to calm them down. Fortunately most of them were too numbed with excitement and exhaustion and fell right off to sleep. A few cried, but she was right there to comfort them.

An hour passed, and two and three, and the hold began to get crowded. On came the refugees until the hold was so packed there was scarcely an inch to move in any direction.

Then they began filling up the deck space topside and when that was crammed they flooded over onto the bridge.

Bill Fry, an American and captain of the ship, came down the ladder and looked over the crush of humanity in the hold and whistled. He was a stocky man with a stubbly beard and an unlit cigar butt clenched between his teeth.

'You know, the Boston fire department would raise hell if they ever saw a room like this,' Bill mumbled.

He stopped talking and began to listen. From the shadows a very sweet voice was singing a lullaby. He pushed his way down the ladder and stepped over the bodies and turned a flashlight on Karen, who was holding a little boy in her arms and singing him to sleep. For an instant he thought he was looking at the Madonna! He blinked his eyes. Karen looked up and motioned him to take the flashlight off her.

'Hey, kid ... you speak English?' Bill's gruff voice said.

'Yes.'

'Where is the section head of these kids?'

'I am the section head and I'll thank you to lower your voice. I've had enough trouble getting them quieted down.'

'I'll talk as loud as I want. I'm the captain. You ain't no bigger than most of these kids.'

'If you run your ship as well as I run this section,' Karen snapped angrily, 'then we will be in Palestine by morning.'

He scratched his bearded jaw and smiled. He certainly didn't look like the dignified Danish ship's captains, Karen thought, and he was only pretending to be hard.

'You're a nice kid. If you need something you come up on the bridge and see me. And you be more respectful.'

'Thank you, captain.'

'That's all right. Just call me Bill. We're all from the same tribe.'

Karen watched as he climbed the ladder, and she could see the first crack of daylight. The *Karpathos* was crammed with as many people as she could hold – sixteen hundred refugees, hanging from every inch of her. The half-rusted anchor creaked up and slapped against the sides of her wooden hulk. The forty-five-year-old engines coughed and sputtered and reluctantly churned into action. A fog bank enshrouded them as though God Himself were giving cover, and the old ship chugged away from the shores of France at her top speed of seven knots an hour. In a matter of moments she was beyond the three-mile zone and into the waters of no man's land. The first round had been won by the Mossad Aliyah Bet! A blue and white Jewish flag was struck to the mast, and the *Karpathos* changed her name to the *Star of David*.

The boat bounced miserably. The lack of ventilation in the overjammed holds turned everyone pale. Karen worked with the Palmach teams feeding lemons and applying compresses to stave off a major epidemic of vomiting. When lemons failed, she went to work quickly with the mop. She found that the best way to keep things quiet was to sing and invent games and tell funny stories.

She had the children under control but by noon the heat worsened and the air grew more rancid, and soon the stench of sweat and vomit became unbearable in the semilit hold. Men stripped to shorts and women to their brassières, and their bodies glistened with sweat. An outbreak of fainting began. Only the unconscious were taken up on deck. There was simply no room for the others.

Three doctors and four nurses, all refugees from La Ciotat, worked feverishly. 'Get food into their stomachs,' they ordered. Karen coaxed, coddled, and shoved food down the mouths of her children. By evening she was passing out sedatives and giving sponge baths. She washed them sparingly, for water was very scarce.

At last the sun went down and a breath of air swept into the hold. Karen had worked herself into exhaustion, and her mind was too hazy to permit her to think sharply. She fell into only a half sleep with an instinctive reflex that brought her awake the second one of her children cried. She listened to every creak of the old ship as it labored for Palestine. Toward morning she dozed off completely into a thick dream-riddled sleep filled with annoying confusion.

A sudden roar brought her awake with a start. She looked up the ladder and it was daylight. Karen pushed her way up. Everyone was pointing to the sky where a huge four-engined bomber hovered over them.

'British! Lancaster Bomber!'

'Everyone return to your places and be calm,' the loudspeaker boomed.

Karen rushed back to the hold where the children were frightened and crying. She began singing at the top of her voice urging the children to follow:

Onward! Onward to Palestine
In happiness we throng,
Onward! Onward to Palestine
Come join our happy song!

'Everyone keep calm,' the loud-speaker said, 'there is no danger.'

By noontime a British cruiser, HMS *Defiance*, appeared on the horizon and bore down on the *Star of David*, blinker lights flashing. A sleek little destroyer, HMS *Blakely*, joined the *Defiance*. The two warships hovered about the old tramp as she chugged along.

'We have picked up our royal escort,' Bill Fry said over the loud-speaker.

By the rules of the game the contest was over. Mossad Aliyah Bet had gotten another ship out of Europe and onto the high seas. The British had sighted the vessel and were following it. The instant the *Star of David* entered the three-mile limit off Palestine she would be boarded by a British landing party and towed off to Haifa.

On the deck of the *Star of David* the refugees hooted at the warships and cursed Bevin. A large sign went up which read: HITLER MURDERED US AND THE BRITISH WON'T LET US LIVE! The *Defiance* and the *Blakely* paid no attention and did not, as hoped, miraculously disappear.

Once her children were calmed, Karen had more to think about. Many of them were becoming quite sick from the lack of air. She went topside and inched her way through the tangle of arms, legs, and knapsacks up to the captain's bridge. In the wheel room Bill Fry was sipping coffee and looking down at the solid pack of humanity on deck. The Palmach head was arguing with him.

'Jesus Christ!' Bill growled. 'One thing we get from Jews is conversation. Orders aren't made to be discussed. They are made to be obeyed. How in the hell you guys going to win anything if you've got to talk everything over? Now I'm the captain here!'

Bill's outburst hardly fazed the Palmach chief, who finished his argument and walked off.

Bill sat mumbling under his breath. He lit a cigar butt and then saw Karen standing rather meekly in the doorway.

'Hi, sweetheart,' he said, smiling. 'Coffee?'

'I'd love some.'

'You look bad.'

'I can't get too much sleep with the children.'

'Yeah ... how you getting along with them kids?'

'That's what I came to talk to you about. Some of them are getting quite sick, and we have several pregnant women in the hold.'

'I know, I know.'

'I think we should have a turn on deck.'

He pointed down to the solid cluster of bodies. 'Where?'

'You just find a few hundred volunteers to exchange places.'

'Aw, look now, honey, I hate to turn you down, but I've got a lot on my mind. It just ain't that easy. We can't start moving people around on this can.'

Karen's face retained a soft sweetness and her voice showed no anger. 'I am going back down there and I am taking my children on deck,' she said. She turned her back and started for the door.

'Come back here. How did a sweet-looking kid like you get so ornery?' Bill scratched his jaw. 'All right! All right! We'll get them brats of yours topside. Jesus Christ, all I get is arguments, arguments, arguments!'

That night Karen led her children to a place on the fantail of the ship. In the cool and wonderful air they fell into a deep and peaceful sleep.

The next day the sea was smooth as glass. Dawn brought more British patrol planes, and the now familiar escort, the *Defiance* and *Blakely*, were still there.

A tremor of excitement ran through the ship as Bill announced that they were less than twenty-four hours from Eretz Israel – Land of Israel. The mounting tension brought on a strange quiet that lasted far into the day. Toward evening the *Blakely* moved very close to the *Star of David*.

A booming British voice cut over the water from the *Blakely*'s loud-speaker. 'Immigrant ship. This is Captain Cunningham of the *Blakely* here. I want to speak to your captain.'

'Hello, *Blakely*,' Bill Fry's voice growled back, 'what's on your mind?'

'We would like to send an emissary aboard to speak to you.'

'You can speak now. We're all *mishpocha* here and we got no secrets.'

'Very well. Sometime after midnight you will enter the territorial waters of

Palestine. At that time we intend to board you and tow you to Haifa. We want to know if you are going to accept this without resistance?'

'Hello, Cunningham. Here's the picture. We've got some pregnant women and sick people aboard here and we would like you to accept them.'

'We have no instructions. Will you accept our tow or not?'

'Where did you say?'

'Haifa.'

'Well I'll be damned. We must be off course. This is a Great Lakes pleasure boat.'

'We will be compelled to board you forcibly!'

'Cunningham!'

'Yes?'

'Inform your officers and men ... you can all go to hell!'

Night came. No one slept. Everyone strained through the darkness for some sight of shore – the first look at Eretz Israel. Nothing could be seen. The night was misty and there were no stars or moon and the *Star of David* danced on brisk waves.

Around midnight a Palmach section head tapped Karen on the shoulder. 'Karen,' he said, 'come up to the wheelhouse with me.'

They threaded their way over the prone bodies to the wheelhouse, which was also packed with twenty of the crew and Palmach section heads. It was pitch black inside except for a bluish light from the compass. Near the wheel she could make out the husky outline of Bill Fry.

'Everyone here?'

'All accounted for.'

'All right, pay attention.' Bill's voice sounded in the darkness. 'I've talked it over with the Palmach heads and my crew and we've reached a decision. The weather off Palestine is socking in solid ... fog all over the coast. We are carrying an auxiliary motor aboard capable of boosting our speed to fifteen knots. In two hours we will be inside territorial waters. If this weather stays bad we've decided to make a run for it and beach ourselves south of Caesarea.'

An excited murmur raced around the room.

'Can we get away from those warships?'

'They'll think this tub's the *Thunderbird* before I'm finished,' Fry snapped back.

'How about radar? Won't they keep us on their screens?'

'Yeah ... but they ain't going to follow us too close to shore. They're not going to risk beaching a cruiser.'

'How about the British garrison in Palestine?'

'We have established contact with the Palmach ashore. They are expecting us. I'm sure they'll give the British an interesting evening. Now all of you section leaders have had special instructions at La Ciotat in beaching operations. You know what to expect and what to do. Karen, and you other two chiefs with children ... better wait here for special orders. Any questions?'

There were none.

'Any arguments?'

There were none.

'I'll be damned. Good luck and God bless all of you.'

Chapter Seventeen

A wind-driven mist whistled around the ancient and abandoned port of Caesarea, Palestine, and its heaps of rubble, broken walls, and moss-covered harbor which was in use four hundred years before the Christian era.

For five long centuries Caesarea – built by Herod in honor of Caesar – had been the capital of Roman Palestine. All that was left was ruin. The wind howled and churned up the water into a swirling foam which dashed against rocks jutting far into the sea.

Here the revolution against Roman tyranny ended with the slaughter of twenty thousand Hebrews and their great sage, Rabbi Akiva, who had called his people to fight for freedom with Bar Kochba, met his martyrdom. The Crocodile River still flowed to the sea where Akiva was skinned alive.

A few yards south of the ruins were the first buildings of a collective Jewish fishing village named Sdot Yam (Fields of the Sea). This night no fisherman or his wife slept.

They were all crouched throughout the ruins and they silently, breathlessly strained their eyes to the sea. They numbered two hundred and were joined by two hundred more Palmach soldiers.

A flashlight signal blinked out from the ancient Tower of Drusus which jutted into the surf, and everyone tensed.

Aboard the *Star of David*, Bill Fry's teeth tightened on a cigar stub and his hands tightened on the wheel of the old ship. He zigzagged her in slowly, inching past treacherous reefs and shoals. On deck the refugees pressed toward the rail and steeled themselves.

The *Star of David* shuddered and creaked as her timbers slashed into a craggy boulder! A single flare spiraled into the air! The melee was on!

Everyone scrambled over the sides, diving into shoulder-high water, and began fighting foot by foot through the surf toward the shore line several hundred yards away.

As the flare burst, the fisherman and Palmachniks scrambled from their cover and waded out to meet the refugees. Many slipped and fell into potholes or were overturned by a sudden wave and went down on slimy rocks, but nothing could stop them. The two forces met! The strong hands from the shore grabbed the refugees and began dragging them in.

'Quick! Quick!' they were ordered. 'Take off your clothing and change into these at once!'

'Throw away any identification papers!'

'Those dressed, follow us ... move ... move ... move!'

'Quiet! No noise!'

'No lights!'

The refugees tore the drenched clothing from their bodies and put on the blue uniforms of the fishermen.

'Mingle ... everyone mingle ...'

On deck of the *Star of David*, Karen handed children down to the

Palmachniks one by one as fast as they could make a trip in and come back out. Strong, sure-footed men were needed to hold the children in the surf.

'Faster ... faster ...'

There were uninhibited cries of emotion from some who fell on the holy soil to kiss it.

'You will have plenty of time to kiss the ground later but not now ... move on!'

Bill Fry stood on his bridge barking orders through a megaphone. Within an hour nearly everyone had abandoned the *Star of David* except for a few dozen children and the section chiefs.

Thirty kilometers to the north a Palmach unit staged a devastating assault on some British warehouse south of Haifa in an effort to divert the British troops in that area away from the beaching operation at Caesarea.

On the beach the fishermen and Palmachniks worked rapidly. Some of the refugees were taken into the village and others to trucks which sped them inland.

As the last of the children was handed over the rail of the *Star of David*, Bill Fry tore down the ladder to the deck and ordered the section heads over the side.

Karen felt the icy water close over her head. She balanced on her toes, treaded water for a moment, and found her direction. She swam in close enough to find footing. Ahead of her, on the beach, she could hear confused shouts in Hebrew and German. She came to a huge rock and crawled over it on all fours. A wave washed her back into the sea. Now she worked to solid ground and pushed in foot by foot against a driving undertow. Downed again on all fours she crawled closer to the shore.

A piercing sound of sirens!

An ear-splitting crackle of rifle fire!

On the beach everyone was dispersing!

Karen gasped for breath as she emerged into knee-high water, holding her side. Directly before her stood a half dozen khaki-clad British soldiers with truncheons in their hands.

'No!' she shrieked. 'No! No! No!'

She hurled herself into the cordon screaming, clawing, and kicking with fury. A strong arm seized her from behind and she was wrestled into the surf. Her teeth sank into the soldier's hand. He yelled in pain and released her. She flung herself forward again fighting like a savage. A second soldier held his truncheon high and brought it down and it thudded against her head. Karen moaned, went limp, and rolled unconscious into the water.

She opened her eyes. Her head throbbed horribly. But she smiled as she looked up into the face of stubble-jawed, bleary-eyed Bill Fry.

'The children!' she screamed, and spun off the cot. Bill's hands grabbed her.

'Take it easy. Most of the kids got away. Some of them are here.'

Karen closed her eyes and sighed and lay back on the cot again.

'Where are we?'

'British detention camp ... Atlit. It was a wonderful show. More than half the people got away. The British are so damned mad they rounded everybody up and herded us off here. We got crew, fishermen, refugees ... everybody mixed up in this mess. How do you feel?'

'I feel horrible. What happened?'

'You tried to whip the British Army singlehanded.'

She pushed the blanket off and sat up again and felt the lump on the side of her head. Her dress was still damp. She stood and walked, a bit wobbly, to the tent opening. There were several hundred more tents and a wall of barbed wire. Beyond the barbed wire were British sentries. 'I don't know what came over me,' Karen said. 'I've never struck anyone in my life. I saw those soldiers standing there ... trying to stop me. Somehow the most important thing that ever happened, happened that moment. I had to put my foot on Palestine. I had to or I'd die ... I don't know what came over me.' She sat down beside him.

'Want something to eat, kid?'

'I'm not hungry. What are they going to do with us?'

Bill shrugged. 'It will be light in a few hours. They'll start processing us and asking a lot of damned fool questions. You know the answers.'

'Yes ... I keep repeating that this is my country to whatever they ask.'

'Yeah ... anyhow, they'll keep you here a couple or three months and then they'll turn you loose. At least you're in Palestine.'

'What about you?'

'Me? Hell, they'll throw me out of Palestine same as they did the last time. I'll get another Mossad ship ... try another run on the blockade.'

Her head began to throb and she lay back but she could not close her eyes. She studied Bill's grizzled face for many moments.

'Bill ... why are you here?'

'What do you mean?'

'You're an American. It's different with Jews in America.'

'Everybody is trying to make something noble out of me.' He patted his pockets and pulled out some cigars. They were ruined by the water. 'The Aliyah Bet came around and saw me. They said they needed sailors. I'm a sailor ... been one all my life. Worked my way up from cabin boy to first mate. That's all there is to it. I get paid for this.'

'Bill ...'

'Yeah ...'

'I don't believe you.'

Bill Fry didn't seem to be convincing himself either. He stood up. 'It's hard to explain, Karen. I love America. I wouldn't trade what I've got over there for fifty Palestines.'

Karen propped up on an elbow. Bill began pacing the tent and groping to connect his thoughts. 'We're Americans but we're a different kind of Americans. Maybe we make ourselves different ... maybe other people make me different ... I'm not smart enough to figure those things out. All my life I've heard I'm supposed to be a coward because I'm a Jew. Let me tell you, kid. Every time the Palmach blows up a British depot or knocks the hell out of some Arabs he's winning respect for me. He's making a liar out of everyone who tells me Jews are yellow. These guys over here are fighting my battle for respect ... understand that?'

'I think so.'

'Well, damned if I understand it.'

He sat beside Karen and examined the lump on her head. 'That don't look too bad. I told those Limey bastards to take you to a hospital.'

'I'll be all right,' she said.

Later that night the Palmach staged a raid on the Atlit camp and another two hundred of the refugees escaped through a gaping hole blown in the barbed wire. Karen and Bill Fry were not among the escapees.

When the full report of the *Star of David* episode reached Whitehall the British realized they had to change their immigration policy. To date, the illegal runners had brought in loads of a few hundred. This ship had carried nearly two thousand, and the greater part of them had escaped in the beaching at Caesarea and the subsequent raid on Atlit. The British were faced with the fact that the French government openly supported the Jews and that one out of every six Jews in Palestine had entered illegally.

And so the British were caught in a tangle. They were as far away from a final answer on the Palestine problem as they ever had been, and so it was decided that the Jews must be turned away from Palestine and not kept at Atlit. The camps on Cyprus were established as a direct result of the pressure of illegal immigration and specifically of the success of the *Star of David* expedition.

Karen Hansen Clement was sent to the island of Cyprus on a British prison ship and interned in the Caraolos camp. But even as the *Karpathos/Star of David* lay wedged in the rocks off the shore of Caesarea and the surf pounded her to bits, the Mossad Aliyah Bet speeded up their operations, planning for more ships and larger numbers of refugees to follow in the wake.

For six more months the young girl stayed in the swirling dust of Caraolos and worked among her children. Her time in the succession of DP and internment camps had done nothing to harden or embitter her. She lived only for the moment when she could once again see Palestine ... Eretz Israel ... The magic words became an obsession for her too.

Many hours had passed when Karen finished telling her story to Kitty Fremont. During the telling a rapport had been established between them. Each detected the loneliness and the need for companionship of the other.

'Have you heard anything further about your father?' Kitty asked.

'No. Not since La Ciotat, and that was very long ago.'

Kitty looked at her watch. 'Goodness ... it's past midnight.'

'I didn't notice the time,' Karen said.

'Neither did I. Good night, child.'

'Good night, Kitty. Will I see you again?'

'Perhaps ... I don't know.'

Kitty stepped outside and walked away from the building. The thousands of tents were still now. A searchlight from the watchtower swept over the waves of canvas. Dust kicked up and blew around her feet and she tightened her coat. The tall figure of Ari Ben Canaan walked toward her and stopped. He handed her a cigarette, and they walked silently over the bridge out of the children's compound. Kitty stopped a moment and looked back, then continued on through the old people's area to the main gate.

'I will work for you on one condition,' Kitty said, 'that that girl does not go on the escape. She stays in this camp with me.'

'Agreed.'

Kitty turned and walked toward the sentry house quickly.

Chapter Eighteen

The plan which David had romantically called Operation Gideon moved into action. At Caraolos a large batch of bills of lading and British army identification cards were forged by Dov Landau and given to Kitty Fremont. She carried them from the camp and turned them over to Ari Ben Canaan.

The delivery of the bills of lading enabled Ben Canaan to complete the first phase of his scheme. During his survey of Cyprus he had become familiar with a large British supply depot on the Famagusta road near Caraolos. It was a fenced-in area containing several acres of trucks and other rolling stock and a dozen enormous warehouses. During the war the depot had been a major supply base for the Allies in the Middle East. Now some of the stock was still being shipped to British forces in that part of the world. Other stock had been declared surplus and had been bought up by private consignees. There was always some measure of movement from the depot to the Famagusta harbor.

Mandria's Cyprus-Mediterranean Shipping Company was the agent for the British Army on Cyprus. In that capacity Mandria had a stock list and numbers of all the materials stored at the depot. He also had a very adequate supply of bills of lading.

On Thursday at 8:00 A.M., Ari Ben Canaan and thirteen Palmachniks, all dressed in British uniforms and carrying British papers, pulled to a halt before the main gate of the depot in a British truck. Zev Gilboa, Joab Yarkoni, and David Ben Ami were in the 'working party.'

Ari, who was carrying papers as 'Captain Caleb Moore,' presented a list of requisitions to the depot commander. Ari's 'working party' had been detailed to gather the listed material and take it to the Famagusta docks for shipment aboard the SS *Achan.*

The forgeries were so perfect that the depot commander did not for a moment remember that Caleb was a spy for Moses in the Bible and that the *Achan*, a nonexistent ship, carried the same name as the man who stole the treasury at Jericho.

The first item the bills of lading called for was twelve trucks and two jeeps. They were rolled out of their parking area and checked out to 'Captain Caleb Moore.' The 'working party' then moved from warehouse to warehouse, loading their twelve new trucks with everything that would be needed for the *Aphrodite/Exodus* to make her trip to Palestine with three hundred escapee children.

Joab Yarkoni, who was in charge of fitting the ship, had drawn up a list of things which included a late-model radio receiver and transmitter, canned foods, medical supplies, flashlights, small arms, water cans, blankets, air-conditioning units, a loud-speaker system, and a hundred other items. Joab was very sad because Ari had insisted he shave off his big black mustache. Zev's mustache met the same fate, for Ari feared this would identify them as Palestinians.

In addition to supplies for the *Exodus*, David took a few tons of the things most urgently needed in Caraolos.

Zev Gilboa nearly went to pieces when he saw the British arsenal. In all his years in the Palmach they had always needed arms, and the sight of so many lovely machine guns and mortars and carbines was almost more than he could stand.

The 'working party' moved with clocklike precision. Ari knew from Mandria's lists where everything was located. Joab Yarkoni rounded out the afternoon's work by taking a few cases of scotch and a few of brandy and a few of gin and a few of wine – for medicinal purposes.

Twelve brand-new trucks crammed with supplies supposedly headed for the Famagusta harbor, where both supplies and trucks would be put aboard the SS *Achan*. Ari thanked the British commander for his excellent co-operation, and the 'working party' left six hours after it had entered.

The Palmachniks were flushed with the ease of their initial victory, but Ari did not give them time to rest or be too proud of themselves. This was but a beginning.

The next stop of Operation Gideon was to find a base for the trucks and material they had stolen. Ari had the answer. He had located an abandoned British camp on the outskirts of Famagusta. It had apparently been used once by a small service unit. The fence was still up, two wooden office shacks and the outhouses remained. Electric wiring from the main line was still in.

During the night and for the next two nights all the Palmachniks from Caraolos came to this camp and labored feverishly pitching tents, cleaning the area, and generally making it appear to be once again in service.

The twelve trucks and two jeeps were painted the khaki color of the British Army. On the doors of each vehicle Joab Yarkoni drew an insignia which could be mistaken for any one of a thousand army insignias and the lettering: 23rd Transportation Company HMJFC.

The 'company' office had enough actual and forged British papers and orders strewn about to give it an authentic look.

In four days the little camp with the twelve trucks looked quite natural and unimposing. They had taken enough British uniforms from the depot to dress the Palmachniks adequately as soldiers and enough of everything else to stock the camp completely.

As a finishing touch Joab Yarkoni put a sign over the entrance gate which read: 23rd Transportation Company HMJFC. Everyone sighed with relief as the sign raising officially dedicated the encampment.

Zev looked at the sign and scratched his head. 'What does HMJFC stand for?'

'His Majesty's Jewish Forces on Cyprus ... what else?' Joab answered.

The pattern of Operation Gideon was set. Ari Ben Canaan had had the utter audacity to form a fake unit of the British Army. Wearing a British uniform, he had established Mossad Aliyah Bet headquarters in broad daylight on the Famagusta road, and he was going to execute the final phases of his plan using British equipment. It was a dangerous game, yet he held to the simple theory that acting in a natural manner was the best cover an underground agent had.

The next phase of Operation Gideon became fact when three Americans from a merchant freighter landed in Famagusta and jumped ship. They were Mossad Aliyah Bet men who had received training during the war in the United States Navy. From another ship came two exiles of Franco Spain.

Often former Spanish Loyalists worked Aliyah Bet ships. Now the *Exodus* had a crew, the balance of which would be filled out by Ari, David, Joab, and Zev.

Hank Schlosberg, the American skipper, and Joab set to the task of refitting the *Exodus* into an immigrant runner. Larnaca was a small port and Mandria certainly knew the right way to produce silence over any unusual activity around the *Aphrodite* at the end of the pier.

First the cabins, holds, and deck were stripped clean of cabinets, bins, shelves, furnishings, and trimmings. The ship was turned into a shell from stem to stern.

Two wooden shacks were constructed on deck to serve as toilets: one for the boys and one for the girls. The crew's mess hall was converted into a hospital room. There would be no formal mess hall or galley. All food would be eaten from cans. The galley was converted into an arsenal and storeroom. Crew's quarters were taken out. The crew would sleep on the small bridge. The loudspeaker system was hooked up. The ancient engine was overhauled thoroughly. An emergency mast and sail were constructed in case of engine failure.

There were Orthodox children among the three hundred, and this posed a particular problem. Yarkoni had to seek out the head of the Jewish community on Cyprus and have 'kosher' food especially processed and canned for them according to dietary law.

Next an exact cubic measurement of the hold was taken, as well as a surface measurement of deck space. Shelves seventeen inches apart were built in the hold. These would serve as bunks and allow each child room to sleep on his stomach or back but not the luxury of rolling over. They computed an average height for the children and allotted four feet, eleven inches per child and marked it off down the shelves. The balance of the deck space in the hold and topside was also marked off, allowing a child just enough room to move an inch or two in each direction while asleep.

The lifeboats were repaired. Large holes were cut into the sides of the ship and wind pipes constructed so that air would be driven into the hold by electric fans. The air-conditioning units taken from the British depot were also fitted in. Air had to be circulated at all times in the packed quarters to prevent mass vomiting.

The work moved along smoothly. The sight of a half dozen men working on the old salvage tub appeared quite natural in the Larnaca harbor.

Loading supplies would pose another problem. Ari did not want to risk sending the khaki-colored trucks onto the dock, as he felt they were certain to attract attention. When the majority of the refitting had been completed the *Exodus* stole out of Larnaca each night to a rendezvous cove a few miles away in the Southern Bay. Here trucks from the 23rd Transportation Company HMJFC would come filled with supplies taken from the British depot. A constant stream of rubber boats moved from shore to ship all night until the *Exodus* was filled, inch by inch.

At the children's compound at Caraolos, Zev Gilboa carried out his part of Operation Gideon. He carefully screened three hundred of the strongest boys and girls and took them in shifts to the playground, where they were toughened up by exercises and taught how to fight with knives and sticks, how to use small arms and to throw grenades. Lookouts were posted all over the playground, and at sight of a British sentry a signal would change the games of war into games of peace. In three seconds the children could stop practicing gang fighting and start singing school songs. Groups not working out on the

playground would be in the classroom learning Palestinian landmarks and the
the depot around the clock and take anything not nailed down. Zev envisioned

At night Zev would take them all to the playground and build a bonfire, and he and some of the Palmachniks would spin stories and tell the children how wonderful it would be for them in Palestine and how they would never live behind barbed wire again.

There was a hitch in Operation Gideon, but it developed among Ari's closest lieutenants: David, Zev, and Joab.

Although David was a sensitive boy and a scholar he feared no man when aroused. He was aroused now. The first expedition into the British depot had gone so well that he, Zev, and Joab felt it was sacrilegious to leave as much as a shoestring in it. He wanted to run 23rd Transportation Company trucks into the depot around the clock and take anything not nailed down. Zev envisioned even taking cannons. They had gone so long on so little that this windfall was too great a temptation.

Ari argued that greed could ruin the whole plan. The British were sleeping but not dead. Twenty-third Transportation Company trucks should appear from time to time for the sake of naturalness, but to attempt to drain the depot would be to hang them all.

None the less he could not hold them down. Their schemes began to sound wilder and wilder. Joab had got so cocky that he even went so far as to invite some British officers to the 23rd Transportation Company for lunch. Ari's patience ran out and he had to threaten to send them all back to Palestine in order to get them into line.

In a little over two weeks after the beginning of Operation Gideon everything was ready to go. The final phases of the plan – Mark Parker's story plus getting the three hundred children to Kyrenia – awaited word from the British themselves. The final move would be made when the British opened the new refugee camps on the Larnaca road and began transferring inmates from Caraolos.

Chapter Nineteen

Caldwell, Sutherland's aide, went into the office of Major Allan Alistair, who was the Intelligence Chief on Cyprus. Alistair, a soft-spoken and shy-appearing man in his forties, gathered a batch of papers from his desk and followed Caldwell down the hall to Sutherland's office.

The brigadier asked Caldwell and Alistair to be seated and nodded to the intelligence man to begin. Alistair scratched the end of his nose and looked over his papers. 'There has been a tremendous step-up of Jewish activity at Caraolos in the children's compound,' he said in a half whisper. 'We analyze it as a possible riot or breakout.'

Sutherland drummed his fingers on the desk top impatiently. Alistair always made him nervous with his quiet, hush-hush ways and now he droned on through several more pages of information.

'Dear Major Alistair,' Sutherland said when he had finished, 'you have been reading to me for fifteen minutes and the theme of your story is that you suspect that some dire plot is being hatched by the Jews. During the past two weeks you have attempted to plant three men inside the children's compound and five men elsewhere inside Caraolos. Each one of your master spies has been detected within an hour and thrown out by the Jews. You have read to me two pages of messages which you have intercepted and which you cannot decode and you allege they are being sent from a transmitter you cannot locate.'

Alistair and Caldwell glanced at each other quickly as if to say, 'The old man is going to be difficult again.'

'Begging the brigadier's pardon,' Alistair said, leaning forward, 'much of our information is always speculative. However, there has been concrete data handed down which has not been acted upon. We know positively that Caraolos is riddled with Palestinian Palmach people who are giving military training on the playground. We also know positively that the Palestinians smuggle their people into Cyprus at a place near the ruins of Salamis. We have every reason to suspect that the Greek chap, Mandria, is working with them.'

'Blast it! I know all that,' Sutherland said. 'You men forget that the only thing that keeps those refugees from turning into a wild mob is the fact that these Palestinians are there. They run the schools, hospitals, kitchens, and everything else at that camp. Furthermore they keep discipline and they prevent escapes by letting only certain people go in and out. Throw the Palestinians out and we would be begging for trouble.'

'Then hire some informers, sir,' Caldwell said, 'and at least know what they are planning.'

'You can't buy a Jewish informer,' Alistair said; 'they stick together like flies. Every time we think we have one he sends us on a wild-goose chase.'

'Then crack down on them,' Caldwell snapped; 'put the fear of God into them.'

'Freddie, Freddie, Freddie,' Sutherland said in dismay, lighting his pipe. 'There is nothing we can do to frighten those people. They are graduates of concentration camps. You remember Bergen-Belsen, Freddie? Do you think we can do anything worse to them?'

Major Alistair was beginning to be sorry that he had asked Fred Caldwell to come in with him. He showed absolutely no latitude in his thinking. 'Brigadier,' Alistair said quickly, 'we are all soldiers here. None the less I'd be less than honest if I reported to you that everything was peaceful at Caraolos and that I thought we'd be wise to continue to just sit and wait for trouble.'

Sutherland rose, clasped his hands behind him, and began to pace the room thoughtfully. He puffed his pipe for several moments and tapped the stem against his teeth. 'My mission here on Cyprus is to keep these camps quiet until our government decides what it intends to do with the Palestine mandate. We are not to risk anything that could bring adverse propaganda.'

Fred Caldwell was angry. He simply could not understand why Sutherland chose to sit and let the Jews drum up trouble. It was beyond him.

Allan Alistair understood but did not agree. He favored a quick counter-blow to upset any Jewish plans in Caraolos. None the less, all he could do was present the information; it was up to Brigadier Sutherland to act upon it. Sutherland, in his estimation, was being unreasonably soft.

'Is there anything else?' the brigadier asked.

'Yes, one more problem now, sir,' Alistair thumbed through his papers. 'I would like to know if the brigadier has studied the report on this American woman, Katherine Fremont, and the correspondent, Mark Parker?'

'What about them?'

'Well, sir, we are not certain if she is his mistress, but the fact that she has gone to work at Caraolos certainly coincides with his entry into Cyprus. From past experience we know that Parker has anti-British leanings.'

'Rubbish. He is an excellent reporter. He did a splendid job at the Nuremberg trials. We made a costly blunder once in Holland and the man found it and reported it. That was his job.'

'Are we correct in assuming, sir, that it is quite possible Mrs Fremont's going to work in Caraolos may have something to do with helping Parker do an exposé of the camp?'

'Major Alistair, I hope that if you are ever brought to trial for murder the jury will not hang you on such evidence as you have just placed before me.'

Little red patches dotted Alistair's cheeks.

'This Fremont woman happens to be one of the best pediatric nurses in the Middle East. She was cited by the Greek government for doing an outstanding job in an orphanage in Salonika. That is also in your report. She and Mark Parker have been friends since childhood. That is also in your report. It is also in your report that the Jewish welfare people sought her out. Tell me, Major Alistair ... you do read your reports, don't you?'

'But ... sir ...'

'I haven't finished. Let us assume that the very worst of your suspicions are well founded. Let us assume that Mrs Fremont is gathering information for Mark Parker. Let us say that Mark Parker writes a series of articles about Caraolos. Gentlemen, this is the end of 1946 ... the war has been over for a year and a half. People are generally sick and tired of, and rather unimpressed with, refugee stories. What will impress people is our throwing an American nurse and newspaperman off Cyprus. Gentlemen, the meeting is concluded.'

Alistair gathered his papers together quickly. Fred Caldwell had been sitting in cold and fuming anger. He sprang to his feet. 'I say we kill a few of these sheenies and show them just who is running this show!'

'Freddie!'

Caldwell turned at the door.

'If you are so anxious I can arrange a transfer to Palestine. The Jews there are armed and they are not behind barbed wire. They eat little men like you for breakfast.'

Caldwell and Alistair walked briskly down the hall. Freddie grumbled angrily under his breath. 'Come into my office,' Alistair said. Freddie flopped into a chair and threw up his hands. Alistair snatched a letter opener from his desk and slapped it in his open palm and paced the room.

'Ask me,' Caldwell said, 'they ought to give the old boy his knighthood and retire him.'

Alistair returned to his desk and bit his lip hesitatingly. 'Freddie, I've been thinking for several weeks. Sutherland has proven utterly impossible. I am going to write a personal letter to General Tevor-Browne.'

Caldwell raised his eyebrows. 'That's a bit risky, old boy.'

'We must do something before this bloody island blows up on us. You are Sutherland's aide. If you back me up on this I'll guarantee there will be no repercussions.'

Caldwell had had his fill of Sutherland. Alistair was a relative of General

Tevor-Browne through marriage. He nodded. 'And you might add a good word for me with Tevor-Browne.'

A knock on the door brought in a corporal with a new batch of papers. He gave them to Alistair and left the office. Alistair thumbed through the sheets and sighed. 'As if I didn't have enough on my mind. There is a ring of organized thieves on the island. They are so damned clever we don't even know what they are stealing.'

General Tevor-Browne received Major Alistair's urgent and confidential report a few days later. His immediate reaction was to recall Alistair and Caldwell to London and to call them on the carpet for what amounted to mutiny; then he realized that Alistair would not have risked sending such a letter unless he was truly alarmed.

If Tevor-Browne was to follow the advice of Alistair and make a quick raid on Caraolos to upset any plans the Jews might have, he had to move quickly, for although he didn't know it, Ari Ben Canaan had set the day, hour, and minute for taking the children out of Caraolos.

The British announced that the new facilities near Larnaca were ready and a general evacuation of many of the over-crowded compounds at Caraolos would begin in a few days. The refugees would be moved by truck at the rate of three to five hundred per day over a ten-day period. Ari chose the sixth day as the day.

No tunnels, no crates, no garbage dumps. Ari was just going to drive up to Caraolos and take the children out in British trucks.

Chapter Twenty

Deliver in person to
Kenneth Bradbury
Chief, ANS
London Bureau

Dear Brad:

This letter and enclosed report from Cyprus are being delivered to you by F. F. Whitman, a pilot with British Inter-continental Airways.

D-Day on Operation Gideon is five days off. Cable me at once that you have received the report. I have used my own discretion on this thing. I feel that it can turn into something very big.

On D-Day I will send a cable to you. If my cable is signed MARK that means that everything went off according to schedule and it is O.K. to release the story. If it is signed PARKER then hold off because that means something went wrong.

I promised F. F. Whitman $500 for safe delivery of this to you. Pay the man, will you?

MARK PARKER

Mark Parker
Dome Hotel
Kyrenia, Cyprus

AUNT DOROTHY ARRIVED SAFELY IN LONDON AND WE WERE ALL HAPPY TO SEE HER. LOOKING FORWARD TO HEARING FROM YOU.

BRAD

Mark's story sat safely in the London ANS bureau, to be released on signal.

Kitty moved from the Dome Hotel to the King George in Famagusta when she went to work at Saraolos. Mark decided to stay put at the Dome in order to be on the spot in Kyrenia when the *Exodus* came in.

He had driven to Famagusta twice to see her. Both times she was out at the camp. Mandria confirmed what Mark suspected. The young refugee girl went to work as Kitty's aide. They were together all day long. Mark became worried. Kitty should have more sense than to try to bring her dead child to life through this girl. There seemed to him to be something unhealthy about it. In addition there was the business of her carrying forged papers out of Caraolos.

There were only a few days left until Operation Gideon moved into the final phase. The tension harassed Mark, and Kitty's strange behavior harassed him even more. He made a date to meet her at the King George in Famagusta.

As he drove to Famagusta his nerves were on edge. It had all gone too easily. Ben Canaan and his gang of bandits had run circles around the British. The British were aware that something was happening but they could not for the life of them seem to find the outside workers. Mark marveled at the finesse and skill of Ben Canaan and the courage of the Palmachniks. The outfitting of the *Exodus*, the training of the children had gone off perfectly. It would indeed be the biggest thing of his career, but because he was part of it all he was very worried.

He reached Famagusta and parked beside the King George Hotel, which was much like the Dome in that it sat on a beach with terraces overlooking the water. He found Kitty at a table looking out at the sea.

'Hello, Mark,' she said, and smiled and kissed him on the cheek as he sat beside her.

He ordered drinks and lit a cigarette and one for Kitty. She was absolutely radiant. She seemed ten years younger than she had that first day in Kyrenia.

'I must say, you look the picture of happiness,' she said in deference to his sour expression.

The drinks arrived.

'Are you on pins and needles for the big moment?'

'Sure, why not?' he snapped.

Their eyes met over the tops of their glasses. Kitty set hers down quickly. 'All right, Mr Parker. You are lit up like a road sign. You'd better start talking before you explode.'

'What's the matter? You mad at me? You don't like me any more?'

'For goodness' sake, Mark. I didn't think you were so thin skinned. I've been working very hard . . . besides, we agreed it would be best not to see too much of each other during the last two weeks, didn't we?'

'My name is Mark Parker. We used to be friends. We used to talk things over.'

'I don't know what you're driving at.'

'Karen ... Karen Clement Hansen. A little refugee girl from Denmark via Germany.'

'I don't think there is anything to discuss ...'

'I think there is.'

'She's just a lovely child I happen to like. She is my friend and I am her friend.'

'You never could lie very well.'

'I don't wish to talk about it!'

'You're asking for trouble. The last time you ended up naked with a marine in bed. This time I think you're going to have the strength to kill yourself.'

Her eyes dropped away from Mark's glare. 'Up to the past few weeks I've been so sane all my life,' she said.

'Are you trying to make up for it all at once?'

She put her hand on his. 'It has been like being born all over again and it doesn't make sense. She is such a remarkable girl, Mark.'

'What are you going to do when she goes on the *Exodus*? Are you going to follow her to Palestine?'

Kitty squashed out her cigarette and drank her cocktail. Her eyes narrowed in an expression that Mark knew. 'What have you done?' he demanded.

'She isn't going on the *Exodus*. That was my condition for going to work for Ari Ben Canaan.'

'You damned fool ... you damned fool, Kitty.'

'Stop it!' she said. 'Stop making something indecent out of this. I've been lonely and hungry for the kind of affection this girl has to give and I can give her the kind of understanding and companionship she needs.'

'You don't want to be her companion. You want to be her mother.'

'And what if I do! There's nothing wrong with that either.'

'Look ... let's stop yelling at each other ... let's calm down. I don't know what you have figured out, but her father is probably alive. If he isn't, she has a family in Denmark. Exhibition number three ... that kid is poisoned like they poison all of them. She wants Palestine.'

Kitty's face became drawn and her eyes showed a return of sadness and Mark was sorry.

'I was wrong not to let her go on the *Exodus*. I wanted to have her for a few months ... to gain her complete confidence ... to let her know how wonderful it would be to go to America. If I could be with her a few months I'd be sure of myself ...'

'Kitty ... Kitty ... Kitty. She isn't Sandra. You've been looking for Sandra from the moment the war ended. You were looking for her in Salonika in that orphanage. Maybe that's why you had to take Ben Canaan's challenge, because there were children at Caraolos and you thought one of them might be Sandra.'

'Please, Mark ... no more.'

'All right. What do you want me to do?'

'Find out if her father is alive. If he isn't, I want to adopt her and get her to the States.'

'I'll do what I can,' he said. He spotted Ari Ben Canaan, dressed as Captain Caleb Moore, coming through to their terrace. Ari walked quickly to their table and sat down. The Palestinian was his usual cold expressionless self. The instant Kitty saw him, her face lit up.

'David just contacted me from Caraolos. Something has come up that requires my immediate attention. I think under the circumstances that you had better come with me,' he said to Kitty.

'What is it?' both Mark and Kitty said together.

'I don't know exactly. The Landau boy, the one who does our forgeries. He is now working on the transfer papers for getting the children out. He refuses to do any further work until he speaks to me.'

'What do you want me for?' Kitty asked.

'Your friend, the little Danish girl Karen, is about the only person who can talk to him.'

Kitty turned pale.

'We must have those papers completed in the next thirty-six hours,' Ari said. 'We may need you to talk to the boy through Karen.'

Kitty stumbled from her chair and followed Ari blindly. Mark shook his head sadly, and his troubled glance remained on the empty doorway for many moments.

Chapter Twenty-one

Karen stood in the classroom that was Palmach headquarters. She stared angrily at the boy with the soft face, blond hair, and sweet appearance. He was a little small for seventeen years and the softness was deceptive. A pair of icy blue eyes radiated torment, confusion, and hatred. He stood by a small alcove which held the papers and instruments he used for his forgeries. Karen walked up to him and shook a finger under his nose. 'Dov! What have you gone and done?' He curled his lip and grunted. 'Stop growling at me like a dog,' she demanded. 'I want to know what you have done.'

He blinked his eyes nervously. No use arguing with Karen when she was angry. 'I told them I wanted to talk with Ben Canaan.'

'Why?'

'See these papers? They are forgeries of British mimeographed forms. Ben Ami gave me a list of three hundred kids here in our compound to be listed on these sheets for transfer to the new camp at Larnaca. They aren't going to the new camp. There's a Mossad ship out there someplace. It's going to Palestine.'

'What about it? You know we don't question the Mossad or the Palmach.'

'This time I do. Our name isn't listed. I'm not going to fix these papers unless they let us go too.'

'You're not sure there is a ship. Even if there is and we don't go they have their reasons. Both of us have work to do right here in Caraolos.'

'I don't care whether they need me or not. They promised to get me to Palestine and I'm going.'

'Don't you think we owe these Palmach boys something for all they've done for us? Don't you have any loyalty at all?'

'Done for us, done for us. Don't you know yet why they're breaking their necks to smuggle Jews into Palestine? You really think they do it because they love us? They're doing it because they need people to fight the Arabs.'

'And what about the Americans and all the others who aren't fighting Arabs? Why are they helping us?'

'I'll tell you why. They're paying for their consciences. They feel guilty because they weren't put into gas chambers.'

Karen clenched her fists and her teeth and closed her eyes to keep herself from losing her temper. 'Dov, Dov, Dov. Don't you know anything but hate?' She started for the door.

He rushed over and blocked her exit. 'You're mad at me again,' he said.

'Yes, I am.'

'You're the only friend I've got, Karen.'

'All you want to do is go to Palestine so you can join the terrorists and kill . . .' She walked back into the room and sat down at a desk and sighed. Before her on the blackboard was this sentence chalked in block letters: THE BALFOUR DECLARATION OF 1917 IS THE BRITISH PROMISE OF A JEWISH HOMELAND IN PALESTINE. 'I want to go to Palestine too,' she whispered. 'I want to go so badly I could die. My father is waiting there for me . . . I know he is.'

'Go back to your tent and wait for me,' Dov said. 'Ben Canaan will be here soon.'

Dov paced the room nervously for ten minutes after Karen had gone, working himself up to greater and greater anger.

The door opened. The large frame of Ari Ben Canaan passed through the doorway. David Ben Ami and Kitty Fremont followed him. David closed the door and locked it.

Dov's eyes narrowed with suspicion. 'I don't want her in here,' he said.

'I do,' Ari answered. 'Start talking.'

Dov blinked his eyes and hesitated. He knew he couldn't budge Ben Canaan. He walked to the alcove and snatched up the mimeographed transfer sheets. 'I think you have an Aliyah Bet ship coming into Cyprus and these three hundred kids are going on it.'

'That's a good theory. Go on,' Ari said.

'We made a deal, Ben Canaan. I'm not fixing these papers for you unless I add my name and the name of Karen Clement to this list. Any questions?'

Ari glanced at Kitty out of the corner of his eyes.

'Has it occurred to you, Dov, that no one can do your work and that we need you here?' David Ben Ami said. 'Has it occurred to you that both you and Karen have more value here than in Palestine?'

'Has it occurred to you that I don't give a damn?' Dov answered.

Ari lowered his eyes to hide a smile. Dov was tough and smart and played the game rough. The concentration camps bred a mean lot.

'It looks like you're holding the cards,' Ari said. 'Put your name on the list.'

'What about Karen?'

'That wasn't part of our deal.'

'I'm making a new deal.'

Ari walked up to him and said, 'I don't like that, Dov.' He towered over the boy threateningly.

Dov backed up. 'You can beat me! I've been beaten by experts! You can kill me! I'm not afraid. Nothing you do can scare me after the Germans!'

'Stop reciting Zionist propaganda to me,' Ari said. 'Go to your tent and wait there. We'll give you an answer in ten minutes.'

Dov unlocked the door and ran out.

'The little bastard!' David said.

Ari nodded quickly for David to leave the room. The instant the door closed Kitty grabbed Ari by the shirt. 'She isn't going on that ship! You swore it! She is not going on the *Exodus*!'

Ari grabbed her wrists. 'I'm not even going to talk to you unless you get control of yourself. We've got too much to cope with without a hysterical woman.'

Kitty pulled her hands free with a fierce jerk.

'Now listen,' Ari said, 'I didn't dream this up. The finish of this thing is less than four days off. That boy has us by the throat and he knows it. We can't move unless he fixes those papers.'

'Talk to him ... promise anything, but keep Karen here!'

'I'd talk till I'm purple if I thought it would do any good.'

'Ben Canaan ... please ... he'll compromise. He won't insist on Karen's going.'

Ari shook his head. 'I've seen hundreds of kids like him. They haven't left much in them that's human. His only link with decency is Karen. You know as well as I do he's going to be loyal to that girl ...'

Kitty leaned against the blackboard where the words: THE BALFOUR DECLARATION OF 1917 IS THE BRITISH PROMISE ... were written. The chalk rubbed off on the shoulder of her dress. Ben Canaan was right; she knew it. Dov Landau was incorrigible but he did have a strange loyalty for Karen. Mark had been right. She had been a damned fool.

'There is only one way,' Ari said. 'You go to that girl and tell her the way you feel about her. Tell her why you want her to stay on Cyprus.'

'I can't,' Kitty whispered. 'I can't.' She looked up at Ben Canaan with a pathetic expression.

'I didn't want anything like this to happen,' Ari said. 'I am sorry, Kitty.' It was the first time he had ever called her Kitty.

'Take me back to Mark,' she said.

They walked into the hall. 'Go to Dov,' Ari said to David. 'Tell him that we agree to his terms.'

When Dov got the news he rushed over to Karen's tent and burst in excitedly. 'We are going to Palestine,' he cried.

'Oh dear,' was all that Karen could say. 'Oh dear.'

'We must keep it quiet. You and I are the only ones among the children who know about it.'

'When do we go?'

'A few more days. Ben Canaan is bringing some trucks up. Everyone will be dressed like British soldiers. They're going to pretend to be taking us to the new camp near Larnaca.'

'Oh dear.'

They went out of the tent, hand in hand. Dov looked out over the sea of canvas as he and Karen walked in and out among the acacia trees. They walked slowly toward the playground, where Zev had a class of children practicing knife fighting.

Dov Landau walked on alone along the barbed-wire wall. He saw the British soldiers marching back and forth, back and forth. Down the long wall of barbed wire there was a tower and a machine gun and a searchlight.

Barbed wire – guns – soldiers –

When had he been outside of barbed wire? It was so very long ago it was hard to remember.

Barbed wire – guns – soldiers – Was there a real life beyond them? Dov stood there and looked. Could he remember that far back? It was so long ago – so very long ago –

Chapter Twenty-two

WARSAW, POLAND, SUMMER 1939

Mendel Landau was a modest Warsaw baker. In comparison with Dr Johann Clement he was at the opposite end of the world – socially, financially, intellectually. In fact, the two men would have had absolutely nothing in common except that they were both Jews.

As Jews, each man had to find his own answer to the relationship between himself and the world around him. Dr Clement clung to the ideals of assimilation up to the very end. Although Mendel Landau was a humble man he had thought out the problem, too, but had come to an entirely different conclusion.

Mendel Landau, like every Polish Jew, well knew what had followed the seven hundred years the Jews in Poland had been subjected to persecution of one kind or another, ranging from maltreatment to mass murder.

The Jews came to Poland originally to escape the persecution of the Crusaders. They fled to Poland from Germany, Austria, and Bohemia before the sword of 'holy' purification.

Mendel Landau, like every Polish Jew, well knew what had followed the original flight of the Jews into Poland. They were accused of ritual murder and witchcraft and were loathed as business competitors.

An unbroken series of tribulations climaxed one Easter week when mobs ran through the streets dragging each Jew and his family from his home. Those who would not accept baptism were killed on the spot.

There was a Jew's tax. Jews were forced to wear a yellow cloth badge to identify themselves as a race apart. A thousand and one statutes and laws aimed at suppressing the Jews stood on the books. The Jews were moved into ghettos and walled in to keep them isolated from the society around them.

In these ghettos something strange happened. Instead of dying slowly, the faith and culture of the Jews deepened and their numbers multiplied. Sealed off forcibly as they were from the outside world, the Jews turned more and more to the laws of Moses for guidance, and these laws became a powerful binding force among them. Inside the ghetto they governed themselves and developed closer-knit family and community ties which continued even after the ghettos were outlawed.

For those who ruled Poland the ghetto was only part of the answer of how to deal with the Jews. Jews were prevented by law from owning land or belonging to dozens of trades and crafts in which they might offer significant economic competition.

The Jews, locked in their ghettos, made ready scapegoats for any Polish disaster. Periodically mobs, goaded by blind hatred and fed on fear, tore into the ghettos and killed and whipped the Jews and smashed their homes and belongings until Jew beating became an accepted, if not honorable, pastime of the Poles.

Four centuries of Jew baiting came to a climax in 1648. During a Cossack uprising half a million Jews were slaughtered; the frenzy of the slaughterers was such that Jewish infants were often thrown into open pits and buried alive.

The Dark Ages, which came to an end in western Europe, seemed to linger on over the Polish ghettos. The enormous tragedy of 1648, together with hundreds of years of continuous persecution, created strange phenomena within the ghetto walls.

Throughout Jewish history, whenever events were black and hope all but vanished, a dozen or so self-styled 'messiahs' would arise among the people and proclaim themselves their saviors. In this darkest of moments after the 1648 massacres a new group of 'messiahs' stepped forward. Each claimed to have been sent in fulfillment of the prophecies of Isaiah. Each had a strong following.

With the messiahs came the Jewish mystics, a cult dedicated to finding Biblical explanations for the centuries of suffering. In their desperation for salvation the mystics concocted weird interpretations of the Bible based on mysticism, numerology, and just plain wishful thinking. They hoped through an involved system called the Cabala to find a way for God to lead them from the wilderness of death.

While the messiahs proclaimed themselves and the Cabalists looked for hidden meanings, a third sect arose in the ghettos: the Hasidim, who withdrew from the rigors of normal life and lived only for study and prayer. By submerging themselves in prayer they managed to lift themselves from the pain of reality into religious ecstasy.

Messiahs – Cabalists – Hasidim – all born of desperation.

Mendel Landau knew all this. He also knew there had been periods of enlightenment when the burden eased and the laws relaxed. Poland's own history was blood-marked. The Poles had struggled for freedom in a series of wars, revolutions, and plays of power. Parts of Poland's borders were torn away, and there was always an invasion – or the threat of invasion. During these Polish struggles the Jews took up arms and fought alongside the Poles, placing the cause of the larger nation above their own.

Much of what Mendel Landau knew was now ancient history. It was 1939 and Poland was a republic. He and his family no longer lived in a ghetto. There were over three million Jews in the country and they formed a vital part of the national life.

The oppression had not stopped with the formation of a republic. It only varied in degree. There was still unequal taxation for Jews. There was still economic strangulation. The Jews continued to be blamed by most Poles for causing floods when it rained and drought when it was dry.

The ghetto was gone, but to Mendel Landau anywhere he lived in Poland was a ghetto. It was a republic, indeed, but since 1936 Mendel Landau had seen pogroms; and anti-Jewish rioting in Brzesc, Czestochowa, Brzytyk, Minsk Mazowiecki; and he knew the snarl of the hoodlums who specialized in smashing Jewish shops and cutting Jewish beards.

And so Mendel Landau and Johann Clement came to different conclusions.

After seven centuries in Poland, Mendel Landau was still an intruder and he knew it.

He was a simple and rather modest man. Leah, his wife, was the plainest of women, a hard-working and devoted mother and wife.

Mendel Landau wanted something to give his children as a heritage. He did not have the fervor of the Hasidim for prayer, nor did he believe in messiahs or in the numerology of the Cabala.

Mendel retained only a measure of faith in his religion. He kept the Jewish holidays as most Christians keep Easter and Christmas. He accepted the Bible for its historical value as a story of his people rather than as a basis for worship. And so he could not offer his children even a deeply rooted religion.

What Mendel Landau gave his children was an idea. It was remote and it was a dream and it was unrealistic. He gave his children the idea that the Jews must someday return to Palestine and re-establish their ancient state. Only as a nation could they ever find equality.

Mendel Landau worked hard as a baker. His world consisted of feeding a family and providing them with shelter, education, clothing, and love. He did not believe, in his wildest moments, that he would ever see Palestine, nor did he believe his children would ever see Palestine. But he did believe in the idea.

Mendel was not alone among the Polish Jews. Of Poland's three and a half million Jews, there were hundreds of thousands who followed the same star, and from them spouted the wellspring of Zionism. There were religious Zionists, labor Zionists, small militant Zionist groups, and middle-class merchant Zionists.

Because he was a trade unionist, Mendel's family belonged to a labor-Zionist group who called themselves the Redeemers. The entire social life of the Landaus revolved around the Redeemers. From time to time there were speakers from Palestine, there was recruiting work, there were books and pamphlets and discussions and songs and dances and endless hope to keep the idea alive. The Redeemers, like other Zionist groups, ran agricultural centers where boys and girls could be trained to work the land. And every so often the Redeemers sent a group to Palestine to cultivate newly purchased land.

There were six members of the Landau family. There were Mendel and his wife Leah. There was the oldest son, Mundek, who was a strapping boy of eighteen and a baker himself. Mundek was a natural leader and was a section head in the Redeemers. There were the two girls. Ruth, who was seventeen, was horribly shy as Leah had been. She was in love with Jan, who was also a leader of the Redeemers. Rebecca was fourteen, and there was little Dov, who was the baby of the family. He was ten and blond and wide-eyed and actually too young to be a member of the Redeemers. He idolized his big brother Mundek, who patronizingly allowed him to tag along to meetings.

SEPTEMBER 1, 1939

After manufacturing a series of border incidents the Germans invaded Poland. Mendel Landau and his eldest son Mundek went into the army.

The German Wehrmacht ripped Poland to shreds in a campaign that lasted only twenty-six days. Mendel Landau was killed in battle along with more then thirty thousand other Jewish soldiers who wore the uniform of Poland.

The Landaus were not allowed the luxury of prolonged sorrow for this was a time of peril. Mundek returned from the gallant but futile defense of Warsaw as head of the Landau family.

The same moment the Germans entered Warsaw, the Redeemers met to discuss a course of action. Most of Poland's Jews, being more hopeful than realistic, felt nothing would happen to them and adopted a 'wait and see' attitude. The Redeemers and other Zionist groups throughout Poland were not so naïve. They were positive that grave danger lay ahead with Germans in occupation.

The Redeemers and many of the other Zionist groups decided to stay together and to take group action which would be binding on them all. Some groups chose to flee to the illusion of safety in the Soviet Union which had moved in to gobble up the eastern half of Poland when the Germans invaded. Other groups began an underground operation, and still others worked on the establishment of an 'underground railway' for escape.

The Redeemers voted to remain in Warsaw and build up resistance inside the city and remain in contact with other Redeemer groups throughout Poland. Mundek was voted the military leader although he was not yet nineteen. Jan, Ruth's secret love, was made Mundek's second in command.

The moment the Germans established themselves in power and Hans Frank became governor, an immediate series of laws were levied against the Jews. Worship, forbidden; travel, limited; taxation, excessive. Jews were thrown out of public office, civil or elective. Jews were barred from bread lines. Jews were barred from public places. Jews were taken out of schools.

There was talk of a revival of the ghetto.

With the restrictive laws the Germans embarked upon a campaign of 'enlightenment' for the Polish population. This campaign fostered the already prevalent opinion that the Jews had started the war; and the Germans claimed further that the Jews were responsible for the German invasion which was designed to save Poland from 'Jewish Bolsheviks.' Warsaw and the other cities were plastered with posters depicting bearded Jews violating nuns and other scenes of Jewish 'depravity.' Beard cutting, profaning synagogues, and public indignities against the Jews were encouraged.

BERLIN, GERMANY

In Berlin the top Nazi officials wrestled with the 'Jewish problem.' Several theories were advanced. Heydrich, the SD Chief, favored holding the Jews for ransom and then deporting them en masse. Schacht, the financial wizard, preferred a slow draining of the financial assets of the Jews. Many ideas were presented and discussed. An old plan of shipping all the Jews to the island of Madagascar was revived for consideration. Others would have preferred to send the Jews to Palestine, but the British blockade made that impossible.

SS Colonel Eichmann had long done 'resettlement' work among the Jews. He had been born in Palestine and spoke fluent Hebrew and therefore seemed the most obvious man to be put in charge of the final solution of the Jewish problem. Headquarters were established at Kurfuerstenstrasse 46. The first thing that was apparent was that until a final solution was reached a mass resettlement program was called for. Most of the Nazis agreed that Poland was the natural place for resettlement. First, there were already three and a half million Jews in Poland. Second, they would encounter little or no public indignation as they would in western Europe.

Hans Frank, the German governor, objected to having more Jews dumped in Poland. He had tried to starve the Polish Jews and he had shot and hanged as many as he could. But Frank was overruled by the top planners in Berlin.

The Germans cast a dragnet all over Poland to catch the Jews. Raiding parties tore into villages and the smaller towns and rounded up the Jews at a moment's notice. They were packed onto freight trains, often without being able to take anything with them, and sent to the large population centers.

A few Jews learned of the roundups in advance and either fled or tried to buy their way into Christian homes. Very few Poles ran the risk of harboring a Jew. Others extorted every penny from the Jews and then turned them over to the Germans for a reward.

Once the Jews were 'resettled,' an edict was issued ordering every Jew to wear a white arm band bearing a Star of David.

Poland wasn't like Denmark. The Poles made no objection to the edict, and the Jews wore the arm band and the Star of David on their backs as well.

WARSAW, WINTER 1939

These were hard and bitter days for the Landau family. The death of Mendel Landau, renewed talk of reviving the ghetto, the resettlement program of the Germans, and the shortages made life very difficult.

One morning, early in 1940, there was a knock on the door of the Landau home. Polish Blue Police who worked with the Germans were outside. They abruptly informed Leah Landau that she had two hours to pack her belongings and move to another section of Warsaw which had been set aside for the Jews. There would be no compensation for the house and barely time to gather together what Leah had saved in over twenty years of married life. The Landaus and all the rest of the Jews in Warsaw were resettled in an area in the center of the city near the main rail line.

Mundek and Jan moved quickly and were able to get an entire three-story building to serve as home and headquarters for over a hundred members of the Redeemers. The Landau family of five had a single room furnished with cots and a pair of chairs. The bathroom and kitchen were shared with ten other families.

The Jews were pressed into a tiny area that ran only twelve blocks in length from Jerozolimksa Street to the cemetery and was a bare six blocks wide. The Redeemers were situated in the Brushmakers' district on Leszno Street. Leah had managed to hoard a few jewels and valuables which might be useful later, although there was no immediate financial need, for Mundek continued to work as a baker and the Redeemers pooled their food resources in a common kitchen.

Jews from the provinces poured into Warsaw. They came in long lines, carrying all they were allowed to take in sacks or wheelbarrows or pushcarts. They unloaded in trainload after trainload at the siding near the Jews' quarters. The small area became packed. Jan's family moved in with the Landau family. There were nine now in the single room. The romance between Ruth and Jan became an open secret.

The Germans had the Jews set up a council to govern their area, but it quickly became an instrument for carrying out German orders. Other Jews who felt it better to 'go along' with the Germans joined a special Jewish police force. The population in the compressed area swelled to over half a million people.

At the end of 1940, one year after the conquest of Poland, the Germans put many thousands of Jews into forced-labor battalions. A brick wall ten feet high was built around the Jewish area in Warsaw. Barbed wire was strung atop the wall. The fifteen exits were guarded by Polish Blues and by Lithuanians. *The ghetto had returned to Poland!* Almost all traffic from the ghetto outside the wall ceased. Mundek, who had held a job on the outside, was now unemployed. Rations inside the ghetto were cut to a level that could barely feed half the population. The only families who seemed to stand a chance of obtaining food were those who held 'labor' cards and worked in one of the dozen forced-labor battalions or industries.

The creation of the ghetto brought panic. Some Jews began to trade their fortunes for food and some tried to escape to Christian homes. But most escape attempts ended in death or betrayal from the other side of the wall. Life inside the wall gradually became a day-to-day struggle to stay alive.

Mundek Landau emerged as a leader. Because of his importance among the Redeemers he obtained a license from the Jewish Council to run one of the few ghetto bakeries. Thus, through a continuation of united action, his group managed to keep alive and fed.

All was not blackness inside the ghetto. A very fine symphony orchestra gave weekly concerts, schools ran on schedule, little-theater groups were formed. There was always a choice of debates and lectures. A ghetto newspaper was printed and ghetto money became a legal means of exchange. Secret religious services were held. The Redeemers played a major part in keeping these services and activities going. Although little Dov wanted to be more active in the Redeemers, the rest of the Landau family forced him to get as much schooling as he could.

MARCH 1941

Eighteen months after the invasion of Poland, the final decision for a solution of the Jewish problem was handed down by Adolf Hitler. The order was verbal. Six weeks later SD Chief Heydrich announced the *Fuehrer*'s decision at a secret conference of SS, SD, and other Nazi officials at Gross-Wannsee.

The final solution was genocide.

SS Colonel Eichmann, the resettlement expert, was put in charge of eradicating the Jews from the face of Europe.

Within a few months the *Einsatzkommandos* – Action Commandos – were mobilized into *Einsatzgruppen* – Special Action Groups – and they swept into Poland, the Baltics, and occupied Russian territory on their mission of genocide. The initial efforts of the Special Action Groups followed a pattern. They rounded up Jews, took them to an isolated area, and forced them to dig their own graves. They stripped them and forced them to kneel beside their graves and shot them in the head.

The climax of the activities of the Special Action Commandos took place in the Russian city of Kiev in a suburb called Babi Yar where thirty-three thousand Jews were rounded up and shot over immense pits in a period of two days.

The *Einsatzgruppen* had a great measure of success because there was no opposition from the local population, which, to some degree, shared the Germans' feelings toward the Jews. The massacre of Babi Yar was carried out midst the cheers of many approving Ukrainians.

It became apparent that the methods of the *Einsatzkommandos* were not sufficient for the over-all plan of genocide. Shooting was slow and clumsy. Furthermore, the Jews were not complying by starving to death in large enough numbers.

Eichmann, Paul Blobel, Himmler, Streicher, and dozens of other top Nazis worked out a huge master plan. The plan called for careful selection of secluded sites near railheads and population centers. Camps to be built on these sites would be designed by the best engineers at the lowest cost so that the executions could be carried out on an assembly-line basis

Top personnel from old established concentration camps inside Germany would be promoted to take over the new establishments.

WINTER 1941

The Warsaw ghetto saw death in numbers that eclipsed even those in the pits at Babi Yar. People by the tens and hundreds and thousands starved or froze to death. Infants too weak to cry died by the hundreds, and old men died by the hundreds too weak to pray. Every morning the streets of the ghetto were strewn with new corpses. The sanitation teams walked through the streets with shovels and stacked the corpses onto pushcarts. Infants, children, women, men: piled up and wheeled off to the crematoriums to be burned.

Dov was now eleven years old. He quit school to prowl for food when Mundek's bakery was closed. Even groups like the Redeemers were in dire straits. Dov learned the tricks of staying alive in a ghetto. He moved about, listened, and acted with the cunning of a wily animal. The Landau kettle was empty for long periods of time. When none of the family or the Redeemers could get together a meal Leah traded off a piece of her hoarded jewelry for food.

It was a long and a cruel winter. Once, when they had gone for five days without food, the Landaus finally had a meal, but Leah's wedding band was missing from her hand. Then their fortunes took an upswing, for the Redeemers got hold of a horse. It was old and bony and forbidden by their religion as food, but it tasted wonderful.

Ruth was nineteen. When she married Jan that winter she was too thin to be really pretty. They spent their honeymoon in the single room they shared with the four other Landaus and three members of his family. But apparently the young couple was able to find some time alone somewhere, for in the springtime Ruth was pregnant.

One of Mundek's major responsibilities as leader of the Redeemers was keeping contact with the outside. Money could be used to bribe the Polish Blue Guards and the Lithuanians, but Mundek reckoned that the money should be saved for more important things. He set out to establish routes in and out of the ghetto 'under the wall' through the sewers. It was dangerous to go into Warsaw, for Polish hoodlum gangs were constantly on the lookout for escaped Jews to extort or turn in for reward money.

The Redeemers had lost five members who had been caught beyond the wall. The last one, captured by hoodlums and turned over to the Gestapo and subsequently hanged, was Ruth's husband, Jan.

Little Dov was wise to the ways of survival. He went to Mundek with the proposition that he be allowed to take up the job of courier through the sewers. Mundek would not hear of it at first but Dov persisted. His blond hair and blue eyes made him the least Jewish-looking of them all. He would be least suspect because of his age. Mundek knew that Dov was cagey and competent, but his heart would not let him let his younger brother do it. Then, when Mundek lost his sixth and seventh courier inside of a few days, he decided to let Dov have a try. Mundek reckoned that they all flirted with death each day anyhow. Leah understood and did not object.

Dov proved to be the best courier in the ghetto. He established a dozen alternate routes 'under the wall.' He became at home in the fetid, slimy, putrid waters that ran beneath Warsaw. Each week Dov took that journey in the blackness through shoulder-high filth. Once 'under the wall' he made his way to an apartment at Zabrowska 99 to a woman he knew only as Wanda. After a meal he would return to the sewer, carrying with him pistols, ammunition, money, radio parts, and news from other ghettos and from the partisans.

When he wasn't making his weekly trip Dov liked to stay at Redeemer headquarters where Mundek and Rebecca spent most of their time. Rebecca's job was forging travel passes and passports. Dov liked to watch her and soon began working along with her. It was not long before it was discovered that Dov had a remarkable aptitude for copying and duplicating. His eye was sharp and his hand was steady, and at the age of twelve he was soon the best forger among the Redeemers.

LATE SPRING 1942

The Germans took a significant step toward the 'final solution' of the Jewish problem by erecting several camps designed for the carrying out of mass exterminations. To handle the Jews from the Warsaw area, thirty-three acres were set aside in a place secluded from general view, called Treblinka. Two main buildings contained thirteen gas chambers. There were quarters here for workers and German personnel and there were enormous field plots for burning corpses. Treblinka, one of the first such camps, was a forerunner of more efficient models that followed.

JULY 1942

July brought a day of mourning for all Jews. Those in the Warsaw ghetto and the other ghettos in Poland mourned perhaps more deeply than other Jews. It was the day of Tisha B'Ab, an annual Jewish holiday commemorating the destruction of the Temples by the Babylonians and Romans in Jerusalem. For the fall of Jerusalem to the Roman invaders nearly two thousand years before had signaled the end of the Jews as a nation. The Jews were thenceforth dispersed to the far corners of the earth. They were, from that day on, a Diaspora.

Tisha B'Ab 1942 coincided with major steps in the 'final solution' of the Jewish problem.

As the Jews of Warsaw mourned both their ancient and present plight German patrols whisked into the ghetto and stopped before the building housing the Jewish Council. To all outward appearances the Germans seemed to be making another roundup for the forced-labor battalions. But this time something sinister was in the air. For the Germans wanted only old people and very young people. Panic swept through the ghetto as oldsters were herded in and the Germans sought out children, most of whom were torn from their mothers' arms.

Those rounded up were gathered at the Umschlagplatz and then marched off to Stawki Street near the rail sidings, where a long line of freight cars stood in readiness. Dazed and shocked crowds gathered. Some frantic parents were kept separated from their children at gun point, and several times the Germans shot to kill.

The children were laughing and singing. The German guards had promised them a picnic in the country. This was an event! Many of them could hardly remember being outside the ghetto.

As the train rolled off toward Treblinka the 'final solution' was at hand. Tisha B'Ab – 1942.

Two weeks later Dov Landau came back from Wanda's apartment at Zabrowska 99 with a shocking report. The report stated that those who had been rounded up on Tisha B'Ab and in five subsequent roundups had been sent off to death in gas chambers in a place called Treblinka. Further information from other ghettos around Poland reported the existence of other such camps: Belzec and Chelmno in the Cracow area, and Maidanek near the city of Lubin were in operation or being readied. It appeared, said the report, that a dozen more camps were under construction.

Mass murder in gas chambers? It did not seem possible! Mundek, as head of the Redeemers, met with half a dozen other Zionist groups in the ghetto and issued a joint decree for everyone to stage an immediate uprising and break through the wall.

The plea was emotional rather than practical. The Jews had nothing to fight with. Furthermore, everyone who held a card in a labor battalion had convinced himself that it was a passport to life.

The main reason that no uprising could be staged was that there was no support for it in Poland outside the ghetto. In France, the Vichy government had absolutely refused the Germans' demands that French Jews be turned over to them. In Holland, the unanimous feeling of all the citizens was to hide their Jews. In Denmark, the King not only defied German edicts but the Danes evacuated their entire Jewish population to safety in Sweden.

If the Poles did not agree to the extermination of their Jews, they did not disagree. If they disagreed, they did nothing to show it. Only a very small minority of Polish people would shelter an escaped Jew.

Inside the ghetto, each different organized group of Jews embraced a different philosophy. The religious and the labor people argued. The conservatives and the left-wingers argued. Jews liked to argue. In ghetto life argument and debate had always been a great pastime. But now the time of greatest peril had come. Mundek's Redeemers joined all the diversified groups in forming a unified command. The combined organizations carried the initials ZOB, and had the momentous task of saving the rest of the Jews in the ghetto.

Dov made one trip after another to Wanda's apartment at Zabrowska 99. On each trip through the sewers he carried a message from ZOB to the Polish underground begging for help and for arms. Most of the messages were never answered. The few answers that were received were evasive.

Throughout that horrible summer while the Germans continued rounding up Jews for Treblinka the ZOB worked desperately to stave off total annihilation.

One day early in September, Dov had a particularly dangerous trip into Warsaw. After leaving Wanda's he was spotted by four hooligans who chased him into a dead-end alley and demanded to see his papers proving he wasn't a Jew. The boy had his back to the wall, and his tormentors closed in on him to pull off his pants to see the circumcision, the sure identification of a Jew. As they set to pounce, Dov took out a pistol he was carrying back to the ghetto and with it killed one of the hooligans and chased the others off. He darted away and soon found the safety of the sewer.

Back at Redeemer headquarters the boy broke down under delayed shock. Mundek tried to comfort him. Dov always felt warm and wonderful with his brother near. Mundek was almost twenty-one now, but he was gaunt and always tired-looking. He had been a good leader and he worked beyond the limits of exhaustion. He had kept almost the entire Redeemer group intact and had never let their fighting spirit flag. The brothers talked quietly. Dov calmed down. Mundek put his arm around Dov's shoulder and they walked from headquarters to their apartment. Mundek talked about Ruth's baby, which was due in a few weeks, and how wonderful it was going to be for Dov to be an uncle. Of course, everyone in the Redeemers would be aunt and uncle to the baby but Dov would be the real one. There had been many marriages in the group and there were already three babies – all new Redeemers. Ruth's baby would be the finest of them all. Things were bright, Mundek told Dov, because they had found another horse and there would be a real feast. Dov's trembling passed away. As they neared the top of the stairs Dov smiled at Mundek and told his brother that he loved him very much.

The instant they opened the door and saw the expression on Rebecca's face they knew disaster had struck. Mundek finally got his sister coherent enough to talk.

'Mother and Ruth,' she cried. 'They were taken out of the factory. Their work cards were invalidated and they were marched off to the Umschlagplatz.'

Dov wheeled around for the door. Mundek grabbed him. The boy screamed and kicked.

'Dov! Dov! There is nothing we can do!'

'Momma! Momma! I want to go to Momma!'

'Dov! Dov! We can't look at her being taken away!'

Ruth, eight months pregnant, cheated the gas chambers of Treblinka. She died in the agony of childbirth and her baby died with her in a cattle car so packed it was impossible for her to lie down.

At Treblinka, SS Colonel Wirth, the commandant, was furious. There had been another breakdown in the mechanism at the main gas chambers and another trainload of Jews was en route from the Warsaw ghetto. Wirth had been proud that Treblinka had the best record for dispensing 'special treatment' of all the camps in Poland. His engineers informed him that it would be impossible to get things into working order again before the train arrived from Warsaw.

To make matters worse, both SS Colonel Eichmann and Himmler himself were due on personal inspection tours. Wirth had planned to hold special gassings in their honor.

He was forced to round up all the old, obsolete gas vans he could find in the area and send them to the rail siding to meet the train. Generally the covered vans could accommodate only twenty people, but this was an emergency. By forcing the victims to hold their hands over their heads the Germans could make space for another six or eight Jews. The Germans discovered that there were still several inches between the tops of the heads and the ceiling of the van. In this space they packed another eight or ten children.

Leah Landau was in a daze of grief over Ruth's death as the train pulled to a siding near Treblinka. She and thirty others were taken from the cattle car and forced with whips, clubs, and dogs to get into one of the waiting vans and hold their hands high. When the van held an absolute maximum the iron door was shut. The truck started into motion, and in a matter of seconds the iron cage was filled with carbon monoxide. Everyone inside the van was dead by the time the trucks entered Treblinka and halted before the open pits where the bodies were unloaded and the gold extracted from the victims' mouths.

At least Leah Landau had cheated the Germans, for her gold teeth had been extracted long before and exchanged for food.

Winter was coming once again and the German roundups were becoming more and more frequent.

The entire ghetto moved into cellars, taking everything of value with them. The cellars expanded and some, like the Redeemers', became elaborate bunkers. Dozens, then hundreds, of bunkers sprouted and connecting tunnels began to weave through the earth.

The sweeps of the Germans and their Polish Blues and Lithuanians netted fewer and fewer Jews for Treblinka.

The Germans became angered. The bunkers were so well concealed they were nearly impossible to locate. At last the commander of Warsaw himself entered the ghetto one day to speak to the leader of the Jewish Council. He was angry and demanded that the Jewish Council assist the Germans in speeding up the resettlement program by locating the cowards who hid from 'honest labor.' For over three years the Jewish Council had been trapped and torn between carrying out German edicts on the one hand and trying to save their people on the other. Now, shortly after the German demand for assistance, the leader of the Jewish Council committed suicide.

It was winter in the ghetto again.

Mundek's Redeemers were assigned to plan the defense of a section of the Brushmakers' district. Dov spent his time either in the sewers or in the bunker forging travel passes. Actually his trips 'under the wall' allowed him one or two decent meals a week at Wanda's. On his trips out of the ghetto he now led old people or others unfit for combat. On his trips in he carried arms and radio parts.

During the winter of 1943 the death rate became appalling. Out of an original five hundred thousand who had been put into the ghetto, only fifty thousand were alive by the end of the year.

One day in mid-January, Mundek and Rebecca took Dov aside before he was scheduled to descend into the sewer on a trip to Wanda's.

'It seems that we don't have much of a chance just to sit around and talk these days,' Mundek said.

'Dov,' Rebecca said, 'we all talked it over here and took a vote while you were in Warsaw the last time. We have decided that we want you to stay on the other side of the wall.'

'You have something special for me to do?' Dov asked.

'No ... you don't understand.'

'What do you mean?'

'We mean,' Rebecca said, 'that we have decided to send certain members out to stay.'

Dov didn't understand it. He knew the Redeemers needed him. No one in the entire ZOB knew the sewer routes as well as he did. If the ZOB was preparing to stage a defense then he would be more valuable than ever. Besides, the papers and travel passes he forged had helped get over a hundred people out of Poland. Dov looked at his sister and brother questioningly.

Rebecca pressed an envelope into Dov's hands. 'You have money there and papers. Stay with Wanda until she can find you a Christian family to live with.'

'You didn't take a vote. This is your idea and Mundek's. I won't go.'

'You will go and that is an order,' Mundek said.

'It is not an order,' Dov answered.

'It is an order from me as head of the Landau family!'

The three of them stood in the tiny earthen room in one corner of the bunker. It was very quiet. 'It is an order,' Mundek repeated.

Rebecca put her arms around Dov and stroked his blond hair. 'You have grown up, Dov. We have not had much chance to spoil you, have we? I have watched you go into the sewers a hundred times and I have watched you bring us stolen food. We haven't given you much of a boyhood.'

'It is not your fault.'

'Dov,' Mundek said. 'Please don't deny Rebecca and me this one thing we want. We have not given you much. You must let us try to give you your life.'

'Mundek, Rebecca. I don't care as long as I am with you.'

'Please . . . please . . . understand us. One of the Landau family must live. We want you to live for us all.'

Dov looked at the brother he worshipped. Mundek's eyes pleaded.

'I understand,' Dov whispered. 'I will live.'

He looked at the package and slipped it into a canvas so that it wouldn't get wet in the sewers. Rebecca crushed his head against her bosom. 'We will meet in Eretz Israel,' she said.

'Yes . . . in the land of Israel.'

'You have been a good soldier, Dov,' Mundek said. 'I am proud. *Shalom, l'hitraot.*'

'*Shalom, l'hitraot,*' Dov repeated.

Dov Landau spent his thirteenth birthday in the sewers beneath Warsaw wading to Wanda's apartment with a heart so heavy it nearly broke. In another day and another world it would have been his *bar mitzvah.*

JANUARY 18, 1943

Three days after Dov left the ghetto for the temporary safety of Wanda's apartment the Germans, Polish Blues, and Lithuanians converged on the ghetto. With only fifty thousand Jews left they began rounding up Jews for the final phase of the 'final solution.'

The Germans and their cohorts ran into a hail of bullets from ZOB defensive positions. They fled, leaving heavy casualties.

The news spread through Warsaw like wildfire!

The Jews were staging an uprising!

That night every ear in Warsaw was tuned to the secret ZOB radio which repeated this appeal over and over and over again:

'Fellow Poles! Today we struck a blow against tyranny! We ask all our brothers outside the ghetto to arise and strike against the enemy! Join us!'

The appeal fell on deaf ears. But from ZOB headquarters on Mila Street the flag of the Star of David was raised. Alongside it fluttered the flag of Poland. The Jews of the ghetto had chosen to fight to the death beneath a banner which had been denied them in life.

Chapter Twenty-three

The Germans were chagrined at having been chased from the ghetto. Konrad, Gestapo chief of the ghetto security detail, reported to Hans Frank, the governor of Poland, that the matter would be cleared up in two or three days. The Polish people, who had been told previously that the Jews were cowards, were now told that the fighting had been the work of a few lunatics and sex deviates – the types who raped Polish girls.

ZOB assumed control of the ghetto and disposed of the Jewish Council. The fighters made a swift and merciless reprisal on all known collaborators and then moved into set defensive positions.

Hans Frank decided he would not play into ZOB's hand by making an attack on the ghetto. The Germans decided to laugh off the attack and minimize it. They cut loose with a propaganda barrage and asked the people of the ghetto to come forth for voluntary resettlement and guaranteed they would be given decent treatment in exchange for 'honest labor.'

ZOB issued an order informing the Jews remaining in the ghetto that they would be shot if they conformed with the German request. There would be no more evacuation.

After two weeks of quiet the Germans moved patrols in once again to round up Jews. This time they came heavily armed and moved with extreme caution. From carefully prepared positions the ZOB opened fire. Again the Germans fled beyond the wall.

The Germans decided to think it all over. Their press and radio were indignant over the Jewish Bolsheviks who were causing all the trouble. While the Germans wailed the ZOB tightened their defensive setups and desperately continued to plead for help from the Polish underground. They expanded their plea to the general public, but no arms came, no underground help came, and only a few dozen volunteers crossed into the ghetto 'under the wall' to fight.

The German staff mapped one big crushing assault to wipe out the remains of the ghetto. The day they picked for the attack was the beginning of Passover, the Jewish holiday celebrated in commemoration of the exodus of the Jews from Egypt under the leadership of Moses.

At three o'clock in the morning, three thousand crack SS troops flanked with Polish Blues and Lithuanians threw a ring around the entire ghetto. Dozens of searchlights criss-crossed to pick out possible targets for German mortars and light artillery. The barrage lasted until daylight.

At dawn the SS launched their assault over the wall. Converging from several sides they penetrated deep into the heart of the ghetto without resistance.

From hidden barricades, from house tops, from windows, the ZOB – men and women – turned loose a barrage of small-arms fire at point-blank range against the trapped and surrounded Germans. For the third time the Germans scurried from the ghetto.

In blind fury the Germans came back into the ghetto with tanks, and the tanks were met with a storm of gasoline-filled bottles which turned the iron monsters into flaming coffins. With the tanks disabled the German SS troops were forced to flee again; this time they left several hundred dead in the streets.

The ZOB fighters rushed out of hiding to take the German guns as well as their uniforms.

Konrad was dismissed and SS General Stroop was called in to take command. He was ordered to destroy the ghetto so thoroughly that no one would ever again dare challenge the power of the Nazis.

Stroop mounted attack after attack, day after day. Each new attack utilized a different strategy and hit from a different direction. Each attack and each patrol met the same fate. They were repulsed by the ZOB, whose members fought like madmen – house by house, room by room, step by step. They refused to be taken alive. Homemade land mines and booby traps, violent counterattacks, raw courage beat the Germans out of the ghetto every time they entered. Ten days passed and the Germans were desperate for a victory. They made a concerted attack on the ghetto's lone hospital – entered, shot every patient, blew up the building, and claimed they had destroyed ZOB headquarters.

ZOB teams dressed in uniforms of German soldiers they had killed and used this device to trick, trap, and ambush their enemy. They crossed out of the ghetto time and time again to hit the Germans from the rear by raiding their arsenals.

The Germans continued their attacks and soon, by the sheer weight of their numbers and arms, made themselves felt. The ZOB could not replace a fallen fighter; once a defensive position was destroyed there was no choice but to retrench; they could not replace ammunition as fast as they were expending it. Still, with the power on their side, the Germans were unable to get a foothold inside the ghetto. ZOB began calling upon many of the Jews not in fighting units to escape into Warsaw, for there were not enough rifles to go around.

Wearing a captured uniform, Mundek led an attack on the Pawiak Prison and freed all the inmates.

The three-day cleanup Konrad had promised had stretched into two weeks. On the fifteenth day after the first German assault Rebecca Landau was fighting in a building in the Brushmakers' district a few blocks from Redeemer headquarters. A direct mortar hit killed every defender but her. Under sustained mortar fire the walls of the building collapsed and she was forced into the street. As the Germans closed in on her and cut off all possibilities of retreat, she reached beneath her dress and withdrew a hand grenade. Running at three Germans, she pulled the pin, and killed them and herself.

After three weeks Stroop was forced to change his tactics. He had drawn heavy casualties and the Nazis were unable to cover up the valiant action of the Jews with propaganda. Stroop pulled his troops back, reinforced the ring of men and armor surrounding the ghetto, and declared a state of siege. He brought in heavy artillery which blasted into the ghetto at near point-blank range in a determined effort to knock down all the buildings which the Jews had used so well as defensive positions. By night Heinkel bombers saturated the ghetto area with incendiary bombs.

Mundek returned to the Redeemer bunker after a staff meeting at ZOB headquarters. He and his fighters were half dead with exhaustion, hunger, and thirst. Many were badly burned. They gathered around him.

'German artillery has knocked down just about every building. What is standing is burning,' he said.

'Have we been able to establish contact with the underground?'

'Oh yes . . . we've made contact, but they aren't going to help us. We cannot expect any more food, ammunition, or water than what we have on hand. Our communications are about ruined. In short, my friends, we can no longer fight according to a fixed plan. Each bunker is on its own. We will try to keep contact with ZOB through runners, but we will each plan and execute our own ambushes and encounters with the Germans when they come back.'

'How long can we hold out like this, Mundek? We have only thirty people left and ten pistols and six rifles.'

Mundek smiled. 'All of Poland held out for only twenty-six days. We have done that well already.' Mundek assigned his guards, rationed what little food was left, and mapped out a dawn patrol.

Ryfka, one of the girls, picked up a battered accordion and began playing a soft, slow tune. In that dank and slimy bunker ten feet beneath the earth the remaining Redeemers sang in a strange and wistful blend of voices. They sang a song that they had learned as children at Redeemer meetings. The song told them that the land in Galilee in Eretz Israel was beautiful and that wheat grew in the fields and the grain bent softly in the wind. In a bunker in the Warsaw ghetto they sang of the fields of Galilee that they knew they would never see.

'Alert!' a sentry called down as he spotted a lone figure weaving in and out of the flames and rubble.

The lights went out and the bunker became black and silent. There was a knock in code. The door opened and closed and the lights were turned on again.

'Dov! For God's sake! What are you doing here?'

'Don't send me away again, Mundek!'

The two brothers embraced and Dov wept. It felt good to have Mundek's arms around him again. Everyone gathered about Dov as he relayed the final tragic news that the Polish underground definitely would not come in and that everyone else on the outside was being very quiet about the uprising.

'When I came back,' Dov said, 'the sewers were filled with people just lying in the muck. They are too weak to stand up. They have no place to go. No one wants them in Warsaw.'

And so little Dov returned to the ghetto and a very strange thing happened. All over Warsaw and the surrounding countryside Jews who had managed to escape and live as Christians were beginning to return to the ghetto for the last-ditch stand. They had concluded that it was a privilege to be able to die with dignity.

MAY 1943

At last the furious bombardment stopped.

The fires went out.

Stroop moved his SS troops in once again, but this time they held all the cards. The Jews had no defensive positions or communications or fixed plans and almost no food, water, or arms. The Germans worked systematically, cutting off one section at a time and cleaning out bunkers one by one with cannon fire and flame throwers until the section was completely destroyed.

They tried hard to capture prisoners to torture into revealing the exact location of the bunkers, but the ZOB fighters preferred to burn alive rather than surrender.

They threw open the sewer lids and pumped the sewers full of poison gas, and soon the slimy waters were filled with bodies.

Still the ZOB fought on. They lashed out of their bunkers on swift and deadly raids when they could find a German patrol. Suicide squads hurled themselves into certain death. German casualties mounted until the number was in the thousands.

Stroop pressed on relentlessly. When the Jews became ineffective as a fighting force they kept going on instinct alone.

On May 14, Mundek held a meeting of the remaining twelve Redeemers in his group. He gave them two choices. One was to remain and fight to the last man. The second was to try the sewers where Dov might be able to lead them to safety and a remote chance of reaching a partisan unit. Dov convinced Mundek he could work around the areas of the sewers that were being gassed.

He made his way in 'under the wall,' but as he approached Zabrowska 99 instinct told him something was wrong. He walked straight past the building. His sharp eye picked out a dozen men who were watching Zabrowska 99 from various vantage points. Dov did not know whether or not Wanda had been taken by the Gestapo but he did know the place was unsafe.

It was late at night when he returned to the ghetto. It was difficult even for him to locate the bunker, for there were no streets or buildings left, only rubble. As he approached he smelled the now familiar odor of burning flesh. He went beneath the ground and lit a candle he always carried in the sewer. Its flickering light bounced off the walls. Dov walked from one end of the bunker to the other and knelt low with his candle each time he came to a body. Direct hits from the flame thrower had charred the still smoking bodies so badly he could not identify them. Dov Landau wondered which of the burned corpses was his beloved brother, Mundek.

May 15, 1943. ZOB radio broadcast its last message: 'This is the voice of the Warsaw ghetto! For God's sake, help us!'

May 16, 1943. Forty-two days had passed since the Germans had made their first attack. Four months had passed since the ZOB arose and chased the Germans out. As a last gesture SS General Stroop dynamited the Great Synagogue on Tlamatzka Street. It had long been the symbol of Judaism in Poland. As the Temple of Solomon once fell to the Romans, so had the Tlamatzka Synagogue fallen. The Germans announced that the problem of the Warsaw ghetto had reached its final solution.

The devastation had been absolute. Nothing stood in the entire area above a man's eye level. Stroop announced the capture of sixteen pistols and four rifles. Further, that the ruins of the buildings would make good material. There were no prisoners.

Even in this most meticulous of massacres there were ZOB fighters who refused to die. Even in the rubble the battle went on. The Jews who had somehow survived began to find each other, and in twos and threes they formed 'rat packs' and attacked German patrols by night. The Germans and the Polish Blues swore the ghetto was haunted by ghosts.

Dov found six other Jews. They went from bunker to bunker until they were all armed. They moved from place to place but the stench and the sight of death was everywhere. At night Dov led them through the sewers 'under the wall' where they made quick raids on food stores.

The Jews were rebelling in a dozen other places around Poland, but their risings all met with the same fate. Too little, too late, no support.

During all the daylight hours Dov and the six others remained below ground in a newly carved-out bunker. For five long and harrowing months neither Dov Landau nor any of his comrades saw the light of day. One by one they died – three on one raid in Warsaw, two by suicide, one of starvation.

Dov was the last one alive. At the end of the fifth month a German patrol found him close to death. His appearance was not even that of a human being. He was revived sufficiently to be dragged to Gestapo headquarters for questionings, which always ended in beatings. The Gestapo could get nothing from him. Dov Landau, age thirteen, ghetto rat, sewer rat, rubble rat, and expert forger, was marked for resettlement. Destination: Auschwitz!

Chapter Twenty-four

Dov Landau was put into an open gondola car with sixty other Jews. The Gestapo refused to believe that he had stayed alive without outside help for five months in the rubble of the Warsaw ghetto. The train moved southward over the icy countryside in the dead of winter toward Auschwitz.

BERLIN, GERMANY, 1940

SS Lieutenant Colonel Karl Hoess entered the office of SS Colonel Eichmann, who had been given the task of carrying out the final solution of the Jewish problem. Eichmann showed Hoess the master plan which was the culmination of the combined brainwork of all the top Nazi officials.

The entire continent of Europe was interlaced with concentration camps and political prisons. Every occupied country was well saturated with Gestapo establishments.

Another network of three hundred 'combination' camps spanned Europe. Half of them were reserved for Jews.

SS Lieutenant Colonel Karl Hoess was impressed with the intricate planning that went into genocide.

Despite all these camps and their carefully chosen locations, the blueprinters felt they were going to run into a special problem, and this was why Hoess had been called to Berlin. The Nazis knew they would have tremendous difficulty trying to run extermination camps in western Europe. Furthermore, Poland was more or less centrally located in relation to the Balkans and western Europe. A final, major camp was needed, one that would serve as a 'master model.' In addition to Jews to dispose of there were Russian, French, and other prisoners of war, partisans, political enemies in occupied countries, religious fanatics, especially Christians of the Catholic faith, gypsies, criminals, Freemasons, Marxists, Bolsheviks, and Germans who talked peace, liberalism, trade unionism, or defeatism. There were suspected foreign agents, prostitutes, homosexuals, and many other undesirable elements. All these had to be eliminated to make Europe a fit place for Aryans to live.

Such a camp as Eichmann spoke of would handle all these people. Eichmann informed Hoess that he was to be rewarded for his years of faithful service as a Nazi by being given command of the new camp. Eichmann pointed on the map to a small Polish town near the Czech border. A town called Auschwitz.

The train bearing Dov Landau and heading south for Auschwitz rolled to a stop at Cracow, a rail center. At a siding on the outskirts many more cars were joined to the train. There were cattle cars holding Jews from France and Greece and coal cars holding Jews from Yugoslavia and Holland and there were open gondolas holding Jews from Italy for resettlement. It was bitter cold. The biting wind and the snow whipped through Dov in the open gondola and all that protected him against it was his torn shirt and some little warmth of bodies packed together.

BERLIN, GERMANY, 1940–41

When the Nazis selected Hoess to command the camp at Auschwitz, the major clearing house and extermination factory, they knew well the caliber of the man they had. Hoess had had a long career in the concentration-camp system beginning way back in 1934 when Hitler first rose to power. More recently he had been second in command of the concentration camp at Sachsenhausen. Hoess was a meticulous man and systematic and he carried out orders without questioning them. Furthermore, he was not bothered by hard work.

Twenty thousand acres of land were cleared of farms and villages in the Auschwitz area and fenced off. The best construction men, engineers, scientists, and transportation experts and the best of the elite storm troopers went to work on the massive project. An area called Birkenau, two miles from the main Auschwitz camp, was selected as the site of the gas chambers. Birkenau was well secluded and had its own rail sidings. The site was picked because of its accessibility by rail from western Europe, eastern Europe, and southern Europe. The little town of Auschwitz was completely undistinguished and lay in a basin of eternal mud at the entrance to the Silesian mining district. In erecting the camp system the Nazis had to overcome a major objection from their own colleagues.

The German Army needed all the railroads and rolling stock it could get its hands on to execute a war on the eastern front. They did not like this nonsense of using valuable rail space to cart Jews all over Europe. The Nazis were just as adamant that the final solution of the Jewish question was as important as running the war. The question was taken to Hitler, who sided with the SS, SD, Gestapo, and other Nazi elements against the German Army High Command.

Hoess assumed command of Auschwitz and traveled to Treblinka to study the methods of extermination. He concluded that Treblinka's commander, SS Colonel Wirth, was a clumsy amateur and said as much. The executions at Treblinka were carried out with carbon monoxide, which was inefficient; the machinery was always breaking down and it used up valuable petrol. Furthermore, Wirth was not systematic and he did not use any measure of deception, so that there were constant rebellions on the part of the Jews. Finally, Hoess felt, Treblinka had been poorly designed if only three hundred people could be executed at one time.

When the chambers of Birkenau were opened at Auschwitz, Hoess conducted extensive tests on the first 'guests.' He and his scientists concluded that

Cyklon B, a crude prussic acid gas, did the job the best. He ordered huge quantities of it from the International Insecticide Company in Hamburg.

The Birkenau chambers were designed to hold three thousand people at one time, and with utmost efficiency ten thousand people a day could be exterminated, depending on weather conditions.

The train bearing Dov Landau was now nearly fifty cars long. It stopped at the town of Chrzanow, the last before Auschwitz. One out of five persons on the train was already dead. Other hundreds were frozen to the sides of the cars and unable to move without tearing off the flesh of arms or legs. Many women threw their children over the rail beds and screamed to the curious onlooking peasants to take them and hide them. The dead were removed and stacked in six new cars added on at the end of the train. Dov, though in very bad condition, was keen and alert. He knew exactly what to expect, and he knew that if he ever used his wits he must use them now. The train rolled on again. Auschwitz was an hour away.

AUSCHWITZ 1941–42

Hoess worked to perfect the operation at Birkenau. First he worked out a system of deception that would keep the victims calm to the very end. Lovely trees, lawns, and flower beds were planted around the buildings which housed the gas chambers. There were signs everywhere in many languages which read: SANITATION CENTER. The main deception used was that the victims were going to be inspected and given a delousing shower before being issued new clothing and sent to labor camps at or around Auschwitz.

Under and around the gas chambers neatly laid-out dressing rooms had been built. There were pegs with numbers for hanging clothing. Everyone was told to 'remember his number.' Hair was cut for 'delousing' and the victims were requested to remove their eyeglasses before entering the sanitation 'shower.'

Everyone was issued a bar of soap with a number on it. They were marched naked, three thousand at a time, down long corridors. A dozen mammoth doors ran along the corridors. The doors opened, revealing enormous 'shower rooms.'

Most of the guests were too numb to realize quite what was happening and entered the shower rooms quietly. Some began to examine the bar of soap and found it was made of stone. Others discovered the shower heads on the ceiling were fake and that there was no drainage for water.

Often a last-minute panic broke out but the Germans were ready now with storm troopers who clubbed and whipped the reluctant into the 'shower rooms.'

The iron doors were bolted shut.

A can or two of Cyklon B was dropped into each 'shower room' and it was all over in ten or fifteen minutes.

Then came the *Sonderkommandos*. These were clean-up squads of inmates from Auschwitz. They emptied the gas chambers and removed the corpses to the crematoriums. Gold teeth were pulled and rings taken before the burnings. These would be melted down and sent to Berlin. Often a well-shaped skull would be taken for sale to the German guards as paper-weights.

Little attention was given to pictures of families or love letters that were found in the clothing. The troopers were most interested in searching through the linings where jewelry was often hidden. Often an infant was found hidden in the clothes and designated for the next 'shower.'

Hoess was good to his troops. They worked hard when a large trainload came to Birkenau and were rewarded with extra rations and schnapps. His system worked with great efficiency and he never seemed fazed. He did not even get upset when Colonel Eichmann unloaded a quarter of a million Hungarian Jews on him practically without warning.

Hoess pressed his scientists and engineers for greater efficiency and lower costs. His architects had blueprinted elaborate expansion plans. One was for a gas chamber with a floor that could be lifted hydraulically like an elevator to another level where the crematorium was situated. Other plans were designed to increase the Birkenau capacity to forty thousand executions a day.

The greatest bottleneck at Birkenau was the disposal of corpses. At first they were taken directly from the gas chambers to open fields and buried in pits and covered with lime. The stench became unbearable. The SS troops forced the Jewish *Sonderkommandos* to dig up all the pits and burn bodies, then crush the bones. Again, open field burning proved too foul-smelling, so inside crematoriums had to be constructed.

The train bearing Dov Landau passed through Auschwitz and came to a halt at the siding at Birkenau.

Chapter Twenty-five

Dov was half dead with hunger and blue with cold, but his years of constant contact with danger and death had sharpened his instincts so that even in this state he was alert to survive. Dov knew that the next hour would spell life or death.

The doors of the cattle and freight cars were opened and those like him in open cars were ordered over the top with harsh guttural commands. The miserable victims dragged themselves onto a long platform and faced a line of storm troopers who stood in readiness with clubs, whips, pistols, and vicious dogs straining at their leashes. The whips cracked out in the cold air and brought screams of pain. The truncheons thudded against skulls, and pistols shot into the bodies of those too weak to walk.

A line was formed, four abreast down the length of the platform, and directed toward a huge station room. The line pressed to the room at a slow but steady pace.

Dov looked around him. To his left were the trains. Beyond the trains on the road outside the station room he could observe a line of waiting trucks. The trucks were not enclosed so they could not be gas vans, Dov assumed. To his right, past the line of guards, Dov could see the neatly groomed lawns and trees around the brick gas chambers of Birkenau. He studied the shapes of the buildings and their conelike chimneys and he knew the area to his right held extermination chambers.

The line pressed on. A nausea born of fear racked him. A man staggered and fell, unable to arise. Two snarling dogs were turned loose and ripped the man to pieces. His shrieks set Dov to trembling. He fought to gain control; he knew that he must show no fear.

His line moved into the station room. The large line was split into four single lines, and each line moved toward a desk set up at the far end of the room. A German doctor sat behind each desk, and around each doctor stood a dozen guards and assistants. Dov fixed his attention on the desk ahead of him to try to find out what was happening.

The doctor quickly looked over every person as he or she stepped to the desk. The doctor would then order the person to go off in one of three directions.

The first way was out an exit on the right side of the room. Dov began counting; seven out of ten people were sent out that way. These people were old or children or appeared in bad condition. Since he assumed the buildings on the right were gas chambers, he came to the conclusion that those being sent out the right exit were going to be put to death immediately.

The second way was out an exit on the left side of the room. This exit led to the outside where the line of trucks was waiting. About two out of ten went that way and all of them appeared fit and well. Dov assumed they were being sent to the labor camp.

The right door meant death and the left door meant life!

There was also a third group. These people, one in ten or even more, were mostly young women, some quite beautiful. A few teen-age boys were ordered to join this group. Dov was certain the girls would be used as German field whores and the boys for homosexual activities with the German officers.

He drew in a dozen deep breaths as his line inched forward. He was a pack of bones and he knew he didn't stand much of a chance of being sent through the left exit to the labor camp.

In the next line a woman screamed and half a dozen guards converged on her and flung her to the ground and ripped away her skirts. The woman had been trying to hide an infant.

'Right . . . right . . . right . . . right . . .' the doctor kept ordering the victims.

Dov Landau stopped before the desk.

The doctor looked up and glanced at him. 'Go to that exit on the right,' he said.

Dov smiled softly. 'You are making a mistake, Doctor,' Dov said with infinite calm. 'I am an expert forger and counterfeiter. Write your name down on that piece of paper and I'll show you.'

The doctor sat back, stunned. Dov's coolness impressed him, for he obviously knew what awaited him. The youngster had put a sudden halt to the monotonous death march. The doctor caught his bearings and a smirk crossed his lips. Two guards grabbed Dov and began to drag him away.

'Wait!' the doctor commanded. He looked at Dov again and ordered him to turn around. For a second he became tired of the foolishness. The boy was making a clever bluff. He was about to order him out of the right exit, but his curiosity got the better of him. The doctor scribbled his name on a pad.

Dov wrote out six duplications of the signature and returned the pad. 'Which one of those did you write?' Dov asked.

Half a dozen guards peeked over the doctor's shoulder and stared in amazement. The doctor looked at Dov again and then whispered to a guard who walked off.

'Stand over here to one side,' the doctor snapped.

Dov stood by the desk and watched the line of people move toward him. He looked at them being condemned at the rate of four a minute.

Dov looked into the eyes of the guards and he looked at their truncheons and at the snarling dogs. He glanced at the right-hand exit and whistled a shaky tune half beneath his breath.

Five minutes passed. Ten minutes passed. The line coming in from the platform seemed never to end.

The guard returned with another man who was obviously a high-ranking officer, Dov thought, for his chest was filled with medals. The doctor handed the pad of signatures to the officer, who studied it for a full minute.

'Where did you learn this?' the officer snapped.

'In the ghetto at Warsaw.'

'What kind of work do you do?'

'Passports, travel cards, any kind of paper. I can duplicate anything.'

'Follow me.'

Dov passed through the left-hand door. As he got into the car and drove off toward Auschwitz a Main he seemed to remember Mundek's words. 'One of the Landaus must live through this.' In a few moments the car passed through the main gate of Auschwitz. The sign over the entrance of the camp read: LABOR LIBERATES.

The main compound was set in an area that wallowed in mud. There was acre after acre of frame wooden barracks which were isolated from each other by high walls of electrified barbed wire.

These acres of barracks fed manpower into some thirty subsidiary slave-labor camps. Each inmate wore a black and white striped uniform and an identification color on his arm and left breast. A pink badge was worn by homosexuals, a black badge by field whores, a green badge by criminals, violet badges for clergymen, red for Russians and Poles, and the traditional Star of David for the Jews.

Dov received another badge at Auschwitz. It was a tattooed number on his left forearm. Dov Landau was now a black and white striped Jew nunber 359195.

LABOR LIBERATES. Dov Landau celebrated his fourteenth birthday in Auschwitz and his gift had been his life. He was quite fortunate for of all the tens of thousands of prisoners at Auschwitz, Dov's small group of forgers were among the elite. His particular section was given the task of engraving and printing counterfeit United States one- and five-dollar bills for use by German agents in western countries.

After a short time at Auschwitz Dov wondered if it would not have been better to have died at Birkenau.

Here the inmates wre underfed, worked into living skeletons, and stacked on shelves for their five hours' sleep a night. Disease ran wild. Prisoners were tortured, driven insane, beaten, and degraded, and every known atrocity conceived by man was committed.

Here each morning found dozens of inmates who had hanged themselves by their own belts or thrown themselves on the quick mercy of the electric wire. The flogging blocks were in constant use and naked buttocks were lashed in public at roll calls.

Here the penal colony lived in single black cells and were fed only oversalted vegetables to induce unquenchable thirst.

Here in Block X, Nazi doctors Wirthe, Schumann and Clauberg kept the human raw material for their pseudo-scientific experiments. Polish prisoner Dr Wladislaw Dering performed castrations and ovarectomies ordered by his German masters as part of their insane program to find a way to sterilize the entire Jewish race.

This was Auschwitz and this was Dov Landau's gift of life. LABOR LIBERATES.

'One of the Landaus must live through this,' Mundek had said. What did Mundek look like? He could hardly remember. Or Ruth or Rebecca or his mother and father? He could not remember his father at all. The memories grew hazier and hazier until he could remember nothing but death and terror and he did not know that there was a life where death and terror did not exist.

A year passed. The trains came in and out of Birkenau. The deaths at the labor camps around Auschwitz from torture and disease and hunger were nearly as appalling as those at Birkenau. Somehow he managed to cling to his sanity and that animal instinct to survive.

Even in this blackest of pits there were some rays of hope. There was the prison orchestra. There was a flourishing underground and they had a radio receiver. Even here a man could find a way to get to a woman.

SUMMER 1944

There was a strange new stirring thoughout Auschwitz. Dov could often look into the sky and see Russian bombers, and the secret radio began reporting German defeats. Hope, however dim, found its way through the muck and torture. Each new Allied victory sent the German guards into a murderous frenzy until the prisoners almost dreaded word of German defeats. At Birkenau activity speeded up until the gas chambers were in operation almost around the clock.

AUTUMN 1944

The feeling now was that Germany was going to lose the war. They were being beaten on all fronts. But as they lost on the battlefield the appetite for extermination grew. Colonel Eichmann threw every possible resource into finishing his mission of genocide.

OCTOBER 1944

The *Sonderkommandos* at Birkenau staged a wild uprising in which one of the crematoriums was blown up. Each day in new uprisings the *Sonderkommando* snatched SS guards and their dogs and threw them into the crematoriums. At last every *Sonderkommando* was executed and a call went out for a new group from Auschwitz.

His back to the wall, Eichmann made a final gesture. Twenty thousand Jews, the cream of Jewry, who had been under guaranteed protection at the Czech camp of Theresienstadt, were ordered transferred to Birkenau for extermination.

The Jewish death toll at Birkenau mounted and mounted until the count reached nearly a million Poles, fifty thousand Germans, a hundred thousand Dutch, a hundred and fifty thousand French, fifty thousand Austrians and Czechs, fifty thousand Greeks, two hundred and fifty thousand Bulgarians, Italians, Yugoslavs, and Rumanians, and another quarter of a million Hungarians.

Each day during the macabre race for total annihilation came a call for more and more *Sonderkommandos*.

NOVEMBER 1944
The counterfeit shop was abruptly closed down in Auschwitz and everyone was sent to Birkenau to work as *Sonderkommandos*.

It was Dov's new job to wait in the corridor of the gas chambers until a gassing was over. He and other *Sonderkommandos* stood by until the shrieks of agony and the frantic pounding on the iron doors stopped. They waited another fifteen minutes for the gas to clear. Then the doors of the gas chambers would be opened. Dov had to go to work with ropes and hooks to untangle the hideous tangle of arms and legs and drag them out for reshipment to the crematorium. After the bodies were removed he had to enter the chamber and hose it down and get the room ready for the next batch of victims who were already in the dressing rooms, being prepared.

For three days Dov worked at this gory task. Every ounce of his strength was sapped, and now that stubborn, defiant will to live that had carried him through seemed to fade. He dreaded that instant when the iron chamber door opened and he was face to face with the tangle of corpses. He dreaded it worse than the thought of the ghetto or the sewers. He knew he would not be able to stand to see that horrible sight much more often.

Then a startling thing happened!

The Germans ordered the crematorium ovens dismantled and the gas chambers blown up! The Allies were advancing from the west and the Russians were coming from the east. Now the Nazis made frantic efforts to cover up their crimes. Pits of bodies were exhumed all over Poland and the bones crushed and scattered. Desperately needed transportation was used to get the Jews inside Germany.

JANUARY 22, 1945
The Russian Army entered Auschwitz and Birkenau and liberated them. The orgy of murder was over. Dov Landau aged fifteen, was one of fifty thousand Polish Jews who had kept alive out of three and a half million. He had kept his promise to his brother.

Chapter Twenty-six

The Russian army physicians who examined Dov were astonished that he had been able to live through the years of privation and punishment without incurring permanent damage. He was weak and undersized and he would never have great stamina but with proper care he could be brought up to reasonable condition.

The injury to his mind was something else. The boy had been kept alive by an indomitable spirit. Now that he could relax after six years of constant strain a flood of memories surged through his brain day and night. He became morose and slipped into melancholia and his mental state approached the thin borderline that separates the sane from the insane.

The barbed wire was torn down and the chambers and the ovens were gone but the memories would never leave him. And the frightful smell seemed always to hang over him. As he looked at his arm with the blue tattooed number he relived that grotesque second when the doors of the gas chamber were flung open. Time and time and time again he saw his mother and his sister Ruth being removed from such a chamber at Treblinka. Time and time again he held that flickering candle close to the smoldering bodies in the bunker in the Warsaw ghetto and wondered which one was Mundek. Over and over again he saw the skulls the Germans used as paperweights as his mother and his sister.

The Jews remaining at Auschwitz huddled together in several barracks. Dov could not comprehend that there was a world of the living without depravity and torture. A world of food and warmth and love was beyond him. Even the news of the German surrender brought no scenes of joy at Auschwitz, for there was no joy in victory.

Dov Landau's memories festered into hate. He was sorry the gas chambers were gone for he could visualize lines and lines of German SS troopers and their dogs being marched into them.

The war was over but no one quite knew what to do or where to go. Warsaw? It was a hundred and sixty miles away and the roads were clogged with refugees. Even if he got to Warsaw, what then? The ghetto was rubble and his mother and father and sisters and Mundek were all gone – all of them were dead. Day after day Dov sat by the window without speaking a word. He stared out at the eternal pall that clung to the Silesian countryside.

One by one the Jews at Auschwitz ventured out to return to their homes. One by one they came back to Auschwitz with a final crushing disillusion. The Germans were gone but the Poles were carrying on for them. There were no cries of Poles for three and a half million murdered. Instead the cities were covered with posters and the people screamed, 'The Jews brought this war on us . . . the war was started so that Jews could make a profit . . . the Jews are the cause of all our troubles!' There were no tears for the dead but there was plenty of hatred for the few survivors. They smashed Jewish shops and beat up Jews who tried to return to their homes and property.

And so – those who ventured out of Auschwitz came back. They sat in the muck-filled compounds, shattered, half mad, and tragically waited to rot together. The memory of death never left them. The smell from Birkenau was always there.

SUMMER 1945

A man walked into Auschwitz and was greeted with suspicious snarls. This man was in his early twenties. He was husky and had a big black mustache and wore a snow-white shirt with the sleeves rolled up above the elbows. He walked with a wonderful step that seemed to tell everyone that he was a free man. An assembly was called on the grounds and they gathered about him.

'My name is Bar Dror, Shimshon Bar Dror,' he called out. 'I have been sent from Palestine to take you people . . . home!'

For the first time in the memory of many there was an outburst of happiness and tears of joy. Bar Dror was mobbed with a million questions. Many fell on their knees and kissed his hands and others just wanted to touch him, to hear him, and to see him. A free Jew – from Palestine! Shimshon Bar Dror – Samson, Son of Freedom – had come to take them home!

Bar Dror took charge of the compound with a vengeance. He told them that it would be some time before they could move out, but until the Mossad Aliyah Bet found a way for them they would do better to live like dignified human beings.

A new surge of life transformed the compound. Bar Dror organized committees to put the place into decent shape. School was started, a theatrical group organized, a small orchestra formed and dances held, a daily news bulletin printed, and endless discussion carried on about Palestine. Shimshon even started a model farm near the compound to begin agricultural training.

Once the new spirit had been instilled and the camp was self-governing, Shimshon Bar Dror set out on treks in search of other Jews to lead them to the base.

As Shimshon Bar Dror and other Mossad Aliyah Bet agents worked untiringly to gather the Jews together and get them out of Poland, another force was working just as hard to keep them in Poland.

Throughout Europe the British embassies and consulates put pressure on every government to keep their borders closed to these refugees. The British argued that it was all a plot of the world Zionists to force their own solution on the Palestine mandate.

As the undercover battle raged between the British and the Mossad Aliyah Bet, the Polish government issued an astonishing edict; it proclaimed that all Jews were to remain in Poland. The Polish government reasoned that if the few remaining Jews were allowed to leave they would confirm to the world that the Poles were continuing their persecution – as indeed they were – even after the German extermination program. Thus the Jews were locked in a country that did not want them and locked out of the country that did want them.

Winter came to Auschwitz and morale broke apart at the seams. All the good work of Bar Dror went for nought. The Palestinian held meetings to try to explain the political battle that raged around them, but the survivors would not listen. They did not care about politics.

In the dead of winter another Aliyah Bet man entered the camp, and he and Bar Dror made a gambling decision. The two men called the section leaders together and told them to prepare to abandon the camp.

'We are going to head for the Czech border,' Bar Dror said. 'It is not too long a journey but it will be difficult. We can only go as fast as the slowest man and we must stay off the main roads.' Bar Dror opened a map and traced a route that would take them through the Carpathian Mountains and the Jablunkov Pass, a distance of seventy miles.

'What happens when we reach the border?' someone asked.

'We have Aliyah Bet men buying off the Polish border patrol. If we can get through to Czechoslovakia we will be safe for the time being. Jan Masaryk is a friend. He will not let them chase us out of Czechoslovakia.'

They left Auschwitz in the middle of the night, striking off the main road – a tragic line of survivors streaming forth, with the strong holding up the weak and carrying the young. The straggling procession pushed over fields of snow, driving their beaten bodies for six harrowing days. Then they drove themselves up into the biting winds of the Carpathian Mountains, with the Palestinians miraculously keeping them all alive and moving them on and on closer to the border.

Along the frontier other Aliyah Bet men worked feverishly to spread bribe money among the Polish guards, and as the ragged caravan pressed to the boundary the guards, with their pockets stuffed, turned their backs and the Jews poured through into Czechoslovakia.

On they marched through the freezing cold until they passed through the Jablunkov Pass and assembled at the bottom, exhausted, feet bleeding, hungry, and in need of medical attention. A special train had been chartered by the Mossad Aliyah Bet. The escapees were taken aboard to waiting warmth, food, and attention. The first leg of the perilous journey was over.

When a Jew entered Palestine legally he surrendered his passport to the Aliyah Bet so that it could be used again. Five hundred such passports were distributed to the escapees from Auschwitz. In addition to the passports the Aliyah Bet had collected visas for Venezuela, Ecuador, Paraguay, and other South American countries. These 'documents' would hold the British at bay for a while.

British CID got wind of the five hundred Jews who had crossed from Poland and relayed the news to the Foreign Office at Whitehall. Whitehall sent an urgent dispatch to the British ambassador in Prague to take the matter up with the Czech Foreign Minister, Masaryk, and have the train stopped. The British ambassador was granted an immediate meeting with Masaryk and demanded that the Jews be returned to Poland. He pointed out that the entire Mossad operation was illegal, contrary to Polish law, and had been sponsored by the Zionists in an effort to force the issue over Palestine.

Masaryk smiled. 'I do not know much about oil pipelines, Mr Ambassador,' he said, 'but I do know about human pipelines.'

Masaryk was known to be outspoken in behalf of the Jews. The ambassador implied that British displeasure could be displayed in a more 'practical' manner.

'Mr Ambassador,' Masaryk said, 'I will not comply with this or any other British threat. So long as I am Foreign Minister of Czechoslovakia the borders of my country are open to the Jews with or without visas and with or without passports.'

The ambassador reported to Whitehall that the train could not be stopped. It rolled on toward Bratislava, the town where the borders of Hungary, Czechoslovakia, and Austria came together.

Again the British attempted to stop it, but this time it crossed into Austria under the personal protection of a sympathetic American military commander.

In Vienna the travelers stopped for much-needed rest and medical attention. They were issued clothing in a giant restaging area that had been established by American Jews to help the European survivors.

In Italy, the next stop, the Mossad Aliyah Bet had the open co-operation of the public and the Italian officials, but movement was hampered by the fact that the country was occupied by the British.

Paradoxically some of the British occupation forces consisted of units of Palestinian Jews. The Palestine Brigade of the British Army and its units stationed all over occupied Italy had long been considered model troops by the British command. Aliyah Bet agents from Palestine integrated with these units, and soon the Palestinian soldiers were busy establishing refugee camps, helping with illegal ships, and the like. For formal purposes the Palestine units were commanded by army officers, but for practical purposes the units were under the command of the Aliyah Bet and Palmach. Shimshon Bar Dror had been an army sergeant in one such unit and used his British army papers to travel back and forth to Poland to round up refugees.

It was springtime when Dov's group of Auschwitz refugees embarked on another train that moved into the Austrian Alps and crossed into Italy through the Brenner Pass.

The train stopped near Lake Como outside Milan at a very isolated siding. Although the refugees had been warned that they would be met by men wearing British uniforms panic nearly broke out. The survivors could not comprehend men in fighting uniform wearing a Star of David on their arm. The Star of David had always been the insignia of the ghetto. No Jews, except in the ghetto uprisings, had fought under a Star of David for nearly two thousand years.

They debarked from the train apprehensively. The soldiers were kind and some spoke Yiddish and all spoke Hebrew and they were gentle but they seemed to be of a different breed of Jew.

A week after their arrival in Milan, Dov's group of a hundred people were taken from a small camp in the dead of night. They were transported in British trucks driven by members of the Palestine Brigade. The convoy dashed to a secret rendezvous point along the coast where it met another three hundred refugees who had assembled from other camps. From nearby La Spezia harbor a tiny vessel moved out to meet them.

The ship dropped anchor offshore and was loaded by rubber boat. It sailed and got out of the three-mile limit and was soon trailed by the ever alert British Navy.

There was something baffling about the *Gates of Zion*. Unlike all the other refugee ships, this one was not heading for Palestine. Its course, instead, was toward the Gulf of Lions on the southern coast of France. Neither the British nor the refugees aboard the *Gates of Zion* had the slightest idea the vessel was a part of a gigantic plot.

Chapter Twenty-seven

Bill Fry sat at a table at Miller Brothers' Restaurant in Baltimore, Maryland. He dropped a handful of oysterette crackers into a big steaming bowl of clam chowder and stirred it. He toyed with the soup for a moment but he had no appetite. 'Jesus Christ,' he thought. 'I wonder if I can get that piss-pot across the Atlantic Ocean.'

Bill Fry had earned a reputation as the most successful captain in the Mossad Aliyah Bet. His beaching of the *Star of David* at Caesarea had opened a new era in the illegal immigration war. It had forced the British to start the Cyprus detention camps. This had been a turning point, for the Mossad had run one shipload after another into Palestine as fast as the British turned them back, and now another crisis was brewing. Mossad Aliyah Bet had run in so many illegals that the camp in Cyprus was bursting.

Flushing with success and determined to break the British exclusion policy, the Mossad dreamed up a wild scheme and chose Bill Fry to execute it.

The largest of the illegal fleet to date had been his *Star of David*, which carried under two thousand passengers. Other ships carried from a few hundred to a thousand. The Mossad figured that if they could run the blockade with a ship holding upwards of five thousand refugees it would be a staggering blow for the British.

Bill was commissioned to find a ship that could do the job, outfit it, and take five thousand refugees from the big center at La Ciotat in southern France. It was felt that the ship should be purchased in the United States or South America where the British would not be suspicious. British CID simply had the European ports too well covered. Mossad agents covered South America while Bill himself searched the Gulf ports and the east coast. It became obvious that they weren't going to get much of a ship for the money they had to spend. So Bill had taken a gamble and now he was worried. He had purchased an overaged, obsolete steamship which had seen service only on the Chesapeake Bay in an overnight run between Baltimore and Norfolk. The ship, the *General Stonewall Jackson*, an oversized pleasure cruiser, had never sailed the ocean. The only thing Bill could think of that was decent about the ship was that it had been bought cheap.

The white-coated waiter hovered over Bill's table. 'Is something wrong with the chowder, sir?'

'Huh? Oh, hell no . . . it's fine,' he mumbled, and shoved a spoonful into his mouth.

Had the purchase of the obsolete bay liner been a mistake? At this moment it was being fitted in Newport News, Virginia, to hold 6850 refugees.

Bill sighed. There was the other side of the picture. Suppose he could get seven thousand refugees out of Europe at one crack! It would just about explode the British policy!

Bill shoved the bowl of chowder away and asked for the check. He picked up the dead cigar butt from the ash tray and relit it and once again read the telegram from Newport News: THE JACKSON IS READY.

At Newport News the next day Bill assembled his crew of Palestinian Palmach and Aliyah Bet, American Jews, sympathetic Spanish Loyalists, Italians, and French. He inspected the ship and ran a short shakedown cruise around the lower bay, then revved up her engines and made for the Atlantic Ocean.

Within three hours the *Jackson* developed engine trouble and had to return to Newport News.

During the next two weeks Bill made three more attempts. The moment the old ship got far from her natural habitat she rebelled and had to be taken back to port.

Bill told the Aliyah Bet people he had made a mistake. The *Jackson* simply could not make it. They urged him to check her over in dock for another week and make one last try.

On the fifth attempt the entire crew held its collective breath as the obsolete steamer chugged past Cape Henry into deep waters of the Atlantic – and continued to chug.

Twenty-two days later the *Stonewall Jackson* wheezed up the Gulf of Lions to the French harbor of Toulon, which stood forty miles from Marseilles and only twenty miles from the big refugee camp of La Ciotat.

There had been a teamster strike in France, and the British CID who were watching La Ciotat relaxed for a moment, assuming that there would be no movement without trucks. Furthermore, there had been no reports of illegal ships coming from any European ports since the *Gates of Zion*, Dov's ship, had landed at Port-de-Bouc several weeks earlier.

The British were caught napping.

They had no advance notice of the *Jackson* because she had been purchased and fitted in the United States and to date no Aliyah Bet ship had been large enough to navigate the Atlantic. When the *Jackson* was due to arrive at Toulon the Aliyah Bet went to the head of the French Teamsters' Union and explained the situation. The Teamsters' head secretly rounded up drivers and trucks and during the middle of their strike they rushed in and out of La Ciotat transporting sixty-five hundred refugees to Toulon – among them Dov Landau.

British CID discovered the secret at the last moment and descended upon Toulon. They passed out enormous bribes to port officials to delay the departure of the *Jackson* long enough for them to contact London for instructions.

Mossad Aliyah Bet men made counterbribes to the officials to get the ship on the seas, and the *Jackson*, now renamed the *Promised Land*, ran the blue and white Star of David to her mast top in open challenge.

Hasty meetings took place at the Admiralty. Chatham House, and Whitehall. The implications of the situation for British policy were clear, and it was obvious that the *Promised Land* had to be stopped at all costs. The British issued angry threats to the French. British warships waited outside Toulon. The French answered by granting permission to the *Promised Land* to sail.

The *Promised Land* set out from Toulon mid the cheers of the refugees aboard her. The instant she passed the three-mile zone she was escorted by two waiting British cruisers, the *Apex* and *Dunston Hill*.

For the next three and a half days Bill Fry steered the *Promised Land* straight for Palestine. Her long thin smokestack puffed and her engines groaned and her decks bulged, and her watchdog cruisers watched.

The *Apex* and *Dunston Hill* kept in constant radio contact with the Admiralty in London. As the *Promised Land* edged to within fifty miles of the Palestine coast, the British broke the rules of illegal blockade. The *Apex* came close to the steamer and sent a salvo over her ancient bows. The cruiser's bull horns blasted and her loud-speaker sent a voice over the water: 'Illegal ship! Stand by to be boarded!'

Bill Fry bit his cigar. He grabbed a megaphone and stepped onto the bridge. 'We are on the high seas,' he shouted. 'If you board us here it will be piracy!'

'Sorry, chaps, just following orders. Are you going to accept a boarding party peacefully?'

Bill turned to his Palmach chief who was standing behind him. 'Let's give these bastards a reception.'

The *Promised Land* turned on full steam in an attempt to sprint away from the cruisers. The *Apex* moved alongside her, then cut in sharply and her steel bow rammed the ancient steamer amidships. The blow splintered deep into the steamer's hull over the water line and she shuddered under the impact. The

Apex sent out machine-gun fire to drive the refugees off the deck and make it clear for a landing party.

British marines, wearing gas masks and carrying small arms, poured over the bow of the *Promised Land* and moved back to the superstructure. Palmachniks unrolled accordions of barbed wire in the path of the British and then loosed a barrage of rocks on them, followed by streams of water from pressure hoses.

The British were swept back to the bow by the attack. They fought off the Palmach with small arms and called for reinforcements. More marines boarded, this time with wire cutters. Another attack mounted toward the superstructure. Again the water hoses pushed them back and again the British returned, under cover of machine-gun fire from the *Apex*. They reached the barbed wire and cut it in time to receive scalding steam jets from the Palmach. Now the Palmachniks jumped to the attack and drove the British back. They overpowered the marines and threw them into the sea, one by one.

The *Apex* stopped the attack to fish their men out of the water, and the *Promised Land*, a huge hole in her side, chugged off once again. The *Dunston Hill* chased her down and pondered the advisability of another ram. The steamer might well go down with one more blow. It was too dangerous to risk. Instead, the *Dunston Hill* poured on heavy-caliber machine-gun fire that raked the decks clean of refugees and Palmach. The *Dunston Hill*'s boarding party came up amid-ships on ladders. A wild hand-to-hand brawl followed. With flailing clubs and an occasional pistol shot, the British pressed the attack toward the ladder leading up to the captain's bridge.

Meanwhile, the *Apex* recovered and raced to the scene again. The two cruisers boxed the steamship in. The *Apex* party boarded again behind a tear-gas barrage, and with the *Dunston Hill* marines pressing from the other direction the Palmach was driven back.

Dov Landau was in the fight. He and other refugees were guarding the top of the ladder near the captain's bridge. They pushed the British down the ladder half a dozen times until the tear gas and, finally, the small arms drove them off.

The British had control of the deck now. They reinforced their position and held the refugees and Palmach off at gunpoint while another party stormed into the wheelhouse to gain command of the ship.

Bill Fry and five of his crew greeted the first three men who entered the wheelhouse with pistols and angry fists. Although he was completely cut off, Bill continued fighting until British marines dragged him from the wheelhouse and beat him unconscious with clubs.

After four hours of fighting, with eight of their men dead and a score wounded, the British gained control of the *Promised Land*. Fifteen Jews were killed, among them the American captain, Bill Fry.

A general order for secrecy was issued at Haifa harbor in Palestine as the *Dunston Hill* towed the *Promised Land* in. The old steamship was listing badly. The entire Haifa dock area was flooded with British troops. The Sixth Airborne Division was there and they were armed to the teeth. But in their attempt at maintaining the secrecy, the British did not know that the Jews had broadcast a full account of the boarding of the *Promised Land* over their radio.

As the ships approached Haifa Bay, the Jews in Palestine called a general strike. Troops and tanks were required in the dock area to form a barrier between the refugees and Palestine's angry Jews.

Four British prison ships, *Empire Monitor*, *Empire Renown*, *Empire Guardian*, and the *Magna Charta* waited to effect an immediate transfer of the refugees from the *Promised Land*. But the very instant the Chesapeake Bay liner was towed into port, the harbor area and the entire city of Haifa shook under the impact of a mighty blast! The *Empire Monitor* was blown to pieces! This act was accomplished by Palmach frogmen who swam in and attached a magnetic mine to the ship's sides.

The *Promised Land* docked and the transfer operation began at once. Most of the refugees had had the fight knocked out of them. They went quietly to delousing sheds where they were stripped, sprayed, searched for weapons, and moved quickly on to the three remaining prison ships. It was a tragic procession.

Dov Landau and twenty-five others locked themselves into a hold, armed themselves with pipes, and defied the British to the very end. The hold was pumped full of tear gas; and Dov was carried from the *Promised Land* by four soldiers, still struggling, cursing, and fighting. He was thrown into a barred cell on the *Magna Charta*.

The prison ships were packed even more tightly than the *Promised Land* had been, and that same night they sailed from Haifa with the two cruisers, *Dunston Hill* and *Apex*, as escort.

If the refugees were sent on to Cyprus to the already crowded camps there, then the Jews would have won their point. Sixty-five hundred more Jews would have been taken out of Europe and added to the ever-growing numbers waiting on Cyprus to go to Palestine.

'The refugees from the so-called *Promised Land* on the *Empire Guardian*, the *Empire Renown*, and the *Magna Charta* are to be returned to their port of embarkation, Toulon, France. Henceforth any other illegal blockade-runners that are caught will also be returned to their ports of origin.'

The Palmachniks and Mossad Aliyah Bet people who were with the refugees on the three ships knew what they had to do. If they debarked and returned to Toulon and if the British rode out the storm, then there would be no more illegal immigration.

The order for secrecy went out in Toulon as the prison ships steamed into the Gulf of Lions and dropped anchor off-shore.

Simultaneously the Palmach chiefs on each of the prison ships handed the British captains a message; each one was to the effect that 'We will be taken ashore only by force.'

The commander of the prison ships radioed to the Admiralty in London for instructions. Whitehall immediately turned on the toughest diplomatic pressure they could, short of breaking the Anglo-French alliance. They warned the French not to attempt to take sides with the Jews and to allow the British to carry out the debarkation by force. For four days messages and instructions flew between London and the prison ships and between Paris and London. Then the French government handed the British its dramatic decision.

'The government of France will not allow or be a party to the forcible removal of the refugees. If the refugees desire to return to France of their own free will, they are most welcome.'

The French had taken a stand with the Jews, even at the risk of rupturing relations with the British. The refugees were exhilarated by the news. To a man, they renewed their vow to stay aboard the ships. The British, recovering from the shock, informed the refugees that they would either debark at Toulon or sit in the Gulf of Lions until they rotted.

Aboard the *Empire Guardian*, *Empire Renown*, and *Magna Charta*, the Jews dug in. The Palmachniks organized schools, taught Hebrew, compiled news, started a theater, and generally tried to keep things going. The French government kept up a daily stream of barges between the ships and Toulon to supply the refugees with good food and medical care. A dozen babies were born. At the end of a week, the refugees were holding fast.

On shore newsmen were getting curious about the three ships and were irate over the curtain of silence. One night an Aliyah Bet man swam ashore from the *Empire Guardian* and gave out the full story to the French press.

The story swept through France, Italy, Holland, and Denmark. Editorial insults were hurled at the British, in all four countries.

London braced itself against the onslaught of public resentment from the continent. They had expected it. They had, in fact, prepared for everything except the doggedness of the refugees. Conditions on the prison ships were of the worst. The atmosphere was sweltering and there was a good deal of sickness. Nevertheless, the refugees refused to come ashore. The British crews, who did not dare venture into the caged sections of the ship, were beginning to get uneasy. At the end of the second week the Jews were still holding fast and the clamor in the press was reaching a crescendo.

Three weeks passed. Four weeks passed.

At last the story began to lose its impetus. Then, the first Jew came ashore without being forced. He was dead. The whole issue was reignited. The captains of the three ships reported that the refugees seemed more determined than ever and the pressure on Whitehall mounted hourly. If more corpses were brought ashore it would be very bad.

The policy makers decided to take another tack. They asked that the refugees send in delegations to talk it all over. Their plan was to try to find a compromise that might let them out of the whole affair without losing face. From all three ships they received the same answer from the Palmach chiefs:

'We will settle for nothing more nor less than Palestine.'

The affair went into its sixth week. When the second corpse was brought ashore the British issued an ultimatum to the Jews either to come ashore or suffer the consequences. It was not clear what those consequences were to be, but when the refugees again remained steadfast the British had to take direct action:

'The *Empire Guardian* and the *Empire Renown* will set sail from Toulon at once. The destination of these two ships will be Hamburg, Germany, in the British occupation zone. The inmates of these two ships will be removed peacefully or otherwise and be detained at Dachau until further notice.'

As the two ships passed through the Straits of Gibraltar on the journey toward Germany, Mossad Aliyah Bet made feverish plans to load up two more ships with fifteen thousand refugees and make a run for Palestine. For as the *Renown* and *Guardian* landed on German soil, world opinion against the British reached a tidal peak. It was a somber victory for the Aliyah Bet.

As a last fact-saving gesture the British let the third prison ship, *Magna Charta*, discharge its refugees at Cyprus, where they were sent to Caraolos. Dov Landau was fortunate to pass his sixteenth year at Caraolos rather than Dachau, but the boy was a study of hate.

Chapter Twenty-eight

Dov Landau spent his seventeenth birthday in yet another prison – Caraolos. He ushered in this birthday as he ushered in every day. He lay on his cot and stared at nothing and spent the day without uttering a word. He had not spoken to anyone since he had been dragged from the hold of the *Promised Land*. During the long weeks in Toulon harbor his hatred had grown.

At Caraolos a dozen welfare people and doctors and teachers and Palmachniks tried to reach him and break through his wall of bitterness, but Dov trusted no one and wanted no one near him.

By day he lay on his cot. By night he fought off sleep, for sleep always brought the recurring dream of that moment the doors of the gas chambers opened at Auschwitz. For hours on end Dov would stare at the blue tattooed numbers on his left forearm: 359195.

Across the path from his tent there lived a girl, and she was the most beautiful girl he ever remembered seeing. Of course, women could not be beautiful in the places he had been. She was in charge of many younger children and she always smiled when she saw him and she did not seem angry and aloof toward him as everyone else did. She was Karen Hansen Clement.

Karen saw Dov and made inquiries as to why he did not take part in school and other activities. She was warned to keep away from him, for he was said to be an 'incurable' and maybe even dangerous.

Karen took this as a challenge. She knew Dov had been in Auschwitz, and her compassion seemed limitless. She had done amazing things with youngsters before, and although she knew it might be better to leave Dov alone her curiosity grew each time she went to her tent and looked over at his.

One day Dov lay on his cot, staring, and the sweat poured from him for it was very hot. He felt someone's presence and jumped up instinctively and tensed at the sight of Karen standing near him.

'I wonder if I could borrow your water bucket. Mine has a leak and the water trucks will be coming soon.'

Dov stared and blinked his eyes nervously.

'I said I wonder if I could borrow your water bucket.'

Dov grunted.

'What does that mean? Yes or no? Can you talk?'

They stood and looked at each other like a pair of gamecocks. For that instant Karen was sorry she had come. She took a deep breath. 'My name is Karen,' she said. 'I am your neighbor.'

Dov still did not answer. He glared.

'Well ... may I use your bucket or not?'

'Did you come here to slobber over me?'

'I came here to borrow your bucket. You are certainly nothing to slobber over,' she snapped.

He spun away and sat on the edge of his cot and chewed his fingernails. Her abruptness disarmed him completely. He pointed to his bucket on the floor and she picked it up. He glanced at her quickly out of the corner of his eye.

'What is your name? I'd like to be able to call you something when I bring your bucket back.'

He did not answer.

'Well?'

'Dov!'

'Karen is mine. Perhaps you can call me that and we can say hello. At least till you learn to smile.'

He turned very slowly but she was gone. He walked to the tent door and watched her moving toward the British water tanker which had just passed through the gate. She was beautiful.

It was the first time in many months that an outside event had been able to penetrate Dov Landau's absorption in himself. This Karen was completely different from the others who had come to see him. She was abrupt and snippy and afraid – yet there was a tenderness that radiated from her too. She did not gush over him or recite words she didn't feel. She was a prisoner at Caraolos but she did not complain or seem angry like all the others. Her voice was sweet, yet it was very stern.

'Good morning, Dov,' Karen said. 'Thank you for the use of your bucket.'

He grumbled.

'Oh yes, you are the one who growls instead of talking. I have a little boy like you in my kindergarten class. But he pretends he is a lion.'

'Good morning!' Dov shouted at the top of his lungs.

Dov knew what time she got up in the morning. He knew when she went to the wash racks and when she came and went from her classes. He slipped into her tent one day and looked around for her bucket and examined it. It had no hole in it at all. He would lie on his cot all day and wait anxiously for the sound of her footsteps coming down the catwalk. He would sneak to the tent door and steal a glance in her direction. Often, Karen would glance at his tent, too, and their eyes would meet for a brief instant. Then Dov would become angry with himself for being taken in and for showing weakness.

The days passed but they were different now. He was still silent and sullen but often his thoughts veered from death and hate and he could hear the children in the playground nearby and he could hear her voice speaking to them. It seemed strange to Dov. In all the time he was at Caraolos he had never heard the children playing until after he met her.

One night Dov stood by the barbed wire and watched the searchlights sweep through the tents. He often stood and looked, for he still did not want to sleep. On the playground the Palmach had built a campfire and there was singing and dancing. Once he used to sing and dance those songs at Redeemer meetings, but he did not want to hear them now. Mundek and Ruth and Rebecca had always been there.

'Hello, Dov.'

He whirled around and saw the dim outline of Karen standing near him. Her long hair blew in the breeze and she tightened a ragged shawl about her shoulders. 'Would you like to come to the campfire with me?' She pressed closer and he turned his back. 'You like me, don't you? You can talk to me. Why don't you go to school and join our gang?'

He shook his head.

'Dov . . .' she whispered.

He spun around and faced her, watery-eyed. 'Poor Dov!' he screamed. 'Poor crazy Dov! You're just like all the rest of them! You just talk prettier!' Dov grabbed her and put his hands on her neck and tightened his fingers on her throat. 'You leave me alone ... you leave me alone ...'

Karen looked him straight in the eye. 'Take your hands off my throat ... this instant.'

He dropped his hands. 'I was only trying to scare you,' he said. 'I wasn't going to hurt you.'

'Well, you didn't scare me,' she said, and walked off.

For a week after that Karen did not look at him or speak to him. He was seized with terrible restlessness. Dov was no longer able to spend the hours in sullen and morbid silence. He paced back and forth all day long. Why did he let the girl break into his thoughts! He had his memories and he had been alone with them! Now he could not think!

One evening Karen was on the playground when one of her children fell in a game and started to cry. She knelt beside him and put her arms about him and soothed away the boy's tears. For some reason she looked up and saw Dov standing over her. 'Hello,' he said very quickly, and walked away.

Despite the continued warnings of many to leave him alone, Karen knew she had penetrated a great darkness. She knew the boy was desperate and trying to communicate and that his 'hello' was his way of saying he was sorry.

A few evenings later she found a drawing on her bed. She held it to the candlelight and saw a picture of a girl kneeling and holding a child, and barbed wire was beyond her. She crossed the path to Dov's tent and when he saw her he turned his back.

'You are a very good artist,' Karen said.

'I ought to be,' he snapped. 'I got plenty of practice. George Washington and Lincoln are specialties of mine.'

He sat on his cot uncomfortably and bit his lip. Karen sat beside him. He felt funny, for he had never been so close to a girl other than his sisters before. Her finger touched the blue tattoo on his left arm. 'Auschwitz?'

'Why do you bother with me?'

'Did you ever think that I might like you?'

'Like me?'

'Uh-huh. You are very good-looking when you aren't sneering, which is quite seldom, I must admit, and you have a very nice voice when you aren't growling.'

His lips trembled. 'I ... like ... you. You're not like the rest of them. You understand me. My brother Mundek used to understand me.'

'How old are you?'

'Seventeen.' Dov sprang to his feet and whirled around. 'I hate these goddam British. They're no better than the Germans.'

'Dov!'

His sudden explosion ended as quickly as it had started.

Yet, it was a beginning. He had blown off steam. It was the first time in well over a year that he had spoken more than one or two words. Karen watched him shrink back into that strange dark world of his.

Dov wanted to see Karen often because she was tender and she could listen to him and understand. He would talk quietly for a while and then burst forth with an impulsive short tirade of hate and then he would withdraw into himself.

Karen began to confide in him and tell him about how she was going to meet her father again in Palestine. Since she had left the Hansens she had always worked so long and hard with the youngsters she had never really formed a close friendship. Dov seemed proud that she would tell him all these things, and it was strange but she rather enjoyed talking to him.

And one day a great thing happened. Dov Landau smiled again.

When they spoke together he wanted to talk about nice things to her. The way she spoke ... about the Hansens ... the Danes ... the children she loved ... about her hope of reunion with her father ... made him want to be able to talk like that too. But he could remember nothing nice, and before the war, 1939, was so long ago he could remember nothing about it at all.

Karen was careful with subjects that Dov did not mention. She never asked about Auschwitz or the ghetto,

After several weeks she came to him one day with a mission. 'Dov, I have a favor to ask.'

Immediately Dov turned suspicious.

'The Mossad people know you were in Auschwitz and they have also found out that you are an expert counterfeiter.'

'So?'

'There is a new man here from Palestine. Joab Yarkoni tells me he wants to talk to you. His name is Ari Ben Canaan. He needs passports and documents and could use your services.'

'So that's it! That's why you made friends! So you could get me to work.'

'Oh, shut up, Dov. You don't even believe that yourself.'

'Well,' Dov grumbled, 'if they want me so badly they can come and ask me themselves.'

'How can anyone ask you anything when you won't even talk to them?'

'And why should I work for them?'

'Because they're working for you.'

'Hell they are. They're working to save themselves.'

'All right. Take your side of it. They are no worse than the Germans, and if you could make American dollars for *them* you can certainly make passports for the Mossad.'

'You're always so damned smart with the answers.'

'Dov. I've never asked a favor of you. What shall I tell them?'

'Tell them I might, but a lot of things have to be made clear.'

Karen took his hand and smiled. 'Why don't you make them clear? Ben Canaan is waiting for you.'

'I'll see him here.'

Dov secretly liked Ari Ben Canaan. He was direct and to the point and let Dov know that if he didn't work he was going to be the last Jew out of Caraolos. But more, Dov liked that quality of leadership in the man – the same quality Mundek had had. He went to work in the Palmach headquarters in one of the schoolrooms. Still, to everyone else in Caraolos but Karen, Dov Landau was incorrigible. He spoke only in anger. She was always called upon to calm his sudden eruptions.

She saw in him things that no other person saw – wonderful strength and pride. There were other things that she could not explain that made her like him very much.

Two and a half weeks after Ben Canaan's arrival on Cyprus, David Ben Ami gave Dov a list of three hundred names of children to be fixed on documents resembling British transfer orders. The three hundred were supposed to be moved from Caraolos to the new compounds near Larnaca. Dov knew that this was the escape! Neither his name nor the name of Karen was on the list of transferees.

Dov told David that he wanted to speak to Ben Canaan, and it was then that he put his demands to Ari that he and Karen be included in the escape. And Ari agreed to his demands.

Chapter Twenty-nine

The final steps in Operation Gideon were twenty-four hours away.

Ari Ben Canaan called a meeting of his chiefs in the home of Mandria, their Cypriot compatriot.

David Ben Ami gave Ari the transfer papers that Dov Landau had just completed. Ari looked them over and commented that the boy was a real artist. The papers could have fooled anyone. David reported that he had taken care of the hundred odds and ends, from security to putting kosher food on the ship for Orthodox children.

Joab Yarkoni, the Moroccan, reported that all the trucks were in ready condition and could be moved from the 23rd Transportation camp to Caraolos in twenty minutes. He gave the elapsed time of trial runs from Caraolos to Kyrenia by several alternate routes.

Zev Gilboa said that the three hundred and two children would be loaded on the lorries in a matter of minutes after the convoy arrived at Caraolos. He would brief the children as to what was going to happen a few minutes before the trucks departed.

Hank Schlosberg, the American skipper of the *Exodus*, said he would take the ship out of its Larnaca berth at dawn and steam up to Kyrenia and be there at least a full hour or two before the convoy was due to arrive.

Mandria reported that he had a system of lookouts posted along the escape route who could notify the convoy of any unusual British activity. He also had watchmen on a half dozen alternate routes. Mandria said that he would wait, as ordered, in Famagusta in his home. The minute the convoy passed through he would telephone Mark Parker in Kyrenia.

Ari rose and looked over his lieutenants. They were nervous, all of them. Even the usually placid Yarkoni was looking at the floor. Ari did not congratulate them or wish them luck. There was time for congratulations. As for luck, they'd make their own.

'I did not want to make the escape for three more days until the British themselves began moving chilren from the children's compound. Nevertheless we have received information that Major Alistair is suspicious of our activities. We even have reason to believe he has gone to London for instructions over Brigadier Sutherland's head. Therefore we must make our break at once. Our trucks arrive at Caraolos at nine o'clock. By ten o'clock I hope we have loaded the children and are passing your house here in

Famagusta. The minute we turn off the Larnaca road we have two crucial hours. We have no reason to believe our convoy will be stopped. Our trucks are well known all over Cyprus. But . . . we must act under the assumption that we are under suspicion. Any further questions?'

David Ben Ami, the sentimentalist, could not let the occasion pass without proposing a toast. Ari tolerated the younger man's frivolity. '*Le chaim*,' David said, raising his glass.

'*Le chaim*,' the rest of them answered.

'I have heard that *le chaim* from you boys often,' Mandria said. 'What does it mean?'

'It means "to life,"' David answered, 'and to Jews that is no small request.'

'"To life."' Mandria repeated. 'That is nice.'

Ari walked up to Mandria and hugged him in the Palmach manner. 'You have been a friend,' he said. 'I must go meet Parker now.'

Mandria stood there with tears streaming down his cheeks for he knew that this kind of affection was reserved for one of their own and to receive it from Ari Ben Canaan meant that he had been accepted fully as one of them.

A half hour later Ari, dressed as Captain Caleb Moore, met Mark on the terrace of the King George Hotel. Mark was a bundle of nerves.

Ari seated himself, refused a cigarette, and ordered a drink.

'Well?' Mark asked impatiently.

'Tomorrow. We will be at Caraolos at nine.'

'I thought you were going to wait until the British started cleaning out the children's compound.'

'It would have been better but we can't wait. A friend at CID tells us that Alistair is on to something. But relax,' Ari said. 'It is almost over. The British still don't know what they're looking for. Now you understand everything.'

Mark nodded. He would send a cable asking for an extension of his vacation. Bradbury in London would know by the signature, Mark, that Operation Gideon had been a success and would turn loose the story Mark had sent with a commercial pilot a week earlier.

'Suppose I don't get a phone call from Mandria at ten.'

Ari smiled. 'Then I'd suggest you get the hell off Cyprus unless you want to cover my hanging.'

'That might be nice,' Mark said. He finished his drink.

'By the way,' Ari said, looking out to the water, 'Kitty hasn't been in the camp since we were forced to put Karen on the *Exodus* list.'

'That's right. She's with me at the Dome.'

'How is she?'

'How in hell do you think she is? She's miserable. She doesn't want Karen to go on the *Exodus*. Do you blame her?'

'I don't blame her but I feel sorry for her.'

'That's nice. I didn't know you felt sorry for anyone.'

'I feel sorry that she has let her emotions get the best of her.'

'I forgot. You don't know anything about human emotions.'

'You're nervous, Mark.'

Mark was angry at Ari's placidness. He remembered Kitty's anguish when she returned to Kyrenia and told him that Karen was going on the ship. 'What do you want? Kitty has suffered more than one person has a right to suffer.'

'Suffered?' Ari said. 'I wonder if Kitty Fremont knows the meaning of the word.'

'Damn you, Ben Canaan, damn you. What makes you think that Jews own a copyright on suffering?'

'Fortunately you're not being paid to like me and I couldn't care less.'

'How could you? You see, I like people with human weaknesses.'

'I never have them during working hours.'

Mark stood up to leave. Ari grabbed Mark's arm in his powerful hand. For the first time Mark saw Ben Canaan shaken from his complacency. There was anger in Ari's eyes. 'What the hell do you think this is? A tea party on the duchess's lawn? We're butting heads with the British Empire tomorrow.'

He released his grip on Mark's arm and regretted the short display of temper. At that instant Mark felt a tiny bit sorry for Ari. Perhaps he had a better way of disguising it but the pressure was beginning to tell on him too.

A few hours later Mark had returned to the Dome Hotel in Kyrenia. He knocked on Kitty's door. She managed to greet him with a half smile, but it could not disguise her red-rimmed eyes.

'Tomorrow.'

Kitty froze an instant. 'So soon?'

'They are afraid the British are on to something.'

Kitty walked to the window and looked out at the pier and the island. It was a crystal-clear evening and she could even see the faint outline of the Turkish coast. 'I've been trying to get up enough courage to pack up and leave Cyprus.'

'Look,' Mark said, 'as soon as this blows over, you and I are going to head for the Riviera for a few weeks.'

'To pick up the pieces? I thought you were supposed to go to Palestine.'

'I doubt if the British will let me in after this. Kitty, I feel pretty rotten about dragging you into this thing.'

'It isn't your fault, Mark.'

'You read that line well but it's not quite true. Are you going to get over this?'

'Yes, I think so. I should have known better. You tried to warn me. At least I knew all the time that I was on thin ice. You know, Mark, it's funny, but we argued the night I met Ben Canaan. I told you there was something different about Jews. They aren't like us.'

'They have an unlimited capacity for getting into trouble. It's their favorite sport,' Mark said, spinning off the bed and rubbing his temples. 'Well ... one way or the other we might as well eat and I'm hungry.'

Kitty leaned against the door frame as Mark splashed his face with cold water. He groped for a towel. She handed him one.

'Mark. It's going to be very dangerous on the *Exodus*, isn't it?'

He hesitated a moment. There was no use trying to fool her at this point. 'It's a floating bomb.'

Kitty's heart sank. 'Tell me the truth. Can they get away with this?'

'They have a fair chance with that mechanical monster, Ari Ben Canaan, running the show.'

The sun went down and it was night.

Mark and Kitty sat wordlessly in her room.

'No use sitting up all night,' he said at last.

'Don't go,' Kitty said; 'I'll just stretch out over the covers.' She reached into the night stand and took out a couple of sleeping pills, turned off the light, and lay back.

Mark sat by the window and watched the surf slap against the shore.

Twenty minutes passed. He looked over at Kitty and saw she had fallen into a restless and thrashing sleep. He walked to the bed and stood over her for several moments, then covered her with a blanket and returned to the chair.

At Caraolos, Dov and Karen sat on his cot, too excited to sleep. They spoke in whispers. They were the only ones among the children who knew what the new day would bring.

Karen tried to calm Dov. He kept whispering what he was going to do when he got to Palestine. How he was going to join the terrorists and kill British soldiers. She hushed him up as only she could and finally induced him to lie down.

As he closed his eyes Karen stood up and a strange sensation swept through her body. Odd and frightening. Dov meant more to her than she had realized until this moment. First it had been pity. Now Dov had a hold on her. She did not understand it. She wanted to be able to go and talk it over with Kitty. But Kitty was gone.

'Karen?'

'I am here, Dov.'

The hours of darkness ticked by.

At the 23rd Transportation Company HMJFC three men lay on their cots wide-eyed.

Zev Gilboa dared think about springtime in Galilee for the first time in nearly a year. He thought of his wife and child and of the farm. His baby had been only a few months old when the Palmach sent Zev to Cyprus.

Joab Yarkoni thought of his farm too. It was different from Zev's, for it hugged the sea just a bit north of the Plain of Sharon. His farm was called Sdot Yam and it meant Fields of the Sea, for its main crop was fish. Yarkoni loved to walk for hours through the abandoned ruins of Caesarea and dig for antiquities, and he hoped that the Palmach might let him return there for a while. He would go out on his trawler fishing and he would see his brother and sister again.

... and David Ben Ami thought of his beloved Jerusalem. He loved Jerusalem almost as much as he loved Ari's sister Jordana. Now he would see them both again until they reassigned him to another mission. The rocky hills of Judea where his six brothers lived and the city rose out of stone. David propped on an elbow and reread the worn letter that Ari had brought him. Jordana! Jordana! His heart raced wildly. Jordana, my love!

The three men knew that their stay in Palestine might be brief because they belonged to the Palmach and Mossad and they might be needed anywhere in the world. But this night they thought of home ...

Brigadier Bruce Sutherland had another of his nightmares. He dressed and went out of his house alone and walked through Famagusta in the depth of night. He walked along the old wall of Famagusta and stared into the old city with its hundreds of churches and cathedrals and ruins of castles and memories of past glory. He walked until he came to Othello's Tower and he climbed it and looked down at the harbor. He was tired, very tired, and he wondered if there would ever be a night again in which he could close his eyes and fall into a peaceful sleep.

Major J. J. Alistair fell asleep over his desk. Most of the night he continued to pore through reports and bits and scraps of information in an attempt to put together exactly what the Jews were up to at Caraolos.

Mandria paced back and forth in the room where the Mossad and Palmach had held so many meetings. Yes, it had been only a few weeks since Ari Ben Canaan and David Ben Ami had stood on that balcony outside and watched a convoy of Jews being taken from their illegal runner, *Door of Hope*. Tomorrow he would stand on the balcony and another convoy would pass. This one would climax Ari Ben Canaan's fantastic scheme. The imagination of the Greek Cypriots had been tremendously stirred by the daring of the Mossad. Those of them, like Mandria, who worked with the Jews, were beginning to think in terms of an underground movement of their own against British rule on Cyprus.

One man slept soundly. Ari Ben Canaan slept like a well-fed baby without a care in the world.

A ray of light fell over Mark Parker's face. He opened his eyes and yawned. He had dropped off by the window with his feet propped on the sill. He was stiff and his mouth tasted foul from cigarettes and scotch. He glanced around and saw Kitty in a deep and quiet slumber on the bed. He pulled the window shade down and tiptoed from the room and shaved and spent several moments under an icy shower and he felt better. He dressed and returned to Kitty's room and sat gently on the edge of her bed and stroked her hair softly. She stirred and opened her eyes slowly. She smiled when she saw Mark and stretched and purred. Then her expression changed to one of fear.

At twenty minutes to nine, Ari Ben Canaan, dressed as Captain Caleb Moore, entered the lead jeep in the convoy of twelve trucks of the 23rd Transportation Company. Each truck had a Palmachnik dressed like a British soldier as driver. They sped out of their camp and twenty minutes later halted before the administration building at Caraolos, outside the barbed-wire compounds.

Ari entered the administration building and knocked on the door of the commanding officer, whose acquaintance he had carefully made during the past three weeks.

'Good morning, sir,' Ari said.

'Good morning, Captain Moore. What brings you up here?'

'We received a special dispatch from headquarters, sir. It seems that they are getting the Larnaca camp ready faster than they expected. They want me to transfer some children today.' Ari lay the forged papers on the officer's desk.

The CO thumbed through the sheets. 'This isn't on the schedule of transfers,' he said. 'We didn't expect to start moving the children for three days.'

'That's the Army for you, sir,' Ari said.

The CO bit his lip and meditated and stared at Ari and looked through the transfer papers again. He reached for the phone. 'Hello. Potter here. Captain

Moore has orders to move three hundred children out of Compound 50. Dispatch a detail to help get them moved.'

The CO picked up his pen and initialed the papers. He signed half a dozen other sheets authorizing entrance into the compound and removal of the children. 'Move them along, will you, Moore? We have another load to be transferred in an hour and the roads could be clogged.'

'Yes sir.'

'Oh, uh . . . Moore. Many thanks, old man, for the whisky you sent up to the club.'

'My pleasure, sir.'

Ari gathered up the papers from the CO's desk. The CO sighed. 'Jews come and Jews go,' he said.

'Yes sir,' Ari said. 'They come . . . and they go.'

The breakfast table was set in front of the window in Mark's room. He and Kitty nibbled at their food. Mark's ash tray brimmed over. 'What time is it now?' Kitty asked for the fifteenth time.

'Almost nine-thirty.'

'What would be happening?'

'If they're running on schedule they're loading the children aboard the trucks right now. Look,' Mark said, pointing out to sea. The salvage trawler *Aphrodite/Exodus* turned and moved slowly toward the harbor entrance.

'Good Lord,' Kitty said, 'is that the *Exodus*?'

'That's her.'

'My God, Mark. It looks like it's ready to fall apart.'

'It is.'

'But how on earth are they going to get three hundred children on her?'

Mark lit another cigarette. He wanted to pace the room but he did not wish to show Kitty how frightened he was.

Nine-thirty.

Nine-forty.

The *Exodus* passed between the lighthouse and the castle, through the narrow opening of the two arms of the sea wall, and into the Kyrenia harbor.

Nine-fifty.

'Mark, please sit down. You're making me nervous.'

'We should be getting a call from Mandria soon. Any minute now . . . any minute.'

Ten o'clock.

Five past ten.

Six past ten.

Seven past ten

'Dammit! Where is that coffee I ordered? Kitty, phone from your room, will you. Tell them to get that coffee up here.'

A quarter past ten. The fresh pot of coffee arrived.

Seventeen past ten. Mark's jitters abated. He knew that if he did not hear from Mandria in the next ten minutes something had gone wrong.

Ten-twenty. The phone rang!

Mark and Kitty looked at each other for an instant. Mark wiped the sweat from the palm of his hand, sucked in his breath, and lifted the receiver.

'Hello.'

'Mr Parker?'

'Speaking.'

'Just a moment, sir. We have a call for you from Famagusta.'

'Hello . . . hello . . . hello.'

'Parker?'

'Speaking.'

'Mandria here.'

'Yes?'

'They have just passed through.'

Mark replaced the receiver slowly. 'He got them out of Caraolos, all right. They're moving down the road to Larnaca now. In about fifteen minutes they'll fork off and make a dash north. They've got about fifty miles, mostly flat country with only one mountain pass if they don't have to use alternate roads. They should be here a little after noon . . . if everything goes all right.'

'I'm almost hoping that something will go wrong,' Kitty said.

'Come on. No use waiting here.'

He took his field glasses and walked with Kitty downstairs to the reception desk and asked for a cable blank.

Kenneth Bradbury
Chief, American News Syndicate
London

HAVING A BALL. REQUEST TWO WEEK EXTENSION OF MY VACATION. ADVISE.

MARK

'Send this through, urgent. How long will it take?'

The receptionist read it over. 'It will be in London in a few hours.'

They walked from the Dome toward the quay.

'What was that about?' Kitty asked.

'My story should be on the wires from London tonight.'

They stood on the quay for several moments and watched the rickety salvage tug tie up at dockside. Mark led Kitty away. They crossed the harbor and climbed to the ramparts of the Virgin Castle. From here they could see both the harbor and far down the coastal road where the convoy was due to pass.

At eleven fifteen Mark focused his field glasses on the coast road. He slowly scanned the road that hugged the shore and wove in and out of the hillls. The mountain pass was too far off to see. He froze! He had sighted a tiny trail of dust and a line of trucks which appeared as small as ants. He nudged Kitty and handed her the glasses. She held them on the trucks as they wove in and out the snake-like turns and inched toward Kyrenia.

'They are about half an hour away.'

They came down from the rampart, crossed the harbor once again, and stood at the end of the quay, which was only five walking minutes from the Dome Hotel. As the convoy passed the hospital at the edge of town Mark took Kitty's hand and started back to the hotel.

In a phone booth at the Dome, Mark put in an urgent call to British Intelligence in Famagusta.

'I wish to speak to Major Alistair,' Mark said, disguising his voice by putting a handkerchief over the mouthpiece and speaking with a British accent.

'Who is calling, please, and what do you wish to speak to Major Alistair about?'

'Look, old boy,' Mark said, 'three hundred Jews have escaped from Caraolos. Now just don't ask any damned fool questions and give me Alistair.'

The phone on Major Alistair's desk rang.

'This is a friend,' Mark said. 'I am advising you that several hundred Jews have broken out of Caraolos and are boarding a ship in the Kyrenia harbor at this very moment.'

Alistair clicked the receiver several times. 'Hello ... hello ... who is this? I say ... hello.' He closed his own phone and opened it again. 'Alistair here. I have a report of an escape of Jews. They are supposed to be boarding a ship at Kyrenia. Sound an alert, blue. Have the Kyrenia area commander investigate at once. If the report is true you'd better advise naval units to move for that area.'

Alistair put down the receiver and rushed down the hall toward Sutherland's office.

The convoy rolled to a stop on the quay. Ari Ben Canaan got out of the lead jeep and its driver drove it off. One by one the lorries rolled up to the *Exodus*. The youngsters responded automatically as a result of Zev's training. They moved quickly and quietly from the truck to the ship. On board, Joab, David, and Hank Schlosberg, the captain, moved them into their places in the hold and on deck. The operation was effected calmly and wordlessly.

Along the quay a few curious onlookers stood and gaped. A few British soldiers shrugged and scratched their heads. As quickly as each truck was unloaded it was driven off toward the mountains around St Hilarion to be abandoned. As of that moment the 23rd Transportation Company had fulfilled its purpose and was going out of existence. Joab left a note in his truck thanking the British for the use of their lorry.

Ari boarded the *Exodus* and went up to the wheelhouse. One by one the lorries discharged the children. It took only twenty minutes to load the boat. Zev, David, Joab, and Hank Schlosberg reported that the boarding had been completed. Ari gave the order to Hank and he cast off and started the engines.

'Get to the children,' Ari said, 'and tell them exactly what we are doing and what will be expected of them. Any child who feels he cannot go through with it will advise me in the wheelhouse and he will be returned to Caraolos. Explain to them that their lives are in danger if they stay. There is to be no pressure from you or the children to induce others to remain who wish to go.'

As the Palmachniks went down to brief the children the *Exodus* backed into mid-harbor and dropped anchor.

In an instant the entire Kyrenia area was alive with the shriek of sirens! Ari turned a pair of field glasses on the hills and coastal road and saw dozens of British lorries and jeeps converging on Kyrenia. He laughed out loud as he saw the trucks of the late 23rd Transportation Company rushing up the hills to be abandoned. They were rushing away from Kyrenia and passed the convoy of British soldiers coming in the opposite direction.

Ari looked below him. The children on deck were calm.

The British poured into the harbor area! Lorry after lorry of soldiers erupted onto the quay. Several officers were pointing at the *Exodus* and shouting orders. Soldiers began racing along both arms of the sea wall and setting up machine guns and mortars at the narrow harbor opening so that if the *Exodus* were to try it could not get out to sea.

More lorries poured into the area. The quay was roped off and curious spectators pushed back. Ari watched the British strength grow by the moment. Inside of an hour the harbor was swarming with five hundred fully armed soldiers. A pair of torpedo boats stationed themselves outside the harbor. On the horizon Ari could see a trio of destroyers rushing to the scene. The sirens shrieked on! The peaceful little town was turning into an armed camp! Then tanks rumbled onto the quay and artillery replaced the machine guns and mortars guarding the harbor entrance.

Another blaze of sirens brought a car bearing Brigadier Sutherland, Caldwell, and Alistair onto the quay. Major Cooke, the area commander of Kyrenia, reported to Sutherland.

'That's the ship out there, sir. It's loaded with Jews all right. It can't possibly get away.'

Sutherland studied the harbor. 'You've got enough here to fight a Panzer division,' he said; 'they must be insane on that boat. Get a public-address system hooked up right away.'

'Yes, sir.'

'If you asked me, we'd blow them out of the water,' Caldwell said.

'I didn't ask you,' Sutherland snapped. 'Cooke . . . get this area cordoned off. Organize a boarding party. Tear gas, small arms, in case they won't come back by themselves. Freddie, hop over to the Dome and inform headquarters I want a news blackout.'

Alistair had remained quiet and was studying the tugboat.

'What do you make of it, Alistair?'

'I don't like it, sir,' he said. 'They aren't pulling a daylight escape like this unless they have something else in mind.'

'Come now, Alistair. You're always looking for sinister plots.'

Mark Parker pushed his way past the guards and approached the two officers.

'What's all the noise about?' Mark asked Alistair.

The instant Alistair saw Mark he knew his suspicion was correct. 'Really, Parker,' Alistair said, 'do be a good sport and tell us. You know, old man, you ought to brush up on your British accent the next time you telephone me.'

'I don't know what you're talking about, Major.'

Brigadier Sutherland was beginning to catch on. He looked from the tug to Parker and to Alistair and he knew that the Mossad Aliyah Bet had caught him unprepared. He flushed. Major Cooke, the Kyrenia area commander, reported. 'We'll have boarding parties formed in ten minutes, sir. Two hundred men and we'll commandeer some trawlers here to take them out.' Sutherland did not even hear him.

'Where is the loud-speaker, damn it all!'

Ten minutes later Sutherland grabbed a microphone. A silence fell over the harbor. The boarding parties stood by to go out into the middle of the harbor after the *Exodus*.

'Hello, out there! This is Brigadier Bruce Sutherland, the commander of Cyprus, speaking,' his voice shot out in a series of echoes. 'Can you hear me out there?'

In the wheelhouse of the *Exodus*, Ari Ben Canaan opened his public-address system. 'Hello, Sutherland,' he said, 'this is Captain Caleb Moore of the 23rd Transportation Company, His Majesty's Jewish Forces on Cyprus. You can find your lorries up at St Hilarion.'

Sutherland turned pale. Alistair's mouth dropped open.

'Hello, out there!' Sutherland's voice snapped angrily. 'We are going to give you ten minutes to return to dockside. If you do not we are going to send out a heavily armed boarding party and bring you back.'

'Hello, Sutherland! This is the *Exodus* speaking. We have three hundred and two children aboard this boat. Our engine rooms are loaded with dynamite. If one of your troops sets foot on this boat or if one round is fired from any of your guns we are going to blow ourselves up!'

At that instant Mark Parker's story was being cabled from London to every corner of the world.

Sutherland, Alistair, and the five hundred British soldiers on the quay stood speechless as a flag was run up on the mast of the *Exodus*. It was a British Union Jack and in its center was painted a huge Nazi swastika.

The battle of the *Exodus* was on!

Chapter Thirty

EXCLUSIVE! DAVID VERSUS GOLIATH: MODEL 1946
BY AMERICAN NEWS SYNDICATE CORRESPONDENT
MARK PARKER
KYRENIA, CYPRUS: [ANS]

I am writing this story from Kyrenia. It is a tiny, jewel-like harbor on the northern coast of the British Crown Colony of Cyprus.

Cyprus has been rich in the pageantry of history. The island is filled with reminders of its vaunted past, from the ruins of Salamis to the cathedrals of Famagusta and Nicosia to the many castles of Crusader glory.

But none of this colorful history can match for sheer naked drama the scene that is being played at this very moment in this quiet, unknown resort town. For some months Cyprus has been a detention center for Jewish refugees who have tried to run the British blockade into Palestine.

Today, three hundred children between the ages of ten and seventeen escaped the British camp at Caraolos in an as-yet-undetermined manner, and fled across the island to Kyrenia where a converted salvage tug of about two hundred tons awaited them for a dash to Palestine.

Almost all the escapees were graduates of German concentration and extermination camps. The salvage tug, fittingly renamed the Exodus, *was discovered by British Intelligence before it could get out of the harbor.*

With its three hundred refugees the ship is sitting at anchor in the center of the harbor, which measures a mere three hundred yards in diameter, and has defied all British efforts to have the children debark and return to Caraolos.

A spokesman for the Exodus *has announced that the hold of the boat is filled with dynamite. The children have joined in a suicide pact and they will blow up the boat if the British attempt to board her.*

LONDON

General Sir Clarence Tevor-Browne dropped the copy of the newspaper on his desk. He lit a cigar and studied the reports. Mark Parker's story was creating a sensation not only in Europe but in the United States. Tevor-Browne had a request for instructions from Sutherland, who refused to take the responsibility of issuing an order to board the *Exodus*.

Tevor-Browne knew that part of the blame was his. He had chosen Bruce Sutherland for the job of commander himself, and he had failed to act on the letter from Alistair which had warned that something was going to happen unless Sutherland was replaced.

Humphrey Crawford entered Tevor-Browne's office. Crawford was a pasty-faced career man in the Middle East section of the Colonial Office, and served as liaison between the army and the policy makers at Whitehall and Chatham House. 'Afternoon, Sir Clarence,' Crawford said nervously. 'It is time for our meeting with Bradshaw.'

Tevor-Browne arose and gathered some papers together. 'Mustn't keep old Cecil Bradshaw waiting.'

Cecil Bradshaw's office was in the Institute of International Relations at Chatham House. For thirty years he had been one of the top men in formulating British Middle East policy.

At the end of World War I, Britain and France competed for influence in the Middle East. When the British got the Palestine mandate, Bradshaw had been one of those, with Winston Churchill, who had pushed for the creation of an Arab state out of half the mandate. The state they were instrumental in forming was Trans-Jordan. The entire purpose for bringing it into being was to turn it into a British military base. British subsidies made possible the establishment of Britain's Arab army, the 'Arab Legion,' and the choosing of a king for Trans-Jordan. He was the Hashimite Arab Abdullah, mortal enemy of Saud of Saudi Arabia.

At the end of World War II the Labour party swept into power with promises – among others – to help establish a Jewish homeland in Palestine and a refuge for the survivors in Europe. Cecil Bradshaw led that strong faction in Chatham House which convinced the new Foreign Minister that these promises were charming but not very practical and that Britain's interests lay with the Arabs. The Arab's ten million square miles were rich in oil and included a vital canal.

General Sir Clarence Tevor-Browne and Humphrey Crawford were ushered into Cecil Bradshaw's office. The latter, a fat man in his sixties, stood looking at the wall with his back to them, his pudgy hands clasped behind him. Humphrey Crawford sat down nervously on the edge of a seat. Tevor-Browne made himself comfortable in a deep leather chair and lit a cigar.

Bradshaw talked to the wall. 'Congratulations, gentlemen,' he said in a voice filled with sarcasm and quivering with anger. 'I see we made the news today.' He turned and patted his rotund stomach and smiled. 'You expected to find me in a lather. No indeed, no indeed. Whitehall called this morning. As expected, the Minister has dumped this *Exodus* business into my lap.' Bradshaw sat behind his desk, glanced at the reports, and snatched off his thick horn-rimmed glasses with a quick gesture. 'Tell me, Sir Clarence . . . was your Intelligence staff dead or merely out for tennis? And I believe you have a bit of explaining to do about Sutherland. He was your idea.'

Tevor-Browne refused to be bullied. 'I believe the establishment of camps on Cyprus was your idea. What is your explanation?'

'Gentlemen,' Crawford said quickly to avert a clash, 'we are faced with a peculiar situation in this *Exodus* affair. This is the first time any publicity has carried into the American press.'

Bradshaw laughed a wheezy laugh. His big apple cheeks reddened. 'With all of Truman's talk the Americans have only allowed ten thousand Jewish refugees into the country since the end of the war. Certainly Truman is for Zionism ... as long as Palestine isn't in Pennsylvania. Everyone talks idealistically but we are still the ones with a million Jews on our hands, a million Jews who could ruin our entire position in the Middle East.' Bradshaw replaced his glasses. '*Star of David, Moses, Palmach, Gates of Zion, Door of Hope*, and now *Exodus*. The Zionists are very clever people. For twenty-five years they have made us the villains in Palestine. They write words into the mandate articles and the Balfour Declaration that were never meant. They can argue a camel into thinking he is a mule. Good Lord ... two hours with Chaim Weizmann and I'm about ready to join the Zionists myself.' Cecil Bradshaw took off his glasses again. 'We know *your* sympathies, Tevor-Browne.'

'I resent the implications, Bradshaw. Perhaps I am one of a few hardheads who say the only way we are going to hold the Middle East is by building a powerful Jewish Palestine. I don't speak of Jewish interest but I speak of British interest.'

Bradshaw interrupted. 'Now let's get to this *Exodus* affair. The implications are absolutely clear. We gave in on the *Promised Land* but this time we will not give in. This boat is in our waters and not in French waters. We will not go on board, we will not send them to Germany, we will not sink them. They will sit in Kyrenia until they rot. Rot – do you hear that, Tevor-Browne? – rot.' His hand began to shake as he grew angrier.

Tevor-Browne closed his eyes. 'We cannot fight this out on moral grounds. We have no cause to keep three hundred children who were raised in concentration camps from entering Palestine. Oil ... canals ... Arabs be damned! We have no cause! We made ourselves look ridiculous by sending the *Promised Land* refugees to Germany.'

'I know your sympathies!'

'Gentlemen!'

Tevor-Browne stood up and leaned over Bradshaw's desk. 'There is only one way we can win this *Exodus* affair. The Jews have planned this whole incident to create propaganda. Turn the tables on them. Let the *Exodus* sail this minute. That is what they don't want.'

'Never!'

'Can't you see, sir, that we're playing right into their hands?'

'That ship will not sail as long as I am in Chatham House!'

Chapter Thirty-one

MARK PARKER
DOME HOTEL
KYRENIA, CYPRUS

STORY GAINING MOMENTUM. KEEP THEM COMING.
KEN BRADBURY, ANS LONDON

KYRENIA, CYPRUS [ANS],
BY MARK PARKER

It is a ridiculous sight. One thousand armed soldiers, tanks, artillery, and a naval task force all looking helplessly out at an unarmed salvage tug.

The battle of the Exodus ends week one in a draw. Both the British and the refugees are holding fast. To date no one has boarded the illegal runner which has threatened to blow itself up, but from the quay it is only a few hundred yards distant and a pair of field glasses bring the boat an arm's length away.

The morale of the three hundred children on the Exodus *seems to be phenomenal. They spent the week in the harbor alternately singing and catcalling to the British troops on the quay and sea wall.*

Mark's reports went out daily, each new one adding new and interesting details.

When Cecil Bradshaw made the decision to make a test case of the *Exodus* he knew there would be a barrage of adverse criticism. The French press staged its usual uproar, although this time the insults were so terrible that the likes of them had not been heard in the history of the Anglo-French alliance. The story spread throughout Europe, and even the British press became split and questioned Whitehall's wisdom in not letting the *Exodus* sail for Palestine.

Bradshaw was a wise politician and he had weathered many storms. This one was a storm in a teacup and it would blow over, he was sure. He sent a trio of friendly journalists to Kyrenia to counter Parker's reports, and a half dozen experts worked full time to explain the British position. The British had a case and it was being presented well, but it was difficult to offset natural sentiment for a group of refugee children.

If the Zionists are so sincere, why are they endangering the lives of three hundred innocent children? The whole thing is a sinister and cold-blooded plot to create sympathy and becloud the real issues of the Palestine mandate. It is obvious we are dealing with fanatics. Ari Ben Canaan is a professional Zionist agitator with a record of years of illegal operations.

Newspapermen from half a dozen countries landed at the Nicosia airport and demanded permission to enter the Kyrenia area. Several large magazines also sent in teams. The Dome Hotel began to look like a small political convention headquarters.

In cafés in Paris the British were denounced.

In pubs in London the British were defended.

In Stockholm there were sermons.

In Rome there were debates.

In New York bookies were laying four to one that the *Exodus* would not sail.

At the end of the second week Ari granted Mark permission to board the ship. Mark picked what he believed to be the ripe moment and arranged it by preset signals. Since he was the first outsider to board the *Exodus* his next three reports were carried by every newspaper on the front page.

EXCLUSIVE INTERVIEW WITH EXODUS SPOKESMAN ARI BEN CANAAN:
KYRENIA, CYPRUS [ANS].

Today I became the first correspondent to interview Ari Ben Canaan, the spokesman for the children on the Exodus. *I confronted Ben Canaan with the barrage of British reports maintaining that he was a professional Zionist troublemaker and with other Whitehall accusations. We spoke in the wheelhouse of the boat, the only place aboard not teeming with humanity. Today the children seem still to be in top spirits but are starting to show physical effects of their two-week siege.*

Ben Canaan, thirty, and a strapping six-footer with black hair and ice-blue eyes, could be mistaken for a movie leading man. He expressed his gratitude to well-wishers around the world and assured me the children were holding up fine. In reply to my questions he answered, 'I don't care about the personal attacks on me. I wonder if the British added that I was a captain in their army during World War II. I admit I am a Zionist troublemaker and I will continue to be one until they keep their promises about Palestine. Whether my work is legal or not is a matter of opinion.'

I pressed him about the British arguments and the importance of the Exodus. *'We Jews are blamed for many things and we are used to it. In anything concerning the Palestine mandate that cannot be explained logically and reasonably they drag out the old excuse that it is some sinister plot of Zionism. I am really amazed that they haven't blamed the Zionists for the trouble they are having in India. Fortunately for us, Gandhi is not Jewish.*

'Whitehall is using that tired whipping boy, the mysterious Zionists, to cover three decades of dirty work, lies to both Jews and Arabs, sellouts, double crosses, and betrayals in the mandate. The first promise they broke was the Balfour Declaration of 1917 which promised a Jewish homeland, and they have been breaking promises ever since. The latest double cross has come from the Labour party, which, before the elections, promised to open the doors of Palestine to survivors of Hitler's regime.

'I am astounded at Whitehall's crocodile tears over our victimizing of children. Every child on the Exodus *is a volunteer. Every child on the* Exodus *is an orphan because of Hitlerism. Nearly every child has lived in either German or British concentration camps for six years.*

'If Whitehall is so concerned about the welfare of these children then I challenge them to throw open the gates of Caraolos to inspection of the newsmen. It is nothing more or less than a concentration camp. People are kept behind barbed wire at machine-gun point with insufficient food, water, and medical care. No charges have been brought against these people. But they are being forcibly detained in Caraolos.

'Whitehall talks of our trying to bully them into an unjust solution of the mandate. There are a quarter of a million Jews in Europe who survived out of six million.

'The British quota of Jews allowed into Palestine is seven hundred a month. Is this their "just solution"?

'Finally, I argue the right of the British in Palestine. Have they more right to be there than the survivors of Hitler? Let me read you something.'

With that, Ben Canaan took a Bible from the desk of the wheelhouse, opened it to Ezekiel, and read:

'Thus saith the Lord God; When I shall have gathered the house of Israel from the People among whom they are scattered, and shall be sanctified in them in sight of the nations, then shall they dwell in their land that I have given to my servant Jacob wherein your fathers abode and they shall abide therein and even they and their children and their children's children forever.'

Ari Ben Canaan put the Bible down. 'The gentlemen at Whitehall had better study their claims further. I say the same thing to the Foreign Minister that a great man said to another oppressor three thousand years ago – LET MY PEOPLE GO.'

The day after his 'Let my people go' report Mark followed up with the inside story of Operation Gideon, including details of how British trucks had been used in the escape. British prestige hit a low-water mark.

On Mark's advice, Ari allowed other newsmen to board the *Exodus* and they clamored to be let into the Caraolos camp.

Cecil Bradshaw had expected criticism, but he had not reckoned on the furor that had been created. Meeting followed meeting, as for that moment in time the eyes of the world focused on Kyrenia harbor. To allow the *Exodus* to sail would be completely disastrous now.

General Sir Clarence Tevor-Browne flew secretly to Cyprus to take command and see whether something could be done.

His plane landed in the small hours of the morning under security measures at the Nicosia airdrome. Major Alistair met him and they quickly entered a staff car and it whisked off toward Famagusta headquarters.

'I wanted to speak to you, Alistair, before I took over from Sutherland. Of course I received your letter and you are free to speak.'

'Well, sir,' Alistair said, 'I would say that the strain has got Sutherland down. Something has happened to the man. Caldwell tells me he has one nightmare after another. He walks all night long, till dawn, and he spends most of his days reading the Bible.'

'Damned shame,' Tevor-Browne said. 'Bruce has been a corking good soldier. I trust what is said will never leave this car. We must protect the man.'

'Of course, sir,' Alistair said.

KYRENIA, CYPRUS (AP)
EXCLUSIVE

General Sir Clarence Tevor-Browne of desert fame landed anonymously at Nicosia airdrome last night. Sir Clarence was dressed in civilian clothes and his arrival was marked by secrecy. Tevor-Browne's appearance on the scene confirms Whitehall's concern over the Exodus. *It could indicate a a change in policy if not a change in command.*

Mark boarded the *Exodus* and asked that Karen be sent to the wheelhouse. He was worried as he pushed his way over the crowded deck. The children were looking gaunt and they smelled bad from the lack of water to wash with.

Ari was in the wheelhouse as placid as ever. Mark gave him cigarettes and a few bottles of brandy. 'How's it going out there?' Ari asked.

'Doesn't look like any change in policy with Tevor-Browne in. The story is still tops all over. Bigger than I expected. Look, Ari, this thing has worked perfectly for you and me both. You've done what you started out to do, given the British a black eye. The word I got is that the British are not going to back down.'

'What's the point?'

'The point is you can top this whole thing off by making a humanity move and taking the ship to dock. We'll make a big story when the British march them back to Caraolos. It will tear the people's hearts out.'

'Did Kitty send you in with this?'

'Aw, cut it out, will you. Just look down there at those kids. They're starting to come apart.'

'They knew what they were in for.'

'There's another thing, Ari. I'm afraid we've hit the mark with this story. We're on top now, but tomorrow Frank Sinatra may unload a left hook on some columnist in a night club and we're off page one.'

Karen entered the wheelhouse. 'Hello, Mr Parker,' she said softly.

'Hello, honey. Here's a letter from Kitty and a package.'

She took the letter and gave Mark one for Kitty. She refused the package as she had refused all the other packages.

'Christ, I haven't got the heart to tell Kitty she won't take the packages for herself. That girl is sick. Did you see the circles under her eyes? You're going to have real trouble on this ship in another few days.'

'We were speaking of maintaining public interest. Get one thing straight, Parker. We don't go back to Caraolos. There are a quarter of a million Jews in Europe waiting for an answer and we are the only ones who can answer them. Starting tomorrow we will declare a hunger strike. Anyone who passes out will be placed on deck for the British to look at.'

'You ghoul ... you stinking ghoul,' Mark snarled.

'Call me what you want, Parker. Do you think I like starving a bunch of orphans? Give me something else to fight with. Give me something to shoot at those tanks and those destroyers! All we've got is our guts and what we believe in. We've had the hell knocked out of us for two thousand years. This is one fight we're going to win.'

Chapter Thirty-two

HUNGER STRIKE
CALLED ON EXODUS!
Children vow starvation rather than return to Caraolos.

After allowing the story to build up over a two-week period, Ari Ben Canaan fooled everyone by launching an offensive. It was no game of 'wait and see' now; the children were forcing a decision.

A huge sign was tied to the sides of the *Exodus* with lettering in English, French, and Hebrew. The sign read:

Hunger Strike/Hour No 1

Hunger Strike/Hour No 15

Two boys and a girl, aged ten, twelve, and fifteen, were brought on the forward deck of the *Exodus* and laid out, unconscious.

Hunger Strike/Hour No 20

Ten children were stretched out on the forward deck.

'For Christ's sake, Kitty, stop pacing and sit down!'

'It's over twenty hours now. How much longer is he going to let this go on? I just haven't had the courage to go to the quay and look. Is Karen one of those children unconscious on deck?'

'I told you ten times she wasn't.'

'They aren't strong children to begin with and they've been cooped up on that ship for two weeks. They have no stamina left.' Kitty pulled nervously at a cigarette and tugged at her hair. 'That man is a beast. An inhuman beast.'

'I've been thinking about that,' Mark said. 'I've been thinking about it a lot. I wonder if we really understand what is driving those people so hard. Have you ever seen Palestine? It's worthless desert in the south end and eroded in the middle and swamp up north. It's stinking, it's sunbaked, and it's in the middle of a sea of fifty million sworn enemies. Yet they break their necks to get there. They call it the Land of Milk and Honey ... they sing about water sprinklers and irrigation ditches. Two weeks ago I told Ari Ben Canaan that the Jews don't have a patent on suffering but I'm beginning to wonder. I swear I wonder. I wonder how something can hurt so badly that can drive them so hard.'

'Don't defend them, Mark, and don't defend those people.'

'Try to remember one thing. Ben Canaan couldn't do this without the support of those kids. They're behind him one hundred per cent.'

'That's what hurts,' Kitty said, 'this loyalty. This fantastic loyalty they have for each other.'

The phone rang. Mark answered, listened, and hung up.

'What is it? I said what is it, Mark!'

'They've brought some more kids up on the deck unconscious. A half dozen of them.'

'Is ... is ... Karen ... ?'

'I don't know. I'm going to find out.'

'Mark.'

'What?'

'I want to go on the *Exodus*.'

'That's impossible.'

'I can't take it any more,' she said.

'If you do this you're finished.'

'No, Mark ... it's different. If I knew she were alive and well I could bear it. I swear I could. I made myself know that. But I can't just sit idly and know she's dying. I can't do that.'

'Even if I can get Ben Canaan to let you on the *Exodus* the British won't let you.'

'You must,' she said fiercely, 'you must.'

She stood with her back to the door and blocked his exit. Her face determined. Mark lowered his eyes. 'I'll do what I can,' he said.

Hunger Strike/Hour No 35

Angry crowds in Paris and Rome demonstrated before the British embassies. Fierce oratory and placards demanded the release of the *Exodus*. Police clubs and tear gas were used in Paris to disperse the mob. In Copenhagen and in Stockholm and in Brussels and in the Hague there were other demonstrations. These were more orderly.

Hunger Strike/Hour No 38

A spontaneous general strike swept over the island of Cyprus in protest against the British. Transportation stopped, businesses shut down, and ports closed, theaters and restaurants locked their doors. Famagusta, Nicosia, Larnaca, and Limassol looked like morgues.

Hunger Strike/Hour No 40

Ari Ben Canaan stared at his lieutenants. He looked into the somber faces of Joab, David, Zev, and Hank Schlosberg.

Zev, the Galilee farmer, spoke up first. 'I am a soldier. I cannot stand by and watch children starve to death.'

'In Palestine,' Ari snapped, 'youngsters this same age are already fighters in Gadna.'

'It is one thing to fight and it is another to starve to death.'

'This is only another way of fighting,' Ari said.

Joab Yarkoni had worked with Ari for many years and had served with him in World War II. 'I have never gone against you, Ari. The minute one of these children dies this whole thing is liable to boomerang on us.'

Ari looked over to Hank Schlosberg, the American captain. Hank shrugged. 'You're the boss, Ari, but the crew is getting jittery. They didn't bargain for this.'

'In other words,' Ari said, 'you want to surrender.'

Their silence confirmed it.

'David, what about you? I haven't heard from you.'

David, a scholar, was steeped in the Torah and in the holy books. He had a closeness to God that none of the rest of them had and they respected it.

'Six million Jews died in gas chambers not knowing why they died,' he said. 'If three hundred of us on the *Exodus* die we will certainly know why. The world will know too. When we were a nation two thousand years ago and when we rebelled against Roman and Greek rule we Jews established the tradition of fighting to the last man. We did this at Arbela and Jerusalem. We did this at Beitar and Herodium and Machaerus. At Masada we held out against the Romans for four years and when they entered the fort they found us all dead. No people, anywhere, have fought for their freedom as have our people. We drove the Romans and the Greeks from our land until we were dispersed to the four corners of the world. We have not had much opportunity to fight as a nation for two thousand years. When we had that opportunity at the Warsaw ghetto we did honor to our tradition. I say if we leave this boat and willingly return to barbed-wire prisons then we will have broken faith with God.'

'Are there any further questions?' Ari said.

Hunger Strike/Hour No 42

In the United States, South Africa, and England mass prayer meetings were being held in synagogues, and in many churches there were prayers for the safety of the children on the *Exodus*.

Hunger Strike/Hour No 45

The Jews in Argentina began to fast in sympathy with the children aboard the *Exodus*.

Hunger Strike/Hour No 47

It was getting dark as Kitty boarded the *Exodus*. The stench was overpowering. All over the deck, in the lifeboats, on the superstructure she saw the crush of humanity. Everyone was lying down and absolutely motionless to conserve energy.

'I want to see those children who have passed out,' she said.

David led her to the bow of the ship where there were three rows of unconscious children, sixty in number. David knelt and held his lantern close to the bodies as Kitty moved from one to the other, feeling their pulses and looking into the pupils of their eyes. Half a dozen times she thought she would faint as her heart pounded and she rolled over a child who looked like Karen.

David led her around the packed deck, stepping over the prostrate bodies. The children stared listlessly at her with dazed eyes. Their hair was matted and dirt caked their faces.

David led her down the steep ladder onto the hold. She nearly vomited as the stink enveloped her. In the half light she saw the ghastly sight of the children packed in shelves one atop the other.

On the deck of the hold they lay piled against each other. She found Karen in a corner, enmeshed in a tangle of arms and legs. Dov was asleep next to her. They lay on a pile of rags and the deck was slimy beneath them.

'Karen,' she whispered. 'Karen, it's me, Kitty.'

Karen's eyes fluttered open. There were huge black circles beneath them and her lips were caked dry. She was too weak to sit up.

'Kitty?'

'Yes, it's me.'

Karen held her arms open and Kitty held her tightly for many moments. 'Don't leave, Kitty. I'm so frightened.'

'I'll be near,' Kitty whispered, releasing the girl.

She went to the hospital and examined the limited supply of drugs and sighed despondently. 'There is very little that can be done,' she said to David. 'I'll try to make them as comfortable as possible. Can you and Joab work with me?'

'Of course.'

'Some of those unconscious are in serious condition. We'll have to try to sponge them to get their fevers down. It is chilly up on deck. We'll keep them covered. Then I want everyone who is capable of working to get this ship clean.'

Kitty laboured feverishly for hours to ward off death. It was like trying to fill an ocean with a thimble. As soon as one child was brought under control three more became seriously ill. She hadn't the drugs, water, or other facilities to do very much. Food, the one weapon, could not be used.

Hunger Strike/Hour No 81

Seventy children in coma lay on the deck of the *Exodus*.

On the quay of Kyrenia harbor there were angry grumbles of insubordination from the British ranks. Many of the soldiers could stand it no longer and asked to be removed, even at the risk of court-martial. The eyes of Cyprus fastened on Kyrenia.

Hunger Strike/Hour No 82

Karen Hansen Clement was carried to the bow of the ship, unconscious.

Hunger Strike/Hour No 83

Kitty walked into the wheelhouse and slumped exhausted into a chair. She had worked for thirty-five straight hours and her mind was muddled and dazed. Ari poured her a stiff brandy.

'Go on and drink,' he said. 'You aren't on strike.'

She swallowed it down, and a second drink brought her to her senses. She stared at Ari Ben Canaan long and hard. He was a powerful man. He showed almost no effects of the siege. She looked into his cold eyes and wondered what thoughts, what plots, what tricks were running through his brain. She wondered if he was frightened or even knew fear. She wondered if he was sad or shaken.

'I was expecting you to come up here to see me much sooner,' he said.

'I won't beg you, Ari Ben Canaan. Ben Canaan and God . . . in that order . . . isn't that right? Well, there are a dozen children on the verge of death. I am merely reporting to you like a good Palmachnik. They're going to die, Mr Ben Canaan. How do you rule?'

'I've been insulted before, Kitty. It doesn't bother me. Is this humanity of yours so great that it cries out for all these children or does it appeal for the life of one child?'

'You have no right to ask that.'

'You are begging for the life of one girl. I am begging for the lives of a quarter of a million people.'

She rose. 'I had better get back to work. Ari, you knew why I wanted to come on board the *Exodus*. Why did you let me?'

He turned his back to her and looked from the window out to sea where the cruiser and destroyers stood watch. 'Maybe I wanted to see you.'

Hunger Strike/Hour No 85

General Sir Clarence Tevor-Browne paced up and down Sutherland's office. The smoke from his cigar clouded the room. He stopped several times and looked out the window in the direction of Kyrenia.

Sutherland tapped out his pipe and studied the array of sandwiches on the tray on the coffee table. 'Won't you sit down, Sir Clarence, and have a bite to eat and a spot of tea?'

Tevor-Browne looked at his wrist watch and sighed. He seated himself and picked up a sandwich, stared at it, nibbled, then threw it down. 'I feel guilty when I eat,' he said.

'This is a bad business to be in for a man with a conscience,' Sutherland said. 'Two wars, eleven foreign posts, six decorations, and three orders. Now I've been stopped in my tracks by a band of unarmed children. A fine way to end thirty years of service, eh, Sir Clarence?'

Tevor-Browne lowered his eyes.

'Oh, I know you've been wanting to talk to me,' said Sutherland.

Tevor-Browne poured some tea and sighed, half embarrassed. 'See here, Bruce. If it were up to me . . .'

'Nonsense, Sir Clarence. Don't feel badly. It is I who feel badly. I let you down.' Sutherland rose and his eyes brimmed. 'I am tired. I am very tired.'

'We will arrange a full pension and have the retirement as quiet as possible. You can count on me,' Tevor-Browne said. 'See here, Bruce. I stopped over in

Paris on my way here and I had a long talk with Neddie. I told her about your predicament. Listen, old boy, with some encouragement from you, you two could get together again. Neddie wants you back and you're going to need her.'

Sutherland shook his head. 'Neddie and I have been through for years. All we ever had between us that was meaningful was the Army. That's what held us together.'

'Any plans?'

'These months on Cyprus have done something to me, Sir Clarence, especially these past few weeks. You may not believe this, but I don't feel that I've suffered a defeat. I feel that I may have won something very great. Something I lost a long time ago.'

'And what is that?'

'Truth. Do you remember when I took this post? You told me that the only kingdom that runs on right and wrong is the kingdom of heaven and the kingdoms of the earth run on oil.'

'I remember it well,' Tevor-Browne said.

'Yes,' Sutherland said, 'I have thought so much about it since this *Exodus* affair. All my life I have known the truth and I have known right from wrong. Most of us do. To know the truth is one thing. To live it ... to create the kingdom of heaven on earth is another. How many times in a man's life does he do things that are repulsive to his morality in order to exist? How I have admired those few men in this world who could stand up for their convictions in the face of shame, torture, and even death. What a wonderful feeling of inner peace they must have. Something that we ordinary mortals can never know. Gandhi is such a man.

'I am going to that rotten sliver of land that these Jews call their kingdom of heaven on earth. I want to know it all ... Galilee, Jerusalem ... all of it.'

'I envy you, Bruce.'

'Perhaps I'll settle down near Safed ... on Mount Canaan.'

Major Alistair entered the office. He was pale and his hand shook as he gave Tevor-Browne a note to read. Tevor-Browne read it and reread it and could not believe his eyes. 'Great God, save us all,' he whispered. He passed the note to Bruce Sutherland.

URGENT

> *Ari Ben Canaan, spokesman for the* Exodus, *announced that beginning at noon tomorrow ten volunteers a day will commit suicide on the bridge of the ship in full view of the British garrison. This protest practice will continue until either the* Exodus *is permitted to sail for Palestine or everyone aboard is dead.*

Bradshaw, with Humphrey Crawford and half a dozen aides, sped out of London to the quiet of a peaceful, isolated little house in the country. He had fourteen hours to act before the suicides on the *Exodus* began.

He had badly miscalculated the entire thing. First, the tenacity and determination of the children on the ship. Second, the powerful propaganda the incident created. Finally, he had not imagined that Ben Canaan would take the offensive and press the issue as he had. Bradshaw was a stubborn man but he knew when he was defeated, and he now turned his efforts to making a face-saving settlement.

Bradshaw had Crawford and his aides cable or phone a dozen of the top

Jewish leaders in England, Palestine, and the United States to ask them to intervene. The Palestinians, in particular, might possibly dissuade Ben Canaan. At the very least they could stall the action long enough to enable Bradshaw to come up with some alternate plans. If he could get Ben Canaan to agree to negotiate then he could talk the *Exodus* to death. Within six hours, Bradshaw had his answers from the Jewish leaders. They answered uniformly: WE WILL NOT INTERCEDE.

Next Bradshaw contacted Tevor-Browne on Cyprus. He instructed the general to inform the *Exodus* that the British were working out a compromise and to delay the deadline for twenty-four hours.

Tevor-Browne carried out these instructions and relayed Ben Canaan's answer back to England.

URGENT

> *Ben Canaan informed us there is nothing to discuss. He says either the* Exodus *sails or it doesn't sail. He further states that complete amnesty to the Palestinians aboard is part of the conditions. Ben Canaan summarized: Let my people go.*
>
> TEVOR-BROWNE

Cecil Bradshaw could not sleep. He paced back and forth, back and forth. It was just a little over six hours before the children on the *Exodus* would begin committing suicide. He had only three hours left in which to make a decision to hand to the Cabinet. No compromise could be reached.

Was he fighting a madman? Or was this Ari Canaan a shrewd and heartless schemer who had deftly led him deeper and deeper into a trap?

LET MY PEOPLE GO!

Bradshaw walked to his desk and flicked on the lamp.

URGENT

> *Ari Ben Canaan, spokesman for the* Exodus, *announced that beginning at noon tomorrow ten volunteers a day will commit suicide ...*

Suicide ... suicide ... suicide ...

Bradshaw's hand shook so violently he dropped the paper.

Also on his desk were a dozen communiqués from various European and American governments. In that polite language that diplomats use they all expressed concern over the *Exodus* impasse. He also had notes from each of the Arab governments expressing the view that if the *Exodus* were permitted to sail for Palestine it would be considered an affront to every Arab.

Cecil Bradshaw was confused now. The past few days had been a living hell. How had it all begun? Thirty years of formulating Middle Eastern policy and now he was in his worst trouble over an unarmed salvage tug.

What queer trick of fate had given him the mantle of an oppressor? Nobody could possibly accuse him of being anti-Jewish. Secretly Bradshaw admired the Jews in Palestine and understood the meaning of their return. He enjoyed the hours he had spent arguing with Zionists around conference tables, bucking their brilliant debaters. Cecil Bradshaw believed from the bottom of his heart that England's interest lay with the Arabs. Yet the Mandate had grown to over half a million Jews. And the Arabs were adamant that the British were fostering a Jewish nation in their midst.

During all the years of work he had been realistic with himself. What was happening? He could see his own grandchildren lying on the deck of the *Exodus*. Bradshaw knew his Bible as well as any well-brought-up Englishman and like most Englishman had a tremendous sense of honor although he was not deeply religious. Could it be that the *Exodus* was driven by mystic forces? No, he was a practical diplomat and he did not believe in the supernatural.

Yet – he had an army and a navy and the power to squash the *Exodus* and all the other illegal runners – but he could not bring himself to do it.

The Pharaoh of Egypt had had might on his side too! Sweat ran down Bradsaw's face. It was all nonsense! He was tired and the pressure had been too great. What foolishness!

LET MY PEOPLE GO!

Bradshaw walked to the library and found a Bible and in near panic began to read through the pages of *Exodus* and about the Ten Plagues that God sent down on the land of Egypt.

Was he Pharaoh? Would a curse rain down on Britain? He went back to his room and tried to rest, but a staccato rhythm kept running through his tired brain ... let my people go ... let my people go ...

'Crawford!' he yelled. 'Crawford!'

Crawford ran in, tying his robe. 'You called?'

'Crawford. Get through to Tevor-Browne on Cyprus at once. Tell him ... tell him to let the *Exodus* sail for Palestine.'

BOOK TWO

The Land is Mine

. . . for the land is mine: for ye are strangers and sojourners with me. And in all the land of your possession ye shall grant a redemption for the land.

THE WORD OF GOD AS GIVEN TO MOSES IN LEVITICUS

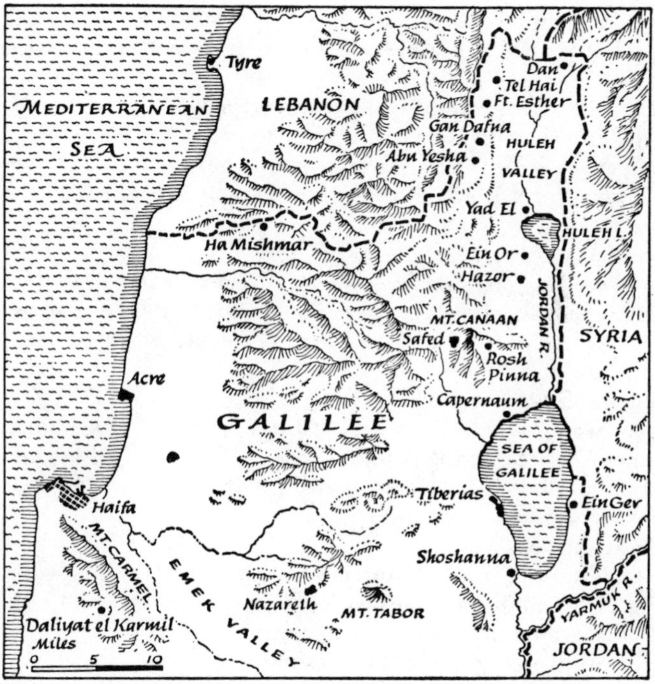

Chapter One

The battle of the *Exodus* was over!

Within seconds, the words '*Exodus* to sail' were on the wires. Within minutes they blazed in headlines around the world.

On Cyprus the joy of the people was boundless and around the world there was one long sigh of relief.

On the *Exodus* the children were too exhausted to celebrate.

The British urged Ari Ben Canaan to bring the salvage tug to dockside so that the children could be given medical care and the ship restocked and inspected. Ben Canaan agreed, and as the *Exodus* pulled in, Kyrenia turned into a mad scramble of activity. A score of British army doctors swarmed onto the ship and quickly removed the more severe cases. A hastily improvised hospital was established at the Dome Hotal. Rations and clothing and supplies poured onto the dock. In addition, hundreds of gifts from the people of Cyprus deluged the ship. Royal engineers combed the ancient tug from stem to stern to patch leaks, overhaul the motor, and refit her. Sanitation teams made her spotless.

After an initial survey Ari was advised it would take several days to get the children strong enough and the ship fit enough to make the day and a half run to Palestine. The small Jewish community on Cyprus sent a delegation to Ari to appeal to him to allow the children to celebrate the first night of Chanukah, the Festival of Lights, on Cyprus before sailing; the holiday was to begin in a few days. Ari agreed.

Only after Kitty had been assured and reassured that Karen's condition was not serious did she allow herself the luxury of a steaming hot tub, a thick steak, a half pint of Scotch, and a magnificent, deep, seventeen-hour sleep.

Kitty awoke to a problem she could no longer avoid. She had to decide either to end the episode with Karen forever or to follow the girl to Palestine.

Late in the evening when Mark came into her room for tea she appeared none the worse for her ordeal. In fact, the long sleep had made her look quite attractive.

'Newsroom still hectic?'

'Matter of fact, no,' Mark answered. 'The captains and the kings are departing. The *Exodus* is day-old news now . . . the kind they wrap fish in. Oh, I suppose we can drum up a final page-one picture when the boat lands in Haifa.'

'People are fickle.'

'No, not really, Kitty. The world just has a habit of moving on.'

She sipped her tea and sank into silence. Mark lit a cigarette and propped his feet on the window sill. He pretended his fingers were a pistol and pointed over his shoe tops out at the pier.

'What about you, Mark?'

'Me? Old Mark Parker has worn out his welcome in the king's domains. I'm going Stateside and then maybe take a crack at the Asian beat. I've had an itch to go there anyhow . . . I hear it runs crosswise.'

'The British won't let you into Palestine?'

'Not a chance. I am held in very low esteem. In fact if they weren't proper Englishmen I'd say they hate my guts. Frankly, I don't blame them.'

'Give me a cigarette.'

Mark lit one and handed it to her. He bided his time, continuing to take target practice with his imaginary pistol.

'Damn you, Mark! I hate that smug way you have of reading my mind.'

'You've been a busy little girl. You went to the British authorities to ask permission to enter Palestine. Being the gentlemen they are, they opened the door for you and bowed. You were just a clean-cut American girl doing her duty. Of course, CID doesn't know about your little rumrunning act for Aliyah Bet. Well . . . are you going or not?'

'God, I don't know.'

'You mean you haven't talked yourself into it yet.'

'I mean I don't know.'

'So which side do you want me to take?'

'You could stop acting like a worldly Buddha looking down on the poor tormented mortals. And you could stop sniping at me, Mark.'

Mark dropped his feet from the window sill. 'Go on ... go to Palestine. That's what you want to hear, isn't it?'

'I still don't feel right around Jewish people ... I can't help it.'

'You feel fine around that girl though, don't you? Doesn't she still remind you of your daughter?'

'Not really, not any more. She is too much of herself to be anyone else. But I love her and want her, if that's what you mean.'

'I've got a loaded question for you, Mrs Fremont...'

'Go on.'

'Are you in love with Ari Ben Canaan?'

Love Ari Ban Canaan? She knew that he affected her whenever he was near or spoke or looked at her or even when she thought of him. She knew she had never met another man exactly like him. She knew she had a certain fear of his dark quietness and his tremendous power. She knew she admired his daring and courage. She knew there were moments she loathed him as she had never loathed another human being. But love...?

'I don't know,' she murmured. 'As much as I cannot walk into it ... I can't seem to be able to walk away from it and I don't know why ... I don't know why.'

Later, Kitty spent over an hour with Karen in the hospital ward that had been set up on the second floor of the hotel. Karen had made a remarkable recovery. In fact, the doctors were amazed with the near magic effect of two words 'Eretz Israel' had on all the children. It was more potent than any medicine. As Kitty sat with Karen she looked out over the faces of the children in the ward. Who were they? Where did they come from? Where were they going? What strange, strange people ... what a strange, strange obsession they carried.

There were long periods of silence between Kitty and Karen in which neither of them dared broach the subject of her coming to Palestine. At last Karen fell asleep. Kitty stared down at the girl. How lovely she was ... how very lovely. She kissed Karen's forehead and stroked her hair and Karen smiled in her sleep.

She walked out to the corridor where Dov Landau was pacing back and forth. They both halted, stared at each other, and Kitty passed on wordlessly.

The sun was setting as Kitty walked out to the quay. Across the street Zev Gilboa and Joab Yarkoni were supervising the loading of materials aboard the salvage tug. She looked about quickly to catch a glimpse of Ari. He was not in sight.

'*Shalom*, Kitty!' they called to her.

'Hi!' she called back.

She walked on down the quay toward the lighthouse. It was getting chilly. She put on her sweater. 'I must know ... I must know ... I must ... I must' she repeated over and over to herself. Out on the edge of the sea wall sat young David Ben Ami. He seemed lost in thought, looking out over the water and flipping pebbles.

She came up alongside him and he looked up and smiled.

'*Shalom*, Kitty. You look rested.'

She sat beside him. For several moments they admired the sea.

'Thinking of home?' she asked.

'Yes.'

'Jordana ... that's her name, isn't it ... Ari's sister?'

David nodded.

'Will you see her?'

'If I am lucky we will have a little time.'

'David.'

'Yes.'

'What is going to become of the children?'

'We will take good care of them. They are our future.'

'Is there danger?'

'Yes, there is great danger.'

Kitty was quiet again for many moments...

'Are you sailing with us?' David asked.

She felt her heart skip a beat. 'Why do you ask?'

'It is beginning to seem natural to have you around. Besides, Ari mentioned something or other about it.'

'If... if Ari is interested then why doesn't he ask?'

David laughed. 'Ari doesn't ask for anything.'

'David,' she said abruptly, 'you must help me. I am terribly puzzled. You seem to be the only one who understands a little...'

'I will help you if I can.'

'... I haven't been around many Jews in my life. You people bewilder me.'

'We bewilder ourselves even more,' David said.

'Can I say something honestly? I feel so much like an outsider...'

'That is not at all strange, Kitty. Most people do. Even those few we call "friends," even though they have a loyalty bordering on fanaticism. Some, I believe, feel guilty for all the crimes committed against us. Others want to be Jews ... although Lord only knows why. We are a confusing lot.'

'But a man like Ari Ben Canaan. Who is he? Who is he really? Is he a real person?'

'Ari is quite real. He is the product of a historic abortion.'

They began walking toward the hotel, for it was suppertime. 'It is difficult to know where to begin,' David said. 'I suppose to really tell the story of Ari Ben Canaan we must start with Simon Rabinsky in the Jewish Pale. The Pale was an area in southwest Russia that included the Ukraine. I suppose we'd have to start before the turn of the century. I think the year of the great happening was 1884.'

Chapter Two

ZHITOMIR, RUSSIA, 1884

Simon Rabinsky was a bootmaker. His wife's name was Rachel. She was a good and a devout woman. Simon had two sons who were his greatest treasures.

Yakov, the younger, was fourteen years of age. He was a fiery lad with a whiplash tongue and a quick mind. He would argue at the slightest provocation.

Jossi, the older of the brothers, was sixteen. Jossi's appearance was distinctive. He was a powerful giant who stood over six feet tall and had a head of flaming red hair like his mother, Rachel. Jossi was as mild as Yakov was wild. Jossi was quiet and meditative and gentle; in fact, Yakov's fertile brain in Jossi's powerful body could well have created a superman.

The Rabinsky family was extremely poor. They lived in that part of western Russia which included Bessarabia, the Ukraine, the Crimea, and parts of White Russia and which was known as the Jewish Pale of Settlement. The boundaries of the Pale were established in 1804 as the only place in Russia where Jews could reside. It was, in fact, one enormous ghetto, with Moscow and Petrograd off limits except to those few wealthy Jews who could bribe their way into sending a son or a daughter beyond the boundaries.

Establishment of the Jewish Pale was merely one event in a long history of discrimination. Jews first settled in Russia in the Crimea area as far back as the first century. The Khazars who ruled in that area were so taken with Judaism that they adopted it as their own religion. The Khazars' kingdom was, in fact, a Jewish state. By the tenth century the Russians in the north had ascended to power and they swept down on the Khazars, dispersed them to oblivion, and began a sordid record against the Jews.

As Russia came to power, the flaming sword of Islam came up from the south. During those periods when the Moslems held parts of Russia the Jews knew their greatest times of peace and prosperity, for Jews had been a potent factor behind the rise of Islam.

With the final defeat of the Moslems, full power over all Russia went to the Czars and to the Greek Church. Jewish 'heretics' were burned at the stake by the hundreds during the Middle Ages. The ignorant peasantry were well instructed in the fable that these Jews were magicians and witches and used Christian blood in their rituals.

Centuries of unrelieved abuse reached a climax during the reign of Catherine I. A series of pogroms – anti-Jewish riots – was unloosed against those who would not accept the Greek Orthodox religion. But attempts to convert the Jews failed utterly, so Catherine I expelled a million Jews from Russia. Most of them went to Poland.

After this came the era of war and conquest in which Poland was conquered and reconquered, partitioned and repartitioned. Catherine II inherited a million of the Jews who had previously been expelled by Catherine I.

These events led directly to the establishment of the Jewish Pale. In 1827 Jews were driven ruthlessly from the smaller villages into the already overcrowded Jewish quarters in the larger cities. In the same year the Czar instituted a quota of Jewish youths to be turned over each year to the army for twenty-five years of military service.

Simon Rabinsky, the bootmaker of Zhitomir, his good wife Rachel, and his sons Yakov and Jossi were prisoners of the Pale and of a unique way of life. There was no social and very little commercial contact between these Jewish communities and the rest of the Russian people. The only regular visitor from the outside was the tax collector who might make off with anything from sacred candlesticks to beds and pillows and shoes. Frequent but less regular callers from the outside were the wild mobs of Cossacks and peasants and students who screamed for Jewish blood.

Divorced from the greater society, the Jews had little or no loyalty for 'Mother Russia.' Their spoken and written language was not Russian but Yiddish, which was a bastard German. Their language of prayer was ancient Hebrew. The Jews even dressed differently. They wore black hats and long gabardine coats. Although it was forbidden by law, many of them wore side curls, and it was a great sport among the Russians to catch a Jew and cut off his curls.

Simon Rabinsky lived the way his father and his father's father had been forced to live inside ghetto walls. Because they were so poor there was endless haggling over a few kopeks. Yet, despite the desperateness of their daily existence, Simon and all other Jews adhered to rigid codes of business ethics inside the ghetto. No man was allowed to infringe on the livelihood of his neighbor or to cheat or to rob.

Community life pivoted around the Holy Laws, the synagogue, and the rabbi, who was at once teacher, spiritual leader, judge, and administrator of the community. The rabbis of the Pale were all great scholars. Their wisdom was far-reaching and their authority rarely questioned.

Within the ghetto the Jews organized their own government under the overall leadership of the rabbis. There were a hundred different lay offices and wardenships. There was a score of Biblical and Talmudic societies. There was an organization for the care of orphans and a society to pay the dowries of the poorer girls. There were societies to care for the sick, the aged, and the lame. There were administrators of marriage contracts and an elected synagogue summoner, as well as a dozen other synagogue posts. There was an ecclesiastical court, there were psalm readers, and administrators over the ritual baths. Indeed, the community moved as one for the existence of all.

The poor donated to the poorer. The poorer – to the poorer yet. Charity was the eleventh, the unwritten commandment. Leading scholars and religious leaders had to be cared for. Nothing was allowed to interfere with the pursuit of wisdom.

Many people said that Simon Rabinsky, the bootmaker, was second in wisdom only to the rabbi himself. In the Pale where nearly everyone was destitute the measure of man's wealth was his knowledge. Simon served as a deacon of his synagogue. Each year he was elected to one or two other high offices in the community. It was Simon's dream to fill his sons with the wonders of the conquest of the mind.

Jews called their Talmud a 'sea.' They claimed it was so vast that one could read it and study it for a lifetime without ever looking at another book and never swim from one side of the 'sea' to the other. The Rabinsky brothers studied this great collection of laws and customs, which contained information on everything from social behavior to personal cleanliness.

In addition to studying the Talmud the Rabinsky brothers spent hours learning the Pentateuch, the first five books of Moses which make up the Torah and were considered the holiest of all works.

They learned the Bible. They learned the oral laws of the Mishnah. They learned the folk legends, wise sayings, and commentary on the Bible of the Midrash. The learned the Cabala, the book of mystics, and they learned the prayers and songs and customs and holidays.

Jossi and Yakov studied the great post-Talmudic scholars – Moses Maimonides and Rashi.

Although the Rabinsky family lived a grim existence it was not entirely a life without hope or joy. There was always talk and debate, a tempting scandal to discuss or a wedding or a death or a confirmation or a birth to celebrate. There were the holidays to look forward to. The matchmakers were constantly busy and there was the Sabbath.

On one night each week, Simon Rabinsky and every other ghetto Jew became a king. The traditional horn would sound in the ghetto, and Simon would lay down his tools and prepare for his day with God. How he loved the sound of the horn! It was the same sound that had called his people to prayer and to battle for four thousand years. Simon would go to the ritual bath while his good wife Rachel lit the Sabbath candles and recited a benediction.

He would dress in his Sabbath finery, a long black silk coat and a beautiful fur-rimmed hat. He would walk proudly to synagogue with Jossi on one arm and Yakov on the other.

At home there was traditionally a family poorer than his in to share the Sabbath meal. Over the candles and the blessed bread and wine he spoke a blessing and a few words of gratitude to God.

Rachel served stuffed fish and noodles and chicken broth, and in the evening they would stroll through the ghetto calling upon the sick or receiving visitors in their shop, as they had no parlor.

On Saturday, Simon Rabinsky prayed and meditated and spoke with his sons and reviewed their lessons and learnings and discussed religion and philosophy.

As the sun set ending the Sabbath, Simon sang the song of the ghetto with Rachel, Yakov, and Jossi: 'Rejoice to Israel . . . banish despair.'

With the day over he returned to the realities of his bitter life. In the dingy cellar he called home and shop, Simon Rabinsky would crouch over his workbench in the candlelight, with his wrinkled hands drive a knife deftly through leather. Simon then said the same lament that had been said by Jews since their captivity in Babylon . . .

'If I forget thee, O Jerusalem, let my right hand forget her cunning . . . let my tongue cleave to the roof of my mouth, if I prefer not Jerusalem above my chief joy.'

There was solace in prayer, and Simon Rabinsky was a believer among men. But even one so devout could not shut his eyes to the misery around and about him. 'How long, O Lord . . . how long . . . ?' he would ask. 'How long must we live in this abysmal darkness?' And then his heart would grow light and he would become exalted as he repeated his favorite passage of the Passover Prayer – '*Next year in Jerusalem.*'

Next year in Jerusalem? Would it ever come? Would the Messiah ever come to take them back . . . ?

Chapter Three

Yakov and Jossi walked home from the seminary. Jossi's head was bowed; he was deep in thought, wondering about the meaning of certain passages of the Torah he had studied that afternoon. Young Yakov danced around on his toes flinging rocks at various objects in the street. He always carried a pocket full of rocks in case they ran into some bullies.

As they approached the corner near home, Yakov grabbed Jossi's wrist. 'There is going to be another meeting tonight in Hacohen's shop,' he said.

'I heard all about it,' Jossi said.

'Will you go this time?'

'No.'

'You should go tonight,' Yakov said; 'there is going to be a real Bilu from Palestine to speak.'

Jossi's heart pounded! A real Bilu from Palestine! How he would love to see and hear someone who had actually been to Palestine. Secretly Jossi envied his younger brother, who had been sneaking off to Lovers of Zion meetings. His curiosity was aroused by this new organization which spoke of the defense of the ghetto and a return to the Holy Land. A real Bilu! No – he would not yield to temptation – never so long as his father objected to the Lovers of Zion.

They turned the corner and entered the shop, first kissing the mezuzah, a tiny prayer scroll nailed to the doorpost. The place smelled strongly of leather. Simon looked up from his workbench and smiled.

'Hello, Papa,' they both said quickly, and drew a curtain over the alcove which served as their bedroom in one corner of the shop. Simon knew by their manner that they had been discussing something in secret and he also knew full well what young Yakov had been up to, but he did not say a word. The boys must have their fling, Simon thought – I will not impose my will on them in this matter nor will I speak to them unless they speak to me first.

Simon could be considered among the more fortunate Jews of the ghetto. His family was in good health and he had a trade which allowed him to exist, however, meagerly. The mortality rate of Jews in the Pale was more than twice that of the rest of the population of Russia.

Not only the Jews were near starvation. Most of Russia, especially the peasantry, hovered on the brink of destitution. The country wallowed in the backwash of feudalism, refused to industrialize, and was exploited by the aristocracy.

Bread, land, and reform movements sprang up all over the nation. Because their own plight was the worst, there were always Jews to be found in any organization which strived to alleviate the wretched conditions.

Unrest mounted throughout Russia. An undercurrent which spelled revolution was brewing. Only then did Czar Alexander II institute some long overdue reforms. His first move was to free the serfs and he relaxed some of the stringent anti-Jewish statutes. The new laws even allowed a limited number of professional and artisan Jews to live in Moscow. In Bessarabia a few Jews could purchase land. However, the reforms were mere crumbs.

In trying desperately to divert the people's attention from the real issue of tyranny, the masterminds behind the Czar found a new and convenient use for the old scapegoats, the Jews. Hatred for the Jew in Russia had been based on religious bias, ignorance, and superstition, coupled with the peasants' blind hostility due to their inferior status. The Russian government decided to make anti-Semitism a deliberate political weapon. They launched a campaign in which the number of Jewish members in the Bread and Land movements was exaggerated and they claimed it was all a plot of Jewish anarchists out to seize the government for their own profit.

It was furthered as the Russian government secretly drummed up, sponsored, fostered, and condoned bloody pogroms in which ghettos of the Pale were sacked, the women raped, and blood flowed freely. As the mobs tore through the ghettos the Russian police either turned their backs or actively engaged in the affairs.

On March 13, 1881, an awesome catastrophe befell the Jews. Czar Alexander II was assassinated by a rebel's bomb, and one of the convicted revolutionaries was a Jewish girl!

This paved the way for years of horror.

The power behind the new Czar Alexander III was the sinister Pobiedonostsev. He handled the weak-minded new ruler like an infant. Pobiedonostsev regarded the principles of equality, bread, and democracy as extremely vulgar and set out to crush them ruthlessly.

As for the Jews, Pobiedonostsev had special plans. As procurator of the Holy Synod he received a silent nod from the Greek Church for his scheme which called for the elimination of the Jewish population. One third would go through government-sponsored pogroms, starvation, and other forms of murder. One third would go through expulsion and exile. One third would be converted.

Easter week, 1881. The coronation of Czar Alexander III was the signal to begin. Pobiedonostsev's pogroms erupted and spread to every city of the Pale.

After the first outbursts, Pobiedonostsev quickly had a dozen laws enacted that either eradicated any previous gains made by the Jews or aimed to destroy the rest of the Jewish population.

In the wake of the awful happenings of 1881 the Jews of the Pale groped desperately for an answer to their problems. A thousand ideas were advanced – each more impractical than the last. In many corners of many ghettos a new voice was heard by a group who called themselves Hovevey Zion – the Lovers of Zion.

Along with the Lovers of Zion came a document from the pen of Leo Pinsker which seemed to pinpoint the causes and solution of the Jewish plight. Pinsker's document called for auto-emancipation as the only way out for the Jews of the Pale.

Late in the year 1881 a group of Jewish students from Romny bolted from the Pale and made for Palestine with the motto on their lips, '*Beth Yakov Leku Venelkha* – House of Jacob, let us go up!' This daring band of adventurers, forty in number, became known far and wide by the initials of their motto, which in transliteration became the 'Bilu.'

The Bilus started a small farming village in the Sharon Valley of Palestine. They named it Rishon le Zion: First to Zion.

The pogroms in the Pale increased in fury, reaching new heights of bloody destruction on Easter morning 1882 in the town of Balta.

As a result new groups of Bilus struck out for the Promised Land and the Lovers of Zion grew by leaps and bounds.

In the Sharon the Bilus founded Petah Tikva: the Gate of Hope.

In the Galilee they founded Rosh Pinna: the Cornerstone.

In Samaria they founded Zichron Yakov: the Memory of Jacob.

By the year 1884 a half dozen small, weak, and struggling Bilu settlements had been begun in the Holy Land.

Each night in Zhitomir and in every other city of the Pale there were secret meetings. Youths began to rebel and to be diverted from the old ways.

Yakov Rabinsky, the younger of the brothers, was swept up in the new ideology. Often during the night he lay awake, staring into the darkness in the alcove of the shop he shared with his brother Jossi. How wonderful it would be to be able to fight! How wonderful to strike out and really find the Holy Land! Yakov's head was filled with the past glory of the Hebrews. Often he pretended he fought alongside Judah 'the Hammer' as the Maccabees swept the Greeks from Judea. He, Yakov Rabinsky, would be there as Judah Maccabee entered Jerusalem and rededicated the Temple.

Yakov Rabinsky would be there with Simon Bar Giora, who held Jerusalem against the might of Rome for eighteen long months. He would be there in chains alongside Giora as the proud Hebrew warrior was led off to Rome to the lions' den.

Yakov would be there with the greatest of them all – Bar Kochba, the scourge of the Romans.

He would be there at the stands at Herodium and Machaerus and Masada and Beitar, where they fought to the last man after several years of siege.

And of all his heroes, Yakov wanted most to be with Rabbi Akiva when he met his martyrdom at Caesarea, for Akiva was teacher, scholar, and fighter all in one.

When the Lovers of Zion came around to Zhitomir, Yakov ran off to the meetings immediately. Their message of auto-emancipation was music to his ears. The Lovers of Zion wanted his brother Jossi because of his size and strength; but Jossi out of respect for his father as commanded by God was slow to move toward these radical ideas.

The day after the Bilu from Palestine spoke in Hacohen's candle shop, Jossi could stand it no longer. He wanted to know everything from Yakov – how the Bilu looked – every word he said – every gesture.

'I think, Jossi, the time has come for you to attend a meeting with me.'

Jossi sighed. It would mark the first time in his life he had openly gone against his father's wishes. 'Very well,' he whispered, and all that day asked forgiveness for what he was about to do.

The brothers told their father they were going to say Kaddish, a mourner's prayer, for a friend who had recently died. They sped off to the shop of Hacohen, the candlemaker. It was a tiny basement shop like their own home. It smelled of wax and sweet scents. Curtains were drawn over the windows. Guards were posted outside on the street. Jossi was surprised at how many familiar faces he saw in the packed room. The speaker was a man from Odessa named Vladimir.

Vladimir neither looked nor acted like them. He had no beard or side curls. He wore boots and a black leather jacket. As he began to speak Yakov became entranced, and around the room a half dozen hecklers started up.

'Are you the Messiah who has come to lead us back?' someone called.

'Did you find the Messiah under your bed when you hid during the past pogrom?' Vladimir rejoined.

'Are you sure you are not one of the Czar's spies?'

'Are you sure you are not one of the Czar's next victims?' Vladimir retorted.

The room quieted down. Vladimir spoke softly. He reviewed the history of the Jews in Poland and in Russia and then expanded his summary to include Germany and Austria as well. Then he spoke of the expulsions from England and France – then of the massacres at Bray and York and Spires and Worms.

Vladimir spoke of how the Pope had called upon the Christians to regain the Holy Land from the Moslems and of how five Crusades over three hundred years were directed against the Jews in the name of God.

Vladimir spoke of one of the most horrible periods of all – the Spanish Inquisition, during which unbelievable atrocities against the Jews were committed in the name of the Church.

'Comrades, every nation on the face of the earth has derided us. We must arise again as a nation. It is our only salvation. Pinsker has seen it and the Lovers of Zion see it and the Bilus see it. We must rebuild the House of Jacob!'

Yakov's heart was pounding as the boys left the meeting. 'See, Jossi! What did I tell you! You saw tonight that even Rabbi Lipzin was there.'

'I must think about it,' Jossi said defensively. But even as he spoke he knew that Vladimir was right and Yakov too. It was their only salvation. The street was quiet and dark and they walked briskly. They reached their home, quickly kissed the mezuzah, and went in.

A candle was burning on Simon's bench. He stood behind it in his long nightshirt with his hands clasped behind him.

'Hello, Papa,' they said quickly, and tried to duck into their alcove.

'Boys!' Simon commanded. They walked slowly before his bench.

Their mother walked into the room and squinted. 'Simon,' she said, 'are the boys home?'

'They are home.'

'Tell them they shouldn't be on the streets so late.'

'Yes, Mama,' Simon said. 'Go to sleep and I shall speak to them.'

Simon looked from Yakov to Jossi and back to Yakov.

'I must tell Mrs Horowitz tomorrow that her husband can surely rest in peace because my sons joined in a minyan for him tonight.'

It was impossible for Jossi to lie to his father. 'We weren't at minyan for Reb Horowitz,' he mumbled.

Simon Rabinsky feigned surprise and held his hands aloft. 'Oh . . . so! I should have known. You boys were courting. Just today Abraham, the matchmaker, was in the shop. He said to me, "Simon Rabinsky," he said, "you have a fine boy in Jossi. Jossi will bring you a handsome dowry from the family of some very fortunate girl." Can you imagine . . . he wants to make a *shiddoch* for you already, Jossi.'

'We were not courting,' Jossi gulped.

'Not courting? No minyan? Perhaps you went back to the synagogue to study?'

'No, Father,' Jossi said almost inaudibly.

Yakov could stand it no longer. 'We went to a Lovers of Zion meeting!'

Jossi looked up at his father sheepishly, bit his lip, and nodded red-faced. Yakov seemed glad it was in the open. He stood defiant. Simon sighed and stared at both his sons for a full five minutes.

'I am hurt,' he announced at last.

'That is why we did not tell you, Father. We did not want to hurt you,' Jossi said.

'I am not hurt because you went to a Lovers of Zion meeting. I am hurt because the sons of Simon Rabinsky think so little of their father they no longer confide in him.'

Now Yakov squirmed too. 'But if we'd told you,' he said, 'you might have forbidden us to go.'

'Tell me, Yakov ... when have I ever forbidden you to pursue knowledge? Have I ever forbidden a book? God help me ... even the time you took the notion into your head that you wanted to read the New Testament? Did I forbid that?'

'No, sir,' Yakov said.

'I think a talk is long overdue,' Simon said.

The candlelight seemed to blend with the red of Jossi's hair. He stood half a head taller than his father and now as he spoke he did not falter. Although Jossi was slow in making up his mind, once it was made up he rarely changed it. 'Yakov and I did not want to hurt you because we know how you feel about the Lovers of Zion and the new ideas. But I am glad I went tonight.'

'I am glad you went too,' Simon said.

'Rabbi Lipzin wants me to sign up for ghetto defense,' Jossi said.

'Rabbi Lipzin departs from so many traditions I am beginning to wonder if he is a Jew,' Simon said.

'That is just the point, Father,' Jossi said. 'You are afraid of the new ideas.' It was the first time Jossi had ever spoken thus to his father and he was immediately ashamed.

Simon walked around the counter and put his hands on his sons' shoulders and led them into their alcove and bade them sit down on their beds. 'Don't you think I know what is going through your minds? New ideas, indeed. There was exactly the same talk about auto-emancipation and ghetto defense when I was a boy. You are only coming to a crisis that every Jew comes to ... to make your peace with the world ... to know your place. When I was a boy I even thought once of converting ... don't you think I know how it feels?'

Jossi was astonished. His father had thought of conversion!

'Why is it wrong for us to want to defend ourselves? Why is it made a sin by our own people to want to better our conditions?' Yakov demanded.

'You are a Jew,' his father answered, 'and being a Jew entails certain obligations.'

'To hide under my bed while people try to kill me?'

'Don't raise your voice to Father,' Jossi admonished.

'No one said it is easy to be a Jew. We were not born on this earth to live from its fruits. We were put here to guard the laws of God. This is our mission. This is our purpose.'

'And this is our reward!' Yakov snapped back.

'The Messiah will come and take us back when He is good and ready,' Simon said, unruffled, 'and I do not believe it is for Yakov Rabinsky to question His wisdom. I do believe it is for Yakov Rabinsky to live by the laws of the Holy Torah.'

There were tears of anger in Yakov's eyes. 'I do not question the laws of God,' he cried, 'but I question the wisdom of some of the men who interpret those laws.'

There was a brief silence. Jossi swallowed. Never had anyone spoken so harshly to his father. Yet he silently applauded his brother's courage, for Yakov was daring to ask the very questions he himself dared not ask.

'If we are created in the image of God,' Yakov continued, 'then the Messiah is in all of us and the Messiah inside me keeps telling me to stand up and fight back. He keeps telling me to make my way back to the Promised Land with the Lovers of Zion. That is what the Messiah tells me, Father.'

Simon Rabinsky would not be shaken. 'In our history we have been plagued with false messiahs. I fear you are listening to one of them now.'

'And how do I recognize the true Messiah?' Yakov challenged.

'The question is not whether Yakov Rabinsky recognizes the Messiah. The question is whether the Messiah will recognize Yakov Rabinsky. If Yakov Rabinsky begins to stray from His laws and listens to false prophets, then the Messiah will be quite certain that he is no longer a Jew. I suggest to Yakov Rabinsky that he continue to live as a Jew as his father and his people are doing.'

Chapter Four

'Kill the Jews!'

A rock smashed through the seminary window. The rabbi hurried the students out through the back to the safety of the cellar. In the streets, Jews scampered wildly for cover ahead of a frenzied mob of over a thousand students and Cossacks.

'Kill the Jews!' they screamed. 'Kill the Jews!'

It was another pogrom inspired by Andreev, the hump-backed headmaster of a local gymnasium – high school – and foremost Jew hater in Zhitomir. Andreev's students swaggered down the streets of the ghetto, smashing up store fronts and dragging any Jews they could find into the streets and beating them mercilessly.

'Kill the Jews . . . kill the Jews . . . kill the Jews!'

Yakov and Jossi raced from the seminary. Using a route through back alleys, they sped over deserted cobblestone streets to reach their home and protect their parents. They ducked frequently for cover and worked away from the sounds of hoofbeats of Cossack horses and from the bloodcurdling screams of the students.

They turned the corner into their street and ran head on into a dozen hoodlums wearing university caps – disciples of Andreev.

'There go two of them!'

Yakov and Jossi turned around and fled, leading the pack of pursuers away from their own home. The students howled with glee as they sprinted after the brothers. For fifteen minutes they wove in and out of streets and alleys until the students trapped them against a dead-end wall. Jossi and Yakov stood with their backs to the wall, dripping sweat and panting for breath as the students formed a semicircle and closed in on them. His eyes gleaming, the leader stepped forward with an iron pipe and swung on Jossi!

Jossi blocked the blow and snatched up the student, spun him around, lifted him over his head, and hurled him at the rest of his companions. Yakov, whose pocket full of rocks was for just such occasions, bounced two stones off the heads of two students, sending them to the ground unconscious. The other students scattered in flight.

The boys dashed home and flung open the door of the shop.

'Mama! Papa!'

The shop was a shambles.

'Mama! Papa!'

They found their mother cowering in a corner in a state of hysteria. Jossi shook her hard. 'Where is Papa?'

'The Torah!' she shrieked. 'The Torah!'

At that instant six blocks away, Simon Rabinsky staggered into his burning synagogue and fought his way gagging to the end of the room where the Holy Ark stood. He threw back the curtains with the Ten Commandments inscribed on them and pulled down the Sefer Torah, the Scroll of the Laws of God.

Simon pressed the holy parchment against his breast to protect it from the flames and staggered back to the door. He was badly burned and choking. He staggered outside and fell onto his knees.

Twenty of Andreev's students were waiting for him.

'Kill the Jew!'

Simon crawled a few yards and collapsed, covering the Sefer Torah with his body. Clubs smashed his skull. Hobnailed boots ripped his face . . .

'Kill the Jew!'

In mortal agony Simon Rabinsky screamed out . . . *'Hear, O Israel . . . the Lord is our God . . . the Lord is one!'*

When they found Simon Rabinsky he was beyond recognition. The Sefer Torah, the laws which God had given Moses, had been burned by the mob.

The entire Zhitomir ghetto mourned his passing. He had died in the noblest way a Jew could meet death – protecting the Sefer Torah. Simon was put to rest along with a dozen others who had been murdered in Andreev's pogrom.

For Rachel Rabinsky, the death of her husband was but another tragedy in a life which had known little else but sorrow. But this time her strength and will were gone. Even her sons could not comfort her. Rachel was taken off to live with relatives in another town.

Jossi and Yakov went to synagogue twice each day to say Kaddish for their father. Jossi remembered how his father had wanted to live as a Jew so that the Messiah would recognize him. His whole mission in life had been to protect God's laws. Perhaps his father had been right – perhaps it was not theirs to live from the fruits of the earth but to serve as the guardians of God's laws. In his sorrow Jossi probed to find a reason for his father's brutal death.

Yakov was different. His heart was full of hatred. Even as he went to say the mourners' prayers, his soul demanded revenge. He seethed and smoldered – he was restless and angry. He muttered time and again that he would avenge his father's death.

Jossi, knowing his brother's state of mind, barely let him out of his sight. He tried to soothe and comfort Yakov but Yakov was inconsolable.

A month after the death of Simon Rabinsky, Yakov slipped from the shop in the middle of the night as Jossi slept. He took from his father's bench a long sharp knife and hid it in his belt and ventured from the ghetto toward the school where Andreev the Jew hater lived.

Jossi awoke instinctively a few minutes later. The instant he saw Yakov was gone he dressed hurriedly and ran after him. He knew where his brother would be going.

At four o'clock in the morning, Yakov Rabinsky pulled the brass knocker on the door of Andreev's house. As the demented hunchback opened the door, Yakov sprang from the shadows and plunged the knife deep into his heart. Andreev emitted one short shriek and rolled on the ground, dead.

A few moments later Jossi rushed onto the scene to find his brother standing hypnotized over the body of the slain man. He pulled Yakov away and they fled.

All the next day and night they hid in the cellar of Rabbi Lipzin's house. Word of Andreev's murder spread quickly throughout Zhitomir. The elders of the ghetto met and came to a decision.

'We have reason to fear that you two were spotted,' the rabbi said when he returned. 'Your red hair, Jossi, was seen by some students.'

Jossi bit his lip and did not reveal that he had only been trying to prevent the crime. Yakov showed no remorse for his deed. 'I would do it again, gladly,' he said.

'Although we understand well what drove you to this deed,' said the rabbi, 'it cannot be forgiven. You may well have started another pogrom. On the other hand . . . we are Jews and there is no justice for us in a Russian court. We have reached a decision you are to abide by.'

'Yes, Rabbi,' Jossi said.

'You are to cut off your curls and dress like goyim. We will give you food and money enough to travel for a week. You must leave Zhitomir at once and never return.'

In 1884, Yakov and Jossi Rabinsky, aged fourteen and sixteen, became fugitives. They used the roads only by night and hid during the day, moving east to Lubny, a distance of a hundred-odd miles from Zhitomir. At Lubny they found the ghetto immediately and sought out the rabbi, only to learn that their notoriety and preceded them. The rabbi and the elders of Lubny met and agreed to give the boys enough food and money for another week's travel. This time their destination was Kharkov, some two hundred miles away, where the search for them might not be so intense. Advance word was sent to the Kharkov rabbi that the Rabinsky boys were on the way.

The entire countryside was on the alert for the Rabinsky brothers. It took twenty days of cautious moving for them to get to Kharkov.

Their fame had spread throughout the Pale, and their capture was being turned into a holy mission. For two weeks they hid in the clammy basement beneath the synagogue in Kharkov, their presence known only to the rabbi and a few elders.

At last the Rabbi Solomon came to them. 'It is not safe, even here,' he said. 'It is only a matter of time until you boys are discovered. Already the police have been prowling around asking questions. But with winter coming on it will be near impossible to move.'

The rabbi sighed and shook his head. 'We have also tried to get you papers to enable you to travel beyond the Pale, but I am afraid that is impossible. You are too well known by the police.'

He paced back and forth. 'We have decided there is but one thing to do. There are some Jewish families in this district who have passed as gentiles and who own small farms. We feel it would be the safest plan for you to hide with one of them until spring at least.'

'Rabbi Solomon,' Jossi said, 'we are very thankful for everything that has been done for us, but my brother and I have made a plan of our own.'

'What is that?'

'We are going to Palestine,' Yakov said.

The good rabbi looked stunned. 'To Palestine? How?'

'We have a route in mind. God will help us.'

'No doubt God will help you but let us not press Him for a miracle. It is over three hundred hard cold miles to the port of Odessa. Even if and when you reach Odessa you cannot get a boat without papers.'

'We are not going by way of Odessa.'

'But there is no other way.'

'We intend to walk.'

Rabbi Solomon gasped.

'Moses walked for forty years,' Yakov said; 'it will not take us that long.'

'Young man, I am well aware that Moses walked for forty years. That does not explain how you are going to walk to Palestine.'

'I'll tell you our plan,' Jossi said. 'We will go south. The police won't be looking for us so strenuously in that direction. We will cross out of the Pale into Georgia and then over the Caucasus Mountains into Turkey.'

'Madness! Insanity! It cannot be done! Do you mean to tell me you will walk over two thousand miles, through the cold of winter, across strange lands and fifteen-thousand-foot mountain ranges without papers . . . without knowledge of the country . . . with the police after you? Why, you are but little more than children!'

Yakov's eyes were burning with passion; he looked at the rabbi. '*Fear not for I am with thee. I will bring thy seed from the east and gather thee from the west. I will say to the north, give up and to the south, keep not back; bring my sons from far, and my daughters from the ends of the earth.*'

And so it came to pass that the Rabinsky brothers who were wanted for murder fled from Kharkov and moved to the east and to the south through an inhumanly bitter winter.

They trudged through waist-high snow during the night, bending their young bodies against howling winds and fighting off the numbness of frostbite. Their bellies rumbled with hunger. They stole from the countryside and in the hours of daylight they hid in the forests.

Through those tortured nights it was Yakov who filled Jossi with the spirit of their mission. It was Yakov who urged another step and another and yet another when all strength was gone. It was Jossi with his powerful body who held his younger brother up. Between their two strengths they somehow managed to keep alive and moving.

Many a night Jossi had to carry Yakov on his back for eight hours because the younger brother's feet were raw and bleeding and he could not walk. Many a day Jossi had to sleep on top of Yakov to pass his warmth on to his weaker brother. Often they crawled the last few yards to a hiding place.

Over the ice and snow they staggered south with but cloth wrappings around their feet – yard after yard – mile after mile – week after week.

In the spring they reached Rostov and collapsed.

They found the ghetto and were taken in and fed and sheltered. Their rags were exchanged for new clothing. They had to rest several weeks before they were fit enough to continue the journey.

Late in the spring they went on again, fully recovered from their winter's flight.

Although they did not now have to contend with the elements they had to move with greater caution, for they had left the Pale behind and could no longer depend on protection, food, and shelter from the Jewish communities. They skirted the Black Sea south of Rostov and moved deep into Georgia. All their food now was stolen from the fields – they never let themselves be seen by daylight.

As winter came on again they were faced with a tremendous decision. To hole up in Georgia, to try to get through the Caucasus Mountains in winter, or – to attempt a boat across the Black Sea.

Each plan had its dangers. Although trying the mountains in winter seemed the most foolhardy their urge to leave Russia behind was so great that they decided to risk it.

At Stavropol at the base of the mountains they staged a series of robberies which completely outfitted them with clothing and food for the assault over the mountains. Then they fled into the Caucasus toward Armenia with the police on their track.

Through another brutal winter they moved deep into the mountains, walking by day, climbing the treacherous passes in the dark, and pillaging the countryside. The first year had hardened them and made them wise – the obsession to get to Palestine was greater than ever and drove them onward. Yakov would babble passages from the Bible by the hour to drive their bodies forward. They made the last part of their push instinctively, in a numbed daze.

And in spring they received their second miracle of rebirth. One day they stood up and for the first time breathed free air – as they left 'Mother Russia' behind them forever. As Yakov passed the border marker into Turkey he turned and spat into Russia.

Now they could move in daylight, but it was a strange land with strange sounds and smells and they had no passports or papers. All of eastern Turkey was mountainous and the going was slow. They went to work in the fields in places where they could not steal food, but twice that spring they were caught and thrown into prison briefly.

Jossi reckoned they would have to give up thievery, for it was too dangerous being caught; they might be sent back to Russia.

In the middle of summer they passed the base of Mount Ararat where the Ark of Noah had landed. They pressed on to the south.

In each village they asked, 'Are there Jews here?'

In some there would be Jews and they would be fed and clothed and sheltered and sent along their way.

These Jews were different from any they had known. They were peasants filled with ignorance and superstition, yet they knew their Torah and kept the Sabbath and the Holy Days.

'Are there Jews here?'

'We are Jews.'

'Let us see your rabbi.'

'Where are you boys going?'

'We are walking to the Promised Land.'

It was the magic password. 'Are there Jews here?'

'There is a Jewish family in the next village.'

Never once were they refused hospitality.

Two years went by. The brothers pressed on doggedly, stopping only when exhaustion overcame them or they had to work for food.

'Are there Jews here?'

They pressed over the Turkish border into the province of Syria and another strange land.

In Aleppo they received their first taste of the Arab world. They passed through bazaars and dung-filled streets and heard Moslem chants from the minarets –

They walked until the blue-green of the Mediterranean Sea burst suddenly before them and the howlings winds and cold of the past years were exchanged for a blistering heat of one hundred and twenty degrees. They plodded down the Levantine coast wearing Arab rags.

'Are there Jews here?'

Yes, there were Jews, but again they were different. These Jews looked and dressed and spoke like Arabs. But yet they knew the Hebrew language and the Torah. Like the Jews of the Pale and the Jews of Turkey, the Arab-like Jews took the Rabinsky brothers in without question and shared their homes and their food. They blessed the brothers as they had been blessed before for the sacredness of their mission.

On into Lebanon they walked – through Tripoli and the wilderness of Beirut – they neared the Promised Land.

'Are there Jews here?'

The year was 1888. Forty months had passed since that night Yakov and Jossi fled the Zhitomir ghetto. Jossi had grown into a lean and leathery giant six feet three inches tall with a frame of steel. He was twenty years of age and he wore a flaming red beard.

Yakov was eighteen and also hardened by the more than three years of travel but he was still of medium height with dark sensitive features and was filled with the same intenseness he had had from childhood.

They stood upon a hill. Below them was a valley. Yakov and Jossi Rabinsky stared down at the Huleh in northern Galilee. Jossi Rabinsky sat down upon a rock and wept. Their journey was over.

'But the Lord liveth,' Yakov said, *'which brought up and led the seed of the house of Israel out of the north country and from all the countries whither I had driven them, and they shall dwell in their own land.'*

Yakov put his hand on Jossi's shoulder. 'We are home, Jossi! We are home!'

Chapter Five

From the hill they looked down onto the land. Across the valley in Lebanon rose the towering snow-capped peak of Mount Hermon. Below them stretched the Huleh Lake and marshes. There was an Arab village nestled in the hills to their right. Jossi Rabinsky experienced the greatest exaltation he had ever known! How beautiful the Promised Land looked from here!

He vowed to himself, as young men will at such times, that he would return someday and from this very spot would look down on his very own land.

They stayed there for a day and a night and the next morning began the descent in the direction of the Arab village. The white-covered mud houses clumped together in a saddle of the hill were dazzling in the morning sun. The farmlands and olive orchards sloped from the village toward the swamp of the Huleh Lake. In the fields a donkey pulled a wooden plowshare. Other donkeys carried small harvest upon their backs. In the vineyards the Arab women labored among the grapes. The village was as it must have been a thousand years before.

The distant beauty of the village faded with each step they took nearer and was soon replaced by an overwhelming stench. Suspicious eyes watched the brothers from the fields and the houses of the village as they entered the dirt street. Life moved in slow motion in the blistering sun. The road was filled with camel and donkey excrement. Swarms of giant flies engulfed the brothers. A lazy dog lay motionless in the water of the open sewer to cool himself. Veiled women ducked for cover into squalid one-room houses made of mud; half the huts were in a state of near collapse and held a dozen or more people, as well as pigs, chickens, mules and goats.

The boys stopped at the village water well. Straight-backed girls balanced enormous urns of water on their heads or were busy kneeling and scrubbing clothing and exchanging gossip.

The appearance of the travelers brought immediate silence.

'May we have some water?' Jossi asked.

No one dared answer. Haltingly they drew a bucket of water, splashed their faces, filled their canteens, and made off quickly.

Further on they came upon a dilapidated shack which served as a coffeehouse. Listless men sat or lay around on the ground as their wives tilled the fields. Some played backgammon. The air was foul with the mixed aroma of thick coffee, tobacco, hashish smoke, and the vile odors of the rest of the village.

'We would like directions,' Jossi said.

After several moments one of the Arabs pulled himself off the ground and bade them follow. He led them out of the main area to a stream; on the other side of the stream was a small mosque and a minaret. On their side was a nicely built stone house set in the shade, and near it a room which served as the village reception room. They were taken to the room, told to enter and be seated. The high walls of the room were whitewashed, and thick, well-placed windows made it quite cool. A long bench ran around the walls. The bench was covered with bright pillows. On the walls hung an assortment of swords and trinkets and pictures of Arabs and visitors.

At last a man in his mid-twenties entered. He was dressed in an ankle-length striped cloth coat and a white headdress with a black band. His appearance immediately indicated that he was someone of wealth.

'I am Kammal, muktar of Abu Yesha,' he said. He clapped his ringed hands together and ordered fruit and coffee to be brought to the strangers. As his brothers went off to carry out the order a cold half silence pervaded the room as the village elders filed in one by one.

To the boys' surprise, Kammel spoke some Hebrew.

'The site of this village is the traditional burial place of Joshua,' he told them. 'You see, Joshua is a moslem prophet as well as a Hebrew warrior.'

Then, following the Arab custom of never asking a direct question, Kammal set out to find out who the visitors were and what their mission was. At last he suggested that perhaps the boys were lost – for no Jews had ventured into the Huleh before.

Jossi explained that they had entered the country from the north and sought the nearest Jewish settlement. After another half hour of roundabout questions Kammal seemed satisfied that the two Jews were not scouting for land in the area.

Then Kammal seemed to relax a bit: he confided that he was not only the muktar and owned all the land in Abu Yesha but the spiritual leader as well and the only literate person in the village.

Jossi somehow liked this man – for what reason, he did not know. He told Kammal about their pilgrimage from Russia and their desire to settle down and farm in the Holy Land. When the last of the fruit had been eaten, Jossi asked his leave.

'You will find Jews thirty kilometers south. You can walk the distance by nightfall if you stay on the road. The place is called Rosh Pinna.'

Rosh Pinna! How exciting! He had heard the name many times in the Pale.

'Rosh Pinna is halfway between the Huleh Lake and the Sea of Galilee. On the way you will pass a large *tel*. Beneath the *tel* lies the ancient city of Hazor... May God protect you on your journey.'

The road took them past the fields of Abu Yesha and skirted the forbidding Huleh swamplands. Jossi looked back over his shoulder. He could see the spot from which they had crossed earlier that day. 'I'll be back,' he said to himself. 'I know I'll be back –'

At midday they came upon the large man-made hill Kammal had described. As they climbed upward they realized that beneath them lay buried the ancient city of Hazor. Jossi was elated. 'Do you realize that Joshua may have been standing on this very spot when he conquered the city from the Canaanites!' Jossi went about collecting bits of broken pottery which were strewn all about. Since his very first sight of the Holy Land, Jossi had been in such a state of joy that he was completely unaware of the bad mood that had been overtaking Yakov. Yakov did not want to spoil his brother's happiness so he remained silent, but his sullenness grew by the minute.

At dusk they reached Rosh Pinna, the Cornerstone, the farthest northern settlement of Jews. Their arrival produced a great furor. In a small building which served as the meeting room they were eagerly questioned. But it was forty months since they had left Zhitomir and they could only say that the pogroms that had started in 1881 were getting progressively worse.

Although both boys concealed their feelings. Rosh Pinna was a terrible disappointment. Instead of flourishing farms they found a rundown village. There were but a few dozen Jews living midst conditions not much better than those of the Arabs of Abu Yesha.

'Sometimes I think it would have been better to have stayed in Russia,' one of the Bilus opined. 'At least in the ghetto we were among Jews. We had books to read, music to hear, and people to speak to ... there were women. Here, there is nothing.'

'But all those things we heard at the Lovers of Zion meetings –' Jossi said.

'Oh yes, we were filled with ideals when we arrived. One soon loses them in this country. Look at it ... so ruined that nothing can grow. What little we do have is stolen by the Bedouins, and the Turks take what the Bedouins leave. If I were you boys I'd keep on going to Jaffa and get on the next boat to America.'

An outlandish idea, Jossi thought.

'If it were not for the charity of Rothschild, De Hirsch, and De Schumann we would all have starved long ago.'

They left Rosh Pinna the next morning and set out to cross the hills to Safed. Safed was one of the four holy cities of the Jews. It sat on a beautiful cone-shaped hill at the entrance to the Huleh area of the Galilee. Here, Jossi thought, their dejection would soon fade because here there were second-, third-, and fourth-generation Jews who lived and studied the Cabala, the book of mystics. The shock of Rosh Pinna was repeated in Safed. They found a few hundred aged Jews who lived in study and from the alms of co-religionists around the world. They cared nothing about the rebirth of the House of Jacob – but wanted only to live quietly, studiously, and in poverty.

The Rabinsky brothers set out again from Safed the next morning, and crossed to nearby Mount Canaan, and stopped to get their bearings. From Mount Canaan the vista was magnificent. From here they could look back at Safed on its cone-shaped hill and beyond it to the Sea of Galilee. To the north they could see the rolling hills of the Huleh from whence they had come. Jossi loved this view – for before him was the land he had first trod. Yes, he vowed again that someday – someday it would be his.

Yakov's bitterness began to show. 'All our lives, all our prayers ... and look at it, Jossi.'

Jossi put his hand on his brother's shoulder. 'Look how beautiful it appears from here,' he said. 'I tell you, Yakov, someday we will make it look just as beautiful from the bottom of the hill as it does from the top.'

'I don't know what to believe any more,' Yakov whispered. 'All through those winters as we walked through the mountains blue with cold ... all through those blistering summers.'

Jossi said, 'Now cheer up. Tomorrow we begin our journey to Jerusalem.'

Jerusalem! The magic word caused Yakov's flagging spirits to soar.

The next morning they came down from Mount Canaan and moved south along the Sea of Galilee into the Genossar Valley, past Arbel and the Horns of Hattin on the plains where Saladin the Kurd had once crushed the Crusaders in mortal combat.

But as they trudged on, even Jossi became dismayed. Their Promised Land was not a land flowing with milk and honey but a land of festering stagnated swamps and eroded hills and rock-filled fields and unfertile earth caused by a thousand years of Arab and Turkish neglect. It was a land denuded of its richness. It was a land that lay bleeding and fallow.

After a while they came to Mount Tabor in the center of the Galilee, and climbed up this hill which had played such a great part in the history of their people. It was here that the Jewish Joan of Arc, Deborah, and her General Barak hid with their armies and swooped down to crush the invading host. Atop Tabor they could see for miles in every direction. Around them stood Crusader ruins and a tiny monastery; it was here that Jesus was transfigured and held communion with Moses and Elijah.

From Tabor they could see the entire sorrowful picture. A fruitless, listless, dying land.

... and they trudged on with heavy hearts. The seeds of the past were all around them. They passed Mount Gilboa where Saul and Jonathan fell in battle and where Gideon lies – and they passed Bethel and Jericho –

As they moved into the hills of Judea their spirits rose again! The ancient terraces still stood from the time when hundreds of thousands of Jews took richness from the earth. There was no richness left, the hills were eroded, but the elation of the Rabinsky brothers could not be dimmed as they ascended higher and higher and higher.

Arriving at the peak of the ridges, Jossi and Yakov saw the City of David!

Jerusalem! Heart of their hearts – dream of their dreams! In that second all the years of privation and all the bitterness and suffering were erased.

They entered the old walled city through the Damascus Gate and wended their way through the narrow streets and bazaars to the mighty Hurva Synagogue.

'If only Father were with us now,' Jossi whispered.

'*If I forget thee, O Jerusalem ...*' Yakov prayed the lament of the captives.

From the synagogue they went to the one remaining wall of their great ancient temple. It stood on the site of the Mosque of Omar, the Dome of the Rock. This wall was the holiest place in all Jewry.

When at last they sought hospitality from the Jews they lost their illusions. The Jews in Jerusalem were Hasidim, ultra-Orthodox fanatics whose interpretations of the Laws were so strict they could be lived up to only by complete withdrawal from the civilized world. Even in the Pale these groups had separated themselves from the rest of the ghetto.

For the first time since they left Zhitomir, Jossi and Yakov were refused the hospitality of a Jewish home. The Jerusalem Jews did not like the Bilus, and the Lovers of Zion were berated for their ungodlike ideas.

The boys then saw themselves as intruders in their own land. They walked away from Jerusalem shrouded in sadness – down from the hills of Judea toward the port of Jaffa.

This ancient port, which had been in constant use since Phoenician times, was another version of Beirut, Aleppo, or Tripoli – narrow alleys, filth, degredation. However, there were a few Jewish settlements nearby at Rishon le Zion, Rehovot, and Petah Tikva. In Jaffa itself there was some Jewish commerce as well as an agency for Jewish immigrants. Here they learned the full story. There were but five thousand Jews in the entire Palestine Province of the Ottoman Empire. Most of these were ancients who lived in study and prayer in the four holy cities of Safed, Jerusalem, Hebron, and Tiberias. The dozen or so agricultural colonies established by Jews were all in dire straits.

They were kept going through the philanthropy of wealthy European Jews, the Barons de Hirsch, Rothschild, and the Swiss multimillionaire De Schumann. Much of the idealism of the Bilus had disappeared. It was one thing to speak of rebuilding the House of Jacob from a cellar in the Pale – it was another to face the realities of the hardships and the complete disintegration that had befallen Palestine. The Bilus were all inexperienced in agriculture. The philanthropists sent over experts to help them, but it was a matter of using cheap Arab labor and settling on two or three crops for export: olives, grapes, and citrus. No attempt at self-labor had been tried nor were there attempts to balance the agriculture. The Jews, in fact, had become overseers.

Both the Arabs and the ruling Turks stole from the Jews mercilessly. Crops were taxed to the limit – there were all sorts of restrictive stumbling blocks. The roving bands of Bedouins looked upon the Jews as 'Children of Death' because of their refusal to defend themselves.

There were, however, a few hundred Jewish boys like the Rabinsky brothers who stayed around Jaffa, and these kept the spark of the Bilu movement alive. They talked night after night in the Arab cafés. The task of regenerating this miserable land seemed nearly impossible, but it could be done if there were only more Jews with a fighting spirit. Jossi reckoned that more Jews had to come to Palestine sooner or later, for there were bound to be more and worse pogroms in Russia and the entire Pale was stirring. Everyone recognized that something was missing that was not in the Talmud or the Torah or the Midrash or the Mishna. Most of the boys, like Yakov and Jossi, had escaped from Russian military service or had fled out of misery or poverty or some idealistic hopes. The Jews already in Palestine treated them as 'outsiders.' Further – they were stateless wanderers.

It took a year for an answer to come back from Rabbi Lipzin. They learned that their mother had died of incurable and bottomless grief.

For the next four or five years Yakov and Jossi grew to manhood. They worked around the docks in Jaffa and in the fields of the Jewish settlements either as laborers or overseers. When the Jews began moving out of the old walled city in Jerusalem with the aid of the British Jewish philanthropist, Moses Montefiore, they worked as stonemasons. Everything in Jerusalem was being built of that hauntingly beautiful limestone quarried from the hills of Judea.

They lived from job to job. Little by little they lost contact with their deep religious training which had been the dominating force of ghetto life. Only on the high holy days did they travel to Jerusalem. Only on the Day of Atonement, Yom Kippur, did they search their souls and their lives – and, too, on the Day of Judgment, Rosh Hashana – the new year. Yakov and Jossi Rabinsky became typical of a new type of Jew. They were young and strong and they were free men tasting of a freedom they had never known in the Pale. Yet they longed for a purpose and they longed for contact with the Jews of Europe.

The years 1891, 1892, and 1893 came and went.

A few more settlers straggled in to burden the pocketbooks of the philanthropists.

But as Yakov and Jossi lived in apparent aimlessness in Palestine, dramatic events were taking place in another part of the world which were to shape their destiny and the destiny of every Jew for all time.

Chapter Six

FRANCE 1894–97

The Jews of France and of most of western Europe were better off than the Jews of eastern Europe. After the massacres and expulsions of the Middle Ages, the vicious side of Jew-hating abated in both France and England.

A great day came for the Jews with the French Revolution. After fifteen hundred years there was at last a country in Europe which accepted them as equal human beings. France was the first country in Europe to grant Jews the full rights of citizenship without qualification. Their position was further enhanced by Napoleon, according to whom Judaism was a religion, not a nationality. So long as French Jews regarded it only as a religion and gave their loyalty to France, they ought to be granted full and equal status.

The early 1800s were the beginning of a golden era for the Jews of France. The Jewish community produced a host of brilliant doctors, lawyers, scientists, poets, writers, musicians, and statesmen who seemed to justify the Napoleonic concept of assimulation.

There were discreet forms of anti-Semitism in France, of course. But the unpleasantness associated with being Jewish were at a minimum there. Never before had Jews in Europe known such freedom or held such a position in society. By the middle of the 1800s they were well integrated into all walks of French life and had formed the powerful Universal Alliance as their voice and philanthropic arm.

Jew hating is an incurable disease. Under certain democratic conditions it may not flourish well. Under other conditions the germ may even appear to die, but it never does die even in most ideal climate.

In France there lived a young career army captain. He came from a well-to-do family. In the year 1893 he was hauled into a military court on trumped-up charges of selling secrets to the Germans. The trial of this man shook the world, and became an irremediable blotch on the cause of French justice. The man was found guilty of treason and sentenced to life on Devil's Island.

His name was Alfred Dreyfus.

In the bitter winter of 1894 Alfred Dreyfus stood in disgrace in a courtyard. In a ceremony of public ostracism the epaulets were cut from his shoulders, his cheeks were slapped, his sword broken, and the buttons pulled from his cloak. He was denounced above an ominous drum roll as a traitor to France. As he was taken off to begin life in a penal hell he cried, 'I am innocent! Long live France!'

Alfred Dreyfus was a Jew.

The dormant disease of anti-Semitism erupted in France. Goaded on by Édouard Drumont, the arch Jew hater, mobs of Frenchmen ran through the streets of Paris screaming the age-old cry – 'Death to the Jews!'

In later years the great novelist Émile Zola took up the case of Dreyfus. In an open letter to the President of France he branded the horrible miscarriage of justice in immortal prose.

A certain man witnessed Dreyfus' hour of disgrace in the Paris courtyard. Although Dreyfus was freed, this man could not forget the cry, 'I am innocent!' Moreover he could not forget the Parisian mobs screaming, 'Death to the Jews!' It haunted him day and night.

The man who could not forget was Theodor Herzl.

Theodor Herzl was also a Jew. He was born in Hungary, but his well-to-do family moved to Austria and he grew up in Vienna. His training in formal Judaism was superficial. He and his family firmly believed in the prevalent theories of assimilation.

Herzl was a brilliant essayist, playwright, journalist. Like so many creative men of his school he was hounded by an incessant restlessness. He was married to a good woman but one completely incapable of giving him the compassion and understanding he needed. Fortunately for Herzl his restless ventures were well financed by a generous family allowance.

Herzl drifted to Paris and eventually became Paris correspondent for the powerful Viennese *New Free Press*. He was relatively happy. Paris was a carefree city and his job was good and there was always that wonderful intellectual exchange.

What had brought him to Paris, really? What unseen hand guided him into that courtyard on that winter's day? Why Herzl? He did not live or think as a devout Jew, yet when he heard the mobs beyond the wall shout, 'Death to the Jews!' his life and the life of every Jew was changed forever.

Theodor Herzl pondered and thought, and he decided that the curse of anti-Semitism could never be eradicated. So long as one Jew lived – there would be someone to hate him. From the depths of his troubled mind Herzl wondered what the solution could be, and he came to a conclusion – the same conclusion that a million Jews in a hundred lands had come to before him – the same conclusion that Pinsker had written about in his pamphlet about auto-emancipation. Herzl reasoned that only if the Jews established themselves again as a nation would all Jews of all lands finally exist as free men. They had to have a universal spokesman – they had to command respect and dignity as equals through a recognized government.

The paper in which he set down these ideas was called 'The Jewish State.'

Galvanized into action by this sudden calling, Herzl drove himself unmercifully to gather support for his ideas. He went to those enormously wealthy philanthropists who were supporting the colonies of Jews in Palestine. They ridiculed the Jewish state idea as nonsense. Charity was one thing – as Jews they gave to less fortunate Jews – but talk of rebuilding a nation was madness.

But the Jewish state idea caught on and spread through a hundred lands. Herzl's idea was neither novel nor unique, but his dynamic drive would not let it die.

Important support began to gather around him. Max Nordau a transplanted Hungarian in Paris with an international reputation as a writer, rallied to his support, as did Wolfsohn in Germany and De Haas in England. Many Christians in high places also expressed their approval of the idea.

In the year of 1897 a convention of leading Jews throughout the world was called in the town of Basle, Switzerland. It was, indeed, a parliament in world

Jewry. Nothing like it had happened since the second Temple had been destroyed. Assimilationists were there and Lovers of Zion were there. Orthodox Jews were there and Socialists were there. No matter what their leanings, they all had a common bond, and to a man they were prepared to stage a rebellion against two thousand years of unspeakable persecution. The Basle convention called for a return of Jews to their ancient historic homeland, for only through the establishment of a Jewish state could all Jews of all lands achieve freedom.

They called the movement Zionism.

As blood riots against the Jews were increasing in Russia, Poland, Rumania, Austria, and Germany and as Jew baiting was reborn in France, the Basle convention made its historic proclamation:

THE AIM OF ZIONISM IS TO CREATE A HOMELAND FOR THE JEWISH PEOPLE IN PALESTINE SECURED BY PUBLIC LAW.

Theodor Herzl wrote in his diary, 'In Basle I established a Jewish State. If I were to say that aloud today, universal laughter would be the response. Maybe in five years, certainly in fifty, everybody will recognize it.'

After the formal declaration of Zionism, Theodor Herzl plunged into the arduous work like a man possessed. He was a dynamic leader and inspired all those around him. He consolidated his support, gained new adherents, raised funds, and built an organization.

Herzl's immediate objective, however, was to obtain a charter or some other legal basis upon which Zionism could be built.

There was a split within Jewry itself. Herzl was constantly harassed by an element which considered his 'political' Zionism impure. Many of the old Lovers of Zion balked. A part of the religious element decried him as a false Messiah, just as another segment had praised him as the true Messiah. But the Herzl train would not and could not be derailed. Hundreds of thousands of Jews carried an imprinted 'shekel' in their pockets as proof of membership.

Still without a charter, Herzl began visiting heads of state to obtain a hearing for his ideas.

Herzl worked beyond his capacities. He depleted his personal finances, neglected his family, and impaired his health. Zionism had become a great obsession with him. At last he obtained an interview with the Sultan of the crumbling Ottoman Empire, Abdul Hamid II, 'Abdul the Damned.' The aging old despot fenced with Herzl and gave half promises to consider a charter for Palestine in exchange for desperately needed money. Abdul was a corrupt human being. His vast holdings in the Middle East ran from the Mesopotamian Province and included Syria, Lebanon, Palestine, and much of the Arabian Peninsula. He tried to play the Zionist proposal off against better gains and finally refused Herzl's appeal. It was a terrible setback.

In the year 1903 matters reached a new low in Russia. In the city of Kishinev the Jews were charged once again with using Christian blood for their rituals, and on Easter of that year the government secretly spurred on a wanton slaughter that left the ghetto of Kishinev in ruins.

Finally England lent a sympathetic ear. At the turn of the century the British were expanding their influence in the Middle East and were already becoming a challenge to the failing Ottomans. They were entrenched in Egypt as well as in half a dozen sheikdoms on the Arabian Peninsula, and they were anxious to gain the favor of world Jewry in order to further their own aspirations. They offered the Zionists a part of the Sinai Peninsula for Jewish immigration and colonization. It was the understanding that this area stood at the door of the Promised Land and the door would open when the British took over. The plan was vague and ill advised and Herzl still hoped to gain a charter for Palestine, so the plan collapsed.

More attempts to gain a charter failed. The pogroms were overrunning a great part of Europe. Herzl became certain that a temporary haven had to be obtained to ease the situation. The British came forth with a second proposal. They offered the African territory of Uganda to the Zionists for Jewish colonization. Herzl desperately agreed to take it up before the next convention.

When the Uganda plan was proposed by Herzl, a fierce opposition developed, led by the Russian Zionists. The basis of their resistance was the fact that they could find no mention of Uganda in the Bible.

Twenty-five solid years of pogroms in Russia and in Poland were now causing the Jews to pour out from eastern Europe by the thousands. By the turn of the century fifty thousand had found their way to Palestine. Abdul Hamid II saw this influx of Jews as potential allies of the British and decreed that no more Jews from Russia, Poland, or Austria would be allowed.

However, the Sultan's empire was rotten to the core. The Zionists had a world headquarters in England and a growing bank to back them up. Zionist bribe money kept the door of Palestine open for all who enter.

This was the First Aliyah of the Jewish exodus!

Along with the return of the exiles to their Promised Land another event was taking place in the Arab world. After centuries of subjugation there was a rankling of unrest among the Arabs that spelled the beginnings of Arab nationalism. In all the Arab world there existed not a single independent or autonomous state.

Arab nationalism sprang first from liberal elements in Lebanon as a progressive movement bent on instituting long overdue reforms. The ideas grew until a first conference was held in Paris and the call was given for the sleepers to awake.

These ideas not only frightened the colonials but they frightened the oppressors within the Arab world, and the well-meaning movement was grabbed up by tribal leaders, sheiks, religious leaders, and effendi landowners, under whose influence the original ideals degenerated into hate-filled dogma as each maneuvered to gain control of the dying Ottoman Empire.

The twentieth century!

Chaos in the Middle East. Zionism! Arab nationalism! The Ottoman's decline and the British ascent! All these elements stewing in a huge cauldron were bound to boil over.

Theodor Herzl's comet streaked over the sky with blinding light and speed. It was a mere ten years from the day he had heard Alfred Dreyfus cry, 'I am innocent!' to the day he dropped dead of a heart attack at the age of forty-four.

Chapter Seven

By the time the Zionist movement came into being the Rabinsky brothers were old-timers in Palestine. They knew almost every corner of the land and had worked at almost every job. They had lost most of their illusions.

Yakov was restless and bitter.

Jossi tried to find a measure of contentment in his existence. He appreciated his relative freedom. Moreover, he never stopped dreaming of the land in the Huleh Valley above Safed.

Yakov held both the Arabs and Turks in contempt. He looked upon them as enemies as he had looked upon the Cossacks and students of the gymnasium. It was quite true that the Turks would not tolerate murder, but everything else against the Jews seemed justified. Many a night Yakov and Jossi sat up arguing.

'Certainly we should obtain land through legal purchase but where are we going to get farmers and what is going to make the Bedouins and Turks leave us alone?'

'We will get farmers when the pogroms get bad enough again,' Jossi answered. 'As for the Turks ... you can buy them. As for the Arabs, we must learn to live side by side with them in peace. This will happen only if we understand them.'

Yakov shrugged. 'One thing an Arab understands' – and he held up his fist and shook it – 'he understands this.'

'Someday they will hang you on the gallows,' Jossi said.

The brothers grew further and further apart. Jossi maintained his desire for peace and understanding and Yakov continued to be a proponent of direct action to counter the injustices against the Jews.

At the beginning of the new century Yakov joined a group of fifteen men who set out on a daring venture. One of the philanthropic funds purchased a small piece of land deep in the Jezreel Valley where no Jews had penetrated for centuries. Here the fifteen pioneers established an agricultural training center and experimental farm. The place was called Sde Tov, Field of Goodness. Their position was extremely dangerous, for they were locked in on four sides by Arab villages and at the mercy of Bedouin tribes who would not hesitate to murder for anything of value.

By 1900 there were fifty thousand Jews in Palestine and a bit more social life for Jossi. Most of those who fled the pogroms wanted nothing to do with the floundering agricultural colonies but were content to become merchants or tradesmen in Jaffa. A few of them settled in the tiny port town of Haifa. However, there were too many coming in for all of them to be absorbed as merchants and there were too many who owned just the clothes they wore; soon there was a good deal of talk of land redemption.

The Zionists opened their first land-buying office, the Zion Colonizing Society, in a dingy run-down hotel in Jaffa which was the local headquarters for Jewish itinerants. Rothschild's Palestine Investment Corporation and the

De Schumann Foundation also stepped up land-buying operations to open new villages for the 'returnees.'

In the middle of 1902 the De Schumann Foundation contacted Jossi Rabinsky and offered him a job as their chief buyer of land. He knew the country as well as any Jew and was noted for his courage in going into Arab territory. Further, he was wise enough to deal with the Turks, for land buying by Jews was severely restricted. Also, one had to be shrewd to trade with the Arab effendis, or landowners. Jossi had his doubts about the new colonies. Living by means of philanthropy and using the fellaheen labor did not seem to him to be the way to redeem the Promised Land, but the opportunity of obtaining land for Jews made him decide to accept the job.

There were other motives behind Jossi's decision. He could get to see Yakov more often this way. He could also learn every inch of the land. Jossi never tired of steeping himself in past glories, and every bit of Palestine held another ghost of the former Jewish greatness. Finally Jossi wanted to be able to travel beyond Rosh Pinna, the last Jewish settlement, to see again the land of the Huleh near Abu Yesha.

Jossi was indeed a handsome figure on his white Arabian stallion. He was a man of thirty now, tall, lean, and muscular. His fiery beard set off the white robes and Arab headdress he was wearing. There were bandoleers of bullets across his shoulders and a bull whip at his side as he rode deep up into the Hills of Samaria and through the Plains of Sharon and into the Galilee to search out land.

Most of the land throughout Palestine was owned by a few dozen powerful effendi families. They charged the fellaheen rent amounting to from half to three quarters of all their crops, and they did absolutely nothing for these poor miserable souls.

Jossi and buyers from the other foundations could obtain land only at outrageous prices. The effendis sold the worst properties – unproductive swamps – to the Jews. They did not believe that anything could or would ever be done with this land, and at the same time the 'Hebrew gold' was a windfall.

Jossi took many trips beyond the last Jewish settlement of Rosh Pinna, often to visit Kammal, the muktar of Abu Yesha. The two men became friends.

Kammal was a few years older than Jossi and a rarity among the effendis. Most of the effendis lived as absentee landlords in pleasure spots such as Beirut and Cairo.

This was not so with Kammal. He owned all the land in and around Abu Yesha and he was absolute monarch within its boundaries. As a youth he had had a tragic love affair with the daughter of a poverty-stricken fellah. His father had ignored his pleas to provide medical care for the girl; she was suffering from trachoma. Kammal's father reasoned that his son could have four wives and innumerable concubines, so why trouble himself with one miserable fellah woman. The girl went blind of the dread disease and died before her eighteenth birthday.

This event made Kammal a hater of his own class. It cut a scar so deep in his heart that he developed a social conscience. He went off to Cairo, not to enjoy its wild pleasures, but to study advanced farming methods, sanitation, and medicine. When his father died he returned to Abu Yesha determined to live among his people and to better their wretched conditions.

Kammal fought a losing battle. The Turks would not give him a school or medical facilities or any social services. Conditions in the village were just about as they had been a thousand years before. Most heartbreaking for the Arab was the fact that he was unable to translate what he had learned into practical applications for his villagers; they were so illiterate and so backward that they simply could not comprehend.

Since he had become muktar, Abu Yesha had fared better than any Arab village in the Galilee, but conditions there were still primitive.

Kammal was puzzled by the strange coming of the Jews to Palestine. Because he wanted to learn its meaning, he intentionally cultivated the friendship of Jossi Rabinsky.

Jossi tried to get Kammal to sell him a parcel of land which was not being worked to begin a colony, but Kammal balked. These Jews confused him. He did not know whether they could be trusted or not, for certainly they were not all like Jossi Rabinsky. Besides, he was not going to be the first effendi to sell land in the Huleh Valley.

Just as Kammal learned from Jossi, so Jossi learned from Kammal. Despite Kammal's enlightenment he was heart and soul an Arab. He never spoke of his three wives, for the servitude of woman was traditional. Kammal was always polite, but he was a great man to bicker when bartering. Jossi watched him exercising his authority. Although he had compassion for his people he could not comprehend any means of rule that was not absolute. On occasion Kammal even consulted Jossi in some typical double-dealing scheme which seemed perfectly legitimate to the Arab.

Through Kammal, Jossi Rabinsky learned about the magnificent and tragic history of the Arab people.

In the seventh century the dogma of Islam had erupted upon the wild semicivilized Bedouin tribes in the deserts. Inspired by Mohammed's divine teachings, they swept out of the sand and with fire and sword spread their gospel from the doorsteps of China to the gates of Paris. During a hundred years of holy persuasion, hundreds of millions of the world's peoples had gathered to the banner of Islam. The heart and soul of Islam were the Arabs, who were bound together by a common language and a common religion of submission to God's will. During the meteoric rise of Islam, Jews held the highest positions of esteem in the Arab-speaking world.

A magnificent civilization arose from the deserts. It was the light of all mankind while the Western world wallowed in the morass of the Dark Ages and feudalism. Bagdad and Damascus became the Athens of their day. The Moslem culture was dazzling. For five hundred years the most advanced thinking, the greatest scientific efforts, the most magnificent artisans belonged to the Arab-speaking world.

Then came the Holy Wars of the Crusaders, who sacked and raped and killed in the name of the very same God who was shared by Moslem and Christian.

After the Crusaders came a century – one hundred unrelieved years – of Mongol invasions. The Mongols swooped in from Asia and the wars were so cruel and so bloody that they defied any known bounds of brutality. Pyramids of Arab skulls stood as the monuments of the Mongols.

The Arabs so exhausted themselves in ten decades of fighting that their once mighty cities were decimated and a dry rot fell on the flowering oases. The beautiful islands of fruit and plenty were eaten up by seas of sand and erosion. The Arabs turned more and more against themselves and a bitter and desperate struggle ensued in which blood feuds pitted brother against brother.

Divided against themselves, their land ruined, and their culture all but destroyed, they were unprepared to defend themselves against the final disaster.

This time it was brought about by fellow Moslems as the mighty Ottomans gobbled up their lands. Five centuries of corruption and feudalism followed.

A drop of water became more precious than gold or spices in the unfertile land. The merest, most meager existence was a series of tortured, heartbreaking struggles from birth to death. Without water the Arab world disintegrated into filth; unspeakable disease, illiteracy, and poverty were universal. There was little song or laughter or joy in Arab life. It was a constant struggle to survive.

In this atmosphere cunning, treachery, murder, feuds, and jealousies became a way of life. The cruel realities that had gone into forming the Arab character puzzled outsiders.

Cruelty from brother to brother was common. In parts of the Arab world thousands of slaves were kept, and punishment for a thief was amputation of a hand, for a prostitute, amputation of ears and nose. There was little compassion from Arab to Arab. The fellaheen who lived in abysmal filth and the Bedouin whose survival was a day-to-day miracle turned to the one means of alleviating their misery. They became Moslem fanatics as elements of the Jews had become fanatics in their hour of distress.

It was small wonder that the Arabs mistrusted all outsiders. The restless movement for freedom originated with the ruling classes, for the Bedouins and fellaheen were far too demoralized even to comprehend freedom and better conditions. The masses were but pawns in the schemes of the effendis and sheiks. They could be stirred into religious hysteria at the least provocation and were thus useful as a political weapon.

Jossi Rabinsky became fascinated by the many-sided Arab character. He could stand for hours around the shops in Jaffa and watch the endless bickering and boisterous trading. He observed as the Arab ran his life as though it were a game of chess. Every move was made with an astuteness designed to outfox those he was dealing with. In the cafés and dens Jossi watched violent passions erupt. During his land-buying expeditions he observed the unscrupulous ethics of the Arab. Yet he enjoyed entering an Arab home where hospitality was unsurpassed. He was confounded by the fantastic reasoning that condoned every crime short of murder. He thought the position of women intolerable; they were held in absolute bondage, never seen, never heard, never consulted. Women often sought quick and vicious revenge by dagger or poison. Greed and lust, hatred and cunning, shrewdness and violence, friendliness and warmth were all part of that fantastic brew that made the Arab character such an enormous mystery to an outsider.

Kammal introduced Jossi Rabinsky to the Koran, the Holy Book of Islam. Jossi learned that Abraham was the father of the Arabs as well as of the Jews. From Ishmael, the cast-out son of Hagar, came the seed of the Arabs.

Jossi learned that Moses, the Jews' great lawgiver, was also the chief prophet of the Moslems, and that all of the prophets of the Bible were also prophets of the Koran. Even many of the great rabbis were looked upon as holy men in Islam.

Kammal eyed the return of the Jews to the Promised Land with suspicion. The Jews puzzled him, for they had come in peace, purchased their land legally, and spoke only in lofty terms of redemption. Kammal, in understanding the basic drive behind the 'return,' admitted to himself that it was a just and true move – but yet his mind could not believe that the newcomers would not eventually engulf and exploit the Arabs as all the others before them had done.

Yakov left Sde Tov. The experimental farm had not been a success. In much the same state he had been in before, Yakov continued to wander around from one end of the country to the other trying to find his niche.

In the year 1905 the revolution long brewing in Russia took place. It was crushed.

The failure of the 1905 revolution was a signal for new pogroms. These were so fearful that the entire civilized world stood aghast. Leo Tolstoy was so moved that he wrote a blistering condemnation of the Czar, his Minister of the Interior Count Plehve, and of the Black Hundreds whose specialty was murdering Jews. The Black Hundreds, protected by the Russian secret police, continued the pogroms until hundreds of thousands of Jews poured out of Russia. Most of them fled to America. Some went to Palestine.

Those who came to the Promised Land were of a new breed. They were not refugees like the Rabinsky brothers nor were they of a mind to become merchants. These were youngsters indoctrinated in Zionism and filled with idealism and a determination to redeem the land.

The year 1905 ushered in the Second Aliyah of the exodus.

Chapter Eight

The need for idealism in Palestine was satisfied by the coming of the Second Aliyah. These newcomers were not content to be merchants in Jaffa nor did they wish to live off the alms of coreligionists. They were fired with a mission to redeem the land.

They set out in groups for the land the effendis had sold and tried to dry up the swamps. It was terrible work. To many of the old-timers the thought of Jews laboring in the fields like Arabs was unbelievable. In Palestine they had been the overseers. In the Old Country they did not work the land at all. Of all the gifts the Second Aliyah brought with them the greatest, perhaps, was the pronouncement of self-labor and the conquest of labor. Through their chief spokesman, A. D. Gordon, labor was made something dignified. Gordon was an older man and a scholar but he gave up scholarship for the greater task of working the soil with his own hands.

These were stimulating days for Yakov. He went out to another new experimental farm in the Galilee called Sejera. In Sejera the excitement never died as the young Jews of the Second Aliyah got down to work. One day Yakov came into Jaffa to see Jossi and he was filled with excitement over a new idea.

Yakov spoke with that fiery exuberance that was his own. 'As you know, the Bedouin tribes use extortion to get our settlements to hire them as guards . . .

against themselves. Well .. they tried it at Sejera. They came in and made threats of what they'd do unless we hired them ... and we didn't. And we've defended ourselves very well. It was precarious for a while, but we set a trap and killed their leader and they haven't come back since.

'We talked it over,' Yakov continued. 'If we can defend one settlement we can defend them all. We have made plans to form a roving guard and we want you to take over one of the units.'

A Jewish guard! What an astonishing idea! Jossi was excited but he answered in his usual way: 'I will have to think it over.'

'What is there to think over?'

'You are making it too black and white, as usual, Yakov. First of all the Bedouins are not going to give up this important source of income without a fight. Then there are the Turks. They will make it nearly impossible for us to carry arms.'

'I'll be blunt,' Yakov said. 'We wanted you, Jossi, because no one knows the country better and no one has had more experience in dealing with both Arabs and Turks.'

'Oh,' Jossi mocked, 'so all of a sudden my dear brother realizes that my years of friendship with the Arabs hasn't been a complete waste of time.'

'What do you say, Jossi?'

'I say I'll consider it. Our own farmers may need a lot of convincing to let us guard them. And one thing that really annoys me ... if we carry loaded guns it may be interpreted to mean we are looking for a fight.'

Yakov threw up his hands. 'Challenging a fight by defending your own property! After twenty years in Palestine you still think like a ghetto Jew.'

Jossi refused to be rattled. 'We came in peace. We have purchased our land legally. We have built our settlements without disturbing anyone. Now if we start to arm, it will be a compromise with the basic idealism of Zionism and don't pretend there is no risk in that.'

'But he stood in the midst of the ground, and defended it ... and the Lord wrought a great victory.'

'Still quoting ...'

'You make me sick,' Yakov snapped. 'Sure, Jossi ... redeem the land under the magnanimous protection of the Bedouin cutthroats. Very well. I shall tell them my brother is deep in meditation. With or without you the Guardsmen are forming. The unit we want you to command is leaving next week for our base camp.'

'Where?'

'On Mount Canaan.'

Mount Canaan! Jossi's heart skipped a beat. He wetted his lips and tried to conceal his excitement. 'I will think it over,' he said.

Jossi didn't think it over. He was tired of buying land for the De Schumann Foundation and of establishing more colonies to live on charity.

A dozen armed Jews who were as hotheaded as Yakov could cause a great deal of trouble. Restraint and wisdom were needed in an armed guard. But the thought of living around Mount Canaan with the chance to spend time in the Huleh Valley proved too great a temptation.

Jossi resigned from the De Schumann Foundation and joined the new group as they arrived at Mount Canaan. They called themselves Hashomer: the Guardsman.

Jossi's company was to work in a circle from Mount Canaan from Rosh

Pinna in the north to the Genossar Valley along the Sea of Galilee in the south and west to Safed and Meron.

Jossi knew that it would be only a matter of time until trouble broke out. As soon as the Bedouins learned they had lost their jobs they were certain to strike. He concocted a plan designed to avert trouble. The most troublesome of the Bedouin tribes in the area was led by an old renegade and smuggler named Suleiman whose encampments were generally in the hills above Abu Yesha. Suleiman extorted one fourth of Rosh Pinna's crops in return for 'protection.' The day after his arrival, before the Arabs were aware of the presence of the Guardsmen, Jossi rode out alone and unarmed to find Suleiman's camp.

He located it late in the evening beyond Abu Yesha, near Tel Hai on the Lebanon side. The camp consisted of goatskin tents scattered about the browned-out hills. These eternal nomads considered themselves the purest and freest of all Arabs. They looked down contemptuously at the lowly fellaheen and the city dwellers. Life was indeed hard for the Bedouin but he was a free man with strong tribal ties, fiercest of the Arab fighters, and the most cunning of the Arab traders.

The sight of the giant red-bearded stranger caused a general alarm. The women, dressed in black Bedouin robes with chains of coins forming masks over their faces, hastened for cover as Jossi rode in.

When he had ridden halfway through the camp a Negro Arab, obviously from the Sudan, came toward him. The Negro introduced himself as Suleiman's personal slave and led him to the largest of the tents near the largest flock of goats.

The old brigand stepped outside his tent. The Arab wore black robes and black headdress. Two magnificent silver daggers hung from his waist. He was blind in one eye and his face was scarred from many battles with men armed with knives and women armed with claws. Suleiman and Jossi sized each other up quickly.

Jossi was ushered into the tent. The earthen floor was covered with rugs and cushions. The two men made themselves comfortable. Suleiman ordered his slave to bring fruit and coffee to the guest. The two men smoked from a long-stemmed water pipe and exchanged meaningless amenities for half an hour. Dishes of curried rice and lambs' testicles were served and they had melons for dessert as they maneuvered the conversation for another hour. Suleiman realized Jossi was no ordinary Jew and on no ordinary mission.

At last he asked Jossi the purpose of his visit and Jossi informed him that Hashomer was taking up his guarding duties. He thanked Suleiman for his past loyal services. The Arab received the news without batting his good eye. Jossi requested a handshake upon a pact of friendship. Suleiman smiled and offered his hand.

Late that night Jossi rode into Rosh Pinna and called a meeting of farmers. Everyone was terrified by the whole idea of the Guardsmen. They were certain that Suleiman would slit their throats when he heard about it. The appearance of Jossi Rabinsky and his promise to remain at Rosh Pinna did much to calm them down.

In the rear of the meeting room a new girl of twenty watched and listened to Jossi Rabinsky. She had only arrived from Silesia in Poland a short time before. Her name was Sarah. She was as tiny as Jossi was huge, and her hair was as black as his was red. She was absolutely entranced as she watched him and listened to him talk.

'You are new here,' he said after the meeting.

'Yes.'

'I am Jossi Rabinsky.'

'Everyone knows of you.'

Jossi remained at Rosh Pinna for a week. He was certain that Suleiman would make a call but he knew the Bedouin was crafty enough not to be reckless. Jossi was in no hurry for the Arab to come, because he was greatly taken by Sarah. But in her presence he became tongue-tied and shy, for he had had little or no experience with Jewish girls in his adult life. The more Sarah teased and prodded, the more he turned into a shell. Everyone in Rosh Pinna, except Jossi, knew that he was a marked man.

On the ninth day a dozen Arabs slipped into Rosh Pinna in the middle of the night and made off with several hundred pounds of grain. Jossi was standing guard and saw them coming and observed every move they made. He could easily have caught them red-handed, but it was no crime to catch a Bedouin stealing. Jossi had a different strategy in mind.

The next morning Jossi rode off once more for Suleiman's camp. This time he was armed – with his ten-foot bull whip. He galloped into the camp at full speed and made directly for Suleiman's tent and dismounted. The Sudanese slave came out and smiled sweetly and welcomed Jossi and invited him to enter. Jossi hit the slave with the back of his hand as though he were flicking a fly from his arm and sent him sprawling to the ground.

'Suleiman!' his big voice boomed out for the whole camp to hear. 'Step outside!'

A dozen kinsmen appeared from nowhere with rifles in their hands and surprise on their faces.

'Outside!' Jossi roared again.

The old brigand took a long time to make his appearance. He stepped from the tent and put his hands on his hips and smiled menacingly. Ten feet of ground separated the two.

'Who is it who howls outside my tent like a sick goat?' Suleiman asked. The tribesmen were seized by a fit of laughter. Jossi did not take his eyes off the Arab for a second.

'It is Jossi Rabinsky who howls like a sick goat,' he said, 'and says that Suleiman is a thief and a liar!'

The smile on Suleiman's lips turned into an ugly scowl. The Bedouins tensed and waited for the signal to pounce on the Jew and devour him.

'Go on,' Jossi challenged softly, 'call all your nephews. Your honor is no greater than a pig's and I hear you have no more courage than a woman.'

No more courage than a woman! This was the deadliest insult he could hear. Jossi had issued him a personal challenge.

Suleiman raised his fist and shook it. 'Your mother is the biggest whore in the world.'

'Go on, woman ... keep talking,' Jossi answered.

Suleiman's very honor was at stake. He drew one of his silver daggers and with a bloodcurdling shriek charged at the red-bearded giant.

Jossi's bull whip whistled out!

It wrapped around the Arab's feet, picked him up, and sent him smashing to the earth. Jossi was at him like a cat. He brought the whip down on Suleiman's back with such terrifying speed and strength that the snap echoed through all the hills.

'We are brothers! We are brothers!' Suleiman cried for mercy at the end of five lashes.

Jossi pointed at his frantic foe. 'Suleiman, you gave me your hand in a bargain of honor and you lied. If you or your kinsmen ever again set foot in our fields I will cut your body apart with this whip and feed the pieces to the jackals.'

Jossi turned and his eyes pierced the astonished Bedouins. They were all too stunned to move. Never had they seen a man so powerful and fearless and angry. Showing utter disdain for their rifles, Jossi turned his back on them, walked to his horse, mounted, and rode off.

Suleiman never touched a Jewish field again.

The next morning when Jossi mounted up to rejoin his company at Mount Canaan, Sarah asked when he would be back. He mumbled something about getting to Rosh Pinna each month or so. As he swung onto his horse, saluted, and galloped off, Sarah thought her heart would burst apart. There was never a man like Jossi Rabinsky – Jew, Arab, Cossack, or king! She swore as she saw him ride away that she would dedicate the rest of her life to loving him.

For a year Jossi commanded his Guardsman company in their territory with such skill that little or no trouble occurred. He never had to resort to firearms. When there was trouble he would go to the Arabs for a friendly consultation and warning. If it happened again – the bull whip. The bull whip of Jossi Rabinsky became as well known through the northern Galilee as his red beard. The Arabs called it 'lightning.'

All this proved too dull for Yakov. He was bored with the lack of action. After six months in the Guardsman he left again to go on the prowl, hoping somehow to fill the constant void in his life.

Jossi was neither sad nor happy as a Guardsman. It gave him more pleasure than buying land and it established an important principle by demonstrating that the Jews could and would defend themselves and were no longer 'children of death.' He looked forward to his northern swing so that he could have a visit with his friend Kammal and then travel up to his hill to keep his dream alive.

Secretly he eagerly anticipated those moments when he rode into Rosh Pinna. He would straighten up to look even more elegant and gallant on his white steed, and his heart would beat more quickly for he knew that Sarah, the dark-eyed girl from Silesia, was watching. But when it came to conversation or action, Jossi was lost.

Sarah was perplexed. She simply could not break down Jossi's shyness. If it had been the Old Country the matchmaker would have gone to Jossi's father and arranged everything. Here there was not only no matchmaker but not even a rabbi.

This went on for a year.

One day Jossi rode into Rosh Pinna unexpectedly. It was all he could do to ask Sarah if she would like to ride with him to see the country north of the settlement in the Huleh Valley.

How thrilling! No Jew but Jossi Rabinsky dared wander up that far! They galloped past Abu Yesha, on up the road, and then into the hills. The trail ended atop his hill.

'I crossed into Palestine right here,' he said softly.

As Jossi looked down into the Huleh Valley he did not need to say another word. Sarah knew how deeply he loved this earth. The two of them stood and gazed for ever so long. Sarah barely reached his chest.

A warm flood of love passed through her. This was Jossi's only way of sharing his most intimate longing.

'Jossi Rabinsky,' Sarah whispered, 'would you please, please marry me?'

Jossi cleared his throat and stammered, 'Ahem ... uh ... how strange of you to mention it. I was about to say something of the sort myself.'

There had never been a wedding in Palestine to compare with Jossi's and Sarah's. They came from all over the Galilee and even from as far away as Jaffa, even though it was a two-day journey to Safed. The Guardsmen came and Yakov came and the settlers of Rosh Pinna came and Turks came and Kammal came and even Suleiman came. Everyone watched as Jossi and Sarah stood beneath the canopy and exchanged vows and drank the blessed wine. Jossi crushed the wine-glass beneath his foot in remembrance of the bitterness of the fall of the Temple. There was food enough for an army and there was dancing and gaiety and celebration that lasted nearly a week.

When the last guest had gone home Jossi took his bride to his tent on the side of Mount Canaan and consummated their marriage.

Jossi took his bride down from Mount Canaan to Jaffa where there was much work to be done for the Zionists. His fame left him well equipped to take charge of settling newcomers and to deal with the many intricacies of this strange land. He signed on with the Zionists as one of the chief men in the Zion Settlement Society.

In the year 1909, Jossi was consulted in a very important matter. Many of the Jews of Jaffa's growing community wanted better housing, sanitation, and a cultural life that the ancient Arab city could not offer. Jossi was instrumental in purchasing a strip of land north of Jaffa, which consisted mostly of sand and orange groves.

On this land the first all-Jewish city in two thousand years was built. They called it the Hill of Spring: Tel Aviv.

Chapter Nine

The agricultural colonies were failing miserably.

There were many reasons. Apathy and lethargy and complete lack of idealism, for one. They still planted only export crops and continued to use the cheaper Arab labor. Despite the influx of Jews and the desire of these Jews to work the land the Zionists could barely convince the colonies to use them.

The over-all situation was discouraging. Palestine was not much better off than it had been when the Rabinsky brothers came twenty years before. There was a measure of culture around Tel Aviv, but all other progress was too small to be measured.

The energy and idealism which had come in with the Second Aliyah was going to waste. Like Yakov and Jossi, the immigrants drifted from place to place without cause and without putting down roots.

As the Zion Settlement Society purchased more and more land it became increasingly obvious that some drastic change in the entire thinking about colonization was necessary.

Jossi and others had long concluded that individual farming was a physical impossibility. There was the matter of security, there was the ignorance of the Jews in farming matters, and, worse, there was the complete wastage of the land.

What Jossi wanted with this new land was villages whose inhabitants would work the soil themselves, plant balanced crops to become self-sustaining, and be able to defend themselves.

The first principle involved was to keep all land in the name of the Zion Settlement Society – all-Jewish land for all the Jewish people. Only self-labor would be allowed on the land: the Jew had to do the work himself and could hire no other Jew or Arab.

The next dramatic step was taken when Jews of the Second Aliyah pledged to work only for the redemption of the land and build a homeland with no thoughts of personal gain or profits or ambition. Their pledge, in fact, came close to later communal farming ideas. The communal farm was not born of social or political idealism. It was based on the necessities of survival; there was no other way.

The stage was set for a dramatic experiment. The year was 1909. The Zion Settlement Society purchased four thousand *dunams* of land below Tiberias at a point where the Jordan River flowed into the Sea of Galilee. Most of it was swamp or marshland. The society staked twenty young men and women to a year's supplies and money. Their mission was to reclaim the land.

Jossi traveled out with them as they pitched their tents at the edge of the marshland. They named their place Shoshanna after the wild roses which grew along the Sea of Galilee.

The Shoshanna experiment on national land could well be the key to future colonization and was the most important single step taken by the Jews since the exodus.

Three clapboard sheds were erected. One was a communal dining and meeting hall. One was a barn and tool shed. The third served as a barracks for the sixteen men and four women.

In the first winter the sheds collapsed a dozen times in the winds and floods. The roads were so muddy they became isolated from the outside world for long stretches. At last they were forced to move into a nearby Arab village to wait it out till springtime.

In the spring Jossi returned to Shoshanna as the work began in earnest. The marshlands and swamps had to be rolled back foot by foot. Hundreds of Australian eucalyptus trees were planted to soak up the water. Drainage ditches were carved out by hand; the work was backbreaking. They labored from sunup till sundown, and a third of the members were always bedridden with malaria. The only cure they knew was the Arab method of cutting the ear lobes and draining blood. They worked in waist-deep muck through the terrible heat of the summer.

By the second year there was some reclaimed land to show for their toil. Now the rocks had to be dragged from the fields by donkey teams and the thick brush hacked down and burned.

In Tel Aviv, Jossi continued to fight to continue support for the experiment, for he was discovering an amazing thing. He was discovering that the drive to build a homeland was so great that there were at least twenty people willing to do this thankless, backbreaking work without pay.

The hardships endured at Shoshanna never ceased, but by the end of two years enough land had been readied to lay in a crop. This was a crucial stage, for most of the group did not know how to farm or what to farm or the difference between a hen and a rooster. They worked by trial and error, and the results were mostly errors. They did not know how to sow or plow in a straight line or how to get milk from cows or how to plant trees. The earth was a gigantic mystery.

They attacked the problem of farming with the same dogged determination with which they had attacked the swampy land. With the swamp water drained off, irrigation water had to be brought in. At first it was carried from the river in water cans on donkey back. Next came an experiment with an Arab water wheel, and after that several attempts at wells. Finally they put in irrigation ditches and built a network of dams to trap the winter rains.

Little by little the land yielded its secrets. On many of his visits Jossi held his breath and wondered and marveled at the morale at Shoshanna. They had nothing but what they wore on their backs and even that belonged to the community. They ate the meagerest of meals in a community dining hall, had common showers and toilets, and slept everyone under the same roof. The Arabs and Bedouins watched the slow steady growth of Shoshanna with amazement. When the Bedouins saw several hundred acres of land under cultivation they set out to dislodge the Jews.

All work in the fields had to be done under cover of armed guards. Along with sickness, overwork – security became a problem. After a torturous day in the fields the tired farmers had to stand guard throughout the night. But they carried on at Shoshanna through isolation and ignorance and threats of attack and swamps and murderous heat and malaria and a dozen other calamities.

Yakov Rabinsky came to Shoshanna to try his luck there.

Joseph Trumpledor arrived. Trumpledor had been an officer in the Russian Army and was famous for his valor in the Russo-Japanese War during which he lost an arm. The call of Zionism brought Trumpledor to Palestine and the path led to Shoshanna. With Trumpledor and Yakov handling security the Bedouin raids soon ceased.

There were more problems in communal living than they had imagined.

There was the governing of the community. This was completely democratic, but Jews were traditionally independent and no two Jews ever agreed on any given subject. Would the governing turn into endless conversation and haggling?

There was the division of work. There was community responsibility for health, welfare, and education. And what of the members who could not or would not do a full day's work? What of those who were disgruntled over their assignments? What of those who objected to the cooking or to living in such tight quarters? What of the clash of personalities?

One thing seemed to overrule all else. Everyone in Shoshanna had a violent hatred for the things which had made him a ghetto Jew. They were going to destroy those things and they were going to build a homeland. Shoshanna had its own code of ethics and its own social laws. They made the marriages and the divorces by common consent. They ran the village in such a way as not to be bound by the old traditions. They threw off the shackles of their past.

So long had their oppression been and so great their desire that here at

Shoshanna was the birth of a true free Jewish peasantry. They dressed like peasants, and they danced the *hora* by firelight. The earth and the building of the homeland had become a noble cause for existence. As time went on flowers and trees and shrubs and lawns were set in and new and fine buildings were erected. Small cottages were built for the married couples and a library was begun and a full-time doctor was hired.

Then came the rebellion of the women. One of the four original women settlers was a stocky unattractive girl named Ruth. She was the leader of the women's rebellion. She argued in the community meetings that the women had not ventured from the Pale and from Poland and certainly not to Shoshanna to become domestics. They demanded equality and responsibilities on the farm. They broke down the old taboos one by one and joined the men in all phases of the work, even plowing the fields. They took over the chickens and the vegetable fields and proved equal in ability and stamina to the men. They learned how to use weapons and stood guard during the nights.

Ruth, the ringleader of the women's uprising, really had her eye on the five-cow dairy herd. She wanted very badly to have the cows. But the votes of the men squashed that ambition. The girls were going too far! Yakov, the most boisterous of the men, was sent into battle with Ruth. Surely she must know that the cows were too dangerous for women to handle! Besides, those five cows were the Shoshanna's most prized and spoiled possessions.

Everyone was astounded when Ruth coyly quit her fight. It was so unlike her! She did not mention another word about it for another month. Instead she slipped out of Shoshanna at every opportunity to the nearby Arab village to learn the art of milking. In her spare time she studied everything she could get her hands on concerning dairy farming.

One morning Yakov went into the barn after a night of guard duty. Ruth had broken her word! She was milking Jezebel, their prize cow.

A special meeting was called to chastise comrade Ruth for insubordination. Ruth came armed with facts and figures to prove that she could increase the milk yield with proper feed and common sense. She accused the men of ignorance and intolerance. They decided to put her in her place by letting her take charge of the herd.

Comrade Ruth ended up as permanent keeper of the cows. She increased the herd twenty-five times over and became one of the best dairy farmers in all of Palestine.

Yakov and Ruth were married, for it was said that she was the only person in the world who could win an argument with him. They loved each other very much and were extremely happy.

The greatest crisis came at Shoshanna with the birth of the first children. The women had fought for equality and gained it and in so doing had become important in the farm's economy. Many of them held key positions. The point was argued and discussed. Should the women quit their jobs and become domestics? Could some other way be found to keep a family going? The members of Shoshanna argued that because they had a unique way of life they could find a unique way to handle the children.

Children's houses came into existence. Certain members of Shoshanna were chosen for the job of raising the children under supervision during the day. This allowed the women to be free to work. In the evenings the families stayed together. Many outsiders cried that this would destroy family life, which had been the saving factor of the Jewish people through the centuries of persecution. Despite the detractors, the family ties at Shoshanna became as powerful as those in any family anywhere.

Yakov Rabinsky had found happiness at last. Shoshanna grew until it had a hundred members and over a thousand *dunams* of the land reclaimed. Yakov did not have money or even clothing to call his own. He had a snippy, sharp-tongued woman who was one of the best farmers in the Galilee. In the evenings, when the day's labor was done, he and Ruth would walk over the lawns and through the flower gardens or to the knoll and look down at the lush green fields – and Yakov was content and fulfilled.

Shoshanna, the first *kibbutz* in Palestine, seemed to be the long-awaited answer for Zionism.

Chapter Ten

Jossi came home one evening from a special meeting of the Vaad Halashon and he was steeped in thought. Because of his position in the community they had made a special appeal to him.

Sarah always had tea ready for Jossi, no matter what time of day or night he returned from his meetings. They sat on the balcony of their three-room flat on Hayarkon Street overlooking the Mediterranean. From here Jossi could look down the curve of coastline to Jaffa which joined Tel Aviv.

'Sarah,' he said at last, 'I have come to a decision. Tonight I was at the Vaad Halashon and they have asked me to take a Hebrew name and speak Hebrew exclusively. I heard Ben Yehuda speak tonight. He has done a tremendous job in modernizing Hebrew.'

'Such nonsense,' Sarah replied. 'You told me yourself that never in the history of the world has a language been revived.'

'And I have come to think that never before have a people tried to revive a nation as we are doing. When I see what has been done at Shoshanna and the other *kibbutzim* ...'

'Speaking of Shoshanna ... you only want to take a Hebrew name because your brother, the former Yakov Rabinsky, has done so.'

'Nonsense.'

'Just what do we call the former Yakov Rabinsky now?'

'Akiva. He named himself after his childhood idol ...'

'And maybe you want to call yourself Jesus Christ after a boyhood idol.'

'You are impossible, woman!' Jossi snorted and stomped in from the balcony.

'If you ever went to a synagogue any more,' Sarah said, following him, 'you would know that Hebrew is for communication with God.'

'Sarah ... I sometimes wonder why you bothered to come from Silesia. If we are to think like a nation, we had better speak like a nation.'

'We do. Yiddish is our language.'

'Yiddish is the language of exiles. Yiddish is the language of the ghetto. Hebrew is the language of all the Jews.'

She pointed her finger up at her giant of a husband. 'Don't recite Zionist propaganda to me, Jossi. You will be Jossi Rabinsky to me till the day I die.'

'I have made the decision, Sarah. You had better study your Hebrew because that is what we will be speaking from now on.'

'Such stupidity, your decision!'

Jossi had been slow in agreeing with Ben Yehuda and the others. Hebrew had to be revived. If the desire for national identity was great enough a dead language could be brought back. But Sarah was set in her ways. Yiddish was what she spoke and what her mother had spoken. She had no intention of becoming a scholar so late in life.

For a week Sarah locked Jossi out of the bedroom. He refused to break down. Then for three weeks he spoke to Sarah only in Hebrew and she answered him in Yiddish.

'Jossi,' she called one night, 'Jossi, come here and help me.'

'I beg your pardon,' Jossi said. 'There is no one in this house by the name of Jossi. If you happen to be speaking to me,' he continued, 'my name is Barak. Barak Ben Canaan.'

'Barak Ben Canaan!'

'Yes. It took much thought to select a proper name. The Arabs used to call my whip "lightning," and that is what Barak is in Hebrew – lightning. It is also the name of Deborah's leading general. I call myself Canaan because I happen to like Mount Canaan.'

The door slammed.

Jossi shouted through it. 'I was happy living on Mount Canaan! I did not have a hardheaded woman then! Get used to it, Sarah Ben Canaan . . . Sarah Ben Canaan!'

Jossi, now Barak, was again locked out of his bedroom. For a solid week neither adversary spoke.

One night, a month after their warfare had started, Barak returned from a grueling three-day meeting in Jerusalem. He came in late at night, exhausted, and looked around, hoping that Sarah might be up to talk things over and have a cup of tea. The door to her room was closed. He sighed and pulled off his shoes and lay back on the sofa. He was so large his legs hung over the arm. He was tired and wished he could sleep in his own bed and was sorry for starting the whole business. He began to doze but was awakened by a crack of light under the bedroom door. Sarah tiptoed to him and knelt by his huge frame and put her head on his chest.

'I love you, Barak Ben Canaan,' she whispered in perfect Hebrew.

Life was busy for Barak Ben Canaan in the brand-new city of Tel Aviv. As the community grew the Jews of Palestine became known by the literal definition of the term – the Yishuv – and Hebrew was revived as the language of the Yishuv. Barak Ben Canaan had risen high among the Zionists and in the Zion Settlement Society. His life was a constant round of meetings and delicate negotiations with the Turks and Arabs. He wrote many papers of importance in the formulation of policy and he and Sarah traveled many times to London to Zionist headquarters and to Switzerland to the international conferences. Yet Barak did not know the true happiness that his brother Akiva had found at Shoshanna. Barak's heart was always north of Mount Canaan in the land of the Huleh Valley. Sarah was a wise and devoted wife. She wanted badly to compensate for his hunger for the land by trying to give him children. This ended in sadness. For five consecutive years she lost children through early miscarriages. It was indeed bitter, for Barak was already in his mid-forties.

Briefly in 1908 there was a rebellion of the Young Turks, who deposed the corrupt old tyrant and despot Abdul Hamid II. The entire Zionist movement was hopeful as he was replaced by Mohammed V as Sultan of the Ottomans and spiritual head of the Moslem world.

They soon learned that the rebellion would have no effect on the granting of a charter. Mohammed V had inherited a collapsing empire, and was known to the world as the 'sick man of Europe.'

From the very beginning, the British had shown the greatest sympathy for the Zionists. Barak felt that Jewish interests and British interests could be brought together, while there was no basis for co-operation with the Turks. The British had offered both Sinai and Uganda for settlement. Many high British officials spoke openly in support of a Jewish homeland. England itself was the headquarters for the Zionists; and further, Dr Chaim Weizmann, a Russian-born Jew, had become the world spokesman for the Zionist movement.

With the rise of the British in the Middle East and the obvious eclipse of the Ottomans, Barak and the Yishuv and the Zionists became openly pro-British.

Mohammed V had lost a series of costly Balkan wars. His position as the 'Shadow of God,' the Moslem spiritual leader, was slipping and the five-century-old Ottoman reign was tottering as the empire came close to economic collapse.

For centuries the Czars of Russia had dreamed of having warm-water ports on the Mediterranean. It had been their eternal ambition to break through the Bosporus and the Dardanelles. With the collapse of the Ottomans at hand, Russia concocted a gigantic power play to carry this out at last. Russia goaded Turkey in an attempt to line her up on the side of Germany. Russia wanted a war with Turkey and she made the ownership of Constantinople the condition of entering that war on the side of the Allied powers. Mohammed V was well aware of what Russia was up to and he studiously avoided a fight. He realized that not only were the Russians going to grab Constantinople but the British, French, and Italians were impatiently waiting to pounce on the empire and split it up among themselves.

World War I erupted!

Mohammed V did not oblige either the Russians or the British by collapsing. Indeed, the Turks showed more fight than anyone had bargained for. The Russian Army was stopped dead trying to cross the Caucasus Mountains; and in the Middle East the Turks lunged out of Palestine, crossed the Sinai Desert, and stood at the very artery of the British Empire, the Suez Canal.

McMahon, the British commissioner in Egypt, began making promises to the Arabs if only the Arabs would rebel against the Ottomans. The British promises implied independence for the Arabs in return for their aid. British agents worked desperately to drum up an Arab revolt against the Turks. They went to the leading Arab prince, Ibn Saud, the powerful Wahabite of Arabia. Ibn Saud decided to wait until he was certain which way the wind was blowing. The balance of the Arab world either fought alongside the Turks or played a game of waiting.

On the Ottoman side, Mohammed V, titular head of all the Moslems, sent out hysterical calls for the entire Moslem world to rise against the British in a 'holy war.' His appeals were met with silence.

The British concluded that the only way to get Arab allies was to buy them. British gold was consequently spread about liberally as bait to hook support. The bait was snapped at. The position of sherif of Mecca was a semi-independent job within the Ottoman rule. The sherif was officially 'Keeper of the Holy Places of Medina and Mecca.' The job was inherited and held for a lifetime by those in the direct line of descent from Mohammed.

The sherif of Mecca was indeed a little man in the Arab world. Further, he was the arch enemy of Ibn Saud. When the British approached him he saw the opportunity to seize power over the entire Arab world if Mohammed V and the Ottomans should fall. So the sherif of Mecca went over to the British, at the price of several hundred thousands of pounds sterling. The sherif had a son named Faisal who was a rarity among Arab leaders, a man who had a social conscience and vision. He agreed to assist his father in getting Arab tribes to 'rebel' against the Ottomans.

The Yishuv in Palestine did not have to be bribed or coddled or bought. The Jews were solidly behind the British. When the war broke out they placed themselves in great peril as avowed friends of the enemies of the Ottomans.

In a swift move, Jemal Pasha the Turk took command of the Palestine province and clamped a reign of terror on the Jewish community.

Barak Ben Canaan had only six hours' warning to flee Palestine. Both he and his brother Akiva were on the extermination rolls of the Turkish police. The Zionist Settlement Society had been forced to close its offices and most Jewish activity had stopped.

'How soon, darling?' Sarah asked.

'We must be gone by daybreak. You are only to pack one small handbag. We must leave everything behind.'

Sarah slumped against the wall and rubbed her hand over her belly. She was six months pregnant and could feel the life in her body as she had never felt it in any of the previous pregnancies ... Five miscarriages, she thought ...

'I can't go,' she said. 'I can't go.'

Barak turned and faced her. His eyes narrowed and his red beard seemed to blaze in the candlelight, 'Come now, Sarah ... we have not time for that.'

She spun around. 'Barak ... oh, Barak' – and she ran into his arms – 'I'll lose this child too ... I can't, I can't ... I can't.'

He sighed deeply. 'You must come with me. God knows what will happen if the Turks get you.'

'I will not lose this baby.'

Barak packed his handbag slowly and shut it.

'Get up to Shoshanna right away,' he said. 'Ruth will take care of you ... stay away from her blessed cows ...' He kissed his wife's cheek gently, and she stood on her tiptoes and clung to him.

'*Shalom*, Sarah. I love you.' He turned and walked out quickly.

Sarah made the perilous journey from Tel Aviv to Shoshanna by donkey cart and there, with Ruth, awaited the birth of her child.

Akiva and Barak fled to Cairo where they met their old friend Joseph Trumpledor, the one-armed fighter. Trumpledor was busy forming a unit of Palestinian Jews to fight in the British Army.

Trumpledor's unit, the Jewish Mule Corps, joined the Anzacs in a mammoth operation. Barak and Akiva were there as the British landed at Gallipoli and vainly attempted to open the Dardanelles and march on Constantinople from the south. In the retreat and debacle that followed the landing, Akiva was wounded in the chest.

The Jewish Mule Corps was disbanded after the Gallipoli disaster. Akiva and Barak continued on to England where Zev Jabotinsky, an ardent Zionist, was busy forming a larger Jewish fighting unit, the 38th, 39th, and 40th Royal Fusiliers, comprising a brigade known as the Judeans.

Akiva had not fully recovered from his wounds and was sent to the United States to lecture in the cause of the Jewish homeland under the sponsorship of the American Zionists, whose leader was Justice Brandeis of the Supreme Court.

When it was discovered that Barak Ben Canaan was among the Fusiliers he was pulled from the ranks at once. Dr Weizmann, the world spokesman for Zionism, reckoned that Barak was too important a figure to carry a rifle.

Barak entered the Zionists' negotiation team in time to hear about a further British disaster in the Middle East, General Maude had launched an attack on the eastern flank of the Ottoman Empire. Using Mesopotamia as a jumping-off point, he planned to come down on Palestine from the north. The route of conquest was to be the Tigris-Euphrates Valley into Bagdad, and then he would wheel and strike for the sea. Maude's legion pressed forward with ease as long as the opposition was Arab troops. The campaign was termed 'brilliant.' Then, at Kut, the British ran into a Turkish division and their forces were beaten to the ground.

The British were reeling! The Ottomans sat on the edge of the Suez Canal and the Germans had torn the Russian first-line army to shreds. British efforts to stir up an Arab revolt against the Ottomans had fallen flat.

Then came the final blow! The Arabs suspected that a secret British-French agreement was in the wind to carve up and subjugate the Arab world.

Dr Weizmann and the Zionists felt the time was ripe to score a point for the Jewish homeland. England desperately needed sympathy and help. In Germany, Jews were fighting for their fatherland as they were in Austria. In order for the Zionists to gain the support of the Jews of the rest of the world, especially those in America, a dramatic decision was needed.

As the negotiations between the Zionists and the British were brought to a close, Lord Balfour, the British Foreign Minister, wrote a letter to Lord Rothschild with the revelation:

> *His Majesty's Government view with favour the establishment in Palestine of a national home for the Jewish people, and will use their best endeavours to facilitate the achievement of this object.*

Thus was born the Balfour Declaration, the Magna Charta of the Jewish people!

Chapter Eleven

Jemal Pasha's police found Sarah Ben Canaan at the shoshanna *kibbutz* just two weeks before her baby was due. Till then, Ruth and the members of the *kibbutz* had guarded her carefully and seen to it that she had rest and comfort to protect the baby.

The Turkish police were not so considerate. Sarah was dragged from her cottage in the middle of the night, locked in a covered van, and driven over a bumpy, muddy road to the black basalt rock police station in Tiberias.

She was grilled without respite for twenty-four solid hours.

Where is your husband? ... how did he make his escape? ... how are you communicating with him? ... you are smuggling out information and we know it ... you are spying for the British. Come now, your husband wrote these papers on behalf of the British, you cannot deny it ... what Jews in Palestine do you contact? ...

Sarah answered the questions directly and without being ruffled. She admitted that Barak had fled because of his British sympathies, for it was no secret. She insisted she had remained only to deliver her child. She made no further admissions to their charges. At the end of twenty-four hours Sarah Ben Canaan was the calmest person in the inspector's office.

They began to make threats, and still Sarah remained calm and direct. At last she was grabbed and pulled into a forbidding-looking room with thick basalt walls and no windows. One small light burned over a wooden table. She was stretched out on her back, pinned down by five policemen, and her shoes were removed. The bottoms of her feet were lashed with thick branches. As they beat the soles of her feet they repeated the questions. Her answers were the same.

Spy! How do you get information out to Barak Ben Canaan? Speak! You are in touch with other British agents ... who are they?

The pain was excruciating. Sarah stopped speaking altogether. She clenched her teeth and the sweat poured from her. Her courage fed the Turks' anger. The whip ripped open the soles of her feet and blood spurted out.

'Speak!' they screamed. 'Speak!'

She quivered and writhed in agony ...

'Jew! Spy!'

At last she fell unconscious.

A bucket of water was thrown at her face. The beating and the questioning continued. She passed out again and they revived her again. Now they held her arms apart and place red hot stones in her armpits.

'Speak! Speak! Speak!'

For three days and three nights the Turks tortured Sarah Ben Canaan. Even the Turks were awed by the woman's endurance. At last they let her go as a token to her courage, for they had never seen anyone endure pain with such dignity. Ruth, who had been waiting and pleading in the station anteroom, carried Sarah back to Shoshanna on a donkey cart.

With the first labor pains she allowed herself the luxury of screaming in anguish. She shrieked for all the times the Turks could not make her cry. Her battered body rebelled convulsively.

Her cries grew dimmer and weaker. No one believed she was going to live through it.

A son was born and Sarah Ben Canaan lived.

She hung between life and death for weeks. Ruth and the farmers of Shoshanna lavished every affection and care upon her. The remarkable courage that had kept the little black-eyed Silesian alive under Turkish torture and the pain of childbirth kept her alive now. Her will to see Barak again was so strong that death could not intervene.

It took over a year for her to mend. Her recovery was slow and filled with pain. It was months before she was able to stand and walk on her battered feet. There was a limp that would never go away.

The child was strong and healthy. Everyone said he would grow up to be another Barak, for already he was lean and tall, although he had Sarah's dark features. With the torment over, Sarah and Ruth awaited their men.

From Cairo to Gallipoli to England to America the brothers wandered. Each day they were tormented with fear for the lives of Sarah and Ruth. They were aghast at the tales being brought from Palestinian refugees of the terror of Jemal Pasha.

Early in 1917 the British Army swept out of Egypt and pushed the Turks back over the Sinai Peninsula to the doorstep of Palestine. At Gaza they were stopped cold. General Allenby then took command of the British forces and under him the British renewed the offensive. By the end of 1917 they had slashed into Palestine and captured Beersheba. On the heels of this victory the ancient gates of Gaza were stormed and Gaza fell. The British knifed up the coast to capture Jaffa.

With Allenby's successful campaign, the long-overdue, much heralded, very costly, and highly overrated Arab revolt began. Faisal, son of the sherif of Mecca, brought in a few tribes from the desert when it was obvious that the Turks were losing. With the Ottomans on their backs, the Arabs dropped their cloak of neutrality so that they could share in the coming spoils. Faisal's 'rebels' made a good deal of noise and hacked up an unguarded rail line but never put it out of commission. Never once did Arab 'rebels' engage in a major or minor battle.

At the ancient city of Megiddo the forces of Allenby and those of the Turks set for a battle. Here was the testing ground for a hundred conquering armies over five thousand years – Megiddo, where the stables of Solomon were to be found and where it was said that the second coming of Christ would take place. Megiddo commanded a ravine to the north which was a natural passageway. It had been the route of conquest since man had begun to record time.

Megiddo fell to Allenby!

By Christmas, less than a year after Allenby assumed command, he led his British forces into liberated Jerusalem!

The British rolled on to Damascus until the Turks were scattered and driven to oblivion. The fall of Damascus was the death knell of the Ottomans.

The Czar of Russia, who had wanted so badly to start a war with the Turks, never lived to realize his dream of a Russian Constantinople. The Russian people rebelled against centuries of suppression, and he and his entire family were shot by a firing squad.

Although his empire was completely crushed and stolen and he had lost his position as the 'Shadow of God' to a billion Moslems, Mohammed V was enjoying life in his harem as the war ended.

Barak Ben Canaan and his brother Akiva came home. The roses were in bloom and the land was alive and green and the waters of the Jordan plunged into the Sea of Galilee as they entered the gates of Shoshanna.

There was white in the great red beard of Barak and there was white in the black hair of Sarah as they stood before each other at the door to her cottage. He held her in his arms very softly, and in that moment all the hardships of the past few years faded away. His little Sarah took him by the hand. She limped slightly as she led him into the cottage. A scrappy, strapping, bright-eyed three-year-old boy looked up at him curiously.

Barak knelt before the boy and held him up in his powerful hands.

'My son,' Barak whispered, 'my son.'

'Your son . . . Ari,' she said.

Chapter Twelve

The Balfour Declaration was ratified by fifty nations.

During World War I the Yishuv population had been cut in half by the Turkish terror. In the wake of the war a new rash of pogroms broke out in eastern Europe.

The times that followed were exciting and vital for the Yishuv. The Third Aliyah was pouring in to escape persecution and filling the decimated ranks of the Yishuv.

For years the Zion Settlement Society had had its eye on the Jezreel Valley which made up the entire southern Galilee. It was mostly swampland with but a few poverty-stricken Arab villages. Most of the Jezreel belonged to a single effendi family, the Sursuks, who lived in Beirut. The Turks would not permit the Jews to buy into the Jezreel, but with the coming of the British and the lifting of land restrictions Barak Ben Canaan and two other land buyers traveled to Beirut and purchased an area from Haifa to Nazareth. The great Jezreel purchase was the first land deal of such magnitude in Palestine and the first one backed entirely by the funds of world Jewry. The Jezreel opened great opportunities for the establishment of more *kibbutizm*.

Old-time *kibbutzniks* unselfishly left their farms to help found new *kibbutzim*. Akiva and Ruth, and their newborn daughter Sharona, left the relative comfort of their beloved Shoshanna to help build a new *kibbutz* just north of Rosh Pinna. The settlement was named Ein Or, the Fountain of Light.

At last the Jews shared part of Barak Ben Canaan's dream. Land was purchased deep in the Huleh Valley near the Syrian and Lebanese borders. They even farmed at his hill and built a *kibbutz*, the village of Giladi, close by Barak's old friend and comrade, Joseph Trumpledor, went up to Kfar Giladi to handle security.

Along with the growth of farming, Tel Aviv and the other cities grew. Jews began buying homes in Haifa above the city on Mount Carmel. In Jerusalem there was building beyond the old Walled City as the needs of the Yishuv called for larger headquarters and the religious elements joined with the Zionists in the spirit of redemption.

The British administration made many reforms. Roads were built. Schools and hospitals were erected. Justice came to the courts. Balfour himself traveled to Jerusalem and on Mount Scopus lay the cornerstone of a new Hebrew university.

To govern the Yishuv, the Jews elected a representative body. The Yishuv Central was a quasi-government to speak for the Jews, deal with the Arabs and British, and serve as a link to the Zion Settlement Society and to the world's Zionists. The Yishuv Central and the Zion Settlement Society both moved to the new headquarters in Jerusalem.

Barak Ben Canaan, a senior respected citizen, was elected to the Yishuv Central, a position he held along with his work with the Zionists.

But there were ominous signs. Palestine was becoming the center of a gigantic power play.

The first act of this play was the publication of the secret Sykes-Picot Agreement, by which the French and the British sought to divide the Middle East between themselves. The paper was first discovered in the files of the Czar by Russian revolutionaries and published to embarrass the British and French.

The Sykes-Picot Agreement directly contradicted earlier British promises to grant independence to the Arabs. The Arabs felt betrayed. Despite British efforts to soothe the situation, Arab fears proved justifed later when, at the San Remo Conference, England and France cut the Middle East pie and England grabbed for herself the lion's share. France snatched the Syrian province and a pipeline from the oil-rich Mosul fields.

Under Ottoman rule the Syrian province had also included Palestine and Lebanon. France felt she was entitled to northern Palestine. The British were adamant. They too wanted a terminal from the Mosul oil fields at Haifa, and they argued that because of the Balfour Declaration and the unique position of Palestine as a promised Jewish homeland it should stay under British rule.

As a result, the French hired several tribes of Syrian Arabs to stir up trouble in Palestine and grab up as much of northern Palestine as possible until fixed boundaries were set.

Those Jews who had ventured into the Huleh to Kfar Giladi were caught in the trap. The French-hired Arabs, in an effort to dislodge them in order to fortify French border claims, attacked Tel Hai, the very hill that Barak and Akiva had crossed to come into Palestine.

Joseph Trumpledor, the legendary Jewish soldier of fortune, made a valiant stand at Tel Hai. He himself was killed but Tel Hai held and the Jews remained at Kfar Giladi and the Huleh Valley remained within the British mandate.

The next of France's troubles came from Faisal, son of the sherif of Mecca and leader of the alleged Arab revolt in World War I. Faisal arrived in Damascus, sat himself down, and declared himself king of a new greater Arab state and the new head of the Moslems. The French chased him out of Syria. Faisal moved on to Bagdad where the British accorded him better treatment. They rewarded their faithful servant by creating a new state out of the

Mesopotamian Province. They called the country Iraq and proclaimed Faisal king.

Faisal had a brother named Abdullah who had to be rewarded too. The British, without authorization from the League of Nations, formed another 'country' from part of the Palestine mandate and named Abdullah its king. This country they called Trans-Jordan.

Both Faisal and Abdullah were arch enemies of Ibn Saud, who had refused to help the British in World War I.

So – the British fared well. They had their puppets in Iraq and Trans-Jordan – two creations. They had Egypt, the Suez Canal, the Mosul oil fields, and the Palestine mandate. In addition they had a dozen 'protectorates' and sheikdoms around the Arabian Peninsula.

The British knew about Arab hate feuds and employed the proved method of 'divide and rule.' Their Arab puppets were kept happy with the latest automobiles and with well-stocked harems.

Palestine was a different problem. It could not be governed by British puppets. The Balfour Declaration had been ratified by the entire world. The articles of mandate further bound the British to create a Jewish homeland. Further, the Jews had presented them with a democratically elected quasi-government, the Yishuv Central, the only democratic body in the entire Middle East.

Barak Ben Canaan, Dr Chaim Weizmann, and a dozen other Zionist leaders entered into a historic negotiation with Faisal, then leader of the Arab world. A mutual friendship pact was signed between Jews and Arabs in which each agreed to respect the aspirations of the other. The Arabs welcomed the return of the Jews and appreciated their historic rights to Palestine and their humanitarian rights to a homeland. Further, the Arabs stated openly that they welcomed the culture and the 'Hebrew gold' the Jews were bringing in. Further, the Arabs in many quarters had proclaimed the Jews as redeemers.

In Palestine as elsewhere in the Arab world, there was no representative Arab government. When the British asked the Arabs to present their government, the usual inner-Arab squabble ensued. The various alliances of effendi families spoke for a small percentage of Arabs.

The most powerful effendi family was the El Husseini clan which owned land in the Jerusalem area. They were so feared by the other effendis that a power block was formed against them that made impossible any form of Arab representation.

The leader of the dreaded El Husseinis was the most vile, underhanded schemer in a part of the world known for vile, underhanded schemers. His name was Haj Amin el Husseini. Haj Amin had once fought on the side of the Turks. Now he saw the demise of the Ottoman Empire as a chance to gain power, just as a dozen Arab leaders in a dozen parts of the Arab world saw it. El Husseini was backed by a clan of devils.

Haj Amin's first move was to grab Palestine. He saw his opening through the position of Mufti of Jerusalem. Jerusalem was second only to Mecca and Medina as a holy Moslem city. Under Ottoman rule the job of Mufti was mostly honorary. Constantinople as head of Islam was the true ruler of all Moslems. With the Ottomans gone and a Christian power ruling Palestine the position of Mufti suddenly became important. Enormous funds poured in from Moslems all over the world for the retention of holy places. Once these funds had been administered by Constantinople but now they would be at the discretion of the Mufti. If Haj Amin could seize the position he could use this money to further his own aspirations. There was another reason why he wanted to be Mufti. The Palestinian fellaheen were ninety-nine percent illiterate. The only means of mass communication was the pulpit. The tendency of the fellaheen to become hysterical at the slightest provocation might become a political weapon.

One thing stood in the way of Haj Amin's desire to become Mufti of Jerusalem. Moslem law declared the position could be held only by someone in the direct blood line of Mohammed. Haj Amin dodged this requirement by marrying a girl in the Mohammed line and holding this as valid enough fulfillment of the prerequisite.

When the old Mufti died, an election was held for the position. The effendis knew of Haj Amin's ambitions and he came in fourth. This did not disturb him, for the El Husseini clan was busy terrorizing the three men who had drawn more votes and 'persuaded' them to withdraw from office.

Haj Amin el Husseini became Mufti of Jerusalem by default.

He saw the return of the Jews as the greatest block to his plans.

On the Moslem holy day which celebrated the birth of Moses, Haj Amin el Husseini whipped up a mob of fellaheen with hatred for the Jews. The mob became hysterical and a pogrom was on!

They did not become so hysterical as to turn their wrath on the cities and *kibbutzim* where the Jews were able to defend themselves. Instead they slaughtered pious old defenseless Jews in the holy cities of Safed, Tiberias, Hebron, and Jerusalem.

Ruth was in Tiberias on her way back to Ein Or from a visit to Shoshanna when the rioting broke out. She and her daughter Sharona were caught and murdered.

Akiva was inconsolable. No one had ever seen a man with such grief. Barak rushed up to Ein Or and took his brother home to Tel Aviv; and as he had done as a boy, he maintained a day-and-night watch. It was months before Akiva came out of his grief. But it left a scar so ugly and deep within him it would never heal.

Many of the settlements had given up their arms to the British when they took over the mandate. Had the Arabs chosen to attack these settlements there would have been a slaughter. The British were responsible for maintaining order and the Yishuv waited for them to bring the Arabs under control and lead the culprits to justice. Such a thing would not have happened under the Turks, for as corrupt as they were they would not tolerate murder.

A commission of inquiry found Haj Amin el Husseini at fault. He was pardoned!

Immediately after the pardon the British Colonial Office issued a White Paper, or declaration of policy, limiting Jewish immigration to 'economic absorption.' It was then that Winston Churchill became instrumental in taking over half the mandate and creating Trans-Jordan from it. For the Yishuv it was the end of an era.

The bubble of British benevolence burst. The Yishuv Central and the Zion Settlement Society called a secret meeting in Tel Aviv which fifty of the leading members of the Yishuv attended.

Dr Chaim Weizmann flew in from London to attend. Barak was there and Akiva, still in a state of bereavement, was there. Itzak Ben Zvi was there. A stocky, short, bushy-browed young leader in the Second Aliyah named David

Ben Gurion was there. Many felt that this fiery, Bible-quoting Zionist was destined to lead the Yishuv.

Avidan, a bald, block-like man of the Third Aliyah, was there. Avidan had come to Palestine after a momentous war record in the Russian Army. He was second in reputation as a fighter only to the martyr Trumpledor, and it was said he was destined to lead Jewish defense.

The meeting was called to order by Barak Ben Canaan. The cellar room was grim and tense as he spoke. A great crisis had fallen. Barak recalled the personal misfortune that all of them had suffered for being born Jews. Now, in the one place they sought freedom from persecution, a pogrom had occurred.

Dr Chaim Weizmann led a group that argued that the British were the recognized authority and had to be dealt with legally and openly. Defense was a British responsibility.

Another group, ultra-pacifists, felt it would only invite trouble from the Arabs to arm the Jews.

At the other extreme, there were the activists led by Akiva, who demanded nothing less than swift and ruthless retribution. They argued that British protection and well meaning was an illusion; the British acted only in self-interest. Haggling, guilt documents, and the like would never take the place of a gun in an Arab's mind.

The debate raged far into the night, never exhausting that endless capacity of Jews to argue. The British were damned and the British were praised. The pacifists begged caution while the activists called Palestine the 'Twice Promised Land' – once to the Jews and once to the Arabs.

Between the two extremes in thinking, Ben Gurion, Ben Canaan, Avidan, and many of the others suggested a realistic middle course. While they recognized need to arm themselves, they wanted to further the Jewish position by legal means.

These men, on behalf of the Yishuv, decided to arm themselves quietly and train a militia in secret. This armed force would be used for one purpose and one purpose alone – defense. While this force existed, the official agencies of the Yishuv were to disclaim all knowledge of it publicly and privately co-operate with its growth. With this silent arm, the Jews would have an unseen partner in restraining the Arabs and in negotiating with the British.

Avidan, the fighter, was voted to head this new secret organization.

They called it Haganah, the Army of Self-Defense.

Chapter Thirteen

The Third Aliyah penetrated the newly purchased Jezreel, the Sharon Valley, and Samaria and into the hills of Judea and the Galilee and even south toward the desert, and called the earth back from its long-naked slumber. They brought in heavy machinery and introduced intensive agriculture through crop rotation and fertilization and irrigation. In addition to the grape, citrus, and olive export crops they raised grain and vegetables, and fruits and flax and poultry and dairy herds.

They experimented with anything and everything to find new crops and increase the yield of the old ones.

They penetrated to the Dead Sea. They went after alkaline land which had not produced a living thing for forty thousand years and they brought it back and made it produce.

They dug fishponds and farmed fish as a crop.

By the mid-1920s over fifty thousand Jews in a hundred colonies worked better than a half million *dunams* of redeemed land. Most of them wore the blue of the *kibbutz*.

A million trees were planted. In ten – twenty – thirty years the trees would fight off soil erosion. Tree planting became an obsession of the Yishuv. They left a trail of budding forests behind them wherever they went.

Many of the new *kibbutzim* and other settlements adopted the name of the Biblical site they occupied. Many new names sprang up over the ancient land and they had the sound of music. Ben Shemen, Son of Oil; and Dagania, the Cornflower on the Sea of Galilee; and Ein Ganim, the Fountain of the Gardens; and Kfar Yehezkiel, the Village of the Prophet Ezekiel; and Merhavia, which means the Wide Spaces of God; and Tel Yosef, the Hill of Joseph. There was Ayelet Hashahar, the Morning Star, which stood at the entrance to Barak's beloved Huleh Valley. There was Gesher, the Bridge; and Givat Hashlosha, the Hill of the Three; and there were more and more being built every month.

The *kibbutz* movement, that unique child of necessity, became the key to all settlement. The *kibbutzim* could absorb vast numbers of new arrivals.

Yet not everyone could adapt to life on a *kibbutz*. Many women who fought for the independence didn't like it once they had it. Others objected to the lack of privacy and others to the children's houses. Although the entire Yishuv subscribed to the idea of national land and the conquest of self-labor, the main reason some could not stand *kibbutz* life was the lack of personal identification with a piece of land one could call one's own. A splinter group broke off from the *kibbutz* movement. It was called the *moshav* movement. In a *moshav* each man had his own piece of land to work and his own house instead of the communal arrangement. As on the *kibbutz* all the civic functions were centrally run and all the heavy machinery were owned by the entire *moshav*. Certain base crops were farmed by the entire community and there was a central agency which did all the marketing and purchasing.

The main difference was the measure of individual freedom and the fact that a man's family was in his own house and he ran his own farm in the way he saw fit. The first *moshav* was in the Jezreel Valley and was named after its Biblical site, Nahalal, the Heritage. The Nahalal pioneers faced the toughest swamp and did a miraculous job of redemption.

The drawback of the *moshav* movement in the over-all scheme was the working for personal profit and the inability of the *moshav* to absorb the numbers of new arrivals the *kibbutz* could; but both movements flourished and grew.

As the Yishuv grew, so did the complexities of the community. Barak Ben Canaan, a respected elder citizen, was never at rest. Zionism had a bulky machinery and there were a dozen different political philosophies inside the Yishuv. The dealings with the Arabs became more delicate after the riots and the dealings with the British became more confusing after their sudden departure from the Balfour Declaration and the articles of mandate. Barak's wise council was sought in every quarter. Although there were no more outbreaks against the Jews, the atmosphere was one of uneasy calm. Every day there was a new story of an ambush, a sniping, or a theft. The tirades from the Moslem pulpit never ended. There was always tension in the air, for the sinister Mufti, Haj Amin el Husseini, lurked in the shadows.

One day in 1924 Barak returned to Tel Aviv after a particularly difficult week at the Yishuv Central in Jerusalem. He was always happy to come home to his three-room flat on Hayarkon Street overlooking the Mediterranean. This time he was delighted and surprised to see his old friend, Kammal, the muktar of Abu Yesha, awaiting him.

'For many years I have been meditating to try to solve the perplexing riddle of how to help my people. It grieves me to say this but there are no greater exploiters than the Arab effendis. They do not want things better for the fellaheen ... it may endanger their own pleasures.'

Barak listened intently. This was a tremendous confession on the part of an Arab and one so enlightened as Kammal.

'I have watched the Jews come back and perform miracles on the land. We have nothing in common in religion or language or outlook. I am not even sure the Jews will not eventually take all the land. Yet ... the Jews are the only salvation for the Arab people. The Jews are the only ones in a thousand years who have brought light to this part of the world.'

'I know this is difficult for you to say, Kammal...'

'Let me continue, please. If we can live side by side in peace although our worlds are far apart then we must eventually prosper from what you have done. I see no other way for the Arab people, Barak, and I don't know if it is right or wrong.'

'We have never given you reason to doubt our sincerity in wanting peace...'

'Yes... but there are powers greater than you and I who could bring us into conflict against our will.'

How true ... how very true, Barak thought.

'Barak, I am going to sell the Zion Settlement Society that land by the Huleh Lake you have always wanted.'

Barak's heart began to beat fast.

'It is not merely benevolence. I have conditions. You must allow the Arabs of Abu Yesha to learn your farming and sanitation methods. This can only be done slowly over a period of time. I want a portion of the village's more deserving boys to be able to attend your school to learn to read and write.'

'That will all be done,' Barak said.

'There is one more condition.'

'And what is that?'

'You must come too.'

Barak rose and rubbed his great beard. 'Me? Why me?'

'As long as you are there I know the conditions will be kept and that we will be able to live in peace. I have trusted you from the first day you entered Abu Yesha as a boy over thirty years ago.'

'I will think it over,' Barak said.

'And what will you tell Kammal?' Sarah asked.

Barak shrugged. 'What is there to say? We can't go, of course. What a shame. For years I have been trying to get him to sell that land. Now if I don't go up there we will never get it.'

'It is a pity,' Sarah agreed and poured some tea.

Barak paced the floor unhappily. 'After all, Sarah,' he mumbled, 'we must face facts. I am needed at the Yishuv Central and the Settlement Society. It isn't as if I was running a candy store on Allenby Road.'

'Of course not, dear,' Sarah said sympathetically. 'You are vital in your work. The entire Yishuv needs you.'

'Yes,' he said, pacing again, 'and we aren't children any longer. I am past fifty and the land is going to be very very hard to redeem.'

'You are right, Barak. We are too old to pioneer. You have done your share in building this country.'

'Right! I'll turn Kammal down.'

He sank into a chair and sighed deeply. He had not succeeded in convincing himself. Sarah stood over him and smiled. 'You are mocking me, woman,' he said softly. 'What's the use?'

She sat on his lap and was almost lost in his greatness. His huge hands were amazingly gentle as they stroked her hair.

'I was thinking of you and Ari. It will be brutal work and the hardships will be great.'

'Shhhh ... drink your tea.'

Barak resigned his position with the Zion Settlement Society, sold his apartment in Tel Aviv, and led twenty-five pioneer families out to the Huleh swamplands to build a *moshav*. They called it Yad El, the Hand of God.

They pitched tents below the fields of Abu Yesha and mapped out their task. No pioneers yet had faced a job so difficult. The Huleh swamp was deep, and full of forbidding tangles of thickly matted unyielding brush and papyrus which towered to heights of fifteen feet. The muck was alive with poisonous snakes, scorpions, and rats and a hundred other creatures. Wild boars and wolves lurked near the isolated base camp. Everything had to be brought in on muleback, including drinking and washing water.

Sarah was in charge of the base camp, the hospital tent, and the kitchen. Barak headed the work gangs which took to the swamps daily with shovels and picks.

In that first scorching summer they worked day after day, week after week, and month after month in hundred-degree heat, in waist- and neck-high water, slogging away the muck to start drainage channels. With machetes they hacked at the jungle growth until they couldn't raise their arms. The women worked right in the swamps along with the men. Young Ari Ben Canaan, ten years of age, one of the three children in the settlement, ran off the pails of sludge and ran in drinking water and food to the workers. The workdays were seven each week. The work hours were sunrise to sunset. Still each night they found the energy to sing a few sons of the fields and dance a *hora* before their six or seven hours of sleep.

At night there was the usual guard against robbers and animals.

It was a race to get the channels in before the winter rains. If the water didn't drain off, the summer's work would be wasted. Hundreds of Australian eucalyptus trees were put in to suck up water. Every *kibbutz* and *moshav* in the area sent over as many workers as they could spare each day to help the pioneers.

At night, by candlelight, Sarah and Barak took turns schooling Ari and the other two children.

The winter downpours came and all but swept the base camp into the swamp. After each downpour they rushed to the channels to keep the slush from blocking the runoff.

Even a man so strong and resolute as Barak Ben Canaan was beginning to wonder if they hadn't attempted too much this time. Each time he looked at Ari and Sarah his heart bled. They were always covered with bug bites or suffering from dysentery or hunger or thirst.

And worse was the ravaging malaria. In that first summer and winter Sarah had five attacks and Ari four. The chills and fevers and deliriums all but killed them. Ari, like Sarah, took his pain in silence.

The swamp broke many of the families. Half the original group quit to return to the city to find an easier way.

And soon – Yad El had a graveyard. Two members died of malaria.

Yad El: the Hand of God. It may have been the hand of God that led them there but it was going to be the hands of men that licked the swamp.

For three solid years they beat back the swamp!

At last there was enough land to make twenty-five farms of two hundred *dunams* each. There was no time to gloat, for there were crops to be planted and homes to be built.

Young Ari Ben Canaan had shaken off the effects of malaria and the other illnesses and had become as sturdy as a rock. At the age of fourteen he could do a man's day's work.

When they moved into their cottage and the fields had been plowed and planted Barak was given a reward for his years of toil. Sarah told him she was pregnant again.

At the end of the fourth year two momentous things happened to Barak Ben Canaan. Sarah presented him with a baby daughter who had flaming red hair like his own. The second occasion was the harvest of the first crop at Yad El.

At last the weary pioneers stopped their labor and took time to celebrate. What a celebration it was! *Kibbutzniks* and *moshavniks* from all over the area who had lent a hand at Yad El came to join in the celebration. Arabs from Abu Yesha came. There was gaiety for a week, each night ending at dawn as weary *hora* dancers collapsed with joy. Everyone came to look at Barak's and Sarah's new daughter. She was named Jordana after the river which flowed past the edge of Yad El.

As the celebration continued. Barak took his son Ari and saddled two horses and they rode up to Tel Hai to that place where he had crossed into the Promised Land from Lebanon forty years before. Tel Hai, the death place of Joseph Trumpledor, was a shrine of the Yishuv. Barak looked down from the hill to Yad El as he had sworn he would long ago.

'I took your mother up here before we were married,' he said to Ari. He put his arm around his son's shoulder. 'Someday there will be two dozen settlements in this valley and it will be green all the year around.'

'Look how beautiful Yad El is from here, Father.'

The irrigation sprinklers were whirling and a school was under construction. They could see an enormous shed where the community had put a dozen pieces of heavy machinery. There were paths of rose bushes and flowers and lawns and trees.

There was sadness, too, for the Yad El cemetery had already claimed five members.

As Kammal had hoped, the establishment of Yad El had a tremendous effect upon the Arabs of Abu Yesha. The creation of the *moshav* was in itself a startling revelation. Barak was true to his agreement and set up special schools for the Arabs to teach them sanitation, the use of heavy machinery, and new farming methods. Their school was open to an Arab youngster of Abu Yesha who would attend. The Yad El doctor and nurse were always at the call of the Arabs.

Kammal's favorite son was a youngster named Taha who was a few years younger than Ari. From the time of his birth Kammal had ingrained into Taha his own great desire to better the conditions of the fellaheen. As the coming muktar of Abu Yesha, Taha spent more time at Yad El than in his own village. He was the personal ward of the Ben Canaan family. Taha and Ari became close friends.

While Yad El and Abu Yesha lived in peace and proved Arab and Jew could exist side by side despite their cultural differences a slow mantle of fear was falling over many of the other effendi families in Palestine. They were becoming frightened at the spirit and progress of the Third Aliyah.

In the beginning the effendis had sold the Jews worthless swamps and rock-filled and eroded hills, eager to get their hands on Jewish gold and certain the land would continue its dormancy. The Jews turned around and performed miracles of redemption. Not only had the farms grown, but cities were springing up all over Palestine.

The example of the Jews could be disastrous. What if the fellaheen began demanding education, sanitation, and medical facilities? What if the fellaheen, God forbid, were to take a fancy to the way the Jews governed themselves by equal votes of both men – and women! It could well wreck the perfect feudal system of the effendis!

To counter the progress of the Jews, the effendis harped on the ignorance, fears, and religious fanaticism of the fellaheen. They pounded the theme that the Jews were invaders from the West out to steal their fellaheen's lands – even though the effendis had themselves sold this land. They maintained tension so that the fellaheen would not come into too close contact with the new ideas.

After many years without a major incident Haj Amin el Husseini moved again. This time he concocted a cold-blooded fraud aimed at driving the Arabs wild. The year was 1929.

The site of the Dome of the Rock or the Mosque of Omar in Jerusalem was worshipped as holy ground by the Moslems as the point where their prophet Mohammed ascended to heaven. On this very site stood the one remaining wall of the Great Jewish Temple which had been destroyed for a second time in A.D. 76 by the Romans. This wall of the Temple was the holiest of all Jewish holy places. Pious Jews gathered before the wall to pray and to weep for the past glory of Israel. From their tears it became known as the 'Wailing Wall.'

The Mufti circulated faked pictures showing Jews at the Wailing Wall preparing to 'desecrate' the Arab holy place of the Dome of the Rock. The fanatic Moslem fellaheen started another outbreak supported by effendi and Husseini Jew baitings. Again the riots hit the defenseless old Jews of the holy cities. The slaughter was far greater than the Mufti-inspired riots of a decade before. The rioting spread against some of the weaker settlements and on to the roads, and casualties mounted into the thousands on both sides. The British again appeared helpless to stop the slaughter.

They sent a commission of inquiry. The commission squarely placed the blame on Arab shoulders. Then, by great paradox, they completely ignored the Balfour Declaration and the articles of the mandate and suggested that Jewish land buying and immigration be restricted to 'soothe Arab fears.'

Chapter Fourteen

In the same year as the riots, 1929, the farmers of Yad El made an agreement with the grain miller of the Arab village of Aata, some ten kilometers away.

Barak gave Ari the job of going to Aata to have their grain milled. Sarah objected to sending a fourteen-year-old boy out on the roads alone with the tension of the riots all around. Barak was adamant on the subject. 'Neither Ari nor Jordana is going to live in fear like ghetto Jews.'

Ari felt very proud of the trust as he jumped onto the seat of the donkey cart. It was loaded with a dozen bags of grain. He set out down the road for Aata.

He was spotted the instant he entered the village by a dozen Arab boys who were lying around near the coffeehouse. They waited till he turned the corner, then trailed him to the miller's.

Ari went about his business, flushed with his own importance. He carried on his transactions in perfect Arabic, which he had learned from his good friend Taha. The grain was crushed to flour. Ari watched closely to make certain that the sacks were filled full and with the same grain, not inferior Arab wheat. The miller, hoping to gain a sack on the deal, was perplexed by the youngster's sharpness. Ari headed back toward Yad El.

The Arab boys who had been waiting quickly made a deal with the miller to steal all Ari's wheat and sell it to him. The boys scampered out of Aata by a short cut and set up an ambush and road block.

In a few moments Ari rode along the road right into the trap. They sprang out from cover, hurling stones at him. Ari whipped the donkey but moved only a few feet before the road block stopped him. He was stoned from the cart and knocked half senseless to the ground. Four of the attackers pounced on him and pinned him down while the others pulled the grain from the cart and made off with it.

The boy returned to Yad El late that night.

Sarah opened the door, took one look at his blood-streaked face and torn clothing, and screamed. He stood there wordless for a moment, then clenched his teeth and pushed past his mother and went into his room and locked the door.

He refused to open it despite her pleas until Barak returned home later from a *moshav* meeting.

He stood before his father. 'I let you down ... I lost the wheat,' he said through puffed and distorted lips.

'It is I who have let you down, son,' Barak said.

Sarah rushed over to Ari and threw her arms around him. 'Never, never, never send this boy out alone...' She led him off to clean him up. Barak did not answer.

The next morning after breakfast, before Barak headed for the fields, he took Ari by the hand and led him out to the barn. 'I have neglected some of your education,' Barak said, and pulled down his old bull whip from a peg.

Barak built a dummy and nailed it to the fence. He showed Ari how to judge distance, aim, and swing. With the sound of the first crack Sarah came running from the house with Jordana in her arms.

'Have you gone mad teaching a boy like that to use a bull whip?'

'Shut up, woman!' Barak roared in a tone she had never heard in over twenty years of marriage. 'The son of Barak Ben Canaan is a free man! He shall never be a ghetto Jew. Now get out of here ... we have business.'

From morning to night Ari practiced using the bull whip. He cut the dummy to shreds. He aimed at rocks and tins and bottles until he could whirl around and split them with a flick of the wrist. He threw the whip so often that by the end of each day he could barely lift his arm.

At the end of two weeks, Barak loaded up the donkey cart with another dozen bags of grain. He put his arm around his son's shoulder and led him to the cart and handed him the bull whip. 'Take the grain to Aata and have it milled.'

'Yes, Father,' Ari said softly.

'Remember one thing, son. You hold in your hand a weapon of justice. Never use it in anger or revenge. Only in defense.'

Ari jumped onto the cart and started for the gate of Yad El toward the main road. Sarah went into her bedroom and wept softly as she watched her son disappear down the road.

Barak did something he had not done for many, many years. He sat down and read the Bible.

The Arab ambush struck again when Ari was a mile outside Aata on his way back to Yad El. This time Ari's eyes were sharp and his body alerted for danger. Remembering his father's words, he remained cold, calm. As the first rocks flew at him he leaped from the cart, spotted the Arab leader, and with a lightning flick sent the mighty bull whip whistling through the air and wrapped it around the boy's neck and flung him to the ground. Then Ari unwrapped the whip and brought down a lash that snapped so sharply it tore his foe's flesh apart. It was all over that quickly.

Barak Ben Canaan's face paled as the sun began to set and Ari had still not come back. He stood trembling by the gate of Yad El. Then he saw the donkey cart coming down the road and his face broke into a large smile. Ari stopped for his father.

'Well, Ari. How was your trip?'

'Fine.'

'I'll unload the flour. You had better go right in and see your mother. She was worried for some reason or the other.'

By 1930 the riots had died down. Abu Yesha and Yad El stayed out of trouble altogether. The majority of villages out of the Mufti's sphere of influence did not participate in the disturbances.

Ari Ben Canaan was not only built like his father but acted very like him too. He was deep within himself and he had Barak's quiet, stubborn ways. He saw the value of learning about his Arab neighbors. Taha was always one of his closest friends and he treated all other Arabs with understanding and compassion.

Ari fell in love with a girl named Dafna whose family had a farm half a mile away. No one was quite sure when it had happened but everyone was quite sure that Ari and Dafna would marry someday, for they had eyes only for each other.

Little redheaded Jordana was a spirited and rebellious girl. In many ways Jordana typified the children being born to the settlers of Palestine. Their parents who had lived in ghettos and had known the fear and degradation of being Jews were determined to purge this horror from the new generation. They bent over backward to give the children freedom and to make them strong.

At the age of fifteen Ari was a member of Haganah, the secret Army of Self-Defense. At the age of thirteen, Dafna could handle half a dozen weapons. For if this was a new generation and a new type of Jew it was also a generation born with a mission even greater than the missions of the Second and Third Aliyah.

The Haganah had grown strong enough to be a restraining force on the Mufti-inspired disturbances, but they were unable to erase the cause of these riots – only the British could do that.

Again British commissions of inquiry came and again the Arabs were whitewashed.

British timidity caused the Mufti to grow bolder.

Shortly after the riots abated, Haj Amin el Husseini called a conference of Moslem leaders to Jerusalem. They arrived from all over the world. He formed a federation, with himself as head, and advertised his fight to save Islam from the British and Jews.

The early friendships, the fact that the Jews had raised the standard of living of the entire Arab community, and the fact that Palestine had lain neglected and unwanted for a thousand years in fruitless despair until the Jews rebuilt it was all forgotten in the face of the Mufti's tirades. The destruction of the Jewish homeland was made a 'holy' mission of Pan-Arabism.

The British were subjected to the next tirade. They had lied about granting independence to the Arabs. They supported the Jews against Arabs. And as the Arab demagogues ranted and raged the British took it all in silence.

In the year of 1933 another great calamity befell the Jews as Adolf Hitler and the Nazis ascended to power. Hitler moved first against the Jewish 'professional' people. The wiser ones among them left Germany immediately and many sought sanctuary in Palestine.

Once again the need for a national home and for Zionism were confirmed. Jew baiting could flare up in any part of the world at any time. Herzl had known it and every Jew knew it.

The German Jews who fled Hitler were different from the ghetto and eastern European Jews. They were not devout Zionists but had largely been assimilated into German society. They were not pioneers and merchants but doctors and lawyers and scientists and artisans.

In 1933 the Arab leaders called a general strike of all Arabs to protest the new Jewish immigration. There was an attempt to stir up more rioting. But both efforts failed. Most Arabs who had done business with the Jews continued to do so for they were economically dependent on one another and many communities like Yad El and Abu Yesha lived in close harmony with each other. Furthermore, the Haganah stood ready to halt a repetition of the 1929 disturbances.

The British solution to the general strike was more talk and more commissions of inquiry. In outright appeasement of the Arab threats the British this time definitely limited immigration and land selling by the Jews. At the very moment when the Yishuv needed open immigration so desperately the British forgot their promises.

The Yishuv Central through the Haganah fought back in the only way they could ... Aliyah Bet.

The Mufti maintained his pressure on the British until the British sent the Royal Navy out to stop Aliyah Bet runners and to set up a blockade of the Palestinian coast.

The strength of Haj Amin el Husseini grew every day. He found a powerful ally for himself – Adolf Hitler. For the Germans, who had their own aspirations in the Middle East, the situation was perfect. What could be more fortunate for the German propaganda machine than to be able to pump the theme that the Jews of Palestine were stealing the Arab lands just as they had tried to steal Germany. Jew hating and British imperialism – what music to the Mufti's ears! The Germans were in luck. And Haj Amin el Husseini saw at long long last the instrument for seizing control of the Arab world.

German money showed up in Cairo and Damascus. The Germans are your friends! Arab lands for Arab people! Throw out the British and their Jewish henchmen! In many high places in Cairo and Bagdad and in Syria the Arabs clasped hands with Nazis in friendship.

As the storm gathered the Yishuv still held one trump card – the Haganah! Although this secret army was officially divorced from the Yishuv Central its existence and strength was an open secret. The Jews pretended it was not there but the British knew it existed. More important, the Mufti knew it existed.

It had grown from nothing to a force of over twenty-five thousand men and women. It was almost entirely a militia with but a few dozen 'paid' full-time leaders. It had a small but deadly efficient intelligence service, which not only had the open co-operation of many British officers but could purchase Arab spies for next to nothing. Every city, village, *kibbutz*, and *moshav* had its Haganah setup. A secret code word could send a thousand men and women to hidden arms caches within minutes.

Avidan, the bald-headed square-built ex-soldier who headed Haganah, carefully built it up in a decade and a half under the noses of the British. The efficiency of the organization was terrifying; they ran a secret radio, carried on the Aliyah Bet immigration, and their intelligence network spread throughout the world where agents purchased arms to smuggle back to the Yishuv.

Arms were smuggled into Palestine in a hundred ways. Hiding them in heavy building equipment was a favorite method. The roller of a steam roller as often as not contained a hundred rifles. Every crate, piece of machinery, and even food tins and wine bottles coming into Palestine were potential munitions carriers. It was impossible for the British to halt the smuggling without inspecting every item, and many British were turning their backs at the docks to let the arms through.

The entire Yishuv was behind the arms-smuggling movement, but even so they could not bring in heavy weapons or sufficient numbers of first-class small arms. Most of what came in were old rifles and pistols discarded or outmoded in other countries. No arsenal in the world contained the conglomeration of weapons the Haganah had. Every known rifle and pistol was represented in some numbers. A thousand ingenious varieties of mortars, Sten guns, and grenades were manufactured in secret. The Haganah arsenal even included walking canes which could fire a single shot.

Once inside Palestine every desk, chair, table, icebox, bed, and sofa was a potential hiding place for weapons. Every Jewish home had at least one false-bottom drawer, hidden closet, trap door, or trick wall.

Arms were moved about inside the spare tires of buses and in market baskets and under donkey carts. The Haganah played on British 'respectability' by having the children run weapons and by using the best hiding place of all – under women's skirts.

In the building of the Haganah the *kibbutz* proved not only the answer to redemption but the answer to Jewish arms. Because of the communal character of the *kibbutz* it was the best place to train young soldiers. A dozen or two dozen could be slipped in easily among three or four hundred members and absorbed by the community. The *kibbutz* was the best place to hide the larger arms caches and the best place to manufacture small arms. It was also the best place to absorb newly arrived illegal immigrants. From the *kibbutzim* came the majority of the outstanding Haganah leaders.

The one great strength of the Haganah lay in the fact that its authority was accepted without question by the entire Yishuv. A Haganah command was a positive order. Avidan and the other Haganah leaders were very careful to use their army only in self-defense. When the 1933 general strike broke out Avidan warned that the Haganah would not try to conquer the Palestine Arabs. 'Palestine will be conquered with our sweat.' It was an army of restraint.

There were many in the Haganah who felt that it should not be held in such restraint. These were activists who demanded swift retribution.

Akiva was one of these. Officially he was a dairy farmer in the *kibbutz* of Ein Or but in reality he was a high man in the Haganah in charge of all defense in the Galilee.

The years had aged Akiva far more than his brother Barak. His face looked tired and his beard was nearly gray. He never fully recovered from the death of Ruth and Sharona. It was a bitterness he carried with him every day of his life.

He was the unofficial leader of the fringe element within the Haganah who demanded more action. As time went on and the trouble heightened, Akiva's group became very militant. Outside Palestine, splinter groups formed from the main Zionist body to support them.

When the British threw the blockade along the coast of Palestine, Akiva could stand it no longer. He called a rump session of his supporters within the Haganah. They were all angry men like himself and they reached a decision that rocked the Yishuv to its core.

In the spring of 1934 Barak received an urgent call from Avidan to come to Jerusalem.

'A terrible thing has happened, Barak,' Avidan said. 'Your brother, Akiva, has withdrawn from the Haganah and taken dozens of our top men with him.

Hundreds of rank-and-file people are beginning to follow.'

When the initial shock had passed, Barak sighed. 'He has threatened to do that for years. I have been amazed at the restraint he has shown till now. Akiva had been smoldering for decades, ever since our father was killed. He has never recovered from his wife's death.'

'You know,' Avidan said, 'that half my work in the Haganah is to hold our boys back. If we let them, they'd make war on the British tomorrow. Your feelings, my feelings, and Akiva's feelings are the same, but he can destroy us all. One reason we have been able to achieve what we have in Palestine is that despite our differences we have acted in unison in our outside dealings. The British and the Arabs have always had to negotiate as though with a single person. Now Akiva has a hot-tempered gang of activists. If they start terror tactics the entire Yishuv will have to answer for his actions.'

Barak traveled back north to Ein Or, which was not far from his own *moshav* of Yad El. Ein Or, like most of the older *kibbutzim*, had been turned into a veritable garden. As senior member and one of the founders Akiva had a separate little two-room cottage of his own which was filled with books. He even had his own radio and toilet – a rarity in *kibbutz* life. Akiva loved Ein Or as he had loved Shoshanna before it. Barak had wanted him to live with them at Yad El after the death of Ruth and his daughter but Akiva loved *kibbutz* life and remained, unheathily, with their ghosts.

Barak talked softly to his brother. Akiva had heard all the arguments before. He was nervous and restless at the prospect of a showdown with his brother.

'So, the gentlemen of Yishuv Central have sent you around to cry for them. They are becoming experts at appeasement.'

'I would have come without their invitation when I heard what an insane thing you have done,' Barak said.

Akiva paced the room again. Barak studied him. He was alive with the same angry fire he had had as a boy. 'All I am doing is something the Yishuv Central recognizes and is afraid to do. Sooner or later even they are going to have to face the facts of life. The British are our enemy.'

'We do not believe that, Akiva. All told we have done very well under British rule.'

'Then you are a fool.'

'I have been wrong before. The British represent the constituted government of Palestine.'

'While they cut our throats,' Akiva mocked. 'The gentlemen of the Yishuv Central carry their brief cases to conferences and read their little notes and findings and bow and scrape while the Mufti and his cutthroats run wild. Do you see the Arabs negotiating?'

'We will achieve our aims legally.'

'We will achieve our aims by fighting for them!'

'Then if we must fight, let us fight as a unified people. You put yourself in the category of the Mufti by starting a band of outlaws. Have you ever thought of the consequences if the British leave Palestine? No matter how bitter your feelings ... and mine ... the British are still our greatest instrument for achieving statehood.'

Akiva waved his hand in disgust. 'We will achieve statehood the same way we redeemed this land ... with our sweat and blood. I refuse to sit around and wait for British handouts.'

'For the last time, Akiva ... don't do this thing. You will only give our enemies an opportunity to point their fingers at us and increase their lies.'

'Aha!' Akiva cried. 'Now we have come to the guts of the matter! Jews must play the games by the rules. Jews cannot be wrong! Jews must beg and appeal! Jews must turn their cheeks!'

'Stop it!'

'God no!' Akiva cried. 'Whatever you do, don't fight! You wouldn't want the Germans and the Arabs and the British to think you are bad boys.'

'I said stop it.'

'Ghetto Jew Barak. That is what you are and that is what the Yishuv Central is. Well, let me tell you something else, dear brother. Here is one Jew who may be wrong but intends to live. So let us be wrong in the eyes of the whole damned world.'

Barak trembled with rage. He sat motionless to try to hide his anger. Akiva ranted on. Was Akiva really wrong? How much pain and degradation and betrayal and suffering must a man take before fighting back?

Barak got out of his chair and walked to the door.

'Tell Avidan and the gentlemen of the Yishuv Central and all the little negotiators that Akiva and the Maccabees have a message for the British and the Arabs ... "an eye for an eye and a tooth for a tooth!"'

'You are never to set foot in my house again,' Barak said.

The two brothers glared at each other for many moments. Tears welled in Akiva's eyes. 'Not set foot in your house?'

Barak was frozen.

'We are brothers, Barak. You carried me to Palestine on your back.'

'And I have lived to regret it.'

Akiva's lips trembled. 'I am a Jew who loves Palestine no less than you do. You condemn me for following the dictates of my conscience...'

Barak stepped back into the room. 'It is you, Akiva, and your Maccabees who have turned brother against brother. Since we were children I have heard your convenient quotations from the Bible. Well ... perhaps you had better read again about the Zealots who turned brother against brother and divided Jewish unity and brought on the destruction of Jerusalem by the Romans. Maccabees you call yourselves. I call you Zealots.' Barak again walked to the door.

'Remember one thing, Barak Ben Canaan,' Akiva said. 'Nothing we do, right or wrong, can ever compare to what has been done to the Jewish people. Nothing the Maccabees do can even be considered an injustice in comparison to two thousand years of murder.'

Chapter Fifteen

Yad El blossomed into a Garden of Eden. The *moshav* continued to push back the swamps so that its cultivable land was increased to bring in another hundred families. There were two dozen pieces of heavy machinery and an experimental station. The entire *moshav* worked the fishponds as a joint crop.

The streets of Yad El were green all year round and there was a blaze of colors in the spring and autumn. Yad El had a primary and secondary school, large community center with a swimming pool, library and theater, and a small hospital with two full-time doctors.

The greatest event of all occurred when electricity was brought in! The celebration throughout the Huleh Valley settlements made all other celebrations look small as the lights went on in Ein Or and Kfar Giladi and Ayelet Hashahar and Yad El simultaneously.

In the same year, the Jews of Yad El helped bring tap water to Abu Yesha, making it the first Arab village in all of Palestine to have it. Yad El extended some of the electric irrigation pumps into Abu Yesha fields to show the Arabs how to farm intensively through irrigation.

To show his gratitude, Kammal gave several *dunams* of a hillside site to the Zion Settlement Society when he learned the Jews were looking for land in the area for a youth village.

Ari Ben Canaan was the pride of his father's heart. By the age of seventeen he was six feet tall and had the strength of a lion. Besides Hebrew and English he mastered Arabic, German, French, and Yiddish, which Sarah slipped back to in moments of anger or excitement.

Ari loved farming.

He and Dafna and most of the *moshav*'s youngsters belonged to a youth group, as did most of the young people in the Yishuv. They would tramp the length and breadth of Palestine to the sites of ancient battles and tombs and cities. They climbed the mountain at Masada where the Hebrews held out against the Roman siege for over three years and they tramped through the desert over the route of Moses and the twelve tribes. They wore the traditional blue shirts and shorts and they were always filled with the songs and dances and ideals of the redemption of the homeland.

Dafna had developed into a buxom, earthy, attractive girl filled with love for the son of Barak Ben Canaan. It appeared that Ari and Dafna would marry at an early age. They would either open a new farm at Yad El or travel out with a youth group to begin a new *moshav* or *kibbutz* as was sometimes the tradition after schooling. But as the troubles mounted in Palestine, Ari and Dafna had less and less time to spend together. Ari had shown remarkable skill and leadership within the Haganah and despite his tender age was considered by Avidan one of the most promising soldiers in all of Palestine. In fact, most of the outstanding soldiers were in their late teens.

By the age of seventeen Ari had set up defenses at Yad El, Ein Or, and half a dozen *kibbutzim* and had done so well that he went into Haganah work almost full time.

When the illegal immigration war with the British began, Ari was called to duty at the sites where Aliyeh Bet ships beached. Ari worked at getting the illegal immigrants hidden in *kibbutzim* and at collecting the visas and passports of 'tourists' who had entered Palestine.

When he had a day or two free he would often phone Yad El and Dafna would hitchhike to Tel Aviv to meet him. They could hear the new philharmonic symphony which had been formed largely with German musicians and whose initial concert was conducted by Toscanini – or they could go to the art exhibits or lectures at the Youth Headquarters – or merely walk along Ben Yehuda Street and Allenby Road where crowds sipped coffee in the sidewalk cafés. Or perhaps they would stroll along the quiet beaches north of Tel Aviv. Each separation became more and more difficult. Ari did not wish to marry until he could get a parcel of land and build a home. With trouble constant and his services more and more in demand it seemed as though that time would never come. They loved each other very much. By the time she was seventeen and he was nineteen she had given herself to him. Now in their rendezvous they spent their few hours discovering the wonder of each other.

The tension which began with the German Aliyah in 1933 hit a peak in the year 1935 when the Jews succeeded in bringing in more immigrants than ever before, legally and illegally. Just as the Second Aliyah brought ideals and leaders and the Third Aliyah brought the pioneers – the German Aliyah resulted in a tremendous cultural and scientific spurt in the Yishuv.

The effendis who were watching the continued progress of the Jews became frantic – frantic enough, in fact, to unite their dissident political groups for the first time and as a unified body make definite demands on the British that all selling of land to Jews and all Jewish immigration be stopped.

Early in 1936 Yishuv Central requested several thousand visas from the British to conform with the growing anxiety of the Jews in Germany. Under violent Arab pressure the British granted less than a thousand visas.

The Mufti, seeing the growing British weakness, made his move at last for control of Palestine. In the spring of 1936 he stirred up a new series of riots. They began in Jaffa with the fable that the Jews were snatching all the Arabs in Tel Aviv and murdering them, and they spread from city to city. As usual, the majority of the victims were defenseless old Orthodox Jews in the holy cities. Immediately after the first outbursts Haj Amin announced the formation of a Higher Arab Committee, with himself as head, for the purpose of 'directing' another Arab general stike in protest against the 'pro-Jewish' British policies.

This time the Mufti moved after careful preparation. The instant the Higher Arab Committee was announced, the El Husseini mob, flanked by hired thugs, fanned out throughout the Arab community to 'enforce' the general strike, and to see that a full boycott was carried out. A wanton rash of assassinations began systematically to wipe out any known Arab opponent of the Mufti. Although the rebellion was supposedly directed against the Jews and the British, its major objective was to kill off all the Mufti's political opponents.

Kammal, the long-time friend of Barak Ben Canaan, and the muktar of Abu Yesha, was made to pay for his friendship with the Yishuv. Husseini's henchmen found the aging muktar kneeling at prayer in the little mosque by the stream in his village – and they slit his throat.

Taha, the son, was whisked away into Yad El to live in the Ben Canaan home where he would be safe. The Mufti's blood orgy continued to enforce the general strike and the boycott of the Jews. Without a market the Arab crops rotted in the fields. The port of Jaffa and the commerce around it ground to a near halt. The strike was paralyzing the Arab population, but they were helpless against the Mufti. Haj Amin el Husseini again used his pulpit to twist the blame upon the Jews; and as the Arab hardship heightened, so did their desperation and anger. Soon the Arabs began to dare to attack settlements and burn fields and steal crops. When an isolated and unarmed Jew was found his murder was always followed by decapitation, dismemberment, eye gouging, and the most primitive brutalities.

As the atrocities increased, Avidan called upon the Yishuv to exercise self-restraint. The Arab population was being victimized, he declared, and no good would come of returning their cruelties.

It was a different story with Akiva and the Maccabees. Soon after the Maccabees broke from the Haganah the British outlawed them and forced them underground. The British, to some extent, turned their backs on the Haganah because they knew about the policy of self-restraint and the fact that the Haganah fought only in self-defense. Furthermore, the Haganah never fought against the British. Not so the Maccabees. They were avowed enemies of the British and they had no intention of exercising restraint. The Maccabees, therefore, had to move into the cover of the three major cities: Tel Aviv, Jerusalem, and Haifa.

Akiva's followers tried to trade terror for terror but they were not large or effective enough to keep pace with the Mufti's thugs. Although they were officially disclaimed by the Jewish leadership, many of the Yishuv were happy over the Maccabee actions.

Once Haj Amin el Husseini had his hands on Palestine's throat, he moved ahead with the next phase of his plan. He sent out a fanatically worded appeal for all Arabs of all nations to join the common struggle to liberate Palestine from the clutches of British imperialism and Zionism.

Husseini gangsters entered Arab villages and demanded fighters for attacks on Jewish settlements. Most of the beleaguered fellaheen had absolutely no desire to fight but they were too terrified of the Mufti to refuse.

From outside of Palestine came an answer to the Mufti's appeal. An Iraqi army officer named Kawukji saw the Palestine 'revolt' as his long awaited chance to seize power and make a fortune as the Mufti's military arm. Kawukji was obsessed with himself; his egomania knew no bounds. He purchased many fine new uniforms with all types of fancy decorations and declared himself generalissimo of the army of liberation. With money extorted from the Palestinian Arabs by the Mufti, Kawukji went about recruiting his army outside the country. He got together a band of thieves, dope runners, white slavers, and the like with the lure of the many Jewish women they could rape and the 'Hebrew gold' they could loot. They were as vicious, degenerate, and brutal a gang as had ever been assembled. Under Generalissimo Kawukji they poured in from Lebanon to save the great Islam martyr, Haj Amin el Husseini.

Kawukji used safe and simple tactics. He would set up a road ambush after first having made certain of an avenue of retreat. When a bus, unarmed vehicle, or party small enough not to fight passed by, the Arabs would spring, loot, and flee.

Soon Kawukji and the Mufti's gangs had the entire country terrorized. The

Arab community was defenseless, the British were inept and reluctant to fight, and the Jews would fight only in self-defense.

Instead of moving to stamp out the Arab attacks, the British were nearly comical in their efforts. A few times they swept in on suspected bandit hide-out villages and assessed collective fines, and once or twice they even destroyed a few villages. But they went into a defensive shell. They built over fifty enormous concrete police forts that encircled all of Palestine. Each fort was capable of holding from a few hundred up to several thousand troops. Each fort was to control its own immediate area. They were designed by a man named Taggart and built by the Jews.

The Taggart forts that ringed besieged Palestine were a system as old as the land itself. In Biblical days the Jews used twelve mountains. A fire from one could be seen by the next and relayed to the next. The Crusaders adhered to the same theory by erecting fortified castles each within sight of the next castle or walled town. Even the Jews now put each new agricultural settlement within sight of a neighbor.

At night the British buttoned up in their Taggart forts and stayed put. By day their raids were ineffective. The moment a convoy was spotted leaving a fort the word was passed along the countryside. Every Arab in every field was a potential spy. By the time the British reached their objective, the opposition had disappeared into thin air.

Yet, under this unbelievable pressure, the Jews continued to smuggle in immigrants and build new settlements for them. On the first day of a new settlement several hundred farmers and builders from all the neighboring settlements would gather on the breaking grounds at sunrise. Between sunup and sundown they quickly constructed a tower with searchlight facilities and generator and a small stockade around it. By night of the same day it would be completed and they would disappear to their own settlements, leaving the new settlers inside the stockade with a small guard of Haganah men.

Ari Ben Canaan, just over twenty years of age, became an expert on the 'tower and blockade' settlements. He generally commanded the Haganah unit which stayed behind to teach the new settlers the trick of handling Arab infiltrators and attackers and how to use their weapons. Almost every new settlement underwent an Arab attack. The presence of the Haganah and their ability ultimately to repulse the attackers was a steadying influence upon the newcomers. Not Ari or any other Jewish leader ever lost a 'tower and stockade' settlement. At the end of a few weeks in one place, Ari would take his unit on to the next new 'tower and stockade' settlement under construction.

The settlers worked out from the stockades slowly, opening up their land a bit at a time. They erected permanent buildings and slowly expanded into full-fledged villages. If the settlement was a *kibbutz* the first building would be the children's house. It was always built in the inner line of defense so that it would be the last building that could be reached by attackers.

Avidan said that the 'tower and stockade' farms were a fulfillment of the Biblical story of the rebuilding of Jerusalem with one hand on the spear and one hand on the trowel. The prophet Nehemiah had said . . . 'half my servants wrought in the work and the other half held the spears.' And so it was that they worked their land and built their homes with a rifleman behind every plow and every carpenter.

The Arabs became so bold that even the British could not go on ignoring the terror. Haj Amin and Kawukji had made them all look like jackasses. At last they plunged into action and broke up the Higher Arab Committee and issued a warrant for the arrest of Haj Amin. The Mufti fled ahead of British police into the Mosque of Omar, the holiest Moslem shrine in Palestine.

The British balked and dared not enter the mosque for fear of inciting a 'holy' uprising on the part of the entire Moslem world. After a week of hiding out, Haj Amin, dressed as a woman, fled and escaped to Jaffa, where a boat carried him to Lebanon.

Everyone breathed a great sigh of relief as the Mufti of Jerusalem left Palestine – especially the Arab community. The riots and attacks abated and the British again renewed their commissions of inquiry and investigations.

The Arabs boycotted the British inquiries except to send a few of their most fanatical members in to read prepared speeches. Although Haj Amin had left the scene, the El Husseinis were still on hand. At the commissions of inquiry the Arabs made more and more outrageous claims against the Jews, who paid eighty-five per cent of all the taxes despite the fact that the Yishuv was smaller than the Arab community.

And so, after another survey of the situation, the British took a new tack and recommended that Palestine be divided into two separate states. The Arabs were to get the lion's share and the Jews a strip of land from Tel Aviv to Haifa and those parts of the Galilee they had reclaimed.

The Yishuv Central, the world Zionists, and the Jews in Palestine were tired of the continued bloodshed, the growing Arab fanaticism, and the ever more apparent British betrayal. Once the mandate for the Jewish homeland had included both sides of the Jordan River – now the British were offering but an iota. Yet, despite everything, the Jews decided to accept the proposal.

The British pointed out to the Arabs that it would be wise to accept, because the area allotted to the Jews couldn't hold many more immigrants. But the Arabs wanted nothing more or less than that every Jew be thrown into the sea. Haj Amin el Husseini was the treasure of Islam and the martyred victim of British and Zionist injustice. From Beirut he renewed the rebellion.

Taggart, who had built the British system of forts, erected an electrified barbed-wire wall along the Lebanese border to stop the Mufti's thugs and arms runners. At intervals he constructed more blockhouse forts to interlace with the wall.

One of the forts on the Taggart wall was erected above Abu Yesha and Yad El at the site believed to be the burial ground of Queen Esther. It became known as Fort Esther.

The Taggart wall slowed the Arab infiltration but could not stop it.

The Haganah, which had contained itself so long, became very restless and the Yishuv began to wonder when the Yishuv Central would let the Haganah fight. Under this growing pressure, Ben Gurion finally agreed to listen to a plan advanced by Avidan. In turn the Zion Settlement Society purchased a piece of land on the northern extremity of the Galilee, right on the Lebanese border, at a point where Haganah intelligence suspected most of the Arab infiltration to be taking place.

Shortly after the land purchase Ari Ben Canaan and two other top young men in Haganah were called to Tel Aviv to Avidan's secret headquarters.

The bald-headed leader of Jewish defense unfolded a map and pointed out the new parcel of land. Its importance to the continuation of the Arab revolt was obvious.

'I want you three boys to take command of a unit to go up to this land and build a *kibbutz* there. We are carefully picking eighty of our top men and twenty women to go with you. I don't have to tell you what to expect.'

They nodded.

'We know the Mufti is going to stop everything else in an effort to run you out. This is the first time we have picked a spot for a *kibbutz* because of its strategic value.'

Sarah Ben Canaan was sick at heart. For years she had not seen her son without a whip or a gun near at hand. Now she feared this mission as she had feared none of the others. A hundred of the best members of the Yishuv were being put into a suicidal position. Ari kissed his mother and brushed away her tears and in his simple way said that it would be all right. He shook his father's hand and said nothing, for the understanding between them was complete.

Dafna knocked on the door and they said good-by to her too.

Dafna and Ari walked out the gates of Yad El and turned to look back briefly at the fields and at the friends who had gathered. Barak sighed and put his arm on Sarah's shoulder as the younger couple disappeared down the road.

'They want so little from life,' Sarah said. 'How long ... how long must we go on giving him?'

Barak shook his great head and his eyes narrowed to catch a last glimpse of his boy and Dafna.

'God asked Abraham to give his son in sacrifice. I suppose we of the Yishuv live in that shadow. We must keep giving Ari so long as God wills it.'

A hundred of the finest young men and women of the Yishuv went up to the border of Lebanon and placed themselves in the path of thieves and murderers. Ari Ben Canaan, at twenty-two years of age, was second in command.

They called the place Ha Mishmar, the Guardpost.

Chapter Sixteen

Ten trucks carrying a hundred Haganah boys and girls and their equipment sped along the coastal road past the last Jewish settlement at Nahariya in northern Galilee and penetrated into territory where no Jew had gone before. A thousand pairs of Arab eyes watched the convoy as it moved up into the foothills of the mountains on the Lebanese border below the Taggart wall.

They stopped, set out guards, and unloaded the trucks quickly. The trucks rushed back to Nahariya before dark. The hundred were alone. Above them the hills were filled with Arab marauder gangs. Behind them were a dozen hostile Arab villages.

They erected a small stockade, dug in, and waited out the night.

By next morning the word had spread from Hebron to Beirut ... 'The Jews have moved into the hills!' Haj Amin el Husseini in Beirut was enraged. It was an open challenge. He swore by the beard of Allah that the Jews would be thrown into the sea.

During the next few days the Haganah force worked themselves to exhaustion tightening the defenses of the base camp at the bottom of the hill against the attack that had to come. Each night when they weren't standing guard, Dafna and Ari fell into exhausted slumber in each other's arms.

On the fourth night the attack came!

The Jews had never undergone anything like it. A thousand Arab riflemen flanked with machine guns poured a steady tattoo of fire into the Jews' stockade for five consecutive hours from the top of the hill. For the first time the Arabs used mortar fire. Ari and his forces lay low and waited for the Arabs to try an assault.

The attack came when Arab thugs began slithering along the ground with knives between their teeth.

Suddenly –

Half a dozen searchlights darted out from the stockade and swept the field. The light caught the Arabs in close. The Jews poured on a deadly counterfire and in the very first burst shot sixty Arabs dead.

The Arabs were paralyzed with fear. Ari led half the Haganah force out from the cover of the stockade in a fierce counterattack which littered the field of battle with Arab dead and wounded. Arabs who survived fled back to high ground screaming in terror.

The Arabs did not attack again for a week. Nothing the Mufti could say or do could make them attack. Kawukji could not make them attack.

In that first night three Haganah boys and one girl were killed in the fighting. One of them was the commander. Ari Ben Canaan stepped up to assume command.

Each day the Haganah moved up the hill a few feet, consolidated the position, and waited out the night. The Arabs watched from their positions above but never attacked during the daylight hours. By the end of a week Ari abandoned the first base camp and had established a second camp midway up the hill.

The Arabs resumed their attacks, but the lesson of the first night was still fresh. They did not try a direct assault but were content to fire at the camp from long distances.

While the Arabs remained indecisive, Ari decided to take the offensive. At the end of the second week at dawn he made his move. He waited until the Arabs were tired from firing all night and their guard was lax. He led twenty-five crack men and ten women in a dawn attack that threw the sleepy Arabs off the top of the hill. The Jews dug in quickly while the Arabs got their bearings and reassembled for a counterattack. Ari lost five soldiers but he held his position.

Quickly he fortified a lookout post on the top of the hill which commanded a view of the entire area. By daylight they worked feverishly to build their foothold into a fortress.

The Mufti was nearly insane with rage! He changed commanders and assembled another force of a thousand men. They attacked, but as soon as they came into close range they broke and fled.

For the first time Jews commanded a hilltop position and the Arabs were not going to dislodge them.

Although the Arabs would not fight at close quarters and would therefore not be able to run the Haganah out, they did not intend to make life easy for the Jews. Ari's troops were constantly harassed by Arab rifles. His force was completely isolated from the rest of the Yishuv. The closest settlement was

Nahariya. All supplies and even water had to come in through hostile territory by truck, and once there everything had to be carried up the hill by hand.

Despite the hardships, Ha Mishmar held fast. A few crude huts were erected inside the stockade and a road was started to the bottom of the hill. Ari began night patrols along the Taggart wall to catch infiltrators and arms runners. The Mufti's underground highway into Palestine was being squeezed shut.

Ninety per cent of the Haganah force were from either *kibbutzim* or *moshavim*. Redemption was so much a part of them that they could not stay long in one spot without trying to grow something. They began farming at Ha Mishmar! The place had been opened in the guise of a *kibbutz*, and by God they were going to make it one. Hillside farming was a new venture for them – and it was especially difficult when there was no natural water except the sparse rainfall. None the less they went at the task with the same vigor with which they had redeemed the swamplands of the Jezreel Valley and the eroded Plain of Sharon. They terraced the hillsides and petitioned the Zion Settlement Society for money for farm tools.

The Yishuv Central and the Haganah were so delighted over the success of the dogged youngsters at Ha Mishmar that they decided that from then on some new settlements would be selected for their strategic value in choking off the Arab revolution.

A second group of pioneers set out for another troublesome spot. This time they were Orthodox Jews. They moved deep into the Beth Shean Valley and built a *kibbutz* at the juncture of the Syrian and Trans-Jordan borders. Their *kibbutz* was called Tirat Tsvi, the Castle of the Rabbi Tsvi. It stood in the midst of a dozen hostile Arab towns and villages. Again the Mufti attempted to dislodge them. But this force of religious Jews was not of the same ilk as the old pious Jews of the holy cities. As at Ha Mishmar, the Arabs could not defeat the Jews of Tirat Tsvi.

Ari was sound asleep in his tent.

'Ari . . . come quickly.'

He threw off his blanket, grabbed his rifle, and ran after them to the south fields which were being terraced for grapevines. There was a gathering. Everyone turned silent as they saw Ari approach. He pushed through and stared at the ground. It was blood-spattered. Parts of a blue blouse were on the ground. A trail of blood led off to the hills. Ari looked from face to face. No one spoke.

'Dafna,' he whispered.

Two days later her body was dumped near their camp. Her ears, nose, and hands had been amputated. Her eyes had been gouged out. She had been raped over a hundred times.

No one saw Ari Ben Canaan weep or even raise his voice.

After Dafna's murder he would disappear for hours at a time, returning chalky-faced and shaken. But he never displayed passion or hatred or even great anger. He never mentioned her name to anyone again. Ari accepted this tragedy in the same way that the Yishuv had learned to accept such things – not by being stirred to violence, but only by deepening his determination not to be thrown from the land. Ari Ben Canaan was all soldier. Half a dozen Arab villages near Ha Mishmar cringed and awaited a revenge attack – but it never came.

The Jews hung on at Ha Mishmar and at Tirat Tsvi and half a dozen other strategically placed settlements. The new tactic was hampering the Mufti's revolt but not stopping it.

Into his hodgepodge came an English major named P. P. Malcolm.

Major P. P. Malcolm had been transferred to British intelligence in Jerusalem at the outbreak of the Mufti's revolt. He was a loner. P.P. dressed sloppily and scorned military tradition. He thought protocol ridiculous. He was a man who could express his feelings openly and violently if need be, and he was also a man given to deep meditation for days on end, during which he might neither shave nor comb his hair. His periods of detachment came at odd times – even in the middle of the formal parades, which he hated and believed a waste of time. P. P. Malcolm had a tongue like a lash and never failed to startle those around him. He was eccentric and looked upon as an 'off horse' by his fellow officers.

Physically P.P. was tall and thin and bony-faced and had a slight limp. He was, all told, everything that a British officer should not be.

When Malcolm arrived in Palestine he was pro-Arab because it was fashionable for the British officers to be pro-Arab. These sympathies did not last long. Within a short period of time P. P. Malcolm had turned into a fanatic Zionist.

Like most Christians who embrace Zionism, his brand was far more intense and rabid than a Jew's. Malcolm learned Hebrew from a rabbi and spent every spare minute reading the Bible. He was certain it was in God's scheme for the Jews to rise again as a nation. Malcolm made detailed studies of the Biblical military campaigns and of the tactics of Joshua, David, and especially Gideon, who was his personal idol. And finally – he became obsessed with the notion that his coming to Palestine had been divinely inspired.

He, P. P. Malcolm, had been chosen by God Himself to lead the children of Israel in their noble mission.

Malcolm drove around Palestine in a battered secondhand jalopy and he hiked on his gimpy leg where there were no roads. Malcolm visited every site of every battle of Biblical times to reconstruct the tactical events. Often Jew and Arab alike were stunned to see this strange creature limping along a road singing a Psalm at the top of his voice and oblivious to everything worldly.

It was often asked why the British command tolerated Malcolm. General Charles, the commander of Palestine, recognized quite simply that Malcolm was a genius and one of those rare types of military rebels who pops up every so often. Malcolm laughed at the British handbooks on war, had nothing but disdain for their strategy, and for the most part thought the entire British Army was a waste of money. No one ever seemed to win an argument with him for he never appeared to be wrong and he was convinced of his own infallible judgment.

One day toward evening P. P. Malcolm abandoned his car when it blew two tires at once and hiked along the road toward Yad El. As he entered the defense perimeter half a dozen guards headed in on him. He smiled and waved at them. 'Good work, chaps,' he called. 'Now be dear lads and take me to Barak Ben Canaan.'

Malcolm paced up and down Barak's living room. His appearance was even more slovenly than usual. For a solid hour he lectured Barak Ben Canaan about the glory and beauty of Zionism and the destiny of the Hebrew nation.

'I like Jewish soldiers,' Malcolm said. 'The Hebrew warrior is the finest, for he fights and lives close to ideals. This land is real to him. He lives with great glories all around him. Your chaps in the Haganah probably constitute the most highly educated and intellectual as well as idealistic body of men under arms in the entire world.

'Take the British soldier,' Malcolm continued. 'He is a stubborn fighter and that is good. He responds to discipline and that is good. But it ends right there. He is a stupid man. He drinks too much. He would sleep with a pig and often does. Ben Canaan, that is what I have come to see you about. I am going to take your Haganah and make a first-class fighting organization out of it. You've got the best raw material I've ever laid eyes on.'

Barak's jaw dropped!

Malcolm looked out the window. He could see the water sprinklers whirling in the fields and in the distance he could see Abu Yesha nestled in the hills below the Taggart fort, Fort Esther.

'See that fort up there – Esther, you call it – stupidity, I call it. All the Arabs have to do is walk around it. The British will never learn.' Malcolm began humming Psalm 98 and singing the words softly in Hebrew. 'I have the Psalms memorized up to a hundred and twenty-six. It comforts me.'

'Major Malcolm. Just what is the nature of this visit?' Barak said.

'Everyone knows that Barak Ben Canaan is fair and non-partisan. Frankly, most Jews like to talk too much. In my Jewish army they won't have ten words to say. I'll do all the talking.'

'You have made me quite aware that you like to do all the talking,' Barak said.

'Humph,' Malcolm grunted, and continued to look at the lush fields of Yad El through the window. Suddenly he swung around and his eyes were ablaze with the same intensity Barak had often seen in his brother Akiva.

'Fight!' Malcolm cried. 'That is what we must do ... fight! The Jewish nation is destiny, Ben Canaan, destiny.'

'You and I are in certain agreement about the destiny of the homeland ... I don't need refreshing.'

'Yes you do ... all of you do ... so long as you stay buttoned up in your settlements. We must go there and start punishing those infidels. If an Arab comes out of his coffeehouse and takes a pot shot at a *kibbutz* from a thousand yards distant he thinks he is a brave man. The time has come to test these bloody heathens. Hebrews, that's what I want ... Hebrew soldiers. You arrange an appointment with Avidan for me at once. Englishmen are too stupid to understand my methods.'

As suddenly as this strange man had appeared at Yad El, he left. P. P. Malcolm limped through the gates singing a Biblical Psalm at the top of his voice and left Barak Ben Canaan scratching his beard and shaking his head.

Barak later phoned Avidan and they spoke in Yiddish in case the line was being tapped.

'Who is this man?' Barak asked. 'He walked in like the Messiah and began preaching Zionism at me.'

'We have reports on him,' Avidan said. 'Frankly, he is so odd we don't know what to make of him.'

'Can he be trusted?'

'We don't know.'

Major P. P. Malcolm now spent all his free hours among the Jews. He candidly observed that British officers were idiots and bores. In a matter of months he was known by the entire Yishuv. Although he moved in the highest circles most of the leaders treated him like a harmless eccentric. 'Our mad Englishman,' he was called with affection.

Soon it became apparent that P. P. Malcolm was not mad. In close discussion Malcolm had the persuasive power to talk the devil out of his horns. Members of the Yishuv came away from his home certain they had been under a magic spell.

After nearly six months of evasions, Malcolm burst into Ben Gurion's office in the Yishuv Central building in Jerusalem one day, unannounced.

'Ben Gurion,' he snapped. 'You are a God-damned fool. You waste all your time talking to your enemies and you haven't five minutes to spare for a friend.'

With that blunt announcement he turned and walked out.

Malcolm's next appointment was with General Charles, the military commander. He argued to convince the general to let him work out some of his theories on Arab warfare with the use of Jewish troops. General Charles was pro-Arab as was most of his staff, but the Mufti's rebellion was beginning to make him look ridiculous. Little by little the British had trained and armed their own Jewish police and had ignored the Haganah arms which supplemented their own forces. The British had failed so badly he decided to let Malcolm go ahead.

Malcolm's jalopy showed up at Ha Mishmar where guards took him up the hill to Ari. The strapping Haganah commander studied the scrawny Englishman before him with puzzlement.

Malcolm patted his cheek. 'You look like a good boy,' he said. 'Listen to me, obey my orders, observe what I do, and I'll make a first-class soldier out of you. Now, show me your camp and fortifications.'

Ari was perplexed. By mutual arrangement the British had stayed out of Ha Mishmar and turned their backs on Ari's patrols. Yet they had every legal right to enter Ha Mishmar. Major Malcolm completely ignored Ari's suspicions and obvious attempt to show him only half the layout.

'Where is your tent, son?'

In Ari's tent, P. P. Malcolm stretched out on the cot and meditated.

'What do you want here?' Ari demanded.

'Give me a map, son,' he said, ignoring Ari's question. Ari did so. P. P. Malcolm sat up, opened the map, and scratched his scraggly beard. 'Where is the key Arab jump-off base?'

Ari pointed to a small village some fifteen kilometers inside Lebanon.

'Tonight we shall destroy it,' Malcolm said calmly.

That night a patrol of eight men and two women crossed over from Ha Mishmar into Lebanon with Malcolm in command. The Jews were astounded at the speed and stamina with which he could push his fragile body through the steep and tortuous hills. He never once stopped for rest or to check directions. Before they left, Major Malcolm had heard someone sneeze and had said he could not go – and that anyone who did not keep up with the pace would be thrashed within an inch of his life. He led them in singing a Psalm and lectured them on the nobility of their mission.

As they neared their objective, Malcom went up ahead to reconnoiter the village. He returned in half an hour.

'As I suspected, they have no security up. Here is what we shall do.' He drew a hasty map to pinpoint what he believed to be the three or four huts belonging to the smugglers. 'I will take three of you chaps into the village and we will open fire from short range and give them a blast or two of grenades to loosen the party up a bit. Everyone will flee in wild disarray. My force will drive them to the edge of the village here where you, Ben Canaan, shall establish an ambush. Be so good as to bring a pair of prisoners, for this area is obviously loaded with arms caches.'

'Your plan is foolish. It will not work,' Ari said.

'Then I suggest you begin walking back to Palestine,' Malcolm retorted.

That was the first and the last time Ari ever questioned the wisdom of P. P. Malcolm. The man's certainty was gripping.

'Never question my judgment again, young man,' he said.

Malcolm's plan was executed. The major led a four-man squad right up to the suspected headquarters. Four grenades were lobbed into the huts and followed by rifle fire. According to Malcolm's prediction, there was a panic. He coolly drove the thugs right at Ari's ambush. It was all over within ten minutes.

Two prisoners were taken to the major.

'Where are your guns hidden?' he asked the first one in Arabic. The Arab shrugged.

Malcolm slapped the Arab's face and repeated the question. This time the Arab pleaded his innocence as Allah was his judge. Malcolm calmly took out his pistol and shot the Arab through the head. He turned to the second prisoner. 'Where are your guns hidden?' he asked.

The second Arab quickly revealed the location of the arms.

'You sons and daughters of Judea have learned many valuable lessons this night,' Malcolm said. 'I will explain them to you in the morning. One thing, never use brutality to get information. Get right to the point.'

The news of Malcolm's raid had a sobering effect on all of Palestine. For the Yishuv it marked a historic occasion. For the very first time the Jews had come out of their settlements to make an offensive action. Many thought it was long overdue.

The British were in an uproar. Most of them demanded that P. P. Malcolm be removed at once. General Charles was not so sure. British methods of fighting Arabs were sorely lacking, and he felt Malcolm had most of the answers.

For the Mufti's thugs and the Husseinis and the Moslem fanatics it was a day of reckoning. No longer could they rove at will and pick their places for attack without expecting retribution.

Ari went out with P. P. Malcolm on a dozen more raids deep into Lebanon. Each raid was more successful than the last. The marauder gangs, the thugs and the gun runners and Kawukji's mercenaries, were shaken from their complacency, for their activities were no longer profitable or safe against the swift merciless raids of the Haganah. The Mufti placed a reward of a thousand pounds sterling on P. P. Malcolm's head.

After Malcolm and his Haganah boys and girls at Ha Mishmar succeeded in quieting down the Taggart line, he moved his headquarters to the *kibbutz* of Ein Or. Malcolm requested from the Haganah a hundred and fifty top soldiers; he specifically wanted Ari Ben Canaan, whom he greatly favored. At *kibbutz* Ein Or, Malcolm formed his Raider Unit.

When the hundred and fifty soldiers had assembled from all over the Yishuv,

Major Malcolm led them on a long hike to Mount Gilboa at the traditional site of the grave of the great Hebrew judge and warrior, Gideon, who was Malcolm's idol. At Gideon's grave he stood before his charges and opened his Bible and read in Hebrew.

'... so Gideon, and the hundred men that were with him, came unto the outside of the camp in the beginning of the middle watch; and they had but newly set the watch: and they blew the horns, and brake the pitchers that were in their hands. And the three companies blew the horns, and brake the pitchers, and held the lamps in their left hands, and the horns in their right hands to blow withal; and they cried, The sword of the Lord and of Gideon. And they stood every man in his place round about the camp; and all the host ran, and cried, and fled.'

Malcolm closed the Bible. He walked back and forth with his hands clasped behind him and seemed to look off into space as he spoke. 'Gideon was a smart man. Gideon knew the Midianites were an ignorant and a superstitious people. Gideon knew he could play on their primitive fears and that they could be frightened by noise and by the night. Gideon knew it ... and so do we.'

The Arabs never knew where or when the Raider Unit would strike next. Their old reliable spy system simply did not work against Malcolm. He would send three units out in three different directions to confuse them. He would pass an Arab village and double back and strike it. He would send a convoy of trucks down a road and drop men off one at a time. During the day they lay hidden in the ditches at the roadside and at night they would assemble.

Every attack that came sounded like a thousand men. He never failed to send his enemy into a panic.

He elaborated on something his Jews already knew – the terrain of Palestine. He taught them the strategic as well as the historic value of every wadi and hill and tree by pointing out how the ancient Hebrew generals had used the land and the knowledge of it to great military advantage.

Ari Ben Canaan became a devoted disciple of this eccentric Englishman, as did all of the Raiders. He went alongside Malcom in a hundred raids against the enemy and never once was Malcom guilty of error. It was almost as though he were divinely guided as well as divinely inspired. He created a flawless text on Arab fighting. He demanded iron discipline and fanatical and unquestioning devotion in payment for victory after victory.

The Raider Unit put a fear into the Arabs which was even greater than that of the Husseinis. With a hundred and fifty men he ripped the rebellion to shreds. The marauders began to flee and Kawukji's grand army of liberation raced back to Lebanon. In floundering desperation the Mufti turned his fire on the oil line which ran from the Mosul fields to Haifa.

'Twenty thousand of those dunderheaded Englishmen could not defend that pipeline,' Malcolm said. 'We will do it with our Raider Unit. Our plans are simple. Each time there is a break in the line the nearest Arab village to that break will be attacked and flattened by the Raider Unit. This will teach the Arab villages to guard the lines against marauders in the interest of their own safety and it will teach them not to shelter those thugs. Reprisal ... remember that, for the Jews are outnumbered ... we must use the principle of reprisal.'

Every time the Arabs moved they got it right back in the teeth. Reprisal, from then on, became the key to Jewish defense.

The Arab revolt petered out and died. It had been a miserable and costly failure. The Arabs had bankrupted their entire community and murdered their foremost spokesmen. Three years of riots and bloodshed had put them on the brink of destitution. In all that time they did not displace a single Jewish settlement or keep some fifty new ones from going up.

With the death throes of the Arab uprising Whitehall made a clean sweep of their government in the mandate.

Major P. P. Malcolm was told he must leave Palestine, for his continued consorting with the Jews now would cause them nothing but embarrassment. Malcolm had been the greatest single instrument in breaking the backs of the Arabs. The Jews he trained were the nucleus of a greater new army – his brilliant tactics their military Bible.

For the last time Major P. P. Malcolm stood before his Jews at Ein Or. The Raider Unit honored by red badges on their blue farmer's clothing stood at attention, and there were tears in the eyes of many.

Malcolm opened his Bible. '... *Gird thy sword upon thy thigh O most mighty, with thy glory and thy majesty. And in thy majesty ride prosperously because of truth and meekness and righteousness.*'

He walked away quickly to the waiting car. His heart was broken. The Yishuv had bestowed upon him the greatest honor they could give a non-Jew. They called him 'the Friend.'

Ari Ben Canaan returned to Yad El after the Raider Unit was disbanded. His heart seemed always on a lonely hill on the Lebanese border where Dafna lay in eternal sleep alongside twenty other Haganah boys and girls who had fallen for Ha Mishmar.

With things quiet and safer, Taha left Yad El, where he had lived all this time under the protection of the Ben Canaan family, to assume the job of muktar of Abu Yessha. Both Barak and Sarah realized that in the eighteen months Taha had lived with them he had fallen in love with Jordana, who was now past her thirteenth birthday. Love of a younger girl was not uncommon among Taha's people. Both of the parents never spoke a word about it and hoped that the boy would get over it without too much pain.

The new British administration, under the command of General Haven-Hurst, came to Palestine. They soon rounded up the Raider Unit men. The latter were hauled into court and thrown into jail for terms of six months to five years! The charge – illegal use of arms!

Ari and a hundred other Haganah members of Malcolm's Raider Unit were locked in the dungeon-like Acre jail. Many of them regarded their plight as rather humorous and spent their days frustrating the British guard by singing Haganah marches and songs of the fields from morning to night. It was a thick-walled old castle – clammy and monstrous and filled with lice and rats and slime and darkness.

Ari was released in the spring of 1939. He returned home to Yad El pale and gaunt.

Sarah cried in the sanctity of her room after she had seen him. What had her son had from birth but a whip and a gun and tragedy? His Dafna was dead and so many of his comrades were dead – how long would it go on? Sarah vowed she would keep her boy at Yad El forever.

With Haven-Hurst commanding Palestine with an iron fist and open anti-Jewish sentiments the stage was set for the final British betrayal ...

There was another commission of inquiry. The three years of Mufti-inspired bloodshed were blamed on Jewish immigration.

Whitehall and Chatham House and Neville Chamberlain, their Prime Minister and renowned appeaser, shocked the world with their pronouncement. The British Government issued a White Paper on the eve of World War II shutting off immigration to the frantic German Jews and stopping Jewish land buying. The appeasers of Munich who had sold Spain and Czechoslovakia down the river had done the same to the Jews of Palestine.

Chapter Seventeen

The Yishuv was rocked by the White Paper, the most staggering single blow they had ever received. On the eve of war the British were sealing in the German Jews.

The Maccabees, who had been dormant, suddenly sprang to life. The White Paper brought Jews into the Maccabees by the hundreds. They lashed out in a series of raids, bombing a British officers' club in Jerusalem and terrorizing the Arabs. They raided a British arsenal and they ambushed several convoys.

General Haven-Hurst completely reversed all previous policies of semi-co-operation with the Jews. The Jewish police were disbanded and the Haganah was driven underground. Leaders of the Yishuv Central and more former Raider men were hauled into court and then thrown into Acre jail.

Ben Gurion again called upon the Yishuv to show the same wisdom and restraint they had shown in the past. He publicly denounced the terror tactics. But even as he spoke there were elements within Haganah who wanted to come into the open and fight. Fearing a showdown would lead to its destruction, Avidan was again forced to hold his army in check.

Barak Ben Canaan was sent to London to join Dr Chaim Weizmann and the other Zionist negotiators in trying to force a reversal of the White Paper. But the men in Whitehall were determined not to revoke it and thereby incite the Arabs.

In Palestine the Husseini mob was busy again, Despite the fact that Haj Amin was still in exile the rest of the clan was still handling opposition through assassination. The Higher Arab Committee was grabbed by the Mufti's nephew, Jemal Husseini.

Within Germany the Jewish situation was beyond despair. The Zionists' organizations were on the verge of collapse as even the most complacent German Jews panicked to get out of the country.

The British were making it as difficult for certain Jews to leave Palestine as for Jews to get in from Germany. They realized that anyone with a Haganah and Aliyah Bet background was a potential agent. When Ari left Palestine on orders from Avidan he had to slip over the Lebanese border at Ha Mishmar and hike to Beirut on foot. He carried the passport and visa of a Jew who had recently arrived in Palestine as a 'tourist.' In Beirut, Ari caught a boat for Marseilles. In another week he showed up in Berlin at Zionist headquarters at Number 10 Meinekestrasse.

His orders were: 'Get as many Jews out as possible.'

When he arrived in Berlin, Zionist headquarters was a scene of panic and chaos.

The Germans were playing the visa market for all it was worth. The more desperate the Jews became, the higher the price for their freedom. Many families turned over entire fortunes for the privilege of being able to escape from Germany. Visas were forged and stolen – visas were life. The first cruel fact of life was that few countries of the world wanted the German Jews. They simply closed their doors. If they did give visas it was with the understanding that the Jews would not come to their countries.

Ari was faced with the decision of deciding who got the visas and who didn't. Each day he was the victim of threats or the object of bribes and desperate pleas. The Zionist rule of thumb was to get the children out. For five years the Jews had appealed to their German numbers to leave Germany.

Along with the children there were essential scientists, doctors, professionals, and artisans, the very cream of the society.

Ari and the Aliyah Bet were moving them in mere hundreds, while thousands were being trapped.

He decided on a desperate gamble in an attempt to get several thousand visas at one time. That way, Ari reckoned, he could at least move the 'essentials' and many children out. He alerted Aliyah Bet in France to be prepared either to receive these thousands – or to expect his own disappearance to a concentration camp.

Ari then went into negotiations with high Nazis to sell them the idea of issuing exit permits in larger numbers. He argued with a strange but fascinating logic. Britain and Germany were both trying to win Arab favor; Ari pointed out that the more Jews who got to Palestine, the more embarrassed the British would be.

How paradoxical that the Aliyah Bet was teaming up with the Nazis in an effort against the British. Ari quickly had training farms set up in the Berlin area under Gestapo protection.

In addition to all the visas he could buy, steal, bribe, and otherwise wangle, Ari built an underground railroad right under the Germans' noses for getting out the top-priority Jews; but these people, mostly scientists, escaped only in two and threes. During the fear-filled summer of 1939 he worked around the clock as the time ran out.

Meanwhile in London, Barak Ben Canaan and the other negotiators worked the clock around too. They spoke to members of Parliament, Ministers, or anyone who would listen to them. But do what they might, the British would not budge from their immigration policy.

In mid-August, Ari received an urgent message from Aliyah Bet in France: LEAVE GERMANY AT ONCE.

Ari ignored the cable and continued his work, for each day now seemed a race against death.

Another cable came. This time it was a Haganah order for him to leave.

Ari gambled on just seventy-two hours more, for he was working on a stack of visas to get a trainload of children into Denmark.

A third cable came – and a fourth.

As the trainload of children crossed the Danish frontier, Ari Ben Canaan made his own escape. He left Germany forty-eight hours before Hitler's Wehrmacht rolled into Poland and ushered in World War II.

Ari and Barak Ben Canaan returned to Palestine from their separate missions. Both men were exhausted and both of them were crushed by despair.

At the outbreak of war it took only ten minutes for the Jewish leaders to announce their course of action. Ben Gurion urged the Yishuv to come forth for duty in the British Army to fight the common enemy.

There was additional encouragement from the Haganah which saw this as an opportunity to train its men legally.

General Haven-Hurst, the Palestine military commander, raised strong objections with the War Office about letting Palestinian Jews into the British Army. 'If we train Jews now and give them combat experience we will only be spiting ourselves, for surely we will have to fight the very same Jews later on.'

Within a week after the war began one hundred and thirty thousand men and women – one out of four in the entire Yishuv – had signed up at Yishuv Central to volunteer for the British Army.

As for the Arabs, most of the Arab world looked upon the Germans as their 'liberators' and waited for them.

It was impossible for the British to ignore the Yishuv's offer. It was also impossible not to heed General Haven-Hurst's warning. The War Office decided upon the middle road of accepting Palestinian Jews but keeping them out of front-line assignments so that they could not get actual weapons training and combat experience. The Palestinians were turned into service units, transportation and engineering battalions. Yishuv Central protested angrily against the discrimination and demanded equal opportunities fighting the Germans.

The Yishuv had presented a solid front, except for the dissenting Maccabees. Avidan decided to swallow his pride and through a chain of underground contacts asked for a meeting with Akiva.

The two men met in a cellar beneath Frankel's Restaurant on King George Road in Jerusalem. It was filled with cases of canned food and bottled goods stacked halfway to the ceiling, and it was dark except for the light from a single light bulb.

Avidan offered no handshake as Akiva entered, flanked by two Maccabees. It had been five long years since the two men had seen each other.

Akiva looked in his sixties and more. The long hard years of building two *kibbutzim* and the more recent years of underground living had turned him into an old man.

The room was cleared of Maccabee and Haganah guards. The two men faced each other.

At last Avidan spoke. 'I have come, quite simply, to ask you to call a truce with the British until the war is over.'

Akiva grunted. He spat out his contempt for the British and their White Paper and his anger at the Yishuv Central and Haganah for their failure to fight.

'Please, Akiva,' Avidan said, holding his temper. 'I am aware of all your feelings. I know exactly what differences there are between us. Despite them, Germany is a far greater enemy and threat to our existence than the British.'

Akiva turned his back on Avidan. He stood in the shadows thinking. Suddenly he spun around and his eyes blazed as of old. 'Now is the time to get the British to revoke the White Paper! Now – right now – declare our statehood on both sides of the Jordan! Now! Hit the damned British when they're down!'

'Is statehood so important to us that we must gain it by contributing to a German victory?'

'And do you think the British will hesitate to sell us down the river again?'

'I think we have only one choice – to fight Germany.'

Akiva paced the cement floor like a nervous cat. Tears of anger welled up in his eyes. He grunted and mumbled to himself – and at last he spoke with trembling softness. 'Even as the British blockade our coast against desperate people ... even as the British create a ghetto inside their army with our boys ... even as they have sold us out with the White Paper ... even as the Yishuv puts its heart and soul into the war effort while the Arabs sit like vultures waiting to pounce ... even with all this the British are the lesser of our enemies and we must fight with them. Very well, Avidan ... the Maccabees will call a truce.'

The air was filled with Akiva's hostility as the two men finally shook hands. Akiva wet his lips. 'How is my brother?'

'Barak just returned from conferences in London.'

'Yes ... conferences ... that would be Barak. And Sarah and the children?'

Avidan nodded. 'You can be proud of Ari.'

'Oh yes, Ari is a fine boy ... a fine boy ... how ... how ... does Ein Or look these days?'

Avidan lowered his eyes. 'Ein Or and Shoshanna show the love and the sweat of the men who built them.' Avidan turned and walked toward the ladder to the trap door.

'*Zion shall be redeemed with judgment,*' Akiva cried from the shadows of the cellar, '*and the destruction of the transgressors and of the sinners shall be together and they that forsake the Lord shall be consumed.* Our day with the British will come!'

Ari had changed. He was melancholy all the time. It was difficult to say exactly what had been the breaking point for him. He had carried arms since he was a boy. The 'tower and stockade' days – Ha Mishmar – the Raider Unit – the Acre prison. The heartbreaking work for Aliyah Bet in Berlin. And the death of Dafna. Ari lived at Yad El and farmed and wanted to be left alone. He scarcely spoke a word.

Even when the war broke out Ari remained at Yad El. Most of his spare time was spent at the Arab village of Abu Yesha with his boyhood friend, Taha, who was now the muktar.

One day, several months after the war had begun, Ari returned one evening from the fields to find Avidan himself waiting to see him. After dinner Ari, Avidan, and Barak retired to the living room to talk.

'I suppose you know why I came,' Avidan said.

'I can imagine.'

'Let me get right to the point. There are a few dozen of our boys that we feel should join up. The British have contacted Haganah half a dozen times and asked for you. They are willing to give you an officer's commission.'

'I'm not interested.'

'They want you badly, Ari. I'm sure we can put you into a position – say, Arab intelligence – where you could be of great value to the Haganah too.'

'That's very nice. I thought they'd have me shoveling garbage with the rest of the Yishuv troops. It's good to know I'm one of the good Jews.'

'Don't make me issue this to you as an order.'

'You may be surprised if you do.'

Avidan, who was an iron disciplinarian, was somewhat taken aback. Ari Ben Canaan had been as reliable and unquestioning a soldier as any in the Haganah.

'I'm glad this is in the open,' Barak said. 'This boy has been eating his heart out since his return from Berlin.'

'Ari . . . I'm afraid we are going to have to insist upon it.'

'Why should I wear a British uniform? So they can throw me into prison again for bearing arms for them.'

Barak threw up his hands.

'All right, Father . . . if you want it in the open. Five years ago Uncle Akiva had the courage to name our enemy.'

'You are not to mention his name in this house!' Barak roared.

'It's about time it was mentioned. I might even have joined the Maccabees except that I would not go against you.'

'But Ari,' Avidan said quickly, 'even Akiva and the Maccabees have called a truce with the British.'

Ari turned and started for the door. 'I'll be playing backgammon at Taha's house. Call me if the Germans invade.'

The German avalanche thundered across Europe. The British suffered one debacle after another. Dunkirk! Crete! Greece! London underwent merciless bombing.

Even as the Yishuv poured its energy into the British war effort it was forced to swallow degradation by the British. A series of unbelievably horrible events occurred which rankled in the hearts of even the most benevolent Jews.

A pathetic, fifty-foot Danube river boat named the *Struma* crept into Istanbul loaded with nearly eight hundred frantic Jews trying to escape from Europe. The boat was unsafe and the people in dire straits. Yishuv Central literally begged the British for visas. The British refused. In fact, they turned heavy diplomatic pressure on the Turkish government to get the *Struma* out of Istanbul. Turkish police boarded the *Struma* and towed it through the Bosporus and cut it adrift in the Black Sea without food, water, or fuel. The *Struma* sank. Seven hundred and ninety-nine human beings drowned. One survived.

Two battered steamers reached Palestine with two thousand refugees and the British quickly ordered them transferred to the *Patria* for exile to Mauritius, an island east of Africa. The *Patria* sank off Palestine's shores in sight of Haifa, and hundreds of refugees drowned.

And so it went – the British clung to the White Paper – the Arabs had to be kept calm!

The war continued badly for the British. By the end of 1941 Palestinian Jews had made their way into fighting units despite General Haven-Hurst's forebodings, for the British were desperate and they were getting no manpower at all from the Arabs. As the Arabs sat, fifty thousand of the cream of the Yishuv wore British uniforms.

With western Europe crushed, German barges waited in the English Channel to invade. England had her back to the wall! And this was the moment of English glory! The Germans, who had beaten the Russians and the Greeks and the Yugoslavs, stood and balked at the showdown with those pale, scrawny wonders – the dogged Englishmen. They feared the English as they feared no others.

As England had carved up the Ottoman Empire, so now the Germans prepared to carve up the British Empire. Rommel's powerful Afrika Korps was building toward a series of strikes that would throw the British out of the Middle East and open a gateway to the Orient and India.

Haj Amin el Husseini moved from Lebanon in search of greener pastures. He landed in Bagdad, Iraq, nominally a British ally but in not much more than name. In Bagdad he was greeted as a great martyr of Islam. He staged a coup with a gang of Iraqi army officers to deliver Iraq to the Germans. The plot failed. But only at the last moment did the British prevent it from succeeding by sending the Arab Legion in to control the country.

Haj Amin fled again. This time he went to Germany where Adolf Hitler greeted him personally as a brother. The two madmen could work through each other for mutual personal profit. The Mufti saw in Germany's military plans a new opportunity to seize power over the entire Arab world. Hitler needed the Mufti to show what a warm and tender friendship could exist between Arab and German. As a Nazi agent, Haj Amin broadcasted over and over again from Berlin to the Arab world; what he had to say he had said many, many times before.

'O, Arabs, rise and avenge your martyrs ... I, Mufti of Palestine, declare this war as a holy war against the British yoke of tyranny ... I know the hatred you feel for them ... I know you Moslems are convinced the British and the Jews are enemies of Islam and plot against the precepts of the Koran ... the Jews will take our holy Islamic institutions ... they even now claim a Temple occupies the site of our most holy Mosque of Omar and surely they will desecrate it as they have tried before ... kill Jews wherever you find them for this pleases God, history, and religion. This saves your honor ... God is with you ... perish Judea!'

As the Mufti spoke, the Arab seemed to heed his words.

Syria and Lebanon were in the hands of Vichy French, and German matériel was pouring in to pave the way for an invasion of Palestine and Egypt.

The Egyptian chief of staff sold secrets to the Germans. King Farouk of Egypt refused to give the British a single soldier for the defense of Egypt against Rommel. Further plots hatched in Iraq.

The only avowed friend of the Allies was the old despot, Ibn Saud, who had been bought with American dollars. But Ibn Saud did not so much as offer a single camel to the British Eighth Army, which was fighting for its life.

In all the Middle East the Allied Powers had but one true fighting friend – the Yishuv!

Rommel, flushed with victory in Libya, stood poised to break through to Alexandria where German flags were being prepared to welcome the 'liberators.'

On the Russian front, the Wehrmacht stood before the gates of Stalingrad!

This was the Allies' darkest hour.

The prime target of the Germans was the Suez Canal, Egypt, and Palestine – the solar plexus of the British Empire. A break-through at Stalingrad could form another arm of a pincer movement to sweep through the Caucasus Mountains and open the doors of India and the Orient.

At last the British came to Yishuv Central and asked the Jews to form guerrilla units to cover the retreat of the British and harass the German occupation. This guerrilla force was called the Palmach. It was later to become the striking arm of the Haganah.

Ari Ben Canaan sat down for supper one evening.

'I enlisted in the British Army today,' he announced quietly.

The next day Ari reported to *kibbutz* Beth Alonim, House of the Oaks, where youths from all over Palestine had assembled to organize the Palmach.

Chapter Eighteen

Kibbutz Beth Alonim stood at the foot of Mount Tabor in the center of the Jezreel Valley. Ari was given a commission in the British Army and placed in charge of operations of the guerrilla units of boys and girls, most of whom were in their teens. Most of the officers were 'old-timers' in their mid-twenties like Ari.

Many of the former Raider Unit men joined the Palmach to indoctrinate the youngsters in the methods of Major P. P. Malcolm.

The troops wore no uniforms nor was there rank below the officers, and boys and girls were treated exactly the same. They were trained with the same sense of Biblical destiny that Malcolm had given his fighters.

Two of the soldiers showed such promise and leadership that they were advanced to lead units directly under Ari. One was a heavy-set *kibbutznik* from Galilee. His name was Zev Gilboa. He wore a big black mustache which later became the badge of a male Palmachnik. The other was a small intense young student from Jerusalem named David Ben Ami. Neither David nor Zev was yet twenty.

One day they were paid a visit by General Haven-Hurst. He was a tall thin blond man in his early fifties. As he inspected the camp he was aware of the coldness which greeted his presence. After the inspection, Haven-Hurst asked Ari to report to the camp's headquarters.

As Ari entered the office, the two men nodded stiffly, neither concealing his dislike for the other.

'Sit down, Lieutenant Ben Canaan,' Haven-Hurst said. 'You are to be commended on your work here with these Palmach troops.'

'Thank you, sir.'

'Matter of fact, I've been studying your record . . . or your case history, if you will. You've been a busy chap.'

'The conditions of my environment and the unfortunate circumstances of my birth have dictated it,' Ari said. 'I am a farmer at heart.'

Haven-Hurst took the rebuff without showing it.

'My main purpose for coming to Beth Alonim today was to ask you to volunteer for a special assignment. I know that when you enlisted it was on the proviso that you could train Palmach troops, but we feel this is urgent enough to alter that.'

'I am a soldier in the British Army, General Haven-Hurst. I will accept any assignment given me.'

'Good. Briefly, here is what it consists of. There has been a large German build-up in Syria. We feel they may attempt an invasion of Palestine this spring.'

Ari nodded.

'We are not at war with the Vichy French and we cannot invade Syria, but we do have sufficient Free French forces to do the job, provided we get flawless intelligence. We have selected you for this job because you know Syria and Lebanon from your Ha Mishmar days, and also because of your mastery of Arabic. We want you to reassemble those lads who were at Ha Mishmar with you and return there to use it as a reconnoitering base. When the invasion begins there will also be special assignments. There will be a captain's rank in this for you.'

'I see one problem, sir.'

'Yes?'

'A great number of my comrades from Ha Mishmar have been thrown into jail by the British.'

Haven-Hurst's face turned crimson. 'We will arrange releases.'

'Yes, sir. One more thing, sir. I have two men here who are exceptional soldiers. I would like to take them to Ha Mishmar with me and have them transferred into the British Army.'

'Very well,' Haven-Hurst said, 'take them with you.'

Ari walked to the door. 'An invasion of Syria at this time is excellent strategy, sir. It will give the British Eighth Army plenty of room to retreat to India.'

Haven-Hurst glared at the Jew. 'I suppose it is unnecessary to say, Ben Canaan, that you and I will be on opposite sides of the fence one day.'

'We already are, sir.'

Arie left Beth Alonim with Zev Gilboa and David Ben Ami as his sergeants and returned to Ha Mishmar on the hill which held such bitter memories for him. Fifty of the original Haganah gang were assembled – some from many parts of the world where they had been serving in the British forces.

Using Ha Mishmar as headquarters, Ari's patrols worked all the way up to Damascus. Extreme caution was needed, for the invasion was to be a complete surprise. Ari's basic method was simple. Most of his people spoke fluent Arabic and were familiar with the territory. He sent them out during the day, dressed as Arabs, and they merely walked along the roads gathering information. Although his intelligence was proving flawless, Ari wanted to get right inside Damascus and Beirut. This was a touchy job, and Ari reckoned it called for an individual foray. The one selected had to be able to move perfectly without raising suspicion. Ari checked with Haganah and they sent him a seventeen-year-old boy named Joab Yarkoni.

Yarkoni was a Moroccan Jew born in Casablanca and could indeed pass for an Arab anywhere. He was small, with saucer-like flashing black eyes and an overabundant sense of humor.

In Casablanca he and his family had lived in a *mellah*, the Oriental-African version of a ghetto. These Oriental and African Jews had little in common culturally with their Russian or German counterparts. Most of them were descendants of ancestors who had fled the Spanish Inquisition. Many still had Spanish names.

In some Arab lands the Jews were treated with a measure of fairness and near equality. Of course, no Jew could be entirely equal to a Moslem. A thousand years before, when Islam swept the world, Jews had been among the most honored of the Arab citizens. They were the court doctors, the philosophers, and the artisans – the top of the Arab society. In the demise of the Arab world that followed the Mongol wars, the demise of the Jews was worse.

There were Jews in Bagdad and Cairo and Damascus and Fez and Kurdistan and Casablanca, throughout the coast of Africa and deep into countries of the Middle East.

The Moslems never went to the extremes of the Christians in the matter of killing Jews. Arab riots were always kept within reasonable bounds – a few dozen murders at a time.

Joab Yarkoni and his family had escaped the *mellah* of Casablanca when he was but a youngster. His family settled down in a *kibbutz* in Samaria that hugged the sea. It was at Caesarea and called Sdot Yam, Fields of the Sea. Many illegal boats beached near Caesarea and it was here that Joab first went to work for Aliyah Bet as a gun runner when he was only twelve years of age.

When he was fifteen he took it upon himself to try a daring feat that spread his fame throughout the Yishuv. Joab walked from Sdot Yam with a donkey to Bagdad. There he stole some of the precious Iraqi date-palm saplings and smuggled them into Palestine. The saplings were sent to Shoshanna *kibbutz* on the Sea of Galilee and were instrumental in opening an entire new export crop for the Yishuv.

Ari's job was easy for young Joab. He walked to Damascus to Beirut to Tyre and returned to Ha Mishmar within three weeks. His information confirmed everything they already knew and further located Vichy strength nearly to a man.

Free French Forces moved quietly into Palestine, to the Galilee, and deployed for the invasion.

Ari's fifty men were bolstered by a special hand-picked group of forty Australians, experts in mines, automatic weapons, and explosives.

This ninety-man force was split into three units of thirty each. Each unit was given a special assignment to cross into Lebanon and Syria ahead of the invasion, advance and hold key roads and bridges against a counterattack until the main body could reach them.

Ari's force had the most dangerous of the missions. He was to lead his thirty men right up along the Lebanese coast, penetrate close to a Vichy garrison, and keep them from getting to half a dozen vital mountain bridges which could halt the Free French advance. Ari took Joab, Zev, and David with him. He had sixteen more Jews and ten Australians.

His unit moved out twenty-four hours before the invasion and sped up the coast with beautiful ease, for they knew every inch of the way. They passed the six crucial bridges one by one.

They stopped three miles from the Vichy garrison of Fort Henried and in a mountain pass mined the roads, set in their machine guns, and waited for the invasion to reach them.

As so often happens in a large-scale battle, an error was made. How, why, who made it is not so important after it occurs. The eastern arm of the invasion crossed from Trans-Jordan into Syria twelve hours ahead of H-Hour. As they moved toward Damascus they tipped off the entire operation.

For Ari it meant he would have to hold his mountain pass for twelve hours plus the additional three or four hours it would take for the main body to reach him.

Within a few hours after the error was made the Vichyites had massed two battalions with tanks and artillery at Fort Henried and started down the coastal road to blow up the mountain bridges.

As soon as Ari saw them coming he realized something had gone wrong. Quickly he dispatched David and Zev back to Palestine to bring help.

The Vichy troops marched blindly into the pass and were pulverized by explosions and crossfire from both sides of the hill. They fell back, reassembled, and sent artillery fire into the pass.

Six unbelievable hours passed before David and Zev came back with a battalion of Free French troops.

All the bridges were intact. There was no break-through. The pass was littered with over four hundred dead Vichyites who had tried to break Ari's position.

Five men of Ari's force were alive when help arrived. Ari Ben Canaan himself was at death's door. His back was filled with shrapnel, two bullets were lodged in his body, and his leg and nose were broken.

The Free French went on to complete the invasion of Syria.

For Ari Ben Canaan the war was over. He was taken back to Palestine for a long slow recovery. The British promoted him to major and he was decorated for his stand at the mountain pass.

Ari had played his role for Allied victory. So had the Yishuv.

Members of the Yishuv were in suicide squads that helped capture Tobruk and Bardia. Later a battalion of Palestinians was at the epic defense of Tobruk.

They fought in Italy and in Greece and in Crete and in the Lowlands. They numbered thousands in the Royal Air Force. They ran the 'death' patrol along the Mediterranean coast. The home guard kept the Arabs under control within Palestine. They fought in the desert in the captures of Sidi Barrani, Sollum, and Fort Capuzzo.

Jewish suicide units were picked for their valor in the campaigns in Eritrea and Ethiopia. Three thousand of the Yishuv joined the Free Forces of Czechoslovakia, Holland, France – and even Poland. A suicide force of Jews went out to destroy the oil refinery at Tripoli. Every member perished. Jews were used by the British for special spying missions. German Jews were dressed in German uniforms and worked right in Rommel's headquarters. Jews guarded the Mosul oil fields against continued Arab attempts to disrupt production.

When the British needed spies in the Balkans they turned to the Jews and trained them as parachutists. They reasoned that any Jew would be protected by the rest of the Jews in the country where he was dropped. Several were parachuted – few returned. One girl, Hanna Senesh, from Joab Yarkoni's *kibbutz* was dropped into Hungary and captured. She became a martyr by refusing to her death to break under the cruelest Nazi torture.

The Yishuv covered itself with glory. Just as in World War I the British glorified the Arab revolt – so they tried to hide the efforts of the Yishuv in World War II. No country gave with so much vitality to the war. But the British Government did not want the Jews to use this as a bargaining point for their homeland aspirations later on. Whitehall and Chatham House kept the Yishuv's war effort one of the best secrets of the war.

Rommel never reached Alexandria – they never broke the defenses of Stalingrad.

As the tide turned in favor of the British the Arabs no longer looked for the Germans to liberate them. Quickly they 'declared war' on Germany. The main purpose behind the Arab declarations of war was to gain a vote at the peace conferences and block the Zionists who had no vote but only the blood of their sons to show for their efforts.

Despite the Yishuv's magnificent record the British did not revoke the White Paper. Despite the Arab treachery and the fact that they did not raise a finger for victory they did not revoke it. Even with the ghastly news of the murder of six million Jews the British would not allow the survivors in.

The Haganah grew restless. Its ranks were filled with experienced soldiers. But it was the Maccabees who called off the truce! A series of terror bombings shook Palestine from end to end and again sent the British into their Taggart forts. The Maccabees, now numbering in the thousands, blew up one British installation after another.

General Haven-Hurst went after the Maccabees. With surprising swiftness he snared and deported several hundred Maccabee leaders to the Sudan. But Akiva's avenging warriors were not deterred.

Haven-Hurst ordered newly captured Maccabees to be lashed. The Maccabees retorted by catching British soldiers and whipping them in public.

Maccabees were hanged. British soldiers were caught and hanged. A dozen Maccabee bullets and grenades found their mark on a dozen of the more outspoken anti-Jewish officers.

Violent and sordid murders were perpetrated by the Arabs in answer to the Maccabees. The Holy Land reeled under the terror.

Haj Amin el Husseini was placed on the list of war criminals by the Yugoslav government. He had made himself spiritual head of the Yugoslav Moslems who had fought for the German Army. He was placed under arrest in France. The British, however, wanted El Husseini alive and ready to stir up trouble when they needed him, so they helped him escape to Egypt where he was welcomed as a Moslem hero. In Palestine his nephew Jemal seized control of the Arab community.

A new phase of history was bringing the United States into focus as the new power in the Middle East. In addition, since most of the European Jewish communities had been wiped out, by mere process of elimination Jews and others in the United States became the world leaders of the Zionist movement.

With America's rise, the British proposed a joint Anglo-American inquiry into the Palestine situation. This joint committee made another exhaustive survey of the Arabs and the Yishuv. They went to Europe to the DP camps. They came to the only human conclusion possible – '100,000 JEWS MUST BE ALLOWED INTO PALESTINE AT ONCE.'

The British balked.

It would only be considered if the Haganah and Palmach were disbanded at once! Preposterous! The British found a dozen more reasons not to follow the commission's recommendations.

The Arabs were as relentless as the Maccabees. Throughout the Arab world there were riots and protests against the Anglo-American commission.

At last the Yishuv Central had had enough. They sent the Palmach and

Haganah on a series of damaging raids on British positions.

The British poured in tens of thousands of front-line troops and turned the country into a police state. In a massive roundup they arrested several hundred prominent leaders of the Yishuv and threw them into Latrun prison.

In a masterful countermove, the Haganah blew up every frontier bridge in and out of Palestine in a single night.

The Aliyah Bet was putting more and more pressure on the British blockade.

Finally the British Foreign Minister burst forth with an anti-Jewish tirade and proclaimed all further immigration stopped.

The answer to this came from the Maccabees. The British had their main headquarters in the right wing of the King David Hotel in Jerusalem. This hotel was in the new city with its rear and gardens facing the wall of the old city. A dozen Maccabees, dressed as Arabs, delivered several dozen enormous milk cans to the basement of the hotel. The milk cans were placed under the right wing of the hotel beneath British headquarters. The cans were filled with dynamite. They set the timing devices, cleared the area, and phoned the British a warning to get out of the building. The British scoffed at the idea. This time the Maccabees were playing a prank. They merely wanted to make fools of the British. Surely they would not dare attack British headquarters!

In a few minutes there was a blast heard across the breadth of Palestine. The right wing of the King David Hotel was blown to smithereens!

Chapter Nineteen

The *Exodus* was declared fit and ready for the run to Palestine.

Ari set the sailing time as the morning after the Chanukah party which the management of the Dome Hotel had arranged on the hotel terrace.

Three hundred places were set. The small Jewish community of Cyprus and the crew of the *Exodus* sat at a long head table. There was tremendous gaiety as the children rushed to the terrace dressed in new clothing and were deluged with gifts from the people of Cyprus and soldiers from the garrison. The children took one gift each for themselves and marked the rest for the detention camps at Caraolos. The tables were bulging with food and the children squealed with delight. The terrible ordeal of the hunger strike was behind them; they had carried their burden like adults and now they could act like happy children with complete abandon. All around the terrace dozens of curious Greeks and British soldiers watched the celebration.

Karen looked around frantically for Kitty and lit up when she saw her some distance away, standing with Mark Parker by the rail.

'Come on, Kitty,' Karen called, 'there is a place for you here.'

'It's your party,' Kitty answered. 'I'll just watch.'

When everyone had opened his present, David Ben Ami stood at the head table. The terrace became very still as he began to speak. Only the steady shush of the sea could be heard behind him.

'Tonight we celebrate the first day of Chanukah,' David said. 'We celebrate this day in honor of Judah Maccabee and his brave brothers and his band of faithful men who came from the hills of Judea to do combat with the Greeks who enslaved our people.'

Some of the youngsters applauded.

'Judah Maccabee had a small band of men and they had no real right fighting so large and powerful an enemy as the Greeks, who ruled the entire world. But Judah Maccabee had faith. He believed that the one true God would show him the way. Judah was a wonderful fighter. Time and again he tricked the Greeks; his men were the greatest of warriors, for the faith of God was in their hearts. The Maccabees stormed Jerusalem and captured it and drove out the Greeks of Asia Minor, who ruled that area of the world.'

A riot of applause.

'Judah entered the Temple and his warriors tore down the idol of Zeus and again dedicated the Temple to the one true God. The same God who helped us all in our battle with the British.'

As David continued with the story of the rebirth of the Jewish nation, Kitty Fremont listened. She looked at Karen and at Dov Landau – and she looked at Mark and she lowered her eyes. Then she felt someone standing alongside her. It was Brigadier Bruce Sutherland.

'Tonight we will light the first candle of the Menorah. Each night we will light another candle until there are eight. We call Chanukah the feast of lights.'

David Ben Ami lit the first candle and the children said 'oh' and 'ah.'

'Tomorrow night we shall light the second Chanukah candle at sea and the night after we shall light the third one in Eretz Israel.'

David placed a small skullcap on his head and opened the Bible. '"*He will not suffer thy foot to be moved; he that keepeth thee will not slumber.*"'

Kitty's eyes came to rest on the head table. She looked at them – Zev Gilboa the farmer from the Galilee, and Joab Yarkoni the Moroccan Jew, and David Ben Ami, the scholar from Jerusalem. Her eyes stopped at Ari Ben Canaan. His eyes were rimmed with weariness now that he had had a chance to relax from his ordeal. David set the Bible down and continued to speak from memory.

'"*Behold!*"' David said, '"*he that keepeth Israel shall neither slumber nor sleep.*"'

An icy chill passed through Kitty Fremont's body. Her eyes were fixed on the tired face of Ari Ben Canaan. '*Behold . . . he that keepeth Israel shall neither slumber nor sleep.*'

The ancient motors of the *Exodus* groaned as she slid back into the center of Kyrenia Harbor and she turned and pointed out to sea in the direction of Palestine.

At dawn of the second day everyone sighted land at once.

'Palestine!'

'Eretz Israel!'

A hysteria of laughing and crying and singing and joy burst from the children.

The little salvage tug came within sight of land and the electrifying news spread through the Yishuv. The children who had brought the mighty British Empire to its knees were arriving!

The *Exodus* sputtered into Haifa Harbor amid a blast of welcoming horns and whistles. The salute spread from Haifa to the villages and the *kibbutzim* and the *moshavim* and all the way to Jerusalem to the Yishuv Central building and back again to Haifa.

Twenty-five thousand Jews poured onto the Haifa dock to cheer the creaky little boat. The Palestine Philharmonic Orchestra played the Jewish anthem – 'Hatikvah,' the Hope.

Tears streaked down the cheeks of Karen Hansen Clement as she looked up into Kitty's face.

The *Exodus* had come home!

BOOK THREE

An Eye for an Eye

... thou shalt give life for life, eye for eye, tooth for tooth, hand for hand, foot for foot, burning for burning.

THE WORD OF GOD AS GIVEN TO
MOSES IN EXODUS

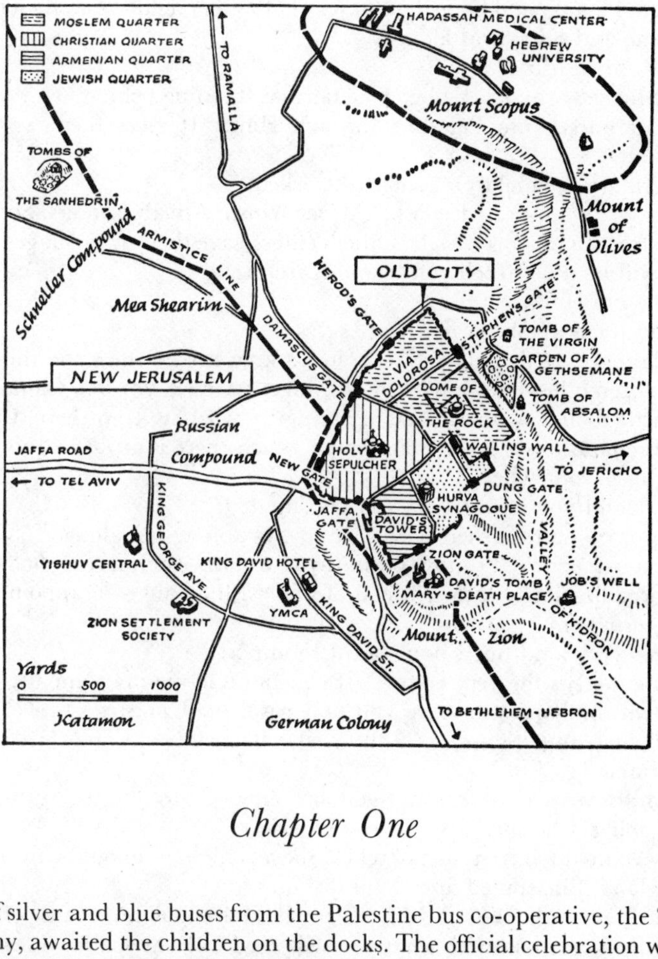

Chapter One

A line of silver and blue buses from the Palestine bus co-operative, the 'Egged' Company, awaited the children on the docks. The official celebration was kept to a quick minimum. The children were loaded aboard the buses and whisked out of the harbor area, convoyed by British armored vehicles. The band played and the crowd cheered as they rolled out of sight.

Karen tugged her window open and shouted to Kitty, but Kitty could not hear her over the din. The buses disappeared and the crowd dispersed. In fifteen minutes the dock was deserted except for a gang of longshoremen and a few British soldiers on guard duty.

Kitty stood motionless by the rail of the *Exodus*, stunned by the sudden strangeness. It was hard to realize where she was. She looked at Haifa. It was beautiful, with that special beauty that belonged to cities built on hills and around a bay. Close to the waterfront was the Arab sector with crowded clusters of buildings. The Jewish sector sprawled all over the long fingerlike slope of Mount Carmel. Kitty looked to her left, just past Haifa, and saw the futuristic shape of the tank and chimney buildings of the immense Haifa oil refinery, the terminus of the lines from the Mosul fields. At a nearby dock she saw a dozen dilapidated, rickety ships of the Aliyah Bet which, like the *Exodus*, had managed to reach Palestine.

Zev, David, and Joab interrupted Kitty's thoughts as they said good-bys and offered thanks and hope that they would see her again. And then they, too, were gone and Kitty was alone.

'Pretty town, isn't it?'

Kitty turned around. Ari Ben Canaan was standing behind her. 'We always bring our guests into Palestine through Haifa. It gives them a good first impression.'

'Where are the children going?' she asked.

'They will be dispersed to a half dozen Youth Aliyah Centers. Some of the centers are located on a *kibbutz*. Other centers have their own villages. In a few days I will be able to tell you where Karen is.'

'I'll be grateful.'

'What are your plans, Kitty?'

She laughed sardonically. 'I was just asking myself the same thing, along with a dozen other questions. I'm a stranger in town, Mr Ben Canaan, and I feel a little foolish at the moment, asking myself how I got here. Oh, Good Nurse Fremont has a solid profession in which there is always a shortage. I'll find a place, somewhere.'

'Why don't you let me help you get situated?'

'I suppose you're rather busy. I'm always able to get along.'

'Listen to me, now. I think Youth Aliyah would be perfect for you. The head of the organization is a close friend of mine. I'll arrange an appointment for you in Jerusalem.'

'That's very kind but I don't want to impose.'

'Nonsense. It's the very least ... If you can tolerate my company for a few days I will be happy to drive you to Jerusalem. I must go to Tel Aviv on business first, but it's just as well ... it will give me a chance to set your appointment.'

'I don't want you to feel that you are obligated to do this.'

'I'm doing it because I want to,' Ari said.

Kitty wanted to give a sigh of relief. She *was* nervous about being alone in a strange land. She smiled and thanked him.

'Good,' Ari said. 'We will have to stay in Haifa tonight because of the road curfew. Pack one bag with what you will need to keep you for a few days. If you carry too much with you the British will be going through your suitcases every five minutes. I'll have the rest of your things sealed and held at customs.'

After clearances Ari ordered a taxi and drove up Mount Carmel into the Jewish section, which spread through the hills on the mountainside. Near the top they stopped at a small pension set in a pine grove.

'It's better to stay up here. I know too many people and they won't let me alone for a minute if we stay in the center of town. Now you rest up. I'll go down the hill and scare up an auto. I'll be back by dinner.'

That evening Ari took Kitty to a restaurant on the very top of the Carmel, commanding a view of the entire area. The sight beneath was breath-taking. The whole hillside was alive with green trees and half-hidden brownstone houses and apartment buildings, all done in a square Arabic style. The weird-looking oil refinery appeared to be but a dot from this height, and as it turned dark a golden string of lights ran down the twisting road from Har Ha-Carmel into the Arab section by the waterfront.

Kitty was flushed with excitement and pleased with Ari's sudden show of attention. She was surprised by the modernness of Jewish Haifa. Why, it was far more modern than Athens or Salonika! Much of the strangeness went away when she was addressed in English by the waiter and a half dozen people who knew Ari and stopped at their table to exchange greetings.

They sipped brandy at the end of the meal and Kitty became solemn, intent on the panorama below.

'Are you still wondering what you are doing here?'

'Very much. It doesn't seem quite real.'

'You will find that we are quite civilized and I can even be charming – sometimes. You know, I never have properly thanked you.'

'You don't have to. You are thanking me very nicely. I can only remember one other place so lovely as this.'

'That must be San Francisco?'

'Have you been there, Ari?'

'No. All Americans say that Haifa reminds them of San Francisco.'

It was fully dark and lights twinkled on all over the Carmel hillside. A small orchestra played some light dinner music and Ari poured Kitty another brandy and they touched glasses.

Suddenly the music stopped. All conversation halted.

With startling speed a truckload of British troops pulled to a stop before the restaurant and the place was cordoned off. Six soldiers led by a captain entered and looked around. They began to move among the tables, stopping at several and demanding to see identification papers.

'This is just routine,' Ari whispered. 'You'll get used to it.'

The captain in charge of the detail stared at Ari's table, then walked over to it. 'If it isn't Ari Ben Canaan,' the captain said sarcastically. 'We haven't had your picture on the boards for a long time. I hear you've been making mischief elsewhere.'

'Evening, Sergeant,' Ari said. 'I'd introduce you if I could remember your name.'

The captain grinned through clenched teeth. 'Well, I remember yours. We're watching you, Ben Canaan. Your old cell at Acre jail is lonesome for you. Who knows, maybe the high commissioner will be smart this time and give you a rope instead.' The captain gave a mock salute and walked on.

'Well,' Kitty said, 'what a lovely welcome to Palestine. He was certainly a nasty person.'

Ari leaned close to Kitty and spoke into her ear. 'He is Captain Allan

Bridges. He is one of the best friends the Haganah has. He keeps us advised on every Arab and British move in the Haifa area. That was all for appearance.'

Kitty shook her head, bewildered. The patrol left with two Jews whose papers didn't appear in order. The orchestra harassed them with a chorus of 'God Save the King.'

The lorry drove away and in a moment it was as though nothing had happened, but Kitty was a little dazed by the suddenness of it and astonished by the calm of the people.

'You learn to live with tension after a while,' Ari said, watching her. 'You'll get used to it. It is a country filled with angry, emotional people. After a while you won't know what to do when you get one of those rare weeks of peace and quiet. Don't be sorry you came just when you are getting...'

Ari's speech was cut off by a shock wave that ran through the restaurant, rattling the windows and jarring some dishes from the tables. In a second they saw a huge orange ball of flame push angrily into the sky. Another series of explosions followed, shaking the place to its foundations.

Shouts arose: 'The oil refinery!' ... 'They've got the refinery!' ... '*Maccabee raid!*'

Ari grabbed Kitty's hand. 'Let's get out of here. In ten minutes the whole Carmel Valley will be crawling with British soldiers.'

The café was emptied in seconds. Ari led Kitty out quickly. Below them oil was flaming madly. The entire city screamed with the frantic siren shrieks of speeding fire trucks and British patrols.

Kitty lay awake half the night trying to comprehend the sudden violent things she had seen. She was glad that Ari had been with her. Would she get used to living with this? She was too bewildered to think about it, but at the moment she felt her coming to Palestine was a sorry mistake.

The next morning the oil refinery was still blazing. A pall of thick smoke hung over the entire Haifa area. The information spread that the raid was Maccabee terrorist work. It had been led by Ben Moshe – Son of Moses – the Maccabee field commander under Akiva, and formerly a professor at the Hebrew University before he rose in Maccabee ranks. The raid was part of a double-pronged Maccabee action. The other strike was against the Lydda airdrome in another part of Palestine, where the terrorists destroyed six million dollars' worth of Spitfire fighter planes on the ground. The action was the Maccabees' own way of welcoming the *Exodus*.

Ari had been able to acquire a small Italian Fiat, a 1933 model. The drive to Tel Aviv took only a few hours under normal conditions. Inasmuch as he had never known conditions to be normal he suggested they depart Haifa early. They drove down from the Carmel and took the coastal road along the edge of Samaria. Kitty was impressed by the greenness of the fields of the *kibbutzim* near the sea. Their color showed more brilliantly by contrast to the drabness of the hills and the dulling glare of the sun. A few minutes' drive from Haifa they met the first roadblock. Ari had warned Kitty to expect it. She watched his reactions. He was apparently not at all annoyed, despite the fact that many of the soldiers knew him and taunted him with the reminder that his amnesty was only temporary.

Ari left the main road and drove to the Caesarea ruins on the sea. A lunch had been packed for them at the pension and they ate it on the ancient sea wall. Ari pointed to the Sdot Yam – Fields of the Sea – *kibbutz* where Joab Yarkoni lived and where he had spent much time with the Aliyah Bet when they beached the illegal runners during the 1936–39 riots. Ari showed Kitty how the Arabs had built their town on ruins, some Roman, some Crusader. The Arabs were experts in building on other people's civilizations and had, in fact, constructed only one wholly new city in all of Palestine in a thousand years. Some of the magnificent Roman statuary and columns had been dragged off from Caesarea and could be found in Arab homes throughout the Samarian and Sharon districts.

After lunch they continued south toward Tel Aviv. The traffic was light. There was only an occasional bus load of either Arabs or Jews or the ever-present donkey cart. Every now and then a speeding, siren-screaming British convoy raced past them. As they passed Arab sections Kitty noticed the contrast of these villages and lands. The Arab women toiled in the fields and the Arab fields were stony and drab. The women walked along the roadside encased in cumbersome robes with enormous loads balanced on their heads. The coffeehouses along the road were filled with listless men sitting motionless or lying down playing backgammon. Below Zichron Yakov – Memory of Jacob – they passed the first barbwire-enclosed ominous-looking Taggart fort. At Hadera, a bit farther, they came to another, and thereafter they seemed to pop up at every town and crossroad.

Beyond Hadera the land around the Plain of Sharon was even more lush and fertile. They drove between enormous archways of Australian eucalyptus trees.

'Everything you see was waste just twenty-five years ago,' Ari said.

In the afternoon they entered Tel Aviv – the Hill of Spring.

Along the Mediterranean coast arose this city so white it dazzled the eye in the afternoon sun. Tel Aviv was like frosting on a cake. Ari drove on broad, tree-lined boulevards between rows of ultramodern apartment houses. The city was alive with bustle and movement. Kitty liked Tel Aviv the instant she saw it.

On Hayarkon Street, right on the sea, Ari checked into Gat Rimon Hotel.

In late afternoon all the shops reopened after the siesta period. Ari and Kitty strolled down Allenby Road. Kitty had to change some currency, purchase a few things, and satisfy a lot of curiosity. Beyond the Mograbi Theater and plaza the road was filled with small shops, the honking and rushing of buses, cars, and people. Kitty had to see every last shop. There were a dozen or more book stores, and she paused to gaze at the cryptic Hebrew letters. They walked and walked, up to Rothschild Boulevard past the main business district. Here was the older town where Tel Aviv had begun as an outgrowth of Jaffa. The closer they came to the Arab city the more run-down the buildings and shops became. Walking along the streets connecting the two cities, Kitty felt as though she were walking back in time. The surroundings grew dirtier and more odorous and the shops grew smaller and shabbier with each step. They circled back to Tel Aviv through a market place common to both Jews and Arabs. The narrow street was a mass of haggling people crowded around the stalls. They returned down the opposite side of Allenby Road, back to the Mograbi plaza and turned into another wide, tree-lined street. This was Ben Yehuda Street and it was filled with sidewalk cafés. Each café had its own distinctive flavor and its own distinctive clientele. There was a café for the gathering of lawyers and there was a café of the socialist politicians and a café of artists and a businessmen's café. There was a café where fellow travelers of the terrorists hung out and there was a café of old retired folk playing never-ending chess games. All the cafés of Ben Yehuda Street were filled and were bursting with chatter and arguments.

The news hawkers of the tiny, four-page newspapers shouted out in Hebrew of the Maccabee raids on Lydda and the Haifa refinery and of the arrival of the *Exodus*. There was a steady stream of people flowing by. There were Orientals in mideastern habit and there were well-groomed women in the latest of fashions from a dozen European countries. Mostly, there were native men in khaki pants and white shirts opened at the necks. They wore thin chain necklaces with a Star of David or some Hebrew pendant. Most of them sported the black mustache which was a trademark of the native born. They were a rugged lot. Many were in the blue of a *kibbutz* with sandaled feet. The native women were tall, angular, and high breasted in plain dresses or slacks or shorts. There was an aggressiveness and pride about them, even in their walk.

Then Ben Yehuda Street became quiet.

It was the same sudden quiet that Kitty remembered from the night before at the restaurant in Haifa.

A British armored sound truck inched down the middle of Ben Yehuda Street. Tight-lipped Tommies manned machine guns on the car.

'ATTENTION ALL JEWS. THE COMMANDING GENERAL HAS ORDERED A CURFEW. ALL JEWS MUST BE OFF THE STREET BY DARK. ATTENTION ALL JEWS. THE COMMANDING GENERAL HAS ORDERED A CURFEW. ALL JEWS MUST BE OFF THE STREET BY DARK.'

A ripple of applause and laughter broke out from the onlookers.

'Watch it, Tommy,' someone called. 'The next intersection is mined.'

When the trucks had passed, the scene quickly returned to normal.

'Let's get back to the hotel,' Kitty said.

'I told you you'll get so that you won't be able to live without excitement within a month.'

'I'll never get used to it, Ari.'

They returned to the hotel with their arms filled with Kitty's purchases. After cocktails in the small quiet bar there was dinner on the terrace overlooking the sea. Kitty could see the sweep of the coast line where the new city of Tel Aviv ran into the ancient city of Jaffa, the oldest port in the world.

'Thank you for a very nice day, British patrols and roadblocks notwithstanding.'

'You'll have to forgive me,' Ari said, 'I must leave after dinner for a while.'

'What about the curfew?'

'That only applies to Jews,' Ari said.

Ari left Kitty and drove from Tel Aviv to the adjoining suburb town of Ramat Gan – the Hill Garden. It was a contrast to the apartment-house city of Tel Aviv in that it was a town of individual homes set in lawns and trees and gardens. The houses were a stucco with red tiled roofs, and they ranged from cottages to huge villas. Ari parked the car and walked about for more than a half hour to make certain he was not being followed.

He came to Montefiore Street 22, a large villa owned by a Dr Y. Tamir. Dr Tamir answered the knock, greeted Ari with a warm handshake, and led him downstairs to the basement.

The home of Tamir was Haganah headquarters.

The cellar held munitions and arms, and a printing press which ground out leaflets in Arabic warning the Arabs to remain calm and keep the peace. In another section of the basement a girl spoke in Arabic into a tape recording machine, repeating the warning of the leaflets. The tape would later be transmitted over the secret mobile radio station, Kol Israel – the Voice of Israel. The manufacturing of hand grenades and the assembly of homemade Sten guns were also among the activities of the underground headquarters.

All activity stopped as Dr Tamir appeared with Ari. The latter was surrounded and congratulated on the *Exodus* affair; questions were fired at him from all sides.

'Later, later,' Dr Tamir pleaded.

'I must see Avidan,' Ari said.

He made his way past the stacked cases of rifles to the door of a secluded office and knocked upon it.

'Yes?'

Ari opened the door and stood before the bald-headed, squat farmer who commanded the underground army. Avidan looked up from the papers on his rickety desk and burst into a smile. 'Ari! *Shalom!*' He sprang up and threw his arms around Ari's neck, shoved him into a chair, closed the door, and slapped Ari on the back with the force of a pile driver. 'So good to see you, Ari! You did a first-class job on the British. Where are the boys?'

'I sent them home.'

'Good. They deserve a few days. Take a few days yourself.'

This was an impressive reward from Avidan, who had not taken a day off for himself in a quarter of a century.

'Who is the girl you came in with?'

'An Arab spy. Don't be so nosy.'

'Is she one of our friends?'

'No, she isn't a friend. Not even a fellow traveler.'

'A shame. We could use a good American Christian.'

'No, she's just a nice woman who looks at Jews as though she were looking into a cage at a zoo. I'm running her up to Jerusalem tomorrow to see Harriet Saltzman about getting her a place in Youth Aliyah.'

'Something personal, maybe?'

'Good Lord, no. Now turn your Jewish curiosity somewhere else.'

The room was stuffy. Avidan pulled out a large blue kerchief and mopped the sweat from his bald pate.

'That was quite a welcome we got yesterday from the Maccabees. I hear the refinery will be burning for a week. Wrecked production.'

Avidan shook his head. 'They did a good job yesterday – but what of the day before yesterday and what of the day after tomorrow? They are making three bad raids to every good one. Every time they resort to brutality or indiscriminate murder the whole Yishuv suffers. We are the ones who have to answer for Maccabee actions. Tomorrow General Haven-Hurst and the high commissioner will be at Yishuv Central. They'll be pounding their fists on Ben Gurion's desk demanding we use the Haganah to apprehend them. I swear I don't know what to do sometimes. So far the British haven't really turned on the Haganah but I am afraid if Maccabee terror continues . . . they've even taken up bank robbery to finance their operations.'

'British banks, I hope.' Ari lit a cigarette and stood up and paced the tiny office. 'Perhaps the time has come to stage a few good raids of our own.'

'No ... we just can't risk the Haganah. We are the ones who must defend all the Jews. Illegal immigration ... that is the way we will fight them for now. One thing like the *Exodus* is more important than blowing up ten Haifa refineries.'

'But the day must come that we commit ourselves, Avidan. We have an army or we don't.'

Avidan took some sheets of paper from his desk drawer and pushed them over toward Ari. Ari thumbed through them: ORDER OF BATTLE, 6TH AIRBORNE DIVISION.

Ari looked up. 'They have three parachute brigades?'

'Keep reading.'

ROYAL ARMORED CORPS WITH KING'S OWN HUSSARS, 53RD WORCESTERSHIRE, 249TH AIRBORNE PARK, DRAGOON GUARDS, ROYAL LANCERS, QUEEN'S ROYAL, EAST SURREY, MIDDLESEX, GORDON HIGHLANDERS, ULSTER RIFLES, HERTFORDSHIRE REGIMENT – the list of British troops in Palestine ran on and on. Ari threw the papers down on Avidan's desk. 'Whom are they fighting, the Russian Army?'

'You see, Ari? Every day I go through it with some young hotheads in the Palmach. Why don't we raid? Why don't we come out and fight? Do you think I like it? Ari ... they have twenty per cent of the combat strength of the British Army here. One hundred thousand troops, not counting the Trans-Jordan Arab Legion. Sure, the Maccabees run around shooting up everything, grabbing the limelight, accusing us of hiding.' Avidan slammed his fist on the desk. 'By God, I'm trying to put an army together. We haven't even got ten thousand rifles to fight with and if the Haganah goes, we all go with it.

'You see, Ari ... the Maccabees can keep mobility and hide with a few thousand blowhards. We have got to stall and keep stalling. We can't have a showdown. We can't get Haven-Hurst angry, either. One British soldier here for every five Jews.'

Ari picked up the list of British troops again and studied it in silence.

'The British dragnets, cordons, screenings, raids get worse every day. The Arabs are building strength while the British turn their backs.'

Ari nodded. 'Where do I go from here?'

'I am not going to give you a command, yet. Go on home, take a few days' rest then report to Palmach at Ein Or *kibbutz*. I want you to assess our strength in every settlement in the Galilee. We want to know what we can expect to hold ... what we are going to lose.'

'I've never heard you talk like this, Avidan.'

'Things have never been so bad. The Arabs have refused even to sit at the same conference table and talk with us in London.'

Ari walked to the door.

'My love to Barak and Sarah and tell Jordana to behave herself with David Ben Ami home. I am sending him and the other boys to Ein Or.'

'I'll be in Jerusalem tomorrow,' Ari said. 'Do you want anything?'

'Yes, dig me up ten thousand front-line troops and the arms to outfit them.'

'*Shalom*, Avidan.'

'*Shalom*, Ari. It is good to have you home.'

Ari grew morose as he drove back to Tel Aviv. Long ago in Cyprus he had told young David Ben Ami that many things are tried in the Haganah and Palmach and Aliyah Bet. Some plans work and some fail. A professional should do his work and not become entangled emotionally. Ari Ben Canaan was a machine. He was an efficient, daring operator. Sometimes he won, sometimes he lost.

But once in a while Ari Ben Canaan looked at it all with realism and it nearly crushed him.

Exodus, the Haifa refinery, a raid here, a raid there. Men died to smuggle in fifty rifles. Men were hanged for smuggling in a hundred frantic survivors. He was a little man fighting a giant. He wished, at that moment, he could have David Ben Ami's faith in divine intervention, but Ari was a realist.

Kitty Fremont waited in the little bar off the lobby for Ari's return. He had been so decent that she wanted to wait up for him and talk some more and have a nightcap or two. She saw him walk into the lobby and go to the desk for his key.

'Ari!' she called.

His face showed the same deep concentration it had showed that first day she saw him on Cyprus. She waved to him but he did not even seem to see or to hear her. He looked directly at her, then walked upstairs to his room.

Chapter Two

Two buses carrying fifty of the *Exodus* children drove past the *tel* of the ruins of Hazor and into the Huleh Valley. All during the drive from Haifa through the Galilee the travelers had been hanging out of the window cheering and waving and pointing in wonder at the sights of their long-promised land.

'Dov! Everything is so beautiful!' Karen cried.

Dov's grumble Karen interpreted as meaning that he didn't see so much to make a fuss about.

They drove deep into the Huleh to Yad El, the home of Ari Ben Canaan. Here a road branched from the main road and ran up into the hills toward the Lebanese border. The children saw the road sign pointing to Gan Dafna; they nearly exploded with anticipation, with the lone exception of the morose Dov Landau. The buses worked up the winding road and soon the Huleh expanded into full vista, carpeted with green fields of the *kibbutzim* and *moshavim*. The rectangular fishponds made a dozen small lakes around the larger swamplands of Huleh Lake.

They slowed as they entered the Arab village of Abu Yesha halfway up the mountains. There was none of the coldness or hostility at Abu Yesha the children had noted in the other Arab villages. They were greeted with friendly waving.

Past Abu Yesha they climbed beyond the two-thousand-foot elevation marker and then on to the Youth Aliyah village of Gan Dafna – the Garden of Dafna. They stopped before green lawn measuring fifty by a hundred yards in the center of the village. The whole place sat on a large plateau. The center green was surrounded by administration buildings and was the hub of the village, which ran off in all four directions. Flowers and trees and green were everywhere. As the *Exodus* children debarked the village orchestra greeted them with a rousing march.

In the center of the green stood a life-sized statue of Dafna, the girl after whom the village was named. The figure was cast in bronze with a rifle in her hands, looking down on the Huleh, much the same as that day at Ha Mishmar when the Arabs had killed her.

The village founder, a tiny man with a slight humpback named Dr Lieberman, stood by the statue of Dafna, smoking a large-bowled pipe as he welcomed the new youngsters. He briefly told them that he had left Germany in 1934 and founded Gan Dafna in 1940 on this land which had been generously given to Youth Aliyah by Kammal, the late muktar of Abu Yesha. Dr Lieberman went to each youngster to speak a few personal words of welcome in a half dozen languages. As Karen watched him she had a feeling that she had seen him before. He looked and acted like the professors at Cologne when she was a baby ... but it was so long ago she could not really remember.

Each new child was attended by a member of the village.

'Are you Karen Clement?'

'Yes.'

'I am Yona, your new roommate,' said an Egyptian Jewess a bit older than Karen. The two girls shook hands. 'Come, I will show you to our room. You will like it here.'

Karen called to Dov that she would see him later and she walked beside Yona past the administration buildings and the schoolrooms to an area of cottages set in a shrubbed pathway. 'We are lucky,' Yona said. 'We get the cottages because we are seniors.'

Karen stopped a moment before the cottage and looked at it with disbelief, then entered. It was very simple but Karen thought it the most wonderful room that she had ever seen. A bed, a desk, a wardrobe and a chair – her own, her very own.

It was evening before Karen had a free moment. After dinner the children were to be given a welcoming show at the outdoor theater.

Karen met Dov on the green near the statue of Dafna. For the first time in weeks and weeks she felt like dancing. The air was so crisp and wonderful and the village was heaven! Karen trembled with happiness. She stood by Dov and pointed to the white clustered houses of Abu Yesha below them in a saddle of the hill. Above them was the Taggart fort, Fort Esther, on the Lebanese border, and down at the floor of the valley were the fields belonging to the village, adjoining the fields of the *moshav* of Yad El. Along the hilltops at the far end of the Huleh was Tel Hai, where Trumpledor fell, and across the valley was Mount Hermon and Syria.

Karen was dressed in olive-drab slacks and high-collared peasant's blouse and she wore new sandals on her feet. 'Oh, Dov! This is the most wonderful day of my life,' she cried. 'Yona is lots of fun and she was telling me that Dr Lieberman is the nicest man on earth.'

She rolled in the grass and looked up in the sky and sighed. Dov stood over her, wordless. She sat up and took his hand and tugged at him to sit beside her.

'Cut it out,' he said.

She persisted and he sat down. He became nervous as she squeezed his hand and lay her head on his shoulder. 'Please be happy, Dov ... please be happy.'

He shrugged and pulled away from her.

'Please be happy.'

'Who cares about it?'

'I care,' Karen said. 'I care for you.'

'Well . . . care for yourself.'

'I care for myself, too.' She knelt in front of him and gripped his shoulders. 'Did you see your room and your bed? How long has it been since you've been in a room like that?'

Dov flushed at the touch of her hands and lowered his eyes. 'Just think, Dov. No more displaced persons' camps . . . no more La Ciotats, no more Caraolos. No more illegal ships. We are home, Dov, and it is even more beautiful than I dreamed.'

Dov got to his feet slowly and turned his back. 'This place is fine for you. I got other plans.'

'Please forget them,' she pleaded.

The orchestra played and the music drifted over the green.

'We had better get to the theater,' Karen said.

Once Ari and Kitty left Tel Aviv and drove past the huge British camp at Sarafand she felt the tension of Palestine again. They passed through the all-Arab city of Ramle on the road to Jerusalem and felt angry Arab eyes on them. Ari seemed oblivious of the Arabs and oblivious of Kitty. He had not spoken a dozen words to her all day.

Beyond Ramle the car turned into the Bab el Wad, a snaking road that twisted up into the Judean hills. Young forests planted by the Jews pushed up from the earth on ravines on either side of the road. Deep into the hills stood ancient terracing that stood out from the denuded earth like ribs of a starving dog. Once these very hills and terraces supported hundreds of thousands of people. Now it was completely eroded. The hilltops held Arab villages clustered in white clumps above them.

Here in the Bab el Wad the magic pull of Jerusalem gripped Kitty Fremont. It was said that none could pass through the Judean hills for the first time and escape the haunting power of the City of David. It seemed strange to Kitty that she should feel it so intensely. Her religious training had been in matter-of-fact midwestern Protestantism. It had been approached with a basic sincerity and a lack of intensity. Higher and higher they drove and the anticipation became greater. She was with the Bible now, and for the first time, in these silent and weird hills, came the realization of what it was to be in the Holy Land.

In the distance a dim outline of the citadels of Jerusalem jutted on the horizon and Kitty Fremont was filled with a kind of exaltation.

They entered the New City built by the Jews and drove down Jaffa Road, the principal commercial spine that passed crowded shops, toward the wall of the Old City. At the Jaffa Gate, Ari turned and drove along the wall to King David Avenue and in a few moments stopped before the great King David Hotel.

Kitty stepped from the car and gasped at the sight of the right wing of the hotel sheared away.

'It was once British headquarters,' Ari said. 'The Maccabees changed all that.'

The hotel was built of Jerusalem stone. It was grandiose in the over-burdened European manner, with its lobby an alleged duplication of King David's court.

Kitty came down to lunch first. She waited on the terrace in the rear of the hotel that looked over a small valley to the Old City wall. The terrace was opposite David's Tower and was set in a formal garden. A four-piece orchestra behind her played luncheon music.

Ari walked out to the terrace and stopped in his tracks. Kitty looked lovely! He had never seen her like this before. She wore a flouncy and chic cocktail dress and a wide-brimmed hat and white gloves. At that moment he felt far away from her. She was all the lovely women in Rome and in Paris and even Berlin who belonged to a world in which women acted in a way he could not quite understand. It was a light year from Kitty to Dafna but she was beautiful, indeed.

He seated himself. 'I have spoken to Harriet Saltzman. We will see her right after lunch.'

'Thanks. I'm very excited about Jerusalem.'

'She has mysterious powers. Everyone is excited on his first visit. Take David Ben Ami . . . David never gets over Jerusalem. Matter of fact he will be sight-seeing with you tomorrow. It is the Sabbath. He wants to take you into the Old City.'

'He is sweet to think of me.'

Ari looked at her closely. She seemed even prettier now than when he entered the terrace. He turned his eyes away and signaled for a waiter, then stared off into space after giving the order. Kitty had the feeling now that Ari had committed himself and was anxious to complete his obligation. No word passed between them for ten minutes.

She picked at her salad. 'Do I bore you?'

'Of course not.'

'Since you came back from your engagement last night you've acted as though I haven't existed.'

'I'm sorry, Kitty,' he said without looking at her. 'I guess I have been rather bad company today.'

'Is there something wrong?'

'There's a lot wrong but it doesn't concern you or me or my bad manners. Let me tell you about Harriet Saltzman. She's an American. She must be well over eighty years old now. If we conferred sainthoods in the Yishuv, she would be our first saint. See that hill beyond the Old City?'

'Over there?'

'That's Mount Scopus. Those buildings make up the most modern medical center in the Middle East. The money comes from American Zionist women that Harriet organized after the first world war. Most of the hospital and medical centers in Palestine come from her Hadassah organization.'

'She sounds like quite a girl.'

'Yes, she is. When Hitler came to power Harriet organized Youth Aliyah. She is responsible for saving thousands of youngsters. They maintain dozens of youth centers all over Palestine. You'll get along fine with her.'

'Why do you say that?'

'Well, no Jew who has lived in Palestine can ever go without leaving his heart here. It's the same way with Americans, I think. Harriet has been here for years but she's still very much an American.'

The orchestra stopped playing.

A silence fell over Jerusalem. They could hear the faint cry of a Moslem muezzin calling his people to prayer from a minaret in the Old City. Then it became quiet again with a stillness that Kitty had never experienced.

The bells from the carillon in the YMCA tower over the street played a hymn and the tones flooded the hills and the valleys. And then – again it became still. It was so peaceful it would have been sacrilegious to speak. All life and all time seemed to stand still in one moment.

'What an utterly wonderful sensation,' Kitty said.

'Those kinds of moments are rarities these days,' Ari said. 'I am afraid that the calm is deceptive.'

Ari saw a small olive-skinned man standing at the terrace door. He recognized the man as Bar Israel, the contact for the Maccabees. Bar Israel nodded to Ari and disappeared.

'Will you excuse me for a moment?' Ari said. He walked into the lobby to the cigarette stand and purchased a pack and then thumbed through a magazine. Bar Israel walked up alongside him.

'Your Uncle Akiva is in Jerusalem,' Bar Israel whispered. 'He wants to see you.'

'I have to go to the Zion Settlement Society but I will be free shortly after.'

'Meet me in the Russian compound,' the contact man said, and hastened through the lobby.

King George Avenue was a wide boulevard in the New City and was lined with administrative buildings and schools and churches. The Zion Settlement Society, a large, four-storied rambling affair, stood on a corner. A long driveway led to the main entrance.

'*Shalom*, Ari!' Harriet Saltzman said, prancing from behind her desk with an agility that belied her years. She stood on her toes, put her arms around Ari's neck, and kissed his cheek heartily. 'Oh, what a job you did on them at Cyprus. You are a good boy.'

Kitty watched quietly in the doorway. The old woman turned to her.

'So this is Katherine Fremont. My child, you are very lovely.'

'Thank you, Mrs Saltzman.'

'Don't make with the "Mrs Saltzman." Only Englishmen and Arabs call me that. It makes me feel old. Sit down, sit down. I'll order tea. Or perhaps you would rather have coffee.'

'Tea is fine.'

'So you see, Ari . . . this is what an American girl looks like.' Harriet made a gesture of tribute to Kitty's beauty with mischief twinkling in her eyes.

'I am certain that not all American girls are as pretty as Kitty . . .'

'Stop it, both of you. You are embarrassing me.'

'You girls don't need me. I have a few things to do, so I'll just beat it. Kitty, if I'm not back for you would you mind taking a taxi back to the hotel?'

'Go already,' the old woman said. 'Kitty and I are going to have dinner together at my flat. Who needs you?'

Ari smiled and left.

'That's a fine boy,' Harriet Saltzman said. 'We have lots of good boys like Ari. They work too hard, they die too young.' She lit a cigarette and offered Kitty one. 'And where do you hail from?'

'Indiana.'

'San Francisco, here.'

'It is a lovely city,' Kitty said. 'I visited it once with my husband. I always hoped to go back someday.'

'I do too,' the old woman said. 'It seems that I miss the States more every year. For fifteen years I have sworn I would go back for a while, but the work never seems to stop here. All these poor babies coming in. But I get homesick. Senility is creeping up on me, I guess.'

'Hardly.'

'It is good to be a Jew working for the rebirth of a Jewish nation but it is also a very good thing to be an American and don't you ever forget that, young lady. Ever since the *Exodus* incident started I've been very anxious to meet you, Katherine Fremont, and I must say I am tremendously surprised and I don't surprise easily.'

'I am afraid that the reports overromanticized me.'

Behind Harriet Saltzman's disarming friendliness functioned a shrewd brain, and even though Kitty was completely at ease she realized how carefully the old woman was estimating her. They sipped their tea and chatted, mostly about America. Harriet became nostalgic. 'I go home next year. I will find an excuse. Maybe a fund-raising drive. We are always having fund-raising drives. Do you know that the American Jews give us more than all Americans give to the Red Cross? So why should I bore you with these things? So you want to go to work for us?'

'I am sorry that I don't have my credentials with me.'

'You don't need them. We know all about you.'

'Oh?'

'Yes. We have a half dozen reports already on file.'

'I don't know whether to be pleased or offended.'

'Don't be offended. It is the times. We must be sure of everyone. You will find that we are really a small community here and very little happens that doesn't come back to these ancient ears. As a matter of fact I was reading our files on you before you came this afternoon and I was wondering why you have come to us.'

'I am a nurse and you need nurses.'

Harriet Saltzman shook her head. 'Outsiders don't come to us for that reason. There must be another one. Did you come to Palestine for Ari Ben Canaan?'

'No . . . of course I am fond of him.'

'A hundred women are fond of him. You happen to be the woman he is fond of.'

'I don't think so, Harriet.'

'Well . . . I am glad, Katherine. It is a long way from Yad El to Indiana. He is a *sabra* and only another *sabra* could really understand him.'

'*Sabra?*'

'It is a term we use for the native born. A *sabra* is the fruit of a wild cactus you will find all over Palestine. The *sabra* is hard on the outside . . . but inside, it is very tender and sweet.'

'That is a good description.'

'Ari and the other *sabras* have no conception of American life, just as you have no conception of what his life has been.

'Let me be very candid. When a gentile comes to us, he comes as a friend. You are not a friend, you are not one of us. You are a very beautiful American girl who is completely puzzled by these strange people called Jews. Now why are you here?'

'It's not that mysterious. I am very fond of a young girl. She came over on the *Exodus*. We met earlier in Caraolos. I am afraid her attempts to reunite with her father may end very unhappily. If she is unable to find her father I want to adopt her and take her to America.'

'I see. Well, you are on the level. Let us talk turkey. There is an opening for a head nurse in one of our Youth Villages in the northern Galilee. It is a lovely place. The director is one of my oldest and dearest friends, Dr Ernest Lieberman. The village is called Gan Dafna. We have four hundred children there and most of them are concentration-camp bred. They need help badly. I do hope you will take this assignment. The pay and the facilities are very good.'

'I . . . I . . . would like to know about . . .'

'Karen Hansen?'

'How did you know?'

'I told you we were a small community. Karen is at Gan Dafna.'

'I don't know how to thank you.'

'Thank Ari. He is the one who arranged it all. Ari will take you up there. It is very close to his home.'

The old woman emptied her teacup and leaned back in her chair. 'Could I give you one last piece of advice?'

'Of course.'

'I have been working with orphans since 1933. The attachment they form for Palestine may be something very difficult for you to understand. Once they have breathed the air of freedom . . . once they are filled with this patriotism it is extremely difficult for them to leave, and if and when they do most of them never become adjusted to living away from Palestine. Their devotion is a fierce thing. Americans take so many things about America for granted. Here, a person wakes up every morning in doubt and tension – not knowing if all he has slaved for will be taken from him. Their country is with them twenty-four hours a day. It is the focal point of their lives, the very meaning of their existence.'

'Are you trying to say I may not be able to persuade the girl to leave?'

'I am trying to make you aware that you are fighting tremendous odds.'

There was a knock on the door.

'Come in.'

David Ben Ami entered, '*Shalom*, Harriet. *Shalom*, Kitty. Ari told me that I could find you here. Am I interrupting anything?'

'No, we've finished our business. I am sending Katherine to Gan Dafna.'

'Splendid. I thought that it would be a good idea to show Kitty around Mea Shearim when the Sabbath starts.'

'An excellent idea, David.'

'Then we had better get started. Will you come with us, Harriet?'

'Lug these old bones around? Not on your life. You have Katherine at my flat for dinner in two hours.'

Kitty stood up and shook hands with the old woman and thanked her and then turned to David. He stared at her.

'Is something wrong, David?' Kitty asked.

'I have never seen you dressed up. You look very beautiful.' He looked at himself awkwardly. 'Perhaps I am not dressed well enough to walk around with you.'

'Nonsense. I was just trying to show off for my new boss.'

'*Shalom*, children. I will see you later.'

Kitty was pleased that David had come for her. She felt more comfortable around him than with any of the other Jews. They walked from the Zion Settlement Society and crossed to the Street of the Prophets. Kitty took his arm, but it seemed as though David was the one who was the sightseer. He was rediscovering everything about Jerusalem and he was as delighted as a child. 'It is so good to be home again,' he said. 'How do you like my city?'

'Are there words? It is overwhelming and a little frightening.'

'Yes, that is the way I have always felt about Jerusalem ever since I was a boy. It never fails to thrill me and to haunt me.'

'It was very kind of you to take time away from your family.'

'We are not all assembled yet. I have six brothers, you know. Most of them are in the Palmach. I am the baby of the family so there will be a reunion. All of us except one ... I will have to see him alone later.'

'Is he ill?'

'He is a terrorist. He is with the Maccabees. My father will not permit him to enter our house. He is with Ben Moshe, a leader of the Maccabees. Ben Moshe was once my professor at the Hebrew University.' David stopped and pointed to Mount Scopus beyond the Hadassah Medical Center and beyond the Valley of Kidron. 'There is the university.'

'You miss it very much, don't you?'

'Yes, of course. Someday I will have the chance to go back.'

The froggy sound of a horn blasted as it turned dusk.

'Sabbath! Sabbath!' a call went up along the streets.

All over Jerusalem the sound of the ancient horn could be heard. David put on a small skull cap and led Kitty to the street of Mea Shearim – the Hundred Gates of the ultra-Orthodox.

'Here in Mea Shearim you will be able to look into the synagogues and see the men pray in many different ways. Some of the Yemenites pray with a swaying motion as though they were riding on a camel. This was their way of getting even, as Jews were not allowed to ride camels because it would make their heads higher than a Moslem's.'

'I am impressed.'

'Take the descendants of Spanish Jews ... During the Inquisition they were forced to convert to Catholicism on pain of death. They said their Latin prayers aloud but at the end of each sentence they whispered a Hebrew prayer under their breaths. They still pray in silence at the end of each sentence.'

Kitty was speechless when they turned into Mea Shearim. The street comprised connected two-story stone dwellings, all displaying iron grillwork on their balconies.

The men were bearded and wore side curls and fur-brimmed hats and long black satin coats. There were Yemenites in Arabic dress and Kurds and Bokharans and Persians in riotous-colored silks. Everyone walked from the ritual bath with a quick-paced bobbing motion, as though swaying in prayer.

In a few moments the street emptied into the synagogues, small rooms for the most part and several on each block. There were congregations from Italy and Afghanistan and Poland and Hungary and Morocco. The Mea Shearim was filled with the chanting of prayers and Sabbath songs and weeping voices of anguished Hasidim who whipped themselves into a furor. Women were not permitted to enter rooms of prayer, so David and Kitty had to content themselves with peeking through iron-grilled windows.

What strange rooms – what strange people. Kitty watched near-hysterical men cluster about the Sefer Torah wailing and moaning. She saw the angelic faces of Yemenites who sat cross-legged on pillows, softly praying. She saw old men weaving back and forth emitting a stream of Hebrew in monotone read from decrepit prayer books. How different and how far away they all were from the handsome men and women of Tel Aviv.

'We have all kinds of Jews,' David Ben Ami said. 'I wanted to bring you here because I know that Ari wouldn't. He and many of the *sabras* despise them. They do not farm the land, they do not bear arms. They shove an ancient brand of Judaism down our throats. They are a force of reaction against what we are trying to do. Yet, when one lives in Jerusalem as I have, we learn to tolerate them and even appreciate the horrible things in the past that could drive men to such fanaticism.'

Ari Ben Canaan waited near the Greek Church in the Russian compound. It turned dark. Bar Israel appeared from nowhere. Ari followed the contact man into an alley where a taxi waited. They got in and Bar Israel produced a large black handkerchief.

'Must I submit to this?'

'I trust you, Ari, but orders are orders.'

The blindfold was tied over Ari's eyes and Ari was made to lie on the floor and was covered by a blanket. For a long twenty minutes the taxi moved in zigzags and circuitous routes to confuse Ari, then headed toward the Katamon district near the former German colony. The taxi stopped. Ari was quickly led into a house and into a room and was told he could remove the kerchief.

The room was bare except for a single chair, a single table which held a single flickering candle and a bottle of brandy and two glasses. It took a full moment for Ari's eyes to adjust to the darkness. His uncle, Akiva, stood opposite him by the table. Akiva's beard and his hair had turned snow white. He was wrinkled and bent. Ari walked to him very slowly and stopped before him.

'Hello, Uncle,' he said.

'Ari, my boy.'

The two men embraced, and the older man had to fight back choking emotion. Akiva lifted the candle and held it close to Ari's face and he smiled. 'You are looking well, Ari. It was a good job you did in Cyprus.'

'Thank you.'

'You came with a girl, I hear.'

'An American woman who helped us. She is not a friend, really. How are you feeling, Uncle?'

Akiva shrugged. 'As well as I can be expected to feel living in the underground. It has been too long since I have seen you, Ari . . . too long. Over two years now. It was nice when Jordana was studying at the university. I saw her once each week. She must be nearly twenty now. How is she? Does she still care for that boy?'

'David Ben Ami. Yes, they are very much in love. David was with me at Cyprus. He is one of our most promising young people.'

'His brother is a Maccabee, you know. Ben Moshe used to teach him at the university. Perhaps I can meet him someday.'

'Of course.'

'I hear Jordana is in the Palmach.'

'Yes, she is in charge of training the children at Gan Dafna and she works on the mobile radio when it transmits from our area.'

'She must be around my *kibbutz* then. She must see a lot of Ein Or.'

'Yes.'

'Does she ... does she ever say how it looks?'

'It is always beautiful at Ein Or.'

'Perhaps I can see it one day again.' Akiva sat down at the table and poured two brandies with an unsteady hand. Ari took a glass and they touched them. '*Le chaim,*' he said.

'I was with Avidan yesterday, Uncle. He showed me the British battle order. Have your people seen it?'

'We have friends in British Intelligence.'

Akiva stood up and began to pace the room slowly. 'Haven-Hurst means to wipe out my organization. The British are dedicated to the destruction of the Maccabees. They torture our prisoners, they hang us, they have exiled our entire command. It is not bad enough that the Maccabees are the only ones with the courage to fight the British, we must also fight the betrayers among our own people. Oh, yes, Ari ... we know the Haganah has been turning us in.'

'That is not true,' Ari gasped.

'It is true!'

'No! Just today at Yishuv Central, Haven-Hurst demanded that the Jews destroy the Maccabees and they again refused.'

Akiva's pacing quickened and his anger rose. 'Where do you think the British get their information if not from the Haganah? Those cowards at Yishuv Central let the Maccabees do the bleeding and the dying. Those cowards betray and betray. Cleverly, yes! But they betray! Betray! Betray!'

'I won't listen to this, Uncle. Most of us in the Haganah and the Palmach are dying to fight. They restrain us until we burst, but we cannot destroy everything that has been built.'

'Say it! We destroy!'

Ari gritted his teeth and held his tongue. The old man ranted, then suddenly he stopped and flopped his arms to his sides. 'I am a master at creating arguments when I don't mean to.'

'It is all right, Uncle.'

'I am sorry, Ari ... here, have some more brandy, please.'

'No, thank you.'

Akiva turned his back and murmured, 'How is my brother?'

'He was well when I saw him last. He will be going to London to join the conferences.'

'Yes, dear Barak. He will talk. He will talk to the end.' Akiva wetted his lips and hesitated. 'Does he know that you and Jordana and Sarah see me?'

'I think so.'

Akiva faced his nephew. His face reflected the sorrow within him. 'Does he ... does he ever ask about me?'

'No.'

Akiva gave a hurt little laugh and sank into the chair and poured more brandy for himself. 'How strange things are. I was always the one who angered and Barak was always the one who forgave. Ari ... I am getting very tired. A year, another year, I don't know how long it will be. Nothing can ever undo the hurt that we have brought to each other. But ... he must find it in his heart to break this silence. Ari, he must forgive me for the sake of our father.'

Chapter Three

A hundred church bells from the Old City and the Valley of Kidron and the Mount of Olives and Mount Zion pealed in chorus to the YMCA carillon. It was Sunday in Jerusalem, the Christian Sabbath.

David Ben Ami took Kitty into the Old City through the ornate Damascus Gate and they walked along the Via Dolorosa – the Way of the Cross – to Stephen's Gate which looked over the Kidron Valley and the tombs of Zacharias and Absalom and Mary and to the Mount of Olives, the scene of the Ascension.

They walked through the narrow streets, through the Arab bazaar and the tiny shops and the scenes of wild bartering. At the Dome of the Rock, the Mosque of Omar, a thousand pairs of shoes covered the steps. Ancient, bearded Jews stood and wept before the Wailing Wall of their great temple.

How strange this place is, again Kitty Fremont mused. Here, so far away in these barren hills, the merging point of a hundred civilizations in its thousands of years. Of all the earth, why this place, this street, this wall, this church? Romans and Crusaders and Greeks and Turks and Arabs and Assyrians and Babylonians and British in the city of the maligned Hebrews. It is holy, it is sacred, it is damned. Everything strong and everything weak, all that is good in man and all that is evil in him are personified. Calvary and Gethsemane. The room of the Last Supper. The last supper of Jesus, a Jewish Passover Seder.

David took Kitty to the Holy Sepulcher, the site of the crucifixion and the tiny chapel lit with ornate hanging lamps and perpetually burning candles over the marble tomb of Jesus Christ. Kitty knelt beside the tomb and kissed it as it had been kissed thin by a million pilgrims.

The next morning Ari and Kitty left Jerusalem and continued northward into the Galilee. They drove through the timeless Arab villages into the fertile carpet of the Jezreel Valley, which the Jews had turned from swamp into the finest farmland in the Middle East. As the road wound out of the Jezreel toward Nazareth again, they moved backwards in time. On one side of the hill the lush lands of the Jezreel and on the other, the sun-baked, dried-out, barren fields of the Arabs. Nazareth was much as Jesus must have found it in His youth.

Ari parked in the center of town. He brushed off a group of Arab urchins, but one child persisted.

'Guide?'

'No.'

'Souvenirs? I got wood from the cross, cloth from the robe.'

'Get lost.'

'Dirty pictures?'

Ari tried to pass the boy but he clung on and grabbed Ari by the pants leg. 'Maybe you like my sister? She is a virgin.'

Ari flipped the boy a coin. 'Guard the car with your life.'

Nazareth stank. The streets were littered with dung and blind beggars made wretched noises and barefoot, ragged, filthy children were underfoot. Flies were everywhere. Kitty held Ari's arm tightly as they wound through the bazaar and to a place alleged to be Mary's kitchen and Joseph's carpenter shop.

Kitty was baffled as they drove from Nazareth: it was a dreadful place.

'At least the Arabs are friendly,' Ari said. 'They are Christians.'

'They are Christians who need a bath.'

They stopped once more at Kafr Kanna at the church where Christ performed His first miracle of changing water to wine. It was set in a pretty and timeless Arab village.

Kitty was trying to digest all that she had seen in the past few days. It was such a small land but every inch held ghosts of blood or glory. At certain moments the very sacredness of it was gripping; at other moments exaltation turned to revulsion. Some of the holy places struck her speechless with awe and others left her with the cold suspicion of one watching a shell game in a carnival. The wailing Jews of Mea Shearim and the burning refinery. The aggressive *sabras* of Tel Aviv and the farmers of the Jezreel. The old and the new jammed together. There were paradoxes and contradictions at every turn.

It was very late afternoon when Ari turned into the gates of Yad El. He stopped before a flower-bedecked cottage.

'Ari, how lovely it is,' Kitty said.

The cottage door opened and Sarah Ben Canaan ran from it. 'Ari! Ari!' She was swept into his arms.

'*Shalom, ema.*'

'Ari, Ari, Ari ...'

'Now don't cry, *ema* ... shhhh, don't cry, don't cry.'

Kitty saw the massive Barak Ben Canaan rush out and throw his arms about his son.

'*Shalom, abba, shalom.*'

The old giant clung to his son and slapped his back again and again, repeating, 'You look good, Ari, you look good.'

Sarah studied her son's face. 'He is tired. Can't you see how tired he is, Barak?'

'I'm fine, *ema*. I have company. I want you to meet Mrs Katherine Fremont. She is going to work at Gan Dafna tomorrow.'

'So you are Katherine Fremont,' Barak said, taking her hand in his two giant paws. 'Welcome to Yad El.'

'Ari, you're such a fool,' his mother said. 'Why didn't you telephone and say you were bringing Mrs Fremont? Come in, come in ... you'll take a shower, you'll change your clothes, I'll make a little to eat and you'll feel better. You're such a fool, Ari.' Sarah put her arm around Kitty's waist and led her toward the cottage. 'Barak! Bring Mrs Fremont's luggage.'

Jordana Ben Canaan stood before the newly arrived *Exodus* children in the outdoor theater. She was tall and straight, with a statuesque carriage and long shapely legs. Jordana, with red hair hanging free below her shoulders, had a striking and classic beauty. She was nineteen years of age and had been in the Palmach since leaving the university. The Palmach assigned Jordana to Gan Dafna to head the Gadna unit which gave military training to all children in the village over fourteen years. Gan Dafna was also one of the prime places for hiding arms and smuggling them to the Huleh settlements. Jordana also worked on the mobile Voice of Israel secret radio when it transmitted in the Huleh. Jordana lived at Gan Dafna, right in her office.

'I am Jordana Ben Canaan,' she said to the *Exodus* children. 'I am your Gadna commander. In the next weeks you will learn spying, messenger work, arms cleaning and firing, stick fighting, and we will have several cross-country hikes. You are in Palestine now and never again do you have to lower your head or know fear for being a Jew. We are going to work very hard, for Eretz Israel needs you. Tomorrow we will have our first hike. We will go over the hills north to Tel Hai. My father came to Palestine through Tel Hai nearly sixty years ago. It is the place where our great hero, Joseph Trumpledor died. Trumpledor is buried there, and a great stone lion near the graveyard looks down upon the Huleh just as the statue of Dafna looks upon the Huleh. On the lion are written the words . . . "It is good to die for one's country." I might add to that: it is good to have a country to die for.'

As Jordana entered the administration building later she was called to the telephone. She lifted the receiver, '*Shalom*, Jordana here.'

'*Shalom!* This is *ema!* Ari is home!'

'Ari!'

Jordana ran from her office to the stable. She mounted her father's white Arab stallion and spurred him through the gates of Gan Dafna. She galloped bareback down the road toward the village of Abu Yesha with her scarlet hair waving in the wind behind her.

She galloped full speed into the main street of the Arab village, sending a dozen people scurrying for safety. The men at the coffeehouse turned and sneered. What a disrespectful prostitute this red-headed bitch was to dare ride through their streets wearing shorts! It was fortunate for her that she was the daughter of Barak and the sister of Ari!

Ari took Kitty's hand and led her through the door. 'Come along,' he said, 'I want to show you some of the farm before it turns dark.'

'Did you have enough to eat, Mrs Fremont?'

'I'm ready to burst.'

'And the room is comfortable?'

'I'm just fine, Mrs Ben Canaan.'

'Well, don't be too long, dinner will be ready when Jordana gets down from Gan Dafna.' Sarah and Barak stared after them, then looked at each other. 'She is a beautiful woman. But for our Ari?'

'Stop being a *Yiddische* momma. Don't go making a *shiddoch* for Ari,' Barak said.

'What are you talking, Barak? Can't you see the way he looks at her? Don't you know your own son yet? He is so tired.'

Ari and Kitty walked through Sarah's garden on the side of the house to the low rail fence. Ari put his foot up on the rail and looked out over the fields of the *moshav*. The water sprinklers were whirling a cooling spray and the orchard trembled lightly in the evening breeze. The air was scented with the fragrance of Sarah's winter roses. Kitty watched Ari as he looked out at his land. For the first time since she had known Ari Ben Canaan he seemed to be at peace. They *are* rare moments for him, Kitty thought, remembering that brief period of peace in Jerusalem.

'Not much like your Indiana, I'm afraid,' Ari said.

'It will do.'

'Well ... you didn't have to build Indiana out of a swamp.' Ari wanted to say much more to Kitty. He wanted to talk about how much he longed to be able to come home and work on his land. He wanted to beg her to understand what it was for his people to own land like this.

Kitty was leaning over the fence gazing at the beauty and proud achievement that Yad El represented. She looked radiant. Ari was filled with a desire to take her in his arms and hold her, but he did nothing and said nothing. They turned away together and walked along the fence until they came to the barn buildings, where the cackle of chickens and the honk of a goose met their ears. He opened the gate, the hinge was broken.

'That needs fixing,' he said. 'A lot of things need fixing. I'm away all the time and Jordana is gone too. My father is away at conferences so much. I'm afraid the Ben Canaan farm has become a village liability. The whole *moshav* has the responsibility. Someday we are all going to be home together ... then you'll really see something.' They stopped by a hogpen where a sow lay panting in the mud as a dozen gluttonous pigs fought to get at her teats. 'Zebras,' Ari said.

'If I wasn't an old zebra expert I'd swear I was looking at pigs,' Kitty answered.

'Shhh ... not so loud. There might be someone from the Land Fund eavesdropping. We aren't supposed to raise ... zebras ... on Jewish national land. Up at Gan Dafna the children call them pelicans. At the *kibbutz* they are more realistic. They are spoken of as comrades.'

They walked beyond the barn, chicken house and machinery shed to the edge of the fields.

'You can see Gan Dafna from here.' Ari stood behind her and pointed to the hills near the Lebanese border.

'Those white houses?'

'No, that's an Arab village called Abu Yesha. Now look to the right of it and farther up where those trees are, on the plateau.'

'Oh yes, I see it now. My, it's really up in the air. What is that building behind it on top of the hill?'

'Fort Esther, a British border station. Come along. I have something else to show you.'

They walked through the fields as it began to turn dusk, and the sun played strange tricks of coloring on the hills. They came to a wooden area on the edge of the fields where a stream rushed past toward the Huleh Lake.

'Your colored people in America sing very pretty spirituals about this stream.'

'Is this the Jordan?'

'Yes.'

Ari moved close to Kitty and they looked solemnly at each other. 'Do you like it? Do you like my parents?'

Kitty nodded. She waited for Ari to take her in his arms. His hands touched her shoulders.

'Ari! Ari! Ari!' a voice shouted from a distance. He released Kitty and spun around. A horse and rider were racing toward them, framed by the dying red sun. Soon they could make out the figure, the straight back, and the flaming hair.

'Jordana!'

She pulled the frothing horse to a halt, threw up both her arms and screamed for joy and leaped down on Ari so hard they both crashed to the ground. Jordana climbed on top of Ari and smothered his face with kisses.

'Cut it out,' he protested.

'Ari! I love you to pieces!'

Jordana began to tickle him and they rolled over wrestling. Ari was forced to pin her down to hold her still. Kitty watched with amusement. Suddenly Jordana saw her and her expression froze. Ari, remembering Kitty's presence, smiled sheepishly and helped Jordana to her feet.

'My overwrought young sister. I think she mistook me for David Ben Ami.'

'Hello, Jordana,' Kitty said, 'I feel as though I know you, from David ...' She extended her hand.

'You are Katherine Fremont. I have heard of you, too.'

The handshake was cold and Kitty was puzzled. Jordana turned quickly and picked up the reins of her horse and led him back toward the house as Ari and Kitty followed.

'Did you see David?' Jordana turned and asked Ari.

'He is in Jerusalem for a few days. He told me to say he would phone you tonight and he will be here by the end of the week, unless you want to go to Jerusalem.'

'I can't with those new children at Gan Dafna.'

Ari winked at Kitty. 'Oh,' he continued to Jordana, 'by the way, I saw Avidan in Tel Aviv. He did mention something or the other about ... now let me see ... yes, about transferring David to the Galilee Brigade at Ein Or.'

Jordana turned. Her blue eyes widened and for an instant she was unable to speak. 'Ari, you mean it? You're not teasing me!'

Ari shrugged. 'Silly girl.'

'Oh, I hate you! Why didn't you tell me?'

'I didn't know it was that important.'

Jordana was about to jump on Ari and wrestle with him again, but Kitty's presence obviously restrained her. 'I am so happy,' she said.

Another dinner was forced upon Kitty, who did her best by it when it became apparent that refusal would come close to creating an international incident. When dinner was done Sarah brought out tables full of snacks for the company that would be arriving.

That evening almost everyone at Yad El came to the Ben Canaan home to welcome Ari and to satisfy curiosity about the American woman. There was, in discreet Hebrew, excited speculation. They were a rugged and friendly lot of people and they went out of their way to make Kitty feel like visiting nobility. Ari hovered near her during the evening with the intent of protecting her from a torrent of questions but marveled at the ease with which Kitty was able to handle the pressing group.

As the evening wore on Jordana became more obvious in the coldness she had shown Kitty earlier. She was hostile and Kitty knew it. She could almost read Jordana's thoughts ... 'What kind of a woman are you who wants my brother?'

It was exactly what Jordana Ben Canaan was thinking as she watched Kitty perform perfectly, charming the curious farmers of Yad El. Kitty looked like all the soft, white, useless wives of English officers who spent their days at tea and gossip around the King David Hotel.

It was very late when the last guest left and Ari and Barak were alone and able to speak. They talked at length about the farm. It was running well despite their absences. The *moshav* saw to it that little was neglected during the protracted leaves of Ari, Jordana, and Barak.

Barak looked around the room for a cognac bottle with something left in it amid the shambles of the welcome-home gathering. He poured his son a glass and one for himself. Both of them settled down and stretched their long legs out and relaxed.

'Well, what about your Mrs Fremont? We are all bursting with curiosity.'

'Sorry to disappoint you. She is in Palestine in the interest of a girl who came over on the *Exodus*. I understand she is anxious to adopt the child later. We have become friends.'

'Nothing more?'

'Nothing.'

'I like her, Ari. I like her very much, but she is not our kind. Did you see Avidan in Tel Aviv?'

'Yes. I will be staying in the Huleh Palmach at Ein Or most likely. He wants to do an assessment of the strength of each village.'

'That is good. You have been away so much it will do *ema* good to be able to fuss over you for a while.'

'What about you, Father?'

Barak scratched his red beard and sipped his cognac. 'Avidan has asked me to go to London for the conferences.'

'I imagined he would.'

'Of course we must keep stalling and fighting to gain a political victory. The Yishuv can't take a military showdown, so I'll go to London and add my bit. I hate to say it but I am finally coming to the conclusion that the British are going to sell us out completely.'

Ari arose and began pacing the room. He was almost sorry that Avidan hadn't seen him away on another assignment. At least when he was working the clock around to complete a mission he did not have time to think of the realities ready to crush the Yishuv.

'Son, you had better go to Abu Yesha and see Taha.'

'I was surprised he wasn't here tonight. Is something wrong?'

'Just what is wrong with the whole country. We have lived in peace with the people of Abu Yesha for twenty years. Kammal was my friend for a half a century. Now . . . there is a coldness. We know them all by first names, we have visited their homes, and they have attended our schools. We have celebrated weddings together. Ari, they are our friends. Whatever is wrong must be righted.'

'I will see him tomorrow after I take Mrs Fremont to Gan Dafna.'

Ari leaned against the bookcases filled with classics in Hebrew, English, French, German, and Russian. He ran his fingers over them a moment and hesitated, then spun around and faced Barak. 'I saw Akiva in Jerusalem.'

Barak stiffened as though he had been struck. In reflex his lips parted for an instant, but he stopped the words that would have asked how his brother was. 'We will not discuss him under my roof,' Barak said softly.

'He has grown old. He cannot live too much longer. He begs for you to make peace with him in the name of your father.'

'I do not want to hear it!' Barak cried with a quiver in his voice.

'Isn't fifteen years of silence long enough?'

Barak stood up to his towering height and looked into the eyes of his son. 'He turned Jew against Jew. Now his Maccabees are turning the people of Abu Yesha against us. God may forgive him but I never will ... never.'

'Please listen to me!'

'Good night, Ari.'

The next morning Kitty said good-by to the Ben Canaan family and Ari drove her from Yad El to the mountain road leading to Gan Dafna. At Abu Yesha, Ari stopped for a moment to have someone inform Taha he would be back in an hour or so.

As their car moved high into the hills Kitty grew more and more eager to see Karen, but at the same time she was apprehensive about Gan Dafna. Was Jordana Ben Canaan playing the role of a jealous sister or was she the forerunner of a kind of people who would be hostile because of their differences? Harriet Saltzman had warned her she was a stranger with no business in Palestine. Everyone and everything seemed to point out this difference. Jordana unsettled her. Kitty had tried to be sociable to everyone but perhaps underneath she was drawing lines and too thinly disguising the fact. I am what I am, Kitty thought, and I come from a place where people are judged for what they are.

As they drove into isolation she felt alone and glum.

'I must leave right away,' Ari said.

'Will we be seeing each other?' Kitty asked.

'From time to time. Do you want to see me, Kitty?'

'Yes.'

'I will try then.'

They turned the last corner and the plateau of Gan Dafna spread before them. Dr Lieberman, the village orchestra, the staff and faculty, and the fifty children from the *Exodus* were all clustered around the bronze statue of Dafna on the center green. There was a warm and spontaneous welcome for Kitty Fremont, and in that moment her fears vanished. Karen rushed up to her and hugged her and handed her a bouquet of winter roses. Then Kitty was engulfed by 'her' *Exodus* children. She looked over her shoulder long enough to see Ari disappear.

When the welcoming ceremony was over Dr Lieberman and Karen walked with Kitty into a tree-studded lane holding the neat little two- and three-room cottages of the staff. They came to a halt halfway down the dirt road before a white stucco house which was deluged in blooms.

Karen ran up on the porch and opened the door and held her breath as Kitty walked in slowly. The combination living room and bedroom was simple but tasteful. The draperies and the spread over the couch-bed were of the thick Negev linen weave and the room was almost buried under fresh-cut flowers. A paper cutout was strung from one side to the other: 'SHALOM KITTY,' it read, and it was from her children of the *Exodus*. Karen ran to the window and pulled the draperies back and revealed a panoramic view of the valley floor two thousand feet below. There was another small room, a study, and a pullman kitchen and bath. Everything had been prepared beautifully. Kitty broke into a smile.

'Shoo, shoo, shoo,' Dr Lieberman said, whisking Karen out of the door. 'You will see Mrs Fremont later ... shoo, shoo.'

'Good-by, Kitty.'

'Good-by, dear.'

'You like it?' Dr Lieberman asked.

'I will be very comfortable here.'

Dr Lieberman sat on the edge of the couch. 'When your children from the *Exodus* heard you were coming to Gan Dafna they worked day and night. They painted the cottage, they made the drapes. They brought in plants ... all the plants in Gan Dafna are on your lawn. They made a big fuss. They love you very much.'

Kitty was very touched. 'I don't know why they should.'

'Children are instinctive about knowing who their friends are. You would like to see Gan Dafna now?'

'Yes, I'd love to.'

Kitty stood a head taller than Dr Lieberman. They strolled back toward the administration buildings. He walked with his hands alternately clasped behind him and patting his pockets, searching for matches to light his pipe.

'I came from Germany in 1933. I guess I knew quite early what was going to happen. My wife passed away shortly after we arrived. I taught humanities at the university until 1940 when Harriet Saltzman asked me to come up here and found a Youth Aliyah village. Actually, I had been longing to do just that for many years. This entire plateau was given to us by the late muktar of Abu Yesha, a most generous man. If only our relations could be a model for all Jews and Arabs ... do you have a match?'

'No, I'm sorry, not with me.'

'Never mind, I smoke too much.'

They came to the center green where the view of the Huleh Valley was the best. 'Our fields are down on the floor of the valley. The land was given to us by the Yad El *moshav*.'

They stopped before the statue. 'This is Dafna. She was a girl from Yad El who died in the Haganah. The sweetheart of Ari Ben Canaan. Our village is named for her.'

Kitty felt a flash of – yes, jealousy. The power of Dafna was there even in sculpture. Kitty could see in the bronze that rugged earthiness of a Jordana Ben Canaan and the other farm girls who were in the Ben Canaan home last night.

Dr Lieberman waved both hands. 'In all directions we are surrounded by history. Across the valley you see Mount Hermon and near it is the site of ancient Dan. I could go on for an hour ... it is filled with the past.' The little hunchback looked fondly around at his creation and took Kitty's arm and led her on.

'We Jews have created a strange civilization in Palestine. In every other place in the world the culture of its people has almost always come from the large cities. Here, it is just the reverse. The eternal longing of the Jewish people to own land is so great that this is where our new heritage comes from. Our music, our poetry, our art, our scholars and our soldiers came from the *kibbutz* and the *moshav*. See these children's cottages?'

'Yes.'

'You will notice how all windows face the fields of the valley so their land will be the first thing they see in the morning and the last thing they see at night. Half of the schooling here is in agriculture. From this village, groups have gone out and started or joined in four new *kibbutzim*. We are self-sustaining in food. We own our own dairy and poultry and cattle. We even weave much of our own cloth. We make our own furniture and we repair our farm machinery in our own shops. All this is done by the children and they govern themselves and very well, too.'

They reached the far end of the green. Just before the administration building the beautiful lawn was abruptly broken by a long trench that circled the entire area. Kitty looked around and sighted more trenches and a bomb shelter.

'It is very ugly,' Dr Lieberman said, 'and there is too much worship of fighters among our children. I am afraid that condition will last until we win our independence and can base existence on something more human than arms.'

They walked along the trench. Kitty became intrigued by an odd phenomenon. The trench works ran past a few scraggly trees. One of the trenches had been dug close to the root system of one of the trees and the roots were bared. The trench revealed layers of solid stone under the topsoil. Sandwiched between the rock there were thin layers of earth, some only a few inches thick. The tree was stunted from trying to grow in such ground but the roots fought a stubborn fight. They ran over and under and about the rock in thin veins, thickening wherever they found a little life-giving soil between the rock strata.

'Look how that tree fights to live,' Kitty said. 'Look how it tries to dig its roots into rock.'

Dr Lieberman observed thoughtfully for a moment. 'That tree is the story of the Jews who have come back to Palestine,' he said.

Ari stood in the high-ceilinged living room of Taha, the muktar of Abu Yesha. The young Arab, his lifelong friend, nibbled on a piece of fruit from a large bowl and watched Ari begin pacing.

'There is enough double talk going on at the conferences in London,' Ari said. 'I think that you and I can talk straight.'

Taha flipped the fruit down. 'How can I explain it, Ari? Pressure is being put on me. I have resisted it.'

'Resisted it? Taha, you're talking to Ari Ben Canaan.'

'Times are changing.'

'Now wait a minute. Our people have lived together through two sets of riots. You went to school in Yad El. You lived in my home under the protection of my father.'

'Yes, I existed because of your benevolence. Now you ask my village to exist the same way. You arm yourselves. Are we not allowed to arm ourselves? Or don't you trust us with guns as we have trusted you?'

'This isn't even you talking.'

'I hope that I never live to see the day that you and I must fight, but you know that passiveness is a thing of the past for all of us.'

Ari spun around angrily. 'Taha! What has gotten into you? All right, then. Maybe you'd better hear it again. These stone houses in your village were designed and built by us. Your children can read and write because of us. You have sewers because of us and your young don't die before the age of six because of us. We taught you how to farm properly and live decently. We have brought you things that your own people would not give you in a thousand years. Your father knew this and he was big enough to admit that no one hates or exploits an Arab worse than another Arab. He died because he knew your salvation was with the Jews and he was man enough to stand for it.'

Taha arose. 'And will you guarantee me that the Maccabees will not come into Abu Yesha tonight and kill us?'

'Of course I can't guarantee it but you know what the Maccabees stand for just as you know what the Mufti stands for.'

'I will never lift my hand against Yad El, Ari. You have my word.'

Ari left, knowing that Taha meant what he said, but Taha was not the man of the strength that his father, Kammal, had been. Even as they promised peace to each other a breach had come between Yad El and Abu Yesha, just as breaches were coming to all the Arab and Jewish villages that had lived together in peace.

Taha watched his friend leave the house and walk to the road near the stream and the mosque. He stood motionless long after Ari disappeared. Each day the pressure grew and there were even voices of dissent in his own village. He was told that he was an Arab and a Moslem and he had to choose his side. How could he turn on Ari and Barak Ben Canaan? Yet, how could he still the voices around him?

He was a brother of Ari. Or was he? This was the tormenting question. From childhood his father had groomed him to lead his village. He knew the Jews had built the great cities and the roads and the schools and they had redeemed the land and they were the enlightened ones. Was he really their equal? Or was he a second-class citizen in his own land, riding on coattails, picking up the crumbs, living in the shadows of Jewish achievement?

Yes, he had benefited from the Jews. His people had benefited more because his father had realized the Jews could give greater benefits than his own Arabs. Yet, was he a partner? Was his equality a real thing or merely a phrase? Was he being tolerated rather than accepted?

Was he really the brother of Ari Ben Canaan or the poor cousin? Taha asked himself this question more often each day. Each time the answer was more certain. He was a brother in name only.

What of this equality the Jews preached? Could he as an Arab ever declare that he had loved Jordana Ben Canaan quietly and with the heartache that comes with long silence? He had loved her since he had lived under their roof and she was but a child of thirteen.

How far did their equality extend? Would they ever accept Taha and Jordana as man and wife? Would all the democracy-preaching members of the *moshav* come to their wedding?

What would happen then if Taha were to go to Jordana and tell her of his love? She would spit on him, of course.

In his heart he felt an inferiority and it tore him apart, despite the fact that the distinction was far less than that between a landowning effendi and the slave fellaheen.

He could not lift his hand against Ari and he could never declare his love for Jordana. He could not fight his friends nor could he resist the force around him which told him he was an Arab and an enemy of the Jew and he had to fight them whether it was right – or it was wrong.

Chapter Four

Dr Ernest Lieberman, the funny little hunchback, was able to translate his tremendous love of people into a living thing at Gan Dafna. The atmosphere was as casual as a summer camp. The children were given complete freedom of movement and thought. School classes were held outdoors, and the children dressed in shorts and lay about on the grass so that even their academic study was close to nature.

Dr Lieberman's children had come from the stink pits of the earth, the ghetto and the concentration camp. Yet, there was never a serious disciplinary problem at Gan Dafna. Disobedience did not exist, thievery was unheard of, and promiscuity between sexes was rare. Gan Dafna was life itself to the children, and they governed and policed themselves with a pride and dignity that reflected their reaction to being loved.

The range of learning and thinking was vast at Gan Dafna; it was difficult to believe the participants were merely teenagers. The library ran from St Thomas Aquinas to Freud. No book was barred, no subject seemed too broad. The children possessed a political awareness beyond their years.

The primary principle the staff and faculty was able to inculcate upon these children was that their lives had a purpose.

Gan Dafna had an international staff, with teachers from twenty-two countries ranging from Iranians to the rugged *kibbutz*-bred *sabras*. Kitty was the only gentile as well as the only American and this proved to be a paradox. She was looked upon with both reserve and affection. Her early fears of hostility proved unfounded. There was an air of intellectualism which seemed to make Gan Dafna more like a university than an orphanage. Kitty was welcomed as a part of a team whose prime concern was the welfare of the children. She became very friendly with many of the staff and was completely at ease in their company. The problem of the Jewishness of the village also proved smaller than she had expected. Judaism at Gan Dafna was founded upon a fierce kind of nationalism rather upon any religious basis. There was no formal religious training or even a synagogue.

They managed to keep tension and fear out of Gan Dafna despite reports of growing violence all over Palestine. The village was physically isolated enough to form some shelter from the realities of the bloodshed. Yet, it was not completely free of the signs of danger. The border was above them. Fort Esther was always in sight. Trenches, shelters, arms, and military training were in evidence.

The medical department building was in the administration area on the edge of the center green. The building had a clinic and a well-equipped twenty-bed hospital and operating room. The doctor was shared with the Yad El *moshav* and came daily. There was a dentist and four trainee nurses under Kitty and a full-time psychiatrist.

Kitty ran her clinic and hospital with machinelike efficiency after completely overhauling the system. She put sick calls and hospital rounds and the dispensation of treatment on a rigid schedule. She demanded and received a respect for her position that created a ripple of talk in the village. She kept a discreet professional distance from her assistants and she refused to operate her section with the informality of the rest of the village. She discouraged the familiarity which most of the teachers encouraged. This was all strange to Gan Dafna. There was a reluctant admiration of her, for the medical section was the most efficient department the village had. In their desire to foster freedom the Jews often leaned too far back from the discipline that Kitty Fremont knew. She was not disliked for the way she ran her department. When Kitty took off her uniform she was the most sought-after companion in Gan Dafna.

If she was firm in running her section, she was the opposite when it came to 'her' children. The fifty *Exodus* youngsters at Gan Dafna continued to keep their identification and Kitty Fremont was always to be identified with them. She was 'Mother of the *Exodus*.' It seemed a natural step that she become personally involved in the cases of some of the more disturbed children from the *Exodus*. She volunteered to work with the psychiatrist in psychotherapy. With the disturbed children Kitty completely dropped her coldness and gave to them all the warmth she was capable of giving. Gan Dafna and Palestine had tremendous curative powers but the horrors of the past still brought on the nightmares, the insecurity, and the hostility that required patience and skill and love.

Once a week Kitty went down to Abu Yesha with the doctor to hold morning clinic for the Arabs. How pathetic the dirty little Arab children were beside the robust youngsters of Gan Dafna. How futile their lives seemed in contrast to the spirit of the Youth Aliyah village. There seemed to be no laughter or songs or games or purpose among the Arab children. It was a static existence – a new generation born on an eternal caravan in an endless desert. Her stomach turned over as she entered the one-room hovels shared with chickens, dogs, and donkeys. Eight or ten people on the same earth floor.

Yet Kitty could not dislike these people. They were heart-warming and gracious beyond their capacity. They too, longed for better things. She became friendly with Taha, the young muktar who was always present on clinic days. Many times Kitty felt that Taha wanted to speak to her about things other than the health problem of the village. She felt an urgency about him. But Taha was an Arab: a woman could only be confided in on certain matters and he never revealed his constant fears to her.

The days passed into the late winter of 1947.

Karen and Kitty had grown inseparably close. The young girl who had found some measure of happiness in the most abysmal places fairly bloomed at Gan Dafna. She had become overnight one of the most popular children in the village. Karen became more dependent on Kitty's guidance through the complex stages of early maturity. Kitty was aware that each day at Gan Dafna would tend to draw Karen farther away from America. She kept America alive in the girl's interest while the search for Karen's father continued.

Dov Landau was a problem. Several times Kitty was tempted to step in between the boy and Karen – their relationship seemed to be deepening. But Kitty, recognizing the possibility of driving them closer together, stayed out of it. Karen's devotion to the boy perplexed her, for Dov gave nothing in return. He was morose and withdrawn. He did talk a little more, but for practical purposes Karen was still the only one who could reach him.

Dov became obsessed with a desire to learn. His education had been almost nothing and now he seemed to want to try to make up for it with a passion. He was excused from both Gadna military training and agriculture. Dov crammed as much into himself as he could absorb. He read and studied day and night. He concentrated upon his natural gift of art with studies of anatomy and drawing and architecture and blueprinting. Occasionally a painting would furnish an escape valve and his drive would come out in effects that displayed his talent and energy. Sometimes he came near breaking through and joining into Gan Dafna society, only to withdraw again. He lived by himself, he engaged in no activities, and he saw only Karen outside classes.

Kitty took the problem to Dr Lieberman. He had seen many boys and girls like Dov Landau. Dr Lieberman had observed that Dov was an alert and intelligent human being who showed great talent. He felt any attempts to force attention on him would work the opposite way: so long as the boy remained harmless and grew no worse, he should be left alone.

As the weeks passed Kitty was disappointed that she did not hear from or see Ari. The statue of Dafna and Yad El *moshav* below always seemed to remind her. From time to time when she had occasion to pass Yad El she dropped in on Sarah Ben Canaan, until the two women became quite friendly. Jordana learned of it and made no effort to disguise her dislike for Kitty. The beautiful young redheaded hellion made it a point to be rude whenever she spoke to Kitty.

One evening Kitty came to her cottage to find Jordana standing before the mirror, holding one of her cocktail dresses in front of her. Kitty's sudden appearance did not bother Jordana. 'It is pretty, if you like this sort of thing,' Jordana said hanging the dress back in the closet.

Kitty walked to the stove and put on some water for tea. 'To what do I owe the honor of this call?'

Jordana continued to look about Kitty's cottage, at the little touches of her femininity. 'There are some Palmach troops training at the Ein Or *kibbutz*.'

'I've heard something about it,' Kitty said.

'We have a shortage of instructors. We have a shortage of everything, anyhow. I was asked to ask you if you would come to Ein Or once a week to give a course in first aid and field sanitation.'

Kitty pulled back the drapes and kicked off her shoes and settled back on the studio bed. 'I would prefer not to do anything that would bring me into contact with troops.'

'Why not?' Jordana pressed.

'Well, I suppose there is no graceful way of refusing you, and I would like it better if the Palmach understood why.'

'What's to understand?'

'My personal feelings. I don't wish to become involved.'

Jordana laughed coldly. 'I told them at Ein Or it would be a waste of time to speak to you.'

'Is it impossible for you to respect my feelings?'

'Mrs Fremont, you can work anywhere in the world and remain neutral. This is a strange place for you to come to work if you want to stay out of trouble. Why are you really here?'

Kitty sprang off the bed angrily. 'None of your damned business!'

The teakettle whistled. Kitty snapped it off.

'I know why you are here. You want Ari.'

'You're an insolent young lady and I think I've taken just about all I am going to from you.'

Jordana remained unmoved. 'I've seen the way you looked at him.'

'If I wanted Ari, you would be the last thing in my way.'

'Tell yourself you don't want him but don't tell it to me. You are not Ari's kind of woman. You don't care for us.'

Kitty turned and lit a cigarette. Jordana came behind her.

'Dafna was Ari's kind of woman. She understood him. No American woman ever will.'

Kitty turned around. 'Because I don't run around in shorts and hike up the sides of mountains and shoot cannons and sleep in ditches doesn't make me one ounce less a woman than you. You or that precious statue. I know what's the matter with you – you're afraid of me.'

'That's funny.'

'Don't tell me what makes a woman – you don't know, you aren't one. You're Tarzan's mate and you behave as though you belong in a jungle. A brush and comb wouldn't be a bad start at fixing what's wrong with you.' Kitty pushed past Jordana and threw open her closet. 'Take a good look. This is what women wear.'

Tears of anger welled in Jordana's eyes.

'The next time you wish to see me you may come to my office,' Kitty said coldly. 'I am not a *kibbutznik* and I like my privacy.'

Jordana slammed the door so hard it shook the cottage.

Karen came to Kitty's office after the dinner sick call and flopped into a chair.

'Hi,' Kitty said. 'How did it go today?'

Karen grabbed two imaginary cow teats and made a milking motion. 'Weak hands. I am a lousy milker,' she opined with teen-age sadness. 'Kitty, I am truly broken-hearted. I must, must, must, talk to you.'

'Shoot.'

'Not now. We have a Gada meeting. We are cleaning some new Hungarian rifles. What a mess!'

'The Hungarian rifles can wait a few minutes. What is troubling you, dear?'

'Yona, my roommate. Just when we are getting to be intimate friends. She's going to join the Palmach next week.'

Kitty felt a stab of dismay. How much longer until Karen came to her and told her she was going to do the same thing? Kitty shoved her papers aside. 'You know, Karen, I have been thinking that there is a real shortage of good nurses and medical aides ... I mean, in the Palmach as well as in the settlements. You've had lots of experience working with the youngsters in the DP camps and I've taken on quite a crowd of the disturbed ones. Do you suppose it would make sense if I asked Dr Lieberman to let you come to work with me and let me train you as my assistant?'

'Would it!' Karen broke into a broad grin.

'Fine. I'll try to arrange it so you skip the agriculture work and report right to my office after school.'

Karen sobered. 'Well, I don't know. It doesn't seem quite fair to the others.'

'As we say in American, they won't be losing a farmer, they'll be gaining a nurse.'

'Kitty, I have a terrible confession to make. Don't tell the Youth Aliyah, the Zion Settlement Society, or the Central Kibbutz Movement but honest, I'm the worst farmer at Gan Dafna and I'd just love to be a nurse.'

Kitty got up and walked to Karen and put her arm about the girl's shoulder. 'Do you suppose that with Yona gone you would like to move into my cottage and live with me?'

The instantaneous look of happiness on Karen's face was all the answer that Kitty needed.

Kitty left Dr Lieberman's cottage early to give Karen the good news. Dr Lieberman had considered their duty to dispense love and not rules and decided the cause would not be hurt with one less farmer and one more nurse.

When she left Karen she crossed the center green and stopped before the statue of Dafna. She felt that she had hurt Dafna tonight, she had won a victory. With Karen near her she could keep the child from becoming an aggressive, angry *sabra* girl. It was good to live with a purpose, Kitty knew. But too much purpose could destroy womanliness. She had hit Jordana in a weak spot and she knew it. Since birth Jordana had been given a mission to carry out without question, at the price of her own personal happiness, career, and femininity. Jordana did not know how to compete with the elegant women coming into Palestine from the Continent and from America. She hated Kitty because she wanted to be more like Kitty and Kitty knew it.

'Kitty?' A voice called out in the darkness.

'Yes?'

'I hope I didn't startle you.'

It was Ari. As he came near her she felt that same now-familiar sensation of helplessness.

'I'm sorry I haven't been able to get up to see you. Jordana gave you my messages?'

'Jordana? Yes, of course,' Kitty lied.

'How are you getting along?'

'Fine.'

'I came up to ask you if you would care to take the day off tomorrow. A Palmach group is going to climb Mount Tabor. It is something that should not be missed. Would you come with me?'

'Yes, I'd love to.'

Chapter Five

Ari and Kitty arrived at the *kibbutz* of Beth Alonim – the House of the Oaks – at the foot of Mount Tabor, shortly after dawn. It was the *kibbutz* which gave birth to the Palmach during the war and the place Ari had trained troops.

Tabor was odd: not high enough to be a real mountain but far too high to be a hill. It stood in the middle of flatlands arising suddenly in the shape of a thumb poking through the earth.

After breakfast at the *kibbutz* Ari rolled a pair of packs with rations, canteen, and blankets and drew a Sten gun from the arsenal. He planned to hike up ahead of the rest of the group during the morning hours when it was cool. The air was crisp and invigorating and Kitty was charged with the spirit of adventure. They passed through the Arab village of Dabburiya at the opposite base of Tabor from Beth Alonim and took up a narrow dirt path. Within moments they could see Nazareth in the hills several kilometers away. It stayed cool and their progress was fast, although Kitty realized her first view was deceptive. Tabor rose to more than two thousand feet; it was going to be a long day. Dabburiya grew smaller and began to look quaint as they put distance between themselves and the village.

Suddenly Ari stopped, and tensed.

'What is it?'

'Goats. Can you smell them?'

Kitty sniffed. 'No, I don't smell anything.'

Ari's eyes narrowed. He scanned the path ahead. It circled out of sight and there was a very gentle slope off to the blind side.

'Probably Bedouins. There was a report about them at the *kibbutz*. They must have moved in since yesterday. Come on.'

Around the turn they saw a dozen haired goatskin tents along the hillside and a flock of little black goats grazing around them. Two rifle-bearing nomads came up to them. Ari spoke to them in Arabic, then followed them to the largest of the tents, which obviously belonged to the sheik. Kitty looked around. They seemed the dregs of humanity. The women were encased in black robes – and layers of dirt. She was not able to smell the goats but she was able to smell the women. Chains of Ottoman coins formed veils over their faces. The children wore dirty rags.

A grizzled individual emerged from the tent and exchanged greetings with Ari. They conversed a moment, then Ari whispered to Kitty. 'We must go in or he will be insulted. Be a good girl and eat whatever he offers you. You can throw it up later.'

The inside of the tent stank even more. They sat down on goat-hair and sheep-wool rugs and exchanged amenities. The sheik was impressed that Kitty came from America and relayed the information that he once owned a photograph of Mrs Roosevelt.

Courses of food came. A greasy lamb leg was thrust into Kitty's hand together with marrow mixed with rice. Kitty nibbled, the sheik watched expectantly. She smiled weakly and nodded to convey how delicious it was. Unwashed fruits were served, and the meal was ended with thick, sickeningly sweet coffee in cups so filthy they were crusted. The diners wiped hands on trousers and mouths with sleeves, and after a bit more conversation Ari begged leave.

They left the camp behind. Kitty emitted a long and loud sigh. 'I feel sorry for them,' she said.

'Please don't. They are quite sure they are the freest men on earth. Didn't you ever see *The Desert Song* when you were a girl?'

'Yes, but now I know the composer never saw a Bedouin camp. What were you two men gabbing about?'

'I told him to behave tonight and not try to collect any rings and watches from the Palmach.'

'And what else?'

'He wanted to buy you. He offered me six camels.'

'Why, that old devil. What did you tell him?'

'I told him that anyone could see you were a ten-camel girl.' Ari glanced at the rising sun. 'It's going to get hot from now on. We'd better get out of these heavy clothes and pack them.'

Kitty wore a pair of the traditional blue shorts from the Gan Dafna stores.

'Damn, you look just like a *sabra*.'

They followed the trail which wove along the southern face of Tabor. Both of them perspired as the sun beat down. The trail broke in frequent places and they were forced to climb. Ari's strong hands led Kitty up the steep inclines. By late afternoon they had passed the two-thousand-foot mark.

The entire top of Tabor was a large, rounded plateau. The south edge of the plateau opened the entire Jezreel Valley to their eyes. It was a staggering sight. Kitty could follow the Jezreel, the square-cut fields, the splashes of green around the Jewish settlements, and the white clusters of Arab villages all the way to Mount Carmel and the Mediterranean. In the other direction was the Sea of Galilee, so that the entire width of Palestine was below them. Through field glasses Kitty followed Ari's pointing out Ein Dor where Saul met the witch and the bald top of Mount Gilboa where Gideon was buried and Saul and Jonathan fell in battle to the Philistines.

'Ye mountains of Gilboa, let there be no dew, neither let there be rain, upon you nor fields of offerings: for there the shield of the mighty is vilely cast away, the shield of Saul . . .'

Kitty lowered the glasses. 'Why Ari, you are poetic.'

'It is the altitude. Everything is so removed from up here. Look over there – Beth Shean Valley. Beth Shean *tel* holds the oldest civilized city in the world. David knows more about these than I do. There are hundreds of *tels* around Palestine. He says that if we were to start excavating them now our modern cities would be ruins by the time we are finished. You see, Palestine is the bridge of history here and you are standing on the center of the bridge. Tabor has been a battleground since men made axes out of stone. The Hebrews stood against the Romans here and between the Crusaders and the Arabs it changed hands fifty times. Deborah hid here with her army and swooped down on the Canaanites. The battleground of the ages . . . You know what we say ? . . . that Moses should have walked the tribes for another forty years and found a decent place.'

They walked over the plateau through a pine forest with relics of Roman, Byzantine, Crusader, and Arab all around. Mosaics, pottery, a wall here, a stone there.

Two abbeys, one Greek Orthodox and one Roman Catholic, stood near the grounds believed to be the place Christ was transfigured and spoke to Moses and Elijah.

Beyond the forest they reached the highest point of Tabor. Ruins of a Crusader fort and Saracen castle occupied the site. They picked their way over the rubble and the walls until they had climbed the eastern rampart which hung over the mountain side and was called Wall of the East Winds. Here the Sea of Galilee came into full view with the Horns of Hattin where Saladin the Kurd demolished Crusader forces.

The wind blew through Kitty's hair as she stood on the wall and the air began to cool again. They sat for over an hour with Ari pointing out the countless points of Biblical history. Finally they retreated to that point on the edge of the forest where it met the castles, and changed back to their warmer clothing. Ari spread their blankets and Kitty stretched out and grunted with a weary happiness. 'It has been a wonderful day, Ari, but I am going to ache for a week.'

Ari propped himself up on an elbow, watched her. Again he felt a desire for her but he held his silence.

By dusk, parties of threes and fours and fives began reaching the summit. There were dark and olive-skinned Orientals and Africans and there were blonds who had immigrated to Israel. There were many girls, most of them straight and high breasted. There were the *sabras* with their large mustaches and the stamp of aggressiveness. It was a reunion. Palmach groups had to train in small units in different *kibbutzim* to remain hidden. This was a chance for both friends from the city and from the same settlements to see each other again and for sweethearts to meet. The greetings were warm, with affectionate hugs and back slaps and kisses. They were a lively bunch of youngsters in their late teens and early twenties.

Joab Yarkoni and Zev Gilboa had come when they learned Kitty would be there, and she was delighted.

David and Jordana came also, and Jordana was provoked by David's attention to Kitty, but she remained quiet to avoid creating a scene.

By dusk nearly two hundred of the young Palmach soldiers had gathered. A pit was dug near the castle wall, while some of them turned to gathering wood for an all-night fire. Three lambs were prepared and spitted for roasting. The sun plunged down behind the Jezreel Valley, the fire was lit with a single bursting blaze, and the lambs were placed over their pits and couples joined in a huge circle around the fire. Kitty, the visiting dignitary, was forced into the place of honor with Joab, Sev, and Ari around her.

Soon the plateau atop Mount Tabor rang with songs. They were the same songs that Kitty had heard the children sing at Gan Dafna. They told of the wonder of the water sprinklers that redeemed the land and they told of the beauty of the Galilee and Judea. They sang of how haunted and lovely was the Negev Desert and they sang the spirited marches of the old Guardsman and the Haganah and the Palmach. They sang a song that said that David the King still walked the land of Israel.

Joab sat cross-legged with his tambour before him. It was a clay drum with goatskin head. With his fingertips and the heels of his hand he beat a rhythm to a reed flute playing an ancient Hebraic melody. Several of the Oriental girls danced in the same slow, swaying, sensuous gyrations that must have been danced in the place of Solomon.

With each new song and each new dance the party quickened.

'Jordana!' someone called. 'We want Jordana!'

She got into the ring and a cheer went up. An accordion played a Hungarian folk tune and everyone clapped in beat and Jordana whirled around the edge of the ring pulling out partners for a wild *czardas*. One by one she danced her partners down, with her red hair flying wildly in her face, framed against the leaping fire. Faster the accordion played and faster the onlookers clapped until Jordana herself stopped in exhaustion.

A half dozen came to the center and started a *hora*, the dance of the Jewish peasants. The *hora* ring grew larger and larger until everyone was up and a second ring formed outside the first. Joab and Ari pulled Kitty into the circle. The circle moved in one direction, then stopped as the dancers made a sudden leap and changed directions.

They had been singing and dancing for four hours and there was no indication of slowing up. David and Jordana slipped away quietly to the Saracen castle and wandered through the rooms until the sounds of the music and the tambour nearly vanished. They came upon a tiny cell set in the Wall of the East Winds and now the sound of the wind from the Jezreel Valley was all they could hear. David spread his blanket on the earth and they embraced and caressed and loved each other.

'David! David!' Jordana cried, 'I love you so!'

The wind died and they could hear wild music ...

'David ... David ... David ...' she whispered over and over as her lips pressed his neck ...

And David repeated her name over and over.

His hand felt for the smoothness of her body. She took the clothing from her to ease his way and they pressed against each other and she asked to be taken and they blended into one.

After their love, Jordana lay in his arms. His fingertips traced over her lips and her eyes and through her hair.

'Jordana.' His whisper thrilled her through her body and soul.

'Do you remember the first time, David?'

'Yes.'

'*I am the rose of Sharon and the lily of the valleys* ...' she whispered. '*For lo, the winter is past, the rain is over and gone; the flowers appear on the earth; the time of the singing of birds is come, and the voice of the turtle is heard in our land.*'

It became so still that each could hear only the other's uneven breathing and the other's heart beating.

'*Take us the foxes, the little foxes, that spoil the vines: for our vines have tender grapes. My beloved is mine and I am his.* Oh, David ... tell me, tell me.'

David whispered with his lips touching her ear, '*Behold thou art fair, my love; behold thou art fair; thou has doves' eyes within thy locks ... thy lips are like a thread of scarlet ...*'

She squeezed his hand that rested upon her breast and he kissed her breast ... '*Thy two breasts are like two young roes that are twins, which feed among the lilies ...*'

And he kissed her lips ... '*And the roof of thy mouth like the best wine for my beloved, that goeth down sweetly, causing the lips of those who are asleep to speak.*'

David and Jordana fell into a bliss-filled sleep, locked tightly in each other's arms.

At four o'clock in the morning the lamb was served, with hot Arabic coffee. Kitty was honored with the first cut. The fervor of song and dance had slowed a little; many of the couples lay in each other's arms. The lamb tasted wonderful.

Joab played his tambour, and the reed flute behind him made a tune as ancient as the land itself. One of the girls who had been born in distant Yemen sang in a voice filled with the mystic and melancholy of the Hebrew, right from the pages of the Bible. Her haunting voice sang a Psalm of David.

Kitty Fremont looked at the faces in the dying firelight.

What kind of army was this? What kind of army without uniform or rank? What kind of army where the women fought alongside their men with rifle and bayonet? Who were these young lions of Judea?

She looked at the face of Ari Ben Canaan and a chill passed through her body. An electrifying revelation hit her.

This was no army of mortals.

These were the ancient Hebrews! These were the faces of Dan and Reuben and Judah and Ephraim! These were Samsons and Deborahs and Joabs and Sauls.

It was the army of Israel, and no force on earth could stop them for the power of God was within them!

Chapter Six

Chatham House
Institute Of International Relations
London

Cecil Bradshaw, the dumpy expert on the Middle East, had been studying the survey reports from a variety of sources. For three days he had been digesting the summaries. The Colonial Office, the Ministry and even Number 10 Downing Street were all bringing pressure on him. The Palestine mandate was in a muddle. A clean-cut new policy had to be formulated. Bradshaw was a man of thirty-seven years' experience in the area. During that time he had gone through a hundred conferences with the Zionists and the Arabs. Bradshaw believed, as most of the officialdom believed, that Britain's interests lay with the Arabs. Time and again he was able to cover up Arab blackmail and threats. This time they had gone completely wild. The current London Conferences were ending in a fiasco.

It is completely obvious that Haj Amin el Husseini, the Mufti, is running the Palestine Higher Arab Committee from exile in Cairo. Our failure to prosecute the Mufti as a war criminal for fear of religious outbursts has now come back to haunt us. The Arab attitude has reached complete unreason. They refuse to sit at the same table with the Jews unless pre-imposed conditions are agreed upon.

Cecil Bradshaw had been at the San Remo Conference when the Middle East was divided between the British and French and he had been there when the Articles of Mandate were drawn and when the Balfour Declaration was issued. Bradshaw worked on Churchill's group that took half the Palestine mandate and created the kingdom of Trans-Jordan. In all the years, in all the Mufti's riots, they had never been up against a band of fighters in the class of the Maccabees. The Jewish terrorists fought with a fearsome conviction.

We have time and again demanded from the Yishuv Central and the Jewish community that they assist the British authorities in stamping out the gangster elements who go under the name of the Maccabees. Whereas the Yishuv claims no authority over these people and they publicly condemn their actions it is known that a large segment of the Jews secretly approve the gangster actions. We have received no co-operation in this matter. Maccabee activities have reached such proportion that we deem it necessary to evacuate all nonessential British personnel and families from Palestine.

Bradshaw read over the reports of the stepped-up terrorist raids which rocked the Holy Land from one end to another.

In addition to the costly gangster raids on the Haifa refinery which stopped production for two weeks, and the raid on the Lydda airdrome, which destroyed a squadron of fighter planes, ten major road ambushes and fifteen major raids on British installations have taken place. There is increasing evidence that the Haganah and its striking arm, the Palmach, is becoming restless and may even be partaking in some of the recent raids.

The leaky tubs, the floating slums of Aliyah Bet, brought loads of illegal immigrants into the shores of Palestine.

Despite increased naval patrol forces there has been a marked step-up in Aliyah Bet activity since the Exodus *incident. The* America, San Miguel, Ulloa, Abril, Susannah, *and* San Filipo *have carried eight thousand illegals from European displaced-persons camps. We have reason to believe two other ships were successful in breaking the blockade and beached. Our embassies and consulates in the Mediterranean countries report that at least five more ships are being outfitted by Aliyah Bet to attempt immigrant runs on Palestine in the near future.*

The British command had powerful forces in Palestine. Fifty-two vaunted Taggart forts spread an interlocking network over the tiny country. In addition, there were border forts such as Fort Esther and there was a regular police force in every town and there was the powerful Arab Legion from Trans-Jordan. Besides the Taggarts the British maintained large bases at Atlit in the Haifa area, the Schneller Barracks in Jerusalem, and the immense Sarafand camp outside Tel Aviv.

We have, in recent months, launched Operations Noah, Ark, Lobster, Mackerel, Cautious, Lonesome, Octopus, Cantonment, and Harp to keep constant pressure upon the Yishuv. These operations basically are for continued screening for illegals, cordons, and arms searches, and counterattacks where our forces have been attacked. Our success has been limited due to the hundred per cent organization and co-operation of every Jew in the Yishuv in their efforts. Arms are hidden in flower boxes, file cabinets, stoves, refrigerators, false table legs, and a thousand other ingenious places, making arms seizure a near impossibility. Arms are transported by women and small children who readily engage in this practice. Our efforts to obtain Jewish informers has met with total failure. On the other hand, the Jews are able not only to purchase Arab spies but are getting information from sympathetic people within the British command. The Jews are manufacturing weapons of improvised nature, and the Sten guns, land mines, and grenades are continually improving in quality and ingenuity. In a recent attempt to uncover a manufacturing plant on a kibbutz *the women poured scalding water on our soldiers . . .*

Bradshaw was not only having his trouble in controlling the mandate. Other outside factors were increasing the pressure. In England, the people were living under the hardships of austerity and the economy was failing badly. The cost of maintaining the Palestine garrison was enormous. The English were sick of bloodshed, too. On the world political scene the American Zionists had definitely caught the ear of Truman and had in him a sympathetic ally.

> *Since our failure to follow the recommendation of the Anglo-American Committee to allow a hundred thousand Jews to enter Palestine, our prestige has fallen greatly among our allies. Also damaging our prestige is the manner of humiliation by the Maccabee terrorist operation. British authority has never been so badly flaunted as in the recent kidnapping of a British judge who passed sentence on a Jewish terrorist.*

Cecil Bradshaw took off his horn-rimmed glasses, wiped his red eyes, and shook his head. What a mess! He thumbed through the reports once more. Jemal Husseini, the Mufti's nephew, was again wiping out Arab opposition within Palestine through assassination. The Haganah through Aliyah Bet and the Maccabees under Akiva had made things impossible. British officers had been horsewhipped in public streets and British soldiers were hung in reprisals. The Jews who had preached and obeyed the rules of self-restraint during the two sets of prewar riots were showing less and less restraint against the Arab acts of aggression.

It was said in official circles that Cecil Bradshaw had lost his stomach for fighting the Jews after the *Exodus* incident. The Palestine mandate was nearing its twelfth hour. The little country occupied a position of tremendous economic and strategic importance. It was the pivot of the empire itself. The Haifa naval base and refinery and the position in relation to the central artery of the Suez made it imperative that it be held.

The intercom buzzer went off on Bradshaw's desk.

'General Tevor-Browne has arrived.'

Bradshaw and Tevor-Browne mumbled cold greetings. Tevor-Browne was one of the few pro-Jews in official circles. It was he who had predicted the end of the mandate in this very office at the onset of the *Exodus* incident and had pleaded that the *Exodus* be allowed to sail before the hunger strike. Tevor-Browne had always felt that the Jews and not the Arabs deserved British support for the reason that the Jews were faithful allies and could be depended upon and the Arabs could not. He had been for the building of a Jewish Commonwealth nation out of Palestine.

General Tevor-Browne's thinking could not sway Bradshaw and the Chatham House crowd or the Colonial Office. Even at this hour they did not have the courage to reverse their drastic mistake but were standing ready to sink with it. The fear of Arab blackmail over the oil fields and the Suez Canal prevailed.

'I have been reading the summaries,' Bradshaw said.

Tevor-Browne lit a cigar. 'Yes, very interesting. The Jews certainly aren't obliging us by marching backwards into the sea.'

Bradshaw tapped his pudgy fingers on the desk top, resenting the general's 'I told you so,' attitude. 'I must give a recommendation in a few weeks.'

'I don't want your needling implications, Sir Clarence. I wanted to speak over the advisability of retaining Haven-Hurst. I think the time has come to get tougher with the Jews.'

'Haven-Hurst is fine for what you want – unless you wish to obtain the services of some SS generals in the war crimes prisons. We still maintain a civil government in Palestine, you know ... we do have a high commissioner.'

Bradshaw turned crimson under the insults. He managed to hold his temper, a temper which was growing shorter and more violent each day. 'I think the time has come to place greater authority with Haven-Hurst.' He handed a sheet of paper over the desk to Tevor-Browne.

It was a letter addressed to the British commander in Palestine, General Sir Arnold Haven-Hurst, KBE CB, DSO, MC. 'The situation has degenerated to such a state that unless means can be recommended for immediate stabilization by you I will be compelled to suggest the matter be turned over to the United Nations.'

'Well said, Bradshaw,' Tevor-Browne said. 'I am certain Haven-Hurst will have some rather interesting suggestions if you are a devotee of horror stories.'

SAFED, PALESTINE

The retirement order came through for Brigadier Bruce Sutherland quickly and quietly after the *Exodus* afair. He moved to Palestine and settled down on Mount Canaan near Safed, the ancient city at the entrance to the Huleh Valley in northern Galilee.

At long last Bruce Sutherland seemed to find a bit of peace and some respite from the years of torment since the death of his mother. For the first time he was able to sleep at night without fear. Sutherland purchased a magnificent small villa on Mount Canaan three miles from Safed proper. The air was the purest in Palestine and a constant fresh breeze kept summer's heat from fully penetrating the area. His home was of white plaster with red tiled roof and granite floor. It was open and breezy and tastefully furnished in Mediterranean décor. Beyond his rear patio there was a terraced hillside of four full *dunams* of land which he converted into a lush garden with four hundred Galilee rosebushes.

The rear garden afforded a breath-taking view of Safed across the valley. From here the city appeared to be a perfect cone in shape. At the wide base of Safed's hill were the beginnings of winding roads which fought up the peak to the acropolis on top, some three thousand feet in the air. Like so many of the hilltops in Palestine, the acropolis of Safed had once been a citadel in the revolutions of the Hebrews against the Greeks and Romans.

He spent his days puttering in his rose garden, considered to be the finest in Palestine, on trips to the holy places, in studying Hebrew and Arabic, or in just wandering through the maze of crooked and aimless alleys that made up Safed. The town was a constant fascination. It was pressed against the hillside with its narrow oriental streets circling up toward the acropolis in no fixed plan, and the houses were jammed together equally haphazardly. These each with its own special design, grillwork, odd-shaped windows, doors, and balconies cluttered the strangled passageways to add up to a strange sort of charm.

The Jewish quarter, a tenth of the city, was inhabited by the poverty-stricken pious who were content to live off the meager offerings of coreligionists. Safed was the center of the Cabala, the Jewish science of mysticism. The ancient ones here spent their lives in study and prayer and were as colorful as the town itself. They ambled along the rows of tiny shops dressed in outlandish oriental costumes and tattered remains of once majestic silks. They were a gentle and peaceful lot, and for this reason the Cabalists of Safed had suffered the most at the hands of the Mufti's riots for they were least able to defend themselves.

Their history in Palestine was one of the longest unbroken records of Jewish habitation of the Holy Land. The Crusaders banished the Jews, but after their defeat the Cabalists returned to Safed and had remained ever since. The cemetery held graves of the great Cabalist scholars with tombs dating back four and five hundred years. The Cabalists all believed that anyone buried in

Safed would go straight to Gan Eden – the Garden of Eden – so pure was the air in Safed.

Sutherland never tired of walking through the tortuous lanes crowded with tiny synagogues and watching the people or filling himself with the folklore and legend of the rabbis and of the Cabala itself.

The Arab section of Safed held the usual broken-down hovels that are found in every Arab city and town in the world. However, the wonderful climate and scenic beauty of Safed attracted many effendi families to build splendid and spacious homes. Mount Canaan had many homes and resorts for the Jews, Arab Safed had the same for wealthy Arabs. Sutherland had friends in both places.

Consistent with the Arab renown for building atop ruins there were, in the Arab quarters of Safed, remains of medieval buildings converted into contemporary housing. The most beautiful example of the architecture was the Mosque of the Daughters of Jacob on the ruins of a Hungarian Crusader convent.

The crown jewel of Safed was the acropolis. The paths that wound up to the hilltop passed the old Knights Templar castle and the ruins of a Hebrew fort. The very peak stood in a pine forest amid a carpet of wild flowers and commanded a view from the Sea of Galilee on the south to the Huleh Lake in the north where one could follow the winding course of the Jordan River. On the horizon was Mount Hermon, and all the valleys and hills of the Galilee were visible beyond Meron on the western side.

On this hill the ancient Hebrews came once each year to light a fire. The signal would be seen and transmitted from hill to hill to indicate the start of the Holy Days. In the days before calendars the Holy Days were determined by calculations of the chief rabbis, and the fires burned on the hilltops from Jerusalem to Tabor to Gilboa to Safed and on to Babylon to where the Jews lived in captivity.

One discordant note jarred the otherwise perfect beauty and visual poetry: a large, ugly concrete Taggart fort stood outside Safed on the road up Mount Canaan and was visible from Sutherland's villa.

Sutherland ventured north to look at the *tel* of Hazor and along the Lebanese border to see the burial places of Esther at the fort and Joshua at Abu Yesha. It was by chance that he happened into Gan Dafna and friendship with Dr Lieberman and Kitty Fremont. For Kitty and Sutherland the renewal of the brief acquaintance made at Cyprus was a welcoming thing. Sutherland was happy to develop into a patron saint of the children. Kitty prevailed upon him to let some of the more disturbed children come with her to visit his villa and Safed. In a short time the two formed a fast friendship.

One afternoon Sutherland returned from Gan Dafna and was surprised to find his former aide, Major Fred Caldwell, awaiting him.

'How long have you been in Palestine, Freddie?'

'I arrived just a bit ago.'

'Where are you serving?'

'Headquarters, Jerusalem, in Intelligence. I'm doing liaison with the Criminal Investigation Division. They've had a shake-up recently. Seems that some of our chaps have been working with the Haganah and even with the Maccabees, if you can imagine that.'

Sutherland could imagine it quite easily.

'Actually, sir, this visit is only partly social, although I certainly intended to drop up and see how you've been getting on. General Haven-Hurst asked me to see you personally because I had worked under you in the past.'

'Oh?'

'As you know we are now in the process of carrying out Operation Polly, the evacuation of nonessential British from Palestine.'

'I've heard it referred to as Operation Folly,' Sutherland said.

Freddie smiled politely at the jibe and cleared his throat. 'General Haven-Hurst wanted to know what you planned to do.'

'I don't plan to do a thing. This is my home and this is where I am going to remain.'

Freddie's fingers drummed impatiently on the table top. 'What I mean, sir, is that General Haven-Hurst wants it understood that once the nonessentials are gone he cannot assume responsibility for your safety. If you remain here it could pose a problem to us.'

Caldwell's speech held obvious devious connotations: Haven-Hurst knew of Sutherland's leanings and was afraid of his working with the Haganah. He was, in effect, advising him to get out.

'Tell General Haven-Hurst I am grateful for his concern and I fully realize his exact position.'

Freddie wanted to press the matter. Sutherland arose quickly and thanked Caldwell for the visit and walked him to the driveway, where a sergeant waited with a staff car. He watched the car drive down toward the Taggart fort. As usual, Freddie had botched his assignment. His delivery of Haven-Hurst's warning had been clumsy, indeed.

Sutherland walked back to the villa and thought it over. He was in physical danger. The Maccabees could easily take exception to a retired British brigadier with Arab friends living alone on Mount Canaan, although the Maccabees would certainly think twice about doing him in. There was no danger from the Haganah. He had a loose contact with them and they were not only discriminate but did not go in for assassination. On the other side there was no telling what Husseini was likely to do: Sutherland had friends among the Jews. Some of them could well have been Maccabees unbeknownst to him.

Bruce Sutherland walked to his gardens. They were bursting with the early spring roses. He looked beyond the valley of Safed. He had found peace and comfort here. The hideous dreams were gone. No, he would not leave tomorrow – or ever.

Caldwell's car entered the Taggart fort a few moments after he left Sutherland. The four outside walls held the offices and barracks. The inner court served as the assembly ground and parking lot for vehicles. He was met and asked to report to CID.

'Are you going back to Jerusalem tonight, Major Caldwell?' the Criminal Investigation Division inspector asked.

Freddie looked at his watch. 'Yes, I plan to. We can make it back before evening if I leave right now.'

'Good. I have a Jew here I want taken back to CID in Jerusalem for questioning. Maccabee prisoner ... dangerous one. There is a chance that the Maccabees know we are holding him here and will be watching for a convoy to transfer him. That is why it will be safer if he goes in your car.'

'Happy to do it.'

'Bring the Jew boy in.'

Two soldiers dragged in a boy of fourteen or fifteen years of age manacled with heavy chains on hands and feet. A taped gag was over his mouth. His face was bruised from a CID third degree. The inspector walked up to the prisoner. 'Don't let Ben Solomon's angel face fool you. He's a ruddy little bastard.'

'Ben Solomon? Ben Solomon? I don't remember seeing his name.'

'Just got him last night. Raid on the Safed police station. They were trying to steal arms. He killed two policemen with a grenade. Yes, indeed, you're a mean little sheeny, aren't you?'

Ben Solomon stood calm with his eyes blazing contempt at the inspector.

'Don't take his gag off, Major Caldwell, or he'll start singing Psalms for you. He's a fanatic little bastard.'

The inspector became annoyed at the boy's steady withering glare. He took a step toward Ben Solomon and smashed him in the mouth, sending him crashing to the floor, bloody and tangled in his chains.

'Get him out of here,' the inspector snapped in a nervous voice.

The boy was shoved on the floor in the back of the car. One armed soldier sat in the back with him and Caldwell sat in front next to the driver. They drove out of the Taggart fort.

'Dirty little bastard,' the driver mumbled. 'Ask me, Major Caldwell, they ought to turn us loose on these Jews 'ere a few weeks. That's what we should do, by rights.'

'Cobber of mine got it last week,' the guard in the back said, 'and a fine bloke he was, too. 'Ad a wife and a new baby. Them Maccabees give it to him right through the 'ead, they did.'

As they drove into the Beth Shean Valley the three men relaxed; they were now in all-Arab territory and the danger of attack was gone until they reached the Jerusalem area.

Caldwell turned around and looked at the prisoner on the floor. The juices of hatred churned in his stomach. He detested Bruce Sutherland. He knew in his heart that Sutherland was helping the Haganah. Sutherland was a Jew lover. Sutherland had intentionally let the catastrophe on Cyprus occur.

Caldwell remembered standing near the barbed wire at the Caraolos camp and a fat Jewish woman spitting out on him.

He looked back at the boy on the floor. The guard sat in the middle of the seat. One heavy boot was planted on Ben Solomon's head and he snickered with amusement.

'Dirty Jew!' Caldwell mumbled under his breath.

He could see a parade of them. The bearded characters in London's Whitechapel and he could smell the smell of pickles. The line of pawn shops – they sat hunched over their benches mumbling prayers. Caldwell could see the little boys on their way to Jew school with the black caps on their heads.

They drove toward the all-Arab city of Nablus.

Caldwell smiled as he remembered the officers' club and the sheeny jokes. He could see his mother leading him into the office of an arrogant Jew doctor.

And they think Hitler was wrong, Caldwell thought. Hitler knew what the score was. It was bloody well too bad that the war ended before he could do them all in. Caldwell remembered entering Bergen-Belsen with Sutherland. Sutherland was sick at what he saw. Well, Caldwell wasn't sick. The more Jews dead, the better.

They passed into an Arab village with a record of known hostility toward the Yishuv. It was an Husseini strong point.

'Stop the car,' Caldwell ordered. 'Now you two men listen to me. We are throwing this kike out.'

'But, Major, they'll murder him,' the guard said.

'I admits I'm put out at the Jews, sir,' the driver said, 'but we got a responsibility to deliver our prisoner, we has.'

'Shut up!' Caldwell barked, half hysterically. 'I said we are throwing him out. Both of you are to swear he was taken by Maccabees who roadblocked us. If you open your mouth otherwise you'll end up in ditches. Am I clear?'

The two soldiers merely nodded as they saw the mad look in Caldwell's eyes.

Ben Solomon was unchained from the floor. The car slowed near the coffeehouse. The boy was hurled into the street and they sped away for Jerusalem.

It worked just as Caldwell knew it would. Within an hour Ben Solomon had been killed and mutilated. He was decapitated. The bodyless head was held up by the hair and photographed with twenty laughing Arabs around it. The picture was sent out as a warning of what was going to happen to all the Jews sooner or later.

Major Fred Caldwell made a disastrous mistake. One of the Arabs in the coffeehouse who saw the boy thrown from the car was a member of the Maccabees.

General Sir Arnold Haven-Hurst, KBE, CB, DSO, MC was infuriated. He paced the office of his headquarters in the Schneller compound in Jerusalem, then snatched Cecil Bradshaw's letter from his desk and read it again.

The situation has degenerated to such a state that unless means can be recommended for immediate stabilization by you I will be compelled to suggest the matter be turned over to the United Nations.

The United Nations, indeed! The tall blond man snorted and crumpled the letter and threw it to the floor. A week before Haven-Hurst had ordered a boycott on all Jewish places of business.

This was to be his thanks after fighting the Jews for five years. He had warned the Home Office in World War II not to take these Jews into the British Army, but no, they wouldn't listen. Now, lose the Palestine mandate. Haven-Hurst went to his desk and began working on an answer to Bradshaw's letter.

I propose immediate adoption of the following points, which in my opinion will stabilize Palestine.

1. Suspension of all civil courts with fines and punishments and prison terms to be dispensed by the military commander.

2. Dissolve the Yishuv Central, disband the Zion Settlement Society and all other agencies of the Jews.

3. Cessation of all Jewish newspapers and publications.

4. Swift, quiet elimination of some sixty top Yishuv leaders. Haj Amin el Husseini has proved this method successful against his political opposition. This phase could be carried out by Arab confederates.

5. Complete use of the Arab Legion of Trans-Jordan.

6. Imprisonment of several hundred secondary leaders in the Yishuv and their subsequent quick banishment to some remote African colonies.

7. Grant the military commander the right to destroy any kibbutz, moshav, *village, or part of a city found with arms. Institute a nationwide screening with all illegals to be deported at once.*

8. Impose fines against the entire Jewish population for every act of Maccabee terror, and place these fines so high the Jews will begin to co-operate in the apprehension of these gangsters.

9. Offer larger rewards for information on key Maccabee terrorists, Aliyah Bet agents, Haganah heads, etc.

10. Hang or execute every apprehended Maccabee gangster on the spot.

11. Institute a series of boycotts on Jewish business, farm products, and halt all Jewish imports and exports. Keep complete control on all the movements of all Jewish vehicles.

12. Destroy the Palmach by armed attacks on kibbutizm *known to be harboring them.*

My forces have been compelled to operate under most difficult circumstances. We have been made to follow the rules and restrain ourselves from the widest and most effective use of our powers. On the other hand the Maccabees, Haganah, Palmach, and Aliyah Bet observe no rules and, indeed, attack our restraint as a weakness. If I am allowed to use my power I assure that order will be restored in short time.

General Sir Arnold Haven-Hurst
KBE, CB, DSO, MC

CHATHAM HOUSE, INSTITUTE OF FOREIGN RELATIONS, LONDON

Cecil Bradshaw's color was a sickly gray when General Tevor-Browne finally reached his office.

'Well, Bradshaw, you asked Haven-Hurst for his ideas. You have them now.'

'Has the man gone mad? Good Lord, his report reads like Adolf Hitler's "Final Solution."'

Bradshaw picked up the twelve-point 'Haven-Hurst Report' and shook his head. 'God knows we want to keep Palestine, but murder, burning villages, hangings, starvation? I cannot recommend this beastly thing. Even if I did I don't know whether you have enough men in the British Army who could carry it out. I've been for the Empire all my life, Sir Clarence, and many's the time we've had to take harsh and unfair measures in our own behalf. But I also believe in God. We're just not going to hold Palestine this way. I wash my hands of the matter. Let someone else endorse Haven-Hurst ... I won't.'

Cecil Bradshaw took the 'Haven-Hurst Report' and crumpled it. He put it in his large ash tray and put a match to it and watched it burn. 'Thank God, we've got the courage to answer for our sins,' he whispered.

The question of the Palestine mandate was thrown open to the United Nations.

Chapter Seven

Now it was the late spring of 1947 and Ari Ben Canaan disappeared from Kitty Fremont's life. She did not see or hear from him after Mount Tabor. If Ari had given any messages to Jordana, Jordana had not delivered them. The two women scarcely spoke a word to each other. Kitty tried to be tolerant but Jordana made even that difficult.

The Palestine mandate issue was handed over for the United Nations to attempt to unscramble it. United Nations machinery was in the process of forming a committee of small, neutral nations to investigate the problem and come up with recommendations for the General Assembly. The Yishuv Central and the World Zionists accepted mediation of the problem by the United Nations. On the other side, the Arabs used threats, boycotts, blackmail, and any other pressure they could find to keep the Palestine issue away from an impartial judgment.

At Gan Dafna the Gadna military training speeded up. The Youth Village became a chief arms depot. Rifles were brought in to be cleaned by the children and then smuggled in village trucks to Huleh settlements and the Palmach. Time and again Karen was called upon to go out on arms-smuggling missions. The assignments were accepted by her and the other children without question. Kitty's heart was in her mouth every time Karen went out, but she had to keep her silence.

Karen doggedly continued to press the search for her father without success. The once bright promise at La Ciotat faded.

The girl retained contact with the Hansens in Denmark. Karen wrote each week, and each week a letter and often a package arrived from Copenhagen. Meta and Aage Hansen had given up all hope of ever getting her back. Even if Karen did not find her father there was something in the girl's letters that indicated she was lost to them. Karen's identification with Palestine and being Jewish became a nearly complete thing. The only qualification was Kitty Fremont.

Dov Landau was taking strange turns. At times he would appear to be breaking out of his reclusion, and in those moments he and Karen added a deeper dimension to their relationship. Then the very audacity of his coming into the clear light would force Dov back into his shell. Whenever he was able to reason about his role he disliked himself for what he felt he was doing to Karen. Then loyalty to him produced self-pity and he at once hated and loved her. He felt he must not contaminate Karen with himself, yet he did not wish to cut off his only link with humanity. The times he would sink back again into bitterness he often stared at the blue tattoo number on his arm by the hour. He would turn to his books and his painting with a savage concentration and close out all living things. Just as he neared the bottom, Karen would succeed in pulling him out of it. His bitterness never quite grew so deep that he could turn on her.

In the time that Kitty Fremont had been at Gan Dafna she had made herself one of the most important persons in the village. Dr Lieberman leaned on her more each day. Looked upon as a sympathetic outsider, she was frequently able to exert the needed extra influence of someone 'outside the family.' Dr Lieberman's friendship was becoming one of the most rewarding she had ever known. She was completely integrated into the life of Gan Dafna; she did splendid work with disturbed children. Yet a barrier still remained. She knew that she was partly responsible for it but she wanted it that way.

Kitty was far more at ease with Bruce Sutherland than she was with the people of Gan Dafna. With Sutherland she was in her own element and she looked forward with increasing impatience to those free days that she and Karen could spend at his villa. When she was with Sutherland it renewed her awareness of the difference between herself and the Jews.

Harriet Saltzman came to Gan Dafna two times. On both occasions the old woman pleaded with Kitty to take charge of one of the new Youth Aliyah Centers in the Tel Aviv area. Kitty was a wizard at organization and a stickler for routine. This, plus her over-all experience and ability was badly needed at places not so well run as Gan Dafna. Harriet Saltzman wisely calculated that the 'outside' influence of a Kitty Fremont would be a tremendous asset to a Youth Aliyah Center.

Kitty refused. She was settled at Gan Dafna and Karen was completely at home. She did not seek a career in Youth Aliyah and had no aspirations.

The main reason, however, was that she did not want to be placed in a capacity where she would have to answer for Gadna activities and arms smuggling. This would put her into the category of a participant. Kitty clung to her neutrality. Her work was going to remain professional and not political.

To Karen Clement, Kitty Fremont was like an older sister who was raising her without the help of parents. Kitty made herself indispensable to the girl. The Hansens in Denmark faded from her life and there had been no progress in finding her father. This left only Dov and Dov gave nothing. Kitty encouraged this condition of dependence – she wanted Karen to need her. She wanted Karen to need her so much the need would defeat the hidden foe, the power of Eretz Israel.

With the passing of the weeks holidays came and left Gan Dafna.

There had been Tuv b'Shevat in the late winter, an arbor day, to perpetuate the fanatical tree planting of the Jews.

Late in the month of March came Hero's Day. Jordana Ben Canaan led the Gadna troops on a hike along the border ridges to Tel Hai where Barak and Akiva had entered Palestine from Lebanon. It was now hallowed ground. At Trumpledor's grave soldiers of the Palmach and the young soldiers of Gadna gathered to pay homage to the new heroes.

The glorious festival of Purim came. Gan Dafna erupted with Mardi gras- and Halloween-like costumes and floats and decorations that turned it into a carnival. The Purim story was told – of how Queen Esther saved the Jews, then in the Persian Empire. The evil Haman, the Amalekite, plotted to have the Jews annihilated but Esther unmasked Haman and saved her people. The grave of Esther was on the border of Fort Esther, where part of the celebration took place. The Purim story was a real thing to the children of Gan Dafna, for almost all of them had been victims of a latter-day Haman named Adolf Hitler.

Passover came and went.

The holiday of Lag Ba Omer occurred on the full moon thirty days after the end of Passover and in time became a memorial to the second uprising of the Hebrews against the Romans. Homage was paid to the great sages buried in the city of Tiberias and in Safed and in Meron. There were the graves of Moses Mainmonides, the immortal philosopher and physician, and of the rabbis, Hiya, Eliezer, and Kahana and of the great revolutionary, Rabbi Akiva. There was the grave of Rabbi Meir the Miracle Maker. All these were in Tiberias where the festival started and whence it moved to Safed. From Safed the pious moved in a great gathering body to Meron and to the graves of Johanan the Sandal Maker and Hillel and Shammai. The ancient synagogue still stood in part at Meron with its door which was supposed to welcome the return of the Messiah.

Of all the rabbis praised on Lag Ba Omer, Simon Bar Yohai received the greatest reverence. Bar Yohai defied the Roman edicts which banned Judaism and he fled to the village of Peki'in where he lived in a cave and where the Lord provided him with a carob tree for food and a stream for water. He lived in hiding for seventeen years. One day each year he came to Meron to teach the forbidden Torah to his disciples. It is said by both Mohammedans and Christians that they owe the life of their religions to those rabbis who kept Judaism alive in hiding. Without Judaism and the Holy Torah neither Christianity nor Islam could have survived, for their roots were in the Torah and their very life and air and blood were in the doctrines of Judaism.

While in hiding Bar Yohai wrote the *Zohar* – the Brightness – which was the standard work of the mystic Cabala. Hasidic and Oriental celebrants converged on the holy cities of Tiberias and Safed from all corners of Palestine and continued on to Meron to spend several days and nights in prayer and song and dance and praise of Simon Bar Yohai.

When the month of May came the rains were gone and the Huleh Valley and the hills of Syria and Lebanon turned a rich green and the valleys filled with carpets of wild flowers and the buds on the spring roses of Galilee burst into magnificent reds and whites and oranges and once again Gan Dafna prepared for a holiday. It was time for Shavuot to celebrate the bringing of the first fruits of the new year.

All holidays concerned with farming were particularly close to the hearts of the Jews of Palestine. Shavuot at Gan Dafna had become traditional for the coming of delegations from the Huleh settlements to the children's village to share in the celebration.

Again Dan Gafna took on the air of a carnival as truckloads of farmers arrived from the Yad El *moshav*. Sarah Ben Canaan came.

They arrived from the border *kibbutzim* of Kfar Giladi up on the Lebanon border. They came from Ayelet Hashahar *kikkutz* on the lake and from Ein Or. They came from Dan on the Syrian border and from Manara on the mountaintop.

Dr Lieberman expressed his disappointment to Harriet Saltzman and Kitty that the Arab delegation from Abu Yesha was only half the usual size and that Taha was missing. The meaning was obvious and saddening.

Kitty managed to see each truck as it arrived. She hoped that Ari Ben Canaan would come and she was unable to mask her disappointment. Jordana in turn watched Kitty, with a cynical smirk.

Some soldiers came from Fort Esher. These were among the 'friends' who always tipped off the village when an arms search was on the way.

The day was filled with merriment. There were athletic contests and open house in the classrooms and laboratories. There was *hora* dancing on the center green, and outdoor tables bent under the weight of food.

At sundown everyone moved to the outdoor theater cut into a hillside, set in the middle of a stand of pine trees. The theater filled to overflowing; hundreds more lay about on the surrounding lawns. As it turned dark multi-colored lights came on, strung through the pines.

The Gan Dafna orchestra played 'Hatikvah' – the Hope – and Dr Lieberman spoke a brief welcome and signaled the parade of Shavuot to begin. He returned to his seat with Kitty, Sutherland, and Harriet Saltzman.

Karen led the parade. The instant Kitty saw her she felt fear. Karen sat astride a large white horse and balanced the staff of the flag with the white field and the blue Star of David. She wore dark blue slacks and an embroidered peasant's blouse and sandals on her feet. Her thick brown hair was done in pigtails and hung on to her small breasts.

Kitty gripped the arms of her chair. Karen looked the very spirit of the Jews!

Have I lost her? Have I lost her? The wind whipped the flag and her horse broke for a second, but Karen turned it into line quickly. She is gone from me as she is from the Hansens, Kitty thought.

Harriet Saltzman was looking at Kitty and Kitty lowered her eyes.

Karen passed out of the spotlight and the parade continued. The five tractors of Gan Dafna were polished and shined. Each pulled a flatcar loaded with fruits and vegetables and grains grown at the village farm.

Jeeps and trucks and station wagons buried under flowers from the gardens passed by. Trucks passed by filled with children in peasants' clothing holding rakes and hoes and scythes and power tools.

The livestock was passed in review, led by the cows, which were decked in ribbons and flowers, and the horses were shiny with manes and tails braided. The sheep and goats were herded past and then the pet dogs and cats and a monkey and white rats and hamsters were led or carried in affectionate display.

Children passed holding cloth of material they had grown, spun, and woven and newspapers they had printed and their art work and baskets and pottery. Their athletic teams marched by.

When the parade was done there was a final rousing cheer from the audience.

Dr Lieberman's secretary slipped alongside him and whispered into his ear.

'Excuse me, please,' he said, 'I have an important phone call.'

'Hurry back,' Harriet Saltzman called after him.

The lights in the trees were turned off, plunging the place into darkness for a moment before a spotlight shone on the stage. The curtain opened and the tambour beat and a reed flute played an ancient melody. The children began to enact the Song of Ruth. It was done in pantomime against the plaintive sound background of the two instruments.

Their costumes were authentic. The dances were the slow and sensuous movements of the days of Ruth and Naomi. Then came performers who danced with wild leaps and a passion like that of the dancers Kitty saw on top of Tabor.

How they lived for the re-creation of their past, Kitty thought. How dedicated they were to regaining the glory of Israel.

Karen stepped onto the stage and commanded an instant expectant hush.

Karen danced the part of Ruth. Her movements told the simple and beautiful story of the Moabite girl and her Hebrew mother-in-law who traveled to Beth Lehem – the House of Bread. The story of love and of one God had been retold at Shavuot since the days of the Maccabees.

Ruth had been a gentile in the land of the Jews. Yet Ruth was an ancestor of King David.

Kitty's eyes were glued to Karen as she enacted Ruth's words to Naomi that she would come to the land of the Hebrews with her.

'*Whither thou goest I will go; and where thou lodgest I will lodge. Thy people shall be my people and thy God my God.*'

Kitty was dismayed as never before. Could she get Karen away from this? Kitty Fremont was the stranger. She would always be a stranger. The gentile among the Hebrews, but she could not say as Ruth had said, '*Thy people shall be my people.*' Would this mean losing Karen?

Dr Lieberman's secretary tapped Kitty's shoulder. 'Would you come to Dr Lieberman's office at once?' she whispered.

Kitty excused herself and slipped from her seat. She walked up to the top of the theater and looked back for a moment to see the children dancing the dance of the reapers and to watch Karen go to sleep at the feet of 'Boaz.' She turned and left the theater.

The path was dark and she had to be careful of trenches. Kitty turned her pocket flashlight on the ground. She crossed the center green and passed the statue of Dafna. Behind her she could hear the beat of the tambour and the cry of the flute. She walked quickly to the administration building, led by the single light.

She opened the door to Dr Lieberman's office.

'Good Lord,' she said, startled at the sight of him, 'what's the matter? You look as though ...'

'They have found Karen's father,' he whispered.

Chapter Eight

Bruce Sutherland drove Kitty and Karen to Tel Aviv the next day. Kitty used the pretext that she had to do some overdue shopping and wanted to give Karen her first look at the big city. They arrived slightly before the noon hour and checked into the Gat Rimon Hotel on Hayarkon Street, on the Mediterranean. After lunch Sutherland excused himself and left. The shops were closed during the midday hours so Kitty and Karen romped along the sandy beach below the hotel, then cooled off from the heat with a refreshing swim.

At three o'clock Kitty ordered a taxi. They drove to Jaffa where one of the faculty at Gan Dafna had recommended some great buys in Arab and Persian brass- and copperware. Kitty wanted some things for the cottage. The taxi took them into a narrow, twisting street in the center of the Jaffa flea market. A row of shops were indentations in a Crusader wall. They stopped before one of the holes in the wall guarded by a fat individual sitting asleep in the doorway, with a red fez tipped over his eyes. Kitty and Karen studied the shop. It was five feet wide and not much deeper and a mess of hanging pots, pans, plates, jugs, vases, urns, candlesticks, and what not. The floor had not been swept for at least ten years.

The fat Arab sensed the presence of customers and awakened from his sleep. He gallantly gestured to the women to enter his domain. He shoved some brassware off two boxes and offered them as seats, then ran outside and called for his oldest son to get some coffee for the honored guests. The coffee arrived. Kitty and Karen sipped it and politely exchanged smiles with the shopkeeper. The son stood by the door, a portrait in stupidity. A half dozen spectators gathered on the outside to observe the proceedings. The attempts to converse soon proved frustrating. There were grunts, gestures, and hand wavings in place of a common language. Whereas Karen spoke Danish, French, German, English, and Hebrew and Kitty spoke English, Spanish, and a smattering of Greek, the Arab was versed only in Arabic. He sent his son out once again to find the flea market interpreter and in another few minutes the intermediary was produced. The interpreter's English was of a pidgin variety, but he was conscientious and the shopping commenced.

Kitty and Karen browsed around the shop blowing dust off encrusted antiques, some with a hundred years' coating of dirt and tarnish to testify to their authenticity. After forty tense minutes of womanly thoroughness, every piece in the shop had been handled by one or the other shopper. They settled on a pair of vases, three long-spouted Arab coffee pots of exquisite delicacy, and an enormous Persian plate with thousands of hand-engraved figures depicting an entire legend. Kitty asked the price for the entire lot, cleaned, polished, and delivered to her hotel. The crowd on the outside pressed closer as the interpreter and the proprietor went into a huddle.

The interpreter turned and sighed. 'Mr Akim, him heart broke. These treasures to depart. Plate, he swear by Allah, three hundred years.'

'Just how much is it going to take to mend Mr Akim's broken heart?' Kitty asked.

'Because lady, your daughter here, so beautiful, Mr Akim make special bargain. Take all, sixteen pounds sterling.'

'It's a steal,' Kitty whispered to Karen.

'You can't pay him what he asks,' Karen said with exasperation. 'Do you want to ruin his day by not bartering?'

'I'm taking it and running,' Kitty whispered. 'That plate alone would cost three or four hundred dollars in the States.'

'Kitty! Please!' Karen cried in disgust. She stepped in front of Kitty and the smile disappeared from Akim's face. 'Nine pounds sterling and not a *grush* more,' Karen announced firmly.

The interpreter reported the counter-offer to Mr Akim. Mr Akim was offended. He went into wails of anguish. He had a large family to feed. Again his kind heart was being taken advantage of. The items picked by these sharp-eyed women they knew were antiques ... on his honor, hs father's honor, and by Allah's beard. Thirteen pounds.

'Twelve and that's final.'

Akim sobbed that he was being cheated but he was a poor Arab so what could he do. He was putty in the hands of these clever women. Twelve and a half.

It was a deal.

The bartering was over and smiles bloomed within and without the shop. There was an extended handshaking ceremony. Akim blessed Kitty and Karen and all their subsequent offspring. She left the name of her hotel and advised Akim he would be paid when the cleaned and polished goods were delivered. She tipped the interpreter and the stupid son and they left.

They walked through the flea market amazed by the amount that could be jammed into the tiny shops and the degree of filth one street could collect. As they approached the end of the street a man who looked like a *sabra* stepped up to Karen and exchanged several words in Hebrew and walked away quickly.

'What did he want?'

'He saw by my uniform I was a Jew. He wanted to know if you were English. I told him who you were and he advised us to return to Tel Aviv. There might be trouble.'

Kitty looked down the street but the man was gone.

'He must have been a Maccabee,' Karen said.

'Let's get out of here.'

Kitty's heart was in her mouth until they were out of Jaffa. They drove to the intersection of Allenby Road and Rothschild Boulevard. Allenby Road was filled with new shops, and Rothschild was a wide street with a center parkway lined with ultramodern three-storied white apartment houses. It was a striking contrast to the flea market of Jaffa. Cars and buses moved in a steady flow and people walked with the big-city gait, all in a hurry.

'It is so thrilling,' Karen said. 'I'm glad I was able to come. It is hard for me to realize that everyone here, bus drivers and waiters and salespeople, are all Jews. They built this whole city ... a Jewish city. You don't understand what that means, do you ... a city in which everything belongs to the Jews.'

Karen's words annoyed Kitty.

'In America we have many important Jews, Karen, and they are very happy and very much American.'

'But it's not the same as a Jewish country. It's not the same as knowing that wherever you go and whatever you do there is still one corner of the earth where you are wanted and that belongs to you.'

Kitty fished in her purse quickly and took out a piece of paper. 'Where would this address be?'

Karen looked at the paper. 'Two blocks down. When are you going to learn to read Hebrew?'

'Never, I'm afraid,' Kitty said, then added quickly, 'I chipped two teeth trying to say some words yesterday.'

They found the address. It was a dress shop.

'What are you going to get?' Karen asked.

'I'm going to buy you a decent wardrobe. It's a surprise from Brigadier Sutherland and me.'

Karen stopped dead. 'I couldn't,' she said.

'What's the matter, dear?'

'There is nothing wrong with what I'm wearing.'

'It is fine for Gan Dafna ...' Kitty said.

'I have all the clothing I need,' Karen insisted.

Sometimes she sounds like Jordana Ben Canaan, Kitty thought. 'Karen, let's not forget that you are a young lady. You won't be betraying the cause if you dress up in something nice once in a while.'

'I am quite proud of ...'

'Oh, quiet!' Kitty said with finality. 'You sound more like a *sabra* every day. When you are away from Gan Dafna with me you are going to make me and Bruce proud of you.'

Kitty appeared angry and sounded adamant. Karen bit her lip and retreated. She peeked out of the corner of her eye at the full-skirted mannequins in the window. 'It isn't fair to the rest of the girls,' she said in a final effort.

'We'll hide the dresses under the rifles if it will make you happy.'

A few moments later she was bouncing before the mirror, happily staging a one-woman fashion show and terribly pleased that Kitty had been insistent. It did feel so wonderful and look so wonderful! How long had it been since she wore nice things? Denmark ... so long ago that she had almost forgotten. Kitty was as delighted as she watched Karen transform herself from peasant to *soignée* teen-ager. They walked the length of Allenby Road, still shopping, and turned into Ben Yehuda Street at the Mograbi Square, loaded with packages. They plopped down at a table at the first sidewalk café. Karen gobbled an ice-cream soda and watched the panorama of passing people with wide eyes.

She shoved a spoonful of ice cream in her mouth. 'This is the nicest day I can remember,' she said. 'It would be perfect if Dov and Ari were here.'

She was adorable, Kitty thought. Her heart was so filled with goodness she wanted only to give to others.

Karen meditated as she sipped from the bottom of the glass. 'Sometimes I think we have picked a pair of lemons.'

'We?'

'You know ... you and Ari. Me and Dov.'

'I don't know what on earth gives you the impression there is something between Mr Ben Canaan and myself, but you are quite, quite, quite mistaken.'

'Ha, ha, ha,' Karen answered. 'Is that why you twisted your neck watching every truck that came in the gate before the Shavuot celebration yesterday? Just who were you looking for if not Ari Ben Canaan?'

'Humph,' Kitty grunted, and sipped her coffee to cover her guilty confusion.

Kitty shrugged as she wiped at her lips. 'Gosh, anyone could tell you are sweet on him.'

Kitty narrowed her eyes and glared at Karen. 'You listen to me, Miss Smarty ...'

'Deny it and I'll run up and down the street and shout it in Hebrew.'

Kitty threw up her hands. 'I can't win. Someday you'll realize a man can be very attractive to us older women of thirty without there being the least bit of seriousness attached to it. I like Ari, but I'm sorry to have to dispel your romantic notions.'

Karen looked at Kitty with an expression that clearly said she was simply not convinced. The girl sighed and leaned close to Kitty and held her arm as though she were going to impart a deep dark secret. Karen's mien took on the earnest sincerity of the teen-ager. 'Ari needs you, I can tell that.'

Kitty patted Karen's hand and adjusted a loose strand of hair in the girl's pigtail. 'I wish I were sixteen again and things were so pure and uncomplicated. No, Karen, Ari Ben Canaan comes from a breed of supermen whose stock in trade is their self-reliance. Ari Ben Canaan hasn't needed anyone since the day he cut his teeth on his father's bull whip. His blood is made up of little steel and ice corpuscles and his heart is a pump like the motor in that bus over there. All this keeps him above and beyond human emotions.'

She sat silent and very still and her eyes looked beyond Karen.

'You do care for him.'

'Yes,' Kitty sighed, 'I do, and what you said is right. We've got a pair of lemons. We'd better get back to the hotel. I want you to dress up for me and make yourself look like a princess. Bruce and I have a surprise for you. We'll take the pigtails down.'

Karen indeed looked like a princess when Sutherland picked them up for dinner. The surprise was attendance at a touring French ballet company's staging of *Swan Lake* at the Habima National Theater, accompanied by the Palestine Philharmonic Orchestra.

Karen leaned forward and sat on the edge of her seat during the entire performance, concentrating intently on the steps of the prima ballerina as she floated her way through the fairy tale. The overpowering, haunting beauty of the score filled her brain.

How beautiful it all was, Karen thought. She had almost forgotten things like ballet were still in the world. How lucky she was to have Kitty Fremont. The stage was bathed in blue light and the music swelled into the finale with the storm and Siegfried defeating the evil Von Rotbart and the beautiful swan maidens turning into women. Tears of happiness fell down her cheeks.

Kitty watched Karen more than she watched the ballet. She sensed that she had awakened something dormant in the girl. Maybe Karen was rediscovering that there was something in the world she once had that was as important as the green of the fields of the Galilee. Kitty resolved again to keep this thing alive in Karen always; as much as the Jews had won her over there was still much of her they could never get.

Tomorrow Karen would see her father and her world would move on in another direction. Kitty won something this day.

They returned to the hotel late. Karen was bursting with happiness. She flung the hotel door open and danced through the lobby. The British officers raised their eyebrows. Kitty sent her up to get ready for bed and repaired to the bar with Sutherland for a nightcap.

'Have you told her about her father yet?'

'No.'

'Do you want me to go with you?'

'I'd rather ... alone.'

'Of course.'

'But please be there afterwards.'

'I'll be there.'

Kitty stood up and kissed Sutherland on the cheek. 'Good night, Bruce.'

Karen was still dancing in their room when Kitty arrived. 'Did you see Odette in the last scene?' she said, imitating the steps.

'It's late and you're a tired Indian.'

'Oh, what a day!' Karen said, flopping into her bed.

Kitty walked into the bathroom and changed. She could hear Karen humming the melodies of the ballet. 'Oh God,' Kitty whispered. 'Why does this have to happen to her?' Kitty held her face in her hands and trembled. 'Give her strength ... please give her strength.'

Kitty lay wide-eyed in the darkness. She heard Karen stir and looked over to the girl's bed. Karen arose and knelt beside Kitty's bed and lay her head on Kitty's bosom. 'I love you so much, Kitty,' Karen said. 'I couldn't love my own mother more.'

Kitty turned her head away and stroked Karen's hair. 'You'd better go to sleep,' Kitty said shakily. 'We have a busy day tomorrow.'

Kitty stayed awake smoking one cigarette after the other and occasionally pacing the floor. Each time she looked at the sleeping child her heart tightened. Long past midnight she sat by the window listening to the waves and looking at Jaffa on the bend of the coast line. It was four o'clock before Kitty fell into a restless, thrashing sleep.

In the morning she was heavy with depression, her face drawn and her eyes showing rings of sleeplessness beneath them. A dozen times she tried to broach the subject. Breakfast on the terrace was in silence. Kitty sipped her coffee.

'Where is Brigadier Sutherland?' Karen asked.

'He had to go out on business. He'll see us later this morning.'

'What are we going to do today?'

'Oh a little of this and a little of that.'

'Kitty ... it's something about my father, isn't it?'

Kitty lowered her eyes.

'I guess I really knew all along.'

'I didn't mean to deceive you, dear ... I ...'

'What is it ... please tell me ... what is it?'

'He is very, very sick.'

Karen bit her finger and her mouth trembled. 'I want to see him.'

'He won't know you, Karen.'

Karen straightened up and looked off to the sea. 'I've waited so long for this day.'

'Please ...'

'Every night since I knew the war was ending over two years ago I've gone to sleep with the same dream. I lay in bed and pretended we were meeting each other again. I'd know just how he would look and what we are going to say to each other. At the DP camp in Caraolos and in Cyprus all those months I dreamed about it every night ... my father and me. See ... I always knew he was alive and ... kept going over and over it.'

'Karen ... stop it. It's not going to be the way you dreamed.'

The girl trembled from head to foot. The palms of her hands were wet. She sprang from her chair, 'Take me to him,'

Kitty took her arms and gripped her tightly. 'You must prepare for something terrible.'

'Please ... please, let's go.'

'Try to remember ... no matter what happens ... no matter what you see ... that I'm going to be right there. I'll be with you, Karen. Will you remember that?'

'Yes ... I'll remember it.'

The doctor sat before Karen and Kitty.

'Your father was tortured by the Gestapo, Karen,' the doctor said. 'In the early part of the war they wanted him to work for them and they made things very hard. They finally gave up. He was unable to work for them even upon threat of danger to your mother and brothers.'

'I remember now,' Karen said. 'I remember the letters stopped coming to

Denmark and how I was afraid to ask Aage about my family.'

'He was sent to Theresienstadt in Czechoslovakia, and your mother and brothers ...'

'I know about them.'

'They sent him to Theresienstadt in hope he would change his mind. After the war he found out about your mother and brothers first. He felt guilty because he had waited too long to leave Germany and had trapped your mother and brothers. When he learned what had happened to them, on top of the years of torture, his mind snapped.'

'He will get better?'

The doctor looked at Kitty. 'He has a psychotic depression ... extreme melancholia.'

'What does that mean?' Karen asked.

'Karen, your father is not going to get well.'

'I don't believe you,' the girl said. 'I want to see him.'

'Do you remember him at all?'

'Very little.'

'It would be far better to keep what you can remember than to see him now.'

'She must see him, Doctor, no matter how difficult it is going to be. This question cannot be left open,' Kitty said.

The doctor led them down a corridor and stopped before a door. A nurse unlocked it. He held the door open.

Karen walked into a cell-like room. The room held a chair, a stand, and a bed. She looked around for a moment and then she stiffened. A man was sitting on the floor in a corner. He was barefooted and uncombed. He sat with his back against the wall and his arms around his knees and stared blankly at the opposite wall.

Karen took a step toward him. He was stubble-bearded and his face was scarred. Suddenly the pounding within Karen's heart eased. This is all a mistake, she thought ... this man is a stranger ... he is not my father ... he cannot be. It is a mistake! A mistake! She was filled with the urge to turn around and scream out ... *you see, you were wrong. He is not Johann Clement, he is not my father. My father is still alive somewhere and looking for me.* Karen stood before the man on the floor to assure herself. She stared into the crazed eyes. It had been so long ... so very long, she could not remember. But the man she had dreamed about meeting again was not this man.

There was a fireplace and the smell of pipe tobacco. There was a big moppy dog. His name was Maximilian. A baby cried in the next room. 'Miriam, see to Hans. I am reading a story for my girl and I cannot be disturbed.'

Karen Hansen Clement slowly knelt before the hulk of mindless flesh.

Grandma's house in Bonn always smelled of newly-baked cookies. She baked all week getting ready for the family on Sunday.

The insane man continued to stare at the opposite wall as though he were alone in the room.

Look how funny the monkeys are in the Cologne Zoo! Cologne has the most wonderful zoo. When will it be carnival time again?

She studied the man from his bare feet to his scarred forehead. Nothing ... nothing she saw was like her father ...

'Jew! Jew! Jew!' the crowd screamed as she ran into her house with the blood pouring down her face. 'There, there, Karen, don't you cry. Daddy won't let them hurt you.'

Karen reached out and touched the man's cheek. 'Daddy?' she said. The man did not move or react.

There was a train and lots of children around and they were talking of going to Denmark but she was tired. 'Goodby, Daddy,' Karen had said. 'Here, you take my dolly. He will watch after you.' She stood on the platform of the train and watched her Daddy on the platform and he grew smaller and smaller.

'Daddy! Daddy!' Karen cried. 'It's Karen, Daddy! I'm your girl. I'm all grown up now, Daddy. Don't you remember me?'

The doctor held Kitty in the doorway as she shook from head to foot. 'Let me help her, please,' Kitty cried.

'Let it be done,' he said.

And Karen was filled with remembering – 'Yes! Yes! He is my father! He is my father!'

'Daddy!' she screamed and threw her arms around him. 'Please talk to me. Please say something to me. I beg you ... beg you!'

The man who was once the living human person of Johann Clement blinked his eyes. A sudden expression of curiosity came over his face as he became aware of a person clutching at him. He held the expression for a tense moment as though he were trying, in his own way, to allow something to penetrate the blackness – and then, his look lapsed back into lifelessness.

'Daddy!' she screamed, 'Daddy! Daddy!'

And her voice echoed in the empty room and down the long corridor – 'Daddy!'

The strong arms of the doctor pried her loose, and she was gently dragged from the room. The door was closed and locked and Johann Clement was gone from her – forever. The girl sobbed in anguish and crumpled into Kitty's arms. 'He didn't even know me! Oh my God ... God ... why doesn't he know me? Tell me, God ... tell me!'

'It's all right, baby, it is all right now. Kitty is here. Kitty is with you.'

'Don't leave me, don't ever leave me, Kitty!'

'No, baby ... Kitty won't ever leave you ... ever.'

Chapter Nine

The news of Karen's father had spread through Gan Dafna before she and Kitty returned. It had a shattering effect on Dov Landau. For the first time since his brother Mundek had held him in his arms in a bunker beneath the Warsaw ghetto, Dov Landau was able to feel compassion for someone other than himself. His sorrow for Karen Clement was, at last, the ray of light that illuminated his black world.

She was the one person he could trust and care for. Why of all people on earth did it have to happen to her? How many times in that stinking camp on Cyprus had Karen expressed her simple, all-powerful faith to him? Now Karen was hurt and her despair was deep pain to him.

What did she have left? Himself and Mrs Fremont. What was he to her? He was a millstone – a nothing. There were times he wanted to hate Mrs Fremont but he couldn't because he knew that she was good for Karen. With Karen's father out of the way perhaps Mrs Fremont would take her to America.

He stood in the way. He knew Karen wouldn't leave him. In Dov's mind there was only one thing to do.

A youth named Mordecai was a secret recruiter fot the Maccabees at Gan Dafna. From him Dov succeeded in discovering where and how to make contact with the underground organization. The cottages of the faculty were never locked at Gan Dafna. He waited one evening until they were all at dinner, then rifled several cottages. He stole a few objects of gold jewelry and fled to Jerusalem.

Bruce Sutherland went directly to Dr Lieberman and got him to urge Kitty to bring Karen to Sutherland's villa for a week or two to allow her to recover from the shock.

Karen bore her grief with the same dignity and courage that had carried her through a life filled with tragedy. Kitty Fremont was wise. She never left the girl's side.

The fate of Karen's father along with the disappearance of Dov Landau added up to a grim victory for Kitty. She felt that in time she would be able to get Karen to America. Kitty thought about it constantly at Sutherland's villa, detesting herself at times for finding consolation in Karen's tragedy, but she could not stop her thoughts. Since she had first seen Karen in the tent at Caraolos her entire life had revolved around the girl.

One day after lunch Ari Ben Canaan came to Sutherland's villa. He waited in the study while the servant fetched Sutherland from the terrace patio. Bruce excused himself and left the girls sunning. The two men spoke for nearly an hour, transacting their business.

'I have a friend of yours here,' Sutherland said after they had concluded their discussion. 'Kitty Fremont is spending a fortnight here as my house guest with the young Clement girl.'

'I heard you two had become great friends,' Ari said.

'Yes, I think Katherine Fremont is one of the finest women I have ever met. You should run up to Gan Dafna and see what she has done with some of those children. There was a boy who didn't even talk six months ago who now has not only opened up but is starting to play a bugle for the school band.'

'I've heard about that too,' Ari said.

'I insisted she come here and bring the Clement girl. The child found her father. Poor chap is completely and incurably insane. It was a terrible shock, needless to say. Come on out to the garden.'

'I'm sorry. I have some other things to attend to.'

'Nonsense, won't hear of it.' He took Ari's arm and led him out.

Kitty had not seen Ari since the Mount Tabor affair. She was startled by the first sight of him. Ari had been neglecting himself.

She thought that Ari was amazingly gentle in his conveyance of condolence to Karen. He showed her a tenderness that he apparently reserved for his own people. He had never treated Kitty that way. Was this because Ari accepted Karen as one of them, Kitty wondered? Then she grew angry at herself. It seemed to her that she was beginning to categorize every word and situation on its meaning in relation to Karen's Jewishness. Now perhaps she was creating meanings that did not even exist.

Kitty and Ari walked through Sutherland's rose garden.

'How is she?' Ari asked.

'She is a very strong and courageous child,' Kitty said. 'It was a shocking experience but she is doing remarkably well.'

Ari looked back to where Karen and Sutherland were playing checkers. 'She is a lovely girl,' he said sincerely.

His words surprised Kitty. She had never heard that tone of appreciation from him before and she had wondered if things of beauty even reached him. They stopped at the end of the path where a low stone wall ran around the edge of the garden. Beyond the wall the valley lay at the bottom of the hill with Safed beyond. Kitty sat on the wall and stared out at the Galilee, and Ari lit a cigarette for himself and one for her.

'Ari, I've never asked a personal favor of you. I am about to do so.'

'Of course.'

'Karen is going to get over her father in time, but there is another thing that she may not get over. Dov Landau has run away from Gan Dafna. We assume he has gone to Jerusalem to join the Maccabees. As you know, she has taken the boy as a personal crusade. The loss of her father has magnified the loss of Dov. She is eating her heart out for him. I want you to find him for us and bring him back to Gan Dafna. I know you have the connections which can locate him. He would come back if you could convince him that Karen needs him.'

Ari blew a stream of smoke and looked at Kitty with curiosity. 'I don't think I understand you at all. The girl belongs to you now. He is the one possible person who stands in your way and he has removed himself.'

Kitty looked at him evenly. 'I should be offended by what you say but I'm not because it's true. The fact is that I can't build my own happiness on her misery. I can't take her away to America with this thing with Dov unresolved.'

'That is very commendable.'

'It isn't honorable intent, Ari. Karen is a wise girl about everything but that boy. We all have our weak spots, I suppose. She will get over him far more quickly if he is at Gan Dafna. With him away in the Maccabees she will magnify his image until it is beyond proper proportion.'

'Forgive me for thinking in simple terms, Kitty. You are shrewd.'

'I love that girl and there's nothing sinister or devious about it.'

'You're making sure she has no place to go but with you.'

'I'm making certain that she knows she has a better place to go. Perhaps you don't believe this, but if I knew it was better for her to stay in Palestine, this is where she would stay.'

'Maybe I do believe that.'

'Can you in all honesty tell me that I am doing something wrong by wanting to take her to America?'

'No . . . it is not wrong,' Ari said.

'Then help me get Dov back.'

There was a long silence, then Ari snuffed out his cigarette on the wall. He peeled the paper, unconscious of his action and scattering the loose tobacco and balling the paper into a tiny knot which he put into his pocket. P. P. Malcolm had taught him never to leave traces of a cigarette. Cigarette butts were glaring signposts to Arabs in search of enemy troops.

'I can't do it,' Ari said.

'You can. Dov respects you.'

'Sure, I can find him. I can even force him back to Gan Dafna and say, "Stay put little boy, the ladies don't want you to get hurt." Dov Landau has made a personal decision that every Jew in Palestine has got to make with his own conscience. The feeling about this is very intense. My father and my uncle haven't spoken to each other for fifteen years over it. Every fiber of Dov Landau's being shrieks out for revenge. He is being driven with an intensity that only God or a bullet can stop.'

'You sound as though you condone the terrorists.'

'Sometimes I am in complete sympathy with them. Sometimes I detest them. Yet I would not want to be the judge of their actions. Who are you and I to say that Dov Landau is not justified? You know what they've done to him. You are wrong about something else. If he is brought back he can only bring more pain to that girl. Dov must do what he must do.'

Kitty got down from the wall and brushed her skirt and they walked toward the gate. 'Ari,' she said at last, 'you are right.'

Sutherland joined them as they walked outside to his car. 'Are you going to be around long, Ben Canaan?' he asked.

'I have a few things to attend to in Safed. I better get them done.'

'Why don't you come back and join us for dinner?'

'Well, I . . .'

'Please do,' Kitty said.

'Very well. Thank you.'

'Good. Come on back up just as soon as you are through in Safed.'

They waved as he drove down the hillside, past the Taggart fort and out of sight.

'*He who guards Israel shall neither rest nor sleep*,' Kitty said.

'Good Lord, Kitty. Have you gotten around to Biblical quotations?'

They opened the gate and walked back toward the patio.

'He looks exhausted.'

'I think he looks fine,' Sutherland said, 'for a man who works a hundred and ten hours a week.'

'I've never seen such dedication . . . or would you call it fanaticism? I was surprised to see him here, Bruce. I didn't know you were mixed up in this business.'

Sutherland stuffed a pipe full of tobacco. 'I'm not really actively engaged. The Haganah came to me and asked me to make an appraisal of the Arab armies' strength outside Palestine. They simply want a professional, non-partisan point of view. See here, Kitty, don't you think it is time you became honest with yourself in this matter?'

'I told you I'm not going to be partial to either side.'

'Kitty, I'm afraid you're acting like an ostrich. You're sitting in the middle of a battlefield and saying "Don't hit my house, my blinds are drawn." '

'I'm getting out, Bruce.'

'Then you'd better do it quickly. If you believe you can stay on much longer the way you have then you are living in a fool's paradise.'

'I can't bring myself to it just yet. I must have a little more time until Karen has recovered from this.'

'And is that the only reason?'

Kitty shook her head. 'I guess I'm afraid of a showdown. There are times when I am sure I have beaten this thing of her and Palestine – and other times, like right now, I'm terrified of putting it to a test.'

From Sutherland's villa before dinner they could see the enormous full moon hanging over the city.

'"*Three great gifts hath the Lord granted Israel, but every one of them will be won by suffering. One of them is the Land of Israel,*"' Sutherland said. 'Those are the words of Bar Yohai two thousand years ago. I would say he was a wise man.'

'Speaking of wise men, I am going to the Sea of Galilee tomorrow. Have you been there yet, Kitty?' Ari asked.

'No, I'm afraid my travel has been rather restricted.'

'You should see it for sure. You'd better go soon. It will be too hot in a few weeks.'

'Why don't you take her?' Karen said quickly.

There was an embarrassed silence.

'That ... that's really a good idea,' Ari said. 'I could work my schedule around to take a few days off. Why don't we all go, the four of us?'

'I don't care to,' Karen said. 'I've hiked there twice already with the Gadna.'

Bruce Sutherland picked up Karen's cue. 'Not me, old chap, I've seen the lake a dozen times.'

'Why don't you go with Ari?' Karen said.

'I think I'd better stay here with you,' Kitty answered.

'Nonsense,' Sutherland pressed. 'Karen and I will get on just fine by ourselves. As a matter of fact it will be a pleasure to get rid of you for a few days, not to mention the fact that Ari looks as though he could stand a bit of a rest.'

Kitty laughed. 'Ari, I smell an underhanded plot. It appears we have a pair of matchmakers trying to make a *shiddoch.*'

'Listen to her!' Karen cried in excitement.

'Shucks, I'm just a *sabra* at heart. It looks as though you're trapped, Ari.'

'That suits me fine,' he said.

Chapter Ten

Early the next morning Ari and Kitty drove to the Sea of Galilee. They entered the Genossar Valley which ran along its northern shores. Across the lake the browned-out hills of Syria loomed over this low point on the earth and the warm, sultry air hung still.

This is God's own sea, Kitty thought. Once again she was alone with Ari Ben Canaan and once again she felt the timelessness of the land close in on her as she had felt it in the Judean hills. Why was she more affected when she was with Ari, she wondered?

At the edge of the sea he took her to the ruins of the synagogue of Capernaum. Here, Jesus walked and taught and healed. Words came to

Kitty's mind that she thought she had forgotten. *Jesus walked by the Sea of Galilee and saw two brethren, Simon called Peter and Andrew his brother casting a net into the sea ... And they went into Capernaum and straight away on the Sabbath He entered into the synagogue and taught.*

It was as though He had never left. On the water's edge fishermen cast their nets into the sea and a small flock of black goats grazed and the ages had not passed.

From there Ari took her to the church which marked the place of the miracle of the multiplication of loaves and fishes a short distance from Capernaum. The floor of the church held a Byzantine mosaic depicting cormorants and herons and ducks and other wild birds which still inhabited the lake.

And then they moved on to the Mount of Beatitudes to a little chapel on the hill where Jesus preached the Sermon on the Mount.

Blessed are they which are persecuted for righteousness' sake: for theirs is the kingdom of heaven. Blessed are ye, when men shall revile you, and persecute you, and shall say all manner of evil against you falsely, for my sake. Rejoice, and be exceeding glad: for great is your reward in heaven: for so persecuted they the prophets which were before you.

These were His words spoken from this place. As she saw the Christian holy places the thought came to confuse her that Ari Ben Canaan and David Ben Ami and her own Karen seemed to live with a closeness to all this that she could never attain.

They sped past the sleeping Arab village of Migdal, the birthplace of Mary Magdalene, and then beneath the Horns of Hattin, which held the tomb of Jethro, the father-in-law of Moses and the chief prophet of the Druses, but Kitty's attention was distracted by her mental turmoil.

Then the car turned away from the plains of Hattin and into a flat field where a burst of scarlet hit their eyes. The field was a red carpet of wild flowers.

'How red it is,' Kitty said. 'Stop the car for a moment, Ari.'

He pulled over to the side of the road and Kitty got out. She picked one of the flowers and as she looked at it her eyes narrowed. 'I've never seen anything like this,' she whispered in a shaky voice.

'The ancient Maccabees lived in caves around here. It is the only place in the world this flower grows. It is called Blood of the Maccabees.'

Kitty examined the red bloom closely. It did look like little droplets of blood. She dropped the flower quickly and rubbed her hand on her skirt.

This land and everything about it was closing in on her! Even the wild flowers will not let you forget a moment. It creeps into you from its very earth and its very air and it is damning and tormenting.

Kitty Fremont was frightened. She knew that she would have to leave Palestine at once: the more she resisted the place the harder it struck back at her. It was all around her and above her and beneath her and she felt stifled and crushed.

They entered Tiberias from the north through the modern Jewish suburb of Kiryat Shmuel – the Village of Samuel – and drove past another large Taggart fort and descended from the hills to the water level, into the Old City. The buildings were mostly of black basalt rock and the hills were filled with the graves and caves of ancient Hebrew greats.

Beyond the city they turned into the Galilean Hotel on the sea. It was very hot in the midday. Kitty nibbled her lunch of Galilee catfish and barely spoke a word. She wished she had not come.

'I haven't yet shown you the holiest of the holy,' Ari said.

'Where is that?'

'Shoshanna *kibbutz*. That's where I was born.'

Kitty smiled. She suspected that Ari knew she was disturbed and was trying to cheer her up. 'And just where is this great shrine?'

'A few miles down the road where the Jordan River runs into the sea. Although I do hear I was almost born in the old Turkish police station in town here. This place is full of tourists in winter. It's a little late in the season. Anyhow, we have the whole lake to ourselves. Why don't we take a swim?'

'That sounds like a really good idea,' Kitty said.

A long pier of basalt rock jutted out beyond the hotel for some forty yards into the lake. Ari was on the pier first after lunch. Kitty found herself looking at his body as she walked from the hotel. He waved to her. Ari had a lean build and looked hard and powerful.

'Hi,' she called. 'Have you been in yet?'

'I've been waiting for you.'

'How deep is it from the end of the pier?'

'About ten feet. Can you swim as far as the raft?'

'You've asked for a race.'

Kitty dropped her robe and put on her bathing cap. Ari inspected her frankly just as she had measured him. Her body had not the angular sturdiness of a *sabra* girl. She was more of the softness and roundness one would expect from an American woman.

Their eyes met for an instant and both of them looked a little abashed.

She ran past him and dived into the water. Ari followed. He was surprised to find that it was all he could do to catch her and get a few strokes ahead. Kitty swam with a graceful crawl and a steady stroke that pressed him to the utmost. They climbed on the raft breathless and laughing.

'You pulled a fast one on me,' he said.

'I forgot to mention it but ...'

'I know, I know. You were on the girls' swimming team in college.'

She lay on her back and took a deep breath of contentment. The water was cool and refreshing and seemed to wash her bad spirits away.

It was late in the afternoon before they returned to the hotel for cocktails on the verandah and then retired to their rooms to rest before dinner.

Ari, who had had little rest in recent weeks, was asleep the instant he lay down. In the next room Kitty paced the floor. She had recovered from much of the agitation of the morning but she was tired of this emotional drain and she was still actually a little frightened of the mystical power that this land held. Kitty longed to return to a normal, sane, planned life. She convinced herself that Karen needed the same therapy more than anything else. She made up her mind to face the issue with Karen without further delay.

By evening it had turned pleasantly cool. Kitty began to dress for dinner. She opened her closet and considered the three dresses hanging there. Slowly she took down one of them. It was the same dress that Jordana Ben Canaan had picked from her closet the day of their argument. She thought of Ari's look on the pier today. Kitty had liked it. The dress was a strapless sheath which clung to her body and emphasized her bosom.

Every male eyebrow in the hotel lifted as Kitty drifted by, and nostrils twitched with the scent of her perfume. Ari stood like a man stunned, watching her cross the lobby. As she came up to him he suddenly became aware of the fact that he was staring at her and quickly found his voice.

'I have a surprise for you,' he said. 'There is a concert at the Ein Gev *kibbutz* across the lake. We will go right after dinner.'

'Will this dress be all right to wear?'

'Uh ... yes ... yes, it will be excellent.'

Most of the full moon of the night before was left for them. Just as their motor launch left the pier it rose from behind the Syrian hills, unbelievably huge, sending a great path of light over the motionless waters.

'The sea is so still,' Kitty said.

'It is deceptive. When God gets angry He can turn it into an ocean in minutes.'

In a half hour they had crossed the water and landed at the docks of the *kibbutz* of Ein Gev – the Spring of the Mountain Pass. Ein Gev was a daring experiment. The *kibbutz* sat isolated from the rest of Palestine and directly below the mountains of Syria. A Syrian village hung above it and its fields were plowed to the border markers. It had been founded by immigrants of the German Aliyah in the year of 1937 and strategically commanded a view of the Sea of Galilee.

The *kibbutz* was set near a basin formed by the Yarmuk River, the border between Syria and Trans-Jordan, and the basin was the site of a cradle of man. Every day the farmers plowed up evidences of human life, some prehistoric. They had found crude plows and pottery thousands of years old, proving the area had been farmed and there had been community life even there.

Right on the border between Ein Gev and the Syrian hills stood a small mountain shaped like a column. It was called Sussita – the Horse. Atop Sussita were the ruins of one of the nine Roman fortress cities of Palestine. Sussita still dominated the entire area.

Many of the German pioneers had been musicians in former life and they were an industrious lot. In addition to farming and fishing they hit upon another idea to augment the *kibbutz* income. They formed an orchestra and bought a pair of launches to bring the winter tourists of Tiberias across the lake for concerts. The idea proved successful and the tradition grew until Ein Gev drew every artist who visited Palestine. A large outdoor auditorium was built into a natural woodland setting on the edge of the lake, and additional plans called for a covered building in years to come.

Ari spread a blanket on the grass at the edge of the auditorium and the two of them lay back and looked up into the sky and watched the enormous Lag Ba Omer moon grow smaller and higher and make room for a billion stars. As the orchestra played a Beethoven concert the tension within Kitty passed away. This moment was perfection. No more beautiful setting could have been created. It seemed almost unreal and she found herself hoping that it would go on and on.

The concert ended. Ari took her hand and led her away from the crowds, down a path along the lake. The air was still and filled with a pine scent, and the Sea of Galilee was like a polished mirror. At the water's edge there was a bench made of three slabs of stone from an ancient temple.

They sat and looked over at the twinkling lights of Tiberias. Ari brushed against her and Kitty turned and looked at him. How handsome Ari Ben

Canaan was! Suddenly she wanted to hold him and to touch his cheek and stroke his hair. She wanted to tell him not to work so hard. She wanted to tell him to unlock his heart to her. She wanted to say how she felt when he was near and to beg not to be a stranger and to find something for them to share. But Ari Ben Canaan *was* a stranger and she dare not ever say what she felt.

The Sea of Galilee stirred and lapped against the shore. A sudden gust of breeze caused the bulrushes at the water's edge to sway. Kitty Fremont turned away from Ari.

A tremor passed through her body as she felt his hand touch her shoulder. 'You are cold,' Ari said, holding her stole for her. Kitty slipped it over her shoulders. They stared long at each other.

Ari stood up suddenly. 'It sounds like the launch is returning,' he said. 'We had better go.'

As the launch pushed off, the Sea of Galilee turned from smooth to choppy with the suddenness of which Ari had spoken. Wisps of spray broke over the bow and whipped back on them. Ari put his arm about Kitty's shoulder and brought her close to him to protect her from the water. All across the lake Kitty rested her head on his chest with her eyes closed, listening to the beat of his heart.

They walked from the pier hand in hand along the path to the hotel. Kitty stopped beneath the willow tree whose branches spread like a giant umbrella, bending clear down into the lake. She tried to speak but her voice trembled and the words would not come out.

Ari touched her wet hair and brushed it back from her forehead. He held her shoulders gently, and the muscles of his face worked with tenseness as he drew her close. Kitty lifted her face to him.

'Ari,' she whispered, 'please kiss me.'

All that had smoldered for months burst into flames of ecstasy, engulfing them, in this first embrace.

How good he feels! How strong he is! Kitty had never known a moment like this with any man – not even Tom Fremont. They kissed and they kissed again and she pressed him and felt the power of his arms. Then they stood apart and walked in quick silence to the hotel.

Kitty stood awkwardly before the door of her room. Ari moved toward his door but she took his hand and turned him around. They stood facing each other wordlessly for a moment. Kitty nodded, and turned and entered her room quickly and closed the door behind her.

She undressed in the dark and slipped into a nightgown and walked toward her balcony, where she could see the light from his room. She could hear him pacing the floor. His light went off. Kitty fell back into the shadows. In a moment she saw him standing on her balcony.

'I want you,' Ari said.

She ran into his arms and held him tightly, trembling with desire. His kisses fell over her mouth and cheeks and neck and she exchanged kiss for kiss, touch for touch, with an abandon she had never known. Ari swept her up in his arms and carried her to the bed and placed her on it and knelt beside her. Kitty felt faint. She gripped the sheets and sobbed and writhed.

Ari lowered the shoulder strap of her nightgown and caressed her breast.

With violent abruptness Kitty spun out of his grasp and staggered from the bed. 'No,' she gasped.

Ari froze.

Kitty's eyes filled with tears and she cringed against the wall, holding herself to stop the trembling. She sagged into a chair. Moments passed until the quaking within her abated and her breathing became normal. Ari stood over her and stared down.

'You must hate me,' she said at last.

He did not speak. She looked up at his towering figure and saw the hurt on his face.

'Go on, Ari . . . say it. Say anything.'

He did not speak.

Kitty stood up slowly and faced him. 'I don't want this, Ari. I don't want to be made. I guess I was just overcome by the moonlight . . .'

'I shouldn't have thought I was making love to a reluctant virgin,' he said.

'Ari, please . . .'

'I don't have time to indulge in games and words. I am a grown man and you are a grown woman.'

'You state it so well.'

His voice was cold. 'I will leave by the door if you don't mind.'

Kitty winced with the sharp crack of the door closing. She stood for a long time by the french doors and looked out at the water. The Sea of Galilee was angry and the moon faded behind a sinister black cloud.

Kitty was numb. Why had she run from him? She had never felt so strongly for anyone and she had never lost control of herself like this. Her own recklessness had frightened her. She reasoned that Ari Ben Canaan did not really want her. Beyond a night of love he had no need of her, and no man had treated her this way before.

Then it came to her that she had been fleeing from this very feeling she had for him, this new desire for Ari which could lead her to stay in Palestine. She must never let it happen again. She was going to leave with Karen and nothing was going to stop her! She knew that she was afraid of Ari: Ari could defeat her. If he were to show the slightest signs of really caring she might not have the strength – but the thought of his steely coldness strengthened her determination to resist, leaving her reassured and yet, perversely, at the same time resentful.

Kitty threw herself onto the bed and fell into an exhausted sleep, with the wind from over the water beating against her window.

In the morning it was calm again.

Kitty threw back the covers and jumped from bed and all the events of the night before came to her. She blushed. They did not seem so terrible now but she was embarrassed. She had created a scene and there was no doubt Ari had thought it pretty melodramatic as well as childish. The whole thing had been her doing; she would set it right by making up with him, sensibly and forthrightly. She dressed quickly and went down to the dining room to await Ari. She thought of the words she would use to apologize.

Kitty sipped coffee and waited.

A half hour passed. Ari did not come down. She snuffed out her third cigarette and walked out to the front desk.

'Have you seen Mr Ben Canaan this morning?' she asked the clerk.

'Mr Ben Canaan checked out at six.'

'Did he say where he was going?'

'Mr Ben Canaan never says where he is going.'

'Perhaps he left a message for me?'

The clerk turned around and pointed to the empty key box.

'I see . . . well . . . thank you very much.'

Chapter Eleven

Dov Landau found a room in a dilapidated fourth-rate hotel on the Street of the Chain in the Old City of Jerusalem. As instructed, he went to the Saladin Café on the Nablus Road near the Damascus Gate and left his name and hotel to be given to Bar Israel.

Dov pawned the gold rings and bracelets he had stolen from the faculty at Gan Dafna and turned to the job of studying Jerusalem. To the ghetto rat and past master of thievery Jerusalem was simple. Within three days Dov knew every street and alley in the Old City and the immediate business districts around it. His sharp eye appraised and his deft hands lifted enough objects of value to keep him sustained. The matter of escape through the narrow alleyways and crowded bazaars was ridiculously easy for him.

Dov spent much of his money for books and art material. He walked along Jaffa Road searching the many bookstores for texts on art, draftsmanship, and architecture.

He locked himself in his room with his books and art material, some dried fruits and bottled soft drinks, and waited for contact from the Maccabees. Dov studied by candlelight. He was unaware of the pageantry that took place outside his window on the Street of the Chain which ran between the Jewish and Moslem quarters to the Dome of the Rock and the Wailing Wall. He would read until his eyes burned and he could read no more, then he would lay the book on his chest and stare at the ceiling and think of Karen Clement. Dov had not realized how badly he would miss her nor that missing her could cause an actual physical pain. Karen had been with him for so long he had forgotten what it was like to be away from her. He remembered every moment with her. Those days at Caraolos and on the *Exodus* when she lay in his arms in the hold of the ship. He remembered how happy she was and how beautiful she looked that first day at Gan Dafna. He remembered her kind, expressive face and her gentle touch and her sharp voice when she was angry.

Dov sat on the edge of his bed and sketched a hundred pictures of Karen. He drew her in every way he remembered her but crumpled each picture and threw it on the floor, for no picture could show how beautiful she was to Dov.

Dov stayed in his room for two weeks, leaving only upon necessity. At the end of the second week he needed some more money and he left his room with some rings to pawn. As he reached the entrance to the building he saw a man standing in the shadows. Dov wrapped his hand around his pistol and walked past, poised to spin around at the first sound.

'Don't move, don't turn,' a voice from the shadows commanded.

Dov froze in his tracks.

'You made inquiries for Bar Israel. What do you want?'

'You know what I want.'

'What is your name?'

'Landau, Dov Landau.'

'Where do you come from?'

'Gan Dafna.'

'Who sent you?'

'Mordecai.'

'How did you get into Palestine?'

'On the *Exodus*.'

'Keep walking out to the street and don't look around. You will be contacted later.'

Dov became restless after the contact was made. He rose to the point of chucking it all and returning to Gan Dafna. He missed Karen terribly. He started a half dozen letters and tore each one up. Let's get it over with ... let's get it over with, Dov said to himself again and again.

He lay in his room reading and began to doze. Then he roused himself and lighted fresh candles: if he fell asleep and the old nightmare came he did not want to awaken in a dark room.

There was a sharp knock on his door.

Dov sprang to his feet, picked up his pistol, and stood close to the locked door.

'It is your friends,' a voice said from the hallway. Dov recognized it as the same voice that had spoken to him from the shadows. He opened the door. He could see no one.

'Turn around and face the wall,' the voice commanded from the darkness. Dov obeyed. He felt the presence of two men behind him. A blindfold was tied over his eyes and two pairs of hands led him down the stairs to a waiting car where he was shoved on the back floor and covered and driven from the Old City.

Dov concentrated on sensing where he was being driven. The car screeched into King Solomon Street, followed the Via Dolorosa to Stephen's Gate. It was child's play to Dov Laudau, who knew his way through a hundred alternate routes in the blackness of the sewers under Warsaw.

The car shifted into a lower gear to make a hill. They must be driving past the Tomb of the Virgin toward the Mount of Olives, Dov calculated. The road became smooth. Now Dov knew they were driving past the Hebrew University and Hadassah Medical Center on Mount Scopus.

They drove another ten minutes and stopped.

Dov accurately pinpointed their position in the Sanhedriya section near the Tombs of the Sanhedrin, the ancient supreme court of Hebrew rabbis, almost to the precise part of the block.

He was led into a house and into a room filled with cigarette smoke where he was made to sit. He sensed at least five or six people. For two hours Dov was grilled. Questions were fired at him from around the room until he began to perspire nervously. As the questioning continued he began to piece it together. The Maccabees had learned through their infallible intelligence sources that Dov had extraordinary talent as a forger, and it was badly needed by them. He had obviously been brought before some of the highest members in the Maccabees, perhaps the commanders themselves. At last they had satisfied themselves that Dov's qualifications and security checked.

'There is a curtain in front of you,' a voice said. 'Put your hands through it.'

Dov pushed his hands through the cloth. One of his hands was placed on a pistol and the other on a Bible. He repeated the oath of the Maccabees:

'I, Dov Landau, do give my body, my soul, my being, without reservation or qualification, to the Freedom Fighters of the Maccabees. I will obey any and all orders without question. I will subordinate myself to the authority over me. Under torture, even to death, I will never divulge the name of a fellow Maccabee or the secrets entrusted to me. I will fight the enemies of the Jewish people unto the last breath of life in my body. I will never cease in this sacred battle until realization of a Jewish state on both sides of the Jordan River, which is the natural historical right of my people. My creed to mine enemies shall be: Life for life, eye for eye, tooth for tooth, hand for hand, burning for burning. All this I swear in the name of Abraham, Isaac and Jacob, Sarah, Rebecca, Rachael and Leah and the prophets and of all the Jews who have been slaughtered and all my gallant brothers and sisters who have died in the name of freedom.'

The blindfold was taken from Dov's eyes and the candles on the Menorah before him were blown out and the lights went up in the room. Dov looked into the eyes of six grim men and two women. They shook hands with him and introduced themselves. Old man Akiva himself was there and Ben Moshe, their field leader, who had lost a brother fighting for the British in the war and a sister with the Palmach. Nahum Ben Ami was one of seven brothers The other six were in the Palmach. These men and women banded together because they were neither capable or desirous of the self-restraint of the Yishuv.

Old Akiva stepped up before Dov. 'You will be of value to us, Dov Landau. That is why we took you without the usual training.'

'I did not join to draw pictures,' Dov snapped.

'You will do what you are told to do,' Ben Moshe answered.

'Dov, you are a Maccabee now,' Akiva said. 'You are entitled to take a name of a Hebrew hero. Do you have such a name in mind?'

'Giora,' Dov said.

There was some laughter about the room. Dov gritted his teeth.

'Giora, is it?' Akiva said. 'I am afraid there are others ahead of you.'

'How about Little Giora,' Nahum Ben Ami said, 'until Dov can become Big Giora?'

'I will become Big Giora soon enough if you give me the chance.'

'You will set up a forgery plant,' Ben Moshe said, 'and travel with us. If you behave and do as you are told we may let you go on a raid with us now and again.'

Major Fred Caldwell played bridge in the main lounge of the British Officers' Club at Goldsmith House in Jerusalem. Freddie was finding it difficult to concentrate on card playing. His mind kept wandering back to the CID Headquarters and on the captured Maccabee girl they had been interrogating for some three days. Her name was Ayala and she was in her early twenties and fetchingly pretty. She had been a music major at the university. At least she was pretty before the questioning started. Ayala had been another tough Jewess and she had spit defiance at the CID. Like most of the captured Maccabees she spent her time quoting biblical passages, predicting their eternal damnation, or proclaiming the righteousness of her cause.

This morning their patience had run out and Ayala began to get the third degree.

'Your play, Freddie,' his partner said across the table.

Fred Caldwell looked at his cards quickly. 'Forgive me,' he said, and played a bad card. His mind was on the inspector standing over Ayala and flailing her with a rubber hose. He heard it thud into the girl's face time and again until her nose was broken and her eyes blacked and swollen almost shut and her lips puffed and distorted. But Ayala would not break.

Freddie considered that he didn't give a damn if Ayala never broke: the thought of the smashing of her Jewish face delighted him.

An orderly walked up alongside the table.

'I beg your pardon, Major Caldwell. There is a telephone call for you, sir.'

'Excuse me, chaps,' Freddie said throwing his cards face down and walking off to the phone on the other side of the lounge. He picked up the receiver. 'Caldwell here.'

'Hello, Major. This is the sergeant of the guard at CID, sir. Inspector Parkington asked me to phone you right away, sir. He says the Maccabee girl is ready to talk and thought you'd best come over to headquarters right away.'

'Righto,' Freddie said.

'Inspector Parkington has already sent a car for you, sir. It will be there in a few minutes.'

Caldwell returned to the card players. 'Sorry, chaps. Have to leave. Duty calls.'

'Bad luck, Freddie.'

Bad luck, hell, Freddie thought. He was looking forward to it. He walked outside Goldsmith House. The guards saluted. A car pulled up to a stop and a soldier jumped from behind the wheel, walked to Caldwell and saluted.

'Major Caldwell?'

'Here, boy.'

'Your car from CID, sir.'

The soldier held the rear door open. Freddie got into the back seat and the soldier ran around, got behind the wheel and they drove off. Two blocks beyond Goldsmith House he pulled the car over to a curb at an intersection. In a second the doors were flung open and three men jumped into the car, slammed the doors, and the car picked up speed again.

Caldwell's throat closed with fear. He shrieked and tried to leap across Ben Moshe. The Maccabee in the front seat turned around and slapped him with a pistol barrel and Ben Moshe snatched his collar and jerked him back into his seat. The Maccabee driver took off the military cap and looked up in the mirror.

Caldwell's eyes bugged in terror.

'I demand to know what this is all about!'

'You seem upset, Major Caldwell,' Ben Moshe said coldly.

'Stop this car and let me out immediately, do you hear?'

'Shall we let you out the same way you threw out a fourteen-year-old boy named Ben Solomon in an Arab village? You see, Major Caldwell, Ben Solomon's ghost called out to us from his grave and asked us to make retribution against the guilty.'

The sweat poured into Caldwell's eyes. 'It's all a lie ... a lie ... a lie ...'

Ben Moshe flipped something on Caldwell's lap and shined his flashlight on it. It was a photograph of the decapitated boy, Ben Solomon.

Caldwell began to sob for mercy. He doubled over and vomited in fear.

'It appears that Major Caldwell is in a mood to talk. We had better take him to headquarters and let him give out with his information before settling Ben Solomon's account.'

Caldwell blurted out all he knew about the British army plans and CID's operations and afterwards signed a confession of the murder of the boy.

Three days after his abduction Major Fred Caldwell's body was found on Mount Zion at the Dung Gate of the Old City. Pinned to his body was a picture of Ben Solomon and a photostat of Caldwell's confession and across it were scribbled the words: *An eye for an eye and a tooth for a tooth.*

Major Fred Caldwell received the same fate that Sisera, the Canaanite, met at the hands of Jael when he fled from the scene of his battle with Deborah and Barak.

Chapter Twelve

The revenge murder of Major Fred Caldwell had a shattering effect. No one seemed to question its justification, but the Maccabee method was more than many could condone.

In England people had become disgusted with the entire situation and were bringing pressure on the Labour government to give up the mandate. Inside Palestine the British garrison was at once enraged and worried.

Two days after Caldwell was found by the Dung Gate, a Maccabee prisoner, the girl named Ayala, died of internal hemorrhages from the beatings she had received during questioning. When the Maccabees learned of Ayala's death, there were fourteen days of wrathful retribution. Jerusalem reeled under the impact of terrorist raids. on the last days the raids were climaxed by an audacious daylight attack on Criminal Investigation Division headquarters.

During 'Hell's Fortnight,' as the Maccabee's wrath came to be designated, Dov Landau had displayed a reckless courage that awed even the toughest of the terrorists. Dov went out four times on raids, the last time as one of the leaders of the final assault against the CID. During Hell's Fortnight a legend of 'Little Giora' was born, in which his name became synonymous with wild fearlessness.

Palestine held its breath waiting for the next blow to fall. General Arnold Haven-Hurst was stunned at first but retaliated against the Yishuv with martial law, cordons, searches, raids, and even executions in a campaign that slowed normal industry and commerce to a crawl. His all-encompassing Operation Squid encircled Palestine.

Caldwell's murder, Hell's Fortnight, and the final raid on CID were obvious mockeries of British authority. As the Maccabees erupted, the Aliyah Bet brought three more illegal ships into Palestine waters. While the illegal immigration runs were not so spectacular they were just as damaging as the activities of the terrorists. British troops patrolled the streets of Jewish cities and the highways with the taut expectancy of ambush any moment.

The United Nations delegation was arriving shortly. Haven-Hurst determined to cripple the Yishuv before they came. The general obtained a list of officers and men who were known for overt anti-Jewish actions. He screened the list personally and selected six of the most vicious: two officers and four enlisted men. The six were brought to his quarters in the Schneller Barracks and sworn in on an ultrasecret mission. For five days the affair was plotted. On the sixth day, Haven-Hurst launched his last-ditch effort.

The six men were disguised as Arabs. A pair of them drove along King George Avenue in a truck loaded with two tons of dynamite. The truck made for the Zion Settlement Building. It stopped catercorner from the building, headed at the long driveway that led into the main entrance. The driver in Arab costume locked the steering wheel, put the truck in gear, and opened the throttle; the two men jumped clear and disappeared.

The truck tore over the street, through the open gate and down the driveway. It swerved for an instant, then careened off the curbing and hit just off the main entrance. A thunderous explosion occurred. The building was demolished.

At the same moment another pair of men in another truck filled with dynamite tried the same maneuver at the Yishuv Central building just two blocks away. A meeting was in session and the building held almost the entire Yishuv leadership.

The truck bore down on the second building. At the last instant it had to jump a curb. In hitting the curb the truck was thrown far enough off course to miss the building and blow up an adjoining apartment house.

The four soldiers were scooped up in two escape cars driven by the last two of the picked team. The cars fled toward the sanctuary of British-controlled Trans-Jordan.

General Arnold Haven-Hurst had attempted in one blow to wipe out the Yishuv leadership and representation. One hundred people died at the Zion Settlement Society. None was killed at Yishuv Central. Among the dead was Harriet Saltzman, the eighty-year-old leader of Youth Aliyah.

Within moments after the explosions, Haganah and Maccabee Intelligence went into action to comb Palestine for the culprits. By the end of the day both of the organizations had identified the six 'Arabs' as British soldiers. They were further able to trace the action directly to Arnold Haven-Hurst, although with no usable proof. Instead of destroying Yishuv leadership, Haven-Hurst's desperate gamble had a reverse effect. It united the Jews of Palestine in a way they had never before been united and it drove together the two armed forces, the Haganah and Maccabees. The Haganah had obtained a copy of the 'Haven-Hurst Report.' With the evidence behind the bombings they knew the general was out to destroy them if they had not known it before. Avidan dispatched Zev Gilboa to Jerusalem to seek out Bar Israel to arrange a meeting between himself and the Maccabee commanders. The procedure was almost unique: the only precedent had been at the beginning of World War II when Avidan asked Akiva to abstain from terror for the duration.

The meeting was held at one o'clock in the morning in an open field on the road from Jerusalem on the site of what was once the Tenth Roman Legion camp. There were four men present: Akiva and Ben Moshe for the Maccabees, Avidan for the Haganah, with Zev Gilboa representing the Haganah's striking arm, the Palmach. There were no handshakes or amenities between the two organizations' representatives. They stood facing each other in the darkness, filled with mutual distrust. The late-night air was cold despite the coming of summer.

'I have asked this meeting with you to see if there is some basis for closer co-operation between our forces,' Avidan said.

'You mean you want us to come under your jurisdiction?' Ben Moshe asked suspiciously.

'I have long given up the idea of trying to control your group,' Avidan said. 'I merely think that times call for a maximum effort. You have strength inside the three cities and are able to operate with a greater degree of freedom than we can.'

'So that's it,' Akiva snapped. 'You want us to do your dirty work.'

'Hear him out, Akiva,' his field commander said.

'I don't like the whole idea. I didn't approve of this meeting, Ben Moshe. These people have betrayed us in the past and they'll do it again.'

Avidan's bald head turned crimson under the old man's words. 'I choose to listen to your insults tonight, Akiva, because there is too much at stake. I count on the fact that despite our differences you are a Jew and you love Eretz Israel.' He handed a copy of the 'Haven-Hurst Report' to Akiva.

The old man gave it to Ben Moshe, who turned his flashlight on the paper.

'Fourteen years ago I said the British were our enemy. You didn't believe me then,' Akiva whispered.

'I won't argue politics with you. Will you or won't you work with us?' Avidan demanded.

'We will try it out,' Ben Moshe said.

After the meeting liaison groups went to work to plot out a joint Haganah-Maccabee action. Two weeks after the explosions the British received their answer for the destruction of the Zion Settlement Society building and the attempted destruction of the Yishuv Central.

In one night the Haganah completely wrecked the railroad system, stopping all rail traffic to and from Palestine.

The next night the Maccabees broke into six British embassies and consulates in Mediterranean countries and destroyed records used in the fight against Aliyah Bet.

The Palmach branch of the Haganah wrecked the Mosul oil pipelines in fifteen places.

With this done, the final measure was plotted by the Maccabees – the elimination of General Sir Arnold Haven-Hurst. Maccabees observed the Schneller compound twenty-four hours a day. They charted movement in and out, logged each car and truck, and diagramed the entire compound.

After four days it began to look like an impossible task. Haven-Hurst was locked in the center of a fortress surrounded by thousands of troops. No one but British personnel was allowed anywhere near his quarters. When Haven-Hurst did move out of the compound it was in secrecy and he was guarded by convoys so heavy the Maccabees would lose a hundred men by attacking it.

Then the first flaw was spotted.

A civilian automobile was logged as leaving the Schneller compound area between midnight and one o'clock in the morning about three times each week, returning to the compound just before daylight. There was only a driver in the car and he was dressed as a civilian. The regularity of the movement of this automobile during such unusual hours made it automatically suspect.

The Maccabee team went to work to find the registry of the owner, who turned out to be a wealthy Arab family. Thereupon the Maccabees decided that the car must belong to someone working with the British on the Arab side and gave it up as a possible device for getting to Haven-Hurst.

Meanwhile reports on Arnold Haven-Hurst's personal background, conduct, and habits were compiled and studied. The Maccabees knew he was an ambitious man who had made an important marriage. The marriage gave him station as well as money and he had never endangered it. Haven-Hurst was considered the epitome of a proper gentleman in his social life; he was considered, in fact, a rather dull bore.

Probing beneath this apparent circumspect surface, the Maccabees discovered that Haven-Hurst had had not one, but several, extramarital affairs. In the Maccabees were people who had served in the British Army under Haven-Hurst years before. Camp rumors always had him with a mistress.

A theory developed that Haven-Hurst could well have been very lonely locked in the compound. Because of his marriage and position he would not dare bring a woman back into the camp. He could possibly be going out to a mistress. The idea was put forward that Haven-Hurst was an unseen passenger in the mystery car and was regularly traveling between the compound and a woman.

It seemed preposterous even to the Maccabees, yet until the mystery car was properly identified it could not be cast away. Who could the mistress of Arnold Haven-Hurst be? There were no rumors to be checked upon. If he had a love nest he had concealed it with great skill. No Jewess would risk living with him, and there were no Englishwomen available. This left only an Arab woman.

To attempt to follow the car would have risked detection and alerting of the quarry. It would have been possible for the Maccabees to waylay the single car traveling late at night, but the command decided that if there were the least chance that Haven-Hurst was a passenger it would be better to discover his destination and catch him at an indiscretion.

They worked from the other direction, the owner of the car. In this family of Arab effendis was a young woman who in beauty, education, and background could qualify as an attraction for a man like Haven-Hurst. The pieces of the puzzle were beginning to fit together.

The Maccabees watched the Arab family house and constantly trailed the girl. On the second night, their persistence paid off. The girl left her home at midnight and made for a house in the rich Arab El Baq'a section of Jerusalem near the Hebron-Bethlehem Road. A half hour after she arrived the mystery automobile pulled up and the Maccabees were able to catch a fleeting glimpse of General Arnold Haven-Hurst rushing from the back of the car to keep his rendezvous.

At three o'clock that same morning Haven-Hurst was awakened by a voice in the darkness which shouted out a bloodcurdling quotation, '*Praise ye the Lord for the avenging of Israel!*'

He leaped from the bed. The Arab woman shrieked as Maccabee bullets raked the room.

Later that morning British headquarters received a phone call from the Maccabees. The British were advised where they could find their late commander. They were further advised that the demise of Arnold Haven-Hurst had been well photographed. If the British brought undue retribution against the Yishuv, the Maccabees would publish the pictures.

Headquarters speculated on the effect of the scandal of one of their generals being murdered in the bed of his Arab mistress. They decided to cover up the entire affair with public announcements that he had died in an automobile accident.

The Maccabees agreed that Haven-Hurst indeed was the victim of an automobile accident.

With the general gone from the scene the terrorist activity dwindled. The pending arrival of the United Nations committee lay an uneasy calm over the land.

In late June of 1947, the United Nations Special Committee on Palestine, known as UNSCOP, arrived in Haifa. The neutrals represented Sweden, the Netherlands, Canada, Australia, Guatemala, Uruguay, Peru, Czechoslovakia, Yugoslavia, Iran, and India.

The odds were long against the Jews. Iran was a Moslem country. India was partly Moslem and its delegate was a Moslem as well as representing a British Commonwealth nation. Canada and Australia were also of the British Commonwealth. Czechoslovakia and Yugoslavia, in the Soviet bloc, had a traditional history of anti-Zionism. The South American representatives, Uruguay, Peru, and Guatemala, were Catholic in predomination and could possibly be influenced by the Vatican's lukewarm feeling toward Zionism. Only Sweden and the Netherlands could be considered fully nonpartisan.

None the less, the Yishuv welcomed UNSCOP.

The Arabs opposed the presence of the United Nations. Inside Palestine a general strike of the Arabs was called, demonstrations were held, and the air was filled with oaths and threats. Outside of Palestine the Arab countries began riots and blood pogroms against their Jews.

Barak Ben Canaan, the old warrior and negotiator, was once again pressed into service by the Yishuv. He joined Ben Gurion and Dr Weizmann on the advisory committee to UNSCOP.

Chapter Thirteen

Kitty and Karen returned to Gan Dafna. Kitty waited for the right moment to have it out with Karen. When the letter from Dov Landau arrived, she decided to delay it no longer.

Kitty poured a lemon rinse over Karen's head and wrung out her long, thick brown hair and rubbed the girl's head briskly with a big towel.

'Phew,' Karen said, taking a corner of the towel to wipe the soap from her eyes.

The water boiled in the teakettle. Karen got up and tied the towel around her head and brewed a pot of tea. Kitty sat at the kitchen table filing her fingernails. She began to paint them carefully with polish.

'What's bothering you?' Karen said disarmingly.

'Good Lord, I'm not even allowed the privacy of my own thoughts.'

'Something is wrong. Something's been wrong since you came back from your trip to the Sea of Galilee. Did something happen between you and Ari?'

'Plenty happened between me and Ari but that's not what is disturbing me. Karen, we have to have a talk about us, and our futures. I guess we'd better do it right now.'

'I don't understand.'

Kitty waved her hands to dry her fingernails. She stood up and lit a cigarette awkwardly. 'You know how much you mean to me and how much I love you?'

'I think so,' the girl whispered.

'Since that first day at Caraolos I've wanted you to be my girl.'

'I've wanted it that way too, Kitty.'

'Then you'll believe that I have thought this all out carefully and what I want to do is for your own good. You must have faith in me.'

'I do ... you know that.'

'What I am about to say will be hard for you to appreciate fully. It is hard for me to come to this, too, for I am very fond of many children here and I have grown quite attached to Gan Dafna. Karen, I want to take you home to America with me.'

The girl stared at Kitty as though she had been slapped. For a moment she did not even understand or believe she had heard it right.

'Home? But ... but this is my home. I have no other home.'

'I want your home to be with me – always.'

'I want that too, Kitty. I want it more than anything. It is so strange.'

'What is, dear?'

'When you said home, in America.'

'But I am an American, Karen, and I miss my home.'

Karen bit her lip to keep from crying. 'That's funny, isn't it? I thought we would go on like we were. You would be at Gan Dafna and ...'

'And you would go off into the Palmach ... and then to some *kibbutz* out on a border?'

'I guess that's what I thought.'

'There are many things I have learned to love here, but this is not my country and these are not my people.'

'I guess I have been selfish,' Karen said. 'I never thought of you as getting homesick or wanting anything for yourself.'

'That is the nicest thing anyone has ever said to me.'

Karen poured two cups of tea and tried to think. Kitty was everything to her ... but leave?

'I don't know how to say it, Kitty, but ever since I was old enough to read in Denmark I've asked myself the question about being Jewish. I still don't know the answer. I only know that I have something here that is mine ... no one is going to take it from me. Whatever it is, it's the most important thing in the world. Someday I might know the words for it – but I can't leave Palestine.'

'Whatever you have, you will still have it. Jews in America and I suppose Jews everywhere have this same belonging that you have. Going away won't change that.'

'But they are exiles.'

'No, baby . . . don't you understand that Jews in America love their country?'

'The Jews of Germany loved their country too.'

'Stop it!' Kitty cried suddenly. 'We are not that kind of people and I will not listen to those lies they fill you with!' She caught herself quickly. 'There are Jews in America who love their country so much they would prefer death to ever living to see what happened to Germany come to America.' She walked up behind the girl's chair and touched her shoulder. 'Don't you think I know how difficult this is for you? Do you believe I would do anything to hurt you?'

'No,' Karen whispered.

Kitty faced Karen and knelt before her chair. 'Oh, Karen. You don't even know the meaning of peace. In all your life you have never been able to walk in the light of the sun without fear. Do you think it will be any better here? Do you think it will ever be better? Karen, I want you to go on being a Jew and I want you to go on loving your land, but there are other things I want for you too.'

Karen turned her eyes away from Kitty.

'If you stay here you'll spend your whole life with a gun in your hands. You'll turn hard and cynical like Ari and Jordana.'

'I guess it isn't fair of me to have expected you would stay.'

'Come with me, Karen. Give us both a chance. We need each other. We've both had enough suffering.'

'I don't know if I can leave . . . I don't know . . . I just don't,' she said with a shaky voice.

'Oh, Karen . . . I want so much to see you in saddle shoes and pleated skirts, going out to a football game in a cut-down Ford. I want to hear the phone ringing and you giggling and talking to your boy friend. I want you full of delicious nonsense as a teen-age girl should be – not carrying a gun in your hands or smuggling ammunition. There are so many things that you are missing. You must at least find out they are in the world before you make your final decision. Please, Karen . . . please.'

Karen was pale. She walked away from Kitty. 'What about Dov?'

Kitty took Dov's letter from her pocket and handed it to Karen. 'I found this on my desk. I don't know how it got there.'

> *Mrs Fremont:*
>
> This letter is being written by someone who knows more better how to say in English than I do but I copy it to show it is my writing. This letter must be sent to you in a special way for reasons you know of. I am very busy these days. I am with friends. My friends are the first I have in a long time and they are real good friends. Now that I am permanent situated, I want to write to you and to say how glad I am not to be at Gan Dafna no more where everybody makes me sick, including you and Karen Clement. I write to say I won't see Karen Clement no more as I am too busy with real friends. I don't want Karen Clement to think I am going to come back and take care of her. She is nothing but a kid. I have a real woman of my own age and we live together and everything. Why don't you go with Karen Clement to America because she doesn't belong here.
>
> DOV LANDAU

Kitty took the letter from Karen's hand and ripped it to shreds. 'I will tell

Dr Lieberman that I am resigning. As soon as we can straighten up matters here we will book passage to America.'

'All right, Kitty. I'll go with you,' Karen said.

Chapter Fourteen

Every few weeks the Maccabee high command changed its headquarters. After 'Hell's Fortnight' and the assassination of Arnold Haven-Hurst, Ben Moshe and Akiva thought it would be best to get out of Jerusalem for a while. The Maccabees were a small organization, a few hundred full-time members and a few thousand part-time with a few thousand more sympathizers. Because they had to remain constantly on the move the headquarters command group carried no more than a half dozen of the top men. Now the pressure was so great that the command split up and only four persons went to Tel Aviv. There was Akiva and Ben Moshe and Nahum Ben Ami, the brother of David, and there was Little Giora – Dov Landau. Dov had become a personal favorite of Akiva. He had gained the inner circle of the Maccabee command by his fame in the raids and by the usefulness of his talents in forgery.

The four moved into a basement apartment owned by a fellow Maccabee, located on Bene Berak Road near the Central Bus Station and the old market, where there was great activity. Maccabee lookouts were posted around the apartment house and an escape route was worked out. It looked ideal – and could have been worse.

For nearly fifteen years Akiva had frustrated CID and British Intelligence. There was a period of amnesty during World War II when Akiva was free, but for the rest of that time he was wanted. He had always evaded them and had escaped many traps that had been set for him. Akiva was the biggest prize in Palestine with the price on his head running to several thousand pounds sterling.

It was coincidence that the CID was observing the activities of another apartment house on Bene Berak Road just three houses away from the new Maccabee headquarters. The suspects were a ring of smugglers who had been storing goods got past customs in the Jaffa port. The alert CID men watching from an observation point in a building across the street spotted the suspicious picket of watchmen regularly near the basement headquarters. With a telescopic lens camera they photographed all the lookouts and identified two as known Maccabees. While stalking smugglers, they had stumbled onto a Maccabee hangout. Their long experience with the Maccabees induced them to raid at once. They organized quickly and moved to effect complete surprise. They still had no idea they were going into Maccabee headquarters itself.

Dov was in one of the three rooms of the basement apartment forging an El Salvador passport. Only Akiva was with him. Nahum and Ben Moshe had gone out to meet Zev Gilboa, the liaison for the Haganah and Palmach. Akiva came into the room.

'Well, well, Little Giora,' Akiva said, 'How did you manage to talk Ben Moshe out of taking you along on today's business?'

'I must finish this passport,' Dov grumbled.

Akiva looked at his watch and then stretched out on a cot behind Dov. 'They should be returning shortly.'

'I don't trust the Haganah,' Dov said.

'We have no choice but to trust them for the time being,' the old man said.

Dov held the passport paper up to the light to study his erasures and see if they could be detected through the water marks and seal. It was a good job. Not even an expert could spot where he had worked over the name and description of the former owner. Dov bent close to the paper and etched in the signature of an El Salvador official, then put the pen down. He got up and paced the tiny room restlessly checking frequently to see if the ink was dry, then resuming his walking, back and forth, snapping his fingers.

'Don't be so impatient, Little Giora. You will find that waiting is the worst part of underground life. Waiting for what, I often wonder?'

'I've lived underground before,' Dov said quickly.

'So you have.' Akiva sat up and stretched. 'Waiting, waiting, waiting,' Akiva said. 'You are very young, Dov. You should learn not to be quite so serious and quite so intense. That was always one of my faults. I was always too intense. Worked day and night for the cause.'

'That sounds strange coming from Akiva,' Dov said.

'An old man begins to see many things. We wait for a chance to wait. If they get us, the best we can expect is exile or life in prison. The hanging and the torture is getting to be standard procedure these days. That's why I say ... don't be so serious. There are many nice Maccabee girls who would love to meet our Little Giora. Have fun while there is time.'

'I am not interested,' Dov said firmly.

'Ah, hah,' the old man teased, 'perhaps you already have a girl you have been holding out on us.'

'I had a girl once,' Dov said, 'but no more.'

'I must tell Ben Moshe to find you a new one and you will go out and enjoy yourself.'

'I don't want one and I'll stay in headquarters. It is the most important place to be.'

The old man lay back again and he meditated. At length he spoke. 'How wrong you are, Little Giora. How very wrong you are. The most important place to be is awakening in the morning and looking out at your fields, working in them – and coming home at night to someone you love and who loves you.'

The old man is getting sentimental again, Dov thought. He tried the paper and found it dry. He fitted the passport photo into place. As Akiva dozed on the cot, Dov began his pacing again. It was worse now that he had sent the letter to Mrs Fremont. He wanted to go on raids. Another raid and another and another. Sooner or later the British would get him and hang him and it would be all over with. They didn't know that his bravery came from the fact that he didn't care. He almost begged to be hit by enemy gunfire. The dream was bad these days and Karen was not there to stand between him and the gas-chamber door. Mrs Fremont would take her to America now. That would be good. And he would keep on going on raids until they got him, because it was no good to live without Karen.

Outside of the apartment fifty plain-clothed British police intermingled with the crowds near the bus station. They moved quickly, picking up the Maccabee lookouts and whisking them out of the area before they could give a warning. Then they cordoned off the entire block.

Fifteen police armed with shotguns, tear gas, axes, and sledge hammers slipped down to the basement apartment and stationed themselves around the door.

There was a knock.

Akiva's eyes fluttered open.

'That must be Ben Moshe and Nahum. Let them in, Dov.'

Dov slipped the chain latch into place and opened the door a crack. A sledge hammer crashed into the door, ripping it open.

'British!' Dov screamed.

Akiva and Little Giora captured!

The word was on every lip in Palestine! The legendary Akiva who had eluded the British for more then a decade was now theirs!

'Betrayal!' cried the Maccabees. They placed the blame on the Haganah. Ben Moshe and Nahum Ben Ami had been meeting with Zev Gilboa. Either Gilboa or some other Haganah person had followed them to learn the Maccabee headquarters. How else could it have been found? The two factions were again at odds. The Maccabees voiced accusations. A hundred rumors circulated purporting to reveal how the Haganah had managed its alleged sell-out.

The British High Commissioner for Palestine moved for an immediate trial to produce a quick sentence which would further demoralize the Maccabees. He felt that swift justice for Akiva would restore British authority and curtail the Maccabee activities, since the old man had long been the spiritual force behind the terrorists.

The high commissioner arranged a secret trial. The name of the judge was withheld for his own safety. Akiva and Little Giora were sentenced to be hanged within a fortnight of their capture.

They were both incarcerated in the impenetrable Acre jail.

In his eagerness the high commissioner had made a disastrous mistake. Newsmen had been barred from the trial, and in the United States in particular the Maccabees had powerful friends and financial aid. The guilt or innocence of Akiva and Little Giora were lost sight of in the passionate outbursts that followed. Like the *Exodus* incident, the sentencing of the pair was being turned into a focus for violent protest of the British mandate. Dov's background of the Warsaw ghetto and Auschwitz was dug up and published, producing a wave of sympathy all over Europe. There was indignation over the secrecy of the trial. Pictures of the eighty-year-old Akiva and eighteen-year-old Little Giora, the prophet and the disciple, captured the imagination of readers. Newsmen demanded to see the pair.

Cecil Bradshaw was in Palestine with UNSCOP. Having seen what could happen in the case of the *Exodus* he quickly went into a conference with the high commissioner and applied to the Home Office for instructions. The incident was creating ill will for the British at a delicate time, when the United Nations Committee was in Palestine. Instead of halting Maccabee activity the affair might trigger a new rash of terror. Bradshaw and the high commissioner decided to move quickly to show the world that British justice was merciful. Using the extreme ages of Dov and Akiva as an excuse they announced that they would allow the sentenced pair to make petitions for mercy and spare their lives. Their action put a halt to the storm of protest.

The high commissioner and Bradshaw themselves went to the Acre prison to see Akiva and Dov and tell them the good news. The latter were brought into the warden's office where the two officials bluntly explained the proposal.

'We are reasonable people,' the commissioner said. 'We have arranged these petitions for you to sign. Officially they are petitions for mercy. However, off the record it is merely a formality ... a loophole, if you will.'

'Now you sign these petitions,' Bradshaw said, 'and we will give you a fair compromise. We'll take you two out of the country. You'll serve a short term in one of the colonies in Africa and in a few years it will have all blown over.'

'I don't quite understand you,' Akiva said. 'What are we serving a sentence in Africa for? We have committed no crime. We are merely fighting for our natural and historical rights. Since when has it been a crime for a soldier to fight for his country? We are prisoners of war. You have no right to pass any sentence on us. We are an occupied country.'

The high commissioner broke into a sweat. The old man was going to be stubborn. He had heard Maccabee fanatics recite that theme before. 'See here, Akiva. This is beyond arguing politics. It is your life. Either you sign these petitions for mercy or we will carry through the sentences.'

Akiva looked at the two men, whose anxiety was fully apparent. He was quite aware that the British were trying to gain an advantage or undo a mistake.

'You there, boy,' Bradshaw said to Dov. 'You don't want to hang on the gallows, do you? You sign and Akiva will sign afterwards.'

Bradshaw shoved the petition across the desk and took out his pen. Dov looked at the document a moment.

He spit on it.

Akiva looked at the two frustrated, half-frightened Englishmen. '*Thine own mouth condemneth thee,*' he snapped.

The rebuff by Akiva and Little Giora of the mercy petitions was carried in headlines as a dramatic protest against the British. Tens of thousands in the Yishuv who had formerly had little regard for the Maccabees were inspired by the action. Overnight the old man and the boy became the symbol of Jewish resistance.

Instead of damaging the Maccabees, the British were well on their way toward creating a pair of martyrs. They had no choice now but to set the hanging date, ten days away.

Every day the tension grew in Palestine. The raids of the Maccabees and the Haganah had stopped, but the country knew it was sitting on a short-fused powder keg.

The all-Arab city of Acre stood at the northern end of an arced bay with Haifa on the southern end. Acre jail was a monstrosity built on Crusader ruins. It ran along a sea wall that stretched from the prison at the northern outskirt of the town to the opposite end of the city. Ahmad el Jazzar – the Butcher – had turned it into an Ottoman fortress and it had stood against Napoleon. It was a conglomeration of parapets, dungeons, tunnels, towers, dried-up moats, courtyards, and thick walls. The British converted it into one of the most dreaded prisons in the Empire's penal system.

Dov and Akiva were placed in tiny cells in the north wing. The walls, ceilings, and floors were made of stone. The cells' dimensions were six feet by eight feet. The outside wall was sixteen feet thick. There was no light and no toilet. A stink of mustiness was present continuously. Each door was a solid sheet of iron with a tiny peephole for viewing, covered from the outside. The only other opening in the cells was a slit two inches wide and twelve inches high cut through from the outside wall, that allowed in a thin ray of light. Through it Dov could see the tops of some trees and the rim of Napoleon's hill, which marked the farthest advance point in the drive to conquer India.

Akiva fared badly. The ceilings and walls dripped, and the clammy damp penetrated his ancient inflamed joints and put him in agonizing pain.

Two or three times each day British officials came to plead for some sort of compromise to prevent the hanging. Dov merely ignored them. Akiva sent them out with quotations from the Bible ringing in their ears.

Six days remained before the hanging. Akiva and Dov were moved to the death cells adjoining the hanging room. These were conventional barred cells in another wing of the prison: four concrete walls, a deep hole under the floor, and a trap door under a steel-beamed rigging to hold the rope. A sandbag of the weight of a man was used in testing; the guards pulled the lever to release the trap door and let the sandbag fall with a crunching thud.

Dov and Akiva were dressed in scarlet pants and shirts, the traditional English hanging dress.

Chapter Fifteen

It was one o'clock in the morning. Bruce Sutherland dozed in his library with his head bowed over a book. He sat up quickly, awakened by a sharp knocking. His servant ushered Karen Clement in to the room.

Sutherland rubbed his eyes. 'What the devil are you doing here this time of night?'

Karen stood before him, trembling.

'Does Kitty know you are here?'

Karen shook her head.

Sutherland led her to a chair. Karen was white and tense. 'Have you eaten, Karen?'

'I'm not hungry,' she said.

'Bring her a sandwich and some milk,' Sutherland ordered his servant. 'Now see here, young lady, what is all this about?'

'I want to see Dov Landau. You are the only one I know who can help me.'

Sutherland snorted and paced the room with his hands clasped behind him. 'Even if I can help you this can only hurt you more. You and Kitty will be leaving Palestine in a few weeks. Why don't you try and forget him, child?'

'Please,' she pleaded. 'I know all the reasons why. I have thought of nothing else since he was captured. I must see him once more. Please help me, General Sutherland, please.'

'I'll do what I can,' he said. 'First, let me call Kitty and tell her you are here. She is probably half out of her mind. You had no business traveling through Arab country as you did.'

The next morning Sutherland called Jerusalem. The high commissioner was quick in granting the request. The British were still trying to get Dov and Akiva to change their minds and were willing to grab at any straws. There was a possibility that Karen's visit could break the armor of Dov's defiance. It was arranged quickly. Kitty left Gan Dafna and was picked up in Safed by Sutherland, whence the three drove to Nahariya on the coast. There from the police station an escort took them directly into Acre jail, where they were taken to the warden's office.

Karen had been in a daze all the way to Acre. Now, in the prison, it seemed even more unreal to her.

The warden came in.

'All right, young lady.'

'I'd better go with you,' Kitty said.

'I want to see him alone,' Karen said firmly.

A pair of armed guards waited for Karen outside the warden's office. They led her through a series of iron doors and into a huge stone courtyard surrounded by barred windows. Karen could see the eyes of the prisoners leering at her. Some catcalls echoed in the hollow yard. She looked straight ahead. They walked up narrow steps into the death wing. They passed through a barbed-wire machine gun emplacement, then came to another door where two soldiers stood with fixed bayonets on their rifles.

She was ushered into a tiny cell. The door was closed behind her and a soldier stood near. He opened a slot in the wall measuring a few inches wide and a few inches high.

'You'll talk to him through that slot there, girlie,' the guard said.

Karen nodded and looked into it. She could see the two cells on the other side of the wall. She saw Akiva in the first and Dov in the other, his scarlet dress. Dov lay on his back, staring at the ceiling. Karen could see a guard enter and unlock his cell door.

'Up, Landau,' the guard barked. 'Somebody to see you.'

Dov picked up a book from the floor and opened it and read.

'You've got a visitor.'

Dov turned a page in the book.

'I said you've got a visitor.'

'I'm not in for any of your good-will ambassadors. Tell them I said to go . . .'

'It ain't one of ours. It's one of yours. It's a girl, Landau.'

Dov's hands tightened on the book and his heart raced. 'Tell her I'm busy.'

The guard shrugged and walked to the slot in the wall. 'He says he don't want to see nobody.'

'Dov!' Karen called. 'Dov!'

Her voice echoed in the death cell. 'Dov! It's me, Karen!'

Akiva looked tensely to Dov's cell. Dov gritted his teeth and turned another page.

'Dov! Dov! Dov!'

'Talk to her, boy,' Akiva shouted. 'Don't go to your grave in the silence my brother has condemned me to. Talk to her, boy.'

Dov set the book down and rolled off the cot. He motioned the guard to open his cell door. He walked to the slot and looked into it. He could see only her face.

Karen looked into his cold, blue, angry eyes.

'I don't want no more tricks,' he said acidly. 'If they sent you here to beg, just turn around and get out. I'm not asking for mercy from these bastards.'

'Don't talk like that to me, Dov.'

'I know they sent you.'

'I swear no one asked me to come. I swear it.'

'Then what are you doing here?'

'I just want to see you once again.'

Dov clenched his teeth and kept his control. Why did she have to come? He nearly died with wanting to touch her cheek.

'How do you feel?'

'Fine ... just fine.'

There was a long silence.

'Dov ... did you really mean what you wrote to Kitty or did you say it just because ...'

'I meant it.'

'I wanted to know.'

'Well, you know now.'

'Yes, I know. Dov ... I ... I'll be leaving Eretz Israel soon. I'm going to America.'

Dov shrugged.

'I guess I shouldn't have come. I'm sorry I bothered you.'

'That's all right. I know you was just trying to be nice. I would really like to see my girl but she's a Maccabee and she can't come. She's my own age, you know.'

'I know.'

'Anyhow. You're a nice kid, Karen ... and ... uh ... you uh ... get to America and forget about all this business here. And good luck.'

'I guess I had better go,' Karen whispered.

She stood up. Dov's expression did not change.

'Karen!'

She turned quickly.

'Uh ... just to show that we are friends ... uh ... we could shake hands if the guard says it's all right.'

Karen put her hand through the opening and Dov pressed it between his own and pressed his forehead against the wall and closed his eyes.

Karen grasped his hand and pulled it back to her side of the wall.

'No,' he said, 'no ...' but he could not resist.

She kissed his hand and pressed it against her cheek and her lips and he felt the tears from her eyes. And then she was gone.

His cell door clanged behind him. Dov flopped on his bed. In all of his lifetime he could not remember shedding tears. But now nothing could stop them. He turned his back to the door so the guards and Akiva could not see his face and he wept softly from his heart.

Barak Ben Canaan was one of the Yishuv advisors who traveled with the

UNSCOP as it inspected Palestine and made its various inquiries. The Yishuv showed its proud record of land reclamations, rehabilitation for the homeless – the progress of the *kibbutzim* and the factories and the cities they had built. The UNSCOP delegates were impressed by the contrast of the Jewish and Arab communities. After the inspection tours formal inquiries were opened in which each side was allowed to present its case.

Ben Gurion, Weizmann, Barak Ben Canaan, and the other Yishuv leaders argued with tremendous skill the morality and justice of the Jewish case.

On the Arab side, the Higher Arab Committee, steered by the Husseini family stirred up bitter demonstrations against the United Nations. They barred the committee from many of the Arab towns where the squalor and primitive factory conditions would turn the strongest stomach. When the inquiries opened, the Arabs officially boycotted it.

It became obvious to the UNSCOP that there could be no middle road in Palestine. On a basis of strict justice the United Nations would have to recommend a settlement in favor of the Jews, but there was the weight of Arab threats to consider.

The Jews had long accepted the theory of compromise and partition, yet they were fearful of the creation of a land ghetto like the Pale.

With the tour of Palestine and the inquiries concluded, the UNSCOP prepared to leave and retire to Geneva to analyze their findings while a subcommittee studied the displaced-persons camps in Europe, which still held a quarter of a million desperate Jews. They would then present recommendations to the General Assembly of the United Nations. Barak Ben Canaan once again accepted a commission to travel to Geneva and continue his advisory capacity.

He returned to Yad El a few days before departure for Geneva so that he might spend some time with Sarah, who, despite his many departures, had never quite got used to them. Neither did she ever get used to Jordana's and Ari's being away.

Ari and David Ben Ami were at the nearby Ein Or *kibbutz*, at Palmach headquarters for the Huleh. They came to Yad El and Jordana came down from Gan Dafna for a farewell dinner.

Barak was preoccupied through the entire evening. He spoke little of the UNSCOP, the coming trip, or of the pressing politics. It was a grim reunion

'I suppose you've heard that Mrs Fremont is leaving Palestine,' Jordana said at the end of dinner.

'No, I didn't hear,' Ari said, masking his surprise.

'She is. She has given her notice to Dr Lieberman. She is taking the Clement girl with her. I knew she would run at the first sign of real trouble.'

'Why shouldn't she go?' Ari said. 'She is an American and the girl is what she came to Palestine for.'

'She never had any use for us,' Jordana snapped.

'That's not true,' David said in defense.

'Don't always take her side, David.'

'She is a nice woman,' Sarah Ben Canaan said, 'and I like her. Many times she passed this way and visited with me. She was very good to those children and they love her.'

'She is better gone,' Jordana persisted. 'It is a shame she is taking the girl with her, but she has the child so spoiled now one would not think she was a Jewish girl.'

Ari stood up and walked from the cottage.

'Why must you make it a point to hurt Ari?' Sarah said angrily. 'You know what he feels for her and she is a fine person.'

'He is well rid of her,' Jordana said.

'And who are you to judge a man's heart?' Barak said.

David took Jordana's hand. 'You promised we would take a horseback ride.'

'You are on her side too, David.'

'I like Kitty Fremont. Come, let's go for that ride.'

Jordana strode from the room and David followed.

'Let them go, Sarah,' Barak said. 'David will calm her down. I am afraid our daughter is jealous of Mrs Fremont as well she might be. Someday our girls may have the time to concentrate on being women.'

Barak played with his tea, and his wife stood behind his chair and laid her cheek on his thick red hair. 'Barak, you cannot go on like this. You must speak or you shall regret it to your grave.'

He patted his wife's hand. 'I will find Ari,' he said.

Ari was near the orchard looking up into the hills at Gan Dafna when Barak came upon him.

'Does she matter that much, son?'

Ari shrugged.

'I rather liked her myself,' Barak said.

'What is the difference? She comes from a world filled with silk stockings and perfume and she is going back to it.'

Barak held his son's arm and they walked through their fields to the place where the Jordan River ran past their farm. They could see Jordana and David riding away and they could hear her laughter.

'You see, Jordana is over it already. How are things with the Palmach at Ein Or?'

'As they have always been, Father. Good boys and girls but too few of them and too little to fight with. We cannot expect to win a war against seven armies.'

The sprinklers began whirling in the fields as the sun started its plunge behind the Lebanese hills near Fort Esher. The father and the son watched their fields for a long time. Each of them wondered if there would ever come a day when the only thing to worry about was the mending of a fence or the plowing of their land.

'Let's go back to the house,' Ari said. '*Ema* is alone.'

Ari turned to go. He felt his father's giant hand on his shoulder. He turned. His father's great head was bowed in sadness. 'I leave for Geneva in two days. I leave with sorrow as I have never known. For fifteen years someone has been missing from our table. I have been a proud and stubborn man but I have paid the price of pride with torment. It is hell for me now. Ari, my son, do not let my brother Akiva hang at the end of a British rope.'

Chapter Sixteen

Jerusalem seethed on the eve of the UNSCOP departure. In the Arab sector inflammatory oratory rang out to the wild chantings of Arab mobs. The city was split into fortified areas, cordoned off with barbed wire, and guarded by Tommies entrenched behind massed guns.

Ari Ben Canaan moved through Jerusalem, crossing from sector to sector to all of the known hangouts of Bar Israel, the Maccabee contact man. Bar Israel seemed to have disappeared. There had been no liaison between Maccabees and Haganah since the capture of Akiva and Little Giora. Ari was not without his sources of information, however, and he found out that Bar Israel was living in a room in the El Katamon district.

Ari went directly to the room and unceremoniously shoved the door open. Bar Israel was engaged in a chess game. He looked up, saw Ari, and returned to studying the chess board.

'Get out,' Ari ordered the other player. He shoved the man through the door and closed it. 'You knew damned well I was looking for you.'

Bar Israel shrugged and lit a cigar. 'You left fifty love letters all over Jerusalem.'

'Then why didn't you contact me? I've been in Jerusalem for twenty-four hours.'

'You've made your dramatic entrance. Now what do you want?'

'Take me to Ben Moshe.'

'We aren't playing with you boys any more. We have an aversion to Haganah commanders learning our headquarters.'

'You're not talking to a Haganah commander. You are talking to Ari Ben Canaan, the nephew of Akiva.'

'Ari, I trust you personally but orders are orders.'

Ari snatched Bar Israel out of his chair, spilling the chess board to the floor. He held the little Oriental by the lapels and shook him as though he were a weightless sack. 'You are going to take me to Ben Moshe or I am going to snap your neck.'

Ben Moshe sat at his desk at Maccabee headquarters in the Greek colony. Beside him stood Nahum Ben Ami. The two men glared angrily at the bewildered Bar Israel and Ari Ben Canaan.

'We all know Ari,' Bar Israel whimpered. 'I took a chance.'

'Get out,' Ben Moshe snarled at the sweating man. 'We will settle with you later. Now that you are here, Ben Canaan, what do you want?'

'I want to know what you plan to do about Akiva and the boy?'

'Do? Why nothing, of course. What can we do?'

'You are a liar!' Ari said.

'Whatever we do it is none of your damned business,' Nahum said.

Ari smashed his fist on the desk so hard it splintered the top. 'It is my business! Akiva is my uncle!'

Ben Moshe remained icy. 'We have had enough co-operation with traitors.'

Ari leaned forward until his face was inches from Moshe's. 'I hate your guts, Ben Moshe, and I hate yours, Nahum Ben Ami. But I am not leaving until I know your plans.'

'You are asking for a bullet through your brain.'

'You shut up, Nahum, or I'll dismantle you,' Ari said.

Ben Moshe took off his glasses, wiped them, and put them back on. 'Ari, you have such a pleasant way of persuasion,' he said. 'We are going into the Acre jail and take Akiva and Little Giora out.'

'That is what I thought. When?'

'The day after tomorrow.'

'I am going with you.'

Nahum started to protest but Ben Moshe held up his hand to be quiet.

'You give your word the Haganah does not know about you being here?'

'You have it.'

'What is his word?' Nahum said.

'I take the word of a Ben Canaan.'

'I still do not like it,' Nahum said.

'That is too bad then. You know what this means of course, Ari. We have mobilized our greatest strength. You have been in the Acre jail . . . you know what it is like. If we can do this thing it will break the British backs.'

'Acre is an all-Arab city. The jail is the toughest stronghold they have in Palestine. Let me see your plans.'

Ben Moshe opened the desk and took out a sheaf of blue-prints. Everything in the Acre area had been covered: there was a layout of the town, the exterior approaches to the prison, the escape roads. The diagrams of the prison's interior were perfect as far as Ari could judge. They must have been drawn up by people who had been prisoners. The guard stations, the arsenal, the main communications center were all pinpointed on the maps.

Ari studied the timetables of the attack. They were masterpieces. Heavy explosives, grenades, and land mines, all manufactured by the Maccabees, were ingeniously employed.

'What do you think, Ari?'

'Everything is perfect – up to a point. I see how you are going to get in and get them outside but the escape from Acre' – Ari shook his head – 'this will never work.'

'We cannot hide conveniently at the nearest *kibbutz*,' Nahum Ben Ami snapped.

'We know the chance of complete escape is very slim,' Ben Moshe agreed.

'It is not very slim. It is nil. Of course I know you Maccabees pride yourselves on being dead heroes. Unless you set up better getaway plans, that is what you're going to become.'

'I know what he is going to suggest,' Nahum said. 'He will suggest we co-operate with the Haganah and the *kibbutzim* . . .'

'That is exactly what I am going to suggest. If you don't you'll have a lot of new martyrs. Ben Moshe, you are brave but you are not crazy. As the matter stands now you have possibly a two-per-cent chance. If you allow me to set up more complete escape plans your chances will become fifty-fifty.'

'Watch him,' Nahum said, 'he talks too slickly.'

'Go on, Ari.'

Ari spread the master map out on the desk. 'I suggest that you take an extra ten or fifteen minutes inside the prison and use that time to free every prisoner in the place. They will scatter in twenty directions and force the British to chase them all and thereby cut the British strength.'

Ben Moshe nodded.

'Now, our own groups should also break up into small units and each unit head out a different way from Acre. I will take Akiva with me and you will take the boy.'

'Go on,' Nahum Ben Ami said. As he listened he realized Ari was making sense.

'For my route I will break for Kfar Masaryk. There I will change transportation to throw them off and use back roads to go up to Mount Carmel south of Haifa. I have trusted friends in the Druse village of Daliyat el Karmil. The British won't even begin to look up there.'

'It sounds good,' Nahum said. 'The Druses can be trusted ... better than some Jews I know.'

Ari ignored the insult. 'The second unit carrying Dov Landau will go up the coast road to Nahariya and split. I can arrange sanctuary in a half dozen *kibbutzim* in the area. I suggest that Landau be taken to Mishmar *kibbutz* on the Lebanese border. I was there at the building of Mishmar; the area is filled with caves. Your brother David was with me at Mishmar in the second world war. We have used it for years as a hiding place for our leaders. Landau will be absolutely safe there.'

Ben Moshe sat like a statue, looking over his plans. Without these hiding places he knew he had no more than a dramatic suicide mission. With Ari's help, there was a chance. Could he risk co-operation?

'Go on, Ari ... set up your escape routes. I do this only because your name is Ben Canaan.'

D-Day minus four.

Four days separated Akiva and Little Giora from a rope. The UNSCOP flew out of Lydda to Geneva. Palestine felt the deathly tense, foreboding calm. The Arab demonstrations stopped. Maccabee raids stopped. The city was an armed camp with British plain-clothes men flooding the area.

D-Day minus three.

A last ditch appeal from the Prime Minister of Great Britain was turned down by Akiva and Little Giora.

D-Day.

Market day in Acre. At daybreak Arab crowds converged on the city from twenty Galilee villages. The market areas were packed with donkeys and carts and produce. The roads were filled with travelers.

Oriental and African Jews, members of the Maccabees dressed as Arabs, drifted into Acre with the influx of the market-day throngs. Each man and woman carried a few sticks of dynamite, caps, wires, detonators, grenades, or small arms under their long dress. The Maccabees dispersed and mingled in the market stalls near the prison and throughout the jammed bazaar.

Eleven o'clock. H-Hour minus two.

Two hundred and fifty Maccabee men and fifty Maccabee women in Arab dress were now dispersed in Acre.

Eleven-fifteen. H-Hour minus one forty-five.

The guard changed inside the Acre jail. Four inside Maccabee collaborators stood by.

Eleven-thirty. H-Hour minus one-thirty.

Outside Acre at Napoleon's Hill, a second unit of Maccabees assembled. Three truckloads of men dressed as British soldiers drove into Acre and parked along the sea wall near the prison. The 'soldiers' quickly broke up into four-man units and walked through the streets as though on security patrol. There were so many other soldiers about that this hundred new people received no attention.

High noon. H-Hour minus one.

Ari Ben Canaan drove into Acre in a staff car dressed as a British major. His driver parked on the sea wall on the west side of the prison. Ari walked out on the big rampart at the north end of the sea wall and leaned against a rusted old Turkish cannon. He lit a cigarette and watched the waves lap against the sea wall below him. The foam swirled around the mossy green rocks worn flat by the waters.

Twelve-five. H-Hour minus fifty-five minutes.

The shops of Acre closed one by one for the two-hour midday break. The sun was getting hot and it blazed down on the Arabs in the coffeehouses, who began to daze as the mournful wails of Radio Cairo blared. The British troops were stifled and groggy in the heat.

Twelve-ten. H-Hour minus fifty minutes.

A Moslem caller climbed the long spiral stairs of the minaret beside the Mosque of El Jazzar. The caller cried out in the stillness and the Mohammedans gathered in the courtyard and inside the huge white-domed house of prayer and knelt in the direction of the holy city of Mecca.

Twelve-twelve. H-Hour minus forty-eight minutes.

The Maccabees move toward their assembly points as the heat beat both Arabs and British soldiers into lethargy.

In groups of twos and threes they moved without apparent purpose through the narrow dung-filled alleys to the assembly points.

Group one gathered at the Abu Christos – Father of Christ – Café. The café sat on the bay and the coffee drinkers watched the Arab boys dive from the rocks for a *grush.* They could see the entire sweep of the bay and Haifa at the far end.

A second large group came together at the mosque. They knelt at the outer fringes of the huge courtyard and joined the Arabs in prayer.

The third unit went to the Khan, a large square that had been used for more than a hundred years as a caravan resting and trading place. They mingled with the camels and the donkeys and the hundreds of market-day Arabs who lay on the ground and rested.

Group four met on the docks by the fishing fleet.

The fifth group assembled at the Land Gate on the sea wall.

At the same time the hundred Maccabees disguised as British soldiers moved for their positions. They had a greater freedom of movement; they went to house tops and blocked alleyways and roads so that they commanded every possible entrance and exit to Acre jail.

Outside of Acre the final unit of Maccabees got into position. These were people with no disguise. They planted land mines and stationed themselves on the highways with machine guns to stop British reinforcements from getting into Acre.

Twelve forty-five. H-Hour minus fifteen minutes.

The soldiers blocking off the jail were in position. The units on the highway outside Acre were in position.

The striking force, the two hundred and fifty disguised as Arabs, moved out of their assembly points in small groups and converged on the attack point.

Ben Moshe and Ben Ami reached the spot first. They watched their people converging. They looked over the roof tops and saw their soldiers in place. They looked at the prison where one of the four 'inside' helpers signaled that all was ready.

Ari Ben Canaan walked to the edge of the rampart and flicked his cigarette out and walked quickly toward the attack point. The driver drifted along behind him in the car.

The attack point was the Hamman El-Basha, a hundred-and-twenty-year-old Turkish public bathhouse. The bathhouse, built by El Jazzar, was attached to the south wall of the Acre jail. In the rear of the bathhouse there was a courtyard used for sunning. A single stairway led up to the roof of the bathhouse and right to the prison wall. The Maccabees had discovered that from their various guard posts inside the prison the British could see every possible approach and detect every possible movement around the jail – except one place: the bathhouse and the south wall, and here was where they would strike.

One o'clock. H-Hour.

The city of Acre was burned into somnolence by the sun.

Ben Moshe, Ben Canaan, and Ben Ami drew deep breaths and gave the signal. The raid of the Acre jail was on.

Ari Ben Canaan led the spearhead of fifty men. They went into the bathhouse and through it quickly to the courtyard in the rear. His group carried sticks of dynamite.

The Arabs sitting in the steaming rooms looked on in utter amazement. Terror seized them and in a second the bathhouse was a confusion of wet scrambling Arabs. A second force moved in and jammed the bathers into one steam-flooded room so they could not escape and give an alarm.

Outside, Ben Moshe received the signal that Ari had reached the courtyard and all the Arabs were trapped.

In the courtyard at the rear of the bathhouse Ari's men raced up the steps, crossed the roof to set their dynamite charge against the south wall of the prison. The explosives and caps and wires came out from under their clothing and the charge was fixed with speed and efficiency. They retreated to the cover of the courtyard and lay flat.

One-fifteen.

An ear-shattering explosion shook Acre. The air was filled with flying rocks. It took a full two minutes for the dust to settle and reveal a huge breach in the jail wall.

With the explosion, the four inside men carried out their assignments. The first threw a grenade on the switchboard, stopping all phone operation. The second grenaded the main switch box, cutting the electricity and, with it, the alarm system. The third man seized the turnkey, and the fourth man rushed to the breach to direct the incoming Maccabees.

Ari's men poured into the prison. The first objective of half his force was to get the arsenal. In a few moments they were all equipped with heavy arms.

The second section of Ari's force cut off the main guard barracks so that these troops could not get out as reinforcements.

At intervals of one minute, Ben Moshe outside fed ten-and twenty-man units into the prison. Each group knew exactly where to hit. Guards were gunned from their positions and the Maccabees tore through the ancient passageways with Sten guns blazing and grenades blasting away obstacles. They fanned out, snatched their objectives, and with the precision of meticulous planning they held the interior of the Acre jail six minutes after the wall had been broken.

Outside the walls the covering force dug in and waited for a counterattack from the British garrison. The troops and plain-clothes men already in the city were stopped by the Maccabees who controlled the entrances from roof tops and alleyways.

When all two hundred men were inside the jail they turned to smashing open the cell doors and freeing the prisoners. The escapees, Arabs and Jews alike, were ushered to the breach in the wall and soon they were running in every direction through Acre.

Ari led five men with the captured turnkey to the death cells and the hanging room. The turnkey began to open the door. Inside the four guards who kept constant watch on the condemned pair began to fire at the iron door. Ari waved the others back, slapped a magnetic mine on the door, and ducked back. The door was ripped from its hinges. Ari stepped into the doorway and hurled a grenade inside and the guards fled to the hanging room.

The party quickly entered, pinned down the guards, and opened the cell doors. Akiva and Dov Landau were rushed from the prison, across the bathhouse roof, and through the bathhouse to the outside.

Dov Landau was pulled aboard a truck filled with men. Ben Moshe waved to them to move out and the truck sped off toward Naharuya. Two minutes later the staff car pulled up and Ari led Akiva into it and they fled in a different direction.

Ben Moshe blew a whistle signal for the Maccabees to begin the withdrawal operations. It was a mere twenty-one minutes since the blast of the wall.

Confused units of the British garrisons attempted to converge on Acre jail. They were stopped by land mines, road-blocks and cross fires. Inside Acre disorganized British units were trying to chase the three hundred freed inmates.

The truck with Dov Landau raced up the coast road. It had been spotted by the British and was not trailed by a motor force that outnumbered its complement ten to one. The truck pulled into the Jewish town of Nahariya. Nahum Ben Ami fled with Dov toward the Lebanese border *kibbutz* of Ha Mishmar while the rest of the force deployed as a rear guard to stall the pursuers. These Maccabees managed to hold the British long enough to allow Nahum Ben Ami to lead Dov to safety, but it was a suicide action: all seventeen men and women of the rear guard were killed.

Akiva and Ari were in the back seat of the staff car. The driver and another Maccabee sat in front. They sped from the Acre area along an inland road toward the *kibbutz* Kfar Masaryk. At Napoleon's Hill, a Maccabee roadblock waved them down and told them to get off the main road, which was mined against British counterattack. This group was holding off two British companies trying to break through to Acre.

Ari made a quick decision.

'Driver. Can you drive through the fields here and get past that British unit?'

'We'll find out.'

They careered off the road and banged and rattled through a field to encircle the area of action. They managed to get past the two British companies and turned again for the highway. A dozen soldiers chased after the car, firing as they ran. Just as the car touched the road again it swerved under the impact of a hail of bullets. Ari grabbed Akiva and held him down on the floor. The whine of bullets was all around them. The wheels of the car spun furiously, digging in the dirt for more traction. The driver threw the car into reverse as more bullets ripped into it. Two soldiers with submachine guns were almost on them. Ari fired through the back window. One of the soldiers dropped. The second opened up with a deadly burst of fire. Ari could see the red flames spit from the mouth of his gun.

Akiva shrieked.

Another burst spewed from the soldier's gun.

Ari fell on top of Akiva just as the car regained the road and raced away.

'Are you all right back there?'

'We've both been hit.'

Ari pulled himself up and examined his right leg. He felt the inside of his leg. It was numb. The bullet had lodged deep. There was no bad bleeding or great pain, only a burning sensation.

He knelt and rolled Akiva over and ripped his bloody shirt open. Akiva's stomach was a gaping wound.

'How is he?'

'Bad ... very bad.'

Akiva was conscious. He pulled Ari close to him.

'Ari,' he said, 'am I going to make it?'

'No, Uncle.'

'Then get me to some hidden place ... you understand.'

'I understand,' Ari said.

The escape car reached Kfar Masaryk where a dozen *kibbutzniks* stood by ready to hide the car and provide a truck to continue the escape. Akiva was gory and unconscious by the time they pulled him from the car. Ari took a moment to pour sulfa into his wounded leg and put a pressure bandage on it. The two Maccabees with him pulled him aside.

'The old man is not going to make it if we go any farther. He must stay here and receive medical treatment.'

'No,' Ari said.

'Are you mad?'

'Now listen to me, you two. He has no chance to live. Even if he did the British would find him here. If we leave him and he dies here it will be known all over Palestine. No one but us must know that Akiva did not escape. The British must never know he is dead.'

The two Maccabees nodded their understanding. They jumped into the front of the truck and Ari got into the rear with his uncle. Ari's leg was beginning to hurt.

The truck streaked south below Haifa. It ascended the narrow roads working up the side of Mount Carmel. Ari held his unconscious uncle in his lap as they bounced on the dirt roads and swayed around treacherous turns, sending up a trail of dust and jolting them unmercifully. Higher and higher into

Mount Carmel they drove until they were in the territory where only the Druses lived in isolation.

Akiva opened his eyes. He tried to speak but he was unable to. He recognized Ari and he smiled and then sagged in Ari's arms.

The truck pulled into a clump of brush a mile before the Druse mountain village of Daliyat el Karmil. Mussa, a Druse Haganah soldier, waited with a donkey cart.

Ari crawled from the truck. He rubbed his leg. He was drenched with the blood of Akiva.

Mussa rushed to him.

'I'm all right,' Ari said. 'Get Akiva. He is dead.'

The tired old body of Akiva was carried from the truck to the cart.

'You two men are Maccabees. You are not to reveal Akiva's death to anyone but Ben Moshe or Nahum. Now get the truck down from here and get it cleaned. Mussa and I will bury my uncle.'

The truck sped away.

Ari got on the donkey cart. It bypassed the village and moved to the highest point on Mount Carmel, the south ridge. At twilight they entered a small forest that held the altar of the greatest of all the Hebrew prophets, Elijah. It was on this ground that Elijah had proved the power of God against Jezebel's priests of Baal.

The altar of the prophet Elijah looked down on the Jezreel Valley. The valley below stood as an eternal reminder that the land had not been forgotten.

Mussa and Ari scratched out a shallow grave near Elijah's altar.

'Let's get that red suit off of him,' Ari said.

The British hanging clothes were removed and Akiva was rolled into his grave and it was filled up and the spot covered with branches. Mussa returned to the cart to wait for Ari.

Ari knelt for a long time over Akiva's grave. Yakov Rabinsky had been born in anger and he had died in sorrow. After so very many years of torment, he could at last find peace. He could find here a peace that had avoided him in life and he could sleep eternally looking down upon the land of the Jews. Someday, Ari thought, all the world will know were Akiva sleeps and it will be a shrine of all Jews.

'Goodbye, Uncle,' Ari said. 'I didn't even get a chance to tell you that your brother forgives you.'

Ari stood up and began to sway. Mussa rushed over to him as he cried out in pain and pitched to the ground in a faint.

Chapter Seventeen

Kitty and Dr Lieberman were both glum as she went over some business in his office.

'I wish I knew the words that would make you stay,' Dr Lieberman said.

'Thanks,' Kitty said. 'Now that the time is here I feel very empty. I didn't realize how attached I had become to Gan Dafna. I was up most of the night going through these files. Some of these youngsters have made remarkable progress in light of their histories.'

'They will miss you.'

'I know. And I will miss them. I'll try to get everything up to date in the next few days. There are a few special cases I'd like to go over with you personally.'

'Yes, of course.'

Kitty stood up to leave.

'Be sure to get to the dining room a half hour early tonight.'

'I would prefer it if they didn't. I don't think the occasion calls for a going-away party.'

The little hunchback held up his hands. 'Everyone insisted. What could I do?'

Kitty walked to the door and opened it.

'How is Karen?'

'Pretty badly upset. She has been since she saw Dov at the prison. I had a bad night with her last night when we heard about the Acre jail raid. Maybe she will learn soon whether or not he escaped. That poor child has been through enough suffering for a lifetime. It may take a while, Dr Lieberman, but I am going to make her very happy in America.'

'I wish it were in my heart to tell you that I think you are wrong for leaving us. I cannot say that.'

Kitty left his office and walked down the corridor thinking about the news that had electrified the world. The Maccabees had lost twenty men and women killed and another fifteen were captured. No one knew how many wounded were in hiding. Ben Moshe had been killed. It seemed like a high price to pay for two lives – until one considered that they were not just any two lives. The raid had been a crushing blow to what was left of British morale and British desire to remain in Palestine.

Kitty stopped before Jordana's door. She hated the idea of confronting Jordana. She knocked.

'Yes?'

Kitty entered. Jordana looked up from her desk coldly.

'I was wondering, Jordana . . . Do you happen to know if Dov Landau made his escape yesterday? I mean, with Karen's attachment to the boy it would make her feel much better if . . .'

'I don't know.'

Kitty started to leave, then turned at the last second. 'Was Ari on the raid?'

'Ari doesn't give me a list of his raids.'

'I thought you might know.'

'How should I know? It was a Maccabee raid.'

'You people have ways of obtaining information about things you want to learn.'

'If I knew I wouldn't tell you, Mrs Fremont. You see, I want nothing to stand in the way of your catching your plane out of Palestine.'

'It would be much nicer if we could part friends but it doesn't look as though you are even going to give me a chance for that.'

She turned quickly and left the office and walked out to the main door. Kitty could hear whooping and cheering coming from a football game on the athletic field. Out on the center green some of the younger children played tag and some of the older ones lay on the lawn studying.

The flowers never stopped blooming at Gan Dafna, Kitty reflected, and the air was forever filled with their scent.

Kitty walked down the steps of the administration building and crossed the green, past the trenches. She stopped by the statue of Dafna. This time she did not feel jealous of Ari's dead sweetheart. She looked down on the Huleh as Dafna always looked down on it and she felt a sudden twinge of loneliness.

'*Shalom, Giveret* Kitty,' some youngsters called to her as they ran past. One of them ran up to her and threw his arms around her waist, and she mussed his hair and sent him along.

As she walked to the hospital she felt very depressed. Leaving Gan Dafna was going to be more difficult than she had thought.

In her office she began to go through her files, discarding some, sorting others.

It was strange, she thought; she had not felt this loss in leaving the orphanage in Salonika. Kitty never really tried to become a 'friend' of the Jews at Gan Dafna. Why was it all catching up to her at this moment?

Perhaps it was because it was the end of an adventure. She would miss Ari Ben Canaan and she would think about him for a long time, maybe forever. But in time things would become sane and organized again and she would be able to give Karen all those things in life she wanted for the girl. There would be good times and wonderful vacations together and Karen would start her dancing lessons again. In time, the picture of Ari Ben Canaan would grow dim as would the memory of Palestine.

It was natural to feel badly, Kitty reasoned. There is a certain regret in leaving any job and moving from place to place.

She began reading through her personal notes on some of 'her' children. Were they impersonal objects of prescribed therapies or were they little lost human beings who were dependent upon her? Did she have the right to take them up and just drop them, or did she have a further duty to them beyond her own personal desires?

Kitty quickly shut her mind to this line of thought. She opened her desk drawer and took out her passport. Karen's British passport was beside her own. There were two tickets – Departure, Lydda – Destination, New York.

Mark Parker was coming in from the Orient to meet them in San Francisco. Dear Mark . . . was there ever a more devoted friend? Mark would help Kitty get situated around San Francisco. Kitty loved the Bay Area. They could live in Marin County over the Golden Gate Bridge or in Berkeley near the university. They would be near the theater and ballet and the wonderland of San Francisco.

Kitty shut her desk drawer.

She picked up the files again and started to replace them in the cabinet. Of course it was right for her to go . . . of course it was. Even Dr Lieberman said so. What did she owe these children? It was a job; nothing more, nothing less.

Kitty closed the drawer to the file cabinet and sighed. Even as she justified it to herself, the shadow of doubt began to creep into her mind. Was she really doing this for Karen or was she going because of her own selfish love for the girl?

Kitty turned and gasped! An Arab was standing in the doorway. He was dressed oddly. He wore an ill-fitting western suit of pin-striped worsted. On his head was a red fez bound in white cloth that gave his head a square look. His black mustache was enormous and waxed to fine points.

'I did not mean to frighten you,' the Arab said. 'I may come in?'

'Certainly,' Kitty said, surprised to hear him speak in English.

She surmised that he was from a nearby village and that someone was sick.

The Arab entered and closed the door behind him.

'You are Mrs Fremont?'

'Yes.'

'I am Mussa. I am a Druse. You know of the Druses?'

She new vaguely that they were an Islamic sect that lived in villages on Mount Carmel, south of Haifa, and that they were loyal to the Jews.

'Aren't you a long way from home?'

'I am Haganah.'

Kitty sprang to her feet instinctively. 'Ari!' she said.

'He hides in my village of Daliyat el Karmil. He led the raid at Acre. He asks that you come to him.'

Kitty's heart pounded wildly.

'He has been badly wounded,' Mussa said. 'You will come?'

'Yes,' she said.

'Do not take medicine. We must be cautious. There are many British roadblocks and if they find medicine they will be suspicious. Ari says to get the truck filled with children. Tomorrow there is a Druse wedding. We tell the British we are bringing the children to the ceremony. I have a truck. Get fifteen children right away and have them pack bedrolls.'

'We will be ready in ten minutes,' she said, and rushed out for Dr Lieberman's office.

It was eighty kilometers from Gan Dafna to Mussa's village, mostly over narrow mountain roads of northern Galilee. The dilapidated truck made slow progress.

The children in the back, delighted with the unexpected holiday, sang at the top of their voices as the truck chugged through the hills. Only Karen, sitting in the front cabin with Kitty, knew the real nature of the journey.

Kitty pumped Mussa for information. All she was able to ascertain was that Ari had received a leg wound twenty-four hours ago, was unable to walk, and was in great pain. He knew nothing of Dov Landau and said nothing of the death of Akiva.

In spite of the instructions, Kitty had packed a small first-aid kit of sulfa, bandages, and iodine, which would appear innocent enough in the glove compartment.

She had known real deep fear only twice in her life. She knew fear in Chicago in the waiting room of the polio wing of the Children's Hospital during the three days and three nights of Sandra's crisis. She knew fear once again as she waited in the Dome Hotel for the news of the hunger strike on the *Exodus*.

She knew fear now. She was oblivious to the children's singing or to Karen's efforts to keep her calm. She was dazed with anxiety.

She closed her eyes and her lips moved and she said the words to herself over and over ... 'Whoever this God is who watches Israel, keep Ari alive ... please, let him be alive.'

An hour passed and two and three.

Kitty's nerves had brought her to a state of near-exhaustion. She laid her head on Karen's shoulder and closed her eyes.

The truck rattled into the turn at Kfar Masaryk, using the roads that Ari had taken in his escape from Acre. As they moved toward Mount Carmel the roads came alive with troops.

They were stopped at a roadblock.

'These children from Gan Darna. We have wedding at Daliyat tomorrow.'

'Out, everyone,' the British ordered.

They combed the truck. All the bedrolls were untied and searched thoroughly; two of them were ripped open with knives. The underneath of the truck was searched and the spare tire torn off the rim. The motor was looked over and the children were searched. The shakedown took nearly an hour.

A second British search took place at the foot of Mount Carmel. Kitty was played out by the time Mussa began to drive up the winding turns along the sides of Mount Carmel.

'All Druse villages are built very high places. We are small minority and need high places to defend against Moslem attacks,' Mussa said; 'we will be in Daliyat in few minutes.'

Kitty pulled herself together quickly as they approached the outskirts and slowed in the narrow streets.

Daliyat el Karmil seemed to sit on the roof of the world.

It was sparkling white and clean in comparison to the filth and decay of most Arab villages. Most of the men wore mustaches and many wore western clothing. Their headdresses were somewhat different from those of other Arabs, but the most dramatic difference was the carriage of dignity and outward pride and the look which suggested that they could be fierce fighters.

The women were exceedingly handsome and the children were bright-eyed and sturdy. The women were dressed in wild colors with white cloths over their heads.

Daliyat teemed with hundreds of visitors. They had come for the wedding from all the Carmel Druse villages, and in addition there were Jews from the *kibbutz* and as far away as Haifa.

The truck inched past the village reception house where solid lines of male guests gathered to congratulate the groom and the village elders. Alongside the reception house a veranda was built over the hillside. It held a twenty-five-yard-long table filled with fruits and rice and curried lamb and wines and brandies and stuffed marrows. The women, balancing dishes of food on their heads, kept a steady stream moving to and from the table.

Mussa stopped the truck beyond the reception house. A half dozen villagers came up to greet the children. The children unloaded the back of the truck and marched off with their bedrolls to their camping area to set up their camp and then return to join in the festivities.

Mussa, Kitty, and Karen drove on down the center street. Here, Druse dancers wearing silver silk shirts and multi-colored embroidered skullcaps were in the middle of a wild performance. They were lined up, each with his hands on the next man's shoulders. Keeping the line straight, they continuously bounced from the ground, holding their bodies rigid, using only their feet as springs. In front of the line the finest Druse dancer in Palestine, a man named Nissim, went through wild gyrations with one knife in his teeth and a pair of knives in his hands.

Nearby, at the sanctuary, a verse maker told a story by calling out extemporaneous chants. Each line of the chant was repeated by a hundred men around him. As his story unfolded, each new line was repeated louder and louder, and as he came toward the end of his legend half the men drew pistols and fired them into the air.

Mussa turned the truck into the main street and took a narrower street down a steep incline. He jammed the transmission into low gear and held his foot on the brake as the vehicle slid down.

At the bottom of the grade, Mussa stopped the truck. The next road was too steep to attempt. The three of them got out quickly. Kitty took the small first-aid kit and followed Mussa down past a block of houses until they were far from the frenzied town activity.

At the last house in the village they stopped. It was closely guarded by a small band of fierce-looking armed Druse men.

Mussa held the door open. Kitty took a deep breath and entered. Inside another pair of guards stood before an inner door. She turned to Karen.

'Stay here. I'll call you if I need you. Mussa, come in with me please.'

The bedroom was almost dark, and it was chilly because of the altitude and the concrete floors. Kitty heard a groan. She walked quickly to the window and threw the shutters open, admitting a stream of light.

Ari lay on a double bed with a brass headboard. His fists were clenched around two of the rungs, which he had bent out of shape as he writhed in agony. Kitty threw the cover from him. His clothes and the mattress were dark with blood.

'Help me take his pants off,' Kitty ordered.

Mussa straightened up with amazement.

'Never mind,' she said. 'Just stand out of my way. I'll tell you when I need you.'

She carefully ripped away his trousers and examined him. His color seemed good and his pulse was relatively strong. She compared the two legs. The bad one did not seem to be unduly swollen nor did it appear that he had lost an excessive amount of blood.

Kitty's manner was brisk efficiency now that she knew Ari was alive and did not appear to be in critical danger.

'Mussa, bring me some soap and water and some clean towels. I want to take a closer look at the wound.'

She washed her hands and wiped around the wound carefully. His thigh was discolored and the blood oozed from the puffy spot where the bullet had entered.

Ari fluttered his eyes open. 'Kitty?'

'Yes, I'm here.'

'Thank God.'

'What have you done for this thing?'

'I put some sulfa on it yesterday. I had a pressure bandage but it didn't seem to be bleeding too much.'

'I'm going to poke around. It's going to hurt.'

'Go ahead.' He grunted and broke out in a cold sweat as she felt the lump. He gripped the brass rungs and shook the bed. Kitty took her hand away quickly. Ari trembled for three minutes. She wiped his face with a wet towel.

'Can you talk to me, Ari?'

'It's going away,' he said. 'It comes and goes. This is a lot of fuss I'm making for a leg wound. Did your Cook County training include this sort of thing?'

Kitty smiled that he should remember. 'Oh, every once in a while somebody's husband caught the boy friend in the act and was dumped at the emergency door.'

'What is it?'

'I can't say for sure. Bullets do funny things. There's no accounting for the way they twist. Your pulse and breathing are good, no shock. Your leg isn't swollen except around the immediate area of the wound.'

'What does that mean?'

'I would say it means you haven't had an internal hemorrhage. The bullet missed a main artery. I can't see any infection, either. I'd say you were rather lucky ... although I'm worried about this pain you're having.'

'I've been passing out every few hours,' he said.

'Hold on. I want to feel around again.'

Ari braced himself but was only able to take the probing for a few seconds. He cried out and bolted up to a sitting position and then gasped and sank down.

'The sonofabitch is killing me!'

He clutched the sheets and rolled over on his face and shook.

He convulsed in pain for ten minutes, then fell limp. 'Kitty ... what is it? ... for God's sake, I can't take much more ...'

'Were you able to walk at all after you were hit?'

'Yes ... what is it, Kitty? Why should it hurt like this?'

She shook her head. 'I'm not a doctor. I can't say for sure. I may be all wrong.'

'Tell me what you do know,' he gasped.

'All right, this is what I think. The bullet entered your outer thigh and hit the bone. It didn't break your leg or you couldn't walk and it didn't pass to the inside of your thigh or it probably would have got an artery.'

'What is it?'

'I think it hit the bone and either chipped or splintered it. That's one of the things that is hurting you. My guess is that the bullet ricocheted back toward the surface. It may be lodged against a nerve.'

'What's going to happen?'

'It has to come out. That pain is either going to kill you or paralyze you. You can't take a trip down the mountain. It may start all sorts of things going ... a hemorrhage, God knows what. You'll have to get a doctor up here in the next few hours – or you're going to be in very bad trouble. That bullet has to come out.'

Ari looked over to Mussa. Kitty turned and looked at the Arab and then quickly to Ari.

'There are wounded men from yesterday's raid hiding all over the Galilee,' Mussa said. 'Every Jewish doctor in Palestine is being watched right now. If I try to bring one back up here for Ari, he is certain to be followed.'

She stared from one to the other again and stood up and lit a cigarette. 'Then you'd better give yourself up and get this taken care of right away.'

Ari nodded to Mussa and the Arab walked from the room.

'Kitty,' he called.

She walked to the side of the bed. He reached out and took her hand. 'They'll hang me. It's up to you.'

Her throat went dry. She pulled away and leaned against the wall and tried to think. Ari was calm now and his eyes were fixed on her.

'I can't. I'm not a doctor.'

'You've got to.'

'There is nothing to work with ...'

'You've got to.'

'I can't ... I can't. Don't you see it will be so painful ... it might put you into shock. Ari ... I'm frightened.'

She slumped into a chair. She thought of Ari's leading the raid and knew he was right about his fate if the British were to find him. She thought of Dov – and how Karen had felt. She knew that she was his only hope; to do nothing was equally courting death. She bit her clenched fingers and stood up quickly. There was a bottle of brandy on the dresser. She took it to him.

'Start drinking this. When this bottle is empty, we'll get you another one. Get drunk ... get as drunk as you can, because I'm going to hurt you like hell.'

'Thanks, Kitty ...'

She opened the door quickly.

'Mussa!'

'Yes.'

'Where can we get some medical supplies?'

'At the Yagur *kibbutz*.'

'How long will it take to get a man there and back?'

'Getting him there is no trouble. Coming back ... he must not use the roads so he cannot take a car. By foot in these mountains will take many hours ... maybe not even till late tonight.'

'Look, I'll write you a list of things that I will want. You get a man to that *kibbutz* as fast as you can.'

Kitty considered. The messenger might get back tonight and he might not get back at all. A *kibbutz* dispensary might or might not have anesthetics but she could not take the chance of waiting. She wrote a note for two liters of plasma, vials of penicillin, morphine, dressings, a thermometer, and some other instruments. Mussa dispatched one of the guards to Yagur.

'Karen, I'm going to need your help but it is going to be very rough.'

'I can do anything.'

'Good girl. Mussa, do you have anything at all in the way of medicine?'

'A few things, not much.'

'Very well. We'll make do with what we have in that first-aid kit. Do you have a flashlight and ... perhaps some unused razor blades or a very sharp small knife?'

'Yes, we can get that.'

'All right, fine. I want the razor blades and the knife boiled for a half hour.' Mussa turned and issued the order.

'Now put some blankets on the floor. The bed is too springy. He will have to be braced solidly. When we move him to the floor, Karen, you get those dirty linens off and change the bed. Mussa, get her some clean sheets.'

'Is there anything else?' Mussa asked.

'Yes, we will need six or eight men in here to move him and to hold him still.'

Everything was made ready. Blankets were laid out on the floor. Ari was drinking steadily. Four of the Druses moved him as gently as possible to the floor. Karen quickly took off the bloody sheets and remade the bed. The blades and knife were brought in. Kitty scrubbed her hands and washed the wound area and painted it with iodine. She waited until the brandy had Ari mumbling incoherently, then placed a pillow beneath his head and placed a handkerchief in his mouth for him to bite on.

'All right,' she said, 'I'm ready. Hold him down and let's get going.'

One man held Ari's head, two men held each arm, two held the good leg and one held the bad one. The eight Druses had Ari pinned solidly to the floor. Karen stood at the edge of the group with the flashlight, brandy, and the meager supplies at hand. Kitty got on her knees and knelt close to the wound. Karen turned the flashlight on it.

Kitty took a razor blade in her fingers and motioned the men to get ready. She pressed the blade against his thigh and lined up her stroke. With one quick hard motion she slit deeply into his flesh and opened it in a two-inch cut over the bullet hole. Ari shook violently. Mucus poured from his nose, and his eyes ran with tears of agony. The men strained to hold him.

Karen saw the blood leave Kitty's lips and her eyes started to roll. She grabbed Kitty's hair and pulled her face up and poured brandy down her throat. Kitty gagged a second and caught herself and took another drink. Ari's eyes rolled back into his head. He fell into blessed unconsciousness.

Karen turned the light on the incision once again. With one hand Kitty held the skin apart. With her other thumb and third finger she dug into his flesh and felt around for the bullet. Her fingernail rubbed the hard object. With a final exertion of strength she gripped it and wiggled it loose from his leg.

She sat on the floor and held the bullet up and looked at it and began laughing. All the Druse men started laughing too. Kitty sobbed half hysterically.

'Mussa,' Karen said, 'get him back on the bed quickly. Don't let anything touch the wound.'

Karen helped Kitty to her feet and sat her down in a chair. She pried the bullet from her hands and wiped them clean. The girl moved over to Ari and poured sulfa powder into the wound and laid a bandage over the top of it lightly. Then she sponged Ari down. Kitty remained crumpled and sobbing.

Karen ordered everyone from the room and poured another drink for Kitty and left.

Kitty sipped the brandy and walked over to Ari and felt his pulse. She pried his eyes open and watched his color.

Yes ... he was going to come through all right ...

She laid her head on his chest. 'Ari ... Ari ... Ari ... Ari ...' she whispered between sobs.

Chapter Eighteen

Ari remained in excruciating pain. The medicines failed to arrive. Kitty was unable to leave him for a second. Several times she had to call Mussa for men to keep Ari from thrashing around and endangering the open wound.

Up the hill in the center of the village the dancing and chanting and hilarity continued. The bride, who had been hidden all day, was taken from seclusion. The groom dressed in a cutaway coat and top hat, mounted a horse and rode to her through a flower-strewn lane flanked with rifle-bearing Druse men.

After the ceremony many of the Jewish visitors, with the children from Gan Dafna, lit a campfire and there were more songs and a *hora*. There was Hebraic dancing to the tambour and flute and the Druse dancers, too, took their turn in the center ring.

Karen remained constantly in the outside room. She came in to spell Kitty for intervals during the long night. Morning found both of them exhausted from the lack of sleep and the prolonged tension. Kitty sat at the edge of the bed and sprang up each time Ari groaned or moved.

By morning the medicines still had not arrived.

'You had better take the children back to Gan Dafna,' Kitty told Mussa. 'Is there anyone else here who speaks English?'

'Yes, I will have him stay here.'

'Good. Can you get another bed set up or a couch or something for me to rest on? I'll have to remain right here for some time.'

'It will be arranged.'

Kitty went into the next room where Karen dozed on a bench. She brushed the girl's cheek gently. Karen sat up and rubbed her eyes. 'Is he all right?'

'No. He is in very bad pain. I want you to go back to Yad El with the children this morning.'

'But, Kitty ...'

'Don't argue. Tell Dr Lieberman I have to stay here until I can get things under control.'

'We are supposed to leave Palestine the day after tomorrow.'

Kitty shook her head. 'Cancel our flight. We can make new travel arrangements later. I have to stay here until they can get someone else up here to take care of him properly. I don't know how long it's going to be.'

Karen embraced Kitty and turned to leave.

'Karen. Get to Safed, will you, and tell Bruce Sutherland where I am. Ask him if he will come to Haifa to meet me. Tell him to stay at the largest hotel. I'll find it, whatever it is. Have him bring some clothes for me.'

By noon the hundreds of celebrants began drifting away from Daliyat el

Karmil. The Druses left for their mountaintop villages and the Jews went back to the *kibbutz* and to Haifa. Mussa took the truckload of children back toward Gan Dafna.

When they were all gone, the Druses relaxed the heavy guard around Ari. The English-speaking Druse stood by in the next room.

Kitty Fremont was alone with him in this strange place. In this first moment of quiet the full impact of these events hit her. She stood over his bed and looked at him.

'God Almighty,' she whispered. 'What have I done?' All the months of fighting him, all the carefully built-up resistance, collapsed in that mad second that had sent her rushing to his side. At this moment she feared this power that Ari held over her.

Late in the evening the messenger arrived with medicines from Yagur *kibbutz*. He had been working his way through the mountains and hiding for long periods of time. British patrols were everywhere looking for the wounded from the Acre jail raid.

Kitty quickly administered a liter of plasma to Ari and filled him with penicillin as insurance against the infection that she feared must be inevitable under the circumstances of the operation. She redressed the open wound and injected morphine to ease the murderous pain.

For the next two days and nights Kitty kept Ari under morphine sedation to block off the pain. She watched his progress from minute to minute. The incision was beginning to bind together. There appeared to be no great crisis. Ari was awake only for brief moments, during which he took some nourishment, but when he was awake he was too torpid to realize what was taking place around him. The Druse villagers marveled at Kitty's nursing efficiency and stamina. The women were particularly pleased with the way she snapped out orders to the men.

By the time Kitty knew Ari was safe, that time was the only requirement, she had become uncertain and filled with anxiety: the question of leaving Gan Dafna was in her mind again.

She pondered again her right to leave the children of Gan Dafna who needed her. Where was the line between professionalism and humanity? And what of Karen? Was Karen coming to America only out of fear of losing Kitty?

Of the thoughts that weighed on Kitty the worst was a factor she could no longer rationalize. Once before she had been drawn into this strange group of people against her will: on Cyprus she had resolved not to work for them – and then she saw Karen. Now, it appeared to be a repetition: on the eve of her departure she was pulled back to Ari. Was this a coincidence or was her fate being shaped by a higher power? As much as her basic common sense resisted the fantastic idea, it kept haunting Kitty. She feared the power of Palestine.

Ari made swift progress under Kitty's ministrations. He was a remarkable man, Kitty reflected. The pain that he had borne could have killed an ordinary human being. By the end of the fourth day she had reduced the morphine sharply. She had also discontinued the use of penicillin, certain that the wound was healing and would not become infected.

Ari awoke on the fifth morning hungry, eager to shave and clean up, and in a cheerful frame of mind. As Ari emerged in renewed vitality, Kitty went into a shell. She adopted an icy, impersonal, clinical attitude. She snapped orders like a sergeant major, prescribing the next week's plans as though he were a complete stranger.

'I hope by the end of this week to have you completely off drugs. I want you to start exercising the leg and give it as much motion as possible. However, you must be very careful about putting too much strain on the incision. It isn't stitched.'

'How long before I'll be able to walk?'

'I can't say without an X ray. I am inclined to think the bone was just cracked and not chipped. If there was a chip you would still be in severe pain. However, I can safely say that you aren't going anywhere for at least a month.'

Ari whistled under his breath as she pulled the sheet up around him.

'I'm going out for a walk,' she said. 'I'll be back in a half hour.'

'Kitty. Just a moment. I ... uh ... look, you've been very kind. You've watched over me like an angel. Since this morning you have seemed angry. Is there something wrong? Have I done something?'

'I'm tired, I'm worn out. I've been up for five nights. I'm sorry I can't do a song and dance for you.'

'That's not it. There's something more. You're sorry you came here, aren't you?'

'Yes, I am,' she said softly.

'Do you hate me?'

'Hate you, Ari? Haven't I made it quite obvious how I feel about you? Please, I'm tired ...'

'What is it? Tell me?'

'I despise myself for caring for you ... Is there anything else you want to know?'

'You can be a terribly complicated woman, Kitty Fremont.'

'I suppose I am.'

'Why do you and I always have to confront each other with our guards up, ready to swing ... ready to run?'

Kitty regarded him steadily for a moment. 'Maybe because I don't live by your simple, uncluttered standards of I-like-you-and-you-like-me-so-let's-go-to-bed. Page four forty-four of the Palmach manual: boys and girls should not indulge in coyness. Women of Palestine, be forthright. If you love him, sleep with him.'

'We aren't hypocrites.'

'I'm not so advanced in my thinking as Jordana or your immortal Dafna.'

'Stop it,' Ari snapped. 'How do you dare to imply that my sister and Dafna were – tramps? Jordana has loved only one man in her life. Is it wrong to give her love when she does not know if either of them will be alive at the end of the week? Don't you think I would have preferred to live in peace at Yad El with my Dafna than have her killed by Arab gangs?'

'I don't live my life as a noble mission. It is very simple with me, Ari. I have to be needed by the man I love.'

'Let's quit this,' Ari said. 'Haven't I made it plain to you that I needed you?'

Kitty laughed shortly with bitterness. 'Yes, you needed me, Ari. You needed me on Cyprus to smuggle forged papers out of Caraolos and you needed me again ... to pull a bullet out of you. It is remarkable, that mind of yours. Even half dead and rolling in pain you could figure out all the angles. You could plot out the course ... fill the truck up with children to avoid suspicion.

You didn't need me, Ari. You needed a candidate to get through the British roadblocks.

'I'm not blaming you,' she continued. 'I am the number-one damned fool. We all have our crosses to bear and I guess you are mine. I just can't take it with the straight-faced unconcern of a *sabra*.'

'Does that make it necessary to treat me like an animal?'

'Yes ... because that's what you are. You're a mechanical animal, too infested with the second coming of the Israelites to be a human being. You don't know the meaning of giving love. You know only of fighting. Well, I'm fighting *you*, Brother Ben Canaan, and I'm going to beat you, and I'm going to forget you, in spades.'

Ari remained silent as she walked to the bed and stood over him with tears of anger welling in her eyes. 'Some bright day you're really going to need someone and it's going to be a terrible thing because you don't have the capacity to truly ask for help.'

'Why don't you take that walk?' he said.

'I'm taking it and I'm going to keep on walking. Good Nurse Fremont is through. Somebody from the Palmach will come up to take care of you in a few days. You'll live till then.'

She spun around and opened the door.

'Kitty, this great vision of man you have ... what do you want?'

'I want a man who knows what it is to cry. I feel sorry for you, Ari Ben Canaan.'

Kitty left Daliyat el Karmil the same morning.

Chapter Nineteen

Bruce Sutherland had been waiting for Kitty at the Zion Hotel in Haifa for two days. It seemed to her that she had never been happier to see anyone. After dinner Sutherland drove up to Har Hacarmel, the Jewish sector of the city which was spread on the slopes of Mount Carmel.

They went into a night club which was built with a view of Panorama Road, where the city below, the harbor, and the sweep of the bay could be seen to Acre and beyond it, to the hills of Lebanon.

'How's the girl?'

'Much better, thank you, Bruce. I do appreciate your coming.' She looked at the view. 'I came up here to Har Hacarmel the first night I was in Palestine. Ari brought me up. I think our conversation had something to do with living with tension.'

'The Jews here have learned to live under the gun the way you Americans live with baseball. It's made them a hard lot.'

'This place has got me so I can't think straight any more. The more I try to reason, the more I am trapped by sentiment and unexplainable forces. I've got to get out of here before it swallows me up.'

'Kitty, we know that Dov Landau is safe. He is hiding up at Mishmar. I haven't told Karen yet.'

'I guess she's got to know. Bruce, what's going to happen here?'

'Who knows?'

'You think the UN will give in to the Arabs?'

'There will be a war.'

There was a fanfare at the bandstand. A master of ceremonies came out and told a few stories in Hebrew and then introduced a tall, handsome *sabra* youth. The young man wore the traditional white shirt opened at the throat and he had a black mustache and a small chain was around his neck with a Star of David pendant. He strummed a guitar and sang a song of passionate patriotism about the Jews coming back to their Promised Land.

'I must know what is going to happen at Gan Dafna.'

'The Arabs can raise an army of fifty thousand Palestinians and perhaps twenty thousand irregulars from over the border. There was a chap named Kawukji who led irregulars in the '36-'39 riots. he's already busy getting another gang of cutthroats together. It is easier to get arms to the Arabs than to the Jews ... they have friendly territory all around them.'

'And the rest of it, Bruce?' Kitty demanded.

'The rest of it? Egypt and Iraq both have armies of around fifty thousand men. There will be some Saudi Arabian troops in the Egyptian Army. Syria and Lebanon will put another twenty thousand men on the field. Trans-Jordan has the Arab Legion ... crack soldiers with the latest arms. According to present-day definitions the Arabs do not have first-class armies; none the less they have many modern units with artillery, armament, and aircraft.'

'You advised the Haganah, Bruce. What did you tell them?'

'I told them to form a defense line between Tel Aviv and Haifa and try to hold that strip of territory. Kitty, the other side of the picture is not pretty. The Jews have four or five thousand Palmach troops and a paper army of fifty thousand in the Haganah, but they only have ten thousand rifles. The Maccabees can put a thousand men out, no more, with light arms. They have no artillery, their air force is three Piper Cubs, and their navy is those illegal-immigrant runners tied up at Haifa. The Jews are outnumbered in soldiers forty to one, in population a hundred to one, in equipment a thousand to one, and in area five thousand to one. The Haganah has turned down my advice and the advice of every military man who has told them to pull in to a tight defense line. They are going to fight it out at every *moshav*, every *kibbutz*, every village. That means Gan Dafna, too. Do you want to hear any more?'

Kitty's voice was shaky. 'No ... I've heard enough. Isn't it strange, Bruce? One night when I was up on Mount Tabor with those young Palmach people I had the feeling that they were invincible ... the soldiers of God. Firelight and moonlight does things to me.'

'It does to me too, Kitty. Everything I've ever learned in my life in the service tells me that the Jews cannot win. Yet when you see what they have done with this land you are not a realist if you do not believe in miracles.'

'Oh, Bruce ... if I only could believe that way.'

'What an army these Jews have! Boys and girls without guns, without rank and uniform, and without pay. The Palmach commander is all of thirty years of age and his three brigade commanders are all under twenty-five. But there are things no military man counts that the Arabs must reckon with. The Jews are willing to lose every man, woman, and child to hold what they have. How much blood are Arabs willing to pay?'

'Can they win? Do you really believe it?'

'Call it divine intervention, if you will, or maybe ... let us say that the Jews have too many Ari Ben Canaans.'

Kitty returned to Gan Dafna the next day. She was surprised to find Jordana Ben Canaan awaiting in her office. The redhead *sabra* girl was ill at ease.

'What do you want, Jordana?' Kitty asked coolly. 'I'm going to be very busy.'

'We learned what you did for Ari,' Jordana mumbled awkwardly, 'and I want to tell you how grateful I am.'

'It seems that your intelligence system is getting information through again. I am sorry I had to delay my departure.'

Jordana blinked but did not answer.

'Don't take this personally,' Kitty said; 'I would have done the same thing for a wounded dog.'

Kitty made plans to leave. Then Dr Lieberman induced her to remain an extra few weeks. Extra personnel had been brought in and needed training to handle a hundred more children who had been smuggled into the country by Aliyah Bet. Housong was being put up as quickly as possible. Many of the new children were in bad shape, having been in DP camps for more than two years.

Once more she made her travel plans. Soon there were but two days left before she and Karen were to depart from Gan Dafna and Palestine.

At the end of August in the year 1947 the UNSCOP announced its majority and minority plans from Geneva. Each of the plans called for partition into separate Arab and Jewish entities with Jerusalem to be an international territory. There was no doubt as to the moral issue, for the United Nations Special Committee on Palestine called for the immediate immigration of six thousand Jews a month from the DP camps in Europe and the resumption of land sales to Jews.

The Jews had begged that the Negev Desert be added to their state. The Arabs had millions of square miles of undeveloped wastelands. The Jews wanted this small piece of a few thousand square miles in the hope that they could redeem it. The United Nations committee agreed.

Weary from a half century of heartbreak and sellout, the Yishuv Central and World Zionists announced acceptance of the compromise. The partitioned area, even with the Negev Desert, was an abortion of a state. It was, in fact, three strips of territory linked together by narrow corridors, resembling a chain of sausages. The Arabs had three strips of territory, larger in area, also linked by corridors. The Jews lost their eternal city, Jerusalem. They kept the Sharon and the parts of the Galilee they had pulled out of the swamplands. The Negev was wasteland. What was the use of fighting it further? It was a monstrosity but they accepted.

The Jews answered.

So did the Arabs. The partition would mean war, they said.

Despite the Arab threats, the UNSCOP resolved to present the partition plan to the General Assembly of the United Nations in New York in mid-September.

Every last detail had been taken care of. Again it was the eve of departure for Kitty and for Karen. At dawn Bruce Sutherland would drive them to the Lydda airport, and in the evening they would fly out to Rome. The heavy trunks had already been shipped ahead by boat. The cottage was ready to be vacated.

Kitty sat at her desk in her office with the final folders to be put away into the files. All that she had to do was to put them in the cabinet, close the drawer, and walk out of the door – forever.

She opened the first folder and picked up the top paper and looked at her notes.

MINNA (SURNAME UNKNOWN), AGE 7. Minna was born in Auschwitz concentration camp. Neither of her parents is known. We presume she is Polish. She was smuggled into Palestine by Aliyah Bet around the first of the year. When she was brought to Gan Dafna she was physically very weak and sick and showed many disturbances . . .

ROBERT DUBUAY, AGE 16. French nationality. Robert was found at the Bergen-Belsen concentration camp by British troops. Robert was thirteen years of age at the time and weighed fifty-eight pounds. The boy had previously been an eyewitness to the death of his mother, father, and a brother. A sister, who later was a suicide, had been forced into prostitution with German soldiers. Robert shows signs of hostility and . . .

SAMUEL KASNOWITZ, AGE 12. Estonian nationality. No known family survived. Samuel was hidden in the basement of a Christian family until he was forced to flee into a forest where he lived alone for two years . . .

ROBERT PUCCELLI, AGE 12. Italian nationality. No known family survived. Liberated at Auschwitz. We found him permanently crippled in his right arm as a result of beatings . . .

MARCIA KLASKIN, AGE 13. Rumanian nationality. No known family. Found at Lachau . . .

HANS BELMAN, AGE 10. Dutch nationality. No known family. Found at Auschwitz. Hidden by Christians . . .

The files went on and on. 'No survivors.'

'. . . this child has the dream so prevalent with those children at Auschwitz. She dreams she is packing a suitcase. This we know is a symbol of death, for suitcases were always packed the night before inmates were transferred to the Birkenau gas chambers.'

'The dream of smelling smoke is symbolic of the smell of burning flesh from the crematoriums.'

Bedwetting.

Overt hostility.

Nightmares.

Belligerence.

Kitty looked at a copy of the letter she had once written to Harriet Saltzman.

My dear friend:

You have asked my opinion of the common denominator, and the reason we are able to get such quick recoveries and dynamic results from those children who are borderline psychopaths. Well, I think you know that answer far better than I. You gave it to me the first time I saw you in Jerusalem. The wonder drug is called 'Eretz Israel.' The spirit is so strong here it seems unnatural. They desire only to live and fight for their country. I have never seen such energy or drive among adults, much less children . . .

Kitty Fremont closed the files.

She stood up and looked around the office for several moments, then quickly snapped off the light and closed the door behind her.

She stopped outside the building for a moment. Halfway up the hill toward Fort Esther she saw a campfire. The Gadna children, the ten- and twelve- and fourteen-year-old soldiers would be singing and dancing a *hora.*

She shined her flashlight on the ground and crossed the green. New trenches had been dug. Larger bomb shelters were being installed by the children's houses.

The statue of Dafna stood its vigil.

'*Shalom, Giveret* Kitty,' a group of youngsters shrilled as they raced to the recreation hall.

She opened her cottage door. The suitcases were all lined up near the door and marked with tags. The room was denuded of the personal little touches that she and Karen had put into it.

'Karen. Are you here, dear?'

There was a note on the kitchen table.

Dear Kitty:

The gang wanted to have a farewell campfire. I won't stay out too late.
Love.

KAREN

Kitty lit a cigarette and paced the room restlessly. She closed the draperies to shut off the view of the lights on the valley floor. She found herself holding the curtains which her children had made for her. Ten of them had already left Gan Dafna to go to the Palmach, that sad little army of the Jews.

It was stifling inside. She walked to the porch. The air was scented with rose blooms. Kitty walked down the dirt path between the rows of cottages all set inside little lawns and hedges and trees. She came to the end of the path and started to go back but was attracted by the light in Dr Lieberman's cottage.

Poor old fellow, Kitty thought. Both his son and daughter had left the university and were in the Negev Brigade of the Palmach, so far away. She walked to the door and knocked. The housekeeper, as old and as quaint as Dr Lieberman, led her to his study. The little hunchback was engrossed in translating some ancient Hebraic on a piece of pottery. A soft background of a Schumann symphony played on the radio. Dr Lieberman looked up and saw Kitty and set his magnifying glass down.

'*Shalom,*' Kitty said.

He smiled. She had never greeted him before in Hebrew. '*Shalom,* Kitty,' he said. 'It is such a nice word for good friends to use to say good-by.'

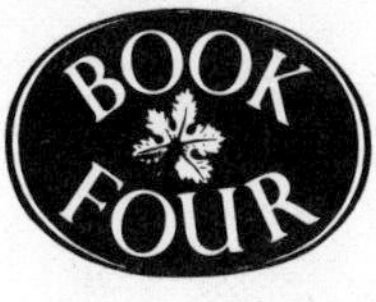

Awake in Glory

Be merciful unto me, O God, be merciful unto me, for my soul trusteth in thee: yea, in the shadow of thy wings will I make my refuge, until these calamities are overpast.

He shall send from heaven and save me; he reproacheth him that would swallow me up . . . God shall send forth his mercy and his truth.

My soul is among lions: and I lie even among them that are on fire, even the sons of men, whose teeth are spears and arrows, and their tongue a sharp sword.

They have prepared a net for my steps; my soul is bowed down: they have digged a pit before me, into the midst whereof they are fallen, themselves . . . Awake up, my glory . . . I will rouse the dawn . . .

THE FIFTY-SEVENTH PSALM OF DAVID

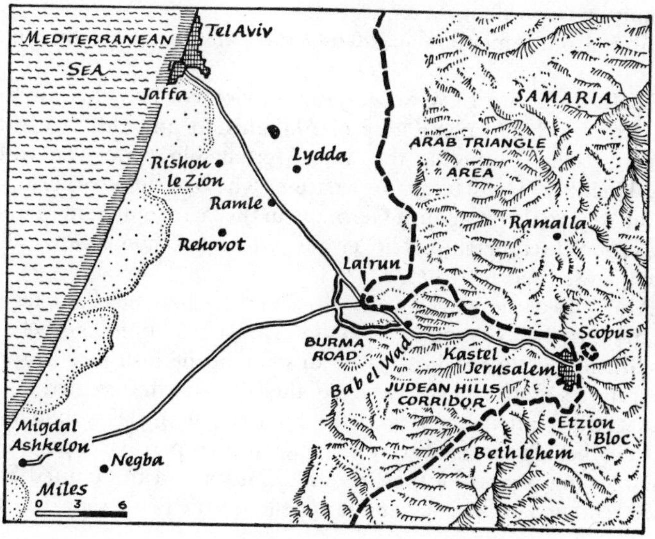

Chapter One

AUTUMN 1947
UNITED NATIONS
FLUSHING MEADOW, NEW YORK

The six-thousand-year-old case of the Jewish people was placed before the conscience of man.

Chaim Weizmann of the World Zionists and elder statesman Barak Ben Canaan led a twelve-man delegation to Flushing Meadow for the showdown. This delegation, seasoned by years of frustration and adversity, held no illusions.

An informal headquarters was established in Dr Weizmann's mid-Manhattan apartment. The delegates were assigned to the task of getting votes. Weizmann took as his personal job the alerting of Jews throughout the world to bring attention and pressure upon their governments.

Barak Ben Canaan worked quietly behind the scenes. It was his job to keep abreast of the hourly shifts in strength, analyze and plug up weak spots, maneuver and reassign his men to meet any sudden changes, and spearhead the committee-room debates.

After initial parliamentary jockeying, the Palestine partition went on the agenda.

The Arabs went into Lake Success sure of victory. They had obtained UN membership for the Moslem state of Afghanistan and the medieval feudal kingdom of Yemen, bringing the Arab-Moslem bloc to eleven votes in the General Assembly. These latter were nations who had sat out World War II in silence and declared war against Germany in the last moment to qualify for the United Nations membership. The Yishuv, which had contributed so richly to the Allied cause, had no vote.

The Arabs used the eleven votes to dangle as bait before delegates from smaller nations. In exchange for a vote against partition, they offered their votes as a bribe to those who aspired to some of the lush jobs in the UN.

The Arabs also took full advantage of the cold war that existed between the two giants, the United States and the Soviet Union, deftly playing off one against the other. From the start it was obvious that passage of partition would need the blessing of both of these nations. Russia and the United States had never before joined on an issue and it appeared little likely that they would do it now.

To win partition a two thirds majority was needed. The Yishuv had to get twenty-two votes merely to offset the eleven of the Arab-Moslem bloc. From that point on they had to obtain two votes to each one the Arabs obtained. Mathematically the Arabs needed only a half dozen additional votes to eliminate partition. With their oil as an additional bargaining factor, it would be an easy matter.

The non-Arab world press generally favored partition. Moreover, Jan Smuts of South Africa and the great liberal, Jan Masaryk of Czechoslovakia, were out on the front of the battle lines. The Danes, the Norwegians, and a few others could be counted upon to the end. Sentiment for partition was strong, but sympathy would not be enough.

Then the Big Four powers, the mighty ones, abandoned the Yishuv.

France, who had been overtly friendly to illegal immigration, suddenly reverted to caution. Arabs in the French colonies of Morocco, Algeria, and Tunisia were rumbling with unrest. A French vote for partition could well trigger an explosion among them.

The Soviet Union had different reasons. For over two decades Zionism had been outlawed. The Russians set out upon a program to erase Judaism by a slow abrasive process. While on paper they granted religious freedom, it was nonexistent in reality. There was no Jewish press, theater, school or community life. Synagogues were limited; there was but one in all of Moscow. No member of a synagogue was allowed membership in the Communist party. By these means the Russians hoped to eliminate Judaism in the new generations. Zionism and the partition of Palestine could serve to remind the Russian Jews that they were Jews, and partition was therefore opposed. With the Soviet Union went the powerful Slav bloc.

The position of the United States was the most disheartening setback the Yishuv suffered. The President, the press and people were sympathetic, but international politics put the United States officially into an equivocal position.

To support partition meant splitting the cornerstone of the Western world by breaking the Anglo-American solidarity. Great Britain still dominated the Middle East; American foreign policy was linked to Britain's. To vote for partition was publicly to rebuff Britain.

More than this, the United States faced a greater threat. If partition was voted, the Arabs threatened war. If war came, the United Nations would be bound to enforce peace, and the Soviet Union or her satellites would put troops into the Middle East as part of an international force. This was America's greatest fear and the reason she chose to hedge on partition.

Of the four major powers, Great Britain struck the most deadly blows against partition. When the British turned the mandate question over to the United Nations they thought that the United Nations could not reach a solution and that Britain would therefore be asked to remain in Palestine. Then UNSCOP went to Palestine, investigated, and reached a decision that censured British rule. Moreover, the world had learned that England's hundred-thousand-man army had not been able to cope with the determined Jews of the Haganah, Palmach, Maccabees and Aliyah Bet, a terrible blow to British prestige.

Britain had to maintain her position of power in the Middle East and to do so she had to save face with the Arabs by scuttling partition. Britain played on America's fear of Russian troops getting into the Middle East by announcing that she would withdraw her garrison by August of 1948. Further, she would not use her force in Palestine to enforce a United Nations decision. Thus checkmating the United States, Britain caused the Commonwealth countries to abstain from voting and applied pressure to those small European countries who were tied to her economically.

The rest of the picture was equally black for the Yishuv. Belgium, Holland,

and Luxembourg bowed before British pressure. Other small countries whom the Yishuv had counted upon began to balk.

The position of the Asian countries was variable. They changed their minds and shifted their votes hourly. However, it appeared that the Asians would side with the Arabs as a gesture to the Western powers of their eternal hatred of colonial imperialism, and as evidence of their purchase of the Arab theme that the Jews were representatives of the West in a part of the world where they did not belong.

Greece had an intense dislike for the Arabs but a hundred and fifty thousand Greek nationals lived in Egypt. Egypt made painfully clear the fate of this minority if the Greeks voted for partition.

Ethiopia had little love for Egypt but was tied to her geographically and economically.

Romulo of the Philippines stood against partition.

The Colombians were overtly anti-Jewish.

The Central and South American countries held one third of the United Nations' fifty-seven votes. Most of these countries were completely removed from the issue and neutral. The Yishuv wanted Jerusalem as the capital of their state; they felt that without Jerusalem a Jewish state would be a body without a heart. The South and Central American countries were predominantly Catholic. The Vatican wanted Jerusalem internationalized. If the Yishuv pressed for Jerusalem there was a risk of losing this vital bloc of votes.

But the Yishuv continued to labor, hoping for the miracle which was obviously needed. Throughout September and October, Dr Weizmann and Barak Ben Canaan were an inspiration to the delegation. They never despaired at the frequent reversals and were never stampeded into errors in strategy.

The greatest weapon the Yishuv had was truth. It was the truth that the neutral UNSCOP had found in Palestine: the truth that Palestine was a tyranny-ridden police state; the truth, seen through the thin veil of Arab deception, of the Arab failure to advance culturally, economically, and socially from the Dark Ages; the truth apparent in the Jewish cities that had sprung from sand and the Jewish fields that had been made to grow from desolation; the truth of industry and ingenuity; the truth – implicit in the DP camps – of the humanity of the Jewish case.

Granados of Guatemala, Lester Pearson of Canada, Evatt of Australia, Masaryk of Czechoslovakia, Smuts of South Africa, Fabregat of Uruguay, and a lot of little men from little nations would not let the truth die at Flushing Meadow.

Finally, in November of that autumn of 1947, 'The Miracle of Lake Success' began to unfold.

First came a cautiously worded statement from the United States in favor of the 'principle' of partition.

Then came a move that rocked the world. After outlawing Zionism for over two decades, the Soviet Union made one of its startling reversals and announced itself as favoring partition. The news was released after a secret caucus of the Slav bloc; Vishinsky orated in impassioned tones of the rivers of Jewish blood shed and the justice of a Jewish homeland.

Behind this humanitarian mask the Russians had made a shrewd political maneuver. First, they openly mistrusted the Arabs. They realized that the Arab anger was merely a verbal expedient; Russia could vote for partition today and buy the Arabs back tomorrow. Meanwhile the Soviet strategy was to brand Great Britain a tyrant, at the same time making a move that could possibly lead to a Russian foothold in the Middle East. Russia knew that if she voted for partition the United States had to follow suit or lose face around the world as a friend of justice. This in turn meant a break in Anglo-American solidarity. Finally, the Soviet Union stood to gain tremendous prestige value from its 'humanitarian' proclamation. And so, inadvertently, the Yishuv suddenly found a strange bedfellow.

As the two great powers made their carefully worded statements for partition, the halls of the United States were filled with rumors that cropped up every hour.

The mammoth chess game went on. In the dramatic maneuverings Granados and Pearson became key figures. After much labor these two succeeded in the momentous achievement of closeting the United States and the Soviet Union in a meeting. They emerged from their conference with an electrifying joint statement of definite support of partition.

The Arabs girded for a last-ditch fight to keep the partition resolution from reaching the floor of the General Assembly. Soon it became apparent that a test vote would take place: to get the resolution to the General Assembly only a majority vote was needed, but this vote would indicate the strength of both sides. The vote came and the move passed and the resolution went to the General Assembly – but the roof caved in on the Yishuv. The count was twenty-five in favor, thirteen against, and seventeen abstentions, with two absent. If the same line-up held on the final vote for partition, the Yishuv would not get its needed two thirds majority. France, Belgium, Luxembourg, The Netherlands, and New Zealand had abstained. Paraguay and the Philippines were absent.

The Arabs saw that many 'sure' partition votes had abandoned the Yishuv, and the Jews did not have the required number. Confident that they could bag an extra vote or two, the Arabs now switched tactics and pressed for the showdown on the assembly floor.

WEDNESDAY, NOVEMBER 27, 1947

The final debates raged. The Yishuv delegation sat in its special section of the General Assembly looking like men prepared for the executioner. The jolt of the test vote had shaken them to the core. As the arguments continued, their prospects turned darker by the hour.

Greece, expected to abstain out of friendship to the United States, declared openly against partition, fearing what the Egyptians would do to their nationals.

The Philippines, expected to follow the United States, reversed again.

Haiti was suddenly without instructions. Liberia went back on the fence and Siam crossed back to the Arabs.

It was 'Black Wednesday' for the Jews.

As the day wore on, the friends of the Yishuv employed a desperation move to talk the clock out and stall the vote. The next day would be American Thanksgiving Day and a holiday. It offered twenty-four precious hours to muster the needed votes. The filibuster went on until an adjournment was called.

The Yishuv delegation assembled quickly in a caucus room. Everyone spoke at once.

'Quiet!' Barak roared. 'We have twenty-four hours. Let's not panic.'

Dr Weizmann came into the room excitedly. 'I have received a message from Paris that Léon Blum is personally interceding to get the French vote. Feeling for partition is running very high in Paris.' It was cheering news, for the former Jewish premier of France was still a powerful voice.

'Can't we appeal to the United States to get Greece and the Philippines into line?'

The delegate who worked with the Americans shook his head. 'Truman has issued absolute orders that the United States is not to pressure any delegation. They won't budge from that position.'

'What a time to become honorable.'

The phone rang. Weizmann lifted the receiver. 'Good ... good,' he said. He held his hand over the mouthpiece. 'Shmuel from downtown. Good ... good ... *Shalom.*' He replaced the phone. 'The Ethiopians have agreed to abstain,' he announced. Ethiopia, under pressure from her neighbor Egypt, had been expected to vote against partition. The abstention decision showed great courage on the part of Haile Selassie.

A newspaperman close to the Yishuv delegation knocked on the door and entered. 'I thought you fellows would like to know that there has been a revolution in Siam and the Siamese delegate has been discredited.' A yell of happiness went up at this Arab loss of another vote.

Barak made a quick run down of the roll call of nations – he knew it by heart – and calculated the vote shifts.

'How does it look, Barak?'

'Well, if Haiti and Liberia go with us and France comes in and we don't lose any more ground, we may just squeeze through.'

It was still too close for comfort. Grimly and tensely they talked over the final assignments. They could not afford to lose a single vote at this stage.

There was a knock on the door and their champion, Granados of Guatemala, entered. There were tears in his eyes.

'The President of Chile has just sent personal instructions for his delegation to abstain. The delegation has resigned in protest.'

'Impossible!' Dr Weizmann cried. 'The President is the honorary chairman of the Chilean Zionists.'

The stark reality, the naked hopelessness of the situation crashed down on all of them. Who knew what pressure had been brought to bear on the President of Chile? Who knew where the screws would be turned in the next twenty-four hours?

FRIDAY, NOVEMBER 29, 1947

The gavel rapped. The General Assembly of the United Nations was ordered into session.

'We shall have a roll call of nations on the partition resolution. A two thirds majority is needed for passage. Delegates will answer in one of three ways; for, against, or abstain.'

A solemn quiet fell over the great hall.

'Afghanistan.'

'Afghanistan votes against.'

The Yishuv had lost the first vote. Barak marked it on a pad.

'Argentina.'

'The government of Argentina wishes to abstain.'

'We have to cut the abstentions down,' Barak whispered; 'they could kill us.'

'Australia.'

Everyone leaned forward as Evatt got to his feet with the first vote of a British Commonwealth nation.

'Australia votes in favor of partition,' Evatt said.

A buzz of speculation went up. Weizmann leaned close to Barak's ear. 'Do you think it might be a trend in the Commonwealth?'

'We'll just have to count them one at a time ... we can't tell.'

'Belgium.'

'Belgium votes for partition.'

Another buzz arose in the great hall. A few days earlier Belgium had abstained on the test vote. At the last minute Spaak had defied British pressure.

'Bolivia.'

'Bolivia votes for partition.'

'Brazil.'

'Brazil favors partition.'

The South American countries were sticking. A vital vote was coming up with the next call. If the Soviet Union had a double cross up its sleeve, the world would know it now, for a satellite, White Russia, was next.

'Byelorussia.'

'White Russia votes for partition.'

In unison the Jews breathed a sigh of relief. The Slav bloc was going to come in. The signs were bright.

'Canada.'

Lester Pearson arose and spoke firmly. 'Canada votes for partition.' The second of the Commonwealth countries had gone against Great Britain.

'Chile.'

Another delegate arose in place of the chief who had resigned in protest to his orders to abstain. 'Chile has been ordered to abstain,' he said slowly.

'China.'

China, jockeying to become the dominant power in Asia, feared to go against the Moslems of India and Pakistan.

'China abstains.'

It was a setback for the Yishuv.

'Costa Rica.'

The Costa Rican delegate had been approached by the Arabs who tried to bribe his vote by a promise to support him for an important United Nations post. He stood and looked at the Egyptian delegation.

'Costa Rica votes in favor of partition.'

The man who would not be bought sat down smiling.

'Cuba.'

'Cuba votes against partition.'

This came as a complete and unexpected shock to the Yishuv.

'Czechoslovakia.'

'Czechoslovakia votes for partition,' Jan Masaryk said.

'Denmark favors partition.'

'The Dominican Republic favors partition.'

'Egypt.'

'Egypt votes against and will not be bound by this outrage!'

The gavel rapped and order came about slowly, following the Egyptian's angry outburst.

'Ecuador.'

'Ecuador votes for.'

'Ethiopia.'

'Ethiopia . . . abstains.'

It was a bombshell! The faces of all the Arab delegates turned to the Ethiopian with stunned expressions. The Syrian delegate shook his fist angrily.

'France.'

The first of the big powers, reluctant France had its turn. Parodi came to his feet slowly. An abstention by France could prove disastrous for the Yishuv. Had Blum and the French people succeeded?

'The Republic of France votes *for* partition,' Parodi said in a voice filled with satisfaction.

An expectant murmur went up. It was the first excited awareness that the miracle might actually take place!

'Guatemala.'

Granados, the champion of partition, spoke. 'For,' he said.

'Greece.'

'Greece votes against partition.'

In the last moment the Greeks had bowed to Egyptian blackmail.

'Haiti.'

Haiti was a key vote that had suddenly been left without instructions in the last two days. 'The government of Haiti has just sent instructions for this delegation to vote in favor of partition.'

'Honduras.'

'Honduras wishes to abstain.'

'Iceland.'

'Iceland votes for partition.' The world's oldest republic had worked to make the world's newest republic.

'India.'

'India votes against partition.'

'Iran.'

'Iran votes against.'

'Iraq.'

'Iraq votes against and we will never recognize the Jews! There will be bloodshed over this day. We vote against!'

'Lebanon.'

'Lebanon votes *against* partition,' Malik said.

'How does the vote stand?' Weizmann asked Barak.

'Fifteen for, eight against, and seven abstentions.'

It was not too encouraging. So far the Jews were running one vote shy of their two thirds, and the deadly abstentions were piling up.

'What do you think, Barak?'

'We will know when they come to the next three South American countries.'

'I think we shall have to start pulling away. We are near the halfway mark and we show no decided strength,' Weizmann said.

'Liberia.'

'Liberia votes for partition.'

'Luxembourg.'

Another small country under duress in the British economic sphere.

'Luxembourg votes for partition.'

And again the British had been directly rebuked. The Yishuv now stood one vote over two thirds.

'Mexico.'

'Mexico abstains.'

The entire Yishuv delegation winced.

'Netherlands.'

'The Netherlands votes for partition.'

'New Zealand.'

'New Zealand votes for.'

'Nicaragua . . . for.'

'Norway . . . for.'

'Pakistan votes against partition.'

The pivot votes were coming up. 'If we get over the next four I think we are in,' Barak said shakily.

'Panama.'

'The Republic of Panama favors partition.'

'Paraguay.'

'Paraguay has just received new instructions not to abstain . . . instead, Paraguay votes for partition.'

'Peru.'

'Peru favors partition.'

'Philippines.'

For a breathless second the world stood still. Romulo had been called away from Flushing Meadow. The alternate stood up.

'The Philippines votes *for* partition!'

A roar went up! The members of the Jewish delegation looked to each other with dazed expressions.

'Dear God,' Barak said, 'I think we have made it.'

'Poland.'

'Poland votes in favor of partition.'

The Jews were beginning to pull away. Poland had paid its small indemnity for the years of persecution.

Siam was not represented.

'Saudi Arabia.'

The white-robed Arab screamed out against partition in a hate-filled voice.

'Sweden.'

'Sweden is for partition.'

And now the Arabs had their backs to the wall as they went into the last ditch.

'Syria, *against*!'

'Turkey votes *against* partition.'

Barak scanned the balance of the roster quickly. The Arabs still had a breath of life. They now had twelve votes with one more certain. If some last-minute change came through it could upset everything.

'Ukraine.'

'For.'

'Union of South Africa.'

'For.'

'Union of Soviet Socialist Republics.'

Vishinsky got to his feet. 'The Union of Soviet Socialist Republics votes for partition.'

'The United Kingdom of Great Britain.'

The hall became silent. The British delegate got to his feet and looked around the room ashen-faced. At this awesome moment he stood alone. The Commonwealth nations had deserted. France had deserted. The United States of America had deserted.

'His Majesty's Government wishes to abstain,' the Englishman said in a shaken voice.

'The United States of America.'

'The United States of America votes for partition.'

It was all over. The reporters scrambled for their phones to flash the news around the world as the last vote was cast. Yemen gave the Arabs their thirteenth vote. Yugoslavia abstained in deference to a large Moslem minority. Professor Fabregat of Uruguay and the delegate of Venezuela gave the partition plan its thirty-second and thirty-third votes.

In Tel Aviv pandemonium broke loose.

In the final analysis, the Jewish victory was crushing. The Arabs had thirteen votes, and eleven of these were Arab or Moslem nations. The twelfth was a vote coerced from the Greeks. The thirteenth vote, Cuba, represented the only nation on the face of the earth that the Arabs were able to convince by force of argument.

Those men who had won this battle at Flushing Meadows and had seen the miracle unfold were realists. The Jews in Tel Aviv celebrated only for the moment. Ben Gurion and the leaders of the Yishuv knew that even a greater miracle would have to take place to win independence for the Jewish state, as the cry 'Perish Judea!' arose like thunder on Arab lips.

Chapter Two

KUWATLY, PRESIDENT OF SYRIA: *We live or die with Palestine!*

AL KULTA NEWSPAPER, CAIRO: *Five hundred thousand Iraqis prepare for this holy war. 150,000 Syrians will storm over the Palestine borders and the mighty Egyptian army will throw the Jews into the sea if they dare to declare their state.*

JAMIL MARDAM, SYRIAN PREMIER: *Stop talking, my brother Moslems. Arise and wipe out the Zionist scourge.*

IBN SAUD, KING OF SAUDI ARABIA: *There are fifty million Arabs. What does it matter if we lose ten million people to kill all the Jews? The price is worth it.*

SELEH HARB PASHA, MOSLEM YOUTH: *Unsheath your swords against the Jews! Death to them all! Victory is ours!*

SHEIK HASSAN AL BANNAH, MOSLEM BROTHERHOOD: *All Arabs shall arise and annihilate the Jews! We shall fill the sea with their corpses.*

AKRAM YAUYTAR, MUFTI SPOKESMAN: *Fifty million Arabs shall fight to the last drop of blood.*

HAJ AMIN EL HUSSEINI, MUFTI OF JERUSALEM: *I declare a holy war, my Moslem brothers! Murder the Jews! Murder them all.*

AZZAM PASHA, SECRETARY GENERAL OF THE ARAB LEAGUE: *This will be a war of extermination, and momentous massacre which will be spoken of like the Mongolian Massacres.*

Other Arab leaders and the Arab press and radio spoke out in equally appropriate words in answer to the United Nations' partition of Palestine.

On December 1, 1947, one day after the UN vote, Dr Khalidi of the Arab Higher Committee in Palestine called a general strike in which inflamed mobs broke out in wild rioting. They crossed into the Jewish commercial center of Jerusalem and burned and looted while British troops stood by idly.

In Aleppo and Aden and throughout the Arab world, other mobs, goaded by their leaders, tore into Jewish ghetto quarters with murder, rape, and plunder in their hearts.

Instead of forming an international police force to full the gap, the United Nations bogged down in the formation of committees and in endless talk. The body seemed to want to believe that partition was going to be enforced without dependence on a single gun.

The Jews were more realistic. A Jewish state had been given an unalterable basis of legality, but if the Jews intended to declare the statehood after the British left, they would have to face the Arab hordes alone.

Could a half million ill-armed people hold back a flood of fifty million hate-crazed Arabs? They would not only have to face the Arabs inside Palestine, all around them on a hundred fronts, but the regular national armies as well.

Chaim Weizmann set out to organize the world Zionist groups to launch fund-raising campaigns for the purchase of arms.

Barak Ben Canaan remained at Lake Success to head the Yishuv delegation and battle out the details of partition and look for arms support.

The great question became, 'Would the Jews declare their independence?'

The Arabs had no intention of waiting until May to find out. Although they held their regular armies back, they went about raising various 'Armies of Liberation' who were alleged volunteers, and they got mountains of arms in to the Palestine Arabs.

Haj Amin el Husseini, the Nazi agent, was back in business. He set up headquarters in Damascus. Money for the Palestine 'volunteers' was extorted from Arabs all over the Middle East. Kawukji, the brigand who had served the Mufti in the 1936-39 riots, was again commissioned 'generalissimo.' Kawukji had been forced to flee Iraq when his part in the coup to deliver Iraq to the Germans was discovered. He spent the period of the war in Germany, acquired a wife there, and along with the Mufti had been pardoned from trial as a war criminal by the British.

Kawukji's agents scoured the stink holes of Damascus, Beirut, and Bagdad recruiting the dregs of humanity, thieves, murderers, highway robbers, dope runners, and white slavers, which he picturesquely dubbed the 'Forces of the Yarmuk,' after a battle the Arabs had won centuries before. These Kawukji 'volunteers' were trained by other 'volunteers,' officers from the Syrian Army. Almost immediately Kawukji's forces began slipping over the Lebanese, Syrian, and Jordan borders into Palestine Arab villages. The main base was set up in Nablus, in a predominantly Arab area in Samaria, north of Jerusalem.

In the meantime, the Jews remained arms-starved. The British continued to blockade the Palestine coast. They even refused to allow immigrants to come from the Cyprus detention camps, where Aliyah Bet agents were speeding military training.

Yishuv agents searched the world desperately for arms.

Then came the devastating announcement that the United States had declared a 'plague on both houses' by an arms boycott of the Middle East. This boycott, reminiscent of the boycott of the Spanish people fighting Mussolini and Hitler, actually worked for the Arabs, who could obtain all the arms they wished.

As the battle lines were drawn, the Yishuv Central confronted the blunt fact that it had only the Palmach of some four thousand fighters fully armed and trained. The Maccabees could raise only another thousand men and could be counted upon only for limited co-operation.

Avidan did have a few things working in his favor. He had several thousand reserves in the Haganah who had been combat trained by the British in World War II. He had settlement defense which had been organized for twenty years and he had a good intelligence system. On the other side, the Arabs had a staggering superiority of manpower and arms, daily augmented by the continual infiltration of Kawukji's bloodthirsty irregulars. The Arabs had at least one excellent commander in Abdul Kadar, a cousin of the Mufti.

As if the Jews did not have enough to contend with, there was the additional factor of the British. Whitehall was hopeful that the Yishuv would send out a mercy call, dropping the partition idea and asking the British to remain. But the Jews would not ask for help on these terms.

In theory, as they withdrew the British were to give the Taggart forts to the side with the greatest population in each area. But as they pulled back from sector after sector the British commander often turned these key places over to the Arabs when they should have gone to the Jews.

Former Nazi soldiers began appearing in the ranks of the 'Forces of the Yarmuk' and other 'liberation volunteers.' For the first time in its existence, the Haganah took off its wraps as the Jews called for a general mobilization.

It was not long until the first shots were heard. In the Huleh Valley, Arab villagers, along with irregulars, fired on the communal settlements of Ein Zeitim, Biriya, and Ami Ad, but the attacks were little more than sniping actions and were repulsed.

Each day the activity increased. There were constant ambushes on the roads so that soon Jewish transport, the lifeline of the Yishuv, was in danger any time it came near or passed through an Arab village.

In the cities the action was even more violent. In Jerusalem the air was filled with flying debris of bomb blasts. The Arabs fired from the sacred walls of the Old City, and the city was divided into battle zones with communications between sections made only on risk of death. In the streets between Tel Aviv and Jaffa sniper posts and barricades appeared.

In Haifa the worst so far of the fighting took place. In retaliation for Maccabee raids the Arabs rioted at the refinery where both Jews and Arabs worked and more than fifty Jews were killed.

Abdul Kadar was able to organize the Arabs in a manner that Kawukji and Safwat in the north could not do. Kadar, working around Jerusalem, formulated a master plan, based on the realization that neither the Palestine Arabs nor the irregulars were organized and skilled enough to carry out sustained attacks. Kadar also realized that the Jews would hang on desperately to every settlement and make the Arabs bleed. He needed easy victories to encourage his people. Kadar settled upon two tactics. First, he would isolate the Jewish settlements and starve them out. Second, he would step up his hit-and-run attacks on transport.

Kadar's strategy proved effective. The Arabs had freedom of movement while the Jews were forced to maintain tight positions. Day by day more Jewish settlements fell under siege.

Abdul Kadar centered his efforts on Jerusalem. The road from Tel Aviv to Jerusalem ran through the perilous Judean mountains and was dotted with Arab villages which commanded several key heights. Kadar wanted to cut off and starve out the hundred-thousand Jews in New Jerusalem. It would be a vital blow to the Yishuv.

To combat the effort, the Yishuv used makeshift armored cars to conduct large-scale convoys. These convoys were vulnerable, and the road to Jerusalem became littered with wrecked vehicles. Inside Jerusalem shortages developed, people had to move about in armored buses and children played inside sniper range.

With Arab strength growing daily in new arms and irregulars and no relief in sight for the Jews, Abdul Kadar was content to play a waiting game through the winter, then lop off the frozen and starved settlements one by one in the springtime.

The Yishuv leaders appealed to the British to patrol the Jerusalem-Tel Aviv road, on the grounds of the inhumanity of starving out a civilian population. The British refused.

This quick Arab action, under a good leader, set the Yishuv down in the initial gambit. The Haganah gave orders to turn every *kibbutz* and *moshav* into a miniature Tobruk. The Jews had paid in blood for their land and if the Arabs were going to take it, it would also have to be in blood.

The battle of the roads opened the first phase of the war. The decision of whether or not to declare independence still hung in the balance.

Ari Ben Canaan made a slow recovery from his wound. This posed a problem for Avidan, who wanted Ari to command one of the three Palmach Brigades. These included Hanita Brigade – the Spearhead – which covered the Galilee. the Hillmen in Judea, and the Desert Rats in the south.

The Palmach commanders from brigade level on down were young men in their twenties, often headstrong, who considered themselves an elite corps. The backbone of the Palmach consisted of boys and girls from the *kibbutzim*. They were communal in nature, even in military structure. Often they were politically opposed to the Yishuv Central and as often as not they resented Haganah authority.

Ari Ben Canaan was mature for his age. He could appreciate the necessity of grasping over-all strategy and carrying out orders instead of waging a private war. Submission to authority as part of a team made him desirable as a Palmach commander, but Ari was simply not yet strong enough to carry the burden. Each brigade covered a vast area in rugged terrain. The Palmach lived under the crudest of conditions. Ari's leg was still too weak.

Avidan instead assigned Ari as Haganah commander to one of the vital places of Palestine, Ari's own Huleh Valley. His command extended from the northern edge of the Sea of Galilee, included Safed, and continued up the valley in a fingerlike jut of land that pressed between the Lebanese and Syrian borders. Slightly south, a third Arab country, Trans-Jordan, bordered it at the Yarmuk River.

Ari's area was one of the chief crossing places for Kawukhi's irregulars. If all-out war came and the regular Arab armies invaded Palestine, the Huleh Valley was certain to be one of the first objectives. The Arabs would attempt a junction of converging forces there, and if they took the Huleh they would use it as a base from which to capture the entire Galilee and to cut the Jews in half by striking between Haifa and Tel Aviv.

There were a dozen or more long-established *kibbutzim* and a few *moshavim* and villages in Ari's area, including his own Yad El, where the tough pioneer farmers could well handle the irregulars and Palestine Arabs. The settlements on the valley floor were close enough together to make it difficult for the Arabs to use their isolation and siege tactics.

The hills on the Lebanese border presented another problem. Here Fort Esther was the key. According to British agreement, Fort Esther was to be turned over to Ari because the Huleh was predominantly Jewish. With Fort Esther in Haganah hands, Ari could maintain excellent control of the border.

Ari's headquarters were in the centrally-located *kibbutz* of Ein Or – the Fountain of Light – which his uncle Akiva had helped establish. He had a few hundred Palmach troops from the Spearhead Brigade; he had David, Zev Gilboa, and Joab Yarkoni as aides. The Haganah organization in each of his settlements was strong: one hundred per cent subscribed in personnel quota and well trained.

The lack of arms was what plagued him, as it plagued the Yishuv all over Palestine. Every day settlement commanders harassed him for guns. He had none, Avidan had none.

There were two glaring weak spots in Ari's area: Gan Dafna and Safed. Ari felt that he would be able to protect the children's village once Fort Esther was turned over to him. So long as the road to Gan Dafna through Abu Yesha stayed open, the village was not in danger.

Safed was a headache. In fact no commander in Palestine had a larger headache. When the Jews made the decision to hold every settlement at any cost there were a few exceptions considered 'untenable.' Safed was one of the exceptions.

The city was an island in a sea of forty thousand Arabs in surrounding villages. Inside Safed the Jews were outnumbered twelve to one. Most of Safed's Jews were the Cabalists who knew nothing about fighting. In all, the Haganah in Safed had but two hundred able-bodied fighters to face more than two thousand Arabs and irregulars.

The Mufti had made Safed one of his first goals. Several hundred heavily armed irregulars had infiltrated and waited only for British withdrawal.

From the standpoint of interior strategy, the Jews were in even worse position. All three key points in the city would be in the hands of the Arabs: a police station right over the Jewish sector, the acropolis atop the town, and the Taggart fort on Mount Canaan would all be turned over to the Arabs.

In arms the Arabs had enough to carry on a war for months. The Jews had forty rifles, forty-two homemade Stens, one machine gun, and one mortar, plus a few hundred homemade grenades. They could arm less than a hundred men.

Safed appeared so obviously indefensible that the British even pled with Ari to let them evacuate the Jews.

Remez, the hotel owner and Haganah commander, paced back and forth before Ari's desk. Sutherland sat quietly in a corner and puffed a cigar.

'Well?' Ari asked at last.

Remez leaned on the desk. 'We want to stay in Safed, Ari. We want to fight it out to the last man. We have decided.'

'Good. I am glad.'

'Give us more arms.'

Ari leaped to his feet angrily. Twenty times a day he heard 'give us more arms.'

'Sutherland, you pray to Christ; you pray to Confucius, Remez; and I'll pray to Allah. Maybe rifles will rain down on us like manna from heaven.'

'Do you trust Major Hawks?' Sutherland asked, speaking of the British commander in the area.

'Hawks has always been a friend,' Ari answered.

'All right, then,' Sutherland said, 'perhaps you'd better listen to him. He guarantees British protection if you evacuate Safed. Otherwise, he guarantees there will be a massacre after he pulls his troops out.'

Ari blew a long breath. 'Did Hawks say when he is leaving?'

'No, he doesn't know yet.'

'So long as Hawks remains in Safed we are relatively safe. The Arabs won't try too much with him around. Perhaps the situation will change for the better before he pulls out.'

'Hawks may have his heart in the right place but his own commanders are tying his hands,' Sutherland said.

'The Arabs have already started sniping at us and are attacking our convoys,' Remez said.

'So . . . ? Are you now going to run at the first shot?'

'Ari.' Remez looked at him levelly. 'I was born in Safed. I have lived there all my life. Even to this day I can still hear the chanting from the Arab quarters that we heard in 1929. We didn't know what it meant until we saw those crazed mobs pouring into our sector. They were our friends – but they were insane. I can see those pitiful Cabalists being dragged into the streets to have their heads cut off. I was only a boy then. We heard the Arabs chanting again in 1936 . . . we knew what it meant that time. For three years we ran and cowed in the old Turkish fort every time a loud noise came from the Arab section. We want to stay this time. We aren't going to run again. Not even the old ones. This time they won't have it easy, believe me . . . but, Ari, there is a limit to what can be asked of us.'

Ari regretted having spoken sharply to Remez. Yes, the decision to remain in Safed took tremendous courage. 'Go on back, Remez. Try to keep things calm. You can count on Major Hawks to keep it from getting out of control. In the meantime I'll give you a priority on everything I get.'

When they were gone Ari sat down and gritted his teeth. What could he do? Perhaps he would be able to send fifty Palmach troops when the British left. It was little better than nothing. What could anyone do? There were two hundred Safeds all over Palestine. Fifty men here, ten men there. If Kawukji, Safwat and Kadar knew how desperate the situation was they would be making frontal assaults all over Palestine. There just wasn't enough ammunition to stop sustained and determined attacks. Ari feared that the first time the Arabs tried one and learned how meager the Jews' arms were, it would become a stampede.

David Ben Ami came in from an inspection tour of the northernmost settlements.

'*Shalom*, Ari,' David said. 'I met Remez and Sutherland on the road. Remez looks a little green around the gills.'

'He has plenty of reason. Well, did you find anything interesting?'

'The Arabs have started sniping at Kfar Giladi and Metulla. Kfar Szold fears the Syrian villagers may try something. Everyone is dug in, all defenses built around the children's houses. They all want arms.'

'Arms . . . what else is new? Where is the sniping coming from?'

'Aata.'

'Good old Aata,' Ari said. 'When the British leave it's going to be my first objective. When I was a boy they tried beating me up when I went to get the grain milled. They've been looking for a fight ever since. It is my guess that half of Kawukji's men are crossing over through Aata.'

'Or Abu Yesha,' David said.

Ari looked up angrily. David knew it was a sore point.

'I have reliable friends in Abu Yesha,' Ari said.

'Then they must have told you the irregulars are infiltrating through there.'

Ari did not answer.

'Ari, many times you have told me that my weakness is allowing sentiment to cloud my judgment. I know how close you are to those people, but you've got to go up there and make the muktar understand.'

Ari got up and walked away. 'I'll have to talk to Taha.'

David picked up the dispatches from Ari's desk, scanned them, and dropped them. He paced beside Ari, then stood looking out of the window in the direction of Jerusalem. A wave of moroseness washed over him.

Ari slapped him on the shoulder. 'It will work out.'

David shook his head slowly. 'Things are getting desperate in Jerusalem,' he said in a doleful monotone. 'The convoys are having more and more trouble getting through. If this keeps up they will be starving in another few weeks.'

Ari knew how the siege of his beloved city was affecting David. 'You want to go to Jerusalem, don't you?'

'Yes,' David said, 'but I don't want to let you down.'

'If you must, of course I'll relieve you.'

'Thanks, Ari. Will you be able to manage?'

'Sure . . . as soon as this damned leg stops acting up. See here, David . . . I don't want you to leave.'

'I'll stay until you are fit.'

'Thanks. By the way, how long since you've seen Jordana?'

'Weeks.'

'Why don't you go up to Gan Dafna tomorrow and look over the situation? Stay up there a few days and take a real good look.'

David smiled. 'You have such a nice way of persuasion.'

There was a knock on the door of Kitty's office.

'Come in,' she said.

Jordana Ben Canaan entered. 'I would like a word with you if you are not too busy, Mrs Fremont.'

'Very well.'

'David Ben Ami is going to come up and inspect the defenses this morning. We would like to have a staff meeting afterwards.'

'I'll be there,' Kitty said.

'Mrs Fremont. I want to speak to you before the meeting. As you know, I am the commander here and in the future you and I will have to work in close co-operation. I wish to express the opinion that I have complete confidence in you. In fact, I consider it fortunate for Gan Dafna that you are here.'

Kitty looked at Jordana curiously.

'I believe,' Jordana continued, 'that it would be good for the morale of the entire village if we set our personal feelings aside.'

'I believe you are right.'

'Good. I am glad we have an understanding.'

'Jordana ... just what is our situation here?'

'We are not in too much immediate danger. Of course, we will all feel better about things when Fort Esther is turned over to the Haganah.'

'Suppose something goes wrong and the Arabs get Fort Esther? And ... suppose the road through Abu Yesha is closed.'

'Then the prospects become very unpleasant.'

Kitty arose and paced the room slowly. 'Please understand that I don't want to interfere in military matters, but looking at it realistically – we may fall under siege.'

'There is that possibility,' Jordana said.

'We have many babies here. Can't we talk over plans to evacuate them and some of the younger children?'

'Where shall we evacuate them to?'

'I don't know. A safer *kibbutz* or *moshav*.'

'I don't know either, Mrs Fremont. A "safer *kibbutz*" is merely a term of relativity. Palestine is less than fifty miles wide. We have no safe *kibbutz*. New settlements are falling under siege every day.'

'Then perhaps we can get them to the cities.'

'Jerusalem is almost cut off. The fighting in Haifa and between Tel Aviv and Jaffa is the most severe in Palestine.'

'Then ... there is no place?'

Jordana did not answer. She did not have to.

Chapter Three

CHRISTMAS EVE, 1947

The ground was sticky with mud and the air was crisp and the first snow of the winter floated down on Gan Dafna. Kitty walked quickly over the green toward the lane of cottages. Her breath formed little clouds.

'*Shalom, Giveret* Kitty,' Dr Lieberman called.

'*Shalom*, Doctor.'

She raced up the steps and into the cottage, where it was warm and Karen had a steaming cup of tea waiting.

'Brrr,' Kitty said, 'it's freezing outside.'

The room was cheerful. Karen had decorated it with pine cones, ribbons, and imagination. She had even got permission to cut down one of the precious little trees, which she had filled with tufts of raw cotton and paper cutouts.

Kitty sat down on the bed, kicked off her shoes, and put on a pair of fur-lined slippers. The tea tasted wonderful.

Karen stood by the picture window and watched the snow fall. 'I think that the first snow falling is the most beautiful thing in the world,' Karen said.

'You won't think it's so beautiful if the fuel ration gets any worse.'

'I've been thinking about Copenhagen and the Hansens all day. Christmas in Denmark is a wonderful thing. Did you see the package they sent me?'

Kitty walked up to the girl, put her arm around her shoulders, and bussed her cheek. 'Christmas makes people nostalgic.'

'Are you terribly lonesome, Kitty?'

'Since Tom and Sandra died Christmas has been something I wanted to forget – until now.'

'I hope you are happy, Kitty.'

'I am ... in a different way. I have learned that it is impossible to be a Christian without being a Jew in spirit. Karen, I've done things all my life to justify something missing in myself. I feel, for the first time, that I am able to give without reservation or hope of compensation.'

'Do you know something? I can't ever tell the others because they wouldn't understand, but I feel very close to Jesus here,' Karen said.

'So do I, dear.'

Karen looked at her watch and sighed. 'I must eat early. I have guard duty tonight.'

'Bundle up. It's very cold outside. I'll work on some reports and wait up for you.'

Karen changed into bulky, warm clothing. Kitty knotted the girl's hair and held it in place while she put on the brown stocking-like Palmach cap so that it covered her ears.

Suddenly there came a sound of voices singing from outside.

'What on earth is that?' Kitty asked.

'It is for you,' Karen smiled. 'They have been practicing in secret for two weeks.'

Kitty walked to the window. Fifty of her children stood outside the cottage holding candles in their hands, singing a Christmas carol.

Kitty put on her coat and walked out on the porch with Karen. Behind the children she could see the lights of the valley settlements over two thousand feet below. One by one the cottage doors opened with curious onlookers. She did not understand the words but the melody was very old.

'Merry Christmas, Kitty,' Karen said.

Tears fell down Kitty's cheek. 'I never thought I would live to hear "Silent Night" sung in Hebrew. This is the most beautiful Christmas present I have ever had.'

Karen was assigned to a post in the outer trenches beyond Gan Dafna's gates. She walked out of the village and down to road to a point where the earthworks commanded a view of the valley floor.

'Halt!'

She stopped.

'Who is there?'

'Karen Clement.'

'What is the pass word?'

'*Chag sameach.*'

Karen relieved the guard, jumped down in the trench, put a clip of bullets into the chamber of the rifle, closed the bolt, and put on her mittens.

It was nice standing guard, Karen thought. She looked through the tangle of barbed wire toward Abu Yesha. It was nice being alone out here with nothing to do but think for four hours and look down on the Huleh Valley. Karen could hear the faint voices of the children floating over the quiet winter air from Kitty's cottage. It was a most wonderful, wonderful Christmas.

Soon the voices were still and it was very silent all about. The snowfall thickened, building a white carpet over the mountainside.

Karen heard movement in the trees behind her. She turned quietly and squinted in the darkness. She sensed something alive moving about. She froze and watched. Yes! Something was there in the trees! A shadow . . . perhaps it is a hungry jackal, she thought.

Karen flicked the safety catch off her rifle, put it to her shoulder, and sighted it. The shadow moved closer.

'Halt!' her voice snapped out.

The figure stopped.

'What is the password?'

'Karen!' a voice called out.

'Dov!'

She climbed from the trench and ran through the snow toward him and he ran toward her and they fell into each other's arms.

'Dov! Dov! I can't believe it is you!'

They jumped down into the trench together and she strained in the darkness to make out his face.

'Dov . . . I don't know what to say . . .'

'I got here an hour ago,' he said. 'I waited outside your cottage until you left for guard duty. Then I followed you here.'

Karen looked around, startled. 'It isn't safe! You'll have to hide from the British!'

'It's all right now, Karen, it's all right. The British can't hurt me any more.'

Her fingers trembled as she felt him in the darkness. 'Dov, you're cold. You haven't even a sweater on. You must be freezing.'

'No . . . no . . . I'm fine.'

The snow fell into the trench and suddenly the moon appeared and they could see each other.

'I've been hiding at the caves outside Mishmar.'

'I know.'

'I . . . I thought you were in America.'

'We couldn't go.'

'I guess you wonder what I'm doing here. Karen . . . I . . . want to come back to Gan Dafna but I took some watches and rings when I left and I guess they think I'm a thief.'

'Oh no, Dov. As long as you are safe and alive that is all that matters.'

'You see . . . I'll pay everyone back.'

'It doesn't matter. No one is angry with you.'

Dov sat in the trench and lowered his head. 'All the time I was in the Acre prison and all the time I was in the caves I thought to myself. I thought: Dov, no one is mad at you. It's just Dov that's mad ... mad at himself. When I saw you in Acre I said then ... I said I didn't want to die any more, I didn't want to die and I didn't want to kill anyone.'

'Oh, Dov ...'

'Karen ... I never really had another girl. I ... I just said that to make you go away.'

'I know.'

'Did you really know it all along?'

'I made myself believe that, Dov, because I wanted to believe you cared for me.'

'That is what is so wonderful about you, Karen. You can make yourself believe things and make me believe them too. I wanted to come back to Gan Dafna and make you proud of me. I wanted to make you proud even though I thought you would be gone.'

Karen lowered her eyes.

'I'll do anything for you,' he whispered.

She reached up and touched his cheek. 'Dov, you are so cold. Please go to my cottage. You can tell Kitty everything. She understands about us. Just as soon as I get off guard duty we will go see Dr Lieberman together. Be careful. The password is Happy Holiday.'

'Karen. I have thought so much about you all the time. I won't ever do anything wrong or anything that would hurt you.'

'I know that.'

'Could I kiss you?'

'Yes.'

Their lips brushed with a frightened searching.

'I love you, Karen,' Dov said, and ran off toward the gates of Gan Dafna.

'International law,' Barak Ben Canaan said angrily to the United States delegate, 'is that thing which the evil ignore and the righteous refuse to enforce.'

Conversation, no matter how well put, made little difference any longer. If the Jews declared their independence on May 15 they would have to face seven Arab armies alone.

Kawukji's irregulars and the Palestine Arabs under the command of Safwat and Kadar increased their activities.

The year 1948, the year of decision, came into being.

Through the first few months the Arabs became bolder and the tempo of the fighting increased as the British dismantled their huge military establishment and pulled back from position after position.

THE GALILEE

Irregulars lay siege to *kibbutz* Manara high in the hills on the Lebanese border. A half dozen other isolated Jewish positions were cut off.

The Arabs launched five straight attacks on Ein Zeitim – the Fountain of the Olives – but each attack was beaten back.

Syrian villagers began to fight. They crossed the Palestine border and attacked the northern Jewish outpost settlements of *kibbutz* Dan and Kfar Szold. Major Hawks, the British commander, dispatched forces to help drive the Syrians back over the border.

Arabs from Aata, helped again by Syrian villagers and irregulars, attacked

Lahavot Habashan – the Flames of the Beshan – Mountains.

Ramat Naftali, named for one of the tribes of ancient Israel, was hit.

Arab activity in Safed increased as the Arabs waited for Major Hawks to withdraw. The blockade against the Jews was beginning to tell as food and water shortages developed in the Cabalist city. Convoys were getting through to Jewish quarters only when the British helped.

HAIFA

The key port of Palestine was a major objective of both sides. For the time, the dock area stayed in British hands, as it was essential for British withdrawal.

In Haifa the Jews has one of their superior positions in Palestine, in Har Hacarmel above the Arab sector. The British commander, openly pro-Arab, continued to force the Jews out of strategic positions they had won.

Maccabees rolled barrel bombs down the slopes of Carmel into the Arab area and the Jews managed to ambush a huge Arab arms convoy from Lebanon and kill the Arab commander.

All normal business between the two sectors ceased. Amin Azaddin, an officer of the Arab Legion, arrived to assume command of the ever increasing irregular force.

The British held the Jews in check to allow the Arabs to build enough strength to launch an attack up Har Hacarmel.

THE SHARON

This central plain, scene of the great Crusader battles, was the most thickly settled Jewish area. It faced the most heavily populated Arab area of Samaria known, from its shape, as the 'Triangle.' Although both sides remained poised, this sector remained relatively quiet.

TEL AVIV-JAFFA

A battlefield appeared between the adjoining cities. Street fighting and patrols continued around the clock. The Maccabees took their place in the center of the Haganah lines. Raids on both sides were constant. The Arabs used a minaret as an observation and sniping post and the position of the intervening British troops prevented the Jews from attacking it.

THE SOUTH

In the sprawling Negev Desert the Jewish settlements were few and widely separated. The Arabs had two large bases, Beersheba and Gaza, of the fame of Samson. The Arabs were able to put a deadly siege on the settlements and slowly starve them. Each Jewish settlement managed to hold out but the Arabs were bold in this area and the pressure steadily increased. The Jewish air force was born. It consisted of two Piper Cubs for liaison contact. Another Piper Cub flew into besieged Jerusalem. These Pipers carried out their first bombing missions by throwing grenades out of their windows.

JERUSALEM

Abdul Kadar tightened his grip on the throat of Jewish Jerusalem. The Bab el Wad, that tortuous and vulnerable road through the Judean hills, was shut tight. The Jews were able to get through only by organizing large convoys and then at heavy price. The British steadfastly refused to keep the roads open.

Outside of Jerusalem to the south, the Jews had four isolated settlements in the Hebron Hills on the road to Bethlehem. These four settlements, manned by Orthodox Jews, were known as the Etzion group. Their position was as bad and vulnerable as Safed's. The Etzion group was completely shut off from Jewish Palestine. To make matters worse, the Trans-Jordan Legion, under the thin disguise of being British troops, blocked the road from Jerusalem to these settlements.

Inside Jerusalem the food and water shortages had become critical. Bombings, sniping, armored-car travel, and open warfare were the order of the day.

The fury reached a peak when a Red Cross convoy from the Hadassah Medical Center on Mount Scopus was ambushed by the Arabs and seventy-seven unarmed Jewish doctors were massacred and their bodies hacked to pieces. Again British troops took no action.

Zev Gilboa reported to Ari's office for the task of receiving Fort Esther from the British.

'We are all ready to go,' Zev said.

'Good. You may as well drive on up to the fort. Major Hawks said he would turn the place over at fourteen hundred. Say, what's this I hear about you and Liora having another baby?'

'That's right.'

'I'll have to stop giving you weekends off if you can't keep out of trouble.' Ari smiled.

Zev ran outside, jumped into the cab of the truck, kicked off the brakes, and drove out of Ein Or *kibbutz*. Twenty Palmach boys and girls rode along to man Fort Esther. Zev drove over the main artery and then took the mountain roads toward the Lebanese border and Fort Esther.

Zev thought about his last visit to his *kibbutz*, Sde Shimshon – the Field of Samson. Liora had told him that they were expecting another child. What wonderful news! Zev was a shepherd when he wasn't on duty . . . but that seemed long ago. How grand it would be to take his sons out with him and laze on the hillsides watching the flock . . .

He switched off thoughts like these; there was much work to do. When Fort Esther was turned over he had to relieve the siege of *kibbutz* Manara and start dispatching patrols along the border to cut down the flow of irregulars.

The big concrete blockhouse dominated the entire Huleh Valley. It would certainly be a relief to raise the Star of David over the fort.

The gang in the back began to sing as the truck spun around the sharp turns on the mountain road. Zev checked his watch. It was fifteen minutes until the appointed time. He turned the truck around the last turn. The huge square building appeared on the horizon a few miles away. Below him, Zev could see the white cluster of Abu Yesha in the saddle of the hill and the green plateau of Gan Dafna above it.

As he drove within a few hundred yards of Fort Esther, he sensed something strange. He slowed down and looked out of the window. If the British were withdrawing it was odd that there was no activity about. Zev looked up to the concrete watch and gun tower. His eyes caught the flag of Kawukji's irregulars on the tower just as a burst of gunfire erupted from Fort Esther.

Zev slammed on the brakes and pulled over to the side of the road.

'Scatter!'

His troops dived for cover. The truck went up in flames. Zev quickly pulled his people back out of firing range, assembled, and began to double-time down the mountain towards Ein Or.

When Ari received the news that Fort Esther had been turned over to the Arabs he rushed to Safed immediately to the Taggart fort on Mount Canaan.

He went directly into the office of the British area commander, Major Hawks, a heavy-set man with dark features. Hawks was haggard from lack of sleep when the angry Ben Canaan entered.

'You Judas!' Ari snarled.

'It wasn't my fault,' Hawks said in a half whine. 'You've got to believe me.'

'No, I can't believe it. Not from you.'

Hawks held his head in his hands. 'Last night at ten o'clock I got a call from headquarters in Jerusalem. They ordered me to pull my men out of Fort Esther immediately.'

'You could have warned me!'

'I couldn't,' Hawks mumbled. 'I couldn't. I'm still a soldier, Ben Canaan. I ... I didn't sleep all night. This morning I called Jerusalem and begged them to let me go back to Fort Esther and take it back.'

Ari glared at the man in contempt.

'Whatever you think of me is probably right.'

Ari continued to stare.

'All right, have it your way ... there was no excuse.'

'It's your life, Hawks. I guess you're not the first soldier who swallowed his conscience.'

'What's the use of talking? What's done is done.'

'This may make you a good soldier, Hawks, but I feel sorry for you. You're the one who has to live with the siege of Gan Dafna on his conscience, provided you've still got one.'

Hawks turned pale.

'You're not going to leave those children on the mountain ... you've got to take them away!'

'You should have thought about that. Without Fort Esther we've got to hold Gan Dafna or lose the whole Huleh Valley.'

'Look, Ari ... I'll convoy the children to safety.'

'They have no place to go.'

Ari watched Hawks beat his fists on the table and mumble under his breath. He had turned Gan Dafna into a suicide position. There was no use of berating him further. The man was obviously sick over what he had been forced to do.

On his way over, Ari's brain had been busy on a scheme, risky at best, but a long gamble that might save the key position of Gan Dafna.

He leaned over Hawks's desk. 'I'm going to give you a chance to undo part of the damage.'

'What can I do now, Ben Canaan?'

'As area commander it is completely within your rights to come up to Gan Dafna and advise us to evacuate.'

'Yes, but ...'

'Then do it. Go up to Gan Dafna tomorrow and take fifty trucks up with you. Put armor in front and behind you. If anyone asks you what you are doing, tell them you intend to evacuate the children.'

'I don't understand. Are you going to evacuate?'

'No. But you leave the rest to me. You just come up with the convoy.'

Hawks did not press to know what Ari had in mind. He followed the instructions and took a fifty-lorry convoy to Gan Dafna, escorted by half tracks and armored cars. The half-mile-long procession moved from the Taggart fort through six Arab villages on the way to Huleh. It drove up the mountain road, through Abu Yesha, in plain sight of the irregulars in Fort Esther. The convoy arrived around noon at Gan Dafna. Major Hawks went through the motions of advising Dr Lieberman to quit the place; the latter, on Ari's advice, officially refused. After lunch, the convoy left Gan Dafna and returned to its base in Safed.

In the meanwhile Ari 'confided' to some of his Arab friends at Abu Yesha that Major Hawks had left tons of arms – from machine guns to mortars – at the village.

'After all,' Ari said in greatest confidence, 'Hawks has been a known friend of the Jews and he was privately doing something to compensate for the Arab occupation of Fort Esther.'

The story was planted. Within hours the rumor had spread throughout the area that Gan Dafna was impregnable. The children were armed to the teeth. This story was lent weight by the fact that there was no evacuation of the children: the Arabs knew the Jews would get the children out if there were great danger.

Ari made a visit to Abu Yesha, once the 'might' of Gan Dafna had been established and proved a checkmate.

He went to see his old friend Taha the muktar in the stone house by the stream. No matter how strained feelings were, a man must be made welcome in the house of an Arab. It was an age-old custom, but despite Taha's going through the motions of hospitality Ari felt a coldness he had never known before from Taha.

The two men shared a meal and spoke small talk. When Ari felt that enough ceremony had been served he turned to the purpose of his visit.

'The time has come,' Ari said, 'that I must know your feelings.'

'My feelings these days are of little concern.'

'I am afraid that I must talk now as the Haganah commander of the area, Taha.'

'I gave you my word that Abu Yesha would remain neutral.'

Ari stood up from the table and looked Taha directly in the eye and spoke words harsh to an Arab ear.

'You have given your word but you have broken it,' he said.

Taha looked at him with a flash of anger.

'We happen to know that Kawukji's men have been passing through Abu Yesha in droves.'

'And what do you expect me of me?' Taha snapped. 'Shall I ask them to please stop coming? I didn't invite them.'

'Neither did I. Look, my friend ... there was once a time when you and I didn't speak to each other this way.'

'Times change, Ari.'

Ari walked to the window and looked out at the mosque by the opposite side of the stream. 'I have always loved this spot. We knew many happy days in this room and by that stream. Do you remember the nights that you and I camped out there?'

'That was a long time ago.'

'Maybe I've got a long memory. We used to talk about it during the riots, how ridicuous it was for everyone else to fight. We took blood vows to be eternal brothers. Taha ... I was up all of last night thinking of what I was going to say today. I began remembering all the things that you and I have done together.'

'Sentimentality does not become you, Ari.'

'Neither does having to threaten you. Mohammed Kassi and the men in Fort Esther are the same kind of men who murdered your father while he was kneeling at prayer. The minute the British leave the area he is going to come down from Fort Esther and get you to block the road to Gan Dafna. If you let him, he'll shove rifles in the hands of your people and order you to attack Yad El.'

'And just what do you expect of me?'

'And what do you expect of me?' Ari countered.

A stony silence ensued.

'You are the muktar of Abu Yesha. You can rally your people just as your father did. You've got to stop doing business with the irregulars.'

'Or what?'

'Or you will be treated as an enemy.'

'*Or what?* Ari?'

'You are going to bring on the destruction of Abu Yesha.'

Neither Ari nor Taha quite believed Ari's words. Ari was tired; he walked up to the Arab and put his hand on Taha's shoulder.

'Please,' Ari said, 'help me.'

'I am an Arab,' Taha said.

'You are a human being. You know right from wrong.'

'I am a *dirty Arab*!'

'It is you who think that of himself.'

'Are you going to tell me I am your brother?'

'You always have been,' Ari said.

'If I am your brother, then give me Jordana. Yes, that is right ... give her to me and let me take her to my bed. Let her bear my children.'

Ari's fist shot out and crashed against Taha's jaw. The Arab was sent sprawling to his hands and knees. He sprang up and instinctively unsheathed the dagger from his waist sash and came at Ari.

Ari stood rigidly, making no move to defend himself. Taha raised the knife, then froze and turned and threw it from him. It clattered over the stone floor.

'What have I done?' Ari whispered. He walked toward Taha with an expression that begged forgiveness.

'You have told me everything that I need to know. Get out of my house, Jew.'

Chapter Four

A terrible turn had taken place at Flushing Meadow. Anticipating the necessity of armed intervention to back up partition, and fearing the Russian position as part of an international force, the United States announced its intention to abandon its stand for partition.

The Yishuv launched a desperate campaign to change the American defeatist attitude. In the middle of these important maneuvers, Barak Ben Canaan received an urgent cable to report at once to France. Because of the urgency of the work at Flushing Meadow, Barak was puzzled by the order, but he left immediately by plane.

He was met by two Yishuv agents. Barak had been called to take part in highly secret negotiations of a vital arms deal. The Yishuv calculated that with the turn of events at Flushing Meadow, arms were the most urgent immediate need, and Barak one of the most able men for such business. It was their friend, Jan Masaryk of Czechoslovakia, who provided the information on sources of weapons in a half dozen European countries.

After several weeks of confidential and ticklish parleying the deals were closed. The problem now became getting the arms into Palestine, still under British blockade.

The first step was to acquire an airplane large enough to haul the arms. In Vienna an Aliyah Bet agent found an obsolete, surplus American Liberator bomber, which was purchased under the name of Alpine Charter Flights, Inc.

Next they had to find a crew; six men, four South African Jews and two American Jews who had flown during the war, were picked and sworn to secrecy.

Finally, the most difficult task was to create a secret airfield in tiny Palestine undetected by the British. An abandoned British fighter-plane base in the Jezreel Valley was selected. It lay in an all-Jewish area and offered the maximum chance of the Liberator's being able to get in and out again.

Meanwhile the assembly of the arms inside Europe was carried out with the same secrecy that hid the true identity of the Alpine Charter Flights, Inc.

It was a race against time. Two weeks would be needed before the first load of arms could leave Europe. The question was whether or not it would be too late.

So far, miraculously, not a single settlement had fallen, but the Jewish convoys were being ripped to pieces. Water lines to the Negev Desert settlements had been cut. In some places the settlers were subsisting on potato peelings and olives.

The focal point of the struggle was Jerusalem, where the isolation-and-starvation tactics were beginning to pay off. The Bab el Wad from Tel Aviv was littered with the wreckage of burned-out trucks. Only occasional huge convoys, mounted at crippling cost of men and matériel, staved off disaster in Jerusalem.

For the first time in the history of Jerusalem, the city was violated by artillery fire, from Kawukji's irregulars.

Kawukji, Safwat, and Kadar urgently needed a victory. The Palestine Arabs were becoming uneasy over the failure of Arab predictions of 'great victories.'

It was Kawukji, the self-styled generalissimo of the Mufti's 'Forces of the Yarmuk,' who decided to grab off the honor of capturing the first Jewish settlement. He picked his target carefully, having no wish to try a nut too tough to crack the first time out.

Kawukji picked what he believed to be a soft spot: Tirat Tsvi – the Castle of the Rabbi Tsvi – was elected for the distinction of being the first Jewish settlement to fall. The *kibbutz* of Tirat Tsvi was made up of Orthodox Jews, many of whom were concentration camp 'graduates.' The *kibbutz* stood in the southern section of the Beth Shean Valley, located there purposely to neutralize an otherwise completely Arab area. South of the *kibbutz* was the 'triangle,' the all-Arab area of Palestine. Within shooting distance stood the borders of Jordan. Slightly north, the hostile Arab city of Beth Shean completed the cutoff of the *kibbutz*.

Tirat Tsvi was one of the Jewish outposts that guarded the Jordan Valley farther to the north.

Kawukji was delighted with his choice of Tirat Tsvi. The religious Jews of the *kibbutz* would crumble before the first massed attack. The brigand assembled hundreds of Arabs at the Nablus base in the Triangle and marched up for the attack.

Kawukji announced his victory in advance; it was published even before he made an attack. When he did move his troops into position, the Arab women from Beth Shean came to the edge of the battlefield and waited with sacks and containers to rush up after the troops and plunder the *kibbutz*.

The attack came with a cloudy dawn. The Jews had one hundred and sixty-seven men and women of fighting age on the battle line, in trenches, and behind rough barricades facing the Arab position. The children were hidden in the centermost building of the *kibbutz*. The defenders had no armament heavier than a single two-inch mortar.

A bugle blew. Arab Legion officers with drawn swords led the charge. The irregulars behind them poured over the open fields in a massed frontal assault calculated to overrun the *kibbutz* by sheer weight of numbers.

The Jews waited until the Arab force was within twenty yards, then on signal they cut loose with a tremendous volley. Arabs went down like mown wheat.

The impetus of the Arab charge carried forward a second, third, and fourth headlong wave. The Jews continued their disciplined fire, blasting each rush as the leaders' feet touched *kibbutz* ground.

The field was littered with Arab dead and the wounded screamed, 'We are brothers! Mercy, in the name of Allah!'

The rest scrambled back out of range and began a confused retreat. Kawukji had promised them easy victory and plunder! He had told them this bunch of Orthodox Jews would flee at the sight of them! They had not reckoned on such a fight. The Arab women on the outskirts of the battle began to flee too.

The Arab Legion officers herded the running irregulars together and stopped the retreat only by firing at them. The leaders reorganized their men for another rush at the *kibbutz*, but the irregulars' hearts were no longer in their effort.

Inside Tirat Tsvi the Jews were in bad trouble. They did not have enough ammunition left to hold off another charge if Arabs came in strong and hard. Moreover, if the Arabs changed strategy and tried a slow attack with flanking movement the Jews could not contain it. They hastily organized a desperation tactic. Most of the ammunition was given to twenty sharpshooters. The rest dropped back to the children's house and prepared for a last-ditch fight with bayonets, clubs, and bare hands. Through field glasses they watched the Arabs mass and saw that there were enough troops left to overrun the *kibbutz*.

The Arabs came over the field more slowly this time, with some of the Legion officers behind the troops forcing them on at gun point.

Suddenly the heavens opened up in an unexpected downpour. Within minutes the open field was turned into a deep and bogging mud. The Arab charge, instead of gaining momentum, began to wallow, just as the Canaanite chariots had done against Deborah.

As the first Legion officers reached the *kibbutz*, the sharpshooters picked them off. Kawukji's noble 'Forces of the Yarmuk' had had enough for the day.

Kawukji was in a rage over the Tirat Tsvi debacle. He had to have a victory quickly to save face. This time he decided to go after big game.

The road between Tel Aviv and Haifa was more important to the Yishuv from a purely strategic standpoint than the road to Jerusalem. If the Tel Aviv-Haifa line could be cut, the Arabs could sever the Jewish dispositions, splitting the Galilee away from the Sharon. There were Arab villages on the main highway which forced the Jews to use alternate interior roads to maintain transportation between the two cities. On one of the vital alternate roads was *kibbutz* Mishmar Haemek – the Guardpost of the Valley. Mishmar Haemek became Kawukji's goal in the ambitious move to separate Tel Aviv from Haifa.

This time Kawukji determined not to repeat the mistakes of Tirat Tsvi. He massed more than a thousand men and moved them into the hills surrounding the *kibbutz*, together with ten 75mm. mountain guns.

With Mishmar Haemek ringed, Kawukji opened a brutal artillery barrage. The Jews had one machine gun with which to answer back.

After a day of the pounding, the British called a truce, entered the *kibbutz*, and advised the Jews to pull out. When they refused the British left, washing their hands of the affair. Kawukji learned from the British that the Jews were relatively weak inside the *kibbutz*. What he did not know, because of his lack of an intelligence system, was that the Emek Valley was alive with men in training for the Haganah. During the second night two entire battalions of Haganah, all armed with rifles, slipped into the *kibbutz*.

On the third day, Kawukji mounted the attack.

Instead of walking into a frightened and cowering *kibbutz*, he ran into two battalions of eagerly waiting and trained men. Kawukji's offensive was smashed.

He rallied his men and tried a slow sustained move. It was equally unsuccessful. He mounted more attacks, but with each the irregulars showed less inclination to fight. They straggled forward halfheartedly and pulled back whenever resistance stiffened.

Toward the end of the day, Kawukji lost control of his troops. They began to walk out of the battle area.

Inside the *kibbutz*, the Jews witnessed the development and poured out after the Arabs. Here was a completely unexpected turn. The Arabs were so startled at the sight of Jews charging that they all fled, with the Haganah literally at their heels. The running fight surged back miles, to Megiddo, site of a hundred battles through the ages. Here, on the historic fighting ground of Armageddon, the Jews completely broke Kawukji's forces. The carnage stopped only when the British stepped in and forced a truce.

The Jews had won their first real victory of the War of Liberation.

In the Jerusalem corridor the Hillmen Brigade of the Palmach performed titans' work to keep the road open. This gang of teen-agers, with commanders in their twenties, patrolled the deep gorges and wilds of Judea, making fierce hit-and-run raids on Arab villages in conjunction with convoy runs. They frequently worked around the clock until they were numb with exhaustion, yet they could always be goaded on to one more patrol, one more raid, one more hike through the fierce country.

'In this wadi King David also lived as a guerrilla fighter!' The bloodshot eyes of the Palmach youngsters recorded fatigue as they roused to still another effort.

'Remember, you are fighting at the place where Samson was born!'

'In this valley David met Goliath!'

'Here Joshua made the sun stand still!'

At night the Bible was read to the exhausted warriors as a source of inspiration for the superhuman efforts the next day would call forth. Here, in Kadar's territory, the fighting was hard and constant and the Arabs had confidence behind a strong leader.

An enormous convoy mustered in Tel Aviv for another all-out effort to save Jerusalem. The Hillmen Brigade's job was to take the Arab village of Kastel, built on a Crusader fort dominating one of the main heights of the highway.

The storming of Kastel became the first Jewish offensive action in the War of Liberation. The brigade made a sheer-guts attack, crawling up the treacherous incline under cover of friendly darkness. They reached the peak of the Kastel bloodied and weary but threw themselves into hand-to-hand combat and threw the Arabs out.

Kastel lifted the flagging spirits of the Yishuv. Following the victory, the huge convoy from Tel Aviv battled every inch of the way through the Bab el Wad, slogged on through to New Jerusalem, and again brought vital relief to the beleaguered Jews.

Kawukji summoned Mohammed Kassi, the Huleh commander of the irregulars, from Fort Esther to headquarters in Nablus.

Kawukji was frantic for a victory. For months he had been writing communiqués boasting of triumph after triumph. As the 'general' of the Mufti, Kawukji had nourished the dream of commanding an Arab army that spread from the borders of Turkey to the Rock of Gibraltar. He blamed 'British intervention' as the reason he had been unable to win a Jewish settlement. When the British pulled out of the Huleh area he had no alibi left.

Kawukji kissed Mohammed Kassi on both cheeks in the accustomed style and they spoke at great lengths of their glorious victories. Kassi told of how he had 'conquered' Fort Esther, and Kawukji described how he had weakened Tirat Tsvi and Mishmar Haemek with brilliant probing tactics.

'I have received a message from his Holiness, the Mufti in Damascus,' Kawukji said. 'On May 15, the day after the British terminate the mandate, Haj Amin el Husseini will make a triumphant return to Palestine.'

'And what a magnificent day that shall be for all of Islam,' Mohammed Kassi nodded.

'His Holiness has selected Safed as his temporary capital until the Zionists are completely exterminated. Now that the dear friend of the Jews, Major Hawks, is gone from Safed, we will have it within a week.'

'I am delighted to hear such news!'

'However,' Kawukji continued, 'Safed will not be truly safe and fit for the return of his Holiness so long as a single Jew remains in the Huleh Valley. They hold a dagger in our backs. We must erase them.'

Mohammed Kassi turned slightly pale.

'The Huleh, I believe, is in your command, my brother. I want you to capture Gan Dafna at once. As soon as Gan Dafna falls we will have the rest of the Huleh Zionists by the throat.'

'Generalissimo, let me assure you that each and every one of my volunteers is a man filled with the courage of a lion and is dedicated to the noble cause of crushing Zionism. They have all vowed to fight to the last drop of blood.'

'Good. They are costing us almost a dollar a month in pay alone.'

Kassi stroked his beard and held up his forefinger with its large jeweled ring. 'However! It is well known that Major Hawks left three thousand rifles, a hundred machine guns, and dozens of heavy mortars at Gan Dafna!'

Kawukji sprang to his feet.

'You cringe before children!'

'I swear by Allah's beard that the Jews have sent in a thousand Palmach reinforcements. I have seen them with my own eyes.'

Kawukji slapped Mohammed Kassi twice across the face. 'You will lay open Gan Dafna, you will level it to the ground, and you will wash your hands in their blood or I will set your carcass out for the vultures!'

Chapter Five

Mohammed Kassi's first move was to send a hundred of his men into Abu Yesha. Immediately some of the villagers went down to *kibbutz* Ein Or to report the fact to Ari. Ari knew that the people of Abu Yesha were predominantly with the Jews. He waited for them to act.

The Arabs of Abu Yesha resented the presence of the irregulars. They had been neighbors of the people of Yad El for decades; their homes had been built by the Jews. They were not angry and had no desire to fight and they looked to Taha, their muktar, to rally them and eject Kassi's men.

Taha kept a strange silence, speaking neither for nor against the coming of the irregulars. When the elders of Abu Yesha urged him to unite the people, Taha refused to discuss the matter. His silence sealed the fate of Abu Yesha, for the fellaheen were helpless without leadership. They quietly submitted to the occupation.

Kassi was quick to capitalize on Taha's passive acquiescence. Day by day his men became bolder and more unruly as Taha continued his silence. The road to Gan Dafna was cut. There was anger in Abu Yesha but it was no more than grumbling on an individual level. Then four Abu Yesha Arabs were caught by the irregulars running food up to Gan Dafna. Kassi had them killed, decapitated, and their heads put on display in the village square as a warning. From that point on Abu Yesha was completely subdued.

Ari had guessed wrong. He had felt sure that the people of Abu Yesha would force Taha to take a stand, especially with the safety of Gan Dafna at stake. Their failure to act and the closing of the road put him in a terrible position.

The road shut, Kassi's ponderous mountain guns began an around-the-clock shelling of Gan Dafna from Fort Esther.

The Jews had trained for this sort of thing at Gan Dafna from the day the place was opened. Everyone knew his job. They switched onto emergency footing quickly and quietly.

All children over the age of ten were assigned to an active part in the village defense. The water tank had been sandbagged and the power generators, medical supplies, arsenal, and food stores had been installed underground.

Life went on as usual in the dank bunkers. School classes, dining, games, and all routine functions continued below the ground. Sleeping quarters were shelf-like bunks in dormitories built inside sections of twelve-feet-diameter concrete water pipes which had been sunk deeply into the earth and covered with yards of dirt and sandbags.

Whenever the shelling outside stopped, the children and staff came out from the bunkers to play, stretch their cramped muscles, and to take care of the lawns and gardens.

Within a week the staff had made it seem that the whistling shells and explosions were merely another minor unpleasantness of daily living.

Down at Ein Or *kibbutz*, Ari faced the problem. All the settlements must depend on their own defense systems, but Gan Dafna held six hundred children and stood in the most vulnerable place, there beneath Fort Esther. There was enough food for a month, and the water supply would be ample if the tank was not hit. Fuel would become a problem. It was extremely cold during the nights in the mountains and Ari knew that Dr Lieberman would rather freeze than cut down the precious trees for burning. Communications from Gan Dafna were maintained by blinker light to Yad El; the telephone line had been cut. The children's village was so completely cut off that the only way it could be reached was by a dangerous and grueling climb up the west face of the mountain, more than two thousand feet, which had to be negotiated by night.

The communication and supply problem, however, was not Ari's main worry. The fear of a massacre was. He could not guess how long it would be until the 'armed might' myth of Gan Dafna would be exploded.

By shaking down his entire command, Ari was able to come up with a dozen Spanish rifles of late 1880 vintage, twenty-three homemade Sten guns, and an obsolete Hungarian antitank weapon with five rounds of ammunition.

Zev Gilboa and twenty Palmach reinforcements were ordered to deliver the new equipment. Zev's patrol were to be human pack mules. The antitank gun had to be dismantled and carried in pieces. The patrol moved out under cover of dark, and through one entire night they climbed up the sheer west slope of the mountain.

At one critical point they passed within a few feet of Abu Yesha's boundary, through a three-hundred-yard draw which had to be negotiated by crawling a few inches at a time. They could see, hear, and smell Kassi's irregulars.

The sight of Gan Dafna was a saddening one. Many of the buildings showed artillery hits, and the lovely center green had been chopped to pieces. The statue of Dafna had been knocked from its pedestal. Yet the morale of the children was amazingly high, and the security system was completely effective. Zev was amused by the sight of little Dr Lieberman coming out to greet the patrol with a pistol strapped to his waist. Sighs of relief greeted the coming of the twenty Palmach reinforcements.

Kassi continued the bombardment for ten more days. The mountain guns knocked down the buildings one by one. Gan Dafna drew its first casualties when a shell exploded near the entrance of a shelter and killed two children.

But Kawukji wanted action. Kassi tried two or three half-hearted probes. Each time his men were ambushed and killed, for Zev had extended Gan Dafna defenses to the very gates of Fort Esther. Palmach boys and girls hid out near both the fort and Abu Yesha to watch every Arab move.

Meanwhile, a courier came to Ari from Haganah headquarters in Tel Aviv. Ari called his settlement commanders together at once. A high decision had been made in Tel Aviv regarding the children in border settlements. It was recommended that all children be moved into the Sharon-Tel Aviv area close to the sea where the situation was not so critical and where every home, *kibbutz* and *moshav* was ready to receive them. One could read between the lines: the situation had become so bad that the Haganah was obviously thinking of eventual evacuation of the children by sea to save them from massacre if the Arabs broke through.

It was not an order; each *kibbutz* and *moshav* had to make the decision for itself. On the one hand, the farmers would fight more fiercely with their children close by. On the other hand, massacre was a horrible specter to contemplate.

The evacuation of the children was a doubly painful thing for these pioneers, for it became symbolic of further retreat. Most of them had fled from former horror to come to this place and their farms were the last line of retreat. Beyond Palestine there was no hope.

Each settlement made its decision. Some of the older and longer-established places simply refused to let their children go. Others vowed they would all stand and die together: they did not want their children to know the meaning of retreat. Others in the mountains already isolated and undergoing hardships managed to bring children out for removal.

Gan Dafna was everyone's responsibility.

Ari's spies reported that Kawukji was bringing unbearable pressure on Mohammed Kassi to make an assault on Gan Dafna. Food was getting low in the village and fuel was all but gone. The water tank had sprung several leaks from near hits. The hardship of bunker life was wearing down the community, although there were no complaints.

The commanders in the Huleh Valley agreed that the younger children had to be taken out of Gan Dafna. The question was – how! A truce would involve a double danger: first, Kassi would never recognize it; second, it would be a costly show of weakness to the Arab commander. If Ari tried a convoy through the roads or an outright attack on Abu Yesha he would have to pull out and mass his entire Huleh strength – then he could be only half certain of success. It was not merely a matter of winning or losing a battle. To lose would lead to the death of the children.

As so many times before, Ari was called upon to evolve a desperation measure to counter crushing odds. And because there was no choice, again he conceived a fantastic plan, this one more daring than anything he had ever tried in his life.

After organizing the details of his scheme, Ari left David to mobilize a task force and he set out for Gan Dafna. The climb up the mountainside was painful every inch of the way. His leg throbbed constantly and collapsed several times during the night. He was able to compensate for the handicap by his intimate knowledge of the route, for he had climbed it a dozen times as a boy. He reached Gan Dafna at dawn and immediately called a meeting of the section heads at the command post bunker. Zev, Jordana, Dr Lieberman, and Kitty Fremont were among them.

'There are two hundred and fifty children here under the age of twelve,' Ari said without introduction or preface. 'They will be evacuated tomorrow night.'

He looked at the dozen surprised faces.

'A task force is now assembling at Yad El *moshav*,' he continued. 'Tonight, four hundred men from every settlement in the Huleh will be led up the west face of the mountain by David Ben Ami. If everything goes according to plan and they are not discovered they should be here by daybreak tomorrow. Two hundred and fifty of the men will each carry a child down the mountain tomorrow night. The balance, a hundred and fifty men, will act as a guard force. I may add that the guard force will be carrying all the heavy automatic weapons in the Huleh Valley.'

Ari's listeners in the bunker stared at him as though he were insane. There was no sound or movement for a full minute.

Finally Zev Gilboa stood up. 'Ari, perhaps I did not understand you. You actually plan to carry two hundred and fifty children down the mountain at night?'

'That is correct.'

'It is a treacherous trip for man by himself in daylight,' Dr Lieberman said. 'Carrying a child down at night – some of them are certain to fall.'

'That is a risk that has to be taken.'

'But Ari,' Zev said, 'they must pass so close to Abu Yesha. It is certain that Kassi's men will detect them.'

'We will take every precaution to see that they are not detected.'

Everyone began to protest at once.

'Quiet!' Ari snapped. 'This is not a forum. You people here are not to speak of this to anyone. I want no panic. Now, get out of here, all of you. I have a lot of work to do.'

The shelling from Fort Esther was particularly heavy during the day. Ari worked with each section head in turn to complete the smallest details of the evacuation and to work out a minute-by-minute timetable.

Each of those dozen people who knew of the scheme went around with hearts heavy with apprehension. A thousand things could go wrong. Someone could slip and cause a panic . . . the Arab dogs in Abu Yesha would hear them or smell them and bark . . . Kassi would discover the move and attack all the settlements in the Huleh realizing they were without their heavy weapons . . .

Yet they knew that there was little else that Ari could do. In a week or ten days Gan Dafna would reach a desperation level anyhow.

As evening approached, David Ben Ami, with the task force in Yad El, sent out a coded blinker message that he would be on the way with the darkness.

Throughout that second night, the four hundred volunteers pushed their way up the mountain and appeared on the outskirts of Gan Dafna before daybreak in a state of exhaustion from the climb and the tension. Ari met them outside the village and hid them in the woods. He did not want them spotted by Kassi's men, nor did he want any wild speculation inside Gan Dafna.

They remained in the woods through the entire day. At ten minutes to six in the evening, exactly forty minutes before the sun was to set, the operation went into full effect.

The children to be evacuated were fed at exactly five minutes to six and a sleeping powder was put in each child's milk. By a quarter after six the children were put into their bunks in the water-pipe shelters beneath the ground. They were led in group singing until they dropped off into a deep drugged slumber.

At six thirty-two the sun set behind Fort Esther.

At six-forty Ari called a meeting of the entire staff outside of the children's bunkers.

'You will all pay strict attention,' he said sternly. 'In a few minutes we are going to begin the evacuation of the younger children. Your name will be called and you will be given an assignment. Everything has been worked out on a tight schedule and any variation of it could endanger the lives of the children and their escorts as well as yourselves. I want no discussion or questions. Any failure to co-operate will be dealt with drastically.'

At six forty-five Jordana Ben Canaan set out a guard around Gan Dafna consisting of the rest of the children. The guard was four times normal strength to make certain there would be no Arab infiltration that might discover the movements inside Fan Dafna. Zev Gilboa and his twenty Palmach troops attached to Dafna pushed out toward the hills on a special covering mission.

As soon as the security around Gan Dafna was reported tight, twenty-five of the Gan Dafna staff went into the bunkers to dress the sleeping children in their warmest clothing. Kitty moved from child to child to make certain that each one had been properly drugged by the sleeping powder. A thick strip of adhesive tape was placed over each child's mouth so that he could not cry out in his sleep. By seven-thirty the unconscious children were dressed and ready. Ari then brought the task force from its hiding place in the woods.

A chain line was formed from the bunkers, and the sleeping little bodies handed out one by one. Improvised strap rigs had been sewn together to form a makeshift saddle seat for the back of the men so that the children could be carried like packs. This would allow each man to have both hands free for his rifle and the climb.

By eight-thirty, the two hundred and fifty men and their small slumbering loads stood a final check to see that the children were strapped in securely. Then the line moved out to the main gate where the protecting force, a hundred and fifty men with automatic weapons, stood ready. With Ari leading the way, they pushed off over the edge of the drop down the side of the mountain. One by one the men and the children dropped down, until the last of them disappeared into the night.

Those left behind stood at the gates of Gan Dafna in silence. There was nothing to do now but wait until morning. They began drifting back toward their bunkers, where they would spend the sleepless night in silence, trembling with fear for the children and for the fate of this strange convoy.

Kitty Fremont stood alone by the main gate for more than an hour after they had gone. She stared vacantly into the darkness.

'It is going to be a very long night,' a voice said behind her. 'You might as well get in out of the cold.'

Kitty turned. Jordana stood next to her. For the first time since they had met, Kitty was actually glad to see the red-headed *sabra*. She had been developing a growing admiration for Jordana since her decision to stay. Jordana was perhaps the one person most responsible for keeping Gan Dafna calm. The girl had instilled the young Gadna troops with an infectious confidence; they behaved like spirited battle veterans. During all the ordeals since the closing of the road, Jordana had remained contained and efficient. It was quite a load for a young woman not yet twenty, but Jordana had that quality of leadership that made those around her feel secure.

'Yes, it's going to be a very long night,' Kitty said.

'Then we can keep each other company,' Jordana said. 'I will tell you a secret. I have a half bottle of brandy hidden in the command-post bunker. I think that tonight would be a perfect time to finish it. Why don't you wait for me at my bunker? I have to bring in the guards. I'll be back in a half hour.'

Kitty didn't move. Jordana took her arm. 'Come on,' she said gently, 'there is nothing we can do now.'

Kitty had been sitting nervously and smoking cigarette after cigarette until Jordana finally got back to the command post. Jordana took the brown Haganah stocking cap from her head, and her long scarlet tresses fell to her shoulders. She alternately held her cheeks and rubbed her hands together to drive out the cold. The brandy was hidden in a loosely filled place in the dirt wall. She took it out and wiped off the bottle and poured Kitty and herself a stiff drink.

'*Le chaim,*' Jordana said, taking a sip. 'That is good.'

'How long will it be before they pass near Abu Yesha?'

'That won't be until after midnight,' Jordana answered.

'I have been telling myself over and over that they are going to come through all right. Then I begin thinking of the thousands of things that can go wrong.'

'It is impossible not to think about it,' Jordana said, 'but it is in the hands of God now.'

'God? Yes, He does special things here,' Kitty said.

'If you don't get religion in Palestine, I doubt that you'll get it anywhere,' Jordana said. 'I cannot remember the time that we have not lived on faith. We actually have little else to sustain us.'

Coming from Jordana Ben Canaan, the words sounded strange, yet – not strange at all. On the surface Jordana did not appear to harbor a deep faith . . . but what else could give her the power to exist under this constant tension if it were not faith?

'Kitty,' Jordana said suddenly, 'I have a confession to make to you. I have wanted very much for us to become friends.'

'Why is that, Jordana?'

'Because I have learned something from you . . . something I have been very wrong about. I have watched you work here with the children and I know what you did for Ari. When you decided to stay I realized something . . . I realized that a woman like you can have just as much courage as . . . our kind of people. I used to believe that to be feminine was a sign of weakness.'

'Thank you, Jordana,' Kitty smiled weakly, 'but I'm afraid I could use a little of your brand of faith or courage or whatever it is right now. I feel as though I'm ready to fall apart.'

Kitty lit a cigarette and Jordana poured her another brandy.

'I have been thinking . . .' Jordana said. 'You would be good for Ari.'

Kitty shook her head. 'We are, as the saying goes, two nice people not made for each other.'

'That is unfortunate, Kitty.'

Kitty looked at her watch. She knew from the discussions that the long column of men would now be approaching the first of the almost straight drops. With the children, they would use ropes easing each man's descent, one by one. It was a thirty-five-foot plunge. From there they would have to slide in loose dirt for a hundred yards.

'Tell me about yourself and David,' Kitty said quickly.

Jordana's eyes lit up. 'Ah, my David . . . my gentle, wonderful David.'

'Where did you first meet?'

'At the Hebrew University. I met him the second day I was there. I saw him and he saw me and we fell in love at that very moment and we have never fallen out of it.'

'That's the way it was with my husband and me,' Kitty said.

'Of course it took me all that first term to let him know he was in love with me.'

'It took me longer than that.' Kitty smiled.

'Yes, men can be a bother about such things. But by summer he knew very well who his woman was. We went out on an archaeological expedition together into the Negev Desert. We were trying to find the exact route of Moses and the ten tribes in the Wildernesses of Zin and Paran.'

'I hear it's pretty desolate out there.'

'No, actually there are ruins of hundreds of Nabataean cities. The cisterns still have water in them. If you run in luck you can find all sorts of antiquities.'

'It sounds exciting.'

'It is, but it's terribly hard work. David loves digging for ruins. He feels the glory of our people all around us. Like so many others . . . that is why the Jews can never be separated from this land. David has made wonderful plans. After the war we are both going to return to the university. I will go for my master's degree and David his doctorate, and then we shall excavate a big, big Hebrew city. He wants to open Hazor, right here in the Huleh. Of course, these are only dreams. That takes lots of money . . . and peace.' Then she laughed ironically. 'Peace, of course, is merely an abstract word, an illusion. I wonder what peace is like?'

'Perhaps peace would be dull for you.'

'I don't know,' Jordana said, with a trace of tiredness in her young voice. 'Just once in my life I would like to see how human beings live a normal life.'

'Will you travel?'

'Travel? No. I do what David does. I go where David goes. But, Kitty, I would like to go out once. All my life I have been told that all life begins and ends in Palestine. But . . . every once in a while I feel strangled. Many of my friends have gone away from Palestine. It seems that we *sabras* are a strange breed made for fighting. We cannot adjust to living in other places. They all come back to Palestine sooner or later – but they grow old so quickly here.' Jordana cut herself short. 'It must be the brandy,' she said. 'As you know, *sabras* can't drink at all.'

Kitty smiled at Jordana and felt her first compassion for the girl. She snuffed out her cigarette and looked at her watch again. The minutes were dragging.

'Where would they be now?'

'Still being lowered down that first cliff. It will take at least two hours to get them all down.'

Kitty sighed weakly and Jordana stared into space.

'What are you thinking?'

'About David . . . and children. That first summer on the desert we found a graveyard more than four thousand years old. We managed to uncover a perfect skeleton of a little child. Perhaps it died trying to find the Promised Land. David looked at the skeleton and cried. He is like that. His heart is sick day and night over the siege of Jerusalem. I know he is going to try to do something foolish. I know it . . . Why don't you lie down, Kitty? It is going to be a long time before we know anything.'

Kitty finished her brandy and stretched back on the cot and closed her eyes. In her mind she saw that long line of men being lowered by rope with the sleeping children dangling from their backs. And then she saw flinty-eyed Arab irregulars lurking near the column, spying on their moves – waiting for them to get close and into a trap.

It was impossible to sleep.

'I think I'll go over to Dr Lieberman's bunker and see how they're doing.'

She put on a wool-lined jacket and walked outside. There hadn't been any shelling all evening. An alarming thought came: perhaps Mohammed Kassi knew something and had moved most of his men out of Fort Esther. She did not like it. The moon was far too bright. The night was far too clear and quiet. Ari should have waited until a foggy night to move the children. Kitty looked up the hill and made out the outlines of Fort Esther. They must have seen, she thought.

She entered one of the faculty bunkers. Dr Lieberman and the rest of the staff all sat on the edge of their cots staring blankly, numb with tension. Not a word was spoken. It was so morbid she could not stand it and she went outside again.

Both Karen and Dov were standing sentry duty.

She returned to the command-post bunker to find that Jordana had gone.

She stretched out on the cot again and covered her legs with a blanket. The vision of the men inching down the mountainside came to her once more. The day had left her spent. She began to doze. The hours passed.

Midnight – one o'clock. Kitty thrashed about on the cot. Her brain was filled with nightmare. She saw the horde of Kassi's men charging out at the column, shrieking, with their sabers glinting. The guards were dead and the Arabs had taken all the children and dug a huge pit for them . . .

Kitty bolted up on the cot in a cold sweat with her heart pounding madly. She shook her head slowly and trembled from head to foot. Then a sound reached her ears. She cocked her head and listened. Her eyes widened in terror!

It was a sound of distant gunfire!

She staggered to her feet. Yes! It was gunfire . . . coming from the direction of Abu Yesha! It was no dream! The column had been discovered!

Jordana entered the bunker just as Kitty rushed for the door.

'Let me go!' she shrieked.

'Kitty, no, no . . . !'

'They're killing my babies! Murderers! Murderers!'

Jordana exerted all her strength to pin Kitty to the wall but Kitty was wild. She lashed out and tore from Jordana's grasp. The *sabra* girl grabbed her, spun her around, and smashed her across the shoulders, sending her to the floor sobbing.

'Listen to me! That gunfire you hear is Zev Gilboa and the Palmach making a diversionary attack. They are hitting the opposite side of Abu Yesha to draw Kassi's men away from the convoy.'

'You're lying!'

'It is true, I swear it. I was told not to say anything until just before the attack. I came here and saw you asleep and went to warn the others.'

Jordana knelt down and helped Kitty to her feet and led her to the cot. 'There is a little brandy left. Drink it.'

Kitty swallowed it, half gagging to force it down. She brought herself under control.

'I am sorry that I struck you,' Jordana said.

'No . . . you did the right thing.'

Jordana sat beside Kitty and patted her hand and massaged the back of her neck. Kitty weakly lay her head on Jordana's shoulder and cried very softly until she had cried herself out. Then she stood up and put on her heavy clothing.

'Karen and Dov will be coming off guard soon. I'll go to my bunker and make them some tea.'

The hours of darkness dragged on and on – a night without end. Out in the blackness the men crawled on their bellies past Abu Yesha while the Palmach made its raid on the other side of the village, and then they plunged quickly down . . . down . . .

Two o'clock. Three o'clock. By now the waiters, even Jordana Ben Canaan, sat drained and empty, in a dazed silence. At five-fifteen they came out of the bunkers. The morning was icy. A thin, slick frost covered the center green. They all walked out of the main gate to that point where the lookout post hung over the edge of the mountain.

The darkness faded from the land and the lights in the valley went off one by one as a musty gray dawn revealed the floor far below.

The sentry looked through the field glasses for some sign of life down the mountain. There was nothing.

'Look!'

The sentry pointed. All of them stared toward the Yad El *moshav*, where dots and dashes blinked out from a signal light.

'What does it read? What does it mean?'

'It says . . . X1416 . . .'

For a moment there was confusion. The message was repeated – X1416.

'They are safe!' Jordana Ben Canaan said. '*But lift thou up thy rod, and stretch out thine hand over the sea, and divide it: and the children of Israel shall go on dry ground through the midst of the sea.* Exodus: fourteen, sixteen.' She smiled exultantly at Kitty.

Chapter Six

Four days after the younger children of Gan Dafna had been evacuated a series of reports filtered in to Ari. His settlement commanders were forwarding information that Arab pressure was lessening. When he learned from friends in Abu Yesha that Kassi had withdrawn half of the hundred men in the village and ordered them back to Fort Esther, Ari knew that the attack on Gan Dafna would come any day.

Ari took twenty more Palmach troops, the last that could be spared anywhere in the Galilee, and once again made the mountain climb to Gan Dafna to assume personal command.

He had forty Palmach troops in all, around thirty staff and faculty members capable of fighting, and Jordana's Gadna youngsters, some two hundred in number. His arsenal showed one hundred and fifty antiquated rifles or homemade Sten guns, two machine guns, a few hundred homemade grenades, mines, and fire bombs, and the obsolete Hungarian antitank gun with its five rounds of ammunition.

Intelligence reports indicated that, opposing him, Mohammed Kassi had eight hundred irregulars with unlimited ammunition and artillery support, plus perhaps another several hundred Arabs from Aata and other hostile villages along the Lebanese border.

Ari's supply of ammunition was critical. He knew that when the attack did come it had to be broken immediately. His one advantage was knowledge of the enemy. Mohammed Kassi, the Iraqi highway robber, had no formal training. He was recruited by Kawukji on the promise of adventure and loot. Ari did not consider Kassi's men a particularly brave lot, but they could be whipped into a frenzy; if they ever got the upper hand during battle they would become murderous. Ari planned to use Arab ignorance and lack of imagination as his allies. He banked his defensive plan on the presumption that Kassi would try a direct frontal assault in the straightest and shortest line from Fort Esther. The frontal attack had been the history of Arab irregulars' tactics since he began fighting them as a boy. He stacked his defenses in one place.

The key spot in Ari's defense was a ravine that led like a funnel into Gan Dafna. If Ari could get Kassi to come into the ravine he had a chance. Zev Gilboa kept patrols in the rocks and brush right outside Fort Esther to observe the Arab movements. He had confirmed the fact that Kassi was massing men.

Three days after Ari arrived at Gan Dafna, a young runner came into his command post with the news that Kassi's men, nearly a thousand strong, had left the fort and were starting down the hill. Within two minutes the 'black alarm' was sounded and every man, woman, and child at Gan Dafna took his post and stood by.

A deep saddle in the mountains could cover Kassi's men until they arrived at a knoll directly over Gan Dafna, some six hundred yards from the north side of the village and two hundred yards from the critical ravine which led in like a funnel.

Ari's men dug in to their prepared positions, became silent, and waited.

Soon heads began popping up on the knoll. Within minutes the point was swarming with irregulars. They stopped their progress and stared down at the ominously quiet village. The Arab officers were suspicious of the silence. Not a shot had been fired by either side.

In the watch and gun tower atop Fort Esther, Mohammed Kassi looked through powerful field glasses and smiled as he saw his horde of men poised atop Gan Dafna. Since the Jews had not fired at them his confidence grew that his men would be able to overrun the place. A cannon fired from the fort as a signal for the attack to begin.

In Gan Dafna they could hear harangues and conversation in Arabic as officers shouted at their men. Still no one moved down from the knoll. The quiet from the village baffled them. More of them began to scream and point down at the village. Their curses and their anger rose in hysterical crescendo.

'They're trying to work themselves into a heroic lather,' Ari said.

The disciplined forces of the Jews showed neither their faces nor their guns, though each man found it hard to remain controlled under the chilling abuse of the Arabs.

After twenty minutes of ranting there was a sudden eruption from the knoll as irregulars poured down with unearthly shrieks, sabers and bayonets flashing a steel silhouette against the sky.

The first phase of Ari's defense would now receive a test. Each night he had sent patrols out to plant homemade land mines which could be detonated from inside Gan Dafna. The mines formed a corridor and were so placed to compress the Arabs toward the middle of the ravine.

Zev Gilboa, in the fowardmost position, waited until the Arab charge was in full fury. When the horde of men reached the mine field, Zev held up a green flag. Inside Gan Dafna, Ari set off the charges.

Twenty mines, ten on each side, blew up at once. The roar shook the mountainside. The mines exploded on the fringe of the mob, which immediately squeezed together and rushed right down the funnel of the ravine.

On the sides of the ravine Ari had placed his forty Palmach troops, the two machine guns, and all the grenades and fire bombs in the arsenal. As the Arabs passed directly under them the Palmach opened up a cross-fire with the two guns and turned the ravine into a gory turkey shoot. Flames erupted from the fire bombs and turned dozens of the irregulars into human torches, while the Palmach hurled a torrent of grenades among them.

In addition the Palmach set off strings of firecrackers, while from loudspeakers in the trees came a recording of bombing explosions. The continued din of the real and artificial arms was deafening and terrifying.

Inside Fort Esther, Mohammed Kassi frantically called for artillery to clean off the sides of the ravine. The excited Arab gunners opened fire and landed half of their shells among their own men. Finally they managed to silence one Palmach machine gun.

The advance Arab force had been cut down like cordwood, but still they poured in. They had been stimulated to such frenzy that their thrust was now that of men insane with fear.

The second machine gun stopped firing when its barrel burned out. The Palmach quit its position on the sides of the ravine and dropped back into Gan Dafna before the unabated onslaught. The Arabs' rush came to within a hundred yards of the village in disorganized knots of screaming men. David Ben Ami had the cover off the barricaded and sandbagged Hungarian antitank gun. The projectiles had been modified and each of the five rounds now contained two thousand shotgun pellets. If the gun worked properly it would have the effect of a battery of men firing at once.

The leading bunched mass of maddened Arabs rolled to within fifty yards ... forty ... thirty ... twenty ...

The sweat poured down David Ben Ami's face as he sighted the gun at point-blank range.

Ten yards ...

'Fire one!'

The ancient antitank gun bounced off the ground and spewed pellets into the faces of the chargers. Bloodcurdling shrieks mingled with smoke, and through it, as he swiftly reloaded, David glimpsed piles of men lying dead or wounded within yards of the gun and others staggering back in blind shock.

The second wave came in behind the first.

'Fire two!'

The second wave went down in slaughter.

'Fire three!'

The barrel blew off the gun and she was finished, but she had done her work. In three shots the buckshot canister sprays had dropped nearly two hundred men. The momentum of the drive was halted.

A last assault was tried. A hundred Arabs again reached the edge of Gan Dafna, to be met by a broadside from Jordana Ben Canaan's entrenched Gadna youths.

Bewildered and bleeding, the Arab survivors now scrambled back up the death-filled ravine. As they retreated, Zev Gilboa yelled out for the Palmach troops to follow him. The shepherd led his forty fighters after several hundred running Arabs. He chased them back up the knoll and continued to pursue them.

Ari looked through his field glasses.

'The God-damned fool!' Ari yelled, 'he's going to try to take Fort Esther. I told him to stop at the knoll.'

'What's the matter with Zev?' David grunted between his teeth.

'Come on,' Ari cried. 'Let's see if we can stop him.'

Ari issued hasty orders for Jordana to have the Gadna children pick up the Arab arms in the field and pull back into Gan Dafna.

His plan had paid off. In less than fifteen minutes he had dissipated the strength of his defense, but nearly half Kassi's troops lay dead or wounded.

When Mohammed Kassi saw his men run back up toward the fort, confusion broke out. Zev Gilboa was twenty-five yards out ahead of the rest of the Palmach when it happened. Arab gunners from Fort Esther began firing toward their own retreating men in order to stop the pursuing Palmach. Some of the Arabs managed to get inside Fort Esther. Those too close to the pursuing Jews were shut out and fired on. Zev had passed the outer accordions of barbed wire only forty yards from the fort.

'Cover!' he screamed at his troops. He threw himself flat and fired his sten gun at the fort until the Palmach fell back out of range. Seeing that his attack was futile, Zev turned and tried to crawl back down the hill. A barrage of bullets came from the fort and he was hit. He stood up and ran and again he was hit, and this time he fell into the barbed wire and became entangled. He was unable to move.

The Palmach had dug in and were preparing to go up to try to bring Zev out when Ari and David crawled up to them.

'It's Zev. He's out there tangled up in the wire.'

Ari looked out from behind a large rock. He was a hundred yards away from Zev across an open field. There were some places he could find cover behind large rocks, but close to Zev he would be fully exposed.

Suddenly the firing from Fort Esther stopped and it became very still.

'What's going on?' David asked.

'They're using Zev for bait. They see he can't move and they hope we'll try to get up there and get him.'

'Those bastards. Why don't they shoot him and get it over with?'

'Can't you see, David? He's lost his rifle. They're going to wait until we leave and try to take him alive. They're going to take it out on him for all the men they lost today.'

'Oh, my God,' David groaned. He jumped out from cover but Ari grabbed him and threw him back.

'Somebody give me a pair of grenades,' Ari said. 'Good. David, take the troops back into Gan Dafna.'

'You're not going up there by yourself, Ari ...'

'Do what I order, damn you!'

David turned quietly and signaled to start a withdrawal. He looked back to see Ari already scuttling up the hill toward Zev.

The Arabs watched Ari move up. They knew someone would try to get the wounded man. They would wait until he got close enough and try to wound him too; then the Jews would send another man up ... and another.

Ari got up, sprinted, and dived behind a rock. The Arabs did not shoot.

Then he crawled again until he got to cover twenty yards from where Zev was tangled in the wire. Ari guessed that the Arabs would wait until he actually reached Zev and was an unmissable target.

'Get back ... !' Zev called. 'Get back!'

Ari peeked around the boulder. He could see Zev clearly. The blood was spurting from his face and stomach. He was completely trapped in the wire. Ari looked up to Fort Esther. He could see the sun glint off the barrels of rifles trained on Zev.

'Get back!' Zev shouted again. 'My guts are hanging out. I can't last ten minutes ... get back!'

Ari slipped the hand grenades from his belt.

'Zev. I'm going to throw you some grenades!' he called in German. Ari locked the pins in so they could not explode. He stood up quickly and threw both grenades to the boy. One landed just beside him.

Zev picked up the grenade and held it close to his torn stomach.

'I've got it ... now get back!'

Ari ran down the hill quickly, catching the Arabs off guard; they had been expecting him to come up after Zev. When they opened fire he was out of range and making his way toward Gan Dafna.

Zev Gilboa was alone now and the life was oozing from him. The Arabs waited for a half hour, watching for a trick, expecting a Jew to come up after him. They wanted him alive.

The gates of Fort Esther opened. Some thirty Arabs emerged and trotted down to surround Zev.

Zev twisted the pin out of the grenade, held it next to his head and let the spoon fly off.

Ari heard the blast and stopped. He turned chalky white and his bad leg folded up under him. The insides of him shook; then he continued crawling down to Gan Dafna.

Ari sat in the command-post bunker alone. His face was waxen, and only the trembling of his cheek muscles showed there was life in him. His eyes stared dully from black-ringed sockets.

The Jews had lost twenty-four people: eleven Palmach boys, three Palmach girls, six faculty members, and four children. There were another twenty-two wounded. Mohammed Kassi had lost four hundred and eighteen men killed and a hundred and seventy wounded.

The Jews had taken enough weapons to make it likely that Kassi would never try another attack on Gan Dafna. But the Arabs still held Fort Esther and controlled the road through Abu Yesha.

Kitty Fremont entered the bunker. She too was on the brink of exhaustion. 'The Arab casualties have all been removed to Abu Yesha except those you wanted for questioning.'

Ari nodded. 'How about our wounded?'

'Two of the children don't look as though they'll make it. The rest will be all right. Here ... I brought you some brandy,' Kitty said.

'Thanks ... thanks ...'

Ari sipped and remained quiet.

'I brought Zev Gilboa's things over to you. There isn't very much here ... a few personal things.'

'A *kibbutznik* doesn't have very much of his own. Everything, including his life, belongs to something else,' he said, with a trace of irony.

'I liked Zev,' Kitty said. 'He was telling me last night how he looked forward to tending his sheep again. Anyhow ... his wife may want these things. She's having another baby, you know.'

'Zev was a damned fool!' Ari snarled. 'He had no business trying to take that fort.'

Ari picked up the handkerchief filled with Zev's meager articles. 'Liora's a good girl. She's tough. She'll come through it.' Ari threw the belongings into the kerosene stove. 'I'll have a hard time replacing him.'

Kitty's eyes narrowed. 'Is that what you were thinking ... you'd have a hard time replacing him.'

Ari stood up and lit a cigarette. 'You don't grow men like Zev on trees.'

'Is there nothing you cherish?'

'Tell me, Kitty. What did your husband's commander do when he was killed at Guadalcanal? Did he hold a wake for him?'

'I thought this was a little different, Ari. You've known Zev since he was a boy. That girl, his wife, is a Yad El girl. She was raised two farms away from yours.'

'What do you want me to do?'

'Cry for that poor girl!'

For a second Ari's face twisted and his lips trembled and then his features sat rigidly. 'It is nothing new to see a man die in battle. Get out of here ...'

Chapter Seven

The siege of Safed had begun exactly one day after the partition vote of November 29, 1947. When the British left Safed in the spring of 1948, as expected, they handed the three key spots over to the Arabs: the police station looking right down on the Jewish quarter, the acropolis commanding the entire city, and the Taggart fort on Mount Canaan just outside town.

Safed was shaped like an inverted cone. The Jewish quarter occupied a slice of about one eighth of the cone, so that the Arabs were above, below, and on both sides of them. The Jews had only two hundred half-trained Haganah men. Their refusal of evacuation and their decision to fight to the last man was in the spirit and tradition of the ancient Hebrews. The Cabalists of Safed, the least capable among the Jews of defending themselves, had been a primary target for the Mufti's riots. They had faced slaughter from Arab mobs before and they had cringed. Now they had made up their minds that they would stand and die. The Jewish quarter, jammed into the narrow twisting lanes, sustained an amazing spirit.

One day after the British left, Ari slipped Joab Yarkoni into the Jewish quarter of Safed with thirty Palmach boys and twenty Palmach girls. A wild celebration marked their arrival. It was the Sabbath and Yarkoni's troops were exhausted from travel through hostile country and they were hungry. For the first time in centuries, the Cabalists broke the Sabbath by cooking a hot meal for the reinforcements.

Kawukji, wanting to secure Safed as the temporary capital for the Mufti, ordered the irregulars to overrun the Jewish quarter. The Arabs tried a few sorties and were thrown back out; they soon realized that they would take the quarter only by a house-by-house, room-by-room fight. They reconsidered and returned to sniping and siege tactics.

The Jews were commanded by Remez and Joab Yarkoni. Brigadier Sutherland had left his villa on Mount Canaan to become the only guest of Remez's resort hotel. He was called upon for advice now and then but conceded that the Jews were doing quite well enough without his help.

Remez took on as his first task the clearing of a definite field of fire. The Arab and Jewish quarters were jammed up against each other, making it easy for Arab patrols to slip through and spread his already thin defensive strength. He wanted space between his forces and the Arabs. Yarkoni took a crew into the Arab quarters, seized a dozen borderline houses, and began shooting from them. Then he withdrew. Each time the Arabs came back, Yarkoni would again attack and take the same borderline houses. Finally the Arabs dynamited the houses to keep the Jews from using them. It was exactly what Remez wanted: it created the space between the two sectors to give the Jews better visibility and easier defense.

With this accomplished Remez and Yarkoni devised the second tactic. Yarkoni set out to harass the Arabs around the clock. Each day he sent three or four Palmach patrols into the Arab sector to move through the maze of alleys or over the roof tops. His patrols would suddenly make a sharp hit-and-run attack, each time at a different place. Whenever the Arabs concentrated their men in one strong point, the Jews were informed of it by spies and thus knew exactly where to strike and what spot to avoid. Like a jabbing boxer the daylight patrols kept the Arabs off balance.

But it was the night patrols of the Palmach that drove the Arabs into a frenzy. Yarkoni had lived in Morocco and he knew his enemy. The Arab was a superstitious man, with an unnatural fear of the dark. Yarkoni used the darkness like extra troops. The Palmach night patrols, merely by shooting off firecrackers, kept the Arab population in a panic.

Remez and Yarkoni admitted that their tactics were desperation measures. They were not strong enough to do real damage to the enemy, and the sheer weight of Arab numbers, position, and arms began to grind them down. A lost Palmach or Haganah soldier could not be replaced. Food was almost as difficult to replace. Ammunition was so critical that fines were levied against any Haganah or Palmach soldier who wasted a bullet.

Even as they were being worn down, the Jews held every inch of their quarter, and the amazing spirit never flagged. A single radio receiver was by now their only daily contact with the outside world, yet schools continued on schedule, the small newspaper never skipped an edition, and the pious did not miss a minute of synagogue. Letters got out by the patrols were fixed with hand-drawn stamps and were honored throughout Palestine by the Yishuv.

The siege carried on through the winter and the spring. Finally one day Yarkoni met with Sutherland and Remez to face bitter reality. The Jews had lost fifty of their best fighting men, they were down to their last twelve bags of flour, and they did not have ammunition to last five days. Yarkoni did not even have firecrackers for his patrols. The Arabs had sensed this weakness and were becoming bolder.

'I promised Ari that I wouldn't bother him with our troubles but I am afraid I must get to Ein Or and talk to him,' Yarkoni decided. The same night he slipped out of Safed and went to Ari's headquarters.

Joab reported in full on the Safed situation. He concluded, 'I hate to bother you, Ari, but in another three days we are going to have to start eating rats.'

Ari grunted. The stand at Safed had been an inspiration to the entire Yishuv. It was more than a strategic position now, it was another invaluable symbol of defiance. 'If we could win Safed we could crush Arab morale in the whole Galilee.'

'Ari, every time we have to fire a bullet, we must go into a debate about it.'

'I have an idea,' Ari said. 'Come with me.'

Ari set up an emergency night patrol to get at least some supplies of food into Safed and then took Joab to the ordnance shed. In an inner room he showed the Moroccan a strange-looking contraption of cast iron, nuts, and bolts.

'What the hell is it?' Joab asked.

'Joab, you are looking at a *Davidka*.'

'A Davidka?'

'Yes ... a Little David, handcrafted by Jewish genius.'

Joab scratched his jaw. In some respects one might say it did appear to be a weapon – of a sort. Yet . . . nothing quite like it existed anywhere else, Joab was sure.

'What is it supposed to do?'

'I am told that it shoots mortar shells.'

'How?'

'Damned if I know. We haven't experimented yet. I have a report from Jerusalem saying that it has been very effective.'

'For the Jews or Arabs?'

'Joab, I'll tell you what I'm going to do. I've been saving this weapon for the proper situation. It's yours, take it to Safed.'

Joab walked around the odd piece of machinery. 'The things we have to resort to to win a war,' he mumbled.

The night patrol carrying emergency rations into Safed also brought along the Davidka and thirty pounds of ammunition. As soon as he arrived, Joab called the Haganah and Palmach leaders together, and through the rest of the night they traded ideas on how the thing was supposed to work. Ten people were present and ten opinions were given.

At last someone thought of sending for Brigadier Sutherland. He was awakened at the hotel and half dragged to headquarters. He stared at the Davidka in disbelief.

'Only a Jew could concoct something like this,' he concluded.

'I hear it was very effective in Jerusalem,' Joab apologized.

Sutherland played with all the levers and handles and switches and sights and in the next hour they evolved a firing procedure which might – or might not – work.

The next morning the Davidka was carried to a clearing and pointed in the general direction of the Arab-held police station and some nearby houses the Arabs used as sniping posts.

The Davidka's ammunition was no less strange in appearance than the Davidka. It was shaped like a mallet, of which the head was an iron cylinder filled with dynamite equipped with detonators. The thick handle allegedly fit down the mortar tube. On firing, the handle was supposed to be thrust out with such force that it would hurl the whole unbalanced load of dynamite at the target. Sutherland had visions of the thing flying for a few feet and exploding in front of them.

'If that warhead merely falls out of the end of the tube – as I confidently expect,' Sutherland said, 'we are likely to lose the entire Jewish population of Safed.'

'Then I suggest we rig up a long line so we can fire it from a safe distance,' Remez said.

'How do we aim it?' Yarkoni asked.

'Aiming this monstrosity isn't going to do much good. Just point it in the general direction and pray for the best.'

The chief rabbi and many of the Cabalists and their wives gathered around the Davidka and carried on a lengthy debate on whether or not it meant doomsday for all of them. Finally the chief rabbi said special benedictions over the weapon and asked the Messiah kindly to spare them for they had indeed been very good in keeping the laws.

'Well, let's get it over with,' Remez said pessimistically.

The Cabalists backed to safety. Firing caps were stuffed down the tube and one of the shells was lifted and the long handle placed inside. The cylinder of dynamite balanced over the end of the tube threateningly. A long line was attached to the firing mechanism. Everyone took cover and the earth stood still.

'Let her go,' Yarkoni ordered in a shaky voice.

Remez jerked and a strange thing happened. The Little David fired.

The handle hissed out of the tube and the bucket of dynamite arched and spun, handle over bucket, up the hill. As it hurled through the air, growing smaller and smaller, it made a hideous swishing sound. It crashed into some Arab houses near the police station.

Sutherland's mouth hung open.

Yarkoni's mustache went from down to up.

Remez's eyes popped out.

The old Cabalists stopped praying long enough to look in astonishment.

The shell exploded like a thunderclap, shaking the town to its foundations. It seemed as though half the hillside must have been blown away.

After moments of stunned silence there was an eruption of shouting and hugging and kissing and praying and jubilation.

'By jove ...' was all Sutherland could say. 'By jove ... !'

The Palmachniks formed a *hora* ring and danced around the Little David.

'Come on, come on. Let's fire another round!'

In the Arab quarters they could hear the Jews cheering, and the Arabs knew why. The very sound of the flying bomb in itself was enough to frighten one to death, to say nothing of the explosion. No one, Palestinian Arabs or irregulars, had bargained for anything like this; each time the Little David fired, a scene of havoc followed. The Arabs quaked in terror as the Jews revenged some of the hundred years of torment.

Joab Yarkoni got word to Ari that the Davidka had the Arabs in a turmoil. Ari sensed an opportunity and decided on a risky attempt to exploit it. He took a few men from each settlement and was able to scrape together two companies of Haganah. He got them into Safed at night with more ammunition for the Davidka.

Swish ... *whoom!*

The bucket of bolts and its hissing bomb was devastating the town. Swish ... *whoom!*

The third day after the Davidka had come to Safed the skies opened and it poured rain. Ari Ben Canaan then made the greatest bluff of the war that counted bluffs as part of the arsenal. He had Remez call all the Arab spies together and he gave them a briefing.

'In case you didn't know, brothers' – Ari addressed them in Arabic – 'we have a secret weapon. I am not at liberty to disclose the nature of the weapon but I might say that you all know that it always rains after a nuclear blast. Need one say more?'

Within minutes the spies spread the word that the Little David was a secret weapon. Within an hour, every Arab mouth in Safed had repeated the appalling news: *the Jews have the atom bomb!*

Swish ... whoom! The Little David roared and the rain turned to a deluge and the panic was on. Inside of two hours the roads out of Safed were clogged with fleeing Arabs.

Ari Ben Canaan led the Haganah on an attack with three hundred men. The attack was more spontaneous than calculated and Ari's men were thrown off the acropolis by irregulars and a handful of angry Safed Arabs. He lost heavily, but the Safed population continued to run.

Three days later, with Safed nearly empty of Arab civilian population and with hundreds of the irregulars deserted, Ari Ben Canaan, Remez, and Joab Yarkoni led a better planned, three-pronged attack and took the acropolis.

The tables were turned. The Jews were on the high ground above the Arab police station. Now those who had for decades tormented and murdered the Cabalists in wild mobs had their chance to stand and fight, but they fled in the face of the Jewish wrath. The police station fell and Ari immediately headed outside of the town to block off the huge Taggart fort on Mount Canaan, the strongest of the Arab positions. When he arrived he was astounded to discover that the Arabs had abandoned the Taggart fort, a position it would have been impossible to take. With the fort in his hands, the conquest of Safed was complete.

The victory of Safed was staggering. The vulnerable position thought impossible to defend had not only been defended but the defenders had conquered the city – with a few hundred fighters and a weird weapon called the Little David.

There were many theories and much discussion on just how this victory came about. Even the Cabalists of Safed were split on the subject. Rabbi Haim of the Ashkenazim or European school was quite certain of divine intervention as foretold in Job:

When he is about to fill his belly, God shall cast the fury of his wrath upon him, and shall rain it upon him while he is eating. He shall flee from the iron weapon . . .

Rabbi Meir of the Sephardic or Oriental school disputed Haim and was just as certain of divine intervention as described in Ezekiel:

Thy walls shall shake at the noise . . . he shall enter into thy gates, as men enter into a city wherein is made a breach . . . thy strong garrisons shall go down to the ground.

Bruce Sutherland returned to his villa on Mount Canaan. The Arabs had desolated it. They had trampled his lovely rose garden to the earth and they had stolen everything including the doorknobs. It did not matter to Sutherland, for it would all be rebuilt again. He and Yarkoni and Remez walked out to his rear patio and looked over the valley to Safed. They drank a lot of brandy and they began to chuckle.

Neither they nor anyone else was aware of it yet, but the stampede of Safed's population had opened a new and tragic chapter – it began the creation of Arab refugees.

Somewhere in the Galilee, an obsolete Liberator bomber piloted by a volunteer crew of South Africans and Americans looked to the earth for a pair of blue flares.

The flares were spotted and they landed the bomber blind, with only a few flashlights marking the airfield. The plane bumped harshly over a pitted runway and skidded to a stop. The motors were cut quickly.

Swarms of people engulfed the plane and emptied it of its cargo, the first shipment of modern arms. Rifles, machine guns, mortars, and hundreds of thousands of rounds of ammunition were snatched from its waist and tail sections and its converted bomb bays.

The working parties stripped the Liberator clean in minutes. They loaded up a dozen trucks, which scattered in as many different directions. In a dozen *kibbutzim* Gadna youths stood ready to clean the weapons and get them out to the embattled settlements. The plane was turned and made a hair's-breadth take-off and flew back to Europe to get another load of arms.

In the morning British troops came to investigate Arab complaints that they had heard an airplane landing in the area. The British were unable to find a single trace of a plane and were certain the Arab imagination was being carried away again.

By the time the fourth and fifth shipment of arms arrived the Jews began to roll up victories. Tiberias on the Sea of Galilee had fallen to the Jews. The huge Gesher Taggart fort was grabbed by the Jews and held off repeated attacks by Iraqi irregulars.

With the fall of Safed, the Jews launched their first co-ordinated offensive, Operation Iron Broom, to sweep Galilee clean of hostile villages. Iron Broom was led by machine-gun-bearing jeeps which blazed into the villages and stampeded the Arabs. Safed had started a crack in the Arab morale that gave Iron Broom a psychological jump.

With a score of local victories behind them and the knowledge that they could mount a successful offensive, the Haganah went after the vital port of Haifa.

The Haganah swept down the slopes of Mount Carmel in a four-pronged attack, each action aimed at an Arab strong point. The Arab troops, consisting of home guards, Syrian, Lebanese, and Iraqi irregulars, mounted a strong defense and were at first able to contain the battle. The British, who still controlled the dock area, called truce after truce to stop the Jewish offenses, and at times took away hard-won vantage points.

The Arabs continued to hold well against the steady Jewish pressure. Then, as the fighting reached a peak, the Arab commander and his entire staff slipped out and quietly fled. Arab resistance became demoralized and collapsed entirely. Again the British called a truce as the Jews swept into the Arab quarters.

At that point a fantastic event took place. The Arabs suddenly announced, to the general astonishment, that the entire population wished to leave. The procedure followed the curious pattern of Safed and many of the villages. It was a strange spectacle to see whole Arab populations stampeding for the Lebanese border, with no one pursuing them.

Acre, an all-Arab city crammed with refugees, fell to the Haganah after a halfhearted and feeble defense that lasted only three days. The infection spread to the Arab city of Jaffa, where the Maccabees held the center of the line and launched an attack which took this oldest port in the world – and the Arabs of Jaffa fled.

In the Jerusalem corridor, Abdul Kadar succeeded in driving the Jews from the vital height of the Kastel, but the Haganah and Palmach came right back and threw the Arabs off in turn. Kadar rallied his people for still another attempt on the Kastel, and in this try he was killed. The loss of their one good commander was a further severe blow to the demoralized Arabs.

May 1948 came into being. The British had only two more weeks left to complete their evacuation and give up the mandate.

On the borders, the revengeful armies of Syria, Yemen, Lebanon, Trans-Jordan, Egypt, Saudi Arabia, and Iraq stood poised to cross and crush the conquering Jews.

The hour of decision – to declare statehood or not to declare statehood – was at hand.

Chapter Eight

Between November of 1947 and May of 1948, the Yishuv had staged a spectacular show by successfully fighting against overwhelming odds with little more than nothing. During that period of time the Jews had converted the Haganah from an underground defense unit into the nucleus of a real army. They had trained new troops and staff men and organized tactical schools, operations, supply and transport and the hundreds of other things that marked the conversion from guerrilla fighting to organized warfare.

The first air force of grenade-throwing Piper Cub pilots had grown to include a few Spitfires manned by Jews who had flown with the American, British, and South African air forces. The Navy had begun with the rickety immigration runners and now had a few corvettes and PT boats.

From the beginning the Jews had appreciated the importance of administration, intelligence, and command. Each day they gained in experience and their victories brought confidence. They had shown they could orgainze and co-ordinate small-scale efforts: the convoys to Jerusalem, Operation Iron Broom, and other local actions.

They had met the challenge and triumphed. Yet they knew that they had only fought a small war, against an enemy who did not have a tremendous desire to fight. The Arabs had little organization of leadership and no stomach for sustained fighting. The Arab debacle proved that it took more than slogans to give a man the stamina and courage to put his life on the block.

The planeloads of small arms had helped to save the Yishuv. As the hour of decision came near the reality came with it that these arms would have to face regular armies with tanks, artillery, and modern air forces.

Those who believed that the Arab countries were bluffing soon got a rude awakening as the Arab Legion of Trans-Jordan wantonly violated every concept of honor. The Legion operated in Palestine as a British police force. This 'British police force' began open action against the isolated Etzion Group settlements on the Bethlehem Road.

The four villages in the Etzion group were manned by Orthodox Jews who chose to stay and fight, as did every settlement in the Yishuv. Led by British officers, the Trans-Jordan Arab Legion shelled the four settlements without mercy and completely cut them off from outside help.

Kibbutz Etzion was the first target of the Legion. After blasting the *kibbutz* apart, the Legion attacked the siege-weary, half-starved settlement. The Orthodox Jews of *kibbutz* Etzion held fast until their last round of ammunition had been fired and only then did they surrender. Arab villagers who had followed the Legion rushed into the *kibbutz* and massacred almost all the survivors. The Legion made an attempt to stop the slaughter but when it was over only four Jews had survived.

The Haganah immediately appealed to the International Red Cross to supervise the surrender of the other three Etzion group settlements, which were also close to being out of ammunition. Only this move prevented mass murder there, too.

In the Negev Desert near the Dead Sea, the Arab Legion of Trans-Jordan attacked again.

This time they hit a *kibbutz* that the Jews had built in the lowest and hottest place on the earth. It was called Beth Ha-Arava – the House in the Wilderness. In the summertime it was one hundred and twenty-five degrees in the shade. When the Jews came to this place no living thing had grown in the alkaline soil in all of history. They washed the soil down, acre by acre, to free it of salts, and by this painstaking process and through the creation of spillways, dams, and cisterns to trap the rainfall, they built a modern farm.

With the nearest Jews a hundred miles away and facing unbeatable odds, Beth Ha-Arava surrendered to the Arab Legion, and as the people walked from the House in the Wilderness the Jews set a torch to it and burned their houses and fields which had been built with inhuman toil.

And so, the Arabs had got their victories at last – Beth Ha-Arava – the House in the Wilderness – and the blood-stained conquest of the Etzion group.

On the night of May 13, 1948, the British High Commissioner for Palestine quietly left embattled Jerusalem. The Union Jack, a symbol here of the misuse of power, came down from the staff – forever.

MAY 14, 1948

In Tel Aviv the leaders of the Yishuv and the world Zionists met in the house of Meier Dizengoff, the founder and first mayor of the city. Outside the house, Sten-gun-bearing guards kept back anxious crowds.

In Cairo, in New York, in Jerusalem, and in Paris and London and Washington they turned their eyes and ears to this house.

'This is Kol Israel – the Voice of Israel,' the announcer said slowly from the radio station. 'I have just been handed a document concerning the end of the British mandate which I shall now read to you.'

'Quiet! Quiet!' Dr Lieberman said to the crowd of children who had gathered in his cottage. 'Quiet!'

'The Land of Israel,' the voice over the radio said, 'was the birthplace of the Jewish people. Here their spiritual, religious, and national identity was formed. Here they achieved independence and created a culture of national and universal significance. Here they wrote and gave the Bible to the world.'

Bruce Sutherland and Joab Yarkoni stopped the chess game in Remez's hotel and, with Remez, listened raptly.

'Exiled from the Land of Israel, the Jewish people remained faithful to it in all the countries of their dispersion, never ceasing to pray and hope for their return and the restoration of their national freedom.'

In Paris, the static on the radio increased and drowned out the voice as Barak Ben Canaan and the Yishuv agents frantically twisted the dials and beat on the receiver.

'Impelled by this historic association, Jews strove throughout the centuries to go back to the land of their fathers and regain their statehood. In recent decades they returned in their masses. They reclaimed the wilderness, revived their language, built cities and villages, and established an ever-growing community with its own economic and cultural life. They sought peace, yet were prepared to defend themselves. They brought the blessings of progress to all inhabitants ...'

In Safed, the Cabalists listened in hope of words to fulfill the ancient prophecies. In the Jerusalem corridor the dog-tired Palmach fighters of the Hillmen Brigade listened, and in the isolated and besieged settlements of the blistering Negev Desert they listened.

'... right was acknowledged by the Balfour Declaration of November 2, 1917, and reaffirmed by the mandate of the League of Nations, which gave explicit international recognition ...'

David Ben Ami rushed into the commander's office at Ein Or *kibbutz*. Ari held his finger to his lips and pointed to the radio.

'... the recent holocaust which engulfed millions of Jews in Europe proved anew the need ...'

Sarah Ben Canaan listened at Yad El and she remembered the first time she had seen Barak ride into Rosh Pinna on a white Arab steed with his great red beard flowing down on his tunic.

'... re-establishment of the Jewish state, which would open the gates to all Jews and endow the Jewish people with equality of status among the family of nations ...'

Dov and Karen held hands quietly in the dining hall and listened to the loud-speaker.

'In the second world war the Jewish people in Palestine made their full contribution to the struggle ... On November 29, 1947, the General Assembly of the United Nations adopted a resolution requiring the establishing of a Jewish state in Palestine ... the right of the Jewish people to establish their independent state is unassailable. It is the natural right of the Jewish people to lead, as do all other nations, an independent existence as a sovereign state.

'We hereby proclaim the establishment of the Jewish state in Palestine, to be called the State of Israel.'

Kitty Fremont felt her heart leap – Jordana smiled.

'The State of Israel will be open to immigration to Jews from all countries of their dispersion; will promote the development of the country for the benefit of all its inhabitants; will be based on the principles of liberty, justice, and peace as conceived by the prophets of Israel; will uphold the full social and political equality of all its citizens, without distinction of religion, race, or sex; will guarantee freedom of religion, conscience, education, and culture; will safeguard holy places of all religions; and will loyally uphold the principles of the United Nations Charter ...

'... In the midst of wanton aggression, we yet call upon the Arab inhabitants of the State of Israel to preserve the ways of peace and play their part in the development of the state, on the basis of full and equal citizenship and due representation in all its bodies and institutions ...

'... we extend our hand in peace and neighborliness to all the neighboring states and their peoples, and invite them to co-operate ...

'... With trust in Almighty God, we set our hand to this declaration at this session of the Provisional State Council, on the soil of the homeland, in the city of Tel Aviv, on this Sabbath eve, the fifth of Iyar 5708, the fourteenth day of May 1948.'

After two thousand years, the State of Israel was reborn.

Within hours, through President Harry Truman, the United States became the first of the nations of the world to recognize the State of Israel.

Even as the crowds in Tel Aviv danced the *hora* in the streets, Egyptian bombers took off en route to the city to destroy it and the armies of the Arab world crossed the frontiers of the infant state.

Chapter Nine

As the individual Arab armies violated the borders of Israel they boasted of immediate victory and began to issue glorious communiques giving vivid descriptions of imaginary triumphs. The Arabs revealed that they had a 'master plan' for throwing the Jews into the sea. If a master plan existed there was no master commander, for each Arab country had its own idea of who should run the armies and each Arab country had its own idea of who should rule Palestine afterward. Bagdad and Cairo both claimed leadership of the Arab world and of a 'greater Arab state'; Saudi Arabia claimed leadership as the country which held the sacred cities of Mecca and Medina; Jordan aspired to Palestine as part of the mandate; Syria had never dropped the claim that Palestine was the southern part of an Ottoman province. And so – the 'united' Arabs attacked.

NEGEV DESERT

A much-heralded Egyptian aggressive force came from bases in the Sinai through Arab-held Gaza along the coast. The first of two Egyptian columns, backed by tanks, armored cars, artillery, and modern aircraft, moved along the coastal road which followed the railroad due north to the Jewish provisional capital of Tel Aviv. The Egyptians were confident the Jewish settlements would break and run before their awesome, overwhelming power.

At the first *kibbutz*, Nirim, the Egyptians made a headlong rush and were hurled out. At the second and third settlements along the way they met the same stiff resistance. This shocking bit of business caused the Egyptian staff to reevaluate the situation. They decided to bypass these tougher spots and continue on up the coast. However, they ran the danger of overextending their supply lines and leaving their rear open for attack from these Jewish pockets: it was mandatory that they stop and fight in certain key places.

Egyptian artillery pounded the settlements to the ground and Egyptian planes bombed and raked them. After furious encounters the Egyptians captured three settlements. The majority of the settlements held and were bypassed.

The most vital strategic settlement in the Egyptian line of march was *kibbutz* Negba – Gate of the Negev – which was located near the intersection of the north road to Tel Aviv and a lateral road that ran inland. This was one of the places that the Egyptians had to capture.

Less than a mile from *kibbutz* Negba stood the Taggart fort of Suweidan – the Monster on the Hill. Suweidan had been handed over to the Arabs by the British. From the fort they were able to shell *kibbutz* Negba to rubble. Negba did not own a gun which could reach the fort.

The farmers of Negba realized the importance of their vital junction to the invaders. They also knew they were not invincible. They knew what to expect; nevertheless, they made the decision to stay and fight. As the guns from Suweidan knocked down every last building and the water ration was reduced to a few drops a day and the subsistence fell to starvation level, Negba continued to hold. Assault followed assault, and each time the Jews threw the Egyptians back. During one Egyptian attack led by tanks, the Jews were down to their last five rounds of antitank ammunition and they knocked out four tanks. For weeks Negba held the Egyptians at a stalemate. It refused to be taken. It fought as the ancient Hebrews of Masada had fought, and Negba became the first symbol of the defiance of the new state.

The Egyptian coastal column left huge forces in Suweidan and continued on up the coast. They moved dangerously close to Tel Aviv.

At Isdud, only twenty miles from Tel Aviv, the Israelis stiffened their defenses. As quickly as arms could be unloaded at the docks, they were rushed to Isdud, along with green new immigrants, to block the Egyptian column.

The Egyptians called a halt to regroup, resupply, and probe in preparation for a final thrust which would take them into Tel Aviv.

The second half of the Egyptian invasion force wheeled inland to the Negev Desert. As they advanced unmolested through Arab cities of Beersheba and Hebron and Bethlehem, Radio Cairo and the Egyptian press hailed 'victory after victory.'

It was intended that this second column join in the 'glorious' conquest of Jerusalem by attacking from the south simultaneously with an attack of the Arab Legion. However, the Egyptians decided not to share the credit and went after Jerusalem by themselves.

Massing at Bethlehem, they assaulted Ramat Rahel – the Hill of Rachel – a *kibbutz* outpost defending the southern approach to new Jerusalem, the place where Rachel once wept for the exiled children of Israel.

The farmers of Ramat Rahel held under the Egyptian attack until they could hold no longer and they fell back slowly into Jerusalem. At the southern outskirt of the city they were met by Haganah reinforcements and they regrouped and roared back into their *kibbutz* and threw the Egyptians out and chased them to Bethlehem.

JERUSALEM

When the British left Jerusalem, the Haganah moved quickly to seize the sections where the British had been and to launch attacks on sections which held Kawukji's irregulars. The fighting consisted of street-to-street engagements, with Gadna children serving as runners and men in business suits leading attacks.

The second objective of the Haganah was to take an Arab suburb which separated the Jews on Mount Scopus from the Jews in New Jerusalem. With this done, a decision had to be made. The Jews were now in a position to win the Old City of Jerusalem. With the Old City in their hands they would have a solid strategic front. Without the Old City they were vulnerable. International politics, the fear of damage to the holy places, and great outside pressures made them decide to leave the Old City alone, although inside the walls was a quarter of several thousand pious Jews.

The Jews abandoned a lookout post in the tower of an Armenian church inside the Old City, at the request of the monks. The moment the Jews left, the irregulars grabbed the same place and refused to leave. Despite this fact, the Jews felt that the Arabs would not dare to attack the Old City, sacred to three religions, and would follow the example set by the Jews in this holiest ground in the world.

The Haganah then became faced with the final bit of treachery. Glubb Pasha, British commander of the Arab Legion, had given solemn promise that the Legion would be returned to Jordan when the British evacuated. But when the British left Jerusalem, the Arab Legion rushed to that city in open violation of the promise. The Legion attacked and was able to gain back part of what the Haganah had taken earlier. The suburb linking New Jerusalem with Mount Scopus had been given to the Maccabees to defend; they lost it to the Legion, thus isolating the forces on Scopus. Then Glubb ordered the Arab Legion to attack the Old City!

The Jews had no illusions left after their years of dealing with the Arabs, but this attack on the most sacred shrine of mankind was the nadir. There was nothing to stop the Legion but a few thousand ultra-Orthodox Jews who would not raise a finger in their own defense. The Jews rushed as much of the Haganah as they could spare into the Old City, and the Haganah was followed by several hundred angry Maccabee volunteers. Once inside the Old City there was no escape for their forces.

JERUSALEM CORRIDOR

The road from Jerusalem to Tel Aviv continued to bear the hardest fighting of the war. The Hillmen of the Palmach had cleared a half dozen heights in the Judean hills. The Kastel was firmly in their hands and they had assaulted and won the Comb, Suba, and enough key places to open the tricky and vulnerable Bab el Wad.

Then the blackest blot on the Jewish record occurred. The Maccabees were given the high Arab village of Neve Sadij to hold. In a strange and inexplicable sequence of events a panic broke out among Maccabee troops and they opened up a wild and unnecessary firing. Once started it could not be stopped. More than two hundred Arab civilians were massacred. With the Neve Sadij massacre the Maccabees, who had proved so valuable, had fixed a stigma on the young nation that it would take decades to erase.

Although the Hillmen Brigade had opened the Bab el Wad, the British made it more convenient for the Arabs to blockade Jerusalem by handing the Legion the Taggart fort of Latrun. Latrun, once a British political prison at one time or another graced by all the leaders of the Yishuv, sat squarely on a junction in the road, blocking the entrance to the Bab el Wad.

Latrun, therefore, became the most important objective of the Israelis. In a desperation plan to capture the fort a special brigade was formed. Most of it consisted of Jewish immigrants freed from Cyprus interment or from the DP camps. The officers were equally unequipped for a major operation. Quickly armed and trained, this brigade was moved into the corridor and a night attack on Latrun was tried. It was ill-planned and badly executed. The disciplined Arab Legion threw it back.

The brigade tried two more attacks on Latrun on succeeding nights with equal lack of success. Then the Palmach Hillmen Brigade, badly overextended by the attempt to cover the long stretch of the Bab el Wad to Jerusalem, nevertheless made an attack on Latrun and almost, but not quite, succeeded in taking the place.

An American army colonel, Mickey Marcus, who used the code name of Stone, had joined the Israeli Army. Now he was sent to the corridor, where his tactical and organizational experience was desperately needed. His efforts there began to bear fruit. In a short time he had reorganized the transportation and amplified the mechanized jeep-cavalry which the Israelis had used in Iron Broom. Marcus was mainly concerned with quickly forming a well-trained and well-led unit capable of carrying out a strategic movement on the Latrun bottleneck. He was close to attaining this objective when another tragedy befell Israel: Marcus was killed.

Jerusalem remained sealed off.

HULEH VALLEY – SEA OF GALILEE

The Syrian Army swept into Palestine from the eastern side of the Sea of Galilee and the Jordan River in several columns, led by tanks and supported by aircraft.

The first Syrian column chose as its objective the three oldest collective settlements in Palestine: the bloc consisting of Shoshanna, the birthplace of Ari Ben Canaan, and Dagania A and Dagania B, where the Jordan flowed into the Galilee.

The Jews were so short of men in that area that they daily drove trucks back and forth from Tiberias to these settlements to make the Syrians believe they were bringing in reinforcements and arms.

The farmers at the Shoshanna bloc had so little to fight with that they sent a delegation up to see Ari Ben Canaan. The Shoshanna bloc was actually outside his command, but they hoped to appeal to a sentimental regard for his birthplace. Ari's hands were full, however, with Kassi at Gan Dafna and at Safed and with another of the Syrian columns. He told the delegation that only one thing might save them – anger. He advised them to make Molotov cocktails and to let the Syrians get inside the villages. If anything could raise the Jews to an inspired defense, it would be the sight of Arabs on their beloved soil.

The Syrians went after Dagania A first. The Haganah commanders ordered the defenders to hold their fire until the tanks leading the attack penetrated to the center of the village houses. The sight of Syrian tanks on their rose gardens enraged the *kibbutzniks* to the point where they loosed their barrage of fire bottles with deadly accuracy from a distance of a few feet and gutted the lead tanks. The Syrian infantry which followed the tanks was no match for the farmers. They fled under the wrath of the Jews and would not return.

The second Syrian column attacked farther to the south in the Jordan-Beth Shean valleys. They managed to win Shaar Hagolan and *kibbutz*, Massada – where the Yarmuk flowed. When the Jews counterattacked, the Syrians burned the villages to the ground, looted everything that could be carried off, and fled. At the Gesher fort, taken earlier by the Haganah, the Jews held and they held at the rest of their Jordan-Beth Shean settlements.

The third column came over the Jordan River in Ari Ben Canaan's area of the Huleh Valley. They overwhelmed and captured Mishmar Hayarden – the Guardpost of the Jordan. Then they regrouped for the thrust that would carry them into the center of the Huleh to link up with Kawukji's irregulars on the Lebanese side. But Yad El, Ayelet Hashahar, Kfar Szold, Dan, and the rest of the tough settlements stiffened and held, patiently enduring the artillery fire which they could not return, then fighting like tigers when the Syrians came within rifle shot. At Ayelet Hashahar a rifleman actually managed to bring down a Syrian airplane, the credit for which was taken by every *kibbutznik* in the settlement.

Across the way, the Lebanese pawed at the Jewish settlements in the hills and at Metulla. The Lebanese, mostly Christian Arabs, had some leaders who were sympathetic to Zionism, and these people had little desire to fight. They entered the war mainly out of fear of reprisal from other Arab nations and to make a 'show of unity.' The first time they ran into stiff resistance the Lebanese seemed to vanish as a fighting force.

Ari had successfully blocked a junction of Arab forces in the Huleh. When he received a new shipment of arms he moved quickly to the offensive. He evolved a 'defense-offense' plan: those settlements not under direct pressure organized offenses and took objectives rather than sitting and waiting for an attack. By this method Ari was able to keep the Syrians completely off balance. He was able to shift arms and men to the hard-pressed places and ease their burden. He built up his communications and transportation so that the Huleh became one of the strongest Jewish areas in Israel. The only major objective left for him was Fort Esther.

The entire Syrian invasion sputtered. It had turned into a fiasco except for Mishmar Hayarden and one or two smaller victories. The Syrians chose to concentrate their efforts on a single *kibbutz* to make up for their losses. Ein Gev, on the eastern shore of the Sea of Galilee, the home of the winter concerts, was the objective.

The Syrians dominated high hills on three sides of the *kibbutz*. The sea was the fourth side. The Syrians held the columnar mountain of Sussita – the Horse – the ancient Roman city which looked right down into the *kibbutz*. Ein Gev was completely cut off from contact except by boat at night from Tiberias across the lake.

As Syrian guns shelled the *kibbutz* without respite the Jews were forced to live underground. There they kept up their schools, a newspaper, and even their symphony orchestra practice. Each night they came out of the bunkers and tended their fields. The endurance of Ein Gev was matched only by the stand at Negba in the Negev Desert.

Every building in the *kibbutz* was blown to pieces. The Syrians burned the fields. The Jews did not have a weapon capable of firing back. They were subjected to brutal punishment.

After weeks of this pounding the Syrians made their assault, sweeping down from their high ground in numbers of thousands. Three hundred *kibbutzniks* of fighting age met the charge. They fired in disciplined volleys, and snipers picked off the Syrian officers. The Syrians rallied time and again and pressed the Jews back to the sea. But the defenders would not yield. There were twelve rounds of ammunition left to them when the back of the Syrian attack was broken.

Ein Gev had held and with it the Israeli claim to the Sea of Galilee.

SHARON, TEL AVIV, THE TRIANGLE

A large bulge of land in Samaria anchored by the all-Arab cities of Jenin, Tulkarm and Ramallah formed the 'Triangle.' Nablus, the early base for Kawukji's irregulars, became the chief base of the Iraqi Army. The Iraqis had made an ill-fated attempt to cross the Jordan River into the Beth Shean Valley but were badly beaten, then had settled down in Arab Samaria.

Opposite the Triangle on the west was the Sharon Valley. It was a vulnerable area – the Jews held only a narrow neck of land along the Tel Aviv-Haifa highway, ten miles inside from the Triangle front to the sea. If the Iraqis could make the break-through they could cut Israel in half.

The Iraqis, however, showed an aversion to combat. When the Jews made badly organized attempts on the Triangle city of Jenin, the Iraqi officers fled, and only the fact that their troops were chained in their positions kept them from running away. The thought of attacking the thickly settled Sharon Valley was distasteful; the Iraqis wanted no part of it.

Tel Aviv itself suffered several air raids from the Egyptians before anti-aircraft equipment arrived to ward off further attacks. In the Arab press, however, there were at least a dozen reports of Tel Aviv being completely leveled by Egyptian bombers.

The Jews managed to get a few planes into operation and scored one big air victory by driving away an Egyptian cruiser which had come to shell Tel Aviv.

WESTERN GALILEE

After six months Kawukji's irregulars were yet to take their first Jewish settlement. Kawukji moved his headquarters to the predominantly Arab area of central Galilee, around Nazareth. Here he waited for that junction with the Syrians, Lebanese, and Iraqis which never came. There were many Christian Arabs in the Nazareth area who wanted nothing to do with the war and repeatedly requested of Kawukji that he remove himself from the Nazareth Taggart fort.

Most of the western Galilee had been cleaned out before the invasion of the Arab armies. Haifa had fallen to the Jews and the Hanita Brigade's Iron Broom had done away with many hostile villages. With the fall of Arab Acre, the Jews held everything up to the Lebanese border. The Galilee was free of the enemy except for Kawukji in the center.

The advertised 'master plan' of the Arabs had become a complete fiasco. The infant Jewish state had borne and blunted the first shock of invasion. Over the world military experts shook their heads in disbelief. The Jews had fought a civil war on a hundred fronts; they had won out over fantastic odds on a dozen more fronts against regular troops.

The Arab victories could be measured. The greatest success had been scored by the Legion which continued to hold Latrun, the key to the Jerusalem blockade. The rest of the Arab armies combined had captured but a handful of settlements and no cities or towns. They had managed to get to within striking distance of Tel Aviv.

Arms poured into Israel, and every day the Jewish military establishment improved. On the day the Israelis declared statehood six new settlements broke ground and throughout the invasion immigrants built more communities. Nation after nation recognized the State of Israel.

Ein Gev and Negba and the hundred other settlements which would not give up, the Palmachniks, who fought for days without food and water, the new immigrants who rushed to the battle lines, the ingenuity employed in place of guns, the raw courage which made extraordinary heroism a commonplace – all these stopped the Arabs.

There was more. Divine inspiration, the destiny foretold by the ancient prophets, the heritage of a people who had fought for their freedom before, the tradition of King David and Bar Giora and Har Kochba, strength and faith from an unseen source – these, too, stopped the Arabs.

Chapter Ten

Barak Ben Canaan had concluded several arms negotiations as well as several diplomatic missions in Europe. He had been sick with anxiety and begged to be allowed to return to Israel. Now past his eightieth year, he had begun to slow up considerably, although he would not admit it.

He arrived in Naples to catch a ship home. There he was met by Israelis who had a headquarters in the city. Most of them were Aliyah Bet agents now working on dissolving the DP camps in Italy as fast as ships could be procured. The manpower of the DP camps was urgently needed in Israel. Those of military age were rushed to training centers as quickly as they landed. A great part of the rest was sent out to build defensive border settlements.

Barak's arrival was the signal for a gathering, and the midnight oil burned in Israeli headquarters. Over many drinks of brandy everyone wanted to hear and rehear Barak's story of the 'Miracle of Lake Success' and of the secret arms deals which he had just concluded.

Then talk turned to the war. There was general dejection over the siege of Jerusalem; news had come through that another attempt to capture Latrun had failed. No one knew how much longer the hundred thousand civilians could hold out.

Around two o'clock in the morning the conversation turned to the private little war the Israelis were having right in Naples over a ship named the *Vesuvius*, a four-thousand-ton Italian motor ship. The *Vesuvius* had been chartered by the Syrians to carry arms to Tyre. The cargo, purchased all over Europe, included ten thousand rifles, a million rounds of ammunition, a thousand machine guns, a thousand mortars, and a variety of other weapons.

A month ago the *Vesuvius* was ready to sail from Naples. The Israelis learned of the ship and cargo from a friendly Italian customs official, and the night before her scheduled departure Israeli skin divers swam along the waterfront, dived beneath the ship, and fixed magnetic mines to her sides. The mines blew three nice holes in the *Vesuvius*'s sides but failed to set off the explosives as they had hoped. The ship did not fully sink, but partly submerged at her berth. From that point on the *Vesuvius* became the center of an involved cat-and-mouse game.

Syrian Colonel Fawdzi, in charge of the multimillion dollar cargo, had the ship raised, dry-docked, and the holes repaired. He brought fifty Arab students from Rome and Paris to guard the area and replaced the twelve-man crew with Arabs. Only the captain and his first and second officers were Italians from the chartering company. The captain, however, could not have disliked the pompous Colonel Fawdzi more and secretly agreed to help the Israelis, provided they promised not to damage his ship again. Again they got word that the *Vesuvius* was ready to sail.

The Israelis could not allow the arms to reach Tyre – but how to stop the ship? They had promised both the Italian officials and the captain that they would not blow her up in the harbor. Once on the high seas the Israeli Navy, consisting of three corvettes, could never find the *Vesuvius*.

Barak Ben Canaan was impressed by the importance of the situation and intrigued by the kind of knotty problem he had faced and solved many times before. Once again he conceived the inconceivable. By dawn he had worked out the details of another of his fantastic plots.

Two days later the *Vesuvius* moved out of the Naples harbor and, as it did, the Italian second officer was relieved of radio duty as an extra precaution by Fawdzi. Radio contact, however, was not necessary to the plotters. The Israelis knew the exact instant the *Vesuvius* left. The ship had barely cleared the harbor area when an Italian customs cutter raced for her with its bull horn blaring.

Fawdzi, who knew no Italian, rushed up to the steering room and demanded to know from the captain what it all meant.

The captain shrugged. 'Who knows?'

'Hello, *Vesuvius*,' the loud-speaker boomed. 'Stand by to be boarded!'

A Jacob's ladder was dropped and twenty men wearing uniforms of the Italian customs service quickly boarded from the cutter.

'I demand to know the meaning of this!' Colonel Fawdzi screamed.

The leader of the boarding party, a giant of a man with a great red and white beard, who bore a remarkable resemblance to Barak Ben Canaan, stepped forward and spoke to Fawdzi in Arabic: 'We have information that one of your crew set a time bomb in one of the holds,' he said.

'Impossible,' Fawdzi shouted.

'We happen to know he was bought out by the Jews,' the leader asserted sincerely. 'We must clear the harbor area before the ship explodes.'

Fawdzi became confused. He had no intention of being blown up with the *Vesuvius*, nor did he like the idea of going out of the harbor with this strange gang of Italian 'customs officials' aboard. On the other hand, he could not show cowardice by demanding to be taken off the ship.

'You will line up your crew,' the man with the big beard said. 'We will find the culprit and he will tell us where he has planted the bomb.'

The Arab crew was assembled and taken into the gallery for 'questioning,' and while they were being questioned the *Vesuvius* passed outside of the three-mile limit and the customs' cutter returned to Naples. The disguised Aliyah Bet agents then produced pistols and locked up Fawdzi and the Arab crew. Later that day, when they had made further distance, the crew was given a compass, a map, and a rowboat and set adrift. Colonel Fawdzi was kept aboard in his cabin. The Israelis took over as crew of the ship as it raced for open sea.

Thirty-six hours later, the *Vesuvius* was met by two corvettes flying skull and crossbones. The corvettes tied up on either side of the motor ship, removed the cargo and crew, and sped off after smashing the radio. The *Vesuvius* then returned to Naples.

Colonel Fawdzi foamed with rage and demanded a full investigation of the high-seas piracy. The Italian customs service, accused by the Arabs of lending the Jews a cutter and uniforms, said it knew nothing about the matter. All cutter movement was clearly logged for anyone to see. The Arab crew followed

Arab practice of never admitting failure and twelve different stories came from the twelve men. Other officials of the Italian government assumed that if there was any piracy, they certainly were not aware of it, for the captain of the ship and the first and second officers swore that the Arab crew deserted because they found out the hold held explosives.

Soon a corps of lawyers had the affair so twisted up with contradictory stories that it was impossible to unscramble the facts. The Israelis in Naples added the final touch of confusion by planting the story that it was actually a Jewish ship stolen by the Arabs and that Fawdzi was a Jewish spy.

Colonel Fawdzi took the only course open. He faked an elaborate suicide and disappeared, never to be heard of again – apparently to the regret of nobody.

Two days after the transfer of arms, the corvettes, now flying the Star of David, brought Barak home in a triumphant entry to Israel.

Chapter Eleven

Ari Ben Canaan received orders to report to Tel Aviv. Headquarters was located in a pension in Ramat Gan. Ari was surprised at the sight of it. The Star of David flew atop the building and uniformed guards of the new army of Israel were everywhere. Identification passes were demanded by the security police before entry was permitted. Outside the headquarters were a hundred jeeps and motorcycles, and there was a military bustle and briskness all about.

Inside, the big switchboard rang constantly. Ari was led through the operations room where huge blown-up maps pinpointed the battle lines and the message center where a battery of radios communicated with the front lines and the settlements. As Ari looked around him he reflected that it was a far cry from the mobile one-desk headquarters of the Haganah.

Avidan, the former head of the Haganah, had given up official command to the young leaders in their mid-twenties and early thirties who had had experience as British officers or were seasoned, as Ari was, in long years of Arab fighting. Avidan now acted in the capacity of liaison between the Army and the provisional government, and although he held no official post he was still a power in general policy as 'commander emeritus.'

He greeted Ari warmly. It was difficult for Ari to tell if Avidan was tired or had just awakened, or if he was morose or happy, for Avidan always wore the same solemn expression. As they went into his office he ordered all telephone calls or other interruptions withheld.

'This is quite a fancy store you have here,' Ari said.

'Not much like the old days,' Avidan agreed. 'It is hard for me to get over it myself. I drive up here many mornings thoroughly expecting the British to sweep down and throw us all into Acre jail.'

'None of us expected you to retire yourself.'

'This army and running a big war is a young man's job. Let me argue policy in my old age.'

'How goes the war?' Ari asked.

'Jerusalem ... Latrun. There is our problem. We won't be able to hold out too much longer inside the Old City. God knows how long the New City can stand it if we don't get through to them soon. Anyhow ... you've certainly done a job for us in your district.'

'We've been lucky.'

'Safed wasn't luck and neither are those magnificent children at Gan Dafna luck. Don't be modest, Ari. We've got children under siege at Ben Shemen too ... the Iraqis won't dare take a try at them. Ari, Kawukji is still in the central Galilee ... we want to get rid of the bastard. That's why I asked you to come down here. I want to extend your command and I want you to take charge of the operation. In a matter of a few weeks we should be able to get a battalion of men up there to you, along with some new stuff.'

'How do you figure it?'

'If we take Nazareth I think we've got it all. We'll have the whole Galilee then, all the roads from east to west.'

'What about the Arab villages in the area?'

'Mostly Christian, as you know. They've already sent delegations down here to see us. They've asked Kawukji to leave. At any rate, they're not interested in fighting.'

'Good.'

'Before we proceed with the planning of this operation we want you to secure your area completely, Ari.'

'Fort Esther?' Ari asked.

Avidan nodded.

'I need artillery to take Fort Esther – I wrote you that. At least three or four Davidkas.'

'Why don't you ask for gold?'

'Look, there are two border villages guarding the approaches to Fort Esther. I just can't get at the place without some long-range pieces.'

'All right, I'll send them up to you.' Avidan stood up abruptly and began pacing the room. Behind him was a large map of the fighting zones. Ari had felt strangely all along about Avidan calling him to Tel Aviv. He had felt there was more to it than the planning of a new operation and he knew that Avidan was leading up to it now.

'Ari,' the bald-headed block of a man said slowly, 'you were ordered to capture Abu Yesha two weeks ago.'

'So that's why you called me down here.'

'I thought it would be best if you and I talked it over before it gets kicked around like a football in general staff.'

'I sent you a report that I didn't feel Abu Yesha was a threat to us.'

'We think differently.'

'As area commander, I believe I'm in the best position to judge.'

'Come off it. Abu Yesha is a base for Mohammed Kassi. It's an entry point for the irregulars and it blocks the road to Gan Dafna.'

Ari stiffened and looked away.

'You and I have known each other too long for equivocation.'

Ari was silent for a moment. 'I've known the people in Abu Yesha since I was old enough to walk and talk,' he said. 'We've celebrated weddings together. We've gone to funerals together. We built their houses and they gave us land to make Gan Dafna.'

'I know all that, Ari. Dozens of our settlements are faced with the same thing. We happen to be fighting for our lives. We didn't invite the Arab armies to invade us.'

'But I know those people,' Ari cried; 'they aren't enemies. They're just plain decent farmers who want nothing more in life than to be left alone.'

'Ari!' Avidan said sharply. 'We have Arab villages who have shown the courage to resist Kawukji and the Arab armies. The people in Abu Yesha made their own decision. It is wishful thinking for you to say it is not hostile. It has to go ...'

'Go to hell,' Ari said and got up to leave.

'Don't go,' Avidan said quietly. 'Please don't go.' The big farmer now actually did appear tired. His shoulders sagged. 'We've begged the Palestine Arabs a thousand times to stay out of this fight. No one wants to drive them from their homes. Those villages that have shown loyalty have been left alone. But the others have left us no choice. They are used as arsenals and training camps and as bases to attack our convoys and starve our settlements. A hundred thousand civilains are starving in Jerusalem now because of them. We talked about this thing for weeks. We have no choice but to kill or be killed.'

Ari walked to the window and lit a cigarette. He stared moodily out of the window. Avidan was right and he knew it. The Jewish settlement had not been given the same choice the Arab had been given. With the Jews it was stand and die ... fight to the last bullet and be massacred.

'I could easily put another man up in your command to take Abu Yesha. I don't want to do it that way. If you feel morally incapable of doing this then I give you the choice of asking for a transfer from your area.'

'To what? Another Abu Yesha by another name?'

'Before you give an answer ... I have known you since you were a baby. You have been a fighter since you were fifteen years old. We haven't enough men of your caliber. In all those years I've never known you to disobey an order.'

Ari turned from the window. His face was lined with worry, sadness, and resignation. He sagged into the chair. 'I will do what has to be done,' he whispered.

'Get together with operations,' Avidan said softly.

Ari shook his head and walked to the door.

'By the way, you are Colonel Ben Canaan, now.'

Ari gave a short sarcastic laugh.

'I am sorry, believe me, I'm sorry,' Avidan said.

Colonel Ari Ben Canaan, his executive officer and his adjutant, Majors Ben Ami and Joab Yarkoni, mapped out Operation Purim for the capture of Fort Esther and the removal of Abu Yesha as an Arab base. It would be the final securing of the Huleh Valley.

The artillery that Avidan had promised never arrived, but Ari really didn't expect it. He brought the faithful Little David mortar from Safed and rounded up fifty rounds of ammunition.

Frontal attack from Gan Dafna of Fort Esther was ruled out without the artillery. Kassi still had some four hundred men in the area and superior arms at Fort Esther plus better strategic position. Ari also knew that Kassi's men would give a better account of themselves fighting a defensive battle inside the concrete barricade.

Ari had three Arab villages to worry about. Abu Yesha was the first on the road to Fort Esther. High up in the mountains on the Lebanese border a pair of villages flanked the entrances to Fort Esther. Kassi had men stationed in both of these. Ari planned his battle to get around to the rear of Fort Esther. In order to do it he had to get past the two flanking villages.

The move on Fort Esther was planned to involve three columns. Ari took the first unit out. At darkness, they went up the mountainside by goat trails to the Lebanese border with the Davidka and its ammunition. His objective was to get near the first of the mountain villages. The going would be hard and tricky. He had to swing wide and travel many extra miles to be able to get at their rear without detection. He had the mountain, the darkness, and the weight of the mortar and ammunition to contend with. Thirty-five men and fifteen girls carried one round of ammunition each. Another fifty men acted as cover.

Ari's leg still gave him trouble but he pushed his column up the mountain in a brutally paced forced march. They had to make their objective by daylight or the whole operation would fail.

They reached the top of the mountain at four o'clock in the morning, exhausted. But there could be no rest now. They continued at a murderous pace along the mountaintop toward the first village. They swung wide of it and made a rendezvous with a patrol from a friendly Bedouin tribe which was acting as a watch on the village. The Bedouins advised Ari the area was clear.

Ari raced his outfit into the ruins of a small Crusader castle two miles past the village. As dawn began to break they scrambled for cover and collapsed into a heap of weariness. All day they stayed hidden, with the Bedouins standing guard.

The next night the two other columns moved out from Ein Or headquarters. Major David Ben Ami led his men up the face of the mountain on the now familiar route into Gan Dafna. He reached the village by daylight and went into hiding in the woods.

The final column led by Major Joab Yarkoni traced Ari's steps in the wide circular route on the goat trails. His men were able to move faster because they did not have the weight of the Davidka and its ammunition. However they had a greater distance to travel as they had to pass the first village where Ari hid, pass Fort Esther and get near the second of the villages. Again the Bedouins met Yarkoni's column on the mountaintop and led them undetected to their objective.

At nightfall of the second day Ari sent the Bedouin leader to the near village with a surrender ultimatum. Meanwhile Ari moved his men out of the Crusader fort and crept close to the village. The muktar and some eighty of Kassi's soldiers thought it was a bluff: no Jews could have got up the mountains and behind them without detection. The Bedouin returned to Ari with the report that the village needed convincing, so Ari had two rounds of the Davidka fired.

Two dozen of the mud huts were blown to pieces. The Arabs were convinced. With the second mortar shot the officers of the irregulars were leading a stampede across the Lebanese border and an array of white flags was going up. Ari acted quickly. He dispatched a small part of his column into the village to guard it and sped on to the second village where Yarkoni had already opened an attack.

Twenty minutes and three Davidka rounds after Ari arrived, the village fell and another hundred of Kassi's men fled to Lebanon. The awesone Little David had again done its job of inflicting terror and destruction. The two villages had fallen so quickly that Fort Esther was completely unaware of it. They assumed the distant sound of the Davidka shells and the firing were their own men firing for pleasure.

At dawn of the third day, David Ben Ami moved his column out of hiding at Gan Dafna and set up an ambush outside Abu Yesha where Kassi had another hundred men. With Ben Ami's men in position to cut off reinforcements from Abu Yesha, Ari and Yarkoni's forces moved to the rear of Fort Esther. When the Little David opened fire Kassi had only a hundred men in the fort. The rest were in Lebanon or Abu Yesha. Round after round of the buckets of dynamite swished and sputtered through the air and exploded against the concrete blockhouse. Each round came a little closer to the mark, the iron rear gate. By the twentieth round, the gate was blown off its hinges, and the next five rounds fell into the courtyard of the fort.

Ari Ben Canaan jumped off with the first wave of attackers, who crawled forward on their bellies beneath machine-gun fire and intermittent blasts of the Davidka.

The actual damage to Fort Esther was superficial, but the noise and the sudden swiftness of the attack was too much for Kassi and his dubious warriors. They made a feeble defense, waiting for reinforcements to come. The only reinforcements left moved out of Abu Yesha and walked right into David Ben Ami's trap. Kassi saw it through his field glasses. He was cut off. The Jews were at the rear gate. The white flag of surrender went up over Fort Esther.

Yarkoni took twenty men into the fort, disarmed the Arabs and sent them packing to Lebanon. Kassi, now quite docile, and three of his officers were led to the jail as the Star of David was raised over the fort. Ari took the rest of the men down the road to where David had set the ambush. They were ready for the final phase of the end of Abu Yesha as an Arab base.

The people of Abu Yesha had seen and heard the fighting. They knew, surely, their village was next. Ari sent a truce team in to give those who were left twenty minutes to evacuate or face the consequences. From his vantage point he could see many of his lifelong friends trudging out of Abu Yesha toward the hills of Lebanon. Ari felt sick in his stomach as he saw them go.

A half hour passed and then an hour.

'We had better start,' David said to him.

'I ... I want to make sure they are all out.'

'No one has left for a half hour, Ari. Everyone is out who is coming out.'

Ari turned and walked away from his waiting troops. David followed him. 'I'll take command,' David said.

'All right,' Ari whispered.

Ari stood alone on the mountainside as David led the men down to the saddle in the hill where Abu Yesha nestled. He was pale as he heard the first sounds of gunfire. David deployed the men as they approached the outskirts. A clatter of machine-gun and small-arms fire went up. The Jews dropped and crawled forward in a squad-by-squad advance.

Inside Abu Yesha a hundred Arabs led by Taha had chosen to make a determined stand. The fight for the village was a rare situation for this war; the Jews had superior numbers of men and arms. A withering barrage of automatic fire was followed by a rain of grenades on the forward Arab positions. The first Arab machine gun was knocked out, and as the defenders fell back the Jews gained a foothold in the town itself.

David Ben Ami conducted the battle by sending out patrols to move street by street, house by house, to clean out pockets of resistance. The going was slow and bloody; these were houses built of stone, not mud, and those who remained fought it out hand to hand.

The day wore on. Ari Ben Canaan did not move from his position on the mountainside. The constant sound of gunfire and the bursts of grenades and even the screams of men reached his ears.

The Arabs of Abu Yesha fell back from position after position as the relentless attack cut off any co-ordination between groups or individuals. Finally all those left were squeezed into one street on the edge of town. More than seventy-five Arabs had been killed fighting to the end in the most dramatic defense the Arabs had made of one of their villages. It was a tragic fight; neither the Jews nor the Arabs wanted it.

The last eight men were pushed into the last stronghold, the fine stone house of the muktar which stood near the stream across from the mosque. David called for the Davidka. The house was blown to pieces. The last eight men, including Taha, were killed.

It was nearly dark when David Ben Ami walked up the road to Ari. David was battle weary.

'It is all over,' David said.

Ari looked at him glassy-eyed but did not speak.

'There were nearly a hundred of them. All dead. We lost ... fourteen boys, three girls. Another dozen wounded are up at Gan Dafna.'

Ari did not seem to hear him. He started to walk down the hill toward the village.

'What is going to become of their fields?' Ari whispered. 'What will become of them ... where will they go ... ?'

David grabbed Ari's shoulder.

'Don't go down there, Ari.'

Ari looked at the little sea of flat roofs. It was so quiet.

'Is the house by the stream ...'

'No,' David said. 'Try to remember it as it was.'

'What will become of them?' Ari said. 'They are my friends.'

'We are waiting for the order, Ari.'

Ari looked at David and blinked his eyes and shook his head slowly.

'I must give it then,' David said.

'No,' Ari whispered, 'I shall give it.' He looked at the village for the last time. 'Destroy Abu Yesha,' Ari said.

Chapter Twelve

David slept in Jordana's arms.

She held his head tightly against her breast. She could not sleep. Her eyes were wide, staring into the darkness.

Ari had given her leave from Gan Dafna so the two of them could travel to

Tel Aviv together and have a weekend alone. After tomorrow, the Lord only knew how long it would be before she saw him again, if ever. Jordana had known in her heart all along that David would volunteer for such a mission. Since the beginning of the siege he had been eating his heart out for Jerusalem. She saw that distant look of sadness and pain each time she looked into his eyes.

He stirred in his sleep. She kissed his forehead gently and ran her fingers through his hair and he smiled in his sleep and became still once more.

It would not be right for a *sabra* girl to tell her lover she was ill with worry for him. She must only smile and encourage him and conceal the fear in her heart. She felt weak with apprehension and she pressed him close to her body and wanted to hold him for a night without end.

It had begun the day partition was voted. The next day the Higher Arab Committee called for a general strike which erupted into the savage burning and plunder of the Jewish commercial center of Jerusalem. While the Arab mobs ran wild, British troops stood by.

The siege of the city began almost immediately with Abdul Kadar using Arab villages along the highway to blockade the Jewish convoys from Tel Aviv. While the titanic battles in the corridor raged for the heights, the Kastel and the other villages, the Jews in Jerusalem were frozen, hungry, and thirsty, and under direct cannonading from Kawukji and Kadar. While the Palmach Hillmen fought to keep the road open, the Yishuv organized the convoys which slugged their way along the Bab el Wad until the Judean hills were littered with wreckage.

Inside the city the fighting started with bombings and ambushes and erupted into full-scale war. The Haganah cleared a huge field of fire from King David Hotel to the Old City wall where the irregulars massed and the wreckage was called Bevingrad. The commander of the Haganah in Jerusalem was saddled with problems beyond mere military matters. He was burdened by a huge civilian population that had to be fed and protected in a situation of siege. He was further burdened by the fact that a large part of his population, ultra-Orthodox and fanatical Jews, not only refused to fight, but obstructed the efforts of the Haganah to protect them. In ancient Israel the commander of Jerusalem had been plagued by the same problems. In the siege against the Romans the fall of Jerusalem was hastened by a division of strength by the Zealots, and it led to a Roman massacre of 600,000 Jews. On that occasion the Jews had held out against the Romans for three years; it was unlikely that they could do it again.

In addition to the problem of the ultra-Orthodox and fanatics who refused to fight, the Maccabees only co-operated part of the time and were frequently concerned with carrying on a private war. When they did support the Haganah, it was not with particular distinction. The Hillmen Brigade of the Palmach was overextended and overworked in the Judean hills and quite reluctant to take orders from the Haganah commander of Jerusalem. It added up to a desperate situation in which the Haganah commander could do no right.

Beautiful Jerusalem became battle scarred and bloody. The Egyptians attacked from the south and shelled the city and bombed it from the sky. The Arab Legion used the sacred walls of the Old City as a stockade. Casualties mounted to the thousands. Again uncommon valor and ingenuity were the keynotes of the Jews' defense. Again the Davidka mortar did yeoman's work. It was moved from place to place to make the Arabs think there were many of them.

Outside Jerusalem, when the Arab Legion took Latrun fort they promised to keep the water pumping station open so that the civilian population would have enough to drink. Instead the Arabs blew up the pumping station and cut off the water supply. Cisterns two and three thousand years old were known to exist under Jerusalem. The Jews located them, tore the covers from them and discovered that, as if by a miracle, they still held water. Until emergency pipelines could be built, these ancient cisterns were all that kept the Jews from dying of thirst.

The days passed into weeks and the weeks into months and still Jerusalem held out. Every home became a battlefield. Men, women, children daily girded to battle with a spirit of defiance that would never be conquered.

David Ben Ami's heart ached for Jerusalem. The siege was on his mind all day and all night.

He opened his eyes.

'Why aren't you sleeping?' he asked Jordana.

'I have enough time for sleeping when I am away from you,' she answered.

He kissed her and told her that he loved her.

'Oh, David ... my David.'

She wanted to beg him not to ask for this mission. She wanted to cry out and tell him that if anything happened to him there could be no life for her. But she held her tongue as she knew she must. One of his six brothers had died at *kibbutz* Nirim fighting the Egyptians and another was dying from wounds received in a convoy to relieve besieged Negba in the Negev Desert. David's brother Nahum of the Maccabees had chosen to go into the Old City.

David heard the rapid beating of Jordana's heart.

'David, love me ... love me,' she pleaded.

In the Old City of Jerusalem, the Arab mobs surged in behind the Legion to destroy a score of synagogues and holy places, and they pillaged and looted every Jewish house that fell.

The pious ones and their Haganah and Maccabee defenders were squeezed back and back until they held only two buildings, one of them the Hurva Synagogue. It could only be a matter of days before they were all wiped out.

Jordana was awakened by the light of day. She stretched and purred with contentment, for her body was pleased with love. She reached out for David. He was not there.

Her eyes opened with alarm and then she saw him standing over her. David, for the first time, was dressed in the uniform of the army of Israel. She smiled and lay back on the pillows and he knelt beside her and touched her hair, which was a scarlet disarray.

'I have been watching you for an hour. You are very beautiful when you sleep,' he said.

She reached out and opened her arms and drew him close and kissed him.

'*Shalom*, Major Ben Ami,' she whispered in his ear, and kissed it softly.

'Darling, it's late. I have to be going,' he said.

'I'll get dressed right away,' she said.

'Why don't I just go right now by myself? I think it will be better this way.'

Jordana felt her heart stop. For a fraction of a second she meant to seize him, then she quickly masked her shock and smiled.

'Of course, darling,' she said.

'Jordana ... Jordana ... I love you.'

'*Shalom*, David. Go quickly ... please.'

She turned her face to the wall and felt his kiss on her cheek and then she heard the door closing.

'David ... David,' she whispered. 'Please come back to me.'

Avidan drove with Major Ben Ami to the flat that Ben Zion, the chief of operations, kept near headquarters. General Ben Zion, a man of thirty-one, was also a Jerusalemite. His aide, Major Alterman, was present when they arrived.

They exchanged greetings and condolences for the death of David's brother at Nirim.

'Avidan tells us you have something of interest,' Alterman said.

'Yes,' David answered slowly. 'Ever since the partition vote, the "lament of the exiles" has been running through my mind, night and day, "If I forget thee, O Jerusalem."'

Ben Zion nodded. He shared David's feeling for Jerusalem. His wife, his children, and his parents were there.

David continued. 'We control the road fairly well up to Latrun. Beyond Latrun, in the Bab el Wad, the Palmach had cleared most of the heights.'

'We all know that Latrun is our greatest stumbling block,' Alterman said crisply.

'Hear him out,' Ben Zion snapped.

'I have been thinking ... I know that area around Latrun like my mother's smile. I have been going over the ground in my mind, inch by inch, for nearly six months. I am absolutely certain Latrun can be bypassed.'

There was a stunned silence for a moment.

'Just what do you mean?' Ben Zion asked.

'If you draw an arc around Latrun from road to road, it is sixteen kilometers.'

'But this sixteen kilometers is merely a line on the map. There is no road. Those hills are wild and impassable.'

'There is a road,' David said.

'David – what on earth are you talking about?' Avidan demanded.

'Over part of the way there is an ancient Roman road. It is two thousand years old and it is completely covered by brush and slide and washout, but it is there. The bed runs through the wadis for about eight kilometers. I know as surely as I stand here that I can follow the wadis for the balance of the distance.'

David walked to the wall map and drew a semicircle around Latrun, linking the roads.

Avidan and Ben Zion stared for several moments. Alterman looked cynical. Avidan, who had already heard some of the plans from Ari Ben Canaan, was critical.

'David,' Avidan said coldly, 'say you are able to find this alleged Roman road and suppose you are able to find a goat path through the wadis – what then? Your are still a long, long way from relieving the siege of Jerusalem.'

'What I propose,' David said without hesitation, 'is that we build another road atop the Roman road and eliminate the need for capturing Latrun by going around it.'

'Come now, David,' Ben Zion said. 'According to the route you have drawn on the map we will have to build this road right under the noses of the Arab Legion at Latrun.'

'Exactly,' David said. 'We don't need much more than a trail. Just enough to accommodate the width of a single truck. Joshua made the sun stand still at Latrun. Perhaps we can make the nights stand still. If one task force builds from the Jerusalem end and another from Tel Aviv and we work quietly by night, I know we can complete the bypass in a month. As for the Arab Legion, you know damned well that Glubb won't bring them out of Latrun to fight. He is keeping them where they are safe from open battle.'

'We aren't so sure of that,' Alterman said. 'He may fight for the road.'

'If Glubb wasn't afraid of committing the Legion to battle, then why hasn't he attacked from the Triangle and tried to cut Israel in half?

It was a question no one could answer. It could only be assumed that David was right. The opinion of the staff was that Glubb was overextended and had no intention of fighting beyond the areas of Jerusalem, the corridor, and Latrun. Besides, the Israelis would welcome the chance to meet the Legion in the field.

Ben Zion and Avidan sat quietly and mulled over David's proposal.

'What do you want?' Ben Zion said at last.

'Give me a jeep and one night to drive through.'

Avidan was worried. In the early days of Haganah, it pained him every time he drew a casualty. It was like losing a son or daughter. In a small, close-knit community like the old Yishuv, each loss was a personal tragedy. Now, with the war, the Jews had casualties in the thousands and for a small country it was a devastating number. Most of them were the cream of the nation's youth, men and women. No nation, no matter how large or small, had David Ben Amis to spare, Avidan thought. It seemed like a suicide task that David was taking upon himself. Maybe David only thought he knew of a route into Jerusalem because he wanted to believe that one existed.

'A jeep and twenty-four hours ...' David pleaded.

Avidan looked at Ben Zion. Alterman shook his head. What David wanted to do was impossible. The burden of Jerusalem weighed every heart, it was the life beat, the very breath of Judaism, yet ... ; Ben Zion wondered if it had not been madness to try to hold the city from the very beginning.

David's parents had suffered enough, Avidan thought. One brother dead and another wounded and a third the leader of the Maccabees suicide squad inside the Old City walls.

David looked from one to the other frantically. 'You must give me a chance!' he cried.

There was a knock on the door. Alterman took a communiqué and handed it to Ben Zion. The blood drained from the face of the operations chief. He handed the paper to Avidan. None of them remembered Avidan's ever losing his composure, but now his hand trembled as he read and tears welled in his eyes.

His voice quivered. 'The Old City has just surrendered.'

'No!' Alterman cried.

David sagged into a chair.

Ben Zion's fist clenched and he gritted his teeth. 'Without Jerusalem there is no Jewish nation!' he cried. He turned to David. 'Go up to Jerusalem, David ... go up!'

When Moses led the tribes of Israel to the shores of the Red Sea he asked for a man with such faith in the power of God that he would be the first to jump into the sea. Nahshon was the name of the man who came forward. 'Nahshon' became the code name of David Ben Ami's venture.

At darkness David left the town of Rehovot south of Tel Aviv and drove toward Judea. At the foothills, near Latrun, David turned off the road into the wilderness, into the steep rock-filled hills and the gorges and wadis. David Ben Ami was driven by an obsession, but his passion was tempered by his appreciation of the gravity of the mission and controlled by his infinite knowledge of the land around him.

The jeep twisted and banged and rebelled against the torture which no mechanical thing was made to take. In compound low gear David drive slowly and cautiously as he came very close to Latrun. The danger of meeting a Legion patrol was great.

His eyes and instincts sharpened as he saw the fort in the distance. He inched the vehicle down a treacherous slope, in search of the Roman road buried under centuries of debris. He followed the contours of washed-down dirt and rocks, and at the junction of two wadis he stopped and dug up some rocks. Their size and texture assured him that the road was there. Once he had established the general direction of the pathway of Roman legions he was able to move along it more quickly.

David Ben Ami swept in a circle around Latrun, pushing himself and his vehicle without mercy. Many times he cut the motor and sat in frozen silence to listen for an imagined enemy sound. Many times he crawled on his belly in the darkness to feel out the route through the dry, rocky wadis. Those sixteen kilometers were the longest David had ever known. The night passed too quickly for him and with its passing the danger of an Arab patrol increased.

At dawn, Ben Zion and Avidan were drowsy from a night of waiting and filled with apprehension. They now knew the folly of David's attempt; they felt in their hearts that they would never see him again.

The phone rang. Avidan lifted the receiver and listened.

'It is the coding room,' Avidan said. 'They have just received a message from Jerusalem.'

'What is it?'

'1358.'

They dashed for the Bible. Ben Zion emitted a long sigh of relief as he read, 'Isaiah: thirty-five, eight: *And an highway shall be there ... no lion shall be there, nor any ravenous beast shall go up thereon ... but the redeemed shall walk there ...*'

Nahshon had arrived in Jerusalem! David Ben Ami had found a bypass of Latrun. Jerusalem still had a chance.

Thousands of volunteers in Jerusalem were sworn to secrecy. They poured out of the city to claw a road through the wilderness along the route that David had found. David returned to Tel Aviv where a second corps of volunteers worked at the opposite end to link up with the Jerusalem people.

The two task forces hid by day and built by night, right under the noses of the Arab Legion at Latrun. They toiled in feverish silence, carrying away by hand each bagful of dirt. Through the wadis and ravines, along the ancient Roman road, the two forces inched toward each other. David Ben Ami asked for permanent transfer to Jerusalem and got it.

Jordana had had a case of nerves ever since she had left David in Tel Aviv. She returned to Gan Dafna where there was a tremendous amount of work to be done rebuilding the wrecked village. Most of the buildings had been hit by artillery fire. The younger children who had been evacuated were now returned. Kitty's cottage had not been too severely damaged so Jordana moved in with her and Karen. The two women had developed a fast friendship. Jordana found herself able to confide in Kitty the things which she could not tell others for fear of showing weakness.

Kitty was fully aware of Jordana's state when she returned from Tel Aviv, though Jordana tried to mask it with an outward show of gruffness. On an evening two weeks after she had parted from David she sat with Kitty in the dining room, having a late snack and tea. As Kitty chatted, Jordana suddenly became pale and stood up quickly and ran from the room. Kitty followed her outside and reached her just as Jordana slumped to the ground. Kitty caught her and supported her, half leading and half carrying Jordana to her office. She stretched the *sabra* on the cot and forced some brandy into her.

It was ten minutes before Jordana came fully around. She sat up in a daze. Kitty made her put her head down. When she had regained her senses Jordana shook her head with disbelief.

'What happened?' Kitty asked.

'I don't know. Nothing like that has ever happened to me. I was listening to you and all of a sudden I couldn't hear you or see you. It turned dark and a cold chill passed through me.'

'Go on . . .'

'I . . . I heard David shriek . . . it was horrible.'

'Now you listen to me, young lady. You've been so tensed up you're ready to explode. I want you to take a few days' rest. Go down to Yad El with your mother . . .'

Jordana sprang to her feet. 'No!' she said.

'Sit down!' Kitty barked.

'It's nonsense. I am behaving shamefully.'

'You are acting quite normally. You wouldn't get yourself into such a state if you would let off a little steam and a few tears occasionally and not try to hold it all inside you.'

'David would be so disgusted with me if he knew I was carrying on so.'

'Oh, stop it, Jordana. Damn your *sabra* pride. I'm giving you a sedative and I want you to go right to bed.'

'No!' Jordana said and ran from the room.

Kitty gave a sigh of resignation. What did you do with a girl who felt that any show of emotion would be construed as a weakness. Years of tension and struggle had built a thick skin on the *sabras*. Their pride was fierce beyond comprehension.

Three days after the incident Kitty came into her cottage one evening after sending Karen over to Dov's. Jordana was working on reports. Kitty sat down before the desk. Jordana looked up and smiled, they turned grave as she saw the expression on Kitty's face. Kitty took the pen from her hand.

Neither of them spoke for several moments.

'David is dead,' Jordana said.

'Yes.'

'How did it happen?' Jordana said in an emotionless monotone.

'Ari phoned a few minutes ago. The details are not clear. It seems that he organized a band of some Palmach, some Maccabees, some Haganah. It was not authorized ... apparently David had been looking at the walls of the Old City and it was more than he could stand. They made an attack to try to win back the Old City. They conquered Mount Zion ...'

'Go on,' Jordana said.

'They didn't have a chance. It was a suicide mission.'

Jordana did not move or even blink her eyes.

'What can I do? What can I say?' Kitty said.

The girl stood up and held her chin high. 'Don't worry about me,' she said in a clear voice.

If Jordana Ben Canaan had tears for her David, no one ever saw them. She disappeared with her grief into the ruins of Abu Yesha. She sat neither moving nor eating nor drinking for four days and four nights. She returned to Gan Dafna. As Ari had done with his sweetheart, Jordana never mentioned David's name again.

One night, a month form the time David Ben Ami found the way to Jerusalem, the 'Burma Road,' the bypass of Latrun, was completed. A convoy rushed through and the siege of Jerusalem was over for all time.

Until that moment no one had known for certain if Israel would live. In the magic instant when the workers from Jerusalem shook hands with the workers from Tel Aviv, the Jews had won their War of Liberation.

Chapter Thirteen

There were many months of the bitterest and most bloody fighting ahead, but the opening of the 'Burma Road' gave the Jews a spiritual lift at a time it was sorely needed.

After the Jews had stopped the first invasion of the Arab armies, the Security Council of the United Nations was able to effect a temporary truce. Both sides welcomed it. The Arabs obviously had to shake up their commands and reorganize. They had lost face in the eyes of the world by failure to overrun the country. The Israelis wanted the time to get in more weapons and increase their operational strength.

The Provisional Government did not have complete control of the situation, for the co-operation of the Palmach, the ultra-Orthodox, and the Maccabees was still a matter of degrees. The Palmach, to their credit, gave up their elite corps and joined the army of Israel en masse, when faced with expulsion from the fighting fronts for failure to take orders from the central command. The Maccabees likewise made up special Maccabee battalions in the Israeli Army, but insisted on their own officers. But nothing could change the unyielding attitude of the fanatics who continued to wait for the Messiah in an absolute literal interpretation of the Bible.

Just as unification of these elements appeared a reality, a tragic event occurred to alienate the Maccabees forever. Maccabee sympathizers in America had purchased a large amount of needed arms and a cargo plane which was named the *Akiva*. Along with the arms, they had several hundred volunteers ready to join the special Maccabee battalions. Under truce conditions, neither side was supposed to rearm nor reinforce any position. Both Arabs and Jews ignore this UN dictate. Both sides secretly moved arms and men around in their build-ups of strength.

The existence of the *Akiva* became known by Israeli people in Europe. The Provisional Government demanded that the *Akiva* and its arms be turned over to it. Israel was one nation now, fighting a single war, they argued, and, after all, the Maccabee battalions were part of the army of Israel. The Maccabees objected. They wanted to keep their identification and they argued that the arms were specifically purchased for use of their members.

The government brought up the question of violation of the truce. If the Provisional Government handled the entry of the *Akiva* the chances of getting the arms in secretly were a hundred per cent better than if the Maccabees tried on their own. The Maccabees countered by claiming that they did not have to recognize the truce order for they were independent of a central command. So the bitter squabble raged, with the Provisional Government asserting that there could be but one central authority and the Maccabees claiming otherwise.

The *Akiva* took off from Europe with its first load of arms and volulteers. The government, which sorely needed both the arms and the men, was forced to order the Maccabees to make the plane return without landing. The Maccabees were enraged at this order.

As the *Akiva* reached Palestine, in defiance of the edict, the airdrome was filled with government officials, Maccabees, and United Nations observers. The government radioed the plane a final warning to return to Europe. The *Akiva* refused. The Provisional Government ordered fighter planes up and the *Akiva* was shot down.

Fighting erupted between army and Maccabee troops. In anger the Maccabees withdrew their battalions from the army. Both sides hurled names and charges and countercharges until all justice in the '*Akiva* incident' was buried under a welter of insults and accusations. The bitterness created in Maccabee ranks was permanent.

The incident did prove to be a final clearing of the air. During the years of the British mandate the Maccabees had been a factor in making the British quit by their constant goading. Once the British were gone, terror tactics lost their usefulness and the Maccabees appeared unable to accept the discipline that a field army required. Thus their value as a fighting force was seriously qualified. Their one great victory had been at Jaffa, a city of crushed morale. In other places they had failed. Their massacre at the village of Neve Sadij remained as the one great black mark against the Jews. The Maccabees were activists with great individual courage but by their very nature they rebelled against authority. After the *Akiva* incident they remained as an angry, defiant, political group whose basic tenet was that force conquered all problems.

For a month talks went on with both sides. Count Bernadotte and his

American aide, Ralph Bunche, working for the United Nations, were unable to bring the sides together. They could not break down in a month what had been building for three decades. Kawukji, in central Galilee, had been constantly violating the truce. Now the Egyptians broke faith by resuming fighting before the truce deadline was up.

It was a great mistake, for it triggered a new Israeli campaign. If the world's military experts had been amazed by the ability of the Jews to withstand the invasion, they were stunned as the army of Israel went on the offensive.

The new phase of the war opened with the Israel air force bombing Cairo, Damascus, and Amman as a warning for the Arabs to quit similar attacks on Tel Aviv and Jerusalem. The Arabs did not bomb Jewish cities from the air again. Israeli corvettes carried the fight to the enemy by shelling Tyre, in Lebanon, one of the key ports for the entry of arms.

At Ein Gev *kibbutz* on the Sea of Galilee, the farmers, who had been under siege for months and who had broken a Syrian attack, now struck back. In a bold night maneuver, they climbed the Sussita mountain and threw the Syrians from it.

In the central Galilee, Ari Ben Canaan went after Kawukji and Nazareth. By pushing his troops to the limit of their endurance and by making brilliant use of his equipment he completely outmaneuvered and outfought the irregulars. The Mufti's personal general took a sould licking and lost Nazareth. With the fall of Nazareth the hostile Arab villages in the central Galilee collapsed and Kawukji led a flight to the Lebanese border. The Israelis commanded the entire Galilee and all its roads.

In the Bab el Wad and the Jerusalem corridor the Hillmen Brigade widened the way and began moving south toward Bethlehem.

In the Negev Desert, the Israelis held the Egyptians in a stalemate. Samson once set fire to the tails of a thousand foxes and turned them loose on the Philistine fields. Now lightning jeep units with machine guns, called 'Samson's Foxes,' made fierce attacks on Egyptian supply lines and Arab villages. The terrible siege of Negba *kibbutz* was lifted.

It was in the Sharon Valley facing the Triangle that the Israelis scored their most spectacular success. Using the jeep units to the fullest and led by the former Hanita Brigade of the Palmach, the Jews swept into Lydda and Ramle, Arab towns that had harassed the road to Jerusalem. They captured the Lydda airdrome, the largest field in Palestine, and then swung into the Samarian Triangle to develop a maneuver to encircle Latrun. On the way they brushed aside the Iraqi forces and relieved the siege of another children's village, Ben Shemen. Just as encirclement of Latrun was near accomplishment the Arabs, in unison, screamed for a second truce.

All the Israeli victories had been scored in ten days.

As Bernadotte and Bunche conducted the second truce talks, the Arab world was frantic. Abdullah of Trans-Jordan was the first to see the handwriting on the wall. He went into secret negotiations with the Provisional Government and agreed to keep the Legion sitting and out of action. This would permit the Jews to turn their full attention to the Egyptians. In exchange, the Jews agreed not to go after the Old City or the Legion-dominated Samarian Triangle.

Again the brigand Kawukji broke the truce by attacking from Lebanon. As the second truce ended, 'Operation Hiram,' named for the Lebanese King in the Bible, blew Kawukji and the Mufti's dreams into smoke, once and for all.

The Israeli Army swept over the Lebanese border on the heels of the shattered and fleeing irregulars. Lebanese villages showed an array of white flags of surrender. With Kawukji banished, the Jews pulled back to their own borders, although there had been little to stop them from going clear to Beirut and Damascus.

With the Galilee clear, the Sharon quiet, and a promise to Abdullah not to attack Jordan-held positions, the army turned its full attention on the Egyptians.

Meanwhile the Arab world scrambled to explain away the series of Israeli successes. Abdullah of Trans-Jordan publicly blamed Iraq for the Arab failure: Iraq had failed to attack from the Triangle to cut the Jews in half and had generally made themselves look ridiculous. Iraq, which dreamed of ruling a Greater Arab Nation in its 'Fertile Crescent' scheme blamed their over-extended supply lines. The Syrians were the most vocal of all: they blamed the Americans and Western imperialism. The Saudi Arabians, who fought in the Egyptian Army, blamed nearly everyone, each Arab country in turn. The Egyptians blamed Trans-Jordan for selling out by Abdullah's agreement with the Jews. However, one of the most spectacular by-products of the War of Liberation was the manner in which the Egyptian press and radio translated Egyptian disasters as victories. So far as the Egyptian public was concerned, their troops were winning the war. The Lebanese and the Yemenites kept very quiet. They were not too interested in the fighting to begin with.

The myth of Arab unity exploded as the Jews continued to administer defeats on the combined Arab strength. The former kisses, handshakes, and vows of eternal brotherhood changed to knife pulling, haranguing, and, finally, political assassination. Abdullah was eventually murdered by Moslem fanatics as he came from prayer in the Mosque of Omar in the Old City. Farouk was thrown out of Egypt by a clique of militarists who spoke the pages of an Arab *Mein Kampf*. Intrigue and murder, the old Arab game, raged at full force.

In the Negev Desert, the army of Israel, now balanced and co-ordinated, brought the war into its closing stages. Suweidan, the Monster on the Hill which had tormented the Negba *kibbutz*, fell. It was at Suweidan that the Egyptians showed their greatest valor.

A bypassed Egyptian pocket at Faluja, which had been under Jewish siege, was later evacuated under truce talks. One of its Egyptian officers was a young captain later to lead the overthrow of Farouk. His name was Gamal Abdel Nasser.

The pride of the Egyptian Navy, the cruiser *Farouk*, had tried to shell a Jewish position a few hours before one of the truces to gain a tactical advantage. It was sunk by Israeli motorboats filled with dynamite which were driven out in the water, set, and rammed into the cruiser's sides.

Beersheba – the Seven Wells, the city of Father Abraham – fell in the autumn of 1948 to a surprise Israeli attack. The Egyptians dug in and built a deep and stacked defense for a stand below Beersheba. The defenses seemed impenetrable. Again the Jews called upon their intimate knowledge of the land. They found a Nabataean path, thousands of years old, which allowed them to encircle the Egyptian defenses and attack from the rear.

From then on it was a rout. The army of Israel lashed out after the fleeing Egyptians. They bypassed the Gaza area and crossed into the Sinai itself.

The Lord has mingled a spirit of perverseness in the midst of her; and they have caused Egypt to go astray in every work thereof, as a drunken man staggereth in his vomit. Neither shall there be for Egypt any work which head or tail, palm branch or rush, may do. In that day shall the Egyptians be like unto women; and they shall tremble and fear because of the shaking of the Hand of the Lord of Hosts, which he shaketh over them.

The words of Isaiah had come true!

At the Suez Canal, the British became alarmed at the Egyptian debacle and the possibility of Israeli penetration near the canal. They demanded that the Jews stop or face the British Army. In warning, the British sent Spitfire fighters into the sky to gun the Israelis. It seemed only fitting somehow that the last shots of the War of Liberation were against the British. The Israeli Air Force brought down six British fighter planes. Then Israel yielded to international pressure by letting the Egyptians escape. The shattered Egyptian Army regrouped and with fantastic audacity marched into Cairo and staged a 'victory parade.'

The War of Liberation became history!

For months there had been truce talk. For centuries there would be arguments over how it all happened. Experts were confounded and realists were confused.

The Arab people of Palestine had long ago accepted the return of the Jews and were prepared to live in peace and benefit from the progress which had been brought after a thousand sterile years. These people simply did not want to fight and never had. They were betrayed by leaders who were first to run in the time of danger. Their courage was mob frenzy. They were confused by catch phrases they did not understand, much less believe in. They were victimized by racist polemics and filled with a fear of a militant 'Zionism' that never existed. Arab leaders exploited their ignorance for their own willful purposes.

Some of the Arabs and their armies fought with valor. Most of them did not. They had been promised easy victories, loot, and rape. They had bolstered each other with a false illusion of Arab unity. Obviously, the 'cause' was not so great it was worth bleeding for.

There never was a question of the Jews' willingness to die for Israel. In the end they stood alone and with blood and guts won for themselves what had legally been given them by the conscience of the world.

And so – the Star of David, down for two thousand years, shone from Elath to Metulla, never to be lowered again.

The aftermath of the War of Liberation involved one of the most widely discussed and thorniest dilemmas of the century – the Arab refugee problem. More than a half million Palestine Arabs had fled from their homes to neighboring Arab states. All discussions of the disposition of these people became bogged down in furious arguments, accusations, confusion, nationalism, and incrimination. The issue became so involved and mired that it turned into a political time bomb.

Barak Ben Canaan was called upon once more to serve his country. The government of Israel asked him to make a complete study of this apparently insolveable situation. He made a painstaking investigation and his findings filled several hundred pages. In a short summary, Barak shed light on what appeared to be a hopelessly confused problem.

* * *

SUMMARY OF THE ARAB REFUGEE SITUATION

The most publicized afterevent of the War of Liberation has been the Palestine Arab refugee problem. It has become the most potent political weapon in the Arab arsenal.

The Arabs have gone to great lengths to describe the plight of these war victims and to keep the refugee camps as working models to demonstrate to the world Jewish cruelty. Indeed, those who visit these wretched souls are certain to be touched by their plight.

The Arabs would have the world believe that the Palestine Arab refugee is unique. Nothing could be further from the truth. Every war man has waged has created refugees, homeless and displaced people. Today in Europe and Asia, five years after the end of World War II, displaced people number in the tens of millions. This is the very nature of war.

Had the Arab leaders obeyed the decision of the highest international tribunal and adhered to the law, there would have been no Arab refugee problem. The refugees came as a direct result of a war of aggression waged by the Arabs to destroy the people of Israel.

The Arabs created the Palestine refugee problem themselves. *After the November 1947 partition vote the Yishuv of Palestine begged the Palestine Arabs to remain calm, friendly, and to respect the unassailably legal rights of the Jewish people.*

Despite wanton aggression the State of Israel, in its Declaration of Independence, held out its hand in friendship to its Arab neighbors, even at the moment her borders were being violated.

The avowed intention of murdering the Jewish people and completely destroying the State of Israel was the Arab answer to law and friendship.

Strangely, most of the Palestine Arabs fled even before the invasion. Jaffa, Haifa, and the Galilee created most of the refugees while the fighting was comparatively light.

The first reason for this was that the Palestine Arabs were filled with fear. For decades racist leaders had implanted the idea of mass murder in their minds. These leaders played on the illiteracy, superstition, and fanatical religious devotion of the fellaheen. These leaders never cared for the fellaheen but only for their own personal ambitions. They completely betrayed the people. Blind fear and ignorance caused the first flight of the Arabs. Was this fear founded upon fact? No! *At one place, Neve Sadij, there was an unforgivable massacre of innocent people. Otherwise, the Arabs who remained in Palestine were completely unmolested. No Arab village which remained at peace was harmed in any way by the Israelis.*

In regard to Neve Sadij we might add that this one example of Jewish excess – in the heat of war, one must remember – pales beside the record of scores of Arab-led massacres in over a three-decade period of nominal peace.

The second major cause of the refugee situation comes from the absolutely documented fact that the Arab leaders wanted the civilian population to leave Palestine as a political issue and a military weapon.

The Arab generals planned an annihilation of the Jewish people. They did not want a large Arab civilian population present to clutter their operational freedom.

The politicians wanted to prove Jewish inhumanity by pointing to the Arab refugees 'forced' from their homes. Lastly, the actual fighting helped create part of the refugee situation. Those few Arab villages which fought against the State of Israel were attacked and the Arabs driven from them. No apologies have to be made for this.

Documented proof exists that the Arabs were promised they could return to their homes on the heels of Arab victories to loot the destroyed State of Israel. No one can question Arab hostility toward Israel since the war. They have blockaded the Suez Canal in violation of international agreement, they have boycotted business, blackmailed foreign firms, raided border settlements, and constantly threatened to come back for a second attempt to destroy Israel. In the light of this it is inconceivable that Israel could even consider resettlement of a hostile minority, pledged to destroy the State. We come now to the most horrible of all the facts concerning the Arab refugees. The Arab nations do not want these people. *They are kept caged like animals in suffering as a deliberate political weapon. In Gaza, to cite one example, the roads are mined and patrolled so that these refugees cannot reach Egypt.*

The United Nations has established a fund of two hundred million dollars for resettlement of the Palestine refugees. There is much lush, fertile, and empty land in the seven million square miles of the Arab world. The Tigris-Euphrates Valley, one example, has some of the richest unused land in the world. It is inhabited by a handful of Bedouins. This section alone could take not only the half million but ten million others as well.

Not one penny of the resettlement money has been used.

On the other hand, Israel, an unfertile land whose seven thousand square miles are half desert, has taken in more than a half million Jewish refugees from Arab countries and stands ready to take in that number again.

The Arabs argue that the Palestine refugees themselves do not want to be resettled but want their farms in Palestine back. This is sheer nonsense. The Arabs have cried crocodile tears over the great love these poor fellaheen have for their lost homes.

The fact is, the Palestine fellaheen were victimized by men who used them as a tool, deserting them, and are victimizing them again. Kept penned up, fed up with hatred, they are being used to keep Arab hatred of Israel at the boiling point.

If the Arabs of Palestine loved their land, they could not have been forced from it – much less run from it without real cause. The Arabs had little to live for, much less to fight for. This is not the reaction of a man who loves his land.

A man who loves his land, as the Arabs profess, will stand and die for it.

The Arabs tell the world that the State of Israel has expansionist ideas. Exactly how a nation of less than a million people can expand against fifty million is an interesting question.

The Arab people need a century of peace.

The Arab people need leadership, not of desert sheiks who own thousands of slaves, not of hate-filled religious fanatics, not of military cliques, not of men whose entire thinking is in the Dark Ages. The Arab people need leaders who will bring them civil liberties, education, medicine, land reforms, equality.

They need leaders with the courage to face the real problems of ignorance, illiteracy, and disease instead of waving a ranting banner of ultranationalism and promoting the evil idea that the destruction of Israel will be the cure for all their problems.

Unfortunately, whenever an enlightened Arab leader arises he is generally murdered. The Arabs want neither resettlement of the refugees, alleviation of their plight, nor do they want peace.

Israel today stands as the greatest single instrument for bringing the Arab people out of the Dark Ages.

Only when the Arab people get leadership willing to grasp the hand extended in friendship will they begin to solve the problems which have kept them in moral and physical destitution.

BARAK BEN CANAAN

BOOK FIVE

With Wings as Eagles

A voice crieth in the wilderness, Prepare ye the way of the Lord, make straight in the desert a highway for our God.

They that wait upon the Lord shall renew their strength; they shall mount up with wings as eagles.

ISAIAH

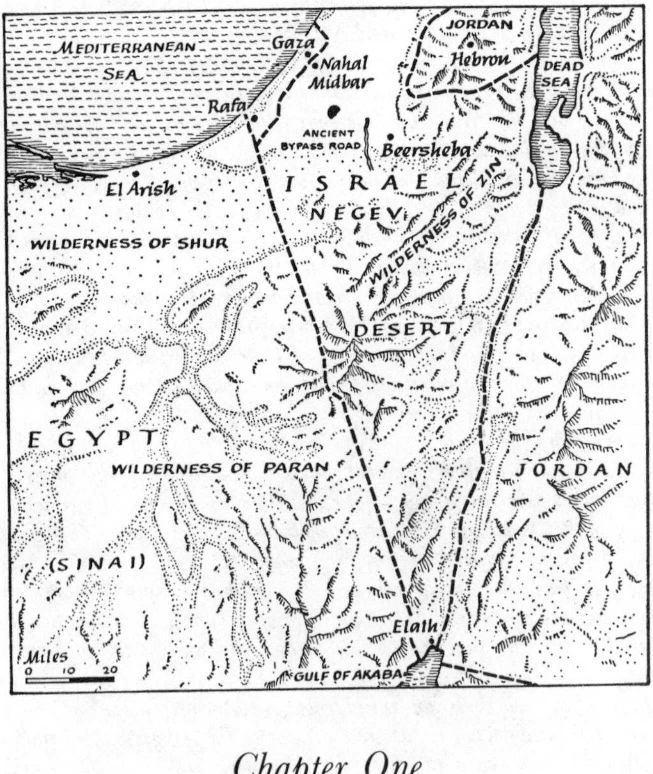

Chapter One

NOME, ALASKA
LATE 1948
The entire flying stock of the Arctic Circle Airways consisted of three army-surplus cargo ships purchased on credit by Stretch Thompson.

Stretch had served in Alaska during the war. He had won renown as a young man with a fertile mind and unlimited imagination when it came to devising means of avoiding honest labor. The nights were long in Alaska and they gave Stretch Thompson much thinking time. Most of his thinking time was devoted to exploiting the untapped riches of Alaska and avoiding honest labor. The longer the nights became, the more Stretch stretched – and thought. And one night he hit it.

Crabs!

The entire coast was lined with virgin beds of Alaskan king crabs, some sixteen inches in diameter. Why, with a little enterprise he could train the American public to drool for king crabs. In a year he would make them a delicacy equal to Maine lobsters, Maryland terrapin, or cherry-stone clams. He could fly the giant crustaceans down to the United States packed in ice. Eager dealers would snap them up. He would be rich. He would be known as Stretch Thompson, the King Crab King.

Things did not work out exactly as Stretch had planned. It appeared that the human race was not advanced enough for his king crabs. The cost of a plane, gas, and a pilot seemed, somehow, always to come out to more than what he could get for his crabs. None the less, Stretch was not a man to say die. With deft bookwork and glib tongue he kept the creditors off his back and he did have an airline, such as it was. With bailing wire, spit, and chewing gum he was able to keep the three crafts of Arctic Circle aloft. Just when things looked the darkest, along came a pay load to keep him in business.

Stretch's one bit of continued good luck was his chief, and sometimes only, pilot, Foster J. MacWilliams, known as 'Tex' for the usual obvious reason. Foster J. had flown the Hump during the war and was, as Stretch put it, 'The best goddam chief pilot any goddam airline ever had.' Such was Foster J. MacWilliams' prowess that no one in Nome would bet against his setting down a C-47 on the tail end of an iceberg in the middle of a blizzard – drunk. In fact, on various occasions Stretch tried to raise enough money to make the bet worth while but something always happened ... either the blizzard slackened or Foster couldn't get drunk enough.

MacWilliams was a tramp. He liked flying. He didn't like the fancy stuff of flying over set routes or with a schedule or with first-class craft. Too dull. The risks of flying Arctic Circle suited him fine.

One day MacWilliams came into the shack at the end of the runway which served as office, operations headquarters, and home for Stretch Thompson.

'Goddam, Stretch,' he said, 'it's colder than a digger's ass out there.'

Stretch had the look on his face of the proverbial canary-filled cat. 'Foster,' he said, 'how'd you like to go to a warmer climate and get *all* of your pay in one bundle?'

'You always did have a gruesome sense of humor.'

'I kid you not, Tex. You'll never guess ...'

'What?'

'Guess.'

Foster shrugged. 'You sold the airline.'

'That's right.'

Foster's mouth dropped open. 'Who'd buy this pile of crap?'

'I didn't ask their life history. I found out their check was good and that was all she wrote.'

'Well, I'll be a sad bastard. That's fine, Stretch, because I'm getting tired of this chicken kacky up here, anyhow. How much you figure you owe me?'

'With the bonus I'm giving you, about four grand.'

Foster J. MacWilliams whistled. 'That will buy a lot of first-class tail. I can stay drunk and laid from here to South America. That's my next stop, Stretch. I'm going to latch onto one of them South American outfits. I hear they pay big dough hauling dynamite over the Andes.'

'There's a hitch ...' Stretch said.

'I figgered as much.'

'We got to deliver the three planes to the new owners. I hired two boys to run the number one and two ships over ... I can't find another one.'

'You mean I'm the only one fool enough to fly the number three ship. Well, that's all right. Where do I deliver it?'

'Israel.'

'Where?'

'Israel.'

'Never heard of it.'

'I was just looking for it on the map, myself, when you came in.'

Stretch Thompson and Foster J. MacWilliams searched high and low on the world map. After a futile half hour Tex shook his head. 'Stretch, I think somebody gave you the rub.'

They went into Nome and asked around the bars where Israel might be. One or two people had heard something or the other about it. Stretch was beginning to perspire in the cold when someone suggested they get the librarian up.

'It's Palestine!' the irate librarian said, 'and midnight is no time to pound on my door.'

After another search on the map they finally located it.

Foster shook his head. 'Goddam, Stretch,' he said. 'It's smaller than a big iceberg. I'm liable to fly right over it.'

Three weeks later, Foster J. MacWilliams landed the number three plane of Arctic Circle Airways at Lydda airdrome. Stretch Thompson had flown over a week earlier and was there to meet him. Foster was ushered into an office which bore the words: PALESTINE CENTRAL AIRWAYS, S. S. THOMPSON, GENERAL MANAGER.

Foster J. MacWilliams smelled a rat.

'How was the trip, old buddy? I'm sure glad to see you.'

'Just fine. Now if you'll give me my back pay, old buddy, I'll just shuffle off to Paris. I got my hooks on a real goer and a month before I hitch a ride to Rio D.'

'Sure, sure,' Stretch said. 'Got the check right here in the safe.'

Stretch watched Foster MacWilliams' eyes bug out. 'Four thousand, five hundred and no zero zero's!'

'The extra five bills is to prove that Stretch Thompson ain't no hog,' Stretch said.

'You're a big man ... always said that.'

'Y' know, Tex, this here is an interesting place. Just about everybody around here is a Jew. Been here a week and I can't get used to it.'

Foster was reluctant to ask why Stretch was here – but he did.

'Name on the door tells the story. Palestine Central Airways. I thought of the name myself. You see, these guys here haven't had too much experience running a first-class line, so they induced me to stay. First thing I told 'em ... boys, I said ... if you want a first class operation, you have to have a first-class chief pilot and I got the best goddam chief pilot any goddam airline ...'

'I'll see you around,' Foster said, standing up quickly.

'What's the fire?'

'I'm on my way to Paris.'

'I got a deal for you.'

'Not interested.'

'Do me the courtesy of listening.'

'I'll listen but I'm not buying. I'm going to Paris if I got to swim there.'

'Here's the pitch. Like I said, everybody around here is a Jew. They bought out the old Arctic Circle so's they could haul more Jews in. Man, I hear they got them stashed everywhere in the world, and they all want in. All we got to do is bring the bodies in. Can't you see it? Every load a pay load. Cash on the line ... per head. This is dream stuff, Tex boy. Stick with me and you'll be bathing in it. You know me, Tex ... I ain't no hog.'

'I know what I'll be bathing in. I'll drop you a card from Rio D.'

'O.K., Foster ... been nice knowing you.'

'Now, don't get mad, Stretch.'

'Who's mad, who's mad?'

'We've had our times in Nome.'

'Sure ... sure ... swell times. I froze my butt off.'

'Well, put her there,' Foster said. Stretch shook his hand half-heartedly.

'Now, what's the matter, Stretch? You act like I'm putting a knife in your ribs.'

'Going to level with you, Foster. I'm in trouble. We got a hot flash that a bunch of these Jews are sitting around and waiting to be picked up at a place called Aden. I had some pilots but they chickened out on me.'

'That's tough titty. You don't con me. I'm going to Paris.'

'Sure,' Stretch said. 'Go to Paris. If I was you I'd go too. I don't blame you. Those other pilots ran like striped apes when they heard there was danger of the Arabs firing on them.'

Foster was on his way out. He stopped and turned around.

'You're right, Foster. No use getting your brains blown out. This is a real rough run ... even rougher than flying the Hump or running dynamite over the Andes.'

Foster J. MacWilliams licked his lips. Stretch went into some more dramatics but he knew that the bait had been swallowed.

'Tell you what I'm gonna, Stretch. I'll make this run for you just to help you off a spot. By the time I'm back you'd better gotten your hooks on some pilots. Just one run. Now where the hell is this Aden?'

'Damned if I know.'

'Well, let's get a map and look for it.'

As Foster J. MacWilliams, American tramp pilot for Palestine Central, nee Arctic Circle, took off from Lydda airdrome he opened a twentieth-century fantasy out of the pages of the *Arabian Nights*.

He flew toward the British protectorate of Aden at the bottom of the Arabian Peninsula, moving right down the Red Sea.

The story actually began three thousand years before Foster's time in ancient Sheba. In the time of the Queen of Sheba, the southern part of the Arabian Peninsula was a land of richness. The people had learned the art of constructing spillways and dams and cisterns to trap and conserve water and with it, created a garden.

After the Queen of Sheba had made her visit to Solomon, some of Solomon's people left Israel to go to Sheba to establish trade routes through the desert, along the Red Sea, and begin a colony. These Jews came to Sheba in Biblical times, hundreds of years before even the fall of the First Great Temple.

For centuries the Jews in Sheba prospered. They colonized well with their own villages; they integrated into the complexities of tribal life. They became leaders of the court and the most prominent of citizens.

Then came the horrible years when the sands slowly and cancerously ate away the fertile land; the wadis dried and the rains disappeared into parched earth. Man and beast wilted and withered under the unmerciful sun, and the fight to conquer thirst was the fight for life itself. Fruitful Sheba and the neighboring states broke up into jealous and hate-filled tribes which warred upon each other constantly.

When Islam first swept the world, the Jews of the ancient religion were given respect and freedom in their ways. Mohammed himself wrote the laws, which all Moslems were to follow, prescribing the kindly treatment of Jews.

This equality of the Jews was short-lived. As in all Moslem lands, all citizens other than Moslems became scorned as infidels. In their own way the Arabs had grudging respect for the Jews, and in their own way granted them a reasonable amount of tolerance. Arab massacres of Jews were never the calculated genocide of Europe, but rather the flaring of a sudden spark of violence. The Arabs had become too busy plotting against each other to be much concerned with the docile little Jews in the land now known as Yemen; centuries of suppression had removed any warlike qualities.

As in all Arab lands, these Jews lived as second-class citizens. There were the usual repressive laws, unequal taxation, persecutions, and denial of the civil rights given to Moslems. The degree of persecution varied with the particular ruler in the particular area.

A standing rule forbade Jews' raising their voices before a Moslem, building a house higher than a Moslem, touching a Moslem, or passing a Moslem on the right side. A Jew must not ride a camel, for the mount would put his head higher than a Moslem's. In a land where the camel was the chief mode of transportation, this was a severity. Jews lived in *mellahs*, Oriental versions of ghettos.

The world moved on and progressed. Time stood still in Yemen. It remained as primitive as the jungle and as remote and inaccessible as Nepal or Outer Mongolia. No hospital existed in Yemen, no school or newspaper or printing press or radio or telephone or highway.

It was a land of desert and vicious mountains linked only by the paths of camel caravans. Hidden cities nestled in twelve-thousand-foot ranges surrounded by hundreds of thousands of square miles of complete waste. Illiteracy was nearly a hundred per cent. Backward, forsaken, wild and uncharted, some of its boundaries were never defined.

Yemen was ruled by an Imam, a relative of Mohammed, and the personal representative of Allah, the Merciful, the All-Compassionate. The Imam of Yemen was an absolute ruler. He controlled the life of every subject. He controlled the gold and the single crop of coffee. He answered to no cabinet. He provided no civil or social services. He held power by dexterously balancing tribal strength, being continually occupied in crushing one tribe or aiding another among the hot desert feuds and the raging jealousies. He kept hostile tribes under control by kidnapping their people and holding them as hostages. He kept hundreds of slaves. He sat in cross-legged pompousness and dispensed justice according to his whim, ordering the noses of prostitutes cut off and the hands of thieves amputated. He scorned civilization and did all in his power to keep it from penetrating his kingdom, although he was forced to yield occasionally from fear of his powerful Saudi Arabian neighbor to the north who dabbled in international intrigue.

Part of the Imam's fear of civilization derived from civilization's desire to subjugate his land. Despite its remoteness it was located in a corner of the world that formed a gateway to the Orient through the Red Sea. Time and again Yemen became a battlefield as colonial expansionists set covetous eyes on it.

The Imam traditionally assumed the role of benevolent despot toward the Jews. So long as the Jews remained subservient they were given some protection. The Imam was cautious: the Jews were the finest artisans and craftsmen of the land. Their generations passed down the arts of silver-smithing, jewelry making, minting, leatherwork, carpentry, shoe-making, and a hundred other trades which most Arabs had not mastered. The latter either farmed or comprised the roving Bedouin bands. Thus skill brought the Jews some measure of protection.

That the Jews of Yemen remained Jews was incredible. For three thousand years these people had no contact with the outer world. Their lives would have been much easier had they taken up Islam. Yet the Yemenite Jews kept the Torah, the Laws, the Sabbath, and the holidays through the centuries of isolation. Many of the Jews were illiterate in Arabic but all of them knew Hebrew. There were no presses; all holy books were written by hand with great accuracy and passed down through the generations.

Direct pressure was often brought to bear to make them convert from Judaism to Islam, but they resisted. When the Imam began to abduct orphans and convert them, the Jews embraced the practice of immediately marrying orphans no matter what their age. There were cases of children only a few months old becoming husbands or wives.

In physical appearance, in dress, in action, and in spirit the present-day Yemenite Jews could have been mistaken for ancient prophets. As in Biblical days, they still practiced multiple marriage. They believed in the evil eye, in ill winds and a variety of demons, against which they wore protective amulets. Their belief in the Bible was absolutely literal.

During the years, the Yemenite Jews never stopped looking toward Jerusualem. They waited through the centuries in patience and devotion for Him to send the word for them to 'go up.' From time to time small groups or individuals managed to get out of Yemen, and they returned to Palestine and established a small community there.

And then, the word came, as the prophets had declared it would!

Yemen declared war upon Israel after the Israeli Declaration of Independence and sent a token force to fight in the Egyptian Army. This action apprised the Jews of the fact that Israel had been reborn. Their rabbis told them it was the message from God. King David had returned to Jerusalem! Their long wait would come to an end! The Haham – the Wise

Ones – told them to rise and go up to the Promised Land on wings of the eagle!

When the first stir of this Yemenite exodus reached the ears of those in Israel, the War of Liberation still raged. Little was known of the number of the Yemenites, of how to get them out, or what to do with them.

The chief Haham went to the Imam and petitioned the All-Merciful to allow the Jews to leave. There were a number of political and economic reasons why the Imam felt it was better to keep the Jews. The rabbi intimated that the Imam had better reacquaint himself with the chapters of Exodus in the Old Testament.

The Imam sat cross-legged in his harem and thought for several days. The rabbi had made his point. The thought of the Ten Plagues was in the Imam's heart. Not long before the chief rabbi had petitioned him a typhoid epidemic had wiped out a quarter of his population. He decided that it was a warning from Allah.

The Imam agreed that the Jews could leave with the condition that all property was left to him, a head tax was paid, and several hundred artisans and craftsmen stayed as hostages to teach the Moslems.

The Jews of Yemen left behind their fields and their homes. They packed what they could carry and began a trek through the wild and murderous mountains, the searing sun, and the vast wastelands scourged by hundred-mile-an-hour winds.

They walked toward the border of the Western Protectorate, this gentle little people with olive skins and delicate features. They were turbaned and wore the same kind of long striped robes that were worn in the palace of Solomon. The women from Sa'na were dressed in black gowns with white fringe and they carried their babies in slings on their backs. They trudged along in the fulfillment of a prophecy, easy prey to the Arab tribes who took their meager possessions as toll for the passage.

The protectorates along the Arabian Peninsula consisted of a complex of large and small Arab kingdoms, sheikdoms and Bedouin tribes which skirted the shores from the Red Sea along the Gulf of Aden on through to the Arabian Sea and Persian Gulf. The British controlled the area by a hundred different treaties which paid tribute in arms or money to the tribes for oil rights. In turn, the British attempted to keep the feuds down and give protection and passage.

The key place in this holding was the Crown Colony of Aden in the Western Protectorate. The port of Aden was a passageway between East and West, settled by Greeks, British, Arabs, and Jews, and a blend of oriental filth, Asiatic exoticness, British rigidity, traces of industrial progress, and the wildness of a port of call. It was at once an exciting and disgusting place.

The port of Aden was the goal of the Yemenite exodus. At first the British did not quite know what to do with these people pouring in over their border in caravans that seemed right out of the Bible. They were still at odds with the Jews over the mandate, yet they could feel no hatred for the Yemenites. The British gave conditional approval to the Yemenites to enter and establish camps, provided the Israelis came down and got them out.

They were tragic figures as they came from Yemen, dressed in rags, filthy and half dead from starvation and thirst. Almost all their possessions had been stolen from them by the Arabs. But each man still carried his Bible and each village still carried the Holy Torah of the synagogue.

A hasty camp was set up at Hashed near the port of Aden. The Israelis covered the border between the Western Protectorate and Yemen. As soon as there was news of another group arriving, they rushed transport to the border to bring them to Hashed. There was a shortage of personnel and supplies at Hashed. The organization badly lagged behind the needs of the numbers coming through.

The immigration people faced the additional difficulty of having to deal with a semiprimitive people. The Yemenites could not comprehend things like water taps, toilets, or electric lights. This was a community who had suddenly caught up with almost three thousand years of progress in hours. Motor vehicles, medicine, western dress, and a thousand things were strange and awesome to them. It was a frightening experience.

The women shrieked as doctors and nurses tried to remove their lice-filled rags to exchange them for clean clothing. They refused to have their bodies examined for sores and diseases, and rebelled against shots and vaccinations. There was a continuous fight against the workers who tried to remove temporarily the infants who badly needed treatment for malnutrition.

Fortunately there was a partial solution that kept the workers and doctors from complete frustration. The camp workers, mostly Israelis with an intimate knowledge of the Bible, quickly learned to go to the Yemenite rabbis with appropriate Biblical passages, and thereby nearly anything could be accomplished. So long as it was written in 'the Book,' the Yemenites would accede.

The Hashed camp grew, and reports along the Western Protectorate frontier told of more Yemeinites coming. Under agreement with the British, the Israel Provisional Government had to get them out of Aden. So Arctic Circle Airways became Palestine Central and Foster J. MacWilliams unwittingly answered an age-old prophecy by dropping from the sky with the first of the great 'eagles.'

The arrival of the plane created tremendous excitement. The first group picked up their Torah and their water bottles and were removed to the airport. They saw the eagle and nodded their heads knowingly: God had sent it as He said He would. But when they were asked to board, they refused. The rabbi in the group remembered it was the Sabbath. A terrible argument ensued. The Hashed camp chief explained that thousands of people were waiting to get to Israel and it was unfair to hold up the eagle for even a day. No amount of arguing could make them break the Sabbath. They sat adamantly under the wings of the eagle and refused to budge. After three thousand years of waiting, they could wait one more day.

Foster J. MacWilliams took one look at these strange creatures, listened to the arguments in the gobbledygook lingo, uttered a short oath to Stretch Thompson and went into town and got very intoxicated.

He was awakened the next morning and carted to the airport with a horrible throbbing hangover from mixing Greek ouzo, rice wine, and Scotch. He watched the Yemenites carrying their water bottles and their Torah aboard the plane.

'Jesus H. Christ,' Foster commented on the procession.

'Captain MacWilliams,' a voice said behind him. He turned and faced a tall, well-shaped *sabra* who introduced herself as Hanna. She was in her mid-twenties and wore the traditional blue of a *kibbutz* and had sandals on her feet. 'I will be flying with you and taking care of the passengers.'

At that point the trip started to become interesting to Foster. Hanna was unconcerned that he was looking her over very carefully. 'Do you have any particular instructions? I mean this is our first experiment.'

'Hell, no. Just keep them gooks out of the pilot's cabin. Of course, *you* are welcome to come in . . . any time. And call me "Tex." '

Foster was watching the loading. The line of Yemenites seemed endless. 'Hey! What's the score? How many of them do you think that plane will hold?'

'We have a hundred and forty listed.'

'What! You crazy? We won't get that thing into the air. Now, Hanna, you just run up there and tell whoever is putting those people on to take half of them off.'

'Captain MacWilliams,' the girl pleaded, 'they are very light people.'

'So are peanuts light. That don't mean that I can haul a billion of them.'

'Please. I promise you won't have any trouble with them.'

'You're damned right I won't. We'll all be dead at the end of the runway.'

'Captain MacWilliams. Our situation is desperate. The British have ordered us to get them out of Aden. They are pouring over the border by the hundreds every day.'

Foster grumbled and studied the weight charts. The Israeli workers nearby held their breath as he calculated. He made the mistake of looking up into Hanna's eyes. He refigured, cheated a bit, and reckoned with luck the old ship could rev up enough steam to get up in the air. Once up, he'd keep her up . . . somehow. 'Hell, leave them in,' he said, 'this is my first and last trip, anyhow.'

The camp director handed him the final manifest. A hundred and forty-two Yemenites were packed into the craft. Hanna got the food and supplies aboard and he climbed up the ladder.

The stench hit his nostrils!

'We didn't have time to bathe them all,' Hanna apologized. 'We didn't know when you were coming.'

He poked his head in the main cabin. It was jammed tight with the little people. They sat cross-legged and frightened on the floor. The smell was horrible.

Foster stepped in and closed and locked the door. Whereupon the unventilated hundred-and-twenty-degree heat began to work on the odors. He worked his way forward an inch at a time. By the time he reached the pilot's cabin he was an interesting shade of green. He threw the window open to get air but instead he got a blast of heat. He ran up the engines and as he taxied down the runway he held his head out of the window and vomited. He continued retching as he gunned the plane down the runway and barely lifted at the last inch. He sucked a lemon as he fought for altitude, and finally, with the coming of cooler air, his stomach came under control.

It was choppy and the plane bounced badly as he tried to get height. He 'turned the corner' at the Strait of Bab el Mandeb and beelined up the center of the Red Sea with Saudi Arabia on one side and Egypt on the other.

Hanna came in and she, too, was green. 'Can't you make this plane stop bouncing?' she said. 'They're all throwing up in there.'

Foster shut off the heat in the main cabin. 'Get in there and open the air vents. I'll try to get a little higher. The cold air will straighten them out.'

His head throbbed from the hangover. Why did he ever let Stretch Thompson talk him into this?

In another half hour, Hanna returned. 'They're all complaining that they are freezing . . . so am I.'

'You got your choice – if I turn on the heat they'll start vomiting again.'

'Let them freeze,' Hanna mumbled, and returned to her passengers.

In a few moments she ran into the cabin shrieking and screaming in Hebrew.

'Speak English!'

Hanna pointed to the main cabin. 'Fire ... they've started a fire to keep warm.'

The plane was on automatic pilot and Foster tore out, throwing bodies to right and left. A small fire was going in the middle of the floor. He stamped it out in a rage and went to Hanna, who sagged limply by the compartment door.

'Do you know how to talk to these people?'

'Yes ... Hebrew ...'

Foster shoved the intercom microphone into her hands. 'Now you tell them the next one who moves out of his place is going for a swim in the Red Sea!'

The Yemenites had never heard a loud-speaker before. When they heard Hanna's voice they all began pointing to the ceiling and, terrified, they cried and cringed.

'What the hell's the matter with them? What did you tell them?'

'They've never heard it before. They think it's God commanding them.'

'Good. Don't tell them no different.'

Things went fairly well for the next few hours. There were a few minor incidents, nothing bad enough to endanger the plane. Foster had just begun to relax when he heard another loud commotion from the main cabin. He closed his eyes. 'Dear Lord,' he sighed, 'I'll be a good Christian from now on. Just let this day end.'

Hanna returned.

'I'm afraid to ask,' Foster mumbled.

'Tex,' she said, 'you are the godfather of a baby boy.'

'What!'

'We've just had a birth.'

'No ... no ... *no*!'

'It's all right,' Hanna said. 'Giving birth is a very routine matter with them. Mother and son are resting well.'

He closed his eyes and gulped.

Nothing more happened for an hour – suspiciously, Foster thought. The little people got used to the sound of the engines of the 'eagle' and began to doze off one by one, tired from their ordeal. Hanna brought a bowl of hot broth to Foster and they began to laugh over the events of the day. Foster asked Hanna a lot of questions about the Yemenites and the war.

'Where are we now?'

Foster, pilot, co-pilot, navigator, and radio operator, looked at the map. 'We'll be turning the corner pretty soon and go up the Gulf of Akaba. On the way down I was able to see the battle lines in the desert.'

'I hope the war will be over soon.'

'Yeah, war's rough. Say, how in hell did you ever get roped into a job like this? Whatever they pay you, it's worth double.'

Hanna smiled. 'I don't get paid for this.'

'Don't get paid?'

'No. I was sent here. I may go out with these people to build a settlement or I may continue this run.'

'I don't dig you at all.'

'It is rather hard to explain. Sometimes outside people don't understand how we feel. Money means nothing to us. Getting these people into Israel means everything. Sometime I'll explain it better.'

Foster shrugged. A lot of strange things were happening. Well, it didn't matter, he thought. It was worth the ride, but once on a run like this was enough.

After a while he pointed ahead. 'That's Israel,' he said.

Hanna ran to the microphone.

'What the hell you doing!'

'Please let me tell them, Tex. They've been waiting for this moment for ... thousands of years.'

'They're liable to tear the plane apart!'

'I promise ... I'll make them stay calm.'

'Well ... go on.'

He set the automatic pilot again and went back to make sure they didn't blow the plane up. Hanna made the announcement.

A fantastic scene of jubilation broke out. Crying, singing, laughing, praying. Whoops of joy – dancing – hugging.

'My God,' Foster marveled, 'they didn't make this much fuss when we beat Georgia Tech in the Cotton Bowl.'

A Yemenite woman took his hand and kissed it. He pulled away and returned to the controls. They continued cheering and singing all the way to Lydda. As the plane touched the end of the runway the din rose above the sound of the engines.

Foster watched them pour out of the plane, fall on their knees, and kiss the ground of Israel, weeping.

'Good-by, Tex,' Hanna said. 'I am sorry you are leaving, but have a good time in Paris.'

Foster J. MacWilliams came slowly down from the plane. He looked at the scene of bustle. Ambulances and buses stood by. There were dozens of girls like Hanna mingling among the little Yemenites, calming them and joining in their joy. Foster froze at the bottom of the steps and a strange new feeling churned inside him.

He did not even see Stretch Thompson rush out for him.

'Good go, Foster baby! How'd the crate hold up?'

'Huh?'

'I said, how'd she fly?'

'Like an eagle.'

A half dozen officials from immigration pumped Foster's hand and pounded his back.

'How'd they behave?'

'Was it a routine flight?'

Foster shrugged. 'Routine,' he said, 'just routine.'

Stretch led Foster away from the scene of jubilation. Foster stopped and looked back for a second and Hanna waved to him and he waved back.

'Well, Foster, you can go to Paris now. I've got my crews in and we dug up another plane.'

'If you're in a jam, Stretch, I *could* take one more run. But it would be my last.'

Stretch scratched his head. 'I don't know ... Well, maybe I can sign you on for one run – to try out the new ship.' Hooked! Stretch said in glee to himself. I got the bastard hooked!

It was the beginning to Operation Magic Carpet.

Stretch Thompson, the erstwhile King Crab King, brought in rough-and-ready American flyers who had flown the Berlin airlift. Each new pilot and crew in turn became obsessed with the mission of bringing the Yemenites to their Promised Land.

Many times the planes were almost ready to come apart. Yet, no craft was ever lost, despite being overworked and underserviced. The pilots on Magic Carpet began to believe that the planes were being divinely sustained so long as they carried Yemenites.

Foster J. MacWilliams never did get to Paris. He flew the Aden run until all the Yemenites were evacuated and then he went on to Operation Ali Baba, the airlift of the Iraqi jews from Bagdad. Foster worked longer and harder hours than any pilot in the history of aviation. As soon as his ship would land at Lydda with a load of immigrants, he would grab a few hours sleep right at the airport while his plane was being serviced. As soon as the plane was ready, he flew out again. In the next few years Foster flew four hundred missions covering millions of miles and bringing in nearly fifty thousand Jews to Israel.

He kept swearing that each trip was his last, right up to the time he married Hanna and took an apartment in Tel Aviv.

Magic Carpet was the beginning. They came from the hinterlands of Kurdistan and Iraq and Turkey.

A warlike lost tribe of Jews in Hadhramaut in the Eastern Protectorate fought their way to Aden.

They poured out of the displaced persons camps in Europe.

Jews came to Israel from France and Italy and Yugoslavia and Czechoslovakia and Rumania and Bulgaria and Greece and Scandinavia.

Across the breadth of northern Africa they arose from the *mellahs* of Algeria and Morocco and Egypt and Tunisia.

In South Africa, the wealthy Jewish community and the most ardent Zionists in the world went to Israel.

They came from China and India where they had settled three thousand years before.

They came from Australia and Canada and England.

They came from the Argentine.

Some walked through burning deserts.

Some flew on the rickety craft of the airlift.

Some came in jam-packed holds of cattle freighters.

Some came in deluxe liners.

They came from seventy-four nations.

The dispersed, the exiles, the unwanted came to that one little corner of the earth where the word Jew was not a slander.

Chapter Two

The trickle became a stream and then a deluge of humanity.

The exodus soon doubled, then began to triple, the population of Israel. The economy, ruptured by war, buckled under the flood of immigrants. Many came with little more than the clothes they were wearing. Many were old and many were ill and many were illiterate, but no matter what the condition, no matter what the added burden, no Jew was turned away from the doors of Israel.

It was not a melting pot, it was a pressure cooker, for they came from every corner of the earth and had lived under every variety of circumstance.

Tent cities and ugly corrugated-tin-shack villages sprang up to blot the landscape from the Galilee to the Negev. Hundreds of thousands of people lived 'under canvas,' in makeshift hovels, breaking down the medical, education, and welfare facilities.

Yet there was an attitude of optimism all over the land. From the moment the downtrodden set foot on the soil of Israel they were granted a human dignity and freedom that most of them had never known, and this equality fired them with a drive and purpose without parallel in man's history.

Every day new agricultural settlements sprang up. The immigrants went out to attack the wastes and the desert with the same fervor that the early pioneers had shown in rolling back the swamps.

Cities and towns seemed to spring up from the earth.

South Africans and South Americans and Canadians poured money into industry. Factories were built until the manufacturing potential reached one of the highest levels in Africa or Asia. General scientific, medical, and agricultural research reached an advanced stage.

Tel Aviv expanded into a bustling metropolis of a quarter of a million people, and Haifa grew into one of the most important ports on the Mediterranean. In both cities, heavy industry sprang up. New Jerusalem, the capital and educational center of the new nation, expanded into the hills.

Chemicals, drugs, medicines, mining, engineering, shoe and clothing manufacturing – the list grew into thousands of items. Cars were assembled and buses were built. Tires were made and airstrips laid down, and a network of highways spanned the nation.

Housing, housing, housing – people needed homes, and the concrete and steel skylines pushed farther into the suburbs almost by the hour. The sound of the hammer, the music of the drill, the concrete mixer, the welding torch never stopped in Israel!

The arts flourished. Bookstores lined Herzl Street and Allenby Road. In every *kibbutz* and in every home and in every *moshav* shelves were filled with books written in a dozen languages. Musicians, painters, writers put this dynamic new society into words and on canvas and into melody.

From Metulla to Elath, from Jerusalem to Tel Aviv there was the electrifying feel and smell of one huge boom town.

Yet life was brutally hard. Israel was a poor and unfertile country and every single advance was made with sweat. Workers labored exhausting hours for little pay. Those out in the settlements fighting the soil toiled under nearly unbearable conditions. All the citizens were taxed to the breaking point to pay for the new immigrants pouring in. Clawing, bleeding, conquering with their bodies and minds, they made the tiny nation live and grow.

A national airline took to the skies.

A merchant marine flying the Star of David began to sail to the corners of the earth.

The people forged ahead with a determination that captured the heart of the civilized world. Young Israel stood out as a lighthouse for all mankind, proving what could be done with will power and love. No one in Israel worked for comfort in his own lifetime: it was all for tomorrow, for the children, for the new immigrants coming in. And in the wake of this drive, the tough young *sabra* generation emerged a generation never to know humiliation for being born a Jew.

Israel became an epic in the history of man.

The Negev Desert composed half the area of Israel. It was for the most part a wilderness, with some areas which resembled the surface of the moon. This was the wilderness of Paran and Zin where Moses wandered in search of the Promised Land. It was a broiling mass of denuded desolation where the heat burned down at a hundred and twenty-five degrees over the endless slate fields and deep gorges and canyons. Mile after mile of the rock plateaus would not give life to so much as a single blade of grass. No living thing, not even a vulture, dared penetrate.

The Negev Desert became Israel's challenge. The Israelis went down to the desert! They lived in the merciless heat and they built settlements on rock. They did as Moses had done: they brought water from the rocks, and they made life grow.

They searched for minerals. Potash was pulled from the Dead Sea. King Solomon's copper mines, silent for eternities, were made to smelt the green ore again. Traces of oil were found. A mountain of iron was discovered. The northern entrance to the Negev, Beersheba, became a boom town with a skyline springing up on the desert overnight.

The greatest hope of the Negev was Elath, at the southern tip on the Gulf of Akaba. When Israeli troops arrived at the end of the War of Liberation it consisted of two mud huts. Israel had the dream of making a port here with a direct route to the Orient, someday when the Egyptions lifted the blockade of the Gulf of Akaba. They built in preparation for that day.

It was here in the Negev Desert that Colonel Ari Ben Canaan volunteered for duty after the War of Liberation. He was assigned the task of learning every inch of this vital place hemmed in by three sworn enemies, Egypt, Jordan, and Saudi Arabia.

Ari took troops over the killing slate fields and through the wadis in places where no human was meant to travel. He devised training so brutally hard that few armies of the world could duplicate it. All officer candidates were sent to Ari to receive some of the most severe physical testing human beings could stand.

Ari's permanent troops became known as 'the Beasts of the Negev.' They were a raw, spirited breed of desert rats who hated the Negev while they were in her and longed for her when they were away. Twenty parachute drops, hundred-kilometer forced marches, road-gang labor, hand-to-hand combat were all part of the experiences that made the Beasts of the Negev men among men. Only the toughest could qualify. The army of Israel gave no medals for bravery – one soldier was considered as brave as the next – but those who wore the shield of the Beasts of the Negev were held in special awe.

Ari's base was Elath. He watched it grow into a town of a thousand hardy pioneers. Water was piped in and the copper mines went into full operation. Paths grew to roads as the Jews worked to strengthen their southern foothold.

There were whispers about the strangeness of Colonel Ben Canaan. He never seemed to laugh, rarely to change his hard expression. There seemed to be a sorrow and longing gnawing at him, forcing him to push himself and his troops too, almost beyond human endurance. He refused to come out of the desert for two long years.

Kitty Fremont had become known as 'the Friend,' a title hitherto conferred only upon P. P. Malcolm, the founder of the Night Raiders. After the War of Liberation, Kitty involved herself in immigration work and soon was the chief trouble shooter for the Zion Settlement Society.

In January of 1949 at the beginning of Magic Carpet, Kitty had been asked to leave Gan Dafna and go to Aden to organize the medical facilities in the children's compound of the Hashed camp. Kitty proved a wizard at the chore. She brought order out of chaos. She was firm in her orders, yet tender in her treatment of the youngsters who had walked from Yemen. In a matter of months she had become a key official in the Zion Settlement Society.

From Aden she went directly to Magic Carpet at Bagdad, an airlift operation twice the size of the Yemenite airlift. Then with things under control in Iraq she rushed to Morocco, where tens of thousands of Jews poured out of the *mellahs* of Casablanca to go 'up' to Israel.

She went from place to place as the *aliyahs* of the exodus formed. She made hasty flights to the European DP camps to break bottlenecks and she scoured Europe to find personnel and supplies. When the high point of the flood receded, Kitty was recalled to Jerusalem, where the Zion Settlement Society assigned her as an official in Youth Aliyah.

She had helped bring the youngsters in. Now she went at the job of getting them integrated into the complex society of Israel. Villages like Gan Dafna were the answers, but they were too few for the numbers arriving. The older ones received an education from the army of Israel, which became the greatest single integration instrument in the country, among other things teaching every new soldier to read and write Hebrew.

Kitty Fremont by now spoke a fluent Hebrew. She was at home flying in with Foster MacWilliams and a load of tubercular children, or visiting a border *kibbutz*. '*Shalom, Giveret* Kitty,' was a password in a hundred places which held her children.

And then something happened that Kitty found both heartwarming and heartbreaking at once. Kitty began to see the infants of the older youths she had known at Gan Dafna who had married and gone to the settlements. Some of them had been her babies in the camp in Cyprus and on the *Exodus*, and now they had children of their own. Kitty had watched the machinery of Youth Aliyah grow until it could handle any emergency. She had helped set up the administration and train the people, from the first harrowing trials of inexperience to the point where they constituted a smooth-functioning organization. Now Kitty Fremont suddenly realized, with heavy heart, that her work was done. Neither Karen nor Israel would need her, and she decided she should leave forever.

Chapter Three

Barak Ben Canaan reached his eighty-fifth year.

He retired from public life and was content to worry about running his farm at Yad El. It was what he had longed for for half a century. Even at his great age Barak remained a powerful man, mentally alert and physically able to put in a full day's work in his fields. His enormous beard was almost fully white, but there were still traces of the old red flame in it and his hand still had a grip of steel. The years after the War of Liberation gave him great contentment. He had time, finally, to devote to himself and Sarah.

His happiness, however, was qualified by the unhappiness of Jordana and Ari. Jordana did not get over the death of David Ben Ami. She was wild and restless. She had traveled in France for a while and she plunged into a few unsatisfying affairs that ended in bitterness. At last she returned to Jerusalem, David's city, and went back to the university, but there was an eternal emptiness about her.

Ari had banished himself to the Negev. Barak knew the reason for Ari's exile, but he was unable to reach his son.

It was just after his eighty-fifth birthday that Barak developed stomach pains. For many weeks he said nothing about them. As he thought of it, he was entitled to a few aches and pains. A nagging cough followed the pains, impossible to conceal from Sarah. She insisted he see a doctor but Barak made light of it. Whenever he did promise, he generally found reason to put off a visit to the doctor.

Barak received a call from Ben Gurion asking if he and Sarah would come to Haifa for the celebration of the third Independence Day and sit in the reviewing stand. It was a singular honor for the old man and he said he would come. Sarah used the occasion of the trip as a lever to make Barak promise to get a full examination. They left for Haifa five days before the celebration. Barak went into the hospital to undergo a complete physical check-up. He stayed in the hopital until the day of Independence eve.

'What did the doctors say?' Sarah asked.

Barak laughed. 'Indigestion and old age. They gave me some pills.'

Sarah tried to press the issue.

'Come on, old girl. We are here to celebrate Independence Day.'

Crowds had been pouring into Haifa all day. They hitchhiked, drove, and came by plane and train. The city was bulging with humanity. All day long people stopped by Barak's hotel room to pay their respects to him.

In the evening a torchlight parade of youth groups started the celebrations.

They passed in review before the green at the City Hall on Har Ha-Carmel and after the usual speeches there was a fireworks display from Mount Carmel.

The entire length of Herzl Street was packed with tens of thousands of people. Loud-speakers played music and every few yards *hora* rings formed. Herzl Street was a riot of whirling feet and music and color. Barak and Sarah joined the *hora* rings and danced to riotous applause.

Barak and Sarah were invited as guests of honor to the Technical Institute where the 'Brotherhood of Fire,' the Palmach fighters during the riots, had gathered. They lit a huge bonfire and Yemenites danced and Druse Arabs danced and a lamb was roasted and Arab coffee was brewed and a chorus sang oriental and Biblical songs. All over the campus of the Technical Institute boys and girls from the settlements slept in each other's arms. The 'Brotherhood of Fire' danced and sang until daybreak.

Sarah and Barak returned to their hotel to freshen up, and even at daybreak the dancing was still going on in all the streets. Later in the day they drove in an open car along the parade route, to thunderous cheers, and went to the reviewing stand alongside the President.

Carrying banners like the ancient tribes, New Israel marched past Barak – the Yemenites, now proud and fierce soldiers and the tall strong *sabra* boys and girls and the flyers from South Africa and America and the fighters who had come from every corner of the world. The elite paratroops in their red berets and the border guards in green marched by. Tanks rumbled and planes roared overhead. And then Barak's heart skipped a beat as the ovation rose in a new crescendo and the bearded, leathery Beasts of the Negev saluted the father of their commander.

After the parade there were more speeches and parties and celebrations. When Barak and Sarah left for Yad El two days later, dancers were still whirling in the streets.

No sooner had they reached their cottage at Yad El than Barak broke into a long, wracking spasm of coughing, as though he had been holding it in by main strength during the celebrations. He sagged into his big chair, exhausted, as Sarah brought him some medicine.

'I told you it would be too much excitement,' she admonished. 'You should start acting your age already.'

Barak's mind was on the tanned, rough youngsters marching in the parade. 'The army of Israel ...' he mumbled.

'I'll made some tea,' she said, fondly mussing his hair.

Barak took her wrist and pulled her down on his lap. She rested her head on his shoulder and then looked at him questioningly, and he turned his eyes away.

'Now that the celebrations are through,' Sarah said, 'tell me what the doctors really told you.'

'I never have been able to lie to you very well,' he said.

'I won't make a fuss, I promise.'

'Please understand that I am ready,' Barak said. 'I think I have known it all along.'

Sarah uttered a short cry and bit her lip.

Barak nodded slowly. 'You had better send for Ari and Jordana.'

'Cancer?'

'Yes.'

'How long?'

'A few months ... a few wonderful months.'

It was hard to think of Barak as anything but a giant. Now, in the succeeding weeks, his age showed frightfully. The flesh had melted from his powerful frame and he was bent with age and his complexion had turned sallow. He was in great pain but he hid the fact and adamantly refused to be moved to a hospital.

His bed was arranged by a window so that he could spend his days looking out upon his fields and up the hills to the border of Lebanon. When Ari arrived he found Barak here, gazing with sadness toward the place where Abu Yesha no longer existed.

'*Shalom, abba,*' Ari said embracing Barak. 'I came as quickly as I could.'

'*Shalom*, Ari. Let me look at you, son. It has been so long ... over two years. I thought you might be at the celebrations with your troops.'

'The Egyptians have been acting up at Nitzana. We had to make a reprisal.'

Barak studied his son. Ari was bronzed from the Negev sun and looked as powerful as a lion.

'The Negev agrees with you,' he said.

'What is all this nonsense *ema* tells me?'

'Don't feel obligated to cheer me up, Ari. I am ancient enough to die gracefully.'

Ari poured some brandy and lit a cigarette while Barak continued to study him. Tears welled in the old man's eyes.

'I have been happy these days, except for you and Jordana. If I could only go and know I am leaving you content.'

Ari sipped his brandy and turned his eyes away. Barak took his son's hand.

'They tell me you could be chief of staff of the army of Israel someday, if you would choose to come out of the desert.'

'There is work to be done in the Negev, Father. Someone has to do it. The Egyptians are forming *fedayeen* gangs of murderers to cross the border and raid our settlements.'

'But you are not happy, Ari.'

'Happy? You know me, Father. I'm not given to making demonstrations of happiness like new immigrants.'

'Why have you shut yourself off from me and your mother for two years?'

'I am sorry about that.'

'You know, Ari, for the first time in my life, these past two years, I have had the luxury of being able just to sit and think. It is wonderful for a man to be able to meditate in peace. And in these last few weeks I have had even more time. I have thought of everything. I know that I have not been a good father. I have failed you and Jordana.'

'Come, Father ... I won't listen to such nonsense. Don't get sentimental on me.'

'No, there's truth in what I say. It seems now I see so clearly. You, and Jordana, and I ... the little time I have been able to give you ... and Sarah. Ari, for a family this is wrong.'

'Father ... please. No son has had the love and the understanding that I have. Perhaps all fathers believe they could have done more.'

Barak shook his head. 'When you were a small boy, you were a man. You stood beside me and worked these swamps when you were twelve. You have not needed me since I put a bull whip in your hands.'

'I don't want to hear any more of this. We live in this country for what we can do for tomorrow. It is the way you had to live and the way I live now. I won't let you torment yourself. We had to live this way because we have never had a choice.'

'That is what I try to tell myself, Ari. I say what else? A ghetto? A concentration camp? Extermination ovens? I say anything is worth this. Yet, this freedom of ours ... the price is so high. We cherish it so fiercely that we have created a race of Jewish Tarzans to defend it. We have been able to give you nothing but a life of bloodshed and heritage of living with your back to the sea.'

'No price is too great for Israel,' Ari said.

'It is – when I see sadness in my son's eyes.'

'You didn't take David Ben Ami from Jordana. It is the price of being born a Jew. Is it not better to die for your country than to die the way your father died, at the hands of a mob in a ghetto?'

'But the sadness of my son is my fault, Ari.' Barak licked his lips and swallowed. 'Jordana has become a great friend of Kitty Fremont.'

Ari started at the mention of her name.

'She has become a saint. She visits us when she is in the Huleh. It is too bad you haven't seen her.'

'Father ... I ...'

'Don't you think I see the hunger in that woman's eyes for you? Is this the way a man gives love, by hiding in the desert? Yes, Ari! Let's have it all out now. You've run and hidden from her. Say it. Say it to me and say it to yourself.'

Ari got off the edge of the bed and walked away.

'What is this terrible thing in your heart that keeps you from going to this woman and telling her your heart breaks for her?'

Ari felt his father's burning gaze at his back. He turned slowly with his eyes lowered. 'She told me once I would have to need her so badly that I would have to crawl.'

'Then crawl!'

'I cannot crawl! I don't know how! Can't you see, Father ... I can never be the man she wants.'

Barak sighed sadly. 'And that is where I have failed you, Ari. You see, I would have crawled to your mother a million times. I would crawl to her because I need her in order to live. She is my strength. God help me, Ari, I have been a party to the creation of a breed of men and women so hard they refuse to know the meaning of tears and humility.'

'She once said that to me,' Ari whispered.

'You have mistaken tenderness for weakness. You have mistaken tears for dishonor. You have made yourself believe that to depend on another person is to retreat. You are so blind that you cannot give love.'

'So, I cannot do what I cannot do,' Ari cried.

'And I am sorry for you, Ari. I am sorry for you and I am sorry for myself.'

The next day Ari carried his father in his arms to his car and drove him to Tel Hai, to the very spot at which he and his brother Akiva had crossed to Palestine more than half a century before.

The graves of the Guardsmen were there at Tel Hai, the first Jews to bear arms at the turn of the century in a roving defense of Jewish settlements against

Bedouins. It was as a Guardsman, Barak was remembering, that he had met Sarah at Rosh Pinna.

The stones of the dead formed two lines, and there were a dozen plots waiting for those Guardsmen still alive. Akiva's remains had been removed from Elijah's Point to this place of honor. The plot next to Akiva was reserved for Barak.

Ari carried his father beyond the graves to where the huge stone statue of a lion stood looking down upon the valley, the symbol of a king protecting the land. On the base of the statue they read the words: 'IT IS GOOD TO DIE FOR ONE'S COUNTRY.'

Barak looked down at the valley. Settlements were everywhere. A town was springing up below them with thousands of new settlers. The father and the son lingered to Tel Hai until darkness fell and they watched the lights go on, ringing the valley with a fortress of determination. Yad El – the Hand of God – stood in their center. A settlement of tough new youngsters had just broken ground at Gonen far below; they lived in tents just a few yards from the Syrian border. The lights of Gonen went on too.

'It is good to have a country to die for,' Barak said.

Ari carried his father down from the hill.

Two days later Barak Ben Canaan died in his sleep and he was taken back to Tel Hai and buried next to Akiva.

Chapter Four

In the last stages of the War of Liberation, Dov Landau joined the army of Israel and took part in Operation Ten Plagues against the Egyptians. His bravery in the storming of Suweidan won him a field commission. For several months he stayed in the desert as one of Colonel Ben Canaan's Beasts of the Negev. Ari recognized the boy's obvious talents and sent him north for tests. The army then asked Dov to go to the Technical Institute at Haifa and study specialized courses for the ambitious water projects being planned for the redemption of the Negev. Dov proved to be a brilliant scholar.

He had completely burst out of his former darkness. Now he was warm and filled with humor and showed uncommon understanding for those people who suffered. Still rather slight in stature, with sensitive features, Dov had become a handsome young man. He and Karen were deeply in love.

The young romance was plagued with constant separations, uncertainty and of course the eternal tension. The land was in a turmoil and so were they; each had his separate serious duties. It was an old story in Israel, it was the story of Ari and Dafna and the story of David and Jordana. Each time they saw each other the desire and the frustration grew. Dov, who worshiped Karen, became the stronger of the two.

When he reached his twenty-first birthday he was a captain in the corps of engineers and was considered one of the most promising officers in his field. His time was spent studying at the Technical Institute and at the Weizmann Research Institute at Rehovot.

Karen left Gan Dafna after the War of Liberation and also went into the Army. There she continued nurses' training. She had gained valuable experience in working with Kitty and was able to finish her basic training quickly. Nursing suited Karen. She wanted someday to follow in Kitty's footsteps and specialize in caring for children. She was stationed in a hospital in the Sharon. It was convenient, for she was able to hitch a ride to Jerusalem to Kitty when Kitty was there and to get to Haifa frequently to see Dov.

Karen Hansen Clement grew from a beautiful girl into a magnificent woman. She was striking perfection, with the tenderness and kindness which had characterized her youth following her into maturity.

In the depths of Kitty's mind the thought sometimes rose that Karen might come with her to America, but it was pure wishful thinking. In more realistic moments she knew that Karen did not need her. She had done her job for the girl just as she had done it for Israel. Karen was a part of Israel now, too deeply rooted to be torn away. And Kitty knew that she did not need Karen now. Once she believed she would never be able to part from the girl. But that void, the emotional starvation in Kitty, had been filled by years of unselfish devotion to 'her children.'

Kitty not only knew she could leave Karen, but she dared hope that normalcy and true happiness awaited her somewhere, sometime, again.

No, for Karen and herself, Kitty had no fears about leaving Israel. But there was one fear – a fear for Israel itself.

The Arabs sat at Israel's borders, licking their wounds and waiting for the day they would pounce on the little nation and destroy her in their much-advertised 'second round.'

The Arab leaders handed their masses guns instead of plow-shares. Those few who saw the light of Israel and wanted to make peace were murdered. The hold harangues poured from the Arab press, from its radio, its leaders, and from the Moslem pulpits.

The Arab people, already bled dry by willful men, were bled even dryer to pay for hundreds of millions of dollars in arms.

The refugee situation was distorted so as to be made insolvable.

Nasser, the one-time army captain who sat in the pocket at Faluja under seige, inflamed the Arab world like a would-be Hitler.

The Suez Canal was blocked by Egypt to Israeli ships and ships of other nations bringing cargo to Israel, in violation of international law.

The Gulf of Akaba was blockaded to keep the Jews from operating a port at Elath.

The Legion of Jordan blatantly ignored the truce agreement whereby Jews were to have free access to Old Jerusalem for worship at the holiest shrine, the Wall of Solomon's Temple.

All Arab nations refused to recognize the existence of Israel; all Arab nations swore to destroy Israel.

Then came the most vicious move. The Arabs, mainly the Egyptians in the Gaza Strip, organized *fedayeen* gangs for the purpose of murdering Israelis. These gangs crossed the border nightly to kill, to burn fields, to cut water-pipe lines, to destroy. Tormented Palestine refugees were used in these gangs, goaded by hate-spewing leaders.

Israel, with all of her other burdens, had to adopt an axiom of reality: 'When Hitler said he was going to exterminate the Jews, the world did not believe him. When the Arabs say it, we in Israel believe them.'

Military training in Israel was compulsory for girls as well as for boys. They learned at early ages to handle arms. All men received training one month out of each year until the age of forty-five. Israel became the most efficiently organized and largest – in proportion to population – standing militia in the world.

The notorious *fedayeen* continued to commit atrocity after atrocity. They reached a new depth by the bombing of children's houses on the border settlements.

At last Israel had no choice but reprisal. The army of Israel swore to kill ten for one. Unfortunately, reprisal seemed to be the only language that the Arabs understood, the only thing that might stop them.

One of the defensive measures used by Israel was the creation of Nahal. Nahal was a militarized intensification of settlements in strategic places. Many youth groups of boys and girls went into the army to take their training as a unit. After basic training they were sent out to the borders to build combined farming and defensive settlements. To build a wall of flesh on the Israeli borders was a partial answer to *fedayeen* terror. The settlements of these youngsters in their late teens were only yards from the frontier; they lived in the jaws of the enemy.

The conditions on the frontier were brutal. The pay rate of the young soldier-farmer was thirty dollars a year. Death lay on one side of them, unfertile land on the other. Yet – still another of the nation's miracles – Israel's youth volunteered to spend their entire lives in border settlements. They went quietly and without heroics. Like Jordana and Ari and David and Joab and Zev ... it was their job. They lived with no thought of material gain for themselves, but only of Israel and tomorrow.

The toughest of these frontiers was the Gaza Strip, the finger of land which was left jutting into Israel as an aborted border at the end of the war. Ancient Gaza, where Samson had lifted the gates, had new gates now, the gates of the Palestine refugee camps. The victimized Arabs were allowed to wallow in listlessness and become wards of world charity while they were pumped full of hatred by Egyptian administrators. Gaza was the principal base and training ground of the Egyptian sponsored *fedayeens*.

It was in this place, less than ten kilometers from the enemy nest, the twenty-two boys and sixteen girls came to build a Nahal settlement.

It was named Nahal Midbar – the Stream in the Desert.

Among the sixteen girls was their nurse, Karen Hansen Clement.

Dov had finished his studies at the Weizmann Institute and was transferred to a water project in the Huleh Valley. He achieved a five-day leave before reporting to his new post so he could hitch a ride to Nahal Midbar to see Karen. They had been separated for six weeks, since she had left with her group.

It took Dov all day to travel to the remote spot in the Negev Desert. A dirt path branched off the main road along the Gaza Strip and ran some four kilometers to the settlement.

Most of Nahal Midbar was still canvas. Only a dining shack, a tool shed, and a pair of guard towers had been built. The water tank and the irrigation pipes were nearly in. Those few buildings stood in the center of a wind-swept, bleak and desolate, sun-baked corner that seemed to be the end of the earth. It was, indeed, on the brink of nowhere. On the horizon could be seen the sinister outline of Gaza. Emplacements of barbed wire and trenches faced the enemy.

The first *dunams* of land were under the plow. Dov stopped at the gate and observed for a moment. Nahal Midbar was depressing. Then, suddenly it turned in his sight into the most magnificent garden on earth, for he saw Karen running toward him from her hospital tent.

'Dov! Dov!' she cried, and raced over the bare brown knoll and flung herself into his waiting arms and they held each other tightly, their hearts pounding in excitement and joy with the feel of each other.

They held hands as Karen took Dov to the water tank; he washed his sweaty face and took a long drink. Then Karen led him away from the settlement to a path which led beyond the knoll where some Nabataean ruins stood. It was the forward outpost, right on the border marker, and the favorite meeting place of the single boys and girls.

Karen gave a signal to the guard that she would take the watch and the guard left knowingly. They picked their way through the ruins until they came to the enclosure of an ancient temple and there they waited until the guard was out of sight. Karen peered out at the field through the barbed wire. Everything was quiet.

They both leaned the rifles they carried against the wall and embraced and kissed.

'Oh, Dov! At last!'

'I've almost died from missing you,' he said.

They kissed again and again ignoring the burning midday desert sun, ignoring everything but each other. Dov led her to a corner and they sat on the earthen floor, Karen lying in his arms, and he kissed her and caressed her and she closed her eyes and purred with happiness.

And then his hands became still and he just gazed lovingly.

'I have some wonderful news,' he said.

She looked up. 'What could be more wonderful than this minute?'

'Sit up,' he commanded teasingly.

'What is it, Dov?'

'You know about me being transferred to the Huleh Project?'

'Yes, of course.'

'Well, I was called in yesterday. They want me to stay up there until the end of the summer only ... then they want me to go to America for advanced studies! The Massachusetts Institute of Technology!'

Karen blinked her eyes.

'America? To study?'

'Yes ... for two years. I could hardly wait to get here and tell you.'

She forced herself to smile – quickly. 'How wonderful, Dov. I am so proud. Then you will be going in about six or seven months.'

'I didn't give them an answer,' he said. 'I wanted to talk it over with you.'

'Two years isn't forever,' Karen said. 'Why, by the time you get back the *kibbutz* will all be built up. We'll have two thousand *dunams* under cultivation and a library and a children's house full of babies.'

'Wait a minute ...' Dov said. 'I'm not going to America or anywhere else without you. We will get married right now. Of course, it will be difficult in

America. They can't give me much of an allowance. I'll have to work after classes but you can study nursing and work too ... we'll make it.'

Karen was very quiet. She looked out and saw the rise of Gaza in the distance and the guard towers and the trenches.

'I can't leave Nahal Midbar,' she whispered. 'We have only started here. The boys are working twenty hours a day.'

'Karen ... you've got to take leave.'

'No, I can't, Dov. If I go it makes it much harder on everyone else.'

'You've got to. I'm not going without you. Don't you understand what this means? I'll come back here in two years and I'll know everything there is to know about water tables and drilling and pipes. It will be perfect. We'll live in Nahal Midbar together and I'll be working around close by in the desert. The *kibbutz* will have my salary. Karen ... I'll be worth fifty times the value I am now to Israel.'

She stood up and turned her back to him. 'It's *right* for you. It's important for you to go to America. I'm more important here, now.'

Dov turned pale and his shoulders sagged. 'I thought I would make you happy ...'

She faced him. 'You know you have to go and you know I have to stay.'

'No, dammit! I can't be away from you for two years! I can't even take it for two days any more.' He stood and seized her in his arms and covered her mouth with kisses and she returned kiss for kiss and both of them cried, 'I love you' over and over and their cheeks were wet with perspiration and tears and their hands felt for each other's bodies and they slipped to the floor.

'Yes! Now!' she cried.

Dov sprang to his feet and stood trembling. He clenched his fists tightly. 'We've got to stop this.'

It was still except for Karen's soft sobbing. Dov knelt behind her. 'Please don't cry, Karen.'

'Oh, Dov, what are we going to do? It is just as though I'm not living when you are away. And now, every time we see each other it ends up the same way. When you leave me I am sick with wanting you for days.'

'It's just as hard on me,' he said. 'It's my fault. We'll be more careful. Nothing is going to happen until we marry.'

He helped her to her feet.

'Don't look at me that way, Karen. I don't want to ever hurt you.'

'I love you, Dov. I'm not ashamed or afraid of wanting you.'

'I'm not going to do what's wrong for you,' he said.

They stood still, eyes shining with love and bodies taut with insistence.

'We had better go back to the *kibbutz*,' Karen said at last, with desolation in her voice.

Kitty had traveled over most of Israel and she had seen the most rugged of the settlements. She knew when she traveled to Nahal Midbar that it was the brink of hell. Yet in spite of preparing for the worst her heart sank at the sight of Nahal Midbar, a bake furnace planted in the path of angry Arab hordes.

Karen showed Kitty around with obvious pride over what had been accomplished in three months. There were a few new wooden shacks, a few more *dunams* of land plowed, but it was a heartbreaking sight. It represented boys and girls working agonizing hours during the day and standing guard during the night.

'In a few years,' Karen said, 'there will be trees and flowers everywhere, if we can only get enough water.'

They walked out of the sun into Karen's hospital tent and each had a drink of water. Kitty looked through the tent flap. Barbed wire and trenches. Out in the fields, boys and girls worked in the sun while others walked behind them with rifles, guarding them. One hand on the sword and one on the plow. That was the way they rebuilt the walls of Jerusalem. Kitty looked at Karen. The girl was so young and so lovely. In a few years in this place she would age before her time.

'So you are really planning to go home. I can hardly believe it,' Karen said.

'I told them I want to take a year's leave. I have been terribly homesick lately. And now, with you gone . . . well, I just want to take things easy for a little while. I may come back to Israel, I am not sure.'

'When will you leave?'

'After Passover.'

'So soon? It will be dreadful with you gone, Kitty.'

'You are a grown woman now, Karen. You have a life of your own.'

'I can't think of it with you away.'

'Oh, we'll write. We will always be close. Who knows, after living in this volcano for four years, I may find the rest of the world too dull for me.'

'You must come back, Kitty.'

Kitty smiled. 'Time will tell. How is Dov these days? I hear he has finished school.'

Karen avoided telling Kitty that Dov had been asked to go to America, for she knew Kitty would take Dov's side.

'They sent him to the Huleh Lake. They are planning a project to dig channels and lower the whole lake into the Sea of Galilee and reclaim it for farmland.'

'Dov has become a very important young man. I hear tremendous things about him. Will he be able to get here for Passover?'

'It doesn't look like it.'

Kitty snapped her fingers. 'Say! I have a splendid idea. Jordana has asked me to come to Yad El for Passover and I promised I would. Dov is working close by. Why don't you come up to Yad El?'

'I really should stay at my *kibbutz* for Passover.'

'You'll be here for many Passovers. It will be a farewell present to me.'

Karen smiled. 'I'll come.'

'Good. Now, how is that young man of yours?'

'Fine . . . I guess,' Karen muttered glumly.

'Did you have an argument?'

'No. He won't argue with me. Oh, Kitty, he is so damned noble sometimes I could scream.'

'I see,' Kitty said raising her eyebrows. 'You are quite the grown-up woman of eighteen.'

'I just don't know what to do. Kitty . . . I . . . I go crazy thinking about him and then every time we see each other he gets noble. They . . . may send him away. It may be two years before we can get married. I think I'm going to break open.'

'You love him very much, don't you?'

'I could die for wanting him. Is it terrible for me to talk this way?'

'No, dear. To love someone that way is the most wonderful thing in the world.'

'Kitty ... I want so much to love him. Is that wrong?'

Was it wrong? Kitty remembered standing over a bed and implying to Ari that Jordana was a tramp for the moments she had stolen with David Ben Ami. Was that wrong? How many times she had regretted her words. David had been dead for three years and Jordana still grieved deeply. Even with that tough shell of *sabra* aggressiveness she would take a broken heart to her grave. Was it wrong? How many tomorrows would Dov and Karen have? That angry host of people beyond the barbed wire – would they let them live?

Karen ... her precious baby ...

'Love him, Karen,' Kitty said. 'Love him with all the love that is in you.'

'Oh ... Kitty!'

'Yes, dear. Love him.'

'He is so afraid.'

'Then help him not to be afraid. You are his woman and that is the way it should be.'

Kitty felt empty inside her. She had given her Karen away forever. She felt Karen's hand on her shoulder.

'Can't *you* help Ari?'

Kitty's heart skipped a beat at the mention of his name. 'It is not love when one person loves and the other doesn't.'

They were both silent for a long time. Kitty went to the tent flap and looked outside. The flies swarmed around her. She spun around quickly and faced Karen. 'I can't go without telling you I am sick about your coming to this place.'

'The borders must be defended. It is easy enough to say let the other fellow do it.'

'Nahal Midbar is three months old. Already you have a boy and a girl in your graveyard, murdered by *fedayeen*.'

'We don't think of it that way, Kitty. Two are lost but fifty more have joined Nahal Midbar and another fifty have come to build a settlement five kilometers away – because we came here. In a year we will have a children's house and a thousand *dunams* of land under cultivation.'

'And in a year you will begin to grow old. You will work eighteen hours a day and spend your nights in the trenches. All that you and Dov will ever have out of this is a single room eight by ten feet. Even the clothes on your back won't belong to you.'

'You are wrong, Kitty. Dov and I will have everything.'

'Including a quarter of a million kill-crazy Arabs at your throats.'

'We cannot be angry at those poor people,' Karen said. 'They sit there day after day, month after month, locked up like animals, watching our fields grow green.'

Kitty sagged down in a cot and buried her face in her hands.

'Kitty ... listen ...'

'I can't.'

'Please ... please listen. You know that even when I was a little girl in Denmark I asked myself why I was born a Jew. I know the answer now. God didn't pick us because we were weak or would run from danger. We've taken murder and sorrow and humiliation for six thousand years and we have kept faith. We have outlived everyone who has tried to destroy us. Can't you see it,

Kitty? ... this little land was chosen for us because it is the crossroads of the world, on the edge of man's wilderness. This is where God wants His people to be ... on the frontiers, to stand and guard His laws which are the cornerstones of man's moral existence. Where else is there for us to be?'

'Israel stands with its back to the wall,' Kitty cried. 'It has always stood that way and it always will ... with savages trying to destroy you.'

'Oh no, Kitty, no! Israel is the bridge between darkness and light.'

And suddenly Kitty saw it all, so clearly ... so beautifully clear. This then was the answer. Israel, the bridge between darkness and light.

Chapter Five

One night above all other nights is the most important for a Jew and that is the religious holiday of Passover. The Passover is celebrated in memory of the deliverance from bondage in Egypt. The Egyptians, the original oppressors, had become the symbol of all the oppressors of all the Jews throughout all the ages.

The high point occurs on the eve of Passover when the Seder – the Feast of Liberation – is held to give thanks for freedom and to offer hope for those who do not have it. For the exiles and the dispersed, before the rebirth of Israel the Seder always ended with the words: '... *next year in Jerusalem.*'

The Haggadah, a special book of prayers, stories, and songs for Passover, parts of which were written three thousand years ago, is read. The story of the Exodus from Egypt is recited by the head of the house.

The Seder was the high moment of the year. The woman of the house had to prepare for it for a month. All dirt had to be chased. Special Passover foods and decorations had to be prepared. All over Israel half-frantic preparations for the Seder took place. In the communal settlements the Seder table would hold hundreds. Other homes had small and simple Seders. As the eve of Passover drew near, the air of anticpation of the great feast grew and grew to a bursting point.

The Seder this year at the Ben Canaan cottage at Yad El was to be a relatively small affair. None the less, Sarah had to carry out the prescribed traditional and rituals to the letter. It was a labor of love and she would not be robbed of it. The cottage, inside and out, was made spotless. On the day of the feast the rooms were filled with enormous Galilee roses. The Menorah – the ritual candlesticks – had been polished to a dazzling gleam. Tens of dozens of special Passover cookies and candies had been made. All the special foods had been prepared and Sarah herself was dressed in her finest.

On the day of Passover Eve, Kitty and Sutherland drove from his villa to Yad El.

'The idea of your leaving Israel is wretched,' Sutherland grumbled. 'Can't make myself get on to it.'

'I've given it a lot of thought, Bruce. It is best. In America we always say, "leave them laughing."'

'Do you really feel that immigration has passed its peak?'

'Well, let's say the first flood is over. There are many small communities of Jews, like the Poles, locked in Europe who want to get out. We suspect the roof may fall in on the Jews in Egypt at any time. But the main thing is that we have personnel and facilities for any emergencies.'

'You mean for little emergencies,' Sutherland said. 'What about the giants?'

'I don't understand.'

'The United States has six million Jews and the Russians have four. What of them?'

Kitty thought deeply. 'Most of those few Jews who have come from the United States are either one of two things; they are either idealists of the old pioneer days or neurotics seeking a false haven. I do not believe that the day will ever come that American Jews must come to Israel because of fear or persecution. If the day does come, I do not want to be alive to see it. As for the Russians, there is a strange and haunting story that not many people know.'

'You have me curious,' Sutherland said.

'Well, you know that they have tried to integrate the Jews by swallowing them up in theories and in evolution. They have tried to make them lose their identity by letting the old ones die out and indoctrinating the young ones from birth. Of course you know that anti-Semitism still rages in Russia.'

'I've heard.'

'It was on the last high holy days that this fantastic thing happened. It proved that the Soviets have failed miserably. The ambassador from Israel went to the only synagogue they permit in Moscow. After thirty years of silence, thirty thousand Jews appeared on the streets just to see and touch the ambassador! Yes, there will be a great *aliyah* from Russia someday.'

'The story struck Sutherland deeply and he was silent. It was the same old story, the concept that arose so often in his mind: ... *the Jew never loses his identity*. And ... there comes that day of truth when he must stand and declare himself. He thought of his own beloved mother ...

They turned from the main road into the Yad El *moshav*. Sarah Ben Canaan rushed from the cottage to meet them. There were hugs and holiday greetings.

'Are we the first here?'

'Dov has arrived. Come in already, come in ... come in.'

Dov met them at the door. He shook Sutherland's hand and embraced Kitty warmly. She held him off at arm's length. '*Major* Dov Landau! You get better-looking every time I see you.'

Dov blushed.

Sutherland was examining Sarah's roses in the living room with a trace of envy.

'Where is everybody?' Kitty asked.

'Jordana went to Haifa last night. She said she would be back early,' Sarah said.

'Karen wrote me that she would leave Nahal Midbar the day before,' Dov said. 'That would be yesterday. She's allowing plenty of time to get here. She may have stayed over at Haifa last night. Anyhow, she may have to hitch a ride beyond Safed.'

'Don't fret,' Sutherland said. 'She'll be here in time for the Seder.'

Kitty was disappointed that Karen had not arrived but made no point of it before the others. Transportation was terrible, especially on a holiday. 'Is there anything I can help you with?' she asked Sarah.

'You can sit down and take life easy. Already there have been a dozen calls for you from the *moshav* office. Your children all over the Huleh know you are coming. They said they would be dropping in during the day before the Seder.' Sarah rushed off to her kitchen.

Kitty turned to Dov. 'I hear some very good reports about you, Dov.'

The boy shrugged.

'Don't be modest. I understand you're planning a Jordan water project.'

'If the Syrians let us, which they won't. Funny, Syria and Jordan stand to benefit from it ten times more than we do. But so long as it puts an extra ounce of water into Israel, they are against it.'

'What is the problem?' Sutherland asked.

'We have to change the course of the Jordan a few kilometers. The Arabs say we are doing it for defensive reasons, even though we welcome their observers. Oh well, we will work it out.'

Dov took a deep breath. He was obviously preoccupied and Sutherland sensed that Dov wanted to talk privately to Kitty, so he drifted to the far end of the room and absorbed himself in the shelves of books.

'Kitty,' Dov said. 'I wanted to talk to you about Karen before she gets here.'

'Yes, Dov, of course.'

'She is very stubborn.'

'I know. I was at Nahal Midbar a few weeks ago. We had a long talk.'

'Did she tell you that I have a chance to study in America?'

'She didn't tell me but I knew, anyhow. You see, I've been in Israel so long I've developed my own spy system.'

'I don't know what to do. She is loyal to her *kibbutz*. I am afraid she will refuse to leave. I ... I just can't leave her for two years.'

'I'll work on her,' Kitty smiled. 'She is weakening by the moment. You'll see, Dov. Everything is going to work out fine.'

The front door was flung open and Jordana, her red hair flowing, held open her arms.

'*Shalom*, everybody,' she called.

Kitty embraced her.

'*Ema!*' Jordana called. 'Come here. I have a surprise for you!'

Sarah rushed in from the kitchen just as Ari walked through the door.

'Ari!'

She reached for her handkerchief and simultaneously burst into happy tears and embraced him. 'Ari! Oh, Jordana, you are a devil with red hair! Why didn't you tell me Ari was coming!'

'Well, I figured that you might have made enough for an extra mouth at the table,' he said, hugging his mother.

'You devils!' Sarah said, shaking her finger at them, and dabbing at her eyes. 'Let me look at you, son. Ari, you look tired. You are working too hard.'

They embraced again and laughed.

Then Ari saw Kitty Fremont.

The room turned awkwardly quiet as both of them stared long and hard. Jordana, who had carefully arranged the meeting, looked from one to the other.

Kitty stood up slowly and nodded her head. '*Shalom*, Ari,' she said softly.

'*Shalom*,' he whispered.

'Make yourselves at home,' Jordana said, grabbing her mother's arm quickly and leading her back to the kitchen.

Dov shook Ari's hand. '*Shalom*, Brigadier Ben Canaan,' he said. Kitty watched Dov. The young man's eyes brimmed with admiration, seeing Ari as the almost legendary leader of 'the Beasts.'

'*Shalom*, Dov. You are looking fine. I hear you are going to bring water down to us in the desert.'

'We will try very hard, Brigadier.'

Sutherland and Ari shook hands.

'I received your letter, Sutherland, and I will be delighted to have you visit us at Elath any time.'

'I am terribly keen to see the Negev first hand. Perhaps we can arrange a time.'

'Fine. And how does your garden grow?'

'Well, I must say, your mother's roses are the first I've found to envy. I say, old boy, I'm not letting you get back to Elath without spending an afternoon at my villa.'

'I shall try.'

Again an awkward silence fell as Bruce Sutherland looked from Ari to Kitty. She had not taken her eyes from Ari. Sutherland walked over to Dov quickly and led him from the room. 'Now, Major Landau, you've got to tell me just how you chaps plan to drop the Huleh Lake into the Sea of Galilee. That's a bit of doing ...'

Ari and Kitty were alone.

'You look well,' Kitty said at last.

'And you.'

And there was silence between them once more.

'I ... uh ... how is little Karen? Is she coming?'

'Yes, she will be here. We are expecting her at any time.'

'Would you ... would you like to take a walk? It is quite fresh outside.'

'Yes, why don't we?' Kitty said.

They walked wordlessly past the fence and along the edge of the fields and past the olive orchard, until they came to the Jordan River. The rebirth of springtime was in the smell and the sight of everything. Ari lit two cigarettes and handed Kitty one.

She was even more beautiful than the memory he held of her.

Kitty became aware of Ari's fixed gaze.

'I ... am really quite ashamed of myself. I have never been to Elath. The commander at Beersheba has offered to fly me down a half dozen times. I should see it, I suppose.'

'The water and the mountains are quite beautiful.'

'Is the town growing?'

'It would be the fastest-growing town in the world if we could break the blockade and open her as a port to the Orient.'

'Ari,' Kitty said seriously, 'what is the situation down there?'

'What it has always been ... as it will always be.'

'The *fedayeen* gangs are getting worse, aren't they?'

'Those poor devils aren't our real worry. They're massing to overrun the entire Middle East from Sinai. We're going to have to hit them first if we expect to survive.' Ari smiled. 'My boys tell me we should cross the border and find Mount Sinai and give the Ten Commandments back to God ... it's all caused us enough trouble.'

Kitty stared at the bubbling stream for a long time. She sighed unevenly. 'I am sick with worry over Karen. She is on the Gaza Strip ... Nahal Midbar.'

'Nasty place,' Ari muttered. 'But they are tough youngsters. They'll make out.'

Yes, that is the way that Ari would answer, Kitty thought.

'I hear you are returning to America.'

Kitty nodded.

'You've become a woman of renown.'

'More of a curiosity,' Kitty said.

'You're modest.'

'I'm sure Israel will survive without me.'

'Why are you leaving?'

'You saw Dov ... Major Dov Landau now. He's a fine young man. Karen is being left in good hands. I don't know ... maybe I just don't want to wear out my welcome. Maybe I still don't fully belong here. Maybe I'm homesick. There are lots of reasons and no reasons. Anyhow, I just want a year to take off and spend the time thinking – just thinking.'

'Perhaps you are doing a wise thing. It is good for a person to think without the pressures imposed by daily living. It was a luxury my father was denied until his last two years.'

Suddenly they seemed to run out of words to say.

'We had better start back for the house,' Kitty said. 'I want to be there when Karen arrives. Besides, I am expecting visits from some of my children.'

'Kitty ... a moment, please.'

'Yes?'

'Let me say that I am grateful for the friendship you have given Jordana. You have been good for her. I have been worried about this restlessness of hers.'

'She is a very unhappy girl. No one can ever really know how much she loved that boy.'

'When will it end?'

'I don't know, Ari. But I have lived here so long that I have become a cockeyed optimist. There will be happiness again for Jordana, someday.'

The unspoken question – the unasked words – hung between them. Would there be happiness for her ... and for him, someday, too?

'We had better go back,' Kitty said.

All through the morning and afternoon Kitty's children came from Gan Dafna and from a dozen Huleh settlements to see her. The people of Yad El came to see Ari. There was a constant flow of traffic through the Ben Canaan house. They all remembered the first time they had seen Kitty, aloof and awkward. Now she spoke to them in their language and they all looked up to her in admiration.

Many of her children had traveled a long distance to spend a few minutes with her. Some showed off new husbands or wives. Almost all of them were in the uniform of the army of Israel.

As the afternoon passed, Kitty became concerned at the failure of Karen to appear. Several times Dov went out to the main road to look for a sign of her.

By late afternoon all the visitors had left to get ready for their own Seders.

'Where the devil is that girl?' Kitty snapped, expressing her worry in annoyance.

'She's probably just a little way off,' Dov said.

'The least she could have done was to phone and let us know she was delayed. It isn't like Karen to be thoughtless,' Kitty said.

'Come now, Kitty,' Sutherland said, 'you know it would take an act of Parliament to put a phone call through today.'

Ari saw Kitty's discomfort. 'Look ... I'll run down to the *moshav* office and put in a priority call to her *kibbutz*. Perhaps they know where she planned to stay en route and we can track her down.'

'I would appreciate that very much,' Kitty said.

Not long after Ari had left Sarah came in and announced that the Seder table was ready for everyone's inspection. This was her moment of triumph after a month of labor. She opened the door to the dining room and the guests self-consciously tiptoed in with a chorus of 'ohs' and 'ahs.' It was a table indeed fit for a Feast of Liberation.

All the silver and dishes glistened. They were used only once a year, on this holiday. The silver candlesticks shone in the center of the table. Next to the candlesticks sat a huge ornate sterling-silver goblet which was called 'Elijah's cup.' It was set there and filled with wine to welcome the prophet. When he came to drink from the cup he came as the forerunner of the Messiah.

Special wine and silver goblets were at each place, to be filled four times during the Seder for the four promises of God: to bring forth, deliver, redeem, and take the Children of Israel. The wine symbolizing joy would also be sipped during the recounting of the Ten Plagues against Pharaoh, and when the Song of Miriam, of the closing of the Red Sea on Pharaoh's army, was sung.

At the head seat there was a pillow, so that the teller of the story of the Exodus might relax. In ancient times only free men relaxed, while slaves were made to sit rigid.

And in the center near the candlesticks sat the gold Seder dish holding the symbolic foods. There was matzos, the unleavened bread to remind them that the Children of Israel had to leave Egypt so quickly their bread was unleavened. There was an egg to symbolize the freewill offering, and water cress for the coming of spring, and the shank of lamb bone to recall the offerings to God in the Great Temple. There was a mixture of nuts and diced apples and *maror*, bitter herbs. The first symbolized the mortar the Egyptians forced them to mix for brick building, and the herbs recalled the bitterness of bondage.

Sarah shooed them all out and they returned to the living room. As they entered, it was Jordana who saw Ari first. He leaned in the doorframe, pale and with a dazed expression in his eyes. Now they all stared at him. He tried to speak but couldn't, and as a moment passed they all knew at once.

'Karen! Where is she!' Kitty demanded.

Ari's jaw trembled and he lowered his head.

'Where is she!'

'Karen is dead. She was murdered last night by a gang of *fedayeen* from Gaza.'

Kitty let out an anguished shriek and slumped to the floor.

Kitty blinked her eyes open. Bruce and Jordana knelt near her. The remembrance hit her and her eyes bulged and she turned and sobbed, 'My baby ... my baby ...'

She sat up slowly. Jordana and Sutherland were in a stupor of shock. They looked haggard and numb with grief.

'Karen is dead ... Karen is dead ...'

'If I could only have died for her,' Jordana cried.

Kitty struggled to her feet.

'Lie down, dear ... please, lie down,' Sutherland said.

'No,' Kitty said, 'no ...' She fought clear of Sutherland. 'I must see Dov. I must go to him.'

She staggered out and found Dov sitting in the corner of another room, hollow-eyed and his face contorted with pain. She rushed to him and took him in her arms.

'Dov ... my poor Dov,' Kitty cried.

Dov buried his head in her bosom and sobbed heart-brokenly. Kitty rocked him and they cried together, until darkness fell upon the Ben Canaan cottage and no one had any tears left.

'I'll stay with you, Dov ... I'll take care of you,' Kitty said. 'We will get through this, Dov.'

The young man stood up shakily. 'I will be all right, Kitty,' he said. 'I'm going on. I'll make her proud of me.'

'I beg you, Dov. Don't go back the way you were because of this.'

'No,' he said. 'I thought about it. I cannot hate them, because Karen could not hate them. She could not hate a living thing. We ... she said we can never win by hating them ...'

Sarah Ben Canaan stood at the door. 'I know we are all broken,' she said pitifully, 'but we should go on with the Seder.'

Kitty looked to Dov and the boy nodded.

They walked in tragic procession toward the dining room. Jordana stopped Kitty outside the door.

'Ari sits alone in the barn,' Jordana said. 'Will you go to him?'

Kitty walked from the Cottage. She saw the lights of the other houses of the *moshav.* The Seder had begun in them. At this very moment, fathers were telling their families the age-old story of the Exodus as it had always been told by fathers and would be told for eternities to come. It began to drizzle and Kitty walked faster, toward the flickering lantern light from the barn. She entered and looked around. Ari sat with his back to her on a bale of hay. She walked up behind him and touched his shoulder.

'Ari, the Seder is about to begin.'

He turned and looked up at her and she stepped back as though from a physical blow. She was shocked by Ari's face, distraught with a suffering that she had never seen in a human being. Ari Ben Canaan's eyes were filled with anguish. He looked at her but he did not seem to see her. He turned and hid his face in his hands and his shoulders sagged with defeat.

'Ari ... we must have the Seder ...'

'All my life ... all my life ... I have watched them kill everyone I love ... they are all gone now ... all of them.'

The words came from profound depths of an unbearable despair. She was awed and half frightened by the almost tangible emotion that tortured the now-strange figure before her.

'I have died with them. I have died a thousand times. I am empty inside ... I have nothing left.'

'Ari ... Ari ...'

'Why must we send children to live in these places? This precious girl ... this angel ... why ... *why* did they have to kill her too ...?'

Ari staggered to his feet. All the strength and power and control that made him Ari Ben Canaan was gone. This was a tired and beaten hulk. 'Why must we fight for the right to live, over and over, each time the sun rises?'

The years of tension, the years of struggle, the years of heartbreak welled up in one mighty surge. Ari lifted his pain-filled face to heaven and raised his fists over his head. 'God! God! Why don't they let us alone! *Why don't they let us live!*'

And his powerful shoulders drooped and his head hung to his chest and he stood and trembled.

'Oh, Ari … Ari!' Kitty cried. 'What have I done to you! Why didn't I understand? Ari, my darling … what you must have suffered. Can I ever be forgiven for hurting you?'

Ari was exhausted, drained. He walked along the edge of a stall. 'I am not myself,' he mumbled. 'Please do not let the others know about this.'

'We had better go in. They are waiting for us,' Kitty said.

'Kitty!'

He walked toward her very slowly until he stood before her looking down into her eyes. Slowly he sank to his knees and put his arms around her waist and laid his head against her.

Ari Ben Canaan wept.

It was a strange and terrible sound to hear. In this moment his soul poured out in his tears and he wept for all the times in his life he had dared not weep. He wept with a grief that was bottomless.

Kitty pressed his head tightly against her body and stroked his hair and whispered words of comfort.

'Don't leave me,' Ari cried.

Ah, how she had wanted to hear those words! Yes, she thought, I will stay, this night and for a few tomorrows, for you need me now, Ari. But even as you show tears and humility for the first time in your life, you are ashamed of them. You need me now but tomorrow … tomorrow you will be Ari Ben Canaan again. You will be all the strong, defiant Ari Ben Canaans who inure themselves to tragedy. And then … you will no longer need me.

She helped him to his feet and dried his tears. He was weak. Kitty put his arm over her shoulder and held him tightly. 'It is all right, Ari. You can lean on me.'

They walked from the barn slowly. Through the window they could see Sarah lighting the candles and reciting a benediction.

He stopped and released her and straightened himself up, standing tall and strong again.

Already, so soon, he was Ari Ben Canaan again.

'Before we go in, Kitty, I must tell you something. I must tell you I never loved Dafna as I love you. You know what kind of a life you must share with me.'

'I know, Ari.'

'I am not like other men … it may be years … it may be forever before I can ever again say that my need for you comes first, before all other things … before the needs of this country. Will you be able to understand that?'

'I will understand, always.'

Everyone entered the dining room. The men put on skull caps.

Dov and Jordana and Ari and Kitty and Sutherland and Sarah. Their hearts were bursting with sorrow. As Ari walked toward the head of the table to take Barak's place, Sutherland touched his arm.

'If you would not be offended,' Sutherland said, 'I am the oldest male Jew present. May I tell the Seder?'

'We would be honored,' Ari said.

Sutherland walked to the head of the table, to the place of the head of the family. Everyone sat down and opened his copy of the Haggadah. Sutherland nodded to Dov Landau to begin.

Dov cleared his throat and read. '*Why is this night different from all other nights of the year?*

'*This night is different because we celebrate the most important moment in the history of our people. On this night we celebrate their going forth in triumph from slavery into freedom.*'

MILA 18

MILA 18

This book is dedicated to
ANTEK-ITZHAK ZUCKERMAN
ZIVIAH LUBETKIN
and the others who participated in an immortal moment in behalf of human dignity and freedom, and to one in particular
DR ISRAEL I. BLUMENFELD

Acknowledgments

Past experience forewarned me that I would be dependent upon the assistance of tens of dozens of individuals and organizations to research this book. Again, I was fortunate to be the recipient of selfless hours by those who transmitted to me their knowledge of this subject.

Without the devotion of the Ghetto Fighters House International Museum and Shrine, the individual members of the Ghetto Fighters Kibbutz in Israel and their comrades in the International Survivors Association, these pages could scarcely have been written.

Sheer weight of numbers precludes my thanking the others, but I would be remiss if I did not acknowledge the contribution of the Yad Vashem Memorial Archives in Jerusalem and the University of Southern California Library.

Within a framework of basic truth, tempered with a reasonable amount of artistic license, the places and events described actually happened.

The characters are fictitious, but I would be the last to deny there were people who lived who were similar to those in this volume.

LEON URIS

BOOK ONE

Twilight

Chapter One

Journal Entry–August 1939

This is the first entry in my journal. I cannot help but feel that the war will begin in a few weeks. If the lessons of the past three years are any barometer, something awesome is apt to happen if Germany makes a successful invasion, what with three and a half million Jews in Poland. Perhaps the tensions of the moment are making me overdramatic. My journal may prove completely worthless and a waste of time. Yet, as a historian, I must satisfy the impulse to record what is happening around me.

ALEXANDER BRANDEL

Drops of late summer rain splattered against the high window which ran from the floor to the ceiling.

The big room was violently Polish, in memory of one of the landed gentry who had kept it as a nest for his mistress of the moment during his visits to Warsaw from his estate. All evidence of female occupants had vanished. It was solid and leathery and masculine. Its former grandeur was somewhat qualified by a practical consideration that the present occupant was a working journalist with the particular slovenliness that goes with bachelorhood.

Christopher de Monti was untidy but rather inoffensive about it. It was almost a pleasure for his housekeeper to clean up after him, for he had immaculate taste in records and books and tobacco and liquor and a wardrobe marked with the finest British labels.

In one corner, next to the window, stood a banged-up typewriter and a ream of paper and an overfull ash tray.

The single bedroom was formed by a deep alcove off the living room which could be isolated by drawing a pair of velvet drapes. A night stand beside the huge bed sported an ancient German table-model radio shaped like a church window. From the radio escaped the sad and foreboding notes of Chopin's Nocturne in A Flat.

That was about all one heard on Radio Polskie these days; Chopin performed by Paderewski . . . nocturnes.

It seemed as though night was again to fall on Poland.

Chris grumbled in a state of half sleep and half wakefulness and stretched his lean, wiry limbs to their full reaches and felt across the bed for Deborah. She was gone. His eyes opened and searched the dark corners of the alcove. Then he quieted as he heard her moving about in the other room.

His hand groped automatically on the night stand and found the pack of cigarettes, and in a moment he watched the smoke laze upward as the nocturne raced to a pulsating crescendo.

Chris rolled over on his side and looked at Deborah through an opening in the drapes. Her half-naked body was bathed in late afternoon shadows. Chris loved to watch her dress. She balanced a foot on the end of a chair and stretched her leg and rolled up her stockings and slipped into her blouse and skirt with effortless grace. Then she stood before the mirror, her fingers darting pins into long raven hair and twisting it nervously into a firm knot. He remembered that first time when he had taken the pins from her hair one by one and watched it fall like black silk. She took her trench coat from the coat tree and buttoned it, never acknowledging that she knew Chris's eyes were on her back, and with determined abruptness walked for the door.

'Deborah.'

She stopped and pressed her forehead against the door.

'Deborah.'

She came into the alcove and sat on the edge of the bed. Chris snuffed out the cigarette, rolled next to her, and lay his head in her lap. Her black eyes filled with melancholy. Her fingers traced his cheek and mouth and neck and shoulders, and Chris looked up at her. How beautiful you are, he thought. She was biblical. Black and olive. A Deborah of the Bible. When she stood, Chris grabbed her wrist and she could feel his hand tremble.

'We can't keep this up. Let me speak to him.'

'It would kill him, Chris.'

'How about me? It's killing me.'

'Please.'

'I'm talking to him tonight.'

'Oh Lord, why does it always have to end like this?'

'It will until you're my wife.'

'You're not to see him, Chris. I mean that.'

He released his grip. 'You'd better go,' he whispered. He turned away, his back toward her.

'Chris . . . Chris . . .'

Pride kept him silent.

'I'll call you,' she said. 'Will you see me?'

'You know I will.'

He threw on a robe and listened to the click-click-click of her footsteps on the marble hall outside. He pulled back the window drapes. The rain had slowed to a miserable drizzle. In a moment Deborah appeared on Jerusalem Boulevard below. She looked up to his window and waved her hand feebly, then ran across the street to where a line of droshkas waited. The horse clip-clopped away from the curb and turned out of sight.

Chris let the drapes fall closed, snuffing out most of the light. He wandered into the kitchen and poured himself a cup of the steaming coffee Deborah had made, then slumped into a chair and hid his face in his hands, shaken by the impact of another parting.

On the radio, a newscaster speaking in nervous Polish recited the latest diplomatic setback in the growing mountain of them.

Chapter Two

Journal Entry

On the news we hear that Russia and Germany are about to announce a non-aggression treaty. It seems impossible that the two sworn enemies on the planet, pledged to destroy each other, have come to this. Hitler's tactics seem logical. He obviously wants to neutralize Russia for the time being to avoid the possibility of a two-front war (that is, if England and France honor their obligations to Poland). I'm willing to wager that the wages being paid to Stalin is half of Poland and I think we are being divided up at some long polished table in Moscow this minute.

ALEXANDER BRANDEL

In embassies, state departments, chancelleries, foreign offices, consulates, ministries, war offices, code rooms, newsrooms, frantic men scurried to all-night conferences, played war games, barked into telephones of flooded switchboards, cursed, prayed, pleaded.

A trail of broken treaties lay strewn about like corpses after a Mongol invasion.

Men of good will were stunned at the warped logic behind which eighty million civilized people rallied and shrieked and strutted like hysterical robots. Hammered into a hypnotic trance by the well-timed tantrums that were the mad genius of Adolf Hitler, the men of good will sank deeper into muck and mire, unable to divest themselves of the all-consuming monster in their midst.

The geopoliticians had drawn and quartered the world into areas of labor and raw material and presented the master plan which stood to make Genghis Khan and every archvillain of every age pale by comparison.

The German masses gave the edict in a terrifying redundance, '*Sieg Heil! Sieg Heil! Sieg Heil!*'

'*Lebensraum* [Land to live]!'

'*Sieg Heil!*'

And they poised ready to act out the role of Teuton war gods to the strains of Wagnerian Fire Music.

'We must save German citizens living under foreign tyranny! A German is always a German!'

'*Sieg Heil!*'

Austria and Czechoslovakia qualified. Flushed with bloodless victories, certain that America, France, and England would not fight, the Nazi cancer spread.

'Danzig is German! Return the Polish Corridor! Return the 1914 borders! Halt the inhuman treatment of ethnic Germans!'

'*Sieg Heil!*'

Once an indifferent world stood by and shrugged as little yellow men fought little yellow men in a place called Manchuria, and once France sputtered feebly as Germany broke the Versailles Treaty and marched into the Rhineland, and once men debated, then sighed as black men in mud huts armed with spears fought for their land . . . a name that children used in games . . . Abyssinia.

A mesmerized world quivered at the proving ground of democratic sterility; the rape of Spain by Italian and Moroccan and German hordes.

Now Austria, now Czechoslovakia, and the righteous cowed and the evil grew bold.

Once the harbingers of peace told their people they had made a bill of peace in a place called Munich. As Poland's hour grew near came that realization that there was no place left to run or to hide, nor words to say, nor treaties to make.

In Moscow, a shrewd chessplayer knew that the long dream of the Allies was to have Russia and Germany maul each other to death. His distrust of England and France was built upon decades of boycott, hard-learned lessons when republican Spain was abandoned, and finally when Russia was not invited to the sellout in Munich.

Hitler, positive of the final timidity of the Allies, positive their string of betrayals would extend to Poland, keyed his war trumpets to shattering highs and was responded to with black drum rolls and pounding boots.

Josef Stalin was no less certain of Allied betrayal. In a desperate bid for time he entered into negotiations with his archenemy. To ensure easy, unimpaired victory for himself, Hitler did business with Stalin, and the Allies cried, 'Foul!'

And in the middle a proud and defiant Poland, which hated Russia and Germany with equal vigor, ended all hope of Allied unity by refusing to petition Russia for help.

Chris sped his Fiat down the rain-slickened boulevard and turned into the shop-lined New World Street. It was gray out. The late shoppers clung close to the buildings and moved with haste past the elegant store windows. At the corner of Traugutta Street, where the line of shops ended, the New World Street changed its name to the Krakow Suburb Boulevard for reasons no one seemed to understand. Chris headed toward the semi-faded, semi-elegant Bristol Hotel. The hotel made a good newsman's headquarters. It gave him a twenty-four-hour-a-day switchboard service and it stood at the apex of a triangle that enveloped the Europa Hotel, the Foreign Ministry, the President's Palace, and Warsaw's city hall. Between them, there was always a constant flood of news.

Chris turned the car over to the doorman and brushed past the turmoil of the rumor-filled lobby to the opened-cage Otis elevator of World War I vintage.

On the balcony floor he entered the door of a suite marked *Swiss News Agency*.

Ervin Rosenblum, photographer and journalist and Chris's indispensable man, stood at the worktable, which was spilling over with photographs, cables, stories, and copy.

Chris walked beside him, wordless, and took a fistful of the late dispatches. One by one he let them flutter to the floor. Ervin Rosenblum was a very homely man who stood five feet five inches and was almost sightless without his thick-lens glasses. As Chris read, Ervin searched Chris's pockets for a cigarette.

'Boy,' Chris mumbled. 'They're surer than hell going to start shooting soon.'

Ervin gave up his search for a smoke. 'Mark my words, Poland is going to fight,' he said.

'Maybe she'll be better off if she doesn't fight.'

Ervin looked at his watch nervously. 'Where the hell is Susan? I've got to get this stuff to the lab.' He picked up his Speed Graphic and jiggled the flash bulbs in his pocket. 'Chris, do you think England and France will help us?'

Chris kept reading the dispatches. 'When are you and Susan getting married?'

'I can't keep her still long enough to ask her. If she's not at the orphanage she's at a Zionist meeting. Did you ever hear of six meetings a week? Only Jews can talk so much. So I'm appointed to the executive council just so I can get dates to see her. Momma asks, are you coming to dinner tonight? She's made potato latkes for you, special.'

'Potato latkes? I'll get there between stops.'

Susan Geller appeared in the doorway. She was as short and homely as Ervin was. Squat, devoid of almost all features which make women pretty. Her hair was pulled back straight and flat and wrapped into a knot under her nurse's cap. Her hands were large and knobby from the life of lifting sick people and changing bedpans, but the moment she spoke the ugliness faded. Susan Geller was one of the kindest creatures on the earth.

'You're a half hour late,' Ervin greeted her.

'Hi, honey,' Chris said.

'I like you better,' she answered to Chris.

Ervin grabbed a batch of negatives, film, bulbs, and his camera. 'It's all yours,' he said to Chris.

'Can you stop by the President's Palace? See Anton. Maybe he can fix us up for five minutes with Smigly-Rydz. He may be changing his tune now that the Russian-German non-aggression pact is official.'

The phone rang. Ervin snatched it off the hook with his free hand. 'Hello . . . Just a minute.' He held his hand over the mouthpiece. 'Wait outside,' he said to Susan. 'I'll be right there.'

Susan and Chris blew good-by kisses to each other.

'Who is it, Rosy?'

'Deborah's husband,' he answered, and handed him the phone and left.

'Why, hello, Paul. How are you?'

'I was asking the same question. I was just saying to Deborah how much we and the children have missed you.'

'Things have been pretty hectic.'

'I can imagine.'

'I do owe you an apology for not calling. How . . . uh . . . is Deborah?'

'Fine, just fine. Why don't you break away for dinner tomorrow?'

Chris was finding it unbearable to keep the masquerade. Every time he saw Paul and Deborah together, every time he thought of them sharing a bed, the revulsion in him grew.

'I'm afraid it's impossible. I may have to send Rosy to Krakow and –'

Paul Bronski's voice lowered. 'It is rather important that you come. I should like to see you on a pressing matter. Say, seven.'

Chris was scared. Paul's tone had the authority of a command. Perhaps Paul Bronski himself would call the showdown that Deborah had avoided. Maybe it was all fantasy. They were good friends. Why not invite him to dinner?

'I'll be there,' Chris said.

Chapter Three

Journal Entry

I have studied the trend of the behavior of the ethnic Germans in Austria and Czechoslovakia. They have done a tremendous job in undermining in advance of the German armies. They have certainly been raising all sorts of hell in Danzig. Just before the Austrian 'Anschluss' they became strangely quiet. This past week their activity here has all but stopped. Could this be on orders? Is this the lull before the storm? Is history about to repeat?

Everyone I know is being called up into the reserve. Smigly-Rydz means to fight. Polish temper and history indicate they will.

ALEXANDER BRANDEL

'We Poles unfortunately got ourselves located between Russia and Germany. The traffic between the two has been busy,' Dr Paul Bronski, dean of the College of Medicine, said to an auditorium overcrowded with students and faculty. 'We have been trampled. We have even ceased to exist, yet Polish nationalism fires a breed of patriot that has always made Poland return.'

A spontaneous burst of applause halted his speech.

'Poland is in trouble again. Our two friends are restless. The situation is so urgent that they have even called upon the senior citizens like this specimen before you ...'

Polite laughter for Paul's overcritical estimation of himself. Although balding and sporting a scholar's stooped shoulders, Paul Bronski had sharp and handsome features.

'Despite the blunder of the High Command in calling me into the army, I predict that Poland will somehow survive.'

In the back of the auditorium, Dr Franz Koenig stood motionless, looking into the sea of faces. Bronski's leaving filled him with an exhilaration he had never known. His long, patient wait was almost over.

'I leave this university both heavy-hearted and joyous. The prospect of war is enormously real and it saddens me. But I am content for the things that we have done here together and I am happy because I leave so many friends.'

Koenig didn't even hear the rest of it. They would all be dripping tears, he knew. Bronski had that faculty to put a tremor in his throat that never failed to move the recipients of his milky words.

They were all standing now, and unabashed tears flowed down young cheeks and even grizzly old cheeks of professors in a sloppy indulgence of sentiment as they sang school songs and anthems, which sounded like school songs and anthems everywhere.

Look at Bronski! Engulfed by his adoring staff. Shaking hands, slapping backs until the end. The 'beloved' Bronski. 'The University of Warsaw without Paul Bronski is not the University of Warsaw.' 'Your office will remain untouched until you return to us.'

Your office, Koenig thought. *Your* office, indeed.

Dr Paul Bronski, the 'beloved' Paul Bronski, had finished the last of his instructions, dictated the last of his letters, and dismissed his weeping secretary with an affectionate buss.

He was alone now.

He looked about the room. Paneled walls covered with the symbols of achievement that one would gather as the head of a great medical college. Diplomas and awards and photos of students and classes. A billboard of glory.

He shoved the final batch of papers into his brief case. All that was left was a photo of Deborah and the children on his desk. He slid that into the top drawer and locked it. And he was done.

A soft, almost apologetic knock on the door.

'Come in.'

Dr Franz Koenig entered. The little gray-haired man with the little gray mustache advanced timidly to the edge of the desk. 'We have been together for a long time, Paul. Words fail me.'

Paul Bronski was amused. A magnificently understated phrase ... a lovely play on words. Dr Koenig was a humorless man who could never believe his sincerity was doubted.

'Franz, I'm going to recommend you fill my office –'

'No one can fill –'

'Nonsense ...'

And more garble ... and another farewell.

Franz Koenig waited in his own office across the hall until Paul left, and then he re-entered. His eyes became fixed on the leather chair behind Bronski's desk. He walked behind it and touched it. Yes, tomorrow he would move in and things would look good from here.

My chair ... dean of medicine! My chair. Bronski gone. Quick-talking, teary-voiced Bronski. Ten years he had waited. The board was blinded by Bronski. They were entranced by the fact they could put a graduate of the university as the dean of medicine for the first time in six decades. That's why they chose Bronski. A whispering campaign against me because I am a German. They were so eager to make Bronski the dean, they even closed their eyes to the fact that he is a Jew.

Franz went to his own office again and got his homburg and tucked his cane over his arm and walked in his half trot down the long corridor. The students nodded and doffed their caps as he sped by.

He approached the big ornate wrought-iron gates. A knot of students blocked his way. For a moment everyone stood still, then the knot dissolved and he passed through, feeling their eyes on him.

How differently they reacted these days, he thought. No longer the vague indifference. He was a man to be respected, even feared. Fear me? The thought delighted him.

Even his fat, nagging Polish wife behaved differently nowadays. He approached the big ornate wrought-iron gates, continuing the fast pace in rhythm to his tapping cane in the direction of Pilsudski Square.

He was happy today. He even made an attempt to whistle. The end of a long, long journey was at hand.

Like most of the million ethnic Germans, Franz Koenig had been born in western Poland in a territory formerly German-occupied, then freed to Poland after the World War. In his youth his family moved to Danzig, which was located in a geographical freak known as the 'Polish Corridor.' It was a finger of land which split East Prussia away from the German mainland in order to give Poland access to the sea. It was an abnormal division. Danzig and the Polish Corridor filled with ethnic Germans and Poles became a thorn in German pride and the object of bickering and threats from the beginning.

Franz Koenig came from a good merchant family. He had received a classical education in medicine in Heidelberg and in Switzerland. He was a man of total moderation. Although raised in the furor of Danzig, he considered himself neither German nor Polish nor much of anything but a good doctor and teacher; a profession, he felt, that crossed the bounds of nationalism.

Franz Koenig was an adequate man. His appointment to the University of Warsaw was adequate. The Polish girl he had married was adequate. He lived his life in a mild and inoffensive manner, delighting most in the privacy of his study with good music and good books. The early marriage ambitions of his Polish wife failed to stir him. She gave up in disgust and grew obese.

When the Nazis came to power, Franz Koenig was embarrassed by their behavior. In an outburst rare for him, he referred to the SA Brown Shirts as 'thick-necked, pinheaded bullies.' He thought himself fortunate to be in Warsaw and clear of the havoc in Germany.

All that changed.

There was a month, a week, a day, and a moment.

The office of dean of the College of Medicine was open. By seniority, competence, and devotion, the position was his. In anticipation of the appointment which should have been routine, he constructed a dull but adequate speech to accept the chair. He never delivered the speech. Paul Bronski, fifteen years his junior, was appointed.

He remembered Kurt Liedendorf, the leader of Warsaw's ethnics, snorting in his ear.

'It's a blow to us – all us Germans, Doktor Koenig. It is a terrible insult.'

'Nonsense ... nonsense ...'

'Now maybe you understand how the Versailles Treaty has made the German people anonymous. Look, you ... Heidelberg ... Geneva. A man of culture. You have been made anonymous too. You are a victim of Jewish cunning. All us Germans are victims of Jewish cunning, Herr Doktor ... Hitler says ...'

Jewish cunning ... Bronski ... Jewish cunning ...

All that Franz Koenig ever wanted for a world he served well was to be the dean of medicine at the University of Warsaw.

'Come and spend the afternoon with us, Herr Doktor. Be with your own people,' Kurt Liedendorf said. 'We have a special guest from Berlin who will give us a talk.'

And the guest from Berlin told them, 'Perhaps the methods of the Nazis are harsh, but to rectify the injustices heaped upon the German people takes men of strong will and vigor. Everything we do is justified because the goal to restore the German people to their rightful way of life is justified.'

'Ah, Herr Doktor,' Liedendorf said, 'Good to see you here. Sit here, sit up front.'

'Hitler has seen to it that the German people are not anonymous any more. If you declare yourself as a German, you will not be anonymous!'

He came home from the fourth meeting, and the fifth and the sixth, and he looked at his fat Polish wife and all that was around him. Feudal gentry, universal ignorance. 'I am a German,' Franz Koenig said to himself. 'I am a German.'

'Doktor Koenig, you should see it in Danzig. Thousands and thousands of Germans fighting for the Führer. Letting the world know that we will not be abused any more.'

How proud he was of the deliverance of the Germans from Austria and Czechoslovakia!

'I've been thinking of it deeply, Liedendorf. I want to join in this work.'

He walked along the edge of the Saxony Gardens, past the blocks of government buildings and palaces and art museums. All this granite and marble were not of his sinew. In the beer halls, in the homes of his own people, German people, was where he belonged. Here Dr Franz Koenig was a respected man. Here they spoke of great things without shame or fear.

He stopped before the Square of the Iron Gates just beyond the Saxony Gardens.

A sickening odor of half-rotted vegetables, unwashed peasants, squalling chickens, haggling, screaming barterers and beggars, and a thousand push-carts pleaded for the zloty in the most primitive form of trade.

'Used neckties, good as new!'

'Pencils!'

'Buy from me!'

Old women squatted on the cobblestones with a few eggs, thieves and pickpockets roamed about, and lines of pushcarts dangled secondhand shoes and greasy jackets. The noise of the iron rims of the carts roared and echoed over the square.

'Buy from me!'

Bearded Jews, bearded Paul Bronskis, argued endlessly to save a half zloty in hand-waving Yiddish, a language cruelly butchering the beautiful German tongue.

A drunken soldier was hurled from a café and fell at Koenig's feet.

Drunk as a Pole – that is what they say, Koenig thought. Drunk as a Pole. Such fitting words.

All of Poland had passed before him in two short squares. How wrong is Hitler's disgust of the Slavs? A nation of thirty million people with only two million newspaper readers. A nation of feudal lords and serfs in this, the twentieth century. A nation which worshiped a black madonna as African Zulus prayed to sun gods.

This was Poland to Franz Koenig. Five per cent Paris, walled behind marble mansions and ruling decadence. Ninety-five per cent Ukrainia . . . abominable ignorance.

What could the good industrious German folk have done with the fertile flat lands and the bursting mineral deposits of Silesia?

'Buy from me!'

Who was this mass of dirty people with their childlike mentality to hold back the German people, who had contributed more to the world's enrichment and knowledge than any other race?

Franz Koenig knew that no matter what small injustices the Nazis perpetrated the final result of a greater Germany justified the means.

Koenig circumvented the confusion of the market place and entered Hans Schultz's bar.

Schultz smiled. '*Guten Tag, Herr Doktor, Guten Tag.*'

'Hello, Schultz. Anything new?'

'*Ja*. Herr Liedendorf is unable to come out these days. He said that our work is done and you should stay home and wait.'

Dr Koenig downed his beer and nodded to Schultz, who smiled as he wiped the bar.

In a few moments he entered his flat and put his hat neatly on the rack and placed his cane directly below it. He looked at his fat Polish wife, whose mouth was sucking in and out like a puckered fish, and he could not hear what she was saying. She walked and her flesh wobbled.

He envisioned her in the bed, which sagged on one side because of her immensity, and he saw her flabby buttocks and her hanging breasts.

Koenig walked to his study and slammed the door behind him.

He turned on the radio. It was always set now on Radio Deutschland.

A rally from Hamburg!

'We Germans cannot tolerate the outrageous treatment of our citizens in Poland, where German women and children are unsafe from Polish vandals . . . where German men are beaten and murdered!'

'Sieg Heil! Sieg Heil! Sieg Heil!'

And soon ten thousand voices shattered the air waves, singing 'Deutschland über Alles,' and Dr Franz Koenig closed his eyes and tears fell down his cheeks, just as they had fallen down the cheeks of his students.

And he prayed that his liberators would be coming soon.

Chapter Four

Journal Entry

Wonderful news! Andrei came home on leave unexpectedly! We of the Bathyran Zionist Executive Council have a lot of things to talk over and decide. With Andrei here it will give us a chance to get together.

ALEXANDER BRANDEL

The army truck came to a halt before the northernmost bridge that spanned the Vistula River from Warsaw to Praga. Captain Andrei Androfski hopped out of the cab, thanked the driver, and walked along the river toward the new northern suburb of Zoliborz. He tilted back the four-cornered cap worn by officers of the crack Ulany regiments and he whistled as he walked and received and returned the smiles and flirtations of young lady strollers. Captain Andrei Androfski indeed cut the classic figure of a Ulan cavalry officer. His leather shined, and the short stiletto at his side glinted when the sun caught it.

He turned away from the river and into a tree-lined street of lovely new homes in an area stamped with upper-middle-class wealth. Andrei spotted a large stone on the sidewalk and began to dribble it with his feet with the dexterity of a trained soccer player, his leg muscles fairly rippling through his trousers. He gave the stone a final swift kick of the boot, speeding it down the street toward an imaginary goal, and turned at the gate of Dr Paul Bronski's house.

'Uncle Andrei!' shouted ten-year-old Stephan as he sprinted over the lawn and leaped on his uncle's back.

'Schmendrick!'

The two 'clashed,' and the big cavalry officer was 'thrown' to the ground, apparently no match for his eighty-pound nephew. He surrendered gallantly, got to his feet, and lifted the victor on his shoulders.

'How is Batory?'

'Batory! The first, the most beautiful, and the most fierce animal in all of Poland.'

'What has he done lately, Uncle Andrei?'

'Lately? This week – well, let me see. I took him to England for the Grand National, and he ran so fast he split the air and caused it to thunder. Well sir, those Englishmen thought it was raining and ran for cover and didn't even see the race. Batory lapped the field four times and was coming up for the fifth time when the second fastest horse crossed the finish line. And those stupid Englishmen who were hiding in the stands thought Batory finished last.'

'Who takes care of Batory when you are gone?'

'First Sergeant Styka, personally!'

'I wish I could ride him again,' Stephan said, recalling the most thrilling incident of his young life.

'You will, just as soon as we clear up some things.'

'Can I jump him this time?'

'Yes, I think so. That is, if heights don't make you too dizzy. When Batory jumps, the world below becomes very small. As a matter of fact, I don't enter him in jumping races any more. Batory jumps so high, the other horses are around the track before he comes down.'

Andrei walked to the house.

'Uncle Andrei!' cried Rachael Bronski. This meeting was devoid of the previous violence, for the voice belonged to an elegant black-eyed fourteen-year-old young lady whose greeting was limited to an affectionate hug.

'Andrei!' cried Deborah, running in from the kitchen, wiping her hands. She flung her arms around her brother's neck. 'You devil. Why didn't you let us know you were coming?'

'I only knew myself last night. Besides, I want to stay clear of Alexander Brandel. He'll call one of those damned meetings.'

'How long?'

'Four whole days.'

'How wonderful!'

Andrei lifted Stephan from his shoulders as though he were weightless.

'What did you bring me?' Stephan demanded.

'Stephan, shame!' his sister reprimanded.

Andrei winked and stretched his arms out. Stephan began fishing through his uncle's pockets, which had been an unfailing source of booty from his earliest memory. He withdrew a gilded Polish eagle, the insignia whose two spread wings held up the front corner of the Ulany cap.

'Mine?' with apprehension.

'Yours.'

'Wow!' and Stephan was gone to alert the neighborhood that his great Uncle Andrei was home.

'And for my beautiful niece.'

'You spoil them.'

'Do me something.'

The girl's fingers quickly worked the ribbon open.

'Oh! Oh!' She hugged him and raced to the mirror to fix the pair of ivory combs into thick black hair which was just like her mother's.

'She's beautiful,' Andrei said.

'Boys are already starting to look at her.'

'What do you mean! What boys!'

Deborah laughed. 'She won't be a wallflower like her mother.'

Rachael walked to her uncle, whom she adored, and kissed his cheek. 'Thank you, Uncle Andrei.'

'My reward, please,' Andrei said, pointing to the piano.

Rachael played her mood. A bubbling étude. Andrei watched a moment, then Deborah took his hand and led him toward the kitchen. He stopped at the door again. 'She plays like an angel – like you used to play.'

Deborah shooed Zoshia, the housekeeper, out and set on some water for tea. Andrei sprawled and loosened his tunic. It smelled good in the kitchen. Deborah had been baking cookies. It was like the old flat on Sliska Street on the day before Sabbath. Deborah took off Andrei's cap and ran her fingers through the array of curly blond hair.

'My baby brother.'

She set before him a large platter of cookies, which were half finished by the time she poured the tea. He took a long sip. 'This is good, this is good. Sergeant Styka brews a lousy tea.'

'How are things on the border, Andrei?'

Andrei shrugged. 'How should I know! They don't consult me. Ask Smigly-Rydz.'

'Be serious.'

'Seriously. I'm home for four days –'

'We're all worried sick.'

'All right, the German concentrations are very, very heavy. Let me give you an opinion, Deborah. As long as Hitler gets what he wants by bluffing, fine. Well, he isn't bluffing Poland and he may damned well back down.'

'Paul has been called up.'

Andrei uncrossed his legs. The mention of Paul Bronski struck an obvious note of discord. 'I'm sorry to hear that,' he said quickly. 'I didn't think –'

'None of us did,' Deborah said. She walked to the sink and began rolling the thin dough for more cookies. 'Have you seen Gabriela yet?'

'I came directly here. She is probably still working.'

'Why don't you two come to dinner tonight?'

'If Brandel doesn't find me first.'

'Try to make it. Christopher de Monti will be over.'

'How is my boy Chris!'

'He has been terribly busy since the crisis. We haven't seen him for several weeks,' she said, rolling the dough at a furious pace.

Andrei walked up behind his sister, turned her around by the shoulders, and tried to lift her chin so she would look at him. Deborah shook her head and spun away.

'Please don't dream things up between Chris and me.'

'Just old friends?'

'Just old friends.'

'Does Paul know?'

'There's nothing to know!'

'Did you raise me for an idiot?'

'Andrei, please . . . please, we have enough to worry about these days. And for God's sake, don't pick an argument with Paul.'

'Who argues with Paul? He always –'

'I swear, if you two get into another fight –'

Andrei gulped down his tea, stuffed a half dozen cookies into his pocket, and buttoned his tunic.

'Please promise me you'll get along with Paul tonight. He's going away. Do it for me.'

Andrei grunted, came up behind Deborah, and gave her a brisk slap on the backside. 'See you later,' he said.

Andrei Androfski stretched lazily on a park bench on the edge of the Lazienki Gardens facing the American Embassy. The statue of Frédéric Chopin hovered above him, patronized by the local pigeons, and the Belvedere Palace of the former Marshal Pilsudski was immersed in the greenery behind him. It was a nice place to laze. He engaged in his favorite pastime of undressing the female pedestrians with his eyes. He dug into his pocket and found the last of Deborah's cookies and munched.

After a while the main door of the Embassy opened. Gabriela Rak came out and walked up the embassy-lined Aleja Ujazdowska. He caught up to her by the time she reached the first intersection. Sensing a masher behind her, Gabriela stepped quickly from the curb.

'Madam,' Andrei said, 'would you kindly give me the name of that fortunate young lady who owns the heart of the most dashing officer in the Ulanys?'

She stopped in the middle of the street.

'Andrei? Andrei?' And she spun into his arms. The traffic policeman raised his hand, sending a flood of vehicles swirling around them. They dodged and honked their horns with the irritated understanding one gives to a soldier and his girl kissing in the middle of a street. At last an unpatriotic taxi driver shouted that they were a pair of jackasses and sent them scurrying to the safety of a park bench across the way.

'Oh, Andrei,' she said, and lay her head on his chest. 'Oh, Andrei,' and she sniffled.

'If I knew that I was going to make you so sad, I wouldn't have returned.'

She dried her eyes and purred with contentment. 'How long?'

'Four days.'

'Oh, I'm so happy.'

'I almost had to find another woman for myself. I thought you would never get out of the Embassy.'

Gabriela toyed with his large hand, which nearly made two of hers. 'I've just been in a meeting. We aren't reopening the American school. All the children have been evacuated to Krakow. Even some of the key personnel are leaving.'

Andrei grumbled something about the traditional cowardice of Americans.

'Let's not talk about it now,' she said. 'We only have ninety-six hours, and look at the time we have already wasted. We can't go to my place. I had it repainted. It smells terrible. I didn't know you were coming home.'

'And if we go to my place, Alexander Brandel and the whole damned executive council will be camping at the doorstep.'

'Let's risk it,' Gabriela said with a low-voiced tremor of want that sent her captain to the curb in search of a droshka.

They drove north past the imposing mansions of the 'new rich' on the Avenue of the Marshals. Gabriela snuggled against him, her fingers feeling his face and shoulders.

Andrei's flat on Leszno Street sat in a middle-class neighborhood that buffered the rich on the south from the wild slums on the north. They climbed the stairs toward his tiny flat, arms about each other. By the time they reached the third-floor landing, Gabriela stopped to catch her breath.

'My next lover has to live on the ground floor,' she said.

Andrei swept her up in his arms and tossed her over a shoulder like a sack of sugar.

'Put me down, you crazy fool!'

He emitted a bloodcurdling cavalry charge and leaped up the final flight of stairs two steps at a time, kicked open his never-locked door, then stood in amazement with Gabriela trying to squirm off his shoulder.

Andrei's eyes went from corner to corner around the flat. He peeked into the kitchen, then looked around again, wondering if he had invaded the wrong apartment. The place was spotlessly clean. For years he had carefully strewn his books and papers about. His desk was always three inches deep in reports. All the wonderful clutter, all the carefully preserved dust – all of the things that make a man a bachelor – were gone.

Andrei kicked open the closet door. Everything pressed and hanging neatly.

The kitchen ... All those lovely unwashed dishes washed.

There were curtains, lace curtains, at the windows.

'I've been evicted!' Andrei cried. 'No, something more horrible than that has happened. A female has been here!'

'Andrei, if you don't put me down I'll scream rape.'

He lowered her to the floor.

'I think you owe me an explanation,' he said.

'I'd sit in my place night after night waiting for Batory to charge down the street bearing my Ulan warrior. All alone with my ten black cats and my memories. And I came here and sat because you were all around me and I wasn't quite so lonely. But! Who can sit in such a mess!'

'I know your type, Gabriela Rak. You're going to try to make me over.'

'Oh, you know it!'

She leaped at him, and he caught her off the floor and held her and sank his lips into hers. And in a moment Andrei had no more talk to make. They were bringing each other from smoldering dormancy with an urgency that heightened every second.

The phone rang.

It stuck them like a knife. They froze.

It rang again.

'Son of a bitch, Brandel.'

It rang again.

'Let it ring, darling,' she said.

And it did ... again and again and again.

Gabriela spun away from him, teary-eyed. 'It has eyes, that phone. It never rang the whole time you were gone.'

'Well, maybe I'd better answer.'

'Oh, you might as well. Every Bathyran in Warsaw knows that Andrei Androfski is home on leave.'

He snatched the phone from the hook. 'Is that you, you son of a bitch, Brandel!'

A soft voice answered on the other end. 'Of course it's me, Andrei. You've been in town for three hours and twenty minutes. Are you snubbing your old friends?'

'Alex, do me something. Go to hell,' he said, and slammed the receiver down. The instant he did, he lifted it again and dialed Brandel's number.

'Andrei?'

'I'll call you later. Tell the gang I'm anxious to see them.'

'I hope I didn't break anything up. Have a nice time. Good Shabes.'

Andrei walked to the edge of the bed, where Gabriela sulked. He leaned over and put his lips into her honey hair, and she closed her eyes, reveling in the sensations his touch caused. Andrei went to the window and pulled down the shade, plunging the room into dusk, and he locked the door.

'Don't be angry, Gaby. I didn't know about your place. I would have gotten a hotel room. Don't be angry.'

'I'm not angry,' she whispered.

They lay beside each other, luxuriating in teasing and touching and whispering.

Suddenly Gabriela broke into a sweat and she was no longer able to control herself. 'Oh God, I've missed you so!'

And they fought awkwardly and furiously to get out of their clothing.

The phone rang.

This time it went unanswered.

Chapter Five

Journal Entry

I think I picked the wrong time to call Andrei. Thank goodness his temper goes down as fast as it rises.

I talked to banker friends this evening. Everyone is frantic to convert their securities to American dollars or Swiss and South American bonds. Whole estates are being liquidated.

With the Russian-German alliance a fact, the German propaganda has gone utterly insane with charges of Polish border violations and maltreatment of ethnic Germans.

Meanwhile, why do we keep a deaf ear to England's and France's pleadings that we negotiate for help from Russia? Does our General Staff really think we can beat the Germans?

ALEXANDER BRANDEL

Dr Paul Bronski filled the large brown envelope with a number of legal and financial papers. There was a will, insurance policies, a variety of securities, some cash in large denominations, and a key to his safe-deposit box. Finally a sealed letter. He scrawled the words, 'In the event of my death,' and put the letter in with the other papers, wet the flap, and rolled it stuck.

In the dining room, young Rachael Bronski pranced about the table helping the large and rapidly aging Zoshia put the finishing touches on a lush setting. The table was overburdened with heavy silverware and gold-rimmed porcelain.

Rachael touched the flowers in the centerpiece and made them just so.

In his study, Paul Bronski listened to the BBC.

'In an exclusive interview with Polish Marshal Smigly-Rydz, Christopher de Monti of the Swiss News Agency, in a story datelined Warsaw, said that the Polish nation remains as always – no thought of a mutual-aid treaty with the Soviet Union. Later BBC confirmed this seemingly unshakable policy in a news conference with Poland's Foreign Minister Beck. Poland's adamance is viewed as bringing war one step closer.'

Deborah, putting the finishing touches on herself, entered the study. Paul placed the envelope face down, turned off the news, and smiled at his wife. In their sixteen years of marriage she had never failed to make herself attractive. No man could ask for a more perfect mate for his career.

'You look lovely,' he said.

'Thank you, dear,' she said. 'Paul ... please try to stay out of an argument with Andrei tonight.'

'Andrei makes that difficult at times.'

'Please.'

'You've got my assurance. Get your brother's.'

'I think for the children's sake – and – well, it should be special tonight.'

The doorbell rang. Rachael answered. 'Hello, Chris, come in.'

'You look more like your mother every day.'

Rachael blushed. 'Momma and Daddy are in the study. Go on in.'

Paul and Deborah stood and looked at the door as Chris came through. Then Deborah studiously avoided his eyes. 'It's been a long time, Chris,' she said.

He nodded. Paul shook his hand, and for the moment the fear of the first moment of the meeting subsided.

'Would you excuse me?' she said. 'I've got to see to dinner. I'll be back with cocktails.'

Paul offered Chris a seat, then returned to his desk and loaded his pipe. 'I've been listening to the news,' he said. 'I hear you got with the old man.'

'Seems strange keeping this position with the clock running out.'

'Both Russia and Germany have pushed us around for centuries. There's actually little to choose between them. Well, the hell with it. Chris, we've missed you. How have you been?'

'Running.'

Much of the tension in Chris had eased. The warm welcome, the small talk. Either Paul was totally ignorant or expedient. Or he was playing some sort of game with great skill. Whatever it was, Paul did not want an ugly scene, and that was a relief.

'I'm leaving tomorrow,' Paul said abruptly. 'Been called up. More than likely I'll be stationed with the surgeon general's staff in Krakow – paper work.

Been so long since I practiced medicine, I begged off line duty for the sake of the army. Works out well, they need administrative help.'

Chris was both glad and sorry at the pronouncement. Nagging thoughts buzzed around inside him. 'See here, Paul,' he wanted to say, 'Deborah and I love each other very much. It's nothing we planned ... just happened. I want you to give her her freedom.'

The words never found their way beyond nagging thoughts. How can you say to a man who is leaving for war, 'I want your wife. Incidentally, have a nice time at the front?'

Why did Paul Bronski have to be such a decent sort? That's what made it so damned lousy. Bronski was a wonderful person. And any desire Chris had to create a scene suddenly melted.

'Chris, you and I haven't known each other tremendously long as some friendships go. You know how it is. With some people you work with them all your life – like myself and Dr Koenig – and never really know them. Another man can walk into a room and in ten minutes you become friends – real friends. I think you and I are that kind.'

'I hope so, Paul.'

'I've been a very lucky man. In addition to my position and my family, my father left me a considerable estate which I have been able to enlarge.' Paul slid the brown envelope across the desk.

'If something should happen to me ...' he continued.

'Oh, come now.'

'Good friends don't have to make small talk, Chris. Poland doesn't have a chance, does it?'

'No – not really.'

'Even if I do get through, which I certainly anticipate, they're going to make it hard on us. With your connections and freedom of movement and with the possibility of an occupied Poland, you are in the best position of anyone I know to convert my estate into Swiss or American holdings.'

Chris took the envelope and nodded.

'You'll find everything in order.'

'I'll take care of it right away. I have a friend leaving for Bern next week. He can be trusted. Any preference in investments?'

'German munitions seem like a good bet.'

They both laughed.

'My bank is good and conservative. They'll know the answers,' Chris said.

'Good. Well ... you hold all my fortunes. One more thing. If anything should happen to me, I know you will see to it that Deborah and the children are taken out of Poland.'

Chris's mouth went dry. All the rest of it was what one friend does for another. But this seemed as though he were willing Deborah to him. Chris looked into Paul's implacable eyes. Revealing, yet not revealing. If he really knew, he had carried it quietly. He had veiled the pain it must have caused. But isn't this the way Paul Bronski would do things? He was a gentle man as well as a shrewd man. Wouldn't he have thought it out and already forgiven both Deborah and him? Or maybe Chris was overdramatizing everything. Perhaps Paul did feel their friendship deep enough to ask this.

Nothing Paul said or did gave the slightest clue to what was really behind his expression.

Chris folded the envelope and put it in his inside pocket. Deborah entered with two glasses of sherry for herself and Paul and a martini for Chris.

'You two look so grim.'

'Chris was explaining the meaning of the news to me, dear.'

'Rachael is playing the piano. Come on into the parlor.'

They stood around the piano, Paul obviously glorying in the extraordinary talent of his daughter. It was the same melody that was coming over the radio.

Chris felt himself back in bed looking at Deborah's body. Paderewski ... Chopin ... a nocturne ...

Deborah lowered her eyes as her daughter's slender fingers danced over the keys. And Chris lowered his.

Paul looked from one to the other. 'Why don't you play, dear?' he said to his wife.

She breathed deeply and slipped beside Rachael and took up the bass. There they were, Deborah and Rachael, beauty and beauty.

The mood of the moment was shattered by a bombastic roar at the door. Uncle Andrei had arrived. He had a second round of battle with Stephan and this time decided to lift fat old Zoshia off the ground and dance her around the anteroom.

'Chris!' he roared, belting De Monti in the back so that he lost half his martini.

Gabriela, filled with the weary happiness of love-making, drifted in almost unseen behind the roaring Ulan. 'Keep playing! Keep playing!' ordered Captain Androfski.

Never known as a man adept in stifling emotions, he greeted Paul Bronski in a way that left little doubt of the iciness that existed between them. The words they exchanged testified they were straining for effect for Deborah's sake.

'I hear you've been called up, Paul.'

'Yes, they're really scraping the bottom of the barrel.'

'No,' Andrei retorted, 'you'll do a good job for them. You always do a good job.'

'Why, thank you, brother-in-law.'

There were 'ohs' and 'ahs' regarding the beauty of the table from Gabriela, Chris, and Paul when dinner was called. Andrei looked up and down for something that was not there. He caught an angry signal from his sister and only then did he seat himself in sulking quiet.

It was a splendid meal, one particularly made to please Andrei. During the gefilte fish and horse-radish the conversation bemoaned the state of the theater in Warsaw. The best plays, always French, were slow reaching Warsaw this summer because of the crisis. Gabriela volunteered that the opera season would suffer too. Rachael hoped that the music would not be affected too much, and Deborah hoped so too, because if things went well the conservatory was going to let Rachael have her debut with a major orchestra.

The chicken soup was loaded with noodles. They talked about the Olympics. Stephan knew almost every statistic. Jesse Owens was great – but Uncle Andrei, who played forward on the Polish soccer team, was greater than Jesse Owens and the rest of the Americans put together. Where would Andrei play this year? Depended upon his situation with the army.

Roast chicken, stuffed helsel and noodle and raisin kugel. Chris reckoned he hadn't had a good Jewish meal in months – he was glad Paul had talked him into coming. Gabriela asked for recipes, which Deborah promised to supply by phone next day. Stephan got restless.

Tea and rice pudding. Reflections of the university. Koenig to the dean's chair? Isn't he mixed up with the Nazis? Well, German or not, Franz Koenig was certainly entitled to the post.

Cognac. Rachael helped Zoshia clear the table. Stephan, who had lost all conversation before and after the Olympics discussion disappeared.

And then, with the children gone, world politics.

All of this conversation, and Andrei Androfski had not uttered a word.

'Chris, Gabriela,' Paul Bronski said, 'we have all endured the silent wrath of my brother-in-law, Captain Androfski. Fortunately it was not great enough to ruin my wife's cooking. In his behalf I wish to ask forgiveness for his bad manners.'

'I agree with you, Dr Bronski,' Gabriela said hastily. 'Your behavior is shameful, Andrei.'

Andrei, suddenly exposed, grumbled a low rumble destined to increase in volume. 'I promised my sister no arguments. I keep my promises despite the inconveniences it causes me.'

'I think it would have been better to argue and get it off your chest rather than sulk like Stephan and try to make everyone at the table as miserable as you,' Paul shot back.

'You promised, Paul. Stop baiting him,' Deborah said.

'Let Captain Androfski speak before he explodes.'

'Paul, you're leaving in the morning. Let's not have an argument tonight?' Deborah pleaded.

'Why, dear? Don't you want me to remember home as it always is?'

'I am a man of my word,' Andrei said. 'But I also remember my home as it always was. Friday night and I sit at my sister's table and there are no candles or benediction.'

'Is that what has been bothering you, brother-in-law?'

'Yes, it is the Sabbath.'

'We stopped facing east a year ago, Andrei.'

'Oh, I knew it was coming. I didn't know you could break her down so quickly. I remember when we lived in the slums on Stawki Street. God, we were poor. But we were Jews. And when we moved to that fancy neighborhood on Sliska Street and Momma died, I had a sister then who was the head of a Jewish house.'

'Andrei, let's stop this here and now,' Deborah said.

Chris and Gabriela were suddenly trapped in the midst of the flying words of a family feud. They looked helplessly at each other as Andrei sprang to his feet and slammed his napkin down.

'Dr Bronski started this. Not I. Deborah, I sat with Stephan and talked to him. He does not even know he is a Jew. What happens when he becomes thirteen? Your only son not given a bar mitzvah. I'm glad Momma and Poppa are not alive to see this day.'

Paul Bronski seemed to be delighted in having opened Andrei up. 'Deborah and I have been married sixteen years. Isn't it about time you got onto the idea we wish to live our own lives without consultation from you?'

'Paul, I am Andrei Androfski, the only Jewish officer in my Ulany regiment. But every man knows who I am and what I am.'

'I am Dr Paul Bronski and they know who I am too. Just a minute, Andrei. I explored your galloping Zionism. It isn't my way to salvation. It didn't appeal to me either.'

'And your name didn't appeal to you either, did it, Paul? Samuel Goldfarb. Son of a Parysowski Place peddler.'

'You are so right, Andrei. Nothing about Parysowski Place appeals to me. Not its poverty or its smells or the weeping and wailing, waiting for the Messiah to come. The Jews are the ones who have caused their own troubles in Poland, and I want to live in my country as an equal, not as an enemy or a stranger.'

'And does that justify your sitting on the council of the Students Union, those dirty little fascists who throw stones through the windows of Jewish booksellers?'

'I didn't back those actions.'

'Nor did you try to stop them. You know why? Well, I'll tell you. You follow a coward's path.'

'How dare you?' Deborah said.

'It is you who is the coward and not I, Andrei, because I have enough courage to say that Judaism means nothing to me and I want no part of it. And you go to your holyroller Zionist meetings not believing what you hear, looking for false salvation.'

The words rained down on Andrei like blows. Paul had struck a nerve and his foe turned white and trembled and the room grew breathlessly quiet, waiting for that short fuse to sizzle to the bomb. But Andrei spoke in a deliberate, trembling rattle. 'You are a fool, Paul Bronski. Being a Jew is not a matter of choice. And one sweet day soon, I fear, it will crash down on you and destroy all your logic and smart talk. God, you're in for a rude awakening, because you are a Jew, whether you want to be or choose to be – or not.'

'Stop it!' Deborah screamed. 'This is my home. You will never do this again if you want to set foot in here, nor will you ever see Stephan or Rachael. Paul is my husband. You will respect him.'

Andrei hung his head. 'I – should do something about my temper,' he said softly. 'I have caused a scene in front of guests. Why should I care, really, so long as you are happy?'

'I am happy,' Deborah said.

'It is only ... Your words – and your eyes do not march to the same tune.'

Andrei walked from the table quickly.

'Andrei!' Deborah called. 'Where are you going?'

'To drink. To drink and drink and drink to Dr Paul Bronski, the king of the converts!'

Deborah started after him. Gabriela quickly stepped from the table and blocked her way. 'Let him go, Deborah,' she said. 'He is all wound up like a piece of spring steel from the tension on the border. You know Andrei, he will be here tomorrow with apologies. Let him go.'

The slam of the front door resounded like a cannon shot throughout the house.

'Chris, keep an eye on him, please,' Gabriela said.

Chris nodded and followed without a word.

When Chris was gone, Deborah sank into her chair, ashen-faced.

Paul Bronski, feeling contented as a Cheshire cat, soothed, 'Don't let him hurt you so, dear.'

Deborah looked up through tear-filled eyes. 'He knew ... he knew. And that is what hurts. My husband is going away and I wanted to light the candles tonight like a Jewish mother – and Andrei knew.'

And all the cunning of Paul's traps slammed in on him in an unexpected and stunning defeat and he sagged and walked toward the door.

'Paul!' Deborah ordered sharply. 'See Gabriela home.'

'No, that's all right, Deborah. Let's you and I have another cup of tea and then I'll find my rampaging cavalier in an hour or so. And don't you worry about Andrei – I am the one who loves him. And sometimes, dear Lord, it is almost worth the pain.'

Chapter Six

The revolutionary activities of Fryderyk Rak had made it increasingly more dangerous for him to live in Poland partitioned between Russia, Germany, and the Austro-Hungarian Empire. He went into self-imposed exile along with many patriots. In France he established himself as one of the leading hydroelectric engineers in Europe.

After the war, in 1918, when Poland had returned to statehood, Fryderyk Rak returned to Warsaw with his wife and daughters, Regina and Gabriela. The new Poland was filled with urgent needs. A hundred years of occupation had left it in a medieval condition. Hydroelectric projects were given an urgent priority. Fryderyk Rak was one of the few Poles with training and experience to cope with the challenge.

He gained neither great wealth nor fame, but a fair measure of each. His most impressive contribution was the part his firm of engineers played in the building of Gdynia. The Versailles Treaty had given new Poland a route to the sea through the Polish Corridor. The only port at the time was Danzig, a so-called 'free city' fraught with political dynamite and largely inhabited by unfriendly Germans. Common sense made the building of a Polish seaport a necessity, and thus Gdynia was created.

In exile, he had become a rabid skiing enthusiast. With the first snowbursts of winter he would pack the Rak family off to the Alps. His doctor warned him there were slopes for thirty-year-olds and slopes for fifty-year-olds, but he indulged in his inbred stubborn Polish pride by defying the advice and finding the most dangerous, swiftest ways to get down the mountainsides. He died at the age of fifty from a heart attack at the bottom of a treacherous run called K-94, aptly nicknamed, 'the butcher,' and left behind him a well-endowed widow and her two daughters.

In her bereavement, Madam Rak turned to the comfort of her only close living relative, a brother in Chicago. She came out of her period of mourning well stocked with suitors of Polish descent and saw little reason to return to the old country, never having shared Fryderyk's passion for it. Regina, the oldest daughter, was a rather plain, rather plump girl who was completely content to marry a nice Polish boy whose family imported Polish hams and become an American housewife with a home in Evanston, within gossiping distance of Mother.

Gabriela, the youngest, was of her father's breed; independent, stubborn, and self-centered. Fryderyk Rak had been a liberal man and an indulgent father. Her uncle, however, had taken his position as head of the family and protector of his widowed sister and her offspring with complete seriousness. He had brought with him from Poland much of the old-country traditions of family tyrant. Gabriela rebelled. Warsaw and life with Father were her happiest memories. She received an impressive education from stern nuns in expensive and exclusive Catholic girls' schools, where she prayed each night that the Virgin Mother would help her get back to Warsaw.

As soon as she was of legal age and came into her part of the inheritance, she made straight back. Gabriela's mastery of English, French, German, and Polish and her American education brought her a job with the American Embassy as a teacher. Later she became a nearly indispensable member of the staff and was the only Polish national permitted to work on classified material.

The allowance from her father's estate and her job allowed her to enter that upper echelon of society which had made Warsaw the Paris of the East. There was a never-ending circle of culture and trivia and romance. Gabriela was an extremely pretty girl. Her calendar never lacked for dates. She was a classic Polish beauty with white-blond hair and sparkling eyes, but a smaller, petite version.

Like many world travelers, she developed a great degree of sophistication, enjoying flirtations and being romanced. Every few months there was a proposal of marriage to weigh and discard. Gabriela enjoyed her freedom. She measured her relationships with a rather cold-blooded shrewdness. She was content in Warsaw. This was the place – it always was. She realized that she would eventually find the man to go with the place, but life was good and she was in no hurry. Her only indiscretion had been a forgivable girlhood fling with an instructor whose after-school instructions were unforgivable.

When Gabriela left the Bronski house, she began her search for Andrei and Chris at Jerusalem Boulevard, knowing that neither of them did any serious drinking south of there. She checked newsmen's and Zionists' hangouts until she picked up their trail. Once on the scent, she quickened her search, as they had left their calling cards in the form of two medium-sized disturbances and one tiny brawl.

She entered the Bristol Hotel and made straight for the little bar inside the entrance of the night club. A new South American band was playing the latest tangos. Tangos were all the rage now. Perhaps, Gabriela thought, if Andrei is not too far gone, I can bring him back here to dance. He is such a lovely dancer when he wants to be.

She adjusted her eyes to the darkness and warded off the advance of a lone male in a crisp, authoritative voice.

'Yes, ma'am,' the bartender said, 'they sure were here. Left about a half hour ago.'

'In what condition?'

'Soused. Mr de Monti a little worse off than his officer friend.'

Well, there go my tangos, Gabriela thought.

'Any idea of where they were going?'

'Mr de Monti usually likes to cap off his benders in the Old Town. Says he likes to drink in Polish folklore.'

Gabriela stopped for a moment in the lobby and stared into the ballroom. It was filled with elegant Polish officers in uniform and elegant ladies in the latest Paris gowns and bearded, beribboned diplomats. It was a high-ceilinged room with dark mahogany paneling twisted into ornate gingerbread and herringbone parquet floors polished to a dazzle. Floor-to-ceiling mirrors alternated with floor-to-ceiling tapestries depicting grim Polish heroes on statuesque white horses with billowing manes leading determined troops into battle. The immense crystal chandelier sparkled, and the elegant ladies and gentlemen hopped around the room in a counterclockwise circle in step with a lively polka. And when the music stopped, the gentlemen bent from the waist and kissed the ladies' hands. Some responded with flirtatious eyes from behind fans and others by looking off in boredom.

It was as though Gabriela looked at two different centuries from the slinky night club to the grand ballroom. The music faded as she walked north to the Old Town. It was balmy out, and the later theater- and movie-goers wandered along arm in arm and the streetwalkers prowled for business and the droshkas rolled by, holding cuddling couples.

She stopped for a moment on the central bridge and leaned on the rail. Far below, the commuter trains loaded up and sped over the river to Praga.

Gabriela hummed the polka to herself and was soon steeped in nostalgia. It was on a warm night like this that she had met Andrei and it was in a big, brilliant ballroom. Good Lord, Gabriela thought, has it been only two years? It seemed hard to recall a life between her father's death and meeting Andrei. Only two years ... only two years.

The Seventh Ulany Brigade held its annual officers' affair at the Europa Hotel. This was the eighth in a line of twenty-six events that illuminated the fall and winter season. The Seventh Ulanys had a particularly long string of great cavalry charges which could trace its beginnings back to the first king, Casimir the Great, in the Middle Ages. Therefore, the Seventh Ulany affair always brought out the cream of Warsaw.

Gabriela Rak, as usual, was nearly crushed by the over-eager band of bachelor officers. They were particularly out of step, more pompous than the Second and Fourth Ulanys combined, and their humor less amusing than that of any regiment of the season.

At the end of the first hour of violent polkas Gabriela retreated to the sanctity of the powder room to rearrange herself for the second round.

Her closest friend, Martha Thompson, wife of her immediate superior at the Embassy, had a cigarette with her. Martha was a clever woman, a mother of three who retained that particular American chic.

Gabriela was bored. The new season was eight grand balls old and nothing was in prospect for even a mild flirtation.

Martha Thompson, on the other hand, was unvarnished in her enthusiasm. 'Aren't they all so beautiful in their boots?' she said.

'Good Lord, Martha, you can't be serious. I've never seen so many fishy-eyed officers in a single brigade.'

'Trouble with you, Gaby, you've driven off all the serious contenders. You're a pampered, spoiled little girl.'

'I've got an abnormal desire to crack some of them over the skull when they bow and slobber on my hand.'

'I kind of like it. Well, young lady, don't wake one morning and find that the only thing left that's any good is much married – or full of complications. Take a stupid one and train him your way.'

Gabriela smiled. 'Come on, Martha, let's have another go at it.'

She braced for the next onslaught and re-entered the ballroom on Martha's arm. Both of them saw him at the same time. In fact, every pair of eyes seemed set on the door as the epitome of a Polish cavalry officer, Lieutenant Andrei Androfski, entered. After that second of awesome silence, which he sensed, he was engulfed by adoring, back-clapping cronies and was soon explaining with bravado how he had performed his latest athletic feat, the winning of the light heavyweight wrestling championship of the Polish Army.

'Isn't he yummy,' Martha said.

Gabriela was still staring.

'Who is he?'

'Forget about him, Gaby. You're really bucking city hall. No one has been able to solve him.'

'So?'

'Some say he's a Tibetan monk who has taken chastity vows. Others say he has mistresses stashed all over Warsaw.'

'Who is he?'

'Lieutenant Androfski.'

'The Tarzan of the Ulanys?'

Martha sighed. 'Well, back to my drab old reliable husband.'

Gabriela took Martha's elbow. 'Have Tommy introduce me to Lieutenant Androfski.'

'Well, well. A new hat at Madam Phoebe's says you can't get him to see you home.'

'I'll meet you there at noon. I know just the one I want.'

When Thompson introduced Andrei to Gabriela, he neither bowed nor kissed her hand. He nodded politely and waited for the usual words – 'So you're the famous Andrei Androfski!'

'I didn't catch your name,' Gabriela said.

A clever opening gambit, Andrei thought. 'I know your name, Miss Rak. Like so many, I am an admirer of the work of your late father, so my name is unimportant. You can just snap your fingers and say "hey you" and I'll know you are addressing me.'

It won't be such a dull evening after all, Gabriela thought.

What a lot of nonsense, Andrei thought, to play Victorian fencing games with spoiled brats.

'I have the next set of dances open, Lieutenant.'

Brother, he thought, this one doesn't even play coy. Works without a fan. Moving in for the kill already. Well, let's look it over. Pretty little thing all right, a little on the lean side ...

'You *do* dance, Lieutenant?'

'As a matter of fact, I am an excellent dancer, but frankly I do it only as an accommodation.'

Well! Does *he* know it.

'If it annoys you so much, why did you bother to come?'

'My colonel ordered me to come. You see, I have covered my brigade with glory.'

Of all the fantastic conceit!

Gabriela was about to walk off but saw Martha Thompson out of the corner of her eye. Martha was nudging Tommy and snickering. The music started.

'I am certain you won't have any trouble finding a partner, Miss Rak,' Andrei said. 'There's a whole line of stags drooling for you over there.'

As he started his retreat Gabriela impulsively snapped her finger and said, 'Hey you.'

Andrei walked toward her slowly, put his arm about her, and whisked her onto the dance floor. He was not boasting about his prowess as a dancer. Every female eye in the room watched them enviously. Gabriela was furious with herself for behaving as she knew a thousand girls had done before. But she liked being in his arms. They were nicer than any pair of arms she had been in for a year. This made her angrier, because he was managing to convey the feeling that he would just as soon be dancing with a broom.

The thought of bringing this egotistical roughrider to heel began to delight her. What a wonderful idea to torment him! How lovely to end the evening giving Lieutenant Androfski just enough to make him plead ... then slam the door in his face. First, the hat from Martha Thompson.

'I should like you to see me home later,' she said at the end of the set of dances.

Her trap was swift and complete. When one is playing the game at a grand ball and one is a Ulan, it would be an unpardonable discourtesy to reject a lady's 'request.'

'Perhaps your escort may take exception,' he answered.

'I came with Mr Thompson of the American Embassy – and Mrs Thompson. I am quite free, Lieutenant – or is it necessary for me to get it in the form of an order from your colonel?'

He smiled weakly. 'I will be delighted.'

As the automobiles were being driven up to the entrance, Mr Thompson offered them a ride.

'It is so nice and balmy out, why don't we walk, Lieutenant?'

'If you'd like.'

'Good night, Tommy. Good night, Martha. Don't forget – Madam Phoebe's at noon tomorrow.'

It was late and the streets were empty except for a few drunks. There was only the sound of their own footsteps and a very distant droshka.

Gabriela stopped suddenly. 'I was terribly silly and rude to you,' she said, 'and I shouldn't have forced you to bring me home. If you would see me to a droshka –'

'Nonsense. I'll be glad to take you home.'

'You don't have to be polite any more – we are off battle limits.'

'Matter of fact,' Andrei said, 'I was a little bit rough on you too. I really don't behave like a pompous ass. I like you better now that I know you work for a living.'

He offered her his arm, and she took it and they crossed the street. She smelled good and she felt good and he was wonderfully aware of her. He whistled softly to hide his feelings.

'I knew you were trying to anger me,' she said. 'I watched you after we danced. You are really very shy and self-conscious, you know.'

'I don't want to sound as if I'm bragging, but – I guess everyone expects me to act a certain way.'

'And you don't really like it, do you?'

'No, not always. Especially at these dances ...'

'Why?'

'Never mind.'

'No, tell me.'

'I don't have very much in common with the people who go to grand balls.'

'A famous Ulan like you – all those adoring men and women …'

'I don't belong with them.'

'Why?'

'I'm not going to spoil your evening with all the serious, complicated things I am.'

They walked in silence for the final block. Both of them had moved too quickly to that strange feeling of helplessness at the discovery that they were suddenly infatuated with each other, and it was frightening for them. The game was over for Gabriela. He had behaved nicely and she did not wish to play the tease but wanted to know more about this man who could be a peacock one moment, then sink into boyishness in another.

Her flat was in a large old mansion on the Square of the Three Crosses facing St Alexander's Church. She stopped before the door and fumbled in her purse for her key and handed it to him. Andrei unlocked the door and handed the key back.

'Good night, Miss Rak,' he said.

They shook hands.

'Lieutenant Androfski. I was brought up in America, as you know, and sometimes we do things a little differently. Would you consider me terribly brash if I said I would like to see you again, very soon?'

He took his hand from hers slowly and became pitifully and awkwardly shy. 'I am afraid not, Miss Rak,' he said quickly, and turned and walked off.

Gabriela was stunned at her own words, more stunned at his action. She ran up the steps, watery-eyed, confused, and hurt and angry.

A large group of American VIPs were flying in from Paris. It included three congressmen and their wives and an advisory board of industrialists for a prospective American loan to build a dam on the Warta River.

'We want to help get this loan pushed through,' Thompson said to Gabriela. 'I've got to be away in Krakow when they arrive. Can you make up their itinerary and handle them for two days till I get back?'

'Anything special you want them to see?'

'The usual junk around Warsaw. Lunch with the Ambassador, press conference, whatever is going at the opera and theater. Meanwhile, draw up a list for their reception.'

'Will do. Don't worry about a thing.'

'Here's all the dope. Look this over. Play it to Congressman Galinowski, big Polish district in Gary. Stay close to Cranebrook; he talks too much.'

'Tommy, the last time we had wives, the Ministry of Information sent over a real creep to escort them around. Why don't we try someone else?'

'Like what?'

Gabriela shrugged. 'Oh, I don't know. Why not – well, get one of those big Ulany officers. The Seventh Ulanys have a dozen real charmers who speak English.'

'Oh, sister,' Thompson mumbled. 'He's already cost me one hat.' He flicked the inter-com and spoke through it. 'Mildred. Call up the commanding general at the Citadel. On that group of VIPs coming in day after tomorrow, we're going to need an escort for the wives. Make it important . . . big loan to Poland involved. See if you can get Lieutenant Andrei Androfski – from the Seventh Ulanys – placed on detached duty for PR. Have him report to Miss Rak.' He flicked off the switch. Gabriela's face was crimson. 'Just call me Cupid Thompson.'

If Andrei was livid with rage, which he was, he did nothing to show it. He reported to Miss Rak and took his orders with complete detachment and oozed Polish charm playing escort to the three elderly but appreciative American ladies. Andrei even managed to hold his temper when one of the ladies discovered he was on the national soccer team and insisted he take off his boots so she could see the muscles in his calves.

At the end of the third day he delivered them to their suites and reported to Miss Rak at the Embassy.

'I must say, everyone is commenting on my master stroke of public relations. You have made a noble contribution to a dam on the Warta River.'

'Thank you,' Andrei said stiffly.

'In fact, Lieutenant, they are so pleased with your company, they particularly asked if you would escort them on a two-day trip to Krakow while the committee surveys the proposed dam site.'

'Miss Rak,' Andrei said, 'I feel I am denying fellow officers a tremendous experience and wish to share this duty with some others –'

'But they particularly asked for you. You *do* want to see that dam on the Warta?'

'Miss Rak. To hell with the dam on the Warta. I hurt your pride the other night and you have made me eat humble pie. You win, I lose. Since I have been taking those – those – nice ladies around Warsaw my brigade has lost an important soccer match and my home is dying of loneliness. You will have to find someone else to assume this pleasurable duty, because it will take a court-martial to bring me back tomorrow.'

'I think that is terribly un-Polish of you.'

'Will you let me return to my brigade?'

Gabriela smiled. 'If you take me home.'

This time when he handed her the key she walked through the door, leaving it open. 'Come on up,' she said.

Andrei followed awkwardly into a small but tastefully and lavishly furnished living room. The luxury seemed to add to his discomfort. She threw open the french doors and stepped out on the balcony overlooking the Square of the Three Crosses. Andrei stood near the front door, fiddling with his hat.

'Close the door and come on in. I won't bite you.'

As he reached the balcony, Gabriela spun around, her eyes ablaze with anger. 'You are very right, Lieutenant. I have never suffered such humiliation.'

'You've had your revenge.'

'No, I haven't.'

'I wish you wouldn't make an affair of honor out of this.'

'I have never chased a man in my life, nor have I ever been rejected.'

'My, what an angry little terrier you are.'

'I made it obvious that I found you attractive. I would like to know exactly why you delight in making me feel like some sort of cheap trollop.'

'I told you. I don't like places like the grand ballroom of the Bristol – or here. I don't belong here.'

'You must certainly know that with a wink of your eye you could obtain the family fortunes of every eligible spinster in Warsaw.'

'I have no desire to be anything but what I am.'

'And what are you?'

'I am a Jew. I am not inclined to do the things necessary to reach a position I don't covet in the first place. To be sure, I'm one of those good Jew boys. I can throw a javelin farther and jump a horse higher than almost any man in Poland. So, you see, there's a gentlemen's agreement in the Ulanys not to mention publicly my tainted ancestry.'

'Is that any reason to treat me as you did?'

'Miss Rak, I don't know how advanced your American education was, but in Poland it is the general consensus we use nice tender young Catholic girls like you for sacrificial offerings.'

Gabriela walked back into the living room and braced herself against a lamp table and blew a long, deep breath. 'Well, I asked for it. I owe you an apology. At least my pride has been served. I thought you disliked me.'

'Not at all. I like you very much.'

'Underneath that layer of bluster you are a very sensitive man.'

'I'm engaged in serious work. I only serve half time in the army.'

'What kind of work?'

'You wouldn't be interested.'

'I think I would.'

'I am a Zionist.'

'Oh yes, I've heard something about it. Redemption of Palestine or something like that.'

'Yes, something like that.'

'Don't be so touchy. What do you do?'

'I'm an organizer and on the executive board of an organization called the Bathyrans.'

'Bathyrans? What an odd name.'

'It was a group of Jewish warriors sent out by Herod to defend against infiltrators ... Look, this doesn't interest you.'

'But it does. And what do your Bathyrans do?'

'We follow certain principles of Zionism, which tells us we must re-establish our ancient homeland in Palestine, and we run an orphanage and have a farm outside Warsaw. On the farm we train youngsters in the rededication to the land. When we are able to raise enough money, we buy a piece of land in Palestine and send off a new group to start a colony.'

'Why on earth would you do that?'

Andrei's patience snapped. 'Because, Miss Rak, the Polish people have not allowed us to own or farm land and –' He stopped short and lowered his voice. 'Let's stop this. You don't give a damn about Zionism and I feel like a fool here.'

'I am trying to be friendly.'

'Miss Rak, between Jerusalem Boulevard and Stawki Street over three hundred thousand people live in a world you know nothing about. Your high and mighty writers call it the "Black Continent." It happens to be my world.'

He put on his hat and walked toward the door.

'Lieutenant. All this – why does all this mean that we can't be friends?'

Andrei walked toward her slowly. 'What do you want from me? I am not interested in a romance.'

'Really . . .'

'Stop this silly damned game. I am a poor man, but I don't mind it in the least because I am doing something that makes me happy. I am and never will be anything you consider important. As far as anything in common, we may as well be living on different planets.'

Gabriela's voice trembled. 'I don't know why I let you get me so angry. You are very presumptuous. Try to be friendly with someone, and immediately they've got illusions of grandeur.'

'I know exactly what's going on in that shrewd little mind of yours and I'll tell you how presumptuous I am. If you annoy me again I am going to rip every stitch of clothing off your body and I am going to make love to you in exactly the way you know I can.'

She was small, but her slap was mighty.

Andrei lifted her in his arms. 'Scream and I'll blacken both your eyes,' he said.

Gabriela was too terrified to know whether he was bluffing or not. He walked in the bedroom to the big canopied, satin-covered bed.

'On the second thought,' he said, 'go out and get a little more flesh on you. You're too skinny for me to trouble with.' He flung her on the bed and left.

'Did he do that!' Martha Thompson exclaimed.

Gabriela nodded and poured tea and sliced the apple cake.

'So what did you do?'

'Do? Nothing. I was absolutely terrified. You can imagine.'

Martha sipped her tea, nibbled on the cake, and sighed. 'Oh dear, why doesn't something like that ever happen to me?'

Suddenly Gabriela pulled out a handkerchief, turned her face, and began to sniffle. 'Why, Gabriela Rak, I've never seen you cry.'

'I don't know what's gotten into me lately. I've been so jumpy since I've met him. All someone has to do is look at me sideways and I start to cry.' And she bawled. 'No one has ever been able to get me so angry,' she sobbed unevenly. 'He's conceited and detestable. Oh God, I hate him!'

Martha sat alongside her on the couch and offered a sympathetic shoulder.

'I hate him!'

'Sure you do,' Martha comforted, 'sure you do.'

Gabriela pulled away and brought herself under control. 'I am behaving like a fool.'

'Welcome to this world of fools. You took a long time joining us, but you're making up for it all at once. You've had this coming to you, Gabriela. You've been running the show all your life.'

'He's a complete opposite of everything I've ever known. Like a stranger from a foreign land.'

'You know what your old Aunt Martha always said. The only good ones are either much married or full of complications.'

'Complications! The terrible part of it is that I'm scared to death of being snubbed again. I've done just about everything but throw myself at his feet, and that, I'll never do.'

'You're going to have to. Alternative, have Tommy send you to Krakow for a long trip.'

Gabriela shook her head slowly. 'I didn't think anything so simple could be so painful. I want to see him so badly I could burst. I just don't know what to do.'

'Well, honey, no matter what this Lieutenant Androfski is, one thing is for certain. He *is* a man.'

Andrei was stretched out on his bed, his feet propped up on the iron bedstead. He stared blankly at the ceiling, ignoring Alexander Brandel, who was fishing through papers at the old round table in the center of the room.

'I am against appointing Brayloff to edit the paper. He is inclined to lean too much toward the Revisionists' point of view. What do you think, Andrei?'

Andrei grunted.

'Ideally, Ervin Rosenblum would be perfect. However, we can't pay him what he is earning on the outside. Maybe, if we could use Ervin in an advisory capacity ... I'll talk to him. Now, Andrei, about the Lodz Chapter – you're going to have to give their problems your attention right away.' Alexander stopped. 'I'm maybe talking to the wall tonight? You haven't heard a thing I've said.'

Andrei spun off the bed, shoved his hands in his pockets, and leaned against the wall. 'I heard, I heard.'

'So what do you think?'

'To hell with Brayloff, to hell with Ervin Rosenblum, to hell with the Lodz Chapter. To hell with the whole goddamned Zionist movement!'

'So now that you've made your great proclamation, maybe you might tell me what is eating you up. You have been uncivilized for a week.'

'I've been thinking. Maybe I'll stay in the army.'

Alexander Brandel muffled his shock at the pronouncement. 'Fine,' he said. 'I'll predict you'll be the first Jew to become Polish Chief of Staff.'

'I'm not joking, Alex. Here I am, twenty-six years old, and what am I? Fighting for a cause that's all but hopeless. Putting on a big front at the time ... working the clock out ... living in rooms like this ... Maybe I'm crazy for not taking the one chance I'll ever have to really be something. I walked today. I walked and I thought. I walked around Stawki Street where I lived when I was a boy, and it scared me a little – maybe that's where I'll end up when all this is over. And I walked to the Avenue of the Marshals and Jerusalem Boulevard. That's where I could be if I set my mind to it.'

'And while you were walking, did you walk along the Square of the Three Crosses and past the American Embassy?'

Andrei turned around angrily.

'Thompson at the Embassy called me up and invited me to lunch today. It seems there is a young lady there almost as miserable as you are.'

'God Almighty! Can't I even have a broken heart in privacy?'

'Not if you're Andrei Androfski.'

'I don't want a lecture about Jewish boys and *shikses*.'

Alex shrugged. 'If a *shikse* was good enough for Moses, a *shikse* is good enough for Androfski. I know all the things you are thinking now. Why am I here? Why am I beating my brains out doing this? But if you are able to believe in Zionism the same way some of the priests and nuns believe in Catholicism and the same way the Hassidim believe in Judaism, then you will find the ultimate reward of peace of mind greater than any sacrifice.'

Andrei knew the words came from a man who could have gained great recognition and economic reward had he not chosen the path of Zionism. Somehow, Alex did not seem to be giving anything up. If only he could believe in Zionism like that.

'Andrei, you stand for something to all of us. We love you.'

'So I will lower myself in the eyes of my friends and I will hurt them by taking up with a Catholic girl.'

'I said we love you. The only way you could ever hurt your true friends is by hurting yourself.'

'Do me a favor and go home, Alex.'

Alexander Brandel put all his papers together and stuffed them into his battered brief case. He stuck his cap on his head and wrapped the muffler, which he wore summer or winter, about his neck, and walked to the door.

'Alex!'

'Yes?'

'I'm sorry. I'll – be off duty in a week. I'll take that trip to Lodz right away. Maybe I should also swing around the country and see the chapters in Lublin and Lemberg.'

'That may be a good idea,' Alex said.

After Alex had left, Andrei poured himself a half glass of vodka, downed it in a single swallow, and took up a caged pacing of the confines of the room.

He stopped and wound up his record player. A scratchy sonata struggled its way flatly out of the sound head. He turned off the lights except the one over the table in the center of the room and walked to his books. He took a book of Hayim Nachman Bialik, the prince of poets of Zionism.

'This is the last generation of Jews which will live in bondage and the first which will live in freedom,' Bialik had written.

He was in no mood for Bialik. Another book. One filled with fury. Here. John Steinbeck, his favorite author.

IN DUBIOUS BATTLE

Innumerable force of Spirits armed,
That durst dislike his reign, and, me preferring,
His utmost power with adverse power opposed,
In dubious battle on the plains of Heaven
And shook his throne. What though the field be lost?
All is not lost – the unconquerable will,
And study of revenge, immortal hate,
And courage never to submit or yield;
And what is else not to be overcome?

Andrei filled his glass again. Now there is a man who understands, he thought. Steinbeck knows of fighting for lost causes. In dubious battle . . . His battle . . .

There was a soft, almost imperceptible knock on the door.

'Come in, it's open.'

Gabriela Rak stood in the doorway. Andrei seized the edge of the table, daring not to move or speak. She walked across the room into the shadow of the books. 'I thought I would take a walk north from Jerusalem Boulevard. I am intrigued by these three hundred and fifty thousand people from the Black Continent.' Her fingers ran over the backs of the books. 'I see you read in Russian and English as well as Polish. What is this here, this odd script? It must be Yiddish, or Hebrew maybe? A. D. Gordon. They have a volume of A. D. Gordon at the Embassy library. Let me see now. "Physical labor is the basis of human existence . . . it is spiritually necessary, and nature is the basis of culture, man's elevated creation. However, to avoid exploitation, the soil must not be the property of an individual." How is that for my first lesson in Zionism?'

'What are you doing here?' Andrei croaked.

She leaned against the books and stiffened, her eyes closed and her teeth clenched, and tears fell down her cheeks. 'Lieutenant Androfski. I am twenty-three years old. I am not a virgin. My father left me a considerable endowment. What else would you care to know about me?'

Andrei's hand pawed helplessly around the table. At last his fist smashed down on it. 'Why don't you leave me alone?'

'I don't know what has happened to me and I don't seem to care. As you can see, I'm throwing myself at your feet. I beg you, don't send me away.'

She turned and wept uncontrollably.

And she felt his hand on her shoulder, and it was gentle. 'Gabriela ... Gabriela ...'

From that moment when she was consumed by his great and wonderful power, all the things she had considered important to her way of life ceased to be important.

Gabriela knew with no uncertainty that there had never been nor ever would be again a man like Andrei Androfski. Those things which society and its religions and philosophies and economies had imposed upon them as great barriers came crumbling down. Gabriela had been a selfish woman. She suddenly found herself able to give with a power of giving that she did not realize she possessed.

For to her, Andrei was like David of the Bible. He was at one time all that was strong and all that was weak in a single man.

He had within him the power to snuff out a life in an angry fit. Yet there had never been a man who could touch her with such a gentleness.

He was a giant who lived his life for a single ideal. He was a helpless boy who became confused or pouted or angered at a seeming trifle.

He was a symbol of strength to his friends. He would get roaring drunk when the frustrations became too difficult.

But with him there were moments of electric flaring of emotions. There were moments of hurt and pain deeper than any she had known except at the death of her father. There were the great expectations fulfilled with the sensuous thrills of pure physical pleasure.

To her friends it seemed that her willingness to become the mistress of a Jewish pauper was a terrible calamity. For Gabriela, the things she surrendered seemed insignificant and indeed no sacrifice for loving a man who made her happier than she had ever been in her life.

Little by little she divorced herself from the treadmill about which she centered her activities. Gabriela accepted the hard fact that her affair with Andrei might never be resolved in a marriage. She understood that she must never step on the dangerous ground of tampering with his work. She knew he would not be changed over to any of her images. Andrei was Andrei, and she had to take him and everything he was as he was.

Andrei had at last met in Gabriela Rak a woman who could match him fury for fury, passion for passion, anger for anger. She often flared into those stubborn streaks of pride which would be resolved only when he humbled himself or blurted an awkward apology. He sat quietly and took without a whimper the wrath of her anger when he had been out on a binge. He instinctively knew when to back down from a conflict. For his reward he found moments he had never known. Moments when she felt his depression and frustrations over the failures in his work. In those moments she was able to reach him with compassion as he had never been reached before.

He knew he had tamed a wild mare, but one who always kept that streak of rebellion. Gabriela demanded her religious identity. He insisted that she not completely withdraw from all those things which had been her life, and he took many of her friends as his.

And they discovered that they had as many things in common as they once believed had kept them apart. They shared a mutual love of music and books and theater. On occasion he would admit he enjoyed dancing with her.

Gabriela did not strain herself for acceptance among his friends but entered part of his strange world and found those closest to him took to her with sincerity.

His trips around Poland and his leaves from the army always brought him home to days and nights of love-making which never wearied or slackened in intensity.

Only two years ago, Gabriela thought. Only two years since I met my Andrei. She watched from the bridge as the last commuter train left for Praga, then walked north again in pursuit of Andrei and Christopher de Monti.

Chapter Seven

Fukier's ancient Wine Cellar in the Old Town was submerged in noises and smoke and smells. The immense casks leaked age-old wines, which blended with the smells of ales and cheeses. The voices of rowdy bohemians were somewhat buffered by thousands of bottles lining the walls. Amid the uproar, the trio of gypsy musicians inched their way from table to table.

The gypsies stopped and hovered over the table, determined to entertain Andrei and Chris. Andrei emptied his mug, belched, and put a coin on the table. The violinist snatched it and downbeated the accordionist and an unwashed tamborine-rattling female vocalist.

'Jesus Christ,' Christopher de Monti mumbled, 'Jesus Christ. Even the gypsies play Chopin.'

'Chopin is a national hero. Chopin gives us courage!'

'Oh balls! He was a tubercular little wart shacked up with a cigar-smoking French whore who cashed in on Polish misery.'

'Is that nice?'

The waitress fought her way to their table, slung down a pair of plates, a loaf of dark rye bread, and a small ham, along with more vodka.

The gypsies played 'O Sole Mio.'

'Christ, that's worse than Chopin,' Chris said.

Andrei gulped down a half pint of vodka and wiped his mouth with the back of his sleeve.

'Let us not digress from our conversation,' he said. 'The Germans attack, we will counterattack, naturally. My steed, Batory, and I will be the first two into Berlin.'

Chris weaved and focused on the ham. He raised his fork, aimed, and plunged it deeply. 'This is Poland,' he announced. He picked up a knife and cut the ham in two. 'One slice goes to Germany. 'Nother slice goes to Russia. No more Poland. All gone. Andrei, tell them goddamn gypsies to blow. So anyhow, all your goddamn poets will write tired sonnets about the good old days when the noblemen kicked the piss out of the peasants and the peasants kicked the piss out of the Jews. Then! Some half-assed piano player will play benefit concerts to the Poles in Chicago. All Chopin concerts. And in a hundred years everybody will say – Jesus Christ, let's put Poland back together – we're sick of hearing Chopin concerts. And in a hundred and two years, the Russians and Germans will start up again.'

Andrei belched again. Chris tried to continue his lecture, but his elbow kept slipping from the table each time he tried to point to Russian Poland. The violin cried. And when a gypsy violin cried in Fukier's, men cried too. 'Chris, my dear friend,' sniffed Andrei, 'take my sister away from that no-good bastard Bronski.'

Chris hung his head. 'Don't mention a lady's name in a bar, sir. Goddamn broad.'

Andrei's sympathetic hand fell on Chris's shoulder. 'Damned broad,' he agreed.

Andrei emptied, then refilled his mug. 'Hitler's bluffing.'

'Hell he is.'

'He's scared of our counterattack.'

'Counterattack, my butt.' Chris's fist struck the table. He spread it clean, shoving bottles and plates and glasses into one corner. 'This table is Poland.'

'I thought the ham was Poland.'

'The ham is Poland *A*. This is Poland *B*. See the table, stupid? See how nice and flat it is? Perfect for tanks. The Germans have them. They got big ones, little ones, fast ones, heavy ones. Tried and tested in Spain. That General Staff of yours had any sense, they'd pull back now.'

'Pull back!' the Ulan officer cried in horror.

'Pull back, I said. Blunt the first German thrust on the Warta River. Then drop everything in back of the Vistula and make your stand.'

'Back of the Vistula! You dare insinuate we give up Silesia and Warsaw?'

'Hell yes. They'll take it anyhow. Chopin or no Chopin. If you can hold a Vistula line for three or four months, the British and French will have to start something on the western front.'

'Oh, big strategist, De Monti – big strategist!'

'Just common sense and vodka.'

Gabriela crossed into the cobblestone square of Stare Miasto, the Old Town. It was surrounded on four sides by perfectly preserved five-story medieval houses that formed the showplace of Warsaw. The historical relics of Poland's glory were preserved in authentic settings. Madam Curie was properly revered in a museum, and shops selling cut glass and national products made it a well-conceived tourist trap as well as a hearthstone of Polish sentiment.

At the far end of the square, Gabriela could hear the noise from Fukier's. She walked in and looked around.

There they were, Chris and Andrei, their elbows on the table, their hands clasped, Indian wrestling. The mob had gathered around them, placing bets and rooting them on. Christopher de Monti was deceptively powerful, a carryover from his basketball days. It was he who was pressing Andrei's wrist down slowly. Andrei was humiliated, as befitted a Ulany officer in a contest with a mere mortal. As Chris poured his strength into his hand and pressed downward, a roar went up from the crowd and the odds shifted quickly. Andrei's face turned first red, then purple with strain, and the veins fairly leaped out of his neck.

Their wrists quivered.

Suddenly the innumerable pints of vodka caught up with Chris. He was unable to make the final pin. Andrei, sensing the weakness of his opponent, called on the reserve strength of a great athlete, and Chris wilted.

Utter silence gripped the mob as Andrei came inching back from the brink of defeat. The sweat rolled down Chris's face as he tried to fight off the inevitable. He collapsed. Andrei made the kill with such speed and power that Chris was thrown right out of his chair and went sprawling into the spectators.

The Ulan officer stood up, wavering, and raised both arms over his head to receive his deserved accolades, then bent down to help his victim to his feet. Bloody, but unbowed, Chris's hand lashed out, caught Andrei by the heel of his shiny boot, and sent him crashing to the floor. They both lay on their backs, convulsed with laughter.

'What in the devil are you doing down there!' she demanded.

'Whadda think I'm doing?' Andrei said. 'I'm trying to get this drunken slob home.'

'It stinks in here,' Andrei said.

'I told you it was painted. Now be careful and don't touch anything. It's still wet.'

Andrei spilled the unconscious Chris on Gabriela's sofa. He landed with a thud, his legs awry.

'You don't have to be so rough,' she admonished. She knelt down and unlaced Chris's shoes. 'Take off his coat and tie. He's so drunk, he's liable to choke.'

Chris blurted out something about flat tables and Polish hams as Andrei fought him out of his clothing. Gabriela placed a pillow beneath his head, covered him with a blanket, and dimmed the lights.

Andrei hovered over him. 'Poor Chris. Do you see the way he and Deborah steal looks at each other? As if they are both going to die of broken hearts. Poor Chris.'

'Get in there,' Gabriela ordered.

He staggered into the bedroom, flopped on the edge of the bed, and held his face in his hands.

'I've got to do something about my temper,' he mumbled. Andrei then berated himself roundly, but it was a monotone soliloquy heard only by himself. Gabriela entered with a large mug of steaming black coffee.

Andrei's head dangled with shame. 'I'm a son of a bitch,' he said.

'Oh, shut up and drink this.'

He stole a guilty look at Gabriela. 'Gaby ... baby ... please don't bawl me out ... please, baby.'

She took his cap off, unbuttoned his tunic, and wrestled his boots off. Andrei had reached that stage of drunkenness where words are thick but thoughts brilliantly clear. The coffee gave him a sudden resurgence. He looked up at his little Gabriela. She was so lovely.

'I don't know why you put up with me,' he said.

She knelt before him and lay her head on his lap. Even in this state, his hands touched her hair with amazing tenderness.

'Are you all right, dear? Can we talk?' she asked.

'Yes.'

'When you've gone away in the past two years, a week to Krakow, or a week to Bialystok, or a week or two on maneuvers, it was never really too bad because I was always able to live for that moment I knew you would come storming up the stairs into my arms. But now you've been on regular duty – you've been gone nearly two months. Andrei, I almost died. At the Embassy we know how bad things really are, Andrei ... please marry me.'

He struggled to his feet, holding one of the four tall posters. 'Maybe you'll hate me the way you hate Paul Bronski for giving up his beliefs, but you mean more to me than being a Catholic does, and I'll give it up and I'll light the candles for you on your Sabbath and I'll try to be all the things –'

'No, Gaby ... no. No ... I'd never ask you to do that.'

'I know how much you mean to other women. I can see the way they look at you. If you were angry with me and should go away for a night or two, I swear I'll never question you or make a scene.'

'You make scenes now. You'd make scenes if we were married. Maybe I wouldn't love you if you didn't make scenes. Dear ... I ...'

'What, Andrei?'

'I have never said this to you, but it would be the proudest thing in my life if I were able to take you as my wife. It is only – I ... tell myself a hundred times a day that it is not true. It will not happen. But Chris is right. Poland is going to be conquered. God knows what the Germans will do to us. The one thing you don't need now is a Jewish husband.'

Andrei's words and their meaning were absolutely clear. 'I see,' she said, deflated.

'God damn it all. God damn everything.' Andrei had that lost look about him that moved Gabriela to forget her own desires, for he was floundering and in trouble and needed her.

'What did Paul Bronski say to you tonight that brought all this on?' she asked.

'That bastard!'

'What did he say to hurt you so?'

Andrei sucked in a deep breath and reeled to the window, where he stared into the darkness. 'He called me a phony Zionist – and he is right.'

'How can you say that?'

'No, he's right, he's right.'

He tried to clear his shrouded thoughts. He looked for Gabriela through bleary eyes. She seemed far away and out of focus. 'You've never been on Stawki Street where the poor Jews live. I can see the garbage on the streets and smell it and hear the iron-rimmed wheels of the teamster wagons on the cobblestones. It was a kind of stink and humiliation that drove Paul Bronski out of there. Who can really blame him?'

Gabriela listened with terrible awe as the drunken outpour increased. Since she had known Andrei he had never spoken a word of his boyhood.

'Like all Jews, we lived through economic boycotts, and blood riots by the same students Paul Bronski leads. My father – you saw his picture?'

'Yes.'

'Just another one of those bearded old religious Jews nobody understands . . . sold chickens. My father never got angry, even when they threw stones through his windows. He always said, "Evil will destroy itself." You don't know the Krasinski Gardens – nice Polish girls don't go there. It's at the north end, where the poor people go on Saturday to look at trees and eat hard-boiled eggs and onions and pass gas while their kids fall into the fishponds. I had to deliver chickens for my father to the Bristol and Europa. I'd cut through the Krasinski Gardens. The gangs of *goyim* hung out there waiting for us little Jew boys. Every time they beat me up and stole my chickens we'd have to eat boiled potatoes for a week. I would ask my father, "Daddy, how long is it going to take for evil to destroy itself?" And all he would answer was, "Run from the *goyim*, run from the *goyim*."

'One day I was making my deliveries. I had a pal from the cheder – that's our parochial school. Funny, I don't even remember his name. But I can see his face so plain. He was skinny – half my size. We crossed Krasinski Square, and the *goyim* trapped us right in front of their goddamned cathedral. I started to run. But this kid – wish I could remember his name – he grabbed me and made me set the chickens down in back of us.

'Funny, not running. When the first one came to me I hit him. I could whip most of the kids in my neighborhood, but I never thought of hitting a *goy*. He went down to the pavement – he got up mad, his nose was busted. I hit him again, and he went down again and just lay there and moaned – and I turned and looked at the rest of them, and they backed up and I kept walking forward and I ran at them and they ran away! I caught another one and beat the hell out of him. Me! Andrei Androfski from Stawki Street had beaten up two *goyim*.'

And he dropped from the elation of the memory of triumph back to his drunkenness. 'That's why I'm a phony Zionist, Gaby. I hate that damned Zionist farm. I don't want to spend my life in little bare rooms over union halls. Bronski knows this – I'm not going to sit in any damned swamp in Palestine.'

'Then why, Andrei – why?'

'Because in the Bathyrans I have a dozen, two dozen friends who are together with me. So long as we hang together, no one can steal our chickens. All I want, Gaby, is to be able to live without running.'

Spent and weary, Andrei lay back on the bed slowly. 'I forced them to make me a Ulany officer. I, Andrei Androfski, a Zionist leader, made them make me a Ulany officer. But I can feel their eyes on my back. Jew, they say to themselves – Jew. But they do not say it to my face . . .'

'Shhh, darling. You are not fighting now.'

'Gaby, I'm so tired. So tired of battling for everyone. I am tired of being the great Andrei Androfski.'

'It's all right, dear. You rest now.'

She dimmed the lights and lay beside him and soothed him until he fell into a fitful thrashing sleep.

What is the best Sehora?
My baby will learn Torah,
Seforim he will write for me,
And a pious Jew he'll always be.

Momma's song. Momma's lullaby. Andrei blinked his eyes open. His fingers felt the pillow. There was a bad taste in his mouth.

What is the best Sehora?
My baby will learn Torah ...

Andrei sat up quickly. He shook his fuzzy head. Gabriela awoke the instant Andrei did, but she lay motionless and watched him swing his legs to the floor, weave his way into his tunic and walk out of the french doors and stand on the balcony. A quiet, sleeping Warsaw was before him.

Seforim he will write for me,
And a pious Jew he'll always be.

'Poppa,' Andrei whispered. 'Poppa.'

Israel Androfski stood before him. His black coat stained and threadbare. His silver-and-black beard ungroomed because of weariness, and his eyes half closed with the strain of the hard life etched into face and posture.

Andrei could smell the poverty of Stawki Street.

'In cheder you will learn to find comfort in the Torah and the Talmud and the Midrash. You go to school tomorrow to begin your swim in the Sea of Talmud and gather the wisdoms which will give you the strength and understanding to live as a good and pious man all your life.'

Little Andrei babbled his excitement in Yiddish, eager to start his training in one of Warsaw's six hundred Jewish schools.

Rabbi Gewirtz stood warming his hands on the fireless stove in a dingy room before a handful of shivering students.

'You see, *Kinder*, we Jews have been in Diaspora since the destruction of the Second Temple and the great dispersion nearly two thousand years ago ...'

... In the Crimea during the Byzantine era, the Khazars, a war-like people, adopted Judaism, but in the tenth century the Khazars were defeated and dispersed by the Russians much as the Jews were driven from the Holy Land. The Russians swept them out and they have never been heard of since, and their empire was consolidated under Christianity of the Greek Orthodox leaning.

Jews suffered maltreatment during the years of their dispersion in all countries of their dispersion from massacres to expulsions. The fever of Jew baiting heightened to a new level during the Spanish Inquisition, when torture and bestiality were as common as daily prayer.

In the Dark Ages the Jews were blamed for the Black Plague and for witchcraft and for ritual murder.

But it was the Crusaders under the flag of Holy Purification and in the name of God who set out to kill every Jew in Europe. The massacres became so bloody that wave after wave of Jews fled from the fountainhead of butchery in Bohemia to the newly emerging kingdom of Poland.

Here the Jews were welcomed and this was their real beginning, along with the beginning of Poland itself. Jews were needed, for there was no middle class between the landed gentry and the peasants. The Jews brought with them their arts, crafts, trades, professions, and ability as merchants.

'And how was cheder today, Andrei?'

'The boys tease me because they say Andrei Androfski is not a Jewish name.'

'Aha! Well, it is a very Jewish name. It appears all down our family line. Our family were very old in France before they emigrated to Poland during the Crusades.'

'Poppa, why must you and Rabbi Gewirtz talk so much about history? I want to know about things happening today. Why do we spend so much time in the past?'

'Why?' Israel Androfski thrust his finger skyward and repeated an old Hebrew phrase. 'Know from where you come. Before you know who you are and where you are going, you must know from where you come.'

And so Andrei learned that a series of Polish kings granted a number of charters guaranteeing religious freedom and protection to the Jews soon after their arrival in Poland from Bohemia.

However, this condition of security was short-lived, and not long after their arrival there opened a sordid, almost thousand-year parade of oppression against the Jews which never stopped but only varied in intensity from time to time.

It began as the Roman Church grew in power and consolidated its position as the state religion. The Jesuits of Posen and Krakow triggered Middle Age riots against the Jews, persisting in the spreading of lies about ritual murder libels.

The Jesuits received help from immigrant Germans who were the competition with the Jews in commerce. With Church help they managed to obtain a Jew's tax, expulsion from competitive crafts and trades and professions. The feudal *pans* kept Jews from owning or farming land.

And so to Poland came the honor of creating one of the world's first ghettos, and enforced separation of the Jews from the rest of the citizens by walling and locking them in.

Banned from participation in national life and from participation in the normal economic life, they were compelled to be a breed apart.

In their ghettos, limited in their means of livelihood, the Jews began their long tradition of self-rule and self-help. Banded together without choice, they intensified their studies of the Holy Books to find the answers to the thousand-year-old dilemma.

'We are like a bird,' Rabbi Gewirtz said. 'We are a long way from home and we cannot fly that far, so we circle and circle and circle. Now and again we light upon a branch of a tree to rest, but before we can build our nest we are driven away and must fly again – aimlessly in our circle . . .'

Polish Jews turned bitter against their homeland. The Poles used the very difference which they had forced on the Jews to prove Jews were not like other people. The Jews had no identity as Poles. They spoke Yiddish, a language carried from Bohemia. They created their own culture and literature apart from the masses around them.

In 1649 the greatest calamity since the fall of the Temples crushed the Jews of Poland. Cossacks of the Ukraine, aided by the Tatars, staged a revolt against the feudal *pans* of Poland. In the wake of gory, savage fighting, the Cossacks became obsessed with the idea of slaying every Jew in Poland, the Ukraine, and the Baltics, the rivers of Jewish blood spurted from the swift-arcing, hissing Cossack sabers. In the frenzy to kill, the Cossacks often buried Jewish babies alive.

And, like the Arab world after the Mongol invasions, the Jews of Poland never recovered from the Cossack massacres.

Numbed from the butchery, they entered an era of desperation and sought a way out of the long black night through their Holy Books.

The cult of the cabala snowballed. The cabala, a study of mystic meanings of the Holy Books, was taught by cabalistic rabbis who preached the Zohar and the Book of Creation. Through cryptic numerology and mystics they sought to overcome the suffering of daily life by finding hidden meanings in the Bible.

Along with the cabalists came a parade of false messiahs. Self declared messiahs proclaimed themselves the anointed leader to take the Jews back to the Holy Land. A desperate, anguished people disposed of reason and flocked behind them.

King of the frauds was Sabbatai Zvi, a Turkish Jew, who through distortions of the cabala 'proved' himself the Messiah. Throughout the world of dispersed Jewry the elders and the rabbis from Amsterdam to Salonika, from Kiev to Paris, argued the validity of Sabbatai Zvi's claims. It was the Polish Jewry who arose, drowning logic with the maddened hope that he could lead them to escape.

A crushing delusion. Sabbatai Zvi was converted to Islam and became a Mohammedan to escape the wrath of the Turkish sultan.

Jacob Frank, a Bohemian rabbi, relit the fires after Sabbatai's death in Albania, but the Frankist sect carried out sex orgies and debasements of the Holy Laws. In the end, Jacob Frank was converted to Catholicism.

And all of the false messiahs fell, and the Jews of Poland sank deeper into a muck of despondency. From the depths of their despair emerged the Hassidim. Israel Baal Shem Tov erupted with yet another new cult which captured the imagination of the enslaved Jews in their ghetto dungeons.

The Hassidim detached themselves from the world of daily tribulation and reality through frenzied prayer that transcended the pain about them. Wild! Leaping! Screaming! Moaning! The joy of prayer!

'Poppa! I don't want to be a tailor or a chicken seller!' Andrei cried. 'I don't want to be a Hassid! I want to be like other people in Warsaw.'

Israel Androfski's face saddened. He stroked his son's curly bush of hair. 'My boy will not be a chicken seller. You will be a great Talmudic scholar.'

'No, Poppa, no. I don't want to go to cheder any more!'

His father raised his hand in anger, but the slap never came, for Israel Androfski was too gentle a man. He looked at the burning in his son's eyes with puzzlement.

'I want to be a soldier – a soldier like Berek Joselowicz,' Andrei whispered.

Poland, partitioned, at constant war with Germany and Russia, ceased to exist as a state time and again in her long and bloody history. At the end of the 1700s she was again in the throes of one of her numerous rebellions, this time against the Russian Tsar on the east and the King of Prussia on the west. Desperate for manpower, the Poles allowed Berek Joselowicz, a Jew of Vilna, and Josef Aronwicz to organize a Jewish brigade, a radical departure from past principle. Five hundred of them took the field in the defense of Warsaw. Twenty of them survived. With the precedent set, the Jews answered the call to arms in Poland's rebellions against Russia in 1830 and 1863, but as Russia gobbled Poland and the state disappeared from the face of the earth, a huge land ghetto was formed called the Jewish Pale of Settlement. Beyond the Pale, no Jew could travel or live.

And through the 1800s the web of economic strangulation, boycott, excessive taxation, and bestial pogroms continued. Murder of Jews was supported by the Tsar and overlooked by the Russian Orthodox Church. The Jews were driven into a position of mass destitution.

A few fumbling calls for reforms were heard, but the voices were far softer than the gangs of roving Jew killers.

And a new generation in the Pale emerged unsatisfied to continue Jewish existence as it had been through the black centuries. The new generation could not find peace in the cabala or the wild prayer of the Hassidim, nor would they follow false messiahs. To them, the old ideas had failed, and during the mid-1800s dynamic new ideas swept the ghettos of the Pale. Young Jews formed self-defense committees to protect the ghetto against the pogroms as they began to emulate the soldier Berek Joselowicz!

Then came the Lovers of Zion, the first practical move to organize colonies in the Holy Land.

The thousand religious groups, led by their rabbis, fought the new radicals who departed from traditional Jewish living, but the brush fires ran wild and each new pogrom made the desire for freedom more intense. Writers, dreamers, angry young men threw off the shackles of the past.

Theodor Herzl molded the hundred different ideas of a thousand years into a simple paper called 'The Jewish State,' setting forth the credo that the Jews would never reach a status of equality until the re-establishment of their ancient homeland was achieved.

Herzl was hailed as a new messiah by some, was scorned as a new Sabbatai Zvi by others, but the father of modern Zionism had planted the seed of the new tree of hope for the Jews of the Pale.

As anti-Jewish riots spread over Europe at the end of the century, the urgency of Zionism heightened.

It was into this world of pogrom and flaming new ideas that Israel Androfski was born at the close of the century. World War I brought freedom to redeclare the state to Poland behind the legions of Pilsudski. Israel Androfski and most of Poland's Jews listened to the words and ideals of Pilsudski and believed that after nineteen hundred years their emancipation had come. The Socialists and idealists rallied all of Poland behind him.

... And then Marshal Pilsudski abandoned the Jews and peasants and the workers of Poland to attain dictatorship with the age-old powers of the feudal gentry, the colonel's clique, and the Church behind him ...

To the Jews, another shattering disillusion as riots and unfair taxation and trade restrictions heightened against them.

'Andrei! What is! You carrying rocks in your pockets and fighting *goyim* in Kransinski Gardens?'

'Poppa, they started it. They attacked me when we began our deliveries.'

'I told you to run from the *goyim*.'

'I will not run.'

'God help me! God help me for a son like this. You listen to me. You will go to synagogue and pray and you will be a good Jew!'

They accepted Andrei outside the Jewish area because he could pit his strength against them and win. But behind his back he knew he was always 'the Jew.' Always the Jew, no matter what he attained. Always the wall between them. Never able to be accepted ... what he craved the most eluded him.

'I have decided to join the Zionists, Poppa.'

'Those radicals! My son, my son. You have not been to synagogue for six months. You are now twenty years of age and you have not found out yet that the price of being a Jew calls for patience and prayer and acceptance of your position.'

'I'll never accept it. Oh, Poppa, I cannot find what I want in the Talmud. I must look for myself ...'

'Andrei,' Alexander Brandel said. 'You must accept the commission in the Ulany. Do you realize what it means to all of us to have one of our boys, a Zionist, a Ulany officer? It has never happened. And pray God you'll make the Polish soccer team for the Olympics in Berlin. Andrei ... do it for us.'

'If they would only accept me ... as ... not some sort of a freak!'

'I know, Andrei, how hard it is to carry this battle for us, but your back is strong and we need you.'

'We are like a bird a long way from home, circling aimlessly ... looking for a place to light and build a nest. But as soon as we cry we are driven from the tree and we must circle again ...'

Israel Androfski lay on his deathbed and rasped to his bereaved boy, 'And have you won your great battle for acceptance? Andrei ... return to a good Jewish life before it is too late ...'

What is best Sehora?
My baby will learn Torah,
Seforim he will write for me,
And a pious Jew he'll always be.

'Know from where you came.'

Dawn cast an ugly light on Warsaw. Andrei's heavy eyes blinked at the sharpening outlines of the rooftops. He felt the presence of someone behind him.

'It is very chilly. You'd better come inside,' Gabriela said.

Chapter Eight

Journal Entry

We are within an inch of war.

The Polish delegation arrived in Berlin for last-minute talks but are without authority to make direct negotiations. It is the consensus that Hitler doesn't really want to negotiate. His pact with Russia puts the Soviet army on the shelf for the time being, and no one is under the illusion that France and England are going to do very much if Germany attacks us.

I was finally able to get hold of Andrei. Ana Grinspan came up from Krakow, so we will be able to hold an executive meeting later this morning.

ALEXANDER BRANDEL

Throughout Warsaw bells pealed. They pealed from the towers of large and small churches and the cathedral. They pealed from St Antoine's and St Anne's and from the Carmelites' and from Notre Dame and the Dominican and Franciscan churches and St Casimir's and the Jesuits' and from the Holy Cross where Chopin's heart is kept in a little black box near the altar.

Warsaw is filled with churches, and all their bells pealed. For it was Sunday.

A smattering of white sails billowed on the Vistula River to test out the first brisk late-summer breeze, and bathers and sunners packed the shore of the beach at Praga Park.

The Poniatowski Bridge and the Kierbedzia Bridge buckled with the heavy traffic to and from Praga as relatives exchanged visits.

Beneath the Poniatowski Bridge was the Solec district. And this was filled with the odor of freshly dropped horse dung, as most of the teamsters lived in Solec and stabled their horses in the courtyards alongside their homes.

In the winding steps beneath the bridge in Solec the police investigated the knifing of a well-known whore. However, the usual smuggling, mugging, fencing, prostitution, pickpocketing, gambling, and thieving which made the Solec the Solec had decreased, for most of the whores and hoodlums were in church.

All of Christian Warsaw, two thirds of its population, piously promenaded in and out of church. The day before, Jewish Warsaw, the other third, had piously promenaded in and out of synagogue.

It was a pleasant day. As Gabriela dressed for Mass she could see beyond her balcony into the square and along the Aleja Ujazdowska, where the elegant promenaded. The men cut fastidious figures with their homburgs and canes and spats and pin stripes, and there were the dashing army officers, and women elegant in Paris hats and Paris dresses and fur pieces.

The new rich paraded along Jerusalem Boulevard and the grand Avenue of the Marshals.

The hopeful young lovers and the soldiers of the rank and their girls promenaded up and down New World Street, looking longingly into the barred shopwindows.

The visitors from the country flooded the Old Town Square to saturate themselves with Polish lore.

The neither rich nor poor filled the Saxony Gardens. And, since the super-nationalistic marshal, Pilsudski, had died, the crowds were allowed to spill into and examine the wonders of his personal botanical gardens in the Lazienki around his Belvedere Palace.

In the Old Town, boys took photographs of their girls posing on the medieval walls.

And the poor people went to the Krasinski Gardens to look at trees and grass and eat hard-boiled eggs and onions and pull their children out of the lake.

Amid squirting fountains and palaces and church bells, Warsaw promenaded and little girls in knee-length white stockings and bows and pigtails walked before parents who felt rather saintly after their visit to the holy domains and little boys ran after the little girls and pulled their pigtails.

In the middle of the broad sidewalks, life centered about the circular-shaped concrete billboard structures upon which handbills were posted announcing cultural events, news, bargains, and Irene Dunne movies.

The monuments of Pilsudski riding his horse, Stefan riding his horse, Casimir riding his horse, Poniatowski riding his horse, and Chopin merely standing were smothered with fresh-cut flowers in the Polish tradition of reverence to her heroes.

Over Pilsudski Square, Warsaw's ground for political and military rallies, stood eleven massive columns forming an entrance to the Saxony Gardens, and in its center the eternal flame to the unknown soldier. This, too, was surrounded with cut flowers.

After church the rich went to the swanky Bruhl House and ate ices and sipped tea after their hour with God, and the poor stared at them from the street through the long, low windows. The rich did not seem to mind.

Not all of Warsaw was so reverent.

The Jews had celebrated their Sabbath a day earlier, and while their Christian brethren purged their sins the Jews quietly cicumvented the stringent blue laws. The center of Jewish gangsterism on Wolynska Street smuggled and thieved, the textile workshops on Gensia bartered for raw material, and the stores of the building-material owners that lined Grzybow Square could be opened with the proper combination of knocks.

In the mixed Christian and Jewish quarters of the smart Sienna and Zlota streets, Jewish professionals and businessmen let their neighbors know they were good Poles and joined in the promenading.

And the bells pealed.

Everything seemed quite in place for a Sunday in Warsaw. That is, if you did not go near the tension-filled ministries or the rumor-riddled lobbies of the Polonia and Bristol and Europa. Or if you were not among those who stopped before the President's Palace and watched and waited for word of a miracle which was not coming. Or if you were not in your home before the radios bringing in voices from the BBC and Berlin and America and Moscow.

For under the normalcy, everyone seemed to know that the bells of Warsaw could well be sounding the death knell of Poland.

The meeting of the Bathyran Council was held in the flat of its general secretary, Alexander Brandel. His place faced the Great Synagogue on Tlomatskie Street and was conveniently near the Writers' Club, which was the meeting place of the journalists, actors, writers, artists, and intellectuals who admitted they were Jewish. The Jewish journalists, actors, writers, artists, and intellectuals who did not admit they were Jewish met in another club a few blocks away.

A dozen routine matters, left unresolved during Andrei's absence, were dispensed with, then the discussion turned to what they should do in the event of war.

'War will bring us to terrible times,' Alex said. 'I do not think it is too premature to set up on an emergency footing. Perhaps even think about what we will do, God forbid, if the Germans come.'

Ana Grinspan, the liaison secretary, was up first. 'The very first thing we should do is close ranks as never before. We must establish a system of communications between all our chapters in case of German occupation.'

Andrei was looking wistfully out of the window. When Ana began to talk, he turned and looked at her. She was still very attractive, he thought. She had been his girl before Gabriela. Funny, she is a lot like Gabriela. Ana was twenty-five and very Polish in appearance. She lived in Krakow and was from an upper-middle-class family. Most half Jews went to one of two excesses – an abnormal hate of their Jewishness or the embracing of it with an abnormal passion. When Ana discovered her father's Jewishness she became a rabid Zionist. It was this obsession that cooled Andrei toward her. There are times when a woman must be a woman and to hell with Zionism. It's too much to hear it going to bed and waking up. At any rate, their parting was completely civilized.

Ana spoke for ten minutes. No arguments about her point of view. Unity forever.

Tolek Alterman was on his feet. Dear God, please don't let Tolek get wound up, Andrei thought. But Tolek was wound up. He was distinguished by a head of bushy hair, a leather jacket, and a leftist point of view. Tolek was the manager of the Bathyran training farm outside Warsaw. He had been to Palestine with a Poale Zion group and, like all of those who had been to Palestine, he had a holy arrogance about it. 'We who have actually been there' was one of his favorite and most-used phrases to press an argument.

'War or no war,' Tolek was chanting loudly, 'we are banded together because of mutual belief in a set of principles.'

Now, Andrei thought, he'll ask us what those principles are.

'And what are those principles?' Tolek said. 'They are the principles of Zionism. Poland and Russia are the well-springs of Zionism because of the desire of our people for a homeland after centuries of persecution.'

Oh, for Christ sake, Tolek – we know why we are Zionists.

'To remain Zionists, we must continue to function as Zionists.'

He's snaking into his weird traps of logic.

'The farm is living Zionism. We must continue to keep the farm going to train our people for their eventual goals – war or no war.'

Tolek then shifted into second gear. There was no denying that he had done a great job as manager of the farm. Before he took over, Andrei thought, we couldn't grow weeds. Since then we've trained three groups of youngsters and they've established successful colonies in Palestine. If only he wasn't so flushed with his sacred mission.

'Having been there myself . . .' Tolek said.

Talk, talk, talk, talk.

Now it was Susan Geller's turn to talk. 'The Bathyran Orphanage in Zoliborz is one of the finest in Poland. We take care of two hundred youngsters. All of them are prospective colonists for Palestine. War will bring us more orphans. Nothing on earth is more important than our children ...'

Tolek wants his farm, Susan wants her orphanage, Ana wants unity forever. Each one argues for his own self-interest. Well, Ervin is yawning. Good old Ervin Rosenblum. Our secretary for information and education hasn't anything to say, thank God. Rosy is a social Zionist; he joined us looking for intellectual company – mostly Susan Geller's. I wonder if they'll ever get married.

Did I tell Styka about Batory's left front hoof? It was a little tender after the last patrol. I'm certain I told him to have the veterinarian look Batory over. Maybe I didn't. My leave came so suddenly.

'So, what do you think, Andrei?' Alexander said.

'What?'

'I said – don't you want to add your opinion?'

'Sure. If the Germans come, we go into the forests and fight.'

Tolek Alterman's bushy hair flopped as he thrust a finger up and said that Andrei had no restraint. Andrei didn't care to argue today – not with Tolek or Ana or Susan or Ervin or Alexander.

'Who can make plans? Who the hell knows what's going to happen!' Andrei said.

Alexander Brandel stepped in quickly and with his great gift for mediation averted the clash of philosophy spurred on by the gushing rivers of words. He pronounced a few well-chosen, all-conclusive benedictions about the great wisdom of Zionism in which everyone's point of view was vindicated, and the meeting broke up on a note of unity, unity forever.

When they were all gone, Andrei remained in the home of his closest friend. He and Wolf Brandel, Alex's sixteen-year-old son, engaged in a chess match while Alex worked at his desk.

'As a cavalry officer, I shall show you how to use your horses,' Andrei said, moving his knight against Wolf's bishop.

Young Wolf lopped the horse off. Andrei scratched his head. It was no disgrace to lose, for the boy was a chess wizard.

Alex looked over from his desk. 'Wolf tells me you commit your horse to battle without proper support. You are a bad officer, Andrei.'

'Hah ... today, schmendrick, you are going to get a lesson.'

The mild and graying Brandel smiled and went back to his papers. Being general secretary of an organization with twenty thousand members and a hundred thousand sympathizers kept him busy night and day. Administrator, fund raiser, recruiter. He was overseer of the orphanage, the training farm, and the publication *Kol Bathyran* – Voice of Bathyran.

More than anything, Alexander Brandel was the philosopher of pure Zionism.

There were many types of Zionism, each with its own variants. Alexander Brandel said there was a different type of Zionism for every Jew.

The largest single philosophy, labor Zionism, emerged from Poland and Russia after terrible massacres of the Jews at the turn of the century. Labor Zionism called for self-sacrifice by a dedicated Jewish labor force as the key to the redemption of Palestine.

The second of the major philosophies was that of the revisionists or activists.

These were angry men whose mold demanded retribution. Often super-nationalistic and military-minded, they wanted the injustices of anti-Semitism atoned by 'an eye for an eye.' From the ranks of the revisionists came many of the terrorists who fought British rule in the Palestine Mandate.

Alexander Brandel's Bathyrans, formed by a small group of intellectuals, were a third group. Their concept was Zionist purity. They believed in a single principle: the establishment of a Jewish homeland was a historic necessity, as proved by two thousand years of persecution.

While the other groups agreed that the Bathyrans indeed had idealism to spare, it was impossible to put ideology into practical use without dogma.

Brandel countered charges that the Bathyrans were an antiseptic social club by taking the best of all the ideas and putting them into practice while being bound by none of them. He did not agree with the restrictions on the individual demanded by the Labor Zionists, nor did he believe in the dedication to force of the Revisionists as a complete answer. Some force and some restrictions – yes, but not completely.

When he had quit his job as an instructor of history at the university to assume leadership of the Bathyrans, the group was struggling and floundering. From chaos he developed concepts and philosophies which brought it into respect.

He lived in abstraction in his personal life. His income was always modest, his person disorganized in a scholar's absent-minded way. The light always burned late in the Brandel flat, for even beyond duty to the Bathyrans, Alexander Brandel was a Polish historian of note.

Wolf knocked off Andrei's second horse when Sylvia, Alex's wife, came in with a pot of tea and some cookies. She was six months pregnant and starting to show very much. Bathyran humor had it that Alex had come home only twice in sixteen years and both times made Sylvia pregnant.

She was the personification of the 'good Jewish girl.' Plain, pretty with dark and plumpish features, she was sharp in mind and the clever homemaker who created ideal conditions which allowed Alex to pursue his work.

To Sylvia, a Zionist from birth, Alex had achieved the pinnacle of accomplishment for a Jewish man. He was a writer and teacher and historian. Nothing could be greater than that. She had attended her first Labor Zionist meeting in her mother's arms before she could walk and she was completely dedicated to her husband's work. She never complained that they were poor or that he was gone half the time.

In his own lackadaisical way Alex loved Sylvia very much. Almost as much as she loved him.

Alex thrived on work. Only once in a while did he seem to need the comfort of a warm bed and his woman's arms and soothing voice. While the world revolved around him in haste and anger and frustration, he never seemed to vary his pace, never raised his voice, never panicked, never seemed torn by those inner conflicts of other men.

Alexander Brandel had achieved that state of heaven on earth which is called peace of mind.

It seemed paradoxical and almost humorous that it was the team of Brandel and Androfski that made the Bathyrans go. Andrei was fifteen years Alex's junior and his opposite in temper and outlook. Andrei was an activist in thinking. Yet they recognized in each other a particular strength the other lacked. The symbol of strength ... the symbol of mind.

'You and Gabriela will stay for dinner,' Sylvia said.

'If you don't go to any trouble.'

'What's trouble? Wolf, the minute you are through with that game, you practice your flute. Money for flute lessons doesn't grow on trees.'

'Yes, Momma.'

'Andrei, it's a good thing your niece Rachael goes to the same conservatory. He would never practice a note.'

Andrei shot a glance at Wolf, who reddened.

So! he thought. You are one of those schmendricks looking over Rachael.

Wolf licked his lips, lowered his eyes, and made a move.

Andrei studied the boy. Gawky, a few straggling hairs on his chin, pimples ... What could Rachael possibly see in that thing? Not a man, certainly, but on the other hand not quite a boy. Known him since he was a baby. He is a good lad. He will respect Rachael ... I think.

'Your move.'

Andrei made an atrocious play.

'Checkmate,' Wolf said.

Andrei glared at the board for three full minutes. 'Go practice your flute.'

He stretched and yawned and meandered over to Alex, who was writing in a large notebook.

'What's this?' Andrei said, lifting the book and thumbing through it.

'Just a journal of events. Fulfilling my natural calling as a nosy person.'

'What do you expect to do with diaries at your age?'

'I don't know if it has any use. Just a wild guess, Andrei, that it might have some importance someday.'

Andrei put Brandel's journal back on the desk and shrugged. 'It will never take the place of the Seventh Ulany Brigade.'

'I wouldn't be too certain of that,' Alex said. 'Truth used at the right time can be a weapon worth a thousand armies.'

'Alex, you're a dreamer.'

Alex watched Andrei grow restless. He was really the only person with whom Andrei could speak from the inner reaches of his mind. Alex pushed his papers aside, took a bottle of vodka from his desk, and poured two glasses, a small one for himself and a large one for Andrei.

Andrei took the glass and said, '*Le'chayim!* – to life.'

'You were quiet at the meeting today,' Alex said.

'The rest of them did enough talking for me.'

'Andrei, I've seen you so unhappy only once before. Two years ago, B.G. – before Gabriela. You've had an argument?'

'I always have arguments with her.'

'Where is she?'

'In the church most likely, lighting candles and asking forgiveness of Jesus, Mary, the Apostles, and forty Polish saints for living in sin with a Jew.'

'It's the coming war, isn't it?'

'Yes, it's the war and it's Gabriela. There are things that a man wants answered before he goes out on a battlefield.'

'We talked about these things today for three hours. You weren't with us.'

Andrei sipped his vodka and shook his head. 'I am a bad Jew, Alex. I am not a Jew my father would have been proud of, may God rest his soul.'

Andrei walked to the window and pulled the curtain back and pointed to the great symbol of eastern Europe's Jewry, the Tlomatskie Synagogue. 'My father could find comfort for any problem in the words of the Torah.'

'But, Andrei, that is why we are Bathyrans and Labor Zionists and Revisionists. We could not find comfort in the Torah alone.'

'That is the point, Alex. I am not even a good Zionist.'

'My goodness, who's been talking to you?'

'Paul Bronski. He sees right through me. I am a phony Zionist. Alex, now listen to me. I'm not a disciple of A. D. Gordon and that crap of love of the soil. I don't want to go to Palestine, now or ever. Warsaw is my city, not Tel Aviv or Jerusalem. I am a Polish officer and this is my country.'

'You told me once very plainly that you don't want anyone to steal your chickens. Isn't that Zionism? Aren't we merely in a struggle for dignity?'

'In dubious battle,' Andrei mumbled. Then he sat and his voice became very soft. 'I want to live in Poland and I want to be a part of this country as though I belong. But at the same time I want to be what I am. I cannot accept Paul Bronski's terms of giving up what I am. I have wanted to run to the synagogue and believe with my father's faith. I want to believe in Zionism as you believe.'

Alexander Brandel tightened the muffler around his neck. He lifted his glass, revealing a big suede patch on his elbow.

'Did you ever read my article when I tried to explain the anatomy of anti-Semitism in Poland? Never mind, it was a bad article.' He closed his eyes to intensify his meditation and recited, 'All of Poland is divided into three classes. The peasant class, the gentry – those who aim to keep them peasants – and the Jews. Ninety-five per cent Ukrainia and five per cent Paris with a few ethnic groups thrown in to make eternal trouble on our eastern and western borders. We Jews came to Poland at the invitation of a Polish king in the Middle Ages fleeing ahead of the holy swords of purification of the Crusades. We came to establish their merchant and professional class.'

'Well said, Professor.'

'Andrei, take that poor miserable peasant scratching out an existence on the land. He is driven to mysticism in his worship in order to justify being able to live in a world he cannot cope with. Now, he has a Jew in his village. The Jew is not allowed to own land, so the Jew makes magic with his hands. The Jew can sew, mend shoes . . . The Jew can read. The Jew reads something in that mysterious script and keeps rituals that frighten the peasant. Or perhaps the Jew becomes the grain merchant. He has to use his wit and cunning to live. He may lend money – this makes him despicable. But what the peasant really does not understand is the Jew who pushes a cart and sells secondhand clothing in order to send his son through college. Now, our peasant goes out once a week to the town and he is very frustrated and confused and he gets drunk. He must hit someone, explode this accumulation of frustration. He cannot hit the nobleman who owns his land and steals half his crop as rent, so he beats up the little Jew who cannot fight back. The nobleman tells him that the Jew who lends the money and is the grain merchant and uses human blood in his rituals has brought him to his state of poverty. He is a victim of Jewish cunning. Now, our nobleman, who robs the peasants blind, does not give them education or medicine or justice, also hates the Jew who is his doctor or lawyer or architect or banker. We are the convenient scapegoat for the serfs and the ones who aim to keep them as serfs.'

Andrei grunted. 'Wanting to be a Pole in your own land is as futile as wanting to be a Jew in your own land. I am not allowed the luxury of either.'

He looked out of the window and saw Gabriela walking toward the flat. At least there is another night with her before I must go back, Andrei thought. At least there is that.

Chapter Nine

The divine feeling which gripped Warsaw on Sunday was, unfortunately, not able to call a truce, to hold back those hands of fate moving toward the twelfth hour. The ministries, the war offices, and the newsrooms were open for business.

Chris turned the bureau over to Rosy and walked to the Foreign Ministry to check out any late announcements in the crisis.

For the moment it was quiet.

He left and, instead of returning to the Bristol, continued past the tall columns of the eternal flame on Pilsudski Square and on into the Saxony Gardens. The Sunday strollers and lazers filled the benches and paths. He passed the big wooden theater which announced the final production of the summer season. New show next week, Chris thought, all German cast. Chris stopped before the lake, checked his watch, and found an empty bench. The warm sun and the gliding swans added to the serenity. He closed his eyes a moment and rubbed his temple. He was queazy and had a slight headache as a result of his binge with Andrei the night before. Lucky Andrei will be going back, he thought, as one more drinking bout with the pride of the Ulanys would do him in.

Deborah appeared down the path. She looked around for him, but he did not signal. For a moment he wanted only to gaze on her. Each time he saw her it was the same as the first. She waved and sat beside him and he quietly took her hand. For a long time they did not speak, nor did they hear the swirl of foot traffic around them or the sounds of giggling from the lake where a soldier stopped rowing his boat and nearly tipped it climbing back to his girl, nor did they hear the swans flutter indignantly to get out of the boat's way.

'I came as soon as I could get away,' Deborah said at last.

'Why wouldn't you come to my apartment?'

Deborah merely shook her head. 'Chris,' she sighed, 'what we have been doing has never been right. Only now it seems even more wrong with Paul away.'

'It's seemed so long. Just listening for you every minute.'

'You know I wanted to come,' she said. Her fingers betrayed her nervousness so badly that she withdrew her hand.

'I'm going off tomorrow,' Chris said.

She was startled.

'Just a few days. I'm going to make a round of the border.'

'I'm glad you called me.'

'Since the other night you haven't been off my mind a minute. Deborah, we're sitting here in the sunlight and we can think. We've just got to have this out with Paul.'

'No, Chris. Not with him in the army.'

'Before that it was another excuse, and before that another. I swear I've been hoping he won't come back.'

'Chris!'

'I know, he's a fine fellow.'

'I've thought a lot about us too, Chris. When I'm with you – it's – I never thought it would ever come to me. But at the same time I am doing something against everything I've believed in. I'm not going to leave Paul.'

'Is there any feeling between you and him?'

'Not the way you mean. There never has been, you know that. There are other ways a man and a woman can be something to each other.'

'Deborah, I'm not leaving you until you throw me out.'

'Then we have come to that. I can't continue to see you and keep what little is left of my self-respect.'

His hand touched her cheek and her neck, and she closed her eyes. 'Don't, Chris, you know how I am when you touch me. Oh, Chris, all I do is give you problems. I'm no good for you.'

She felt his lips touching her face. 'Come on up to my place,' he whispered. 'I'll undress you and we'll lie in bed and listen to music and open a bottle of champagne . . .'

'Chris . . . get up and walk away . . . please.'

'I will if you really want me to.'

'You know I don't.'

The afternoon was filled with a hundred kisses and endearments and a hundred more. Their love-making carried with it an intense sort of desperation, and when they had exhausted each other they fell into deep, glorious naps. When they awoke, Deborah was happy. She bathed and roamed around the kitchen, all but lost in Chris's big terry-cloth robe, and fixed the steaks and iced the champagne while he soaked in a steaming tub.

'Wash my back!' she heard him call.

When she came into the bathroom, his feet were up on the edge of the tub and he was singing a Verdi aria, trying for a high C, which he missed by a full six notes. Deborah whimpered sensuously as she knelt beside the tub and rubbed the soap over his back. He tried to open her robe.

'No peeking,' she said.

She grabbed his hair and dunked him, then covered his wet face with kisses.

Toward evening it grew chilly and he lit a fire. They finished their meal and lay contentedly on the big sofa, sipping warming cognac. Deborah opened the robe and closed it over the two of them, and his hand traced the lines of her body from her shoulders to her knees.

'Would you believe that I was such a terrible prude and such a good girl? What have you done to me, Mr de Monti?'

Deborah Androfski was only eleven when her mother died. She had to assume the role of homemaker for her father and little brother, Andrei. Before and after school, her job never ended. She had to cook and clean and do laundry and shop. They were poor as only a Polish Jew could be. She had to spend hours bargaining and haggling in the filth and poverty of Parysowski Place to save every zloty.

It seemed that all Deborah could remember of her mother after a time was an image of a tired and pain-filled woman waiting for the redemption of death to take her away from the smells and the dirt of Stawki Street. Momma always held her back and groaned as she climbed the stairs. Momma always had a new ache in a never-ending assortment of them.

Israel Androfski was able to find respite from the struggle of existence in the comforts of a deep-rooted Jewishness which bordered on fanatic joys through prayer. He could detach himself from the misery around him at synagogue. This was denied Momma, for everyday prayer was a privilege of men.

Being a 'good Jewish wife' imposed rigid rules of life. As Deborah grew older, all the little vignettes and mosaics began to take form and meaning. Why Momma always complained especially on the Sabbath eve when Poppa came home from synagogue, for a good Jewish wife was supposed to reconsummate the marriage every Friday night. And this was painful and unpleasant for Momma. Momma lost three children by miscarriage; one other died from disease when a year old. This came from what Momma and Poppa did on the Sabbath eve, and it always ended up in pain and suffering.

When Andrei was born, this brought on a new set of ills to Momma's insides.

'Be careful of the boys,' Momma told Deborah. 'They will make you pregnant and you'll spend your life scrubbing floors and washing and over an oven and giving them babies. Boys are no good, Deborah – boys are no good.' Momma went to her grave decrying the suffering connected with being a woman.

Momma's prophecies were borne out when Deborah had to scrub and clean and cook and wash and shop. It was like a voice from the grave always on her shoulder.

By the time she had reached fifteen, her father had worked his way out of the slums and moved the family to the nice Sliska Street neighborhood where Orthodox Jews of means resided.

Although Israel Androfski was a rather kindly man, in the back of her mind Deborah always blamed him for her mother's death. And when she came of an age to understand why her father visited certain women with bad reputations, it further proved, in her mind, the sordidness of what men and women did in bed. Family responsibility had imposed upon her a passive nature. She was always lonely, as long as she could remember, except for Andrei. Her one solace was the piano.

When the burden of being a homemaker lifted after they moved to Sliska Street, Deborah threw all the latent hurts into it, bringing about an artistry that moved her close to dizzying heights of mastery.

Then, as suddenly as she had plunged into it, she rebelled against it when her father demanded she spend more and more time in its study.

A strange and unexplainable phenomenon stirred within her which overpowered the fears of night. A desire for freedom. She wanted to explore that strange world beyond. An instinct of survival let her know she was drowning in a mental ghetto.

In her first act of defiance Deborah quit the piano and demanded to go to the university to study medicine. Her first look at the outside world gave her her first true friend, Susan Geller, a nursing student.

Deborah Androfski was eighteen years old when she met Dr Paul Bronski, the brilliant young professor for whom every female student in the university carried a secret torch. Deborah was an uncommonly beautiful girl, and as uncommonly naïve as she was beautiful.

Paul Bronski, who had been rather meticulous in every move he made in his life, wanted her for his wife. She had every quality – intelligence and beauty – and would be the perfect mother and hostess. She could supply the needs of a man when he desired, and she would be good for his career.

Deborah stepped into the big wide world too fast. She was completely without sophistication or experience in that game of boys and girls. She was swept off her feet. With shattering accuracy, Momma's dire prediction came true. She was pregnant.

'I love you very much,' Paul said. 'I want you to become Mrs Paul Bronski.'

'I think I would die if you didn't want me.'

'Not want you? Deborah ... dear ... only ... now, we must do something about your pregnancy.'

'What –'

'I know this will be difficult for you, but our future depends on it. We are going to have to give you an abortion.'

'Paul ... take our baby ...'

'Dear, you're eighteen years old. You are one of my students. Think of what kind of scandal there will be if you are married in your condition. Not only the shame for you and your family, it would ruin my career.'

'But ... an abortion ...'

'It will be done carefully – and don't worry. We will have children, lots of them.'

The result mired her deep in guilt. Momma was right. Sex was ugly and painful. Her deep religious roots made her bear losing the child as a penance for her sin. She married Paul Bronski and became to him all the things he wished. She was the perfect mother and the clever hostess and she filled his needs as a man.

But it was in darkness in their bed that she served her sentence. The guilt of the sex act was deeply embedded, and she practiced the discipline of pretending to enjoy in order not to offend her husband. She experienced neither fulfillment nor the smaller pleasures of love-making. She was entirely frigid.

What strange and wonderful thing was it that drew her to Christopher de Monti? He took her hand as though she were a little girl and led her through the black evil forest to the golden castle that sat on a cloud.

There was that first frightening time they were alone in his apartment and everything between them that had gone before had led to the moment when a man and a woman have nowhere left to go in their relationship but to bed.

She threw an angry tantrum over a seeming trifle. Chris completely understood that she was in reality angry with herself over her fear of an inability to perform.

So many times Chris held her face in his hands.

'Deborah, my love ... your mother is dead. You are not going to disobey her by letting yourself have the pleasure of a normal woman.'

And all the years of frustration burst out when Chris unlocked them and drove them from her.

'I didn't know ... I didn't know it could be like this.'

* * *

Deborah blinked her eyes open. The fire was in embers. Chris was rattling around in the kitchen. She looked at her watch. It was very late. He came in, rumpled and smiling, wearing a battered old pair of khaki trousers and holding two cups of coffee.

As wild and wonderful a woman as she had been, Chris watched her change into someone else before his eyes. She fumbled for the telephone and dialed in a nervous, jerky manner. 'Hello, Rachael. This is Momma. Darling, I'm sorry I didn't call you. I got held up. Did Zoshia make you a good dinner? Practice your piano, darling. Tell Stephan I'll be home in a little while.'

She set the phone down slowly. Chris offered her coffee. She shook her head, avoiding his eyes, and walked away quickly toward her clothing.

'Do we have to play out another remorse-filled scene?'

'Don't.'

'But I do –'

'I woke up just now with a terrible start. It is terribly clear that we have done something sinful in the way we have lived. I know we are going to be punished –'

The phone rang.

'It's me, Rosy.'

'Yes, Rosy.'

'You'd better get down here, right away.'

'What's up?'

'Everything out of Berlin has stopped cold. I called Switzerland. They say all the lines from Germany have been cut at the Polish border.'

Chapter Ten

August 31, 1939
To: Commander, Company A, Reinforced
From: Commander, 7th Ulany Mounted Brigade – Grudziadz
Subject: Patrol Assignment

Proceed north on the Tczew road at 0700. A special detachment of intelligence scouts has been detailed to your command for the purpose of detecting unusual movements, changes of disposition, or additions of strength to the German Third Army.

Send reports to us by rider in a routine manner.

When you reach Tczew, join your battalion and continue with them to Gdynia.

No later than 0600 tomorrow you will encounter Company B coming from Tczew in a patrol which will be the reverse of yours. Send your dispatch with them.

It is emphasized that we are at peace with Germany and an unprovoked incident could have serious repercussions. However, under extraordinary circumstances you are authorized to use your judgment.

Signed: Zygmunt Bozakolski, Brigadier in Command, 7th Ulany Mounted Brigade – Grudziadz.

Captain Andrei Androfski moved Company A out of the large headquarters base at Grudziadz at 0700. It was scheduled as a routine patrol that called for a two-day ride along the eastern border of the Polish Corridor, along a road that ran parallel to German East Prussia. He was to meet another company of his battalion the following morning. For several weeks his brigade had been engaged in these roving patrols covering the area from the Baltic port city of Gdynia to the Grudziadz base. The patrols had been singularly dull and uneventful.

The late-summer day in Pomerania was warmish, and as Company A galloped north they were completely detached from the frantic business taking place in Berlin several hundred kilometers away. The land was green and quiet and, as soldiers do, they looked forward to a blowout in Gdynia.

Berlin, Germany: August 31, 1939

Sir Nevile Henderson, the British Foreign Minister, asked for and received a list of demands from the German Chancellery upon which war could be averted. The demands were read to him in a quick unintelligible language. He then demanded to see them in writing. They did not come.

The Germans, instead, demanded direct negotiations with the Polish peace mission upon terms the Poles did not know.

The Polish mission was not authorized to take on a direct negotiation. In last-ditch desperation Sir Nevile Henderson pleaded with the Poles to get authorization from Warsaw. The Poles attempted to comply, but when they tried to telephone their capital they discovered the phone lines had been cut.

Sir Nevile Henderson, raw-nerved from the tension and lack of sleep, angrily demanded to know why the lines were down. The Germans answered that it was the work of Polish bandits, furthering the already 'intolerable' situation and 'proving the Poles wanted war.'

Berlin was white-hot with war fever. The population was barraged with tales of Polish attacks along the border, of Polish aircraft firing on German commercial planes flying over the corridor, of Poles committing murder and atrocities against 'innocent German ethnic families,' of Polish mobilization, and of Polish war hysteria.

By the evening of August 31, Captain Androfski's company had made an uneventful ride along the Polish-Prussian border. They came to a halt for the day opposite the German town of Marienwerder, setting up a bivouac in a small woods a few hundred meters from the road. After the evening meal, it turned dark. Normal security was established, then Captain Androfski called together the special detachment of intelligence scouts who had been assigned to him.

In addition to the routine patrol orders, Andrei had also received verbal orders from the brigade intelligence commander concerning the German massing of armor along the corridor in that area, and Andrei's patrol carried the secondary purpose of scouting it. The special detachment of ten men, dressed as civilians, crossed unarmed into Germany with instructions to circle the Marienwerder area during the night and return to camp before dawn. Their observations would be assessed and the data given to Company B.

August 31, 1939
TOP SECRET
To: Commander, Armed Forces
Directive No. 1
... inasmuch as we can find no peaceful means to solve the intolerable situation on the Eastern Frontier ... the attack on Poland is to be carried out in preparations made in CASE WHITE.
Date of attack: September 1, 1939
Time of attack: 0445
Signed: Adolf Hitler

While the men of Company A slept in a wooded area in the Polish Corridor, the epilogue to peace was written hundreds of kilometers to the south, where Germany and Poland faced each other at Gleiwitz and Katowice.

German SS troops, dressed as Polish soldiers, crossed the frontier into Poland, then recrossed into Germany and blew up their own German radio station at Gleiwitz. Therefore, in Nazi logic, a reason had been created to stamp the war as 'official.'

When First Sergeant Styka shook the men of Company A out of their sleep, they were unaware of CASE WHITE. To them it was to be another boring day of soldiering. They grumbled into wakefulness, cursing as they moved about.

There had been only snatches of sleep for Captain Androfski and First Sergeant Styka. They waited out most of the night until the ten scouts had returned safely. Andrei sifted their information and wrote this dispatch.

September 1, 1939
To: Commander, 7th Ulany Mounted Brigade – Grudziadz
From: Company A, mobile border patrol

Last night we encamped at position L-14 opposite Marienwerder. The area was scouted by the special detachment in accordance with verbal orders.

Abnormal German strength is evident in this area. In addition to units we have previously identified, we have identified two new regiments of armored infantry and at least a portion of a division of Panzer tanks (22nd and 56th Infantry and 3rd Panzer Tanks).

Two battalions of this Panzer tank division moved out of Marienwerder this morning at 0300, apparently for disposition in a southerly direction.

Company A will continue north today. We expect to join the balance of the battalion at Tczew tonight.

Signed: Andrei Androfski, Captain, Company A

Andrei folded the dispatch, then opened it on a sudden impulse. Across the bottom of the paper he scrawled the words, 'Long live Poland!'

First Sergeant Styka trotted his mount to Andrei and snapped a salute. 'The company is eating, sir. We should be ready to move out in a half hour.'

'Any sign of Company B yet?'

'No, sir. No sign of them.'

Andrei looked at his watch and wondered. It was half-past five. The deadline was 0600. A half hour to go. Trouble up north? Well, no use speculating about it.

'Morning, sir,' the officers said as he moved into their circle.

'Morning.'

He and Styka sat off to one side and ate. Goddamned ham. My father would roll over in his grave if he could see me eat ham.

'Styka, when the hell are you going to learn to brew tea?' He flipped the contents in the bottom of the cup to the ground.

'I'm afraid never, sir.'

'Have the company saddle up and stand by.'

'Yes, sir.'

Andrei walked to the edge of the woods and stared long and futilely up the empty road, straining to see a telltale whiff of dust or hear the welcome sound of hoofbeats.

0600, the maximum hour, passed. No Company B.

Suddenly the entire movement of the company stopped, and all the men were staring up the road. Andrei walked back to the bivouac area. 'Styka!'

'Yes, sir.'

'Send me a rider. Make it Tyrowicz.'

Company A's best rider, Corporal Tyrowicz, reported.

'Tyrowicz, ride hard back to Grudziadz. I want you back there by noon. Use fields – stay off the main road. Can you do it, lad?'

'I'll try hard, Captain.'

'Hand-deliver this dispatch to Brigadier Bozakolski. Tell him that Company B did not show up. We are proceeding north.'

'Yes, sir.'

He watched Tyrowicz spur out, driving his horse. He wheeled to Styka. 'Move the advance scouts out. First platoon take the point. Use flank guards. Be on the road in five minutes, column of twos. Shake it up.'

'Yes, sir.'

It was chilly in the dawnlight. The men beat warmth into themselves, and darts of frosted air spurted from their mouths. The first rays of light penetrated the woods, changing the world from ugly gray. Up and down, the crisp orders to mount up. There was no cursing or griping. A sobering tension filled them all. Some of the more pious were on their knees saying quick Hail Marys. Strange, Andrei thought, this isn't much of a praying company. He looked at his watch again. It would be fully light in another forty minutes. Where the hell was Company B! Where the hell were they!

Andrei's stomach knotted in much the same way as it did before a soccer match. Was this quiet morning and Styka's bad tea war?

The first sergeant returned. 'We are formed up, sir.'

Andrei nodded and watched the sergeant trot off out to the road.

The woods was empty now. Andrei checked the saddle buckles on Batory. He chewed a piece of black bread, sipped from the canteen, and slipped it back into the saddlebag. He looked up at his magnificent black beast. The horse was nervous.

Andrei pressed his forehead against Batory's neck. 'We render thanks unto Thee for our lives, which are in Thy hands, and for our souls, which are ever in Thy keeping.'

Why did I pray? I have not prayed since I was a boy. Batory whinnied and went up on his hind legs. 'You feel it too, don't you, boy? Steady, fellow.' Andrei swung astride his horse and soon had him calm and trotted out to the road.

'Move out!' Styka barked.

The forward platoon galloped off. The flanks fanned out, and the communicators positioned to keep contact. They advanced in a slow trot, transfixed by the brightening day. North for an hour, then two, three, and each kilometer filled them with greater uneasiness. There was no sign of Company B. It was beyond normal limitations. Either they had had their orders changed or ... trouble.

Styka heard it first. The column stopped without a command. Everyone's eyes went upward. There was a distant hum in the sky. Then black specks appeared high, high overhead, almost beyond sight.

'Off the road,' Andrei ordered quietly.

They went into the ditch on the Polish side of the border road, dismounted, and held their restless horses still. Two hundred pairs of eyes fixed on the sky.

'... sixty. Sixty-one, sixty-two ...'

The humming overhead grew louder and louder. And soon the sky was pocked with masses of black spots moving in perfect formation in what appeared to be slow motion.

The only sound in the stunned company was Styka's voice continuing a toll in monotone. '... two hundred thirty-four, two hundred thirty-five ...'

They had never seen such a mass of planes. The awesome display passed and disappeared from sight and sound. Three hundred fifty airplanes. For a very long time no one uttered a sound.

'Captain,' Styka said in a cracked voice, 'aren't they flying over our territory?'

'East-southeast,' Andrei answered.

'Where would the captain say they are heading?'

'Warsaw.'

The eyes of every man went from the sky to Captain Androfski. 'Well, gentlemen,' he said, 'the store is open for business.' Nervous laughter greeted him. 'Styka, bring my officers in and get Private Trzaska from the First Platoon.'

They huddled around the map. 'Trzaska,' Andrei said, 'you were a farmer near Starogard, weren't you?'

'Yes, sir.'

'Where can we find good cover and an elevation overlooking the road?'

Private Trzaska studied the map a moment, then slid a dirty fingernail up the border road and stopped. 'There's a small forest here, sir. Runs several hundred meters in all directions and sits on a knoll.'

'How far from the road?'

'Oh ... maybe three hundred meters.'

They could make it an hour of good riding. It was the nearest point with decent cover. 'This is where we're going, gentlemen,' Andrei said. 'Have your men combat-ready, and move single file and stretched out. Quick trot all the way. Second Platoon, take the rear guard and drop your last man a kilometer back. Let's move.'

'Mount up!'

'Combat-ready. Load them up.'

'Single file. Don't bunch up like a flock of pigeons.'

The scouts moved out at a gallop.

This time Captain Androfski was first on the road. He put on his steel helmet, buckled the chin strap, cocked his pistol, and swung Batory up ahead of the company.

Styka's large mustache drooped.

'How you doing, Sergeant?' Andrei asked.

'I'm so scared I could crap my pants,' Styka answered.

'Stay close to me. We'll get through today. They say after the first one it's not so bad.'

Styka faced the company. 'Ride hard!'

Company A moved north again and within an hour found the woods which Private Trzaska had promised. Andrei was pleased. He had cover and an excellent view of the road.

He ordered each of four men to ride out a kilometer in different directions and observe. They were issued flares for warning. Then he sent one rider north to continue to look for Company B and a second rider south back to the Grudziadz base.

By midafternoon a second flight of planes, as large as the first flight in the morning, again blackened the skies, heading toward central Poland.

Andrei sat away from his men, trying to evaluate his situation and its implications. The new German Panzer power they had discovered, the seven hundred airplanes, and the lost Company B – all indicated war had started.

What move?

To continue to Tczew and join the battalion even though there appeared to be trouble up north?

To stand pat and wait for the sign of Germans?

What if the Germans showed up? He had good cover. Should he button up and wait for dark and head back to the main base?

No, impossible. The nature and breeding of the Ulany made the idea of both running and hiding repulsive. He smiled to himself as he thought of Chris. Too bad he won't be the first into Berlin. No doubt we are massing for a huge counterattack into Germany now.

As often happens in war when men are in the field, the decision is made for them.

'Captain,' Styka said, 'riders coming in from the north!'

Andrei trained his field glasses on them. There were two. One was his, the rider he had dispatched earlier. Another, a stranger. They pulled into the forest with frothing mounts. The stranger was bloody and half senseless.

'Back up, dammit,' Andrei said. 'Give the man breathing room.'

'He's from Company B, sir,' Andrei's man said.

'Can you talk, soldier?'

He nodded and gasped. 'Holy Mother ... oh, holy Mother, Captain.' Andrei pumped some water down his throat. 'Oh, Jesus. We never knew what happened. The Germans ... heading south ... right down the road.'

'Take this man and keep him calm. Lieutenant Vacek, plant your contact mine on the road. Lieutenant Zurawski, set up all four machine guns in a U-shaped cross fire around the mine. Use the ditches on both sides of the road for cover. Dzienciala, can we use our mortars effectively from this distance?'

'I think so, sir.'

'Keep your squad in the woods here as a covering force. The rest of you line out for a single-file charge. I'll lead. If our luck goes right, we can ambush the first batch of them. I want only limited pursuit. Pull back here to the forest for regrouping.'

'If we don't pursue, they'll know where we are, Captain.'

'Hell, they'll know in Berlin where we are ten minutes after the first shot.'

'What does the captain plan to do after we regroup?'

'Sit our asses right here and keep them from getting south on this road. As soon as it turns dark we'll go north to find the battalion.'

The single land mine was planted on the road and a cross fire of machine guns established within minutes. The two mortar squads set up in the forest and zeroed in on the road. The rest of Company A stretched nearly the length of the woods ... and they waited.

A warning flare arched up from the northern advance guard.

'Here they come, Captain.'

Out of the north there arose a billow of dust. Andrei lifted his field glasses and watched the cloud of dust grow larger until it could be seen by everyone. And then, the sound of motors. He counted them as they turned a bend into the straight flat stretch of a kilometer and a half directly below him.

'Troop carriers, twenty-two of them. Must have two companies.'

And then he could see the swastika markings on their sides. The trucks rambled down the road in an undeterred race. Andrei reasoned that the Germans must have felt there would be no opposition after they had overrun the battalion and Company B.

'Steady the line, dammit!'

He held the glasses to his eyes. He could see the face of his enemy! In the lead truck the driver looked to be a boy. For some crazy reason he thought of Wolf Brandel at that second, and Batory went up on his hind legs.

'Stand by!'

The lead truck was armored. It struck the mine, and the earth shook and splattered and the truck disintegrated. The second truck, filled with soldiers, attempted to stop short and it careened off the road, rolling into the ditch, bursting into flame. The third and fourth trucks slammed into each other. And then! Rat-a-tat! Rat-a-tat! Streaks of tracers leaped from the machine guns, catching the Germans in a deadly cross fire. German soldiers poured out of the trucks in wild disarray, trying to organize under the frantic shouts of their officers.

Andrei brought his hand down. 'Charge! Charge! Kill the sons of bitches! Charge!'

A bloodcurdling battle cry erupted from Company A as they poured down the knoll behind their captain. The horsemen tore into the confused enemy, ripping, hacking, trampling them into a gory massacre.

Unable to organize, the Germans began fleeing on foot, to be run down, shot down, smashed down.

The tail end of the convoy, the last five trucks, were able to turn around and flee back north. The mortars in the woods found one truck, turning it into a torch. The other four escaped.

It was over in ten minutes. A hundred dead and dying Germans lay strewn about the road and the ditches, and the air hot with the burning of the shattered vehicles. Andrei pulled his men back into the forest.

He climbed from Batory and fell to his knees and doubled over to catch his breath. There were howls of the delight of victory among his dripping wet, exhausted men. The first smell of combat had been victory.

Andrei climbed to his feet and leaned against his horse, who was wet with sweat too but excited over the stimulation of carrying his master to a kill.

'Styka, we're not going to throw a victory ball. Calm them down, we've work to do. Medic, what were our casualties?'

'Four dead, sir. Trzaska, Lieutenant Zurawski – I think he got it from our own cross fire – and Wajwod and Lamejko.'

'Wounded?'

'Six – one bad.'

'Horses?'

'Ten, Captain,' Styka said. 'All have been executed.'

Andrei looked at the wreckage on the road. Nothing could pass. The Germans could not detour, for the ditches were too steep.

'Any orders, Captain?'

'Get the machine gunners back here. No use having them exposed. Just stand by – they'll be back. Let me take a look at the wounded.'

The victory had done much to pass the first terrible fear of contact. They waited.

Andrei stood at the farthest edge of the forest, holding Batory's reins. 'Well, boy, we're in it now,' he said to his horse. 'That wasn't so bad after all the times we've practiced it, was it? Too damned easy, if you ask me. Wish we had an alternative to this position ... Well, we're committed now. Have to hold them off this road. Think we can keep this position? Sure we can. They'll never get another attack organized today. Easy, boy.'

Blam!

An explosion went off at the foot of the knoll, very close to the road, and another and another.

'Styka!'

It was long-range cannon fire. Where? A half dozen more shells exploded, walking up the knoll. Andrei looked at his watch. Only forty-eight minutes since he had regrouped for the attack.

Blam! Blam! Blam! Blam!

'Over there,' Andrei said. He pointed in the direction of East Prussia. A dozen iron-treaded monsters were crossing the field, their cannons probing the forest. Andrei grunted. Radio communication and long-range guns had turned a good defensive position into a trap within minutes. Was he going to pay with interest for his ambush? He looked at his pair of puny mortars. They would be unable to reach the tanks until they were fairly near the road. The Germans could lay back out of range and blast them to pieces if they chose. Break for it, maybe? No, dammit, never!

The cannon fire began to find the edge of the woods. The line of horsemen began to waver. 'Steady there!'

Two of the tanks reached the road.

'Mortar fire!'

The mortar shells bounced around the tanks. One scored a direct hit. They did nothing to deter the German barrage.

Good God! Andrei thought. How can I stop them?

... four-five-six-seven-eight-nine-ten-eleven-twelve. All the tanks were in position now, hitting them from three hundred meters.

'Dismount! Take your horses back and hitch them! Form a staggered firing line.'

Blam! Blam! Blam! Blam!

Barks of thin trees burst into flame. A dozen horses cried in terror and several broke from the woods. Company A hid behind the cover of the trees.

Only Captain Androfski and Batory stayed forward to observe.

The German tanks groaned into motion toward the bottom of the knoll. 'Machine gunners! Give it to them. Shoot for the turrets!'

The machine guns hit into the tanks, and their bullets bounced off like annoying little ant pricks.

'Captain! Airplanes!'

The black vultures streaked over the treetops and screamed down on the woods. The planes flew low, dropping fire bombs, and the woods went up like a torch. A second flight of planes vomited ten thousand machine-gun bullets into them. The instant they passed, the tanks started again. Now truckloads of infantry unloaded, forming up behind the tanks.

'To your horses!'

Gagging and choking and bleeding, what was left of Company A found what was left of their mounts.

'Charge!' Andrei screamed. Batory, his black mane flying in defiance, led the broken and pathetic line of Ulanys down the knoll and into the German tanks. Andrei's terrible anger could see only the infantry men behind the tanks. I'll get them! I'll get the bastards!

His men were blasted from their saddles before they had gone fifty meters. Andrei whipped around and dragged them to their feet and pulled them on their horses and tried to reorganize the attack. There was nothing left. It was a rout. They went back into the forest, with their captain after them, cursing them to make one more try.

Now the tanks inched forward up the knoll, German infantrymen crouched low behind their iron cover. The line of steel came within a hundred meters – point-blank – and let go again, and the infantry fanned out between the tanks.

In the woods there was the smell of burning flesh and burning wood and the sounds of screaming men and screaming horses. All was havoc. For ten, fifteen, twenty minutes Andrei was able to rally his men to hold the German infantry. He kicked them to their feet and tried to set them on their horses again, but they were bombed from the saddles and gunned and burned with methodical indifference.

And then he staggered around blindly as a cloud of smoke hit him in the face, and he cried for Batory and felt his horse and struggled into the saddle. 'Come on, boy! Let's get them!'

He spurred the animal toward the Germans, then he whirled about and the world began to spin, and when he opened his eyes he felt as though his chest were being crushed and all he could see was the blue sky above him and the tops of the burning trees whirling and whirling. Andrei thrashed about on his hands and knees, semi-conscious, crawling to Batory. 'Batory! Get up! Get up, boy! Don't lay there! Get up! Let's kill them!'

First Sergeant Styka knelt over Andrei and shook him violently. 'Captain, we are finished! Get up, sir! I have two horses. We must make a run for it, sir!'

Andrei lifted the dead horse's head in his hands. 'Batory! Get up!'

'Sir, your horse is dead! Nearly all the men are dead!'

The big soldier dragged Andrei to his feet. Andrei broke loose from his grip and kicked his lifeless animal. 'Get up, God damn you! Get up! Get up! Get up!'

Chapter Eleven

Humanity had been endowed by the German people with their Beethovens and Schillers and their Freuds and the dubious gifts of a Karl Marx. Now the German people presented humanity with a new set of authors – General von Bock, General von Küchler, General von Kluge, General von Rundstedt, General von Blaskowitz, General List, General Halder, General von Brauchitsch, General von Reichenau. The book they wrote presenting mankind with a new innovation of German culture was called *Blitzkrieg*, lightning war.

Poland formed a huge bulge which fitted into the open jaws of Germany, with Prussia on the north, a common border of many hundred kilometers from the Baltic to Krakow, and in the south newly raped Czechoslovakia beyond the Carpathian Mountains.

The jaws bit down, and saber teeth in the form of armored columns tore deeply into the flesh of Poland. The Poles, arrogant and stubborn and filled with foolhardy national pride and an offensive-minded Polish Staff, doomed whatever small chance there may have been for some sort of stand.

Forgoing logic, Poland did not fall back on her few natural defensive river barriers. Instead, she dreamed in vain of holding a fifteen-hundred-mile border whereon the enemy chose his points of attack. She had further vision of making a counterattack in the form of a hell-bent-for-leather cavalry charge.

Poland's forces were all but immobile, armorless and antiquated, her arsenal better suited to war five decades earlier. Sustained by raw courage, Poland asked the horse to fight the tank.

German land forces ran double and triple envelopments, executed picture-book tactics; massacred, trapped, overwhelmed, sliced, overpowered the near-defenseless but proud enemy. The new book called for the disregard of even the token humanities customarily observed in the organized art of murder known as war.

Death spewed from the skies.

Within hours of the German border violations, the Polish air force, tiny and outdated, was shot to pieces on the ground. Within hours, rail lines were ripped up and supply dumps smoked skyward and hot bridges sizzled as they buckled into rivers. Cities and villages without so much as a gun to fire were leveled into smoldering rubble heaps.

The Luftwaffe, which had learned to violate open cities in Spain, turned all of Poland into one big turkey shoot. It shot down Polish troops fleeing for cover and Polish peasants working in the fields and Polish children in the schoolyards and Polish women nursing in maternity hospitals and Polish nuns at Mass.

Through the Carpathians from Czechoslovakia, List shoved his armor through the mountain passes and turned the Krakow flank at that place where the Gleiwitz radio station hoax was perpetrated. In the center, Reichenau was given the honor of unleasing the greatest mass of iron-treaded monsters, and on his left Blaskowitz enveloped a pocket on the flatlands near the industrial heart of Poznan. And Von Bock and Von Küchler lashed out from northern flanking positions in Prussia and Pomerania and there was no more pesky Polish Corridor.

Indeed, the book had been rewritten. It was the ultimate in mechanical and technical murder. The butchery of Poland – the slaughter of two hundred thousand of her army and scores of thousands of her civilians and the rape of her land – was a new German masterpiece.

Captain Andrei Androfski was knocked senseless by his first sergeant and dragged from the scene of the flaming death of Company A. With a half dozen survivors, they found horses and managed to get back to the Grudziadz base, where an even greater catastrophe had befallen the Ulanys. At Grudziadz, one third of Poland's forces had been foolishly concentrated for a counterattack which was never delivered. The Germans enveloped them with ridiculous ease and, having trapped them, chopped them to bits. The large Westerplatte Saliant was formed by a double envelopment trapping the Polish marines. Soon, the last of Poland's cavalry charges was made. With the Polish eagle still waving in defiance, a foolhardy attack tried to break the ring of iron around them. The Germans ungallantly ripped the Ulanys to shreds. The Westerplatte Saliant collapsed. The remaining Ulanys staggered back from Grudziadz to Torun. And ... a last weak gasp, one more charge at Wloclawek, and they were done.

There was no rest, for the German monster clamped its jaws tighter and the saber teeth pressed toward Warsaw at the end of only a week.

Captain Andrei Androfski had four horses shot out from under him in seven days. He was gored with arm and leg wounds and his body covered with bruises and filth. He and First Sergeant Styka were two of a handful of survivors when the brigade finally surrendered after Wloclawek.

On the night of September 7, before the Germans could fully organize prisoner compounds and complete the disarming of the Poles, Andrei, Styka, and four others broke out of their area and under cover of darkness gambled they could swim the treacherous upper Vistula River.

Two of them drowned. The remaining four hid in a forest the next day and at night crawled along the ditches of roads filled with German patrols.

At dawn on September 9 the four found refuge in a peasant's hut on the outskirts of Plock, a third of the distance back to Warsaw. Beyond normal exhaustion, hunger, thirst, and close to death from his festering wounds, Captain Andrei Androfski allowed himself the luxury of collapsing.

Styka sent the other two men into Plock to fetch a doctor. He hovered over Andrei, who was terribly still and a chalky yellow shade. Andrei had spent the last ounce of reserve strength pulling Styka across the swift river. The soldier's muddled mind remembered snatches of the past week since dragging Andrei from the burning forest. He saw the vision of his captain leading charge after charge and fighting on even after the end had occurred. He had never seen such anger in a man's eyes as when they were put into the prisoner compound even though Andrei was barely able to stand. 'We're swimming the river, Styka, as soon as it turns dark.'

The peasant brought Styka bread and lentil soup. The soldier was too weak to lift the spoon or bite through the bread. He lay his head on Andrei's chest. Yes, there were still heartbeats. His eyes began to shut. Must not sleep until the doctor comes ... must not sleep ...

'Who is he?' the doctor asked.

'My captain,' Styka answered through thick lips. His mind was fuzzy. An ignorant man, Styka was almost illiterate and too exhausted to put into words the horror he had seen in the past week. Only when the doctor promised to remain with Andrei did he fall on the floor by Andrei's bed and drop off to sleep.

When Andrei blinked his eyes open twenty hours later, Styka was hovering over him. Styka managed a small smile. The doctor from Plock had gone and returned. Andrei managed to rise up on his elbows, looked around the cottage, and flopped back on the bed.

'We were wondering if you were ever going to wake up,' the doctor said.

'Sure he would! I knew it all along!' Styka roared.

The peasant's wife crossed herself innumerable times and wailed that all her prayers to the Blessed Virgin Mother had been answered.

'What's the scorecard on me?' Andrei asked.

'The wounds are under control. The assortment of cuts and bruises will vanish. Your state of exhaustion will require rest. You are as thoroughly beaten up as any man I have ever examined. You have the constitution of a bull. I don't see how you ever swam the river in your condition.'

Styka and the doctor helped him sit up. He took a stiff drink of home-brewed vodka and stuffed a half a loaf of bread into his stomach. Despite everyone's objections, he remained sitting.

'Where are we?'

'Plock.'

'What is happening?'

'The news is bad all over. We are being beaten everywhere,' the doctor said.

'What about Warsaw?'

'The Germans have not reached Warsaw yet. Radio Polskie says Warsaw will fight.'

Andrei tried to stand. His legs buckled and he tottered. 'Where are the other two, Styka? They got across the river with us – where are they? We must get back to Warsaw and fight.'

The doctor and Styka exchanged glances.

'Well, where are they?'

'They have surrendered.'

'Surrendered?'

'The Germans have crossed the river in strength. All roads to Warsaw have been cut. I stayed here only until I knew you were all right, Captain, but there is no chance of reaching Warsaw. Every hour we stay here we put these good people in danger. The Germans have been shooting everyone harboring an escaped soldier.'

'I am a Pole,' the peasant announced. 'I will never close my door to a Polish soldier.'

'Your sergeant is right,' the doctor said. 'Now that he knows you are alive, it would be best for him to turn himself in. As for you, I can find you a hiding place for a few days until you get a little of your strength back, and then you must surrender yourself too.'

Andrei looked at all four of them. The woman was crossing herself and praying again. 'If you will be kind enough to spare me a loaf of bread, a canteen of water, and perhaps some cheese, I will be on my way. I am going to Warsaw.'

Styka flopped his arms about helplessly. 'Captain, we can't make it.'

Andrei managed to walk to his sergeant and put a hand on his shoulder. Styka lowered his eyes. 'Look at me, Styka – look at me, I said. You would surrender?'

The big homely man had been a good soldier for fifteen years. Dirt encrusted his once-proud mustache, and beads of sweat broke through the caked mud on his eyebrows and unshaved face. His face dropped in complete dismay. 'Yes, sir,' he whispered.

'Now you listen here,' the doctor said. 'Warsaw is a hundred kilometers, the roads are cut, and the place is swarming with German patrols. If you were the strongest and healthiest man in Poland you could not make it. In your condition you won't be strong enough to go ten kilometers.'

Styka began to cry, something Andrei had never seen him do. 'Captain, sir. We have fought the best we know how. We have not disgraced ourselves.'

A sudden dizziness overcame Andrei. He pitched into Styka's arms, then pushed himself free and stumbled into a chair.

Seven days and their war was over. Their fine beautiful brigade pulverized into a disorganized bloody pulp. The vision of the glazed eyes of the soldiers came to him, and he saw the line of thousands of corpses stretched beside the road outside Torun after their cavalry charge and the fields of lifeless horses.

The memory of battle ran together without day or night, beginning or end. The smells and the burns and the agonies. Kicking men to their feet to fire one more round . . . one more round . . . ear-splitting shellbursts and the tank treads cutting into walls of flesh and the cries of the wounded . . . The little village north of Rypin. What was its name? He had organized fifty strays for an attack. They stopped in the village for water. The children ran out of the school into the village square to cheer them. The priest came out and the women came out with bread in their hands.

No one heard the airplane, it came so fast. Rat-a-tat-rat-a-tat – and it was gone, and five children lay bleeding in the square. The priest knelt over them, saying prayers, and the women wailed. The little girl dead, clutching the rag doll. Rat-a-tat – and planes came in again.

'We have fought with honor,' Brigadier Zygmunt Bozakolski said. 'I am surrendering the Seventh Brigade. I expect you gentlemen to conduct yourselves as Ulany officers.'

The prison pen. The accordions of barbed wire. The crisscross of German guards. 'Styka, as soon as night falls we are going through the wire and swim the river.'

'I'm with you, Captain.'

Styka fell on the wire and made himself a human bridge, and the other five ran over the top of him. He followed after them. When they reached the riverbank the air was filled with whistles and sirens and shouts in German.

Flashlights probed the darkness.

The river was swift and pulling them back to shore. The lights streaked over the water. Blam! Blam! Swim for your life! Swim for your life!

A scream! One of them hit. He is dragged by the current like a limp rag.

'I'm going under, Captain. I can't make it.'

Styka gurgled and thrashed hopelessly. 'Relax, Styka – relax.' Andrei's

hand was under his chin, his free arm driving at the water.
'I'm drowning! I'm drowning! Mother of God!' Styka screamed.
'Stay calm, you son of a bitch ...'
Andrei pulled him up on the bank and knelt over him and pumped the water from his lungs and slapped his face until he came around.
... And then ... what happened then?

Andrei looked up. The peasant and his wife. The doctor. And Styka, crying.
'If you wish to surrender, Sergeant, you have my permission.'
'What about you, sir?'
Andrei shook his head.
'You are a damned fool!' the doctor said.
'Then I guess I am a damned fool too,' Styka said.
'You're going with him? You know he can't make it. Why?'
Styka tried to think. It was hard for him. He shrugged. 'Because he is my captain,' he said.

Chapter Twelve

For the first few days after the war began, England and France desperately tried to get the German army to withdraw, ready to impose another Munich sellout on Poland. When Germany refused, England and France had to do what they should have done years before; they declared war. With Poland's doom more certain each day, the British and French embassies in Warsaw turned over much of their papers and duties to the neutral Americans.
The Americans were short-staffed, but the spirit remained excellent even with extra burdens.
Well into the second week, complete catastrophe for Poland was evident.

Gabriela left the Embassy after a shift of fourteen hours. Thompson insisted she get some rest. Instead, she got one of the marine guards to drive her to Zoliborz to see the Bronski family, with whom she had lost contact for several days. When she arrived, Zoshia told her that both Rachael and Deborah were at the Bathyran Orphanage. She followed after them.
The bombing raids had increased in intensity as the German armies moved in on Warsaw. The city was determined to fight on. At the orphanage, Susan Geller had sent out an emergency call for help to move the facilities underground so they would at least have food, medicine, and sleeping places during the air raids. Gabriela worked alongside Deborah, Susan, Rachael, and Alex and Sylvia Brandel through the night and all the next day, helping move supplies underground, catching only a few naps whenever they could. She returned to the Embassy. Things had slowed down, and Thompson sent her home again.
She had reached a state of numbness. She looked up at her flat from the street. It was so lonely there. Several buildings near and on the square had

been hit by bombs. She found herself doing what she always did when she was lonesome – she walked north to Leszno Street and climbed the four flights to Andrei's flat. As always, the door was open. Just as she arrived the air-raid sirens began. She stood by the window, strangely fascinated by the leaping flames from the slums only a mile away. Some of the fire appeared to be coming from the Old Town. What a tragedy if anything happened to the old square, she thought.

An hour earlier the bombers had started the incendiary attacks to light their way over Warsaw during the night. This time the raiders were hitting acres of workers' homes in Praga across the river.

On the streets below she could hear the confusion as firemen rushed to the slum area, where the houses were so tightly packed and inflammable that the fire could spread all over Warsaw if not contained quickly.

Dull booms from Praga.

There was neither a Polish gun nor a Polish plane to stop the Germans. But the raiders kept coming back to smash the will of the people to resist.

She shut the window and taped the blackout paper into place, then lit the room with a single lamp beside the bed and stretched out to read herself to sleep with Walt Whitman's *Leaves of Grass*.

A knock on the door startled her.

'Come in.'

Alexander Brandel entered the room. She was glad he had come. 'I didn't mean to startle you,' he said. 'I went to the Embassy and your place first.'

'Is everything all right at the orphanage?'

'Fine, fine. The children are so wonderful. We try to keep it like a game. I think they are smarter than we are.'

'How is it outside?'

'The whole northern end is burning. Praga is catching hell. So, Mayor Starzynski says to fight on – so, we fight on. Could I have some cognac?'

Gabriela took a bottle from the cabinet and looked at Alex with suspicion. He was mostly a teetotaler, except when Andrei was around. He drank it down very quickly. He coughed as the fire hit his stomach. Perhaps just the air raid, Gabriela thought. It is enough to make anyone nervous. Then Alex began to mop his brow. There was something serious on his mind.

'What is it?' Gabriela said.

'Andrei is in Warsaw.'

She closed her eyes and held her stomach as though she had been hit. She tried to ask questions, but her lips would not form words.

'Let me first say that he is all right.'

'You swear . . . you swear it now?'

'I swear it. He has been wounded, but it is not serious. Please sit down.'

'Where was he wounded, Alex?'

'I tell you it's not serious and I beg you to be calm.'

'Where is he?'

'Will you please get control of yourself?'

'Where is he!'

'Gabriela . . . please . . .'

'You're lying! He's been hurt.' And then she fought herself into control. 'All right, tell me.'

'God only knows how he was able to get back to Warsaw. It was a miracle. No one will ever know what he has been through.'

'Alex ... I beg you ... the truth. How badly is he hurt?'

'His heart is broken, Gabriela.'

'Where is he?'

'At the bottom of the stairs.'

She lunged for the door, screaming his name. Alex caught her and clamped his hand over her mouth. 'Now listen to me, Gabriela! He is broken, without spirit. You are going to have to be a very brave girl.'

'Andrei, Andrei,' she whimpered.

'He came to me first and asked me to come to you because ... he does not want you to look at him the way he is. Do you understand that?'

She nodded.

'Then make the room dark and I will send him up.'

She left the door open and turned out the light. There was a tiny ray from a hall light downstairs. Gabriela listened at the landing for Alexander to reach bottom. She heard Alex's voice. She tensed, waiting for another sound. It seemed like forever. She fought off the agonizing desire to scream out his name and bolt down after him. Then ... a slow, clump, clump, clump. It labored up and up, each step seeming more painful than the last. Clump ... clump ... clump ... clump ...

Gabriela fell back into the room, her heart throbbing violently.

Clump ... clump ... clump ... Dragging and then a deep wheezing breathing.

His hulk cut a shadow on the landing. He stood wavering on his legs and fighting for his breath. He moved for the door, groping in the darkness.

'Andrei?' she whispered.

He groped into the room, stumbling like a blind man, and found the bed and crawled on it and groaned with pain and weariness.

Gabriela burst with desire to turn on the lights, but she dared not. She leaned over the bed quickly and her hand felt around his face. His eyes, his ears, his nose, his mouth. They were all there. Arms, hands, fingers, legs. All of him was there!

He smelled putrid from the smokes of battle and dried blood and sweat, and his hair was matted with dirt. He lay and groaned weakly.

And then Gabriela became calm. She sat on the edge of the bed and lifted his head to her lap and petted him gently. His face burned with fever and he gripped the bedcover and convulsed.

'It's all right, dear, it's all right now.'

'Gaby ... Gaby ...'

'I'm right here, dear.'

And Andrei cried. 'They killed my beautiful horse,' he sobbed. 'They killed Batory.'

The shrill screams of the air-raid sirens erupted from Bielany to Rakowiec and from Praga to Kolo as new flames were about to be added to the old as the rape of Warsaw heightened.

'They killed my horse ... they killed my beautiful horse ... they killed him ...'

Chapter Thirteen

Journal Entry – September 17, 1939

The pie has been cut. Poland, the historic whipping boy, is again acting out its ancient historical role. Hitler has paid off in his deal with Stalin. The Soviet armies have jumped us from the rear, obviously moving to pre-set borders.

The German invasion has awed the most advanced military thinkers. Smigly-Rydz, the government, and the foreign legations have fled. They say some of our army has been able to escape.

Somehow Warsaw continues to hold out, but I wonder if Polish courage does not prove that the bloodless collapse of Austria and Czechoslovakia was the better way out?

ALEXANDER BRANDEL

Dateline, Warsaw
September 21, 1939
by Christopher de Monti
(Swiss News)

How long can Warsaw hold out? How long can Mayor Starzynski keep this city rallied? This is the question asked ten thousand times a day.

It is a strange battle, a commuters' war. Soldiers and those civilians pressed into labor battalions take up their positions on Warsaw's outer defense perimeter. When their relief comes, they catch a trolley car back to town to their homes.

Often the front lines begin where the trolley lines end. Troop movements are by red and yellow street cars, taxis, horse-drawn droshkas, and teamster wagons.

On the perimeter there is a strange conglomeration of humanity in the labor battalions digging trenches and preparing fortifications. Old bearded Orthodox Jews, secretaries, housewives in gaily colored babushkas, students in university class caps, children, bankers, bakers.

All over Warsaw long lines queue up for their ration on ever-worsening shortages. Water, in some sections, is doled out by the bucketful. Water priority must go to the fire department for its round-the-clock fight to keep the city from going up in flames.

The women waiting in lines stay put despite artillery fire and air raids. Yesterday nearly a hundred were buried by a collapsing wall.

Around the city, both famous and unknown buildings and landmarks are pocked with shell holes. Warsaw's only skyscraper, the fifteen-story Prudential building, a visible target for German long guns, has suffered better than eighty hits. It still stands intact, although only a single window on the tenth floor remains unshattered.

Poland's pride, the Stare Miasto, the Old Town Square with meticulously preserved Renaissance houses and historic shrines, is being leveled lower each day.

Statues of Poland's heroes which adorn her many squares and parks are now headless, armless, and swordless. The magnificent fountains of the Saxony Gardens and the Lazienki are dry; the swans that filled their lakes have fled, and no one seems to know where.

Despite the situation, a strange calm has fallen over the city. There are amazing semblances of normalcy, and the Poles have not lost their traditional sense of humor. Two papers manage to get published each day. Radio Polskie plays Chopin around the clock between dramatic urgings from Mayor Starzynski. The long-awaited German frontal assault must come sooner or later. How long can Warsaw hold?

Chris pulled his report from the typewriter, hastily marked over the errors with a green grease pencil, and put it into a large envelope.

When the phones went out a week before, Chris was able to obtain a wire until that was broken, then radio. Now Warsaw was completely cut off from communication with the outside world except for the one Radio Polskie station operating for the city on an emergency basis.

There was a sudden break for Chris when arrangements were made for a two-hour truce the next day to allow the balance of the American Embassy personnel to evacuate to Krakow. Chris went to Thompson, who agreed to carry out his reports and Rosy's photos in a diplomatic pouch. Both of them worked feverishly, Rosy shooting up film and Chris doing a series of articles not requiring a dateline but which could run as an 'eyewitness' account in papers around the world even after Warsaw's fall. It would stand as a great scoop for Swiss News.

Rosy handed Chris a stack of photographs, and he went through them, marking them and checking their captions. Pictures of broken houses and twisted girders dangling in grotesque shapes and stunned mothers kneeling beside dead children and stunned children kneeling beside dead mothers. War's harvest, a photographer's field day. Dead, bloated animals whose curious expressions asked what they did to be caught in the middle of man's folly, and the images of old ladies praying to Gods and Virgins who do not hear them and trench diggers and exhausted bucket brigades.

Ervin Rosenblum's camera did justice to war. Chris put the pictures into folders.

'Where're the rest of them?' he asked.

'The Kodak lab just went out of action. I'm going to see if I can't get enough junk to rig up a darkroom in my basement.'

'Well, if you can't make prints, you'll have to let me send your negatives.'

Rosy grumbled. The most horrible thought to any photographer was to surrender exposed film which could not be duplicated if ruined. But Chris was right. It would probably be the last chance to get the pictures out of Warsaw.

Rosy went into his familiar routine of jiggling flash bulbs in his pocket and playing with the shutter stops on his camera. 'It's going to be rough on the morale, watching the last of the Americans leave tomorrow,' he said. 'It will affect us worse than a half dozen bombing raids. You know how it is – everyone has an uncle in Gary or a brother in Milwaukee.'

'Yeah,' Chris agreed, 'it will be rough all right.'

'How come you're not evacuating?'

'Why should I? I've got an Italian passport and this is a Swiss News Agency bureau. Switzerland isn't at war. Maybe I want to be on the welcoming committee for my liberators.'

'Chris, you don't even make a third-rate Fascist. You think those fellows at the Italian Embassy are going to vouch for you? You're so American you may as well be wearing a sign.'

'It happens that America isn't at war either. I'm keeping the bureau open.'

'I'll tell you what I know,' Rosy answered. 'I know that within two weeks the Germans will put us out of business.'

'I'll get around it somehow.'

'Why?' Rosy persisted. 'You won't be able to get any news out but watered-down potato soup.'

'You know damned well why I'm staying!' Chris said angrily.

Rosy set his camera down and walked up behind Chris's chair and put a sympathetic hand on his shoulder. 'It's not like I don't want you to stay, Chris. I have a good job. I'd really have to struggle if the bureau closed. But . . . when a friend is in trouble, sometimes you don't think too much about yourself. That's why I tell you, pack up and leave with the Americans tomorrow.'

'I can't leave her, Rosy.'

'My Susan has known Deborah Bronski since college days. When two people like you and she come from different ends of the earth there has to be a great ability on both parts to be able to give. She is controlled by inner forces that make it impossible to change, even if she wanted to.'

'It's not true. Bronski has been cutting away at her beliefs for a decade.'

'Only on the surface. When the final showdown comes she'll return to them. She doesn't have the ability to do otherwise, and that is why you are walking down a blind alley.'

'Oh hell – women in Italy and Spain and Mexico and India and half the damned world are driven to a wall of mysticism and superstitions in order to be able to keep existing in a world which fights them every inch of the way. The trouble with you Jews is that you make yourselves believe you have the priority on suffering –'

'But there is a difference, Chris. In all of the world, no matter how sordid the life, no matter how evil and bare and fruitless, almost every man can open his eyes in the morning in a land in which he had his beginning and a heritage. We can't. And I know what this does to women like Deborah Bronski. I know too many like her.'

'No, you're wrong, Rosy. If you really know Deborah, then you'd understand that I am unable to ever leave her.'

The bell rang. Rosy answered. It was Andrei. In only a week he had made a remarkable recovery. Much of the pain was still with him and his face showed great weariness, but he pulled himself together for that last battle which had not been fought.

Two days after his return to Warsaw he reported to the commander at the Citadel and was given a spot promotion to the rank of major and placed in charge of a battalion on the southern perimeter. The truce to evacuate the Americans was to take place at his position.

'How is it out there?' Chris asked.

'The same,' Andrei answered. 'The bastards won't attack.'

'Why should they?' Chris said. 'They can sit back and blast the city till kingdom come.'

'I want to get one more look at them,' Andrei said.

'We may be looking at them for a long, long time,' Rosy said. 'And how are you feeling, Andrei?'

'Never better,' he answered, lifting the glass filled with scotch whisky that Chris had poured. 'I'm only in for a few hours. I've got to get back. Something has come up that may be of interest to you on that truce tomorrow morning to evacuate the American Embassy personnel.'

They both nodded.

'The Germans contacted us a few hours ago by radio. One of our officers just finished speaking to them personally beyond the lines. The Germans have asked for a trade of prisoners of war at the same time the Americans are evacuated.'

'How many Germans do you have here?'

'A few hundred, more or less. Most of them are ethnics.'

'Seems like a normal procedure,' Chris said.

'No, there's something fishy about it,' Andrei said. 'The Germans are offering us five to one.'

'Why would they do that, I wonder?' Rosy asked.

'I don't know – but something's wrong with the whole business.'

'We might as well go down there and cover the truce,' Chris said. 'There may be a story, although God knows when we'll be able to get it out of Poland.'

Chapter Fourteen

The American Embassy was closed except for a half dozen token personnel. There had been a final tear-filled farewell with Thompson, who was to evacuate during the truce in the morning, and then Gabriela went to Andrei's flat to wait for him as she had waited for two harrowing nights through shellfire and air raids.

It was just turning dark when he arrived after leaving Chris. They embraced wearily. He slumped into the big armchair while Gabriela poured the last of the vodka. The liquor felt good and warm going down. Gabriela stood behind him and rubbed the knots out of the muscles in his neck.

'I managed to save a large pail of water,' she said. 'You will feel better when you have washed.'

He clumped into the bathroom and dunked his head, trying to wash away the exhaustion, then shaved with a cup of heated water.

Gabriela had the food ready. He shoved some stale bread into a bowl of beans.

'I'm sorry there isn't more to eat,' she said. 'When we closed down at the Embassy I came straight here. I didn't want to risk standing in line and possibly miss you if you came in. I'll go out and get some things at Tommy's house later and fix you a good warm meal.'

'It's fine,' Andrei muttered. 'I can only stay a few hours anyhow.'

He chewed the hard bread without speaking. Gabriela became uneasy.

'You'd better take a little nap. You look as if you're ready to cave in.'

'Stop nagging me!'

The air-raid sirens cried out. Gabriela turned quickly from his testiness to draw the curtains and put out half the lights.

'Bastards,' Andrei mumbled. He pushed the bread through the beans. 'Bastards.'

In a moment the sky was crackling with the sounds of the motors. Andrei listened for the first whistling screams of the dives and then bombs. He did not have to wait long.

'Mokotow,' Andrei said to himself, 'the airdrome. Only there's no airdrome left. They're methodical. Every part of Warsaw is like a number on the clock. Mokotow, then Rakowiec, then Ochota, then Wola. Why not? We know where they're coming, but we can't shoot back. Why not? I've seen those sons of bitches face to face. I'll see them again before this siege is over. They won't break us with air raids – they're going to have to make an attack, and when they do –'

'Stop it, please.'

Andrei ate and listened. The Germans were passing in from the north, starting their unimpeded diving patterns into the southern fringe of the city from directly over his apartment. As the Stukas and Messerschmitts screamed down on the undefended city, Gabriela became shaken. A miscalculated bombing run dropped a rack just a block away from Leszno Street. Andrei's flat shook from the blast. 'Perhaps we'd better get to the basement,' Gabriela said.

'Do I look like a mole or a gopher? I will not live under the ground.'

'That arrogant Polish Ulany pride will get us killed.'

'Go to the basement, then!'

'No!'

'Well, make up your mind.'

It was not a long raid, for there was nothing of military value left to bomb in Warsaw. The Germans had had their sport for the day and departed. Gabriela examined the empty vodka bottle with disappointment. Andrei drew the curtains and watched the dancing flames in the distance. He turned back to her, and she became frightened. He had a strange look on his face that she had never seen before.

'I came to say good-by, Gabriela,' he said. 'Go home and pack your things. You are allowed one suitcase. You are leaving with the Americans tomorrow.'

'I . . . don't believe I understand you.'

'Don't make a scene.'

'How am I to get through the German lines? Perhaps I should sing "Swanee River" for them to show them I am an American.'

'I spoke to Thompson. He has already made out an American diplomatic passport for you. There is no better way to travel. Tommy will get you to Krakow.'

'My, you've been a busy man. Here I thought you were defending Warsaw, and you've been out making diplomatic missions.'

'I said I don't want a scene!'

'I'll make up my own mind where and when I want to go.'

'So maybe I've condemned you to purgatory! America is such a horrible place? Only a crazy damned fool would want to keep their skinny neck in this city.'

'Since when do you tell me what to do?'

'Since now!' he answered, slamming his fist on the table with such force it rattled the bottles and dishes.

Gabriela watched his terrible temper with a bit of fright and a bit of awe. He seemed to be issuing an ultimatum that if she stayed he would not see her again. She dared not ask. Her eyes were filled with hurt. She whispered, 'Andrei, what have I done to make you so angry?'

'You have a mother and a sister in America. That is where you are going.'

'Is this good-by?'

'One way or the other ...'

She waited for him to make some move, some sign. He stood like a lump, glaring at her, unwavering in his intensity.

'All right,' she whispered. She picked up her coat and put it on slowly and walked toward the door, waiting, praying for Andrei to call her name. He did not move a muscle or blink an eye. She opened the door and faced him. He was like a stranger. This cruel man was not Andrei ... to dismiss her as a nobleman dismisses a peasant.

If I walk down these steps I will die, Gabriela thought.

She closed the door and walked across the room to him. She put her arms around him and lay her head on his chest, but he remained emotionless.

'Don't try any female tricks on me.'

'All right,' she said, 'but I didn't believe the day would come when you would not touch me. I will leave you, but you cannot make me leave Warsaw. This happens to be my home too.'

'You must leave!'

'Don't shout, Major Androfski. You may frighten away the Stukas.'

Andrei flopped his arms hopelessly, and the look of humanity returned to his eyes. 'Goddamn but you are one stubborn woman,' he said. 'I only tried to do it this way because, if I threatened never to see you, you might go. Now let me plead with you. This isn't our country any more. God only knows what the Germans are going to do with three and a half million Jews. I cannot live knowing that because of me harm will come to you. If you love me, then give me my pride. Let me know I have given you life, not taken it from you.'

'Oh, Andrei, I should have seen through you right away. I love you. I don't know any other way to love. I cannot leave because I cannot do what I cannot do.'

'Oh God ... Gabriela. I don't want you hurt.'

'Shhh, darling, shhh.'

'You are a little fool – a terrible little fool.'

Chapter Fifteen

Warsaw gagged. Clouds of smoke billowed from the ground and then rained down a billion bits of dust and ground-up brick and mortar. An unearthly silence mingled with the fumes of war.

Christopher de Monti and Ervin Rosemblum were already interviewing the evacuees when Major Androfski drove up.

Thompson was the first to reach Andrei.

'Where is Gaby?'

Andrei beat his shoulders to ward off the pre-dawn cold and shifted his feet about. 'She wouldn't come, Tommy. Honest to God, I tried.'

'I really didn't think she would. Take these papers, she may be able to use them later.'

'Thanks, Tommy. Thanks for everything. Gaby sends her love to Martha.'

'Take care of her . . .'

The second-in-command, a captain, approached them, and Andrei assumed a formal pose.

'Have you checked the credentials of all your people?' the captain asked Thompson.

'I have.'

'What's the count?'

'Twenty American personnel. Fifteen personnel from mixed neutral embassies, and twelve civilians, miscellaneous.'

'Get back with them.' Andrei looked at his watch, then strained to see in the darkness. 'It will be light in about fifteen minutes. Be ready to move out if everything goes well.'

Thompson nodded. They grasped hands, and the American turned and trotted back to the courtyard behind a shattered farmhouse where the evacuees huddled.

Andrei turned to his captain. 'How many Germans?'

'We managed to get eighty of them.'

'Has this information been radioed to the Germans?'

'Yes, sir. They said they will return three hundred ninety of our people.'

Andrei walked down the road to where the German prisoners stamped around restlessly in the cutting chill. They were glum and humiliated. Their faces wore masks of hatred and arrogance. Andrei stared at them for a while. They looked like people he had known all his life. A baker . . . a gentleman with children . . . a teacher . . . What was it that had brought them to this place?

He turned on his heels, followed by the captain, and walked briskly to the forward trenches.

The distant thump-thump-thump of artillery never quit. It was still too dark to see across the field. Another eight minutes. Andrei gave a series of security commands.

Chris climbed down into the trench alongside him.

'Gaby staying?'

'Yes.'

'It was a safe bet.'

'I tried ...'

'Don't blame yourself. Be thankful. Find out anything about the prisoner exchange?'

'They're still paying us almost five to one. We're watching for a trick. Lord knows what they're up to.'

The thumping stopped.

All eyes strained for the sight of something moving in the ugly grayness over the field. Andrei held his field glasses up and crossed back and forth over the horizon ... back and forth.

There! A shadow emerging from the clump of trees. Barely make it out. Definitely coming into the field. He waited for five minutes while the figure grew more visible.

You son of a bitch, Andrei thought. How I'd like to blow your filthy head off! The figure stopped. He was holding a makeshift white truce flag.

Andrei jumped out of the trench and walked toward the German over what had once been a potato field. It was pocked with holes and littered with wreckage. From both sides, ten thousand eyes were on them. Andrei stopped a few feet from the German. He was a colonel, but neither beetle-browed nor blond Aryan, but rather nondescript. He seemed uneasy in his exposed position. He and Andrei stared at each other for several moments without a word.

'You are in charge?' the German said at last.

'Yes.'

'What is your situation?'

Although Andrei spoke conversational German well, he addressed the colonel in Yiddish. He rattled his Yiddish, staring directly at his enemy.

'We have forty-seven mixed neutral nationals, American Embassy personnel, and eighty of your people. Credentials have been checked.'

'Bring them out here. I will escort them through our lines.'

'You owe us three hundred ninety Poles. I will bring the evacuees to this point when you bring my people here.'

Andrei's implication that he mistrusted the Germans was obvious. There was more the two men wished to say to each other. Andrei longed to break the German's neck with his hands, and the German's eyes told a message of 'don't let me find you when we enter Warsaw, Jew boy.'

But this part of war was by the rule book. Restraint. The victor had to show majesty. The loser was given his pride.

'I have a message from our commander. He urges surrender of Warsaw to avoid further useless bloodshed.'

'I have a message from our mayor in the event that your commander asks Warsaw to surrender. No.'

The German broke off the conversation, looking at his watch. 'It will take me approximately six minutes to have your people moving here. They have been assembled in the small woods there.'

'I'll wait.'

The German snapped his heels together, made a curt short bow from the waist, and walked back across the field.

Andrei stood alone. He heaved a terrible sigh and bit his lip. He watched the figure of the German grow smaller and smaller, and now the thousands of eyes were on him alone. The last of the proud Poles . . . erect as a statue. Still cursing beneath his breath, still praying for his enemy to fight him face to face.

Six minutes passed to the second. The German was efficient. Clusters of men began to emerge slowly from the woods and cross the field toward Andrei. Andrei turned to his own lines and raised his hand.

They came from his side in two groups, one led by Thompson, the other by a German officer in command of the German prisoners. The distance was far shorter to Andrei than to the woods. They came at a trot and were formed up quickly.

Andrei looked toward the woods again, annoyed by the slowness of the Polish prisoners in returning.

'Something is wrong out there,' Thompson said.

Andrei lifted his field glasses, and his hand dropped. He kicked a potato on the ground viciously. He lifted the glasses again, and his face contorted with quivers of rage.

'No wonder they wanted to give us five to one,' he said. 'They're sending back nothing but amputees.'

'Oh dear God.'

'Must they torment us!' Andrei cried.

'Maybe,' Tommy said, 'if they torment enough, we will wake up and get off our dead prats in America. Can we leave, Andrei?'

'Go ahead, Tommy. Move slowly. I want to be sure those men are safely in before you reach the woods. They may ... try something if they were left exposed.'

The Americans walked toward the enemy lines, turning their eyes from the macabre marchers coming in the opposite direction.

Andrei returned to the trench.

'What's going on out there?' Chris said.

'Look for yourself.'

He took Andrei's glasses. Nearly four hundred armless or legless men straggled toward Warsaw. Men with one arm used their other to carry stretchers of men with no legs, and men with one leg hobbled and fell in the pitholes.

Andrei turned to the captain. 'Get out there and help those people,' he said.

Polish soldiers dropped their weapons and ran over the field and the two forces came together, and in the distance the thump-thump-thump of the cannonading began once more and overhead the first flights of German warplanes ushered in a new day.

It was night when Christopher de Monti reached the Bronski home in Zoliborz. As he approached the house, the familiar sound of music reached his ears. Rachael was playing the piano. How wonderful! How wonderful that Deborah was able to keep them together and functioning, holding back the fear and gloom. Chris was a welcome face these days. Young Stephan let out a large sigh of relief when Chris hugged him, for he knew the duties of 'manhood' would be relieved for the time he was there.

Deborah was in the kitchen with Zoshia, who wailed in uncontrolled grief, her fat body wobbling as she cried. Deborah looked up at Chris.

'Poor thing. Her sister was killed in the raid today.'

Chris went to the study and found some cognac and made the woman drink it. They helped Zoshia to her feet and led her to Deborah's own bedroom and forced her to lie down and fetched Rachael and Stephan.

'Sit with her, children. Don't let her get up.'

Zoshia cried out that she wanted to go to her sister.

'No, dear. It is not safe there. The walls are all tumbling. Now rest ... rest.'

Deborah found a sedative in Paul's study among the medicines he kept for family use and after great difficulty got the maid to drink it. In a while her wails died down to a weaker cry.

Chris led Deborah to the study and locked the door, and for a moment he held her and soothed her. 'Poor thing,' Deborah said, 'poor thing. Her only sister. All she has left is that no-good son, and she may not even have him. Not a word since the war.'

'She has you and the children.'

Chris poured her a drink, but she refused it. 'The children have been so brave – how long can this go on?'

'I talked with Mayor Starzynski just now. It may end at any moment.'

'Sometimes I think I will be glad when it is over. Even with the Germans in Warsaw it can't get worse. Have you seen anybody?'

Chris nodded.

'I was at the orphanage,' Deborah continued. 'Susan Geller is worried about Ervin. She hasn't seen him in three days.'

'Rosy is all right. I just left him a few minutes ago.'

'That's good. And Gabriela? Did you tell her to come out here with us? It's much safer than in the center of town.'

'She won't leave Andrei's apartment. You know that.'

'Andrei?'

'I was with him this morning, Deborah. The evacuation truce took place through his position on the line. You heard?'

'Yes,' she whispered, 'they gave us back limbless men ... I heard.'

'Deborah ... your husband was one of them.'

The long storage corridors beneath the National Museum were a crush of cots and mattresses stretched out on the floor. The depth of the cellar gave protection from the shelling. It was converted hastily into a hospital. The power in that section of Warsaw had been blasted out. Even the emergency generators were gone. The musty halls were dimly lit by kerosene lamps. It was damp and it smelled moldy and it was clammy-cold and the smell of wounded flesh and antiseptics mingled with the other smells, and there were the sounds of nurses moving in a gliding kind of silence and there was the sound of continual prayer and moans and now and then a shriek of agony.

In the makeshift maternity ward, infants sucked at empty breasts and screamed angrily at what life had dealt them in their few hours on earth.

Chris led Deborah through the maze of corridors, threading his way among the sick and the dying. He went down another dozen steps into a long corridor storing medieval armor from other, less efficient wars. Here lay the amputees and here knelt their bereaved relatives. A nurse held a flashlight close to Paul Bronski's face.

'Paul ...'

'He is under heavy sedation.'

'Paul ...'

A legless man next to Bronski spoke. 'I was there when he did it. He had operated on about twenty or thirty of us ... he was working with a flashlight only . . . then he got it . . . direct hit . . . he was the only doctor left alive. He was conscious the whole time, directing the soldiers how to take his arm off . . .'

'Paul . . .'

Paul Bronski blinked his eyes open. They were glazed, but a small smile cornered his lips to say he knew she was there. She held his hand until he fell back into the drug-induced sleep.

'You Mrs Bronski?' a doctor asked.

She nodded.

'Lucky he is a doctor. There's every chance he'll get through without infection or serious complication. He's out of shock. He'll pull through all right.'

Deborah walked from the house of misery.

Chris waited at the main door of the museum. There were sudden flashes of light, like summer lightning, from the cannon fire on the horizon. The shells arched above them, plunging down on the workers' shacks across the river.

'Let's get out of here,' he said, taking her arm to lead her to his car.

She jerked free of him.

'Come on, Deborah. We'll talk about it at home. If one of those shells falls short we'll be blown to kingdom come.'

'Get away from me,' she snarled.

The skyline lit up in quick, brilliant flashes and he saw her face. Her eyes were those of a madwoman. He grabbed her hand.

'I want to die!'

'Control yourself!'

'We did this to Paul!'

Chris shook her till her head bobbed. 'We didn't make this war!'

'God is punishing me! Murderers! We are murderers!' She tore herself out of his grip and ran off into the darkness.

BOOK TWO

Dusk

Chapter One

Journal Entry – September 27, 1939, Warsaw surrendered.

Poland has been divided into three parts. Germany annexed western Poland to the pre-1918 borders. Soviet Russia has grabbed eastern Poland. The third part has been designated as the General Government Area, which the Germans are going to administrate. It appears this has been set up as a buffer zone against Russia.

The streets of Warsaw trembled beneath the treads of hundreds of tanks moving up Jerusalem Boulevard and the Third of May Boulevard in parade array. These were followed by tens of thousands of goose-stepping soldiers moving in absolute precision, and overhead, squadron after squadron of planes flew in elements at house-top level.

It was an awesome display. The curbs were lined with stunned people. A few German flags fluttered from the homes of ethnics or cowards.

I think that Andrei and I were the only two of Warsaw's three hundred thousand Jews who watched. The rest sat behind drawn curtains and locked doors. I could not resist the temptation of seeing Adolf Hitler. He glowered at us from an open Mercedes. He looks just like his pictures.

I had to watch after Andrei. He was so enraged I was afraid he might try something foolish and get himself killed. He behaved.

Well, we're in it now, brother.

ALEXANDER BRANDEL

Franz Koenig wiped the peak of his cap with his sleeve to enhance the shine. What a pity Herr Liedendorf was not here for this moment. Liedendorf, long the leader of Warsaw's ethnics, had been caught shining lights during German night-bombing raids and was shot by a Polish firing squad. He died a true son of Germany.

Franz Koenig, a brand-new official, had applied for Nazi membership. He was pure in birth, German all the way down to his great-grandparents. He was certain his membership would come through. He admired himself in the mirror and attached the swastika to his right sleeve and went into the bedroom to collect his plump Polish wife. She was too afraid to laugh when she saw the potbellied little professor decked out in a comic-opera uniform. Franz had changed since he began taking up with the Germans a few years before. Once she had had ambitions for him when he was at the university. She prodded him to try to win the chair of medicine. Now he had suddenly become a powerful man and was showing her a dark side she never knew existed, and she did not particularly like it.

Koenig's wife looked like an overdecorated Christmas tree or perhaps a clove-garnished pig ready for the oven. She made nearly two of him. Franz circled her, reckoned she would have to do, and they went out of their flat to the staff car waiting to take them to the grand ballroom of the Europa.

When they arrived the room was filled with uniformed generals of the land forces and admirals of the sea forces and generals of the sky forces and pin-striped, swallow-tailed, beribboned members of the diplomatic forces. Franz saw many old friends, also in new uniforms, and they looked neither more nor less ridiculous than he did, nor did their wives. There was a fantastic amount of heel clicking, square handshakes, bowing and hand kissing, glass clinking, and merry congratulations to the tune of soft Viennese waltzes ludicrously rendered by a German army band. Bottles popped and there was laughter and monocles. There was an entourage of new Polish mistresses, quick to serve new masters, and they were sized up for bed duty by the new administrators of Warsaw.

The orchestra stopped between two notes.

A single drum roll.

Everyone scrambled to set down his drink and line up on either side of the sweeping staircase.

Adolf Hitler appeared at the top of the stairs and as he stepped down, followed by a mass of black-uniformed men, the orchestra rendered a soul-stirring 'Deutschland über Alles.' It was indeed a moment for German backs to be ramrod-stiff and German hearts to pound. Unable to contain himself, an overenthusiastic officer of lower rank cried out, *'Sieg Heil!'*

Hitler stopped and nodded and smiled.

'Sieg Heil!' cried the officer again.

And the room broke into spontaneous rhythmic chanting, right arms thrust forward.

'Sieg Heil! Sieg Heil! Sieg Heil!'

Tears of joy streamed down the cheeks of Dr Franz Koenig, the enthralled and the hypnotized.

Like the ethnic Germans of Austria and Czechoslovakia, the ethnics of Poland lined up for their reward for the service of spying on Poland and helping to destroy the country of their residence in advance of the German army. In the months before the invasion Dr Koenig had grown powerful in the movement, second only to the late Liedendorf. He was made a special deputy to the new Kommissar of Warsaw, Rudolph Schreiker.

'Dr Paul Bronski is here to see you, sir,' a secretary told Koenig.

Koenig looked up from his massive, gleaming desk in his new office in the city hall.

'Show him in.'

Paul was ushered in. Koenig pretended to be deep in meditation of a paper before him. He allowed Bronski to stand, neither offering recognition, a handshake, a seat, or sympathy for his missing right arm.

Paul Bronski had made a good recovery, but he was still very weak and in constant pain. He stood before Koenig's desk for a full five minutes before the German looked up. He realized that Koenig was basking in the glory of retribution. Koenig looked around the lavish environment, as if to point out the distance he had traveled from the tiny cluttered room he had had at the university.

'Sit down,' Koenig said at last. He lit his pipe, rocking his chair back and forth, back and forth. Then, after another few moments, after insatiable sensations oozed from every pore, the delightful pleasures of revenge faded.

'Bronski, I summoned you here because we are in the process of forming a new Jewish Civil Authority. We are disbanding the old Jewish Council as of this afternoon. I am appointing you as deputy in charge of Jewish professionals.'

'But ... Franz ... my position at the university ...'

'As of tomorrow, there will be no more Jews at the university.'

'I have no choice?'

'That is correct. If you carry out our directives and cooperate, you will be much better off than the other Jews in Warsaw, I can assure you.'

'I ... don't know what to say. It would certainly do no good to plead that ... I have been divorced from all things Jewish for many years.'

'The directives from Berlin clearly state that all new laws regarding Jews refer also to converts to Catholicism and people having one Jewish parent, grandparent, or great-grandparent. Active or inactive practice of Judaism is not a matter of consideration.'

'Franz ... I ... it is hard to believe what I hear.'

'Times have changed, Dr Bronski. Get used to it quickly.'

'We have been friends a long, long time ...'

'Never friends.'

'Professional colleagues, then. You have always been a compassionate man. You were here this last month. You saw what happened. You are an intelligent human being. I cannot believe that you have completely lost feeling for us.'

Koenig set his pipe down. 'Yes, Bronski, I have made peace with myself, if that is what you mean. You see, I have been lied to by all those philosophers of righteousness who speak of truth and beauty and the triumph of the lambs. This is real, here and now. It is a victory of lions. Germany has given me in one instant more than a thousand years of piddling through mediocrity and finding comfort in the quotations of false wisdoms.'

'Franz ...'

'Just a minute, Bronski. Your way puts me below your cunning. This way makes me your master. I take it you will serve on the Jewish Civil Authority.'

Paul laughed ironically. 'Yes, I'll be happy to.'

'Very well, then. Tomorrow at ten you will report here to receive your first instructions from the Kommissar, Rudolph Schreiker.'

Paul stood up slowly and extended his hand.

Koenig refused it. 'It would be wise if you got into the habit of dispensing with amenities which heretofore made us appear as equals. You will address me as Dr Koenig at all times and otherwise show the respect due a superior.'

'Times have changed,' Paul said. He started from the room.

'Bronski. One more thing. The Zoliborz suburb is being commandeered for the exclusive use of German officials and officers. Jews are no longer permitted. I shall be moving into your house in about ten days, so you have that length of time to resituate yourself. Before you start crying, I might say that out of deference to past relationships I will make a reasonable settlement on your property, a courtesy that most of the other Jews in Zoliborz will be denied.'

Bronski felt weak. He leaned against the door to support himself, then opened it quickly.

'Tomorrow, here at ten to meet Rudolph Schreiker.'

Chapter Two

Journal Entry

Warsaw has blossomed with German uniforms of all colors. One must have a program to tell who is über *who. The biggest uniform apparently belongs to the new Kommissar, Rudolph Schreiker. We don't know too much about him, but obviously he is not going to try to win a popularity contest here. The old Jewish Council, a quasi-religious government, has been disbanded. A new instrument called the Jewish Civil Authority has been formed. Emanuel Goldman, the musician and a good Zionist, asked me to serve on the executive board. I ducked him because this so-called Civil Authority doesn't seem quite kosher to me.*

ALEXANDER BRANDEL

Rudolph Schreiker, the new Kommissar of Warsaw, had come from a small town in Bavaria. He did not wish to spend his life at a cobbler's bench as had his father, his grandfather, and his great-grandfather. It was doubtful that Rudolph would have made a good cobbler, anyhow, for he wasn't very good at very much.

He reached maturity in that post-war Germany bitter over defeat, jobless, confused, floundering for direction. A malcontent in a time of malcontentment, he spent his energy berating a world he did not understand and was unable to cope with. Schreiker's mediocrity left him with two divorces and four children and debts and alcoholic tantrums.

There were rumblings in Bavaria in the twenties which were music to Rudolph Schreiker and all of his breed. Obscure and insignificant people were being offered a status in life they could never have attained for themselves. His failures were explained to him in a way he liked to believe. He was not responsible for his plight but a victim of conspiracies by the world against his people. He became a Nazi at once.

This new status and this brown uniform and this striking insignia and this man who posed as the Christ of Germany did not demand that he earn his way through labor or through study or wisdom. If these had been demanded, then all the Schreikers would have remained anonymous and Nazism's voice would not have sounded so jewel-toned, and that is why Nazism's voice had such jewel-like tones to him.

All he had to do was exert brute force, the same kind of brute force he used in beating his wives. With little in the way of personality or mental capacity he was yet able to understand clearly that his only hope for success or recognition in the world lay in casting his lot with the Nazis.

He instinctively grasped the one basic rule: absolute obedience. In true German tradition he responded to discipline and power. As a drunkard and wife beater, he had demonstrated his absence of personal morality, so morality posed no problem.

All Rudolph Schreiker really wanted was to be somebody, and Adolf Hitler gave him that chance.

The Nazis took bullies and bums and made them heroes. In exchange, the bums gave absolute obedience. There was no qualm or remorse or inner conflicts of conscience when Schreiker was asked to destroy a synagogue or murder an enemy of the party.

And the Nazis did what Hitler promised. Germany became powerful and feared and, as it expanded, the loyal Schreikers were given their rewards. He had served unquestioningly for nearly two decades, and for this he was made the Kommissar of Warsaw in the General Government Area.

This was a large position for a man who had always been a deputy and whose greatest forte was following commands. Certainly Schreiker was no mental giant and a great deal of the orders would come from Berlin or Krakow or Lublin, where his superiors held office. Nonetheless, it called for more administrative ability and more initiative and authority than he had ever believed he would possess. He did not want to fail. If he were a success in Warsaw, there might be no limit to how far he could advance.

Schreiker learned many lessons intuitively as a Nazi. One of the purest axioms was that intellectuals were weak men. They espoused noble ideas which he did not understand. They argued ideals, but they were not ready to die for them as he was for Nazism. These so-called thinkers were exactly opposite of what they posed to be. They were all talk. They were cowards.

He, Schreiker, could rule them because he could bully them. And they would not fight back. Moreover, he could use them to accomplish for him what he could not do for himself.

The moment he arrived in Warsaw he examined the lists of ethnics who had supported the Germans. Dr Franz Koenig. Perfect. Middle-aged, physically inept, proven loyalty. A doctor and professor, highly educated, lover of classics, reader of philosophers. An intellectual who was completely controllable. Rudolph Schreiker gave Dr Franz Koenig a uniform, a title, and nearly unlimited range and power in his operations.

A good little puppy dog who would help him rule his district.

Paul Bronski was led by Koenig through a series of connecting offices to that of the Kommissar of Warsaw. Rudolph Schreiker sat behind the desk. His personal vanity made him a striking figure. He was a large, strong man with square black German features. Franz Koenig took his place at Schreiker's right.

'They are all here,' Koenig said.

Paul Bronski recognized the other men. Silberberg, the playwright. There was Marinski, who controlled most of the leather factories around lower Gensia Street, and Schoenfeld, the most brilliant of Warsaw's Jewish lawyers and a former member of the Polish Parliament. Seidman, an engineer, was there and Colonel Weiss, one of the highest-ranking Jews of the Polish army. Goldman, an outstanding musician who had at one time taught both Deborah and Rachael. He was known as a strong Zionist among the intellectuals. Finally, there was Boris Presser. Presser seemed out of place in an otherwise distinguished gathering. He was a merchant, the owner of a large department store, but completely unnoted politically or socially in Warsaw.

The eight of them fidgeted before Schreiker's desk. The Kommissar looked from one to the other slowly, examining each and playing the game of invoking his power and authority by deliberate mannerism.

'For reasons of racial inferiority,' Schreiker said, 'we deem it necessary for the Jews to govern themselves separately from the other citizens, under our directives. You eight men have been selected as the executive board of the Jewish Civil Authority. Each one of you will be responsible for a specific department – welfare, health, professions, properties, and so forth. Which of you is Goldman?'

The famed musician and idealist stepped forward. Although aged, Goldman showed the flash and color of a virtuoso.

'You will be in charge, Goldman. You will report directly to me. You others will receive your directives from Dr Koenig.'

Koenig spoke. 'You will occupy the premises at Grzybowska 28 immediately and set up offices. Your first task will be to take a census of the Jews in the Warsaw district. As soon as each Jew registers with your Civil Authority he will be issued a *Kennkarte*, which will also serve as a basis for a ration book. Any Jew found at the end of three weeks without a *Kennkarte* will be punished by death.'

'I expect this registration to be carried out efficiently,' Schreiker added, 'or there will be a new Civil Authority in short order. You will be advised of further directives. You are dismissed.'

They shuffled for the door, dazed.

'One more thing for now,' Schreiker said, standing up and walking around to the front of his desk. He was a large and obviously powerful man and wanted to make certain the others saw it. 'We have thousands of young virile soldiers in our garrison who require diversion. You will supply a list of women who will take care of their requirements. We will need at least fifty or sixty to start; the choice ones will be fortunate to serve in an officers' brothel.'

They looked from one to the other, desperate for one of them to have the courage to speak out.

Schreiker snatched a paper with their names. 'Who is Silberberg?'

Silberberg stepped forward, trembling. All his courage went into the words he wrote. 'You are a playwright! You must know actresses.' Silberberg's thin chest was pained with fear. He drew a deep breath and spit on the floor. Schreiker ran across the room and stopped in front of him. The playwright closed his eyes, waiting for the blow. It came across the bridge of his nose. He sank to his knees, holding his gory face in his hands, temporarily blinded. Goldman knelt beside him quickly.

'Get away from him!'

'Go on, hit me too, you brave man,' Goldman challenged.

Schreiker spun around quickly, looking over the others. 'You, cripple!' he said, pointing to Bronski. 'You will take personal charge of getting the whores!'

'I am afraid I cannot serve under these conditions,' Paul Bronski said.

Franz Koenig sensed that Schreiker had gone too far, too fast. He stepped in quickly. 'We shall discuss this in due time,' he said. 'Now get out, all of you.'

Schreiker wanted to beat them all up, but he knew Koenig's move was to save him from bumbling. He must not bumble. After they left he paced the room, livid with rage, and cursed every oath he knew, then slumped behind his desk, swearing he would show who was the authority. When he calmed down, Koenig spoke softly and calmly. 'Herr Schreiker,' he said, 'we have touched upon a very sensitive point.'

'But they defied me!'

'Herr Kommissar, never mind. Let us not give them issues to unify them. After all now, we have selected them to do a job for us – right?'

'They are privileged!'

'Yes, yes, exactly,' Koenig said. 'In order for them to carry on for us, they must have a certain amount of authority and weight among the Jews. If we destroy their authority by forcing them to do something to make them lose face with the people – then they can't do the job for us.'

Schreiker thought about that. Yes, he had done a stupid thing. He was going to create a power, then destroy it in the same blow. Koenig was shrewd. Intellectuals could always see those things. He would keep Koenig close at hand so he would not make mistakes.

'There are other ways to supply women for brothels,' Koenig said. 'I suggest we drop the matter so far as the Civil Authority is concerned. That will make them think they have some importance.'

'Yes, of course,' Schreiker said. 'I was only testing them to see if they had enough personal courage to carry out our directives – just testing them.'

Journal Entry

Well, we certainly did not have to wait long to find out what is in store for us and what kind of a man Rudolph Schreiker is.

The seat of the government for the General Government Area has been set up in Krakow, which is a surprise. We were certain it would be in Warsaw. A chap named Hans Frank is running the show down there. Each day he publishes a four-page paper called the General Government Gazette. *Pages one, two, and three cover an assortment of things. Page four is dedicated to the 'Jewish Problem.' We certainly are making news these days.*

ALEXANDER BRANDEL

DIRECTIVE

ALL JEWS MUST REGISTER IMMEDIATELY AT THE JEWISH CIVIL AUTHORITY AT GRZYBOWSKA 28 FOR ISSUANCE OF KENNKARTEN AND RATION BOOKS. FAILURE TO DO SO IS PUNISHABLE BY DEATH.

DIRECTIVE

THE ZOLIBORZ SUBURB IS OUT OF BOUNDS FOR FUTURE JEWISH RESIDENCE. THOSE JEWS LIVING IN ZOLIBORZ MUST FIND OTHER QUARTERS WITHIN ONE WEEK.

DIRECTIVE

FOR CLARIFICATION. ALL FUTURE DIRECTIVES PERTAINING TO JEWS ALSO PERTAIN TO THOSE WITH ONE JEWISH PARENT OR GRANDPARENT. JEWS WHO HAVE CONVERTED TO OTHER RELIGIONS ARE CONSIDERED JEWS.

DIRECTIVE

JEWS ARE FORBIDDEN IN PUBLIC PARKS AND MUSEUMS.

JEWS ARE FORBIDDEN IN PUBLIC RESTAURANTS IN NON-JEWISH DISTRICTS.

JEWS ARE FORBIDDEN TO RIDE ON PUBLIC TRANSPORTATION.

JEWISH CHILDREN ARE TO BE WITHDRAWN FROM PUBLIC SCHOOLS IMMEDIATELY.

DIRECTIVE

THE PRACTICE OF THE JEWISH RELIGION IS FORBIDDEN. ALL SYNAGOGUES ARE OUT OF BOUNDS. JEWISH RELIGIOUS SCHOOLING IS FORBIDDEN.

DIRECTIVE
THE FOLLOWING TRADES AND PROFESSIONS MAY BE PRACTICED BY JEWS ONLY AMONG THE JEWISH POPULATION: MEDICINE, LAW, JOURNALISM, MUSIC, ALL GOVERNMENTAL POSITIONS, ALL MUNICIPALLY OPERATED INDUSTRIES.

DIRECTIVE
JEWS ARE FORBIDDEN TO ATTEND THEATER OR CINEMA IN NON-JEWISH AREAS. JEWS ARE FORBIDDEN TO ENTER NON-JEWISH HOSPITALS.

As the registration commenced, each *Kennkarte* was stamped with a large *J*. A directive came out quickly, lowering the ration of Jews. This brought on a scramble to obtain illegal and false Aryan *Kennkarten*. In Zoliborz and other areas confiscated for German officials, the dispossessed Jews were forced to abandon their properties without compensation.

Each day a new directive.

Meanwhile Rudolph Schreiker returned to work with which he was more familiar. The old street fighter of the early Nazi days in Bavaria organized gangs of Polish hoodlums and put them on the German payroll with the order to terrorize the Jewish population. Within a few weeks of the German entry into Warsaw there was a rash of unmolested window smashing, shop looting, and the beating up of bearded Jews.

On the streets, loudspeaker trucks rolled up and down the Jewish areas, barking out the latest directives and page four of the *General Government Gazette*, and orders from the Warsaw Kommissar and the Jewish Civil Authority were plastered on walls on every street.

A special detachment of SS troopers rounded up people most likely to resist, Jews and non-Jews alike, who had been fingered in advance by Dr Franz Koenig and other ethnics. They were marched into Pawiak Prison and shot down by firing squads.

On the radio, round-the-clock saturation to educate the Polish public on the causes of the war.

'Germany has come here to save Poland from Jewish war profiteers.'

And the billboards which once announced Irene Dunne movies found her replacement with drawings of bearded Jews violating nuns, bearded Jews using the blood of Christian babies for their rituals, bearded Jews sitting atop piles of money and knifing good honest Poles in the back.

For the most part, the German program met with universal success. The Polish people, who could not strike at their noblemen who had now vanished, nor at the Russians who had betrayed them, nor at the Germans who had massacred them, were willing to accept the traditional Jewish scapegoat as the true cause of their latest disaster.

Chapter Three

DIRECTIVE
ALL JEWISH TRADE UNIONS, PROFESSIONAL SOCIETIES, AND ZIONIST ORGANIZATIONS ARE, AS OF THIS DATE, ILLEGAL.

Journal Entry

The Bathyran Executive Council held an emergency session today to prepare to go underground. I must find some loopholes in the German directives which will keep us together and functioning, perhaps under a 'front' organization.

Ana Grinspan

has made the most progress. She reports the Krakow Chapter is unified. She has a lot of spunk, that girl. Despite the new directives restricting travel by Jews, Ana has already obtained false travel papers (as a nonexistent Tanya Tartinski). Ana's non-Jewish appearance will help her to move around unchallenged. She has contacted Tommy Thompson at the American Embassy now in Krakow, and he has agreed to receive American dollars from our people outside Poland (and especially our chapters in America) and pass the money on to her. Thank God for Tommy. He is a true friend. Ana is going to travel to all our major chapters at once to set up a system of underground communications which we have worked out.

Susan Geller

has the most urgent situation. She estimates that thirty thousand Jewish soldiers were killed in the invasion. (This figure seems fairly accurate. To the best of our estimates, a Polish total of two hundred thousand soldiers were killed, many thousands escaped over the border, and there are uncounted thousands in prisoner-of-war camps.) In addition, hundreds of children were left parentless during the siege of Warsaw. We must take our share of them. Susan has committed the Bathyran Orphanage to take in another two hundred children, which doubles our present capacity. Needless to say what this does to the budget. We need personnel. That means taking our best people off their outside jobs and sending them to work in the orphanage. God knows how we will manage it. With the cut in rations for the Jews, we must have an extra fifty ration cards from the Jewish Civil Authority for the children.

Tolek Alterman

after his usual speech on Zionism, promised Susan that he will open new acreage at the farm to take up the ration cut. He must be encouraged to increase production if the price of food gets out of hand. But to increase the farm's load will take personnel too.

Ervin Rosenblum

is still working for Swiss News on the technicality that it is a neutral agency, while the letter of the German directive forbids Jews to work on non-Jewish Polish papers. (We expect the Jewish press will be closed down any minute, although Emanuel Goldman, the Authority chairman, sold the Germans on letting it run as a means of mass communication to implement German directives. How long can he hold this point?) Ervin does not believe that either he, Swiss News, or Chris de Monti will be around for long. It will be a great loss, because Ervin is very close to news sources and several times already has given us tips that gave us twenty-four hours of grace to set up defenses. One very sour note. I am distressed that Andrei was not present. I lied to the others, saying he was in Bialystok on business. Three or four members have reported he is planning to do something which will hurt us desperately. I must stop him. I close my entry now in order to find him.

ALEXANDER BRANDEL

Gabriela Rak opened the door for Alexander Brandel at her flat on the Square of the Three Crosses.

'Come in, Alex.' She closed the door behind him and took his overcoat and cap.

'Is he here?'

Gabriela nodded and pointed to the balcony.

'Before I see him ...'

She shook her head. 'I don't know, Alex. Some days he paces like an animal and curses. Other days, like today, he sits and sulks and drinks without a word. Yesterday and today he has been out seeing people. I don't know what for. He won't confide in me.'

'I know,' Alex said.

'I have never known anyone could take defeat so hard, Alex. He has such a fierce pride – it seems as though he is taking it upon himself to suffer for thirty million Poles.'

She walked to the french doors and opened them. Andrei was looking aimlessly out at the battered ruins. 'Andrei,' she called a half dozen times before she got his attention. 'Alexander Brandel is here.'

He walked into the room. He was unshaven and bleary-eyed from too much drinking and too little sleep. He went directly to the liquor cabinet and poured himself some vodka.

'I'll go fix you some tea, Alex,' Gabriela said nervously.

'No,' Andrei ordered, 'you stay. I want you to hear the great dissertations of Zionist logic. Pearls of wisdom are about to drop like spring rain. We should have a bucket so we could catch them all.' He downed the vodka and poured himself another. Gabriela uncomfortably edged into a chair while Alexander walked to Andrei and took the glass out of his hand and set it down.

'Why weren't you at the executive council meeting today?'

'Haven't you heard? There are no more Bathyrans. Directive twenty-two by order of the Kommissar of Warsaw.'

'It was a terribly important meeting. We have to set up mechanisms to go underground.'

Andrei smacked his lips and clapped his hands together and walked to Gabriela. 'Gaby, shall I tell you what they said today, verbatim? Let me see now. Susan Geller cried the loudest because the war gave her lots and lots of new orphans and our girl Susy is going to take them all in, each and every one. So tomorrow Herr Schreiker will issue a directive outlawing orphans. But! Don't underestimate us. Our Alexander Brandel will bypass the directive ... he is a wily man. He finds loopholes in everything. "From now on," declares Alex, "we will call the orphans novitiates and the Bathyran Orphanage will become St Alexander's Convent." Now then, Tolek Alterman sprang to his feet. "Comrades," he said, "I will increase the production of the farm tenfold because it is living Zionism." And then Ana . . . dear old Ana. "I would like to report that the Krakow group is singing 'Solidarity Forever.'"'

'Have you finished?'

'No, Alex. I've had a few meetings of my own.'

'So I hear. Very interesting plans you've made.'

'What plans?' Gabriela said.

'Why don't you tell her, Andrei?' Andrei turned his back. 'No? Well, then I'll tell her. He is planning to take fifty of our best people and leave Warsaw.'

Andrei spun around. 'Let Alex and the rest of that pack of idiots continue their debating societies while the Germans squeeze the life out of them. Yes, I'm taking fifty people and I'm going over the border to Russia and get arms and return and write a few little directives of my own on the Germans' supply lines.'

'Why didn't you tell me this?' she demanded.

'I told you to go to Krakow with the Americans. Well, I still have your papers. It will be my present to you when I leave.'

'But why didn't you tell me!'

'So you'd team up with him and schlogg me to death with arguments?'

'No one is going to argue, Andrei,' Alex said. 'Here it is, straight and proper. You are forbidden to do what you plan.'

'Listen to him! The new Kommissar has issued a directive.'

'You are not going to take fifty of our best people. We need them desperately to keep other people alive.'

'Sing, Brother Brandel!'

'Through us and other Zionist groups the people have organizations prepared to function in their behalf. If you and a hundred others like you take fifty men and women away, you're stripping three and a half million Jews of the only buffer they have to protect them.'

'Alex, try and stop me.'

'We have worked together for a long, long time, Andrei, but I will not hesitate to throw you out of the Bathyrans in disgrace.'

'Then you'll have to throw out the other fifty, because they will follow me.'

They stopped suddenly, each building to a point of no return. There was anger in Andrei that defied logic. Alex was stunned. He turned to Gaby, who threw up her hands in helplessness.

'I prayed to God that my son Wolf would be half the man Andrei Androfski was. When I saw you crawl in on your hands and knees from battle I said, "This is the most gallant man who ever lived. No matter what happens in the days to come, we will pull through so long as Andrei is with us." Now . . . I see you for what you are. A man without true courage.'

Gabriela threw herself between them, looking from one to the other in desperation, and suddenly it was Alex who received her wrath. 'How dare you say that to him!'

Alex brushed by her and slapped Andrei across the face. He did not even blink.

'Stop it!' Gabriela cried.

'It's all right, Gaby. He hits like a woman and he knows I will not strike him back.'

'But the Germans do not hit like women and you do not have the courage to take their blows and keep your hands at your side.'

Andrei walked across the room to the sofa. 'I will not let it be said that I destroyed the Bathyrans. Keep them here. I will go alone. There are a hundred thousand Polish soldiers who escaped over the borders who will fight again. There will be one more.'

Alex hovered over him. 'You are a selfish, vengeful man with only desire to fill this great thirst of yours for personal revenge. Forget the woman who loves you ... forget your sister and her children ... forget your friends ... forget the people to whom you're obligated. When we need you the most, run off to join your roving band of Robin Hoods. Hail and farewell to the gallant Major Androfski of the Seventh Ulanys.'

'Stop tormenting him,' Gabriela cried.

'For God's sake, Alex,' Andrei screamed. 'I cannot fight your kind of war. I am not a traitor! I cannot fight your kind of war!'

'You have fought your war your way and it was no good. Now the battle is even more unbalanced. This is not strong men against strong men. We are a few people who have in our hands the responsibility of three and a half million helpless people. We have no weapons but faith in each other. Andrei, you've always wanted to know what Zionism is. This is Zionism, helping Jews survive. You must give yourself to us. We cannot do without you.'

Andrei sighed and grunted. 'Jesus Christ,' he mumbled, 'what kind of a battle is this?' He looked up at them. 'In all those years I carried the pose of being the great Androfski – and I know why. Because we were fighting a hypothetical battle. Everyone was our enemy – yet, no one. We talked about a dream, we talked about our longings, but now ... I am no longer in a dubious battle. Can't you understand I have seen the enemy face to face? I want to fight him with these,' he said, holding up his hamlike fists. 'I want to smash in the faces of those German bastards.'

'Will that keep us alive?'

'I don't know if I have the courage you speak of, Alex – to watch murder and not lift my hand.'

'Don't leave us, Andrei.'

Gabriela knelt beside him and tried to comfort him. 'Alex is right,' she said. 'You must stand by your people.'

'Didn't you know, Gaby, Alex is always right – didn't you know?'

Andrei looked from one to the other. Yes ... his war was over. In his war he had been trampled and humiliated. Now he must try to fight Alexander Brandel's war.

'I will try,' he muttered at last. 'I will try.'

Chapter Four

As a member of the executive board of the Jewish Civil Authority, Paul Bronski had several privileges and immunities. The ration for his family was equal to that of a Polish official, half again as much as the Jewish ration. Franz Koenig convinced Kommissar Schreiker that such generosity to the JCA would pay off.

Paul was able to secure a lovely apartment on Sienna Street, which was a mixed district of upper-middle-class professionals and long one of the fashionable streets in Warsaw. Bronski was not truly discomfited by the German occupation. His fortune was intact in Switzerland, beyond German reach, and he had quickly achieved the top status the new society allowed. So long as Chris stayed in Warsaw, it was an easy matter for him to advance Paul money which he was able to import on Swiss News accounts.

Nevertheless, moving day brought a terrible uneasiness in him. Deborah seemed delighted at the idea of leaving Zoliborz to move into a predominantly Jewish area. It was as though their forced identification as Jews gave her some sort of victory. While the boxes and crates were piled high, Paul closed himself in his study because he could not stand another question from the children.

On his desk were armbands his family had to wear from now on. The Germans were so damned thorough, he thought. Their directive called for the armband to be white in color with a blue Star of David no less than three centimeters in height. Paul laughed at the irony of it all and put the armband on, feeling that at least he cheated somewhat by losing the specified arm and having to wear the band on his left arm.

There was a knock on the door and Andrei entered.

'Well, hello, brother-in-law,' Bronski said. 'Deborah is about the house somewhere, packing.'

'As a matter of fact, I came to see you, Paul.'

'To gloat over your victory? To tell me how foolish I look wearing a Star of David? To raise your finger and tell me how your ill-fated prediction came to pass – "Bronski, you are a Jew whether you want to be or not" – or to ask if I gave the Germans a lesson on galloping Zionism, which I abhor, and tried to convince them I wasn't really a Jew? Dammit all, the most difficult part of having one arm is trying to load and light a pipe – that and buttoning your fly.'

Andrei struck a match and held it over the bowl of Paul's pipe while he drew in the fire.

'How do you feel, Paul?'

'Fine. I discovered I'm still a hell of a good doctor. Did you ever give directions to a corporal on how to amputate your arm by flashlight? Good trick if I say so myself. You look fine. Mere bullet wounds wouldn't annoy you.'

'How are Deborah and the children taking this move?'

'Deborah? I think she's delighted. The Lord is making divine retribution for the years I forced her to be an agnostic. I am going to brush up on my Hebrew, read the Torah nightly, and spend the rest of my life saying, "I shall be a good Jew," so help me Stawki Street.'

'I came here to ask you if you and I shouldn't call a truce.'

Paul looked surprised. 'You are a gallant winner, sir.'

'No, it's just that times have grown so serious we don't have the luxury of battling each other for a point already proven. You're sitting in the JCA. You know just how bad things are.'

'Oh, no doubt they are bad. It is going to be a rough transition.'

Andrei had his opening. He pressed his point. 'Are you certain it is only a transition? No one really knows what the Germans are up to or when they will quit.'

Paul looked at Andrei with suspicion. The truce was merely a mask behind which he was operating. 'And?' he asked.

'Now that the Jews, the half Jews, the converts, and the unadmitting Jews have been labeled, there is a tremendous need to unify all the loose ends.'

'Go on,' Paul said.

'Paul, we are trying very hard to get a meeting together of every faction of the community, regardless of philosophy, to map out some sort of master policy. You are sitting in one of the key positions. We want to know if you can be counted in.'

'Counted in on what?'

'We can't stand by idly and let the Germans keep pouring these directives at us and beating up our people in the streets. We must go to them as a single body to let them know we are going to resist further abuse.'

Paul sighed and lay his pipe in the ash tray and rocked his chair back and forth, back and forth. 'I might have known you'd still be trying to lead a cavalry charge.'

Andrei, who swore to himself he would not get angry, held his temper. 'How much do you have to take from them before you show your spine? Where are all your fine students now? Where are all your colleagues from the university now?'

'Andrei,' Paul said softly, 'you are not the only one who has meditated about this problem. When I lost my right arm, my body underwent a shock but, as you see, I am well recovered. So, the Jews in Warsaw are losing their right arms. It is painful, but the shock will pass and they will live. Not so well as before, perhaps, but that is the way things are, and nothing we can do will change them.'

'Are you willing to guarantee me that the Germans are going to stop at merely taking an arm? Can you tell me honestly the directives won't take the other arm, then both legs?'

'I'll tell you what I am willing to do, Andrei. I am willing to accept life for what it is. The Germans are the law. They have won a war. I see no alternative.'

'You really think you can do business with them?'

'I really think I have no choice, Andrei. Andrei ... Andrei ... You are always charging windmills – you are always looking for the mystical enemy. Before the Germans, you fought Poland. You cannot accept life for what it is. Yes, I've compromised, but I know reality. I've not chased ghosts. I compromise now because I was suddenly made a Jew again and I have no alternative. Andrei, I've been put into a position of responsibility to this community. Didn't ask for it – didn't want it. But I must, you see. I also have a wife and two children to keep alive –'

'And for that you'll forfeit your soul and honor!'

'Try out the catch phrases elsewhere. I know what you are up to. Insurrection . . . agitation . . . an underground. Break your head against a wall just as you did before the war. I know the reality of what is here now and I'm going to bring my family through it.'

Andrei was about to roar that Paul was a coward, always looking for the easy path out. The cat who always lands on his feet. The first to sell his soul. It took all the strength he had, but he restrained himself.

'And, so long as we are talking about it, Andrei, your activities are bound to be known. For the safety of Deborah and the children, it may be best if you stay away from us.'

'Let my sister decide that!'

'Oh, nothing her darling brother does can be wrong.'

Andrei spun around on his heels and stamped out. He was unable to resist slamming the door as a sign that he had not entirely lost his restraint.

Paul tapped the pipe against his teeth and shook his head. There he goes, Paul thought. Still looking for a fight. Still at the head of a cavalry charge. How long would Andrei last in this atmosphere before he was dragged up before a firing squad?

But then, Andrei would laugh at them while he was being shot. And for a moment Paul was envious of that reckless courage that was unable to give quarter. He, Paul Bronski, had shown an instinctive courage in a single instant when the German bully Rudolph Schreiker demanded Jewish women for prostitutes. There would be other moments of crisis in the days ahead. How he would like to be Andrei Androfski in those moments. Would he be defiant when the challenge came the next time? He did not know. If only he could store that second of courage in a little box and open it again when he needed it.

A ruckus from the direction of the kitchen sent Paul running from his study. Deborah was standing over Zoshia, yelling at her.

'What is going on here?'

'Zoshia stole our silver. Rachael saw her pass it over the fence to that rotten son of hers.'

Paul stepped between the two of them.

'Is this true, Zoshia?' he demanded.

'It is true and I'm not sorry,' Zoshia screamed.

'She is a dirty thief,' Deborah snarled.

'It is mine and more than mine for the years I have cleaned your Jew dirt.'

'Oh, dear Lord,' Deborah said, 'we have treated you kinder than your own son, whom we've bailed out of jail every time he went into one of his drunken rages. I paid the doctor bills for you and your sister when you couldn't work.'

'You brought the Germans to Poland,' Zoshia cried. 'The priest told us so! It is all the fault of the Jews!' She spit in hatred in their faces and waddled from the room.

Deborah leaned against Paul and cried softly, and he tried to comfort her. 'I can't believe it,' she murmured. 'I can't believe it . . .'

'There is nothing we can do. The Germans are encouraging them to do what she did.'

One of the moving men came in.

'We have a wagonload. You said you wanted to come with us to Sienna Street and show us where the things go.'

'Mrs Bronski will be out in a moment. She will follow you over.'

The teamster tipped his cap and left.

Deborah dried her eyes. He walked to his office and returned with the armbands. 'You and the children will have to wear these,' he said.

She took them and stared at them, then put one on her right arm. 'Isn't it a shame,' she said, 'that the first time we really must tell the children they are Jews ... it must be like this ...'

Chapter Five

Journal Entry

Andrei warned me that we could not depend on Paul Bronski. How right he was. We continue to canvass the Jewish community to see who among us will come together for a leadership meeting. We are picking up strength, but not fast enough. A few more of these German directives will do more to convince them than any of our arguments.

I am going to see Rabbi Solomon. If we can win his support, it could well put us over the top.

ALEXANDER BRANDEL

The Rabbi Solomon's name was most often preceded by the word 'great.' He was one of the most learned men not only of Warsaw but of all Poland, and that constituted the heartland of religious Jewry.

He was a humble man who was beloved for giving his life to study and devotion and teaching. His rulings set the vogues among the religious Jews.

Not the least of the man's many qualities was a political agility. When one came to earth from Talmudic and ethical writings to things real, deftness was required in order to be able to get along with all the diversified factions of Jewish opinion and philosophy. It was because of this wizardry that he was often called upon to use his good offices to mediate between extreme thinkers, from Communists to neo-fascists.

All organized Zionists believed that only they were the true standardbearers of Zionism and that the others outside their ranks were merely pseudo Zionists. It was the same with Rabbi Solomon. His Zionism, he felt, was certainly the purest form, for it came from the books of the Bible which told him a 'Messiah' would return to earth and lead the scattered children of Israel back to their 'Promised Land.' This was not so much Zionism to him but rather fundamental Judaism.

All the new ideas – revisionist, socialist, communist, intellectualism – were merely expedient and radical ideas which took the place of the true basic faith.

Although he did not agree with the new ideas, he was compassionate toward them. He understood that it took enormous inner strength not to be able to rebel against the abuses the Jews had suffered. These new forms of Zionism, therefore, were rebellions by weak men who could not suffer in silence and dignity, to pray and to accept as part of life the penalties imposed by God for being worthy of being the chosen guardians of the Holy Law.

After the Germans shut his synagogue, he worked harder than ever keeping up the morale of his people. During the storm of directives his quiet strength and counsel were constantly sought.

It was after such a strenuous day that Alexander Brandel arrived in his study. The old man looked forward to the relaxation and verbal swordplay with the learned Zionist historian.

They recounted the terrible things of the day with mutual sadness, went through all the accepted amenities, then Alex got down to business.

'We feel the urgencies of the day call for us to set aside the things which divide us,' Alex said carefully, 'and unite in those upon which we agree.'

'But, Alexander, two Jews never agree on anything.'

'On certain things, Rabbi Solomon. On taking care of orphans. On helping each other.'

'And what shall we do on those things which you claim we agree?'

'We shall first hold a meeting. I have many diversified leaders who have agreed to attend. If you would come, it would be a signal for most of the rabbis in Warsaw to follow suit.'

'Do you have support from the Bund?'

'Yes.'

'And the Federation of Labor Zionists?'

'Yes.'

'And the Communists?'

'Yes.'

'Such a meeting will be a mess.'

'There is another intention.'

'Aha.'

'We must try to present a unified front to stop these German directives.'

'So? Well, Alexander, I am not a social worker. I am also not a politician. I am merely a teacher. As for civil problems, we have a Civil Authority to cope with most of the problems which you pose.'

Alex promised himself not to become discouraged. He started again. 'The Jewish Civil Authority was hand picked by the Germans. We feel they merely wish to use it as an instrument to carry out their policy.'

'But surely with good Zionists like Emanuel Goldman and Schoenfeld and Silberberg on the Authority –'

'But, Rabbi, they are truly without power. These are extraordinary times and call for extraordinary measures.'

'What is so extraordinary about these times, Alex?'

'We could be possibly engaged in a struggle for our very survival.'

The old man smiled and stroked his big bushy white beard. How dramatic these young people were! 'Alexander. Tell me, learned historian, when in the history of the Jewish people has survival not been an issue? Sometimes the degrees varies. What is happening today in Poland has happened many times in our history. Now tell me, Brandel the historian, have we not outlived every tyrant in the past?'

'I think there is a difference.'

'So?'

'From the time of the First Temple we have been massacred because of scapegoatism, expedience for the ruling politicians, passion outbursts, ignorance. The Crusades, the Inquisition, the Worms massacre, the Cossack uprisings. Never before have we been faced with a cold-blooded, organized, calculated, and deliberate plot to destroy us.'

'And how does the learned historian know this to be true?'

'I read Adolf Hitler.'

'Aha. Tell me, Alexander, what do you suppose the Germans stand to gain by destroying the Jews? Will they gain territory? Will they gain more than token wealth? What can be the ultimate goal in doing away with some of the world's finest doctors, musicians, craftsmen, scientists, writers? What is the point that they will win by doing it?'

'It is not the matter of winning a point. They started on us the same way a hundred others started on us, but in the case of the Germans, I do not know if they will be able to stop themselves. Like no other people in history, they are psychologically geared to destroy merely for destroying.'

'So, what you are saying is that the Nazis are evil. As a historian, surely you know that evil destroys itself.'

'It may also destroy us while it is destroying itself. Where does it say in the Talmud and Torah, Rabbi, that we are not supposed to defend ourselves?'

'But we do defend ourselves. We defend ourselves by living in the faith which has kept us alive all of the centuries. We defend ourselves by remaining good Jews. It will bring us through this hour as it has through all the rest of our crises. And the Messiah will come, as He has promised.'

'And how do you suppose we will recognize Him?'

'It is not if we recognize Him. It is if He will recognize us.'

The argument was at a dead end. The old man would not budge.

Alex took his armband off and held it in front of the Rabbi's eyes. 'Can you wear this with pride?'

'It was good enough for King David.'

'But he did not wear it as a badge of humility!'

'Alexander, why must all Zionists shout? The gates of heaven are barred to those who pick up weapons of death. That is what will come ultimately to you if you form a band of rabble. Learn to suffer in humility and faith. That alone will be our salvation.'

Chapter Six

DIRECTIVE
ALL GOVERNMENT PENSIONS FOR JEWS ARE HEREBY SUSPENDED.

DIRECTIVE
JEWS ARE FORBIDDEN TO PATRONIZE NON-JEWISH FOOD MARKETS AND DEPARTMENT STORES.

DIRECTIVE

TRAVEL PERMITS ARE REQUIRED FOR JEWS LEAVING WARSAW. JEWS ARE RESTRICTED TO SPECIAL COACHES MARKED 'JEWISH.'

DIRECTIVE

JEWS ARE FORBIDDEN TO STAND IN RATION LINES EXCEPT AT SPECIFIED JEWISH STATIONS.

Alexander Brandel's quest for solidarity was frustrating. There was confusion among the people. Most of them were not connected with organizations. They wanted merely to be able to take care of their families. The few men whose power and influence could have rallied everyone were marched to Pawiak Prison and shot.

Mayor Starzynski, who had made the epic fight for Warsaw and was one of the few Poles in high positions to give the Jews credit for their contribution to the defense of the country, disappeared. Like many another, he was taken off in the middle of the night without explanation and never returned.

Alex watched his fellow intellectuals disintegrate. These men who had once gushed forth waterfalls of idealism seemed unable to put their words into practice.

He courted Rodel, the Communist, who controlled an important organization. The baldheaded, chain-smoking leader of the Communists spent most of the time explaining how the Soviet Union truly saved eastern Poland by jumping her from the back while the Polish army fought for its life. Rodel was always amusing to Alex. He had an amazing range of verbal dexterity and political acrobatics. In the spring of that year Rodel had been violently anti-Nazi. In the summer, after the Russian-German pact, he decided the Germans weren't so bad, after all – it was the Western powers who had really sold everyone down the river. Now he was violently anti-German once more but spent most of his time explaining away Russian treachery. Rodel had no use for Zionism simply because he had no use for anything that was not communism. Nonetheless, Alex needed Rodel. To ignore the Communists would be worse than to be refused by them. The Communists, with their non-Jewish members, boasted the closest-knit group for the Jews. But Rodel was having his hands full. The Communists were being hounded by the Nazis even more unmercifully than the Jews. The Gestapo had a single order covering them: FIND THEM AND SHOOT THEM.

Alex couldn't even get to talk with the leader of the Revisionists, Samson Ben Horin. They were traditionally loners who wanted no part of a plan committing them to act with the group. Alex reckoned they were girding for street fighting.

The businessmen were racked with problems. Shelves were bare, prices were rising, there was a continuing pressure by the new directives. They considered Alex's quest for unity as asking for charity. For them, anything outside of normal business activities was deemed 'charity.' Charity could be considered only after profits, and they were doubtful these days.

The largest single entity, the religious community, simply refused to budge. They took their cue from Rabbi Solomon to resort to the traditional weapons of prayer and patience.

The Jewish Civil Authority treated Alex as though he were a leper. He was branded as a harbinger of doom by Silberberg, the playwright, who had had all the fight knocked out of him by the single blow delivered in the office of Rudolph Schreiker. Silberberg, whose plays had once reeked with slogans of courage ... The rest of them were jealous of their stations. Only Emanuel Goldman, the pianist, could be counted on.

Outside the Jewish community, pickings were lean. The gentile intellectuals were as terrified as the Jewish intellectuals. Paul Bronski proved a classic example. From the time he returned to Warsaw till the time he moved to Sienna Street, he did not receive a single call from his colleagues or students at the university.

The majority of the population wanted no part of the German-Jewish war. A minority were actively against the Jews.

The one great voice of power and conscience, the Church, remained silent.

As a clever tactician, Alexander realized early that unity was impossible, so he carefully formulated a secondary objective. When it was all thought out, he called together three of the most reliable strong men. These were people who understood the urgency without being preached to and who, like him, were groping for a way to hang together and bypass the dreaded directives.

The four of them picked each other's brains in a series of secret meetings.

There was Alex, and there was Simon Eden, the iron-handed ruler of the Joint Federation of Labor Zionists. He alone was able to form and control ten different middle-to left-wing factions. His Joint Federation accounted for more than sixty per cent of all organized Zionists. Simon had the best qualities of Alexander and Andrei combined and few of their faults. Like Andrei, he had been an officer in the army and was a large and strong man who could rise to fierceness. Like Alex, he was a cool and deliberate thinker. Andrei respected Simon more than any man in Warsaw except Alex.

The third man was Emanuel Goldman, the aging but still flamboyant artist of the piano who had been appointed head of the Jewish Civil Authority.

Goldman was Dr Franz Koenig's one error in judgment. Koenig believed correctly that the famed musician had a 'name' value to the Jews but certainly underestimated his devotion to humanitarian causes. Goldman was realistic. He knew he could not last long on the Civil Authority. The Germans wanted a weak man to carry out their orders. He was grimly determined to find a route for the community before he was dispossessed.

The fourth man was David Zemba, director of the American Relief Society, an organization supported by American Jews. Zemba, a Polish Jew, was small in stature, with a closely cropped beard and a mild manner, but he was utterly fearless and brilliantly shrewd. With Poland occupied, the American dollars which he controlled had to be one of the foundations of any adventure.

Together, they worked out a formula.

Stage one: Emanuel Goldman, as head of the Jewish Civil Authority, received an appointment with Dr Franz Koenig.

'We are faced with a problem, Herr Doktor. By tradition, we Jews have always taken care of our own. Social work was formerly handled by the old Jewish Council, which has been disbanded. As you know, the war has compounded this problem. We have no legal instrument through which to take care of welfare problems.'

'I take it you are petitioning me to set up a welfare department in the Jewish Civil Authority?'

'Not exactly. The Authority does not have either trained personnel or funds and we are too busy taking the census.'

'I am certain you did not come here without a proposal.'

'So. My proposal is such. There are many professional do-gooders. They can collect the money – they can find the people – they can run orphanages and old-age homes.'

'Are you suggesting an independent agency?'

'I am.'

'Not as a branch of the Civil Authority?'

'Correct.'

'Why?'

'On matters of self-help the Jews are nearly always unified, no matter what their philosophy. Having this traditional service operated by a government agency would cause tremendous grumbling among diverse elements. The raising of funds would be extremely hard, for people are naturally suspicious of government. There would be untold confusion, duplication of work, and administrative hassles which could be avoided by establishment of an independent agency.'

Koenig saw sense in Goldman's arguments. He could assign the Civil Authority to watch over this new agency. On the other hand, if the Civil Authority were running welfare work he would always have Goldman fighting with him for more funds. Yet it was not all so black and white. Dr Koenig was learning that Goldman was a man of character, and although it appeared on the surface that it was a simple matter, he was not coming in with a proposal that would benefit the Germans.

Emanuel Goldman also knew he was not up against a robot like Schreiker. Koenig was probing, looking for a trap.

'Who do you propose to head this new agency?'

'Oh, there are lots of people. Mainly, we must find a man acceptable to all elements. Say, Alexander Brandel.'

'Brandel? With his Zionist background?'

Goldman shrugged. 'The Bathyrans as a group never achieved Brandel's personal stature. They are disbanded now. He is mild and inoffensive and quite trusted.'

'Suppose I let you have your agency, but on one condition?'

'And that condition, Herr Doktor?'

'Brandel does not run the agency.'

They had come to the impasse. Goldman had hoped he could push it through without this moment. Now he had to make his gamble. He reached inside his breast pocket and placed a small envelope on Koenig's desk. 'The full plans for the agency are in here, Herr Doktor,' he said. 'I beg you to study them carefully and give me your answer tomorrow.'

The old man left the city hall, not knowing whether he was about to spend his last day on earth.

When Koenig opened the envelope he took out five one-thousand-dollar bills.

It was quite clear to him. The Jews wanted to run this agency away from prying eyes. His first inclination was of anger. He snatched the envelope from the desk and started for Rudolph Schreiker's office. Then he stopped. Schreiker would laugh at him and pocket the money.

The very idea that a good German official would accept a bribe! He walked back to his desk slowly. The last few weeks had plunged him from the dreamworld to Teutonic purity. At this moment Schreiker was organizing hoodlum gangs to begin looting Jewish-owned warehouses.

Why shouldn't the Jews play the game also? But where did he fit in? Five thousand dollars! More in a snap of the finger than he had made in an entire year at the university.

While everyone was playing cutthroat, wouldn't it be utterly ridiculous for him to stand alone as a paragon of virtue? And if he did, how long would he last with Schreiker? Schreiker had been playing him for a fool.

Think it over, Franz. Schreiker needs you. You can make yourself indispensable to him. And this game. It is a rough game. The war was rough. The business here is rough.

He paced the floor of his home taken from Bronski in the Zoliborz suburb. Everyone is scheming and conniving. But he, Koenig, was in a key position. This is only the beginning. He was in a position to amass fantastic wealth in the days ahead.

Play the game ... five thousand dollars ... play the game ... Bit by bit the moral foundations upon which Dr Franz Koenig had built his life had been nibbled away. From the moment he had cast his lot with the ethnics before the war he began compromising and rephrasing the wisdoms and rethinking the thoughts and justifying.

The next day.

'Emanuel Goldman is here to see you, Herr Doktor.'

'Send him in.'

'I have spoken to the Kommissar. I was able to convince him that a separate agency for Jewish welfare cases would be the best solution for all concerned. Your Civil Authority is authorized to issue a license for its operation.'

Goldman nodded.

'I have taken under consideration the appointment of Alexander Brandel. I think he is an excellent choice. He will deal with me directly on matters of rations, personnel, and privileges.'

Goldman nodded again. Dr Koenig was cutting himself in for a nice big slice, he thought. Now he could not back down. Koenig had pocketed the first bribe. He could be had. The gamble was won. In the future the money would come harder to Koenig, for the five thousand dollars had not only bought his silence but had stuck his neck out. There will be some more for you, you rat, Goldman thought, but not so much as you think, or we may tell your friend Schreiker how you have been stealing from him.

Stage two: Formation of the Orphans and Self-Help Society. Alexander Brandel was made its director.

Stage three: American Relief turned over tens of thousands of dollars of emergency funds to Brandel. In the name of the Orphans and Self-Help Society he leased fifteen pieces of property in the northern section of the Jewish area of Warsaw, where it was less expensive.

The houses were set up as soup kitchens, ration stations, aid and medical stations, orphanages, and for whatever welfare work came under the society's jurisdiction.

Although these places functioned legitimately, each one in fact served the secondary purpose as a screen for the continued activities of the Zionist groups, which the Germans had ordered disbanded.

The Zionists had successfully changed their name but in fact were still intact. Personnel for the Orphans and Self-Help Society were all key people from the Zionist groups. They were given special armbands and special immunities. Another thousand dollars to Dr Koenig made certain the Orphans and Self-Help Society staff was not screened.

One of the master reasons for the Orphans and Self-Help Society was to get money from American Relief to its welfare objectives without first passing through the hands of the Jewish Civil Authority for disbursement. Goldman was certain that if the Authority touched the money it would become an object of graft.

Brandel now had bases of operations, the Zionists intact, money to pay personnel to run the farms, to increase the capacity of the former Bathyran Orphanage, and to get the hungry and homeless fed and clothed.

There was a final purpose. Only some of the houses were used for welfare work. Brandel was able to get choice jobs for his people, and many of them moved into the headquarters house and worked under the authority of the Orphans and Self-Help Society and donated their wages back into a communal pool. This, Tolek Alterman proclaimed, was 'living Zionism.'

Journal Entry

The Orphans and Self-Help Society is a reality. All of our key people in Warsaw are working for us.

I took the five-story building at Mila 19 as our headquarters. Twenty of our Bathyran youngsters have left their homes and are living on the premises and donating all their earnings into a communal. This makes me terribly proud! Six of the buildings were handed over to Simon Eden's Federated Zionists as 'Orphan and Self-Help Agencies' ... Simon chose Leszno 92 as his headquarters. He also reports communals in all six of his places. We are reserving the other places, for we are certain some of the reluctant divergent groups who did not want to unify will come over to us now.

Self-help has always been our one great source of unity in the past. It will bring us together now. Incidentally, at my last meeting I asked Goldman, Zemba, and Eden if they would mind jotting down notes on things they see and hear. So many things are happening these days I cannot keep track of them all. I want their impressions to set down in the journal. May I say that they are tolerant of this historian. They all promised to collect notes and turn them over to me at our weekly meetings.

ALEXANDER BRANDEL

Chapter Seven

Journal Entry

I had a long talk today with Ervin Rosenblum. I wanted his opinion about what the Germans were really up to and who was actually running Poland.

Ervin says Hans Frank, the Governor General of Krakow, is not the real boss. His background indicates he is a civil administrator mainly here to exploit Poland for the German economy.

Lublin, not Krakow, is the real capital. The German political police, concentration-camp administrators, criminal police, special-duty squads, and all of that personal Nazi contingent of Hitler's, independent of the German army, have their organizations and duties so intermixed it is nearly impossible to determine where one ends and the other begins. We do know that there is one boss in Lublin of SD, SS, and Gestapo for the General Government Area. He is Gruppenführer Odilo Globocnik. He is an Austrian (like Hitler) and has a background as a Jew baiter. As an SS major general, he has only to answer to three people over him – Hitler, Himmler, and the SD chief in Berlin, Reinhard Heydrich.

I think Ervin is right. It is a cinch he has more power than Hans Frank.

As for the true aim of the Germans? There is a Department 4B of the Gestapo in Berlin which handles 'Jewish Affairs.' It is being run by a Lieutenant Colonel Adolf Eichmann, who, I understand, has been to Palestine and speaks Hebrew. Ervin is sure the directives are all part of a master plan coming from Department 4B from blueprints drawn up by Reinhard Heydrich.

It certainly appears they are going to start draining Jewish wealth systematically, throw the leaders and intellectuals into concentration camps. No one doubts but that the Germans will strike again. Like Pharaoh and Rome, they will need slave labor. I believe the three and a half million Jews in Poland are marked for this.

Ervin thinks Swiss News will be closed any day. Among the new arrivals is a Nazi named Horst von Epp, who will run the Department of Propaganda and Press. It is only a matter of time until Chris de Monti's credentials are checked.

ALEXANDER BRANDEL

Horst von Epp joined the influx of Nazi officials to Warsaw in the winter of 1939. Completely unlike most of his fellow Nazis, he was a sophisticated man with continental charm and a sparkling sense of humor. He did not wear any of the several choices of uniforms but had tailor-made clothing in the latest fashions and bemoaned the fact that war with England caused him to lose his Bond Street clothier.

The scion of a wealthy family of former nobility, he had little in common with fellow Nazis. He found their violent methods personally distasteful, had little regard for their mentality, and thought all the nonsense of super-men theories, geopolitics, land to live and joy through labor completely ridiculous.

He was far more at home in Paris, on the Riviera, or in New York than in Munich (but he adored Berlin). Yet he was a devoted Nazi and promoted the very principles he abhorred. Denied most of his family holdings by mismanagement and overspending, he was shrewd enough to recognize the irresistible and unstoppable surge of Nazism in the early thirties and simply drifted into the stream. He had few ideals and convictions to deter him from the pursuit of his own pleasures. He wanted the most for the least exertion of effort. He knew the bumbling mentality of most of the early Nazis would call for men like him to think for them.

He was a good-looking man in his early forties, a first-rate libertine who was never faithful to his wife for more than a month or so, and he was a genuine snob, intellectually superior to the majority of his confederates.

Horst von Epp grated the nerves of men like Rudolph Schreiker. He made them feel insignificant, and no Nazi should be made to feel that way. Many would have loved to get rid of Von Epp, but those in power realized he was needed for his particular talents and therefore worth the annoyance he caused.

The German propaganda instrument had effects which had never been duplicated. They knew the basic premise that if a lie was repeated often enough even those who knew it was a lie would soon regard it as truth. Then there were half truths based on masterful distortions of facts. Horst von Epp had helped engineer for Josef Goebbels one of the most brilliant propaganda coups of any age during the Spanish civil war, which was no civil war at all. He was able to clutter the true issues so neatly that the world soon came to believe that the Loyalist government was a Communist government and therefore the Spanish war was a war against communism.

While the Propaganda Ministry poured out fantastic distortions, it became Horst von Epp's job to water down the vitriol. In Berlin, clever and unsatisfied newsmen from the outside world always stood ready to pounce on the validity of the Progaganda Ministry's statements and charges. It was impossible to evict all of the journalists who questioned them and still keep world opinion in check.

Horst stilled the troubled waters. He became the pal of the newspapermen. He was always the swell guy, despite the fact that he was a Nazi. The Nazis were never known for being personality boys, so Horst's personal charm was a luxurious departure from the Nazi bureaucrats. He became the front man who shielded the curious from the inner circle. Horst von Epp could fix anything for a journalist, from a speeding citation to a fräulein, any size or specification – for his friends.

Warsaw became a focal point of world observation. World opinion had to be kept in bounds.

During the winter of 1939, France and England engaged in a make-believe war with Germany on the western front. Not a single shot was fired by either side. Trains moved along the border unmolested. Germany embarked on a massive campaign to try to talk England and France out of continuing the war, now that the 'Polish issue was settled.'

It therefore became a priority issue in the Propaganda Ministry to keep adverse news from getting out of Poland, which could upset their plans. Legions of neutral journalists had descended on the General Government Area from Italy, Switzerland, Sweden, the Orient. A few Americans and South Americans got in. A slick operator like Horst von Epp was needed to 'keep things quiet.'

He arrived in Warsaw and established an elaborate headquarters in the Bristol Hotel, commandeering half a floor. He stocked his personal suites with the best liquors and foods. Within two weeks he had a line on every model and actress in Warsaw who was not stricken with Polish nationalism and made the propositions very attractive to them. Twenty-five of the most ravishing specimens were set aside for the pleasure of the top foreign newsmen and diplomats. He made up a second-string team of coeds from the university, secretaries, professional women, and attractive wives seeking to augment their incomes.

After the humorless, dull, blustering Rudolph Schreiker, Von Epp was making things bearable for the foreign journalists. Everything was conducted in a rather informal atmosphere, which both eased the tension and tranquilized the extent of their probing.

Chris was just finishing dressing when the doorbell of his flat on Jerusalem Boulevard rang. He opened the door, and Horst von Epp stood before him. The man was immaculately dressed and wore a pleasant smile.

'Hello there,' he said. 'I am Horst von Epp.'

'Come in.'

The German looked around. 'Lovely ... lovely. Ah! That jacket you are wearing.' He looked at the label. 'Feinberg of Bond Street. The finest tailor in London. I was his customer right up to the war. Of course I had to switch the labels because he's Jewish, but most of those lunkheads can't tell a fine piece of material when they see one. Uniforms! Uniforms! The tailors in Berlin are butchers. Do you suppose you could get me a few things through Switzerland from Feinberg?'

'You didn't come here for that.'

'No. I had a reception for the foreign press corps yesterday. I was particularly looking for you.'

'Sorry, I was driving back from Krakow. I phoned in my regrets.'

'No matter.'

'I just finished reading your love letters,' Chris said, referring to the new set of censorship regulations and procedures for filing dispatches.

'Oh, that,' Von Epp scoffed. 'Nazi bureaucracy. You see, we have to put a hundred people to work making orders and then another hundred countermanding them. Another hundred sorting paper clips. That pays off our obligations to the party faithful. We shall rule the world in triplicate. Cigarette?'

'Matter of fact, yes. I drove back from Krakow so fast I forgot to buy some.' Chris was impressed with the package of American Camels.

'I'll send you a case, my compliments. I've also made arrangements for certain members of the press corps to draw food supplies, personal articles, liquor, and so forth, from the SS officers' stores at the Citadel.'

Well, Chris thought, this *is* something new in Nazi public relations. He studied Von Epp. Why had he been singled out for special treatment? He had heard Von Epp was coming to Warsaw and was a regular guy. Smooth – very smooth. Yet certainly likable.

'I didn't mean to break in on you,' Von Epp said, 'but I did want to get acquainted and I have a few matters to take up with you.'

'Shoot.'

'If you want to keep your offices in the Bristol, I probably can arrange it, but frankly, the place is overrun with Nazis. Needless to say, we must put men to work tapping switchboards and phones, but you'll probably be more comfortable elsewhere.'

'I can work right here in my apartment. There's an empty storeroom connected to my kitchen. It will work fine.' Chris was relieved at the idea that Von Epp was going to let him stay in Warsaw. He had dreaded this moment. Now it had come and gone – just like that.

'Now, the phone lines are open to Switzerland. I'll get you a direct connection with your agency – Swiss News, isn't it?'

'That's right.'

'Fine agency. I know your boss, Oscar Pecora, quite well. We're putting up a message center for the press corps at the Bristol so you'll be able to have twenty-four-hour service – you might as well let us see your incoming messages first, because we'll see them sooner or later. Now, anything particular that you want?'

'What's the price?'

Horst von Epp smiled. 'You're a big boy – you know what you can and can't do. All I want is your gentleman's agreement to keep within reasonable limitations. I don't want to work hard, and the best way to make things easy for myself is to make them easy for you. What do you say?'

Chris shrugged. 'I've never had it better.'

'I am afraid there is one unpleasant bit of business on the agenda. So far as I am concerned a Jew can take a photograph as well as a blond Aryan and certainly report a story – but –'

'Rosenblum.'

'I'm afraid so.'

'He offered to quit several days ago. He knew this would happen.'

Horst von Epp flopped his arms. 'I wish I knew what to do. It appears that Berlin simply won't let me have room to maneuver on Jewish matters.'

Chris wanted to press the point. Rosy knew it would happen. But Rosy had been wrong about the Germans closing out Swiss News. Better hold his tongue . . .

'It's not your fault,' Chris said.

'I have an idea. How about dinner tonight? My suite?'

Chris shrugged. Why not? He had nothing better to do.

'Perhaps . . . a little company later on?'

Chris walked to the window. So many times he had seen Deborah standing before that same window . . . had watched her from the alcove. The last time he had looked at Deborah her eyes were mad and she plunged into darkness. Sienna Street was only four blocks away. So near . . . so damned near. She was there with Paul now, on Sienna Street. Another lonely night, and another, and another. Would there ever be a moment of peace for him? He didn't want to face the darkness alone again. Nagging, longing. Lonely. He would stand at the window and look toward Sienna Street and think about her. Rosy told him he was a fool, she would never leave Paul Bronski.

Chris turned and faced the German. 'Ladies? Sure, why not? That's just fine with me.'

Chris approached the dinner engagement with Horst von Epp with suspicion. It had all come too easily. He thought he would be on a train to Switzerland by this time, booted from Poland. Instead, he and Swiss News were still alive and operating in the middle of a German occupation.

Chris suspected that Horst von Epp would be a perfect host. He was. In fact, he was more comfortable with the German than he had been with anyone for months. Horst knew all the latest stories and had vast amounts of gossip about mutual friends in the newsmen's world. Chris's suspicions began to fade as the evening wore on. For a while he hung on every word, looking for some telltale sign of what Von Epp really wanted from him. The German would not tip his hand. Further, Chris was constantly amazed at Von Epp's open expressions of disdain for many Nazis.

'Well,' Von Epp said, 'speaking with realism, I am committed to Hitler's policies. If he wins, I shall be an enormous man. If he loses, I'll become a gigolo on the Riviera. I have one terrible aversion, and that is to perform honest labor. I'll do anything to avoid it, and frankly, I'm not suited for much.'

Chris admired his candor.

'Now!' Horst said. 'I have a surprise for you. Surprises should always go with dessert.'

The German handed a *Kennkarte* over the table. Chris opened it. It was a document signed by Kommissar Rudolph Schreiker. Ervin Rosenblum was to be allowed to continue his position with Swiss News. He was not obliged to wear an armband with a Star of David.

'I don't know what to say.'

'Please understand that I can't guarantee that this won't be revoked, but . . . for the time being . . .'

Chris waved away the after-dinner cognac and loaded his glass with scotch. He pocketed Rosy's *Kennkarte* with amused perplexion. The inevitable cigar smoke came from the direction of Von Epp.

'Herr von Epp,' Chris said, raising his glass, 'I salute a perfect but confusing host. You know, I am a professional observer of the cat-and-mouse game that diplomats play. I am first rate at deciphering the meaning of double talk. Yet here I am in the middle of a squeeze play and I am completely puzzled. Pardon me for not being subtle, but what the hell are you up to? What's your deal? What are the strings? What do you want from me?'

'Bravo, De Monti. All journalists must be suspicious by nature.'

'Are you queer? Do you have designs on me?'

Von Epp roared with laughter. 'God, no – but confidentially, the city hall is loaded with them. Chris, you see these Nazi clots around here. They bow stiffly from the waist, kiss a lady's hand like a pig, and walk in those ridiculous uniforms as though they had broomsticks up their rectums. You are my kind of man. We drink scotch and have the same tailor in London. I believe your handshake is better than a Nazi pact. I want to be friends.'

'No orders?'

Horst shrugged. 'You have friends among the Jews. I would guess that everyone in Warsaw does. Just use a reasonable amount of common sense.'

'What do your files say about De Monti?' Chris asked.

'Well, now, let me see. According to your passport, you are an Italian national. Your mother is an American. We are certain your leanings are American. The gentlemen at the Italian Embassy think you are a bad Fascist. However, you've covered both the Ethiopian and the Spanish affairs from the Italian side of the lines. You are cautious not to editorialize but only to report news. That is commendable. What else would you like to know about yourself?'

Chris flipped his napkin on the table. 'I'll be a son of a bitch! You take the cake.'

'Do we understand each other, Chris.'

Chris smiled and held his glass up in salute. 'To friendship.'

'A good toast.'

The ladies of the evening arrived.

They were, as Horst promised, two of Warsaw's loveliest courtesans. Chris knew both of them, in bed. They were minor European film actresses and belonged to a small social clique that ran in a continual circle in Warsaw. Hildie Solna was a striking blonde. He had had an affair with her before he met Deborah. The other one . . . a few one-night adventures . . . her name slipped his mind – Wanda something-or-other.

Horst von Epp kissed their hands in the accepted fashion. Chris was amused. Yes, he thought, Hildie would be quick to jump on the band wagon and switch masters. He wondered if Von Epp knew how shopworn Hildie was under the paint. Well, she still had enough tricks left to get her through one more war.

'Darling!' Hildie cried in delight at seeing Chris. Dear Hildie . . . the body without a soul. Soft words without meaning. He looked at her. Could he lie in bed tonight with her or Wanda something-or-other and not cry out for his true love?

No . . . It was better to spend the night in agony, longing for Deborah, than with one of them. He turned quickly to Von Epp and spoke in Italian. 'I think I will take a rain check. Pretend that I am not your guest. I am sure you can dig up a good German officer to take my place. I shall act as though I were an intruder and beg my leave.'

'Go ahead,' Von Epp answered. 'I will arrange everything.' Horst watched Chris pat Hildie's cheeks and tell her he was sorry he could not stay, but another time . . . Why would he run off, Von Epp thought? It is as I surmised – De Monti has something going for him here in Warsaw and he does not want to leave – almost certainly a Jewess. If it is so, I have found his price.

Chapter Eight

Ervin Rosenblum was homelier than usual when he opened the door to let Chris in. Aroused from a deep sleep, he yawned and stretched in a half-tied monstrous old robe and paddled to the mantel clock in a pair of worn slippers. He squinted at the clock.

'My God, past midnight! Something terrible has happened?'

Chris handed him the *Kennkarte*. Ervin was nearly blind without his glasses. He held it to his nose but could not read it. 'Wait, I'll get my glasses.'

He returned from the bedroom with a look of complete puzzlement.

'How in the name of God did you arrange this? I thought sure you had come to tell me good-by.'

Momma Rosenblum was up with a monstrous old robe to equal Ervin's. She kissed Chris on the cheek. 'Bad news?'

'No, Momma, good news. Chris will be able to keep the agency open, and I have a special work permit.'

'A miracle . . . a miracle.'

Chris knew better than to try to stop her from making tea and putting out a feed.

He recounted the day with Horst von Epp to Ervin. Rosy kept looking at the *Kennkarte*, shaking his head.

'You're the analyst, Rosy. What do you make of it?'

'Well, you have covered the Italian side of two wars. You have never been caught slipping reports out to the free press, but a man like Von Epp should surely know you pass tips and information to others who can use them. Maybe he is neutralizing you. He knows your word is sound and you won't double-cross him.'

'I've thought about that. But why would he let me stay here in the first place?'

'To get you on his side. To make a deal with you sooner or later. To use you, somehow.'

'That's possible too. He put on a real show for me. Even tried to soften me up with Hildie Solna tonight.'

Rosy laughed. 'Hildie sure has good instincts. The smoke from battle has not yet cleared and the old girl is in German headquarters. So you had a party?'

'I pulled out.'

'Before or after?'

'Before. I begged off.'

'Maybe that wasn't so smart, Chris.'

'Hildie's a good lay, but – you know.'

'And by this time so does Von Epp. Why does an unattached bachelor walk out on a party with the most expensive whore in Warsaw? Because he's carrying a torch for a woman. You might as well be wearing a sign.'

The whistle of the teakettle sounded from the kitchen. Momma Rosenblum summoned them in. There was enough on the table for ten men to eat.

'I'm sorry, I didn't know you were coming. There's practically nothing here,' she said.

'You shouldn't be so extravagant with the ration on, Momma Rosenblum,' Chris said.

'I'm only serving an iota of what you've sent over to us the past month. You could stand a little babying.' She knew that Chris and Ervin wanted to speak in confidence and took her leave.

Ervin stirred his tea slowly. 'The trouble with a man like Von Epp is that you never know what is really going on in his head. We all know what Schreiker wants and what he is. Von Epp is twice as dangerous.'

'No one – positively no one – knows about me and Deborah but you. Perhaps Andrei and Gabriela suspect. Perhaps even Bronski suspects, but no one really knows.'

'Don't be lulled to sleep by Von Epp's smooth talk. He's a Nazi. If he ever knew, he could blackmail you into doing anything for him. He'll let you stay on now because he thinks he's discovered a blind spot and he wants to know what it is. Keep away from his parties, and for God's sake be careful when you see Deborah. You'll have to find another place to meet.'

'Rosy, I haven't seen her for over a month. Can't you see I'm going out of my mind!'

'I know, Chris, but I also know you're going to try to see her.'

'Have you seen her?' Chris whispered.

'Yes. She works most of the day at the orphanage in Powazki. Susan is with her most of the time.'

'Does she . . . ask for me?'

'No.'

Chris gave a hurt little laugh. 'Funny, damned funny. I make secret meetings with Paul Bronski to give him his money – funny, isn't it, Rosy?'

'Not particularly. From now on you'd better give me the envelopes to deliver to him.'

'Maybe you're right. Rosy, see her for me. She's got relatives in Krakow. She could make an excuse to see them. I've got to go there in a few days. Sorenson from the Stockholm Press has a place there. He'll let me use it.'

Rosy gripped his arm and stopped him. 'If you were my own brother I couldn't love you more, Chris. Don't ask me to do this.'

Chris pulled away. 'I'll wait. I've got time on my side now. Something will happen.'

'Drink some tea. Momma will be offended.'

Chris drank slowly, drowning his churning anger.

'So long as you are going to Krakow, would you see Thompson at the American Embassy? He has a package for us.'

'I wish you wouldn't ask me to carry any more packages,' Chris said sharply.

'I don't think I understand you.'

'I made a deal with Von Epp.'

'My, you're a regular boy scout. You don't mind being a messenger boy for Paul Bronski.'

'That's different. It's coming through on company funds – it can't be traced.'

'So what are we doing with the money from Thompson? Feeding orphans. This has become a crime?'

'Rosy, this Bathyran business is your own fault. I don't want to know anything about it. I'm not getting involved.'

Chris got up from the table. Rosy wanted to rip the *Kennkarte* in half and throw it in his face, but he could not. It was too important to all of them. He had to continue working on the outside as long as he was able.

'See you in the office in the morning,' Chris said.

'Good night, boss.'

Chris flopped on his bed and gazed into nothingness. The soft melodiousness of Chopin on Radio Polskie had been largely replaced by a thumping, clanging Wagner. Chris snapped the radio off.

He walked to the window. Only a few blocks away from Deborah. What was she doing now? Combing Rachael's hair ... keeping time as Rachael played the piano ... helping Stephan with his studies? No, it was late. Almost one o'clock. She and Paul would be in bed together.

He closed the curtains abruptly.

He lay back on the bed again. Andrei! Good old Andrei! We'll hang one on! He rolled over and had a hand on his phone. No ... wait. Andrei was wearing that damned Star of David. He couldn't go into any of the hotels or bars. What's the difference? Andrei could take off the armband. They could hit some dives, have a real blow out. Hell, Andrei would get mad and try to take on the German army. He let his hand drop from the phone.

Maybe I should have stayed with Von Epp, Chris thought. Hildie Solna is good for a few laughs. Von Epp is good company. If I had met Von Epp anywhere else in the world, we would have been friends. Isn't that reason enough to trust a man? No ... Von Epp couldn't be trusted.

Just how much does he really know about me? He knows about mother ... They must have a file on me a foot thick.

Chris's thoughts began to drift back and back and back in time. All the way back to the beginning.

Chapter Nine

Flora Sloan had been described at various times as enchanting, fetching, witty and gay, terribly, terribly chic, charming, clever, empty-headed, flighty, hyperthyroid, and so forth. All of these descriptions fitted in one way or another, at one time or another. She was never still long enough for a comprehensive composite to be made.

Her background was mysterious. Midwesterner, most people thought. Indiana . . . small town in Wisconsin . . . or something like that.

No one knew when she came to Manhattan or about her early failures and affairs. She was suddenly there. Eminently successful as a fashion executive, a financial wizard, a magazine editor, and later as the queen bee in a hive of social-climbers.

The most successful of her profitable ventures was a pair of marriages and subsequent divorce settlements, first with her magazine-publishing husband, then with a real estate operator from whom she extracted a commendable hunk of mid-Manhattan. After the second coup she retired to become a patron of the arts and grand matron of the Flora Sloan clique.

She did nothing worthy with her independent wealth, but Flora had the ability to do nothing in extremely good taste. Her only true dedication was to keep her face unwrinkled and her body beautiful. She ran through a succession of lovers, with whom she became bored in days, weeks, and occasionally months. The moment they began to ooze around to talking stocks and bonds, they were through.

It was inevitable that sooner or later she would get a pasting. She fell in love with a young artist. His paintings showed a rather sketchy talent, but he did have a positive talent in bed. For the first time in her life she behaved silly, lavished her lover with expensive gifts, became fiendishly jealous, and allowed herself to be pushed around. She sponsored a one-man art show at a time when her expression of like or dislike was a command, and he became a 'rage.'

Everyone seemed to know that Flora was being had, but how does one tell a queen bee? She woke one rainy morning to find her lover flown from the nest after skinning her out of a small mint. When the detectives dragged him back for a tear-filled showdown, there came the revelation that he had a wife and three children 'somewhere in Maine.'

Comforting friends soothed her. A trip to Europe would be the remedy for her shattering experience. She pulled herself together for 'their' sake. Yes, they were right. An ocean voyage and the long-overdue grand tour to put the broken pieces together.

Flora, her traveling companion, secretary, Irish maid, and two poodles got no farther than the second stop, Monaco. In barreled the Count Alphonse de Monti at a hundred and twenty miles per hour in a red Ferrari. He saddled up to a chair opposite her at the Casino and began throwing around ten-thousand-lira notes like kleenex at the baccarat table.

From the second he bowed and kissed her hand Flora knew what a hell of an elegant gentleman he was. And with a title to boot. She shrieked with exhilaration as he buzzed around hairpin turns in his red Ferrari. She listened breathlessly as he whispered his way through Verdi love arias.

'God damn,' she told her traveling companion, 'this continental charm is the living end. I checked his financial rating and the bastard's loaded to boot.'

Since European titles and rich American divorcees were fascinating subjects, when Flora became the Countess de Monti it almost knocked the World Series off the front pages.

The glitter lasted through two spaghetti dinners. She found that Italians had very very funny ideas about their womenfolk. His old Kentucky home outside Rome was big and marbly enough, but although she had investigated his solvency she had failed to check into a stable of mistresses stashed in villas all over southern France. Now that she was properly the Countess de Monti, his charm became reserved for rivers yet uncrossed.

In fact, in many respects, he proved a slob.

He had peculiarities that she had not tested before in men. He was saturated with pride from head to foot. He bathed in old tradition. He professed to be deeply religious. And, like many normal and healthy Italian men of means, he fully expected his wife to stay in the old Kentucky home and get quietly plump while he barreled around Europe in his red Ferrari.

One more thing! An heir! Italians considered the production of a male offspring as some sort of monumental feat. With Flora as his mate, it was – but he managed.

She went into wild scenes about her treatment. Alphonse was proud because his wife was so spicy. But when she blurted out her plan to get rid of the unborn baby, it was another matter. He promptly slapped her into a private apartment under lock and key and the watchful eyes of a pair of matrons, then barreled off in his red Ferrari.

The result of this happy union was Christopher de Monti.

The proud father came home and celebrated long and hard. In fact, he dropped his guard so low that Flora was able to bundle Chris up and flee to the United States.

This time the divorce and custody battle did knock the World Series off the front pages.

Final judgment. Momma got another splendid settlement, mostly in olive groves. Chris was to spend summers with Poppa in Italy.

Flora never quite forgave little Chris for lowering her breasts, ruining her eighteen-inch waistline, and turning her stomach muscles to jelly. Unfortunately a society larger than her personal clique imposed certain conditions which called for her to be a 'good mother.' She smothered Chris in a sea of motherliness – in full view of her friends.

He remembered being displayed by Flora, led into the parlor where she held court, listening to the 'ohs' and 'ahs' from the waxen-faced people posed about the room. Momma would tussle his hair. Momma would squeeze him. He hated that, because she was always nervous when he was around and her fingernails always dug into his flesh.

But summer! That was different! In summer he would get on a big ship with his current 'Nana' and cross the ocean to Italy and Poppa. He traveled with Poppa in the red Ferrari, and they went to museums and the opera and to the Riviera. He loved his father deeply. He did not think he loved his mother. He cried and Poppa cried when summer was over and he had to return to America to school. Flora took Alphonse's pleas to keep the boy as a personal vendetta against her 'motherliness.'

And so Chris was kept in America nine months of the year. A veteran Atlantic traveler by the age of twelve, he was also an habitué of fashionable schools with names that all sounded like either Exeter or Briarwood.

He was a very quiet boy and a determined student. His true character was formed by teachers who taught in a day when political liberalism, sense of social conscience, and ideals were not frowned upon. He loved Poppa more than anyone in the world – but somehow, Italy was always a playland.

He read Lincoln and Paine and Jefferson. He completely identified himself as an American. He did not like the way the rich people treated poor people in Italy.

The American dream – the American ideal – became the guidepost in his life.

When he was old enough, Chris overlooked Poppa's weakness for women, and often a new mistress formed a threesome on their travels in the summer. And as he grew older he began to see his father's human frailties. Poppa was vain. Poppa was a snob. Poppa was unmoved by the poverty in Naples. Poppa guarded the iniquities of the class system.

Poppa was a Fascist.

Chris did not know what it meant at first, but each year it came more and more into focus and it rubbed against the grain of his American education.

Poppa would get a little drunk and talk about Benito Mussolini returning them to the glory of ancient Rome. Chris knew Mussolini – a pompous ass – but he never said anything to his father about that. The Italian people were warm and kind and they liked to sing and eat and drink and strut and believe they were great lovers. Years of privation as a second-rate power had allowed evil men to perpetrate the hoax of fascism upon them.

Chris was seventeen. At the end of the summer he would return to America and begin college.

Poppa was particularly perplexed. 'I was hoping that your mother would let you study here. She promises her usual scandal if you don't return.'

Chris said nothing. He wanted very much to return to America to study.

'I think it is time you and I had a long and serious talk about many things. Although an American education will be satisfactory, it is not really what I hoped for you. Where are you planning to go?'

'Columbia University in New York City.'

'Hmmm. I trust they have a good college in business administration and law. For the next four years you should be preparing yourself to take over our estates. I have only done a so-so job. I count on you to make the De Monti fortunes what they were when your grandfather was alive.'

'Poppa, you don't understand. I am going to Columbia because of their school of journalism.'

'Journalism? But what good will journalism do you in running the De Monti estate?'

'Journalism is one of the greatest ways to translate your ideals. It is a way to bring truth to the world.'

'What kind of nonsense is this? You are my son. You will take over my duties just as I took them over from my father and his father before him. And while you are about it you will join the Young Student Fascist League in your college. It is important you begin to identify yourself as a good Italian boy.'

'But I don't believe in fascism.'

Alphonse de Monti shrieked. He ranted angrily at Flora for what she had done to the boy's education. 'You will understand, Chris, what Mussolini has done for us. The Italian people have work now. He will lead us to a grandeur we have not seen in two thousand years!'

Chris held his tongue. He knew that Poppa didn't give a damn about the Italian people working, and Chris felt that fascism would lead them to destruction.

'You are my son and you will do as you are ordered!'

'I'm sorry, sir,' Chris said. 'I am going to be a journalist.'

Alphonse struck Chris across the face . . . then again . . . and again and again. The boy stood rigid but unflinching. And then his father began to cry. 'Since you were a baby, all I have wanted is for my son. My Christopher – a nobleman – to take over our great traditions – to live to see you as an officer in the Italian army bringing us back our glory – all I wanted is for you, Chris.'

What traditions? Those poor bastards slaving in Poppa's olive groves? Whoring all over Europe in ten-thousand-dollar cars? Sitting at the Casino, a portrait of decadence? Trying to resurrect a ghost of ancient Rome which would take them on a path to hell?

Chris was sad because he loved his Poppa so.

'Chris . . . Chris . . . my bambino,' the old man pleaded.

'I am sorry, Poppa, that I cannot be the son you want.'

Even in anguish there was that deep stubborn pride. 'Get out of my house and never come back!'

Chris was a brilliant student in journalism at Columbia. He wrote many letters to Poppa, but they were all returned unopened. He knew the deep pain he had caused his father and he hated himself for it, but he knew that he could not live as an instrument of a thing he hated. He was cut off without a cent.

In his junior year things brightened with an athletic scholarship. He was a first-rate forward on the varsity basketball team and highly successful in the new, experimental one-hand shots.

And Flora? She had taken a dumping in the stock market, but Chris didn't want a thing from her, anyhow. Christmas passed without so much as a greeting from her. She did not like to have Chris around at all these days because he served as a reminder that she was turning ripe fast. She had lovers almost as young as her son.

Eileen Burns was a commercial-art major as vibrant as Chris was quiet. She was completely taken by the lean, handsome right forward on the basketball team and his grimish ways.

Perhaps Chris was far more intense about Eileen than a college romance would have implied, but with her all his lonely years and frustrations seemed to pour out. There had been other girls before. He was fifteen when he started with the daughter of one of Poppa's housekeepers.

But with Eileen he could talk about things he only remembered speaking about to instructors in private schools a long time ago. It was different, because Eileen became a part of his hopes. He could say, 'I want to be a great journalist – it's a wonderful way to serve mankind.' And Eileen understood – she understood so well.

In his senior year Chris met Oscar Pecora. Oscar was standing by the window in his room when he came in from basketball practice late one evening. Pecora was a strange-looking little fellow. Stiff Hoover collar, four-in-hand cravat, bowler hat, pin-striped suit. He had the stamp of a European all over him.

'I hope you will forgive me,' Pecora said in Italian. 'Your door was open.'

Chris looked at him for a while. Ten to one he was from the Italian Legation. 'If you're here to ask me to join the Student Fascist League, don't waste either of our time.'

Pecora opened his wallet neatly and snapped a card to Chris. OSCAR PECORA: INTERNATIONAL DIRECTOR, SWISS NEWS AGENCY, GENEVA.

Chris flung the dirty laundry off one of the room's two chairs. 'Sit down, sir.'

'You are familiar with Swiss News?'

'Yes, sir.' He knew it was a small agency with one of the very best reputations for journalistic standards in the world.

'I shall get right to the point. We are expanding our operations in America. We will need an extra man for overloaded work in our New York and Washington bureaus. If you are familiar with Swiss News you know we select our people carefully. We find you are one of three students in this country whom we wish to train and put on our staff. When you graduate you will immediately leave for Geneva for a training course to get rid of the bad habits you've picked up in college.'

Chris and Eileen were married three days before graduation. A week later they were aboard ship for a honeymoon trip.

No more idyllic four months were ever lived by two people. They loved each other with an energy reserved for the young in a fairyland setting of snowy mountains and roaring fireplaces. Although half oblivious with thoughts of Eileen, Chris managed to learn the practical methods of journalism taught by the veteran Swiss News staff.

At the end of the schooling Chris was assigned, as promised, as a relief man between New York and Washington. Eileen was homesick to return, which seemed entirely natural for a girl who had lived her life in New Jersey.

There was but one short detour he had to take home, and that was through Rome.

The Count Alphonse de Monti had aged. He was a somewhat seedy representative of faded nobility. Yet he put up a lavish front: the cars and the servants and the women were still there. So were the debts. All his failures seemed to make him a more devout Fascist, for it was easy to blame enemies who did not exist.

Alphonse de Monti was a gentleman to the core. He was polite to his son and his son's bride, but his coolness made it completely obvious he would never accept the fact that his son would not be the things he wanted.

Chris left Italy with a feeling that he might never see Poppa again.

Chris and Eileen became members of those faceless legions of Manhattan cliff dwellers who rushed to dinner and theater, washed down too many martinis at lunch, and made certain their 'new love and independence' would not be marred by the sudden announcement that a child was on the way. Chris thrived on all of it.

Eileen didn't tell Chris how lonely it was when he was away in Washington. He was happy – so happy. And a new marriage is something large and powerful, the little flaws and cracks often invisible in the over-all magnitude. Each reunion after a week in Washington buried the loneliness.

Six months of it. Then, while he was away in Washington, he was suddenly called to a conference in Denver. Next time she tried tagging along in Washington. It was worse than staying in New York. She was in his way. A journalist had to have mobility and no limitation on hours, no worries about a wife waiting in a hotel room.

'Chris honey, why don't I take a job? You know, Mom and Dad did spend a fortune getting me through Columbia and –'

Enough of the old-country pride had rubbed off on him to make the idea of a De Monti wife working unthinkable.

Oscar Pecora arrived just in time.

'You are one of our bright young stars, Christopher. We have an extraordinary opportunity. Bureau chief in Rio de Janeiro.'

Rio! And less than a year with Swiss News!

Chris was so happy that Eileen covered her disappointment, as a good wife will do. This was his life and it was a great opportunity. She was planning to have a talk with Chris about buying a place in Jersey, near Mom and Dad. Maybe starting a family. They'd had their fun ...

But Eileen held her tongue and packed and went along.

Chris fitted in every newsmen's bar and in the lobbies of the capitols and in the offices of prime ministers and at the scenes of the disasters. Hours of light and darkness and light and spaces of great distance had lost meaning to him when a story was involved.

They had a beautiful apartment on the Avenida Beira Mar that hugged the bay. She came to learn every corner of it and how many squares were in the marble of the entrance hall and how many different colors there were in the drapes.

She tried very, very hard to assimilate herself into that circle of diplomats who seemed to spend their entire lives holding a cocktail glass for the incoming attaché of culture or the outgoing second secretary.

Eileen got a pair of cats and stroked them and paced the floor in lounging pajamas and waited until Chris got back.

And then one day she broke. He wrote:

Dear Oscar,

I must resign this bureau for personal reasons. I should like to return to New York if you've a spot for me there. Otherwise, I am afraid I must quit the agency and find a job in New York.

Dear Christopher,

I understand your plight and I sympathize with it. Try to understand mine. Hold on another six or eight weeks and I'll get things shifted around so that you can break someone in and I'll make an opening in New York.

'Honey, why don't you go on back to the States ahead of me? See your folks. It will do you good.'

Eileen was relieved and frightened at the same time. It was an omen, she knew it. The little flaws were turning to deepening cracks.

And Chris was worried, too, because when Eileen left he did not miss her as much as he believed he should. At first he dreaded the thought of coming back from a trip with Eileen not there. But ... it wasn't so bad. There was always a poker game going at the press club or the Embassy, always a party in session with an open invitation to him.

Dear Chris

I have taken a job in an advertising firm here. I know how much you are against this, but you won't be when you see how happy I am. It won't interfere with a moment of our being together ... I made that clear to them. But, I just can't keep on feeling so useless. Please, darling, don't be angry.

Chris swallowed his pride. Why not? Eileen was too vital to be locked up in a lonely flat. She was too sensible to become a partner to a wasteland of women's clubs. That's one of the things he admired about her from the first. Her desire to be useful – not like his mother.

When he returned to New York there was a wonderful reunion. Oscar Pecora had given him the New York Bureau permanently! He had enough help so that he would have to make only an occasional trip to Washington. For a moment they seemed to have recaptured those first days of their marriage.

And then, the scene:

'Eileen, be reasonable, honey. The conference in Quebec is one of the most important international meetings of the year.'

'You promised and Oscar promised. No more traveling.'

'Eileen! Dan is sick. He can't work. He's in the hospital.'

'Then let them send someone else.'

'Swiss News is a small outfit. We haven't got that many men.'

'You don't need any more. Good old Christopher de Monti will always go.'

'Don't make it so dramatic. It's only ten days.'

'Ten days in Quebec ... ten days in Washington ... ten days in San Francisco. Do you know what it's like alone here for ten days? I don't ask terribly much, Chris – to work until we decide to have a home and a baby – but what's the use of having a baby who won't know his father! We have so much fun together when you're here. I don't ask much, Chris –'

'Christ! You're making a world revolution out of this. How can you ask me to let Oscar down after all he's done for me?'

'How about me, Chris? Haven't I done something for you too? Do you ever think about letting me down?'

Chris didn't answer. He went into the bedroom.

Eileen trailed in slowly. 'Your things are all packed,' she said with tears falling into the corners of her mouth. 'Your gray suit didn't get back from the cleaner's in time.'

'Eileen ... honey ...'

'Hurry, Chris. You'll miss your plane.'

When he returned from Canada his reception was one of polite coldness. For the first time in their marriage Eileen did not want to be loved when he returned from a trip. It was doubly bad when she played out the role of the accommodating wife.

'I guess we're in a lot of trouble,' Chris said the next morning.

Eileen's silence was answer enough.

'I thought about it all during the time in Quebec. About us and where we are going. I've been pretty damned selfish. I guess I've done all the taking ... none of the giving.'

'That's not true, Chris. You've tried. So have I. I really wanted to be the kind of woman you need.'

'Do you still love me?'

'Yes . . . and I think, in your way, you love me too. But I'm kind of jealous, I guess, because what you have away from me means more to you that I ever will. It's not your fault or mine.'

'Let's try, Eileen, please let's try. I know most of this has been my fault.'

'Don't let that Italian pride of yours compound a mistake.'

'Why don't we take a ride over to Jersey and look at some of that real estate? Then I'll get a letter off to Oscar –'

'Chris . . . Chris. I do love you, but if I take you away from that world of yours out there you'll grow to hate me.'

Both of them tried hard to pull it together. Eileen never did buy that house in New Jersey and she was terribly cautious about having a child.

Restraint and all its murderous aspects came between them.

There were more trips – there always would be, but she never made another scene or shed another tear – and there were no more wild reunions.

For a year they drifted and grew more and more indifferent to each other.

And one day Christopher de Monti had to face that moment when a man's pride grovels to its lowest depths. He found it out by accident, by returning home from a trip early and taking a phone call not meant for him. Eileen had begun sleeping with another man.

Chris never spoke to her about it. He waited until a weekend when she was visiting her parents, and he packed his things and left with only a brief note.

Dear Eileen,

I have learned about you and Daniels at your office. There is absolutely no use of discussing anything. For my part of the guilt, I am sorry, but it will be best for us both if I never see you again. If you will arrange the divorce as quickly and quietly as possible on some semi-civilized grounds, I would be obliged.

After a month of trying to drown his pride across every bar in England and Europe, Chris got himself steamed out and reported to Oscar Pecora in Geneva.

'That's quite a little bar bill you've run up, Christopher. It's a wonder you have a liver left,' Pecora said.

'Oh, for God's sake, Oscar, save the sermon.'

'Tell me, Chris. Was the pain because you loved Eileen so much, or has your Italian nobility been offended?'

'I don't know, Oscar.'

'If you still love Eileen you can have her back. She's written to me a half dozen times. Of course you've got this stack of letters you've never opened. She'll come to you on any condition – on her hands and knees. Now, if your love is so great, it must find forgiveness for her.'

'I don't know if I can, Oscar. Besides, the same thing will happen again. She's a fine woman, Oscar. She really tried. I've got no right to butcher her life up –'

'And deep in your heart you really don't want her back. Except for the blow to your vanity, you are happy to be free.'

For a moment Chris looked offended.

'That's hitting below the belt, Oscar.'

'Truth does not offend you, Christopher.'

'I guess you're right.'

'Well, there's no use of both Eileen and me losing you. I saw it coming for a long time. One of us had to be the big loser, and I'm glad it's not me.'

'Let me get back to work, Oscar, right away.'

'Fine. How does Ethiopia sound? The legions of Rome are on the march. That Italian passport of yours will come in handy.'

'You know how I feel about the Fascists. I can't stomach covering their side of a war against defenseless little black men with spears.'

'You are a journalist, Christopher. Leave your personal politics out of it. We can get you attached to the Italian command. Get the best you can out of the latitude they give you to operate.'

Chris walked slowly to the big wall map behind Oscar Pecora's desk. 'Ethiopa? Why not? That's about as far away as I can get from the goddamned mess I've made.'

Chapter Ten

Mussolini's campaign in Ethiopia was a pleasant little war. Sort of reminded one of when the colonizers of the last century directed their armies from campaign chairs in the shade of banana trees with a tall, cool gin and tonic in their hands as they brought 'civilization' to the Zulus.

It was, indeed, good practical experience for the aspiring new legions of Rome. The little clay townships made excellent targets for the artillery gunners. The infantry could zigzag about the tall brush, boning up on their efficiency without too much danger, for the natives were mostly armed with spears and the few Ethiopian riflemen were dreadful shots.

Chris made peace with himself and played it straight. He could stand nearly everything except when he interviewed the bragging, strutting aviators after they had returned from their missions of bombing and strafing undefended villages of thatched huts.

Ethiopia was not the real battleground.

The British fleet ordered a muscle-flexing maneuver in the Mediterranean. Mussolini called the bluff. There were indignant pickets in Paris and New York and London against Italian legations by people who had learned only in the last month or so that there was actually a country named Ethiopia.

For one fleeting moment the world had a twinge of conscience. An embargo was called against Italy, but it was really not an embargo at all.

Then, for all its inept and ill-fated existence, the League of Nations was honored by one great moment of human dignity. A small black man who was named the Lion of Judah, Haile Selassie, the Emperor of Ethiopia, made a plea to the souls of men for his people. But Ethiopia was a long way from about everywhere, and who the hell really cared about Addis Ababa?

Apathy of free men. This was the real victory. The scent of blood made the legions of Rome hungry.

On the Yangtze River an American gunboat named the *Panay* was sunk. Some Americans were able to convince other Americans that the *Panay* had no right being there in the first place. Yellow men in the Orient were battling yellow men – but that was far away too.

There followed the era of appeasement. The Versailles Treaty was broken by the tramping of German boots into the Rhineland.

The bullies grew brave.

The crucible: Spain.

'Christopher, you did a magnificent job in Ethiopia. Your restraint was remarkable. Now, Christopher! Your Italian passport is really going to come in handy,' Oscar Pecora said. 'I've gotten you credentials to cover the Insurgent side in Spain.'

Christopher de Monti went to Spain on the Fascist side as a man obsessed with a mission. This was the climax of his life. This was the meaning of every word he had read about freedom and truth. Spain was not Ethiopia. Now the world would listen!

He joined Franco's forces just after the conquest of Málaga. He became a man with a split personality. On the surface, Christopher de Monti sent out routine dispatches and stories expected of a competent journalist.

All his skill and ingenuity were used in smuggling stories to the free world. Using daring and cunning, he risked his life time and again to get reports over the border to the 'neutral' embassies in self-exile in France.

Christopher de Monti secretly reported the arrival of millions of tons of German and Italian war materials – cannons, tanks, airplanes.

Christopher de Monti secretly reported the arrival of the first contingents of German and Italian aviators fighting for Franco.

Christopher de Monti secretly reported that Germany and Italy were using Spain as a testing ground for personnel and equipment.

Christopher de Monti secretly reported the arrival of masses of Italian ground forces.

Christopher de Monti secretly reported the atrocities committed by Franco's Moroccan hordes and wrote the true reports that the ranks of the Catholic Church were, in actuality, with the Loyalist government.

Christopher de Monti was the first to send through a secret report that the 'unidentified' submarines blockading Loyalist ports were Italian.

He was the first to send through documentary evidence that the Italian air force was murdering women and children in undefended open cities.

And he watched his work drown in a cesspool of German propaganda. The rape of Spain, the first of the great sellouts in an age of sellouts, left him a disillusioned man. Fainthearted democracies hid behind shallow words and non-intervention pacts and embargoes which penalized a democracy fighting for its life.

The world did not want to hear what Christopher de Monti risked his life to tell them.

Oscar Pecora kept a close eye on Chris and finally decided that he could not go on smuggling out his stories from the Franco side. Afraid for Chris's life, he recalled him from Spain early in 1938.

Christopher de Monti, a quiet boy who had formed a love of truth long before he was a man, had been betrayed by his mother and disillusioned by his father. He had destroyed his own relations with a fine woman and he hated himself for that. But this was to be the cruelest disillusion of all.

He left Spain with his faith in the human race gone.

Chris had always been a sensible and hard-working journalist. He was particularly sober and responsible in a fraternity of the not-so-sober and sometimes irresponsible. His one binge had been with reason – when he broke his marriage with Eileen.

His second was worse. Oscar Pecora bailed him out of a Paris police station after a month's solid drinking and packed him off to his villa on the lake at Lausanne.

Oscar Pecora was a patient man who loved Christopher. Christopher was his own protégé. Like a son, Chris sulked bitterly until the boiling within him could not be contained.

And one night it all exploded.

Chris was drunk. Madame Pecora, Oscar's beautiful former-opera-singing wife, had retired. They were sitting on the balcony and there was a full moon on the lake and Chris was coming to the end of a fifth of scotch whisky.

'Why, Oscar, why! Why did they do that?'

'Tell me about it, Chris.'

'Saw them killing women and children. Dirty bastard Italian fliers sitting in their dirty bastard clubs bragging about it ... Watched them torture soldiers. Ever seen a Moroccan torture someone? By putting his testicles in a squeezer ... Oscar ... God dammit ... I got all that over the border to the Americans!'

'Christopher. Every report that you sneaked out of Spain was planted in newspapers and wire services. All we can do is give the facts to the people. We cannot force them to stage a rebellion in righteous wrath.'

'You are so right, Oscar. The whole goddamned human race sat on its hands and watched them murder Spain. Lemme tell you something, brother. They'll pay for not stopping Mussolini and Hitler in Spain. Pretty soon they'll run out of hiding room and, Jesus Christ, will they get clobbered!'

Oscar Pecora's sympathetic hand fell on Chris's shoulder. 'We journalists are like garbage cans, Chris. Everybody sends us their filth. Through us comes all that is rotten in man. Christopher, what you are going through now ... You were a single small voice that cried out for justice in a dark and angry sea and no one heard you. Until a man is struck in his own face he does not want to believe the attack on his brother concerns him.'

Chris stumbled for his chair, staggered to the rail, and hung onto it. 'Shall I tell you why I became a journalist? Do you know Thomas Paine? "The world is my country, all mankind are my brethren ... to do good is my religion."'

Oscar Pecora recited, '"In a chariot of light from the region of day, The Goddess of Liberty came. Ten thousand celestials directed the way. And hither conducted the dame. A fair budding branch from the gardens above, Where millions with millions agree, She brought in her hand as a pledge of her love, And the plant she named Liberty Tree ... from the east to the west blow the trumpet to arms! Through the land let the sound of it flee; Let the far and the near all unite, with a cheer ... in defense of our Liberty Tree."'

'Bravo, Brother Pecora! Bravo! And now I give you William Lloyd Garrison ...' Chris stood upright and thrust his finger into the air. '"With reasonable men, I will reason; with humane men I will plead; but to tyrants I will give no quarter ..." Now how's that for a goddamn quote?'

Chris reeled into his sea. 'Little Jefferson ... we need a little Jefferson to round it out ... Oscar, I'm drunk ... God damn I'm drunk.'

'Come, Christopher. You're tired. You have lost a hard battle, but you are my best soldier and tomorrow we must go out to the field again.'

'She's in Jersey ... married that guy. They've got two kids ... nice little home, I hear. Me ... I'm the real winner, Oscar. I get to bring truth to the people.'

Chapter Eleven

The next afternoon, after Chris awoke from a deep sixteen-hour slumber, he found his way to Oscar Pecora's study sheepishly.

'Boy, did I hang one on,' he said in an apologetic voice.

'For talent, nearly anything can be forgiven.'

'It has all been a pretty startling lesson, Oscar. I can see why the men in our business turn crass and cynical. We sound the great trumpet and no one hears us. Free men with full bellies don't want to believe that a black native in Ethiopia concerns them or that the bombing of an open city in Spain is the prelude to the bombing of London.'

'Christopher, you've eaten my food, drunk my liquor, and now Madame Pecora is giving you flirtatious glances. I think it is high time you got back to work.'

'Doing what, Oscar? Can I go on being a journalist under these conditions? I have learned now that truth is not truth. Truth is only what people want to believe and nothing more.'

'But you will continue to seek it as a journalist or as a streetcar driver in Geneva. You have lost sight of the fact that there is a world of decent human beings and a lot of them are listening. They depend on the Christopher de Montis to be their eyes. You are not a man to abandon the human race because you have lost a battle. Now, what do you say, Christopher?'

Chris laughed ironically. 'When you come right down to it, I'm not much good for anything else. I can't even operate a streetcar.'

'I've called in men from our European bureaus for the past month. We are trying to determine how events will shift. What do you think, Christopher?'

Chris shrugged. 'Spain is Italy's show, mainly. The republican government will fall sooner or later. Franco is it.' Chris looked at the wall map behind Oscar. 'Hitler will start up next.'

'Bergman in Berlin thinks so too. How does Warsaw sound to you? We have a small bureau there.'

'If you still want me, why not? One place is as good as another.'

'Settled. You go to Poland. We have a free-lance man we've been using off and on. An Ervin Rosenblum.'

'Photographer, too, isn't he?'

'Yes, a good man. Take him on with you and try him out. Christopher, don't try anything foolish in Poland. Keep us in business as long as you can there.'

'You don't have to tell me. I've had my fill of playing cops and robbers. It won't do any more good in Poland than in Spain. Don't worry, Oscar. All you'll get are the straight reports.'

Dear Oscar,

Warsaw has been like a tonic. I'm glad one of us had some sense and I thank you. It's like a little Paris here.

Ervin Rosenblum is a crackajack. I want to keep him on permanently. The bureau is in good shape. The usual government red tape, but nothing earth-shaking. Next week I hope to have a direct phone connection to Geneva. That will speed things up considerably.

Although I'm getting along O.K. in French and English, I'm taking an hour a day of Polish. And – can you believe it? – I've taken on the hobby of coach of several of the army basketball teams.

Chris blew a whistle. He talked to Andrei Androfski in French, and Andrei translated into Polish that the basketball practice for the day was over. The members of the newly formed Seventh Ulany Brigade team thanked their coach and trotted from the floor of the Citadel gymnasium.

Andrei, the team captain, worked with Chris for another half hour. He was intrigued by Chris's wizardry in dribbling and hook shooting. Chris showed him the variations of passing the ball while being guarded and how to fake his pass moving in one direction, flipping the ball in the other.

They sat down drenched with sweat after the brisk workout. Chris wiped his face with a towel and lit a cigarette. 'I'm pooped. I haven't done this in years.'

'Those cigarettes are no good,' Andrei said. 'They wind you. Such a wonderful game. I did not realize there were so many fine points to it. But what can I do with these dumb oxen? They have no finesse.'

'They're coming along fine. By the end of the season they'll play like the Harlem Globetrotters.'

Chris slapped Andrei's knee. 'Well, to the showers.'

'I think I'll practice foul shots for a while,' Andrei said. 'Say, by the way, what do you have on tonight?'

'I can be had.'

'Good. My colonel gave me his box at the opera. *La Bohème*.'

Opera! It struck a note of joy in Chris. He had neglected it so much lately. It had been a religion with him in New York and with Poppa in Italy.

'You'll have dinner with Gabriela and me and then we'll pick up my sister. She would join us for dinner, but she wants to bring the children and her daughter has a late piano lesson.'

'I didn't know you had a married sister.'

'Yes, my one and only.'

Chris hedged. 'Look, I'll be a third wheel breaking in on a family party.'

'Nonsense. Her husband is in Copenhagen at a medical convention. Besides, the children will be thrilled to have a real live Italian explain the libretto to them. Settled! Be at Gabriela's apartment at six.'

'This is my sister, Deborah Bronski. And my niece Rachael, and the schmendrick is Stephan.'

'How do you do, Mr de Monti.'

'Call me Chris . . . please.'

It was the most strange and awesome sensation Chris had ever experienced.

Even as he walked from the car to the house he felt it come over him. The instant he saw her eyes she understood that he was reading a message of a deep inner sadness and frustration.

Good God, she was beautiful!

Chris was an experienced, sophisticated man. He was too wise to be felled suddenly like this. Yet his stability seemed shot. This strange feeling had never happened – not even with Eileen.

During the opera they were both uncomfortable in their awareness of each other. It was as though ectoplasm were leaping from the body of one to the other. There was a quick succession of stolen glances. There was the first accidental brushing of arms that made them twinge. And a few less accidental touchings.

Between the second and third acts Chris and Deborah found themselves standing away from the others, oblivious of the pomp and finery around them. Deborah turned completely pale as they stared wordlessly at each other.

The bell rang and the audience began to drift in to their seats.

Deborah suddenly broke and turned. Chris automatically touched her elbow. 'I must see you,' he blurted. 'Please phone me at Swiss News at the Bristol.'

Andrei called across the lobby for them to hurry.

Four days passed.

Chris started each time the phone rang. Then he began to resign himself to the fact that she would never call him and that he had done something foolish. Flirtations were flirtations, but this wasn't. There was in this none of the game men and women play. It was something serious from the very first second. Even though he realized she would not call, he could not shake that strange feeling.

'Hello ...'

'Is this the Swiss News Agency?'

'Yes ...'

'Christopher de Monti?'

'Speaking.'

'This is Deborah Bronski.'

Chris's hand became wet on the phone.

'I will be in the Saxony Gardens in an hour, along the benches beside the swan lake.'

They were both quiet and confused and feeling guilty and foolish as they found themselves sitting opposite each other.

'I feel absolutely silly,' Deborah said. 'I am respectfully married and I want you to know I have never done anything like this before.'

'It is all so strange.'

'I cannot lie about the fact that I wanted to see you again and I don't know why.'

'You know what I think? I think that you and I are a couple of magnets made out of some sort of unique metal. I think I was irresistibly pulled to Warsaw.'

And then they were awkwardly quiet, groping for a logical thought.

'Why don't we take a walk,' Chris said, 'and talk about things?'

She lay awake that night. And she met him again and she lay awake again. All of those little things that make a romance the most wonderful exploration of one human by another had been denied Deborah. Now suddenly she was flooded with them. Flooded with emotions she never believed she would have or knew existed.

The touch of a man's hand. The little duels of small talk to inflict small hurts on each other. The instantaneous thrill the moment he appeared coming down the path. The pangs of jealousy. The color of eyes, the way his dark hair fell over his forehead, the long strong hands, the sensitive expressions, the lanky careless stature.

The pain of being away from him.

The first kiss. She did not know what a kiss was. She did not believe feelings from a kiss were part of the human experience.

'Deborah, I love you.'

Each new adventure was like nothing that had ever happened to her before.

'I am not quite certain I knew what love is, Chris. I do know that seeing you is wrong and we will get into trouble if we keep it up. But I know I want to see you, regardless. Because ... being away from you is becoming more and more unbearable. Is this what love is, Chris?'

Chapter Twelve

Journal Entry

Today, my son was born. Susan Geller was in attendance with Dr Glazer from our orphanage. Sylvia came through beautifully for a woman of forty.

Outwardly, I must exhibit unabashed joy. Inwardly, I am worried. This is a bad time for a Jewish child to be born.

Moses is a common name, but I think the historian in me weighed my decision. The first Moses was also born in an era of duress, and when Pharaoh ordered all Jewish male infants slain he was hidden in the bulrushes. With this sentimentality and much luck, Moses Brandel will come through the difficult days ahead.

ALEXANDER BRANDEL

Despite the austerity and the outlawing of religious ceremonies, nothing could diminish the collective happiness of the Bathyrans. Moses Brandel was born to be spoiled by them all. He was their baby, and they were damned well going to have a blowout at the *bris*.

Tolek Alterman closed down the farm and brought in all the workers, thirty boys and ten girls, to Warsaw with an extravagance of food.

Momma Rosenblum took charge of cooking the traditional dishes. Rabbi Solomon would personally conduct the prayers at the ceremony.

The event took place at the Writer's Club on Tlomatskie Street, near Alex's flat, which the Orphans and Self-Help Society had 'leased' as an agency.

On the eighth day after his birth Moses Brandel was passed around on an ornate velvet pillow from relative to relative, from Bathyran to Bathyran, and finally ended up in the arms of his godfather, Andrei Androfski.

Down the street, the Great Tlomatskie Synagogue was boarded up at the doors and windows and guards posted around it, but in the Writer's Club a covenant with God was made by this child in a ceremony over four thousand years old from the command in Genesis, 'He that is eight days old among you shall be circumcised, every male throughout your generations.'

As in ancient times when Abraham circumcised Isaac, symbolic of a covenant with God, so did Finkelstein, the professional mohel, circumcise Moses Brandel. It is probable that Finkelstein did a better job, as he had had far more practice. He had been mohel at some two thousand *brisim.*

Little Moses lost his composure and shrieked.

'Blessed are you, Lord our God, Master of the Universe, who have made us holy with your commands, and have commanded us to bring Moses, the son of Alexander and Sylvia, into the covenant of Abraham our father,' chanted Rabbi Solomon.

When Moses' ordeal was over, the infant was returned to his mother in their flat down the street and the celebration began.

'*Mozeltoff?*' everyone congratulated the proud father.

'*Mozeltoff!*'

And the toasts began.

And singing.

And dancing.

And soon the Writer's Club reeled under the impact of a dancing hora ring. The 'proud father' was pulled into the center, and one by one the young Bathyran girls whirled with him around the circle in unison with the clapping and stamping. He danced and danced until he could dance no more. It didn't take much wine to get him high; he had been heady since the birth of the baby.

At last he staggered from the dance floor, sweating and gasping for breath.

Ervin Rosenblum and Andrei hooked their hands under Alex's arms and dragged him off to a side room, where he flopped down, wiped his face, and fanned himself.

'Why do Jews have to make such a tsimmes about the birth of a son?' Alex asked.

'Our kids have been pent up so long, they are about to explode with tension,' Rosy said. 'This party is doing everybody good.'

'So!' roared Andrei. 'How does the new father feel now?'

'At my age, to have a son is an unexpected bonus.'

Then he looked up glumly from Andrei to Ervin. They could hear the hilarity outside, but they were never a second away from the times. Even in the middle of the celebration it lurked in Alex's mind. 'Have you seen the new set of German directives?'

They nodded.

'So, they may as well celebrate tonight.'

'Why don't you forget it for a night too, Alex?' Andrei said.

'I've been doing a lot of thinking. I am at the headquarters at Mila 19 most of the time now, day and night. As soon as Sylvia is on her feet she'll be working at the orphanage again. I think we will give up our apartment and move to Mila 19. Susan Geller has indicated she'll move over too. I think it will be encouraging for our youngsters to have us living there. We are only using the first floor for offices and the dispensary. We could divide the place into dormitories for boys and girls and bring in another sixty or seventy people.'

'I'll move in if I can bring Momma,' Ervin Rosenblum said.

'No. So long as you are able to work on the outside, it would be better not to be too closely identified.'

Alex looked slyly at Andrei. Andrei Androfski at Mila 19 would be a great boost to everyone's morale.

'What are you doing with the basement?' Andrei asked.

'Storage.'

'Have you thought about an underground press?'

Andrei had behaved very well for the past weeks. He had shown great restraint, but he was going to be a problem as things grew worse, Alex thought. Ana Grinspan had started publication of a weekly sheet in Krakow. Alex didn't want to face the situation. Discovery of an underground printing plant could destroy the entire Orphans and Self-Help organization.

'I'll help you with your press, Andrei, but not at Mila 19.'

'Then you really don't need me there, do you?'

'We had better get out to the dance floor,' Ervin said quickly.

The forgotten man – or the forgotten boy – at the *bris* of Moses Brandel was his sixteen-year-old brother, Wolf. He seemed bewildered by everything. When everyone said '*Mozeltoff*' to him, he wondered why he was being congratulated. He was a bit forlorn over the attention the new baby was getting and more confused at suddenly becoming a brother. Wolf was rather shy, anyhow, and leaned against a wall and watched the others dance. Rachael watched him while she played the piano.

Poor Wolf, she thought. He is like a lost soul. When her mother relieved her at the piano she drifted over to him.

'Would you like to dance?' she asked.

'Uh-uh.'

'Come on.'

'No, I don't care to. Besides, I get all tangled up with my feet.'

There was an electrifying moment as the evening reached its highlight when Emanuel Goldman entered the room and it was announced that he would perform at the piano.

He had been in retirement for several years, and his hands and reflexes had become slowed and his technique rusty, but there was still that great personal charm of a real virtuoso. Tonight he had made an exception and was going to perform. The hall became breathless with anticipation as he seated himself at the upright and burst into a thundering polonaise.

Rachael Bronski went out to the balcony where Wolf Brandel stood alone, looking at the Tlomatskie Synagogue down the street. His hands were shoved forlornly into his pockets.

'Don't you want to hear Emanuel Goldman play?' she said.

'I can hear him fine from out here.'

She walked up behind him, and that made him uncomfortable. He moved a few feet away, still keeping his back to her.

'What's the matter, Wolf! I've never seen you so unhappy.'

He turned and shrugged. 'Everything, I guess. Mostly the way things are today. Wearing this,' he said, touching the Star of David on his arm. 'Not being able to go to school. Are you still taking piano lessons?'

'Momma teaches me now. I have a lot of time to practice when I'm not working at the orphanage. Are you still taking flute lessons?'

'No. I never liked it, anyhow.'

'I thought you did.'

'No, I just said that.'

'Why?'

'To make Momma happy. It wasn't really too bad. I kind of used to look forward to Tuesdays. Sitting in the park with you after lessons.'

'I miss that too,' she said softly.

'Well, you'll get over that. I'm not much.'

'Why do you always pull yourself down?'

'Look at me. I get more stupid-looking every day.'

'It's not so, Wolf. You're turning into a man and you will be very, very handsome.'

He shrugged. His voice alternated from high to low, and now he had much trouble holding it steady. He cleared his throat formally. 'I should like to visit your brother Stephan,' he said. 'I realize that you and your mother are schooling him, but he needs older masculine company. Someone he can look up to. I could teach him chess and many other things.'

'That would be very nice. Stephan does need an older ... man. Uncle Andrei is not around much, and Father works very late.'

'Good. I will come to see him. Rachael ...'

'Yes?'

'Do you think – I mean – with all the joy around here now – What I mean to say is that everyone is kissing everyone. Do you think it would be proper if we expressed our joy too? I mean, properly. For little Moses.'

'I don't know. Seeing how happy everyone is, it might be all right, don't you think?'

He pecked at her cheek and pulled back abruptly. 'That was stupid,' he said. 'It wasn't a real kiss. Have you ever had a real kiss, Rachael?'

'Once,' she answered.

'Did you like it?'

'Not too much. I really didn't like him. I only wanted to see what a kiss was like. It was sort of mushy. Have you ever had a real kiss?'

'Lots of them,' he threw off nonchalantly.

'Did you like it?'

'You know how it is. I can take it or leave it.'

Rachael and Wolf looked at each other for ever so long, and their breathing became irregular. There was a burst of applause inside and spontaneous calls for the master to play more. Then the shouts died down. Goldman played a soft Beethoven sonata.

Rachael was becoming frightened at the strange feeling she had all over her body. 'We had better get inside,' she said.

'Could I – for real?'

She was too scared to talk. She nodded her head and closed her eyes and lifted her chin and parted her lips. Wolf braced himself and leaned over slightly and touched his lips to hers.

He lowered his eyes and jammed his hands in his pockets.

'That was very good,' Rachael said, 'nothing at all like the other time.'

'Could we do it again?' he asked.

'Maybe we shouldn't ... Well, just once more.'

This time Wolf pulled her gently to him and they felt each other and it was even more wonderful. Her arms reached around him and held him against her and it was so good. 'Oh, Wolf,' she whispered.

She tugged away from him and walked toward the door.

'Rachael.'

'Yes?'

'Shall I see you soon?'

'Yes,' she said, and ran inside.

Chapter Thirteen

Paul Bronski generally brought his work home from the Civil Authority after hours. The census had been a demanding task. There had been a wild scramble for 'Aryan' *Kennkarten* not stamped with the demanding *J*. Many of the Jewish population were trying to buy their way out of the country or otherwise make the census count very difficult. Three hundred and sixty thousand Jews had registered with the Civil Authority.

It was the new directives and continual organizational work that kept Paul busy until late each night.

Deborah, who spent the days at the orphanage and the evenings schooling her children, took time out from their studies to make tea for Paul.

When she entered the study he was slumped over the desk, his eyes red from reading, and he was pale with fatigue. As he sipped the tea she stood behind him and massaged his neck. It always felt so good when Deborah did that.

'Anything bad?' she asked.

'Just weary,' he answered. 'This stump aches. Acts up in the damp weather.'

'Can't you take anything?'

'Don't want to get into the habit of too much pain killer.'

'Paul, you've been working too hard. Why don't we take a few days off together? We can slip off somewhere. You can get a travel pass.'

'I wish I could. My belated responsibilities to the Jewish community are rather time-consuming.'

She sat on the desk. He smiled and pushed his papers back. 'We aren't spending much time together,' she said. 'Orphanage during the day – but they're so short-handed – our children's lessons at night. I'll cut off a few hours at the orphanage.'

'No,' Paul said. 'I won't be able to get home earlier, anyhow. Besides, it makes a good impression to have the wife of a Civil Authority member volunteering in the Orphans and Self-Help program.'

There was something Deborah didn't like about that. Paul had reacted with a sense of duty to his new status, but he was still groping for prestige – still thinking in terms of doing the proper thing.

'When is all this going to end?' Deborah said glumly. 'Once I was foolish enough to think nothing could be worse than during the siege.'

'Well, no one really knows what the Germans are up to. But even they only can go so far. It will level off.' He switched the subject quickly. 'I saw Chris today.'

'Oh ...'

'He's been able to transfer most of our accounts to American banks.' Paul laughed ironically. 'There's a paradox for you. We are getting richer all the time.'

Deborah worked hard to mask the sudden shock at the mention of Chris's name. 'How is Chris?' she said quickly.

'Fine – fine.'

'I didn't know that he would be allowed to continue here. Susan Geller told me Ervin Rosenblum was concerned about a possible closing of Swiss News.'

'Seems he has gotten himself in thick with this Von Epp fellow. Naturally, his agency wants him to keep operating as long as the Germans let him. Incidentally, we decided that for mutual interests we shouldn't see each other except in emergency. There's no use alerting the Germans that we have business, and I could endanger Chris's position here. We don't need the funds, fortunately, and if we do we can always work through Rosenblum.'

'Yes,' Deborah said, 'that's sensible.'

'Dear,' Paul said, 'while we're about it, I want to speak to you about this business of sending Stephan to Rabbi Solomon for study. Let me say that I am in sympathy with your motives, but it's dangerous business.'

Deborah's sweetness suddenly vanished. 'Dangerous for whom?'

'For the boy himself.'

'Have you thought about the shock he has received in the past few months?'

'Of course I have. Deborah, be sensible. We are very lucky. We have been spared all the harrowing things going on in Warsaw.'

'Is that really it, Paul?' she said sharply. 'Protecting our position?'

'Did you ever think what would happen to us if I'm thrown off the Civil Authority? I'm not a criminal for wanting to protect my family.'

Paul had never seen Deborah look so stubborn. Almost always he had been able to talk her around in the past.

'Our son is being humiliated and persecuted because he is a Jew,' Deborah said. 'He should at least have some moral fortification to withstand these shocks. We cannot let him stumble through this without knowing why he is a Jew.'

Deborah wanted to say more. She wanted to tell Paul that if he assumed his responsibility as a Jewish father he would give his son instruction and training as other Jewish fathers were doing since the outlawing of the cheder schools. But what she said carried an authority he had never heard from her before. She let it stop there because Paul was tired and confused and she did not wish to hurt him.

The doorbell rang.

Paul opened it. Gawky Wolf Brandel dangled before him. 'Good evening, sir,' he said, his face reddening.

Paul smiled slightly. He quickly tried to change the atmosphere of the argument. 'Good evening, Mr Brandel. Did you come to visit with Stephan or Rachael?'

'Rachael – I mean Stephan, sir.'

'I will let you have them both for the price of one chess game.'

Oh darn, Wolf thought. Bronski was a tough chessplayer. It would take an hour to beat him. Then a lovely thought occurred. He would throw the game on purpose. This would kill two birds with one stone – please Dr Bronski's vanity and allow him to see Rachael quicker.

That night Deborah lay awake. The mention of Chris had stirred a restlessness in her. She ached for him. She closed her eyes and began to remember moments of coming up the path in the Saxony Gardens ... his touch, the warmth of him. The music in his room as they lay in the shadows. She squirmed about the bed.

She had run from him in anger and fright. But always in the back of her mind she knew she would see him again. Now ... cut off, completely. Not even a stolen glance ... a touch ... not even his voice on the phone. He must have been terribly, terribly hurt. But he is still in Warsaw ... he is still here. She wanted him to touch her. Oh, Chris ... Chris ... Chris ... please touch me.

Her tears fell on the pillow.

Paul reached out for her, and her body turned tense and rigid as it always did. Deborah forced the tears to stop and breathed deeply several times to make herself relax, and she rolled over to her husband.

Paul was in trouble. He was walking a tightrope. In the old days before the war he was so sure of himself, so independent and clever. He was floundering and now he had to lean on her more and more.

'You aren't angry about what I said about Stephan? If it means so much to you, then we will chance it. We'll let the boy continue with Rabbi Solomon.'

His hand went beneath her waist. She put her arms about him as he lay his head on her breast.

'I need you so much,' Paul said.

After sixteen years of taking her for granted, it was the first confession he had ever made.

Chapter Fourteen

Journal Entry

Something new has been added. As if we don't have enough to worry about, we were presented with Sturmbannführer Sieghold Stutze. Despite the lowly rank of SS major, it looks as if Stutze holds great power.

He came from Globocnik's SS, SD, Gestapo capital in Lublin. Like Globocnik and Hitler, Stutze is an Austrian. He arrived with a detachment of SS troopers who are billed as 'specialists in Jewish affairs.' We are learning that Globocnik and not Governor General Hans Frank is the real boss of Poland. It may hold true then that Stutze and not Rudolph Schreiker will be the real boss of Warsaw.

Whereas Rudolph Schreiker has shown himself to be a plain and simple pigheaded bully, Stutze is exhibiting a maniacal lust for cruelty. He is small in stature, thus a Napoleonic complex. He is slightly deformed in one leg and has a limp. This is a clue to his sadistic delight in inflicting pain. We are very concerned about this development.

ALEXANDER BRANDEL

Although religious study had been banned, this merely meant it would be carried on in secret places, as had been done by the Marranos during the

Spanish Inquisition and a hundred times in a hundred places where it had been banned during Jewish history.

Stephan Bronski had entered a most impressionable age. After a lifetime of immunity, the sudden branding of being a Jew made his trips to Rabbi Solomon's home part of a great adventure of discovery. He liked the secrecy of it. He was fascinated by the strange cryptic scrawlings in Hebrew and much awed by the infinite wisdoms of the rabbi. The gradual understanding of the two thousand years of unspeakable persecution did much to alleviate the confusion within him.

His class had six other boys. They studied in the basement beneath the home of Rabbi Solomon. They spoke in whispers. All about them were the treasures taken from the synagogue for safekeeping. The synagogue's library of many thousand books of Talmudic and Jewish literature was there. The menorah, the sacred candelabra, were there. The heart of Judaism, the Torah scrolls from the ark of the synagogue, were there.

The boys learned Hebrew prayers, ethics of the fathers, and prepared for the bar mitzvah.

The old man would walk from one to the other and pick up the chant of their prayer, pat one on the head, twist another's ear who was lagging. Although he was ancient, the boys could not put anything over on him, for it seemed he could see in back of his head and hear all seven of them at the same time.

Stephan Bronski asked the rabbi if he could be excused for a moment and it was granted. He stood up, and then he saw them!

There were three Nazis in black uniforms in the doorway. Major Sieghold Stutze stood before the other two.

'Rabbi!' Stephan cried.

And they all froze in terror.

Sieghold Stutze limped into the room. 'Well, well, well, what do we have here?'

The children flocked behind the rabbi, quivering in fright. One vomited. Only Stephan Bronski stood in front of the old man. His eyes burning with anger, he looked at that moment very much like his Uncle Andrei.

Stutze brushed Stephan aside as he tried to 'protect' the old rabbi and grabbed him by the beard and flung him to the floor. He took the dagger from his belt, straddled the fallen man, and cut off the earlocks worn by religious Jews because King David had worn them.

The other two Nazis broke into laughter. They walked around the room, throwing the books to the floor, overturning the desks, trampling on the symbolic ornaments from the synagogue.

'These will make a lovely bonfire,' Stutze said. His eyes searched the room carefully. 'It is here, somewhere – now where is it?' He walked to a large canvas. 'Could it be beneath here?'

'No!' shrieked the rabbi.

'Aha!' Stutze said, pulling the canvas away, revealing the Torah scrolls.

'No!' shrieked the rabbi again.

Stutze took off the breastplate, tore off the velvet cover, and took out the scrolls which formed the heart of Judaism, Christianity, and Islam – the five books of Moses. Genesis, Exodus, Leviticus, Numbers, and Deuteronomy. 'Here it is, the prize.'

The rabbi crawled to the Nazi and threw his arms about his knees and begged him not to harm the scrolls. Stutze answered by sending his boot thudding into the old man's ribs.

As he dangled the tree-of-life lambskin Torah before Solomon's nose the old man cried prayers.

Stutze laughed and his troopers laughed. 'I understand old Jews often die for this trash.'

'Kill me, but do not harm the Torah!'

'Shall we have some amusement? You! Boys! Line up against the wall! Hold your hands over your heads and put your faces to the wall.'

The boys did as they were ordered. Stutze dropped the Torah to the floor. Rabbi Solomon crawled quickly to it and covered it with his body.

Stutze took out his pistol and walked to the boys. 'All right, old Jew, dance for us. Right on the Torah.'

'Kill me first.'

The Austrian cocked his pistol and placed the barrel against the back of Stephan Bronski's head. 'I shall not kill you, old Jew. Let me see how many of the boys I will have to kill first. Now dance for us.'

'Don't do it, Rabbi!' Stephan shouted.

Stutze went into a spasm of hysterics. 'Sometimes when I play this game we have to kill two or three before they do their dance.'

The old man got to his knees, grunting in anguish.

'Now dance for us, old Jew.'

As Stutze tantalized the boys by placing the pistol against their skulls they cried, 'Rabbi! Rabbi!'

The tears streamed down the old man's cheeks.

He brought his foot down on the Torah and shuffled a grotesque dance on the sacred lambskin.

'Faster, old Jew, faster! Wipe your feet on them!'

'Now, old Jew – piss on them! Piss on them!'

While the Nazis convulsed in laughter at the desecration of the Law, Stephan Bronski had in the flash of a second made a lightning dash for freedom.

Chapter Fifteen

Journal Entry

Never a dull moment since Sturmbannführer Sieghold Stutze has honored us with his presence. He calls his SS detail the 'Reinhard Corps' after Reinhard Heydrich, the SD chief in Berlin. This gives us a clue to the chain of command. Hitler, Himmler, Reinhard Heydrich, Globocnik, and, in Warsaw, Stutze. In this week's meeting with Emanuel Goldman, David Zemba, and Simon Eden, they gave me a raft of notes for my journal.

The Reinhard Corps swept into the northern Jewish area in large trucks and emptied Jewish stores of all their merchandise.

The Reinhard Corps has been going into individual homes and taking clothing, pots, pans, lamps, books – which are burned – pillows, blankets.

The Reinhard Corps has emptied supplies from Jewish warehouses, including Zemba's American Relief supplies. This has created shortages in medicine and food. Then Dr Koenig sold us back the things that Stutze had stolen at a six-hundred-per-cent markup.

Fuel ration has brought on pneumonia this winter, Emanuel Goldman tells me. He says another cut in food ration was ordered by Schreiker yesterday.

Not to be outdone by the Reinhard Corps, Rudolph Schreiker has hundreds of thugs from Solec and even mobs of children and students to roam the Jewish area and smash store windows, beat up Orthodox Jews on the street, and loot. It is understood that no Pole will be punished for a crime against a Jew. Special rewards are offered to Poles who turn over Jews with 'Aryan' Kennkarten.

Rabbi Solomon's synagogue was burned to the ground, as he was caught by Stutze teaching cheder in his basement. (I could have sworn young Bronski was receiving instructions. Maybe not. He did not show up among those turned in at Pawiak Prison.) Rabbi Solomon's congregation was fined twenty thousand zlotys to free the boys and to pay for petrol which the Germans used to burn the synagogue. Zemba's American Relief put up half the fine in American dollars.

All teen-age orphans in our orphanage in Powazki and a dozen other orphanages were forced to donate blood to the German army. Does Hitler know his Aryans will be transfused with impure blood?

Simon Eden says the trade in poison is getting large. Everyone is carrying a capsule for suicide. No one gets more than a few hours' sleep these nights. Whistles, rifle butts, pounding boots. We sleep with one eye open. A hundred different rape cases reported. 'Juden 'raus [*Jews, come out*]!' *is heard every night, all night.*

If we are to hand out prizes for ingenuity, Stutze's Reinhard Corps must win. They force the old Orthodox to scrub sidewalks under bayonets. They have made them dance naked. They make them exercise with heavy cobblestones. They make them beat each other with galoshes. They make them crap their pants. Still, through it all, I am proud of these Jews. They refuse to shave off their beards or earlocks. They walk with their heads erect in great dignity despite the fact that their very appearance will bring them abuses. They are stubborn and honorable and of Rabbi Solomon's breed, and we Zionists could learn a thing or two from them.

Schreiker, jealous of Stutze and not to be outdone, turned loose mad Gerta, an ethnic with a psychopathic hatred of Jews. She has been allowed to wander through the northern quarters with a lead pipe.

A.B.

Chapter Sixteen

Journal Entry

The German hand is being revealed more each day. The Krakow Gazette *keeps hammering on the theme of 'segregation of the Jews on reservations.' That is fancy talk for ghettos.*

More talk about sending Jews from Austria, Czechoslovakia, and Germany into Poland.

Yesterday it became true. A ghetto was decreed in Lodz. Chaim Rumkowski was appointed chairman of a Council of Elders. Ana Grinspan is there now to see if we can organize a 'self-help house' like Mila 19. There are around two hundred thousand Jews in Lodz.

At yesterday's meeting with Emanuel Goldman, David Zemba, and Simon Eden, Goldman thinks we are heading into a week of crisis in Warsaw. He says that all the abuses up to date have been merely to soften us up. A new Nazi, Oberführer Alfred Funk, has arrived, and that means trouble because Funk is the direct liaison between Berlin and Globocnik in Lubin and is no doubt carrying a pocketful of candy on new German policy.

ALEXANDER BRANDEL

SS Brigadier Alfred Funk was the young blond blue-eyed Aryan about whom Adolf Hitler bragged. He was an intelligent and industrious man who cut a smart figure and would have been successful in any capacity he sought in life. He was shrewd and astute and dependable, unlike the bumbling bully Rudolph Schreiker, the timid conforming opportunist Franz Koenig, the half-mad Sieghold Stutze, and the cynical, lazy Horst von Epp.

Like Von Epp, he calculated that the rise of Nazism was unstoppable. Unlike Von Epp, he felt that Hitler could bring the German people to their peak position in history. Like most of the German people, he willingly chose to be a part of this 'march to destiny.' He accepted the traditional German obedience to authority without question. He desired to be a large and important man and he became what he desired. Alfred Funk had a few qualms at first about Nazi methods but soon realized that the political tyranny of the concentration camps, the abolition of civil liberties, and the destruction of the intellectual opposition were merely fundamentals clearing the path for this Greater Germany. He became a deputy of tyranny with conviction. The tools of tyranny were not questions in his mind – only the best methods of using them.

Golden hair, trim body, Alfred Funk was a man of undeniable strength who was able to impose his authority. As the master blueprints came from Berlin from Heydrich and Eichmann of the 4B section of Gestapo, Oberführer Funk received the position of special liaison to Globocnik in Lublin.

When Emanuel Goldman was summoned to the city hall to see Oberführer Alfred Funk, he had already surmised Funk's mission in Warsaw.

Funk spoke impassively. 'We are concerned about the unsanitary habits of Jews. Your homes are filled with lice. Lice cause typhus.'

Funk was, indeed, starting on an interesting tack, Goldman thought. 'I am not a doctor like the eminent Franz Koenig,' Goldman answered curtly, 'but your regulations denying us sanitary facilities are the cause of the outbreak of lice.'

Funk stared. He did not blink or budge. The old man is tough.

The Nazi picked up a paper. 'Our facts scientifically prove otherwise. Everyone knows Jews are filthy. Look at those bearded people. A perfect nesting place for lice.'

'We didn't have a bit of trouble with them in the past,' Goldman answered.

'But there's trouble now, isn't there, Goldman? Now, Goldman, I want your Civil Authority to help us protect the citizens of Warsaw. Have this Orphans and Self-Help Society of yours set up delousing sheds. Each Jew will get a stamped card when he is deloused. He will have to have the card in order to receive rations. We will carry out extensive inspections of personal dwellings in order to stamp out this scourge.'

You mean looting parties under guise of medical inspection, Goldman thought.

'In order to control this condition which the Jews have brought on Warsaw, we have blacked out certain areas of the city which will be under quarantine.'

Goldman knew ... here it comes.

'All Jews must move into the quarantine area within two weeks under punishment of death.' He shoved a map of Warsaw over his desk at the old man. It was blacked out from the northern rail bridge below Zoliborz down to Jerusalem Boulevard. The eastern boundary was a zig-zag line past the Saxony Gardens, and the western boundary roughly in a line with the Jewish and Catholic cemeteries. Funk was watching him. There was no use arguing with the German.

'Goldman,' Funk continued, 'you do agree we are at war with the Jews.'

'I cannot disagree.'

'Therefore, we consider that Jewish property, personal and otherwise, is legitimate booty – spoils of war. Therefore, when the move is completed into the quarantine area, you will begin a registration of all Jewish property. I have appointed Dr Koenig as registrar and custodian of Jewish property. That goes for business inventories, bank accounts, jewels, furs, et cetera, et cetera.'

Koenig! My, he has come up in the world ...

'One final thing, Goldman. Because you Jews have imposed these deplorable dangers and have consistently disobeyed our directives, we are fining all the Jews three hundred thousand zlotys. We are holding fifty people in Pawiak Prison to assure payment of the fine within a week. Your Civil Authority is expected to make the collection. You are to draft directives covering the things we have discussed and you will return here tomorrow for me to study them.'

When Goldman returned to the Civil Authority building at Grzybowska 28, he summoned the board immediately. Goldman relayed his conversation with Brigadier Alfred Funk to seven pasty-faced men.

'The quarantine order is merely a thin disguise for a ghetto. If we collect this mass fine for them, there will be others. Registration of property. I don't have to explain that to you. The most dreadful part of their whole scheme is to make us issue the orders. Now, we on the Civil Authority believe we could be of some service to the community and be a protective wall between the community and the Germans. The Germans are converting the Civil Authority into their own tool for carrying out their dirty work.'

The room was stricken with fear. Everyone knew what the Germans were up to. Everyone also knew he was facing a moment when he had to search the depths of his own soul to see if it held a hidden reservoir of courage. So long as they carried out German orders, they and their families were safe. Defiance could bring them instant death. Was this worth dying for? Emanuel Goldman, their chairman, thought it was.

One by one they revealed themselves. Weiss, who had been an army officer all his life, had never been much of a practicing Jew. He considered himself an assimilated Pole. He was angry. He banged his fist on the table. 'Certainly, as conquerors, they will give us the choice to withdraw in honor,' he said.

What nonsense, Goldman thought. Weiss is still playing colonel. 'These are not soldiers, but Nazis,' Goldman said. 'I do not know if they will let us resign.'

Now Silberbert. Once he had written plays in which vaunted ideals bounced from the rafters of the theaters. He had been terrified into conformity. He sulked. He hated himself for it. 'We are not collaborators,' he said, finding his reserves of strength.

Seidman, the engineer, was Orthodox. 'Misery is nothing new for the Jewish people. We have lived in ghettos before.'

As he talked he began to sound like Rabbi Solomon, but Goldman knew that Seidman spoke from conviction and not fear.

Marinski, the factory owner. He had spent a lifetime building his leather-works. The new orders would end in confiscation of his factories, he was certain of it. He had to calculate. As a member of the Civil Authority, can I save my factory or shall I gamble that the Germans will back down if we have a show of strength? There was another thing worrying Marinski. He was a just and proud man. The right and wrong seemed clear. 'We must make a stand,' he said.

That was the way Schoenfeld felt too. He was a brilliant lawyer. 'No matter how complete the occupation. No matter how strong their authority, they have to base every action on cause. They gave you a cause with the excuse of a quarantine. A determined effort by us, and I am certain we can force them to adhere to the rules of basic decency. Make them negotiate.'

And Paul Bronski spoke. 'We have no choice. To whom can we appeal? An outside world who won't listen to us? Schoenfeld, you are a fool if you think we can negotiate them out of a ghetto. They want it, they've ordered it in Berlin, and they'll have it. There is nothing we can do.'

'Yes there is,' Goldman answered. 'We can behave like men.'

Boris Presser, the merchant, who had an art of being anonymous, said nothing except to vote with Paul Bronski and Seidman against making a protest to the Germans.

'It is voted five to three that we protest to Funk.'

A sudden wave of nausea hit Paul. He stumbled to his feet. 'We are under no bylaws stating that we can vote. We are merely independent department heads. If you want to go to Funk with a protest, do it in the name of the others – not me.'

Was it an outburst of cowardice? Was it an outburst of self-preservation? Goldman wondered. He wondered if it was not all a useless gesture. There would be fifty more men like Paul Bronski to replace them and fifty more to replace *them*. What good would a protest do? Bronski was the realist there. The Germans would have what they wanted, regardless.

Emanuel Goldman was very tired. He was seventy-three years old. His children were all married. He lived alone with only his housekeeper.

He had had a good rich life. He had traveled and brought fame to his people and his country. A quirk of fate had put him into a position he did not wish, but he had accepted the position without protest. He had been made the chairman of the Civil Authority because Franz Koenig thought he was a weak man. Goldman was far from weak. He was an idealist who did not know how to back down from the things in which he believed.

He spent the night tying up all the loose ends of his business and took them to his friends, David Zemba of American Relief and Alexander Brandel. He left them knowing he would probably not see them again.

In the morning he reported to Oberführer Alfred Funk. He sat opposite the German very calmly, a picture of self-assurance, with the old flamboyance still in his mannerisms. Funk knew the moment Goldman entered the room, but his icy blue eyes did not betray the thoughts whirling behind them.

'You have drafted the directives?'

The old man shook his head.

Funk registered neither surprise nor anger.

'I won't put my name on a ghetto order,' Goldman said.

'Do you speak in behalf of the entire board?'

'I suggest you ask them,' he retorted.

'I am curious,' Funk said. 'Why are you doing it?'

Goldman smiled. 'I am more curious. Why are you doing it?'

It was Funk who broke off the staring contest.

Goldman arose, bowed slightly, sending his long white silken hair awry. 'Good day,' he said, and left.

Alfred Funk thought for a moment about the various possibilities, then shrugged to himself and methodically lifted his desk phone. 'Find Sturmbannführer Stutze. Have him report to me instantly.'

Journal Entry

Emanuel Goldman was murdered last night. It appears to be the personal handiwork of Sturmbannführer Sieghold Stutze. He was beaten to death with a pipe. His body was dumped on the streets before the Civil Authority building as a clear-cut message.

Boris Presser, whom none of us know, has been appointed Civil Authority chairman and Dr Paul Bronski given wider powers.

I must now deal with Bronski on all matters concerning the Orphans and Self-Help Society. We cannot expect from Bronski anything near what Goldman did for us.

ALEXANDER BRANDEL

Chapter Seventeen

Journal Entry

It is summer of 1940 already. News from the outside world, our one great source of hope, lists one disaster after another. Norway and Denmark have fallen. The Low Countries and the debacle at Dunkirk. Italy has been dragged into the war. German power is still on the rise, unchecked. France has paid for a decade of appeasement.

Rudolph Schreiker has no more trouble with the Jewish Civil Authority with Boris Presser as chairman. Paul Bronski's co-operation with the Orphans and Self-Help Society is rigidly guided by German directives.

The poor Jews have had their personal property stripped and carted away. They have no choice but to register for slave labor in one of the dozens of new German factories and enterprises springing up all over the Warsaw area. Dr Franz Koenig owns three or four factories outright. When short of labor they merely pull people off the streets in roundups and they simply disappear.

The rich are able to do better. There is wild trade in gold and jewelry and false Aryan papers. Everyone in the upper classes scrambles for himself. As for our countrymen, we do get superficial help from certain classes, but the bulk of the Poles show us nothing but apathy.

Any questions about who runs Poland? They are answered. SS Gruppenführer Globocnik in Lublin. It is known that Governor General Hans Frank protested to Hitler about having Jews deported from all over Europe into Poland. He was overruled. They are pouring in by the tens of thousands to the sixteen Jewish 'reservations' in that curious master plan in Berlin calling for 'resettlement' of all Jews in occupied countries.

Some of the German and Austrian Jews are pretty haughty. They have been able to rent themselves nice flats and look down upon us poor Polish Jews as inferior. However, the vast majority arrive destitute. Dr Glazer, who heads the medical staff of the Orphans and Self-Help, fears epidemic conditions and possibly mass starvation if we get another ration cut. Can Dave Zemba's America Aid keep up with the massive new problems we face?

What is the ultimate aim of the Germans' master plan? As German victories increase, their fear of world opinion lessens. I hear that the 4B section of the Gestapo on Jewish affairs under Adolf Eichmann on the Kurfürstendamn in Berlin is an empire within an empire.

A.B.

It was getting more dangerous for Andrei each time he traveled outside Warsaw. On his last trip he had a close call when a sudden inspection was pulled at a siding. He slipped the Pole who spotted his fake travel pass a three-hundred-zloty bribe and it worked. He always carried the bills folded and placed in his papers so the inspector could be bought on the spot.

When Emanuel Goldman headed the Jewish Civil Authority, Andrei was issued travel permits under the guise of Orphans and Self-Help business. Now that Paul Bronski was the liaison, he shut off all but legitimate permits.

Andrei had to travel with false papers as a non-Jew. His *Kennkarte* read 'Jan Kowal.' Normal hazards were increased by bands of hoodlums who hung out around the train depots detecting hidden Jews, whom they either extorted or turned over to the Gestapo for rewards.

Andrei's Aryan appearance and obvious physical prowess had got him through six false-permit trips. How long he could evade capture was a moot question.

He arrived at the central terminal on Jerusalem Boulevard and walked directly toward Mila 19 to report to Alexander Brandel. He had gone only a few blocks when he stopped and watched the surge of humanity pouring into the Jewish quarantine areas. First they had come from other parts of Warsaw, then from the surrounding countryside. Now they were being transported in from outside Poland. Barbed-wire accordions were laid across dozens of streets and placed under guard to define the quarantine districts.

A stream of miserable dazed human beings filled the street from the northern terminal for several blocks south. Iron wheels on the cobblestones set up a din. Some of the wealthier of the new arrivals had their belongings on horse-drawn wagons. Others had their goods piled high on bicycle-driven porter carts, still others on hand push-carts. Most carried their possessions wrapped up in a single blanket slung over their backs.

Hawkers tried to sell them armbands, pots, pans, books – anything. Self-Help workers were trying to organize the chaos.

'Where are they from?' Andrei asked another onlooker.

'Belgium.'

No matter how many times Andrei saw it, the sight disgusted him. Anger churned him into a hot flush. He abruptly turned away from the direction of Mila 19 and walked quickly to Leszno 92, the headquarters of Simon Eden.

Leszno 92 had a line of refugees outside it that ran for a block. Volunteers were aiding in registration and working the soup kitchen for the new arrivals. He walked past the line. They became a blur of faces.

He entered the main room and was recognized immediately.

'I want to see Simon,' he whispered to one of the girls behind the counter.

Because Simon Eden was the most powerful Zionist in Warsaw, he lived in semi-seclusion in the attic. Three buzzes would let him know a friend was coming up. A different signal would send him to the safety of the rooftops for hiding.

Andrei climbed the ladder into the attic. Simon pulled him up the last step. They slapped each other on the back and went into his small garret quarters. It was wilting from the midday heat which had come through the roof and settled in the airless room. Andrei opened his shirt and took off his hat. Simon smiled as he saw that Andrei was still wearing his boots in symbolic defiance of the enemy.

Simon opened and closed a half dozen desk drawers until he discovered a half-filled bottle of vodka. He took a swig and passed it to Andrei.

'How was the trip?'

Andrei shrugged. 'Good and bad.'

'Did you see any of my people?'

'Krakow. The underground press is getting important. At least it keeps the people aware of German motives.'

'What about the ghetto in Lodz?'

'I don't know if we can set up Self-Help houses there. This bastard Chaim Rumkowski is acting like a mad emperor. He walks around with a pair of German guards.'

Simon grunted. Andrei relayed the rest of the events, city by city, and a pall of gloom as thick as the heat settled on them. Simon needed no expert to disseminate the news. His dark rugged features strained with the words of a uniformly worsening situation.

'What does Alex have to say about all this?'

'I haven't seen Alex yet,' Andrei answered. 'I came straight here from the terminal.'

Simon looked at him curiously.

'What's on your mind, Andrei?'

'You were an officer in the army, Simon. We've been friends since I can remember. Out of everyone in this whole business, you and I think the most alike. When all this started I wanted to cross the border and get arms. Alex talked me out of it. I've gone along with everything, but . . . after this last trip . . . Simon, we've got to start hitting back.'

Simon took another nip of vodka from the bottle and scratched his unshaven jaw. 'Not a day passes by that my stomach doesn't turn over. It is all I can do to keep from exploding.'

'If I go to Alex he'll talk me out of starting a resistance movement. He can talk a leopard out of his spots. But if you and I went to him – you, speaking for Federated Zionists – and issued him an ultimatum, he'd have to start giving us some of the funds from American Aid to buy arms. We've got to do it now. Thompson is afraid the Germans are watching him. If they send him out of Poland, one of our chief sources to get dollars in is gone.'

Simon Eden wiped the sweat from his forehead with his sleeve and walked to the tiny window which looked straight down for six stories. Hundreds of impoverished refugees lined up before Leszno 92 for a bowl of soup and a *Kennkarte* which would give them the 'privilege' of joining slave labor.

'What about them down there?' Simon asked. 'We are all they have.'

'How long can you get slapped in the face without raising your hand!'

Simon spun around from the window. 'What the hell can we do!'

'Kill the bastards! Make life hell for them!'

'Andrei! Denmark, Norway, Poland, France, Belgium, Holland! Will they give in to us? Twenty, thirty, a hundred to one in reprisal for every one we kill, and they'll murder women and babies and old men. Can you take that responsibility?'

'You're a damned fool, Simon, and Alex is a damned fool. Do you really think they will stop with ghettos and slave labor? They mean to wipe us off the face of the earth.'

The two giants glared at each other, portraits of anger and frustration. Simon shook his head.

'One of these days we will be at the twelfth hour, and by God you'll know then there is no way but to fight our way out,' Andrei said.

Andrei left Simon Eden in a huff. He did not go to Mila 19 to see Alexander. There would be hours of reports and bickering. Alterman and Susan and Rosy would listen to his monotonous repetitions of the fear of new ghettos, the continued murder of intellectuals, the slave-labor camps, the unbelievable abuses. And they would try to put up a new Self-Help house in Bialystok or

Lemberg. They would try to print a one-page paper. They would put up a few bags of sand to hold back a rising, rampaging river.

Andrei walked fast for Gabriela's flat, trying to shut out the sight and the sound of the agony around him. Many people were becoming anonymous in Warsaw these days. Gabriela was one of them. It was an unwritten code that if you ignored a friend who recognized you in a public place it was understood.

Gabriela had moved from her flat to a smaller one on Shucha Street. Through Tommy Thompson she sent messages to her mother and sister that it would be dangerous for her if they were to communicate with her. She stopped her allowance from coming into Poland and took an inconspicuous job as a tutor in French and English in the small, exclusive school in the Ursuline Convent.

Andrei stopped before her flat on Shucha Street. Across the street stood Gestapo House. It was ironic, but he thought Gaby's flat was probably in the safest place in Warsaw. It was early. She would not be home yet. He dashed off a note and put it in her mailbox so she would not be startled.

Andrei threw off his cap and flopped into a big armchair and fought with himself to relax the burning pains of tension in his chest. It had been a terrible trip. He did not realize until this moment that he had not slept more than a few hours in three days. His eyes closed and he rolled his face into the sun's rays to catch its warmth, and he dozed quickly.

... The sound of footsteps brought him sharply awake. Gaby had read his note. She was running up the steps. The door to the flat flung open and closed quickly, and she set down her parcels of food and looked for him in the evening shadows. She curled up on his lap and lay her head on his chest, and they clung to each other with no sound except for her deep sighs of relief and no movement except for her trembling.

She looked at him. His face was so drawn and tired. Day by day she watched the energy being sapped from him. After each trip he was drained. He was eating himself away inside.

Now, at this moment, she could transfuse life back into him. Andrei smiled with pleasure at the feel of her fingertips tracing the lines of his face and her lips brushing his eyes and ears and neck.

'It was very bad this time,' he said. 'I don't know how much longer I can take it.'

'I'll take care of you, dear ...'

She unbuttoned his shirt and felt his chest and shoulders, and the knots of tension slowly melted away.

'I'll take care of you,' she whispered.

'Gaby ...'

'Yes, darling ...'

'When you touch me like this it all seems to go far away. Why are you so good to me?'

'Shhh ... shhh ... rest, darling ...'

'Gaby, when will they stop? What do they want from us?'

'Shhh ... shhh ... shhh.'

Chapter Eighteen

Journal Entry

Don't hide your gold ring, Mother,
Your chances are quite nil,
That if the Germans do not find it,
Kleperman, the *goniff*, will.

That verse is attributed to Crazy Nathan, a half-wit who roams the ghetto making rhymes and some rather clairvoyant observations. No one knows where Crazy Nathan comes from, who his parents are, or even what his last name is. He wears filthy rags and sleeps in alleyways and cellars. Everyone looks upon him as a harmless goof and treats him with benevolent tolerance. Crazy Nathan shows up at the best cafés in the Jewish districts and, after a few new verses, earns his meal. He prefers fish so he can share it with the dozen or more alley cats who follow him. He has named his cats after the board members of the Jewish Civil Authority.

A.B.

Max Kleperman was a product of the slums. He learned at a tender age that it was easier to live off his fellow man than, God forbid, bend his back in honest labor.

By the age of five Max was a fast-hand artist. He could wander through the smelly, noisy trade in Parysowski Place and rifle wares off the pushcarts of the old bearded Jews with dazzling deftness. By the time he reached seven he was an expert in fencing his stolen goods.

While good Jewish sons like Andrei delivered chickens for their fathers and were robbed and beaten by hoodlums, naughty Jewish sons like Max Kleperman showed a natural aptitude as middlemen. He would purchase all stolen chickens and other goods from the hoodlums and resell them on the Parysowski open market at stunning markups.

By the age of fourteen he had been a guest of the Pawiak Prison three times. Once for theft. Once for extortion. Once for swindling.

By the age of sixteen he went to his natural habitat, to live in the Smocza area populated by the Jewish underworld of Warsaw.

At seventeen he was accepted as a full-fledged member of the Granada Night Club, the most notorious hangout for thugs and gangsters in Poland.

As Max grew older his varied talents expanded. He became the head of a gang of strong-arm men who muscled in on the building-trade area on Grzybowski Square. The square was lined with building-material shops, craftsmen, contractors, teamsters, ironworks, and brick shops. Plying his talent as a middleman with the help of husky friends, Max elbowed his way into the square until his 'clearance' became standard for most normal operations. Only the opposition of the labor unions kept him from absolute czardom.

His hand was in every pie from blueprint to finished product. His little finger bore an eight-carat diamond and his cigar ashes dripped on half the building deals made in Warsaw.

Max was at home at the Granada Night Club or even with the *goyim* underworld in Solec, where he was respected; but strangely, he reached a point in life where he began to wonder what all his hard labor was for. He was, in fact, nothing but a bum.

Max Kleperman did not want to be a bum. He wanted to be as respectable as the 'new rich' who promenaded on the Avenue of the Marshals on the Sabbath. He could not muscle himself into their affection, and this annoyed him. So he set about to purchase respectability. First the beautiful old mansion of a nobleman living in France. It did not help. His neighbors looked upon him as a social leper.

Max was determined. He hired an expensive lawyer with a three-word dictum, 'Make me respectable.'

The lawyer's first move was to buy a pair of seats in the Great Tlomatskie Synagogue. Max could parade in during the High Holy Days when the synagogue was filled to capacity and uniformed police held back the mobs of onlookers who 'ohed' and 'ahed' at the elite.

Max was put on a program of philanthropy. He donated to the poor and he patted orphans on the head and sponsored scholarships for students who never did amount to much.

His work was so good that he was accepted into membership by a half dozen professional societies. Then followed a series of lavish parties.

Soon Max Kleperman was so respectable he fired his lawyer.

To consolidate his hard-won position, Max had to get rid of his ignorant wife, who was constantly a source of embarrassment. She was delighted with the settlement. Max then shopped around through the professional matchmakers for a nice homey girl from a good religious family.

One was found for him. Sonia Fischstein filled the bill. Her family was Orthodox, respectable, traditional, and acceptable to a settlement on their daughter. Rabbi Solomon was called in to negotiate the terms.

Rabbi Solomon saw right through Kleperman's fraud. Max was enraged at the rabbi's attitude. He even invited the notion of having him rubbed out. Then he learned that Rabbi Solomon was really respectable – in fact, the most respectable man in Jewish Warsaw. He set out to cultivate the great man.

Rabbi Solomon was not fooled. He considered everything. Max would never change, but his quest for respectability would keep him in check and there was some hope that a little of the decency he was exposing himself to would rub off on him. Besides, Sonia Fischstein was quickly running out of chances to marry. So he agreed to the match.

Rabbi Solomon became the earthly custodian of Kleperman's soul. Max realized under his puffy jowls that his one link with the Maker was through the rabbi.

When the Germans invaded Poland, Max was sad because no one liked Germans. However, he was a realistic man. His past made him perfect for the type of business that was flourishing – black market, smuggling, money exchanging. In fact, opportunities were never so great. Moreover, the Germans could be dealt with. Before the smoke of battle had cleared, Max Kleperman got in touch with Dr Franz Koenig and impressed him that his organization would be indispensable to the Germans.

At that time, Dr Koenig had the problem of opening brothels for German soldiers, a venture in which the Jewish Civil Authority had refused to co-operate. Eager to prove his own mettle to Rudolph Schreiker, Dr Koenig gave Max his first assignment, the rounding up of a hundred whores. Max had pimped in his younger days but not since he became respectable. Nevertheless, his contacts in the Solec were still active and he came through for Koenig in two days.

Dr Koenig knew he had a real ally.

With a license to operate, Max Kleperman gathered around him the most immoral gang of chiselers in Warsaw. His tentacles spread everywhere.

When the Germans introduced slave labor, Max had at long last broken his enemy, the labor unions. He grabbed firm control of the building-trade industry and from there poached on dozens of legitimate businesses. With the strong arm of the Germans behind him, it became realistic to do business with Max and his partners.

The main windfall was the sale of protection. If a father or son was picked up off the street in a German roundup and taken to the slave-labor camps outside Warsaw, Kleperman could arrange a release for a price.

It was in this area that he posed as a benefactor of the people. When they came to him for a release of a relative, Max treated them with great sympathy, all the while appraising them for how much he could shake them down. He would tell them it took a lot of money to make a fix with the Germans. There is honor among thieves. Max refused compensation until he arranged the release. Dr Koenig, Sieghold Stutze, and Rudolph Schreiker had also hit a windfall in kickbacks.

Max's interests became so large that he and his six minor partners leased a building on the corner of Pawia and Lubeckiego streets, opposite the Pawiak Prison, to direct their enterprises. The organization became known as the Big Seven.

When the Germans ordered registration of Jewish property, Dr Franz Koenig became custodian of all Jewish-owned dwellings in Warsaw. The Big Seven became the agent for Koenig.

During the quarantine directives, Jews had to move from all parts of Warsaw into the new restricted area. Eighty thousand Christians who lived in the quarantine area were to be replaced by a hundred fifty thousand incoming Jews. In the two weeks of the move, with a quarter of a million people suddenly upheaved, the Big Seven made a killing.

Amid the frantic turmoil and the endless streams of wagons and pushcarts, there was a frenzied scramble to find living quarters for a hundred fifty thousand people in an area designed to hold eighty thousand.

Property was at a premium for the Jews. As agent for Koenig's office, Kleperman was able to rent and sell at astronomical figures, even 'doing a favor' to those wealthy enough to afford it.

Property values again jumped when the mass deportation of Jews from occupied countries into Poland began.

Dr Franz Koenig and the other German heads preferred to deal with the Big Seven mostly because of the language barrier that existed with the Poles. Most Jews spoke Yiddish.

Toward the end of the summer of 1940, Max Kleperman was summoned to the city hall to the office of Dr Franz Koenig. When he was ushered into the office he was surprised to find Rudolph Schreiker and Oberführer Alfred Funk there also. Max did not mind doing business with Koenig, but he did not like Schreiker and he knew that when Funk was in Warsaw trouble was brewing, for Funk carried the messages from Berlin. No matter how decent Max was to Schreiker, Schreiker always bullied him around. Kleperman had made a large donation to the German Winter Relief, yet this did not placate Schreiker.

Max betrayed his nervousness by incessantly squeezing his cigar. He deftly slipped the eight-carat diamond into a vest pocket lest it end up in German Winter Relief.

He had never met Funk before. Funk was arrogant. Max could see immediately the disdain Funk held for him.

Max's upper lip dampened with perspiration, and ashes dropped on his trousers.

Rudolph Schreiker opened a map of Warsaw on a conference table. Max mopped his brow and studied it. A heavy black grease-pencil line was drawn encircling the areas which the Germans had placed under quarantine. Much of it followed the route of the barbed-wire rolls in 'epidemic' streets.

'I have studied the past several weeks Warsaw and I am aghast,' Alfred Funk said. 'You Jews have been guilty of the most blatant infractions of our regulations. We have notified the Jewish Civil Authority that the Jews are fined three million zlotys and they must collect it within a week.'

Kleperman nodded and squeezed his cigar.

'As you know, you are a filthy people,' Funk continued. 'We cannot seem to do anything about your sanitation habits. Typhus is reaching epidemic proportions despite our delousing operations. Therefore, for the protection of the people of Warsaw, and in order to further segregate you dirty Jews, we have decided to build this enclosure around the quarantine areas.'

Max dared not take his eyes off the map.

'General Funk is willing to consider having an outside building group construct the enclosure. I suggest the Big Seven, provided your bid is in order,' Dr Koenig said.

Max was able to pick up all the meanings of Koenig's statement. Kickbacks down the line for the Germans. A continuance of the pattern of forcing the Jews to carry out German directives and thereby justifying the German claim that 'Jews were doing this to Jews.'

Max had an infamously gained knowledge of construction. He clamped the cigar in his teeth, and his fat finger ran down the lines marked by the Germans.

'What type of an enclosure do you have in mind?'

'A brick wall, ten feet high. Triple strands of barbed wire on top.'

Max licked his dry lips. The line ran for eleven or twelve miles, more or less. He jotted down a page of figures to approximate the number of bricks, miles of barbed wire, mortar needed.

'About labor costs?'

'The Jewish Civil Authority will recruit three battalions of labor.'

Good, Max thought. Slave labor. They worked for rations. He went back to work on his figures. With slave labor, inferior materials, salvaged brick, he could bring it well under the fine of three million zlotys with a huge profit for himself.

'With the price of the zloty,' Max whined. 'It was five to one – now it is a hundred to one and still climbing.'

'Don't steal so much and it may go down,' Rudolph Schreiker snapped.

Max toyed with the figures and looked from one to the other. 'I am sure I can come up with a satisfactory figure,' he said.

'Yes, I am sure you will,' Funk agreed.

Journal Entry

In ancient days Jewish slave labor built monuments to Egyptian glory. Now we build one to German glory. We pay for it with a fine. We watch it happen with a strange fascination. A lot of people are relieved that the ghetto is coming. Safety in numbers. Well, we've got numbers. The population has swelled to over a half million and they are still pouring in.

Each morning labor battalions are formed in various parts of the quarantine area. They split into a dozen or more smaller groups, all working in different places.

A row of bricks here ... a row of bricks there. Two rows, three rows. It seems aimless, without a plan. Now and then two groups connect.

The Krakow Gazette *has stepped up its tirades on page four with the campaign about the uncleanliness of Jews, asserting that we 'sub-humans' must be segregated.*

The wall grows higher. Two feet, three, four. It follows a weird, unexplainable course. From the slums of Stawki Street and Parysowski Place, which is crammed with refugees, it follows south along the Jewish cemetery and stops at the fashionable Sienna Street, running there to Wielka Street, north again.

The wall is shutting off the Saxony Gardens and the Great Tlomatskie Synagogue. We are even denied the squalid Krasinski Gardens. I do not believe there will be a single tree in the ghetto.

For eleven crooked, reasonless miles. Who planned this? In some places the wall cuts right down the middle of the street, putting half of the houses in the ghetto and half outside. On Leszno Street it slices right through the middle of the courthouse. Chlodna Street is a finger of land on the Aryan side, splitting the ghetto into two parts. The big ghetto is on the north. A smaller ghetto is to the south, and this holds the elite – members of the Civil Authority, Militia, wealthy, German and Austrian deportees. A bridge covered with barbed wire crosses Chlodna Street, connecting the two ghettos. It has been named the 'Polish corridor.'

Seven, eight, nine, ten feet. The wall is connected in all parts. Tens of thousands of jagged pieces of glass have been cemented on top to rip off the hand of anyone who tries to scale it. A triple strand of barbed wire is on top of the glass.

There are thirteen gates. Never has the unfortunate number had a more sinister use. There are guards at each gate. A few of the Reinhard Corps bossing the unarmed Polish Blue Police. There is a rumor that a Jewish police force will be formed inside the ghetto.

Irony. One Catholic church on Leszno has been included in the ghetto. The Catholics have put it to work. Franciscan Father Jakub has been sent to take care of Jewish converts who are forced to live as Jews now but still carry on Catholic ritual.

Statistics? The ghetto is a thousand acres, or one hundred square blocks, or fifteen hundred buildings. Any way you cut it, it's pretty rough to find places for half a million people.

On November 7, 1940, the Big Seven had completed the wall and the ghetto was declared. In a fell swoop tens of thousands who were working at jobs outside the quarantine area were jobless.

Sieghold Stutze's Reinhard Corps had the task of ghetto security. True to early rumor, a Jewish Militia was formed. On paper it was under the direction of the Jewish Civil Authority, a guise in keeping with the German policy of trying to create the illusion that the Jews were imposing this upon each other. Stutze was the ruler of the Jewish Militia.

He chose as his chief a former sub-warden of the Pawiak Prison named Piotr Warsinski, who had a long-time reputation of brutality to prisoners, especially Jewish prisoners.

Piotr Warsinski was squat, bald, and sported an immense mustache. A tormented youth filled with fear of a brutal father had left him impotent and seething with hatred. Warsinski blamed his demented soul on being a Jew. He converted. Conversion left him with an unreasonable hatred of Judaism. Now the Germans forced him to be a Jew again and it intensified his hate.

Warsinski gathered about him the dregs of Jewish society. Men and women with limited mentality, criminal records, without conscience. They were given truncheons, special armbands, blue caps, and they were issued black boots, the symbol of power. They were given preferential rations and quarters for themselves and their families.

There was one condition. Warsinski made it utterly clear that their personal survival depended upon complete obedience.

As 1940 closed, a half million people in the Warsaw ghetto formed the largest human stockyard the world had ever known. They were at the complete mercy of the greatest military power ever experienced by man. The Germans had craftily carried out their master plan by forcing Jew to rule Jew through the impotent Jewish Civil Authority backed by the potent Jewish Militia under the sadist Warsinski. To augment their problems, the Big Seven continued their legalized swindles.

All that was left to protect this swell of humanity was a thin line of Zionists, Socialists, and the Orphans and Self-Help Society with American Aid.

Chapter Nineteen

Journal Entry

I think that Susan Geller will die of a broken heart. The Germans have ordered her to abandon our orphanage (and pride and joy) in Powazki and move inside the ghetto. Their directives order Susan to leave all equipment attached to the floors and walls, and that constitutes some of our most expensive things. Even the Orphans and Self-Help Society has a hard time renting property these days. Space is at a premium. We were able to find Susan a building on Niska Street, which she must completely convert. It is hardly comparable to the place in Powazki.

Thank the Lord for my dear Sylvia and for Deborah Bronski. Between the two of them, they kept Susan from a breakdown on moving day. It is so strange how different Deborah and Paul Bronski are. Yesterday I had to argue for three solid hours to convince Paul Bronski to petition the Germans to allow us to keep our farm in Wework running. You never know how the Germans will react. Paul just phoned me that the farm will be allowed to operate. Tolek Alterman will be overjoyed.

I am sending my son Wolf out to the farm in Wework. It will be good for him out there.

We have received our first group of Dutch Jews. The trip to Poland was very hard. They were jammed in cattle cars. Where can we put them? I don't know. The ghetto has over five hundred fifty thousand people in it now.

Mila 19 has been divided up by the Bathyran Council. On the first floor we have the ghetto administrative offices of the Orphans and Self-Help. We have a soup kitchen that can be entered from the back alley (Orphans and Self-Help now runs sixty soup kitchens), and we have a dispensary for minor ailments and a delousing shed as demanded by our German friends.

Second story. Bathyran families. Our rule is one family to a single room, regardless of the size of the family. The kitchen for the entire house is also on the second floor.

Twenty-one families ... sixty-two occupants, including Sylvia, me, and baby Moses (now that Wolf is gone).

Third floor. Walls have been broken through. Our dormitory for single girls. We have thirty. Divided right down the middle; fifteen work in the dispensary and soup kitchen and fifteen are hired out as domestics in the small ghetto on the southern end. I cheat by supplying our domestics with green armbands denoting a Self-Help employee in order to allow them to move about unmolested by Warsinski's overeager Jewish Militia.

Fourth floor. Fifty of our boys have a dormitory. Twenty of them work in Mila 19. Thirty work at various jobs around the ghetto, mostly as bicycle porters and riksha drivers.

The problem is shaping up. Of our eighty 'kids,' most have left families to live with us in the communal. How many members of their families can we take in – the aged, the ill? This is going to become serious.

In the attic we have cut up a dozen cubicles for the married couples. They are living on the second floor, mostly more than two to a room, so they must have a place where they can duck off for a few hours to have privacy. There are pre-set signals on the doors to advise whether the cubicles are in use or not. Sylvia and I are fortunate. With Wolf gone and the baby still an infant, we manage very well in our room.

The unmarried who wish privacy have to work it out for themselves. We neither officially encourage nor discourage it. Off the record, the unmarried know that the basement is available to them.

Irony. David Zemba, who wins more and more respect from me all the time, went in to see Schreiker and demanded that American Aid be allowed to open an office in the ghetto. So, he gets it. The dollars he receives from American Jews are our main support, but we can't keep up with the flood of refugees, mass fines, and confiscations.

Dr Glazer says the typhus death rate is becoming alarming. Pneumonia, TB, and malnutrition will be critical problems.

We are able to get passes in and out of the ghetto with relative ease. We know the situation won't last long, so we are lining up people in the Jewish Civil Authority and the Jewish Militia who control passes who can be bribed in the future.

Orphans and Self-Help with American Aid money has taken over another important function, running all the Labor Zionist farms and ours at Wework. We have managed to open two more farms and we can also buy food and transfer through this farm system. The over-all operation is called Toporol.

A straw in the wind? Perhaps, I don't know. For all the astute planning for which the Germans are famous, they are pulling an enormous blunder. In the ghetto we have thousands of building-trade people, craftsmen, tailors, engineers, etc. If used properly, these people would be of tremendous value to the German war effort. There is no rhyme or reason for the way people are slapped into slave-labor battalions. Carpenters are sent to the Brushmaker's factory, doctors are set to digging ditches and building airfields (for an attack on Russia?), and this inconsistency draws me to two conclusions.

1. *The Germans are not quite certain why they are herding Jews into Poland.*
2. *A 'final solution' of their 'Jewish problem' has not been decided.*

ALEXANDER BRANDEL

In the winter of 1940 and the spring of 1941 Wolf Brandel worked on Toporol Farm 2 situated northeast of Warsaw, near the village of Wework.

Each time the produce and milk were taken in to the ghetto the farm workers sent letters in to their loved ones. Wolf wrote to his mother and father and Stephan Bronski, who looked up to him very much. And he wrote to Rachael Bronski.

Dear Rachael,

It is sure different out here on the farm. Like in another world away from the ghetto. There are seventeen girls and thirty of us fellows. I'm one of the youngest. We live in dormitories (separate, boys and girls).

Tolek Alterman, who has been to Palestine, keeps us hustling. He gives a continual lecture about living Zionism almost every night and we have slogans posted everywhere about keeping production up and getting milk and fresh vegetables in to the children in the orphanage.

We work very hard. I'm milking cows. I'm lousy at it. I like everything, including Tolek. He needs a haircut, however.

Would you write to me? Your mother can give your letters to Susan Geller and they will reach me. Also, please have Stephan write.

Your sincere friend,
WOLF BRANDEL

Dear Wolf,

It was nice to hear from you. I will write to you regularly. Stephan studies you know what and you know where and he is getting good at it. He misses you. He admires you greatly. I am very happy for you being out of here – if you know what I mean.

With fondest regards,
RACHAEL BRONSKI

Dear Rachael,

I'm milking better. However, the real important work in the winter is the hogs and I've asked to be transferred. Whatever you do, don't tell anyone we are raising hogs. The rabbis would raise h--- if they knew, but with meat so scarce, we must. I'm certain that God will let the kids at the orphanage into heaven, anyhow.

At night it is swell here. We have a kind of game room. We have a community meeting to talk about production, farm problems, and division of work. Then a lecture by Tolek. Afterward we can debate, hear music, study and read and play games. (I'm chess champion.)

Almost always before bedtime we start up a song fest and sing the songs that the Bathyran pioneers sing in Palestine and we dance horas.

We don't even have to wear the Star of David unless we go to the village.

Please write.

Most sincerely,
WOLF BRANDEL

Dear Wolf,

It sounds nice on the farm and I'm so glad for you. Winter here has been – well, you can imagine. Momma says things are very bad at the orphanage. We have 100% too many children and 50% too little rations and medicine. That is why your job is important. I suppose you hear about the things happening in the ghetto. I don't want to write you about them, you'll worry.

Fondly,
RACHAEL BRONSKI

Dear Rachael,

Hey, guess what! I am learning to play the accordion and the guitar. Tolek Alterman is teaching me. He knows all the Palestine pioneer songs, as he has been there. I'd like to teach them to you.

Warmest personal regards and kind wishes and thoughts.

WOLF

Dear Wolf,

I would indeed like to learn your songs. But when? When will I ever see you? I mean, Stephan misses you.

I am busy with my music too. I play recitals all the time and quite a few concerts. Sometimes eight or nine a week. I have learned about fifty children's songs and singing games (also in French and German) so I can go around to all the orphanages and entertain them.

Do you dance with the girls? I think I am envious.

Very fondly,
RACHAEL

Dear Rachael,

We are celebrating Succoth in memory of Moses and the ancient tribes in the wilderness and giving thanks for the first fruits of the harvest.

You lived in Zoliborz before the war and they don't allow celebrations now, but ask your mother about how Succoth used to be. Almost all the upper balconies and courtyards in Jewish homes had little 'succah' huts built of branches and twigs and leaves to commemorate the way the Jews lived during their wandering.

Out here we have constructed a giant 'succah' and it is covered with hundreds of fruits and vegetables and we have all our meals under it. Don't worry, we are sending all the food in to the orphanage just as soon as the holiday is over.

To answer your question candidly – I do dance with girls. However, I play the accordion most of the time for them while they dance.

Most sincerely,
WOLF

Dear Wolf,

Hanukkah has passed. The holidays in the ghetto were terribly gloomy. Everyone spoke of the old days when the Tlomatskie Synagogue was jammed with people in fancy dress and there was an air of gaiety everywhere. Now we can't even see the Tlomatskie Synagogue. Hanukkah seems almost like a mockery. Silly, celebrating the Maccabees storming into Jerusalem, throwing out the tyrants and rebuilding the Temple, when we are cowered in a ghetto.

I think the worst of all was Yom Kippur, earlier. We were all sitting and meditating and atoning for our past sins. The stillness this year was horrible. There was no breath of movement anywhere. Everyone was really asking God what we have done so terrible as to deserve this punishment.

Sorry to be so glum.

RACHAEL

Dear Rachael,

I worry about things in the ghetto all the time. Tolek keeps telling us we are front-line soldiers and how important the farm is. I try to make myself believe him.

I think about you often.

With affection,
WOLF

Dear Wolf,

I think about you, too, but I guess you're really not too lonesome with all those girls out there. If you know what I mean.

Also, with affection,
RACHAEL

Dear Rachael,

I will be frank with you.

I have had offers (not exactly offers) to kiss and play around, but I am not interested. Most of the girls like to neck. I think one or two even will do more (so it is rumored).

I don't know how you will take this, but I miss you more all the time. I didn't think I would, but I do. This sounds awful, but I think mostly about those four different times we kissed and held each other. You'll probably stop writing to me and I won't blame you.

WOLF

Dear Wolf,

You didn't write anything bad at all. I wish you were here right now so I could kiss you.

With deepest affection,
RACHAEL

Dear Rachael,

I sure don't know why anyone would want to kiss me. Especially someone like you, so beautiful. I never said it, but I have always thought so. You are very beautiful.

I look at your picture every chance I get and I memorize your letters. The once or twice they didn't come in I was pretty miserable.

Candidly speaking, I am pretty certain I am in love with you.

Love,
WOLF

Dear Wolf,

I am not certain what love is, so I can't be sure. I do know that I have a funny feeling inside me when I think about you and that is almost all the time. I know, too, that it hurts me to be apart. I didn't know anything could be so painful. I cry at night sometimes. That's because I'm a girl, I guess.

Isn't it curious? I liked you very, very much before you left (I wouldn't want you to think I'd kiss a boy I didn't like very, very much), but since you've been away I guess it must be love or something very close to it.

RACHAEL

Dearest Rachael,

If two people feel the same way about each other and are forced to be apart and nothing was decided upon before they parted, then they find they miss each other more and more all the time, I think an understanding could be reached.

I would like you to be my girl, candidly speaking. I promise I won't have another girl or fool around until I see you. I wouldn't impose the same conditions on you except to ask you to promise you will let me know immediately if you feel seriously inclined toward anyone else. Then, when we see each other, we can decide how we really feel.

WOLF

Dearest Wolf,

I think your idea is wonderful, but you can be sure that I am not and won't be interested in anyone else. The thought of any other boy than you touching me makes me shudder.

Love,
Your girl,
RACHAEL

A great deal of that calm and witty shrewdness that was the mark of Dr Paul Bronski's personality had vanished. It seemed as though he was worried all the time. At home he was often irritable and many times he snapped at the children for trifles. Deborah tried hard to compensate by comforting him, but Paul's burdens were running ahead of her powers to transmit sympathy. As the deputy under the chairman, Boris Presser, Paul had to carry out the German directives, deal directly with both Piotr Warsinski as well as the Orphans and Self-Help Society, and was often the scapegoat for all sides. He got little or no support from Boris Presser, who was a complete robot of conformity.

Deborah waited several days after she and Rachael had had their confidential talk in order to find Paul in a proper restful mood. As they prepared for bed one night, Paul had let it be known by the innuendoes married couples develop that he desired sex. Deborah, as always, prepared to comply. It was in that moment that he seemed a little relaxed as he sat in the big chair near the bed and sipped tea and watched her put up her hair as she sat before the mirror.

As he looked at her he thought it amazing how she managed to keep herself so beautiful. Deborah worked eight, ten, twelve, and often fourteen hours in the orphanage on Niska Street. She had kept up Stephan's studies and Rachael's piano and she had been a good and comforting wife. There was not a line in her face, no gray in her hair, no telltale sagging of her body.

Perhaps there was envy on the part of Paul. Once Deborah had been retiring and obedient and passive. Now she seemed the stronger of the two. Paul resented his growing need for her.

Deborah twisted the long black strands of hair into tight curls on her forehead and deftly darted pins into them to hold them in place. Then she picked up the hairbrush and went into her nightly stroking exercise.

'Paul, dear.'

'Yes?'

'I have been thinking that, with both of us gone a good part of the day and conditions as they are, wouldn't it be nice if Rachael were able to get away for a change of scenery? I could take Stephan along with me to the orphanage. There are dozens of boys his own age and he enjoys it there ...'

Bronski furrowed his brow. 'It would be nice if all of us got a change of scenery. What about your plans for Rachael to debut with the symphony? Besides, this is so much nonsense. There is no place she could go but to another ghetto.'

She watched him in the mirror out of the corner of her eye. 'We could send her to the Toporol farm in Wework.'

He put his cup down. 'Wework? The damned place is just a front for Zionists. The whole place is staffed by former Bathyrans.'

'But it's healthy and there are girls her age and she will have a chance to look at trees and flowers and something other than misery.'

'You know the morals of these Zionist children.'

'No, I don't,' snapped Deborah.

'They're very loose.'

'Has it occurred to you that Rachael is nearly as old as I was when I met you?'

Bronski paled at the verbal slap. Then his eyes narrowed. 'Just a minute. Isn't that where the Brandel boy is?'

'Yes. And before you say another word, I think he is a fine young man who would be overly aware of not violating her. Besides, it's something that they will have to work out for themselves whether we like it or not.'

'My, listen to the voice of modern sophistication. Have you become a free-love advocate? Are you going to spend the rest of your life throwing up to me your debauching?'

'Paul, she happens to be in love with the boy. Lord only knows they have little or no chance for a normal life, and I cannot see that it is a sin for her to want to be near him.'

He stood up abruptly. 'There are other considerations. The Toporol farms are open only on a technicality. We have no guarantee the Germans won't take a notion to raid them and ship everyone off to labor. If she is caught out there, I won't be able to help her.'

Deborah lay down the hairbrush and spun about on the vanity bench. 'Is there a guarantee they won't come in here in the next ten minutes and haul us away? Living itself is a plain and simple day-to-day risk.'

The issue was clear. Paul would continue to retrench, to play it close, cautious. Deborah was willing to let her daughter take the risk to pursue a normal, healthy impulse.

Compromise, Paul, compromise! Caution! She had done everything but call him a coward.

He paced the floor, then spurred into one of his more frequent tantrums. 'Dammit! There are nearly six hundred thousand people in this ghetto! I have to find a place for four thousand new families by the end of the week! There is no space! People are sleeping in courtyards, alleyways, basements, attics, warehouses, hallways.'

'I don't see what one has to do with the other.'

'Everything has to do with everything! I'm sick and tired of being chastised by my own wife for trying to protect my family. Isn't it enough that I let Stephan keep on with this whim of yours to study with Rabbi Solomon? He barely escaped with his life once. Do you know one of those children caught was shot? It could have been your own son. I am still the head of this family, and that girl is not going to Wework.'

She nodded and turned and picked up the brush again and stroked her hair. More and more she saw him going down. So long as Mrs Bronski, wife of the JCA deputy chairman, works in an orphanage and so long as his daughter plays in morale-building concerts and the status is not besmirched, that was all that really mattered. The words never left her lips. She wanted to cry that there had to be an end to the price he was willing to pay for his skin – but she merely stroked her hair and said, 'Yes, Paul.'

Chapter Twenty

Journal Entry

Wolf wants to come home. I don't know why. I thought he would be happy on the farm. Tolek says he is one of the best people out there. What could it be?

The brief marriage of convenience between Germany and the Soviet Union has been abruptly annulled. Russia was attacked last week (June 21, 1941). This year's casualties have been Greece, Yugoslavia, Crete, and North Africa. Rumania and Bulgaria have declared war against the allies. (What allies?) The news reports that Britain is getting a fearful bombing by the Luftwaffe. London is catching it even worse than Warsaw did. Hard to believe.

The prospects of four to six million Jews in the Soviet Union in the path of Germany's unchecked onslaught is a terrifying prospect.

ALEXANDER BRANDEL

Old Rabbi Solomon entered the headquarters of the Big Seven on the corner of Pawia and Lubeckiego streets opposite the prison. Many of the sleazy characters around the anteroom were accomplished rabbi baiters. They stared at the old man. He carried a holy dignity in his stature, almost as though he had a mystic power to invoke God's wrath.

'Announce me to Max Kleperman,' he ordered sternly.

'Ah, my rabbi,' beamed Max. 'My own holy rabbi,' he cooed to the personal guardian of his soul. Max rushed from behind his desk and pulled the old man in by the elbow, shoved him into a chair, and raced to the door and shouted, 'I am with my rabbi. I am not to be disturbed for anyone. Not for a fire – not even for Dr Franz Koenig!'

He winked to relay his fearlessness. Rabbi Solomon let him play out the role. 'What can I get you? Maybe a chocolate. Hershey's from America – or coffee, Swiss Nestlé's, personal stock.'

'Nothing at all.'

'You have received my food packages?'

Solomon nodded. Large bundles arrived each week with butter, cheeses, eggs, bread, fruits, vegetables, meats, candies. They were promptly turned over to the Orphans and Self-Help Society.

The rabbi said he wouldn't mind if Max smoked in his presence, so Max went through the ritual of nipping the end of a cigar, coddling it, squeezing it, lighting it, puffing it, admiring its taste, pointing it. 'Confidentially, I wanted to speak to you, Rabbi. You have been forgetful. This business of teaching Talmud Torah after you were caught twice, and then that Passover seder you conducted in prison yet. Your last trip to Pawiak Prison cost me sixty thousand zlotys in gifts to the German Winter Relief. They take winter relief in the middle of the summer, those *goniffs*.'

The old man did not dignify Max with an answer. It seemed as though lightning shot out from his eyes, and his white beard fairly bristled in anger.

'Rabbi, can't you take a joke? You know Max Kleperman stands behind you.'

'I should like Max Kleperman to stand beside me. The situation in the ghetto is degenerating. The plight of the street urchins anguishes me. Many of them are starving. Without families, they will turn into wild animals.'

'It is terrible, terrible,' Max agreed, his forefinger fishing around up his nose. 'Confidentially, Rabbi, I and my partners are bringing a few things into the ghetto to alleviate the situation. For this I ask no thanks, mind you. And my sweet wife Sonia, God love her soul, spends every day working in an Orphan and Self-Help soup kitchen.'

Rabbi Solomon's bony hand slammed down on the desk top. 'Stop this mockery, man! You have not seen your wife for two months, and in that time you have lived with eight different prostitutes.'

'So, I have a few minor weaknesses! You are supposed to tend to my spiritual needs, Rabbi ... Only yesterday two of my men were shot at the wall of Muranowski Place trying to bring flour into the ghetto for food for babies.'

'I am certain you will arrange appropriate funerals, and when their funeral vans return to the ghetto they will be filled with black-market food which you will sell at a thousand-per-cent profit.'

'Shut up, old man!' Max raged suddenly.

'Smuggler, liar, thief!'

Max raised a bulky paperweight. His veins popped from his neck. He grew purple. He would not tolerate such talk from anyone but the Germans. No, not even from Piotr Warsinski. He had warned Warsinski that if the Jewish Militia touched any Big Seven business he would personally break his skull like an eggshell. Warsinski knew Max was not kidding. Why take these insults from this bearded old bastard! Crack his head in! What was this strange power the old man held over him? What was this fear of the beyond Max had?

He slid into his chair and wilted.

'Do you think our God is so shallow in His wisdom that He does not detect your scheme to bribe your way into heaven through me?'

'Rabbi,' Max whined, 'you don't understand the fundamentals of business matters. Business is business.'

He avoided Rabbi Solomon's eyes, mumbling about how misunderstood he was. Suddenly his hand turned the desk key and he withdrew an iron box and opened the lid. Sweat rolled down his face as he dipped his fat hand into the till and peeled off a large number of American dollars.

'Give this to the sick in the name of Max Kleperman!'

'You dare bribe me with this pittance?'

'Pittance! These are American dollars. Two hundred zlotys apiece!'

Rabbi Solomon stroked his beard thoughtfully as he looked at the money. Max watched him, praying that he would pick it up.

Which was the wiser of the decisions? Leave the money and leave Max to fry in hell for eternity? Or take back some of what Max had stole? After all, nothing could make the man change his ways, and this could do so much for so many children.

'Is there enough here to open up an orphanage to take a hundred children off the streets and feed them?'

'An entire orphanage? My partners ... the price of the zloty ...'

Max's cigar billowed with the fury of a locomotive.

'It would do much to alleviate some of the unpleasant talk about you and the Big Seven. An orphanage named for Max and Sonia Kleperman.'

Max had to think about that. It would look good. He would again become a benefactor of the people. Besides, his new smuggling operations were reaping a fortune. 'How much would it cost?' he asked with caution.

'Two thousand dollars a month.'

Max slammed his hand on the table. 'Done.'

'That is, two thousand a month, taking it for granted that the Big Seven will supply food and medicine.'

'But – but – but –'

'But what?'

'But of course.'

'Now, if you'll be so good as to make a lease assigning one of the properties you manage, I shall make arrangements with Alexander Brandel.'

'My own property!'

'I think the house at Nowolipki 10 will be the most suitable.'

'Nowolipki 10! Rabbi, you're a worse *goniff* than Dr Koenig!'

Max Kleperman whined through all the tortures of losing one of his most formidable properties. He, personally, would have to kick back the lease money to Franz Koenig from his own pocket.

Goddamned little orphan bastards! Goddamned old rabbi bastard! God shook you down worse than the Germans did, Max thought.

Rabbi Solomon snatched the money and the papers from Max Kleperman's desk, stuffed them into a big pocket in his long black frock, and asked the good Lord to please forgive his dubious methods.

Alexander Brandel shook his head in disbelief.

'How in the name of God did you manage to shake Max Kleperman down for this property?'

'You're right. It was the name of God.'

Alex grunted at the irony. He tied the muffler around his neck as though he had a chill, even though it was the middle of summer and the room was like a furnace. No one, including Alex, seemed to know why he wore the muffler.

'It's a miracle,' Alex said. 'A hundred children. We will find room there for two hundred – it is a miracle.'

'God works miracles, Alex. Believe a little more in him and a little less in Zionism.'

Alex put the papers and money in the desk. He had not seen Rabbi Solomon since the *bris* of Moses. The old man seemed in fine fettle. He commented upon it.

'I am kept alive by the Almighty so that I may carry my share of today's burdens,' the rabbi answered.

But Alex did not look so good. Rabbi Solomon said nothing. Alex had always been a bit untidy. He was seedy now. He did appear as good as a man could be expected to on three or four or a luxurious six hours' sleep a night. He sat behind that desk day and night, bargaining, pleading, juggling lives, juggling *Kennkarten* and rations, juggling medicine. Fencing with the crushing pressures from all sides. Debating for hours on end with Paul Bronski to wheedle an extra gram on the rations.

'Why have you done this, Rabbi? I came to see you once and asked you to help us unify and you refused.'

'I do not question the word of God. I merely follow his instructions.'

'Are you saying you have done this out of divine revelation?'

'I say that I find nothing in the Torah or the Holy Laws which commands me not to help starving children. It is hard for me to walk in the streets and see them these days. I studied the situation for many hours and I searched my soul as well as the word of the Law. I concluded that self-help has always been a God-meant key to Jewish survival. For some strange reason God has picked a *goy* like you and a *goniff* like Max Kleperman as his instruments of self-help. Mind you, I still do not subscribe to these radical theories or Zionism and physical resistance.'

As usual, Alex thought, Rabbi Solomon has all the answers. Perhaps he has an answer that has been nagging at me for weeks now. For a long time Alexander longed to show someone his journal. He desired a concurrent opinion that his notes and hours of work at it really had some significance. He knew that Simon Eden and David Zemba had been more or less indulgent of a former historian. Time and again he was tempted to take someone into his confidence. But whom? Rabbi Solomon? Beneath that crustiness lay a shrewd and brilliant mind. One thing was certain – the man could be trusted. Alex started to clear his throat for the proclamation.

'Alex. Already, what is on your mind? You are like a little boy with a secret. *Nu?*'

Alex smiled and walked to the door and bolted it. He went to the big floor safe behind his desk, dialed the combination, and pulled the heavy iron doors open and took out three volumes of thick notebooks wrapped in a large canvas cloth and placed them before the old man.

'*Nu?*' said Solomon, putting on his thick glasses. 'What is the great mystery?' He bent his face down so that his nose nearly touched the page to give vision to his semi-blind eyes. 'Alex, you are a *goy*. You even write in Polish.'

'You will find some in Yiddish, some in Hebrew.'

'Hummm – let me see. Let me see what is so important. "August 1939. This is the first entry in my journal. I cannot help but feel that war will begin in a few weeks. If the lessons of the past three years are any barometer, something awesome is apt to happen if Germany makes a successful invasion . . ." ' He looked up quickly to Alex and back to the book, and only his mouth moved, forming the words as he read more rapidly.

Rabbi Solomon seemed spellbound as he turned page after page. It was all there. From the first declaration of Alexander Brandel's intuition of a unique event to the daily record from the moment of occupation. There were limericks by Crazy Nathan, gossip, German directives, his personal diary, events of the world outside, ghetto poems, songs, poetry. The names and number of Yiddish theatrical productions. The recording of the sudden departure of friends. The constant groping for an answer.

At the end of the first hour, when he had closed the initial volume of the journal, Rabbi Solomon knew he had read a remarkable history of his people going through another siege of Rome and Greece and Babylon.

His eyes stung and were watery, but he quickly opened the second volume and thumbed through page after page with pulsating wonder.

Then he stopped.

'Who knows about this?' he asked in a hush.

'Eden. Zemba. Emanuel Goldman, before his murder.'

The rabbi was on his feet. 'When have you had time?'

'At night, in my room.'

'Amazing! Your intuition of a holocaust. Your wisdom in putting it all down on paper before the events occurred.'

Alex shrugged. 'Time and again Jews have written secret histories from intuition.'

'Intuition? I wonder. The Lord works in His own ways. Moses was a *goy*, like you. Alex, you must not leave this about. Not even in the safe. Hide it.'

'Rabbi, I have never seen you so excited. Are you certain of its importance?'

'Certain! This will sear the souls of men for centuries to come. This journal is a brand that is to be stamped on the German conscience so that a hundred of their unborn generations will have to live with these words with guilt and shame!'

Alex sighed and nodded with contentment. He knew now that all those hours through the night when he had been drugged from lack of sleep and forced his hand to write out another line had not been in vain.

'May God forgive me for saying this, Alex, but that journal is like a new chapter of the "Valley of Tears Chronicle." '

Journal Entry

Rabbi Solomon has an infectious enthusiasm for the journal and he has paid me the most magnificent of compliments. He calls it a new chapter in the 'Valley of Tears Chronicle!' (The 'Valley of Tears' lists fifteen centuries of Jewish martyrdom, par-

ticularly detailing the massacres and suffering of the Jews under the Crusaders during the Middle Ages. The lifework of Rabbi Yosef Hacohen was discovered by Rabbi Eibeschutz in 1850 and translated and has become a part of our lore, prayer, and tradition.)

Rabbi Solomon insists I expand the journals and that it should be hidden more carefully and even duplicated in case of the destruction or German discovery of the original. Such precautions! He and I have gone to the basement of Mila 19 and made a hiding place by moving bricks. I think it is nonsense, but so long as it pleases him . . .

We have formed a secret society of contributors. We call ourselves the Good Fellowship Club. Simon Eden and David Zemba are left over from the original contributors.

All of the executive council of the Bathyran (except Andrei Androfski) are members of the Good Fellowship Club; i.e., Susan Geller, Ervin Rosenblum, Tolek Alterman, and Ana Grinspan.

Other members:

Silberberg, the former playwright, who is on the Jewish Civil Authority and our closest ally there.

Rodel, Communist leader in the ghetto. He has been in semi-hiding since the occupation but has been valuable in both children's aid and contacts on the Aryan side.

Dr Glazer, chief of medical staff of Orphans and Self-Help.

Rabbi Solomon, of course.

Father Jakub, priest of the Convert's Church. I have known him since 1930. He is one of the few who has had a long record of sympathetic understanding toward us. (Incidentally, Orphans and Self-Help does not have much to do with converts. The converts and half Jews fare much better than most in the ghetto. It seems as though the Catholic Church is determined to take care of 'their' Jews.)

From time to time we will vote in new members to the Good Fellowship Club.

Ervin Rosenblum, who still works on the Aryan side and has less demands on his time than we do, has agreed to spend his spare time classifying and cataloguing the information now pouring in.

Rabbi Solomon is making duplicate copies of the first three volumes (in Yiddish and Hebrew only.) In the Jewish tradition, special scribes write all our Torah scrolls by hand. That is why they have been so accurate for millennia. Seeing Rabbi Solomon copying the journal reminds me of that.

It is thrilling to see this come alive and the belief that the work is important.

I must admonish everyone to write more neatly, especially Father Jakub.

ALEXANDER BRANDEL

Chapter Twenty-one

'Rachael.'

'Wolf!'

They stood facing each other in the hallway outside the main recreation room of the new Max and Sonia Kleperman Orphanage on Nowolipki Street.

Children swirled around them before herding nurses who clapped their hands sternly.

'Wolf, this is such a surprise, seeing you.'

'I didn't know I was going to be able to come in. I didn't have any time to write.'

'How did you find out where I was?'

'Stephan told me. I was with him all morning. I've been here for an hour. I was watching you give the recital from out here. You were very good.'

'Why didn't you come in?'

'I don't know. I got to watching you singing and playing and watching the kids all laughing ...'

The hallway suddenly became empty. It was shadowy and hard for them to see each other, and they were wordless as the impact of the sudden meeting lessened.

'It's nice to see you again,' Wolf said.

'Will you be here long?'

'That depends. I don't know.'

Wolf looked about and grunted. 'Could we take a walk or something? Here, let me hold your music.'

'All right.'

Wolf tried to think. There was no place to walk in the ghetto, nor bench to sit upon, nor nightingale to hear. There was only misery and beggars and stone and brick without a leaf of grass or the green of a tree.

'I'd like to sit and talk someplace,' Wolf said.

'So would I. We have so much to talk about.'

'Where can we go?'

'If we go to my place Stephan won't leave you alone. Then Momma and Daddy will come home and Daddy would make you play chess.'

'Sure can't go to Mila 19. The minute we walked in the door there'd be all kinds of gossip. Besides, there's no place there to be alone.'

'We can't stand here.'

'I'd sure like to talk to you.'

'We could try Uncle Andrei's place. I stop there often to talk to him. Most of the time he isn't there and his door is never locked.'

'Boy! If he caught me there with you he'd break my neck.'

'Oh no. Uncle Andrei's bark is much worse than his bite.'

'Well ... all right.'

They did not see each other on the entire walk to Andrei's. Wolf's eyes were cast down, looking at the pavement, and Rachael had learned to walk through the streets looking dead ahead to shut out the terrible things happening on all sides. The beggar children were more pathetic every day, and in the last week corpses of starved persons were beginning to appear in the gutters.

Suddenly they found themselves all alone in Andrei's flat. Wolf turned on the light over the table in the center of the room while Rachael caught her breath from the climb up the stairs.

Now they could see each other. Wolf had changed. His elongated, gangly body had filled out and his white, blemished skin was unblemished and deepened to a tan from working in the wind and the sun, and the scraggly hair on his chin had turned to a hard beard which could legitimately be shaved every other day and the shaky voice was now a steady baritone.

Rachael had changed too. She had been more like a girl before. Now she was much different. Round and soft, like her mother. Her eyes were filled with sadness and weariness.

Wolf suddenly turned his back and scratched his head. 'Heck! This isn't the way I figured it would be,' he blurted.

'It's very strange, isn't it? Almost as if we were just meeting each other for the first time.'

Wolf sagged into a chair, disappointed at his own weak performance. How many nights he lay awake at the farm thinking about this very moment when he would see Rachael again and simply sweep her off her feet. Now both of them seemed like strangers to each other and both wondered about all the passion and promises they had written.

'Wolf, you're disappointed.'

'Just at myself. Candidly speaking, I'm not one for fancy talking.' He stood up slowly, towering over her. 'I have missed you,' he managed to say. Rachael leaned against him slightly and he put his arm around her shoulders. Her arms found their way about him and she began to tremble, and as they held each other close the terrible uneasiness inside them ebbed. Wolf audibly gulped and sighed with relief. They searched each other out and kissed and then they were both calm.

Rachael and Wolf stood before the window, watching darkness come. They looked down on the street, and from this height they could see beyond the wall into the 'Polish corridor' which separated the big and little ghetto and they could see the dome of the forbidden Tlomatskie Synagogue. His arm was about her waist and her head was on his shoulder.

'This is wonderful,' Rachael said.

'It sure is.'

'You have become terribly handsome and mannish.'

Wolf shrugged. 'Rachael, I meant all the things I wrote to you.'

'So did I. I know that now.' She pulled away from him. 'Wolf . . .'

'What?'

'Would you answer one thing, honestly?'

'Sure.'

'Did you have any girls on the farm?'

'Heck! What kind of a stupid question is that?'

'I think I'm a terribly jealous kind,' Rachael answered.

'I'm sure not much to be jealous about.'

'You didn't answer me.'

'I messed around a little.' Then he added quickly, 'But that was before we made promises.'

'Messed around?'

'You know, messed around.'

'More than . . . kissing?'

Wolf patted his flat chest to demonstrate. 'Messed around.'

'Oh.'

'Before we made promises.'

'Did you do any other things?'

'Rachael . . .'

'I think I should know everything before we can be certain of our relationship. What else have you done?'

'Rachael, I'm a boy and boys are different, and if I tell you you're liable to get very mad.'

'I'm sixteen, almost seventeen. I've been a woman for several years. I know about these things – I mean, Momma and I have had long talks about growing up.'

Wolf was flustered. Rachael was adamant.

'Wolf . . .'

'What?'

'Have you ever . . . done it?'

'You sure ask a lot of questions. This isn't something a man wants to discuss with his girl.'

'If we are really sweethearts, the way we say we are, then there shouldn't be any secrets.'

'I tried it once,' Wolf croaked. 'Even before I went to the farm. It was on my birthday. My sixteenth – almost two years ago. You don't want to hear about it.'

'Yes, I do.'

'Well, I was with three of my pals. One of them was older – he was nineteen – and he knew a woman in Solec. One of those kind of women.'

'What kind?'

'Who does it for money.'

'Oh . . . one of *those* kind.'

'So, anyhow, it was my birthday and all that and we were at this guy's house and he snitched a bottle of vodka from his parents' liquor cabinet. I never drank before, except a sip now and then. I got to laughing and couldn't stop. Then we started talking about . . . things, and he said he knew this woman in Solec. Next thing you know, it was a dare and I was feeling pretty good.'

'And you went there?'

Wolf nodded.

'And you did?'

'Well, it wasn't so hot. I got scared as hell and I didn't know what to do. Boy, I'll bet you hate me now.'

'No. I admire your honesty. Now I know that you will always be honest with me.'

'You're not mad?'

'Momma explained that certain things are very normal for boys – that is, men. And she says I should not suppress my emotions and feelings too much because that can lead to frustration.'

'She's sure smart.'

'Sometimes I think she says it to me because she's frustrated. I can feel that she hasn't been too happy with Daddy.'

'That's too bad. My folks are happy. Poppa doesn't seem to need it too much because he works all the time, but I know he and Momma are happy. Rachael, you sure are understanding.'

'Wolf . . . do you ever think about us . . . doing it?'

'Yes . . . I never would try or force my attention on you or ever do anything to hurt you. But it's not my fault that I can't help thinking about it. It's supposed to be a sin to think about it, but I can't help it.'

'I think about it too,' she whispered.

'I . . . didn't know that girls thought about it. The way boys do.'

'Yes . . . the same way. All the time you were away I began to wonder if I would see you again. And I knew that if there wasn't a war and a ghetto and the awful things that are happening, I would grow up a little slower, like we're supposed to. And we could play coquette like girls are supposed to. But this fear hanging over us all the time ... Waking up in the middle of the night when the whistles are blowing outside during roundups and walking the streets when their sirens blow and the loudspeakers shout ... Now, those little children dying in the streets – it all made me change. I'm terribly aggressive, aren't I?'

'I think you are the most wonderful person who ever lived.'

Rachael threw her arms about Wolf and clutched him desperately. 'I love you in a different way than Momma loves Daddy. She is trying to tell me. Wolf, I don't want to die unhappy like Momma!'

This kiss was different from all others, for in the instant of its impact they reached manhood and womanhood, and they wanted each other and there was neither restraint nor control. Her eyes closed and her cheeks were damp with the wonderful feel of him and her teeth found his shoulders and her hands clawed at his back and his fingers fumbled for the buttons on her blouse ...

The door slammed!

They looked in terror at Andrei across the room. He took two, three menacing steps toward them.

'You little son of a bitch,' he hissed.

Wolf stepped in front of Rachael, and she buried her face against his back and wept.

Andrei looked from one to the other, the fury twitching his face.

'Get out of the room, Rachael,' Wolf said softly.

'He'll kill you!' Rachael cried.

Andrei stopped. Wolf Brandel abusing my niece. But look. It is not Wolf any longer. A tall, strong young man waiting like a fool for me to tear him apart. And Rachael ... Strange. Not until this moment did I realize that she is a woman. Wolf Brandel. I diapered him when he was a baby. Has he ever been anything but a fine person? God, Andrei! What is the matter with you? These two love each other!

Andrei relaxed.

'In the future,' he said, 'if you leave your armbands in the mailbox I'll know you are up here and won't disturb you. And for God's sake, lock the door.'

Chapter Twenty-two

The next day Wolf Brandel returned to Andrei's flat.

'I want you to know,' he said to Andrei, 'that I am not messing around with Rachael. I feel more deeply for her than I've ever felt for anyone. I love her. I'm sure not much, but she feels that way about me too.'

Andrei nodded. 'I thought about it. I believe you.' He poured himself a short drink of vodka. 'Do you drink this stuff?'

'I had it a few times at the farm. I don't care too much for it. I want you to know that – well, how much we appreciate your confidence. There's hardly a place where two people can be alone in the ghetto.'

'It was a shock, all of a sudden seeing someone you thought as a little girl in the arms of someone you thought of as a little boy. Under normal conditions things would have happened more slowly. One has to grow up quickly these days, there is no choice.'

'Andrei, I don't really want to do anything to her.'

'I appreciate your good intentions, but they will become lost in the heat of the moment one day. Just be as gentle as you can and make her be careful.'

Wolf blushed violently. 'I think I'll try a little vodka.' He sipped and made a face as it burned its way to his stomach. 'I wanted to see you about something else too. I'm not going back to the farm.'

'Oh? Tolek Alterman tells me you are the best worker. I am certain he can arrange for you to come in once a week with the milk so you can see her.'

'That's not really why.'

'What is it?'

'Life is easy out there. I think I ought to be doing more.'

'Don't be so noble.'

'I'm not noble. It would be easier if you left Warsaw, but you stay.'

'Look, Wolf. Be happy your father is in a position to put you on the farm.'

'That's just my point. I'm getting preferential treatment because I'm Alexander Brandel's son. That's not right. I talked to Momma and Poppa last night after I took Rachael home. I told them I wasn't going back.'

'How did they take it?'

'Momma cried. Poppa argued. You know how he can argue. Between him and Tolek Alterman I've heard enough Zionist logic to last for six lifetimes. Anyhow, I may not look it, but I can be stubborn. When Poppa knew I wasn't going back he began to blame himself for not being a good father and not spending more time with me. He always does that. So, the baby started screaming and all four of us were going at once. Then later we sat in his office, just the two of us. We don't do that too often. He's convinced that I'm right by wanting to stay. He told me to come to see you. You would have work for me.'

'Did he say what kind of work?'

'No. But I know that you must be mixed up in important things. I want to be a runner.'

'What makes you think you can be a runner?'

'Well, I don't look too Jewish.'

'We use women as runners, Wolf.'

'I can do the job as well as a woman.'

'You said you don't look Jewish. I say you do. Know what would happen if you got picked up? They'd march you to Gestapo House on Shucha Street and unbutton your pants. Your father put you in a covenant with God when he had you circumcised so that God would recognize you as a Jew. Only trouble is that the Germans use that for recognition too.'

The thought did not appeal to Wolf.

Andrei looked the boy over. Eighteen. Tall, strong. Smart – smart as a whip. The shyness was a decoy. Wolf Brandel had mastered his studies as a brilliant scholar. Ideals. Wonderful. So many people without them, these days. Taking the hard road to satisfy an inner desire to do right. A good soldier in any army.

'Come on, let's take a walk, son.'

They walked down Leszno Street past the Convert's Church and the huge new complex of houses forming a factory to make and repair German army uniforms. 'A Franz Koenig Enterprise,' the big sign said. Koenig also had part ownership of the woodwork factory in the little ghetto and of the huge Brushmaker's complex at the extreme northern end. Dr Koenig had become a millionaire.

They waited on the corner until a red and yellow street-car came along and hopped on the back of it. Its sides and tops showed large Stars of David. The Ghetto lines were operated by the Big Seven.

At Smocza and Gensia, Andrei got off. Wolf walked alongside him until they reached the wall that ran down the middle of Okopowa Street. He was filled with the adventure of it all. They walked up the street to the middle of the block. Over the wall was the Jewish cemetery. This was a neighborhood for a lot of smuggling. People could hide in the cemetery with black-market goods. In this area the wall was heavily guarded. Andrei stopped at the old abandoned Workman's Theater. Before the war it had been one of the showplaces of the vital Yiddish stage. Now the lobby had been converted into yet another soup kitchen. The rest, empty.

Down the alleyway to the stage door. Andrei looked about quickly, thrust the door open, and shoved Wolf inside. They were on the stage. It took a moment to adjust their eyes to the darkness and their noses to the musty smell. Andrei whispered to be careful of cables and obstacles. The house was ghost-like. The hard-back seats in a state of disrepair. A faded backdrop of a Polish gentry's garden hung behind them.

Andrei listened. He could make out very dim sounds from the soup kitchen. He tiptoed to the light cage and threw a switch. Wolf was entranced. Nothing lit up. Some sort of signal, he was certain.

Above them a trap door opened. Andrei scooted up it quickly, the boy behind him. They were in a large loft. The trap closed after them.

'Ladies and gentlemen,' Andrei said, 'you all know our newest worker.'

Wolf's mouth hung open in awe. There were four people present, all former Bathyrans who lived at Mila 19. Adam Blumenfeld was at a radio receiver with earphones on. 'Hello, Welvel,' he greeted the boy by his nickname.

Pinchas Silver worked at a box of hand-set print. Beside the small press were copies of the underground paper, *Liberty*. Pinchas smiled and welcomed Wolf in. A forgery table and camera were in one corner.

The Farber sisters, Mira and Minna, were there, studying to become runners.

'Any news?'

Adam Blumenfeld took one earphone off. 'I've got BBC. Something about American destroyers being loaned to England.'

'How about the Home Army?' Andrei asked in reference to the quickly growing Polish underground force.

'They keep changing frequencies. Unless we can get their schedule, we can only pick them up hit or miss.'

Andrei grunted. His most urgent job was to set up a solid liaison with the Home Army, but he had been unsuccessful. He turned to Wolf. 'Two lessons. First, live with access to the top floor. In danger, we go the rooftops. Second, this work is neither romantic nor exciting. It is dull and exacting.'

For the next few weeks Wolf learned to stand radio watch and work the printing press. Then Andrei made him memorize the entire Jewish Militia and know which police would 'play' for bribes and how much. One by one he learned the secret rooms behind bakeries, in abandoned synagogue basements, where Simon Eden and Rodel, the Communist, and the small nucleus of the underground carried on their sub rosa business.

His prime duty: to distribute the copies of *Liberty*. Dump them in the market places, drop them at secret rooms, post them on conspicuous walls. As Andrei had warned, it was exacting and tedious work. The streets were more dangerous to travel each day. Piotr Warsinski's police were pulling people in by the hundreds for the continued feeding of the slave-labor factories.

Dr Franz Koenig took a quick trip to Berlin to be received by Himmler, personally, and brought back with him a contract for a great portion of the German army's brushes. The Brushmaker's complex in the north had to be tripled. When there were no people on the streets, Warsinski ordered indiscriminate raids on homes or the bulging refugee compounds for workers.

Wolf accepted his duties without protest. He envied the Farber sisters. Blond and blue-eyed, they fitted the bill as 'Aryans.' Learning the paths of a runner was only a small part of the training.

They had to learn the Catholic Bible forward and backward, how to pray in Latin, how to pray with the rosary. They had to learn to go deaf to the sounds of Yiddish and German, the languages with which they had been raised, in order to 'prove' they were not Jewish.

There was one more regular who worked in the loft of the Workman's Theater, and that was Berchek, a former commercial artist. From time to time 'Aryan' *Kennkarten*, travel papers, and even passports were obtained. These had to be doctored for use by underground members. Berchek taught Wolf the principles of forgery and allowed him to work on the simpler tasks of fixing photographs on the papers.

Andrei was terribly proud of his protégé. The boy learned quickly and responded to orders without question. In one or two tight spots while distributing *Liberty*, he kept himself out of trouble by quick thinking.

When Wolf went off duty he spent part of the time at home with his parents and his baby brother at Mila 19. Some of the time was with his 'adopted' brother, Stephan Bronski. He taught the younger boy his Hebrew and tutored him in basic subjects and played chess and answered a thousand searching questions.

And two or three nights a week he would meet Rachael in Andrei's flat.

Each time they met, they brought their relationship one step closer to culmination. Each time they chastised themselves and groped and damned. They wanted to try it, desperately. First Wolf, then Rachael took turns in being the stronger to resist. Each time they parted, they parted heartsick but eager for the next rendezvous.

The thought of seeing each other kept them alive. It was able to make them somewhat oblivious of the horror around them. More and more terrible things were happening. So long as there was that electric second when he ran up the final flight of steps into her arms, the rest did not matter so much.

Journal Entry

Last night the Good Fellowship Club met to discuss the latest disaster.

Yesterday morning twenty-five Reinhard Corps Nazis, under the personal direction of Sieghold Stutze, entered the ghetto at the Zelazna Gate. Their barracks are directly outside the wall, so there is little or no warning. They proceeded directly to Nowolipki

24 and surrounded the house. Fifty-three occupants – men, women, and children – were pulled out and loaded aboard two army trucks.

As they drove off, the Jewish Militia posted signs all over the building that it was 'contaminated by typhus, rodents, etc. ...'

The fifty-three were taken to the Jewish cemetery. On the north wall they were forced to dig a huge ditch, undress, and stand on its edge. They were shot in the back and, after they fell into the ditches, were bayoneted.

The Militia entered the Nowolipki property and carted off every single belonging.

We have had mass executions at the cemetery before. Usually a group accused of 'criminal' activities or intellectuals. Never have fifty-three people been indiscriminately lopped off without excuse.

Although the property was 'condemned as contaminated,' I was able to lease it this morning as an orphans' home. Now I hear that the Germans are going to do a series of legal explanations of their actions to 'justify' the executions. 'Fear of epidemic' is their main reason as well as the catchfall phrase 'criminal activities.'

We in the Good Fellowship Club are rather certain this mass execution was a test case.

Other distressing signs. A further ration cut was ordered this morning. Dr Glazer says this puts us below starvation level. This means that anyone obtaining enough food to live is a 'criminal,' according to Nazi logic. Who figures these things out for them?

It is in the Soviet Union where the real terror is going on. More and more word comes back about special SS 'Action Kommandos' massacring Jews all over the Baltics, White Russia, and the Ukraine just as quickly as the German army presses forward.

We heard something about a plan to send all the Jews to the island of Madagascar. (It might be a vacation.)

Hans Frank has lost his battle, once and for all. Not only are Jews still pouring into the General Government Area, but criminals, homosexuals, gypsies, 'Slavic types,' political prisoners, prostitutes, and others deemed as 'sub-human.' So, the General Government Area has become the 'cesspool' for Germany's non-Aryans. Several huge new concentration camps are under construction. One in particular, Auschwitz in Silesia, I hear, is mammoth.

The Good Fellowship Club reasons that this transporting of Jews and 'sub-humans' is a burden on the rail system, especially for the German army on the Russian front. It is taking tens of thousands of their manpower also.

Conclusion: The Germans have reached their decision for a 'final solution' for us. *I fear further executions until they reach the desired level for slave labor.*

The phone interrupted Alex.

'Hello, Alexander Brandel, here.'

'Alex. *Shalom aleichem,*' a voice on the other end said. It was a greeting from a contact named Romek on the other side of the wall.

'*Shalom,*' Alex answered.

'Alex, I hope you didn't forget we have a lunch date.'

'Ach, what a stoop I am. I forgot to mark it down.'

'Yetta's house at two o'clock.'

'Good, good, I'll be there.'

Alex quickly locked the volume of the journal in the safe and went upstairs to his room. Wolf was playing with baby Moses on the floor.

'Son,' Alex said, 'get Andrei at once. Wanda has arrived from Krakow with a package. Tell him to send one of the Farber girls to the Old Town Square. He'll understand. Time is important. Wanda will pass at two o'clock.'

When Wolf arrived at the loft over the Workman's Theater, only Adam Blumenfeld was there on radio watch.

'Where is everyone? A runner is in from Krakow.'

'Lord,' Bumenfeld grunted. 'She wasn't expected till tomorrow. Andrei, the Farber sisters, and Berchek are all on the Aryan side. Pinchas Silver can't go. Get back to your father and tell him right away. He'll know what to do.'

Alex drummed his fingers on the desk top, trying to think. It was one o'clock. Only an hour to the pickup. It was so unexpected that all four of the Bathyran runners were on the other side.

Think, dammit, think, Alex said to himself.

His usual unalterable calm became thready. Eight to ten thousand dollars were in the package. Nice, wonderful, untraceable dollars from Thompson at the American Embassy.

He looked at the phone. Call up Romek over the wall. No, that would be breaking the cardinal rule. Never phone a contact on the Aryan side under any circumstances.

What if Wanda saw there was no contact? They had completely lost one package like that.

Alex lifted the phone and dialed the Orphans and Self-Help Division at Leszno 92, Simon Eden's headquarters and asked to speak to Atlas.

In several moments Simon Eden was on the phone.

'Atlas, here.'

'Brandel.'

'Yes?'

'I got an invitation from Romek to be at Yetta's house for lunch at two o'clock. I simply can't get away from my desk. Could you keep it for me?'

'That's less than an hour. Hold on a moment and I'll see if I can rearrange my appointments.'

Three more precious minutes ticked off. It was twelve after one.

'Alex.'

'Yes!'

'Can't do it. Impossible.'

Alex put the receiver on the hook slowly. Lost! The package is lost! He looked up slowly and saw his son at the edge of the desk.

'I'll go, Poppa.'

'No.'

'I've got false papers and I've been in training –'

'I said no!'

'Poppa ...'

'It's damned well bad enough I let you talk me into this business of leaving the farm. It has nearly killed your mother.'

'I swear,' the boy said softly, 'I'll never talk to you again.' Wolf turned and walked toward the door and unbolted it.

'Wolf, for God's sake, don't ask me to –' He knew his boy. Gentle but stubborn. Even more stubborn than Andrei. Alex steadied himself. 'All right. Leave everything identifying you on the desk. Take only your false papers. Time is running short. You'll have to go out of one of the three northern gates – there should be a guard "playing" at one of them.' Alex opened a drawer. 'Here, twelve hundred zlotys, mixed notes. That will get you in and out of the ghetto. Go to the Madam Curie Museum in the Old Town Square. Buy some blue violets on the way and wrap them in a newspaper. Wanda is Rebecca Eisen. You know her.'

'Anything else?'

'If . . . anything happens . . . you are not Wolf Brandel.'

'Don't worry, Poppa. Nothing will happen.'

'Son, we haven't spent enough time together – now, all of a sudden –'

'Poppa, you mean so much to so many people. I've always been very proud of you.'

Wolf walked briskly for the closest gate at Dzika and Stawki streets, only a few blocks from Mila 19. He made a false run past the gate to study the Jewish militiamen on guard. He did not recognize any of the three, so it was certain they did not know who he was.

He walked to the man of highest rank and snapped out his *Kennkarte*. The guard unfolded the three-part document and deftly palmed the folded hundred-zloty note. The guard studied the document. It was obviously a false paper, for it was not marked with a *J*. A clue that this was underground work or smuggling. He'd try for more.

'My old mother is very sick,' the guard said.

'She should see a doctor,' Wolf answered, slipping the man another hundred zlotys.

A windfall. 'What time are you coming back?'

Bastard wants more, Wolf thought. 'Few hours.'

'Too bad. I won't be on duty. Try my cousin Handelstein at the Gensia Gate. Tell him you spoke to Kasnovitch.'

'Thanks,' Wolf said.

Fifty zlotys on the other side of the gate took care of the Polish Blue Police.

Wolf walked rapidly for the Old Town Square. Time was running out.

For several weeks the Gestapo had been watching the movements of Tommy Thompson at the American Embassy in Krakow. They knew his sympathies and were relatively certain he was passing money and information to the Jews. The Gestapo allowed him to continue, in the hope that they could trail his contacts successfully and break up the ring at the Warsaw end.

Recently Thompson started a new activity. The Home Army, a large Polish underground, was forming and growing quickly and he had been working with them. This was a more serious matter. He was earmarked to be thrown out of Poland shortly.

The Gestapo decided to make an arrest of the next runner who left Thompson. From the moment that Thompson passed a package of eight thousand dollars to Wanda, the Bathyran runner, they were on her.

Trained and alert, Wanda became suspicious when there had been a dragnet at the Warsaw railroad terminal and she was allowed to pass through the inspection far too easily, her fake papers not scrutinized and her package unchallenged.

She entered the Old Town Square with the intuition she was being tailed. The square was not badly crowded – only thirty or forty people. Yet it was impossible to spot a stake-out because the quadrangle of five-story buildings could have hidden a hundred pairs of searching eyes. She entered on purpose from the corner opposite the Madam Curie Museum and walked cater-corner over the cobblestones. From the corner of her eye she glanced at the partly bombed-out museum. A lanky young man leaned against the wall. She came closer, still moving diagonally, calculated to pass him at a distance of some twenty or thirty meters in order to study him.

Click-click-click went her heels on the cobblestones.

Blue violets wrapped in newspaper. She shot a glance upward. It was Wolf Brandel. Smart boy, Wanda thought. He sees that I am going to pass him by.

Now Wanda had put a block and a half of open space behind her. If she was being tailed they would have to show themselves in the vast square or face the danger of losing her. She wanted to look back but dared not. She could not make her contact with Wolf until she was certain.

Wanda spotted a grate next to a sewer hole. Perfect! She walked over the grate and intentionally jammed her high heel into it so it would stick. She knelt down to free herself and in doing so stole a look behind her. Two men stopped dead in their tracks halfway over the square.

Trap!

Wolf was watching her closely. He saw the men trailing her. He saw her quickly throw the package into the sewer, pull her heel loose, and walk from the square. In a moment the place was flooded with Germans rounding everyone up. Wolf held fast.

'Violets for your mother, sonny?'

Wolf looked into the eyes of a pair of waiting Gestapo.

Chapter Twenty-three

As a matter of standard operational procedure, any Jew caught on the Aryan side was personally interrogated at Gestapo House by the chief, Gunther Sauer.

A few moments after Rebecca Eisen, known as Wanda, disposed of her package of dollars she was arrested and the forty-two people in the Old Town Square were rounded up and hauled in for questioning. Four hidden Jews were found among them.

Gunther Sauer's appearance was deceptive. Pouchy, elderly, and of medium build, he owned an extraordinarily high forehead with a widow's peak of neat silver hair. His eyes were a bit puffy and half closed and his voice was gentle.

One would easily mistake him for a kindly grandfather instead of a Gestapo chief. He was, indeed, an adoring grandfather.

And Gunther Sauer loved animals. A bright-eyed dachshund named Fritzy sat beside his desk in a cushioned basket all the time. Sauer would break from his work at intervals and go into spasms of laughter when Fritzy performed for a tidbit.

He was, first and last, a policeman utterly devoted to his job, a master of his profession, and living in that world apart, as policemen often do. Sauer was a master at political terror, which became the prime job of the state police after the Nazis took power. The eradication of political and intellectual opposition was a dogma which had to be executed with ruthless objectivity.

He was also a master of the psychological warfare that one uses to break down the nerves and will of the opponent. Intellectuals were putty. Business competitors of the Nazis even easier. The intelligent application of fear could win the battle of a hundred armies.

Unlike many of his Gestapo compatriots, Gunther Sauer never used terror or torture for its own sake, but as a tool of the trade to gain an end. Torture did not always work on some people, nor did psychological fear tactics. In his estimation, it was a waste of time and energy to dismember someone who was not going to help you solve your 'police' problem. Sauer abhorred the brutality of Sieghold Stutze, who received personal pleasure from inflicting pain.

One had to be completely objective about his victim. After a study of a person he could fairly well establish the limit of his moral endurance. He never used torture on prisoners whom he knew would not break under torture.

On the other hand, he never hesitated when he spotted weakness. And it never annoyed him that he resorted to torture more often than not. Once or twice, early in his career, he had spent sleepless nights after torturing a child in front of its mother, but he learned to harden himself to it as part of a day's work.

Sauer interrogated the first three Jews. All of them were nervous and talky. The first was a smuggler who implied a bribe and friends in high office.

The second, a fool who had escaped from Lemberg, a vagrant.

The third, one of the many thousands of 'hidden' Jews living as Christians in Warsaw on the Aryan side. This man gave such a garbled version to cover his tracks and contacts that he was most suspect as the contact for Rebecca Eisen.

Wolf Brandel was shoved into the office. Sauer was leaning over his desk, scratching Fritzy's chest. The dog whined and begged as Sauer teased the animal by opening and closing the drawer containing the box of tidbits. Fritzy won his prize, ran in a happy circle, then settled on the rug and crunched the hard biscuit.

Wolf snatched his cap from his head and stood at attention.

A quick appraisal. Eighteen or so. Not too Jewish in appearance. Strong, well fed, therefore resourceful. A perfect size and shape for a runner. He shifts from one foot to the other, nervously, but his eyes are innocent. He looks forward at me.

'Jew?'

'Yes, sir, I got caught.'

'Name?'

'Hershel Edelman.'

'Where are you from, Hershel?'

Watch his sweet talk, Wolf. They had the line on Sauer. Deceptive. He'll tie you in knots.

'I'm from Wolkowysk.'

'How did you get to Warsaw?'

'My family was taken to the ghetto in Bialystok. I hid in the church during the roundup. After, I walked to Bialystok to look up a friend of my father outside the ghetto.'

'What was the name of the church in which you hid?'

'St Casimir's.'

'What was the name of the priest?'

'I don't know, sir. He didn't know I was hiding there.'

'Go on.'

'So I saw this friend of my father. He used to do business with him.'

'What is his name?'

'Wynotski.'

'What's your father's business?'

'*Schoychet.*'

'I beg your pardon?'

'It's a man who kills chickens and cows so the meat will be kosher.'

'Fritzy, bad boy. Now get in your bed and stay there . . . But, Hershel, you said Wynotski did business with your father. If Wynotski sold kosher meat, wouldn't he be in the ghetto?'

'No, sir. Wynotski has a gift shop. You see, sir, my father carved chessmen in his spare time and sold them to Wynotski. If you lived around Wolkowysk and Bialystok, you'd have heard about my father's chessmen.'

'Go on.'

'So, anyhow, Wynotski got me this Aryan *Kennkarte* and travel pass.'

'I take it Wynotski is not Jewish.'

'Half Jewish, I think. Anyhow, his house and gift shop was lousy with crucifixes and rosaries and Bibles and stuff like that.'

'Where did Wynotski get the Aryan *Kennkarte*?''

'Most likely bought it from a family where someone died and it wasn't recorded. Anyhow, I didn't ask questions. I mean, sir, under the conditions, you just take it and don't ask questions.'

Clever young man, Sauer thought. Either a magnificent fake or entirely honest.

'Continue,' Sauer said.

'So, I came to Warsaw.'

'Why?'

'Why not? It's the biggest city in Poland. I figured I'd have the best chance to stay hidden because I don't know anybody here and wouldn't get recognized.'

'How long have you been here?'

'Three days.'

'Where have you stayed?'

'I found a loose window in back of the men's room at the railroad station. Anyhow, it's like a storeroom for mops and buckets and stuff and I've been sleeping there.'

'What were you doing standing in front of the Old Town Square statue?'

'The Madam Curie Museum,' Wolf corrected. 'Waiting for someone.'

'Who?'

'Well, you can imagine. I've got to figure something out. I start prowling around. My money is running low and stuff. So, pretty soon you hear talk and stuff, and so I went to the Solec because they said you can get fixed up there for just about anything. I went to the Granada Club. Sure got tough guys in there, and I met this – well – whore.'

Sauer was entranced.

'So, I find out she is Jewish. Selma is her name. I'm sure it is a fake name. So, anyhow, I'm cautious at first because I think she may be helping look for runaways like me, but it's kind of funny how two Jews can spot each other. So,

Selma says she knows someone who can help me but for me not to come back to the Granada because the hoodlums in there are looking for hidden Jews and to meet her next day at the Old Town Square.'

'What were you doing with violets?' Sauer snapped.

Wolf scratched his head and blushed. 'This whore was sure nice to me, sir. I just wanted to buy her violets.'

Sauer talked softly to Wolf for two hours. The questions were masked in huge traps. Every so often Wolf would whimper, 'Sir, if you are trying to confuse me, you sure are succeeding. I'm getting mixed up trying to remember the honest truth.'

That night Wolf Brandel spent alone in a cell. The screams of torture pierced his eardrums from down the hall.

Gunther Sauer, in his meticulous, grinding way, listened to wire playbacks of the interviews with the four Jews. He was oblivious of the cries of pain coming from Rebecca Eisen in the main interrogation room.

In the morning Sauer called Gestapo in Bialystok. In the afternoon they phoned him back. Yes, there was a gift shop run by a half Jew named Wynotski who had disappeared. There was a record of a *schoychet* from Wolkowysk who was sent into the ghetto and who had a son who had escaped. Edelman was, in fact, famous for his hand-carved chessmen.

The whore in Solec? Untraceable. The moment the Nazis approached the Granada Club no one would know anything. Even their informers could not be counted upon. Whores had dozens of names. Selma could be Elma or Thelma.

The weeks of meticulous training were put to the acid test. Each of the underground assumed an identity of an actual person who could not be traced. The identities were taken from information supplied by Bathyran runners in other cities. Wolf Brandel's story had been carefully worked out for weeks before he was given the name of Hershel Edelman. The real Edelman was obviously masquerading as someone else, somewhere in Poland.

'Bring back Hershel Edelman,' Sauer said.

The boy seemed no more frightened than a night at Gestapo House would demand. Sauer played for the one possible loophole. He opened his desk drawer and pulled out a chessboard and a set of chessmen.

'Sit down.'

'Yes, sir.'

'Black or white?'

'Your preference, sir.'

'I have seen you defend yourself, Edelman. Now I should like to see your attack. Take the white.'

'Sir,' Wolf said haltingly. 'Sir, this is very awkward. I mean, under the circumstances, I'm rather afraid to win.'

'You had better win, young man.'

Wolf did. In nine moves.

He was sent into the main interrogation room to sit alone on the single chair beneath the spotlight. There was nothing else in the room. Gunther Sauer had hit a dead end. His only choice was shock identification – or resort to torture. He was puzzled by the boy and not certain he would break down. Even if he did break down, he might have been telling the truth and could reveal nothing.

Sauer proceeded to the booth next to the interrogation room. There, through an arrangement of mirrors, he could watch the interrogation without being seen. Sensitive microphones piped sounds back to him, refined to pick up heartbeats.

'Bring in that woman,' Sauer ordered.

He watched closely as Wolf sat fidgeting in the hard chair. All Wolf could think of now was to keep his mind on Rachael and keep thinking of her and keep saying to himself that she would be proud of him, no matter what happened.

The iron door creaked open.

Wolf looked toward it slowly. Two Gestapo men stood on either side of the figure of a woman, holding her up. They let her go. The woman staggered, then fell face first to the floor.

Wolf edged out of the chair toward her.

Sauer watched and listened ...

He knelt and rolled the woman over. It was Rebecca Eisen. Her face was bloated and distorted. One eye was locked tight, a multitude of colors, and blood gushed from her broken mouth and her torn fingernails. She quivered the other eye open. They recognized one another.

'Lady,' Wolf said, 'lady, are you alive? I wish I could do something for you, lady.'

'Boy ... boy ... water ...'

A small smile crossed Gunther Sauer's lips. If they were actors, they had played it to perfection. Hershel Edelman was obviously clean, but the story was so pat – so untraceable – the boy mystified him so ...

'What do you think, sir?' an assistant asked.

'They don't know each other,' Sauer said. 'On the other hand, they don't have to if he was actually a contact. The violets – I'm not sure of the violets.'

'Shall we send a dog in there?'

'Let me think about it.'

The Club Miami on Karmelicka Street inside the ghetto was the Jewish counterpart of the notorious Granada Club in the Solec as the center of smuggling, fencing, and prostitution. At the moment, members of Max Kleperman's Big Seven were the ruling gentry.

The Club Miami had a unique distinction as a 'free trading zone.' All activities within the bounds of this unholy sanctuary were looked upon as 'off the record.' This confidence was respected even by the Germans. The Nazis realized that, as often as not, they too would need the facilities of a 'free trading zone' and thus allowed the operation to exist. A half dozen rooms in back of the main bar were used to carry out transactions which were never taped, nor were the transactors followed or photographed. Unwritten law, gentlemen's agreement, honor among thieves.

Max Kleperman knew that something strange was afoot when he received a phone call from Rabbi Solomon to go to the Club Miami.

Max arrived, filled with eager anticipation of a huge deal. The bartender advised him his contact waited in one of the back rooms. He entered and closed the door. Andrei Androfski turned and faced him. Max's inevitable cigar smoke billowed around the room. Extraordinary for Androfski himself to come to him.

'One of our people has been picked up,' Andrei said.

Max grunted in disappointment. From time to time the Zionists had come to him to arrange releases for those stupidly picked up by Piotr Warsinski for the labor battalions. Kleperman had made one big killing when Rodel, the Communist, was thrown into Pawiak. It may be a big one again, Max hoped. After all, Rabbi Solomon personally made the call and Androfski personally made the contact.

'Who?'

Andrei halted for a moment. 'Wolf Brandel.'

Max whistled. It was getting interesting. He polished his outlandish ring hastily on his vest.

'Where is he?'

'Gestapo House.'

Max put his cigar down and shook his head. Work camps ... easy to make a fix. Pay off a few shnook guards. Koenig's factories in the ghetto, a little harder. The money went right to Koenig and cost more. The Jewish Militia, hadn't found one yet who wouldn't go for two hundred zlotys. Pawiak Prison – difficult, but he always came through.

'Gestapo House,' Max said. 'Brandel's boy. I don't know.'

Max calculated the pros and cons quickly. He could rat on the Brandel boy and endear himself to the Germans. It would be genuine proof of his honesty and sincerity. Question was, would they appreciate it? On the other hand, the Big Seven and the Orphans and Self-Help Society were doing more and more business with him all the time. He could lose a lot of face in the ghetto if word of a sellout got around. But ... suppose he tried to get the Brandel boy out and failed or the Germans got wind of it. He'd be out on his ass, but good.

Max stood up quickly. 'Leave me out of it. Hands off. I'll forget everything you said.'

'Sit down, Max,' Andrei said softly. 'Max, that order of flour for the Orphans and Self-Help – just cancel it. We're opening up a new source.'

Max slipped into his chair. 'Damn you, Androfski, I went to a lot of trouble to ship that wheat in here. I brought in so goddamned much flour that half the bakeries on the Aryan side had to close.'

'Just talking off the top of my head, Max, but forty or fifty of our own people think we can run the smuggling operation just as effectively.'

The message was clear. The Brandel boy had to be freed at any price. Androfski was one of those bastards who didn't bluff. Max opened his wallet and took out his estimation pad and began to scratch figures down.

'It will cost plenty.'

'We'll pay.'

'I'll have to work in gold or dollars. We can only move through high-class people.'

'I've only got zlotys,' Andrei lied.

'So have I got zlotys. A warehouse full of them. They aren't worth the goddam paper they're printed on. Gold or dollars, three thousand dollars.'

'Three thousand dollars!'

'Your hearing is excellent.'

Andrei's eyes watered in anger. He turned his back on Kleperman to conceal the rage inside him. Filthy stinking scum. Bargaining for a life as if it were a secondhand suit on the Parysowski market. Goddamned son of a bitch, Kleperman. Rachael's eyes. Day and night she waited in his flat. Could he look at Rachael's eyes again?

'It's a deal,' he whispered.

'Let's have the details.'

Andrei sat down opposite Max and held his face in his hands. 'He got picked up in the Old Town Square carrying an Aryan *Kennkarte* made out for a fictitious Stanislaw Krasnodebski. He was sent out as a contact for a pickup from one of our girls from Krakow. Now the Germans hauled in forty, fifty people. Mass questioning. No doubt they've looked at his penis and know he's Jewish. We've got reason to believe several Jews were grabbed in the dragnet.'

'One of my boys was taken in on the same roundup,' Max said, and added ironically, 'He isn't as lucky as Brandel. Doesn't have his friends.'

'So, he goes on a story of being Hershel Edelman from Wolkowysk. If we're lucky, he hasn't been identified.'

'He'll need more than luck with Sauer working him over. I'll find out what his status is. If he is under suspicion we can't touch him at Gestapo House. That will only endanger him. Sauer doesn't take bribes. Just hope the boy doesn't crack. We have to wait until he is transferred.'

Andrei nodded. Max stood up.

'Max ... I know the Big Seven can put us out of business, but if there's a double cross you'll get it first from me, personally.'

Chapter Twenty-four

Eight days passed.

Rachael Bronski waited in her Uncle Andrei's flat twenty-four hours each day, resisting consolation, eating only enough to keep her alive.

Each time Andrei walked in and shook his head the shock recoiled through her like the jagged glass on the top of the wall. She kept her eyes open in vigil until she collapsed from exhaustion, and then only a few nightmare-filled hours' respite could be found.

She twitched and sweated on the bed and woke up with her heart thumping and the sweat pouring into her eyes, and Wolf would be standing there at the foot of the bed, gory and dismembered, and she would cry out the horror within her and then start her slow, zombie-like pacing of the room.

All of this silly war of morality I fought with him. All this modesty – all this fear ... Wolf was locked up in that terrible place. I have sent him to his grave, unloved. I have sent him to his grave, unloved. If Andrei comes through the door and tells me Wolf is dead, then I must die too.

Rachael developed a superhuman sharpness for sound. From four flights up she could hear the door of the lobby open and close. Each time it did she would walk to the door of the flat and lean against it and begin to count footsteps.

It took sixty steps to get to Andrei's flat.

She would count. Sometimes the sound of footsteps would stop on the first landing or the second or third. She could tell if they were climbing stairs or walking in a corridor.

She could tell if their sound was taking someone up or down.

The ninth day.

She washed her face with cold water and fixed her hair and sat by the window. The door opened and closed in the lobby. Rachael listened and began her count.

... ten ... eleven ... twelve ...

The footsteps had reached the first landing.

... sixteen ... seventeen ... eighteen ...

She was able to distinguish between footsteps as they rose higher. The flat, weary shuffle was a man. The sharp sound was a woman's heels. The soft sound, the child.

... thirty-three ... thirty-four ... thirty-five ...

Two men! Two men walking up slowly. Everyone walked slowly these days.

... forty-three ... forty-four ... forty-five ...

Her heart began to race. Two men on the third-floor landing. Oh God! Please don't let them go into a flat down there. Please, God! Please make them come up to this floor. Please, God! I have never heard two men come up to the fourth floor! Please! Please!

... fifty-one ... fifty-two ... fifty-three ...

Rachael backed away.

... fifty-nine ... sixty

The door opened

Andrei walked in ... someone behind him.

'Wolf!'

He walked in slowly and took off his cap. Rachael pitched forward into his arms and fought off the consuming blackness that took hold of her.

For many, many moments she was too terrified to look up. Was this another dream?

No ... no ... no dream. She looked up. He was fine. Just a scar on his cheek. And then she allowed herself the luxury of breaking wide open in convulsive tears.

'Rachael,' he whispered, 'I am all right. Please don't cry. I am all right ...'

Andrei left them, closing the door behind him.

Alex and Sylvia sat in their room, ghost-faced, drained of life. Neither of them had spoken a word for an hour since Wolf had left to go to Rachael.

Andrei knocked softly and entered.

'Dr Glazer examined him. None of the dog bites are infected. He'll be all right.'

The bit of information brought forth a new burst of crying from Sylvia. And then the baby shrieked and Sylvia picked him up and clutched him to her breast and rocked him back and forth, oblivious of Alex's words of consolation.

Alex nodded to Andrei to leave Sylvia alone. He tiptoed from the room, both of them retreating to his office. Alex began berating himself.

'Stop sniveling,' Andrei demanded. 'He is a courageous boy.'

'Where is he now?'

'Don't you know?'

'Should I?'

'He is with his girl.'

'His girl?'

'My niece.'

'Oh, I didn't know.' Alex began berating himself again for being such a bad father that his own son would not confide his love life.

'Shut up, Alex, the boy is alive and safe.'

Alex kept rambling. 'All these eight horrible days I said it was right to get Wolf out. We have bought freedom for our people before. Rodel cost us nearly two thousand when they took him to the Pawiak Prison, and he isn't even one of ours. The Communists didn't even pay me back for Rodel's release. It was all right, buying Wolf out. We would have done the same for any of our people.'

'You want to hear it, I'll tell you!' Andrei raged. 'It was not all right! You should have left your son to die before crawling in front of Max Kleperman!'

'Don't talk like that, Andrei!'

Andrei snatched him from his chair and grabbed his lapels and shook him as though he were weightless. 'Grovel! Beg Max Kleperman for mercy! That three thousand dollars could have bought guns to storm the Gestapo House and take your son out like a dignified human being!'

Alex fell against him and wept, but Andrei slung him into his chair. 'God damn you, Alex! God damn you! Open your goddamned precious journal and read to me about the Jewish massacres in the Soviet Union!'

'For God's sake, leave me alone!'

'I want money! I want to buy guns!'

'No – never. Never, Andrei. We keep twenty thousand children alive – not one zloty for guns.'

Alexander Brandel gasped violently for air as the room whirled around him. He had never seen the anger of the big man who glowered over him. Cornered and beaten, his soul cried out instinctively for the lives of the children.

'I'm through,' Andrei hissed.

'Andrei,' Alex cried pathetically.

'Roast in hell!'

'Andrei!'

The door slammed on his plea.

Andrei Androfski wandered in a fog, aimlessly through the ghetto streets. It was done. There was no turning back. He walked and walked and walked in a daze that shut out the sight of corpses and the pitiful moans of the child beggars or the brutal clubs of the Jewish Militia.

And he found himself standing in the lobby of his apartment house before the bank of mailboxes. His hand groped instinctively in slot 18. He pulled out two armbands. Two white armbands with blue stars of shame. The kids were still upstairs. Wolf and Rachael. He shoved the armbands into the slot and dug around in his pocket. Two bills. A hundred zlotys each. Always when he plunged lower and lower one word kept him from reaching the bottom – 'Gabriela.' Two hundred zlotys. Enough to get him to the Aryan side. He needed her desperately.

'I have quit,' Andrei said.

'What are you going to do?' Gaby asked.

'Try to contact the Home Army. They'll give me a command. The Home Army needs men like me. They won't argue and quibble, they'll fight – tired of all this damned arguing – all this dealing with Kleperman.'

Gaby watched him mumble aimlessly.

'Roman. That's the name of the commander of the Home Army in the

Warsaw district. Roman. I'll get to him somehow. You'll stick with me, Gaby?'

'You know I will.'

He put his arms about her waist and buried his head in her belly, and she stroked his hair. 'Are you certain?'

'I am certain – absolutely certain.'

Rachael and Wolf lay side by side on the bed, awed by the magnificence of their experience.

Wolf was completely exhausted. Rachael held him and petted him, and her lips sought him again and again.

She felt so elated from the wonderment of fulfillment.

It was not ugly or difficult. She felt no shame when they saw each other for the first time. Wolf had been so gentle and tender. He knew the awkwardness in her.

He was happy. She had made him happy. He was tired, but he wanted her to touch him.

Poor dear Wolf, Rachael thought. He is so shy he cannot say words he wants to, but I feel every word he wants to tell me by the way he touches my breast and kisses me and whispers to me.

It felt good ... so good ... and I am so proud I was able to be a woman for his sake. Now anything can happen and it won't be quite so bad.

I am so sleepy ... Uncle Andrei must be furious. I hope he went to see Gabriela, because I'm not going to leave. I'm going to snuggle close and sleep for a little while, then I'll wake him up and try it again ...

Chapter Twenty-five

Journal Entry

No one has seen Andrei for ten days. We assume that he is living on the Aryan side. After so many years of working together, it is difficult to believe he is really gone. None of us knew till now what a symbol of security he was. It has been a terrible blow to the morale here at Mila 19.

We now operate ninety soup kitchens and have some twenty thousand children under the care of Orphans and Self-Help.

Dr Glazer tells me we have a new trouble, venereal disease. Before the war, prostitution was never a Jewish social problem. Nowadays I hear more and more of wives and daughters, many from fine old Orthodox families, taking to the streets.

For a family to get a daughter married to a Jewish militiaman is an achievement.

Tommy Thompson has been evicted from Poland. We have lost a dear friend. However, we have been expecting it for a long time. Ana Grinspan has already made a new contact to pass in American Aid funds. Believe it or not, a chap named Fordelli, who is the second secretary at the Italian Embassy. Although he is a good Fascist, he takes exception to the German treatment of the Jews. Is Ana having an affair with him?

ALEXANDER BRANDEL

Alex was instinctive about bad news. The moment Ervin Rosenblum walked into his office he knew something had gone wrong. Ervin paced and wrung his hands.

'Out with it.'

'My pass to the Aryan side has been revoked.'

'Has De Monti protested?'

'He left for the eastern front four days ago. He doesn't know yet.'

'Confidentially, it is just as well you are inside the ghetto with us.'

'But all the contacts on the Aryan side ...'

'It was getting more difficult for you to see anyone, and De Monti refused to co-operate. You were being watched every minute. Ervin, I've been thinking. You can fit right in here at Mila 19. We need you in several positions.'

'Like for example?'

'Orphans and Self-Help cultural director. *Nu*, don't shrug and make faces. The arrangement of debates, concerts, theater, chess tournaments becomes more and more important to give the people something to think about other than misery. What do you say?'

'I say that you are a good friend.'

'Another thing. The Good Fellowship Club. I can't keep up with all the material coming in to the journal. I have been thinking for a long time. Build a secret room in the basement. With you putting time in, we could really expand the archives.'

Ervin shrugged at what he felt was charity.

'Think it over, Ervin. Let me know.'

That evening Susan Geller came to Ervin's flat. Since the ghetto, they had had little time for each other. Susan was nearly completely married to the orphanage and Ervin was on the Aryan side most of the time. They met about once a week at Good Fellowship Club meetings, usually too weary to pursue personal pleasures. Their unofficial engagement seemed destined to go unresolved.

'Susan!' Momma Rosenblum cried with delight.

'Hello, Momma Rosenblum.'

'You heard?'

'Yes.'

'So maybe cheer him up a little.'

Ervin sat on the edge of his bed, staring glumly at the hole in the toe of his bedroom shoe. She sat beside him, creaking the bed.

'So maybe you've come to pray over the corpse,' he said.

'Shut up. Alex has offered you a responsible position. So, stick up your nose. Be a martyr.'

'I am glad you stopped by to cheer me up with your tender consolation.'

'Ervin, you'll take the job?'

'I have a choice, maybe?'

'Stop krechtzing. Alex is very excited about the plans for a secret room in the basement. You know how important the work on the journal is.'

'All right, all right. I'm bubbling with happiness.'

'Confidentially, Ervin, I am just as happy that you don't go to the Aryan side any more. I have been afraid for you, even with your fancy super-official papers.'

'That's something. I didn't think you had time to think about me.'

'Ugh, you are in a mood. Of course I think about you.'

'I'm sorry.'

'Ervin,' she said, taking his hand, 'on the way here I was giving this all a great deal of meditation. We're not getting any younger and God knows I'll never grow pretty. With conditions as they are and so forth and so forth and so forth, perhaps we should consider getting married. In addition to the fact that already we should be having a little pleasure now and then, there are very practical reasons. For example, you'll be working at Mila 19 most of the time. It will be difficult for you to keep up this flat. So, why should we waste space? If we are married, Alex will give us our own room on the second floor, and you can move Momma in and so forth and so forth.'

He reached over and kissed her on the cheek. 'How can a man resist a proposal like that?'

Journal Entry

Ervin and Susan were married yesterday by Rabbi Solomon. It is about time.

ALEXANDER BRANDEL

Chapter Twenty-six

Chris returned to Warsaw from the eastern front to find Rosy gone, his office and apartment thoroughly searched and filled with hidden microphones, and his private line to Switzerland unavailable.

He dialed Rosy's number in the ghetto, to learn the phone was disconnected; then stormed to the Press Division at the Bristol Hotel, where his attempt to see Horst von Epp was thwarted by a minor bureaucrat.

'I am sorry, Mr de Monti. Herr von Epp is in Berlin for a conference.'

'When will he be back?'

'I am sorry. I don't have the information.'

'Well, where can I reach him in Berlin?'

'I am sorry. I don't have that information.'

A second minor official was equally sorry and uninformative about the revoking of Ervin Rosenblum's credentials, and a third minor official was sorry about the suspension of Chris's wire to Switzerland.

'Sorry, Mr de Monti. Until further instructions you will have to file all dispatches here at the Bureau for Censorship.'

Chris was tired and his head was fuzzy from the long trip back from the front lines. He stifled his irritation, knowing nothing could be done until he could put the pieces back in place. A hot bath and a tall drink and the things that a man looks forward to after living in the mud were in order.

While he soaked and sipped he decided not to pursue it any more until he could get his mind straight after a night's sleep.

Chris hid himself at a corner table at Bruhl House to avoid conversation and nibbled his way halfheartedly through a leather-tough schnitzel. The room was filled with guttural sounds of talk about the eastern front, the voices sharp with confidence.

'You are not hungry tonight, Mr de Monti?' the waiter asked patronizingly as Chris gave up. 'It is getting more and more difficult to put together an eatable menu. They ... get it all.'

Chris signed the bill and wandered out into the street. Warsaw was a gay place these days. The city was filled with German troops having their last fling before shipping to the eastern front. Although the Polish people were open in their hatred of the enemy, there were enough women not annoyed with patriotic considerations to give the German lads a good time. Brothels reaped a fortune, beer and vodka and goldwasser flowed in the taverns, and even the ancient streetwalkers struck an unexpected vein of gold.

Most of Warsaw's musicians were Jews. German soldiers and their girls slipped into the ghetto to dance and live it up in one of the fifty night clubs, mainly operated by the Big Seven, for the music on the Aryan side was dreadful.

Chris walked for several blocks. He was weary and unsettled from the shocks of war and hung in limbo by the sudden turn of events in Warsaw.

From the taverns, there was riotous singing from Germans as drunk as Poles and from Poles as drunk as Poles. In order to avoid further accosting by the streetwalkers, he crossed at Pilsudski Square and stopped to get his bearings.

Back to his car and home? No. Damned apartment gave him the creeps.

Track down a party? A good bender and maybe a little action afterward? No.

Chris looked around, then found himself walking up a footpath in the Saxony Gardens, which seemed more delightful with every step because it put the sounds of Warsaw behind him. It grew darker and dimmer as he walked. All he could hear now were occasional squeals from the bushes by roomless couples consummating their deals. Now and then a self-conscious pair emerged from the thickets or down the path, avoiding his eyes.

Chris walked past the swan lake. So often he had waited there for Deborah ... sitting on the bench ... waiting for her to appear. That first wonderful instant he would see her ... That moment never changed, never dulled.

Damned fool, sitting here. Deborah isn't coming up the path – there won't be a tryst. No beautiful Deborah to see through the velvet curtains. Only a roomful of microphones and hidden eyes.

Chris was magnetically drawn to the ghetto wall. He crossed the Saxony Gardens and wandered along Chlodna Street, which divided the big and little ghettos. On both sides of him was the wall. The night lights caught the broken glass cemented on the top, causing it to sparkle like the sudden glint of a rat's eyes.

So dark ... so quiet. It was hard to comprehend that six hundred thousand people lay in silence on the other side. All that could be heard was the sound of his own steps, and all that could be seen of life was his shadow, which grew longer and longer as the light contorted the angle of his movement.

He stood underneath the bridge. It was covered with barbed wire. He had come there many times during the day and stared at it, watching the Jews cross from one ghetto to the other over the 'Polish corridor,' hoping beyond hope he could catch a glimpse of Deborah.

He stood for a half hour.

What the hell, he thought, and walked away quickly.

From the corner of his eye he detected movement in an indentation in the wall ahead of him. Quickly two men stepped out and blocked his path. Chris stopped and looked over his shoulder. Two more men were behind him. He could not distinguish their faces, but the bulky cut of their clothing and leather workers' caps and their size intimated that they were thugs.

'Waiting for somebody under the bridge, Jew boy?' a voice came from one of the figures.

Hoodlums out Jew hunting. Big sport, these days. Good source of income. What to do? Show his papers and pass through?

'Come on, Jew boy. Two hundred zlotys or you'll take a walk to Gestapo House.'

Chris's blood boiled. 'Go to hell,' he snapped, and walked straight at the pair ahead of him.

One from behind hooked his arm and turned him around. Chris drove his fist into the figure's mouth and the man fell backward, hit the curb, and landed on the flat of his back.

Damn! Damn my temper!

Two leaped on him, and while he struggled to free himself the third brought a blackjack to the side of his cheek.

A surge of raw strength threw the men from him. As he shook himself free, the first one got up and caught him in the eye with a hamlike fist, and for an instant Chris was blinded. He reeled, then stopped abruptly as his back hit the ghetto wall.

Chris grunted as the blackjack found its mark again. He sank to his hands and knees and wobbled on all fours and the ground spun around him.

'Get up, Jew boy!'

Chris looked up. They hovered over him. One with the blackjack, another with a jagged broken bottle. Another, bloody-mouthed from his blow. He could not see the fourth man.

His head cleared and the ground steadied. Chris lurched up, ramming his shoulder into the one with the glass bottle to crack out of the ring. With the air suddenly smacked from his lungs, the hoodlum fell and sat on the ground, gasping.

And then Chris sank under a rain of fists and boots. He was jerked to his feet and propped against the wall, his arms spread-eagled as in the position of a crucifixion. The leader could not resist one last smash into the stomach of his helpless victim. A light was held to Chris's face. His dark Italian features were studied. 'He's a Jew, all right.'

Chris's head rolled up and his eyes opened and he snarled. The leader pressed the jagged glass close to his eye, so he dared not move.

Chris brought his knee up into the man's groin and the man shrieked and staggered back, then came forward, enraged and intent on cutting up his face.

'Wait. He fights too good to be a Jew. We had better make sure he is.'

'What's the difference now? Just take his money.'

'Holy Mother! Look at these papers! He isn't a Jew.'

'Let's get out of here.'

Footsteps ... faded ... they're gone ...

Chris slipped down to the ground, bloody, and pawed around to pull himself up.

Someone stood over him. He managed to hold his head up enough to see the faces of a frightened middle-aged couple.

'Help me ...'

'Don't touch him, Poppa. Can't you see he's a Jew? He jumped over the wall. Leave – leave before the guard comes.'

Chapter Twenty-seven

A week passed before Horst von Epp returned to Warsaw. He entered the Holy Cross Church, spotted Chris kneeling in the first row, and knelt beside him.

'Good Lord,' Horst said, 'what happened to you?'

'I was mistaken for a Jew.'

'Bad mistake, these days.'

'You should have seen me a week ago.'

'I thought we'd better meet out of the office,' Horst said, nodding in the direction of the little black box on the altar containing Chopin's heart. 'Let's take a walk. That box may have a microphone hidden in it. Matter of fact, I bit into a microphone planted in my breakfast bun this morning.'

They shaded their eyes from the sun. Chris put on dark glasses to cover the bruises, and they strolled down New World Street. Across the street a pair of men began to follow them, and Von Epp's car drifted alongside at a crawl. 'Lovely system,' Von Epp said. 'This way no one knows exactly who is watching who. How did you find the Russian front?'

'Nothing but victory for the Fatherland. Trouble is, I'm having a time getting my dispatches through about your glorious achievements.'

'Sorry about that. Your line to Switzerland was restored this morning. Bloody blockheads. I knew the moment I left Warsaw there would be a panic.'

'Restoring Rosenblum to me too?'

They crossed the street.

'Your silence is deafening, Horst,' Chris pressed.

'Be reasonable.'

'He's like my right arm.'

'I told you I didn't know how long I'd be able to keep him out of the ghetto.'

They walked in quiet unison for the rest of the block, then stopped at the junction where Jerusalem Boulevard turned into the Third of May Boulevard. A screaming set of sirens froze all movement. A pair of motorcycles followed by a command car followed by a convoy of a hundred trucks filled with fresh soldiers poured past them. From two or three of the trucks they were able to catch a note or two of a marching song. The convoy swept toward the newly reconstructed bridge to Praga.

Meat for the eastern front, Chris thought. The blitzkrieg had swept over the steppes. The fantastic military machine was slicing up the vastness of Russia from the Black Sea to the gates of Moscow. Horst and Chris drifted in the wake of the convoy to the bridge, and they stopped in the middle and leaned on the rail.

'Schreiker called me in and questioned me about Rosenblum. They were all on me about him. For both of your welfares it is better this way. It is impossible to have him out of the ghetto without casting all sorts of suspicion on you. Obviously he's mixed up in some sort of contacts around Warsaw and probably two steps ahead of being hauled into Gestapo House. Now don't press me on this matter, Chris.'

Von Epp was right. Rosenblum was in thick as a courier. The Germans would be fools to allow him to continue to run loose.

'If you need another man, for Christ sake, find yourself a nice untainted Aryan.'

Chris nodded. The Vistula River was filled with barges bearing the tools of war for transfer to the eastern front.

'Any of all this bother you, Horst?'

'Everyone knows the Jews started the war,' Horst recited from the principal dogma.

'I saw a few things out there behind your lines that may be pretty hard to explain.'

'Believe me, Goebbels will find explanations. And the rest of us? Hell, we'll all shrug with blue-eyed innocence and say, "Orders were orders – what could we do?" Thank God the world is blessed with short memories.'

'Where does it end?'

'End? We can't stop until we either own it all or get blown up into a billion pieces. Besides, don't be too hard on us. Conquerors have never won any prizes for benevolence. We are no worse than a dozen other empires when they ran the show.'

'Does this make it right?'

'My dear Chris, right is the exclusive property of the winning side. The loser is always wrong. Now, if I were you, I'd string along with us for awhile because the way things are going we may be Rome, Babylon, Genghis Khan, and the Ottomans combined for many hundred years.'

'Christ, what a prospect.'

Horst laughed and slapped Chris on the back vigorously. 'Trouble with you, you bastard, you've been out on the front looking at the seamy side of things. Warsaw is the warriors' reward. Unbend a little. How about a private party tonight? You, me – a pair of ladies. Hildie Solna said you were rather nice to her last time out.'

'Once in a while my chemicals get out of balance. Hildie restores them. Usually when I'm tailing off a drunk.'

'Tell you what. To hell with Hildie. Tonight I'm lending you number one from my private stock. Eighteen, built like a ripe peach. And where this dear girl picked up so many tricks in her short life – fantastically beautiful muscle control, and she does a thing of rubbing on baby oil . . .'

A roaring truck blotted out further dissertation on the orgy.

Chris again became entranced by the river barges. Horst von Epp was correct. 'Right' was the winning side. He sure was with the winner. Five hundred years of Germany? Could be. The trip to the eastern front was the clincher. No matter how dark things had been in Spain, in Poland he always felt that the pendulum would swing back the other way. But would it? A breakthrough in Egypt would put Rommel on an unstoppable path to India. Moscow was digging in for a siege. The frantic preparations in America – too little, too late. He had seen the German power unleash a fury that made the conquest of Poland look like child's play. Kiev, a half million Russian soldiers trapped. What could stop them?

Chris looked at Von Epp, who was enjoying a cigarette. Orders are orders. A wall of indifference built around him that shut out a struggle of good and evil.

And then . . . the thoughts of the massacre outside Kiev seared into his mind. Chris had to make his move. Make it soon. Now . . . now . . .

And Horst von Epp was his only chance.

Do it, Chris prodded himself, do it – tomorrow may be too late.

'I want to go into the ghetto,' Chris said quickly, fearing his own courage.

'Come now, Chris,' Von Epp said, concealing his delight. 'It will put us both in a bad light.' All of Horst von Epp's patience was beginning to pay off now. Chris had held a card up his sleeve from the beginning. His desire to stay in Warsaw at any cost. His reluctance to join the parties after a reputation as a lothario in other places at other times. Chris wanted something. Von Epp knew that from the start. Now the card was being played with caution.

'I've got to see Rosenblum and clean up a lot of odds and ends.'

'If you insist on this . . .'

'I insist.'

Von Epp threw up his hands in 'defeat.' 'All right.' He glanced at his watch. Enough for one day, he thought. He looked for his car, which had trailed them and parked at the foot of the bridge. 'Can I drive you into town?'

'I'll walk. I'll see you later.'

'Try to change your mind about going into the ghetto.' Horst turned briskly as he started for his car.

'Horst!'

The German turned to see Chris walking grimly toward him, on the brink of a terrible decision.

'Suppose I want to get someone out of the ghetto?'

'Rosenblum?'

'No.'

'A woman?'

'And her children.'

'Who?'

'My grandmother.'

Horst von Epp smiled. Christopher de Monti had played his card. Every man had his price. Von Epp always found it. With most, petty bribes . . . favors. That was for petty people. Christopher de Monti? Tough. An idealist in the throes of conflict. Blackmail often worked. Almost everyone had dirty tracks they tried to cover. Von Epp found them too.

No matter how tough, how idealistic, how clean, every man had his price. Every man had his blind spot.

'How important is this?' Horst asked.

'Everything,' Chris whispered, culminating the decision, putting himself at the mercy of the German.

'It can be done, I suppose.'

'How?'

'She can sign papers that she isn't Jewish. We have handy form letters for all occasions, as you know. Marry her, adopt the children. A ten-minute detail. Then send her into Switzerland as the wife of an Italian citizen.'

'When can I pick up my pass for the ghetto?'

'After we settle on the price.'
'Like Faust? My soul to the devil?'
'That's right, Chris. It will be steep.'

Chapter Twenty-eight

Andrei waited for two restless, mood-filled weeks before he could corner the man known to him as Roman, the Warsaw commander of the fledgling underground Home Army.

Time and again Andrei had to stifle his desire to go back into the ghetto with his friends. He drank heavily in the evenings, and when his mind became fuzzed he was filled with remorse. He had been intolerant of Alexander Brandel's struggle. He had acted wrongly to friends who believed in him.

He thought about everything since the war had come. Bullheaded . . . angry. Perhaps he was no good for a command again. There was a time when he had settled down and moved about Poland on mission after mission. He had pieced together a secret press. He had acted with a cool head and a quick mind.

But always, anger surged. Rebellion against tyranny. He was overpowered by this drive to throw off his containment and fight.

And Gaby. He was remorseful about her too. What kind of life had he given her? He had taken her from a world in which she thrived and placed demands upon her, giving little or nothing in return. When the command in the Home Army comes, maybe I will get away from Warsaw. Then perhaps she can forget about me slowly and find the thread of a decent life.

At long last the word came back through super-cautious networks of information that Roman would see him. It was with an immense feeling of relief that he followed out the instructions. A contact in Praga. A blindfolded ride back over the river. Two dozen false turns to throw off his sense of direction. Men whispering, leading him up a dirt path. A door, a room. Where was he? He did not know exactly.

'You may take off the blindfold,' a high tenor voice said in immaculate Polish.

Andrei adjusted his eyes to the shadows of the room. They were in a large shed. Crude curtains shutting out light. A kerosene lantern on a shelf. A cot. A few garden tools.

Roman's face came across the flicker of light. He had seen the prototype of Roman a thousand times in a thousand places. Tall, erect, blond, high forehead, curly hair. He wore the unmaskable glower of perpetual arrogance of a Polish nobleman. It was the sneer of a Ulany colonel, the innuendo of superiority, the thin mocking lips. Andrei could almost tell Roman's story. The son of a count. Landed gentry. Misused wealth. Medieval mentality. Roman most likely lived in the South of France before the war. He cared damn little about Poland except to bleed his estate dry with the blood of legalized serfdom. He saw damned little of Poland except during the social season.

Andrei's estimation was deadly accurate. Like many of his ilk, Roman had become suddenly smitten with latent Polish 'nationalism' after the invasion. He joined the government in exile in London because it was the fashionable thing to do. London was jammed with Poles who gathered to hear Chopin and recite poetry and live memories of Warsaw in the 'good old days.'

He parachuted into Poland to work with the Home Army, a play of immature romanticism. Despite the guise of workman's clothing, Roman's frailties shone like a beacon. 'You are persistent, Jan Kowal,' Roman said to Andrei.

'Only as persistent as you are evasive,' Andrei answered.

'Cigarette?' American, of course. He'd rough it later with the local product. No use carrying nationalism to extremes.

'I don't smoke.'

Roman did. With a long cigarette holder.

'You're Androfski, aren't you?'

'That's right.'

'I remember seeing you in Berlin in the Olympics.'

Andrei began to have that uneasy feeling he had had a thousand times in the presence of the Romans. He could read the thoughts hidden behind Roman's eyes.

... Jew boy. We had Jewish families on our estate. Two of them. One was the village tailor. Had a little son with earlocks. I beat the hell out of him with my horsewhip. He wouldn't fight – only pray. The other Jew ... grain merchant. Thief. Cheat. Always had my father indebted to him. The inbred hatred of centuries could not be belied by Roman's small, tight smile.

'I am afraid,' Roman said, 'that our position is such that you cannot expect too much co-operation from us at the present time. Perhaps later, as we are better organized ...'

'You mistake my mission,' Andrei said. 'I represent only myself. I wish to place myself at the service of the Home Army. A fighting command, preferred.'

'Oh, I see. That puts a different light on everything.' Roman's slim elegant fingers caressed the long cigarette holder. 'The Home Army does not work under conditions of a peacetime military force, naturally. All our people are volunteers. The maintenance of discipline cannot be as simple as a day in the guardhouse or the loss of pay. Discipline is life and death.'

'I don't understand what you are trying to say.'

'Merely this. We wish to avoid in advance the creation of unnecessary problems.'

'Such as?'

'Well, we don't solicit your services. It may be impossible to get our men to respond to your leadership. And ... you might feel rather uncomfortable with us.'

'No room for Jews!'

'As a matter of fact, yes.'

'Your army represents the government of Poland. Thirty thousand Jewish soldiers died in Polish uniform during the invasion.' Andrei stopped. He knew his arguments were falling on deaf ears. Roman's eyes now said, 'If it weren't for the Jews we would not be in this situation.' Oh, they'd have a few Jews all right, Andrei knew. A nice quota system like all the quota systems he'd lived with all his life.

'I'll make you a counteroffer. I know my way in and out of all sixteen ghettos. Let me organize my own unit of the Home Army.'

Roman turned his back on Andrei. 'My dear – er – Jan Kowal. That would only increase the friction. Can't you see?'

'It is disgusting,' Gabriela snapped.

'No, I should have known.'

'What now?'

'There is no turning back. I am leaving in the morning for Lublin.' Gaby's face became drawn. Sooner or later Andrei would reach a fearful conclusion. 'The Bathyrans there have a good collection of foreign passports and visas. For old times' sake they will give me one and enough money to travel. I'll pick up the underground railway. We have sent a number of people out of the country that way. Goes into Germany to Stettin. From Stettin it will be a relatively easy matter to make a deal for a boat to Sweden. From Sweden I'll get to England, then join the Free Polish Forces. If they refuse me a command, I'll join the British army.'

Gabriela listened to every word with mounting fear. Andrei stopped his pacing. 'Someone in this world must let me fight.'

She nodded. She knew. There would never be peace for him again until he was able to strike back.

'What about us?' she whispered.

'Go to Krakow to the Americans. Thompson is gone, but you still have friends there. They will get you out. We will meet in England, Gaby.'

She bit her finger and brushed the hair back over her shoulder nervously. 'I don't want to be parted from you.'

'We can't travel together.'

'I'm afraid of it all, Andrei.'

'There is no choice.'

'Andrei, it is such a wild scheme. So many, many things could go wrong. If you leave tomorrow and I never see you again –'

He put his hand over her mouth gently, then wrapped his arms around her in his wonderful way, which he had not done for a very, very long time. 'And when we meet in England, do you know the first thing we will do?'

'No.'

'Get married, of course, woman!'

'Andrei, I'm so afraid.'

'Shhh.' He petted her hair and rubbed the back of her neck and she purred and smiled weakly. 'I must go into the ghetto. There are a few things in my flat. Nothing of value but sentimental. I should like Rachael and Stephan and Deborah to have them.'

He broke from her and put on his cap. 'Strange ... I wanted so badly to see Stephan have his bar mitzvah. Well – no matter now.'

'Hurry back, darling ...'

The return to the ghetto after his absence was shocking. In the few weeks he had been away the situation had collapsed with fearful speed. With winter coming on, the sight of corpses in the streets was commonplace and the smell of death, the low moan of misery, and the tautness of expectant doom cast a pall of gray in the midday sun.

Andrei shoved his hand into the mail slot in the hope that Rachael's and Wolf's armbands would be there. He might be able to speak to them ... say a few words ...

The flat was as he had left it. He looked about. The library. Some to Wolf, some to Stephan to read later – if there would be a later. The trinkets which once had been shined to a dazzling polish and adorned his uniform were tarnished. He threw them with his medals into a box. Stephan would want these.

The records and the player for Rachael.

What else was there? Very little. A Zionist organizer had no time for the accumulation of personal wealth. It was a shame that there were so few bits of tangible evidence of what this shabby room had meant. There had been much happiness here once.

The photograph album. The brown oval-framed pictures of Momma and Poppa. The pictures of his own bar mitzvah. Deborah would want these.

Should he see Alex? Rosy? Susan Geller? He heard Rosy and Susan were married. He really should. Hell, saying good-by is a rotten business. Just skip it. This was no bon voyage.

He sat at the table and wrote a note, which he was certain that Rachael and Wolf would receive, dividing his things and saying farewell.

He blotted and folded it.

The door creaked open and closed. Simon Eden was in the room with him.

'Bad news travels fast,' Andrei said.

'We have had a twenty-four-hour watch here. We hoped you'd come back.'

Andrei didn't want to get into a discussion with Simon. He wanted nothing to sway his mind, throw him into turmoil, challenge his loyalty, play on his sympathy. He had made his decision.

'I've spent my life arguing,' Andrei said quickly. 'I don't want one now.'

Simon Eden was acquainted with the reality of Andrei's words. Two Jews in a room will give you three opinions. His life had been an endless debate. Minute interpretations. Interpretations of interpretations. The kinds of Zionism, the variations of Judaism. Every man an eminent literary and musical critic. Every man having the personal answer to every problem. Debate ... talk, talk, talk, talk.

'I didn't come to argue. Just to ask you what you are going to do. My people on the Aryan side tell me you made a contact with Roman. Did he give you a commission in the Home Army?'

'They don't want anyone but tenth-generation red-blooded Polish Catholics.'

'I could have told you that. Jews in the ranks of the partisans are getting murdered for their boots and guns. And I could have told you the Home Army won't back Jewish units. Going to make a run for it?'

'I think so.'

'Strange damn thing about us, Andrei. We are a race of individuals like none other. We are savage about our right to seek truth as individuals. We are ridiculous sometimes at the numbers of answers we have to the same problem or how we can confuse a simple issue with conversation.'

'It was the lack of unity that lost us Jerusalem in ancient times,' Andrei said. 'It is the same damned thing that will destroy us here.'

Their talk was without anger. Simon was one who was always held in esteem by Andrei for his strength and for his unique ability to hold together a dozen factions of Jews engaged in ideological differences. 'You say individualism is a weakness. I agree that it has been, at times. At the same time, it is also our greatest source of strength. The constant search for truth by a single man has been the key to survival.'

'Don't trick me, Simon. I said I did not want to argue. Now you are trapping me into an argument on my right to argue.'

'Can I say that you have expected too much?'

'I? All I've ever wanted to do is –'

'I know damned well what you've wanted to do. Did it ever occur to you that we don't have six hundred thousand Andrei Androfskis in the ghetto? They are just ordinary people clinging to a thread of life. They cling to a magic *Kennkarte* which allows them to work in slave labor. Some even sell their daughters' bodies – they beg and plead –'

'Without leaders!' Andrei snapped.

'Do you forget that this country was trampled and its leaders killed? Do you dare say Alexander Brandel is not a leader? And Dave Zemba? Do you think Emanuel Goldman was not a leader? Are you ashamed of the courage of Wolf Brandel? Andrei, Alex hears nothing and sees nothing but the cry of hungry children. His only dogma is to put food into their bellies. And damn you, he has fought a hell of a war in his own way.'

Andrei shoved out of the chair. 'Thanks for the lecture.'

Simon grabbed his arm. 'Hear me out for one more minute.'

Andrei pulled his arm free. Simon was not begging or pleading. He had too much respect to slough Simon off.

'Go on.'

'You have begged to die stupidly, irrationally, unheard, in vain. No underground army will form until the people want one. We're coming to the end of 1941, and in 1942 the people will want an army. They hear about the massacres in the east and they see the death rate climb to a hundred a day in the ghetto and they are not so afraid of reprisal any more and not so certain that Brandel has the answer for survival. Andrei, every idea, every man's thinking is good or bad because it comes at the correct time. It was not the correct time for a fighting force before. Now it is becoming the correct time. People are thinking about it more. They are talking about it. They are starting to plot. To think in terms of guns.'

Andrei slipped back into the chair. Simon hovered over him, burning his arguments home with intensity.

'So much has been lost,' Andrei whispered. 'So much to do.'

'Recontact Roman.'

'That bastard.'

'Never mind your personal feelings. Press him for arms.'

'Hell, you're crazy, Simon. It's too late. The Home Army will give us nothing but evasions. Piotr Warsinski has a gang of ghouls, and the Gestapo has a thousand informers. Our contacts on the Aryan side are flimsy. There is no real unity. We have no source for arms.'

'Did you ask for victory or the right to fight?'

'Are you with me now, Simon? Are you really with me?'

Simon dug into his pocket and pulled out a fat wad of bills. Hundred-zloty notes. 'Buy guns,' he said.

From the moment that Gabriela heard the lightness in his steps, she knew that something wonderful had happened. He flung open the door, his face beaming, and he threw the money on the table and picked her up and whirled her around and around.

For the first time since the war Andrei seemed at peace. There was much to do and his own people would be battling him all the way, but, by God, they were thinking his way. They knew, in some degree, that they had to find means to defend themselves.

Too little ... too late ... it did not seem to matter.

Chapter Twenty-nine

Chris parked his car opposite the ghetto gate facing the Square of the Iron Gates. An unshaven Polish Blue policeman picked his teeth with his little fingernail as he examined Chris's pass and waved the barrier up.

A few steps inside the wall Chris was challenged by a pair of huskies in long gray coats and mirror-polished boots of the Jewish Militia.

Chris oriented himself quickly. He knew from Rosy where Deborah was most likely to be. His best chance to see her alone would be at the orphanage on Niska Street. The ghetto was filled with spies and informers, yet he felt that Horst von Epp was both too clever and sophisticated to use the crude tactics of having him tailed. Horst had Chris boxed in, anyhow. If he were to force his luck, the German risked scaring his prey to cover.

Chris walked along the wall beyond which the 'Polish corridor' split the big and little ghettos. The streets were sticky with unswept dirt, and the pungent odors of filth filled his nostrils.

He approached the bridge which ran over the 'Polish corridor' to the big ghetto. He stopped. There! On the foot of the bridge steps. The corpse of an emaciated woman. Enormous ghastly circles formed on the skin pulled taut by protruding bones. Chris backed away. He had seen corpses on the eastern front by the thousands – he remembered the massacre – but ... here ... dead of starvation. It was different. Foot traffic moved around the dead woman with no one paying the least attention.

Chris edged up the steps to the top of the bridge. He was imprisoned in barbed wire. He looked down into the 'Polish corridor.' He had stood down there on the street so many times, looking up to where he now stood, hoping for a look at Deborah. He had been caught down there and beaten. He continued quickly over the bridge and down the steps into the big ghetto.

High barbed-wire walls surrounding Dr Franz Koenig's uniform factory greeted him. Slow movement on the other side of the wire by half-starved slave laborers. Brisk, arrogant movement along the guard posts by the Jewish Militia.

Each step now made him catch a vignette of squalor, of pain. Each step churned his queasy belly close to a vomit. A lice-riddled ragged remnant of what had once been a human being lay in front of him.

The mosaic of misery, the montage of horror became blurred. He was walking on a small square.

'Armbands! Buy armbands!'

'Books for sale. Twenty zlotys a dozen.' Spinoza for a penny, Talmud for a dime. A lifetime collection of wisdom. Buy it in gross lots for kindling ... keep my family alive one more day.

'Mattress for sale! Guaranteed lice-free!'

Two children blocked Chris's way. Warped, inhuman. 'Mister, a zloty!' one whined. The second, a smaller brother or sister too weak to cry for food. Only the lips trembled.

'Do you want a lady's company? Nice virgin girl from a good Hassidic family. Only a hundred zlotys.'

'My son's violin. Imported from Austria before the war ... Please, a beautiful instrument.'

'Mister, how much for my wedding ring? Solid gold.'

A long line of scraggly, ragged humanity getting a dole of watery broth at a soup kitchen. The line pressed forward, stepping wearily over a corpse of one who had died en route to the soup.

An old man collapses in the gutter with hunger. No one looks.

A child sits propped up against a wall, covered with sores and lice bites and burning with fever, moaning pitifully. No one looks.

Loudspeakers boom. '*Achtung!* All Jews in Group Fourteen will report tomorrow to the Jewish Civil Authority at 0800 promptly for deportation for volunteer labor. Failure to report for volunteer labor is punishable by death.'

The 'kings' from the Big Seven with flour and meat and vegetables make their barters quietly, in whispers against the walls, in the alcoves, in the courtyards.

A Nazi sergeant from Sieghold Stutze's Reinhard Corps stands in the middle of Zamenhof Street. Bike rikshas, the basic mode of transportation, swirl around him. Each riksha comes to a halt before the 'master' and doffs his cap and bows.

Clang! Clang! The bulging red and yellow streetcar with the big Star of David on its front and sides.

'*Achtung*! Jews, listen! Green ration stamps are hereby ruled invalid.'

Another corpse ... another ... another.

Billboards filled with directives. BY ORDER OF THE JEWISH CIVIL AUTHORITY the building at Gensia 33 is declared contaminated.

Walls hold torn corners of posters and publications of the underground press ripped down by the Jewish Militia.

The Jewish Militia. Fat and brutal, beating a herd of hapless girls with their clubs as they push them north to their destination in the Brushmaker's factory.

Chris doubled over in the seat before the desk in Susan Geller's office at the orphanage. His face was chalky, his stomach churning, ready to rebel at one more sight, one more smell.

Susan closed the door and stood over him. He stumbled to his feet.

'I'm sorry I couldn't get here sooner,' Chris said. 'I got back from the front and ran into a pile of trouble. You know it's very difficult for me to get in here.'

Susan was immobile, wordless.

'I tried to get Rosy back.'

'I'm sure you did everything you could,' she said coldly. 'It is just as well for him to be in the ghetto. With Ervin's Jewish nose, the hoodlums would always attack him, even with his fancy immunity papers.'

'Where is he, Susan?'

'We live at Mila 19 with the others.'

Chris grunted. 'Lord, I didn't even bring you a wedding present.'

'It isn't necessary.'

'Susan, is there anything I can do? Anything you want or need?'

She walked to the glass door which overlooked a sea of cots jammed together holding a hundred typhus-riddled children. Do? 'Surely that must be the understatement of all time.'

Her coldness reached him. 'Susan, what have I done?'

'Nothing, Chris. There is one thing you can do. It will be a very fine wedding present for me and Ervin. You know what kind of work Ervin does. I beg you not to betray him to the Germans.'

'I am sorry that you feel it necessary to say that to me.'

Susan turned on him. 'Please, Mr de Monti. No lectures about honor and humanity.'

'Rosy is my friend –'

'Horst von Epp is also your friend.'

Chris sank into the chair, shattered.

'I am sorry for the unpleasantries, Chris. These are unpleasant times. When a person is trying to survive he is apt to be rude to an old friend. Now, if you'll let me go back to work . . .'

'I want to see Deborah Bronski.'

'She isn't here.'

'She is here.'

'She doesn't want to see you.'

'She is going to have to.'

'I'll give her your message.'

'Susan, before you go . . . You've been close friends for many years –'

'We were the only two Jewesses allowed to study in a class of fifty nurses. We clung together for self-preservation.'

'Do you know about –'

'Ervin is my husband. He confides in me.'

'I have a chance to get her and her children out of Poland.'

Susan Geller turned from the door. Her homely face was clearly puzzled. There were many things she did not like about Christopher de Monti. There was something about him that reminded her of a Polish nobleman despite his loyalty to Ervin. The one thing she had no doubt about was his love for Deborah Bronski.

'Can you influence her?'

'I don't know,' Susan answered. 'Strange things happen to people under this pressure. Most people will do anything to survive. Many completely lose their souls, their sense of morality is shattered, they turn to weak masses of jelly. A very few seem to find sources of unbelievable strength. Deborah has become a single symbol of humanity to many dozens of children. I would say that a lesser woman would grab the chance to flee . . .'

'Tell her that I am waiting,' Chris said.

It took all the restraint he owned to contain the overpowering drive to sweep

Deborah into his arms. She was thin, and the signs of weariness were in her face. But she was more beautiful than he remembered. Her eyes spoke a compassion that one can gain only through suffering. They stood before each other with lowered heads.

'I have never stopped hungering for you for a minute in all these months,' Chris blurted.

'This is hardly the time or the place for a balcony scene,' she answered stiffly. 'I only agreed to see you to avoid an embarrassing argument.'

'All of this great pity you give. Is there none for me? Is there no word of consolation for the hours I've stood beneath the bridge praying to get a glimpse of you? Is there no iota of sympathy for all those nights I've drunk myself into a stupor from loneliness?'

The hardness flowed out of her. She had been cruel. She sat down and folded her hands in her lap, and they rested like a Mona Lisa's.

'Listen to me without haste or anger,' Chris pleaded. 'I can get you and the children safely out of Poland.'

Deborah blinked her eyes and frowned as though she really did not comprehend what he was saying. She stole a glance at him.

'Do you understand what I am saying?'

'There's so much work here. Every day we lose two or three or four of our babies.'

'Deborah, your own people encourage escape. It is no sin. You owe the gift of life to your children.'

She became confused; she tried to piece together a line of logic. 'My children are strong. We will fight this out as a family. Rachael and I have work . . .'

He knelt before her. 'Listen to me. I was at the capture of Kiev. Within a week after the German army entered, Special Action Kommandos rounded up nearly thirty-five thousand Jews. They were dragged out of basements and closets and barns. The Ukrainians helped hound them down for an extra ration of meat. Then they were marched to a suburb called Babi-Yar – Grandmother's Pits. A thousand at a time they were stripped naked – men, women, children. They were lined up at the edge of the pits and shot in the back. Then bayoneted, then covered with lime – then another thousand were marched in. Thirty-three thousand in three days, and the Ukrainians cheered every time the guns went off. An insanity has taken over the Germans.'

Deborah was glassy-eyed with disbelief.

'I saw it with my own eyes!'

'Paul will keep us alive.'

'Paul has brought you to this. He has dishonored himself and sold himself to them so completely, they will never let him out alive.'

'Paul has only done this for us!'

'You don't believe that yourself. He has done it for Paul. Now, listen. You're leaving. I'll have you picked up and forced out beyond your choice before I'd let you die.'

'You'll never touch me again.'

Chris nodded and stood. 'I know that,' he said weakly. 'I have already resigned myself to the fact that I will never see you. I know that there can never be a life for us if Paul is left here. That doesn't matter to me – all I want is for you to live.'

'I can't leave him,' Deborah said.

'Ask him! I think he will let you and your son and daughter die before he faces this alone here.'

'That's not true.'

'Ask him!'

Deborah tried to push her way to the door, but Chris grabbed her arms with a vise-like grip. She started a useless resistance. Then she stiffened.

'I'll haunt you, Deborah. Every day and every night I'm waiting beyond the wall.'

'Let me go!'

'Haven't we been punished enough? Do you want the death of your children as part of the penance too?'

'Please, Chris,' she begged.

'Tell me you don't love me and you're free of me.'

Deborah leaned against him and put her head on his chest and sobbed softly, and his strong arms folded about her gently. 'That is my greatest sin,' she cried, 'still loving you.'

Chris's arms were empty. He watched her disappear among the cots in the ward.

Paul dozed in the overstuffed chair. She was sick with worry about him since the Germans closed the Civil Authority and moved their headquarters to the big ghetto at Zamenhof and Gensia, in the former ghetto post office. They would have to move soon, too, she was certain. House by house, the Germans were emptying the little ghetto on the south.

Deborah watched him over the top of her book. Sometimes his mind would go blank in the middle of a sentence and he would stare aimlessly, then try to mumble his way back to reality. He wanted to sleep, only to sleep. He was taking greater doses of pills to block from his mind the torment of the German directives.

The children never said it, but she knew. She knew they were ashamed of him.

God, why did I have to see Chris? No rational human being could avoid being swayed by the thought of leaving this chamber of horrors. There was less and less she could do about the wails of the pitiful ragamuffins. Babi-Yar . . . Would it happen in Warsaw? Did she have the right to deny a try for life for Stephan and Rachael?

She doubted that Rachael would leave. She had sent her own daughter to a woman's bed at the age of seventeen. She felt it would be the greater sin to yield to society's dogmas of morality and find some morning the boy was gone forever and her child bear a lonely and unfulfilled cross. They had so little and so little time. But Rachael would not leave the boy. Deborah knew that as surely as she knew she would not leave Paul.

Perhaps she should send Stephan away by himself. He was a tenacious little boy, so much like his Uncle Andrei. So eager to fight. He would rebel.

Suppose she asked Paul. Would he let them go, or would he let them die first? Was Paul's weakness for survival at any price so consuming that he would bring his family to doom out of sheer fear?

Paul blinked his eyes open and saw Deborah's black eyes searching him questioningly.

'I must have dozed,' he said groggily. 'Dear, what is it? Why do you look at me that way?'

She started at the realization that she had not heard him.
'Is something wrong, Deborah? Is there something you want to ask?'
'No,' she said. 'I have the answer.'

Chapter Thirty

Journal Entry

If you want to be in movies,
You don't have to travel far,
The ghetto is like Hollywood,
All here, have a STAR.

COMPLIMENTS OF CRAZY NATHAN

Ervin Rosenblum has done a magnificent job as cultural secretary of Orphans and Self-Help. We now have a full Ghetto Symphony Orchestra, fifteen theatrical productions in Yiddish and Polish, a secret school for both primary education and religious training in each orphanage; art exhibitions, debates, poetry readings, etc., etc. Several individual artists perform in roving troupes. Most well known is Rachael Bronski, who has made her debut with the symphony playing Chopin's Second Concerto. She is called the 'Angel of the Ghetto.' A pity Emanuel Goldman was not there to see her great talent.

But ... our situation continues to degenerate. The death rate, mainly from typhus and starvation, climbs upward: July, 2200; August, 2650; September, 3300; October, 3800. So far in November, 150 a day. Strange, the suicide rate continues to drop. Conclusion: The weaker ones have killed themselves already. The rest are determined to survive. Each morning families deposit new corpses on the sidewalk. No money for funerals. The 'sanitation teams' come along with hand pushcarts, shovel the corpses up, twenty or thirty to a cart, and wheel them to the cemetery for burial in mass graves. The spectacle of death and starvation no longer impresses anyone. We must immunize ourselves. How crass.

Food comes in daily to Transferstelle. There is simply not enough to feed everyone. The Big Seven has shoved prices so high, Orphans and Self-Help is barely able to get bare minimum rations. The Big Seven has a virtual control on the licensed bakeries. The bakers are the 'kings' of the ghetto.

Smuggling has become a way of life. No one can stop it. Napoleon tried and failed. The Germans cannot stop it. Even if they were scrupulous and honest, it would be impossible. Every guard is corrupt, Jewish Militia on the inside, the Polish Blues and the Germans on the outside. They all 'play' for the right price. Why should the Germans even try to stop smuggling? Payoff money is lining the pockets of their top officials.

Smuggling runs from primitive forms to highly organized operations. In its most basic form, small, quick children dart about and move through small cracks in (or one of a half dozen tunnels under) the ghetto wall. Some of these children are sole providers for their families. They risk going into the Aryan side to scavenge in the garbage cans, barter if they have anything to barter, beg at the squares, or steal. One poor child was stuck in a crack in the wall. He was beaten by police on both sides of the wall.

The main transfer point of smuggled goods is outside the ghetto where the Jewish and Catholic cemeteries have a common wall. It has been breached in a dozen places and is a sort of 'free trading zone.' Grave-diggers who work the detail for mass graves are the main contact people. However, one must be in the upper bracket of smugglers to work the cemeteries.

Needless to say, the Big Seven has the most profitable and highly organized operation. They have paid off all down the line. However, every once in a while the Germans put on a show and catch a Big Seven smuggler and shoot him. It makes Kleperman appear not to be in league with the Germans. I'm certain he knows in advance.

The Big Seven built an underground pipe under the wall to pipe in milk from the Aryan side. Sacks of flour and other goods are thrown over the wall at given times in given places. Portable ladders come up out of nowhere, go against the wall, and in three or four minutes, while the guard turns his back, in come the goods. The Big Seven has even constructed a portable ramp and brought in a live cow on it.

Epitome of the smuggler's art is the large funeral (which only the wealthy can afford). The Big Seven controls the undertaking licenses. Their funeral vans always re-enter the ghetto with a ton or so of goods. When business is slow, I hear the Big Seven stages fake funerals with empty coffins.

To control prices, the Big Seven sells only part of its goods; a shortage raises prices. Food is stored all over the ghetto in basements. I hear that Mila 18, directly across the street from us, holds one of the largest caches. An 'independent' smuggler, Moritz Katz, runs a band from Mila 18.

Oddity. Along Leszno Street is the freak boundary of the 'Polish corridor.' The wall slices the courthouse in half, so it can be entered from both sides. Jews enter from the ghetto through a basement. Poles use the main entrance on the Aryan side. Meetings are held in certain chambers, offices, and corridors. Kleperman's 'authorized' representatives have space in the courthouse much like one buys a seat on the Stock Exchange (or a London prostitute has a station). For a broker's fee, Kleperman's 'authorized' representatives trade gold, dollars, and precious stones.

The most horrible of all sights in the ghetto are the 'snatchers.' Starved children prowl near the bakeries and, driven by hunger, grab bread from people as they leave. They eat it on the run. Often children have been beaten half to death while cramming the bread into their bellies.

The Good Fellowship Club appointed a special committee to analyze the always elusive mystery of what the Germans are really up to. Information from the massacres in the east. There are definitely four main groups of 'Action Kommandos,' SS men trained for massacre.

Group A. Commanded by SS Major General Franz Stahlecker in the Baltic-Leningrad area.

Group B. Commanded by SS General Artur Nebe, White Russia.

Group C. Otto Rasch (rank?) in Kiev on the southern front. The Babi-Yar massacre of thirty-three thousand in three days seems to be his brain child.

Group D. SS Major General Otto Ohlendorf (is he the noted engineer of pre-war times? Hard to believe) in central Russia.

The method is basic. Roundup, victims dig their own graves, are stripped, shot in the back. This apparently amuses the local populations, who are giving full co-operation. The SS have augmented their ranks with Ukrainians and Lithuanians.

Reports of massacres so far at Rovno, Dvinsk, Kovno, and Riga. They say seventy thousand have been shot at Wilno.

We are trying to determine what the shifts in general German policy are and how these massacres will apply to us in Warsaw and the General Government Area. Have the Germans established the number of people they will need to run their slave-labor factories? Obviously the action groups were formed in advance of the invasion of Russia.

Ervin Rosenblum develops the theory of the German 'apologetics.' They go to extraordinary lengths to prove their 'innocence' and establish their 'justifications.' This, of course, means they know they are doing something evil and feel they must cover their tracks.

The German language has been bastardized by the Nazis with their 'joy through labor' ... 'Aryan-master race' ... 'land to live' ... 'German destiny' ... 'the true ones' ... 'folk people' ... 'führer' ... 'inhuman treatment of ethnics,' etc., etc.

The whole text on behavior toward Jews also has been compounded in this new 'language.' The basic 'theory' is that the Jews have always been the enemies of the German people and are therefore trying to destroy them, so the Germans must destroy the Jews purely out of 'self-defense.' They point up to the economic competition with classic portraits of the cunning Jew who has 'always hated the German' and robs the German of his right to make a living.

Here are examples of their new double-meaning language:

Reservation – ghetto.

Legitimate war booty – wealth stolen or confiscated from Jews.

Contaminated – to be confiscated.

Sanitation measures – an excuse for mass executions.

Unpleasantness – the carrying out of mass murder.

Shot while trying to escape – a common phrase for someone killed in prison.

Resettlement – deportation with confiscation of all property.

Voluntary labor – slave labor.

Sub-humans – Jews, Slavs, gypsies, political and criminal prisoners, clergy, homosexuals (other than German), and others unfit to breathe Aryan air.

Mongrelization – the excuse to 'get rid of sub-humans' who will contaminate the pure German blood lines.

Bolshevik-profiteer-warmonger – almost always used before or behind the word 'Jew' to pound in the identification.

Now then, theorizes Silberberg, the playwright, the Germans go to fantastic trouble to make themselves truly believe what they are saying. The verbal acrobatics are played out. Basis: In order to live in the ghetto, one must break the law. Therefore, everyone who is alive is a criminal in the German lexicon and can legally be executed. Incredible?

Here are some of their 'proofs':

They will go to great trouble to hold a kangaroo court trial, documented fully, to punish a common thief or vagrant. They will make an exhaustive investigation over a single typhus death to 'prove' their interest in human lives. They will show 'shock' at the brutality of the Jewish Militia, which must be brutal to enforce their rule.

They allowed a few schools to reopen to 'prove' German love of freedom of education. Because we are unable to support many schools, have no textbooks, fuel, facilities, and the children are too sick and weak to attend, this 'proves' the sub-human Jews will not educate their children.

Ghettos have been made to 'isolate' the warmongers and filthy Jews from the Poles.

And to protect the Jews from the vengeance of the Poles once the Poles understood what the Jews had brought upon them.

More 'proof' of the German case: Special SS film units have entered the ghetto. They film the delousing sheds. Have you ever seen a man fifty pounds underweight, freezing cold, and hairless? German narration shows this is a 'sub-human' disease carrier, and the appearance portrays just that.

Bearded rabbis are forced to pose in the warehouses at Transferstelle beside tons of food while the narration 'proves' how the Gestapo located secret caches which these old bearded Jews hoarded while their neighbors starved.

The Jewish Militia is always willing to oblige with a show of brutality which, when captured on film, finds the obvious commentary of Jew destroying Jew.

Their prize exhibits are the smugglers' orgies. The smugglers are mostly men of low mentality, lower morality. At their clubs they gladly pose gorging food, drinking, brawling, in orgies with prostitutes. The Germans then plant garbage cans filled with scraps outside the clubs and photograph beggar children clawing around in them.

Most sinister move in the German master plan is the creation of the illusion that the Jews are doing all this to one another. The dregs of society in the Jewish Militia, the emasculated Jewish Civil Authority, the smugglers. This is 'final vindication' for the Germans – of themselves.

What is next on the Nazi blueprint? Who knows? Nothing out of Berlin comes in the form of written orders (further indication of their knowledge of their evil). SS General Alfred Funk carries it all in verbally. Two phrases in the German lexicon appear more and more. We do not know what they mean and they terrify us.

1. En route to unknown destination.

2. Final solution of the Jewish problem.

ALEXANDER BRANDEL

Only a man of Rabbi Solomon's stature would dare risk walking the ghetto streets alone at midnight. He turned the corner into Mila Street in a half trot, then slowed to a walk when his ancient legs rebelled, then took up the trot again.

At Mila 19 he grunted up the steps and pounded on the door. The girl on night watch opened it, alarmed. 'Rabbi, what are you doing out this hour of night?'

'Where is Alexander Brandel?' he gasped, fighting to regain his wind.

'Come in.'

Through Alex's office, down the corridor to the basement landing. The girl scratched a match and lit a candle and took the old man's hand. They went down a step at a time. The stairs creaked beneath their weight. He squinted to adjust his eyes to the sudden blackness. The basement was musty and dark. An aisle cut through two rows of packing cases all marked with supplies for the Orphans and Self-Help Society. She led him down the row and stopped before a particular crate some four feet in height. She knocked on the case with six short raps, then pulled open a false door, lowered her head, and entered the secret room where Alexander and Ervin Rosenblum looked up from the voluminous notes being prepared for entry in the journal.

'Rabbi! What on earth ...'

'The news! I have just heard the news on the radio. America is in the war!'

BOOK THREE

Night

Chapter One

Journal Entry

Since Pearl Harbor, events have occurred with stunning rapidity. Our first natural impulse of gladness has faded to bitter reality. America is being badly beaten in the Pacific. Suddenly we are cut off from our main source of income, American Aid. Our cash reserve can only hold us for days. We are frantically trying to find new avenues of revenue.

Two days after Pearl Harbor, detachments of Waffen SS from Trawniki Concentration Camp carried out a swift roundup raid at our farm at Wework. In a fell swoop we have lost fifty of the cream of our youth. Was I wrong to keep the farm in operation, knowing this might happen? Where could we have put fifty extra people at Mila 19? I do not know. After the roundup they were put on a cattle car (along with a trainload of deportees from the Baltics).

Then unfolds a most unusual tale. The train took a crooked, uncertain course toward Germany. Obviously slave labor at the end of the line. By some miracle, Ana Grinspan was working in the ghetto of Czenstochowa at the time the train stopped there. (Second thought, Czenstochowa is quite a site of miracles; i.e., Christian versions. This is the home of the 'Black Madonna,' the 'Luminous Mountain,' and the 'Miracle of the Mount.') Ana (traveling as the Aryan Tanya Tartinski) learned somehow that there were Bathyrans in one of the cattle cars. She followed the train into Germany. The internees were put up at a temporary relocation camp near Dresden. Ana entered the lager armed with false papers, a tall story, and Jewish hutzpah *and managed to bring out Tolek Alterman and ten of our youngsters.*

This girl, Ana Grinspan, is fantastic! This is the fourth time she has crossed into Germany, walked into concentration camps, and freed key people. Her own story is recorded fully in Volume 4A of the journal. Someday when it is read I wonder if her exploits will be believed?

Tolek and Ana got back here to Warsaw. Tolek immediately went to work for Andrei. The other ten who escaped are scattered. Shall we ever hear from them again? Or the ones in the Dresden lager?

Tolek tells one story of the trip into Germany that I must record here. The train was all open cars; everyone half froze to death. It was a torturous, stop-and-start trip. It took three days to reach the town of Radomsk near the German border, where they stopped again at a siding to give priority to a military train for the eastern front. Dozens of curious peasants gathered about the train. Our people, who had not eaten or drunk for three days, were near dead with thirst. They begged the peasants to pass

them a few handfuls of snow to quench the thirst. The peasants first made them throw out their rings, money, and valuables. Then ... they got a handful of snow.

Mira and Minna Farber were captured on the Aryan side of Warsaw along with our major contact, Romek. Both girls died under torture at Gestapo House. Romek is still alive, but I understand he is blind and badly crippled. This shatters our major contact on the Aryan side. I am sick about the Farber girls. They were wonderful, sweet, quiet girls. Twenty-two or -three, I believe. Cursed with non-Jewish faces which made them natural 'runners.' Thank God their parents are both gone.

Ana Grinspan is staying in Warsaw to try to reset our shattered runner system. Things are black in Krakow, anyhow. Bathyran House was raided and the underground press there seized.

The day after our farm was raided at Wework all the Toporol farms were closed. We lost several hundred of our best people and irreplaceable food supplies.

A.B.

Wolf Brandel, eighteen, wisened and toughened, became the first lieutenant of Andrei Androfski. Although Andrei and Alexander made peace with each other, a certain coolness had developed between them.

Alexander had enough of a sense of history to realize that the initiative and his philosophy were slowly slipping from his control. Andrei's approach to resistance was creeping over them. From time to time Alexander held a line, but if Andrei pressed an issue he retrenched. At first Alexander would permit no illegal activity at Mila 19. Now Andrei demanded a second secret room in the basement of Mila 19 be dug for the manufacture and storage of arms. Alex avoided a showdown, afraid of the growing power that Andrei could gather behind him. He allowed the room to be built.

This second room was carved out so that it ran beneath the center of Mila Street. Andrei brought in Jules Schlosberg, a pre-war chemist of note, for the purpose of creating weapons which could be made cheaply with accessible components. Jules' first weapon was a bottle bomb requiring only low-grade fuel, a wick, and a plastic detonation cap. It was a foolproof fire bomb. Next Schlosberg worked to perfect a more complicated weapon: a grenade which could be built inside the casing of an eight-inch length of water pipe and exploded by contact percussion.

On the Aryan side, arms were difficult to obtain. As soon as they came into demand, the price spiraled. The Home Army had the money and the contacts to corner the market. Roman evaded the frantic efforts of Simon Eden and the Jews to obtain a share of weapons.

Each purchase of a pistol became a large, involved project. A weapon such as a rifle was almost unheard of. A machine gun did not exist. For his arsenal Andrei concentrated on Schlosberg's 'inventions,' which were manufactured by Bathyrans in hidden rooms around the ghetto. While Rodel, the Communist, co-operated on matters of Self-Help, he was jealous of his arms sources. The Revisionists at Nalewki 37 remained aloof on both self-help and arms. Andrei was able to obtain ten pistols of six different calibers, each with only a dozen rounds of ammunition. Although it seemed completely ridiculous in the face of a German army that had conquered all of the world it sought, Andrei was content with his work and had a rather pleasant attitude that at the right time and the right place his microscopic might would cause a mighty roar.

Andrei's main source of pistols was a small ordnance shed near the main train depot on Jerusalem Boulevard, where wounded German officers were transferred from the eastern front back to Germany. Their sidearms were checked in for reissue, and in a rush a few could conveniently be 'lost' by the German sergeant in charge of the detail.

Immediately after American Aid folded, Alexander Brandel got a radio message to the two Jewish members of the Polish government in exile in London, Artur Zygielboim and Ignacy Schwartzbart, with a plea for emergency funds. A message in Hebrew was radioed back using passages in the Bible as reference to advise them that the funds were being flown in by British aircraft and would be parachuted to the Home Army. A later confirmation of the parachute drop came, and Tolek Alterman was dispatched from the ghetto into the Aryan side to receive the money from Roman.

When Alterman returned to the ghetto, Andrei and Ana Grinspan were called to Alexander Brandel's office.

Tolek came in and took off his worker's cap, appearing strange to them, as they had not yet adjusted to the shaved head. The long floppy hair that had been his trademark had been ordered shorn to give him a more Aryan appearance.

Tolek dramatically placed a bundle of American dollar bills on Alexander's desk. 'I was only able to get one third of the amount that was parachuted in for us,' he announced.

Alex's face sagged.

Andrei sat with his legs stretched out, the heel of one boot balanced on the toe of the other. He stared at the tip of his toe.

'That arrogant son of a bitch Roman,' Tolek snorted in growing rage.

'Don't waste your time chewing up the furniture, Tolek,' Andrei said softly. 'The fact that you were able to contact that bastard Roman and even get him to admit he received the money, much less turn any of it over to you, was an accomplishment.'

'I'll tell you why he turned over part of it,' Ana Grinspan said. 'So we would not stop future parachute drops. Roman knows that so long as we get a crumb we'll keep the money coming.'

Alex rubbed his temples, tried to think. 'We need more so badly. When will the British fly in more?'

'Ten days. Two weeks,' Andrei answered. 'As quickly as it arrives from America.'

'Then, Andrei, we have to get one of our people there when it is dropped.'

'Forget it. Roman won't permit that. Take what he gives us and keep our mouths shut.'

'But we can't hold the line,' Alex cried. He was about to accuse Andrei of skimming too much off for his fool weapons inventions in the basement but thought better of it. 'Dave Zemba told me this morning that he has a plan to obtain zlotys here in the ghetto,' he said with desperation in his voice. 'But we must have the other money.'

'One thing is obvious,' Ana Grinspan said. 'With Romek gone, we must have a new contact on the Aryan side. As soon as we do we must get in direct contact with our people in London and arrange our own drops.'

Andrei looked up from the toe of his boot, sensing Ana's thoughts, anticipating her next words. She stood over him. 'What about Gabriela Rak?' she asked.

Andrei did not flick an eye. He shrugged. Why not?' he said. 'I'll ask her.'

He left the meeting knowing what he must do. Andrei had always felt that someday he must lose Gabriela, that his time with her was borrowed time. When the ghetto was formed he knew, too, that it would be only a matter of time before someone brought up her name for underground work. The moment had arrived. He had carefully rehearsed for it so that when her name was mentioned he would show no evidence of concern.

Andrei sat alone in his flat, meditating and gathering himself for the task ahead. He began collecting memories of her from that first moment at the grand ball of the Ulanys. It was so very long ago. He had been sitting right here at this table reading – what was it? – Steinbeck, when Gabriela came through the door and begged for the right to love him. And he remembered all the individual episodes of the warmth and comfort always there when he plunged into depths of despair.

The next day, still showing no outward sign to his friends, he went to the basement of Mila 19 where Jules Schlosberg had completed his first pipe grenade. Andrei, of course, was most anxious to test the weapon somewhere in an open field away from the ghetto. He tied the pipe to his left forearm. It had been designed so that it could be hidden on a man, fitted between the elbow and wrist. He told Ana that he would see Gabriela about setting up her place on Shucka Street as a contact point, then left the ghetto.

At Gabriela's apartment, the moment he saw her he thought he would falter. She wore that same expression that told of the strain of listening for him, anxiety, relief at the sight of him. The weak smile. The trembling embrace. When she touched him he thought he would die before being able to go through with it.

'Come, dear,' she said, 'I have some dinner.'

'Sorry. I can't stay.'

'You'll be back later tonight?'

'No.'

'You look so strange, Andrei. What is it?'

'I want to talk to you about something.' He managed to look placid, almost bored. 'We've had to do a lot of reorganizing. It's getting more and more difficult for me to get in and out of the ghetto. Today I had to tag onto a labor battalion going out as a road gang. Anyhow, everyone feels I should stay in the ghetto,' he lied. 'Besides, it's getting extremely dangerous for me to see you. It would be only a matter of time until I'm trailed here.'

'Then I'll come into the ghetto with you, of course,' she said.

'Well, as a matter of fact, that wouldn't be suitable.'

'You never did make a good liar,' she said. 'What's really on your mind?'

'This is the last time I'll be seeing you, Gaby. I came to say good-by. It's not easy –'

'Why? I have a right to know.'

'I don't want a scene.'

'I assure you there will be no scene.'

He sucked in a deep breath. 'Ana has been in Warsaw since a week after Pearl Harbor. We've had a lot of business together and naturally have been seeing a lot of each other.'

'Go on.'

'I wish you wouldn't insist.'

'I do insist.'

'Very well. The night that Romek and the Farber sisters were taken to

Gestapo House she was at my flat. Ana was pretty tired and upset, as you can imagine. Well, one thing led to another ...'

Andrei watched Gabriela's back stiffen with the hurt from his words and he watched her eyes grow watery. 'I don't have to draw you a diagram. You know that Ana and I were once ... Well, she's older and better now. All things equal, it is a very good arrangement for both of us.'

He stopped when she abruptly slapped his face. Then he shrugged. 'I don't see why you have to take that attitude. Frankly, let's admit it. We are getting a little tired of each other. At least I am. Well, that's life. We should be civilized and shake hands and wish each other luck. After all ...'

'Get out!'

Andrei walked briskly down the street, knowing that her eyes were on his back. He turned the corner out of her sight and stopped and leaned against the building and touched the place where she had slapped him and choked back the tears. Insurmountable grief overcame him, and he sank to a sitting position on the pavement and dropped his head into his arms, which were drawn around his knees.

'Drunk,' several people commented, passing him by.

A pair of Polish Blue policemen hovered over him. 'Get to your feet,' one ordered, prodding him with the club.

'Leave me alone,' Andrei mumbled, 'just leave me alone.'

They bent down on either side of him, grabbed him under the armpits, and pulled him to his feet. 'Let's see your *Kennkarte*!'

Andrei grabbed them by the scruffs of their necks and banged their heads together. Both of them reeled about, bloody and half-senseless. Andrei staggered down the street, blinded by his own tears.

Across the street a pair of German soldiers crisscrossed in square movements before the iron gates of the home of a high Nazi. Andrei became aware of the pipe grenade tied to his arm. His right hand fished up the sleeve of his left arm and pulled it free.

He waited until the Germans approached each other and timed his throw to hit at their feet as they crossed. The pipe arched end over end, hit the sidewalk, gave one short clatter. Then a flash and a racket and then screams.

Ana waited in Andrei's flat. His dazed eyes, his incoherent movement alarmed her.

'Andrei!'

He shook his head hard, spiraling back to reality.

'What happened? What's wrong? What did she say?'

Andrei lurched for the cabinet holding his hoard of a half bottle of vodka. A stiff drink straightened him up. 'What would you expect her to say when I broke in unannounced and found her and her Polish lover rolling around on the bed?'

'Oh, Andrei! I am sorry.'

'Never mind – never mind. I've been suspecting it for a long time. No matter. Tomorrow I'll go out and start setting up other contacts.'

In the days after, Andrei suffered a torment he did not realize existed. Throughout the nights he sulked in agony, trying to find a secret source of strength to keep him from crawling back to Gabriela. He was unable to eat. He became weak. He slept only when drugged exhaustion came over him, and his sleep was in snatches filled with teasing, hurting dreams. Each memory of his Gabriela plunged him to a new depth of torment. He moved about the ghetto with a listlessness that matched the listlessness of life around him. It was as though the will to live had left him for the first time.

A few days before Christmas, Andrei dragged himself up the stairs to his flat.

Gabriela Rak stood behind the table. He had seen her in dreams with haunting reality. But now – a hallucination in the middle of the day! The end was coming. He knew he was losing his mind. The vision refused to disappear. 'Gaby?' he said, half frightened.

'Yes,' she answered in a voice so crisp as to dispel the illusion.

'What the hell are you doing in the ghetto!' he roared. 'How did you get in?'

'You are not the sole custodian of cleverness in the human race.'

'I demand to know –'

'Kindly don't shout.'

'– how you got in.'

'I work for the Ursuline Sisters, remember? The convent has a church. My good friend Father Kornelli is the priest. Father Kornelli told me that Father Jakub at the Convert's Church needed more candles for Christmas day, so I volunteered to bring them. Wasn't that nice of me?'

Suddenly Andrei felt the presence of someone else in the flat. He turned his eyes slowly to the kitchen. Ana stood in the doorway. 'Hello, Andrei,' she said.

He looked from Ana to Gabriela to Ana to Gabriela. He turned crimson. Caught red-handed!

'Really, Andrei,' Ana said, 'you have become a frightful liar. I should be angry, for you assault my honor.'

'Which do you think is worse, Ana, Andrei's story about you and him or the story about me rolling around in bed with my Polish lover?'

'Actually, both are corkers. By the way, Andrei, did you ever get around to telling Jules Schlosberg that his grenade works? Fortunately for us, the Gestapo has blamed it on Home Army.'

'All right – all right,' Andrei said, 'enough fun. Ana, tell Gaby how Mira and Minna Farber died.'

The mood of foolery burst.

'Go on, tell her, Ana. No? Well, I will. After the Gestapo finished with them they were turned over to the Reinhard Corps barracks for sport. Stutze led the parade. A hundred more of his sportsmen followed. They continued raping them for hours after they were dead. Raping their corpses. Ana sent me to ask you to take their place in Warsaw.'

'That would never happen to me, dear. I carry a vial of poison.'

'I don't want any of it to happen to you. None of it!'

'You're shouting again.'

'Ana, for God's sake – tell her.'

'I'll tell *you*, Andrei,' Gabriela said. 'I'll tell you I have watched the only man I have ever loved come to me time after time after time with his heart eaten away because of the indifference of the Polish people. I am ashamed and I am humiliated for the way they have turned their backs on this terrible thing. Now you ask me, too, to be indifferent. I am going to carry my share of this. I am going to work with Ana, whether you forbid it or not.'

Andrei turned his back on both of them and stared glumly, blankly, out of the window.

'I guess you don't need me here,' Ana whispered to Gabriela. Gabriela saw her to the door. They touched cheeks and she left. Gaby drew the bolt on the door and walked to the center of the room. Andrei continued his sulking for a long, long time, berating himself for the rotten break he had given Gabriela by ever meeting her. Finally he turned around.

Gabriela had taken her dress off. It lay on the floor at her feet. She whisked her slip over her head in a delicate motion and let it crumple on top of her dress.

'Why, Andrei, you're blushing.'

'For God's sake, this is no time for ...'

She retreated to the bed and lay down and beckoned him with her forefinger. 'Come,' she said, 'let me show you how I take care of my other lover.'

Andrei Androfski surrendered unconditionally.

It was night. Gabriela came out of her sleep laughing. Andrei sat up, startled. When his heart stopped racing he turned to her. 'What's so damned funny at two o'clock in the morning?'

'I forgot to deliver the candles to Father Jakub!'

And Andrei roared. 'Hell! They're only converts. In a pinch they can dekosherize some of Rabbi Solomon's stock.'

They settled into each other's arms and spoke with that particular endearment known only to those who are very much in love and who feel they have discovered something unique in the universe.

'We have had something, Gaby. More than most people have in a lifetime.'

'There is only one Andrei Androfski. He makes me very sad and he makes me very happy, but I am so glad he is mine. I have more wonderment – more fulfillment – than a hundred ordinary women have in their hundred ordinary lives.'

'No regrets?'

'No regrets. I have been happier with you than a woman has a right to expect.'

'I feel that way about you, Gaby. I wonder why God has been so good to me.'

'Promise me, Andrei, you'll never again try to send me away.'

'I promise – never again.'

'Because I am prepared to take anything. Whatever lies ahead, we go it together, and if the very worst comes, I am happy.'

'Oh, Gabriela ... Gabriela ... Gabriela ...'

'Love ... love ... love ... love ...'

Chapter Two

Journal Entry

Gabriela Rak has given us all a shot in the arm. Why didn't we use her earlier? I guess because Andrei tried to shield her. A natural, forgivable impulse. Her first action was to have Father Kornelli organize a dozen young priests about Warsaw who agreed not to register the deaths in their parishes with the authorities. In this way Gabriela (through the priests) can purchase the Kennkarten *from the families of the deceased. We estimate in the neighborhood of twenty thousand hidden Jews on the Aryan side. With Aryan* Kennkarten *they can at least get ration books.*

The Ursuline Sisters have always been sympathetic and have taken as many children from us as they possibly can. They have enlisted similar help from the Sisters of the Order of the Lady Immaculate and the Sisters Szarytki of the municipal hospitals in Warsaw.

Gaby has rented flats for three more of our runners (code names: Victoria, Regina, Alina), whose main job is to supply money to hidden Jews.

Andrei tells me her flat on Shucha Street contained a windowless alcove two meters deep. A bookcase was built across it on hinges. Andrei says it is impossible to detect there is a hidden room behind the bookcase.

Zygielboim and Schwartzbart in London radioed us that fifteen thousand dollars had been dropped for us to the Home Army. Tolek Alterman was able to get only $1650. We have put an urgent priority on establishing our own direct contact with England.

Gabriela traveled to Gdynia (where her father was a key engineer in building the port) to see an old friend, Count Rodzinski. He is almost unique, a sympathetic nobleman. His estate includes several kilometers of coast line and he owns several boats. He made a successful trial run to Karlskrona, Sweden. This could be an enormous break for us. From his estate we can smuggle out key people, and from Sweden we can bring in American funds as well as visas and passports. (Our forgeries here are expensive and crude.)

What could we accomplish with a thousand Poles like Gabriela Rak – or a hundred – or two dozen?

ALEXANDER BRANDEL

Of the two, Father Kornelli was far more nervous than Gabriela Rak as they sat in the anteroom of the office of Archbishop Klondonski. The room had a bare, cold, dark, musty appearance. The walls were lined with expressionless statues.

Father Kornelli was young and highly excitable, one of a handful of priests moved to action by the happenings in the ghetto. To him it was a simple basic rule that the saving of lives was the carrying out of Christ's work.

Monsignor Bonifacy opened the door to the archbishop's office. 'His Grace will see you now.'

Archbishop Klondonski studied them from behind his desk. He was a square, squat man with blond hair, blue eyes, and rugged features that revealed his Slavic peasant ancestry. He was deceptively simple in appearance.

The monsignor, on the other hand, was a thin, gaunt man with slender, even delicate features and dark, penetrating eyes which hinted a shrewd, probing mind.

Gabriela and Father Kornelli kissed the archbishop's ring, and he waved them into chairs opposite him. Monsignor Bonifacy slipped into a chair across the room, watching, listening, unnoticed.

'Gabriela Rak!' Klondonski said expansively, in the manner of a politician running for office. 'By chance the daughter of Fryderyk Rak?'

'Yes, sir.'

'A fine man. A great Pole. I remember him when he was one of the engineers building the port of Gdynia. I was a young priest at the time, not much older than Father Kornelli. Gdynia was my first parish.'

Gabriela studied his open pleasantness and calculated it was a ruse with which he disarmed his visitors.

'If I am not mistaken,' the churchman continued, 'he met an untimely death in Switzerland.'

'Your Grace has a phenomenal memory.'

'And your mother – and sister, was it?'

'They live in America.'

'A good place these days. Great Pole, your father. Now, tell me about yourself, young lady.'

'After finishing my schooling I returned to Warsaw and until the war I worked as an aide in the American Embassy. I am now teaching at the Ursuline Convent.'

'Ah, yes.' He leaned back in his chair, smiling like an amiable Friar Tuck, reasonably assured her request would be nominal and in the nature of a personal favor. 'And your problem, my child?'

'I am here to speak to Your Grace in behalf of the Jewish Orphans and Self-Help Society in the ghetto.'

The momentum of the conversation stopped. Klondonski's blue eyes lost their sweet sparkle. He covered his temporary puzzlement by tapping his fingertips together in mock meditation.

'There is imminent peril that thousands of children will die of starvation in the next few months unless immediate help is forthcoming.'

Bonifacy spoke quickly. 'Your Grace has studied the report on the situation.'

'Oh, yes,' he said, taking the cue. 'Yes, we have been concerned, naturally.'

'While His Grace expressed concern,' Bonifacy continued to refresh his superior's memory, 'and we concluded in our report that there are hardships in the ghetto, it is a reflection of the times in Poland.'

'Yes, my dear,' said Klondonski, 'we are all undergoing hardships.'

'It is difficult to comprehend,' Gabriela answered swiftly, 'that Your Grace could study an impartial report and fail to discern the difference between mass starvation and rampant disease in the ghetto and mere privation out here. People are dying off in there at a rate of over five thousand a month.'

Bonifacy spoke in a slow measured whisper now. 'Our reports are based on examinations of the ghettos in Poland by a responsible international body, a commission of the Swiss Red Cross. They will be in Warsaw again next week. To date their reports do not bear out your contentions. We feel that the Jews are inclined to a natural tendency to exaggerate.'

Gabriela looked to Father Kornelli for support. Willful cowardice? Closed minds? Fear? A crass expression of anti-Semitism?

'Your Grace ... Monsignor ...' Father Kornelli said unevenly. 'You must necessarily realize that any Swiss report is based on expediency and fear. While I do not have the details of their investigations I am quite certain they are seeing only what the Germans wish seen, listening only to those with whom the Germans will let them speak. Switzerland is vulnerable to German invasion and defenseless. They have everything to lose by getting the Germans angry. If you wish the truth, I suggest you call in Father Jakub, who heads our Convent's congregation inside the ghetto.'

'You *do* want the truth, Your Grace?' Gabriela asked bluntly.

The round Polish face of Archbishop Klondonski reddened. He did not want the truth. He simmered down and weighed his words with astute care, for his adversaries were sharp and persistent. 'We do have a natural humanitarian concern. Yet the Catholic Church is not a political body, a welfare agency, or an underground. Whether or not we like the present occupants of power is a moot point. The fact is, they do constitute the government of Poland. We have a clearly outlined duty to perform. We cannot enter the Church into any schemes in wholesale defiance of authority.'

'It seems to me, Your Grace, that our Church was born in defiance of the authority of Rome,' Gabriela said. 'If you would only see the cardinal in Krakow. If we could organize a thousand convents to take five children each ... If ...'

The archbishop held up his hand. 'I have closed my eyes and turned my back and shut my ears to those priests and nuns who have engaged in these activities. But my office is for the spiritual welfare –'

'Your Grace, this is basic Christianity we are pleading for.'

'– the spiritual welfare of the Polish people,' he finished, ignoring the interruption.

'Those are Polish people behind the wall.'

'Not really, Miss Rak. The fact of the matter is, we could do more for them if they agreed to conversion. Now, if they allowed us to give their children instructions in Catholicism –'

Gabriela came to her feet. 'Your Grace! I am shocked! You cannot demand what God has decided.'

'I will overlook your rudeness and forgive because of the tensions of the times. I suggest penance.'

What was left of Gabriela's restraint exploded. 'I will not forgive yours. And I suggest penance for you, sir! For every child who dies within your power of saving.'

The archbishop was on his feet, as was Monsignor Bonifacy. A frightened Father Kornelli knelt and kissed the archbishop's ring. He held it in Gabriela's direction.

She looked at his hand. 'You are not the representative of the Jesus Christ my father taught me of,' she said, and walked from the room.

Chapter Three

Journal Entry

Strange studies are being initiated. Dr Glazer told me six months ago that he had cancer and his time was limited. A few weeks ago he became very ill. Subsequent examination also revealed a severe case of malnutrition. Glazer has chosen to starve to death so that the Orphans and Self-Help doctors can initiate through him the world's first comprehensive medical study on starvation. There is a mania to have some good come out of even this basest form of human death. Each day the doctors meet and hold forums on the mental and physical changes of those dying of hunger. Most all of them have malnutrition themselves and discuss their own cases. (The full study of starvation is carried as a separate volume of the journal, 9A). Dr Glazer dictates his symptoms, his mental changes. The patterns are shrinking flesh, gauntness, skin changing color, weakness, running sores, depressions, hallucinations, gnarling bones, bloating stomachs. A Jewish gift to posterity – a detailed account of what it is like to starve to death.

Irony. This week a shipment of wheat and tons of potatoes poured in to Transferstelle and was distributed without cost to the orphanages. Our orphanage on Niska Street also received medicines we no longer thought existed and even chocolates (which no one has seen for two years). Then a school was licensed and textbooks arrived. The orphanage was painted; new bedding arrived. Then we discovered why we were being killed with kindness. Elaborate preparations were for the benefit of a delegation of Swiss from the International Red Cross who had arrived to investigate ghetto conditions. Our orphanage was designated as 'typical and representative.'

The Swiss carried out the sham to a T. They called a committee together at the Jewish Civil Authority building and called witnesses. The JCA, led by Boris Presser and Paul Bronski, dutifully testified to 'bettering-leveling' conditions. (Truth: December death by starvation went over 4000.) Silberberg, the last friend left on the JCA board, tried to get to the Swiss to give them the truth. He was hauled off to Pawiak Prison as a 'Bolshevik agitator.' I was invited to testify and declined. What could I say? Could I endanger these life-giving shipments when I know that the moment the Swiss leave it would all return to as before.

We decided to get Andrei over to the Aryan side to reach Christopher de Monti. It is known that De Monti is escorting the Swiss about Warsaw. Andrei reasoned that it would be better not to attempt to get to De Monti, for even if he were to turn in our report the Swiss would not submit it. It is doubtful the Swiss would stick their necks out or suddenly make overt moves in behalf of humanity. I conceded that Andrei was correct. The Swiss do not wish to anger the Germans. They treat the entire war with indifference. We hear of numerous examples of courage by the Danes, Dutch, French, et al.*, in behalf of their Jewish communities. Even the Swedes, who are neutral, are harboring thousands of Jewish refugees. Could it be that ghettos could exist only in Poland, the Baltics, and Ukrainia? Our Bathyrans in Hungary and Rumania tell us that Adolf Eichmann is even having trouble extracting the Jews there. Ervin Rosenblum works in the basement, filing more and more documents. It seems that everyone is writing diaries these days. There is a terrible fear that we will be forgotten.*

Jules Schlosberg continues to build weird weapons in the next room to Ervin. I am certain we'll be blown up someday.

ALEXANDER BRANDEL

It became dangerous in the streets in the winter of 1941 after the American entry into the war. The only regulars on the streets were the corpses deposited each morning for the sanitation squads. Even the sanctity of the Club Miami became suspect.

Andrei seldom showed up in public these days, so when a feeler was sent out by Paul Bronski for a meeting, Bronski was led through a series of blind alleys before he was finally allowed to come face to face with his brother-in-law in a basement somewhere near the Gensia Gate. Bronski's blindfold was removed. He adjusted his eyes to the candlelight.

Andrei stood over him, thinner and wearier. He studied Paul. Paul had aged with a sudden sagging of his face muscles. The thin face was prune-like, he shook with constant tension, and his fingers were yellow with tobacco stains.

They changed amenities without feeling.

Paul took out a cigarette and went through one-armed contortions of lighting it. 'This business of arms smuggling and underground press is putting the entire population in grave danger,' he said.

'Go on.'

'No matter what you think about us on the Civil Authority, we try our best under very limited conditions. If your activities increase it will only antagonize the Germans.'

'Shut up, Paul! For Christ sake – antagonize the Germans. Do you think this death on the streets is a result of any underground? Are you so damned naïve after two years of this as to think the population is in any less danger whether there is an underground or not?'

Bronski shook his head. 'I told Presser it was useless to argue with you. Andrei, there is no magic formula for getting rid of the Germans. Your activities are costing us millions of zlotys in fines and the lives of hundreds in reprisals.'

'And what about the fines and the executions before the underground existed?'

'I'm trying to do the best I can,' Paul whined.

Andrei could not even bring himself to hate Paul Bronski. Once, before the war, he had had a reluctant admiration for the penetrating mind and sharp wit that could run him through mental acrobatics. The thing before him was a mumbling shell.

How very strange, Andrei thought. Little Stephan Bronski had begun as a runner between the orphanage and the Self-Help headquarters over a year ago and increased his sphere of operation each month. The youngster idolized Wolf Brandel, who taught him the routes around the ghetto over rooftops, through courtyards and basements, and all the secret hiding places. Stephan pressed to be given more responsible missions, even begged to be allowed to go to the Aryan side. Stephan was not yet thirteen years old. How can a boy demand to walk like a man and his own father crawl through the mud?

'Andrei, think what you will of me, but the people here only want to survive. You know that, Andrei – survive. The best way to live is through the Civil Authority. No one has answered your call to arms, Andrei. Your way would be mass suicide. Andrei – now listen – Boris Presser and I have been negotiating with Koenig. Koenig is a reasonable man and he can maneuver Schreiker. Koenig promises that if we can get the underground to stop its activities they will make a settlement with us on rations, medicine, and the disposition of the labor force.'

'Good God, Paul. Can you believe your own words?'

'It's our only chance!'

There was nothing more to be said. Andrei could not mask his contempt. He handed Paul Bronski a blindfold. 'I don't know anything about an underground.'

Bronski took the blindfold. 'You'll have to tie it on ... I can't do it with one hand.'

Ervin Rosenblum worked in the musty room below Mila 19, sorting the notes of the Good Fellowship Club. A rap on the false packing crate which served as an entrance made him douse the lights and freeze. Ana Grinspan entered.

'Susan has just come back,' she said. 'Get up to your room.'

'Is anything wrong?'

'Go on.'

Ervin felt his way through an aisle lined with packing cases. In the main office on the first floor he saw everyone staring. Alexander Brandel stood by the door of his office, shaking his head.

Ervin raced up the stairs to the second floor carefully. The rail was gone, chopped up for firewood weeks earlier. Down the corridor to that cell which he shared with his wife and mother.

Momma Rosenblum lay on a cot beneath a pile of quilts. It was icy. There was no heat in the house. The room was ugly and bare except for Momma's cot, double bed for Ervin and Susan, and a single table and two chairs.

Susan's face was distraught. Ervin felt a catch in his heart. Susan had always seemed resilient to tragedy, plodding on, doing her job regardless. He had never seen her like this. He wiped his glasses nervously, trying to adjust his vision to the change of light from the cellar.

'Tell me,' he said at last.

'Dr Glazer,' she groaned.

In a way, Ervin was relieved. They had been expecting Glazer to go. Another death, another, another. Key people dying in droves. Glazer had been like a father to Susan from the day she graduated from the university. Little Bernard Glazer who had brought so many children into life had watched them die, helpless to save them. Glazer was better off, Ervin thought. But God, he'd be missed. He was the best man in his field.

Ervin flopped his hands. 'Too bad,' was all he could say.

Susan slung a sheaf of papers on the table. 'A farewell present to you, Ervin. A minute-by-minute account of his death.'

What a legacy! Ervin stared at the yellowish papers but did not touch them.

'Take it, Ervin!' Her voice rose sharply. 'It's Dr Glazer's gift to you!'

'Susan ... Susan ... please.'

'Damn you!' she shrieked. 'People die and you write in your lousy journal! God damn you, Ervin!'

Momma Rosenblum stirred. '*Kinder, Kinder,*' she said weakly, 'don't shriek at each other.'

Susan sat beside the old woman and felt her forehead automatically. 'I'm sorry, Momma. I didn't mean it, Ervin.'

'It's all right, Susan, I understand.'

'God, I don't know what to do with Dr Glazer gone. God ... Ten children died today ... God ...' Her breath darted out in streams of frosty air.

Journal Entry

As the population is decimated the Germans close off the little ghetto in the south. As soon as a bit of room becomes available in the big ghetto, houses are closed off in the south. Crossing the bridge over the 'Polish corridor' are the fancy Jews from Germany, the Jewish Civil Authority people, and the Militia and wealthier smugglers and members of the Big Seven. Only one major factory complex is left in the small ghetto, and that is the woodwork shops. As the small ghetto is abandoned it has become a no man's land where Wild Ones without Kennkarten *hide so they will not have to submit to slave labor. The abandoned ghetto has become a rendezvous for smugglers and to carry on prostitution for those still decent enough in appearance to sell their bodies. Raiding parties cross into the little ghetto at night and rip up wooden floors, doors, rails, and anything else that can be used for firewood and cart it off. In the big ghetto the crowding is worse than before. People sleep in hallways, cellars, in outside courtyards.*

We continue to attempt to get dollars from British parachute drops, but it is hit-and-miss. With our dollar supply shrinking, the zloty has inflated again. David Zemba has made a simple plan. Through our people in London we have gotten American Aid to deposit several hundred thousands of dollars in Swiss accounts. Many of the smugglers have enormous collections of zlotys virtually unspendable and useless to them. We buy the zlotys by transferring Swiss dollars into their personal accounts in Geneva. We are able to get a good rate and with enough of these zlotys can buy essentials. We try not to deal with the Big Seven, but it is certain that Max Kleperman has his people in on this. Also, we can make direct barter with our Swiss money for houses, rooms, gold, food, and medicine with those smugglers who have caches. This latter is preferable to the zloty exchange. David Zemba is in conferences, trading for our Swiss dollars all day, every day. He has saved hundreds of lives.

Three major slave-labor factory complexes remain in the ghetto, all belonging to Franz Koenig. In the small ghetto there is a woodwork plant. In the north, the Brush-maker's district. This latter supplies a major part of the brushes for the German army. Most of the people, in their desperation to live, still maintain that a Kennkarte *stamped for labor is the key to life.*

From the third factory we hear something that is a ray of hope, however faint. It is the uniform factory. Although the Germans claim to be at the gates of Moscow, we sense their first great defeat of the war. Nearly a hundred thousand bloody uniforms have arrived from the eastern front. In the factory the slave laborers clean, patch, and weave them and make them ready for reissue in Germany.

A hundred thousand German casualties? Good news.

ALEXANDER BRANDEL

Chapter Four

Rachael raced through rapid passages of Chopin's Second Concerto in preparation for a concert with what was left of the Ghetto Symphony Orchestra to be held in Franz Koenig's uniform factory.

She turned to the slow lilt of the andante, and her mind strayed from her work. Three more members of the orchestra had died. There were only forty musicians left and they were listless. A spasm of tension gripped her stomach. Wolf had been gone five days this time. It was the third time in a month that Andrei had sent him to the Aryan side. They said they wouldn't, but they needed Wolf, even at the risk. What were they to do? She longed to marry him, but her father would be violently opposed. Wolf's father had once been an active Zionist and many people knew about Wolf's work. Poppa would allow nothing to besmirch his position on the Civil Authority. He was completely unreasonable about it.

In the bedroom, Stephan lay on his stomach studying the Haftorah, a reading from the Prophets, in preparation for the coming bar mitzvah. He always remembered the sound of music from his mother and sister. It had a magic quality of transcending him beyond all harm and all ugliness. Rachael stumbled on a passage, then fingered her way through the next bars.

Stephan automatically stopped reading and rolled off the bed and walked to the window. They had just moved to this new place in the big ghetto. He had to share a bedroom with Rachael, and it was a pretty run-down place but far better than most people had. Just across the street stood the old post office building where the Civil Authority had been housed since the Germans closed the place on Grzybowska Street. His father worked in there. In front of the large square, columned structure stood the only tree and plot of grass in the ghetto. It felt cool and soft to roll in.

The music stopped.

Stephan walked back to his bed and flopped on his belly, waiting for Rachael to begin playing again so he could resume his studies.

He had always had an unspoken communication with his sister. They wanted to talk to each other now. She sat on the edge of his bed and mussed his hair. He rebelled slightly.

'How can you read that chicken scratch?' she said, referring to the Hebrew text.

'It's no worse than the chicken scratch you read at the piano.' Stephan closed the book, 'I wish Wolf would get back and help me with my lessons. Rabbi Solomon – well, we have to be perfect. He's tough.'

'Stephan?'

'Yes?'

'Wolf told me you tried to get him and Uncle Andrei to let you distribute the underground paper.'

The boy did not answer.

'Is it true?'

'I guess so.'

'Does Momma know?'

'No.'

'Don't you think you'd better tell her?'

He spun off the bed, away from her inquiries.

'What would we do if anything happened to you?'

'Don't you understand, Rachael?'

'With Wolf and Uncle Andrei doing their work, I can't lose all of you.'

'If only Poppa –' Stephan stopped short. 'Nothing.'

'You can't make up for him, Stephan.'

'I'm so ashamed. For a long time I tried to believe what he was telling me.'

'Don't be too hard on Poppa. No one knows how much he has suffered. You must be kind.'

'How can you say that? If it weren't for Poppa you and Wolf could marry.'

'He's still your father, Stephan, and I know that Rabbi Solomon would be the first to tell you to honor him, always.'

'Rachael . . . Momma and Poppa don't love each other any more, do they?'

'It's only because of the times, Stephan.'

'That's all right. You don't have to try to explain.'

She changed the subject quickly. 'So, you're going to be a real man next week. Well, let me see if you have a hair on your chin yet.' Rachael wrestled him to the floor. He gently allowed himself to be pinned down. Her fingers dug into his ribs and he squirmed, half angry, half laughing.

'Quit it, Rachael! I can't wrestle with you any more.'

She bared her claws. 'And why not?'

'Because you're a girl and I may grab something by mistake.'

'Well! Stephan Bronski! You *are* becoming a man!'

In a moment she went back to the andante movement. Stephan slipped beside her on the bench and rested his head on her shoulder. Rachael put her arm about her brother and kissed his forehead.

'It won't be much of a bar mitzvah for you, will it?'

'Just taking the oath to live as a Jew is important,' he answered.

'You are a little man.'

'Don't be afraid, Rachael. Wolf will be back. I heard you cry last night. Don't be afraid. Rachael, I think I understand everything about you and Wolf and I want you to know I'm very glad because next to Uncle Andrei he's the finest man who ever lived. He has explained lots of things to me . . . about being a man . . . like things Poppa should have explained . . .'

Rachael blanched, then smiled. 'I wish he would come back. I wish he would come back . . .'

'He said he'd get back for my bar mitzvah. He will, Rachael.'

Alexander Brandel's office was converted into a makeshift synagogue, just as a million other places had been converted for illicit worship for two thousand years. Rabbi Solomon donned the ancient vestments of the rabbinate and opened the Torah scroll and chanted to the room where Ervin Rosenblum and Andrei and Alex and three Bathyrans stood near what represented an altar. Beyond Alex's desk, Rachael and Susan and Deborah and many of Stephan's friends jammed together. The shell of the man who was once Dr Paul Bronski was alone by the door.

Stephan Bronski fidgeted slightly as his mother brushed her hand over the tallis which had belonged to her own father. Since no new shawls had been made since the occupation, the rabbi ruled it fitting for the boy to wear this symbol of one generation passing a tradition to another. Stephan's months of study were coming to a culmination.

He looked about toward the door, hoping that Wolf Brandel would come through it in the last moment, but all he saw was his father. He smiled slightly at Rachael.

Rabbi Solomon faced the assemblage. Another boy was ready to accept his duties as a son of the commandment, a guardian of the Laws, and take upon himself the terrible burden of Jewish life. Only a week earlier there had been another bar mitzvah. The son of Max Kleperman had reached the age of thirteen. He was given the symbols of manhood in a large hall at the Big Seven headquarters amid gluttonous revelry. The old man wanted to turn his back on Kleperman's mockery and walk away, but he didn't, for he was merely the administrator of God's will and not its judge.

His thinning high voice asked the candidate to step forward.

Stephan took a last sigh and felt his mother's hand squeeze his shoulder. He walked forward to receive his new social status. The boy was slight and small like his father.

'Bless the Lord Who is to be praised.'

'Praised be the Lord Who is blessed for all eternity,' the men in the room answered.

'Blessed art Thou, O Lord our God, King of the universe, Who didst choose us from among all the peoples by giving us Thy Torah. Blessed art Thou, O Lord, Giver of the Laws,' Stephan chanted.

The boy and the old man turned to the Torah scrolls which lay on Alexander Brandel's desk. With the tassels of the shawl, Stephan touched the Torah, kissed the shawl, and read from the Laws of Moses. From the benediction he went to the climax of his studies, the chanting of the Maftir Aliya from the Book of Prophets, one of the most difficult of all Hebrew readings.

Stephan faced the room and chanted from memory. His voice was small and high, but it carried with it that cry of anguish born of the oppressions of many Pharaohs in many ages. The room was awed as the lad displayed the full mastery of his accomplishment. Even Solomon delved into memory to try to recall when a young man had read the Haftorah with greater authority, grace, and musical perfection.

When the closing benediction was done, the Torah scrolls were closed, to be taken and hidden from desecration by the Germans.

Stephan Bronski faced the room. Uncle Andrei winked. Stephan looked about, hoping that Wolf might have come in, but he hadn't. He cleared his throat. 'I would like to thank my mother and father,' he said in the traditional opening of the valedictory, 'for bringing me up in the Jewish tradition.'

The pronouncement seldom failed to bring tears to women. Deborah and Rachael proved no exception. But in the rear of the office the words struck Paul Bronski like a stiletto. He lowered his eyes as his son continued.

'I realize that becoming a son of the commandment is just a token of manhood. A lot of people told me how sorry they were that I couldn't have my bar mitzvah in peacetime when the Great Tlomatskie Synagogue would have been almost full and relatives would have come from all of Poland and there would have been a large celebration and presents. I thought a lot about all that, but I am really glad to have my bar mitzvah in a place like this room, because in places like this the Jewish faith has been kept alive during other times of oppression. I think, too, it is a special privilege to have your bar mitzvah in bad times. Anyone can live like a Jew when things go well, but to take an oath to be a Jew today is really important. We know that God needs real Jews to protect His laws. Well . . . we have survived everyone who has tried to destroy us before because we have kept this kind of faith. Our God will not let us down. I am very proud to be a Jew and I will try hard to uphold my responsibilities.'

Rabbi Solomon held the tallis on Stephan's head and chanted the closing priestly blessing. The room pressed forward to converge on the boy and congratulate him with hearty '*Mozeltoffs*.' Paul Bronski left the place quickly and quietly.

'I guess you are satisfied now,' Paul snapped at Deborah. 'You've put on your little circus. You've won your battle. You've showed me up as a damned fool in front of the whole ghetto.'

Deborah tried to contain herself. His eyes were filled with that half-wild look again.

'Grinding salt into my wounds,' he continued. 'Making me look ridiculous.'

'Stephan did not have a bar mitzvah as a vendetta against you.'

'Like hell.'

'Paul, let's go to sleep,' she pleaded.

'Sleep?' He laughed sardonically. 'Who sleeps?'

He tried to light a cigarette, but his hand trembled so violently that he was able to accomplish it only with her steadying hand. 'Well, Deborah, now that our son is properly a Jew and you have won your crusade for his holy purification for my sins –'

'Stop it!'

'– now perhaps we can discuss a family matter. We *are* still a family, you know.'

'If you speak like a civilized person.'

His outburst was done now. He calmed himself. 'You've got to give up working at the orphanage and Rachael has to stop giving concerts. As for Stephan, he spends entirely too much time on the streets.'

She merely narrowed her eyes at his pronouncement.

'We must reappraise all our friends. A continued association with Brandel, Rosenblum, and Susan could become dangerous. Everyone is aware of their past affiliations and no one is sure they are not part of this underground.'

'Now you just stop where you are, Paul –'

'Let me finish, dammit, let me finish! I can't guarantee your immunity because of the likes of your goddamned brother and his agitators. They've pulled in the entire family of one of our board members and are holding them all at Pawiak Prison as a warning for us to break up this underground.'

All that was left of a desire for honor seemed to drain out of him in that instant. His skin was a horrible gray. 'We have decided –'

'What?'

'We have decided that our families have to come to work inside the Civil Authority building and never be out of our sight.'

'Oh, my God, it's come to this.' Deborah held her hand over her eyes for only a few tears. 'All through this,' she whispered, 'I have waited patiently for . . . Paul, at first I tried so very, very hard to make myself believe that what you were doing was really the right thing. But each day as you degrade yourself lower and lower you have ceased to be a human being.'

'How dare you?'

'Good God, Paul! Didn't you hear your son today? Can't the courage of a little boy touch you, move you?'

'I won't listen!'

'You will listen, Paul Bronski! You will listen!'

He knelt before her desperately and grabbed her arm and shook it. 'We can talk aesthetics until hell freezes, but what I am saying to you is reality.'

The tears fell down her cheeks. 'Reality? My poor man, you are the one who has been hiding from reality. I'm going to tell you what reality is. Your daughter is sleeping with Wolf Brandel, and I sent her to him because her marriage would endanger her father's precious position as a collaborator.'

'That son of a bitch –'

'Good! At least you have the decency to show anger. But he is a fine young man and I thank God she is able to find a few moments of happiness in this hell. Shall I tell you more reality? I am working on manufacturing bombs in the cellar of the orphanage, and your son Stephan is delivering the underground newspaper.'

Paul Bronski stood up and grunted like a confused, dying animal.

'Do you know why, Paul? He came to me and pleaded – "Momma, I'm going to be thirteen . . . Momma, someone in our family has to be a man."'

Paul crumpled into a chair and sobbed. She stood over the groveling, shaking cur, and the disdain ebbed into a terrible weariness. 'I only did it for you,' he wept, 'only for you.'

'I'm tired, Paul . . . I'm all done in.' Suddenly, without plan, the words found their way through her. 'I have a chance to leave the ghetto with the children.'

He looked up at her, blinking. 'De Monti . . . De Monti.'

She nodded.

'You'd do this to me?'

'I have made my atonements. I have paid, repaid a thousand, thousand times, and I swear I don't know if I was ever wrong even in the beginning. But if I was, I have been punished by you. I promise you, Chris will never touch me. All I want is to find a hole someplace to crawl into where I can't hear starving children cry. Maybe a patch of grass . . . that's all I want . . . just . . . a patch of grass.'

Paul slid to the floor on his knees and doubled up before her feet. 'Please don't leave me,' he wept, 'please don't leave me . . . please don't leave me . . .'

Chapter Five

Spring of 1942.

The awesome winter was done, but the smell of death lingered. The little ghetto on the south was all but shrunken. Polish families inched back in as the Jewish decimation increased. All that remained in the south were a few streets of Jews, the woodwork factory, and Wild Areas. The big ghetto became more crammed than ever.

With the reinforcement of the Waffen SS guard, the ghetto fell into a grip of fear worse than any it had experienced. The smug Elite Corps with their lightning streaks on black uniforms entered Warsaw fresh from their jobs as Kommandos in the Special Action massacres on the eastern front. Placed under Sieghold Stutze, they were wild, drinking louts, turned into savages by the sight of the blood of their victims. They filled the barracks at 101 Leszno Street just beyond the ghetto wall, opposite Koenig's uniform factory.

A second set of guards arrived. Latvians and Lithuanians wearing uniforms of Nazi Auxiliaries with insignia of skull and crossbones on their epaulets. These peasants from the Baltics had carried out their share of the eastern massacres with relish.

A third force came in from Globocnik's headquarters in Lublin. Ukrainians. Their men's choir, sober or drunk, sang with such harmony they were dubbed the Nightingales. The Litts, Latts, and Nightingales took the red brick building cater-corner to the SS barracks.

Each night the sounds of drunken revelry heightened the fear.

SS General Alfred Funk, courier of the verbal messages on 'Jewish problems,' arrived in Warsaw as a harbinger of doom. Fresh from conferences with Heydrich, Himmler, and Hitler in Berlin, he arrived with Adolf Eichmann, Gestapo 4B, Jewish affairs.

The Krakow *Gazette* increased its build-up of the 'final solution to the Jewish problem.' Around Poland, the feverish activity of building new camps brought in German experts in transportation and construction. But these new camps were different. They were neither for slave labor nor for the containment of enemies of the Reich. They were built in great secrecy in out-of-the-way locations, and their structures had odd shapes unlike any ever seen.

By midwinter Alfred Funk concluded his conferences in Warsaw and returned to SS headquarters in Lublin with further verbal instructions for Globocnik.

Early in March one of Ana Grinspan's runners reached Warsaw with the information that an Operation Reinhard, named after Heydrich, was taking place for the liquidation of the Lublin ghetto. The ghetto occupants as well as transports of Jews from outside Poland were being sent to a camp named Majdanek on the outskirts of the city.

When Funk came back to Warsaw everyone speculated wildly on the meaning, but after the winter just past no one believed things could get worse.

* * *

Rabbi Solomon sat on the floor in another of the makeshift synagogues before his emaciated congregation, which had once been a proud group recognized in the religious circles of Poland. The few stragglers who remained represented the heart of European Jewry. Stephan Bronski, the rabbi's favorite pupil, was near the learned one.

It was the ninth day of the Hebrew month of Ab, the day on which the greatest disasters had befallen the Jews. On Tisha B'Ab the First Temple of Solomon was destroyed by the Babylonians, and centuries later, on the same day, the Second Temple fell to the Romans, starting a series of events which eventually spread the seed of Abraham to the corners of the world as damned and eternal wanderers and strangers.

On Tisha B'Ab an angry Moses had come down from Sinai and smashed the tablets of the commandments upon sight of the reveling tribes of Israel worshiping an idol. It was as though he had cast an eternal curse upon them, for this night of Tisha B'Ab the lights burned late in the offices of Gestapo House, Reinhard Corps headquarters, and the offices of Rudolph Schreiker.

Rabbi Solomon read from the 'Valley of Tears' and the Holy Torah was revealed and he swayed and cried Jeremiah's prophecies of doom.

'And the Lord shall scatter you among the nations and ye shall be left few in number.'

A mournful response followed his words.

'We looked for peace, but no good came; and for a time of health and behold trouble! For, behold I will send serpents among you which will not be charmed and they shall bite you, saith the Lord ... the harvest is past, the summer ended and we are not saved ... for death is come up to our windows and is entered into our palaces to cut off the children from without, and the young men from the streets ... the carcasses of men shall fall as dung upon the open field.'

As Rabbi Solomon lamented, the overture to the most horrible catastrophe in a catastrophe-filled history was playing out.

Black Friday ushered in the Big Action.

The Nazis called in members of their networks of informers and bled them for information during the night. By dawn a swift, merciless sweep was plotted to denude the Jews of the last of their leadership.

With sirens screaming in hideous harmony to the rabbi's prayers, the SS and their Litts, Latts, Polish Blues, Jewish Militia, and Ukrainians swept in from every gate and scoured the ghetto, smoking out the resistance people from secret rooms.

Tens of dozens were marched unceremoniously to the cemetery and shot by a firing squad of Nightingales.

Ana Grinspan, Andrei Androfski, and Tolek Alterman had the fortune to be on the Aryan side. Other Bathyrans hid in the basement of Mila 19 with Jules Schlosberg and Ervin Rosenblum amid journals of the Good Fellowship Club and homemade fire bombs. Simon Eden spent the day crossing rooftops, and Rodel, the Communist, cringed in a hidden closet.

Alexander Brandel and David Zempa were among the fortunate not on the roundup list.

But dozens of people from the Bathyrans and the Labor Zionists and Revisionists and Bundists were not so fortunate. Black Friday shattered the ghetto and it sank to its lowest depths.

On the Sabbath following the massacre the ghetto was plastered with terrifying orders and the loudspeaker trucks roamed up and down, up and down, booming the edicts.

ORDER OF DEPORTATION NOTICE

1. By order of the German authorities all Jews living in Warsaw, without regard to age or sex, are to be deported to the East.

2. The following are excluded from the deportation order:

(a) All Jews employed by German authorities or in German enterprises who have their *Kennkarten* properly stamped.

(b) All Jews who are members and employees of the Jewish Civil Authority as of the day of this notice.

(c) All Jews belonging to the Jewish Militia.

(d) The families of the above-mentioned. Families consist only of husband/wives and children.

(e) Jews employed by social welfare agencies under the Jewish Civil Authority and Orphans and Self-Help Society.

3. Each deportee is entitled to take fifteen kilograms of personal possessions as baggage. All baggage over the weight will be confiscated. (All valuable articles such as money, jewelry, gold, etc., should be taken in order to use if for an orderly resettlement.) Three days' food should be taken.

4. Deportation commences on July 22, 1942, at 11 A.M.

5. Punishments:

(a) Jews in the published lists not reporting will be shot.

(b) Jews undertaking activities to evade or hinder orderly deportation will be shot.

JEWISH CIVIL AUTHORITY, WARSAW
Boris Presser, Chairman

ANNOUNCEMENT

Each deportee who reports voluntarily will be supplied with 3 kg. bread and 1 kg. marmalade. Food distribution will be held at Stawki Square.

Staging center for deportation will be the process center at Stawki 6–8 on the Umschlagplatz.

JEWISH CIVIL AUTHORITY, WARSAW
Dr Paul Bronski, Deputy Chairman

ANNOUNCEMENT

Each day deportations will be clearly posted and announced for the proceeding day. Deportees for July 23 shall come from the following areas:

Elektoralna St No. 34–42
Chlodna St No. 28–44 inclusive
Orla St No. 1–14 and 16–34
Leszno St No. 1–3, 7–51, 57–77
All Biala Street

BY ORDER OF PIOTR WARSINSKI
Jewish Militia of Warsaw

Chapter Six

The underground recoiled from Black Friday and set out to determine what was behind the deportation.

For the first three days the Germans had an unexpected success. Wild Ones who lived in hiding without *Kennkarten* left their secret hovels, unable to resist the temptation of the three kilograms of bread and one kilogram of marmalade promised by the Germans. There were more volunteers than could be processed at the Umschlagplatz.

The deportation center was in a gray four-story concrete structure at Stawki 6-8, just beyond the northern gate. It was out of view of both the ghetto and the Aryan side. Once a school, it had later been an Orphans and Self-Help hospital.

Waffen SS Hauptsturmführer Kutler, in charge of the detail, was a member of the Kommandos who had carried out the massacres on the eastern front. Kutler was in a state of drunkenness, tormented by a continuous nightmare of blood. His gory dreams were shared by most of the other Kommandos, who kept themselves going on liquor and dope.

A pair of thick iron doors hung across the entrance. Inside, a half dozen Nazis made selections, standing in front of the never-ending lines of humanity. A few were returned to the ghetto for labor. Most were passed along to the immense cobblestone yard surrounded by a high wall.

The courtyard detail was composed of Nightingales and their Litt and Latt compatriots under the direction of a few SS men who held various Alsatian dogs at leash end.

A brick train shed and platform some two blocks in length ran to the extreme end of the courtyard. A train of forty-four cattle and freight cars stood in readiness.

As the selectees came in, their belongings were ransacked for jewelry, money, valuables of any kind. In order to make room for more people on the cars, most of the clothing they carried was confiscated.

A detail of Jews from Koenig's labor pool carted the clothing across the street to a building which served as a warehouse. Linings of coats were ripped apart for hidden valuables. Personal mementos – family letters, pictures, keepsakes – were burned in a large oven alongside the building.

When six thousand people had been gathered, they were loaded on the trains. At three o'clock promptly each afternoon the train pulled out for an 'unknown eastern destination.'

The Wild Ones who had volunteered in the first days of the Big Action had been cowed to such a state that they offered almost no resistance. But anyone who balked inside the Umschlagplatz courtyard was pounced upon immediately, mercilessly, by the guards.

Outside the courtyard, Polish Blues and Jewish Militia kept order in the lines feeding people into the selection center.

The aged, cripples, and those obviously unfit for labor were taken from the Umschlagplatz and shot by SS firing squads at the cemetery several blocks away. In this way the Germans 'proved' they were taking only the healthiest people to the new labor camps.

Despite the passivity of the Orthodox community, men like Rabbi Solomon continued to wield great influence over the people. As more and more rabbis went to an unknown fate, diminishing the numbers leading the Orthodox Jews, the remaining inherited more responsibility.

On the fourth day of the Big Action the remnants of the underground had the Umschlagplatz under observation and scurried desperately around Warsaw trying to learn the destination of the trains.

Alexander Brandel visited Rabbi Solomon in an attempt to convince him to go to the Jewish Civil Authority. The old man had drawn a rigid circle binding his duties. The Civil Authority, he argued, was beyond his sphere of activity. Through Talmudic reasoning and arguments Alex weakened his stand by drawing parallels with ancient exiles. Finally the rabbi agreed to a rabbinical court and allowed Alex to plead before the five rabbis they were able to assemble.

They decided it was morally correct for Rabbi Solomon to petition the Civil Authority.

The old man was partly blind, able to see only in shadowy images. Months before, he had been forced to give up his work on the Good Fellowship notes and Brandel's journal. He entered the Civil Authority building at Zamenhof and Gensia streets on the arm of Stephan Bronski, his favorite student.

Paul Bronski was more nervous than usual. The sight of Stephan with the rabbi in broad daylight in a place which was a rats' nest of informers unnerved him. Stephan was sent home. Although Solomon could not see Paul, he was able to sense the uneasiness in the man's voice.

'Dr Bronski, there has been much talk about these deportations. In fact, little else is spoken of.'

'That is certainly understandable.'

'We hear that there are continuations of the eastern massacres in death camps.'

'Nonsense. Can't you see it is the same group of agitators we have had to contend with since the first day of the occupation? We have only their propaganda that there have ever been massacres in the east.'

'Has the Civil Authority ever questioned the Germans about the validity of the stories of the eastern massacres?'

Of course not. Paul clamped his teeth together. Sightless though the old man was, none of the keen edge had gone from his mind, nor had he lost the acid manner of setting verbal traps.

'My dear Rabbi Solomon, no one claims that life in the ghetto has been easy. We are the losers in a war in which we have been chosen as the scapegoat. Yet, through orderly process, the fact is that we have kept most people alive and here.'

'Then, Dr Bronski, I assume you are ready to assure us that most of us will still be alive and here in three or four weeks?'

Paul had spoken about the deportations only to Boris Presser. His own hopes were that within a week or two the Germans would restock their labor camps and the deportations would stop.

'I am waiting for an answer, Dr Bronski.'

Paul was afraid to take a position. Suppose he said the deportations would stop and they did not. Suppose the rumors of death camps were true and the Civil Authority had taken no stand on them. He had run out of maneuvering room. For two years and seven months he had found one more escape, and one more, and one more. This was the dead end.

'I am reasonably certain the deportations will stop as soon as the Germans decongest the ghetto. Decongestion of the ghetto will alleviate many of our problems here, and the population shifts to strengthen their labor pool closer to the eastern front will obviously satisfy the Germans.'

'Would the Civil Authority ask the Germans if your reasonable certainties are reasonable certainties with them also?'

Rabbi Solomon's trap sprang shut. Paul wanted no more of the man. He mumbled quickly that the matter would be pursued.

Boris Presser had performed his duties as chairman of the Jewish Civil Authority almost as a nonentity. He was a quiet little man whose forte was an extraordinary ability to stay out of people's way and to carry out his office in a mechanical manner, without emotional attachment. The murder of Emanuel Goldman, the first Civil Authority chairman in the early days of the occupation, clearly outlined the limitations of his power.

Presser dexterously avoided clandestine meetings with the underground, the social agencies, or the smugglers. He was learned at knowing nothing, seeing nothing, hearing nothing. He kept himself untainted through deftness. He was, in fact, the perfect tool in the Nazi logic which pointed up that Jews were killing each other off. When boxed in from time to time, Presser could always justify the existence of the Civil Authority. Without it, he explained, conditions would be far more severe. He made himself believe it was an instrument of survival.

When Paul Bronski confronted Boris with the ground swell of apprehension over the deportations Presser would not be talked into a meeting with the Germans. As he had done a hundred times before, he delegated Paul Bronski.

The choices? Schreiker and the Reinhard Corps were impossible to speak to. Could he move through Max Kleperman? No, the Big Seven wanted to know nothing about the deportations. Move through Brandel and David Zemba? No, it was they who brought the pressure on the Civil Authority.

Dr Franz Koenig was his only choice.

Koenig's new residence was a forty-room palace, the latest confiscation in his capacity as chief of confiscations. In a few short years he had become a multimillionaire.

Koenig had grown abnormally obese. His body resembled a pear and his head a puffy tomato with an obnoxious flat clipping of fuzz on top.

Power was unbecoming. After the first sweet taste of revenge and fulfillment, he came to loggerheads with the reality that he had placed himself in league with men of a bestiality he did not believe could exist among civilized people. His wonderful Germany, his land of the gifts of culture, was being run by maniacs and sadists. He remembered his very first discussion of the mass murders. Now he wondered what he had done. Yet, irresistibly, he rose higher and higher. Himmler himself received him regularly. All that Franz Koenig had known of truth and beauty was abandoned by him. A victim of fear, he had been purchased – soul, heart, and mind.

Paul's throat was caked dry as he stood before Dr Koenig. It was a long way from the university to this forty-foot office. Yet Paul's presence always had the disconcerting effect of making Koenig remember that he had once been content to read Schiller and listen to Mozart in the sanctity of his study, away from his fat Polish wife.

Paul managed to blurt out the message of apprehension over the deportations.

'You have a militia at your disposal. Use it,' Koenig snapped in irritation.

'But if we use it more than we already have to implement the deportations, it will only serve to confirm the people's suspicions.'

Koenig rocked back and forth in his outsized chair. He could turn the matter over to Rudolph Schreiker for a flat and brutal closing of all discussion. Was this wise? Only a few days and the stream of volunteers for deportation had all but dried up. There was risk of a hardening resistance with the growing underground. Koenig had a dozen factories both in and out of the ghetto which needed a constant supply of labor. Schreiker had not changed an iota from his blundering, stupid ways. He had learned to manipulate Schreiker, to make his own position firm by the feeling that he was indispensable. Schreiker was deep in his debt through bribes and loans.

Paul Bronski and Boris Presser had been obedient servants. If they were replaced in a swift purge, it could upset the well-controlled balance he maintained over the ghetto.

'It is reasonable,' Koenig said in measured terms, 'that the Jewish Civil Authority assure the people of our good intentions.'

When Paul had gone, Koenig went to the city hall to convince Rudolph Schreiker of the importance of having the Jewish Civil Authority make a public proclamation for the continuance of orderly deportations. Schreiker was, as usual, too confused by the issues to do other than mumble for Koenig to go ahead.

The next day Paul Bronski, Boris Presser, and the entire board of the Jewish Civil Authority were whisked out of the ghetto for an inspection at Poniatow, Trawniki, and dozens of eastern labor camps which existed to supply road gangs constructing air strips and manufacturing munitions. The railroads had received their first Russian bombings. Gangs of Jews put them back into working order.

The superficial inspection was parallel to the 'inspections' held for the Swiss Red Cross in their investigation of ghetto conditions. Yet it served as a face-saving gesture for Presser and Bronski. At the end of the tour, which showed or proved nothing, Koenig distorted it into Nazi logic. The inspection 'proved' that the deportations from Warsaw were for the announced purpose of dispersing and decentralizing industry and moving it closer to the eastern battle line.

Neither Boris Presser nor Paul Bronski was able to allow himself the luxury of pursuing the truth. On their return to Warsaw, Koenig had prepared statements for their signature. They affixed their names to documents declaring their satisfaction that the deportations were for the stated reasons and under tolerable working conditions and further urged co-operation in orderly departures.

Copies of the documents were plastered on a thousand walls, but despite them the streams of volunteers had completely dried up by the sixth day of the Big Action.

* * *

'Juden! 'Raus!'

'Jews! Outside!'

Whistles! Sirens! Deserted streets. Taut fear behind the drawn shades.

The Nightingales who sang in such beautiful harmony poured from their trucks in another of the sudden strikes to block off a building and pour in and smash down doors and drag the struggling occupants into the streets.

Wolf Brandel slipped into his trousers and shirt at the sounds of the screams across the way and peered from a corner window in Andrei's flat to the scene of horror in the courtyard. Rachael wrapped herself in the bed sheet and tried to look, but Wolf held her back at arm's length.

A drama of violence erupted amid the confusion as a man attempted to break through the cordon of Ukrainians to reach his wife and was bloodily clubbed to the pavement for his efforts. He lay groaning and twitching, drenched in his own blood. Another outburst. A frantic young mother lurched at a huge guard, clawing his face, biting his hand, as she tried to get back her infant. The guard roared with laughter, grabbed her by the hair, and flung her into a circle of flailing clubs. The cordon pushed their captives up the street toward the Umschlagplatz with a steady tattoo of truncheon smashes.

Wolf buttoned his shirt clumsily and replaced his pistol in his belt. Rachael forgot her modesty and let the sheet fall from her, but the blood-burst on the streets had broken the spell of love-making. Wolf braced his back against the iron bedstead and dropped his face on his knees while she dressed. She cuddled up next to him, laying her head on his lap, and they stayed numbed and quiet until the last of the cries faded from their hearing.

'Where are the trains going?' she whispered shakily.

He shook his head.

'My father says they'll stop soon, but I don't believe him. There's talk about death camps.'

She began to tremble, and her face and hands felt icy. He tried to comfort her.

'I don't mean to be like this ... It was only – I was so frightened when you didn't come back in time for Stephan's bar mitzvah. I'm always dreaming of the trains. I dream they're taking Stephan. Wolf, he's taking too many chances. Make him stop.'

'How can I argue with him to be against what we are trying to stand for?'

'What do we stand for? What in God's name do we stand for?'

'I don't know, really. My father might be able to put it into certain words. So can Rabbi Solomon. I just want to live and I want you to live. I guess that's all I really stand for.'

In a little while she became calm.

'Someday it will all be over, Rachael. It must end sometime.'

'If I could only be your wife. If I could only have your baby. Wolf, if either of us goes on the trains, I want you to know how very much I love you.'

'We're going to come through this ... Rachael.' Then his voice saddened. 'My father talked to Rabbi Solomon about marrying us secretly, without your father knowing. He won't do it.'

'Why? It's only because my father would never agree –'

'To Rabbi Solomon it would mean he would be taking the side of the underground against the Civil Authority. You know how the Orthodox are about finding hidden meanings in hidden meanings. Besides, I would want the world to know you're my wife.'

'I try so hard to remember my father the way he used to be, but I think I hate him. I swear, sometimes I almost wish he were –'

'Shhhhh . . .'

Sounds on the roof sent them into a grip of fear. Wolf rolled off the bed, yanked Rachael off, and shoved her behind him into an alcove. Someone was rattling about overhead. An indistinguishable figure appeared at the skylight in the kitchen ceiling. It tugged at the trap door. Wolf withdrew his pistol, cocked it, and aimed it on the skylight. The trap door groaned open, sending in a burst of light and air. A pair of legs lowered and a figure dropped to the floor.

'It's Stephan.'

Stephan got to his feet, rubbing his wrist, which was tingling from the impact of breaking the fall. 'I'm sorry to have to come here,' he apologized, 'but Uncle Andrei needs you right away, Wolf.'

'Where is he?'

'At the loft over the stage, Workman's Theater.'

Wolf fought his way into his shoes, slapped his cap on, and peered out of the window. Nightingales patrolled the street below.

'You'll have to go over the roofs,' Stephan said.

'You two get on the roof and stay till after dark,' Wolf ordered.

Rachael obeyed silently, fearing words would bring on a betrayal of tears. A kitchen table was shoved under the skylight. Wolf climbed on, leaped up, caught hold, and struggled through. He closed his eyes for a moment as he saw the sheer drop. The sharp heights always brought on dizziness. He lay flat on his belly and reached down into the kitchen. Rachael hoisted Stephan into Wolf's hands. She came through last. Wolf closed the skylight and pointed to cover behind a chimney. Stephan and his sister crouched behind it and watched Wolf disappear over the top of the ghetto.

It took him an hour to negotiate the mile over the roofs, down stairs, sprinting through exposed courtyards and over intersections, diving into the cover of friendly basements.

Wolf knew instantly it was a very important meeting, for Simon Eden was there with Andrei and Tolek Alterman. Andrei and Simon had kept apart to lessen the chance of their both being captured. It was the same with the other leaders. They came together under an urgency, for the informers had unearthed dozens of hiding places on Black Friday.

Simon spoke to Wolf and Tolek. 'The Germans are lying about the deportations. One of my people has been able to observe the Umschlagplatz. For six days now the same forty-four cars have come and gone. Figure it. The trains pull out every day at three o'clock. They return by eight o'clock the next morning. Seventeen hours' travel. Eight and a half going. Eight and a half coming back. Subtract an hour's unloading time. Subtract an hour to turn the train around. Consider today's travel conditions.'

'Summary,' Andrei said. 'It is our educated guess this train is not traveling more than seventy or eighty kilometers beyond Warsaw.'

Tolek rubbed his jaw, drew a mental picture of Warsaw's environs. 'There is no labor camp or combination of them inside this radius which can continue to take six thousand new people every day.'

'Exactly.'

'As you know,' Simon continued, 'my runner system was almost shattered on Black Friday. I lot almost all my people on the Aryan side.'

Andrei handed Wolf and Tolek packets of money. 'There's a guard playing at the Tlomatskie Gate. Go out in fifteen-minute intervals at six o'clock and meet at Gabriela's flat. She will have a railroad maintenance engineer there. He will place you in observation positions along the rail line.'

When they had gone Simon Eden asked Andrei about new arms. It was the same story. No arms. No money. No help from Roman or the Home Army. Evasions. Frustration. They had only five hundred soldiers left after Black Friday.

Andrei looked at his watch and said it was time for him to leave too.

'Must you go to Lublin?' Simon asked.

'Yes.'

'If there was a way to command you not to go . . .'

'No, Simon.'

'Are you certain you can get into this camp?'

'I don't know for certain. Ana tracked down my old company sergeant. A good soldier, that Styka. I have faith in him. He has been working on it for two weeks, Ana brought the message that he can get me in.'

'Andrei, if we lose you . . .'

'What's to lose, Simon?'

Simon flopped his big hands to his sides. 'What's to lose? I've been in a fog for over two years. I try to tell myself all this is untrue. It is not happening. I'm numb, but we survive on instinct.'

Andrei slapped his back.

'Well,' Simon said, 'wishing you luck inside Majdanek is rather ludicrous these days. Does Gabriela know?'

'No. I promised her not to keep secrets, but I cannot bring myself to talk about this trip to Lublin. But the minute I come through the door tonight, she will no longer be fooled.'

'I envy you, Andrei, having that kind of love. Andrei, for God's sake, get back here safely. I can't keep going without you.'

'See you around, Simon.'

Chapter Seven

Andrei rubbed his eyes wearily and brought them to focus beyond the unwashed window. The train poked past a hamlet of thatched shanties surrounded by the rye fields of the flat Lublin Uplands. It was a long, slow trip. Late afternoon before he would reach Lublin. Good old Styka. He had come through.

Simon's words ran through his mind: 'I've been in a fog . . . I'm numb, but we survive on instinct.' On those nights before a dangerous assignment Gabriela, too, was instinctive. She had held him all night with her eyes wide open and without a word.

Andrei allowed himself the reward of a sigh and an inner rebellion of his nerves over another close call. There had been an unexpected siding of the train and an inspection. Life and death hinged on an exchange of glances with one of the Polish police, who returned later for his bribe.

Freedom and capture had hung by a thread so many times, he could not count them any more. Every day fate or luck or a proper instinctive move was the difference between life and death. Each night at Mila 19 the Bathyrans related a series of stories of the day's close brushes and miraculous escapes.

Andrei took a canteen from his knapsack and sipped a swallow of water and bit off a small hunk of the staling bread. It was painful to put food into his stomach, which, shrunken by the lack of food, rebelled at the sudden stretching.

The train passed a hamlet. The tracks split a large field in half where men and oxen strained against plow leashes and women bent double in stoop labor. Burly leathered men and wrinkled women in drab black rags carried on in a primitive way, almost unchanged from feudal times. Peasants puzzled Andrei. He wondered how they could go on in poverty, superstition, ignorance, with a complete lack of desire to make either their land or their lives flourish.

Andrei remembered a Bathyran meeting long ago. Tolek Alterman had returned from the colonies in Palestine and, before the national leadership, exalted the miracles of drying up swamps and irrigating the desert. A fund-raising drive to buy tractors and machinery was launched. Andrei remembered that his own reaction had been one of indifference.

Had he found the meaning too late? It aggravated him. The land of the Lublin Uplands was rich, but no one seemed to care. In the unfertile land in Palestine humans broke their backs pushing will power to the brink.

He had sat beside Alexander Brandel at the rostrum of a congress of Zionists. All of them were there in this loosely knit association of diversified ideologies, and each berated the other and beat his breast for his own approaches. When Alexander Brandel rose to speak, the hall became silent.

'I do not care if your beliefs take you along a path of religion or a path of labor or a path of activism. We are here because all our paths travel a blind course through a thick forest, seeking human dignity. Beyond the forest all our paths merge into a single great highway which ends in the barren, eroded hills of Judea. This is our singular goal. How we travel through the forest is for each man's conscience. Where we end our journey is always the same. We all seek the same thing through different ways – an end to this long night of two thousand years of darkness and unspeakable abuses which will continue to plague us until the Star of David flies over Zion.' This was how Alexander Brandel expressed pure Zionism. It had sounded good to Andrei, but he did not believe it. In his heart he had no desire to go to Palestine. He loathed the idea of drying up swamps or the chills of malaria or of leaving his natural birthright.

Before he went into battle Andrei had told Alex, 'I only want to be a Pole. Warsaw is my city, not Tel Aviv.'

And now Andrei sat on a train on the way to Lublin and wondered if he was not being punished for his lack of belief. Warsaw! He saw the smug eyes of the Home Army chief, Roman, and all the Romans and the faces of the peasants who held only hatred for him. They had let this black hole of death in Warsaw's heart exist without a cry of protest.

Once there had been big glittering rooms where Ulanys bowed and kissed the ladies' hands as they flirted from behind their fans.

Warsaw! Warsaw!

'Miss Rak. I am a Jew.'

Day by day, week by week, month by month, the betrayal gnawed at Andrei's heart. He ground his teeth together. I hate Warsaw, he said to himself. I hate Poland and all the goddamned mothers' sons of them. All of Poland is a coffin.

The terrible vision of the ghetto streets flooded his mind. What matters now? What is beyond this fog? Only Palestine, and I will never live to see Palestine because I did not believe.

By late afternoon the train inched into the marshaling yards in the railhead at Lublin, which was filled with lines of cars poised to pour the tools of war to the Russian front.

At a siding, another train which was a familiar sight these days. Deportees. Jews. Andrei's skilled eye sized them up. They were not Poles. He guessed by their appearance that they were Rumanians.

He walked toward the center of the city to keep his rendezvous with Styka. Of all the places in Poland, Andrei hated Lublin the most. The Bathyrans were all gone. Few of the native Jews who had lived in Lublin were still in the ghetto.

From the moment of the occupation Lublin became a focal point. He and Ana watched it carefully. Lublin generally was the forerunner of what would happen elsewhere. Early in 1939, Odilo Globocnik, the Gauleiter of Vienna, established SS headquarters for all of Poland. The Bathyrans ran a check on Globocnik and had only to conclude that he was in a tug of war with Hans Frank and the civilian administrators.

Globocnik built the Death's-Head Corps. Lublin was the seed of action for the 'final solution' of the Jewish problem. As the messages from Himmler, Heydrich, and Eichmann came in through Alfred Funk, Lublin's fountainhead spouted.

A bevy of interlacing lagers, work camps, concentration camps erupted in the area. Sixty thousand Jewish prisoners of war disappeared into Lublin's web. Plans went in and out of Lublin, indicating German confusion. A tale of a massive reservation in the Uplands to hold several million Jews ... A tale of a plan to ship all Jews to the island of Madagascar ... Stories of the depravity of the guards at Globocnik's camps struck a chord of terror at the mere mention of their names. Lipowa 7, Sobibor, Chelmno, Poltawa, Belzec, Krzywy-Rog, Budzyn, Krasnik. Ice baths, electric shocks, lashings, wild dogs, testicle crushers.

The Death's-Head Corps took in Ukrainian and Baltic Auxiliaries, and the *Einsatzkommandos* waded knee-deep in blood and turned into drunken, dope-ridden maniacs. Lublin was their heart.

In the spring of 1942 Operation Reinhard began in Lublin. The ghetto, a miniature of Warsaw's, was emptied into the camp in the Majdan-Tartarski suburb called Majdanek. As the camp emptied, it was refilled by a draining of the camps and towns around Lublin, then by deportees from outside Poland. In and in and in they poured through the gates of Majdanek, but they never left, and Majdanek was not growing any larger.

What was happening in Majdanek? Was Operation Reinhard the same pattern for the daily trains now leaving the Umschlagplatz in Warsaw? Was there another Majdanek in the Warsaw area, as they suspected.

Andrei stopped at Litowski Place and looked around quickly at the boundary of civil buildings. His watch told him he was still early. Down the boulevard he could see a portion of the ghetto wall. He found an empty bench, opened a newspaper, and stretched his legs before him. Krakow Boulevard was filled with black Nazi uniforms and the dirty brownish ones of their Auxiliaries.

'Captain Androfski!'

Andrei glanced up over the top of the paper and looked into the mustached, homely face of Sergeant Styka. Styka sat beside him and pumped his hand excitedly. 'I have been waiting across the street at the post office since dawn. I thought you might get in on a morning train.'

'It's good to see you again, Styka.'

Styka studied his captain. He almost broke into tears. To him, Andrei Androfski had always been the living symbol of a Polish officer. His captain was thin and haggard and his beautiful boots were worn and shabby.

'Remember to call me Jan,' Andrei said.

Styka nodded and sniffed and blew his nose vociferously. 'When that woman found me and told me that you needed me I was never so happy since before the war.'

'I'm lucky that you were still living in Lublin.'

Styka grumbled about fate. 'For a time I thought of trying to reach the Free Polish Forces, but one thing led to another. I got a girl in trouble and we had to get married. Not a bad girl. So we have three children and responsibilities. I work at the granary. Nothing like the old days in the army, but I get by. Who complains? Many times I tried to reach you, but I never knew how. I came to Warsaw twice, but there was that damned ghetto wall ...'

'I understand.'

Styka blew his nose again.

'Were you able to make the arrangements?' Andrei asked.

'There is a man named Grabski who is the foreman in charge of the bricklayers at Majdanek. I did exactly as instructed. I told him you are on orders from the Home Army to get inside Majdanek so you can make a report to the government in exile in London.'

'His answer?'

'Ten thousand zlotys.'

'Can he be trusted?'

'He is aware he will not live for twenty-four hours if he betrays you.'

'Good man, Styka.'

'Captain ... Jan ... must you go inside Majdanek? The stories ... everyone really knows what is happening there.'

'Not everyone, Styka.'

'What good will it really do?'

'I don't know. Perhaps ... perhaps ... there is a shred of conscience left in the human race. Perhaps if they know the story there will be a massive cry of indignation.'

'Do you really believe that, Jan?'

'I have to believe it.'

Styka shook his head slowly. 'I am only a simple soldier. I cannot think things out too well. Until I was transferred into the Seventh Ulanys I was like every other Pole in my feeling about Jews. I hated you when I first came in. But ... my captain might have been a Jew, but he wasn't a Jew. What I mean is, he was a Pole and the greatest soldier in the Ulanys. Hell, sir. The men of our company had a dozen fights defending your name. You never knew about it, but by God, we taught them respect for Captain Androfski.'

Andrei smiled.

'Since the war I have seen the way the Germans have behaved and I think, Holy Mother, we have behaved like this for hundreds of years. Why?'

'How can you tell an insane man to reason or a blind man to see?'

'But we are neither blind nor insane. The men of your company would not allow your name dishonored. Why do we let the Germans do this?'

'I have sat many hours with this, Styka. All I ever wanted was to be a free man in my own country. I've lost faith, Styka. I used to love this country and believe that someday we'd win our battle for equality. But now I think I hate it very much.'

'And do you really think that the world outside Poland will care any more than we do?'

The question frightened Andrei.

'Please don't go inside Majdanek.'

'I'm still a soldier in a very small way, Styka.'

It was an answer that Styka understood.

Grabski's shanty was beyond the bridge over the River Bystrzyca near the rail center. Grabski sat in a sweat-saturated undershirt, cursing the excessive heat which clamped an uneasy stillness before sundown. He was a square brick of a man with a moon-round face and sunken Polish features. Flies swarmed around the bowl of lentils in which he mopped thick black bread. Half of it dripped down his chin. He washed it down with beer and produced a deep-seated belch.

'Well?' Andrei demanded.

Grabski looked at the pair of them. He grunted a sort of 'yes' answer. 'My cousin works at the Labor Bureau. He can make you work papers. It will take a few days. I will get you inside the guard camp as a member of my crew. I don't know if I can get you into the inner camp. Maybe yes, maybe no, but you can observe everything from the roof of a barrack we are building.'

Grabski slurped his way to the bottom of the soup bowl. 'Can't understand why the hell anyone wants to go inside that son-of-a-bitch place.'

'Orders from the Home Army.'

'Why? Nothing there but Jews.'

Andrei shrugged. 'We get strange orders.'

'Well – what about the money?'

Andrei peeled off five one-thousand-zloty notes. Grabski had never seen so much money. His broad flat fingers, petrified into massive sausages by years of bricklaying, snatched the bills clumsily. 'This ain't enough.'

'You'll get the rest when I'm safely out of Majdanek.'

'I ain't taking no goddamned chances for no Jew business.'

Andrei and Styka were silent. Grabski looked from one to the other, snarling, bullying. He quickly realized that the men before him were as large and tough as the Death's-Head Corps. He knew, too, Styka would kill him. Grabski grunted, cursed, and shoved the money into his pants pocket. 'Be here in the morning at six. We'll get started on the work pass.'

A sudden northeast breeze blew the sack curtains into the room, bringing in a terrible stench, nauseating the men. Grabski shoved away from the table and slammed the window shut. 'Every time the wind blows we get that smell from Majdanek.'

Andrei and Styka stood behind Grabski. Styka pointed to the skyline a few kilometers away where grayish smoke fizzled from a tall chimney.

'That's it,' Styka said, 'Majdanek.'

'Only way the Jews leave that camp is through the chimney,' Grabski said. Amused at discovering himself a humorist, he broke into a fit of laughter.

Chapter Eight

Horst von Epp waited with an infinite, knowing patience for Christopher de Monti to unravel after he had made his visit to the ghetto. Horst played it like a puppet master, confident that Chris was sinking closer to that point where he would be abandoned by the ever-shrinking voices of morality within him. As the weeks and months went, Horst saw his calculations coming to pass.

Chris drank hard these days, and women he had once resisted with bored ease were now constant bedmates. He became a perpetual guest at the perpetual parties he once shunned. As the heaviness inside him compounded, that point of no return would soon be reached. A week, a month, two, it did not matter to Horst, for Chris's downfall had become inevitable in his calculation. One day he would come to Horst and babble a plea for the life of the unknown Jewess inside the ghetto, and the piper would be paid.

Dr Franz Koenig's parties were uninhibited affairs that generals recalled with affection during the long cold winter nights on the Russian front. Koenig kept an international flavor, spicing the invitations to include the diplomatic corps, the press, and the stars of the moment, as well as the top Nazis. Nothing was spared by Koenig in the pursuit of gluttony and revelry. In addition to Warsaw's courtesans, Koenig continually imported new, young, slim, high-cheekboned blondes from Berlin, playing the role of a degenerated industrialist with great finesse.

Dr Koenig premiered the newly remodeled ballroom as the first large midsummer event of 1942. It had been redecorated in unabashed elegance. Amid tinkling glasses, bowing, kissing of hands, rumors ran rampant and deals and bribes and barter were made. Much of the talk was about the new depth of the German armed penetrations. El Alamein in North Africa stood before Rommel's magnificent Afrika Korps, and on the Russian front the Don River had been reached. The Japanese guests had an air of cocksure confidence. The Americans had not recovered from the devastation of Pearl Harbor. The Japanese General Staff was positive America had no stomach to make the sacrifice necessary to displace them from the Pacific islands. It was a night for Axis gaiety. America had come into the war with too little, too late. The glitter of Dr Franz Koenig's new ballroom made the participants so heady, there was even talk of a German breakthrough to India, which had been the long-forbidden dream of a dozen empires in a dozen ages.

Toward one o'clock the more strait-laced had made their departures and the party broke into splinter groups drifting to one of the many lush parlors adjoining the ballroom.

In another hour the guests would include only Dr Koenig's intimate circle of ten or twenty and the new imports from Berlin. The serious business of an orgy would begin.

Chris's cup had run over. He was in that state of inebriated calm when all of the tensions within him seemed gone for the moment. In the library he rested his head on the shoulder of a young German model. She was delighted to have found an Italian and he said that it was some time since he had had a German girl, so it should be fun. The room was quite dark, lit only by candelabra and some light filtering in from the main ballroom.

His German girl was approached by Koenig's aide and spoke so rapidly that Chris could barely decipher it through the alcoholic haze. Apparently she was essential to an act and could not be dispensed with. She eased away with apologies and promises. Chris yawned and shut his eyes for a moment.

He opened them, smacked his lips, and looked around for a servant. A figure of a small woman framed the doorway. Chris tried to think. He had seen the girl from a distance several times during the evening. He was positive he knew her from somewhere, and it seemed as though she were watching him.

She walked into the library, moving to the uninhabited corner by the candelabra. Chris walked up behind her. 'Do I know you?' he asked.

She turned and faced him, holding her chin up to the candlelight. 'Once you did.'

He squinted, trying to make her out in a sliver of light.

'Gabriela!'

She nodded. He turned chalky.

'What the hell are you doing here! What do you want?'

'An old friend wants to see you. He is in a desperate situation.'

'Andrei?'

'Yes.'

Chris mopped his wet forehead. 'Impossible. What's more, it's dangerous for you to be here. Dangerous for both of us.' He grabbed her arm. 'Wait. Let me think.'

'Hello there, Chris! I've been looking for you.'

Chris spun around to see Horst von Epp glower past him, staring at Gabriela. 'Sorry, I wasn't able to get here till late, but I understand it was rather dull – up to now, that is. This makes it all worth while. By God, Chris, you have an unfailing talent to find the most magnificent creatures.'

Gabriela played her role, acknowledging his interest with a coy smile.

'Well, aren't you going to introduce us, Chris?'

'Yes – certainly.'

'I am Victoria Landowski. I've just come to Warsaw from Lemberg for a visit with my cousin. From the many descriptions, I take it you must be Baron von Epp.'

'Madam,' Horst said, taking Gabriela's hand. He kissed it with a touch and look which embraced all the connotations, and she let her eyes answer him just enough to let him know she understood and welcomed his intentions.

'And where will you be staying, Miss Landowski?'

'I am not quite certain yet, Baron. Why don't I reach you as soon as I'm settled?'

Horst bowed and backed off gracefully, yielding the girl to Chris with her promise of a future relationship. 'It should be a wonderful fall season . . . I say, Chris, are you ill?'

'Dr Koenig is too generous with his liquor. I think I've had one too many.'

'Why don't we get a breath of air, Chris?' Gabriela said.

'Good idea.'

Horst von Epp watched them leave, intrigued with the pretty little thing. He sized her up for bed. Koenig's busy aide whispered in his ear that he was invited to the conservatory, where the girls were about to amuse them.

The doorman closed Chris and Gabriela into his Fiat. He fumbled for the ignition switch. 'You're a damned fool walking into this nest,' he mumbled.

Chris drove aimlessly at a crawl, checking the rear-view mirror constantly to see if he was being followed.

'What I want to say is, things have changed.'

'I should say that's rather obvious.'

'Gaby, you don't understand.'

'I do understand, quite well. I told Andrei it was a waste of time and that you wouldn't come.'

'Gaby ...'

'If you gave a damn for him you wouldn't have let two and a half years go by,' she said.

Chris wanted to tell Gaby he had tried to see her during the past year but had lost track of her when she changed flats. But he could not say it.

'Where is he?' Chris blurted impulsively.

'A hotel room near the yacht club in Saska Kempa.'

Chris sucked in a lungful of air, grunted, looked in the rear-view mirror once more, then made a U turn and drove on the Third of May Boulevard directly for the Poniatowski Bridge. In Saska Kempa, Chris concealed his car in a teamster's stable several blocks from the shabby hotel.

A meek handshake, an avoiding of Andrei's eyes. Unbearable small talk. Chris sagged into a hard-backed chair, studying the designs in the linoleum on the floor.

'How have you been?'

'Just fine.'

'Seen Deborah?'

'Yes, She is all right.'

'The children?'

'They are all right.'

'Do you have a glass of water? I'm all dried out.' He sipped and looked up at them. 'A hell of a reunion, isn't it? Well, I'm here. Gaby said it was something desperate.'

'We've needed you many times in the past two and a half years,' Andrei said. 'But I wouldn't come to you unless it was something so important we had to come to you.'

He watched Chris go through uncomfortable mannerisms. 'What is it?' Chris looked to Gabriela, but she gave no solace in her expression.

'Chris,' Andrei said in a voice filled with an unfamiliar pleading, 'tens of thousands of people are being murdered every day in extermination camps. We have put together an authentic report, detailing the locations, the names of the personnel and commanders, the method of operation. We have gone to the Home Army and begged them to get this out to the government in exile, but they won't help us. Every day means twenty, thirty, forty, fifty thousand human beings. Chris – you've got to carry this out for us and get it into the world press. We've got to stop this blood bath. This is the only way.'

Chris pulled himself to his feet. 'I've heard this talk, but I don't believe it. Germany is a civilized country. The Germans aren't capable of doing what you claim – it's a lie.'

'I've just come from inside Majdanek. If you care to interview your friend Baron von Epp, I'll gladly supply you with some very leading questions.'

Chris sank back into the chair again in a stupor. Andrei lay a typewritten book of a hundred pages before him. Chris glanced at it out of the corner of his eye but pulled his hand back. 'I'm not your man,' he whispered.

'Chris, you and I have spent too many hours together putting this lousy world under our microscopes. I know how you've been pulled apart these last two years, but I've always known with all my soul that in the crucible you are unable to walk away from the cries of the anguished without destroying yourself as a human being.'

'I told you, no! Why the hell did you ask me here?'

'Chris! Chris! Chris! You and I believe in the final nobility of man! You can't turn your back on us!'

Chris's fist drummed against the table with a monotonous thudding repetition. 'I've cried for justice before, Andrei! I cried rape and murder in Spain and it fell on deaf ears.'

'My God, Chris! Men have always destroyed each other. They always will. You can't pull out because you've been hurt once.'

'Do you really believe that goddamned world out there is going to be moved by this report? It's you who is the fool, not me. No one's going to care about murdered Jews or starving Indians or floods in Holland or earthquakes in Japan so long as their stinking bellies are full! Your goddamned conscience of man is a myth, Andrei.'

Andrei hovered over Chris. He shook Chris's shoulders, but the man would not unbend. Andrei slowly sank to his knees. 'Chris, I beg you on my knees to help us.'

Gabriela jerked angrily at Andrei. 'Get off your knees!' she commanded. 'Get off your knees! You will never do this again before any man!'

Chris turned his sweaty face up to her enraged expression. He tried through bleary eyes to beg her to stop.

'You sanctimonious son of a bitch,' Gabriela quivered. 'You sit up there on your throne and watch all us little ants scramble in fright to survive and you make your terse comments and your snide observations. I present to you, Chistopher de Monti – champion of the press! Oh God, no. Don't dirty your precious hands with our blood.'

'All I ever wanted is for Deborah to live – that's all – that's all I've ever wanted. I know she'll never see me again, but I want her to live – that's all I've ever wanted.'

'Your sister is a very fortunate woman, Andrei. In a single lifetime she has had two upstanding men like Paul Bronski and Christopher de Monti who would sell their souls for her.'

Andrei was limp with weakness and humiliation. 'My sister is a woman,' he whispered. 'She will take her life and the life of her children before she allows you to save her at the expense of a betrayal to the Nazis.'

'That's enough, Andrei,' Gabriela said. 'Look at him. He is completely degenerated.'

Andrei gave up. He walked to the door. 'You were right, Gabriela. We should not have asked him. I'd like to spit on you, Chris, but I must save my strength.'

Andrei left the room.

'You're not worthy of his spit,' Gabriela said, and followed.

Chris slumped over the table, weeping, choking on his own saliva and tears. His hand fell on the report. He pulled his head up. He gained control of himself and turned the first page.

COMBINED JEWISH ORGANIZATIONS' REPORT ON EXTERMINATION CENTERS IN OPERATION WITHIN THE GENERAL GOVERNMENT AREA OF POLAND, JULY 1942

We are able to authenticate firmly the existence of four centers in the General Government Area created for the sole purpose of conducting mass exterminations. In addition, two combination concentration-extermination camps are in existence. There are five hundred labor camps in Poland, of which a hundred and forty are reserved for Jews. All of them contain some sort of murder facilities.

The only conclusion to be drawn is that a master German plan is in effect for the absolute destruction of the Jewish people. In the beginning, mass starvation, disease, and executions decimated the various ghettos by tens of thousands. After the invasion of Russia, Kommandoes of four Special Action groups massacred additional hundreds of thousands. The culmination of this plan is now assembly-line murder. The master plan, it must be concluded, comes from Hitler through Himmler and Heydrich. The actual execution is performed by the so-called 4B section of the Gestapo (Jewish affairs) under the direction of SS Sub-Colonel Adolf Eichmann.

The extermination centers are located at railheads and generally in secluded sites. They are guarded by Waffen SS and Ukrainian and Baltic Auxiliaries. A staggering amount of planning, material, and manpower is being used to carry out this operation at a time when Germany is conducting a war on many fronts. For example, rail cars are at an urgent premium for the purpose of shipping war materials to the Russian front, yet importation of Jews from German-occupied countries into Poland seems to have taken a priority over army needs. In addition, thousands of engineers, scientists, and key personnel are tied up in this operation as well as desperately needed manpower. We can safely estimate that from two to three hundred thousand men are directly or indirectly involved. All of this effort testifies to the insane will of the Nazis as well as to the urgency of our situation.

These camps follow a basic pattern. Deception is carried out and secrecy maintained. This certainly indicates the Nazis are aware of the evil they are perpetrating. At each camp, deportees arrive and are weeded at selection centers. A few are set aside for slave labor. The rest, including women and small children, are moved to a 'sanitation center' under the illusion of receiving a disinfectant shower. Hair is shorn. The guards play out the game to the end by issuing bars of soap (which later turn out to be made of stone), and victims are asked to remember the number of the peg on which their clothing is hung. Many women attempt to hide children in their clothing or throw them off trains to peasants, but they are almost always found out.

When the occupants are in, an iron door is sealed and an attendant carries out the gassing. The first gassings were from the carbon monoxide exhaust of engines. This method proved slow and petrol costly, therefore a prussic acid mixture called Cyclon B was developed by the Hamburg Insecticide Company. Death is in minutes.

Jewish slave laborers clean the chambers and remove the corpses to crematoriums, where they are burned. At first cremation was in open pits, but the stench was unbearable. The Jewish laborers generally last only a few weeks before losing their sanity.

There are many variations, but this is the general pattern. Gold teeth are pulled from the corpses before burning. Anything of value is taken for the German war effort. Everything else – clothing, eyeglasses, shoes, artificial limbs, even dolls – is stored in warehouses, then scrutinized for hidden valuables. Hair is baled and shipped to Germany for use in the manufacture of mattresses and to waterproof submarine periscopes. In one camp, bodies have been boiled down for their fat content, to be used in the making of soap.

In addition to the Polish camps, we have reason to believe several camps in Germany have extermination facilities. Dachau, among others, is used as an 'experimental medical' center. Humans are compelled to undergo experiments, such as the grafting of bones, transplanting of organs, testing beyond human limitations in freezing, electrical shock, etc. In all camps, extermination and labor, the indignities, abuses, torture, and rape are universal. These are amplified in the attached supplementary reports.

The German extermination facilities are capable of murdering a minimum of a hundred thousand persons a day in Poland. We do not have the additional numbers who are killed inside Germany. The Polish camps are currently working at full capacity. New gas chambers and crematoriums are being constructed to increase the rate.

The Polish camps are:

LUBLIN DISTRICT

Belzec – Located on the Lublin-Tomaszow rail line near Rawa Ruska, handling Jews from the Lwow-Lemberg area with a capacity of ten thousand a day.

Sobibor – Near Wlodawa, between Wlodawa and Chelm. Capacity believed to be six thousand a day.

Majdanek – An early concentration camp in the Lublin suburb Majdan-Tartarski under the personal direction of Odilo Globocnik, SS Gruppenführer of Poland. Capacity in excess of ten thousand a day.

WESTERN POLAND

Chelmno – The oldest extermination center (in operation at the end of 1941), nine miles from Kolo, on the rail line between Lodz and Poznan, exterminating Jews in western Poland.

CENTRAL POLAND

Treblinka – Most recently discovered by underground efforts, located in the Sokolow Podlaski province near Warsaw, liquidating Jews from the Warsaw ghetto as well as Radom, Bialystok, Grodno, the Baltics, Czenstochowa, Kielce.

SOUTHERN POLAND

Auschwitz – Located just outside the Silesian village of Oswiencim. The concentration camp has some fifty satellite labor camps. Extermination facilities are in a compound named Birkenau. Capacity in excess of forty thousand a day. Gypsies, Russian POWs, political, criminal, and other prisoners are liquidated here as well as Jews.

SUPPLEMENTARY REPORT No. 1

by 'Jan' on the Majdanek extermination camp in Lublin

I was able to enter Majdanek disguised as a Polish laborer, one of hundreds who work on construction jobs in the outer compounds.

At 0700 I left Lublin by horse and cart with a party named 'Leopold.' We were halted at a rail terminal approximately one kilometer from the main gate of the camp. The terminal is adjacent to the main highway. We sat and waited while several thousand Rumanian Jews were herded over the highway on a march to the camp gate.

A line of Red Cross vans waited alongside the terminal building. German guards loaded these vans with aged, cripples, infants and others unfit to walk the mile. Leopold told me these Red Cross vans are actually sealed, escape-proof cabins. Once they are in motion, the carbon monoxide from the exhaust is routed back into the van so that by the time they reach Majdanek the occupants are dead.

> (*Note:* This same method was used in both Chelmno and Treblinka but ruled out as too slow and costly. It is used only to supplement the main extermination facilities.)

I entered the outer compound at 0800 through a gate which bore a sign: LABOR BRINGS FREEDOM. My crew was working on a brick barrack in the outer camp, fifty meters from the inner camp, for use by a new guard contingent. I was able to place myself on the third-story roof in a hidden spot and in a position of observation through a pair of field glasses which I brought in in my lunch box.

I should estimate that the entire camp area covered six or seven hundred acres. At its closest point it was only a kilometer and a half from Lublin. The outer camp contains guard barracks, the commandant's home, a general store, garage, and other service buildings of a permanent nature.

The inner compound is composed of forty-six barracks made of wood of the type used as German army stables. Air and light came through a narrow row of skylight windows. I was told that each barrack holds nearly four hundred prisoners. Obviously they are crammed with room only for slabs for beds and a narrow passageway to the main door.

The inner compound is surrounded by double walls of barbed wire five meters high. Between the two walls is a continuous patrol by Ukrainians with Alsatian dogs. I am told that the inner wall is electrified at night.

High guard towers with floodlights and machine guns stand every twenty-five meters along the outer wall.

Leopold called my attention to the set of barracks nearest us. He told me these are warehouses. The Rumanian Jews whom I had seen earlier at the rail terminal were already filing into the first barrack, which is a selection center. Only a few were taken into the camp. The rest trekked over an open plot to a concrete building marked by signs I could clearly identify as SANITATION CENTER.

The 'sanitation center' is very pretty, with lawns and trees and flowers planted around it.

When four hundred people had gathered, the line from the warehouse was halted and the group ordered into the 'sanitation center.' In approximately ten minutes I heard a burst of hideous screaming which lasted only ten or fifteen seconds. The building was then besieged by Jewish prisoners (*Sonnderkommandos*) who, I am told, clean out the chamber and remove the personal belongings to the second warehouse for sorting.

Ten minutes after the first gassing, the Jewish prisoners brought the corpses out. I saw them clearly. They were the same four hundred who had gone in twenty minutes before. Six to eight corpses were piled on a welded sledlike affair, and each 'sled' was pulled by Jewish prisoners. The *Sonnderkommandos* passed out of the inner-camp gate to a side road which ran one kilometer up a hill to a large building with a tall smokestack. I was able to see this clearly also through my field glasses.

The entire gassing process took thirty minutes for four hundred people. On the first day of my observation there were twelve separate gassings, or approximately forty-eight hundred persons. On the second day there were twenty gassings, or eight thousand, and on the third day seventeen gassings, or sixty-eight hundred. I have been told that upward of forty gassings have been accomplished in a twenty-four-hour period and never less than ten.

Leopold and other laborers have worked both in the repair of the gas chamber and crematorium. He tells me the chamber is a low-ceilinged room of four meters by twelve. It resembles a shower room in every detail except that the shower heads are false. An SS man is able to control the volume of gas through a barred observation window. Leopold and a crew of workers must enter the chamber every few weeks in order to resurface the concrete, which is torn up by victims clawing to get out.

Leopold was also instrumental in building the crematorium after open-pit burning of corpses was abandoned because of the stench. After the sleds are run to the crematorium the corpses are placed on a table and examined for gold teeth and slit open (and bled through a drainage pipe) to see if any gold or valuables had been swallowed. Then the corpses are taken into the adjoining room and placed in one of five ovens that hold five to seven corpses apiece. Extending arms and legs are hacked off. Cremation lasts minutes. The bones are removed from grates from the opposite side. Through my field glasses I was able to make out hills of bones some two stories high. Leopold tells me that recently when he went to repair the ovens a bone crushing machine had been installed and the bone meal sacked and shipped to Germany for fertilizer.

Christopher de Monti held his head between his legs and began to vomit. He vomited until his guts screamed with pain. Page after page it went. The full report of Andrei Androfski, the reports of a handful of survivors of Treblinka and Chelmno and the labor camps.

'God! What have I done?' he cried in anguish. 'I am a Judas! I am a Judas!'

The puke and the tears and the pain and the liquor crushed on him and he fell to the floor in a dead faint.

Chapter Nine

FELLOW JEWS! WARNING!

DO NOT REPORT TO THE UMSCHLAGPLATZ FOR DEPORTATION! THE DESTINATION IS A DEATH CAMP LOCATED NEAR THE TREBLINKA VILLAGE! HIDE YOUR CHILDREN! RESIST! THIS IS A SIGNAL FOR AN UPRISING! JOIN US!

JOINT FORCES

Journal Entry

Oh, my God, why have your forsaken us! How has man reached such depravity? We are at the bottom of a swill pit, and it is midnight! In all of the long tortured history of our people we have reached the moment of greatest degradation.

ALEXANDER BRANDEL

The immediate result of the relevations brought the long-sought unity among the diversified elements in the ghetto. Simon Eden and the Labor Zionists already had a working agreement with Andrei and the Bathyrans. Now the Communists and many religious fringe groups and individuals went under the single banner of Joint Forces. The Revisionists agreed to a non-binding working agreement. Simon Eden was declared commander and Andrei Androfski his deputy, with the Communists taking charge of activity beyond the wall. Although they were weak inside the ghetto, the Communists on the outside gave them the closest set of allies of any other group on the Aryan side. Wolf Brandel was sent into the Brushmaker's district to organize a fighting unit inside the factory complex.

The Joint Forces counted sixty pistols, thirty-four rifles, and a single automatic weapon.

The guns were of so many different calibers and varieties that some had only a half dozen rounds of ammunition. The tiny arsenal was reinforced somewhat by several thousand homemade bottle bombs and grenades manufactured from water pipes perfected by the chemist, Jules Schlosberg, in the cellar of Mila 19.

The total combat force stood at five hundred sixty young men and women, mostly in their early twenties, almost entirely without military training.

Journal Entry

The call for a rebellion has fallen on deaf ears. How can the people rebel? What do they have to rebel with? What help will they receive from the outside? In a final banality of the German language, the Nazis refer to the exterminations as 'dispensation of special treatment.' The desire to survive has become so intense that the people will not allow themselves to believe there is a death camp at Treblinka. The

Jewish Militia and members of the Civil Authority rip down underground posters as quickly as they are put up. Kennkarten *stamped for slave labor are still believed by the people to be some sort of magic key to life.*

It is amazing how the people will submit themselves to a living death worse than death itself. Even the most decadent societies in past history have understood that a basic minimum must be accorded for a slave or even an animal to be able to produce a reasonable day's work. The Germans have even made an innovation on this by turning all of Poland into one big slave-labor pool. With millions of extra laborers who cannot exist otherwise, the competition for the right to become a slave is fierce.

The slaves in Dr Koenig's brush and uniform factories are separated from their families, numbered, stamped, beaten at their work. They labor in abysmal conditions for sixteen to eighteen hours a day. There is almost no heat in winter or ventilation or light. They exist with no personal property or human rights. They are terrorized and starved so that the fight for food among them is a further struggle to live. Their sleeping quarters are unfit to be pigsties. Every slave of every time has dreamt of freedom, and every tyrant of every time has recognized that dream. Here the only alternative is death. The slightest defect by protest or sickness brings immediate liquidation and replacement by another who scrambles for the right to be a slave.

The Big Action enters its second week. Yesterday no volunteers showed up at the Umschlagplatz. The Militia and Nightingales surrounded Koenig's Brushmaker's factory and selected half the workers for deportation. Today the Civil Authority called for volunteers to fill thefactory openings. It was oversubscribed! Of course this newest German ruse will not last long, but it is fantastic that the people continue to allow themselves to be tricked.

Crazy Nathan stands near the Umschlagplatz and laments and prophesies that he will be the sole survivor in Warsaw. His latest psalm:

The Germans are so good to us.
They even make a raid
To give us free vacations,
With all expenses paid.

ALEXANDER BRANDEL

On the ninth day of the Big Action, Alexander Brandel walked into the barracks of the Jewish Militia, cater-corner to the Civil Authority building at Zamenhoff and Gensia streets. The police who had bullied the ghetto around for nearly two years became uneasy at the presence of Brandel. He was more disheveled than ever. His slight stature certainly posed no threat of physical harm, yet they feared him. He was one of the few untouchables. Harm to him would bring savage retribution to them. But more, they feared his calm. He asked to see Piotr Warsinski.

Warsinski, the convert, whose hatred of Jews matched the viciousness of the Reinhard Corps, also feared Alexander Brandel. The flesh on the backs of his hands were always crimson from a nervous itch. At the sight of Alex entering his office, his fingernails dug into them, turning his skin to bleeding scales.

'What do you want here?' he growled.

'I should like to go into the Umschlagplatz and I want a dozen of my nurses around the selection center.'

'You're crazy.'

'I'll pay for the privilege.'

'Get the hell out or you'll be taking a train ride yourself.'

That goddamned smile on Brandel's face! That son of a bitch! What he hated more than anything was Brandel's calm. Brandel's refusal to argue. When he had been sub-warden at Pawiak Prison he liked to watch the prisoners cringe, broken at his feet. Then one like Brandel would show up. unafraid. He hated unafraid bastards. Warsinski's itch worsened and his slitty eyes watered.

This morning he had beaten a woman prisoner to death with his hands. Women pointed up his impotence, his inability to be a man even when he paraded them around naked and made them perform obscenities with male prisoners.

He dropped his hands below the desk and tore at them with his fingernails.

'What do you want?'

'To see Haupsturmführer Kutler and Sturmbannführer Stutze. There are certain people who are taken to the Umschlagplatz whom we want to buy back.'

'What are you paying with?'

'American dollars.'

'I'll take the message to them. How much a head?'

'Six dollars.'

'Whatever deal is made, add on another dollar for the Militia.'

'Fine,' Alex said, shoving away from the desk, hiding his revulsion. What pearls of wisdom had he gathered in a lifetime of study to pierce the heart of Piotr Warsinski? Seven dollars per life. Warsinski's cruel eyes told him that one day he would stand on a platform and watch Alex ride off to Treblinka in a cattle car.

Haupsturmführer Kutler was sloppy drunk when Warsinski reached the SS barracks. The sight of Warsinski's bloody hands triggered a quicker guzzling. The nightmare had been particularly bad for several days as Kutler relived the massacre of Babi-Yar and woke up screaming from a dream of drowning in blood. Now his sleep was tormented by visions of little animals tearing at his flesh. Sturmbannführer Stutze tried to pull the captain to his feet. Stutze was sickened at the weak fiber of the Germans who had been Kommandos in the Action Squads. They constantly drank themselves to the DT's and pumped their veins full of dope. Austrians such as he and Globocnik and Hitler were made of sterner stuff. When the war was won, the Austrians would dominate the weaker German species. Kutler was in no condition to talk. Stutze had him taken to his room by a pair of guards, then turned to Warsinski.

'So,' Stutze said, 'he offered you six dollars a Jew head. How much did you add on for yourself?'

'Only a dollar a Jew. Herr Sturmbannführer, and much of that must be spread among my police.'

The crippled Austrian meditated. 'Hummm. What is the difference? Let them buy the Jews. We'll get them all back anyhow. Only . . . Jews barter. You are a Jew, Warsinski. Barter.'

Warsinski winced at being called a Jew.

'I want ten dollars a Jew, payable at the end of every business day,' Stutze said.

'Yes, sir.'

'And, by the way, let us keep this transaction between us.'

'Yes, sir.'

At the final price of eleven dollars and fifty cents a head, Alexander Brandel and his nurses were allowed into the Umschlagplatz. In the next few days they snatched out a few writers, scientists, musicians, poets, historians, teachers, children, engineers, doctors, actors, and rabbis from among the thousands jammed into the daily train.

The ruse of taking factory workers failed because volunteers refused to take their place any more. The next clean-up was a systematic dragnet of the ghetto to bag the thousands of beggar children, Wild Ones, and homeless for deportation. Crazy Nathan was among those picked up, but Alexander Brandel purchased his life, for he was a sentimental historian and the 'crazy' one had filled his journals with hundreds of poems and anecdotes.

In these days the lines of deportees were not so orderly as in the beginning. Bribe money flashed all over the Umschlagplatz. When there was no money, the deportees offered the guards watches, rings, furs – anything – to buy their way back into the ghetto for another day, another hour. And each day the marches to the trains were halted dozens of times by frantic bursts for freedom which only intensified the brutality of the guards.

And each day when the trains pulled out at three o'clock there were leftovers in the square. These prisoners were taken to the top floor of the selection building, to be first in line for deportation the next day. Each night the Ukrainian guards stripped the prisoners, searching them for valuables. Women were taken to the lower floors of the building and raped.

On the twelfth day of the Big Action, the Bathyran Council met and demanded from Alex that he stay out of the Umschlagplatz. Tolek and Ana pleaded that a whim of Kutler or Stutze would cancel their deal and threaten his own life. Alex would have none of it, not even their orders nor, finally, their threats to restrain him. For so many years he had battled to breathe life into the dying. He could not hold back the flood, but he was frantic to salvage the product of a great culture.

And on the next day he milled in the courtyard of the Umschlagplatz, as usual.

'Alex! Come quickly. Rabbi Solomon has passed from the selection center. They're taking him to the cemetery for execution.'

Alex raced over the square, stumbling, gasping, into the building, down the corridor, past the guard, into Kutler's office. The captain was more than halfway through his first bottle of schnapps and it was not yet noon. Alexander completely lost his composure.

'The Rabbi Solomon!' he cried.

'Don't push your luck, Jew boy,' Kutler blurted.

Alex panicked.

'A hundred dollars!'

'Hundred?' He began to laugh. 'Hundred for that old Jew carcass? God damn. The price for old Jews is good today. He's all yours, Jew boy.'

As Alex sighed and reeled out, Kutler reared back and laughed until the tears came to his eyes.

In the middle of the night Sylvia Brandel tiptoed down to Alexander's office. Mila 19 was asleep except for the guards. Earlier in the day she had tried to go to him, but his door was locked. He refused to answer her calls. She did not know whether to be angry or hurt or to try to approach him with sympathy or to leave him alone. It was indeed strange behaviour for Alex. She rattled on the doorknob and knocked again. He opened it and walked away from her.

Sylvia stared at his back, trying to adjust to the awesome experience, for Alexander was not like other men. He had always been a strong stone lighthouse for people to look up to find light and shelter. In twenty years of marriage she could not remember him floundering or crying for help. At first she was troubled that he did not seem to need the compassion that other men needed, but she learned to revere him and to live to serve him. Alex lived in his own world, a strange mixture of ideals and ideas, and he functioned with inexhaustible reservoirs of patience and courage. It was frightening to see him derailed.

'How is Rabbi Solomon?' he asked.

'We have a cot set up for him in the Good Fellowship room in the cellar. Ervin will stay with him tonight. Alex, will you eat something? There is some soup left in the kitchen.'

'I'm not hungry,' he whispered.

'It's almost three o'clock. Please come up to bed.'

He flopped at his desk, and his face dropped into his hands in utter defeat.

'Alex, I have never questioned your decisions, but I beg you – don't go to the Umschlagplatz again. There is a limit to what I can stand too.'

Tears welled in the corners of his eyes and rolled to nothing halfway down his cheek.

'No man can continue as you have without breaking up.'

'I've failed,' he whispered, 'I've failed.'

'You're a human being, Alex. You've given your life to other people. I can't stand to see you let yourself be destroyed.'

'I've failed,' he mumbled, 'I've failed.'

'Alex, for God's sake!'

'I lost my head today. I'll lose it again.'

'You're tired ... so tired.'

'No. It's just ... that I knew today ... everything I've stood for ... everything I've tried to do has been wrong.'

'Oh no, darling.'

'My way? Keep one more body alive for one more day. All my cunning to save a single man, and now thousands flood to their deaths and there is nothing I can do ... nothing.'

Sylvia gripped him awkwardly. 'I won't hear you berate yourself after all you have done.'

'Done?' He laughed. 'What have I done, Sylvia? Trade with swindlers and Nazis? Use trickery and cunning? Done?' He took her hands and he was again gentle Alex. 'They are going to destroy our entire culture. How can I preserve a few voices to show the world who we were and what we have given them? Who will be left?'

He walked away from her. 'We don't speak of it here in Mila 19, but Andrei and I have had little to say to each other since the war. Do you know why? When the Germans came here he wanted to take our people to the woods to fight. I stopped him. I took the guns and the bullets from him. My way – I had to have my way.'

'Alex, please!'

'Wrong! I am wrong and I've always been wrong! Not my journal or Rabbi

Solomon's prayers will deliver us. Only Andrei's guns, and it is too late and I did this to him.'

Like the catacombs of Rome, an underground city was clawed beneath the ghetto of Warsaw. Every person capable of working joined in a frantic race to build hiding places.

Fifty thousand trap doors, fifty thousand secret entrances led to false rooms in sub-floors, closets, behind bookcases, in attics. In the stores and bakeries they hid in unfired ovens, under counters. They made hiding places by removing the stuffing in couches, under tubs, in garbage dumps.

They lived a second away from their escape hatches. Walking in the streets became a memory. Communication was by rooftop. Behind loose tiles, stoves, toilets, pictures, lay entrances to secret rooms.

Cellars were good to hide in, for they could hold larger stores of food and their entrances were easily concealed, but attics had the advantage of the best escape routes.

The epitome of ingenuity did not deter the Big Action from bagging their quotas for the deportations. The cry of children, the keen noses of trained dogs, the spying of informers continued to flush more and more secret places. Guards in the streets watched guards upstairs break every window in a house, for unbroken windows revealed the presence of a hidden room.

At Mila 19 and at Leszno 92, Andrei and Simon took attic rooms where an alarm bell would send them to the rooftops, where the guards were not so anxious to follow.

The entrance through the packing crates to the secret rooms in the basement of Mila 19 was abandoned as not safe enough, and a false water closet was constructed on the main floor. By removing a loose floor bolt the lavatory swung away, revealing a hole in the wall large enough for a man to crawl through. A ladder led to the new parts of the basement dug out since the Big Action and holding a dozen people Alex had snatched from the Umschlagplatz as well as the archives and arsenal rooms. An exit tunnel was dug to tie into the large drainage pipe which led many meters beyond Mila 19. The underground complex spread until it was halted by the main line of the pipe which ran directly down the middle of Mila Street. The sound of rushing sewage was constantly heard.

At the end of the third week in August the Big Action suddenly ground to a halt. The roundups stopped.

Chapter Ten

Max Kleperman had not only one of the few Jewish telephones in the ghetto, he had two, the second a direct line to Dr Franz Koenig, with whom a vast amount of business was transacted. The license to buy and sell gold, agent real estate, smuggle, inform were exclusive rights granted the Big Seven.

Max Kleperman's private phone rang.

'*Ja, Herr Doktor ... Ja, Herr Doktor ... Ja, Herr Doktor.*'

After several more '*Ja, Herr Doktors,*' Max hung up and called for his secretary. 'Dr Koenig wants to see all the partners here in my office in an hour. Get hold of them right away and have them wait here. I go now to see him at his residence and I will come back with him for the meeting.'

Max checked out his appearance, took the diamond ring from his little finger, and clapped hands for his chauffeur and bodyguard. They drove from the ghetto through the Krasinski Gate. Max liked to drive to the Aryan side. He enjoyed looking at the trees. There was only one tree in the entire ghetto, and that was in front of the Civil Authority. That particular tree annoyed him, for he always considered the Civil Authority in competition with the Big Seven. Many times he toyed with the idea of planting a half dozen trees in front of his headquarters on Pawia Street but decided it would be provocative.

Max had a particular affection for the Krasinski Gardens. As a boy he had started his career there, hiring Polish hoodlums to steal from the Jewish delivery boys and reselling the merchandise at Parysowski Place. Parysowski Place was closed to trade these days, since the deportations.

Max heaved a sigh of relief now that the deportations had stopped. Even he and the Big Seven people were getting edgy. Certainly the Germans had accomplished what they wanted. Max's mind turned to visions of a new plum awaiting him at Dr Koenig's. With the deportations over, some new venture was cooking. I've come a long way since the old days, he thought.

Dr Koenig was the best of the Germans to deal with. He didn't shout or berate one, nor did he try to steal arms and legs off in a deal. All Dr Koenig wanted was a fair share. A fine man, Dr Koenig.

Max was ushered into Koenig's office. He sat down and squeezed his cigar in excited anticipation and, when Koenig nodded that it was all right for him to smoke, lit it with the silver lighter on the desk.

'Are your partners waiting at the Big Seven?' Dr Koenig asked.

'They will be there as ordered, Herr Doktor.'

'Now, Max, let's talk a little business.'

Kleperman opened his arms graciously. 'I am your humble servant.'

Koenig put on a pair of bifocals, opened a file, and lifted a sheet of paper and studied it. 'You've made quite a killing in the last few years, Kleperman.'

The smile vanished from Max's face. Over his shoulder he caught a glimpse of a pair of SS Waffen guarding the door. Max cleared his throat and leaned on his elbow. What was Koenig up to?

'I must say, you were very clever. Bilking us out of a quarter of a million dollars.'

Max thrust out his hand in protest. 'A terrible exaggeration!'

'One of your partners volunteered the information.'

Max's big fingers tugged away to loosen his collar as Dr Koenig read a terribly correct accounting of his fancy footwork. 'And finally,' Koenig said, 'you have given inflated zlotys to the welfare people through agents in exchange for dollar deposits in Swiss banks. Buildings for which you have acted as agent have been leased to Orphans and Self-Help for dollars also. Now, Max, you know all of this is illegal.'

Kleperman was way ahead of Koenig. He looked over his shoulder to see if the guards had miraculously disappeared. They hadn't. The *hutzpah*, the gall of Koenig to sit there with this holier-than-thou attitude when it was he, Kleperman, who set up most of the deals for the Germans. They had wallowed together in the muck, and now Koenig was going into an act of righteousness. Nothing on earth was worse than a righteous thief!

'As Kommissar of Jewish property,' Koenig said, 'I am appalled at the state of the affairs conducted by you. You have blatantly betrayed the trust of the occupation authorities.'

Think fast! Max Kleperman, you are in a bad position. His brain raced. He'd have to go for a deal. He'd play with the Swiss money and save the South American money. No one knew about the South American money.

'I am in a bad bargaining position,' Max smiled.

'I thought you would comprehend the situation.'

'But, as always, Max Kleperman is a reasonable man.'

Max nodded in the direction of the SS men. Koenig ordered them to wait outside.

'Now, Kleperman, let's make a clean breast. How much do you have sitting in Swiss banks, and which banks?'

'I have forty thousand dollars on demand,' Max confided.

'Which banks?'

Max wiped his forehead with his sleeve.

'May I conclude, Herr Doktor, that the various contracts between you and the Big Seven are about to be terminated?'

'You may conclude whatever you wish to conclude.'

Max cleared his throat and leaned over the desk to dispense a great confidence. 'The fact is, I have a few dollars more. Fifty thousand. Frankly, I am weary of business. I should like to enjoy the fruits of my labor. Now – we make a final deal. I'll sign half this money to you now and half when I arrive in Bern with my family.'

Koenig rocked in his chair and smiled tightly. 'Ready to jump ship, eh, Max.'

Max winked.

'How about your partners?'

'Believe me, I've tolerated those thieves as long as it is humanly possible. I think this is a reasonable way for two honorable men to end a long and fruitful association.'

'But, Max, how will you live?'

'Somehow, I'll struggle by.'

'Perhaps with the money in the National Bank in Geneva?'

'Oh – oh yes, I did have an account there.'

'And the Bank of South America in Buenos Aires, and the Grain Exchange in Rio de Janeiro.'

'*Herr, Herr, Herr ...*'

Koenig spread six documents before Kleperman and handed him a pen. 'Just sign these, Mr Kleperman. We will fill in the details.'

Max's face twitched violently. A belch of misplaced cigar smoke gagged him. 'The other partners have money over the border too. If I sign these papers and give you the information on them, do I get a passport?'

Koenig smiled. 'You've made yourself a deal.'

Max scrawled his signature on the papers, giving away over two-hundred thousand ill-earned dollars. Droplets of sweat dripped on the transfers as he signed.

'When I arrive in Switzerland I will give you the information on the others.'

Koenig nodded. 'We knew we could depend on your co-operation, Max.

You will receive information about your departure shortly.'

Max was sick, but he still had his life. The pair of SS men led him out of Koenig's palace. He had money in eight banks. There were two places that that righteous thief Koenig had not discovered. Max flopped in the back seat of his car, removed his hat, and fanned himself and groaned.

His eyes bulged in terror! His cigar fell from his mouth. His chauffeur had been replaced by an SS man, and his bodyguard was gone. Before he could budge, a pair of SS were on either side of him and the car whisked out of the driveway. It stopped six minutes later at the entrance to the Jewish cemetery.

Max was white with terror at the sight of Sturmbannführer Sieghold Stutze. The SS men had to help him walk. Stutze tapped a length of pipe in his open palm as Max was dragged before him. Kleperman took off his hat. 'Your excellency, Sturmbannführer ... I ... I ...'

Stutze spoke. 'I wanted to be here for you personally, Kleperman. You are the filthiest of all the filthy Jews. I have always admired that ring of yours. No, don't bother to give it to me now. I'll get it after the execution.'

'Ah, then ... you did not receive the word. Dr Koenig and I made a deal. You are in for a hundred thousand dollars ... you see ...'

'Shut up. You didn't really think we would let you out of Poland with what you know?'

'My lips are sealed. I swear it.'

'You don't have to swear it. We are going to seal them for you.'

Six powerful hands gripped him. He dropped to his knees. They began to drag him.

'Wait!' the Austrian said. 'Let him crawl.'

'Excellency. There is more money. I didn't tell Koenig. You ... me ... a private deal ...'

The lead pipe caught Kleperman behind the ear. He pitched face down on the dirt and crawled to Stutze and threw his arms around his knees. 'Mercy! Mercy! Mercy for Max Kleperman!'

The pipe came down and down, again, again, again, until Max's face was squashed like an overripe watermelon. Stutze broke into a sweat. He kicked with his gimpy leg and screamed and ranted until he had exhausted himself on the blood orgy and had to be held upright by his SS troopers.

Max Kleperman's lifeless body was dragged down the long path lined with desecrated grave markers to the west wall and unceremoniously flung into a ditch twenty feet long and twelve feet deep.

Along the edge of the ditch the partners and fifty members of the Big Seven were lined up. They cried, begged, bartered. Below them, Kleperman lay in a bed of lime.

Some fell to their knees and cried for God and for mother. Whoremasters, thieves, informers.

'Mercy!'

'Fire!'

The sound of rifle fire was a cliché within these walls. The Jewish gravediggers watched impassively as the bodies plunged to the bottom of the ditch and stared up at them from grotesque positions. The firing squad advanced to the edge of the ditch and poured gunfire into the twitching bodies until they were still. Shovels of lime were spread. Another batch of Big Seven people was hauled in.

PROCLAMATION!

IT HAS BEEN DISCOVERED THAT THE BIG SEVEN COMPANY HAS BEEN GUILTY OF INNUMERABLE CRIMES AND WERE THE MAIN PERPETRATORS OF MUCH OF THE JEWISH SUFFERING. IN THE NAME OF COMMON JUSTICE THE GERMAN AUTHORITIES HAVE DISPOSED OF THESE CRIMINALS AFTER INVESTIGATIONS AND TRIALS.

AS OF THIS DATE ALL FURTHER DEPORTATIONS ARE CANCELED. SPECIAL SCHOOLS MAY REOPEN AND AUTHORIZED PUBLIC MEETINGS WITHIN THE GHETTO ARE PERMITTED. THE CURFEW IS AGAIN EXTENDED TO 7 P.M.

BY ORDER
RUDOLPH SCHREIKER
KOMMISSAR, DISTRICT OF WARSAW

Chapter Eleven

Rachael thumbed through a stack of sheet music, selected several numbers, and slipped on her Star of David armband. Deborah, dressed in a gown and robe, entered the room, yawning and stretching.

'Are you certain it is safe to give a recital today? I feel uneasy about it.'

'Momma, there haven't been any deportations for four days. Ervin is arranging programs all over the ghetto to get people's minds off the past three weeks. Besides, I'll be playing at your orphanage on Niska and nothing will happen there.'

'Well, I suppose it is all right.'

'I may see Wolf today. It's been ten days.'

Deborah fussed with her daughter's hair. 'I wish you wouldn't go to Andrei's.'

'We can't any more, Momma. It's being watched all the time.'

'You can come here. Your father won't be home till late.'

As Rachael turned and faced her mother, Deborah realized for the first time that her child was as tall and mature as she. 'Thanks, Momma, but Wolf is terribly proud about that. Besides, it's not the most important thing any more. Just being able to see each other for a few minutes and talking is all we really want.'

Deborah patted her cheek.

Stephan burst into the apartment. 'Hey, come on. Aren't you ready yet?'

'Be careful, children. Keep your Civil Authority *Kennkarten* handy and forgive me for not coming. I'm dog-tired. I have to get a few hours' sleep before going back to the orphanage. Tell Susan I'll take the night shift.'

Stephan and Rachael pecked kisses on Deborah's cheek.

Rachael opened the door and stopped. 'Strange,' she said. 'Being able to walk in the streets again.'

'Be careful,' Deborah repeated.

The assembly hall in the Niska Street orphanage was capable of holding most of the four hundred children. It was one of the twenty-eight institutions under Alexander Brandel's Orphans and Self-Help Society which somehow managed to feed and secretly educate over twenty thousand parentless youngsters. Unlike the rest of the ghetto, these homes had no hiding rooms, for it would have been impossible to construct them secretly. After all, Brandel concluded, these were children, and he had to believe in the final mercy of the enemy to leave them alone.

Rachael Bronski was the very favorite of the children. They crammed together, filling all the benches, sitting in the aisles and on the floor before her piano on the platform at the end of the hall. The nurses, teachers, and social workers stood along the back wall.

Rachael looked continually to the back door through which Wolf might appear. A long time ago when he returned from the Bathyran farm at Wework, he had come to her during a recital in this very place. Perhaps he would come again today.

Rachael held up her hands for attention and told the children what her first number would be. It was a new one in which she narrated the life of Chopin behind a sampling of waltzes, nocturnes, and etudes, ending with the patriotic crescendo of a polonaise.

The next number was a medley of Yiddish songs. She watched the faces of the children searching their memory for a faint voice in the past which had sung to them.

'Should I be a rabbi?
I don't know my Torah,
Should I be a merchant?
I have nothing to sell.

'And I have no hay,
And I have no oats,
And I'd like a drink of vodka,
But my wife will curse me,
So I'll find a big rock,
And I'll sit me down and cry.

'Should I be a *schochet*?
I cannot use a *chalef*,
Should I be a *melamed?*
I don't know an *alef*.

'Should I be a cobbler?
I don't have any last.
Should I be a teamster?
I have no cart or horse.

'Should I be a blacksmith?
I won't have any anvil,
Should I run a tavern?
No, my wife would get too drunk.'

'What would you like to hear next?'
'Palestine!'
'Rachael! Sing to us about Palestine!'
'Palestine!'
'Palestine!'

> 'The roses bloom in Galilee,
> And the land rejoices.
> Round the day and through the night,
> We lift our thankful voice.
>
> 'We love you, our Galilee,
> Your land makes our hearts sing.
> We guard it dear with soul and gun
> And fear not what fate brings . . .'

Susan Geller entered at the rear of the hall. She looked around quickly, then whispered to her second nurse. The woman looked startled for an instant, then nodded and whispered to another nurse.
'All together now, children!'

> 'The roses bloom in Galilee,
> And the land rejoices . . .'

Susan Geller looked around once more and spotted Stephan. She wove through the pack of children, took his hand, and led him to a side door. 'Make no outcry, Stephan. The building is surrounded by Militia. Get upstairs. There are twenty-five or thirty children in an attic classroom. Do you know where it is?'
Stephan nodded.
'Take them over the roof to Mila 19. Tell Alexander Brandel to get to the Umschlagplatz quickly.'
Rachael frowned as she saw Stephan slip out of the hall.

> 'We love you, our Galilee,
> Your land makes our hearts sing . . .'

Susan sat on the bench beside Rachael. 'At the end of this song I will make an announcement. You keep playing. We want no panic. Do you understand?'
'Oh God . . .'
'Keep playing, Rachael, keep playing.'
'I . . . understand . . .'
Susan stepped before the piano and held up her hands. 'Children!' she said. 'Aunt Susan has a most wonderful surprise! Today we are going to the country on a picnic!'
The announcement was greeted with 'ohs' and 'ahs' of disbelief.
'We are all going on a train ride out of the ghetto and we will see all of those things we have talked about – trees and flowers and farms. All those wonderful things which you have never seen before. This is going to be the greatest experience of your life. Now we will all file out of the hall and to the street. Don't be frightened of the soldiers, because today they are there to help us. Now, Rachael, would you play something while we march out?'

Susan stepped into the corridor just as Piotr Warsinski entered the building. She blocked the door to the assembly hall.

'We are quite ready,' Susan said. 'If you will kindly tell your men not to alarm the children we will keep them calm.'

'We just want the children, not you.'

'We choose to go too.'

Warsinski shrugged. 'Have it your way. Get them out into the streets.'

'Quickly,' Stephan Bronski ordered two dozen six-year-olds in the attic classroom. Ghetto life had conditioned them to respond to his order with unqualified discipline. Stephan was first up the escape ladder to the roof. He nudged the trap door open an inch and peered around.

A Ukrainian on the roof!

Stephan signaled for the line behind him to be still. The guard paced back and forth, sweating in the heat through his dirty brown, black-sleeved shirt. He turned. Stephan could see his face and the epaulets with the skull and crossbones and the big knobby hands gripped around a rifle.

The guard stopped near the corner of the roof. The ridge was built up fifteen inches over the roof level. The guard knelt on it, peering past a steep tile roof which partly blocked the view to the street five stories down.

Clump ... clump ... clump ...

The man looked around at the thing flying over the roof at him. Before he could gather his wits or straighten up it was on him at a dead run. Stephan slammed his body at the Ukrainian at the same instant the man tried to stand up. It threw him off balance. His legs buckled and he fell onto the overhang, dropping his rifle on the roof.

In a frantic grab he snatched the top of the ridge. Stephan lifted the guard's fallen rifle and with its butt smashed the clinging man's hands.

A shriek!

The guard slid down the tiles, flailing in panic for something to grab. His body swooped over the edge and became smaller, smaller, smaller, until it stopped suddenly on the pavement.

'Quick!' Stephan cried, ruling out fear or revulsion at his deed. One by one the children climbed onto the roof.

Rifle fire cracked from the street. Shouts below! '*Juden Kinder!* Jew children!'

The ghetto rat knew his way well. He fled over the ceiling of the city with the knowledge of a craftsman. Then a dead end.

The line of buildings dropped from five stories to four. A chasm four feet wide separated the buildings. Stephan looked for the mattress which had been laid on the lower roof to break the falls. It had been removed! The decision was already made for him. He could neither stay nor turn back.

'Now we are going to have to jump over to that roof. We will have to stand on the very edge so we can reach the roof. When you land, land on your feet and use your legs as though they were big giant springs. Bend and then throw yourselves on your tummies.'

A little girl wept in fear.

'You,' he said to the largest youngster, 'you be my assistant commander. You stay till last. Everyone choose a partner.' He quickly took the crying girl by the hand. 'You will be mine.' Before she could register a protest they leaped over the drop onto the next roof.

* *

Piotr Warsinski reported to Haupsturmführer Kutler.

'How is it?' Kutler asked.

'The most successful "kettle" we have ever made. Every orphanage is cleaned.'

'How many?'

'Maybe ten, twelve thousand heads.'

'That's a lot of Jew babies. Well – they've got no valuables. Start loading them up. Send the leftover bastards to the top floors for storage till tomorrow and the day after. I want all your people around the Umschlagplatz on guard tonight. Bastards in the ghetto liable to try something.'

Warsinski turned to leave. 'Good job, Chief,' laughed Kutler.

Kutler walked out to the selection desks and frowned at the sight of the nurses mingling with the children. 'Warsinski!'

'Yes, sir.'

'What are all those people doing here?'

'They wanted to come with the children.'

Susan Geller came up to them. 'Surely you cannot object to having us resettled with our wards,' she said.

Kutler sneered. He did not like her homely face. He glanced around at the other nurses, teachers, doctors, and workers holding their tiny flocks together. Goddamned Jews, Kutler thought. They got some kind of strange love for dying like martyrs. He remembered the fathers holding their hands over their sons' eyes on the edge of the pits at Babi-Yar at Kiev.

'You people aren't wanted in this transfer,' Kutler said.

'The children will enjoy their picnic in the country so much more if they have us with them to explain everything. You see, many of them do not remember being out of the ghetto.'

Kutler turned his eyes way from Susan Geller's insistent stare. 'What have you got in that bag?' he asked.

'Chocolates. I've been saving them for a wonderful occasion like this.'

Kutler cracked. 'Be heroes,' he muttered, and dashed back to his office and closed and bolted the door. He yanked viciously at a desk drawer, unable to open it quickly enough, and smashed the top of the schnapps bottle, guzzling until a hot wave of alcohol flooded his blood and crashed into his brain, dulling his thoughts. 'Heroes ... martyrs ...'

The courtyard bulged with ten thousand ragged, emaciated children with a sprinkling of nurses who kept up a play of gaiety. Some of the older children who knew where they were going kept it to themselves.

'Jew babies, start moving up the ramps!'

'Well, children, now begins our wonderful picnic in the country.'

'Aunt Susan, when will we come back?'

'Oh, probably later tonight.'

'Keep moving down to the end of the platform to the first car!'

The engine warmed up with a few puffs of steam.

The line of tykes straggled up the ramps. Curses and kicks moved them quicker.

Kutler, in a thick drunk, staggered out to the courtyard and watched the march. He snarled semi-intelligible sounds, screaming to hurry it up. He sighted a dozen small children leaning against a far wall, doubled up from exhaustion and hunger, too weak to drag themselves to their feet. Kutler wove toward them. 'Up, you Jew babies!' he shrieked.

Two of the three nurses converged on them, helping them to their feet.

A rachitic girl of three clad in filthy rags toppled to the cobblestones, dropping a torn baby doll which had neither arms nor legs. Her little hand reached for it.

Kutler's shiny black boot stomped on the doll.

The ragamuffin stared curiously at the tall black-uniformed man hovering over her. 'My baby,' she whined weakly, 'I want my baby.' Her hand tugged, trying to pry it from under the Nazi's boot. His Mauser pistol came out of the holster.

A pistol shot echoed.

'Let me through! Let me through! cried Alexander.

A half dozen bulky Jewish militiamen restrained the desperate Brandel before he could get into the selection center. He was dragged screaming and fighting across Stawki Street to the warehouse where Warsinski had the Umschlagplatz detail office.

'I demand to be allowed in the Umschlagplatz!'

Warsinski let Alexander babble, plead, coax, argue. Then he spoke. 'Your immunity is running short, Brandel. Take him back to the ghetto.'

Clickety-clack, clickety-clack the train rolled over the countryside.

'Now, children,' Susan Geller said, 'I have another surprise. Chocolates!'

'Chocolates!'

She passed the bag of poisoned candy about the car.

'Doesn't that taste wonderful?'

The train rolled on.

'Let's all sing together.'

> 'Onward, onward,
> On to Palestine.
> Onward, onward
> Join the happy throng ...'

'I'm sleepy, Aunt Susan.'

'Well, why don't you lie down and rest?'

'I'm sleepy too, Tante Susan.'

'Well, all of you take a nap. It must be the excitement and the fresh air.'

One by one they closed their eyes. Susan Geller snuggled between a pair of her babies and held them close to her and slowly swallowed the last square of chocolate.

> *Shluf mine faygele,*
> *Mach tzu dine aygele*
> *Eye lu lu lu,*
> *Shluf gesmak mine kind,*
> *Shluf un zai-gezund,*
> *Eye lu lu lu.*
>
> Sleep my little bird.
> Shut your little eyes,
> Eye lu lu lu,
> Sleep tight my child,
> Sleep and be safe,
> Eye lu lu lu.

Chapter Twelve

Sturmbannführer Seighold Stutze was adept at aping his God, Adolf Hitler, down to the slightest gestures. Thumbs in belt, he limped up and down the courtyard holding the massed assemblage of Jewish Militia. He stopped before a microphone and glared at his captive audience with seductive authority. The board of the Jewish Civil Authority was lined up on his right and a company of his Reinhard Corps on his left.

Throwing a hand above his head, he shrieked in a high pitch which echoed off the stones of the yard. 'Fat Jews! You are fat because we have rewarded you too much. Despite our loyalty to you, you continue to permit publication of lies about us! You allow these Communist agitators to exist under your noses! They will be found and destroyed! Because of these lies we have not received a single volunteer for four days for orderly deportation for honest labor in the east!' Stutze whirled around to Warsinski. 'Read the new orders!'

Warsinski opened a document. '"From this day forward every member of the Jewish Militia has a personal daily duty to bring three people to the Umschlagplatz for deportation for honest labor. In the event a militiaman fails to meet his quota, he and his family will be deported immediately."'

The respite in the Big Action, the show of 'common justice' by executing the Big Seven, and the reopening of the schools, all became part of a master scheme to lure the people into relaxing their vigil long enough for the Germans to reorganize for the next onslaught.

A terrorized Jewish Militia under Warsinski's obedient haranguing had long ago sold their souls; now they sank to a new depth of decadence. It became a common sight to see them dragging their own relatives to the Umschlagplatz for deportation when they were unable to fill their quotas.

Ghetto *Kennkarten* stamped for labor were long believed to be a magic key to life. In a stroke of the pen they were all declared invalid. All but a handful of people in the ghetto had lost their immunity to deportation.

Each day new 'kettles' and 'pots' were executed. Streets or blocks of houses were hermetically sealed off and methodically raked from cellar to attic for occupants.

The constant fountain of trickery spouted. The lure of food was used to gain new spies. Children were tortured before the eyes of their mothers to reveal the locations of secret bunkers.

An immunity to tragedy became normal. Yet the roundup of the orphans accomplished what the master planners knew it would. It seemed to crush whatever morale and will to exist remained.

Alexander Brandel, long the symbol of love and dignity, long the symbol of food and medicine, turned into a morose, depressed man overnight. Speechless day followed speechless day. He no longer functioned as the dynamic force for survival.

Rabbi Solomon sat in the dank cellar next to the sewer pipe under Mila 19 and wailed ancient Hebrew prayers day and night to the sound of rushing sewerage.

Deborah Bronski was the sole nurse remaining from the Niska Street orphanage to take care of the two dozen boys and girls Stephan had led over the roofs to Mila 19. Yet another room was dug out alongside the pipe and fitted with bunks and a classroom.

Deborah flicked on the light in her bedroom. She opened the dresser drawers one by one and filled a suitcase. An item or two came from the jewelry box. A few things of a personal nature. Everything else was to be left. She checked the children's room for the mementos they wanted, then walked down the long hall.

There was a light from Paul's study. She entered and could see the back of his head as he sat in his swivel chair in front of his desk.

'I am leaving you, Paul. I should have done so long ago. Stephan and Rachael will be with me.'

Paul was motionless.

'Good-by, Paul.'

As she turned to go, she saw that his hand hung limply over the arm of the chair, a crumpled sheet of paper in his fist. On the floor lay a bottle. She recognized it as his sleeping pills. The bottle was empty. It had been filled only a few days earlier. Deborah walked slowly to the front of the desk. Paul was rigid, his eyes closed. She set down the suitcase and felt his hand. It was icv. There was no pulse.

Paul Bronski was dead.

'May God forgive me,' she said, 'but I wish I could say that I am sorry.'

She pried the paper loose from his hand. 'My dear Deborah,' the note read, 'I wish I knew what to say or what I have done to deserve this scorn from you. Boris Presser has an envelope explaining various affairs which I'm sure you'll find in order ...' And there the scrawling stopped.

The top of the desk was tidy. Paul was meticulous in his habits. Everything would be in order. Even his death. He had closed out a business day by suicide simply because there was no alternative.

Deborah shook her head in a final bewilderment. She looked squarely into his sallow, lifeless face. 'Oh, Paul, Paul, Paul. Even this had to be done so properly. Why didn't you write a message for your son and daughter? Why didn't you make this act an outcry for justice and protest? Paul, Paul ... Why?'

She picked up her suitcase. Without remorse, without tears, without regret, without pity, she left everything that had been between them, forever.

'We must have help!' an impassioned Andrei cried.

Roman, the Home Army commander in Warsaw, listened with head cocked, eyes lazily half shut. The nobleman placed a cigarette in the long holder delicately and lit it. A frustrated Andrei waved off Roman's offer of a smoke.

'Jan Kowal,' Roman said softly, 'just last week we sent you thirty-two rifles.'

'Of six different calibers with a hundred and six rounds of ammunition. One of the rifles becomes obsolete the moment it fires its three bullets.'

'If there is suddenly a downpour of heavy-caliber automatic weapons from the skies, I'll be the first to let you know.'

Andrei smashed his fist on the table.

Roman got up and clasped his hands behind him dramatically. 'Just what do you want?'

'We haven't the strength to mount an attack without help from outside. If you had three companies of the Home Army make simultaneous diversified strikes in the suburbs, we can push out of the ghetto.'

Roman sighed with frustration. Despite the rigors of living ungerground, he had lost none of the fine edge that characterized a French-bred snob. 'It is impossible,' he said.

'Can you be that much of a Jew hater to watch us cooked alive?'

Roman leaned against the window sill and bit on the ivory holder with the studied gestures of one who knows he is on stage. His eyebrows raised on his high forehead. 'Shall we get coldly realistic? What if I carry through your plan? Where will you go? How many will you break out?'

'As many as you can make provisions for.'

'Ah,' beamed Roman, 'that is the rub. Ninety per cent of the peasants would turn in a Jew for a bottle of vodka. Ninety per cent of the city people are quite certain this war is being fought because of international Jewish bankers. Not my personal feelings, mind you, but I am in no position to carry out a program to educate the Polish people.' Roman was deadly accurate again.

'Then at least let the fighting force find its way out with the children.'

'Children? Those convents and monasteries which take Jewish children are filled to the brim. Most won't. The few others want ten thousand zlotys a head in advance with the right to convert them to Catholicism.'

Andrei closed his eyes.

Roman warmed up to his arguments, sliding his tongue over his teeth as he paced. 'I cannot allow partisan units made up of Jews. I do not command an army on discipline. The underground depends upon secrecy and loyalty. You know full well you will be betrayed just as you were betrayed when you gave us the report on extermination camps. It was sold by someone to the Gestapo.'

'At least – at least give us guns and money. At least the money you've stolen from us.'

Roman frowned and sat at the table, lifting some papers to read to demonstrate he was too busy for further bickering. Andrei snatched them out of his hand and flung them to the floor.

'All right, Jan!' Roman snorted. 'Your precious report was smuggled out of Poland by someone or other and has been published in London. Have you heard the heads of state make impassioned cries for justice? Has the world suddenly stormed to its feet in indignation? Jan Kowal, no one really gives a damn.'

Andrei pushed back from the table. 'Don't slop your Polish garbage on the rest of the world, Roman. This is the only corner of the world where extermination camps could exist. The German army doesn't have enough divisions to guard against the people if they tried it in London or Paris or New York. Only in your goddamned Warsaw! All over this continent men and women are behaving with basic Christian decency. You are a Christian, aren't you?'

Roman went through arrogant gestures of indulgent disgust.

'You won't walk away from this free. They're already starting to gas Poles at Auschwitz only because you let them get away with it with us. March into the chamber with your chin up, Roman, your turn is coming.'

Andrei stormed out.

Roman broke the shortened cigarette from the holder and squashed the tip out. He looked up at a stunned aide. 'If those blasted Jews try to contact me again, I am not to be reached, do you understand?'

'Yes, sir.'

'Jews are so emotional. Oh well, at least we won't have a Jewish problem when the war is over.'

Simon Eden smashed his fist into his open palm as Andrei related the meeting with Roman. The attic room fell into gloom. Tolek, Alexander Brandel, Ana, Ervin, Wolf Brandel, Simon Eden. A ghastly morbidity crushed them. It was all over. Everyone thought the same thing at the same moment. It was all over . . . done.

The alarm bell sounded five short rings to indicate a 'friend' was coming up. Rodel, the Communist, entered. For an instant everyone looked eagerly with a flickering of hope beyond hope that some miracle had happened. Rodel shook his head. 'They can give us four armed men, no more. They can't even really spare that.'

Tolek droned the names of writers, doctors, actors, journalists, and Zionists who had been taken to the Umschlagplatz in the last few days. He went on and on, moaning a death march.

'Be quiet,' Andrei said.

But he droned on. The last of the rabbis – one saved by the Catholic Church as some sort of relic of a past civilization, the other was in their cellar. The rest, dead. 'Dead, all dead,' Tolek said. 'Farm gone . . . farm gone . . . everyone is dead.'

'Shut up,' Andrei repeated.

Ana Grinspan, an unwavering symbol of strength, a figure of daring, collapsed and cried hysterically. There was no one in the room who could comfort her.

'Say something, Alex,' Simon Eden pleaded.

But Alex said nothing these days.

'Dead . . . all dead. *Nishtdoo, keiner, keiner nishtdoo.*'

'Stop your goddamned crying!' Andrei screamed.

Ervin licked his dry lips. Tears wet his thick glasses, so that the people before him were blurred images. Within five days he had lost his wife Susan and his mother. He had tried gallantly to carry on for Alexander Brandel after the children were rounded up. 'Simon . . . Andrei . . . Comrade Rodel . . . I . . . have taken all the notes and volumes of the Good Fellowship Club and hidden them in milk cans and steel boxes. I had occasion to speak to your committees today. They are in full accord with me that if this last try for help was unsuccessful we should burn the ghetto and commit mass suicide.'

'You have no right to hold meetings behind my back,' Simon said without conviction.

'We had no times for rules of procedure,' Ervin said.

'Who among us hasn't thought of suicide?' Ana cried.

And then silence. There were no arguments.

'As a Labor Zionist . . . as a Labor Zionist,' Simon mumbled. He brushed the hair back from his eyes. 'As a Jew and Labor Zionist,' he floundered and fumbled. Oh God, he thought, death would be so sweet, so very sweet. 'As commander of Joint Forces, I cannot and will not give an order for a suicide pact. But if this is the wish of everyone, then I will resign my command and also abide by the decision.'

Andrei stared up at his comrade. Simon had been a soldier. Simon had been a strong man. Simon had been a leader. His innards were shot. The fine features of his dark face sagged with the loss of will.

Wolf Brandel, the youngest commander in the ghetto, walked slowly toward the door. 'I will not obey that order,' he said. 'My girl and I are going to live, and if we're captured we are going to make them pay. If they want me,' Wolf cried, 'let them come in and try to get me!'

He slammed the door behind him.

'Well,' Andrei whispered, 'one of us is left with enough strength to want to live.'

Tolek fell on his knees. 'Oh God! God! God! Please help us! What have we done? What have we done?'

No one looked at the other. Their faces fell into their hands. All through the night they sat wordless until the dawn broke them with weariness and they dropped off into snatches of nightmare-filled sleep.

And then, as suddenly as it began, the Big Action ended. On September 16, 1942, there were no more deportations or 'kettles.'

The Warsaw ghetto, the largest human stockyard in man's history, once held nearly six hundred thousand people. That number was decimated by starvation, disease, executions, deportation to slave labor, and finally assembly-line murder in Treblinka. When the Big Action ended, less than fifty thousand remained.

Chapter Thirteen

Horst von Epp cut the classic conception of the ramrod German baron as he stood framed before the tall window of Chris's flat, transfixed by the first snowfall of the winter, and the strains of a Chopin record.

Chris came in from the outside, slapping the cold from his bones. He nodded to Horst, denoting he was pleased at the unexpected visit.

'Hope you don't mind my breaking in and helping myself to the whisky?' Horst said, fixing a scotch for Chris.

'Why should I mind? There's nothing in this apartment your friends haven't examined twenty times.'

The Chopin record came to the end. 'I like Chopin. All those blockheads play is Wagner. A tribute to Hitler in absentia. Isn't there something enormously enchanting about the first snow?'

Chris threw open the drapes to the alcove bedroom, tugged off his shoes and wet socks. He fished around under the bed for his slippers.

'O the snow, the beautiful snow.
Filling the sky and the earth below,
Over the housetops, over the street,
Over the heads of the people you meet,
    Dancing,
    Flirting,
    Skimming along,
Beautiful snow, it can do nothing wrong.'

'Ye gods, Chris, that's horrible.'

'James Whittaker Watson, 1824–90. My recitation for the second-grade graduation. My mother didn't come to the graduation. I never forgot snow, beautiful snow.'

Horst handed him a tall drink. They clinked glasses. '*Fröhliche Weihnachten* – Christmas cheer,' he said.

'I'll be a sad bastard. Christmas. I forgot all about it.'

'I toast those poor misled Aryans laying on their wet bellies in snow, beautiful snow on the eastern front for the glory of the Fatherland,' Horst said.

'Amen. Well, how does it feel to get clobbered?'

'We are going to lose at Stalingrad, aren't we, Chris?'

'It's going to be a catastrophe, Baron. Your Chief of Staff should have read Napoleon's memoirs and taken a lesson of what mother winter does to trespassers.'

'I had it about a week ago. The sudden realization Germany is going to lose the war. It is making a mess out of all the Christmas parties. Everyone is so damned glum. Stalingrad, El Alamein, the landings in North Africa. But you know what really confounds me is those Americans. Guadalcanal. Now there's a romantic name. Everyone underestimates Americans. Why?'

'The mistaking of gentleness as weakness is like underestimating a Russian winter.'

'Next year,' Horst said, 'Berlin is going to be bombed. What a pity. Oh dear, how they are going to pay us back. Well, Christmas cheer.'

Horst set down his drink and again became enchanted with the falling snow. 'Chris,' he said, looking outside, 'a report has just been published by the Polish government in exile in London. A nasty White Paper detailing alleged extermination camps operating in Poland. Heard about it?'

'Something or other.'

'Tell me,' Horst said, 'how did you smuggle it out of Poland?'

Chris made only a nominal attempt to cover his deed. 'What makes you think it was me?'

'My male vanity. When a beautiful piece of tail, Victoria Landowski from Lemberg, turns out not to be a piece of tail and not even Victoria Landowski, my masculinity was offended.'

'Find the woman. They are behind all sinister plots.'

'The trouble was, I couldn't find the woman. My friend Christopher de Monti had become deliciously decadent, a quivering alcoholic mass of sponge. Then Victoria Landowski enters and Christopher undergoes a magic transformation. He returns to being – what do you call it? – a clean-cut All-American boy. I began to add this sudden spiritual resurrection. It was not difficult to figure the rest of it.'

'By God, Horst, you're downright clairvoyant. Well, does Gestapo Chief

Sauer put his dogs on me, feed me a quart of castor oil, or use testicle crushers to make me talk?'

'Oh, cut that nonsense out. Those dreary people at the Gestapo won't figure this thing out for months. How did you get the reports out? Italian diplomats?'

'Something like that,' Chris answered.

'See! I told Hitler personally not to trust the Italians. Those people are far too romantic to really carry out a first-class war of annihilation. As soon as we come to the acid tests, they abandon us.'

Chris laughed. 'I'm only an Italian by passport. Come to think of it, I'm really not much of anything. But I do know the Italian people. They were sold a bill of goods that they were a reincarnation of the noble Romans, twenty centuries removed. So why in hell shouldn't they believe it? All they really wanted was to be somebody again.'

'On German coattails.'

'The bride awoke to find her maidenhead broken, but the Teutonic god she married had turned into an ugly black gorilla. Sort of a beauty and the beast in reverse. Horst, the Italian people have no stomach for what you are doing in Poland. It was no chore at all getting five men to carry out five separate copies of the extermination-camp report.'

'Archetype German villain that I am,' Horst said, 'I cannot comprehend why those who are utterly crushed insist on dying gestures of defiance. Martyrs are dreadful. I watched you sink to degeneration. What was that voice that called you out of Satan's arms? What did it say to you?'

'It told me ... I must become worthy enough to receive the spit of a man who was once my friend.'

'Morality.' Horst shook his head. 'Just before the war I saw that big hammy American baritone – what was his name? – Tibbett. Lawrence Tibbett. He sang in Paris. After a song about mother's southern-fried cake he bellowed some more dreadful poetry. Somehow, the damned verse keeps going through my mind these days.

'Out of the night that covers me,
Black as the pit from pole to pole,
I thank whatever gods may be ...'

'"For my unconquerable soul,"' Chris said. 'To William Ernest Henley, 1849–1903.

'Under the bludgeonings of chance
My head is bloody, but unbowed.

'This immediately brings to mind the question of why all poets have three names and why wasn't my mother at the fifth-grade commencement ceremonies, either?'

'It will never replace Schiller or Heine – that is, before Heine became a Jew. I know, you cannot put man's soul in a ghetto or gas his spirit at Treblinka. It looks fine in the hands of poets but puzzling when it really happens. Why did you do it, Chris? A few sermons by minor bishops, a few editorials by minor newspapers, a few pasty statements by minor politicians, a few protest suicides by minor idealists. What did you hope to gain? *Ach.* Now I have to spend the whole winter writing counterpropaganda.'

'I'm sorry it's making you lose so much sleep, Horst. I thought perhaps the report itself might annoy you.'

'Don't give me that snide journalist's sneer. I know – how could we do this? The fine, cultured German people, after which I rattle off the names of musicians, poets, doctors, and list all our gifts to mankind. How could we do this? It will take the great philosophical and psychiatric brains a hundred years to find a standard of morals to explain this behavior.'

'I'll simplify it,' Chris said. 'You're a pack of beasts.'

'Oh no, Chris, we are not even to be classed with beasts. Man is the only animal on this planet which destroys its own species. But how in the devil did I get involved in this? I'm no more guilty than you are. Less, perhaps. I'm trapped. But you, dear Chris, are all the moralists in the world who have condoned genocide by the conspiracy of silence.'

'The conspiracy of silence,' Chris mumbled. 'Yes, I buy that.'

'Hell, my own skin isn't important. After the war all this business will be unearthed and mankind will register a proper shock and horror. Then they will say, "Let us all forget about the past. Let bygones be bygones." And all over Germany you'll get a chorus of "Amen." What will the song be? There was nobody here in Germany but us anti-Nazis. Extermination camps? We knew nothing about them. Hitler? Always did think he was crazy. What could we do? Orders were orders. And the world will say, "Look at all the good Germans." They will string up a few Nazis as showpieces, and all the good German folk will slink back to their cobblers' benches and sulk and wait for the next Führer.' Horst broke into a sudden sweat and lost his composure. He downed a shot of whisky quickly.

'What's eating you, Horst?'

'The Jews. They'll pin a curse on us. They'll make us a scourge among men for a thousand years.'

'History is written by survivors. There will be no Jewish survivors,' Chris said.

'Hell! They're uncanny. They have this maddened, insatiable desire to put words on paper. This mania to document their torment.' Horst calmed and thought. 'Last time they documented their destruction we got a Bible, then a "Valley of Tears" – now what? You know, Chris, my brother was in a Knight Templar colony in Palestine before the war. Every winter he would climb around in caves near the Dead Sea looking for ancient Hebrew letters.'

'Why, Horst, you're afraid of your hereafter. I wouldn't have dreamed it.'

'I have a crawling suspicion that inside the ghetto wall are ten thousand diaries buried beneath the ground. And that is what is going to crush us. Not the allied armies, not a few tokens of retribution, but the voices of the dead, unearthed. From this stigma we can never … Forgive me, Christmas has a habit of putting me in a mood.'

'What are you going to do with me?' Chris asked sharply.

'I've given it a lot of thought. I can't let you out of Poland. I mean, after all, we have to play the game. We both played fairly and I lost. I made a bad guess. On the other hand, no use letting Sauer get his hands on you. I am a believer in grandiose gestures! Pack a bag!'

Horst steered his auto down Jerusalem Boulevard. About them a dismal attempt to find Christmas cheer was being made by the Poles and despondent German soldiers.

'Chris, one thing I must know. This Victoria Landowski. Was she a good piece?'

'The truth? I wouldn't know.'

'Amazing. Simply amazing. Well, we will find her one day.'

'When you do, do me one last favor. Give her a chance to finish herself off before Sauer roughs her up.'

'Chris, you're asking entirely too much.'

'She is very important to me.'

'Oh well, it is Christmas. My promise. By God, I'm forgetting all my good German training and turning into a downright sentimentalist.'

The car stopped before the ghetto gate opposite the Tlomatskie Synagogue. Horst handed Chris a *Kennkarte* and special papers. 'Into the ghetto. These papers will keep you out of police hands until you find your friends. In three days I'll turn in a report you are missing. That should give you enough time to get buried in there.'

'I am afraid I have no friends left,' Chris said.

'Don't be too sure. Jews have an infallible intelligence system. They will somehow know how the extermination-camp report was spirited out of Poland.'

Chris got out of the car. 'You're one for the books.'

'Well, three cheers for the final triumph of morality in men. If we ever run across one another after the war, put in a good word for me. There is always a demand for ex-German barons as gardeners, bartenders, villain parts in movies. I am a man of many talents.' He sped away.

The ghetto streets were devoid of life. Chris turned up his coat collar and walked aimlessly through the swirls of snow. Eyes were on him from the rooftops the instant he entered. He wandered until he grew weary. Where to go? Whom to see? What a strange ending. Were there people behind the stillness? Was there life left?

Where to go? Where to turn?

'You!'

Chris whirled about. He saw no one in the courtyard from which the voice came.

'You!' it called again.

Chris walked toward the voice. It was coming from an indentation in the building.

'Turn around and walk,' the voice commanded. 'Don't look around. I will give you directions.'

He sat alone on the cot in the attic of Mila 19. Andrei Androfski entered.

Finally Chris stood up and turned his back on Andrei. 'Divine retribution. The sinner has come to face his makers. Poetic justice in its purest form.'

Andrei sat at the wooden table and placed his elbow in the center. 'Want to hand-wrestle? I haven't eaten as well as you, but I can still beat you.'

'Don't you know me, Andrei? I stood by with my hands in my pockets and my ears deafened to the cries of the dying.'

'Must you be so dramatic? All I want to do is hand-wrestle.'

'Andrei ...'

'We know how that report reached London, Chris. Thank you.'

Chris bit his lip to hold off tears.

'We got a horse over the wall this morning. Steaks tonight. Take this pistol. Later I'll show you how to move around. I'll put up another cot here for you. When you hear five alarm bells in short rings, it is a friend. Long dashes, we go to the roof. We must be very careful. The roofs are icy.'

'Andrei ...'

'Never mind. I understand.'

Chris was alone. He peered out of the slanting garret window. The snow had stopped, revealing the spires of churches beyond the wall. The churches would be filled with kneeling, praying, singing people. Meager gifts would be exchanged, and for an instant the spirit of goodness would pass through people. Would they think for a fleeting moment of those inside the ghetto? Would they remember that Jesus was a Jew? Chris was flooded with a strange, wonderful, warm sensation, and peace filled his body and his heart. It was a comfort he had never known in a restless, searching life. Now he had captured it.

Five short rings.

'Deborah ...'

'Don't say anything. Just let me hold you, Chris. Don't speak ... don't speak ... Just let me hold you.'

BOOK FOUR

Dawn

Chapter One

Journal Entry

Alexander Brandel continues to be morose and uncommunicative. He has barely spoken to any of us all winter. The Orphans and Self-Help Society still 'legally' exists and carries immune Kennkarten. *I have assumed Alexander's duties, such as they 'officially' remain. There is still much intercourse with the Civil Authority on rations, etc.*

The ghetto is like a morgue. It is impossible to believe that the face of the moon could be more quiet and deserted than the ghetto streets. During the Big Action the women going to the Umschlagplatz for deportation wanted to carry their silk comforters and feather beds, but they were too bulky. So they cut them open and dumped the feathers and goose down on the roofs so they could carry the outer cover (in hopes of finding something to refill them with at their destination). In some places the feathers are ankle-deep on the roofs, and when a wind blows it looks like snow coming down. Always, feathers drift down to add to the haunting stillness.

We think there are forty thousand of us left. Several thousand are at the Brushmaker's and the uniform factory. There are some of us 'authorized' personnel left, a thousand or so. (Why, we do not know.) Mostly there are Wild Ones. The ghetto has been transformed into an underground city with mazes of tunnels, hidden rooms, and cellars dug under cellars. The Militia and Nightingales wrecked all the vacant houses, so they are thoroughly uninhabitable.

We are completely shut off from the little ghetto, which has been devoid of Jews for almost a year, except for the woodwork factory, which has now closed. Poles are moving back into the former little ghetto, scrambling for the fine houses on Sienna and Sliska streets, which they are able to get without compensation to the departed occupants.

This winter we have concentrated in getting key people into the Aryan side. David Zemba reluctantly left the ghetto with his family, but I hear he continues to live in Warsaw, refusing to leave the country. We have been able to place six of the children (who escaped the Niska orphanage and live in the cellar of Mila 19) in the Franciscan Sisters' convent in Laski.

Joint Forces has about seven hundred fighters in training, learning street-fighting tactics, the handling of our various weapons, and the routes over the roofs. We have twenty so-called battle companies, about one third armed. There are seven Labor Zionist companies, two Bund, four Communist, two Bathyran, and religious and

mixed groups. The Revisionists outside of Joint Forces have a well-armed group of fifty, or more of their bunker under Nalewki 37.

Arms, food, and medical stores are hidden in dozens of alternate store bunkers all over the ghetto. Our standard weapon is the Polish 35 rifle. We have about thirty of these with a thousand rounds of ammunition. Next in importance are the fifty-six various models of 9-mm pistols (German Mausers, Parabellums and Swedish Lahtis). The odd weapons are a nuisance, but we take them despite the difficulty and cost in obtaining ammunition. We have a few Italian Berettis (cal 32) and Glisentis 10.35. The two Hungarian Baby Frummer .380's have only eight rounds between them. (A round of ammunition for the Baby Frummer costs two hundred zlotys apiece, wheras 9-mm ammo runs from eighty to a hundred and twenty zlotys.)

We have several thousand fire bottles and nearly a thousand water-pipe grenades manufactured from a formula by our genius, Jules Schlosberg. We have also three dozen Polish grenades and assorted knives.

Schlosberg's newest concoction is a tin can filled with nuts and bolts. The open end of the can is sealed with plastic percussion caps and covered with a light wax. The theory works. We tested four of them in empty houses. The impact was so great that some of the bolts shot clear through the plaster walls into the next rooms. We call this 'weapon' the 'matzo ball.'

Joint Forces operates out of our primary bunkers. Simon Eden's headquarters (Leszno 92) under Bund House, Gensia 43, and our bunker at Mila 19 (which now holds almost a hundred people, including eighteen children) form the 'Central Command.' Rodel has a series of small bunkers at the southern end around the uniform factory. His main bunker is under the Convert's Church! Father Jakub hears nothing. A good friend. The other command in the Brushmaker's district is held by Wolf Brandel, who is barely twenty years old. Wolf amazes us all with his imagination and complete calm. His main bunker is at Franciskanska Street, almost at the ghetto wall and under two parts of the factory complex. Rachael Bronski, now a soldier, has gone to live at the Franciskanska bunker. Stephan Bronski, incidentally, is considered the best runner in the ghetto.

The Brushmaker's factory still turns out six thousand brushes a day for the Wehrmacht. This means, of course, a constant flow of raw supplies in from the outside. Wolf has capitalized on this by paying off a few key people in shipping and receiving. Food cans and supplies coming in can be easily marked and used for smuggling in pistols and ammunition.

Before David Zemba went over to the Aryan side we held a final meeting of the Good Fellowship Club (half our original number are left). It was decided that everything except the current volume in progress should be hidden immediately. Fifty completed volumes have been stuffed into fourteen milk cans and sealed and buried in fourteen different places. Ten more milk cans and iron boxes contain unclassified or unentered material, such as photographs, diaries, poetry, essays. Only six people know where the twenty-four cans and boxes are hidden: David Zemba, Andrei Androfski, Gabriela Rak, Alexander Brandel, Christopher de Monti, and myself. David, Andrei, Gabriela, and Alex each know where part of the cache is located, so if captured they cannot possibly reveal the entire archives.

Only Christopher de Monti and I know the location of all the cans and boxes. We have placed the most urgent priority in getting Chris out of Poland, for he alone is our greatest hope of bringing world attention to the holocaust which has befallen us. However, there is an unparalleled man hunt for him on the Aryan side, and getting him out of Poland will be nearly impossible.

One bit of good news. Although Finland is an ally of Germany, she has adamantly refused to turn over her Jewish community (of two thousand) to Eichmann. In fact, old Marshal Mannerheim has threatened to use the Finnish army to protect the Jews. We hear similar reports of defiance, particularly from Denmark. Also, we hear that Bulgaria and Rumania will not yield Jews to Eichmann's fanatical pressure. Lord, Lord, what couldn't we do with the protection of the Polish Home Army, which now has a quarter of a million men!

With the Good Fellowship Club archives hidden, I feel that my work has come to an end. I am so lonely without Susan and Momma. I am almost blind from the years of working in the cellar in bad light with these notes. My hands and shoulders are swollen with arthritis from the dampness. I am in pain all the time. How much longer can we go on? How many of us will escape? Two? Five? Fifty? How many? And what of Joint forces? A fool's army. No one in their wildest dreams believes we can hold out against assault for more than two or three days. So what is the use? When will we fight? Or will we fight? Who among us will dare to fire that first shot against them? Who?

Entered as the first entry of a new volume by Ervin Rosenblum on January 15, 1943.

Chapter Two

Blond, blue-eyed, trim, intelligent, industrious SS Oberführer Alfred Funk stood, posture correct, at the head of a polished table. Listening in rapt attention on his left sat Rudolph Schreiker and Dr Franz Koenig. Opposite them, Gestapo Chief Gunther Sauer and Sturmbannführer Sieghold Stutze, newly appointed as security police head for all of Warsaw. Not so rapt in his attention, Horst von Epp, bored, stared out of the window at the opposite end of the table.

Funk had carried verbal orders from Berlin to Poland on the 'Jewish question' for so long that meanings were understood beyond their thin veils. He spoke in an uninspired monotone.

'Those who remain in the ghetto are Communists, criminals, perverts, and agitators.'

Four of them agreed. Von Epp played with a paper clip.

'Himmler has decided that for the sake of common justice we must erase this blot. We will proceed shortly with the final phase of the liquidation of the ghetto.'

Each of the men immediately translated the order into his own personal sphere of action.

For Rudolph Schreiker the removal of the Jewish problem in his area would be a relief. It was getting far too complicated for him to understand; besides, many of his business dealings could be buried in the ghetto.

Franz Koenig had been way ahead of it, anticipating the ghetto-liquidation order. He had already negotiated new war contracts, using labor at Trawniki and Poniatow.

Sauer took the order with unconcern. A policeman is always busy. Old problems are solved, new ones pop up. The Gestapo never rests, never will rest. Put out one fire, two more ignite. It did not matter.

Horst von Epp wanted the meetings to break up so he could get to a telephone and check to see if the new girls had come in from Prague.

Stutze was the most outwardly concerned. To him would fall the actual job of digging the vermin out. The Jews had shown great ingenuity in hiding themselves, and with an entire winter to dig in he would need more help.

'You are, of course, aware that the Jews are subterranean,' Stutze said. 'One can walk in the streets of the ghetto for hours without a sign of life. They live like moles. According to their Civil Authority records, there are forty to fifty thousand of them left. And one cannot overlook the fact that they have been arming themselves.'

Funk cut Stutze short. 'You do not suggest that Jews will fight?'

'Of course not, Oberführer,' the Austrian said too quickly. 'But you yourself said that criminals and Communists have taken refuge in the ghetto.'

'I have full faith that your Reinhard Corps will be more than equal to the situation,' Funk concluded abruptly.

Stutze blanched. Funk had put him in such a position that he could not request additional troops. 'Of course, Oberführer.'

'Fine ... fine,' Funk said. 'Tomorrow evening I should like to hear your plans for completion of the liquidation.'

'Of course, Oberführer.'

'You, Dr Koenig, shall submit your requirements to have the machinery in your factories transferred.'

Koenig nodded.

'Until tomorrow evening, gentlemen.'

They came to their feet sharply.

'Heil Hitler.'

'Heil Hitler.'

'Herr Sauer ... a moment please.'

The Gestapo chief returned to his seat. Horst von Epp also remained. When the others were gone, Funk turned to Sauer.

'On this matter of the archives in the ghetto of which I spoke to you on my last visit. What have you been able to ascertain?'

'Not too much. The Jews protect these historians with an uncommon devotion. Not even their Militia will inform on them. Fear of retribution, I suppose.'

'What's this about?' Horst asked.

'The Jewish mania for diaries. We have unearthed thousands of them in reservations around Poland and particularly in the special-treatment camps. We have long been aware of an entire organization here writing records.'

Well, well! Horst thought.

'We cannot proceed with the final liquidation of the ghetto until these records have been found,' Funk continued. 'Hitler himself gave me specific instructions to see that these Jew lies are found. We cannot permit their distortions to be published.'

Sauer was unmoved by Funk's double talk. The general sensed it. 'Isn't it enough,' Funk pressed, raising his voice to a sharper pitch, 'that this filthy pack of lies about our labor camps was smuggled out of Poland?'

'Perhaps,' Sauer said softly, 'the Führer should take the matter up with our Italian friends to learn how this was done.'

'It is the job of the Gestapo to learn these things and stop them before the crime is committed.'

Horst became fascinated at the sudden sharpness of argument. Someone had to give.

'We want positive information on these ghetto archives,' Funk snapped.

'Certain people,' Sauer answered, 'were in such a hurry to cover their business transactions, they did away with the Big Seven prematurely and in a single fell swoop destroyed my entire system of informers.' The implication was obvious. Half of Warsaw's Nazis wanted Max Kleperman's lips sealed.

The policeman rubbed his eyes and meditated, speaking as if to himself. 'If anyone in the ghetto knows about these papers it would be Alexander Brandel, but he has not been seen all winter. We know there is a bunker under Mila 19. We have not been able to determine the entrance.'

Funk, anxious to oversimplify the matter and get rid of Sauer, whom he could not bully, made an abrupt decision. 'I shall have Stutze find this Brandel immediately. Then we can proceed with the liquidation of the ghetto.'

Later that evening Horst walked down two flights in the Bristol Hotel to where a brace of SS guards flanked the door leading to Alfred Funk's suite. Funk's orderly let him in.

'The Oberführer is taking a bath,' the orderly said. He mixed a drink for Von Epp and disappeared into the bedroom.

Funk bathing again. Funk bathed before and after all conferences. Some days he took five or six baths. Often, when a good party was moving into its second stages and the women were getting deliciously vile, Funk would excuse himself and run off to a shower.

Reading the Jew Freud was legally banned, but Horst had brought several volumes to Warsaw nevertheless. Freud's interpretations afforded him a never-ending, amusing list of clues to the strange behavior of his Nazi cohorts. Alfred Funk's mania for cleanliness, he concluded, was an unconscious effort to wash his soiled soul with soap. However, the ersatz soap was of a very poor quality these days.

Horst reflected on the bizarre reactions at the earlier conference. He had attended many conferences at long polished tables where Funk and other Nazis announced dogma and sent everyone on his merry way with crisp 'Heil Hitlers.' But today there was a roomful of unusual performances. The first cracks. The minute trace of doubt and fear.

Rudolph Schreiker loosened with a dozen audible sighs of relief that the ghetto was to be liquidated.

One could see the wheels of Koenig's mind spinning to shift his fortune to Argentina, which alone showed a friendship for the Nazis.

Stutze was afraid to execute the final liquidation. In a moment he showed outright cowardice.

Sauer. A fine chap, like myself. Sauer never wavers. Knows his job. Plods on. He and I are true stalwarts.

It was Funk who had put on the real show, reflecting Berlin's panic over some obscure Jewish archives. Funk had backed down from Sauer, something he had never done before.

Funk bundled himself into a large towel robe and padded, still dripping, into the living room.

'You look tired, Alfred,' Horst said. 'I have just the relaxation the doctor ordered.'

Funk's orderly was all over him, trying to dry his master's hair. He dismissed the man curtly and lit a cigarette and flopped into a big chair, stretched his legs and arms, opening the top of his robe enough to reveal the double streaks of lightning tattooed under his left armpit, the mark of an SS Elite.

'I've got a pair of Czech sisters just in from Prague. They come highly recommended. They're not much to look at, but I understand they do fantastic contractions.'

'Good. I need a little sport.'

Funk left the room with a drink, leaving the bedroom door ajar so that they could speak.

In the beginning of their relationship, Funk had detested Horst von Epp. His cynical attitude, his snide mockery and obvious lack of sincere devotion to Nazi ideals and his constant barbs at the conferences irritated Funk no end. Then Horst began to grow on him.

Horst von Epp ran his office with enviable German efficiency. Moreover, he was the best officers' pimp in Europe, and once one got used to his sense of humor it lost much of its offensiveness. Funk came to understand that Von Epp was actually berating himself most of the time through his jokes.

He liked Von Epp for another reason too. He was reluctant to admit it, but he liked to talk to Horst. Since he had joined the party in 1930 he was in a league of tight-lipped, humorless men who considered it dangerous to speak one's inner thoughts or even admit to having them. He had taken vows as harsh as those of a monk in one of those silent ecclesiastical orders.

After the first shocks of Von Epp's curt observations of the Nazis subsided he found himself looking forward to coming to Warsaw. With Von Epp he could share thoughts, speak, fence verbally, confide frustrations. He could indulge himself in a way he dared not, even with his own wife and children.

Horst leaned against the doorframe while Funk primped himself to his blond Aryan best before the mirror.

'How is our defeat at Stalingrad being taken in Berlin? Graciously, I hope.'

Funk dropped the hairbrush and spun around angrily, then contained himself. 'We will break through at Stalingrad.'

'That is what I was afraid of. You spoilsports will be too bullheaded to see the handwriting on the wall. And the crushing of our Afrika Korps in Tunis?'

Funk quickly spouted the line of Nazi logistics. The Russians would collapse soon. America was too weak-spined to fight a sustained war, give up her sons and her luxuries and make the sacrifices necessary for victory. England? Washed up.

'Oh, for Christ sake, Alfred,' Horst said, sitting on the edge of the bed. 'I wrote most of that nonsense after Dunkirk. Know what I've been doing lately? Soul-searching. Do you ever soul-search?'

'That is a dangerous avocation reserved exclusively for those whose advanced age makes them otherwise useless. I gave it up twelve years ago when I joined the party.'

Funk pulled up his suspender straps and assured his servant he was capable of buttoning his own tunic. Horst followed Funk back to the living room, where they settled down to await the arrival of the sisters from Prague.

'Why is Hitler suddenly concerned over a few Jewish writings? Is it guilt? Is there a realization that Germany will lose the war unless they break through to Stalingrad? Does Hitler liken these writings to the other book the Jews wrote which has tormented the conscience of man for two thousand years? Does he fear two millennia of a Jewish curse gnawing at the souls of unborn German generations, thwarting their growth? Is it a fear of divine retribution?'

'Nonsense,' Funk snapped. He was about to recite the Nazi line about the war's being fought because of international Jewry but decided to spare Horst, or rather spare himself from Horst's retorts.

'Would you say this strange desire to find a few books when you own half the world points out that the pen is indeed mightier than the sword?'

'Nothing of the sort. Every conqueror has justified his actions. In our case the obliteration of the Jews is our holy mission, just as the obliteration of other peoples has been a holy mission for other empires.'

'Would you say that this desire to find the archives is more like a dog scratching frantically to cover up his dung pile?'

'Put it away, Horst. You talk as though the German people have committed some sort of crime.'

'Haven't they?'

'Of course not. Precedent is all around us. Even the ancient Hebrews destroyed their enemies . . . attributed to the commands of their God. Mongols made pyramids of skulls. The Chinese used human bodies as mortar to build the Great Wall. Napoleon had his Gestapo and the Russians have theirs. We are merely making variations on an ancient theme. Every man wants to be the best. The drive to rule is a completely natural expression of human behavior. In an individual the drive finds its expression by pushing the writer's pen to create a book, by driving the athlete to strain his heart and his muscle. When the drive becomes a national expression it takes the form of conquest. Every people in every age have taken their turn. The world has only one standard for proof that one is better than the other, and that is conquest.'

Horst grunted at Funk's cruel but accurate logic. 'Granted,' he said, 'that the desire to dominate is an unalterable trait in the human being. Let us take it a step farther. A woman wants to commit adultery. She has a family, children, position in the community. Does she walk naked in the streets to her lover and perform sex acts in a store window? No. Why? Adultery is a sin we all indulge in, but the woman finds a secluded place, deceives her husband, and avoids scandal. She plays by the rules. You see, Alfred, even the game of sin must be played by the rules. So must war be fought by the rules.'

Funk set his glass down. 'What you are saying is that when the sloppy aim of the Luftwaffe kills women and children in London it is permissible. When it is deliberate we break the rules. Isn't that a hypocritical double standard? Is it a greater sin for a submarine to kill a man on a ship without warning or to blast him, gentlemen's style, off a battlefield? Your rule says "Kill soldiers." Is the killing of an armed man really less a murder than the killing of a child? We have learned that other conquests have failed because one cannot go to war with compassion. Total war means total death. If victory means reducing Poland to a pool of cultureless serfs, then that is what must be done.'

'Then why not use poison gas on their armies?'

'This is not a decision of compassion but of expediency. We would certainly not hesitate if we knew they would not do the same to us. You cannot measure brutality by degrees. All conquerors justify their aims on a political theory. In our case the Nazis provide our various frills. No country goes to war without the belief in its own justice – we take it a step farther. We act out what others only theorize. In the concentration camps we reduce our political enemy until he takes the physical appearance of a sub-human. This makes us supermen by comparison.'

'Alfred, does any of this ever annoy you as an individual?'

'No. I decided by 1930 that you either become a Nazi or drown. My personal views on this Jewish business fail to be important. Horst, have you witnessed a gassing?'

'No.'

'I'll arrange one for you.'

'Thanks, anyhow.'

'The first time I witnessed one it was with a sense of complete fascination. I slept very well that night. The only thing that annoyed me a little was some of the Jewesses carrying their children into the chambers who looked at me with a mocking Mona Lisa smile.'

Horst was sorry he had brought the whole subject up.

'I shall tell you why the German people will be able to achieve what others have failed. It is because we are capable of the perfect state of mind necessary. We can give absolute obedience, respond to total authority, like no others.'

Horst spun the ice cubes with his forefinger. He glanced up into Funk's face. The Oberführer was in a state of detachment, the cruel and impersonal monster qualities dominating his appearance.

'Others talk of love of country. We act it out through absolute obedience. Four years ago I was commandant of the Waffen SS youth training school at Dachau. We got boys at the age of sixteen for a year's indoctrination, complete with live prisoners to experiment with. The entire course was geared to teach absolute unquestioned obedience to the Fatherland. Each boy was given an Alsatian puppy of six to eight weeks of age when he entered training. During the year part of their study was to train the animal, live with it, compete it against the other dogs. We encouraged them to develop the natural affection a boy does for a dog.'

Funk clasped his hands behind him.

'The last graduation test to see if the boy was worthy to become an SS officer was by calling him into a private room with his dog. As he stood before me at attention with his dog at his side I would say, "Hans, I order you to strangle your dog this instant."'

Horst thought he was going to vomit.

'Oh, a few were unable to do it. Some even broke and cried. But! Almost all of them, without a trace of remorse, without a second of hesitation, said, "*Jawohl, Herr Kommandant,*" and proceeded to snap the dog's neck without a trace of emotion. And this, Horst, is the supreme state of absolute obedience which we Germans have attained.'

Horst poured himself a triple drink. 'Heil Hitler,' he said.

Sturmbannführer Sieghold Stutze paced his room in the barracks wildly. Gestapo Chief Sauer had just left him with orders to set up a massive pot around Mila 19 and not to leave until the underground bunker was located and Alexander Brandel found.

It was just like that bastard Prussian, Alfred Funk, to give him the dirty work, he fumed. Where was his promotion to Standartenführer? He had more than earned his colonelcy. It was all part of the German plots against the Austrians.

All winter the Jews had been arming in the ghetto. No telling what those crazy Jews were liable to do. He broke into a sweat.

Damned if he'd walk into a trap on Funk's whim. Funk simply didn't understand how dangerous it was.

And then the idea came to him as he heard a shriek down the hall. It was that damned Kutler and his nightmares again. Wait! Kutler. That drunken beast was becoming completely useless. Yes! That was it. Kutler would lead the force into the ghetto. Kutler would set up the kettle. Good idea ... good idea.

Chapter Three

'Aha!' Andrei cried with fiendish delight, rubbing his hands together. 'Aha, you stupid man. You have made a fool's gambit!' Andrei moved his knight over the chessboard. 'Check!'

Chris coutered immediately, lopping off an exposed castle, putting Andrei's chessmen in an impossible position. 'Fool's gambit, all right,' he said, 'but you have the wrong fool.'

Andrei studied the board a moment and cursed under his breath.

Chris pulled back from the table and paced the tiny garret room restlessly.

'What's the matter, Chris?'

'I'm hungry, I want a smoke, I'm sick of being cooped up – I want to see Deborah.'

'I have yet to hear the first person speak in favor of ghetto living,' Andrei said.

'It has its advantages. It got me out of some bad drinking habits.' Chris patted his stomach. 'And notice how slim I've become.'

'What's bothering you?' Andrei asked again.

'To go or not to go. Hell, I know how important it is to get out of Poland knowing where the archives are buried, but it was impossible to leave Deborah before, even believing she hated me. Now, I swear, I don't know if I have the strength to leave.'

'Women,' Andrei grunted, 'they have a way of getting under one's skin.' He walked up behind Chris and put one hand on his shoulder. 'I am confident that when the time comes you will make the correct decision, and if you are very lucky the decision will be made for you.'

Both men froze at the same instant, trying to hear something that alerted a sixth sense beyond their normal waves of hearing. A few seconds later the alarm bell erupted in a series of dashes.

'I'll never get used to that goddamned bell,' Chris said.

Wolf Brandel came in carrying a large suitcase. He looked at the chessboard. 'Who played black?' he asked. Chris jerked his thumb at Andrei. Wolf grimaced and went 'Tsk, tsk, tsk.'

'Got a cigarette?' Chris asked.

'Don't smoke.'

'Hell.'

'Hey, Andrei. Three Kar 98's came in with seventy rounds of ammo. Pretty good. We got a line on four Mauser 9-mm's day after tomorrow.'

'Good work,' Andrei said. 'At this rate we'll have weapons for half our force in another few weeks. How is Rachael?'

'Fine.'

'What do you have in the suitcase?'

'I want to get some matzo-ball grenades to take back to my bunker. We tested one yesterday. Blam! Nuts and bolts everywhere. I want to talk to Schlosberg about designing a real big matzo ball.' Wolf held his hands out to indicate a four-foot diameter. 'Something like a land mine we can detonate with a hot spark. Something packed with a couple thousand nuts and bolts.'

'Good idea,' Andrei said.

Wolf put the suitcase on the table. 'Take a look.'

Andrei opened the lid, not knowing what to expect. He unfolded a blanket. An automatic weapon and five clips of ammunition burst into view.

'My God,' Andrei said, not believing what his eyes saw, 'my God! A Schmeisser machine pistol. My God!' Andrei licked his lips; his hands trembled to pick up the weapon but feared it would disappear like a mirage. 'Where on earth did you get it, Wolf?'

'German tank sergeant, lost a leg on the eastern front. Sold it for only four thousand zloys.'

'My God!'

'Go on, Andrei, pick it up.'

Andrei lifted the weapon out of the suitcase. He patted it with a gentleness reserved only for Gabriela. He slipped the bolt, sighted in, cradled it against his hip, clicked the trigger.

'It's yours,' Wolf said.

'Mine?'

'A gift from the Brushmaker's command.'

'I couldn't accept it.'

'We had a meeting and a vote. We decided in a democratic manner it would be most effective in your hands. Of course most of the voters were Bathyrans.'

Andrei was seized with emotion. 'I love it so much there is only one name for her. Gaby! Perhaps Gaby will fire a shot heard around the world! Wolf, I love you!'

The alarm bell sounded again. Simon Eden came in.

'Got a smoke?' Chris asked.

'Only German ersatz, but they're yours.'

Chris retreated to the cot, caressing the pack of cigarettes with the same affection Andrei had shown for the Schmeisser.

'Look!' Andrei said, showing Simon the machine pistol.

'Yes, I know,' Simon said. 'As commander of Joint Forces, I was given the nominal courtesy of being allowed to cast my vote with the Bathyrans for its disposition.'

It was immediately clear to Andrei that Simon's dark eyes were trying to shield trouble.

'What's on your mind, Simon? You're a worse faker than I am.'

'Funk arrived in Warsaw last night.'

It had been long expected. Everyone knew it would come and what Funk's arrival meant. Final liquidation. Yet the silence was long and frightened.

'Alfred Funk,' Chris said at last. 'The harbinger of spring. The messenger of peace and light.'

Andrei patted his Schmeisser. 'Gaby, dear girl, you arrived just in time.'

The tall, angular commander looked doubtfully from Wolf to Andrei to Chris, then exploded his message. 'I am making a change in strategy,' he said. 'I am pulling our companies out of their exposed positions, breaking them up and putting them into bunkers.'

'Why?' Andrei demanded. 'To have them wait in the ground like shivering dogs to be hunted down and butchered bunker by bunker?'

Simon shook his head in defeat. 'I have reappraised our strength. We cannot make a street fight.'

'What? Wasn't it Simon Eden who came to me a year ago oozing Zionist purity from every pore, saying, "Don't fight now, Andrei. Wait! Make your shots heard! Do not die in silence!"'

'God damn it, Andrei. Do you think I like this decision?'

'Why did you lie to me?'

'Because ... because I believed with all my soul that we would gather an angry army of ten thousand soldiers. We can't last more than two or three days. There will be no help from the Aryan side. Nothing ... nothing.'

He unfurled a large blueprint and flattened it on the table. 'Look,' Simon continued, 'a city engineer's map of the sewer system under Warsaw. We move our companies into bunkers which can connect to the sewers. I have sent Rodel over the wall to buy trucks and get drivers. The Communists will set up escape routes and hiding places in the forests. We go under the wall a group at a time and move through the sewers, and we will come up five or six miles beyond the ghetto in prearranged locations.'

Andrei snatched the blueprint off the table and crumpled it.

'Do we destroy ourselves with a futile three-day gesture?' Simon screamed. 'Or is it our duty – yes, our duty – to get a handful of survivors out? If we stay, we die – all of us. At least this other way a few may get through to tell the story.'

'He's right, Andrei,' Chris said, stepping between them. 'This story must be told.'

Andrei looked slowly to Wolf Brandel.

'I don't know,' Wolf pleaded.

Andrei sat down slowly and contained his temper. 'What story will they tell, Simon Eden? Will they unearth the Brandel journals and read about how five hundred thousand sheep walked silently, without protest, to their deaths and the high-sounding idealists who stood for honor crawled out on their hands and knees through crap-filled sewers to tell the world our heritage? What story, Simon? What story? Have you no shame? Have you no anger to avenge dead children? Simon! One week! Let us stand and fight like men for one week!'

'We cannot hold a week. It is impossible.'

'Betar! Masada! Jerusalem! We must show them Jews can still fight, Simon!'

'It is our duty to try to survive,' Simon said.

Andrei turned to Wolf. 'Order the Bathyrans back to Mila 19. We will not be a partner to this final debasement of our people.'

'Don't pull your people out of the command,' Simon pleaded.

'Do you hear me, Wolf? I have given you an order!'

Wolf looked again from one to the other in utter confusion.

Ring! Ring! Ring! screamed the alarm bell in long dashes. Ring! Ring! Ring!

Wolf stole a glance at the street. 'It's swarming with SS.'

The four men quickly checked their weapons and bolted out to the ladder to the roof. Andrei was the last one through. He closed the trap door behind him and rubbed his arms in the sudden burst of January cold.

'Down through Mila 5,' Andrei said. 'Be careful not to stir up those feathers and give our position away.'

They crouched low and stepped on the feathers as though they were walking on eggs. Chris's foot hit a hidden ice slick and he crashed down, unable to contain a pain-racked scream.

'My knee!' he cried, torn with pain.

'What is it?'

'Trick basketball knee. Fine time to jump out.'

'Look over the side,' Andrei said. Wolf crawled off with Simon.

Chris grimaced as he tried to slip the loose cartilage back into place. It cracked as it found the slot. Chris turned white-lipped.

'Can you move?'

'Wrap it up in something so it won't jump out again,' he grunted.

Andrei whipped off his leather jacket, then tore the sleeve from his shirt and with it deftly locked Chris's kneecap into place.

At the edge of the roof Wolf and Simon peered down on a street swarming with Germans. The kettle was set up all the way from Nalewki to Zamenhof streets with the main force concentrating on the Orphans and Self-Help headquarters at Mila 19. They slipped back to Andrei.

'We're boxed in,' Simon said.

'Can we make a break for your headquarters?'

'No,' Simon answered. 'We'd have to cross an open courtyard at Mila 5. We'd never make it.'

'Can't stay here,' Wolf said. 'They'll be all over the roof in minutes.'

'I have a hiding place up here,' Andrei said. 'I think it will hold all four of us.'

Chris struggled to his feet. Simon and Wolf draped an arm over his shoulders and Chris was able to hobble. Andrei led them to the last house at Mila and Zamenhof.

The roof slanted at a sharp pitch for fifteen yards to the rain gutters. Near the very edge, before the overhanging eaves, was a large chimney.

'We've got to get down there to the chimney,' Andrei said. 'Lie absolutely flat and move in a direct line with the chimney so you won't be observed from the street.'

Andrei went on his belly, headfirst down the steeply angled tiles, the Schmeisser cradled in his elbows. Inch by inch he wiggled his body downward. Watch the ice, he said to himself, dig your toes in, don't look at the edge – that's a five-story drop – easy ... easy. The blood poured into his head and made him giddy for a moment, and he was suddenly struck with the weakness of three days without food. The tile nails jammed into his legs and belly and sliced his leather jacket, and the cold cramped his body. A few feet more ... just a few feet. Andrei lined up the chimney and rolled against it.

With his back braced against the chimney, he waved for the next man to come down. Simon went over. Andrei removed a loose tile nail, the first key to a Chinese puzzle. He slid a tile out and loosened five more, which he set down into the sub-roof. He had made a hole just large enough for a man to get into the sub-roof and eaves.

Simon made the mistake of coming down feet first. Although he was in a better position to grab with his hands, he could not see his direction or the ice slicks and could conceivably miss the chimney, for Andrei was unable to shout up directions without drawing attention from the street. Midway down, Simon had to turn his body so that he would come headfirst.

Come on, Simon. Come on, for Christ sake, Andrei muttered to himself. Time drawled on. Come on, Simon. If they get on top of us, we'll be clay pigeons.

Simon Eden reached the chimney, put his back against it, and dropped his head between his legs, close to tears of sheer fright.

Next Chris. Wolf crouched in a rear guard, watching the rooftops.

Chris was racked with pain, dragging the game leg, but he came down fast and without hesitation. Andrei dared a peek around the corner of the chimney to the street. Luck was with them so far.

'Simon, get down there. Crawl forward as far as you can go. Stay on the crossbeams. The flooring under it is rotted away. Chris, follow him in. Move up as close against him as you can so there'll be room for all of us.'

Simon went headfirst into the hole. He slid his body over the beams. The joists formed a sharp angle at the beams, so a large man like Simon Eden was all but wedged in a vise. He pushed forward with the greatest effort until he came to a dead end.

Chris followed him, struggling with the painful leg.

Andrei looked up the roof to Wolf and waved for him to begin his descent. Wolf hated the roofs. They made him dizzy. He had moved a few yards when all he could see was the edge below him and all he could think of was his body hurtling down a sheer plunge of five stories to the pavement. He closed his eyes. Everything began to spin. He froze on the spot. Andrei and the chimney seemed miles away.

Andrei snarled. He wanted to shout up to Wolf, curse him, prod him, order him. Time was running out. Should he crawl up after Wolf? No, that would certainly attract attention from the street. But if he allowed Wolf to stay where he was, Germans would be above him at any second.

'Come on, lad,' Andrei prayed. 'Come on. Move, boy, move.'

The sweat in Wolf's eyes turned icy. He lifted his head. 'Got to . . . got to . . . got to . . .' He crawled an inch . . . another . . . 'Got to . . . got to . . . got to . . .' Closer, closer, closer. Andrei scampered up, snatched his hand, and dragged him down the last six feet. Wolf was shaking.

'Get down there,' Andrei said, hurling him headfirst into the hideaway.

Andrei went into the roof last. He was greeted by an accumulation of sixty-five years of filth and cobwebs. He stretched his body downward until he was stopped by Wolf's feet, then eased his upper half down. He lay flush against the chimney. Andrei lifted the tiles from his prone position and slipped them back into place. When the last tile was fitted, the eaves were plunged into darkness.

The four men were locked in a lightless coffin. They lay inside a triangle formed by beams, rafters, and the wall. Each man lay on three two-inch boards which supported his body at his calves, thighs, back, and shoulders. Beneath the beams was a rotted floor, part of which extended into the eaves, directly over the street.

The face of one man touched the feet of another end to end. Their movement was limited to a few inches. They could turn over from back to stomach only with a slow effort.

'Everybody all right?' Andrei whispered.

They answered in the affirmative.

'How's the leg, Chris?'

'Going up like a balloon.'

'Painful?'

'Let me suffer in peace.'

A bug bit Wolf under the eye. 'How long did you stay here, Andrei?'

'Once for six hours.'

'Holy Mother.'

'Of course I didn't have such nice company. Don't lie on the sub-floor. It's rotted. Pieces may fall down on the street. And reach up and rub your partner's feet so his blood will circulate.'

Andrei tucked the Schmeisser firmly into the apex of the joist and beam and saw a slit of light at the extreme end of the eaves. By the most difficult of straining and contortion, he could lift his head and put his eye to it.

'By God. Some boards are split. I can see the pavement.' He worked the blade of a pocketknife back and forth between the boards, separating them a half inch. 'I can see Mila 19.'

'What's going on?'

'It's swarming with Germans. They must be looking for the bunker.'

Wolf and Simon felt Chris writhe as spears of pain lashed up and down his leg. Chris's leg twitched against Wolf's face. Simon handed Chris a handkerchief. 'Bite on this,' he said.

Luminous eyes peered at the four strangers who had invaded their home. A scraping of claws.

'Rats!'

'Get out of here, you bastards!'

'Oh God, I hate rats,' Wolf moaned.

'You'll find them quite friendly in a few hours,' Andrei said. 'It's the bats at night that get you.'

Wolf's skin crawled as he felt the animal dash over his chest and brush up against his face. 'Oh God damn it,' he cried, 'I hate rats.'

They became silent. The sound of guttural orders bounced off the deserted houses in the street below and echoed up to them. They had found a Jew on Mila Street and were torturing him for the location of the Mila 19 bunker.

Cries of agony below settled them down to adjust to their own discomfort. And then the automatic silence when one breathes only with controlled quiet, for there was movement on the roof above them.

'No Jews down this way, Sergeant!'

'You can never tell where the vermin hide. Post a guard here and one at the opposite end of the roofs.'

'Yes, sir.'

Andrei calculated that the guards were at that point where the roof began its pitch, some fifteen yards away. From their speech, they were Ukrainians.

The beams cut into their bodies, but no one dared change his position. The slightest sound now could give them away.

They muted themselves into a deeper stillness at the sound of noises in the attic under them. A smashing of glass. The sound of hatchets and sledge hammers bursting the walls and doors. The building was undergoing a dismantling for secret hiding places.

Each of them touched his weapon at the same instant for a comfort which did not really exist.

Curses penetrated their tomb from the frustrated, grunting hunters.

Screaming whistles in the street. Another Jew had been located, cringing in a courtyard sewer.

More men were on the roof above them.

Chris's body convulsed in pain. His eyes rolled back in his head. He clamped his teeth into the cloth in his mouth. Simon was trying to decide whether or not to knock Chris unconscious with the pistol barrel, but at that moment Chris straightened out and was still.

Chris saw his father kneeling at the altar next to the library in their villa outside Rome. So funny to see his father praying. Poppa was a hypocrite! He drank, he gambled, he was a libertine . . . he was a Fascist. But Poppa prayed. Poppa told him to learn to pray. I've wanted to pray but I couldn't. I just couldn't without damning myself.

Oh Mary, Mother of God! Help me! I'm going to scream! My leg! Jesus! Jesus! Help me!

'Have your men smash holes in the roof. Jews hide in the roofs!'

They could feel the vibration of the sledge hammers as they splintered the tiles. The ancient beams rattled under the pounding and shot needles of fear through their bodies. Wolf wept softly to himself. Each new blow brought the enemy closer and closer to the edge of the roof.

All Chris could see was his father's chapel.

Andrei had no thoughts but of that moment when the hammer would burst through and reveal him. He would fire the gun into their rotten faces.

Simon Eden was calm. It did not matter much any more, Simon thought. His parents, his sister and brother were gone. The years as a Labor Zionist organizer had taught him that when the fountains of idealism ran dry one weighed the odds without emotion and accepted reality. This was the end. Trapped in a coffin with rats and spiders. There had been no sweetheart, really. A marriage ended in failure. To be the wife of a Zionist organizer, one had to be a woman like Sylvia Brandel. There had not even been a sweetheart like Gabriela. He envied Andrei. Simon's only marriage was to Zionism.

They were coming down the roof with ropes around their waists. Andrei prayed as he held his machine pistol ready, his finger quivering on the trigger. There was only one hope. Perhaps we are so far out on the edge they won't come down, he thought.

An hour passed. Then two, then three.

At last the hammering above and below them stopped.

The relief from the tension brought on a new realization of physical agony. Their bodies had been cut to a blissful numbness. Chris mumbled hallucinations. They stretched one by one and shifted their positions slightly and massaged themselves and each other to restore circulation.

They had to be quiet; the Ukrainians were still up there. The terror on the streets was unabated.

Wolf played a chess game in his mind. It was the most magnificent jeweled board one could imagine. The black squares were made of solid gold and the white of ivory, each pawn and piece carved of a different precious gem. Move the pawn . . . no, the bishop. He tried to think. Then the board would become muddled and the opponent's chessmen turned to rats and spiders. Why can't I keep the board straight? Why? I've played blindfolded before! The rats ate his chessmen and he could not move his hands to help them. Stop eating my chessmen! Rachael ... Please don't let me think of Rachael. I'll cry if I do.

Andrei licked his lips. Food! Oh, look at it. Deborah, you shouldn't have cooked so much. You cook just like Momma. The gefilte fish is just right. So tasty.

Andrei sniffed. He came out of his trance slowly. Smoke! The brick chimney next to him was becoming warm. German efficiency. Many fireplaces in the ghetto had false coveys for hiding places. This was countered by burning fires in them so any bricked-up Jews would be smoked out. Their hiding place turned into a stifling furnace. The sweat gushed from their bodies, driving them deeper into agony. Whiffs of smoke slithered into the eaves through the crumbled mortar. Andrei gagged and twisted his head to the slit in the eaves to try to suck in a whiff of pure air.

'The smoke is coming through that one down there!' he could hear someone shout. 'Mark it off the list.'

Andrei closed his eyes again and dreamed of food.

The high-pitched multi-thousand-cycle cries of bats.

Simon's dream of cold and wet made him urinate.

Andrei opened his eyes. He could hear the flapping wings and the vibrations. Dream or real? Dream or real? Dream or real? Oh God, I'm hungry. Tiny droplets of light sparkled off and on, off and on. Andrei looked through the slit in the boards. Outside, a glaring, artificial light. He turned over again and watched the sparkling overhead. They were beams of searchlights pushing through cracks in the roof. It must be night. He listened for several moments. He could hear nothing on the roof.

'Simon!' Andrei dared whisper. 'Simon!'

'Andrei!'

'Chris!'

'He is unconscious,' Simon said. 'He passes out and comes to, passes out and comes to.'

'Wolf!'

Andrei was answered by a feeble groan. Andrei kicked against Wolf's shoulder. 'Wolf!'

The return was an incoherent babbling.

'Must be night. They're using searchlights.'

'That's the way I figured it,' Simon said.

Andrei looked through the boards again, squinting to see through the glare. There was still a concentration of SS at Mila 19. He groped around for his weapon and toyed with the idea of breaking out of the entombment and firing at the searchlights. No, he'd be shot off the roof in seconds.

'I guess we're no worse off than those poor bastards in the bunker,' Andrei said. 'At least they're not looking for us.'

'Nothing to do but wait,' Simon said.

'Yeah ...'

And then quiet once more as they heard the steps of men patrolling the roof over them, complaining about their bad fortune of nighttime duty.

Nothing to do but wait. Andrei slumped back, hoping for a misty dream to take him where there were plates piled with food.

'I didn't catch your name.'

'I know your name, Miss Rak. Like so many, I am an admirer of the work of your late father, so my name is unimportant. You can just snap your fingers and say, "Hey you," and I'll know you are addressing me.'

'You do dance, Lieutenant?'

'As a matter of fact, I am an excellent dancer, but frankly, I do it only as an accommodation.'

Gaby! Gaby! I am afraid! Gaby! I am so afraid!

Whistles!

Andrei forced his eyelids apart. I must be dead, he told himself. I am nowhere. In the sky. In hell. I am dead. There was no movement in his body. No feeling. No pain.

But then the cold sent a chill through him and his stomach knotted with hunger.

Like hell I'm dead! He tried to move his arms. Numb. Neck and shoulders without feeling from the pressure of the beams. First my fingers . . . just my fingers first. He drew them up like claws, back, forth, back, forth; then he shook his wrists. His fingers scratched against his leg and sides, over and over to make some feeling return. His body tingled as he tore at it harder and harder. He pinched himself again and again and slapped his face. Inch by inch circulation flowed.

'Simon!' he croaked.

'Andrei!'

'The others?'

'Out cold. Neither of them has spoken for two hours. I've been counting seconds. It must be day again.'

'I don't know.'

'Can you see down on the street?'

His head felt like a lead ball. He pushed it to the crack. The searchlights were gone. It was misty out. Germans were still all over the street.

'They're still down there.'

'I think they've left the roof. I heard them ordered down. No sounds for over fifteen minutes.'

'Think it may be a trick?'

'We've got to take a chance,' Simon said. 'We can't hold out here another day.'

Andrei rolled over on his back. Sharp needles of pain greeted his effort to raise his arms over his head. He fished around for the key tile and wiggled it. He tugged desperately. It slid away, letting in a show of light, nearly blinding him. Andrei pulled the other five tiles loose. He drew himself up on all fours, his knees resting on a pair of beams, and shoved the upper part of his body through the hole.

'Clear! Simon, it's clear!'

He pulled himself outside to the roof and crouched against the chimney, reaching in until he found Wolf's head. Straining with every sinew, he slid Wolf over the rafters until his body appeared beneath the opening. Next Chris was pushed by Simon until Andrei could hook onto him.

Simon jammed past the two unconscious, prostrate bodies. Simon and Andrei looked at each other. Their faces were swollen and misshapen by bug bites, their clothing ripped to shreds. Blood and bruises were everywhere, and layers of filth hid their features. They stared like strangers.

'Do you look like hell,' Andrei said.

'You're no lily of the valley, Androfski.' Simon looked at his watch and held it against his ear. 'Thirty hours we've been in there.'

Andrei looked at Simon again and began laughing. And Simon laughed too. They burst into a hysterical, uncontrolled laughter in each other's arms until they ached and tears fell down their cheeks. And it ebbed slowly, each shaking his head alternately. Andrei wiped his Schmeisser clean and counted the clips of ammunition, then got to his knees and reached down and slapped Wolf's face.

'Is he alive?'

Andrei slapped him again and again.

Wolf groaned convulsively and sucked at the air. He blinked his eyes, shrank away from the light.

At the same time Simon worked on Chris.

Wolf came to enough to look up at his comrades and smile at the sight of them.

'Listen, Wolf. Stay here with Chris. Massage yourself and keep massaging him. There are holes all over the roof, so this one won't draw further attention.'

'Where are you going?'

'Up to take a look. They've stopped patrolling the roof, but they're still in the streets. Stay here until we come back for you with ropes.'

Andrei crawled up, with Simon close behind him. When the roof flattened, they inched to the edge to get the best possible look down on Mila Street.

Andrei's fists tightened around the Schmeisser, enraged at what met his eyes. A double cordon of bayonet-wielding SS Reinhard Corps men formed a corridor and circle around people straggling out of the building, flushed from the bunker. He saw Rabbi Solomon thrown to the ground. Alex knelt over to help him up. Sylvia Brandel held the child, and Tolek and Ana and Ervin stood by Deborah, keeping the children calm.

Kutler barked orders, clapping his hands in delight that the search was over.

'Schnell!'

'Move quickly, Jews!'

Andrei backed away slowly. 'Come on, Simon,' he said.

'Where are you going?'

'Where do you think?'

'You'll destroy us all,' Simon snapped. He stood up quickly and blocked Andrei's path.

'Let me pass,' Andrei hissed.

'You're a damned fool,' Simon said, grabbing his shirt.

Andrei's fist smashed into Simon Eden's mouth. The big man went flat on his back. Before Andrei could make a step, he found himself looking into the muzzle of Simon's Luger leveled at his heart.

They glared, neither daring to move.

'Jews ... move out!'

Simon's face went slack. His pistol hand dropped. 'I'm coming with you,' he said.

The two men moved swiftly over the rooftops to Mila 5. The stairs were clear. They ran down, jumping half a flight at a time, and stopped in the courtyard.

'It's clear.'

They sprinted through the courtyard, down into the basement of Mila 1, and into a tunnel that came up on the edge of Muranowski Place. A fast straight run down Niska Street brought them to the intersection ahead of the slower-moving cordon.

Andrei flattened his back against the corner house, gasping for air, his legs wobbly. He looked around the corner. Kutler strutted, laughing and jovial, with a dozen SS men in the lead of the quarry, SS men on either sidewalk, and Nightingales in the rear.

Andrei beckoned Simon to get close to him. 'Kutler and some SS men are in front of our people – about ten yards. Let them get past us. We'll hit them from behind.'

'How many guards?'

'Hundred.'

He shoved a clip of ammunition into the Schmeisser and threw the bolt. Simon unclicked the safety lock on his pistol.

Step by step, as in a funeral procession, the bagged game of Mila 19 walked for the Stawki Gate to the Umschlagplatz. Alexander Brandel stood tall and brave despite the ordeal in the bunker. He walked like a patriarch toward Calvary, and those behind him found courage in his presence.

A dozen black uniforms passed the corner of Niska Street.

Rat-a-tat-tat-a-tat!

A flame erupted from the end of Andrei's machine pistol. Kutler pitched forward on his face, the back of his head shot away. Four of his cohorts tumbled around him.

Rat-a-tat-tat!

Wham! Simon Eden's pistol crackled with deadly accuracy. Wham! Wham! Wham! Shrieks, Germans toppled to the ground.

Andrei stepped into the intersection and blasted at the row of flanking guards.

A wild melee. The Nazis broke and scattered.

'Run, you sons of bitches! Run! Run! Run!'

Rat-a-tat! Rat-a-tat!

'Run, you lousy bastards! Run! Run! Run!' Andrei screamed, spewing death into them.

A calmer Simon Eden picked his shots, sharp-shooting the stunned Germans. A hidden fire bomb came out of Tolek Alterman's shirt and arched into an alcove filled with cowering SS. They shrieked out into the streets, trying to put out the flames devouring them.

'Scatter!' Simon commanded. 'Alex! Tolek! Ana! Move, everybody! Go!'

The captives fled from the street.

'Sons of bitches!' Andrei screamed. 'Sons of bitches! Die!' He tore down Zamenhof, looking for the terrified enemy. Bullets came back at him. He knelt and poured fire.

And then he was whirled around with a sudden impact that cracked his head on the side of a building. He slid to the sidewalk. On hands and knees he tried to fight to his feet, but he could not get up and it all became a blur. His face hit the sidewalk . . . blood oozed from the corners of his mouth . . . oblivion.

Chapter Four

'Idiot!'

SS Oberführer Funk slapped Sturmbannführer Sieghold Stutze across the mouth. The Austrian winced, then came stiffly to attention.

'Imbecile!' He slapped Stutze again, leaving streak marks on his cheek. Stutze stood at an even more ramrod posture.

'Swine!' Another slap.

'Herr Oberführer,' Stutze whined.

'Chased by Jews! Eleven SS men killed!' Whap! Whap!

'Herr Oberführer. We were attacked by fifty madmen!'

'Liar! Coward! Assemble your officers at the barracks immediately.'

'*Jawohl, Herr Oberführer!*' Stutze snapped his heels together. 'Heil Hitler!'

'Get out of my sight, you worm.'

Horst watched the performance, somewhat amused. 'It seems,' he said when Stutze had left, 'that I detect flaws in the lofty theories of absolute obedience. Oh, I grant you that the German people are the most likely to succeed as robots, but we are still riddled with human frailties. Stutze is a coward, Schreiker a damned fool, Koenig a thief, and myself – well, I'd rather not go into that.'

Funk didn't hear a word. He was too immersed in his own sudden dilemma. 'Has the world gone entirely mad?' he said. 'First Reinhard Heydrich is assassinated by Czech bandits, and now – this.'

'Yes, dear Reinhard. We shall all miss his noble soul,' Horst said.

Funk kept talking aloud to himself. '*Ach!* Himmler will have a wild tantrum when he learns about this.' He lit a cigarette and pressed his fingertips together in a rapid motion, noticing the nails needed trimming and cleaning. Better get it done. Dirt annoyed him. 'Tomorrow I personally will direct operations to begin the liquidation of the ghetto.'

'Do you think that's wise, Alfred?'

'What?'

'To go into the ghetto tomorrow.'

Funk took it as an immediate affront to his courage. He was no Stutze!

Before he could answer the challenge Horst held up his hand. 'Just a moment. Today the Jews have burst another one of our pet theories like a bubble. They have discovered that we are not supermen at all. Hit a German with a bullet he will drop dead like any other man. This delicious taste of blood after three years of torment will obviously spur them into greater efforts.'

'I have no time for your nonsense today,' Funk cracked back with the full cruelty revealed in his eyes. He was incensed with the very idea that the sub-human rabble could present an obstacle, but he did not wish to argue, for Horst had a needle under his skin and was prodding him.

'Do you have any idea of the Jewish strength?' Horst asked.

'What difference does that make!'

'A good general should know the weight of the enemy forces.'

'Enemy forces, indeed! Since when do we recognize Jews as a fighting force?'

'I should say that as of today would be a good time.'

Funk slammed his fist on the table. Horst refused to be intimidated and obviously was not going to be slapped around like the Austrian. Funk recalled why he had hated Horst von Epp in the beginning. That attitude of knowing something Funk did not know. That ability to operate on a level of shrewdness that eluded the stern, dogmatic, rigid SS devotion. Funk smiled faintly in an attempt to play the game with Von Epp. 'And what do you propose might happen if I take the Reinhard Corps into the ghetto tomorrow?'

'I don't propose it, nor do I suggest it. I know it,' Horst said. 'You will lead three hundred men into a massacre.'

'And I say they will flee and bury themselves at the sight of us. Jews won't fight.'

'How unfortunate that you have become victimized by our own propaganda. Oh yes, I know. You have proof. We have translated our theories by acting out our superiority on helpless people. You'll find another caliber of man left inside those walls.'

'Do you really believe that I would hesitate in the face of Jews?'

'When I was in the ministry in Berlin I spent week after week inventing and expounding the theories of Jewish cowardice, Alfred. The plain and simple fact of the matter is – we are liars.'

Funk's entire face reacted with shock.

'I doubt if any warriors in the world were as furious in battle as the ancient Hebrews, nor did any people in man's history fight harder for freedom. Not once, but many times, they made Rome totter. And since their dispersion, because they have not had the opportunity to fight under a Jewish flag, we have been able to isolate them into individual units and riddle them with inferiority complexes. German torment has taken these segregated masses and jelled them together as a people for the first time in two thousand years. We cannot measure their determination to acquit themselves, but we can make an educated guess that we'd better be damned careful from this point on.'

Funk sprang to his feet. 'I will not listen to this anarchy. You defile the noble purposes of the Third Reich!'

'Oh, stop shouting, Alfred. I invented half the noble purposes of the Third Reich.' Horst walked to the window and drew the curtains apart. Across Krakow Boulevard and beyond the Saxony Gardens some of the ghetto roofs could be seen. 'Who is left in that ghetto is the one man in a thousand in any age, in any culture, who through some mysterious workings of forces within his soul will stand in defiance against any master. He is that one human in a thousand whose indomitable spirit cannot bow. He is the one man in a thousand who will not walk quietly to the Umschlagplatz. Watch out for him, Alfred Funk. We have pushed him to the wall.'

Oberführer Funk became confused. Von Epp, one of the very creators of the Aryan myth, was ripping it apart. Suddenly it became clear to him. 'I have been ordered by Himmler to have the ghetto liquidated, and that is what shall be done,' he snapped.

Horst flopped his arms to his side in disgust. 'Simple, eh? Orders are orders.'

'Naturally.'

'Alfred, you represent that confounding German idiocy which is unable to improvise from a fixed plan. Forget that orders are orders before you perform a monumental blunder.'

'You know, Horst, I really should report your conversation to Himmler. I really should. What possible blunder can I make by fulfilling orders? Say that these noble creatures do fight. So what? We shall destroy them.'

'For a decade we have been preaching a gospel of Jewish cowardice. It is Nazi dogma. What happens if the Reinhard Corps is wiped out tomorrow in the ghetto? How shall we explain it to the world? Shall we say that Jews fight, after all? How would we look to those whom we have impressed as supermen to be forced even to admit that Jews were standing up against us?'

'I hadn't thought of that,' Funk admitted.

'Suppose this defiance in the ghetto lasts a week ... ten days ...'

'Impossible.'

'But suppose it does. It could ignite rebellions all over Poland. "See," the Poles would say, "the Germans have lied to us. Let us take a crack at them too." Perhaps the Czechs and the Greeks may like to have a crack at superman hides. You invite insurrection.'

Funk sank to the seat, completely confused now. 'Hitler will be out of his mind with rage,' he mumbled.

'Get back to Berlin immediately,' Horst said. 'We must put across to them that this liquidation can be completed only if it can be carried out with no further armed conflict. We could invite a dangerous precedent, otherwise. And for this unfortunate incident today, I will say that it was a band of Communists or bandits. You know, minimize it with the usual stories. Then we proceed carefully. We outwit them. We use cunning to lure them out.'

'Very well,' Funk agreed, 'very well.'

Andrei's eyes fluttered open. He was in a bunker cell somewhere. Someone hovered over him. It was Simon.

'My gun!'

'It's under the cot. No ammunition left, mind you, but the gun is there.'

Andrei closed his eyes. He tried to separate the blur of events that all ran together. He remembered seeing Kutler fall in the street, parts of the agony in the rafters, snatches of things that might have been dreams or might have happened. Simon fed him a drink of water. Half of it spurted out of his mouth, unable to penetrate the thick dry caking lining his throat. He sipped again.

'What happened?'

'We put on quite a brother act. We make a colorful pair.'

'Where is everyone?'

'Scattered in a half dozen bunkers.'

'Did Alex get away?'

'He's in the cell across the passage.'

'My sister?'

'At the Franciskanska bunker with the children.'

'Chris ... Wolf ...'

'They are safe.'

Andrei forced himself up on his elbows. He ached all over. He pushed himself to a sitting position on the edge of the cot and was stricken with a spell of dizziness. He lowered his head between his legs to let blood circulate.

Simon moved a small crude table beside the cot and placed a bowl of gruel on it with a hunk of stale bread. It was the first food Andrei had eaten in nearly five days. His stomach growled and his hand trembled as he sloshed the bread in the bowl to soften it. The food was taken slowly, carefully.

'Where am I? At your bunker?'

'Yes.'

'How did I get here?'

'I scraped you off the sidewalk. You fell short in your one-man effort to annihilate the entire German garrison, but not too bad, eleven SS killed, two Ukrainians. You're the rage of the ghetto.'

Andrei felt his pain-racked body. 'Did I get hit?'

'Grazed. The doctor said that normally it wouldn't have stopped you from playing soccer an hour later, but combined with hunger, exhaustion, and a few other discomforts, you fainted.'

'Fainted? What a ridiculous thing to do. Only women faint.' He mopped the bread around in the bowl more rapidly, cleaned the dish, and licked his fingers. Simon was acting strangely, he thought. His voice rang with bitterness and he was avoiding Andrei's eyes. Simon never did that. He could win most of his arguments by his penetrating look alone.

'One of our people didn't make it,' Simon said. He set a familiar notebook on the cot beside Andrei. Andrei recognized it as a volume of the Good Fellowship Club's study. Simon laid a pair of thick-lensed glasses on top of the book.

'Ervin?'

'Yes. Stray bullet. He lived long enough to tell me where he had hidden this volume. It was the one he was working on. We went to the Mila 19 bunker immediately to find it. Rest of the bunker is destroyed, but we were able to find many hidden things. We salvaged all the arms stores.'

Tears welled up in Andrei's eyes. 'You would think that we would get used to our friends dying after a time. I loved Ervin. Lot of years together.' Andrei bit his lip, but the tears fell anyway. 'Quiet, gentle little man. Believed in what he was doing without shouting, breast-beating. He just stayed in the cellar month in and month out, working on the archives. He never said why. He just did it because somebody had to. Ever see how swollen his hands were from the damp? Blind as a bat, but he stayed and kept working after they took Susan. He stayed and went about his business ... never raised his voice.'

The cot groaned as Simon sat beside Andrei. Simon picked the book up, opened it, and turned the pages, then pulled the candle on the table directly to him. 'This was his last entry.' He read, '"When will we fight? Or will we fight? Who among us will dare to fire that first shot against them? Who?"' He closed it and set it down. He hunched his massize frame forward and rubbed the knuckles of one hand against the palm of the other. 'I don't deserve to be the commander. I want you to take over.'

'No, Simon, no.'

'Don't humor me, Andrei. I was the man who was planning to send our companies through the sewers to escape. You were the one who fired the shot – and I pointed my pistol at your heart to stop you.'

'Don't you think I know how torn up you are to have to give an order that will turn us into a suicide force?' Andrei said.

'You don't understand,' Simon snapped, standing up abruptly with his back to Andrei. 'I aimed that pistol at your heart because I was afraid to go down on the street. I was afraid, and I'll be afraid again.'

'You were afraid, but you went anyhow, and while I was in a blind rage you brought them to safety, because when the moment was needed you were calm and deliberate, as a good commander must be.' Andrei walked up behind him and put his hand on Simon's shoulder. 'I had a lot of time to think while we were up in the rafters. I found answers to many questions. I guess when one is close to his Maker many perplexing problems suddenly become amazingly clear and simple. Who fights what kind of war? The quiet courage it took to be a soldier like Ervin Rosenblum. Simon ... I ... I'm no damned good for anything but leading cavalry charges.'

'Perhaps,' Simon whispered, 'if you stuck close by me to knock me flat on my back ...'

'I don't think it will be necessary again.'

'There were too many mistakes today,' Simon said with a quick surge of excitement. 'We have to have scouts in observation posts so that nothing can get into the ghetto before we can move our companies into battle position.'

Andrei nodded in agreement.

'And we have to teach them that the cardinal rule is to pick up enemy weapons and strip their uniforms. We missed on that today.'

Andrei nodded again and smiled slightly at the knowledge that Simon was again in full control and eager.

'I'm thinking. We should find a new bunker close to the central area for a command post.' Simon stopped abruptly, watching Andrei look at the volume of the journal and Ervin's glasses. 'Andrei, what made you go into the streets?'

'I don't know. Just that this was the moment which could not pass. It wasn't even seeing my sister. It was Alex. I couldn't let them take Alexander Brandel to the Umschlagplatz.' Andrei picked up the book. 'So damned much time has gone by, and Alex and I have barely talked to each other. I wish I knew how to apologize.'

'Why don't you try?'

'What can I say for being a damned fool?'

'Come,' Simon said.

Andrei trailed him haltingly out of the cell and across the narrow passageway to the opposite cell. Simon pulled back the sack curtain. The three of them were there. Sylvia with her little boy on her lap. Moses Brandel at the age of four was disciplined to the silence of underground living; pale, scrawny from the lack of sun and air and nourishment. Alexander gazed emptily at the floor in much the same way as he had since the children were taken to the Umschlagplatz. Sylvia stood and put the boy down. She blocked Andrei's way, but Simon nodded for her to leave the room. She looked from Andrei to Alex, then took the child and led him out.

Andrei hulked helplessly over the dejected man, groping for words. He knelt slowly beside Alex. Alex turned his face, recognized Andrei and hung his head.

'I ... uh ... wanted to give you this,' Andrei said, showing the book. 'They ... uh ... were lucky enough to salvage it from Mila 19.'

Alex did not answer.

'I think that – well, with Ervin gone, you'll want to take up the work again.'

Again, nothing.

'It's very important that the archives be continued and – Look, I know something I didn't know. What I mean to say is, it takes many kinds of men and many kinds of battles to fight a war.'

Andrei reached out and touched his shoulder, but Alex shrank away.

'Please look at me, Alex,' Andrei whispered. 'You must hear what I'm saying. Alex, once I told you that the Brandel journal would never take the place of the Seventh Ulany Brigade, and you answered that truth is a weapon worth a thousand armies. I never understood that till now. It's true, all of the divisions of the German army can't defeat these words.'

Alex shook his head slowly.

'You ... you were right. You've won a great battle with this,' Andrei said.

The mouth in Alex's bearded face fumbled to form words in a cracked, wavering voice. 'I called my dearest friend a man who thirsts for personal revenge. I ... took the weapons from your hands. I am the vengeful man. Your way has always been the only way.'

'You're wrong about that, Alex. My way hasn't been the only way. I would have destroyed us all long ago. You see, only because of men like you and Simon has a moment like today been possible for men like me.'

'The children are gone ... Everyone is gone ... I have failed.'

Andrei clutched Alex's arms hard and pleaded with fervor. 'Listen to me!' he cried. 'We've all done the best with what we've had. No man has ever fought a better fight than you! And it was the only fight. It was, I swear it.'

'Don't patronize me, Andrei. It is I who should be on my knees to you.'

Andrei released his grip and stood up slowly, and his voice mellowed with softness. 'All my life I have believed I walked in the darkness, battling windmills, crying for lost causes, living a life in dubious battle. My father gave me a country which hated me, and you have given your sons a ghetto and genocide. God only knows what kind of a world Wolf will hand to his sons. We enter this world in the middle of a war that is never won. It has always been this way – this endless war. No one of us ever really wins in his life. All you have the right to ask of life is to choose a battle in this war, make the best you can, and leave the field with honor.'

Alex mumbled, 'Make your battle ... leave the field with honor.'

'You've fought your good fight. Now the war goes on. I must fight my way now.'

'Oh, Andrei, stop! What is there left but doom?'

'Left? We have a lot left. We can go out like men ... "What though the field be lost? All is not lost – unconquerable will, the study of revenge, immortal hate ... The courage never to submit or yield," I never understood those lines till now. But I know – it is not a dubious battle.'

Alexander picked up the book, and his fingers caressed it lovingly. He opened it, glanced up at Andrei quickly, then thumbed hungrily through Ervin's notes. He came to the last entry. 'Who will fire the first shot?' Alex took out a pencil, and his hand wrote:

Journal Entry

Today a great shot for freedom was fired. I think it stands a chance of being heard forever. It marks a turning point in the history of the Jewish people. The beginning of return to a status of dignity we have not known for two thousand years. Yes, today was the first step back. My battle is done. Now I turn the command over to the soldiers.

Chapter Five

Piotr Warsinski slammed the phone receiver down. He scratched his scaly hands. Again he had pleaded in vain with Sieghold Stutze to issue firearms to the Jewish Militia. After the outbreak of January 18, Warsinski was positive that the Germans would return to the ghetto immediately with an overpowering force. Instead, several days had passed in silence and his police were becoming afraid to patrol the streets.

Warsinski scoffed at the idea that the ambush at Niska and Zamenhof streets was anything but an insane gesture by a madman. He knew there was no real planned insurrection. He had no fear of this so-called Joint Jewish Forces. But he was afraid of what would happen if Sieghold Stutze decided he was no longer able to command the Militia effectively.

Piotr growled in frustration and became restless. He decided to leave the barracks and go to the Pawiak Prison. A girl had been brought in earlier who was suspected of being a member of the Joint Forces. He would work her over, and that would relieve the tension. Perhaps he could force from her the location of Eden or Andrei Androfski or Rodel. If he could deliver such a prize to Sieghold Stutze it would reaffirm his ability.

But, Piotr mused, it was getting more and more difficult to beat information out of these people as time went along. Those who were left simply could not be tortured for information. But what the devil, he could rip the clothing from the girl and smash her up. That would be a good evening's sport

Piotr was not afraid to go into the streets alone. He told his men so. Yet it was stupid to invite another attack from a madman. He called in his personal bodyguards, six fat, faithful huskies, to escort him to the Pawiak Prison a few blocks from the barracks.

When he arrived at the ugly reddish brick structure a phone call awaited him. He took it in his office.

'Sturmbannführer Strutze here,' the Austrian said.

'Yes?'

'Warsinski, I have been thinking over your request for arms. Perhaps we can supply some guns for a special squad of your men – in exchange for certain new duties.'

'When can we talk about it?'

'Tomorrow.'

'Fine. I shall expect you at the barracks, then?' Warsinski asked.

'No, no, no,' Stutze said quickly. 'We meet outside the ghetto at the Stawki Gate at noon.'

'Noon, Stawki Gate.'

Warsinski unbuttoned his long gray coat and hung it up. He took off his jacket and lowered his suspenders. His big belly, released from restraint, poured over the top of his trousers. His hands itched. He scratched them until they pained, then opened the desk drawer and wiped a thick oozy green salve over them. The ointment stung tears into his eyes. He stretched back on his cot, holding his hands under his head, his underwear gray with sweat stains under the armpits.

What was Stutze up to? Warsinski's bulgy face became mobile with thoughts and counterthoughts. He had to keep the appointment. Was it a trick? Perhaps Stutze was a coward afraid to come into the ghetto, and wanted the Militia to carry out Reinhard Corps duties. Why else would he give arms? Had Stutze decided that a convert like Warsinski wasn't really a Jew and therefore could be trusted with guns, like the Ukrainians? He brushed his long handle-bar mustache. Why not arm him? He had been loyal. But ... the Big Seven had been loyal too.

Crash!

A splintering sound bolted him to a sitting position. He saw the door fly open with such impact that it nearly tore off its hinges.

'What the hell!'

Three pistols were leveled at him. One man closed the door, the second went to the desk and tore the phone wire out. Warsinski squinted at the third. Knew him from somewhere. Alterman ... Tolek Alterman from the Bathyrans.

Warsinski scowled at them fearlessly.

'I have the pleasure of carrying out the judgment of Joint Forces to execute you as a traitor to the Jewish people,' Tolek said.

Warsinski laughed in contempt. 'Guards!' he roared. 'Guards!'

'They don't hear you, Piotr Warsinski. They are all locked up. Pawiak Prison is in the hands of Joint Jewish Forces. The prisoners are being freed at this moment.'

The smirk came off Warsinski's face. The guns on him were in steady hands. He folded his hands and closed his eyes and lowered his head. 'I don't beg like Jews,' he said. 'Go on. I am ready.'

'It is not so simple,' Tolek said. 'There are a lot of questions you are going to answer first.'

Warsinski snarled at them. He thought so. Yellow Jews unable to carry out the execution. It is all a bluff. Talk ... negotiate ... bargain ...

Tolek's boot suddenly came up into Warsinski's fat stomach, sinking in from toe to heel. The air left Warsinski. He sank from the bed to his knees. A second kick caught him alongside the jaw, thudding his head against the wall. He sat dazed. Tolek nodded to his two comrades. The first, Pinchas Silver, tossed a thumbscrew and a pair of pliers onto the desk. Adam Blumenfeld revealed a barb-tipped whip.

'We picked up a few of your toys from the interrogation room, Warsinski. Get up and sit at the desk.'

Warsinski did not move.

The lash cut through his underwear. Piotr crawled quickly on his hands and knees to the desk and sat.

'Thumb ... let's have your thumb.'

The lash ripped once more over his neck.

'Thumb!'

He extended a green-ooze-covered paw. Tolek locked Warsinski's thumb into a screw and slowly turned the top bolt to apply steady pressure.

'You've got no guts for torture,' Warsinski snarled in defiance, 'no real guts for it. Jews are too weak!'

Tolek slipped his pistol into his belt, grabbed Warsinski's out-sized mustache in his fist, and ripped it from his face.

'Yaaaaaahhhh!' Warsinski screamed, clutching a gory upper lip with his free hand.

Tolek slipped the pliers onto a big dirty fingernail of Warsinski's free hand.

'Adam, tighten the thumbscrew. Warsinski can loosen the bolt if he wants to reach for it. It will cost him a fingernail to try.'

Adam Blumenfeld tightened the bolt, crunching the vise into Warsinski's knuckle. He gasped. The sweat poured from his face and turned his underwear to a soggy rag. Adam turned the thumbscrew a quarter turn.

'Yahhhh!'

Warsinski suddenly tried to reach for the screw, but Tolek held the pliers tight and a fingernail tore loose.

Mucus spurted from his nose, and his eyes ran.

'Will you co-operate?'

'Stop! Stop! I'll talk!'

As his thumb was freed he stumbled blindly around the room, wailing and bouncing off the walls. He sank in a blubbering, groaning hulk to the floor. A mass of sweaty ugliness.

Tolek and the other two looked down at him with disgust, and Tolek was sick to his stomach with himself for his brutality, but he knew he could not puke in the presence of an enemy who regarded it as a weakness.

'He didn't even last five minutes,' Pinchas said. 'I didn't think he would.'

They dragged him to the cot and flung him on it.

In a few minutes Alexander Brandel came in and after shuddering at the first sight of Warsinski grilled him for twelve hours from questions and knowledge gained from the Good Fellowship archives. Piotr Warsinski revealed his own crimes, the crimes of his officers, his own fortunes, the places of hidden stores, information about Stutze, Schreiker, Koenig, the Nightingales, and the Reinhard Corps.

Next morning Piotr Warsinski was killed in accordance with the Joint Forces' judgment by a single bullet through the back of his head.

Chapter Six

The immediate problem facing Joint Forces was locating a new command bunker in the central area. The other bunkers were already jammed to capacity, and the hundred people from Mila 19 added to the problem. To build a suitable underground complex for two to three hundred people would take weeks.

Alexander Brandel's knowledge through his past dealings became invaluable. By one means or another he knew of most hiding places in the ghetto.

Alex suspected there was a large bunker under Mila 18, across the street from his own former headquarters.

He had often done business with a smuggler named Moritz Katz, a rotund little chap who in pre-war Warsaw had been a furrier. His business was always considered on the fringe; a tightrope between the legal and the unlawful. It was difficult to come right out and say that Moritz fenced stolen goods. His clientele was always high class. He carried an ethical concept with him into the ghetto. He was a decent fellow, as smugglers went. After all, smuggling was an honorable necessity in ghetto life. Moritz bought and sold at reasonable prices. Moreover, he was softhearted. When things got particularly desperate, Alex could always get Moritz to make an urgent delivery of essentials at cost price.

Moritz had two distinguishing features. He was in a never-ending card game, and his mouth always chewed sweets, fruit, cake, candy. For the latter frailty, he was known as Moritz the Nasher.

The Bathyrans who guarded the rooftops around Mila 19 detected Moritz the Nasher entering and leaving Mila 18 so many times that it had to be suspected as his headquarters.

These suspicions were advanced after the bunker at Mila 19 was expanded until its rooms stretched to the sewer under the middle of the street. Deborah Bronski had the room next to the sewer pipe with the children from the orphanage. Many times they heard foreign sounds coming from either the inside of the pipe or beyond it.

From this Alex concluded that Moritz the Nasher had a bunker under Mila 18, separated from his own by the twelve-foot pipe. He discussed this possibility with Simon and Andrei.

'I am positive there is a bunker under Mila 18, and if it is what we think, it will be a large one.'

'It would be a perfect location for a command post,' Simon said. 'Particularly since the Germans have located and wrecked Mila 19, they'd never suspect we'd be in another location so close.'

'But,' Andrei said realistically, 'how the hell do you find the entrance? Moritz Katz is the shrewdest smuggler in the ghetto.'

'Can we get a message to him?' Alex suggested.

'No one has seen him for weeks, since his gang was caught at the Gensia Gate and taken to the Umschlagplatz.'

They mused and pondered. The idea of a large, readymade command post was terribly appealing.

'Well. What's to lose if we cut a hole through the children's room and make another on a direct line across the *Kanal*? If we're lucky we might hit the bunker.'

'You know how tricky sound is in the sewers. The children may have been hearing an echo coming from a hundred meters away.'

'What the hell?' Andrei said. 'Let's cut through and look around. Nothing to lose.'

Simon shrugged a dubious okay. No one had a better suggestion.

'I think I'd better go in alone,' Andrei said. 'If Moritz is still down there he will panic if he sees an army coming after him.'

Later that day Andrei entered the shambled Orphans and Self-Help building at Mila 19. He went to the converted water closet where the false lavatory once covered the secret entrance to their underground rooms. The lavatory was smashed, but the pipe leading to the cellar was still intact.

Andrei tucked a flashlight and short-handled pick and sledge hammer into his belt, strapped the Schmeisser 'Gaby' on his back, and slid down the pipe. He flicked on the light. The beam probed over mounds of wreckage. The retaining walls and overhead crossbeams had been knocked loose, caving in the main tunnel in many places. Andrei inched forward, digging away the blockage with his hands.

He came to the room which had belonged to the children. It was a shambles. The layers of bunks had been wrecked with axes and the books torn to shreds and the few toys smashed. Andrei moved along a ten-foot wall which lay against the *Kanal* pipe. Seepings oozed through. He could hear the flow of sewage. He calculated in order to line up Mila 18.

Any decision would most likely be wrong. 'Well, I've got to start someplace.'

He fixed the flashlight on a single spot, sank his pick into the dirt wall, and hacked away until it crumpled to the outer shell of the pipe.

Andrei smoothed a place big enough for him to carve out a manhole and bashed at the concrete with a sledge until it cracked under the beating. Once through the outer layer, he jarred loose enough bricks from the inner lining of the pipe so that he could fit through.

He wiped the sweat from his eyes and refixed the tools in his belt, cursing that he was on a wild-goose chase, then knelt at the hole and looked into the *Kanal* with his light. It was not too bad. The tide on the Vistula River was low, as he had calculated, so the sewage was only waist-high.

Andrei squeezed through the hole into the sewer. His feet skidded in the slime. He pulled the strap of his weapon several notches tighter so it would ride higher on his back and not get wet. In both directions dim streaks filtered through the manholes, sending an eerie bluish light glistening on the bricks.

He waded to the middle and looked behind him so he would remain in a line with the children's room. On the opposite side of the sewer he thrust his ear against the brick, hoping for sound. There was none.

His flashlight moved first in one direction for several yards, then another.

Andrei splashed down a dozen yards. A cluster of bricks were not laid in the same pattern as the rest, as though they had been knocked loose and replaced. Could it be! He felt with his fingers. The bricks were definitely not cemented in. There was room for a man to fit through if they were removed. Was there a bunker on the other side? Were the children hearing smugglers coming in and out of the sewer?

Andrei hit his sledge against the bricks for a sounding. Hollow ring! It was not solid on the other side. There was a room!

He picked at the bricks. They came out easily.

It was hollow on the other side. Andrei shone the light in.

He crawled in and moved his light in a complete circle. 'Holy God!' he muttered, and whistled with disbelief. He stood at his full height in a huge subterranean room. It was the most magnificent underground structure he had ever seen. Along one wall were sacks of rice, flour, sugar, salt. There were crates of medicine. Salted meats. Cases of tins of food. A bin of dried vegetables. Beautiful couches, easy chairs, furniture, bed.

'Holy God!'

He found the exit into a corridor and inched down it. Five more large rooms were on either side of the corridor, and each as big as the first one and each held stores. Overhead an electric line with light bulbs.

Andrei came to the end of the corridor. It turned into a smaller tunnel holding a series of cells.

'Don't move,' a voice behind him commanded. 'Hands over your head. High!'

Andrei lifted his arms. It had all been too good to be true. He cursed himself for forgetting to unstrap his weapon in the excitement of locating the bunker.

'Put both your hands on the wall,' the voice commanded. Andrei did as he was told. 'Now turn your face.'

He looked into a blinding light.

'Andrei Androfski?'

'Is that you, Moritz?'

'How in the hell did you figure out where this bunker was?'

'We added two and two. Put that goddamned gun away and take the light out of my eyes.'

'Don't rush me into any decisions. I'm not sure whether I have to kill you or not.' He shifted the light toward one of the cells. 'Step into my office. What I'm holding on you, for your information, is a shotgun.'

Moritz lit a lantern and settled in back of his desk. He had a grizzly beard and an anemic color. Much of his chubbiness had shrunk away. Underground living had been hard on him. Moritz kept the shotgun leveled at Andrei's chest. Andrei was too busy being awed by the office. In addition to electrical wiring, there was a phone on the desk and a low-wattage radio transmitter.

'What a setup.'

Moritz shrugged modestly at the compliment. 'We tried to give our customers good service. Only trouble is that we've got no more customers. We got no one. Most my boys were grabbed on a haul. Just me and my wife Sheina and a few others. You've met Sheina? She's asleep in the other room. She sleeps through anything, that woman. Even your banging holes into my bunker. She's sick. She needs a doctor. Change of life.'

'How in hell do you run the lights – the radio?'

'Generator, what else? Used to be able to send messages to my contacts on the Aryan side. Simple code.'

'Telephone?'

'One of my boys worked for the phone company. There's a million ways to screw the phone company. We tied in on a Ukrainian line from the guards at the Brushmaker's and we speak Yiddish. They've never been able to figure it. No, Andrei. I'm sorry you had to find this place because I've always held you in high esteem. You were a very smart man to locate my bunker, but naturally I've got to kill you.'

'Not so fast, Moritz. Obviously I wouldn't pull a move like this without a cover. You've heard of Joint Jewish Forces?'

Moritz screwed up his face. He suspected he was about to be taken. 'I still get around.'

'They know I'm here and what I'm looking for.'

'Oh crap!' Moritz the Nasher said. He lay the shotgun on the desk in disgust. 'Minute I saw you barreling through the sewer into the bunker I said to myself that this bastard is too smart to come in exposed. Now you talk to Alexander Brandel. He'll tell you I've been right down the line with his Orphans setup. I always did business on the square with him.'

'Moritz, for God's sake, stop apologizing. Do you hear me pushing you around?'

Moritz the Nasher was hungry. He opened the top desk drawer and took out a packet of German chocolate, unwrapped it, nibbled, and decried the lack of fresh fruit. 'You want my bunker, no doubt.'

'No doubt.'

'And seven hundred thousand zlotys' worth of food.'

'I feel bad, Moritz – believe me.'

'What a kick in the ass life is. If one thief doesn't get you, another will,' Moritz opined.

Andrei sympathized with him. Moritz the Nasher was a gambler, a smuggler, a man who existed by wit. But he was also a supreme realist. He knew that he had been caught flat. At least Andrei Androfski and the Joint Forces held him no malice. Maybe he was lucky, after all. Had the Germans or the Militia found him first . . . curtains . . . Umschlagplatz. He had hoped that he and his wife Sheina could ride the war out in Mila 18. They had enough supplies and medicine to see through a year or two without ever coming up. But . . . what kind of life was it for a man? Never to see the sun. Nobody to play cards with. Candy running out. Always in fear that the next minute or the next or the next those goddamn German dogs would sniff him out.

'Let me ask you something, Androfski,' Moritz asked. 'This here Joint Forces – you the ones who blasted the SS men at Zamenhof and Niska?'

Andrei nodded.

'You the ones who fixed up Warsinski?'

Andrei nodded again.

'You guys really mean business?'

Andrei nodded for the third time.

'Let me tell you something. You work, you live, you do your best, but you never quite get onto the idea of the way they're kicking you around. In the last week – since the ambush – for the first time in my life I'm proud to be a Jew.'

'That's the way we all want to go out.'

Moritz shrugged. 'So, maybe I'm glad you found me first. Obviously, you realize you have me over a barrel.'

'Obviously,' Andrei agreed.

Moritz munched on another square of chocolate, somewhat relieved that his long, taut vigil was over.

'Moritz,' Andrei said, 'the one thing that Joint Jewish Forces really needs is a quartermaster.'

'What's a quartermaster?'

'Someone high class to get in supplies.'

'You mean a smuggler?'

'No. Quartermaster is a respectable position. Every army has them.'

'What's the cut?'

'Well, a regular army – like ours – doesn't work on cuts.'

'*Oy vay!* What a day this has been. All I've ever done is run a nice clean business.'

'Moritz, you're too much of a gambler to ride this war out in a hole. We've got doctors. Sheina will get treatment. You'll have lots of interesting people here to share this bunker.'

'I bet I will. Tell me honest, Androfski. This post of quartermaster. It is important? I mean, like a Ulany colonel?'

'In our army,' Andrei said, 'it's the most important.'

Moritz sighed in resignation. 'One condition. No one inquires into my past finances.'

'Done,' Andrei said.

They clasped hands, Moritz pulled a faded double deck of cards, shuffled, and began to deal. 'Before you move in, one game of sixty-six.'

Chapter Seven

An ant line of laborers in a Brushmaker's building bent their backs, pushing large clumsy carts. The line moved in an endless circle from the lumber store to the lathe room to the assembly room.

An emaciated slave named Creamski, who had kept alive somehow for ten months, loaded the cart with finished toilet-brush handles from the lathe room. He grunted down the corridor, pushing the load at a snail's pace.

The assembly room consisted of ten long tables, each forty feet long. Each table had a series of varied drilled holes to stuff bristles, tie the wires, and attach the handles. Fifty men worked each table.

Creamski pushed his cart to table number three; toilet brushes. A 'leader' stood at the head of each table. 'They are here,' Creamski whispered to the 'leader.'

He pushed his cart along the table, placing several handles before each bench.

'They are here,' he whispered.

'They are here.'

The word passed down the line and over to the next table and the next – 'They are here.'

'You there!' the German foreman shouted from the balcony. 'Hurry up!'

Creamski moved faster, emptying the cart. He turned it about and pushed it out of the room, down the corridor, past the lathe room, and into the lumber warehouse.

While his cart was being loaded with boards he stepped into the checker's office.

'Now!' he said to the checker. The two of them shoved the desk aside, revealing a trap door. Creamski pulled it open.

'Now!' Creamski called down into the black hole.

Wolf Brandel's head popped out of the tunnel. He moved quickly out of the checker's office, scrutinizing the long high stacks of lumber. 'Move them out,' the beardless commander ordered. One by one, forty Jewish Fighters emerged from the underground passage. The Franciskanska bunker a few blocks away connected to the *Kanal*. Wolf's company had followed the sewer to a point inside the Brushmaker's complex and dug the tunnel into the checker's office.

With hand signals he dispersed his force of ten women and thirty men to pre-fixed positions. They ducked behind the lumber with their weapons ready. Wolf blew a long breath and nodded for Creamski to return to the assembly room.

Creamski grunted and strained to put the loaded cart into motion. As he turned into the lathe room he gave a hand signal which could be seen by a table 'leader' in the assembly room. Every eye in the room was on the 'leader.' He nodded.

Clump! Clump! Clump! Clump!

The feet of the inmates thumped against the floor in unison.

Boom! Boom! Boom! Boom!

They took their wooden handles and banged them on the tables, setting up a din.

'What's going on!' shrieked the foreman through a megaphone from his balcony cage. 'Stop this noise! Stop it! Do you hear!'

Clump! Clump! Clump! Clump! Boom! Boom! Boom! Boom!

The clatter from the building swelled over the compound.

'Guards!' the foreman shouted into his alarm phone. 'Guards! Building number four! Quick!'

Alarm sirens erupted all over the complex in a series of short whistles to draw the guards to assembly building number four.

The foreman locked the barred door of his office. He snatched the pistol from his desk and looked down at the five hundred pairs of maddened eyes staring up at him.

Clump! Clump! Clump! Clump!

'Krebs dies! Krebs dies! Krebs dies! Krebs dies!' they chanted his name.

Ukrainians, Latvians, and Estonians poured out of the guard barracks with whips, guns, and dogs, racing for the spot of the insurrection.

Part of Wolf Brandel's force, hidden around the outside of the building, let them pass through. There was only one entrance, through the main corridor. He watched the first of the guards pass into the assembly room from his position in the lathe room.

'Now!'

Wolf and ten of his Fighters stepped into the corridor and faced a mass of guards. The Ukrainians had trapped themselves. A pipe grenade shattered in their midst, followed by a tattoo of pistol fire.

The Ukrainians outside plunged backward for the exit, but the Jewish Fighters outside moved in to cut them off. A massacre ensued.

A half dozen guards reached the assembly room. The slaves leaped from their benches. In pent-up wrath they attacked their tormentors and their tormentors' dogs with bare hands. Within seconds the guards and dogs were pummeled to death and their bodies smashed with spit and kicks and disembowelment and decapitation.

Benches were overturned and smashed, lathes broken up by sledge hammers.

'Krebs! Krebs! Krebs! Krebs!'

The foreman was bug-eyed, insane with fright, locked in his own prison. They were coming up the balcony after him. No way of escape!

'Krebs! Krebs! Krebs! Krebs!'

He placed the barrel of the pistol in his mouth and pulled the trigger as the outstretched arms of the slaves reached through the cage for him.

Ana Grinspan, with a company in the central district, was the highest-ranking woman commander in the ghetto. Her company was the most integrated of the various parties and final proof that unity had been achieved. Thirty-two Fighters came from the Bathyrans, Poale Zion, Gordonia, Dror, Communists, Akiva, Hashomer Hatzair, Hechalutz, and the Bund. She even had four members from religious Zionist Mizrachi who could no longer stomach the passive attitudes of the Orthodox Agudah.

The secondary objective at Brushmaker's was the confiscation of the fleet of five trucks. The instant Brushmaker's was secured Wolf turned the trucks over to Ana, who put into operation a pre-set plan. Each truck had a driver, four fighters, and liberated Brushmaker's slaves.

They struck at every known remaining warehouse, store, shop, medical station, bakery, and private cache in the ghetto, holding anything usable for Joint Forces. Loading rapidly under the protective guns of the Joint Fighters, they whisked off to a series of small bunkers scattered all over the ghetto.

No protest or conversation was permitted.

'Load! Move!'

And away.

Every sack of flour, every grain of food was carted off.

One of the bunkers in the central command was located almost beneath the Jewish Militia barracks, where the Fighters kept the barracks under scrutiny. Simon Eden ordered a raid to bring back a half dozen militiamen.

They were dragged off to the new command center at Mila 18 to confront Alexander Brandel, who had drawn up a list of dozens of persons suspected of collaboration, concealing wealth, and illegal operations. The captured militiamen were quick to sing out all they knew about the location of these people.

Squads of Jewish Fighters made forays, unearthing one person after another on the list. The most notorious of the collaborators were executed. The others were fined.

'You are fined ten thousand zlotys for passing information to the Germans.'

'You are fined twenty thousand zlotys for collaboration with the Jewish Militia.'

'You are fined ten thousand zlotys for failure to protect Jews taken to the Umschlagplatz within your power to warn them.'

These fines were collected on the spot, on pain of death, without argument or equivocation.

Rodel, the squat, blocklike commander of the southern area, had been a member in good standing in the Communist party most of his adult life. He deemed it ironic that his command bunker was located under the Convert's Church with the open knowledge of Father Jakub.

Moreover, the war had compelled him to enter strange alliances with Labor Zionists holding completely diverse political views. Zionism was the drug of the Jewish people, he had said on numerous occasions. However, he worked not only with Labor Zionists but Jabotinski Revisionists, whom he considered fascists, and religious elements, whom he considered mentally inept. It was a strange war to Rodel, but no stranger than the Soviet Union and America fighting as allies.

From the moment of Warsinski's assassination, Rodel ordered the workers in the uniform factory to sabotage the product. In the following days, uniforms left Warsaw with flies, armholes, and neckholes sewn shut, buttons with no buttonholes, and seams that would rip away under the slightest stress.

An hour after Wolf Brandel captured Brushmaker's, Ludwig Heinz, the manager of the uniform factory, sent a message to Rodel through Father Jakub that the Lithuanian guards had fled. Heinz, an ethnic German, was one of an infinitesimal number who displayed a measure of humanity toward the slave labor under him. Within the strict limitations permitted, Heinz was credited with saving a number of lives. He walked untouched to the corner of Nowolipki and Karmelicka streets to open the main gates and allow the Jewish Fighters in.

'I'm glad my part in this is over,' Heinz said to Rodel.

Rodel shook his shiny, hairless head. 'It is a strange war,' he said. 'You've been decent within your means. Joint Forces has ordered me to see you safely through the ghetto gates.'

'I'm glad it's over,' Ludwig Heinz repeated.

'Let's go,' Rodel said, pointing in the direction of the Leszno Gate two blocks away.

As Ludwig Heinz turned, Rodel whipped out his pistol and struck the man across the back of the ear with the barrel. Heinz pitched forward to the street, unconscious. Rodel leaned down and ripped part of his clothing off and bloodied his face with a series of blows.

'All right,' he ordered two fighters, 'take him to the Leszno Gate and dump him. I'm sorry I had to beat him up, but it's for his own good. If he walked out unharmed, the Germans would suspect him. This way they may get the impression he barely escaped.'

As they hauled Heinz away, he shook his head again. 'Strange war,' he said.

Samson Ben Horin, commander of the Jabotinski company of Revisionists, had remained outside the jurisdiction of Joint Jewish Forces, but the events of the day compelled him to look upon Eden's army with a new respect. He dispatched a runner to Eden with an offer to keep runner contact with their bunker and join in limited co-operation.

Simon soon found an assignment much to Ben Horin's liking.

On the last day of January, Samson Ben Horin led a combined company, half Revisionists, half Joint Forces, through the sewer pipes under the wall into the Aryan side. He picked the hour of the Vistula's lowest tide, when the sewage was only knee-deep. Using Simon's engineer's map of the sewer system, he had only a mile to negotiate. Ben Horin's party came to a stop beneath a manhole close to Bank Square near the Ministry of Finance.

Three Aryan side contacts waited. One was dressed as a sewer worker, the second sat in the driver's seat of a parked teamster wagon, and the third watched at the corner in a position to observe the German Exchange Bank on Orla Street.

It was the day before payday for the German garrison. At precisely noon an armored truck from the ministry would stop to deposit part of the payroll at the Exchange Bank.

The watchman signaled the arrival of the armored truck.

The horse-drawn wagon moved from the curb and stopped beside the manhole. A long ladder was taken from it and set down in the sewer. Samson Ben Horin led his party out of the sewer. They scattered with startling rapidity so that both ends of the block-long Orla Street could be sealed.

A dozen German soldiers formed a guard around the armored truck before the bank. They passed the money sacks in.

Samson Ben Horin arched a homemade matzo-ball grenade. It landed at the right front tire of the truck.

Nuts and bolts flew everywhere, ripping into the bodies of the Germans.

A second grenade.

A third.

Half of the Germans were on the ground, groveling with iron in them. The truck was disabled, but guards inside fired back.

A fire bottle splattered against the side of the truck, igniting into flame and driving the defenders out.

Samson Ben Horin signaled for his men to converge. They pressed in from both ends of Orla Street. The Germans were pinned against the wall and the flaming truck. A few plunged into the bank for safety.

Half of the raiders grabbed every money sack in sight. The other half pushed into the bank and forced the vaults open. Within eight minutes of the time they had come from the sewer, they disappeared the same way with more than a million zlotys.

Simon Eden referred to the actions as practical field training to teach his army that the invulnerable enemy was indeed vulnerable.

Within a week after Andrei's ambush at Niska and Zamenhof streets which signaled the uprising, Joint Jewish Forces had purged the ghetto of collaborators, added millions to their treasury, controlled the streets, confiscated tons of food, wrecked the two major slave-labor factories, and freed the workers.

There were two large jobs left. The Jewish Militia, who cowered in their barracks, and the Civil Authority. The act of mere vengeance: doing away with the Jewish Militia was overruled by more practical considerations of settling with the Jewish Civil Authority.

On February 1, 1943, a hundred fifty men and women of Joint Forces surrounded the Jewish Civil Authority building at dawn. Simon Eden broke down the doors and entered with fifty more Fighters.

From his office on the third floor Boris Presser watched the scene below with Marinski, his assistant.

'Get into the outer office,' Presser said quickly. 'Stall them. Keep them out of here.'

Presser sat behind his desk and tried to think. Every day he had been phoning Rudolph Schreiker to report on the rampaging of the Joint Forces. Murder in the streets, assassinations, looting, extortion. Boris was positive the actions would result in a murderous reprisal from the Reinhard Corps, but another day passed and another and another and nothing happened.

Each day his people cringed in the Civil Authority building with their families, trying to push him into a decision. Boris didn't like decisions or involvements. He had made a career of evasiveness. The Germans had always told him what to do. He did it. He had the ready-made excuse of throwing up his hands and saying, 'What could I do?'

Marinski bolted into the room, crying semi-coherently, 'Stop them! They're taking our families!'

'Stop shouting. Shouting will do no good. Get out there and delay Eden from coming in.'

Boris locked the door and ran to the phone. First Schreiker, then the Militia. The line was dead. He clicked it desperately. Nothing. Presser rubbed his throbbing temples and slipped to the window. Women and children, families of the Civil Authority, were being prodded out into the street at gun point. A ruckus in the outer office. Authoritative knocks at his door.

Stall ... play for time ... debate ... stall.

He unlocked the door. Simon Eden stood before him. Black-eyed; long, wiry frame; intense. Simon hovered over the smaller man, shoved the door wide, and looked around the office. He stepped inside the room and closed the door behind him, shutting out Marinski, who was too terrified to protest the abduction of his wife and daughter.

Boris backed up, bringing everything within him to the fore to maintain control and not show fear. 'I protest this humiliation of the Civil Authority,' he said.

Simon ignored him; his eyes showed almost boredom.

'You have no right to barge in here and kidnap our families. You have no right to treat us like collaborators.' Boris prodded to find a point of argument.

Simon would not argue. 'History will pass judgment of the Civil Authority,' he said dryly.

Careful, Presser said to himself, careful. Don't anger him. 'You must realize,' Boris fenced, 'that I have no personal authorization to grant you recognition.'

'Just recognize what comes out of the end of this muzzle. It is quite simple. We have your families. We want your treasury.'

Beads of perspiration popped out on Boris Presser's upper lip. To refuse would be to admit that he was truly a puppet of the Germans, for in fact Joint Jewish Forces now represented the authority in the ghetto. But if he did recognize Eden, the Germans would eventually punish him when they returned. Boris was in a vise. He opened his arms benevolently. 'Surely, Simon, as a man who knows organizational structure, you are aware that I do not control our very insignificant treasury. I have no way of acting.'

'Find a way,' Simon interrupted. 'In an hour we shall deposit three corpses at the doorsteps of this building. One will be a member of your own family. Each hour thereafter, three more hostages will be shot until you deliver two million zlotys to Joint Forces.'

Marinski, eavesdropping, burst in, 'Give him the damned money!'

Boris was dying to drink a glass of water to relieve his parched throat, but he knew that if he lifted a glass his hand would spill it with trembling. 'Let me discuss this with my board,' Boris said, continuing the role of a reasonable man. 'There are many touchy legal problems. Mind you, I am certain they can be solved, but this is rather sudden. Let us thrash it out. We will come up with a suitable compromise.'

Simon Eden looked down at him with final disgust. 'You have no alternative,' he said, and before Boris Presser could speak again, Simon left.

An hour later the two million zlotys were turned over to Simon, half from the denuded treasury and half confiscated as ransom from personal fortunes.

'I was in favor of dumping you at the Stawki Gate with Piotr Warsinski,' Simon said impassively. 'But Alexander Brandel is a dreamer. He believes in the poetic justice of making you and your people burrow into the ground and live like rats ... as the rest of us have.'

The Jewish Fighters released the hostages. Boris Presser's action ended any further use the Germans may have had for the Civil Authority.

Boris Presser and the rest who had served as message boys of the Germans were cast loose to spend the rest of their days despised and scorned by both their own people and the enemy.

The next morning posters were nailed over the front door of the abandoned Civil Authority building and posted on the walls throughout the ghetto.

ATTENTION!
AS OF TODAY, FEBRUARY 1, 1943, THE JEWISH CIVIL AUTHORITY IS DISBANDED.
THIS GHETTO IS UNDER THE SOLE AND ABSOLUTE AUTHORITY OF JOINT JEWISH FORCES. ORDERS ARE TO BE OBEYED WITHOUT RESERVATION.
SIGNED:

Atlas, Commander, Joint Jewish Forces
Jan, Executive Commander

Chapter Eight

Journal Entry

The Star of David flies over the Warsaw ghetto!

On February 2, 1943, the German Sixth Army surrendered at Stalingrad. We feel for the first time that Germany will lose the war. But how quickly will the flood-waters recede?

None of us are so foolish as to believe we will ever live to see a Jewish state in Palestine, but we have sounded the great trumpet of the return. A Jewish army controls the first autonomous piece of Jewish land in nearly two thousand years of our dispersal. Our 'nation' is only a few square blocks and we know we shall not hold it long, but, as Tolek Alterman says, 'This is living Zionism.' No matter what happens hereafter, for this moment we are a proud and free people.

The first 'capital' of our 'Jewish state' is Mila 18. I shall describe it. There are six main rooms. These are named for the six Polish extermination camps. Rooms: Belzec *and* Auschwitz *hold a hundred and twenty fighters of two companies, one Bund and one Bathyran. This group is under Andrei's personal command (in addition to his other duties).*

Majdanek *is the room which runs alongside the* Kanal. *Joint Forces had voted to keep this room (and several others around the ghetto) for the exclusive use of as many children as we can care for. We have rounded up forty. Nothing takes priority over the continuation of the Orphans and Self-Help tradition. As soon as we can place these children on the Aryan side we find others to bring into* Majdanek. *Although Rachael Bronski lives at the Franciskanska bunker (under Wolf's command – I am very proud of him. To think such a soldier and leader is my son), she spends a great deal of time on the 'children' operation. We keep a program of schooling and games. At night they can go out for exercise and fresh air. Pray God a few of them will survive. They are our harvest.*

Treblinka *holds food stores and is the 'hospital' for the central command (two doctors, four nurses.)* Sobibor *keeps relatives of the Fighters and those few intellectuals we have been able to salvage. A smattering of writers, scientists, artists, theologists, historians, and teachers, who represent the last voice of our dying culture.*

Chelmno *is the arsenal and munitions works. Jules Schlosberg and a dozen workers manufacture and store fire bombs and grenades. (Actual weapons – i.e. pistols, rifles – are as scarce as ever.)*

The second hallway is filled with small cells which are also named in 'honor' of the lesser camps.

Stutthof *is a closet holding the generator;* Poniatow *has the office and living quarters of Simon, Andrei, Tolek (operations and training officer), and Christopher de Monti.* Stutthof *holds two other cots for the radio and telephone operator on watch.* Trawniki *is a tiny cell for the exclusive quarters of Rabbi Solomon. He is the last rabbi left in the ghetto. Father Jakub tells me the Church is hiding Rabbi Nahum, probably to preserve as a historic relic.* Dachau *is shared by Moritz and Sheina Katz and Sylvia and me. (What privileged characters we are!)*

Our number varies, but two hundred and twenty persons is the limit. We could not fit another in sideways. Thanks to the ingenious engineering by Moritz the Nasher's departed gang, circulation through air vents is not too bad. We use the generator for lights, sparingly. Petrol is hard to get and is needed for fire bottles. Candles are used most of the time. But candles burn oxygen.

Mila 18 has six entrances: the sewer through the children's room, a removable stove in the house above, and four tunnels in different directions running one hundred to three hundred feet away from Mila 18.

Expansion of our army is almost nil. Few left in the ghetto are fit to fight. Secondly, the arms shortage is as bad as ever. Our forces, combined with the three Revisionist groups at Nalewki 37 (Jabotinski, Chayal, and Trumpeldor), gives us a total of six hundred soldiers. Less than one in three has a firearm. The operations of the last week have seriously depleted our ammunition. We average less than ten rounds per weapon.

Our 'quartermaster,' Moritz the Nasher, made his first major acquisition yesterday – several hundred pairs of boots. Boots, long time a symbol of German oppression, have become a symbol of our defiance. In Poland only strong men wear boots these days. Simon knew that the boots would be a great morale factor.

The Joint Jewish Forces work in three operations. One third: duty on the rooftops watch and in roving patrols. One third: constructing underground bunkers. One third: in training. The commanders (Eden, Androfski, and Rodel, sometimes Ben Horin) have set up a system of rooftop fighting based on ambush tactics. Each company has alternate bunkers, so that we continually shift our positions. The key is a continued building of a skilled runner system to keep communications intact. Although we have had simulated combat drills for several days, the main question is yet to be answered. Can this rabble army with few weapons maintain discipline under fire? Is there enough individual courage and ability to improvise among these unskilled soldiers to really tell upon the greatest military power the world has ever known?

The task of holding for a week seems impossible, but there is an unmistakable air of optimism. Morale is splendid. A new feeling of dignity among the surviving population is infectious.

We await the enemy. We hope that this fight for freedom is entirely without hope. But does the fight for freedom ever really end? Andrei is right. All we have left is our honor and the historic duty to make our battle at this moment.

ALEXANDER BRANDEL

An ingenious phone circuit had been rigged from Mila 18 through the sewers directly to the other command posts at Wolf Brandel's Franciskanska bunker and to Rodel beneath the Convert's Church. A half dozen phones, mainly in German factories, were used on occasion for contact beyond the wall, along with the low-wattage radio transmitter.

Tolek Alterman dozed on his cot next to the phone in the commander's office in Poniatow at Mila 18.

The phone rang. Tolek swung to a sitting position. He had let his hair grow long again since he stopped going to the Aryan side. He brushed it out of his eyes and fished for the receiver.

'Jerusalem,' he said. 'Roberto speaking.'

'Hello, Roberto. This is Tolstoy in Beersheba.' Tolek recognized the bullhorn voice of Rodel. 'Get me Atlas.'

Andrei, who was standing behind Tolek, walked quickly around the el of the corridor to Chelmno, where Simon fretted over the plans of the matzo ball-land mine being designed by Jules Schlosberg.

'Phone,' he said. 'Rodel.'

'Hello, Beersheba. This is Atlas in Jerusalem.'

'Hello, Atlas. Tolstoy, Beersheba. My angels see the Rhine Maidens and their Swans at Stalingrad. One thousand bottles. It looks as if they are coming through the Red Sea.'

'Don't take any wine unless it's offered.'

'*Shalom.*'

'*Shalom.*'

Simon set the phone down and looked up at Tolek and Andrei.

'I heard,' Andrei said. He went quickly to Belzec and Auschwitz. 'All right! Let's go! Up to the roofs!'

The Fighters snatched their weapons and crowded to the ladder which would take them through the stove into Mila 18.

'Move along, move along,' Andrei prodded.

Alexander Brandel stumbled from his cell, coming out of a deep sleep. 'A drill, Andrei?'

'No drill. They're coming.'

'Runners!' Simon Eden barked.

A dozen swift, daring boys in their teens clustered around the entrance to Poniatow. Simon towered over them. 'The Germans are massing before their barracks with their Auxiliaries. We expect them through the Zelazna Gate. One thousand in number. Alert all companies. Hold fire unless fired upon. Move out!'

The ghetto rats scampered through the six exits to alert the scattered bunkers.

Andrei watched the last of his men go up the ladder to the stove upstairs. Stephan, Andrei's personal runner, followed his uncle as though he were glued to him. Andrei poked his head into Poniatow. Simon was afraid. Andrei slapped Simon's shoulder hard. 'We won't fire until we can smell their breath,' he said. 'Don't worry.'

'We'll soon find out,' Simon said. 'I wish I could be up there with you.'

Andrei shrugged. 'Such are the fortunes of a commander,' he said, and was gone with Stephan close behind him.

Tolek ran up and down the tunnel. 'Stop the generator! Combat conditions! Deborah, keep the children quiet. Rabbi, I'll have to ask you to pray silently. Moritz, card game's over for now. Button up, everyone – button up!'

Adam Blumenfeld at the radio threw a switch to put the receiver on batteries as the generator ground to a halt and the lights went out.

Beep ... beep ... beep ... beep ... he heard in his earphones. He pulled the headset off and called out in the darkness.

'Are you there, Simon?'

'I'm here.'

'Radio confirmation. The Germans are moving.'

Beep ... beep ... beep ... beep ... warned the mobile transmitter from the Aryan side.

Simon struck a match and found the candle on the desk. He cranked the phone handle.

'Haifa ... hello, Haifa.'

'This is Haifa.'

'This is Atlas in Jerusalem. Let me speak to Chess Master.'

'Chess Master speaking,' Wolf Brandel answered from the Franciskanska bunker.

'The Rhine Maidens and their Swans are at Stalingrad. One thousand bottles. They're coming through the Red Sea. Don't drink any wine unless it's offered.'

'Oh boy!'

Simon hung up. He could see Alex and Tolek on the fringe of the candle glow. Now was the commander's agony. Waiting in the dark. The acid test was here. It was deathly still. Even the endless prayers of Rabbi Solomon trailed to a silent movement of the lips.

Across vacant courtyards, flitting over rooftops, sloshing through sewage, darting up deserted staircases, the runners from Mila 18 flashed from cover to cover to alert the Fighters. The companies moved in ghostlike silence to their positions behind windows, on the roofs, from sewer cover. Yes, it was all quite like a drill.

The streets had a stillness like the face of the moon. Some feathers fluttered down from the rooftops in sudden gusts of wind. Hidden eyes watched the ethereal stillness.

A dim sound of heels cracking against cobblestones. Clump ... clump ... clump ... clump ... clump.

The SS at the Zelazna Gate, barricaded behind machine-gun nests, darted out to remove the barbed-wire gate blocking the entrance.

Rodel looked from the window in the uniform factory out to the picket fence where the black-uniformed marchers flickered past with the broken motion of a film running to a halt. The bootless brown uniforms of the Auxiliaries made a softer tread. Rodel watched, his teeth tightening in his moon-shaped face. On and on they passed.

'Hello, Beersheba,' Rodel phoned to his bunker. 'This is Tolstoy. Advise Jerusalem that the Rhine Maidens and their Swans have passed the Land of Goshen. Brunhilde is leading them. They are going up the Jordan River.'

Andrei Androfski looked up and down the rooftops at his dispersed Fighters. He was satisfied that they were deployed properly. Once on the roofs, the Joint Command was able to keep their companies in communication by signal posts from roof to roof. A message was relayed from Ana Grinspan's company that the Germans were marching up Zamenhof Street almost at the same moment that Rodel's command had phoned the information to Simon Eden.

Andrei crawled on his belly to the corner overlooking the intersection of Mila and Zamenhof streets, with Stephan at his heels. He wiggled into a position to observe Zamenhof Street through a pair of field glasses.

Andrei grumbled to himself and sharpened his focus. 'Brunhilde himself,' he said. 'Stutze. How nice.'

Clump! Clump! Clump! Clump! The boot heels cracked, their echoes reverberating off the hollow shells of the buildings.

'Halt!'

The SS, Wehrmacht, and Auxiliaries broke ranks and scattered at the corner of Zamenhof and Gensia streets under the eyes and guns of Ana Grinspan's company.

With the enemy three blocks away, Andrei shifted his position, risking a little more exposure to get a better view. He saw the Germans surrounding the Civil Authority building and the Jewish Militia barracks. SS men smashed into the abandoned Civil Authority. In a few minutes Andrei watched a confused command meeting in the middle of Zamenhof Street. Stutze pointed and ranted.

'Hello, what's this?' Andrei whispered.

Jewish militiamen appeared in the streets for the first time since they had been terrorized into their barracks, but now they came at the end of Wehrmacht bayonets. Several Jewish militiamen, obviously of rank, were pulled from the herd and beaten into the Civil Authority building.

The sounds of machine pistol shots split the air.

'Runner!' Andrei snapped. Stephan crawled alongside him.

'Get a message to Simon. The Germans are rounding up the Jewish Militia. Some of them are being executed in the Civil Authority building. Apparently the Germans don't know that the Civil Authority had defected. We can anticipate the Germans taking the Militia straight up Zamenhof to the Stawki Gate and the Umschlagplatz. We want instructions.'

Stephan repeated the message, then scooted down the middle of the roof for the short run through the skylight of Mila 18 and down the stairs to the bunker. Stephan appeared at the same moment that Ana Grinspan's runner appeared with an identical message.

Simon looked to Tolek and Alex.

'Andrei wants instructions,' Stephan said.

The Germans would march the Jewish Militia under the massed guns of Andrei's companies and a company of Wolf's Fighters near the Stawki Gate. There were a thousand Germans in the street. They would be sitting pigeons. Should the rebellion begin on a note of saving Jewish traitors? Would it not be poetic and historic justice to see those ghouls marched off to the Umschlagplatz just as they had taken their own blood and flesh? An outburst which would give these bastards a chance to spread and hide would all but deplete the ammunition stores of the Joint Forces.

Command decision! God. If only Andrei were down here to knock me on my back. Tolek and Alex continued to watch him in the dim light. Simon sucked in a deep breath, then another. The Germans were in a box such as they might never be caught again. But . . . did it not take just as much courage to make the decision to let them pass out of the ghetto to give his Fighters a day, a week, ten days to find more ammunition?

'Tell Andrei . . . to keep absolute discipline. Let them pass.' He spun the cranks of the phone to confirm his opinion, to assure himself. 'This is Jerusalem. Atlas speaking. The Rhine Maidens are at Herod's Palace and are taking Korah and Absalom to Egypt. Let them pass.'

In the bunker of the Revisionists at Nalewki 37, Samson Ben Horin faced the commander of his Chayal group who were spread along the roofs over Zamenhof near Ana Grinspan's company. The Chayal officer, Emanuel, snorted at Ben Horin.

'We will not let them pass!'

Samson Ben Horin stroked his newly grown beard. He liked it. The liaison runner from Eden's headquarters looked from Ben Horin to his officer.

'We are not obliged to carry out orders from Eden,' the officer prodded.

'You are obligated to take my orders,' Ben Horin answered. 'By coincidence they are exactly the same. Let the Germans pass through.'

Emanuel was enraged. 'The Germans are in a box!'

Ben Horin shrugged.

'You are a flunky of the Labor Zionists,' Emanuel cried.

'I shall relieve you of your command this instant if you cannot obey,' Ben Horin threatened angrily.

Emanuel sulked, simmered, calmed, and was returned to his post, distressed that Ben Horin had taken a position concurrent with that of the Joint Forces.

Clump! Clump! Clump! Clump!

Andrei crawled as close to the roof's edge as he dared. He looked over his people. Their sweaty hands tightened around their weapons. Black eyes blazed from hidden corners. Andrei poked his fist into the air in a 'hold fire' signal.

Beneath him the Germans took the Jewish Militia toward the Umschlagplatz and Treblinka.

Andrei licked his lips. He sighted 'Gaby,' the Schmeisser, on Sieghold Stutze's heart. 'Ah,' he whispered to himself. 'What a lovely, magnificent target. So full of nice plump syphilitic blood.' He clenched his teeth, pulling his itching, wiggling finger off the trigger.

The Fighters strewn out above Zamenhof Street looked down on their tormentors, gnawing pains of restraint holding them from unleashing their wrath.

'Look at that juicy Austrian. Ah, Stutze . . . Will I ever get such a lovely shot at you?' Andrei half cried to himself. 'What a goddamn war!'

'Hello, Jerusalem,' Wolf Brandel said. 'The Angel from Lebanon advises us that the Rhine Maidens have taken Korah and Absalom into Egypt. They are boarding the train for hell. All is clear.'

As the tail end of the German force disappeared out of the Stawki Gate, the hands gripping the guns and grenades and bottle bombs relaxed and their bodies slumped in exhaustion, drained by tension.

A waving of signal flags, rooftop to window, window to rooftop to street. A scampering of the runners. 'All is clear.'

The generator in Mila 18 sputtered and spun into life. The lights flickered on. The children in Majdanek, lying tightly against Deborah on the floor, resumed their reading game and Rabbi Solomon lifted the chant of his prayer and Moritz the Nasher cut the double deck of cards for another round of sixty-six and Alexander wrote down the notes in the journal.

Simon Eden was doubled over the desk with exhaustion. Andrei came in and slammed him across the back. 'Simon! Did I have that syphilitic Austrian in my gun sights! I ached from head to toe to blast his head off. What discipline! Not a whisper up there! Not a sign. Not for a single second did Stutze know he was under our guns! Simon! Simon! By God, we have an army!'

Simon nodded weakly.

'You know,' Andrei whispered confidentially, 'I will wager anything you own that we can hold them for a week.'

Chapter Nine

Oberführer Funk arrived in Berlin somewhat regretful that he had allowed Horst von Epp to muddle his thinking. It was preposterous to suggest a new set of tactics for the liquidation of the ghetto. He should have followed orders and returned with heavily armed men the day after the January 18 act of banditry. But it was too late. He had no choice. When Funk proposed Von Epp's theory of pacifying the Jews he was chagrined that Himmler thought it an excellent idea. In fact, it was so well received that Funk took full credit for thinking up the entire scheme.

In Berlin, problems were cropping up everywhere. The shock of the catastrophe at Stalingrad rocked the High Command, which was now facing a mammoth Russian winter counteroffensive.

In North Africa, Rommel's magnificent Afrika Korps was engaged in furious actions with the ever-strengthening Allied Forces. A second disaster seemed in the making.

Italy was all but militarily impotent. One could smell that Italy was about to defect politically, as well.

In the air, the Luftwaffe had failed in its mission to crush the morale of the dogged Englishmen, and now all of England was being transformed into a gargantuan air field poised to return German bombs tenfold.

In the Pacific, the Americans had wrested the initiative. They seized island after island, which the Japanese had been certain was beyond the stamina of the American fighting men. The Japanese had not reckoned the extent of the uncommon valor of the United States Marine Corps.

Throughout the German Empire one could sense the restless awakening of the conquered. Despite brutal reprisals for underground activities, secret armies continued to grow. Indeed, Yugoslavia was gathering a force potent enough to divert badly needed German divisions off the eastern front. The policing of Greece and Poland required men and arms needed elsewhere.

To a lesser degree, sabotage, assassination, harassment, espionage flared up from Prague to Copenhagen to Oslo to Amsterdam to Brussels. Pin pricks, indeed, but enough stings were causing a painful swelling. Even in northern Italy a partisan army was forming.

This was the sudden realization of the brute who thought himself invincible being felled and stunned for the first time and crawling to his feet with a new appraisal of his adversary. Germany was stunned and smarted. The contemptuous smile was wiped from his lips. He was in pain.

Funk's visits with Eichmann at Gestapo 4B showed that Eichmann was still going about his job of rounding up the Jews with uncommon zeal, but he was hitting stone walls. Finland flatly defied German orders to turn over the Jews and threatened to use the Finnish army to defend them. A second flat refusal came from the Bulgarians. Then Denmark. King Christian of Denmark responded to the German order for Jews to wear the Star of David by putting on the first one himself and ordering all Danes to follow suit in a display that one Dane was the same as the other.

In France and Belgium and Holland, Jews were hidden in convents and attics, and even the Rumanians balked and the Hungarians split on the issue. Italy refused to become a partner to genocide.

Although Eichmann's agents were able to flush out Jews, get them through subterfuge and threat and strong-arm methods, nowhere in western Europe were they for sale for extra rations as they were in Poland, Ukrainia, and the Baltics.

Funk arrived in Berlin during a period of agonizing reappraisals. Himmler, Eichmann, and those most interested in the final solution agreed that the Warsaw ghetto, largest symbol of European Jewry, had to be liquidated quietly. It would indeed be a terrible propaganda setback for Berlin to admit the Jews were capable of fighting. It would be worse if Jews were to conduct the first rebellion against the Nazis that could start a chain reaction among the restless undergrounds.

Alfred Funk returned to Warsaw just long enough to turn the matter of peaceful liquidation over to the district Kommissar, Rudolph Schreiker. He left immediately for Denmark, where the pesky Danish underground was chopping the rail system to bits and leading in British bombers. Denmark, symbol of the 'little Aryan' brother, was behaving badly.

Throughout February 1943, Rudolph Schreiker bumbled through a fruitless campaign to lure the forty thousand survivors out of the ghetto. Joint Jewish Forces had a standing order that anyone volunteering for deportation or attempting to leave under German auspices would be shot.

Joint Jewish Forces allowed small numbers of Germans to enter the ghetto unmolested. Schreiker's emissaries went to the factories, attempting to win 'labor transferrals' by guaranteeing good working conditions in Poniatow or Trawniki. To back up his intentions of good faith, Schreiker shipped in some food and medicine.

A few prominent Jews in prison in Warsaw were sent into the ghetto to form a new Jewish Civil Authority to open schools and hospitals and resume cultural activities.

But no one budged from his hiding place.

In a week Schreiker realized the new Civil Authority was powerless and in an angry rage over his own failure had them executed in the bloody Civil Authority building.

The newspapers and the radio decried the lack of Jewish co-operation in the resettlement for 'honest labor.' The Polish people were fed a line that it was Jewish behavior that was to blame for the Polish misfortunes, for if Jews reported for 'honest labor,' then Poles would not be needed. It was a 'logic' the Poles accepted.

Simon Eden had the one thing he wanted most, time. It was time he had played for when he held fire when the Militia was taken to the Umschlagplatz. Time gave him the chance to augment his meager forces.

The Revisionists made firm contact with a small right-wing underground group, the ND Brigade, on the other side. Through the ND Brigade, the Revisionist groups – Chayal, Jabotinski, and Trumpeldor – were the best-armed company in the ghetto.

The Communist underground People's Guard was ill armed and could not spare a bullet for the ghetto, but they gave Joint Forces a strong liaison on the Aryan side with radio contact and hiding places in Warsaw.

By March of 1943 the tiny Jewish Forces were deeply hidden in the catacombs of the ghetto, were quick in their response to discipline, had as good observation and communications and contacts as circumstances allowed. The small teams of Fighters had shown extraordinary restraint in holding fire and maneuvering without being seen and had developed leadership to such a degree that even the pessimistic Simon Eden was beginning to feel they could hold the Germans at bay for a week.

Mid-March. Two months had passed and the Jews still held the ghetto. Alfred Funk roared into Warsaw, locked Rudolph Schreiker in his office, and berated him with obscenities for an hour. Schreiker was stripped of the duty. He was allowed to retain his post, for the Nazis could not admit failure in in Jewish matters, but ghetto liquidation was turned over to Horst von Epp and Dr Franz Koenig.

On March 17 a single German staff car drove through the Leszno-Tlomatskie Gate with a pair of large white flags attached to either fender. It moved at a crawl up Zamenhof Street and stopped before the Civil Authority building. A single soldier without rank stepped from behind the wheel and held up another white flag.

The car was under observation by Jewish Fighters the instant it entered the ghetto. The soldier shifted nervously from one foot to the other, unnerved by the quiet.

Heads began popping out from behind doorways, crevices, windows, courtyards, in a circle around him. He waved the white flag vigorously. Then his eyes narrowed as a woman holding a German rifle and wearing German boots approached him, leading a dozen men.

Ana Grinspan had seen Germans in her rifle sights before, but this was different. The mutual curiosity of enemy looking at enemy. The practical application of Andrei's continued lectures that these were not supermen. Hit them with a bullet and they will go down. The soldier was clearly puzzled at the face of his enemy. The 'sub-human' was a tall handsome woman leading men whose prowess he had no desire to contest.

'I have a message for your commander from Dr Franz Koenig representing the German authorities,' he recited.

'Runner,' Ana commanded, 'go to Atlas in Jerusalem and tell him that Pharaoh has sent a messenger under truce. We will hold him at Herod's Palace.'

A runner dashed off down Zamenhof Street.

'Blindfold him,' Ana ordered.

Moments later Simon Eden spoke to the back of the soldier. 'I am the commander,' he said.

'Dr Koenig wishes to have a meeting under truce with you and your command. He guarantees complete safety –'

Simon interrupted. 'Tell him that if he wishes a conference he will walk alone through the Leszno-Tlomatskie Gate holding a white flag and he will stop before the Civil Authority building. He will come between twelve and twelve-ten o'clock.'

The single obese figure of Franz Koenig waddled into the unearthly stillness. He quaked with fear, waving an oversized white flag back and forth with each step.

Down the middle of the empty street. The eerie sensation that a thousand pair of eyes were on him. Hidden. Looking at him. He stole glances at the windows and the roofs. Not a stir. How could anything be so deserted?

Koenig had wanted to wear civilian clothing, but he feared the Nazis would think he was afraid to wear a uniform. He did slip off the swastika armband the instant he was inside the ghetto. No use antagonizing them, he thought.

He inched farther up the street, past Dzielna, past Pawia. Still no sign of life. He stopped at the intersection of Gensia and looked in all four directions. Nothing. Only a snowfall of feathers. The structure of the Civil Authority building was behind him.

'Anyone here?' Anyone here ... anyone here ... anyone here? echoed his voice.

'Hello!' Hello ... hello ... hello.

Ten minutes passed. Koenig was numbed with fear.

'Koenig!'

He looked for the voice.

'Koenig!'

The front door of the Civil Authority building was ajar. He walked gingerly up the steps and shoved the door open. It groaned. He narrowed his eyes to slits to see down the shadowed corridor and waved the white flag.

'Truce!' he called. 'Truce!'

The door slammed behind him. He turned and looked into the bearded face of Samson Ben Horin.

'Hands up,' Ben Horin said. He frisked Koenig. 'March!' Down the corridor. The walls were stained with dried blood from German executions. The plaster chipped away. Debris everywhere.

'Turn in there. Sit.'

Franz didn't like the sordid room. It was overturned and smashed. It smelled bad. He swallowed to loosen his throat and stared at the table, afraid to look into the eyes of Samson Ben Horin. Samson smirked.

'So you are a superman,' he said.

Koenig felt inept before the lean, fierce, black-eyed young Jew who could obviously rip him to shreds. Samson sat in the window sill and swung his leg back and forth. 'So you are a superman,' he repeated.

The door opened. Simon Eden towering over six feet three inches and like a band of steel, Andrei Androfski with the power of a lion, Rodel with the build of a tank – all came in and leaned against the wall.

Koenig knew instantly that not only were the Joint Forces not a myth, but the survivors were a fierce breed.

Alexander Brandel helped Rabbi Solomon into the room. He and the old man sat opposite Koenig.

'Stand up in the presence of our rabbi,' Andrei said, 'and cover your head.'

Koenig pushed the chair back from the table and arose.

Rodel did not particularly subscribe to the idea of having Samson Ben Horin and Rabbi Solomon attend the conference. To him, Ben Horin's Revisionists were akin to fascists. Moreover, Ben Horin would not bind himself to Joint Forces. As for Solomon, it was sentimentality and nonsense. But for the sake of unity he did not protest.

'Talk,' Simon said.

'On behalf ... on behalf of the German authority, I am authorized to negotiate a settlement of our difficulties.'

The pronouncement was made without reaction. Koenig cleared his throat and continued.

'We would like to put the past behind us. Let bygones be bygones. I mean, there is no use dragging out old skeletons in the closet. Let us forget yesterday and talk about tomorrow.'

Still no reaction from the six men he faced.

'What we wish to do is complete the resettlement of the ghetto. Now, before you say anything, let me assure you that I came here fully prepared to guarantee excellent working conditions at camps you are free to examine.'

Ben Horin swung his leg back and forth from his seat in the window. Rodel glared hatred. Simon and Andrei looked aimlessly at the floor. Only Alex registered some amazement.

Koenig cleared his throat again.

'We are prepared to sign a pact. Our word. A treaty, if you please . . .' He stopped. All six pairs of hard eyes were on him now, registering disdain. He was making no progress whatsoever and he was getting more nervous.

'All right. I ask you, under what conditions will you consider abandoning the ghetto?'

There were no German tricks left, no more cunning or wile or ruses.

'You must consider it,' Koenig continued. 'Mind you, I am not making threats, but surely you must know that your position is impossible.'

Still no reply. Koenig had come to barter, prepared to fall back to a line of retreat to get what he wanted; peaceful liquidation. Their continued silence had left him with no choice but to make the final offer at once.

'You men here represent the leadership of what we estimate to be forty to fifty thousand people. To show you we mean business, we are prepared to pay you a handsome indemnity. Several hundred thousand zlotys. We will deposit it in Swiss francs, American dollars, or however you desire, and we will give you two thousand visas to Sweden. We guarantee safe conduct under Swedish or Swiss auspices. If you wish, you can leave in lots of one hundred and arrange coded messages to assure each other of safe arrivals. Now, gentlemen, what could be fairer than that?'

Koenig's offer was absolutely clear. It was a bribe for freedom. They would allow the leaders and part of the Jewish Forces to escape and, not only that, pay them to escape in exchange for leaving the rest of the survivors undefended and at the mercy of the Germans. Without Joint Jewish Forces there would be no further danger of resistance. The rest would go quietly.

'Don't keep Dr Koenig waiting, Alex,' Simon said. 'I'm sure you have an answer for him.'

Alexander Brandel stood up face to face with Franz Koenig. He expectorated a large wad of spit which landed on Franz Koenig's nose and dribbled down the German's lips and chin.

'Get out,' Simon hissed.

Samson Ben Horin jumped down from the window sill and cocked his pistol. 'Let's give the Germans a real answer.'

'No,' Rabbi Solomon said. 'He has entered our house under truce. We are bound to protect him.'

'Rabbi! This is Pharaoh! The blood of Jewish slaves is on his hands. His fat pockets bulge with gold from Jewish sweat.'

'No, Samson,' the rabbi admonished softly, 'As elder of this community, I will not permit it.'

Samson jammed the barrel against Koenig's temple and snarled. Neither Andrei nor Simon nor Rodel cared to stop him.

'Only one side in this war is the Nazis'. Let this miserable cur crawl out of here with the memory of honorable men engraved on his wretched soul living in fear of the moment the wrath of God will avenge us!' Solomon said.

Simon heaved a sigh and grasped the gun barrel and lowered it from Koenig's temple. 'Let him go,' he said.

Samson Ben Horin whirled around and smashed the wall with his fist.

'Get out before I change my mind,' Simon said to Koenig.

Franz Koenig bolted out of the room, tripped and tumbled from his awkward fat, and crawled halfway down the corridor in a panic to escape. He ran out into the street, waving the white flag.

'Truce! Truce! Truce!'

Andrei put his hand on Alex's shoulder. '*Nu*, how does it feel to be a man of violence?'

'Not bad, Andrei. Not bad at all.'

'A week,' Simon whispered. 'Let us hold for just one week.'

Chapter Ten

Journal Entry

For the entire month of March the Germans have made a frantic effort to lure Jews into the open. The Gestapo has initiated a 'visa' scheme designed to make 'foreigners' register at the Polonia Hotel. The unwritten understanding is that Jews in hiding will be given passage to Sweden if they can purchase their freedom.

The Gestapo has gone to extraordinary lengths to make the visa selling appear legitimate. A fake Red Cross unit is at the Polonia to administrate the plan. (Note: Fake Red Cross establishments have been used again and again by the Germans throughout Europe to bait escaped prisoners of war and others in hiding. They also use fake undergrounds with collaborators operating them.)

Apparently they are allowing a few of the visa purchasers to reach Sweden to 'prove' to the others that this is the real thing.

We were astonished to learn that David Zemba has put so much credence in the visa scheme that he has come out of hiding and is actually at the Polonia Hotel for the purpose of contacting world Jewry to get money to buy visas. Visas go at from ten to twenty thousand zlotys each.

We are certain it is an over-all scheme to lure us into complete complacency. The leopard does not change his spots. We are even more sure the visa scheme is a fraud and that most of those who register will end up in Treblinka.

Strange that a man with the experience of David Zemba could be duped so easily. I suppose the desperation is so great that people are ready to fool even themselves with a slim hope there may be a thread of truth.

Consistent with the German 'peace' offensive, we have not had an overt act against the ghetto in two and a half months. There is still electricity in many areas and tap water is available. Food deliveries continue to the factories, although the factories no longer are productive. Smuggling goes on with comparative ease. Moritz Katz has built a 'Quartermaster Corps' with a dozen former smugglers. They have stocked enough food for a two-week supply for the Fighters and our immediate dependents. We store water for drinking purposes as quickly as we can find containers and storage space. (We estimate we have a ten-day supply.)

One thing is certain. The Germans do not wish to fight with us. The ghetto is plastered with 'peace' posters urging the people to come out and report for labor. Joint Forces continues to warn of the dangers. We permit no volunteers for deportation.

How long will the Germans continue to tolerate our behavior? It is already the first week in April. We expect the ax to fall at any moment.

ALEXANDER BRANDEL

Dusk, the quiet transition to darkness, brought Deborah Bronski and forty children from the ages of three to ten years through a tunnel beneath Mila 18 to a courtyard near Muranowski Place.

They emerged singly from beneath the earth, gasping deeply to fill their lungs with pure air, and they blinked at the intensity of the dying daylight.

Jewish Fighters on the roof above them crisscrossed back and forth to guard the precious ones from a sudden attack. Sylvia Brandel was the last to emerge. They ran and jumped and rolled around and skipped and clapped hands with the joy of the release from bondage. Soon ... soon it would be springtime.

In a few moments the children played games that children play in a ghetto. They played the game of 'smuggler,' hiding an object from the searching 'Nazis and Nightingales.' They played 'escape,' weaving in and out of passages of the abandoned house to reach the 'Aryan side' past the 'Polish Blues.' They played Jewish Fighters and Germans,' peppering each other with imaginary bullets and bombs.

Everyone wanted to be Atlas and Jan and Chess Master and Tolstoy. The girls wanted to be Tanya, like Ana Grinspan, or Rachael Bronski. No one wanted to be Pharaoh or Brunhilde or Nazis or Nightingales or Polish Blues.

'Bang! Bang! I caught you, Jew!'

A little boy tripped and fell in the courtyard and his nose bled. He did not cry although he was in pain, for he was taught not to cry when he was hurt. Nazis and their dogs listened for crying children, to find hiding places.

Deborah hugged the boy and stopped the bleeding. In a moment he darted up the steps to resume the game.

She looked at her watch. In a moment Rachael would be coming. Strange, Deborah thought, that after a time a person would begin to take on the characteristics of a rat or a mole. Living beneath the earth should dim human values. Tragedy should immunize one to pain. Darkness should ease loneliness. It was not that way at all. Her heart ached again and again when the Fighters brought a warped little body to the children's room in Mila 18. A whimpering skeleton salvaged from the cold sidewalk or dark alley or abandoned, shattered room. Deborah cried when it was dark for their wild little eyes and their sharp nails which lashed out like those of frightened animals. She cried at the slow, torturous inability to respond to tenderness.

How she missed Rachael. That loneliness never left her.

And Stephan. The gnawing fear each time he left the bunker with Andrei.

How many times can a person die without the nerves dying too?

If only Rachael could stay with her. It was dangerous for the girl to come out of the Franciskanska bunker at night to visit. But Rachael should be with Wolf. There was no room for the children other than at Mila 18.

'Saska Kempa,' a Fighter called down from the roof.

'Grochow,' a girl's voice called up from the street, answering the password.

Rachael was coming diagonally across the courtyard. Deborah could not distinguish her face from the distance. She wore new knee-length boots and a leather jacket criss-crossed with a pair of bandoliers. Grenades were hooked into the belts, a rifle was slung over her shoulder, and her black hair was knotted up under a worker's cap. In her hand she carried Wolf's guitar. Despite the subterfuge, it was still Rachael. Nothing could keep her from walking like a woman. Nothing could taint her softness.

'Hello, Momma.'

'Hello, darling.'

They kissed cheeks.

'Where is Stephan?'

'Out with Andrei. Why isn't Wolf with you?'

'He's holding pistol drill at the factory.'

'Maybe you shouldn't come out alone at night.'

'Momma, I'm a soldier.'

Deborah took off her daughter's cap and unpinned her hair and let it fall down on her shoulders. 'Don't be a soldier for a while,' she said.

Rachael nodded.

'I caught you,' cried the voice of a child. 'Off to the Umschlagplatz!'

'Such wonderful games they play,' Deborah sighed. She sat down with her daughter on the top step and watched the children dart in and out of the courtyard. 'You look fine!' Deborah said aimlessly.

'You don't, Momma. Are you sick?'

'No. Just that ... every once in a while this unreality becomes real and you stop working long enough to think. You're in a hole under the ground, and the only way out is death. When I have time to think I become frightened. Just plain frightened.'

Rachael patted her mother's hand. 'It's strange, Momma, but being with Wolf ... He has a way about him. I've always the feeling that we will get through.'

'That is a good way to feel,' Deborah said.

'Yes,' Rachael said quickly. 'He makes everyone around him feel that way. I can hardly believe it sometimes because he's just like a little boy. He didn't let me go on the Brushmaker's raid, but everyone told me afterward how he was. Calm – like ice. A real leader. I just know we can get through anything together.' Rachael stopped short. What was she saying? Speaking of the hope of freedom to her mother, when her mother's position was hopeless. 'I'm sorry, Momma ... I didn't mean ...'

'No, dear. It's nice to hear a voice filled with hope.'

'Tell me about it, Momma.'

'With Susan gone, I have no girl friends to talk to. You are my best girl friend now.'

'I'm glad.'

'Simon and Alex and Andrei are moving heaven and earth to get Chris out of the ghetto. He's the most important man here now. Alex calls him our passport to immortality. One day he will have to run for it. He must go alone, of course. It's killing him, and it's killing me.'

Deborah lay her head on her daughter's shoulder and sobbed softly, and Rachael comforted her.

How terrible for Momma to love without hope. Each day a hell of torture and the knowledge of inevitable doom. The inability to combat it, cry out against it. With Wolf there was hope, always hope.

'It's all right, Momma ... it's all right ...'

Deborah was wound up like a spring.

'It's all right, Momma ... it's all right ... shhh ... shhh.'

'I don't know what's come over me. It's just that being shut in that bunker all day with the children ... pretending to them ... making believe everything will be all right. They know I'm an awful liar.'

'Tante Rachael!' Moses Brandel cried at discovering the visitor from Franciskanska.

'Tante Rachael is here!'

Children converged toward them from all corners of the building. Deborah dried her eyes. 'It's time for us to get back,' Deborah said.

They crawled through the tunnel into the Majdanek room. Rachael and Sylvia and Deborah lifted the children into layers of straw bunks and tucked them in. They lay close to the edge, tiny little faces looking to the lone candle on the wooden table near Rachael. Rachael strummed Wolf's guitar, and her thin voice sang about a never-never land of milk and honey.

And soon they fell asleep and Rachael left and Deborah dozed, waiting for Andrei and Stephan to return.

'Deborah.'

She blinked her eyes open. Andrei stood over her. She smiled.

'Stephan is asleep in my office,' he assured her at once. 'Come out into the corridor. I want to tell you something.'

From the rooms of the Fighter companies, the voices of singing, joking, storytelling. A beep-beep-beep from the radio. A howl of laughter as Moritz the Nasher slapped the cards of a winning hand of sixty-six on the table.

Andrei and his sister found a quiet place just inside one of the escape tunnels.

'Chris is waiting for you,' he said. 'Muranowska 24. There's a guard at the other end of the tunnel on the lookout for you.'

'Thanks,' she whispered.

'Before you go, Gabriela found places for three more children. You'll have to make a selection. It's an excellent place with a childless couple. Woodcutter and his wife.'

Make a selection! Deborah hurt at the thought. She felt as though she were at the selection center in the Umschlagplatz. The power to give three children the right to life. How to choose? Three sick ones? Three with the saddest eyes? Three with the most pitiful wails? How do you choose? By seniority as subterraneans?

'Their chances of survival are excellent. Pick strong children,' Andrei said.

'Very well.'

She and Andrei looked at each other and passed thoughts without words. Both of them had the same instantaneous impulse. Send Stephan. No one would blame them or accuse them of favoritism. The boy had more than earned his right to freedom. But Deborah and Andrei were trapped by the very things with which they had infused Stephan. How do you tell your son that dignity and honor are things for other people to die for?

Thoughts which never became words.

Andrei patted his sister's cheek and handed her a flashlight.

'Will Chris be leaving soon?'

'Any day,' Andrei answered.

She plunged into the tunnel, inching along with the dim light poking ahead of her through the narrow dirt walls beneath the dead ghetto above. The last twenty yards were on hands and knees.

The Fighter on watch at Muranowska 24 pulled her through the trap door and helped her to her feet. She caught her breath and wiped the perspiration from her cheeks and stretched her back.

'Is there water here?'

He pointed to the storage basins. It was a ghetto and it was war, but Deborah was a woman about to go to her lover and she was going to make herself desirable. She washed the streaks of dirt from her face and brushed her hair and fixed it the way Chris liked it and was extravagant with a drop of a gram of perfume that Gaby had sent in with Andrei. Then she ascended the stairs to find him.

When Chris had first returned to her Deborah was riddled with a feeling of sordidness. She was ashamed she could desire Chris in such a place. Their trysts were in cellars and attics, cold-straw, oppressive heat, in hidden tunnels or on floors. In the torn-up bunker at Mila 19, next to rushing sewer waters. Bodies sweaty or shivering and pimpled with cold.

She was ashamed of the sensuous pleasures. The shame never faded, but neither did her desire for those pleasures.

Deborah pushed open the attic door.

Chris watched the lights of Warsaw blink on one by one as darkness swept the city. She slipped beside him quietly and watched them too.

'A zloty for your thoughts,' she said.

'My thoughts? They aren't worth a zloty, even with today's inflation.'

'Then a kiss for your thoughts?'

Chris smiled a smile that was not a smile. 'I've been thinking of man, God, and the universe – all those damned things no one ever really understands.'

'That is worth a kiss,' she said.

Chris could not be appeased. 'Today, in a bunker at Mila 18, Christopher de Monti of Swiss News listened to two men arguing philosophy over a minute point to which each adamantly clung. They clung to their points, although it will never make a bit of difference. It will never affect the price of tea in China. Alexander Brandel argues for Rabbi Solomon to make a statement in support of Joint Forces as a morale factor for the survivors of the ghetto. Rabbi Solomon quotes the Torah, Midrash, and Mishna opinions that an act of vengeance is a form of suicide which is roundly forbidden. So there you have it, Deborah. Two men in a hole in the ground debating a question that is going to be solved for them anyhow. Frankly, man, God, and the universe give me a large pain.'

'My, you *are* in a mood. Here I get all prettied up to make myself alluring and I cannot even seduce a kiss from you.'

'Sex should never get in the way of man, God, and the universe. I think right now I'd give up sex forever for a cigarette and a good belt of scotch.'

Chris walked away from the window, patting his pockets for cigarettes that were not there. 'Why the hell doesn't Andrei bring in a few packs of cigarettes from Gabriela?'

'Some of us have been living this way for quite a few years now,' Deborah answered sharply.

Chris sagged to the cot and mumbled that he was sorry.

'What's really bothering you, Chris?'

'Don't you know?'

'Perhaps we'd better talk about it.'

'I don't want to.' He shook his head slowly. 'I just don't want to.' They were at a dead end. In a few days Gabriela would find a route for him to take out of the country. Deborah would be left behind. There was no way for her to leave the children or Rachael or Stephan. There was no way for her to take them. He had to go and she had to stay. Simple and absolute.

'I never felt sorry for those poor bastards I preyed upon for my bread and butter. The generals, the admirals, the heads of state. The great doers. Many of them looked upon themselves as pawns of fate. Not me. I said to myself: They deserve everything they get. They really crave this destiny bit. They beg for martyrdom. So, now I feel sorry for them. Look at me, Christopher de Monti, the great white hope of the battered tribes of Israel. I am the voice beyond death which must not be stilled.'

'None of us has a choice, Chris. Be grateful you may be able to walk in the sun again.'

'Without you ... Deborah ... All I want is to come home at the end of a day to you. I'm not made of the sterner stuff of Andrei and Alex and Rabbi Solomon.'

'You'll find it when the time comes.'

'I cannot reconcile myself to what I have given you, Deborah. Torment. Love in the catacombs. I can't make peace with it.'

'Chris, listen to me. When I die –'

'Stop it!'

'When I die, Chris, dying will be very painful. I will want to live because I have known what ecstasy is. If we had never met, there would be no regrets. How lonely and empty it would be never to know giving and receiving love and, yes, all the pain it brings.'

Deborah knelt beside him. He lifted her face in his hands and smiled. 'And on flows the Vistula,' he said.

'For these moments we can make it stand still. You and I have the magic power to transcend the flowing river and the guns and the cries. Right now love ... they are all far away ... far away.'

Chapter Eleven

Alfred Funk looked down at a blown-up map of the ghetto and rubbed his hands together with childlike glee and anticipation. He lifted a magnifying glass and moved it about, stopping at the displacement of troops, armor, and artillery marked with various colored pins. He changed a pair of pins indicating high-powered searchlight batteries.

He was honored that Berlin was forgiving enough to give him the chance to vindicate himself. This time there would not be failure.

His plan was simple. Every seven meters around the wall he would alternate a 'foreign racial watchman' with a Polish Blue policeman. An SS officer would patrol each section of two hundred meters behind the Ukrainians to make certain their weapons could not be purchased by the Jews. The circle of soldiers around the ghetto wall would make a breakthrough impossible and reduce the possibility of a single man sneaking through.

The city engineers as well as army engineers advised him against blowing up the sewers. The huge *Kanal* pipes could cave in parts of the city as well as wreck the drainage to the Vistula. Instead, every manhole leading out of the ghetto would be under watch. Accordions of barbed wire would be dropped down the manholes. This would not impede the flow of sewage but would trap the Jews trying to escape through the sewers. Poison-gas smoke candles would be used both in the sewers and the bunkers inside the ghetto.

With all the exits blocked, Funk would then move in the Reinhard Corps, Wehrmacht, and Waffen SS with armored pools held in readiness. Most of the forty thousand Jews were in the factory compounds. He would nip these off quickly and get them on the way to Treblinka.

The magnifying glass stopped at a bank of searchlight positions pinned on the map on the Aryan side near Muranowski Place. Master stroke, Funk complimented himself on the night lights. By working two shifts of troops day and night, the Jews would not have a chance to rest or alternate their positions. Once the factory workers were gone, he'd move in the dogs and special sound detectors to flush out the bunkers with dynamite, flame throwers, or poison gas.

Water and electricity would be shut off the same night his troops moved into position.

It was a marvelous, simple, and efficient foolproof plan.

Everything was ready at Treblinka to give 'special treatment.' The entire process would take three to four days. Five at the absolute most.

Now, about the Jewish Forces, he thought. He wanted them to open fire first and commit themselves to combat. This way he could clean them out in a few hours. Once they were gone, the liquidation of the rest would be much easier. But would they fire at heavily armed troops? Damn it, no – they'd cower.

If these Jews did open fire it would cost him troops. Ten or twenty casualties. Should he send in Ukrainians the first day and let them take the casualties? No. The honor had to go to the Reinhard Corps! Shame to risk blooding the Elite Corps, but such were the fortunes of war. They would be insulted if they did not enter the ghetto first.

He ran over the map again, replaced his tanks for reserve, and set his artillery in positions to effect better cross fire, then set the magnifying glass and picked up the roster of troops being placed at his disposal.

SS UNITS
SS staff and officers, Warsaw
Reinhard Corps, Warsaw
Special Waffen SS, Trawniki and Poniatow
SS Panzer Grenadier Battalion
SS Mobilized Cavalry Battalion
SS Police Regiment, Lublin
SS Dog Company, Belzec
All Gestapo units, Warsaw

WEHRMACHT UNITS
Battalion, Infantry
Engineer companies, detached
Flame-throwing companies, detached
Battalion plus battery, artillery
Special detachment anti-aircraft searchlight units
Medical Corps company

LOCAL UNITS All companies, Polish Blue Police
All companies, Polish fire brigades

FOREIGN RACIAL GUARDS
One battalion mixed, Baltic guards
One battalion, Ukrainian guards

Alfred Funk sighed with contentment. His special brigade of eight thousand men was being assembled rapidly. Those from outside the Warsaw district were en route. It was a nicely rounded force. He muttered his unhappiness at having to expose SS people to the first fire, but ... no choice ... simply no choice.

Horst von Epp returned from his regular four-day monthly trip to Krakow with the knowledge that Oberführer Funk had been in Warsaw for three days. The instant he entered Funk's office the Oberführer snapped up from his desk. 'Aha!' Funk cried with obvious delight, 'Aha! Enter Neville Chamberlain, the great negotiator. The great appeaser!'

'From the tremors of joy in your voice, I should say that you have come on a mission of annihilation.'

'Look!' Funk said, proudly pointing to the map. 'I am grateful for this chance to vindicate myself.' He clasped his hands behind his back snappily and paced with a jaunty step. 'The instant I returned from Denmark, Himmler called me in. "Enough of this nonsense," Himmler told me. "Der Führer commands you to obliterate the Warsaw ghetto immediately. This symbol of Jewry must be wiped off the earth. You, Alfred, have priority on all troops in the General Government Area."'

Horst von Epp grimaced and swung open the liquor cabinet.

Funk had his knuckles on the desk and bent forward rigidly, his blue eyes alive with vehemence. 'You know, Horst, you actually had me fooled for a moment with your silly talk. Negotiate with the Jews, indeed! I was a fool to listen to you. I should have carried out my orders to the letter in January.'

One quick jigger of scotch roared down Von Epp's throat, and a second followed, and a third was poured. Then he turned and faced Funk and began to laugh ironically. Funk's face quivered as his expression changed from anger to puzzlement.

'"With reasonable men, I will reason; with humane men I will plead; but to tyrants I will give no quarter ..."'

'What in the name of hell are you babbling about, Horst?'

'As a good propagandist, I studied the art of another good propagandist. We should all study our predecessors, don't you think?'

'I don't recall the phrase, nor do I see the occasion for your laughter.'

'I give you William Lloyd Garrison, master American propagandist.'

The muscles in Funk's face knotted with anger. 'Perhaps it would be more fitting if you quoted Nietzsche.'

'Ah yes. That great humanitarian, Friedrich Wilhelm Nietzsche. To enter into a higher civilization, a super-race must ruthlessly destroy the existing inferior civilizations. We must divest, purge, cleanse ourselves of Judeo-Christian perversions in order to achieve this ultimate form of life. Now, how's that for Nietzsche, Alfred?'

'It is men like you, who compromise with sub-human forms of life, who will keep the German people from reaching their goals.'

Horst flopped his hands. 'Here we go, underestimating the Americans again. A chronic, incurable illness of ours, underestimating Americans.' Horst settled opposite Funk's chair, tilting the bottle of scotch once more. 'I paraphrase an underestimated American. Reasonable men reason. Compassionate men show mercy. Tyrants destroy. We destroy because we must destroy because we must destroy.'

'You are playing dangerous games with this radical thinking, Horst. Take my advice. Change your tune. Berlin is not so happy over some of your attitudes.'

'Save it, Alfred. You will need apologists around like me after the Third Reich is crushed to expound the theories of apologetics. What shall I say? Ah yes, there was no one here but us anti-Nazis. What could we do? Orders were orders.'

'You speak treason against the Fatherland,' Funk said menacingly.

Horst jumped up from his seat and slammed the bottle on the desk. It was the first show of temper Alfred Funk had ever seen him make, and he was clearly startled into silence.

'Damn you!' Horst cried. 'I am neither damned fool nor coward enough to keep smiling and pretending and clicking my heels and bowing from the waist in the face of absolute disaster. Say it, Alfred! Germany has lost the war!'

Funk's eyes bulged with disbelief.

'We have lost the war! We have lost the war! We have lost the war!' Horst bellowed.

Funk paled and sat down.

'Now we have the opportunity to soften the blows of defeat if we have the intelligence to recognize defeat and prepare for it carefully. So, what do we do? Step up the murders at Auschwitz. Five thousand more Poles and Slavs a day . . . We respond to the reality of defeat by throwing open the doors for our own destruction.'

Funk mopped his brow and smiled weakly. He thought he had better change the subject. Von Epp always tied him in knots when they argued. He was like the devil himself! One lovely day Himmler would tell him to get rid of Von Epp. What a pleasure that would be.

Alfred Funk cleared his throat. 'One of the things I discussed with Goebbels concerns you. Next week we are to meet in Lublin and design a campaign to minimize the unpleasantness in Poland. We start by understating the numbers of Jews involved in the final solution. Then we deny the special-treatment camps have facilities for other than labor. Bone-crushing machines are being installed in all special-treatment centers to eliminate the evidence. In fact, those given special treatment by firing squads are being exhumed for cremation. Eichmann has full-time staffs at 4B making a duplicate set of records – court trials, epidemics, and such – which can account for a good part of the deaths. In Czechoslovakia, at Theresienstadt, we have established a model camp for Jews and invited the Red Cross to inspect it . . .'

'Shut up, Alfred! We scratch like dogs to cover dung piles while we proceed to drown ourselves in our own vomit.'

Alfred Funk had that queasy feeling in his stomach again. He tested his words carefully. 'The world has a short memory.'

'I think this time they are not going to forget. Jews have a long memory. They weep for temples lost two thousand years and they repeat old wives' stories of liberations and rituals from the dawn of time. Do you know what an old Jew rabbi told me once when I asked him about Jewish memory?'

'What?'

'The words "I believe" mean "I remember." Even Nietzsche is puzzled over their ability to outlive everyone who has tried to destroy them. I believe . . . I remember. So you see, Alfred, a thousand years from now old Jews will wail in remembrance of the Nazi pharaoh who held them in bondage in Warsaw.'

Terrifying thoughts ran through Alfred Funk's mind. Damn Eichmann and his mania for rounding up Jews. Damn Globocnik! Damn Himmler! Damn Hitler! They had all gone too far with this Jewish business. But what could he say? What could he do? He looked at the map on the desk. In a few days his army would be assembled. Perhaps . . . perhaps when he destroyed the last of the Jews he could enter into the higher form of life the Nazis promised. He restored his calm. To hell with Horst von Epp!

'Shall I tell you something, Alfred?' Horst said, bleary from a rapid emptying of the bottle. 'You are a man who understands the mathematics of checks and balances. We Germans respect mathematics. The punishment always balances the crime. We have only eighty million Germans. It is not a sufficient number to bear our guilt. To balance the scale, we pass on our sentences to be served by a hundred unborn generations.'

Alfred Funk began to shake visibly. Words he dared not speak but thoughts he could not squelch were being hammered at him.

'Our names will be synonymous with the brotherhoods of evil. We shall be scorned and abused with no more and no less an intensity than the scorn and abuse we have heaped upon the Jews.'

Alfred Funk pushed away from his desk. He was perspiring badly. He had to take a bath.

Chapter Twelve

Andrei sat in the back row of the small church of a village on the northern fringe of the Lublin Uplands.

Gabriela Rak knelt before the altar, whispering prayers before a crudely hewn image of a bleeding Christ on the crucifix. She stood, lit a candle on the right side of the altar, knelt at the aisle, crossed herself, and retreated back to Andrei just as Father Kornelli entered.

'The children were exhausted,' Father Kornelli said. 'The two girls fell right to sleep. The boy is waiting for you,' he said to Andrei.

'When will they leave?' Gabriela asked.

'In the morning Gajnow and his wife will come and fetch them. It is about ten miles into the forest to their home. Gajnow is a good man. The children will be safe with him. You must of course tell them that they have to learn Catholicism for their own protection.'

'I have told the girls,' Gabriela said. 'They are bright children. They understand.'

'I'll talk to the boy now,' Andrei said.

'You will find him in my room,' Father Kornelli said.

Andrei crossed a dirt courtyard filled with flitting geese and wallowing pigs. He entered the priest's home. The door to the bedroom was ajar. He opened it a bit wider and looked at the two sleeping girls. One child had only a name they had invented for her. She did not know her name when they had found her. The other was a twelve-year-old daughter of one of the members of the Civil Authority. Deborah had been right. Children were children. This one deserved to have the second chance for life. Andrei shut the door and walked down the short hall to the sitting room and entered. A bed had been made on the couch, but his nephew Stephan was still dressed.

'It has been a long day, Stephan,' Andrei said. 'You should get some sleep.'

Stephan looked at him with suspicion.

'Tomorrow you and the girls will be taken on the next stage of your journey.'

'What about you, Uncle Andrei?'

'I must be getting back to Warsaw with Gabriela.'

'You said I had a mission. What is it?'

'Yes ... I've come to give you your orders now. Your orders are to survive.'

'I don't understand you, Uncle Andrei.'

'Stephan, you and the girls will be staying in the forest at the home of a very wonderful old couple.'

'Staying?'

'Yes, Stephan. I've come to say good-by.'

The boy's eyes grew wide with astonishment. 'You tricked me!'

'I told you to obey orders without question. That is not trickery.'

'You tricked me. You promised me you were taking me on a special mission.'

'You have a very special mission.'

'No. I won't stay. I'll run away if you don't take me back to Warsaw!'

'This was a decision of your elders, Rabbi Solomon and Alex.'

Andrei walked to the boy slowly and put his hand on his shoulder. Stephan twisted away from him abruptly. 'You lied to me, Uncle Andrei! I'll get back to Warsaw myself!'

'I overestimated you, Stephan. I thought you were a good soldier. I guess you're still a little boy.'

'I am a good soldier! I am as good as any runner in the ghetto!'

Andrei shrugged. 'Not really. A good soldier knows how to obey orders even though they may not please him.'

'It is not a soldier's assignment to hide in the woods like a coward.'

The boy was too clever to fool with games of words. Andrei had no alternative but to give him the hard facts in all their naked cruelty. Perhaps he should have done so earlier.

'Are you man enough to hear the truth? Can you take it, Stephan?'

'I can take it,' the boy answered firmly.

'Your momma is going to die. There is no way out for her.'

'No!'

'Truth, Stephan. Momma is going to die. She cannot leave those children and she cannot get them out. She is trapped and she is doomed.'

'Momma will live!'

'Only if you survive and preserve her memory.'

'I'll go back and die with Momma!'

'I said are you man enough to hear the truth? I have not finished.'

Stephan's eyes burned with an anger that told his uncle he had the courage to see it through. Andrei pointed for him to sit down on the sofa.

'Your sister and Wolf and I are in an impossible situation. The odds on reaching a star are better than the odds on any of us coming through. Do you think I lied to you when I told you I have a mission? It is the job of your mother and your sister and me to die for the honor of our family. It is your job to live for our honor. I say this with all my soul, Stephan. It is you who has the more difficult mission. You must go from this battle to fight your way into Palestine, and you will have to fight again for your freedom.'

Stephan looked up at his uncle, who was pleading for a sign of affection. The boy bit his lip hard to hold back the tears, but his eyes still showed anger.

'Stephan, one of us must get through this to show who we were and what we stood for. It is a big, big job, son! Only the best soldier can do it. You must live for ten thousand children killed in Treblinka and a thousand destroyed writers and rabbis and doctors. It's a hell of a big mission.'

Stephan flung his arms around his uncle's waist and buried his head on Andrei's chest, and Andrei patted his head. 'I'll try,' Stephan wept.

Andrei comforted him and knelt beside him and held his tear-stained cheeks in his hands and winked. 'You won't let me down, Stephan ... I know it.'

Andrei removed the large gold ring which had been given to him as a member of the Polish Olympic team. 'To seal the bargain,' he said.

Stephan looked at it in disbelief and tried to slip it on a finger. It was even too large for his thumb.

'Well now, don't worry about that. Once you get at that woodcutter's cottage and get fresh air and food and exercise, that damned ring will be too small for you. See if I'm not right.'

Stephan tried to smother his tears, but he could not. He wept convulsively. 'I'll try . . . I'll try . . .'

'Come on now, let's get you undressed. It's been a long trip for any soldier.'

Stephan submitted as his uncle unbuttoned his shirt and trousers and lifted him in his arms and carried him to the sofa. He clutched the ring in his fist and buried his head in the pillow.

'Now there are parts of the orders which you will understand as a good soldier whose duty it is to survive. You've got to learn all this Hail Mary business, but it's not so bad as you may think. You know Gabriela has been doing it all her life and she is a fine woman. We Jews have had to pray like that before – during the Inquisition, to fool the Spaniards –'

Andrei stopped short. The pillow was wet with the boy's tears.

'Tell me about Batory.'

'Batory! Hah! Now there's a horse for you. The blackest, fiercest animal in all of Poland. Only a few weeks ago I took him to England for the Grand National and he ran so fast he split the air and caused it to thunder. Well, sir, those Englishmen . . .'

Father Kornelli and Gabriela waited in the tiny vestry. The priest poured two fingers of kirschwasser. She sipped it with controlled slowness, capturing its warmth.

'I was filled with unpriestly forlorn when the archbishop exiled me to limbo or purgatory or what have you. May the Holy Mother forgive me, but I am quite certain that the Lord won a battle with the archbishop. My little church has become a vital link to the partisans in the forests.' He winked with slyness. 'There are grenades stored beneath the altar.'

'Shame on you, Father.'

'Gabriela Rak! I was delighted that I was able to make contact with you. I want to find places for more children. Dozens of them. Gajnow is a good man. I must find others.'

Suddenly Gabriela grimaced, paled, and drank the rest of the cherry brandy in a single swallow.

'Is anything wrong?'

'Just a little queasy spell.'

'Do you think you should be making such strenuous trips in your condition?'

Gabriela was startled at the sudden unmasking. 'I didn't realize I was being so obvious.'

'There is nothing in my vows which says I cannot recognize a pregnant woman when I see one. The first month or two is always the worst, I understand.'

Gabriela fumbled nervously with the empty glass. He poured her another drink. 'I don't want a sermon, Father. I don't seek forgiveness, nor do I confess to sin.'

'I am offended that you look upon me as an old fishwife in whom you cannot confide.'

'I'm sorry, Father. Yes, I would like to hear my own voice speaking the thoughts I've held locked for so long.'

'Having a child under your circumstances is a very difficult task.'

'I'm fully aware of the consequences.'

'Does Andrei know?'

'Perhaps and perhaps not.'

'I don't understand.'

'We have had to adapt our lives to each other in a strange way. It's full of unsaid things.'

'It is a constant source of amazement,' Father Kornelli broke in. 'The capacity of the human being to live with tension. The way nerves can be controlled, thoughts and fears locked –'

'Not really, Father. Andrei and I know each other's thoughts. A look, a touch, a sigh. A way he avoids my eyes. A way I avoid his. We read each other's fears, though we never speak them. The sound of his breath in the darkness, the touch of his fingers are all silent couriers.'

'What a wonderful experience to be able to communicate with another human being that way.'

She sighed deeply, unevenly, and sipped the drink once more. 'Yes, I suppose he knows that I am carrying his child.'

'He should hear it from your lips.'

'No, Father. It's all part of silent understandings. Andrei returns to the ghetto now, and he will never leave it again. I accept it. I don't challenge it and I cannot burden him with worry about me.'

'You speak against every concept we hold sacred. You cannot live without hope. That is a sin.'

Her eyes brimmed with sadness. 'I know it and he knows I know. But we have never said it and we never shall. My Andrei is a man so full of pride it would be utterly impossible for him to leave so long as there is a bullet to be fired, and when the last bullet is fired he will fight them with his fists. That's my Andrei, Father.'

The priest patted her hand. 'My dear. My poor child.'

She shook off his sympathy and her own self-pity. 'Don't feel sorry for me. I don't think you understand. I'm deliberately having this baby.'

His expression betrayed the idea that he was immune to shock.

'I planned this with cold-blooded, meticulous calculation. Each time we part there has always been the gnawing fear that this is the last time. But you even harden to that. Now that the end has really come it is almost anti-climatic. This is the last time. I think he was hoping I'd do this, and I think he's proud of me.'

'Do you realize what you're doing!' he cried in panic.

'I must have his life in my body. I cannot let Andrei be destroyed. This is the only way to preserve his life. I regret I cannot bear him a hundred children.'

'This is not an act of love. It is an act of vengeance.'

'No, Father. It is an act of survival. I will not let Andrei be destroyed!'

He studied the animal fury in her eyes. She was a savage with the most basic of all instincts. And then he was puzzled. Had the absence of a prescribed ritual made their union less pure? Could a man and a woman cherish each other more deeply, sacrifice, give fidelity, truth, with a greater ability because of a prescribed ritual? Had not Andrei and Gabriela behaved in a manner completely sacred to the eyes of God? He did not like these questions of himself.

Gabriela stood and turned her back to Father Kornelli as the defiance ebbed from her, and her voice was shaky. 'I have one terrible regret. I must leave the Church. Andrei's child must be raised as a Jew.'

He was dazed and hurt, but at the same moment of anger there was admiration for the completeness of her giving. He walked to her. 'I cannot condone that and I cannot be your priest,' he whispered. 'But I can be your friend and I want you to know that I will help you.'

She nodded and remained rigid, then suddenly spun around and faced him in anguish. 'Will I be forgiven?'

'I shall pray for you and your child as I have never prayed before.'

Andrei suspected that Gabriela and Father Kornelli would be immersed in a deep and intimate conversation. When he left Stephan he made sufficient noise upon entering the church to alert them of his presence. He entered the vestry chalky-faced.

'How is Stephan?'

'How? His heart is broken.'

'What is he doing now?'

'He's trying very hard to be a man, but he's doing what any fourteen-year-old boy would do. He's crying himself to sleep.'

'Please know, Andrei, that Gajnow will protect those children. I will personally do everything in my power.'

He patted the priest on the shoulder. 'I am very grateful, Father.'

Father Kornelli changed the tone by opening the curtain to the storage closet for his vestments. He took out a bottle of vodka. 'Look! I have been saving this for a special occasion. Take it, Andrei.'

'Father ... I couldn't ...'

'No. Go on. I want you to have it.'

Andrei looked toward Gabriela, who nodded that it was all right.

'You two children look completely done in. Now Count Borslawski's hunting lodge is vacant and at your disposal. Just a mile into the woods. The horse cart is hitched up. You'll find a roaring fire in the fireplace and a meal for royalty. Be off! Go on, get out of my sight.'

'By God, Father Kornelli,' Andrei said, 'if there were a few more priests like you around, I'd seriously consider becoming a convert!'

Chapter Thirteen

Journal Entry

All week detachments of special troops have been arriving in Warsaw from Globocnik's headquarters in Lublin, the labor camps of Trawniki and Poniatow, and the extermination camps. They are staging in Praga over the river. Oberführer Funk has issued them extra schnapps and promised a mere three to four days' work in liquidating the ghetto. They have named themselves the Death's-Head Brigade after Globocnik's Lublin butchers.

Strange. The two extreme political philosophies in the ghetto have been able to get the closest co-operation on the Aryan side. The Communists and the People's Guard on the left, the Revisionists and ND Brigade on the right are in close alliance.

Unfortunately both undergrounds are small and semi-effectual. We can expect no further help from the Home Army.

The ND Brigade is even discussing trying to get the Revisionists out of the ghetto to form a partisan unit. (It would weaken our forces badly if they left, but they are not under our command.)

The Communists have two trucks in hiding in the Targowek suburb. We have heard rumors of Jewish partisan units forming in the Machalin Forest. The Communists have agreed to transport any people we can slip out of the ghetto to the forest.

We have two short-range transmitters. One is at Mila 18 and the other at the Franciskanska bunker. We only transmit messages in case of emergency. We know that German direction finders are trying to get bearings on our bunkers when we transmit, so we must go through the cumbersome business of taking the radios out of the bunkers and moving them from place to place in order to send messages. As a last-ditch measure we have worked out a series of codes with the People's Guard, who stand radio watch on the Aryan side. We transmit on a low frequency which can be received by an ordinary radio. Our code tells them the number of people coming through the sewers and through which manhole. Andrei informs me that Gabriela Rak is in contact with the People's Guard in the hopes she will find places for more children. She stands a radio watch of several hours a day also.

The Germans have dropped barbed wire into the sewers at most of the manholes leading from the ghetto. However, the sewer networks are so vast and tricky, we can bypass the wire. We have also formed a special squad called the 'Sewer Rats,' whose duty it is to duck beneath the running sewage and cut the barbed wires in the main sewers.

Jules Schlosberg delivered the land mine to my son Wolf. It took longer than expected to manufacture because Wolf was adamant about wanting to be able to control the detonation. Wolf reasons he can get the maximum number of the enemy this way. It is fixed to be discharged by a spark from a hundred and fifty yards' distance. The mine is a true curiosity; flat and nearly five feet in diameter. Jules says it has the power of a one-ton bomb, and there are so many nuts and bolts stacked in it that he calls it the 'kasha bowl.' I think Jules likens all of his inventions to food simply because he is hungry; the pipe grenade is called 'long strudel,' the nut-and-bolt grenade 'matzo ball,' and the fire bottles 'borscht soup.'

Simon, Andrei, and Wolf argued lengthily over the placement of the 'kasha bowl.' Wolf wants to plant it under the Brushmaker's main gate. He reasons that the Germans are too arrogant to enter the factory in spread formations and they'd march right on top of the mine. Both Andrei and Simon, who are military men, doubt if the Germans have such a lack of judgment. But Wolf won out. Under the gate it goes. Wolf is quite stubborn in his own quiet way – like his mother.

We have not been able to find a safe route for Christopher de Monti. We cannot take any chances of his being captured. He is fit to be tied; particularly because he must stay with the 'women and children' in the bunker when the Fighters go to the roofs on alerts. Simon assures him it is far more difficult to stay than be upstairs. Simon almost dies with tension during the alerts.

Optimism continues, but my own personal view is that we cannot hold for a week in the light of the power the Germans have massed in Praga.

ALEXANDER BRANDEL

Oberführer Alfred Funk glowered majestically before the assemblage of officers of his Death's-Head Brigade. The swastika and the skull and crossbones were in evidence everywhere. With pointer in hand, he crisply explained the disposition of troops.

'Are there questions?'

Naturally, there were none.

'I read you now a message from Reichsführer Heinrich Himmler.'

Everyone leaned forward in anticipation.

' "This is a page of glory in our history, which has never been written and is never to be written. We have the moral right, we have the duty, to our people to destroy the sub-humans, who want to destroy us. Only through the ruthless execution of our duty will we attain our rightful place as masters of the human race." ' Alfred Funk breathed deeply, awed by the words. He folded the document and placed it in his breast pocket. 'Sturmbannführer Sieghold Stutze. You will step forward.'

The Austrian limped crisply to the general and cracked his heels together with vigor.

'To your Reinhard Corps has fallen the great honor of leading the Death's-Head Brigade into the ghetto to initiate its liquidation. Befitting this monumental occasion of the obliteration of the largest European Jewish reservation, I am pleased to notify you that you have been promoted from Sturmbannführer to Obersturmbannführer!'

Stutze was hit with a wave of nausea. Not even for the rank of Obergruppenführer did he wish to enter that ghetto first. For weeks he had been thinking of ways and means to attain a transfer to an extermination camp. He snapped his heels together once more, bowed to Funk, and then drew himself up straighter. 'I am honored!'

'Heil Hitler!' barked Funk.

The room stormed to its feet. 'Heil Hitler!' they responded.

Moved by the enormity of the moment, several officers burst into a spontaneous singing of the 'Horst Wessel' song.

'Close ranks! Raise the swastika!
Storm troops, march with calm determination!
Soon Hitler's flags will fly over all!
Soon Germany will take its rightful place.'

'Hello, Jerusalem. This is Tolstoy at Beersheba.'

'Atlas in Jerusalem. What is it, Tolstoy?'

'Water and electricity have been cut off in our sector.'

'We have the same report from Haifa. We are awaiting an Angel from Canaan for a full report. Have your Angels give a blue alert.'

'*Shalom* and ... good *yontof*.'

'Happy holidays to you too.'

Simon set down the phone. Strange, he thought, that Rodel, a Communist and devout atheist, should wish him a 'good holiday' for Passover. Simon faced Andrei, Tolek, Alex, and Chris. 'Power and water are off in Rodel's area too. He wished us a happy Passover ... Tolek, send out the runners. Spread a blue alert.'

It became abysmally glum. The last-minute decision to bring in another forty children crammed Mila 18 beyond its capacity. Air circulation sufficient for two hundred twenty persons was inadequate for nearly three hundred packed into the catacomb. The rooms had no place for movement. The corridors were crushed with sweaty bodies, stripped to undergarments, sucking at the oxygen scarcely enough to keep the candles lit.

'Passover,' Andrei said sardonically. 'The feast of liberation. What a damned joke.'

Simon nodded in agreement. 'Oh, where is Moses to lead us through the Red Sea and drown Pharaoh's army! The only pillars of fire are the ones that will devour us.'

'Well,' Andrei said, 'we have to have the seder.'

Chris shook his head. 'You Jews astonish me. In the pits of hell, about to be destroyed, and you mumble rituals to freedom.'

'Doesn't one cry out more desperately for freedom when it is taken from him? What better time can there be than tonight to renew faith?' Alexander Brandel said.

'Come now, Alex,' Chris prodded. 'Andrei, you, Simon ... most of those out there are not renewing a faith they've ever kept. Rodel, the Communist, wishes you well. What was his synagogue?'

'Yes, Chris, you are right in a way. And it is very strange that we who have not lived like Jews have chosen to die like Jews.'

'There is no reason and there is every reason,' Simon said. 'We only know ... we must have the seder.'

Passover. The night of the seder. The retelling of a story from the ancient Hagada as old as recorded history. The liberation from Pharaoh's bondage.

How Jewish Warsaw would have reverberated with the weeks of unabated excitement before the war! Alex tried to remember the Tlomatskie Synagogue ... crowds jammed to watch the elite fill the marble temple.

In the homes of the poorest, brass and silver candlesticks shone to a glisten and the white tablecloths and shining dishes dazzled the eye and the kitchens smelled of baking and candies prepared with the very soul of the homemaker.

The tables were fixed with special foods symbolizing the suffering of Moses and the tribes. The diced nuts and bitter herbs for the mortar of Pharaoh's bricks which the Jews laid in bondage.

What the hell kind of better vetch could there be for the ghetto in the future, Alex thought! What symbol would there be for sewer water!

Watercress for the coming of spring, and the egg for the symbol of freedom. Well, spring was coming to Warsaw. There was no egg, no watercress. Forty thousand terrified people mumbling ancient prayers, begging to an unhearing God to fill His promises to bring forth ... to deliver ... to redeem ... to take the tribes of Israel. In six hundred bunkers the ritual was repeated in numbed and tear-filled voices while the Polish Blue Police took their positions around the ghetto walls every seven meters.

But ... the story had to be told. Was it ever to be told with greater futility? Alexander wondered. Still ... it had to be told.

A tiny bench stood at the junction of the two corridors of Mila 18. They held a pair of candlesticks Moritz Katz had managed to salvage. Substitutes took the place of the prescribed symbolic foods.

Alexander pushed his way past the jam of humanity into Rabbi Solomon's cell.

'We are ready to begin the seder,' he said. He helped the old man to his feet. Solomon was no longer able to see except in shadowy outlines, nor was he able to read. But that did not matter. His voice was yet clear and he knew the Hagada by memory. He was led to the bench and seated upon a pillow, for the pillow symbolized the free man who relaxes while he feasts. From rooms Auschwitz, Belzec, Chelmno, Majdanek, Treblinka, and Sobibor, the Fighters and the children pressed to the door in bated breath to hear – Zionists plain and fancy, infants, Communists, Bundists, Orthodox, and smugglers.

One could hear gasping in the silence. The air was putrid and the heat oppressive.

The silver goblet in the center of the bench was called Elijah's cup. When the Prophet who had foretold the second coming of Israel drank from the Passover goblet, the prophecy would be fulfilled. Solomon's ancient hands felt over the bench for the cup. He lifted it and jiggled it. It was empty, for there was no wine.

'Perhaps,' he said, 'this is a way we are being told that Israel will come again. Perhaps Elijah has come and drunk.'

Someone began to sob, but one sob was melted into another. All a shimmering mass of bodies. Another sobbed, and another.

'A learned man walks through a maze searching for rooms marked "truth." Bits of the puzzle are given us in our Torah and our Mishna and the Midrash and the Talmud. But how strange that the real clues come to us at a time when we least expect them.'

'Momma ... Momma,' a child wept.

Another began praying, and another and another.

The old man's voice cried out again. 'Why are we in this place? What is God trying to tell us? Why have I been spared when all my colleagues are gone? Is there a message for us here?'

Alexander Brandel had never heard Rabbi Solomon rant like this. Why? The weeping was becoming universal. People were remembering glistening candlesticks and tables bending beneath the weight of food. People remembered the faces with smiles of tenderness and lullabies. Sister ... brother ... lover ... they remembered ...

'Remember the stories of our people!' cried Rabbi Solomon. 'Remember Betar and Masada and Arbel and Jerusalem. Remember the Maccabees and Simon Bar Kochba and Bar Giora and Ben Eliezer! No people upon this earth have fought for their freedom harder than we have. Tonight we are on the eve of another fight. Forgive an old man who told you not to use arms, for he realizes now that the truest obedience to God is the opposition to tyranny!'

The bunker was galvanized. Yes! Yes! Alexander trembled. He has found a great key to all of life – to obey God is to fight the tyrant!

The bony hand lifted Elijah's cup. 'Elijah has drunk our wine tonight. Israel will come!' He chanted a prayer of the ages, and the bunker trembled.

And then it was silent once more.

'Let us begin the seder,' he said. 'Let us begin our feast of liberation.'

The youngest fighter in Joint Jewish Forces, an eleven-year-old runner named Benjamin, opened the Hagada to ask the questions.

He asked, 'Why is this night different from all other nights of the year?'

And Rabbi Solomon answered firm and unwavering, 'This night is different because we celebrate the most important moment in the history of our people. On this night we celebrate their going forth in triumph from slavery into freedom.'

The Fighters in the Franciskanska bunker were tired and dreamy. Wolf and a squad of his people had just finished planting the 'kasha bowl' mine in the middle of the Brushmaker's Gate and returned in time to conduct a symbolic seder. After the seder, the not-yet-twenty-year-old commander announced a great treat.

When he had captured the Brushmaker's he had found a case of schnapps in the office of Krebs, the disposed overseer. Wolf had hidden it for just such an occasion. Almost all of the eighty Fighters at Franciskanska had no knowledge of liquor, only passing forays with wine and vodka. It was not long before they were all suffused with a lovely, peaceful glow. Wolf, cross-legged on the earthen floor of the main room, began the song fest, playing his accordion. A squad of Communists attached to his command insisted upon singing Russian folk songs hailing victories of the proletariat. Wolf had to show impartiality to his command. He played for them and what they lacked in numbers, they made up in vigor. The Zionists answered with songs of how the pioneers in Palestine had redeemed eroded land. They played and they sang until they were hoarse, and then they hummed nostalgically. Wolf's accordion was very beaten up and wheezed along with great effort.

The guard changed. Everyone was at peace. The phone rang.

Wolf retreated to his small three-by-six 'office.' He lifted the receiver. 'Haifa. Chess Master speaking.'

'This is Atlas at Jerusalem. Is the "kasha bowl" in place?'

'Yes, sir.'

A pause at the end of the line. 'Chess Master, the Angel has just returned from Canaan. Blue boys are all around the walls of Jericho. We expect the Rhine Maidens to come at dawn. Change the alert from blue to gray. *Shalom.*'

'*Shalom.*'

Wolf hung up. They were crowded about his office. Eighty pairs of eyes on him. 'Runners. Change the alert to gray. Polish Blue Police have the ghetto surrounded. We anticipate the Germans at dawn.'

As the runners scampered off to warn the satellite bunkers, the stunned soldiers continued to stare at him. Wolf nonchalantly shrugged, picked up his accordion again, and began to play.

'Havenu shalom aleichem!
Havenu shalom aleichem!
Ve-nu ve-nu
Shalom aleichem!'

And with a snappy hora he got everyone to clap in rhythm and he passed around the last four bottles of the schnapps he had been hoarding. When the shock had passed, they became mellow again and dreamy. Wolf set down the accordion.

'We'd better get some sleep. We want to be wide awake for our house guests.'

He walked around the bunker, quietly checking last-minute details, giving looks and smiles of encouragement. In one part of the bunker he had to kneel, for he was too tall to stand straight.

The fighters were dozing off one by one. Only emergency candles at the exits. It was still . . . Those awake were at least fighting the battle within them in silence.

Being commander had its small compensations. Wolf had his own private cubbyhole off the main bunker and a sacking curtain over it. It was large enough to contain a table for the phone, a chair, and a bed of straw.

Rachael's rifle was propped against the wall. She unloosened her hair and let it fall. Wolf knelt in the straw, then squirmed his way close to her. With a free hand he snuffed out the candle. They had learned to lie together so tightly that when either spoke only the other could hear.

'I'm so proud,' Rachael said. 'You are so brave.'

Wolf didn't answer. He felt icy. He crushed even more tightly against her.

'Don't worry, Wolf. You will get us through. Everyone trusts you . . . Did you see the way they all calmed down after being so frightened?'

Even in their room, privacy was limited. At any instant a messenger could poke a flashlight in. She carefully unbuttoned her blouse enough to draw his head against her breast, and she wrapped him in her arms and soothed him. As a commander, he never showed fear before his Fighters. But now, alone with her, he was cold and he trembled and it was she who was not afraid. Wolf would get up in the morning and lead them to their positions as though he had not a care in the world. Her fingers stroked his hair and his face . . .

'I'm scared,' he said.

'Shhh . . . shhh . . . shhh . . .'

Chapter Fourteen

Five o'clock. The first light of day. The only movement, a snowfall of feathers cascading from the roofs.

Andrei wiggled up to his forward observation point and through binoculars scanned the intersection. His four companies were well concealed. Less than half of them were armed. Cardinal rule: take guns from the enemy or from a fallen comrade. Distant sounds beyond the wall. Andrei took a borscht bomb-fire bottle from his jacket and shook it to wet the wick. It would be the signal to open fire if the Germans came into his area.

Andrei heard movement behind him. he looked over his shoulder. A figure moved in his direction. Andrei put the binoculars on the figure. 'Dammit! What's he doing here!' he muttered as Alexander Brandel, on hands and knees, muffler straggling, crawled toward him.

'Who told you to leave the bunker?' Andrei snorted as Alex came alongside him.

'Since I have become a man of violence, I was certain you would not deny me the pleasure of this moment.'

'Get down below.'

'Please let me stay, Andrei.'

'Write your journal.'

'It's up to date.'

'Shhh . . . here they come.'

'I don't hear anything.'

'Well . . . it's too late to send you down. Stay close to me and keep quiet.'

Andrei signaled to his people, then strained to hear.
'I don't see them,' Alex whispered.
'Shhh . . . shhh.'
Clump! Clump! Clump! Clump!
Andrei looked around for a return signal. A blue flag waved in a window on Zamenhof Street. 'They're coming down Gensia Street between the factory compounds. I hope Wolf lets them pass.'
Clump! Clump! Clump! Clump!
Andrei fixed the binoculars at the intersection of Gensia and Zamenhof, site of the abandoned Jewish Civil Authority building. The first of the black-helmeted, black-uniformed troops appeared. Stutze was leading them. They would be under the guns of Ana Grinspan's company now. He signaled over the roof to hold fire, guessing they would come up Zamenhof into the central area.
'Halt!' The command broke the silence.
'Daggers ready!' The Nazi knives were unsheathed.
'Parade march!'
Clump, clump, clump, clump, they goose-stepped up Zamenhof Street.
'Look at those arrogant syphilitic whores,' Andrei hissed. 'All bunched up like a rat pack, goose-stepping. We'll scatter them, eh, Alex?'
Clump! Clump! Clump! Clump!
Andrei handed Alex the binoculars. He pushed his glasses up to his forehead and focused on the black waves of uniforms filling the width of Zamenhof Street, pouring around the corner at them in row after row. Alex felt a knotting of his stomach. he wished he had stayed in the bunker. Andrei was more concerned with the discipline of his troops. So far no one had moved or made a sound.
On they came around the corner of Gensia. The line of Nazis stretched for a block, and still they came.
'Sing!'
A thousand hairy hands thrust a thousand daggers skyward. Clump, clump, clump, clump, they goose-stepped.

'When Jewish blood is squirting from our
daggers!
Only then the Fatherland will be free,
When Jewish corpses rot and putrefy,
We'll glory in Hitler's victory.'

Clump! Clump! Clump! Clump!
Their voices and their boots grew louder, and the marrow of the Jews was chilled.

'When Jewish blood squirts from our
daggers!
It shall make us doubly glad,
When Jewish skulls are stacked to the sky,
Good Germans shall not be sad.'

'Halt!'
The massed Reinhard Corps stopped at the intersection of Zamenhof and

Mila streets. Sieghold Stutze called his officers together and huddled over a map and discussed the first phase of the operation. They stood directly below Andrei and Alexander. The Reinhard Corps was in the gun sights of the four companies of Jews awaiting the signal.

Andrei took out a pack of matches. He began to light the bottle but stopped. 'I am a sentimentalist, Alex. I believe in historic justice. Have you ever lit one of these bottles?'

'Me? God in heaven, no.'

'I hereby commission you to signal the uprising,' Andrei said, thrusting the bottle into Alex's hand.

Alex merely stared at it. 'Well ... what do I do?'

'Light the wick and throw the bottle down on the street.'

'Light ... and throw ...'

'Yes, it's very simple. You're bound to hit one of those syphilitic whores. But hurry, before they disperse.'

Alex licked his lips. The challenge was too tempting, the honor too great. 'I'll try,' he said shakily. He carefully placed the bottle flat and struck a match. The wind blew it out.

He struck another and tried to touch the flame to the wick hurriedly, and the wind blew that one out too.

'Come along, Alex. Men of violence must act deliberately.'

Alex struck a third match and sheltered the flame by cupping his hands, but his hands trembled so violently that he could not steady it on the wick.

He gave up. 'We all battle in our own ways. I can't do it.'

'Try once more,' Andrei said.

Alex clenched his teeth, fired with determination, and struck the match. Andrei held his wrists, steadying his hands like a kindly father, and the flame touched the wick. It fizzed.

'Throw it!'

Alex flung it over the edge like a hot rock and it spiraled down to the street.

Whommmmmmm! Plow! Fzzzzzzzztttt!

The bottle smashed on the helmet of an SS man and erupted!

'Yaaaaaaahhhh!' the human torch screamed. The ranks around him split apart and became transfixed on him as he twitched and kicked and rolled in the streets, being consumed by fire. 'Yaaaahhhh! Yahhh! Yaaaaaaahhhhh!'

They all looked up to the roofs simultaneously.

Blam! Blam! Blam! Blam!

Blue flames spurted from hidden rifles and pistols, behind windows, doorways, the roofs.

Wissshhhh! Whoom! blew the fire bombs.

Sieghold Stutze's eyes looked upward as Jewish guns vomited into their midst, spewing three years of pent-up rage. 'Hans!' Stutze shrieked. 'Look! A woman is firing!' He pitched forward on his face as a bullet tore at his chest. He crawled on his knees. The earth rumbled with deafening shocks of grenades. Nuts and bolts blew apart Sieghold Stutze's stomach. He clutched at his guts spilling into the street. A fire bomb fell at his feet and whisshed up his boots, and he groveled and screamed and gagged and died. Human torches and bullet- and grenade-riddled Germans turned the intersection into a pond of carnage.

Oberführer Alfred Funk soaked luxuriously in a deep warm sudsy tub and sniffed the rising scented steam. The tones of Wagner's *Tannhäuser* 'Overture' crashed in from the phonograph in the living room. Between low points in the crescendo Funk could hear the sound of gunfire from the ghetto. He hummed in tune. 'Da dam dam dam.'

His orderly lay a tray containing his shaving gear on the rim of the tub. Funk sharpened the razor, looking up with disdain at the orderly, who never did it properly. He flicked his thumb over the edge and was satisfied. 'Dum de dum dum,' he sang, 'dum de dum dum dum dum dum . . . de da da da,' as he lathered his face.

'Hold the mirror still,' he snapped.

'*Ja*, Herr Oberführer.'

Horst von Epp appeared in the doorway, bleary-eyed, wearing a dressing gown over his pajamas. Funk looked contemptuously at him and snorted. 'What gets you up at this hour of the morning?'

'You'd better drink this,' Horst said, thrusting the glass of schnapps forward.

Funk screwed up his face. 'At six o'clock in the morning? Never. Dum de dumm. Da da da.' He stretched his skin so the razor could bite off the stiff chin hairs.

Horst took the mirror out of the orderly's hand. 'Alfred, put the razor down. You're liable to cut your throat after what I tell you.'

Funk merely glowered.

'The Reinhard Corps has been massacred. Your men have been thrown out of the ghetto.'

'Damn you, Horst! This is the last of your nonsense I am going to tolerate!' He lifted the razor to resume shaving.

Horst lowered Funk's hand slowly. 'We have succeeded very well in drawing their fire. A hundred SS men have been killed. At least that number wounded. Our forces have fled beyond the wall.'

Funk blinked in disbelief, then smiled weakly. 'There must be a mistake. Those are Jews in there.'

'I have prepared a press release that it wasn't Jews but that we discovered gangs of Polish bandits hiding in the ghetto and have gone in to clean them out. The gunfire was not from Jews but from the bandits, et cetera, et cetera, et cetera.'

'Jews? Jews threw the Reinhard Corps from the ghetto? Jews?'

'Jews,' Von Epp answered.

Funk threw over the tray and slushed to his feet, half slipping. He leaped from the tub and ran into the living room. A bloody, trembling officer stood before him.

'Untersturmführer Dolfuss,' he said, snapping his heels before the naked, dripping general.

'Speak, God damn you!'

'We were caught in a terrible cross fire.'

'Where!'

The confused lieutenant tried to find Zamenhof and Mila streets on the table map filled with pretty colored pins. Funk's orderly threw a large towel over his master.

'What the good officer is attempting to say, Alfred . . . it was here,' Von Epp said.

'So,' he snarled. 'So. They want the taste of the whip.' He lifted the phone.

'Get me field headquarters . . . Hello . . . Oberführer Funk here. Send the tank officer to my suite immediately.'

Noon.

Six medium panzer tanks rumbled through the Swientojerska Gate and hugged the wall as they proceeded toward Zamenhof Street and into the central area. Their cannons and machine guns pointed at the buildings.

Their motors set up a din, and their weight caused the street and the buildings to tremble.

The Fighters of Ana Grinspan's company became frozen with fear at the sight on the street. What could one do with pistols? The panzers passed under the muzzles of ineffective guns and turned into Zamenhof Street.

The gun turrets swung menacingly and aimed at the upper stories of the buildings on both sides of them. Gunners peered through the slits, looking at the lifeless, motionless windows and roofs. Now where was this army of the Jews? Now let them fire!

Andrei tried to think as the tanks rumbled toward his area. If they blasted his people to cover or if his people cowered, the Germans would own the ghetto immediately. But how to stop tanks? For an instant an agonizing thought tantalized him. Perhaps we are cowards. Perhaps all the fight was gone from us after the first ambush.

As the tank rolled over the intersection of Kupiecka Street a lone figure darted out into the street so quickly that the German gunners could not train their guns on it. The figure ran directly in front of the lead tank.

Andrei watched the single Jewish Fighter attack the panzer. The Fighter's cap fell off, revealing a long head of flaming red hair. It was a girl! With the tank almost on top of her, she jammed a pipe grenade into its treads. The tank rolled on the grenade and exploded it. With a resounding shudder the tread unsnapped and lashed from its moorings and the tank spun around, helpless. The redheaded girl was crushed.

Fighters watching on both sides turned the panzers into iron coffins. As from the tops of ravines, they rained down a hailstorm of borscht bottles. The tanks spun crazily, firing wildly at the enemy they could not see, trying to wipe the pricks of fire from their steel skins, but the rain of bottles increased. The tanks became engulfed in flame and turned into infernos. Fighters crept up close to make their hits more certain.

One by one the hatches were thrown open and gagging, blinded, burned Germans stumbled out onto the streets, to be raked by cross fire.

Dusk.

The German corpses were stripped of uniforms and guns and ammunition and stacked at the curbstones as Jewish corpses had once been stacked in the ghetto.

The tanks were silent and smoldering and wrecked.

The streets became quiet again.

Tolek Alterman was the first up from Mila 18. He shouted at the top of his lungs, 'The Germans have quit! The Germans have quit! Condition green!'

'Condition green!' a voice echoed.

Hand signals . . . runners flashed from block to block.

'Hello, Haifa. The Germans have quit the ghetto! Condition green!'

'Beersheba! Condition green!'

The cries of joy and whoops bounced from building to building.

A Fighter appeared in the street, running up and down, calling the all-clear.

They poured out of the buildings and threw arms about each other and skipped and somersaulted and hugged each other and cried and shouted and wept for joy.

In a few moments hora rings were dancing in the middle of the street and civilians cringing from the sounds of battle came up one by one in shock and amazement and kissed the Fighters.

Andrei and the other commanders were tolerant of the breakdown in discipline. Nothing could dim the exultation of those who had waited three years for this moment of triumph.

Gabriela Rak heard the voice of Alexander Brandel on her radio, as did all of Warsaw. 'Fellow Poles. Today, April 19, 1943, we have struck a blow for freedom as the first to rebel againstNazi tyranny. By ejecting the Nazi butchers from the ghetto, the Joint Jewish Forces tonight hold the only piece of Jewish sovereign Polish territory. In the past we have begged you to join us, and we beg you again. The Germans are murdering Polish citizens at a staggering rate in the gas chambers at Auschwitz. They intend to reduce Poland to a slave-labor pool by murdering more than half its citizens. No matter what our differences have been, the struggle for survival is mutual. Join us. Help us destroy the tyrant!'

In Warsaw, things were rather gay. For a while there was concern over the noise and shooting from the ghetto, but the newspapers quickly explained that bandit gangs were hiding there and the Germans had begun action to get them out. The Germans confessed to a half dozen or so casualties, but the noise was certainly nothing to get excited about. As for this repeated broadcast from a clandestine radio – well, it was typical Jewish exaggeration and really, who cared, anyhow?

Chapter Fifteen

The weary Fighters of Joint Forces slept deeply with delicious dreams of their victory. It was a victory largely belonging to a single girl who threw herself beneath a tank at the right moment to galvanize them into action, but she had done it and they had won the day. Tomorrow or the tomorrow after they would be asked to do the same as the redheaded girl, but tonight it did not matter. Victory is a balm. Alexander Brandel, a man of violence, celebrated longer and harder than anyone. He said he had two thousand years of defeats to make up for.

While the rabble army slept, their commanders worked far into the night on more practical matters than celebrations. They assessed the day. It had been a good day mostly. Only six of the twenty-two battle groups had been committed to action. Casualties from stray bullets were nominal. They had captured sixty rifles and pistols from fallen German soldiers. They had administered a wicked defeat to the best of Hitler's Elite.

Yet the balance sheet added up to a minus based on one simple fact. Joint Fighters had expended more ammunition than they could replace. There would not be many more victories like today's. It was a war of diminishing returns. A rather sober judgment said they'd shoot themselves out of business quickly. The victory broadcast from the ghetto failed to stir the population or the Home Army. A dozen Polish youths tried to get into the ghetto to help but were shot for their effort.

Tomorrow ... another day. The commanders guessed that the Germans would go for the factories. Here was the largest pool of Jews in the most vulnerable place and the most difficult to defend.

Simon shifted two companies under Andrei to help Wolf at Brushmaker's. Ana took her company from the central area and Tolek brought three groups down to Rodel at the uniform complex.

They argued till dawn. Simon and Andrei demanded that Wolf remove the kasha-bowl land mine. The Germans surely would not dare march through the gates in close formation again after the lesson of the first day. Wolf reckoned differently. He was certain they had not learned or would not admit respect for the Jewish fighting force. Wolf filibustered until it was too late to replant the mine.

The second morning.

Andrei and Wolf lay side by side in a second-story window which looked down at Brushmaker's main gate. The plunger to set off the kasha bowl was at Wolf's hand. He trusted no one else with the mine ignition switch.

Half of Wolf's Fighters crouched inside the main factory buildings behind barricades placed there for the protection of the workers. Their position was vulnerable, for they had to meet a German attack head on. The second half, along with Andrei's two companies, were scattered in a ring around the Brushmaker's in order to hit the Germans from the rear. The gamble was completely upon the guess that the Germans would make a try for Brushmaker's.

Ten o'clock in the morning.

'What's holding them up?' Wolf wondered.

'Confusion. They're making their plans outside this time,' Andrei said. 'Germans can't improvise too well. They must fix their plans.'

Wolf patted the handle of the plunger. 'We'll unfix them.'

'A waste. They'll never come in through the main gate.'

'We'll see.'

At eleven o'clock runners reached them with the word that the Germans had concentrated a large force in the Krasinski Gardens. Eden had anticipated properly. The Germans were out to snip off the northeastern corner of the ghetto containing the Brushmaker's complex.

By eleven-fifteen runners reported movements outside the wall along Bonifraterska Street and opposite Muranowska Street. A ring of soldiers on the entire sector.

'Hello, Jerusalem. This is Haifa. Troop concentration to cut off Brushmaker's. They'll be entering at any moment.'

'This is Jerusalem. I have two companies ready to move at their backs if you need them.'

'Hold them.'

The Germans entered the ghetto in three places: the two Swientojerska gates opposite the gardens and at the Przebieg Gate touching Muranowski Place.

They strung out quickly on Nalewki Street from the gardens for two blocks to Muranowski Place. The Brushmaker's compound was completely cut off. Its eastern boundary was the ghetto wall along Bonifraterska Street.

'They've a positive talent for walking into traps,' Andrei said. The Revisionists were also on top and behind the Germans. Andrei dispatched a runner to Ben Horin to hold fire.

Now deployed, the Germans moved toward the main gate. A company down Gensia Street, a company up Walowa set to converge.

Opposite the main gate, the Germans took cover near the buildings. A loudspeaker unit was set up.

'*Juden 'raus!* Jews come out!'

Five minutes passed. There was no movement from inside the factory. Fixed bayonets, battle ready, the Germans edged for the main gate.

'See?' Andrei snorted. 'I told you they wouldn't march in.'

'Wait.'

With caution a squad poked inside the gate. A courtyard of forty meters of open space awaited them before they could reach the main building. They edged into the courtyard unmolested, but squarely in the sights of the barricaded fighters inside.

A second squad of Germans followed into the courtyard. They fired blindly into the main building. Glass shattered, brick chipped away, bullets echoed. No fire was returned. They fired again and again. No return.

A third squad entered and set up a machine gun pointing at the main building, and the other two deployed to give cover to the main German force.

'I'll be goddamned!' Andrei said as he watched a German battalion mass to march in.

The protection squads gave an all-clear signal.

Clump! Clump! Clump! Clump!

Trawniki SS unsheathed their daggers and marched at the gate. The first line passed over the kasha bowl ... the second ... the third.

Andrei licked his lips and looked at the ignition plunger. Wolf's hands toyed with it.

'Now ... now,' Andrei said.

'Just a few, few more,' Wolf said. 'Just ... a ... few ...' His hand thrust the plunger down.

Warsaw bounced from the impact.

Blood and sinew and muscle and shrieks soared skyward. Nuts and bolts erupted like an angry volcano. Disintegrated bits of a hundred Germans floated back to earth. The near living, the half living whimpered with shock, and the neatly deployed living were terrified.

The three German squads in the courtyard were met with a barrage from the factory, but the land mine had already thrown them into disarray.

From the rooftops Samson Ben Horin's Revisionists – Chayal, Jabotinski, and Trumpeldor – poured a murderous fire at the backs of the Germans stretched out along Nalewki Street.

It was a rout!

Fighters from Andrei's and Wolf's commands tore into the streets at the fleeing enemy with a vengeance. Confused Germans guarding the ghetto gates fired into their own troops pouring out. Other Germans tried to leap the ghetto walls. Their hands were sliced to ribbons on the cemented broken glass, their bodies tangled in the barbed wire.

Wolf's judgment on the planting of the kasha bowl was confirmed.

Chapter Sixteen

Journal Entry

THE THIRD DAY

Today we administered to the Germans their most humiliating defeat of our infant rebellion. I shall describe it.

The Reinhard Corps who survived the first day and Ukrainians, Litts, Latts, and Estonians assembled at their parade ground off 101 Zelazna Street and crossed and marched along the wall along Leszno Street, apparently to enter at Tlomatskie Gate. Rodel has been anticipating such a move against the uniform factory. The Germans moved in the former 'Polish corridor,' a slot between two sets of walls. Rodel's Fighters had rounded up twenty ladders. With the Germans singing and marching in the 'protected' corridor, they rushed the ladders against the wall, climbed, and pelted pipe grenades down on the Germans. The enemy never even got into the ghetto!

Later in the afternoon Germans poured through four gates behind heavy machine-gun and mortar barrages. Our strategy: let them in. Their protective barrage must lift quickly after their troops penetrate. Then we hit them from the rear. All four times we drove them out.

Two events to hearten us! The first Russian bombers passed overhead for an air raid (on Germany, we hoped). We cheered them wildly!

Tonight the Germans admit on the radio broadcasts that the 'Polish bandits' have been joined by Jewish gangs (perverts, subhumans, nun rapists, etc., etc.). This admission that they are fighting *Jews is bound to have an impact on the people.*

THE FOURTH DAY

Our friends arrived at dawn. This time they neither sang nor marched in formation. They moved in dispersed, heavily, armed formations. After artillery, mortars, and machine guns drove us to cover, they came in slowly. They crept along in the shadows of the building. We no longer suffer from fright. It is they who show fear. We allow them to get deep into the ghetto, and then we hit them with cross fires at intersections, hurl fire bombs and grenades down from the roofs, shout at them in German to confuse them, jump them from the rear.

Today they concentrated on the uniform factory. We estimate they used a thousand troops to seal it off. Rodel's forces harassed them unmercifully, but they managed to get a few hundred workers out. Frantic for a victory, they blew up a hospital near Pawiak Prison. All but the bed patients had long been evacuated.

THE FOURTH NIGHT

Banks of floodlights in tall buildings over the wall lit up large sections of the ghetto.

Their troops moved in to continue with a night attack on the uniform factory. Simon and Andrei have spoken of this possibility (night action) for some time. Simon tried our most daring foray. Broken into three groups, our people dressed in German uniforms taken from the factory and trimmed (leather belts, helmets, even decorations) from fallen enemy. Group 1 was led by Andrei, Group 2 by Simon, and Group 3 by Tolek Alterman. Our 'Germans' merely marched out of the ghetto. The enemy mistook us. We got them completely off guard. Simon's group attacked the floodlights and artillery. They wrecked twenty floodlights and five cannons. Tolek's group raided the arsenal at SS barracks, captured a machine gun and twenty rifles and several thousand rounds of ammunition (desperately needed).

Group 3, Androfski split into two parts. Part one raided the central market and 'confiscated' three trucks loaded with food. The second unit raided the Citadel Hospital for medical supplies.

We know we have reached our high-water mark. We cannot use German uniforms at night again, as they will undoubtedly think of using a password to prevent future occurrences. (Further testimony to their respect for us as a fighting force.) Nevertheless, we can continue to confuse them in the day by sudden attacks, wearing their uniforms.

THE FIFTH DAY

We took inventory. Ammunition is very, very low. Schlosberg has manufactured four more smaller versions of the kasha bowl. We have planted them at key intersections, hoping for the best.

Simon called in all commanders and called for less concentrated fire on the enemy and more 'individual improvisation.' Translated, this means more acts of individual heroism.

Our Fighters responded today with incredible acts of courage. A tank blew up on one of the planted mines on Nowolipki, but another tank and armored car were stopped literally barehanded. A Fighter from Rodel's command leaped on the tank, threw open the hatch, and hurled a bottle inside! The armored car was stopped by Fighters leaping on it from a second-story window with grenades in their hands.

The Germans sense we are running short of ammunition. They are pressing us harder. Thank God they have not been able to replace the floodlights we destroyed. Tonight the ghetto was dark. Our fighters need sleep desperately.

THE SIXTH DAY

Incredible acts of heroism continue to save the day. Wolf's command reports the following:

Two Fighters without guns leaped on a German squad with knives; killed two, three fled. They took the weapons.

Rachael Bronski was caught by a squad of Germans as she tended a wounded Fighter. She reached inside her skirt and flung a hidden grenade at them.

In the central area, Andrei tells me that his people are making the Germans fight house by house, room by room. We start at the ground floor and make the Germans pursue us up, step by step, to the roof. We hurl bombs and grenades on them and we continue to fight clear up to the roof. The Germans quit. They will not come on the roofs.

From Rodel's command: Saul Sugarman, an old-time Bundist, was badly wounded. He refused to die until he crawled back to his bunker and gave his rifle to his brother.

Simon has called for hit and run only when we are behind the Germans; not to meet them head on. We don't have the ammunition. We should adjust our positions so that we can retreat and lead them into the dead ends to use our bottle bombs with the most effect.

The Germans have managed to unearth a few bunkers of civilians. They have been marched out of the ghetto. I hear that Boris Presser and his family were taken to the Umschlagplatz today. Well? What can one say? Has there ever been a doubt of Jewish courage? I suppose we all have wrestled with that. Andrei confided to me that it crossed his mind on the first day when he saw the six tanks come up Zamenhof Street. I hope these past six days answer that question forever. Sacrifice is commonplace. Not a single Fighter has surrendered.

THE SIXTH NIGHT

Still no replacement for the destroyed floodlights. The Germans press in on night patrols to keep us from sleeping. We butchered them.

Our Fighters shout in the darkness and the Germans fire blindly at our voices, revealing their positions and their fear.

A report from the Aryan side tells us that Funk asked for SS Volunteers for night patrols and no one volunteered!

The report also says that the Polish people are awed by our fight. To hell with awe! Less awe and more help is what we need.

As I write this I realize that tomorrow begins the seventh day of the rebellion. The four days' work Alfred Funk promised the Death's-Head Brigade has proved false. This week we have prayed for will come to pass. God! Will we get help!

THE SEVENTH DAY

Simon Eden spoke to his commanders before dawn. We are to drop back to even more desperate tactics. We are to stay in hiding until the German is so close we can smell his breath, count the hairs on his head. Attack by knife, leap on him barehanded, and choke him to death. Fire only at point-blank range. We cannot afford the luxury of missing a single round. We cannot make a bad throw of a single grenade. We must constantly shift our positions at night to alternate bunkers. Finally, a further cut in rations. Water: one glass per day per Fighter.

Today the Germans finally cleaned out the uniform factory. Rodel's people did not have the fire power to stop them. We had managed to take most of the laborers from the Brushmaker's factory into buildings and bunkers.

The bunkers are becoming unbearable. Mila 18 has four hundred people (*capacity 220*)*. It is only an iota above suffocation level. The thermometer today read 140 degrees.*

THE SEVENTH NIGHT

The Germans have had enough of the ghetto in the dark. We own the night. We are the kings of darkness? *They do not come in here out of sheer cowardice and fear. Like college boys making drunken vows, we have fulfilled our 'goal' of holding the ghetto for a week. Israel reborn has lived for seven days under fire. Ridiculous, isn't it. We are perilously low on ammunition. Food and water are not going to improve. We cannot replace a fired round of ammunition. We cannot replace a killed Fighter. Our wounded die quietly with no complaints about the little aid we can give them. But I am ashamed of my past cynicism. I have never seen morale so high. I have never been so proud to be a Jew. At night we walk tall and straight as free men. We sing and we dance. We tell jokes about our hunger and we laugh about our fear. Strange, so very strange, how a hopeless cause can be the cause of the most exhilarating experience I have ever known* (*forgive me, Sylvia*).

ALEXANDER BRANDEL

Chapter Seventeen

Simon Eden was chagrined. A week was over and his army was still intact and full of fight. Simon, who had dreaded the burden of command, had reacted to a hundred cries without hesitation. When in doubt, he personally led his troops on foray after foray. He had become transformed into a symbol of leadership.

The week's end called for a reappraisal. His Fighters no longer had the luxury of concentrating gunfire. This meant that the Germans could cut off and fine-comb surrounded areas with a determined effort. No longer able to protect the civilians in the southern area, Simon ordered Rodel to abandon a suicidal position and pull his Fighters into the central area.

Wolf was ordered to cut and destroy the phone line between Mila 18 and the Franciskanska bunker despite the fact that runners often needed hours to negotiate a few blocks during the daytime. There was too great a risk of the Germans finding the phone line and using it to lead them into the bunkers.

A new standing order: all Fighters were to scour for food and water during the night in bunkers which the Germans had discovered during the day.

In his favor was his continued night control of the ghetto, plus the fact that the Germans gave up using tanks and armored cars. And Andrei Androfski, his workhorse, his nonpareil warrior. The sight of Andrei nearby never failed to calm him.

Simon worked throughout each night, having developed a remarkable facility to sleep in short snatches. Rodel came to Mila 18, to the first floor, where Simon stayed during the night to escape the heat of the bunker.

Rodel reported that all his Fighters were moved and deployed in the central area.

'Good. Get some sleep,' Simon said. 'It's four o'clock in the morning.'

'I wanted to talk to you about something else. I hear rumors that Samson Ben Horin is taking the Revisionists out of the ghetto.'

'That's right,' Simon answered. 'I'm going to see him now.'

'Take me with you.'

'Why? You and Ben Horin haven't passed a civil word to each other for five years.'

'They've no right to leave!' Rodel roared.

This was what Simon had expected of the hotheaded Communist. No matter how many times a man must come to a decision, there is no immunity to the shock of a new decision. This was the most difficult he had faced the entire week.

'The Revisionists are not obligated to our command,' Simon answered softly.

'But they do have a duty.'

'What is their duty, Rodel? Glorious death? They've fought well. We've all done what we set out to do. We can no longer protect civilians – you know that.'

'But each day we can hold out, our monument grows higher. With the

Revisionists here we can buy time. A day ... two ...'

Simon did not know how to answer. 'I've thought about this moment long and hard. There is a line which we cross when it is no longer our duty to die but to live. Each man has his line set in a different place. I cannot command what a man must choose for himself.'

'All right then, but you don't have to help them by approval. Simon, think! You're setting a dangerous precedent. Others may decide to go.'

'Yes ... I know ...'

The rendezvous with Samson Ben Horin was held at Nalewki 37 in a lantern-lit room. It would be daylight in two hours. Samson's neatly trimmed beard was in straggly disarray, and his hollow features made his weariness more pronounced.

'Did you bring me a map of the sewers?'

Simon spread it on the table. 'Do you still plan to try it before dawn?'

'Yes. It shouldn't take more than an hour to reach the Vistula. They'll have a barge waiting for us.'

'I don't want to interfere, but you're taking your people right under the heart of Warsaw by staying in the main line. It's dangerous. I seriously suggest that you consider using smaller cross lines ... here ... here ... here ...' he said, pointing. 'This way you come out a few miles north in Zoliborz.'

'We can't change plans now. They'll be waiting for us.'

'Delay it for a day. Recontact your people on the outside and set up a safer route.'

Samson hemmed and hawed, then sprang from his seat. He had thought of a safer route, but it would cost him twenty-four hours. 'It's a greater risk to stay,' he said. 'We don't think we can hold for another day.'

Simon showed no reaction to the shock he felt. 'Do you have a compass?'

'Yes.'

He penciled in the route. 'It's almost perfectly straight. Watch for barbed wire here. Tides won't be too bad. Hold hands, keep conversation down. Be careful with lights.'

Samson Ben Horin studied the map for several moments, then folded it and put it in his breast pocket. Simon arose. 'I've got to get back to my bunker,' he said. 'We have a meeting scheduled in ten minutes. Our German friends are bringing up another battalion of artillery.'

'Thanks for everything, Simon. Listen, I want you to know. What I mean to say is ... this is a group decision to leave.'

'No explanation is necessary.'

'It's not as if we are running away.'

'No one has accused you of that.'

'Simon, when the ghetto was started we had five hundred people in Warsaw. There are fifty-two of us left. I want you to know that I personally voted to remain. But ... as their leader, I am obliged to take them out to the forests.'

'I figured it was that way.'

'Eleven of my people have decided to remain with you. We have also voted to leave you half our guns and eighty per cent of our ammunition. You'll find it all in our bunker.'

He extended his hand. Simon shook it. Samson Ben Horin, a rebel among rebels, headed quickly for his bunker.

* * *

In ten minutes the forty-one remaining Revisionists were in the main sewer line under Gensia Street. They passed near Wolf's Franciskanska bunker, under the Brushmaker's compound, and they were beneath the wall. Every ten yards Samson flicked on his flashlight for a two-second bearing. A chain, hand to hand, moved silently.

The light found the barbed-wire trap.

Five men with wire cutters bit their pliers into the barrier and worked it apart slowly.

Samson peered at his watch. It was going too slowly. It would be light in fifty minutes. 'Hurry,' he whispered.

'It's very thick.'

'Hurry!'

They grunted as their rusty instruments tried to break the wire. Samson flashed his light again. They were only a third of the way through. He pushed past the wire-cutting team and with his hands squeezed the accordions flat. The barbs tore his flesh in a dozen places, but he batted at the wire until there was a partial clearance. They slugged through. The wire ripped their flesh and their clothing and they were bloodied and in pain.

Overhead, a Polish Blue policeman patrolling the area was drawn to the manhole by foreign sounds. He knelt and lay his ear against the manhole, then darted off to the Citadel gate only a block away, where the Wehrmacht had a camp.

'There are people in the *Kanal*. I'm sure of it. I could hear them grunting.'

The last of the Revisionists passed the entanglement. Their bloody legs were washed with sewage. The manhole cover behind them clunked open. A blasting light probed in. German voices! The Revisionists flattened against the slimy side of the bricks, just out of reach of the beams.

'See? Some of the wires have been cut!'

'Get a ladder!'

Samson was dizzy. Simon's warning about going through an arterial flashed through his mind. Trapped in a black fetid coffin. Oh God! He could feel the tremors of fear running up and down the line. Stay? Fight when they come into the sewer after us? Run back to the ghetto? Bolt for the river?

'Let's go, we can't stay here!' He pushed on down Franciskanska Street, slushing as fast as his feet could hold in the slime and muck. Samson wanted to flash his light to study the map and find a small connecting *Kanal*, but there was no time to stop. Two mains converged. Freta Street. Large intersection. We are halfway there. The sewage ran swiftly.

Behind them they could hear the Germans lowering a ladder and they could see a crisscross of lights searching for them.

'We have to change our course,' Samson said.

'No.'

'Yes, I say. Up Freta Street.'

'No. We won't make the river.'

'Come on. Up Freta Street!'

'Samson!' someone shrieked at the end of the line.

'Samson! Poison gas!'

Samson turned on his flashlight and saw the billows of smoke rolling at them.

There! A built-in iron ladder leading up to the street! Coughing, screaming at the end of the line! Samson climbed the ladder and put his shoulder against the manhole and shoved the lid off. He poked his head out, then squirted onto the street. Two, three, four, five, six, seven, they fled after him.

Blinding lights!

Red streaks of tracer bullets from an arc of German machine gunners shot them down. Some scampered back to the sewer and were shot down the hole into the poison gas. And then, after a few more shattering screams as the gas converged from four directions, it was still.

The long-sought German breakthrough came just before dawn on the eighth day with the destruction of the Revisionists whose attempt to break down a main *Kanal* proved as foolhardy as Simon had feared.

On the eighth day the Germans roared into the ghetto, inspired by the victory. It had had a strange reaction on the Jewish Fighters. It brought them a full and final realization that there was no escape, that the fight would have to be fought to the very end on this ground. The Jews turned savage, hurling themselves into German ranks as living grenades and torches. Cornered, out of ammunition, they fought with rocks and clubs and bare hands.

Each step the Germans took into the central area, they paid more heavily. The Jews were on top of them, behind them, beneath them, and they fought like maniacs.

On the eighth day they drove the Germans out.

The calculated concealment of news of the uprising burst apart. The word rolled over the length and breadth of Poland.

Jews have rebelled in the Warsaw ghetto!

Jews have been holding against onslaught after onslaught for over a week!

Tales of the fanatical Jewish courage dribbled out. The myth of Jewish cowardice was burst.

Berlin was shocked.

Jews fighting, routing the Elite Corps! It was catastrophic, a humiliation as bad a propaganda defeat as Stalingrad was a military defeat.

On the ninth day Funk mounted his most furious assault, using six thousand troops, and at the end of the ninth day he received his officers, who babbled stories of yet another defeat.

'Herr Oberführer, they strike like phantoms!'

'And you strike like cowards,' Funk shouted. 'You disgrace the SS, the Fatherland. You disgrace the Führer, Adolf Hitler.'

Funk threw them all out except Horst von Epp. He loathed the man personally but had to rely on him more and more in the past days. Von Epp could make up the most magnificent excuses.

Funk sat at his desk to write his report. Six hundred Jews had been taken out of the ghetto on this, the ninth day. In all, only eight thousand removed in ten days and most of them from the uniform factory. There were still over thirty thousand of them hidden, and it was getting more difficult to locate them each day. At this rate it could take forever. His promise of four days to liquidate the ghetto was haunting him like a joke – Göring's promise that no bomb would drop on Germany. He could sense the disdain of the officers. No, they would not dare replace him, for that would be admission that the Jews had defeated the SS.

Horst concentrated heavily on which woman to bring in for a weekend. Alfred Funk wrote his daily report. The report was concise and boasted of progress which had not been made and exaggerated enemy strength and expanded the myth of a large army of Polish bandits helping the Jews. Crisp, dull, military. Copies to Police General Kruger in Krakow, to Globocnik in Lublin, and to Himmler. Ultra-secret.

Horst walked over to him in a turmoil between a redhead and a blonde and lifted the report and scanned it. 'Have you ever heard of the Ass of Balaam, Alfred?'

'The what of what?'

'The Ass of Balaam in the Bible.'

'Of course not.'

'The Ass of Balaam attempts to curse the sons of Israel and ends up praising them. I think the Americans call it a left-handed compliment.'

'Must you always talk in riddles?'

'Look at these phrases in your report. You refer to the "enemy." Since when do we admit the Jews are a military enemy? And here – "Jewish disregard for death and the unshakable decision to resist" – why don't you recommend we decorate them with Iron Crosses?'

Funk took the report and tore it in half. 'I'll do it over.'

'They tell me it's like a nightmare in there,' Von Epp said.

'I don't understand this at all. Most of these troops have performed well on the eastern front . . . I simply don't understand it.' Horst's mind was back on the women. Alfred Funk's was not. 'We have to get them off the roofs,' he said. 'Must get them down on the ground . . .'

The phone rang. Funk answered. He turned sallow and clapped his hand over the mouthpiece. 'Himmler calling from Berlin.' Alfred Funk lifted his latest reports and read passages, spoke of German devotion and courage, gave assurances. Then he became quiet and listened and listened. His shading turned to crimson and then to gray. He placed the receiver on the hook very, very slowly.

'News of this insurrection has spread all over Europe. Hitler has been in a rage all day.'

Horst von Epp's hand clutched his throat unconsciously.

'Damn! Damn!' Funk walked to the window in a violent anger. 'Damn their filthy Jew souls!'

He whirled to Horst. His face was a mask of evil. Von Epp was frightened.

'What are you going to do, Alfred?'

'I'll get these filthy animals down from the roof. I shall burn the ghetto to the ground!'

Chapter Eighteen

'Heinkel bombers!' cried the Fighters on the roofs.

The German airplanes swooped in at a height of two hundred feet over the Brushmaker's and slowed their speed. Tons of black bombs fell from their opened wombs on the crush of buildings. They hurled down, tore through the roofs, splattered on the streets, ignited.

The incendiaries smoldered and their groping flames licked around for fuel. The wood spurted into sudden fire and roared up the stair wells to the roofs.

'The ghetto is burning!'

The Heinkels zoomed in on a second and a third pass. There was nothing to shoot back and deter their 'drill' with human targets. Palls of smoke billowed and spiraled heavenward and flames leaped on the roofs, turning them into frying pans. Glass windows exploded and scattered on the streets, and orange-and-red fingers of flame leaped violently through the windows.

A scorched runner spilled into the bunker at Mila 18, holding his blackened hands, and another with wild eyes came in, and another. All of them had the same story.

'We have to abandon the roofs.'

The ghetto burned crisply, concisely, and helplessly, for there was not so much as a single drop of water to stop the conflagration. Fire, a hungry beast, devoured all that would succumb and relentlessly searched for more.

Warsaw's fire brigades surrounded the ghetto with power hoses ready. Orders: keep the flames locked in on the Jews. Occasionally an angry spark would leap the wall and ignite on the Aryan side. These fires beyond the wall were quickly stamped out. Not a single drop of water went into the ghetto.

At the end of the tenth day of the uprising the northern quarter of the ghetto was in flames.

On the tenth night the new artillery battalions went to work. They poured five thousand rounds of artillery fire from the mouths of their cannons over the wall at point-blank range. Debris flew in the wake of the shell fire. Walls that refused to fall to fire were blasted apart.

Blam! Blam! Blam! Blam! bellowed the German guns.

The earth shook and windows rattled and the muzzles flashed lightning and no one slept in Warsaw.

Blam! Blam! Blam! Blam! they reached out at the silhouettes outlined in the fire. Blam! Blam! Blam! Blam! until daylight.

And then the Heinkels came back and showered more coals into the inferno, and the fire raced from house to house, leaped over intersections, block to block. The tightly packed poor Stawki area raged, and the fire raced down Zamenhof, up Niska, along Mila, along Nalewki, devoured the Brushmaker's complex.

Immense belches of violently twisting columns of smoke streamed skyward and turned into yellow-black clouds and blocked the sun and turned day into night. Showers of soot rained down thickly, covering the city with a snowfall of ashes. Everything was an ugly disintegrating gray.

One by one Simon called his groups down from the roof. The very key to their defences were burned from under them. Fighters whom the Germans had been unable to force down were driven out by the ever-probing, darting flames.

The wall of fire billowed down Zamenhof and encircled and ate the Civil Authority building and ran down Gensia, once a commercial artery of Warsaw, and the Pawiak Prison erupted like an immense torch.

Easter Sunday!

The mighty organ of the cathedral bellowed a tribute to the resurrection of the Son of God. The confines of the cathedral and of every church in Warsaw were overrun with pious who knelt, crossed, prayed, Hailed Mary, dipped holy water. Choir boys with shiny faces sang out to the glory of the Lord in falsetto voices.

The flames from the ghetto warmed them and caused the pious to perspire profusely, but they pretended no discomfort, for this was a joyous time.

'Hail Mary, full of grace ... Mother of God ...'

Gabriela Rak knelt in the last row of the mighty tabernacle. She had wept until she had no more tears. A coughing broke out in the cathedral as a wind shift sent gusts of smoke from the ghetto racing down to the altar.

Gabriela looked up at the bleeding, limp Christ. The archbishop chanted prayers rapidly in Latin.

'Oh my God,' Gabriela whispered to herself. 'My hatred for these people around me knows no bounds. Help me, God. Help me not to hate them ... help me not to hate ... please let my children live. My child must live, but I am afraid because of my hatred. O Jesus ... how can you do this to your own people?'

Gabriela knelt alone after the cathedral was empty.

It was a bad day for an Easter Sunday. The gardens and the Vistula River and the places where one celebrates the resurrection and the coming of spring were simply unbearable because of the damned fire inside the ghetto. Soot poured down on their clothing, and it was humid and dark. A perfectly wonderful day was being ruined.

'O Jesus, Jesus, Jesus. Why are you making them suffer?' Gabriela moaned. 'Help me, help me. Help me not to hate.'

In deference to the holy day, the fire brigade poured their water jets over the ghetto wall to keep the Convert's Church from falling to the flames as they reached the southern boundary.

Easter night.

Fires lit the sky from the Convert's Church on the south to Muranowski Place on the north; from the cemetery on the west to the Brushmaker's on the east. All of the ghetto blazed.

Horst von Epp stood transfixed before his window and watched. A naked oil-covered girl lolled on the bed behind him. He was drunk as he had never been drunk. He hung onto the curtain.

'Fire is fascinating,' the girl observed.

'That is no fire. That is hell. That is hell the way the devil meant it to be!'

'Horst, be a good boy. Close the curtain and come to bed.'

'Hell!' He poured a drink sloppily. It ran over the edge of his glass and down his arm. 'I salute our thousand-year empire! See it! See it! We shall live in fires like that for a thousand years! We are cursed!'

He turned and looked at the girl wildly. 'Cursed, damned ...' The shadows of the flames crisscrossed her body.

'You frighten me,' she whimpered.

'Get out, you slut!'

Inferno! Inferno! Inferno!

Large beams devoured by the fire plunged from the roofs through floors. Choking, gagging, blinded Jews scrambled dazed into the streets and walked in helpless circles. Jews hurled their children from the windows and then themselves. Jews were crushed and buried under collapsing walls.

On the thirteenth night of the rebellion the artillery began again to make up for its one-day Easter holiday.

Jews were charred into unrecognizable smoldering corpses.

Jews were roasted in bunkers which were turned into coffins by wind shifts and downdrafts.

Jews were choked to death in clouds of smoke which crushed their lungs.

Jews leaped from their hiding places into the sewers and were boiled to death in bubbling, sizzling waters.

On the fifteenth day the ghetto burned.

On the sixteenth day the ghetto burned.

On the seventeenth day it burned. Pillars of smoke continued to reach for the sky, and for miles in every direction it was black. Undraped skeletons defiantly remained standing.

Searchlights picked out the dissenters and the guns rankled and the walls fell.

Because of the extreme depth of Mila 18, it had been spared direct contact with the fire. But the bunker was a continued scene of the epitome of agony. Heat reached 170 degrees. Naked people collapsed atop each other in exhaustion. The Treblinka room, the central area hospital, was loaded with groaning, charred ruins of human beings. Many were burned beyond recognition. Deborah Bronski and the other nurses had no salve for their wounds and but a drop of water for their parched lips. Day and night they begged to be put to death to escape their misery, but not even a bullet could be spared for that.

And when they died they were taken through the Majdanek room, the children's part of the bunker connected to the sewer. Their bodies were floated out in the sewer to make room for more near death to be brought down from the inferno above.

His voice grew weaker and weaker, but day and night Rabbi Solomon wailed in a stupor the chant 'Eli, Eli.'

> 'My God, my God, why hast Thou forsaken me?'
> In fire and flame our race did they burn,
> With shame our masses brand.
> Yet none turned away from Thee.
> Not from Thee, My God, nor Thy Torah . . .

On the nineteenth day nearly everything that could be burned had burned. Now was a time for smoldering. Iron beams sizzled out their stored-up heat. Pavements could not be walked on. The boiling sewers ran cool again.

And when the sizzling slowed on the twentieth day, the Germans returned to probe the enemy strength, hoping that their work had been complete.

But most of the Fighters lived and throughout their agony begged to see the face of the enemy once more. Rodel and ten of his people moved behind the broken walls, searching out bunkers of Fighters, when the Germans came in.

He hid his men in a rubble pile as a patrol advanced toward him along Lubecka Street.

The Germans moved cautiously, fearfully, hopefully expecting every Jew would be gone.

An officer pointed to his sub-machine gunner to check the rubble pile on his right.

Rodel had a quick decision to make. The Germans had twenty men spread on the street. His people did not have the equipment to attack them. Yet the soldier would surely discover them if he kept coming. Rodel tightened his fat lips and felt his pistol. His eyes became glued to the soldier's weapon. A lovely sub-machine gun, and then he saw the soldier's water canteen.

The German had almost reached Rodel's group.

'Stay under cover,' Rodel ordered, and in the same instant leaped out of the rubble.

'Jew!' screamed the startled German in his last word. Rodel's knife slit him in half. He snatched the sub-machine gun, jerked off the ammunition belt, and drew the German patrol away from his own Fighters.

'After him!'

The Waffen SS fired.

Rodel dropped back into the skeleton of a building. Half its walls had fallen away, exposing the stairway up to the top floor, which was still burning. He crouched and let go a burst which scattered them and he began to climb the exposed stairs. Half of the twenty Germans raced in after him, and the second half stayed in the street and fired into the denuded building.

Up one flight, up two. He crouched and shot down on his pursuers.

His own Fighters used that moment to make their escape.

Rodel came to the top floor. The rooms were burning. He retreated to a dead end. Fire lapped all around him. The Germans came up the steps and forced him to break ground with a grenade lobbed at his feet. He reeled back, his machine pistol spewing defiantly. Curses poured from his mouth. The fire caught his shirt and flared up his back. He snarled and moved into his tormentors and fired, and they began retreating down the stairs, awed by his rage.

A human torch spit at them from a landing. His gun went empty. He pulled his pistol out and fired.

A German bullet struck him, two, three. He staggered and crashed out of the building, flaming down to the sidewalk, and his body smashed on the pavement. With broken bones protruding from his body, he kept crawling toward the Germans on the street and firing his pistol.

On the twentieth day the Germans returned with sound detectors, engineers, and dogs. Thirst-crazed fighters leaped at them with vengeance, but the tide of war had turned unalterably.

While the ghetto burned, Oberführer Funk meticulously planned the block-by-block extermination of what remained of the ghetto. With military efficiency the Germans set up barricades over a block and then took it apart house by house, room by room. They were able to unearth one bunker after another and find people cowering in the rubble. Once a bunker was located, the engineers moved in efficiently and set dynamite charges in them. The blasts were followed up by teams of flame throwers, and finally the last of the 'experts' pumped poison gas in.

Manhole covers were thrown open and poison gas filled the sewers. They were flooded to the height of the pipes. Soon the putrid waters were clogged with corpses entangled in the barbed-wire traps.

On the twenty-first and twenty-second days, bunkers fell by the dozens. Still the pesky, arrogant Jewish Fighters continued their attacks. The Germans detested running into the Fighters because it called for a struggle to the death.

By the twenty-third day a hundred and fifty bunkers had been methodically located.

A new tactic was tried.

Five-gallon cans of drinking water and freshly baked bread were set up by the Germans at intersections to lure the starved, thirst-crazed survivors into the open. Once a child was captured, he was tortured before his mother to reveal the location of a bunker. The bestial dogs forced their share of confessions.

Fifteen thousand near dead were uncovered and marched to the Umschlagplatz by the end of the twenty-third day.

On the twenty-fourth day the Germans were certain they had won the hardest battles and it was now a downhill fight. During the night Andrei Androfski, whose job was to reorganize the Joint Fighters after each day, pulled together two hundred sixteen fighters and the entire stock of firearms and waited for the enemy. Fighting out of rubble, they audaciously threw the Germans out of the ghetto in a series of ambushes, captured the planted food and water, and crashed through the Gensia Gate into the Aryan side, where they raided a small arsenal and threw the arms over the wall to their waiting comrades. They had captured enough food, ammunition, and water to sustain them for another angry gasp.

Sylvia Brandel was killed in this action, trying to tend a fallen Fighter.

So great was Oberführer Funk's frustration, he shot one of his officers to death in a rage.

'German patrol overhead.'

Mila 18 went into a familiar pattern of silence. Deborah Bronski kept the remaining twenty children quiet. The Fighters did not breathe. The wounded prayed silently, daring not to shriek out their pain.

An hour passed ... two ...

The Germans still hovered over them, pressing in to find the elusive headquarters of the Joint Fighters.

On the third hour Rabbi Solomon began to weep prayers. Simon Eden nearly choked him to death to silence him.

Overhead, dogs sniffed up and down Mila Street; sound detectors begged to hear a cough, a cry.

At the end of the third hour the tension became unbearable. Heat added to the stillness. One by one they pitched forward in dead faints. Christopher de Monti yanked Deborah's hair to keep her awake.

And then a cry!

Simon and Andrei and Tolek Alterman pistol-whipped the weepers into silence before a mass outbreak of hysteria.

Five hours ... six ...

The utter collapse as the Germans left the street.

Journal Entry

Tomorrow our battle goes into its twenty-fifth day. I want death to take me. I cannot stand more of it. Till yesterday I managed, but now Sylvia is gone and Moses is close to death. What has he had? What has he had?

Our boys and girls still fight fiercely. The enemy cannot claim the ghetto. I will die with pride. There is only one thing I wish now. Christopher de Monti must be taken out of the ghetto. He alone knows where the entire works of the Good Fellowship Club are buried. We cannot risk keeping him here any longer. I have not prayed in synagogue since I have been a boy. I have taken a position of convenience by calling myself an agnostic. I therefore did not have to submit to the hypocrisy of dogma, but on the other hand it spares me from exposing myself by saying I am an atheist and do not believe in God. Yes, a true position of convenience. Now I ask God to prove Himself. I beg him to let Christopher de Monti live so that this history will not die.

ALEXANDER BRANDEL

Chapter Nineteen

Andrei rolled his tongue over his gritty teeth and peered out from behind the rubble pile. Muranowski Place before him was lit up with arc lights. It looked like day. Andrei thought, this night life is killing me. There was no chance of getting into the bunker from the Muranowski entrance. The square had at least two companies of Germans in it. He scratched his beard. Got to remind Simon to trim my beard tomorrow. I looked like hell in the mirror. Come to think of it, I owe Simon a trim too.

Andrei patted the Schmeisser, 'Gaby,' and sized up the opposition. He had only one clip of twenty bullets and a grenade. Poor Gaby, Andrei said to himself. I can't keep you clean any more. I'm all out of oil. Your pretty little sights are all rusted. Sorry, Gaby, we simply can't take on a hundred of these whores by ourselves.

Well, they're not moving, Gaby, so we'd better move, because I'm tired. I'd love to brush my teeth again before I die.

Each night since the beginning of the rebellion Andrei made a round of the Joint Fighters' positions and reset them with orders for the next day. After the Germans were driven out of the ghetto in the first days the job was not too difficult. He could travel walking upright with runners at his side. During the fires it was nightmarish. Leaping flames, crumbling walls, and those damned artillery shells.

Now the communications between bunkers was all but broken. Two days ago he carried an order from Simon that each group was independent to act and improvise against the conditions in the immediate area. Each commander was responsible for forming his own hit-and-run attacks and, even more urgent, finding the food and ammunition and medical supplies to continue the fight.

Each night Andrei left Mila 18 to regroup the diminishing army. The Germans were getting bolder and bolder. Their night patrols increased. It took Andrei almost all night to find his scattered people, although their area was becoming smaller and smaller. Caution every damned step of the way. The Germans owned the southern end of the ghetto. Now at Muranowski Place they had a foothold in the north. On arterials like Zamenhof and Gensia, they dug in with permanent positions.

Joint Fighters shrank their area. Two bunkers holding half the force formed the extreme boundaries. At one end was Mila 18 and at the other end Wolf Brandel in the Franciskanska bunker.

Between these two bunkers the balance of the Joint Fighters had an interlacing network of a dozen smaller bunkers and two hundred people.

Ana's company pulled back into Franciskanska. Tolek Alterman was sent out of Mila 18 to take over Rodel's command of the small bunkers on the northern fringe.

Tonight Andrei pulled them in tighter again.

A month was coming to an end. It was a miracle, but over half the Joint Fighters were alive and armed. They had captured enough to sustain the rebellion into a second month!

'Filthy whores,' Andrei grunted, realizing the Germans had a permanent hold in Muranowski Place. His mind ventured the thought of a hit-and-run attack on them tomorrow night. He was very weary. He slid out of his hiding place and crept over the rubble piles down Nalewki Street through a puzzle of broken walls. He prowled with the deftness of a large cat playing with shadows and sped in his search to find one of Mila 18's six entrances out of sight of the enemy.

The entrance from Muranowski Place was out of the question. The drainage pipe on Nalewki 39 was too close to German activity to try. He went for the third entrance in what had been a courtyard in the rear of a house on Kupiecka Street, which had a tunnel connecting to an air-raid shelter. Andrei peered out from the wreckage at the shelter. It looked clear, then he narrowed his eyes.

Something out there ...

Andrei's eyes could penetrate the darkness with the sharpness of the large cat he was when he moved in the night. He saw the outlines of German helmets. They were in an emplacement of some kind past the courtyard and they were facing Mila Street with their backs to him.

Andrei calculated the odds. If he ran for the air-raid shelter and its tunnel entrance, there was every chance he would make it without being sighted. But any risk involving German discovery of Mila 18 had to be avoided.

His choice was to move on to the fourth entrance on Zamenhof Street or the sewers. Neither choice appealed. Zamenhof Street would be filled with the enemy, and the sewers were dangerous. He decided to have a closer look at the German emplacement.

Andrei slithered on his belly over the courtyard and crept up behind the enemy. Andrei observed what seemed to be a squad of six men fixed in an emplacement which looked over part of Mila Street from behind a barricade of fallen bricks.

He studied the area around them. On their left, a fallen building. On their right, a partially standing building. Andrei calculated that if he could reach the half-ruined structure he could get over the top of them, but any movement beyond his present position would be detected.

He felt about for a brick and threw it to the left. It skittered over the rubble.

'What was that!'

The Germans turned a machine gun on it.

Rat-a-tat! Rat-a-tat!

Andrei sprinted in the opposite direction. He made a flying belly flop in the ruined structure and began to climb up while the Germans continued to be occupied with the decoy.

'Stop your fire. It is only falling rubble,' someone ordered.

'Yes. Don't be so nervous.'

The Germans laughed jumpily.

Andrei was above them now. He inched up so he could count the helmets.

Four . . . five, six. Bastards! Whores! They had set up a machine gun to cover part of Mila Street as a permanent emplacement. Filthy whores! Andrei squinted. Regular army, Wehrmacht. Good, they were less willing to die bravely than the SS. It was a stupid position. What audacity to put up this gun without flanking cover, he thought. Well . . . I shall have to give them a lesson on how to be soldiers. Too bad they shall not be around afterward to benefit. Look at the fools, all clustered up as if they were at a Hitler rally. How lovely.

Andrei unhooked the hand grenade from his belt, placed the handle in his teeth, and with his free hands slipped his clip of ammunition into the machine pistol. Now, Gaby, don't you be a naughty girl and jam on me.

He calculated his moves. I'll have to hit them very fast. Unfortunately my grenade will ruin their machine gun. I must throw at the fat one and go for the three on the right with my machine pistol. Remember, Andrei . . . first I go for their pistols and the privates with their rifles. Then I yank off their ammunition belts, then their water. One, two, three, four; pistols, rifles, ammo, water. He looked back over his shoulder to the air-raid shelter. A twenty-five-yard dash back. Won't have more than a half minute to do the job. Okay . . . ready . . .

He pulled the pin from the grenade, steadied the machine pistol, and counted . . . one . . . two . . . three . . . and lobbed the pineapple down on the fat soldier on the left.

Startled shrieks! A flash! Men held ripped faces!

Andrei counted . . . one . . . two . . . three . . . four . . . while the bits of the grenade spent their wrath, and he leaped.

Straight down, fifteen feet, into the writhing Germans. Gaby spit a blue flame at the three soldiers on the right side of the machine gun, and they were still. The gun jammed before he could turn it on the other three.

One lay groaning under the gun, and a second leaped wounded into Mila Street, screaming, 'Jews! Jews! Help! Help!'

The last soldier was knocked against the wall. He crawled to his feet. Andrei pulled the trigger of his weapon. It was jammed. He hit it with his fist, but it was stuck tight. The soldier jerked his pistol out of his holster. Andrei flung his weapon at the helmetless redheaded enemy, and the barrel cracked against his skull and caused him to fire wild. Andrei's fist smashed the German's mouth and shattered his jaw. A kick in the groin, and he sank to his knees, and Andrei brought the flat of his hand on the German's neck and broke it with a loud pop.

He was dead.

The wounded soldier crawled for a pistol. Andrei's boot smashed into his jaw and he too was still. Half a minute gone. Hurry! Pistols, rifles, ammo, water . . . Where's that goddamned rifle? Can't find it.

The sounds of boots converging from both ends of Mila Street. Andrei tried to turn the machine gun on them, but the grenade had wrecked it.

He leaped out of the wrecked emplacement and scampered into the air-raid shelter and into the secret entrance to Mila 18.

'Where in the hell have you been?' Simon Eden greeted him with relief and anger.

Andrei shrugged. 'It's slow moving up there.'

Then Simon saw the guns and belts and water canteens draped over Andrei. 'What happened?'

'Nothing much. Just routine.' Andrei treated himself to a couple of swallows of water, took enough ammunition to fill three clips, and turned the rest over to Simon, grumbling that he wished he could find some oil to lubricate the Schmeisser.

After seeing Deborah to tell her Rachael was all right, he saw Alex to report that Wolf was fine, then went upstairs with Simon to a small closetlike room which they felt was safe during the night hours, and there they rehashed their diminishing position. Over three hundred Fighters remained, but the circle of bunkers was shrinking. There was enough food and water to hold out for another five or six days. Ammo? One sharp encounter and they would be depleted. What to do when the ammo was gone? Dig deeper and hide? Suicide? No thought of surrender. Attempt escape or fight bare-handed.

'Maybe Moritz Katz will come in with ammunition,' Simon said, hoping beyond hope.

Andrei yawned. 'Moritz will do it if anyone can.'

'If he brings in a couple of hundred rounds, I want you to make a raid on the Przebieg Gate. There's a field kitchen and some loose arms supplying the troops in Muranowski Place.'

Andrei stretched out on the floor. 'Przebieg Gate ... good idea. Holy Mother, I've got to get some sleep. Tomorrow you have to clip my beard. I'm a mess. Wake me up at daybreak.'

It seemed to Andrei that he had no more than closed his eyes when he felt a sharp slap across the soles of his boots. He and his machine pistol awoke at the same instant. Simon was over him. His finger slid off the trigger. 'What ... hell ... Simon ... it isn't daybreak yet.'

Then he rubbed the thick cakes of sleep out of his eyes and saw Alexander Brandel next to Simon. Andrei propped up on an elbow. 'What's wrong?'

'Moritz and two of the smugglers got captured very close to the Kupiecka entrance to the bunker. They were taken away alive.'

Andrei was fully awake in a second. 'We'd better start moving the Fighters to some of Tolek's bunkers.'

'Can't,' Simon answered. 'Mila Street is crawling with Germans. Movement is impossible. We've been lying frozen all night. I'm afraid hysteria is going to break out down there any minute.'

'De Monti,' Andrei said.

'That's right,' Alex answered. 'We've got to get Chris moved immediately.'

'Have you heard anything from the Aryan side? Any word from Gabriela?'

'No, but we can't wait. The Germans are all but breathing on Mila 18. I want you to take Chris over to Wolf's bunker. We'll try to reach the Aryan side to set up an emergency hiding place for him.'

'What time is it?'

'Almost five o'clock.'

'It's going to be a tricky business getting him over there in daylight.'

'I think we're out of extra chances, Andrei.'

Andrei nodded.

'Get him over there and get back here.'

Andrei was already on his feet.

Chris and Deborah stood in the tunnel exit through the Auschwitz room which led to Nalewki Street. Farther down the tunnel Andrei probed about to make certain there were no Germans near the entrance. Chris tucked his pistol into his belt and flicked the flashlight a couple of times and knelt and tightened the rags wrapped around his feet which would assure greater silence in their movements. And then there was nothing left to check and he was forced to search for Deborah's face in the half darkness.

'It's so terribly, terribly strange' – his voice trembled – 'how do you wait for a moment and dread it. You dread it every living moment of the day and night. Now it is here. Somehow I'm almost glad – it's almost better to bear the agony than live with the tension.'

'I've always known,' Deborah said, her fingers feeling for his face and tracing the contours of his lips and chin. 'I've known you'd be able to do it, Chris.'

'Oh God, Deborah ... help me ... help me ...'

'I've always known you'd be able to make the right decision. Chris ... you must ...'

Then all she could hear were deep futile sighs. 'My anger against them is nearly as great as my love for you. All day and all night I've memorized the places where the journals are buried. I'll be tormented until I can unearth them and hold them up for the world to see. I'll never rest, Deborah ... it's like a brand seared on my soul.'

They felt a closeness of each other and were softly holding each other.

'Thanks for everything,' Chris said.

'Thanks for ... life,' she whispered.

They could hear the shuffle of Andrei's rag-covered boots coming toward them and they seized each other desperately. Andrei cleared his throat.

Deborah gasped and spun out of Chris's arms and bit her hand hard. Chris grabbed her from behind and she sagged and writhed to keep from breaking down.

'We have to go,' Andrei said sternly.

Chris still held her. 'Go,' she cried, 'please go!'

'Christ!' Chris wailed.

'We have to go,' Andrei repeated. He took Chris's arms from Deborah and she plunged out of the tunnel into the Auschwitz room of the bunker. Chris started after her, but Andrei grabbed him and his hold was like a vise.

'Steady, Chris.'

Chris collapsed and buried his head in Andrei's chest. 'Steady ... steady,' Akdrei said as he dragged the grieving man up toward the entrance.

It was turning light outside. They poked their heads out of the drainage pipe in the Nalewki 39 courtyard and sprinted to cover. Around them, fires continued to sizzle. They could hear a rumble of trucks assembling in Muranowski Place.

Andrei gestured that they had to move along under cover to the intersection of Nalewki and Gensia, a single block. They were almost completely hidden by the few walls, shell holes, immense rubble piles.

At the intersection they were in for trouble. It was a main cross street which ran parallel to the ruins of the Brushmaker's and was filled with patrols and movement. It would be hell to get across the street without being seen.

Andrei crept along a few feet, signaled Chris to follow, crept another few feet, signaled Chris again.

They inched along for fifty yards. It took two hours.

Clump! Clump! Clump! Clump!

They lay flat as a company of soldiers passed. The boots seemed to be only inches away from them.

A hundred feet north, the Germans had discovered a bunker of civilians. A little emaciated boy and two girls no more than six years old crawled out of a pile of bricks, holding their hands over their heads. They stood trembling under the guns and bayonets of the German soldiers, who were amused with their find. An officer ordered the children to hold their hands higher so he could properly photograph his 'prisoners.'

Dogs were moved into the area along with sound detectors.

Freeze or go? Andrei did not like his present position. His only cover was out toward Nalewki Street. The Germans were fanning out and would be behind him. He nudged Chris and pointed to a shell hole a few yards away.

Andrei slid up to it cautiously. It was perfect. The bottom was covered with fallen timber, mud, and muck. He plunged down six feet headfirst and Chris made his move in a leap and dive atop him. They squirmed under the charred timbers to cover their bodies. And they lay.

An hour passed. The sounds of activity overhead never faded.

Grrrrrrr! Grrrrrrr!

They heard a dog's claws padding around, sniffing. Andrei opened an eye just a slit.

A dog crouched on the rim of the shell hole. He could see fangs. The animal sniffed and growled.

'What do you see, Schnitzel?' a soldier said.

'Jews down there, Schnitzel boy? I see nothing.'

The animal poked his nose through the boards and sniffed. Chris felt the dog's wet nose against his face. The animal's jaws opened and the teeth pressed close to Chris's throat.

'Schnitzel! Up here, boy!'

'Up here I say!'

The dog backed slowly off the buried bodies. The soldier hooked his leash again and knelt and squinted into the shell hole. He called another soldier.

'Schnitzel smells Jews down there. Do you see anything?'

'No . . . Wait. Is that a hand?'

'Where?'

'In the mud there.'

'Ah yes . . . I see it now.'

'It looks like they are dead.'

'Well, let's make certain. Stand back. I throw a grenade.'

. . . the grenade slowly rolled down the hole.

Andrei lifted his head, snatched the grenade in a lightning motion, and threw it back up.

Blam!

The dog yelped.

'Jews!'

'Move your ass, Chris! Move your ass!'

Chapter Twenty

The Germans were in Mila 18, directly over a bunker, smashing around to find the entrance.

In the dark catacomb the hidden could hear guttural orders being snapped, the clumping of boots, the crashing of axes. Simon Eden slipped from the cot to the floor. The cot creaked too much. It could send up a sound. He propped his back against the dirt wall, and his bleary black-ringed eyes went upward in his head. Alex sat against the wall opposite him, bent double with tension, exhaustion, and grief for his wife. The stunted, lily-pale boy Moses Brandel who had spent most of his life in silence, was silent again.

For five hours the enemy prowled in Mila 18. In this endless agony the hidden tried to make their breathing soundless and their hearts stop, for surely the detectors would catch a sound of life. Alex raised his head long enough to look at his watch. It was three more hours till darkness.

Oh Lord ... what then? Even when darkness comes they would be locked in this, their tomb, their final coffin. Four hundred lungs gasped for the meager ration of air. Four hundred of the damned – numbed, sweaty, half naked, half dead.

The sixty Fighters who remained still had enough anger in their hearts to spoil for the making of a gesture of defiance.

Simon tried to rationalize. It was difficult to do that any more. The sewers were deadly and filled with bloated gassed corpses. There was no door open to them beyond the wall. We are finished, anyhow. Why not take my Fighters up and make a final attack? What would happen to the children and the civilians if we went up? What would happen to them?

Either way, doomsday was at hand. Well, Simon, make the choice, he said to himself. Be baked alive in this catacomb or destroy some of the enemy along with us? So hard to think. So hard. I wish Andrei would get back.

The noise above them stopped. For that instant everyone's heart in the bunker stopped too. They waited ... a moment ... two ... three.

'They're gone,' Alex whispered ever so softly. 'Do you suppose Chris and Andrei got to Wolf?'

Simon didn't hear Alex. His stomach churned with anger. The instant Andrei returned he would split into two forces. He would take one and Andrei the other, and they would throw every last grenade, fire every last shot in a suicide attack. Goddamn Germans! Dirty bastard animals! Dirty bastard animals!

Deborah Bronski slipped into the cell. They learned to speak and hear the other by barely whispering. 'Will I be able to take the children up tonight? They've been lying still for two solid days and nights without speaking. They must have some air ... some water ...'

Simon was detached. Alex and Deborah tried to speak to him, but he was in his own fuzzy world of logistics, trying to organize an attack with knives against cannons.

'Simon, don't do it,' Alex begged. 'Don't do what you're thinking.'

'At least we'll die looking at the sky,' Simon said.

Oberführer Alfred Funk's field headquarters were in the Citadel, a few blocks from the northern gates of the ghetto. His goading obsession for several days had been focused on a blown-up sectional map of the central area filled with markings where sounds had been detected along Mila Street. Trails of underground sounds indicating tunnels, all in the proximity of the middle of the block. He knew it led to the Jews' main bunker. Two entrances had been located. One in an air-raid shelter on Kupiecka Street, the other in a house on Muranowski Place. But he could not attack yet, for there were certain to be three or four more entrances and the Jews could either escape or hide in the other exits.

A large black grease-pencil mark was drawn around the houses from Mila 16 to Mila 22.

Funk walked to the second-story window and looked at his handiwork. Most of the ghetto had been leveled. Engineers were systematically dynamiting the standing buildings one by one to flush out those Jews who had hidden themselves in sub-floors. It had gone well in the last few days. Since the final action more than twenty thousand Jews had been taken to the Umschlagplatz and another five thousand were known dead. How many were burned or gassed? Impossible to tell, but the total indicated that victory over the invisible army of the Jews was at hand. He could not foolishly declare victory until the Mila Street bunker had been found.

Funk was desperate to find it quickly, for soon the rebellion would be in its second month and that would look very, very bad. Polish Home Army activity had been spurred by the Jewish rebellion, and unrest among the occupied countries could be felt as a direct result. He simply had to finish it off before it went over a month's duration.

A knock on the door.

'Enter.'

An eager young Waffen SS officer from Trawniki entered, snapped his heels together, unable to contain his joy. 'Heil Hitler!' Untersturmführer Manfred Plank crackled.

'Heil Hitler,' Funk grunted.

'Herr Oberführer! We are certain we have located another entrance to the main Jew bunker!'

'*Ja?*'

'*Jawohl!*'

Funk showed the man the map. The young officer snapped off his cap and tucked it under his left arm, and his right forefinger shot out and pointed to the location of Nalewki 39. 'Here we have discovered a drainage pipe. It runs in this direction ... so. Along with the tunnel on Muranowski Place and the tunnel on Kupiecka Street, it converges on the same location ... here ...'

'Mila 18.'

'We may also have found the location in Mila 18 itself. A large removable oven on the first floor of the building which still stands is extremely suspicious. We did not wish to take action until we received your personal orders.'

Funk rubbed his hands together eagerly. 'Four possible entrances. Good.'

In a few moments Oberführer Alfred Funk emboldened his troops by another of his personal appearances in the ghetto. Surrounded by two squads of sub-machine-gun-bearing Nazi guards, he marched alongside the exuberant Untersturmführer Plank until they came to a place which had once been a building, now a rubble heap. Manfred Plank showed where the drainage pipe had been uncovered.

'We sent a man twenty meters deep into it. It becomes a tunnel at that point and turns sharply toward Mila 18.'

Funk looked at his watch. Two and a half hours of daylight left.

A staff car at the Przebieg Gate whisked him across town to Shucha Street and Gestapo House. Gunther Sauer was in a foul mood. His dog Fritzie had developed a cataract and was going blind. Moreover, his wife wrote complaining letters about the shortages of butter and meat developing at home.

Now Funk. These SS people were impossible. Himmler's saving grace was his love for animals. Poor Himmler couldn't bear to see a dog hurt. It was confided to him at one of the gassings at Treblinka that he had attended with Himmler. Himmler despised Göring, who was cruel to animals.

Sauer gave Fritzie an affectionate pat on the head and looked up to Alfred Funk in his grandfatherly way.

'I want to see the three Jews from the bunker. The Moritz Katz man and the others.'

'So?'

'We have located three entrances to their precious bunker. Faced with these facts, perhaps they will talk.'

Sauer reached in the drawer and gave the dog a tidbit. 'Can't see them,' he said.

'And why not?'

'They're dead. Tried to break them down. Turned them over to the dogs last night. There, Fritzie ... good boy ... good boy.'

'Simon, come quickly.'

He pushed down the dark corridor. Alex opened the curtain to Rabbi Solomon's cell. The last doctor left in the ghetto knelt over the old man's prostrate body. The rabbi presented little more than a weightless bag of bones. His eyes were opened like a defiant Elijah doing combat with the wicked priests of Jezebel. His bony fingers clutched Torah scrolls.

Simon lifted his body and placed it on the cot and closed Rabbi Solomon's eyes, and he looked inquiringly at the doctor.

'Don't ask me why he died. Old age, lack of air ... grief ... who knows?'

'Last night he told me he would die today,' Alex said.

'And what did he say?' Simon snapped. 'To fight tyrants is to honor God?'

'No ... in fact, he said he wished he were like King David with a young wench to warm his bed.'

Simon spun around and into the corridor. 'Fighters up!' he called. 'We're moving up for an attack!'

'Fighters up!'

'Fighters up!'

A hideous shriek came from the arsenal in the Chelmno room simultaneously with an explosion of the stored munitions.

Jules Schlosberg's body was hurled into the corridor.

'Germans!'

Simon plunged over bodies of confused, frantic civilians into the turn of the corridor. The bunker was in a dark panic. He smashed his way into the

Belzec room, where half of the Fighters were housed. A blinding light probed through the secret entrance from the tunnel up to Kupiecka Street.

'Germans!'

'*Juden 'raus!*' a voice commanded from the other end of the tunnel.

Simon dived over the corridor to the Auschwitz room. Another light penetrated from the tunnel at Muranowski Place.

Mass screaming and wailing and praying and crushing broke loose among the scrambling, aimless ants who battered forth from the tunnels. Simon and the Fighters used pistols and clubs on them to force them back and into silence. He was crushed against a wall. A dozen broke out in the Auschwitz room up the tunnel.

'We surrender,' they cried.

Rat-a-tat! The German machine gun blasted them down.

Simon kicked his way clear and drove into the Majdanek room, where a dozen of his Fighters already blocked the room to keep the children from getting trampled.

Simon handed his flashlight to Deborah and pulled the bricks away which led into the sewer. He poked his head through and flashed the light up and down. There were no Germans, but billows of poison gas floated in from both directions.

With Alex and a dozen Fighters forming a chain across the *Kanal* to Mila 19, Simon and Deborah passed the children out of the room one by one to the old bunker across the *Kanal*. Some of them were swept up by the rushing sewer waters. Others doubled over, gagged and blinded, as the could of gas enveloped them.

Outside Majdanek, frantic people tried to batter past the bayonets of the Fighters to get to the dubious safety of the death-filled sewers.

'Hold your breath, children. Duck under the water! Keep your eyes closed!'

German machine gunners at the head of the entrances shot down the panicked civilians, and then poison gas and lashes of fire from flame throwers ate up what little oxygen was left in Mila 18 and the bunker became a huge gas chamber filled with a screaming, frantic doomed mass.

Chapter Twenty-one

Chris and Andrei froze for the rest of the day in the second floor of a gutted structure from which they could watch the Germans methodically move over the area inch by inch, dragging the dregs of humanity from beneath the ground. The Germans were finding bunkers quickly now. Thirst-maddened people who had to live in silence for days on end broke.

Often at dusk there was a respite as the Germans pulled their forces off the streets and out of the ghetto to give it a working over with artillery, picking out for target practice the diminishing number of skeletons of buildings.

Andrei used this lull to make the final lunge for the Franciskanska bunker.

Andrei always looked forward to seeing Wolf, for there was always an air of frivolity, jokes, songs, poems.

Not this night.

When Chris and Andrei arrived, Wolf and Rachael and Ana were sprawled glassy-eyed on the floor of the big room. Andrei looked around. There were only twenty-odd Fighters present. Everyone seemed only half conscious. There was no greeting for them. There had been no guard at the bunker entrance.

Wolf's head hung between bunched-up knees, and Rachael lay on the floor beside him, her face in his lap. Ana looked up for an instant and half recognized Andrei and sagged again.

'What happened?' Andrei demanded.

No one answered.

Andrei turned to Ana. He didn't like looking at her these days. All the tall fine hard round woman that had once been Ana was gone. She was wasted.

'Ana! What happened!'

Ana sniffled and mumbled incoherently.

'Momma ... Daddy ... Momma ... Daddy ...' wailed a woman Fighter. 'Momma, I'll be with you soon.'

Andrei turned abruptly in all directions. Living dead.

He reached down and jerked Wolf Brandel to his feet. Wolf slumped at the end of Andrei's arms like a rag doll. Andrei shook him. Wolf blinked his eyes.

'Fool's gambit,' he mumbled. 'Fool's gambit ... fool's gambit.'

Andrei's hands let Wolf go, and Wolf fell to the ground again and he lolled on the floor, smacking his lips for water. Rachael groveled for her canteen, turned it over. It was empty. Wolf pulled Rachael to him and propped his back against the wall and looked up at Andrei.

'What the hell do you want?' Wolf said. 'The canteen is empty. We have no ammunition left.' His hand flopped and hit the accordion beside him. 'Even this thing won't work any more.'

'Get on your feet, you son of a bitch,' Andrei bellowed in a tone that shook the bunker. 'Get on your feet! You're a commander of the Jewish Fighters!'

Wolf Brandel was shocked back to life. He dragged himself up and hung laboriously before Andrei Androfski, swaying back and forth ... back and forth.

'Now, what happened?'

Wolf licked his lips. 'Germans ... got close to the bunker ... we all came up. We were committed to fire by a fool who opened up on them. In ten minutes we were out of ammunition ... not a thing left ... so we started throwing stones! Know how well stones stop the German army! Know that, Andrei! Stones! Stones!' Wolf caught his breath and puffed to fill his lungs with air. 'They hit us with mortars and flame throwers. I watched ... I watched while they turned my soldiers into torches and I threw stones at them ...'

'Leave him alone, for Christ sake,' Christopher de Monti demanded.

Andrei kept at Wolf. 'Is this what is left?'

Wolf blinked like a drunkard and looked at his people. Last night seventy-four of them had sat in the bunker and laughed about wanting to take a bath and how the twenty girls could hardly service the men and if only the men had money what fortunes could be made! And they sang about the Galilee until the accordion broke.

Only a few scraggy scarecrows left ...

'Stop it!' Ana screamed. 'Stop it, Andrei!'

Andrei lifted her up and slapped her across the face with a sound that struck everyone in the bunker.

'Stand up, damn you all!' he bellowed unrelentingly. 'Stand up, you bastards.'

One by one they struggled to their feet.

'Now hear me. So long as your lungs breathe, you fight. We move back to Mila 18 and we find weapons.'

Christopher de Monti was paralyzed by Andrei's wrath. Yes, Andrei had the mystic power to take this punch-drunk crowd for yet one more attack.

'Ssshhh ... someone is coming!'

Silence.

Tolek staggered into the bunker. His long hair was caked with innumerable layers of dirt and muck. He looked like a wild hairy ape from another age. His clothing was torn and his head was bloodied from the reopening of an old wound. He wavered to Andrei and jerked his head toward the commander's cell.

Andrei and Tolek were alone in Wolf's room.

'They've got Mila 18,' Tolek said.

'Are you sure!'

'Yes. I am sure.'

Simon! Deborah! Rabbi Solomon! Alex! Andrei covered his face in his hands and bit his lip so hard that blood poured from it and he shook so hard that Tolek grabbed his hair and wrenched it. 'Hold on, Andrei ... hold on ...'

And then things became very, very clear.

'How many Fighters do you have left, Tolek?' he asked softly.

'A hundred thirty-two.'

'There must be twenty or thirty more on the southern boundary,' Andrei said quickly, his mind calculating and making decision upon decision. He fished around the table top for Wolf's duplicate map of the sewer system. He marked in a routing ...

'I'm going back to Mila 18,' he said. 'You stay here. At four o'clock I will have rounded up your people and any survivors around Mila 18. We are going to make a diversionary attack on the western side of the ghetto to draw the Germans away long enough for you to take to the sewers. There is only one thing important now. Christopher de Monti must be saved.'

'I'll go with you to Mila 18,' Tolek said. 'Wolf will take them through the sewers.'

'We've got no time for this nonsense. You'll take them through the sewers!'

Tolek clenched his teeth and nodded in obedience.

'At four o'clock when we make our attack you will break radio slience and send a message to the Aryan side that you will be coming out at Prosta Street.'

Tolek's eyes narrowed.

'Prosta Street! But ... through this course it is over five miles through small connecting pipes! It's impossible. It will take six or seven hours!'

'Every damned fool who tries the sewers obliges the Germans by walking down main lines. These small laterals are your only chance.'

'The Vistula is running high. We'll have to go on our hands and knees in the small pipes. We'll drown.'

Andrei punched Tolek on the shoulder. 'You'll make it, Tolek. Living Zionism, you know.'

Tolek took the map from Andrei. 'I'll try.'

Andrei stepped out to the main room. He collected the half dozen bulletless guns and pistols and strapped them on his back and tucked them into his waist.

'Well,' he said, 'you go to the sewers at four o'clock. Tolek and Wolf will take you through a new route. Have a good trip. See you next year in Jerusalem.'

Wolf and Chris and Rachael stood at the ladder leading out of the Franciskanska bunker, blocking Andrei's way.

'We heard,' Chris said. 'Mila 18 has been attacked. We're going back with you.'

'Uh-uh,' Andrei answered.

'Don't try to stop us,' Chris threatened.

In a single motion Andrei jerked Chris's pistol from his belt and knocked Wolf Brandel flat on his back and shoved his niece sprawling.

'Tolek!' he said, flipping the pistol to him. 'If either of these two move, use the pistol. You have my orders to put one through Wolf's brain. As for Chris, just wing him – but not too seriously, or else he will be a horrible burden dragging through the sewers.'

Chris made an angry pass at Andrei, but Tolek was between them and the cocked pistol was leveled on him. There was no doubt in Chris's mind that Tolek would follow Andrei's orders. He snarled, then backed off.

'Chris ...' Andrei said softly. 'Don't forget where those journals are buried ... will you?'

'I won't forget,' Chris answered hoarsely. 'I won't forget.'

Andrei took two steps up the ladder.

'Uncle Andrei!' Rachael cried.

He stepped down for an instant, and she flung her arms around him and wept.

'It is good,' Andrei said, 'that even in this place we still have tears left for each other and broken hearts. It is good that we are still human. Rachael ... you will go from this place and become a fine woman.'

'Good-by, Uncle Andrei.'

Outside, Andrei wrapped the rags on his feet tightly and began darting over the rubble, playing cat-and-mouse with the crisscrossing searchlights, flopping flat ahead of the hurling bombs. A few things left that would burn seared and sizzled. A wall tottered behind him and crashed, sending flying debris about his head. He groped and stumbled and fell and ran in the holocaust.

In an hour he reached Mila 18.

The Germans were gone. As always, they left a bunker after they had poured gas and gunfire and bullets into it, returning in two or three days to send in their dogs before they dared enter themselves. Andrei climbed down the main entrance from the demolished Mila 18. The poison gas had spent its fury.

He was in the small corridor lined with tiny cells. He was standing on a mass of entwined corpses. His flashlight played over them. He pushed into the commander's cell. It was empty. He found Rabbi Solomon in his cell, still stretched on his cot, a Torah in his waxy hands.

Andrei stepped over the bodies into the main corridor. The Chelmno room with its ammunition stores was a sight of devastation. Bodies were charred, unrecognizable from the explosions of the bottle bombs.

Wait!

Coughs!

Weak ... weak coughs!

Sounds of gagging and gasping from the Majdanek room.

Andrei plunged over the bodies.

'Simon! Deborah! Alex!' his lone voice called in the dark.

His light sped frantically over the bodies in Majdanek. Two or three of them were breathing with the desperation of fish out of water.

'Simon!'

Andrei rolled over the body of his commander. Simon Eden was dead. And then the light fell on the lifeless face of Alexander Brandel holding his infant Moses against his chest.

He turned the corpses over one by one. Fighters who had tried to hold back the civilians. Children ... children ... children ... and the light poked at the bricks removed to the sewer.

'Deborah!'

He knelt behind the body of his sister, who hung half in, half out of the room, stricken down while passing a child through the sewer to the safety of Mila 19. As he touched her she gasped. There was yet life!

'Deborah!'

'Don't ... Don't ...'

'Deborah ... you're alive!'

'Don't ... look at me ... I am blind.'

'Oh God! Deborah ... oh, my sister ... oh, my sister ...' He lifted her in his arms and found a corner and held her and rocked her back and forth and kissed her cheeks.

She coughed and gagged in terrible pain. 'Some children are alive in Mila 19,' she rasped.

'Ssshhh ... don't talk ... don't talk.'

'Chris ... Rachael ... Wolf ...'

'Yes, darling ... yes. They have escaped. They are safe.'

She made a sound of relief and groaned as the sharpness of the gas jabbed her lungs.

'Andrei ... pain ... children in pain. Kill them ... put them out of their misery ...'

'Deborah! Deborah! Deborah!'

'So good ... you holding ... me ... Andrei ... I lost my pill ... please ... give ... me ... one.'

Andrei reached in his breast pocket and took a small cyanide capsule and put it against his sister's parched lips.

'So good ... you holding me ... I was afraid I'd be alone. Andrei ... sing Momma's song ... when we were children ...'

> 'What is the best Sehora?
> My baby ... will ... learn the Torah ...'

Chapter Twenty-two

Gabriela bolted upright in bed, her heart pounding unmercifully. A dream of a chill wind passing through the room was unfounded. She perspired from the clarity of the nightmare. Andrei was a ghost floating over the smoldering rubble of the ghetto. She rolled to one side and squinted to read the luminous dial of the bedside clock. Three forty-five.

She flicked on the radio automatically, as she always did during the waking hours. Perhaps there would be a radio signal from the ghetto transmitter today. There had been none for twenty-six days, since the last time they fetched four children out of the sewers and took them to Father Kornelli. Twenty-six days of silence.

She slipped into a dressing gown and walked out to the fifth-story balcony. Far from the dream of cold, it was warmish out, fighting its way into late spring. Moonlight threw light on the ghetto. She watched for ever so long, just as she had stood and watched for hour after hour during the day. She had taken the new apartment because of its view of the ghetto.

The artillery fire had stopped. Almost nothing remained standing. The moonbeams played on disorganized heaps of brick.

Beep ... beep ... beep ...

A weak sound came from her radio.

She ran into the room.

Beep ... beep ... The signal faded and became drowned in static and re-emerged. Beep ... beep ... beep ... beep.

It stopped.

She sat with bated breath for a repeat. There was no further sound.

Then from the ghetto a sudden crackle of gunfire startled the stillness. She ran once more to the balcony but could see nothing. The gunfire sounds heightened.

Gabriela closed the balcony door, pulled down the black-out curtain, and flicked on the lamp beside the phone stand. She hedged for several moments, hoping that the transmission from the ghetto would be repeated. She lit a cigarette and pulled at it nervously, then with an impulsive spur of decision dialed a number.

A half-sleeping voice answered at the other end of the line.

'Kamek. This is Alena,' Gabriela said.

'Yes?'

'Did you hear it?'

'Yes, but I could not understand it.'

'Neither could I,' Gabriela said. 'What should we do?'

'There is nothing we can do until after curfew. Come over to my place as soon as it turns light.'

Oberführer Funk blinked sleepily over the report. It was almost four o'clock in the morning, yet he wanted it for Kruger, Globocnik, and Himmler, finished and en route by dawn. It was precariously close to the one month marking the uprising. He wanted to give assurances that the bulk of action was over. Any further action was merely the formality of a mop-up. Soon, quite soon, victory could be formally declared.

Four o'clock.

Funk untied his silk night robe.

The sound of gunfire! What the devil! It was not possible. He had ordered the artillery to cease fire at two-thirty and for the patrols to resume their fixed positions.

He tied his robe quickly and started to lift the phone, then let his hand drop. A sudden grip of fear encompassed him. Could it be possible that the Jews were attacking? No . . . it was . . . discovery of another bunker, that was all. Don't let your imagination run wild. Calm . . . calm, now. Another large belt of schnapps and he sat slowly behind his desk again.

The crackling gunfire was sharper now. His hand once more touched the phone, fell from it. He licked his dry lips, sagged in the chair, and waited. The report to Berlin, Lublin, and Krakow lay face up before his eyes.

From: The SS and Police Führer, Warsaw District, Special Actions.
Ref. NO: 1 ab/ST/Gr-1607-Journal No. 663/43 SECRET
Re: Large-scale Ghetto Operation
To: Reichführer Der Schutzstaffel Himmler, Berlin
SS Obergruppenführer, Police General, Krakow
Gruppenführer General Government SS, SD, Lublin

I beg to advise the following information:

1. A total to date of 34,795 Jews and other sub-humans caught for deportation, 7,654 known destroyed in former residential area. Estimate another 11,000 destroyed in bunkers by asphyxiation, flames, etc.

Conclusion:

Except for sporadic resistance from the few remaining Jews and sub-humans, we have succeeded in our mission.

2. Account of reduction of Jewish residential compound.

(a.) 612 bunkers destroyed.

(b.) So-called Jewish residential area is nonexistent. Three buildings remain standing; that is, the Convert's Church, parts of the Pawiak Prison, the *Jewish Civil Authority building* (former post office convenient for us to make immediate on-the-site executions of those we do not desire to transport).

3. Booty captured to date:

(a.) 7 Polish rifles, 1 Russian rifle, 7 German rifles.

(b.) 59 pistols of various calibers.

(c.) Several hundred hand grenades, including Polish and homemade.

(d.) Several hundred incendiary bottles.

(e.) Homemade explosives and infernal machines with fuses.

(f.) A variety of explosives, ammunition of all calibers. (In destroyed bunkers we were not able to capture further booty, which was destroyed. The captured hand grenades were used by us against the bandits.)

Furthermore, I beg to report

1. 1200 used German uniforms (tunics) and 600 pair of used trousers. (Some uniforms were equipped with medals.)

2. Several hundred assorted German helmets.

3. Four million zlotys (from deportees). Fourteen thousand dollars, nine thousand dollars in gold; an undetermined value in gold, rings, watches, jewelry.

I beg to report that today the principal Jew-bandit bunker was located at a place known as Mila 18 and it was summarily destroyed by gas, flame throwers, dynamite, and small-arms fire.

The ruins of the Jewish residential reservation will give us vast amounts of scrap material and used brick which can be salvaged for future building projects.

May I make mention of the valiant SS Waffen and Wehrmacht troops attached to this command whose uncommon devotion in the face of the 'invisible' enemy has brought about this success. They went into the sewers, crawled into bunkers, and otherwise exposed themselves to the gunfire of the enemy. These comrades will not be forgotten.

Under separate cover I recommend the following decorations:

Iron Cross, Second Class – SS Haupsturmführer Zisenis.

Cross of War Merit, Second Class with Swords – SS Untersturmführer Manfred Plank, SS Rottenführer Joseph Blesche.

IT IS MY FIRM OPINION THAT I WILL BE ABLE TO ADVISE YOU OFFICIALLY OF THE FINAL EXTERMINATION OF THE JEWS IN WARSAW WITHIN SEVENTY-TWO HOURS.

Heil Hitler!

Signed:
SS Oberführer Alfred Funk

Certified copy:
(Jesuiter)
SS Sturmbannführer

Horst von Epp entered the room but did not speak. The two of them listened and listened and listened for nearly an hour until the gunfire in the ghetto stopped.

Five o'clock.

The moments before dawn of the second month of the uprising came. Neither Alfred Funk nor Horst von Epp dared lift the telephone. A knock.

'Enter!'

Untersturmführer Manfred Plank, showing the effects of battle, stood wild-eyed before his general. 'Heil Hitler,' he said with somewhat less than his usual vigor.

'Heil Hitler,' Alfred Funk answered.

'What happened out there?' Horst von Epp asked.

It seemed as though Plank's fine young Aryan body would collapse.

'Speak!' ordered Funk.

Plank's lips quivered. 'We were moving into our fixed position at the western end of Niska Street ...'

'Speak!'

'Like ... like ghosts, they leaped out of the ruins on us! They did not fight like human beings ...'

'Speak!' Funk screamed again at the faltering man.

'We were compelled to abandon our positions.'

'Swine!'

'Herr Oberführer!' cried Manfred Plank. 'I have been decorated twice for valor on the eastern front. As a result of my fearless attitude in combat I was sent to SS Waffen training. I tell you, sir . . . I tell you . . . there are supernatural forces in there!'

'Get out,' Funk hissed.

He did not hear the Untersturmführer click his heels and make his squarely conceived exit.

Funk's hands were so slippery with sweat, he could not hold his drink. He took his report promising victory and dropped it in the wastebasket after tearing it to shreds, and he looked up at Horst with dazed puzzlement.

'Even from their graves . . .'

'Tonight we have really lost this battle.'

On his hands and knees, his shoulders rubbing against the top of the pipe, Wolf Brandel crawled first into the sewer pipe that cut diagonally down the eastern end of the ghetto. Rachael, second in line, grabbed his ankle with one hand and followed. Tolek, next in line, took Rachael's ankle and Chris took Tolek's and Ana took Chris's. The chain spread down for the twenty-three who left the bunker after sending the radio signal to the Aryan side.

Eight beeps, a pause, six more beeps. Repeat the message twice. Decoded, it meant: 'Twenty coming through the Prosta Street manhole.'

Ten seconds after Andrei started his diversionary attack in the western ghetto, Wolf and Tolek began their perilous journey.

The lateral pipes connecting to the large ones were slightly more than a yard in diameter, and to move in them one had to crawl laboriously on hands and knees.

Silence – absolute, complete, utter silence – was commanded by the leaders.

They inched into the pitch-blackness while overhead Andrei leaped out at Manfred Plank's SS company and threw the Germans into confusion to draw attention from the evacuees. Andrei had chosen the desperation route carefully. No one was apt to watch the smaller laterals under the ground simply because it was not believed that a human could move for long through them.

They came to Nalewki Street. Their small pipe dumped into the big *Kanal*. Wolf halted the line and sloshed around in the darkness, feeling the walls to find the continuation of the small pipe on the other side. Corpses floated swiftly down and hit against him and knocked his feet from beneath him and he went under in the sewer water. He got to his feet after being swept ten or twenty yards and again slogged upstream to feel for the lateral. An hour passed before his hands found it.

He recrossed the *Kanal* and took Rachael's hand. Hand in hand, the chain crossed the big line and re-entered the lateral on their hands and knees.

For another agonizing hour of step by step, the chain pressed on in measured progress. Their backs were breaking, their knees raw and bloody from the dragging. The stench blinding and numbing.

The pipe ran into the Zamenhof *Kanal*.

Three tortured hours had passed since the beginning.

Again Wolf had to cross alone and grope around from memory.

Another hour passed.

When he had gotten the chain over the Zamenhof *Kanal* the lateral pipe was running high and fast. They crawled on hands and knees, ever southward, with the sewage splashing up to their chins, floating into their eyes and noses and ears and hair.

Six hours later they were under the Convert's Church and the site of the demolished uniform factory ... now under the wall in the 'Polish corridor.'

Along the chain one Fighter after the other fainted. They had to stop long enough to slap them into consciousness and drag them further. Silence could not be broken even when someone pitched flat into the sewage and drowned. The line tightened. There were twenty-two left instead of twenty-three.

Another went under and another.

After they crawled eight hours on hands and knees the pipe widened. They were able to stand bent over. The water running in this direction was only a few feet high. Wolf did not give them a chance to glory in the respite. He drove them on while the chance for making progress was good. The strong dragged the weak to their feet. Pain ... nausea ... numbness ... half sanity ... half life ... they trudged on, on, on through the bilge and filth, until in the ninth hour they had passed out of the ghetto and the 'Polish corridor,' and now they looked for the main *Kanal* which would take them down Zelazna Street.

Somehow in the darkness they had taken a wrong turn and veered back north. Then they splashed around in aimless circles. Wolf stopped them, trying to find his bearings and the main *Kanal*. Without compass, light, conversation, and using only a hazy memory of a few hours' study, he was utterly and completely lost. There was no use pushing on. Three more had fainted, including Ana. Unless he gave them a rest they would all be done in. Wolf crawled back to Tolek and broke the nine-hour silence.

'Rest,' he said.

Rest ... rest ... rest ... the magic word fired back along the line.

They sat in the pipe with the sewage waters swirling around their chests and they gasped and groaned with hunger and thirst and weariness and bloody hands and knees.

Tolek and Chris held the head of Ana, who was unconscious from falling into the water.

Wolf crawled away alone, counting each step carefully until he came to a large *Kanal*. He was utterly confused, for the Twarda Street line veered into the system at an angle. He could not understand. They were more than a mile away from the designated Prosta Street manhole and completely confused as to direction, but the big *Kanal* had ledges and would give them a place to recover their strength.

Wolf retraced his steps and led them to the Twarda main, and they crawled on the ledges and collapsed.

Wolf and Tolek and Chris stayed half awake, trying each in his own mind to comprehend the situation, and the same set of questions crossed their minds without conversation. Had their message to the Aryan side been received? Would someone be waiting for them on Prosta Street ... if they reached Prosta Street?

As commander, Wolf Brandel had other decisions to reach. He tried to reason out their proximity. He guessed rightly that they were under the former little ghetto area which was now largely reinhabited by Poles. The area, he knew, was under close watch of the police because of its proximity to the ghetto. Overhead they could hear motor vehicles and the marching of soldiers. Perhaps we are near Grzybow Square, Wolf thought. It was an assembly point for the Germans to enter the southern end of the ghetto.

Daylight showed through manholes on either end of their ledge. Wolf looked his people over. It was a battle of endurance against exhaustion more than anything at this point. One by one his people had passed out into semi-consciousness. If his guess of location was right, they would now be safe from poison gas and out of reach of the prying sound detectors. The tides were going high again. Water splashed over the ledge. Nothing to do but wait until darkness ... nothing to do but wait.

Kamek's house in Brodno was the first stop in the underground railway to the Machalin and Lublin forests. Gabriela arrived shortly after the morning curfew was lifted.

'They're down there!' she cried.

Kamek was unexcitable. He put his hands behind his back and deliberately pieced everything together. 'Where are they? We do not know. Neither you nor I got the signal clearly. It could be one of fifteen manholes.'

Gabriela pressed her temples and tried to reason.

'Moreover,' Kamek continued, 'both of our trucks are gone. The Gestapo raided our headquarters last night; our people are dispersed.'

'The Home Army ... Roman ...'

'We cannot depend upon them. Someone may sell out.'

Gabriela knew he was right. She winced. Kamek, once Ignacy Pownicki, had been a journalist and an ardent supporter of both the ruling colonel's clique and the reactionary pre-war noblemen's casts. Events during the war changed his thinking. Humanity overpowered nationalism. Kamek was one of the few who were revolted by and ashamed of the behavior of the Polish people toward the things happening in Poland's ghettos. He did not embrace the leftists' philosophy personally, but he joined them, for they were the ones who gave the fullest support to those in the ghetto. Kamek lost his identity as Ignacy Pownicki to immerse himself fully in the underground work of the People's Guard.

He was a cool man, seeming almost lazily detached from the urgency.

'They're under there somewhere,' Gabriela mumbled again.

'Keep calm, Gabriela. You and I are the only two who are aware of it and who are left in a position to help. The Jewish Fighters' leaders all know your address. Certainly they will attempt to contact you. The best thing you can do is go home and wait.'

The cuckoo chirped the hour. 'Ah, time for the news.'

Kamek flicked on the radio and closed his eyes to concentrate on the true meanings, for the real news was between the lines and filled with cryptic clues. The war since Stalingrad continued to go badly for the Germans, and their double talk could not fully cover it. There was not a single mention of the ghetto action. This also was a good indication, for they were quick to brag of victories. He flicked off the radio.

Gabriela was already on her feet, walking toward the door.

'Keep calm,' he said once more.

The light filtering through the manholes was turning dimmer and dimmer. Wolf watched it fade. Soon it would be night again. He slipped off the ledge and inched along where the nineteen survivors lay entwined like a net full of freshly caught fish. During the day they had passed out and awakened, slept in snatches and gained back an ounce of strength from what they lost during the terrible crawling of the night before.

Wolf satisfied himself that all of them could be marched again. The instant darkness fell he alerted them to stand by. Soon the movement overhead thinned to silence and then, a break. Ack-ack guns in the distance popped at another Russian air raid. This would keep the Germans busy in the streets.

'Let's go,' he said.

The water ran chest-high. Wolf first, Tolek second, Chris third, they pushed against the current, moving southward in a direction which they knew was leading them away from the ghetto. Some of the shorter girls had to go up on tiptoes to keep the sewage out of their mouths and noses.

Hand in hand, they inched down the *Kanal* hoping desperately to find another arterial. Wolf counted steps.

In three hours, he estimated, they had moved two and a half blocks. Someone was always slipping or collapsing or breaking silence.

And then the luxurious sound of loud rushing water farther down the line met his ears. It meant another large *Kanal*! This sound spurred the half-dead line of marchers to another effort. The two sewer lines merged in swirls and whirlpools battering together.

Wolf halted the line. From his memory of the maps, he tried to remember where two such intersections merged at such an angle. There was no place like it in the ghetto. A *Kanal* the size of the one before him must be near the Jerusalem Boulevard area. If so, they were entirely beyond both the big and little ghettos. Wolf decided to gamble with his flashlight. It was soaked and unworkable. Chris had dry matches in a pipe pouch.

A single match sent a dullish yellow glow on the moist bricks. It also revealed the shocking condition of his people. Wolf knew the race for life had to be speeded, more gambles taken. He lit a second match and sloshed nearer the intersection. A third match found him what he was looking for, an iron ladder leading to the street.

'Hold the line still,' Wolf told Tolek and Chris. 'I'm going up to find out where we are.'

'Wolf . . . don't . . .' Rachael cried.

'It will be all right. There's an air raid going on up there.'

He climbed the ladder and shoved hard to wiggle the manhole cover loose. It gave after a fifth renewal of effort. He held it open just enough to look out to the streets. Good luck! Pitch-black in a blackout! Streets deserted!

'Help me lift this manhole cover.'

Chris, Tolek, and Wolf hung on the narrow ladder and grunted together and dislodged it. Wolf darted for the cover of a building, worked toward the corner, and sprinted back, replacing the lid. He huddled with Tolek. Chris was too occupied holding Ana and Rachael erect. Rachael fainted again. Ana had been in a bad way for hours.

'We are directly under the intersection of Twarda and Zelazna.'

'That means we are just two and a half blocks from Prosta Street.' Would someone from the People's Guard be waiting for them there? Both agreed that it was a small chance. It was twenty-four hours since they had sent the signal and entered the sewer. Moreover in daylight this present intersection would be too crowded. Wolf decided to try a push for the quieter Prosta Street and at the same time send Tolek to Gabriela's flat.

'Careful, and bring back water.'

Tolek and Wolf once again dislodged the manhole cover and shoved it back into place.

Wolf lowered himself once more and went back to the other sixteen.

'We are three hours from Prosta Street. We can make it by daylight if everyone tries with all they have. Tolek has gone out for water. He will be waiting for us.'

'No! No!' a girl shrieked. 'We'll never make it! No!'

'Keep her quiet,' Wolf barked.

'No!' the girl screamed again. She began drinking the sewage in her thirst madness.

Wolf went back and lit a match and fished for her head and jerked it out of the contaminated bilge. The girl was insane. In a moment the poison hit her stomach and she gave a last two or three writhes of agony and was dead.

Wolf let her loose, and she was washed into the merging waters, spun in a whirlpool, and swept into the larger *Kanal*.

'Listen, all of you! We're going to live! I promise you we'll live! Two more hours and there will be water to drink! Fight! Live!' he pleaded.

They took hands and pressed north into the whirlpools. The rushing water broke their line, and before they could pull it together another Fighter who was moving in a coma was swept under and drowned.

'Together!' rasped Wolf. 'Hands together ... push ... push ... we'll be through this intersection in a minute.'

They pressed north again in foggy oblivion. Each agony-filled step, each one called upon God unknown.

'I'll live ... I'll live ... I'll live ...'

'Survive ... survive ... survive ...'

'God help me live ... live ... live ...'

Chapter Twenty-three

Tolek Alterman wove his way through the streets of Warsaw with the skill of an alley cat. Years of moving around in the ghetto, later in rubble and flame and falling walls, made this trek seem like child's play by comparison.

It was four-thirty in the morning when he stopped before an apartment door on the top floor of Dluga 4. The name read 'Alena Borinski.' He knocked sharply. The door opened a crack, stopped by the night latch.

'Who is it?' Gabriela asked cautiously from the other side.

'Don't scream when you see me. I've been in the sewers.'

Gabriela flung the door open. Tolek tumbled in and looked around desperately for the kitchen. He stumbled to it and turned on the water faucet and let the water spill into his throat and guzzled it like a lunatic. She locked the door behind her and looked at the scene of madness. He emitted animal-like grunts as the water found its way to his caked innards.

A gray stinking creature from another planet, unrecognizable as human, sucking at the faucet. He drank too fast and began vomiting in the sink and drank again, and sharp pains hit his belly. At last he was appeased and he slipped to the floor, weeping hysterically.

Gabriela ran to the phone. 'Kamek! Come to my flat as soon as the curfew is over. Bring clothing and any food you have.'

'Have they arrived?'

'Yes.'

Gaby dipped a rag in alcohol and wiped Tolek's forehead and comforted him.

'I'm sorry,' he whispered. 'I'm sorry ...'

'Please tell me about it ... please.'

'Twenty-two or twenty-three of us went into the sewer ... Did you get our signal?'

'Yes, but we couldn't distinguish it. Good Lord, have you been in the sewer for twenty-four hours?'

'Yes. Maybe sixteen, seventeen left. Few went crazy from thirst ... drank the sewage ... told them not to ... some others drowned.'

'Where are they now?'

'Trying to make Prosta Street. We've got to get water to them.'

'There's nothing we can do for another hour and a half, until it turns light and the curfew is lifted. Kamek will be here by then.'

Gabriela studied the thing before her. 'Your voice. Don't I know you?'

'Tolek.'

'Oh, my poor dear. I didn't even recognize you.'

'Don't suppose anyone could.'

'Who else is down there?'

'Christopher de Monti. We must get him out.'

She nodded and her eyes widened. 'Who else?'

'Rachael ... Wolf ... Ana ...'

He stopped, and the pained expression she bore both asked the wordless question and answered it. She stood up and walked to the kitchen chair and sagged into it. She bit her lip. The last tears she had left in her trickled down her cheeks. Andrei was still out there in the ghetto ... leading cavalry charges ... Andrei would never come out. She knelt beside Tolek once more and helped him to his feet.

'Come,' Gaby said, 'let's steam you out so you look presentable.'

Gabriela filled the last of four shopping bags with bread, cheese, and bottles of water. Each bag had a rope tied to the handles so it could be lowered quickly into the *Kanal*.

Kamek was a picture of his usual calm. 'Today is Sunday,' he recited for his own benefit. 'Sunday is trouble. We cannot ride through the streets with a load of hay on Sunday. I must get a covered truck and try for the best.'

Tolek came in from the bathroom. He had been soaking and scrubbing for two full hours. It brought him back to the semblance of a man. He tucked a short crowbar into his belt for lifting the manhole cover quickly and took two of the shopping bags from Gabriela.

'I hope they made it,' Tolek mumbled. 'They were in a bad way when I left them.'

Kamek stood up. 'After you get that food and water down to them, wait in the café down the street. Watch for my truck.'

'Hurry with that truck,' Gabriela said. 'They've been down there almost thirty hours.'

'Leave it to Kamek,' Kamek said.

'It's day,' Wolf said, looking up to the manhole cover atop him. 'It's day and we're at Prosta Street. Today we'll be saved.'

Weeping ...

'Our Father which art in heaven.'

'O Merciful God ... save us ... save us ...'

Christopher de Monti leaned against the bricks. He held Ana with one arm and Rachael with the other. Both of them were semi-conscious.

Death closed in with each passing second. There were only twelve left.

'O help us, merciful God ...'

'Today we'll be saved,' Wolf cried. 'Today we'll be saved.'

Christopher skidded to his knees and struggled to his feet, pulling the girls up. Feverish fire tore through his body.

Shadows over them!

'Shh ... someone's up there ... silence ...'

'Merciful ... merciful ...'

'Sshhh!'

Their eyes looked up in terror. The cover slipped off. 'It's me, Tolek! It's me, Tolek! Are you down there? Are you down there?'

'Help ... help ...'

'Tolek ... help ... us ...'

'Thank God! They're alive. Listen, down there. We are lowering bread and water. We will remain close by until the truck arrives. Do you hear me?'

'Water ... water ...'

'Water!'

'Water!'

'Water!'

'Quiet,' Tolek commanded. The bags were lowered. 'There is smelling salts in one of the bags.'

Mass weeping broke out as the bottles were opened and they gurgled and wetted their dehydrated bellies. They tore at the bread and the cheese with the savagery of starved animals and grunted and wept and prayed.

Even the calm Kamek was worrying. He was running out of chances. Two covered-truck owners had their vehicles in repair. Three others were out of the city in the countryside to bring in food from villages.

It was almost eleven o'clock.

Church bells pealed. The pious were coming and going to Mass.

Kamek walked into the Solec to the house of Zamoyski, the teamster of thieves. He did not like to do business with Zamoyski. He was a slimy crook. Kamek had no choice. From time to time on desperate occasions the People's Guard used Zamoyski's truck ... for a price.

When Kamek came to his house Zamoyski was in his usual Sunday pose – coming out of a bombastic Saturday-night hangover.

'Sunday?'

'Special load.'

Must be important, Zamoyski thought. I'll take him for plenty. He grunted disdainfully. 'It's heathen to drive on Sunday. Besides ...'

A roll of green American dollars from Kamek's pocket to the center of the table cut short the oration and bargaining.

'Wait till I get my shirt on.'

'Bring a ladder.'

'A ladder?'

'Yes. The guns we are running are up in a loft.'

Noon.

Gabriela and Tolek drank their fourth cup of tea in a café on Prosta Street. Bells pealed. Tolek was a nervous wreck.

The pious paraded in their finery after their hour with God. 'What the hell is holding Kamek up?' Tolek sputtered. 'They've been down in that hole almost thirty-six hours.'

Gabriela patted his hand. 'Kamek won't let us down,' she said.

In the sewer the food and drink had restored the twelve survivors to a state of consciousness and gave them enough strength to cling to life for another few hours.

They could hear the church bells.

Children played in the street almost directly above them. The children stood in a circle and threw a ball and sang a song and clapped hands.

'*Raz! dwa! trzy!* One! Two! Three!'

The ball was thrown.

'The Roman king had many sons,
Until one born became a Caesar,
Low to the ground, high to the air,
Raz! dwa! trzy! One! two! three!
Yes he was, yes he was,
The great Caesar.'

Zamoyski's truck rumbled up Jerusalem Boulevard.

'Where to? he asked.

'Prosta Street.'

He turned up Zelazna, then into Prosta.

'Where?'

'Stop by the manhole halfway up the block opposite the café.'

Zamoyski's face opened with the sudden discovery. 'What's this all about, Kamek? I don't like this business. Wait a minute. Jews! I'm not getting mixed up in Jew business!'

Zamoyski felt something cold against the side of his face. It was the barrel of Kamek's pistol.

The truck screeched to a halt beside the manhole. Kamek held Zamoyski at bay. Tolek and Gabriela sprinted out of the café. Tolek knocked the cover off the manhole, ran to the back of the truck, and pulled the ladder off. Gabriela took a short-barreled shotgun from inside her trench coat.

The burst of light from the street blinded those in the *Kanal* for an instant. Chris held one side of the ladder, Wolf the other. They dragged the other ten and literally threw them up. Tolek reached down and pulled them through.

'*Raz! dwa! trzy!* One! Two! Three!
The Roman ...'

The children stopped and gawked at the things emerging from the sewer. Gabriela's shotgun menaced them back.

People stopped their Sunday stroll and looked at the sight.

Stunned customers of the café gaped in amazement.

Zamoyski cried and cursed. 'I am ruined! I am trapped! Holy Mother! I am dead!'

Wolf Brandel tumbled out last and hobbled heavily. He was thrown bodily atop the others in the back of the truck, and within two minutes of their stopping they sped away toward the bridge and Brodno.

Chapter Twenty-four

Journal Entry – December 1943

I, Christopher de Monti, shall make the final entry in the Brandel journals of the Good Fellowship Club. After months of hiding I have arrived here in Sweden with Gabriela Rak, whose child is due at any moment. She does not want it to be born on Polish soil. I shall see to it that neither she nor her child shall ever want.

Little is known here about the uprising despite the fact that Artur Zygielboim, a Jewish member of the Polish government in exile in London, committed suicide last June in protest to the world's indifference to the genocide of his people.

What of the Warsaw uprising? How does one determine the results of such a battle? Jewish casualties were in the tens of thousands while the Germans merely lost hundreds.

I look through the books of history and I try to find a parallel. Not at the Alamo, not at Thermopylae did two more unequal forces square off for combat. I believe that decades and centuries may pass, but nothing can stop the legends which will grow from the ashes of the ghetto to show that this is the epic in man's struggle for freedom and human dignity.

This rabble army without a decent weapon held at bay the mightiest military power the world has ever known for forty-two days and forty-two nights! It does not seem possible, for many nations fell beneath the German onslaught in hours. All of Poland was able to hold for less than a month.

Forty-two days and forty-two nights! At the end of that time SS Oberführer Alfred Funk ordered the Great Tlomatskie Synagogue dynamited to the ground to symbolize the destruction of Polish Jewry. He received the Iron Cross for valor.

But Alfred Funk failed, just as all the other Pharaohs failed.

The new year will see Nazi Germany crushed. Germany's cities are destined to be dismantled brick by brick and her people to perish in flames in much the same way as they destroyed the Warsaw ghetto.

What of the murderers? What of Horst von Epp and Franz Koenig? No doubt their ilk will die in bed of old age, for the world is a forgiving world and they will say they were merely following orders. And the world will say ... let us forget the past. Let bygones be bygones. Even the Alfred Funks may escape. Already we hear the verbal gymnastics of the Polish government in exile spouting theories of apologetics in behalf of their people who committed the conspiracy of silence.

I, Christopher de Monti, swear on the eternal soul of my late friend, Andrei Androfski, that I shall not let the world forget. I shall return to Poland. I shall find the Brandel journals and I shall make it a brand on the conscience of man forever.

Wolf Brandel and Rachael Bronski, Tolek Alterman and Ana Grinspan are fighting in a Jewish partisan unit near Wyszkow. Stephan Bronski is alive and well in the home of a woodcutter named Gajnow in the Lublin Uplands. We shall all meet again someday.

I shall close this final entry with the words of the man who wrote the first entry and who is responsible for the historical documents of the Good Fellowship Club. On our last night together in the bunker of Mila 18, this is what Alexander Brandel told me:

'If the Warsaw ghetto marked the lowest point in the history of the Jewish people, it also marked the point where they rose to their greatest heights. Strange, after all the philosophies had been argued, the final decision to fight was basically a religious decision. Rodel would decry my words; Rabbi Solomon would be outraged if I told him this. But those who fought, no matter what their individual reasons, when massed together obeyed God's covenant to oppose tyranny. We have kept faith with our ancient traditions to defend "the laws." In the end we were all Jews.' And Alexander Brandel, always mystified by ways of God and strange ways of men, shook his head in puzzlement. 'Isn't it odd that the epitome of man's inhumanity to man also produced the epitome of man's nobility?' Alexander Brandel told me something else. 'I die, a man fulfilled. My son shall live to see Israel reborn. I know this. And what is more, we Jews have avenged our honor as a people.'

CHRISTOPHER DE MONTI

QB VII

QB VII

I dedicate this book to my darling wife
JILL
On her twenty-third birthday.
And to
CHARLIE GOLDBERG

Aspen, Colorado
April 16, 1970

Author's Note

The English legal profession adheres to an extremely formal protocol and a rigid etiquette. I have not attempted to bind myself to all these customs but have used a reasonable literary license so long as the novel remains within a framework of basic truth and credibility. The characters contained herein are purely fictitious.

LEON URIS

BOOK ONE

The Plaintiff

Chapter One

November 1945 – Monza, Italy

The corporal cadet stepped out of the guard hut and squinted out over the field. A shadowy figure ran through the knee-high grass toward him. The guard lifted a pair of binoculars. The man, half stumbling, carried a single battered suitcase. He waved and gasped a greeting in Polish.

It was a familiar sight these days. In the backwash of the war, all of Europe had become a tangled river of refugees, east going west, west going east, and burgeoning refugee camps all but collapsed under the swell. Hundreds of thousands of liberated Polish slaves roamed about desperately seeking contact with their countrymen. Many wound up here in Monza at the Fifteenth Free Polish Fighter Wing of the Royal Air Force.

'Hello! Hello!' the man shouted as he crossed out of the field and over a dusty road. His run had slowed to a limp.

The corporal cadet stepped up to him. The man was tall and slender with a high-boned face capped with a head of solid white hair.

'Polish, Free Polish?'

'Yes,' the guard answered, 'let me take your suitcase.'

The man leaned against the guard to stave off fainting.

'Easy, father, easy. Come, sit down inside my hut. I will call for an ambulance.'

The guard took him by the arm and led him. The man stopped suddenly and stared at the flag of Poland which flew from its staff just inside the gate and tears came to his eyes. He sat on a wooden bench and held his face in his hands.

The corporal cadet set the suitcase down and circled the handle of the field phone. 'Post number four, send an ambulance. Yes, a refugee.'

As the man was driven into the confines of the camp, the guard shook his head. Ten a day? A hundred some days. What could be done but put a few hot meals into their shrunken bellies, scrub them, give them shots against the raging diseases, a set of ragged clothing, and then dispatch them to a refugee center girding for a terrible winter. Europe would be one large house of death when the snows came.

The bulletin board in the officer's club carried a daily list of refugee arrivals. These Free Polish sought the miracle of contact with a relative or even an old friend. On some rare occasions there would be an emotional reunion of old schoolmates. Almost never was there a meeting of loved ones.

Major Zenon Myslenski entered the club, still dressed in flight jacket and fur-lined boots. He was warmly greeted, for Myslenski, with twenty-two kills of German aircraft, was one of the few quadruple aces of the Free Poles and a legend in a time of legends. He stopped automatically at the bulletin board and glanced at the new orders, the list of social events. There was a chess tournament he must enter. He was about to turn away when he was drawn to that frustrating catalogue, the new refugee list. Only four arrivals today. It was so futile.

'Hey, Zenon,' someone called from the bar. 'You're late.'

Major Myslenski froze, eyes fixed on a name on the refugee list. Arrived, November 5 – Adam Kelno.

Zenon knocked once, then burst the door open. Adam Kelno was half asleep on the cot. At first Zenon did not recognize his cousin. God, he had aged. At the outbreak of the war he didn't have a gray hair in his head. He was so bony and drawn. Through a haze, Adam Kelno felt the presence of someone. He groggily propped on an elbow and blinked his eyes.

'Zenon?'

'Cousin –'

Colonel C. Gajnow, Commander of the Fifteenth Fighter Wing, poured himself a stiff shot of vodka and lifted the pages of a preliminary interrogation of Dr Adam Kelno, who had petitioned to be allowed to join the Free Polish Forces.

ADAM KELNO, M.D. – Born near the village of Pzetzeba, 1905. Educated – University of Warsaw, Medical College. Entered practice as a physician/surgeon in 1934.

There was testimony by his cousin, Major Zenon Myslenski, that Kelno was always identified with Polish Nationalist movements even as a student. At the beginning of World War II, with Poland occupied by the Germans, Kelno and his wife, Stella, immediately went into the Nationalist underground.

After several months their activities were discovered by the Gestapo. Stella Kelno was shot to death by a firing squad.

By a miracle Adam Kelno was spared and sent to the infamous Jadwiga Concentration Camp located midway between Krakow and Tornow in the southern region of Poland. It was an enormous manufacturing complex to feed the German war machine and manned by hundreds of thousands of slaves.

The report continued on that Kelno became a leading figure among the prisoner/doctors and did much to lift the primitive medical facilities. Kelno personally was a selfless and dedicated physician.

Later in the war when extermination facilities were introduced into Jadwiga, Kelno was responsible for saving thousands of lives from the gas chambers by falsifying reports and death certificates, through the underground and by his medical skill.

He became so prominent that toward the end of the war, the chief German medical officer, SS Dr Colonel Adolph Voss, took Kelno, against his will, to help him run an exclusive private clinic in East Prussia.

At the end of the war, Kelno returned to Warsaw, where he ran into a shattering experience. The Polish Communists had betrayed that country to the Soviet Union. During his stay in Jadwiga, as a member of the Nationalist underground, he was constantly in a life and death struggle with the Communist underground. Now, many Communist doctors, most of them Jews, had rigged a conspiracy against Kelno with statements that he had collaborated with the Nazis. With a warrant out for his arrest, Adam Kelno fled immediately and made his way across Europe to Italy, where he made contact with the Free Polish.

Colonel Gajnow set the report down and called for his secretary. 'On the Kelno matter,' he said, 'I am declaring a commission of inquiry to be composed of five officers with myself as chairman. We shall inquire immediately to all Free Polish Forces and organizations which may have knowledge of Kelno and we shall convene for consideration in three months.'

When Poland fell in World War II and was divided between Germany and the Soviet Union by pact, many thousands of soldiers were able to escape. A government-in-exile was formed in London and fighting units put into the field and in the skies under British command.

During the war many thousands of other Polish officers fled to the Soviet Union, where they were interned and later massacred in the Katyn Forest. The Soviets had designs to take over Poland and naturally a Nationalist officer corps stood as a threat to this ambition. At the end of the war, the Soviet Army stood at the gates of Warsaw and did not budge to assist the Nationalist underground in an uprising but allowed the Germans to destroy them.

The Free Poles were to remain in England, rightfully bitter, tightly knit, and forever fanning the dream of a return to their homeland. When the call went out on the matter of Adam Kelno it quickly reached the entire Polish Community.

On the face of it, things seemed clear enough. Dr Adam Kelno was a Polish Nationalist and when he returned to Warsaw he was to be eliminated by the Communists just as the officer corps had been in the Katyn Massacre.

Within days of the launching of the inquiry, sworn statements began to come back to Monza along with offers of personal testimony.

I HAVE KNOWN DR ADAM KELNO FROM 1942, WHEN I WAS SENT TO JADWIGA CONCENTRATION CAMP. I BECAME ILL AND TOO WEAK TO WORK. HE HID ME AND SAVED ME FROM THE GERMANS. HE SAVED MY LIFE.

DR ADAM KELNO OPERATED ON ME AND NURSED ME BACK TO HEALTH WITH GREAT CARE.

DR KELNO HELPED ARRANGE MY ESCAPE FROM JADWIGA.

DR KELNO OPERATED ON ME AT FOUR O'CLOCK IN THE MORNING WHEN HE WAS SO TIRED HE COULD HARDLY STAND UP. I DON'T THINK HE EVER SLEPT FOR MORE THAN A FEW HOURS AT A TIME.

HE SAVED MY LIFE.

On the day of the commission, the camp was visited by Leopold Zalinski, a legendary figure of the Polish Nationalist underground during the occupation. His code name, Kon, was known by every Pole. Kon's testimony erased any doubts. He swore Adam Kelno to be a hero of the Nationalist underground before his imprisonment and during his years as a prisoner/doctor at Jadwiga. With letters and testimonies from two dozen others without conflict, the commission cleared him.

In a moving ceremony at Monza attended by many Polish colonels of the Free Forces, Dr Adam Kelno was sworn in as a captain and his pips were pinned on him by his cousin.

Poland had been taken from these men but they continued to remember and dream.

Chapter Two

The Sixth Polish Hospital.
Foxfield Cross Camp.
Tunbridge Wells, England – March 1946.

Major Adam Kelno walked slowly from the surgery tugging at his rubber gloves. Sister Angela untied his surgical mask and dabbed the perspiration from his head.

'Where is she?' Adam asked.

'In the visitor's lounge. Adam?'

'Yes.'

'Will you come to my flat?'

'Yes, all right.'

'I'll wait.'

As he walked the long dim corridor, it was obvious Angela Brown's admiration was more than professional. It had been but a few short months that they had worked together in surgery. From the onset she was impressed by his skill and a kind of dedicated zeal in which he performed half as many operations again as most of his colleagues. His hands were magnificent.

It all happened rather plainly. Angela Brown, a common-place sort in her mid-thirties, had been a capable nurse for a decade. A first short marriage ended in divorce. The great love of her life, a Polish flyer in the RAF, was shot down over the Channel.

Adam Kelno was nothing like her fighter pilot so it became a new kind of love. A rather magic spot in time the instant he peered over his mask and caught her eye as she placed instruments in his hands, his quick decisive hands and the closeness of spirit as they worked together as a team to save a human life. The exhilaration of a successful operation. The exhaustion of a failure after a difficult battle.

They were so lonely, both of them, and so it happened in a very undramatic but lovely manner.

Adam entered the visitor's lounge. It was very late. The operation had lasted more than three hours. There was a look of stunned anticipation on Madame

Baczewski's face. Afraid to ask. Adam took her hand, bowed slightly and kissed it, then sat beside her.

'Jerzy has left us. It was very peaceful.'

She nodded, but dared not speak.

'Is there anyone I should call, Madame Baczewski?'

'No. There was only us. We are the only survivors.'

'I think we had better put you in a room here.'

She tried to speak but her mouth went into a trembling spasm and tiny little grunts of agony emerged. 'He said ... get me to Dr Kelno ... he kept me alive in the concentration camp ... get me to Dr Kelno.'

Angela arrived and took charge. Adam whispered to have her put under.

'When I first met Jerzy Baczewski he was so strong like a bull. He was a great Pole, one of the foremost dramatists. We knew the Germans were out to destroy the intelligentsia and we had to keep him alive at any price. This surgery was not that difficult. A healthy man would have gotten through this, but he had no stamina left after two years in that putrid hell hole.'

'Darling, it was you that told me a good surgeon has to be impersonal. You did everything ...'

'Sometimes I don't believe my own words. Jerzy died a betrayed man. Lonely, his country taken from him, and a memory of unbelievable terror.'

'Adam, you've been in surgery half the night. Here, darling, take your tea.'

'I want a drink.'

He poured a stiff one, tossed it down, and poured another. 'All Jerzy wanted was a child. What kind of a damned tragedy are we? What kind of curse is on us? Why can't we live?'

The bottle was empty. He chewed at his knuckles.

Angela ran her fingers through that thicket of white hair. 'Will you stay tonight?'

'I would like that. I don't want to be alone.'

She sat on the footstool before him and lay her head in his lap. 'Dr Novak called me aside today,' she said. 'He told me to get you out of the hospital for a little rest or you're going to break down.'

'What the hell does August Novak know. A man who has spent his life fixing oversized noses and transplanting hair for balding British gentry in his singular quest for knighthood. Get me another drink.'

'My God, turn it off.'

As he began to arise she grabbed his hands and held him, then looked pleading and kissed his fingers, each one.

'Don't cry, Angela, please don't cry.'

'My auntie has a lovely little cottage at Folkestone. We're welcome there if we want to go.'

'Perhaps I am a little tired,' he said.

The days at Folkestone all went so quickly. He was renewed by long quiet walks along the leas on the cliffs overlooking the sea. France was across the Channel in shadowy outline. Hand in hand in silent communication they walked wind-blown along the shrub-lined rosemary path to the harbor and in the distance the sounds of the band concert at the Marine Gardens. The narrow little streets had been bombed out but the statue of William Harvey, the discoverer of the circulation of the blood remained. The steamer to Calais left daily again and soon there would be vacationers for the short summer season.

The evening chill was dulled by a crackling fire that threw odd shadows over the old low-beamed ceiling of the cottage. The last lovely day had ended and tomorrow they would return to the hospital.

A sudden moroseness came over Adam. He drank rather heavily. 'I'm sorry it's over,' he mumbled. 'I don't remember such a beautiful week.'

'It need not end,' she said.

'Everything for me must end. I can have nothing that is not taken from me. Everyone I have ever loved has been taken from me. My wife, my mother, my brothers. Any who have survived are in virtual slavery in Poland. I can make no commitments, never again.'

'I've never asked for one,' she said.

'Angela, I want to love you, but you see, if I do, I'll lose you too.'

'What's the difference, Adam. We'll end up losing each other without even giving it a chance.'

'There's more to it, you know that. I am afraid for myself as a man. I have this deadly fear of impotence and it's not the drinking that does it. It's ... so many things that happened in that place.'

'I'll keep you strong, Adam,' she said.

He reached out and touched her cheek and she kissed his hands. 'Your hands. Your beautiful hands.'

'Angela, would you give me a child right away?'

'Yes, my darling darling.'

Angela became pregnant a few months after their marriage.

Dr August Novak, executive surgeon of the Sixth Polish Hospital, returned to private practice and in a surprise move, Adam Kelno was moved over a number of seniors to be named head of the hospital.

Administrative work was not what Adam desired but the enormous responsibilities at the Jadwiga Concentration Camp had trained him for it. Along with budgets and politics, he managed to keep his sure hand in as a surgeon.

It was so good to come home these days. The Kelno cottage in Groombridge Village was a few miles from the hospital at Tunbridge Wells. Angela's belly was filling beautifully with their child and in the evenings they would walk, as always, hand in hand in communicative silence up the wooded path to Toad Rock and take their tea at the quaint little café. Adam drank much less these days.

On an evening in July he signed out at the hospital and his orderly put the groceries in the rear seat of his car. He drove to the center of town and in the Pantiles Colonnade he bought a bouquet of roses and made for Groombridge.

Angela did not answer to his ring. This always gave him a start. The fear of losing her hovered behind every tree of the forest. Adam juggled the grocery sack and fished for his key. Wait! The door was not locked. He opened it.

'Angela!'

His wife sat on the edge of a chair in the living room, ashen-faced. Adam's eyes went to the two men hovering over her.

'Dr Kelno?'

'Yes.'

'Inspector Ewbank, Scotland Yard.'

'Inspector Henderson,' the second man said, holding out his identification.

'What do you want? What are you doing here?'

'I have a warrant for your arrest, sir.'

'My arrest?'

'Yes, sir.'

'What is this all about? What kind of joke is this?'

Their sullen expressions denoted it was no joke.

'My arrest ... for what?'

'You are to be detained at Brixton Prison pending extradition to Poland to stand charges as a war criminal.'

Chapter Three

The setting was London but the room seemed something out of Warsaw. Angela sat in the anteroom of the Society of Free Poles where walls were adorned with enormous sterile paintings of Pilsudski, Smigly-Rydz, Paderewski, and a gallery of Polish heroes. It was in this place and others like it around London that the hundred thousand Poles fortunate enough to escape perpetuated the dream of Poland.

Angela's pregnancy now showed heavily. Zenon Myslenski comforted her as she wrung and knotted a handkerchief nervously. A tall door opened from an inner office and a secretary approached them.

Angela adjusted her dress and waddled in on Zenon's arm where Count Anatol Czerny came from behind his desk. He greeted Zenon as an old friend, kissed Angela's hand, and bade them be seated.

'I am afraid,' the dapper little aristocrat said, 'valuable time has been wasted by contacting the government-in-exile. England no longer recognizes them, and we were unable to get any information from the British Home Office.'

'What in the name of God is it all about? Someone has to tell us something,' Angela emoted.

'All we know is that about a fortnight ago a certain Nathan Goldmark arrived from Warsaw. He is a Jewish Communist and a special investigator for the Polish Secret Police. He has a number of sworn statements from ex-inmates of Jadwiga, all Polish Communists, making various allegations against your husband.'

'What kind of allegations?'

'I have not seen them and the Home Office is most secretive. The British position is this. If a foreign government with whom they have a mutual pact requests extradition and establishes a prima facie case, they treat the matter as routine.'

'But what possible charges could there be against Adam. You've read the testimony from the investigation in Monza. I was there myself,' Zenon said.

'Well, we both really know what is happening, don't we,' the count answered.

'No, I don't understand it at all,' Angela said.

'The Communists feel it necessary to keep up a constant parade of propaganda to justify their seizure of Poland. Dr Kelno is intended as a sacrificial lamb. What better way than to prove a Nationalist was a war criminal.'

'What in the name of God can we do?'

'We will fight this thing, of course. We are not without recourses. It will take a few weeks for the Home Office to review the matter. Our first tactic is to get a delay. Madame Kelno, I want the liberty of engaging a firm of solicitors who have been most helpful to us in these matters.'

'Yes, of course,' she whispered.

'Hobbins, Newton, and Smiddy.'

'Oh, my poor darling Adam ... Oh, dear God.'

'Angela, please.'

'Are you all right, Madame Kelno?'

'Yes ... I'm sorry.' She pressed her white folded knuckles to her lips and drew deep sighs.

'Come now,' Count Czerny said. 'We are in England. We are dealing with a decent, civilized people.'

The Austin taxi stopped in the center of the Pall Mall, found an opening in the opposite flow of traffic, and did a swift U-turn in a circle no larger than a halfpenny, stopping before the Reform Club.

Richard Smiddy jammed his bowler on tightly, tucked his umbrella under an arm, opened a tattered change purse and carefully doled out the exact fare.

'And a sixpence for you,' he said.

'Thank you, governor,' the cabbie said, putting on his FOR HIRE light and pulling away from the curb. He shook his head as he pocketed the frail tip. Not that he wanted the war, mind you, but he wished the Yanks were back.

Richard Smiddy, son of George Smiddy and grandson of Harold Smiddy of that fine old law firm marched the stairs to the entrance of the Reform Club. He was rather pleased about getting an appointment with Robert Highsmith in less than a week. As protocol required, Smiddy's clerk wrote a hand-delivered note to Highsmith's clerk at Parliament and arranged the meeting. Smiddy did have his man denote that the matter had some urgency. For a passing moment Richard Smiddy had contemplated by-passing tradition and picking up the telephone but only the Americans did business that way.

He deposited his umbrella and bowler with the hall porter and made the usual remark about the foul weather.

'Mr Highsmith is expecting you, sir.'

Smiddy trotted up the stairs to that place where Phileas Fogg began and ended his trip around the world in eighty days, then into the lounge off to the right. Robert Highsmith, a heavily set fellow indifferently tailored, moved his largeness from a deep leather chair that was cracked with age. Highsmith was somewhat of a colorful character having bolted a family of landed gentry to be called to the bar. He was a dazzling barrister of extraordinary skill and, at the age of thirty-five, recently elected to the House of Commons. A zealous crusader by nature, Highsmith always seemed to have his finger in some pudding of injustice. As such he headed the British office of Sanctuary International, an organization devoted to the defense of political prisoners.

'Hello there, Smiddy, sit down, sit down.'

'Good of you to see me so soon.'

'Not soon enough. I had to put a lot of pressure on the Home Office to hold things off. You should have phoned me for an appointment with time so short.'

'Well yes, that did occur to me.'

Highsmith ordered a whisky neat and Richard Smiddy ordered tea and cakes.

'Well, I've got the gist of the charges,' Highsmith said. 'They want him for just about everything in the book.' He balanced his specs on the end of his nose, brushed back his disheveled hair, and read from a single sheet of paper. 'Giving fatal shots of phenol to prisoners, collaboration with the Nazis, selecting prisoners for the gas chambers, participating in experimental surgery, taking an oath as an honorary German. And so forth, and so forth. Sounds like a bloody monster. What kind of a chap is he?'

'Decent enough sort. A bit blunt. Polish, you know.'

'What's your office got to say about all this?'

'We've gone over the matter very carefully, Mr Highsmith and I'd wager my last quid that he's innocent.'

'Bastards. Well, we're not going to let them get away with it.'

Sanctuary International
Raymond Buildings
Gray's Inn
London WC 1

The Under Secretary of State
Home Office
Aliens Department
10 Old Bailey
London EC 4

Dear Mr Clayton-Hill,

I had advised you earlier of the interest of Sanctuary International in the matter of Dr Adam Kelno, now being detained in H.M. Prison at Brixton. As a matter of procedure, our organization looks with suspicion on any demands for political prisoners being extradited to Communist states. Dr Kelno is clearly a political victim.

On further scrutiny it is our belief that the charges against Dr Kelno appear to be totally without foundation. The affidavits against him are either from Polish Communists of Communist-oriented persons.

In no event has anyone claimed to have personally witnessed any wrong doing by Dr Kelno. These affidavits are based on the loosest kind of hearsay that would be inadmissible evidence in any court of law in the Western world.

Furthermore, the Polish government has been unable to produce a single victim of Dr Kelno's alleged cruelty.

In our opinion Poland has absolutely failed to establish a prima facie case. Those persons who are able to testify to Dr Kelno's magnificent behavior in Jadwiga cannot go to Poland and under no circumstances will the man be given a fair trial. If this extradition is permitted it would be tantamount to a political murder.

In the name of British fair play, Sanctuary International pleads for the unconditional release of this blameless man.

Yours faithfully,

ROBERT HIGHSMITH

Hobbins, Newton & Smiddy
Solicitors
32B Chancery Lane
London WC 2

The Under Secretary of State
Home Office
Aliens Department
10 Old Bailey
London EC 4

Re: DR ADAM KELNO

Dear Mr Clayton-Hill,

Further to the matter of Dr Adam Kelno. I have the pleasure of enclosing twenty more statements from former inmates of the Jadwiga Concentration Camp on behalf of our client.

We are appreciative of your granting a delay which has allowed us to bring forth over a hundred affidavits. However, Dr Kelno has been in prison for nearly six months without a prima facie case against him.

We shall be obliged if you will inform us whether you are now satisfied on the evidence we have produced and can arrange to release Dr Kelno or if we are to go to further expense and labor.

May I call your attention to an honorary tribunal consisting of representatives of all the Free Polish organizations which has not only exonerated him but cites him as a hero.

Faithfully yours.

HOBBINS, NEWTON & SMIDDY

In the House of Commons, Robert Highsmith gained support from his fellow members and exerted growing pressure for the release of Kelno. A rash of opinion was growing against the obvious injustice.

Yet, equally insistent was a feeling of anger from Poland that a beastly war criminal was at large and being protected by the British. From their point of view it was a Polish matter and England was bound by treaty to return him for trial.

Just as it seemed that Sanctuary International was turning the corner, Nathan Goldmark, the Polish investigator who was in England pressing for the extradition, found an unexpected witness.

Chapter Four

The skyline of Oxford was punctured by a hundred spires and towers. Nathan Goldmark of the Polish Secret Police nibbled on his knuckles and pressed close to the train window as fellow passengers pulled their luggage down from the overhead rack.

Oxford, he had read on the ride up from London, dated back to the twelfth century and had grown to its present conglomerate of thirty-one colleges with assorted cathedrals, hospitals, institutions, all joggled about in winding ways, a terribly romantic stream, Gothic richness, fluted ceilings, ancient quadrangles, and the chancellors, and masters, and readers, and students, and choirs. Colleges such as the Magdalenes and Pembrokes and All Souls counted their history and their heroes in hundreds of years. The Nuffields and St Catherine's in mere decades. All of it was filled with the roll call of immortals that was the greatness of England itself.

Nathan Goldmark found the taxi stand and handed the driver a slip of paper that read, Radcliffe Medical Center. He lowered his window despite the chill drizzle as they drove toward a flood of bicycles and jaunty students. On an ancient wall in paint in red letters were the words, JESUS WAS A FAIRY.

In the sterile sanctuary of the medical center he was taken down a long corridor, past a dozen laboratories to the tiny, disheveled office of Dr Mark Tesslar, who had been expecting him.

'We will go to my place,' Tesslar said. 'It is better to speak there.'

Tesslar's apartment was a few miles from the center of Oxford in the countryside, in a converted monastery at Wytham Abbey. It took only a moment or so for Dr Mark Tesslar and Nathan Goldmark to size each other up, for they were both members of the same unique club, the few and far between Polish Jews to survive Hitler's holocaust. Tesslar had matriculated through the Warsaw Ghetto, Majdanek and Jadwiga Concentration Camps. Goldmark was a graduate of Dachau and Auschwitz. The rivulets of deep furrows and sunken eyes betrayed the past of one to the other.

'How did you find me, Goldmark?' Tesslar asked.

'Through Dr Maria Viskova. She told me you were in Oxford working on special research.'

The mention of Maria brought a smile to an otherwise rigid, bony face. 'Maria ... when did you see her last?'

'A week ago.'

'How is she?'

'Well, in a favorable position but, like all of us, trying to find out where life is again. Trying to understand what happened.'

'I begged her, when we were liberated and returned to Warsaw, to leave Poland. It is no place for a Jew. It's a graveyard. A vast, hollow place filled with the smell of death.'

'But you are still a Polish citizen, Dr Tesslar.'

'No. I have no intentions of going back. Never.'

'It will be a great loss for the Jewish community.'

'What Jewish community? A smattering of ghosts sifting through the ashes.'

'It will be different now.'

'Will it, Goldmark? Then why do they have a separate branch of the Communist Party for Jews. I'll tell you. Because the Poles won't admit to their guilt and they have to keep what is left of the Jews locked in Poland. See! We have Jews here. They like it here. We are good Poles. And people like you do their dirty work. You have to keep a Jewish community in Poland to justify your own existence. You're being used. But in the end you'll find out the Communists are no better for us than the Nationalists before the war. Inside that country we are pigs.'

'And Maria Viskova . . . a lifelong Communist?'

'She will be disenchanted too, before it's over.'

Goldmark wished to disengage the conversation. His face pinched nervously as he sucked at one cigarette after the other. As Tesslar made his attack, Goldmark became more restless.

Mark Tesslar limped slightly as he took the tray of tea from his housekeeper. He prepared it and poured.

'The reason of my visit to Oxford,' Goldmark said, 'concerns Adam Kelno.'

The mention of Kelno's name brought an instant visible reaction. 'What about Kelno?'

Goldmark smirked a little, chomping with the sudden importance of his revelation. 'You've known him a long time?'

'Since we were students in 1930.'

'When was the last you saw of him?'

'Leaving the Jadwiga Concentration Camp. I heard he came to Warsaw after the war, then fled.'

'What would you say if I told you he was in England?'

'Free?'

'Not exactly. He is being detained at the Brixton Prison. We are trying to get him extradited to Poland. You ought to know the situation here in England with the Polish fascists. They have made a cause célèbre out of him. They've managed to attract enough attention in high places to make the British do a fence-sitting act. You knew him intimately in Jadwiga?'

'Yes,' Tesslar whispered.

'Then you must be aware of the charges against him.'

'I know he committed experimental surgery on our people.'

'How do you know this?'

'I saw it with my own eyes.'

The Under Secretary of State
The Home Office
Alien's Department
10 Old Bailey
London EC 4

Hobbins, Newton & Smiddy
Solicitors
32B Chancery Lane
London WC 2

Re: DR ADAM KELNO

Gentlemen:

I am directed by the Secretary of State to inform you that he has carefully considered all the circumstances including information furnished by the Polish government. With the recent sworn statement of Dr Mark Tesslar the Secretary of State considers that a prima facie case has been established. It is not within our jurisdiction to comment on the right or wrong of Polish law but to comply with treaties in effect with that government.

Therefore, the Secretary of State has decided to enforce the deportation order by sending Dr Kelno to Poland.

I am, gentlemen,

Your obedient servant,

JOHN CLAYTON-HILL

Chapter Five

The guard led Adam Kelno into the glassed consultation room where he was seated opposite Robert Highsmith and Richard Smiddy.

'I'm going to come right to the point, Kelno,' Highsmith said, 'we are in a nasty bind. Nathan Goldmark has obtained a very damaging affidavit against you. What does the name Mark Tesslar mean to you?'

Fear was evident in him.

'Well?'

'He is in England?'

'Yes.'

'It is all very clear. Once the Polish government could not establish a case against me, they sent one of them after me.'

'One of whom?'

'The Communists. The Jews.'

'What about Tesslar?'

'He swore to get me almost twenty years ago.' Kelno hung his head. 'Oh God, what's the use.'

'See here, man, you pull yourself together. There is no time for sinking spells. We have to keep our wits.'

'What do you want to know?'

'When did you first meet Tesslar?'

'Around 1930 at the university when we were students together. He was dismissed for committing abortions and he claimed I was the one who turned him in. At any rate, he concluded his medical training in Europe, Switzerland, I think.'

'Did you see him when he returned to Warsaw to practice before the war?'

'No, but he was a well-known abortionist. As a Roman Catholic it was difficult for me to recommend abortions, but a few times I felt it best for the life of the patient and once a close relative was in trouble. Tesslar never knew I sent people to him. It was always done through a blind party.'

'Go on.'

'By some insane quirk of fate I met him again in Jadwiga. His reputation proceeded him. Late in 1942 the Germans took him from the Warsaw Ghetto and removed him to Majdanek Concentration Camp outside the city of Lublin. Here he was charged by the SS doctors to keep the camp prostitutes free of disease and to perform abortions when necessary.'

Smiddy, who had been writing notes quickly, looked up. 'How do you know this?'

'Word of this sort spreads quickly even from one camp to another. The doctors were in a very small community and a few transfers here and there would give us all the news. Also, as a member of the Nationalist underground I had access to this kind of information. We all knew about Tesslar when he arrived in Jadwiga in 1943.'

'You were the chief medical officer, so you must have had close contact with him?'

'No. It was not the case. You see, there were twenty-six barracks in the medical complex but Barracks One to Five were where the SS doctors conducted secret experiments. Tesslar lived down there. It is he who should be standing trial, not me. I warned him he would have to answer for his crimes, but he was under protection of the Germans. When the war was over, Tesslar became a Communist and joined the secret police as a medical officer in order to save himself. That is when he swore those lies against me.'

'I want you to answer this very carefully, Dr Kelno.' Highsmith accentuated. 'Did you ever perform any amputations of testicles and ovaries?'

Kelno shrugged. 'Of course. I performed ten thousand, fifteen thousand operations. Large ones, small ones. A man's testicle or a woman's ovary can become diseased like any other part of the body. When I operated, I did it to save a patient's life. I recall cancers and tumors of the sexual glands. But you see how such things can become distorted. I never operated on a healthy man.'

'Who accused you of that?'

'I know all of Tesslar's accusations. Do you want to hear them? They are stamped on my brain.'

'Very well,' Highsmith said. 'We were able to get a short delay in order to give you time to answer Tesslar's statement. You must go about it coldly, dispassionately, and honestly and don't inject your personal animosity against him. You must answer every charge, point by point. Here, study this statement tonight with great care. We will be back tomorrow with a shorthand writer to take your answer.'

'I categorically deny that I boasted to Dr Tesslar the performing of fifteen thousand experiments in surgery without anesthetic. Too many people have testified to my good behavior to make this anything but the wildest sort of slander.'

'I categorically deny I ever performed surgery on a healthy man or woman. I deny I was ever inhumane to my patients. I deny ever taking part in any experimental surgery of any sort.'

'It is a pure fabrication that Dr Tesslar ever saw me perform surgery. He was never, at any time, in any theater where I operated.'

'Too many of my patients are alive and have testified in my behalf to give validity to the charge that my operations were badly performed.'

'It is my sincere conviction that Dr Tesslar made these charges to take the onus of guilt off himself. I believe he was sent to England as a part of a conspiracy to destroy all remaining traces of Polish nationalism. The fact that he has asked for asylum in England is merely a Communist trick, is not to be trusted.'

As the time of decision drew close, Adam Kelno went into a deep depression. Even the visits from Angela failed to lift his spirits.

She handed him a set of photographs of their son, Stephan. Adam set them down on the table without looking. 'I can't,' he said.

'Adam, let me bring the child so you can see him.'

'No, not in a prison.'

'He's only an infant. He won't remember.'

'See him ... so I can carry the tortured remembrance of him through a mock trial in Warsaw. Is that what you are trying to tell me?'

'We are fighting just as hard as ever. Only ... I can't see you like this. We've always drawn strength from each other. How easy do you think this has been on me? I work all day, try to raise a child by myself, come to see you. Adam ... oh, Adam ...'

'Don't touch me, Angela. It is becoming too painful.'

The special basket of food she brought to Brixton four times a week had been inspected and passed. Adam was disinterested.

'I have been here almost two years,' he mumbled, 'watched over like a condemned man in solitary confinement. They watch me at meal times, at the toilet. No buttons, belts, razors. Even my pencils are taken away at night. I have nothing to do but read and pray. They're right ... I have wanted to commit suicide. Only the thought of living to see my son as a free man has kept me alive but now ... even that hope is gone.'

John Clayton-Hill, the Under Secretary, sat down at the table across from the Secretary of State, Sir Percy Maltwood, with that damnable deportation order between them.

Maltwood had called Thomas Bannister, King's Counsel, into the Kelno affair on behalf of the Home Office to see if his opinion differed from Highsmith's.

Thomas Bannister in his early forties was a barrister of stature equal to Highsmith's. A man of average build, prematurely grayed, and ruddy English in complexion. All that seemed extraordinarily placid leaped into exquisite and brilliant action within the walls of a courtroom.

'What will your report say, Tom?' Maltwood asked.

'It will say that there is a reasonable doubt as to either Kelno's guilt or innocence and therefore the Polish government is obliged to produce more evidence. I don't think they have established a prima facie case because what it all boils down to is Tesslar's word against Kelno's.'

Bannister gracefully moved into a seat and rifled through the now heavy records. 'Most of the affidavits supplied by the Polish government are based on pure hearsay. We have come to know, have we not, that Tesslar is either lying to save himself or Kelno is lying to save himself. Both of them obviously dislike each other. What happened in Jadwiga happened in total secrecy so we don't really know if we would be hanging a political victim or freeing a war criminal.'

'What do you think we ought to do, Tom?'

'Continue to hold him in Brixton until one side or the other comes up with concrete evidence.'

'Off the record,' Maltwood said, 'what is your opinion?'

Bannister looked from one to the other and smiled. 'Come on, Sir Percy, you know I won't answer that.'

'We are going strictly on your recommendation, Tom, not your hunches.'

'I think Kelno is guilty. I'm not sure of what, but he's guilty of something,' Tom Bannister said.

The Polish Embassy
47 Portland Place
London, W 1
January 15, 1949

The Secretary of State

Sir:

The Polish ambassador presents his compliments to His Majesty's Principal Secretary of State for Foreign Affairs and has the honor to inform him of the Polish government's attitude on the subject of Dr Adam Kelno. The Polish government holds the view that:

It has established beyond doubt that Dr Adam Kelno, now under custody in Great Britain in Brixton Prison, was a surgeon in Jadwiga Concentration Camp and is suspect of having perpetrated war crimes.

Dr Kelno is listed as a suspect war criminal by the United Nations War Crimes Commission and the governments of Czechoslovakia and the Netherlands as well as Poland.

The Polish government has supplied all required evidence to His Majesty's government sufficient for a prima facie case.

Further evidence should be preserved for the proper Polish courts.

The government of the United Kingdom must now comply with requests for the extradition of war criminals under existing treaty.

Furthermore, public opinion in Poland is outraged by this undue delay.

Therefore, for finalizing once and forever the fact that Dr Adam Kelno should be deported to Poland, we shall produce a victim of Dr Kelno's brutality and will, in accordance to British jurisprudence, bring forth a man who was castrated by Dr Kelno in a brutal manner as a part of a medical experiment.

I am, sir,

Most faithfully,

ZYGMONT ZYBOWSKI,
Ambassador

Chapter Six

Opposite glorious old Covent Garden stood that grim gray stone Palladian edifice, the Bow Street Magistrate's Court, most noted among London's fourteen police courts. A line of chauffeured limousines parked before the station testified to the importance of the occasion taking place behind the closed doors of a large, drafty, shabby conference room.

Robert Highsmith was there, hiding his tension behind a strewn posture. The proper Richard Smiddy was there, nibbling at his lower lip. The Magistrate, Mr Griffin, was there. Nathan Goldmark, the dogged hunter, was there. John Clayton-Hill of the Home Office was there and so were officers of Scotland Yard and a shorthand writer.

Someone else was there. Thomas Bannister, K.C. Doubting Thomas, one might say.

'Shall we proceed, gentlemen,' the magistrate said. Everyone nodded. 'Officer. Bring in Dr Fletcher.'

Dr Fletcher, a nondescript man, was ushered in and asked to take a seat opposite the magistrate at the end of the table. He gave his name and address to the shorthand writer. Magistrate Griffin proceeded.

'This hearing is rather informal so we shan't bind ourselves with too many rules unless counsel become argumentative. For the record, Mr Goldmark and Mr Clayton-Hill, may ask questions. Now, Dr Fletcher, are you a registered medical practitioner?'

'I am, sir.'

'Where do you practice?'

'I am the senior medical officer at His Majesty's Prison at Wormwood Scrubbs and I am senior medical adviser to the Home Office.'

'Have you examined a man named Eli Janos?'

'I have, yesterday afternoon.'

The magistrate turned to the reporter. 'For the sake of identification, Eli Janos is a Hungarian of Jewish ancestry now living in Denmark. At the instigation of the government of Poland, Mr Janos volunteered to come to England. Now, Dr Fletcher, would you be so kind as to inform us as to the findings of your examination in particular regard to Mr Janos's testicles.'

'Poor devil is a eunuch,' Dr Fletcher said.

'I should like that stricken,' Robert Highsmith said unfolding himself quickly. 'I don't think it's proper to inject such personal observation and editorial comment as "poor devil."'

'He's damned well a poor devil, isn't he, Highsmith?' Bannister said.

'I should like the Learned Magistrate to inform my learned friend here . . .'

'All of this is rather unnecessary, gentlemen,' the magistrate said with a sudden show of the authority of British justice. 'Mr Highsmith, Mr Bannister, will you stop this immediately?'

'Yes, sir.'

'Sorry, sir.'

'Please continue, Dr Fletcher.'

'There is no trace of testicles in the scrotal sack or the inguinal canal.'

'Are there scars of an operation?'

'Yes. On both sides, just a bit over the inguinal canal, which I would deem orthodox scars for the removal of testicles.'

'Can you tell the Learned Magistrate,' Bannister said, 'if you have an opinion as to whether or not the operation on Janos's testicles was performed in a normal, skillfull way?'

'Yes, it appears to be proper surgery.'

'And,' Highsmith snapped, 'there is nothing to show abuse, bad surgery, complications, that sort of thing?'

'No . . . I would say I saw nothing to indicate that.'

Highsmith, Bannister, and the magistrate asked a number of technical questions about the manner of the operation after which Dr Fletcher was properly thanked and dismissed.

'Bring in Eli Janos,' the magistrate ordered.

Eli Janos had many of the manifestations of a eunuch. He was fat. When he spoke, his high pitched voice was broken. Magistrate Griffin personally escorted Janos to his seat. There was a beat of awkward silence.

'It is quite all right if you wish to smoke, gentlemen.'

There was fishing through pockets for the relief of tobacco. Pipe, cigar, and cigarette smoke bellowed out, then drifted to the high ceiling.

Magistrate Griffin glanced through Janos's statement. 'Mr Janos, I take it you speak sufficient English so you will not need an interpreter.'

'I can pass.'

'If there is anything you don't understand, do ask us to repeat the question. Also, I realize that this is an ordeal for you. If, at any time, you become upset, please let me know.'

'I have no more tears left for myself,' he answered.

'Yes, thank you. I should first like to review some of the facts in your affidavit. You are Hungarian by birth in the year of 1920. The Gestapo found you in hiding in Budapest and transported you to the Jadwiga Concentration Camp. Before the war you were a furrier and at the concentration camp you worked in a factory making German uniforms.'

'Yes, that is correct.'

'In the spring of 1943 you were caught smuggling and taken before an SS tribunal. They found you guilty and sentenced you to have your testicles removed. You were then removed to the medical compound and interned in a place known as Barrack III. Four days later the operation was performed in Barrack V. You were forced at gun point to undress and were prepared by prisoner/orderlies and thence castrated by a Polish prisoner/doctor whom you accuse of being Dr Adam Kelno.'

'Yes.'

'Gentlemen, you may question Mr Janos.'

'Mr Janos,' Thomas Bannister said, 'I should like to establish a little more background. This charge of smuggling. What was this about?'

'We were always in company with the three angels of Jadwiga, death, hunger, and disease. You have read what has been written of these places. I do not have to elaborate. Smuggling was a normal way of life ... normal as the fog of London. We smuggled to stay alive. Although the SS runs the camp we are guarded by Kapos. Kapos are also prisoners who earn their favor with the Germans by collaboration. The Kapos can be as brutal as the SS. It was a simple matter. I did not pay off certain Kapos so they turned me in.'

'I should like to know if any of the Kapos were Jewish?' Bannister asked.

'Only a few from every hundred.'

'But most of the labor was Jewish?'

'Seventy-five percent Jews. Twenty percent Poles and other Slavs and the rest criminals or political prisoners.'

'And you were first taken to Barrack III.'

'Yes. I learned that in this barrack the Germans kept the raw material for medical experiments ... and then I was taken to Barrack V.'

'And forced to undress and shower?'

'Yes, then I was shaved by an orderly and made to sit naked in the anteroom.' Janos fished for a cigarette and his story slowed and his voice varied now with the pain of memory. 'They came in, the doctor with an SS colonel. Voss, Adolph Voss.'

'How do you know it was Voss?' Highsmith asked.

'He told me, and he told me that as a Jew my testicles would do no good because he was going to sterilize all the Jews so I would be serving the cause of science.'

'In what language did he speak to you?'

'German.'

'Are you fluent in German?'

'In a concentration camp, you learn enough German.'

'And you claim,' Highsmith continued, 'that the doctor with him was Kelno.'

'Yes.'

'How did you know that?'

'In Barrack III it is known and said Dr Kelno was the head of prisoner medicine and often performed surgery for Voss in Barrack V. I heard of no other doctor's name.'

'Dr Tesslar. Did you ever hear of him?'

'At the end of my recovery a new doctor came to Barrack III. It may have been Tesslar. The name sounds familiar, but I never met him.'

'Then what happened?'

'I became panicked. Three or four orderlies held me down and another gave me an injection in the spine. Soon my lower body became dead. I was strapped to a trolley and taken into the operation room.'

'Who was there?'

'The SS colonel Dr Voss and the Polish doctor and one or two assistants. Voss said he was going to time the operation and wanted the eggs removed quickly. I begged in Polish for Kelno to leave one testicle. He only shrugged and when I screamed he slapped me and then . . . he took them out.'

'So,' Bannister said, 'you had ample time to see this man without a surgical mask.'

'He wore no mask. He did not even wash his hands. For a month after, I almost died from infection.'

'To be absolutely clear,' Bannister said, 'you were a normal healthy man when you were taken to Barrack V.'

'Weak from the concentration camp life but normal sexually.'

'You had no prior treatment of X ray or anything else that could have damaged your testicles?'

'No. They only wanted to see how fast it could be done.'

'And would you describe your treatment on the operating table as less than gentle.'

'They were brutal to me.'

'Did you ever see the Polish doctor again after the operation?'

'No.'

'But you are absolutely certain you can identify the man who operated on you.'

'I was conscious the entire time. I will never forget the face.'

'I have no further questions,' Bannister said.

'No questions,' Highsmith said.

'Is the inspection line-up ready?' Magistrate Griffin asked.

'Yes, sir.'

'Now, Mr Janos. You understand what a police identification parade is?'

'Yes, it has been explained.'

'There will be a dozen men behind a glassed-in room, dressed in simulated prison clothing. They are unable to see into the room where we shall be observing. One of the men is Dr Kelno.'

'I understand.'

They filed from the conference room, down a rickety stair. Each man was still full of Janos's tale of horror. Highsmith and Smiddy, who had fought so bitterly for Adam Kelno, felt an unavoidable twinge of apprehension. Had Adam Kelno lied to them? The door of Barrack V had been opened for the first time giving a glimpse of its horrible secrets.

Nathan Goldmark's chest nearly burst. The moment was at hand for vengeance for the death of his family, for justification to his government. The orgasm of victory. From here, there could be no further delays. The fascist would be brought to heel.

Thomas Bannister took all of this with the apparent dispassionate calm that stamped his personality and career as a human refrigerator.

To the man who had suffered the most, it mattered the least. Eli Janos would still be a eunuch when it was over and it did not matter one way or the other.

They were seated and the room darkened. Before them was a glass-paneled room with a height marker on the rear wall. The men in prison uniform were marched in. They blinked from the sudden shower of light. A police officer directed them to face the dark room beyond the glass.

Adam Kelno stood second from the right in a mixture of tall and short and fat and thin people. Eli Janos leaned forward and squinted. Immediate identification eluded him so he started at the left side of the line-up.

'Do take your time,' Magistrate Griffin said.

All that broke the silence was the deep wheezing of Nathan Goldmark and it was all he could do to restrain himself from jumping up and pointing at Kelno.

Janos's eyes stopped for a long search of each of them, probing for recognition of that terrible day in Barrack V.

Down the line. One, then the other. He came to Adam Kelno and hunched forward. The officer inside ordered everyone to turn left profile, then right profile. Then they were marched out and the light turned on.

'Well?' Magistrate Griffin asked.

Eli Janos drew a deep breath and shook his head. 'I do not recognize any of them.'

'Have the officer bring in Dr Kelno,' Robert Highsmith said in a sudden, unexpected flare.

'It's not required,' the magistrate said.

'This bloody business has been going on for two years. A blameless man has been in prison. I want to make completely certain of this.'

Adam Kelno was marched in and made to stand before Eli Janos and they stared at each other.

'Dr Kelno,' Highsmith said, 'would you speak to this man in German or Polish.'

'I want my freedom,' Adam said in German. 'It's in your hands,' he concluded in Polish.

'Does the voice mean anything?' Highsmith said.

'He is not the man who castrated me,' Eli Janos said.

Adam Kelno sighed deeply and bowed his head as the officer led him out.

'Are you willing to swear a statement?' Highsmith asked.

'Of course,' Janos answered.

There was a formal letter that His Majesty's government regretted any inconvenience to Adam Kelno for his two year detention in Brixton Prison.

As the prison gate closed behind him, the patient and loving Angela rushed to his arms. Behind her, in the alleyway that lead to the entrance, his cousin Zenon Myslenski with Count Anatol Czerny, Highsmith, and Smiddy. There was someone else. A little boy who wavered cautiously under the prodding of 'Uncle' Zenon. Then he toddled forward and said ... 'Daddy.'

Adam lifted the child. 'My son,' he cried, 'my son.' And soon they passed down the long high brick wall into a rare day of sunlight in London.

The conspiracy had been beaten, but Adam Kelno was filled with an even greater fear without the protection of prison walls. He was on the outside now and the enemy was relentless and dangerous. He took his wife and son and fled. He fled to the remotest corner of the world.

Chapter Seven

'Adam! Adam!' Angela shrieked.

He tore over the veranda and flung the screen door open at the same instant Abun, the houseboy, arrived. Angela had flung herself over Stephan to shield the child from the cobra coiled near the bed, tongue flicking, head bobbing in a death dance.

Abun motioned Adam Kelno into stillness, slowly unsheathed his parang. His bare feet slipped noiselessly over the rat mat.

Hisssss! A flashing arc of steel. The snake was decapitated. Its head bounced off and the body crumpled after a short violent tremor.

'Don't touch! Don't touch! Still full poison!'

Angela allowed herself the luxury of screaming, then sobbed hysterically. Young Stephan clung to his mother and cried as Adam sat on the edge of the bed and tried to calm them. Adam looked away from his son guiltily. The boy's legs were still full of welts from leeches.

Yes, Sarawak in the northern corner of Borneo was about as far away as a man could run and deep as a man could hide.

A few days after his release from Brixton Prison and in a state of overwhelming fear the Kelno family booked secret passage for Singapore and from there a rotting tramp steamer took them over the South China sea to the end of the earth ... Sarawak.

Fort Bobang, a classic pesthole, stood on a delta formed by the Batang Lampur River. The outpost held a hundred thatched huts on hardwood stilts that nestled on the river's edge. A bit inland, the town consisted of two muddy streets of Chinese-owned shops, warehouses for the rubber and sago exports, and a dock large enough to accommodate the ferry that shuttled to the capital at Kuching and the long boats that traveled the endless rivers.

The British compound was a smattering of peeled, faded white-washed buildings scalded by the sun and beaten by the rain. In the compound was an area commissioner, a police station, a few banished civil servants, a clinic, and a one room schoolhouse.

A few months prior to the incident with the cobra, Adam Kelno had been interviewed by Dr MacAlister, the Chief Medical Officer of Sarawak. Kelno's credentials were in order. He was a qualified physician and surgeon and men who desired to come to this place were not asked too many questions about their past.

MacAlister accompanied the Kelnos to Fort Bobang. Two male nurse assistants, a Malayan and a Chinese, greeted the new doctor without particular enthusiasm and showed him through the shoddy clinic.

'Not exactly the West End of London,' MacAlister understated.

'I've worked in worse places,' Adam answered tersely.

Adam's trained eye photographed the meager inventory for drugs and equipment. 'What happened to the last man?'

'Suicide. We get quite a few of them out here, you know.'

'Well, don't have any thoughts like that about me. I've had the opportunity. I'm not the type.'

After the inspection, Adam curtly ordered a thorough scrubbing and cleaning of the building, then retreated to his quarters on the opposite side of the compound.

Angela was disappointed but did not complain. 'A little touching up here and there and everything will be just lovely,' she said, convincing herself least of all.

The view from the screened-in veranda was to the river and the docks below them back up to the hills that rose behind the town. It was all in low palm and an incredibly deep luscious green. As their drinks arrived, the sounds and smells of dusk invaded and a blessed blade of coolness cut through the wet suffocating heat of the day. As Adam stared out, the first drops of rain sprinkled down in prelude of the daily torrent to follow. The usual power failure of the compound's generator flicked the lights off and on, off and on. And then the rain came for fair, gushing and hopping off the ground as it hit with trip hammer impact.

'Cheers,' said MacAlister. His time-wizened eyes studied the new man. Old Mac had seen them come and go, so many of them. The drunks and the dregs, and those filled with the false hope of bettering mankind. He had long forgotten his own missionary zeal, which was squashed by his mediocracy, the crown's bureaucracy and finally wrung out by the hot wet jungle and those savages down the river.

'The two boys you have with you are quite good. They'll help you learn your way about. Now that Sarawak has become a crown colony, we're going to have a bit more to spend on medicine. Spruce things up, here and there.'

Adam stared at his own hands and flexed them and wondered. It had been so long since they had held the surgeon's tools. 'I'll let you know what I'll need and what changes I plan to make,' he said abruptly.

Rather a cheeky sort, MacAlister thought. Well, he'll get all that beaten out of him. He had watched them withdraw and grow cruel and cynical by the month, once they realized the unthinkable situation.

'A bit of advice from an old Borneo hand. Don't try to change things here. The people down the river will thwart you on every turn. They're only just a generation or two removed from being head-hunters and cannibals. Life is hard enough here, so take it easy on yourself. Enjoy our meager comforts. After all, you've brought a woman and child to this place.'

'Thank you,' Adam said, not really thanking the man at all.

Stinking Sarawak. Hidden from humanity in a corner of Borneo. It was peopled by a conglomerate of Malayans who were the Moslems and there were Kayans and the tribes of Land Dayaks and the Ibans, who were the Sea Dayaks, and, of course, the omnipresent Chinese, the shopkeepers of the Orient.

Its modern history came about a bit over a century ago when trade over the China Sea between the British colony of Singapore and the Sultanate of Brunei on Borneo increased to such an extent that it became a prime target of pirates.

The Sultan of Brunei was not only raided by the pirates but constantly plagued by uprisings within his own kingdom. Law and order arrived in the person of James Brooke, a swashbuckling English soldier of fortune. Brooke stamped out the rebellions and sent the pirates packing. As a reward, the grateful Sultan ceded to him the province of Sarawak and James Brooke became the first of the fabled 'white rajahs.'

Brooke ruled his own domain as a benevolent autocrat. It was a steamy little state, with but a few miles of dirt roads. Its highways were the rivers which poured down from the hilly thick forests into the deltas of the South China Sea. It was a land blanketed in tropical foliage, inundated by two hundred inches of rain a year, and co-inhabited by crocodiles, rats, snakes, bats, and wild pigs. Its natives were beleaguered and decimated by leprosy, elephantiasis, worms, cholera, smallpox, dropsy.

Oppression was their lot. With pitiful little farm land, their meager crops were under constant attack by pirates and neighbors or taken by taxation.

They made war on each other and went into battle resplendent in feathered dress, and the head of the vanquished hung in the home of the victor. Those who were not murdered were sold into the slave markets.

Over a period of time, James Brooke and his nephew, who succeeded him as rajah, established some form of order so that one merely had to concern himself with the task of survival against the land.

The third and final white rajah, Sir Charles Vyner Brooke, ended the hundred and five year reign of his family after the Second World War. During the war the Japanese occupied Sarawak for its oil fields at Miri and when the war ended, Brooke ceded the state to the British crown and Sarawak along with Brunei and North Borneo became crown colonies.

Sir Edgar Bates, the first governor of Sarawak, was to take over a state that had grown to fifty thousand square miles and held a half million people. Most of these were the Ibans or Sea Dayaks, the former head-hunters of uncertain origin. Some say they were seagoing Mongols.

Sir Edgar, from the upper middle civil servants, did his best toward education and eventual self-rule. But all of those things passed over in the time of the white rajahs had taken its toll. The new Sarawak-Orient Company explored for oil and minerals and attempted to exploit the unending forest. Yet, progress was measured as the snail crosses the land and bogged in a quagmire of ancient pagan taboos.

When Adam Kelno arrived in 1949, he became the thirtieth doctor in Sarawak. There were five hospitals. This was the facility for half a million persons.

He was assigned to Fort Bobang in the Second Division of Sarawak, in the land of the Ibans, the tattooed head-hunters of Borneo.

Chapter Eight

Adam Kelno's boatmen deftly maneuvered the thirty foot thatched roof dugout over the bubbling rapids where the Lemanak tributary rushed into the Lampur River. It was not difficult to tell the doctor's boat for it had the largest outboard motor of any that pushed up the Lemanak. It smoothed and they glided past a brace of sleeping crocodiles. The sound of the motor sent them slithering down the sandbank into the water. A tribe of monkeys shrieked at them leaping along the treetops.

For ten miles up the Lemanak tributary there were a series of long houses of the Ulu Tribe of Sea Dayaks. Each of the houses was a communal village unto itself built on hardwood poles and housing from twenty to fifty families. The long houses running up to lengths of over two hundred feet hugged the river front. A pull-up ladder, once a defensive measure against attacking neighbors, served as a stairs to the common veranda. Facing the river, were a long uncovered drying platform and communal kitchen and work area. In the rear of each house there were small private rooms for each family. It was all roofed in palm leaf and shingles and beneath it pigs and chickens ran wild amid human feces and mangy curs struggled for existence.

Fifteen such long houses formed a tribal unit of the Ulu's under the rule of a chieftain named Bintang, after the stars.

The arrival of Dr Kelno's boat was greeted by the clap of gongs, the usual welcome for any visitor. During the day, as Dr Kelno held clinic, the Turah's, the heads of the other long houses of the tribe, arrived for the council meeting that Bintang had promised the doctor.

By evening they had all assembled, bedecked in woven jackets of blazing colors, cone-shaped hats topped with feathers, and assorted arm and leg bracelets. They were olive-skinned men of five feet in height, with seminegroid features mixed with that of Oriental. Their shiny black hair was pulled back to buns behind their necks and their shoulders, legs, and hands bore heavy tattoo markings. Some of the older Turahs sported such tattoos awarded to a warrior for his kills as a head-hunter in days not so long past. From rafter beams, all about the long house hung dozens of heads, all scraped clean as the inside of pumpkins. As the Turahs gathered Bintang offered them hot rice beer and they drank and chewed betel nuts and puffed cheroots in a corner of the common veranda.

Beyond them on the drying deck, the women went about their business of cooking, weaving rattan mats and bright cloth, making jewelry and curing the sago, a starchy food from tree trunks. Beneath their bare breasts they wore corsets made of many brass rings encircling the entire body and these adornments were decorated with coins and chain jewelry, and their ear lobes were deformed by heavily weighted earrings.

The mood of the Turahs, which had been lively, changed to somber as the dour Dr Kelno and his translator joined them. Feelings about him were definitely mixed. Bintang bade them to place their highly colored and ornamented seat mats on the rattan floor. Dr Kelno and his translator, Mudich, sat opposite them all. Bintang and his chief magician Pirak, the Manang of the tribe, sat off to a side. Pirak was one of the hereditary fakirs called by the spirits to administer health and the wisdom of the gods. There were numerous categories and ranks of the Manangs. Pirak, a wrinkled old specimen, was of a special breed known as Manang Bali, a male in female's dress and behavior. He was a seductress of young males but bisexual as well. Pirak received exorbitant fees of gifts and food for performance of his mystic hokum. Too old to inherit chiefdom from Bintang, Pirak was determined to hold his exalted position and felt that Dr Adam Kelno presented a threat.

Meaningless amenities flowed and then the translator began the business, as the half-starved dogs snapped up the remains of the plates of delicacies.

'Dr Adam say,' Mudich began, 'that monsoon season is almost upon us and and river will swell. Dr Adam not come back for long time. Last year during monsoon, cholera very bad. This year Dr Adam wants no such. He ask to give medicine through needle to save from cholera. Only twenty families in all of the long houses agree. Why is this so, say Dr Kelno.'

'Because Wind Spirit, Sea Spirit, Forest Spirit, and Fire Spirit are chosen by the Chief Spirit, Patra, to rule over sickness. We have prepared birds to sacrifice and will beat gongs four nights after first monsoon. Tell Dr Adam, we have many way to fight sickness.'

'Many, many way,' Pirak the magician added, pointing to his bag of omens, healing stones, and herbs.

A murmur of agreement arose among the Turahs.

Adam drew a deep breath, controlled himself, and leaned over to his translator. 'I want you to ask Bintang the following. I will give my medicine to families that want it. If, after the monsoon season is over, the families I have treated are all well but many others who were not given my medicine are dead from fever will that prove that the gods favor my medicine?'

Mudich pretended not to understand. Adam repeated it slowly. The translator squirmed, then shook his head. 'I cannot ask such question of Bintang.'

'Why not?'

'It will embarrass chief before his Turahs if you prove to be right.'

'Well, isn't he responsible for the health and well-being of his people?'

'Bintang also responsible to keep the legends. Sickness come, sickness go. Legend remain.'

All right, Adam thought to himself, I'll get at this another way. He once again explained carefully to Mudich the question he was posing.

'Dr Adam say to Bintang, why is burial ground so close to river? Dr Adam say it must be moved because it make water unclean and bad water cause sickness.'

'No true,' Bintang answered. 'Spirit cause sickness.'

Again the Turahs all nodded in agreement.

Adam saw the anger in Pirak's eyes. The Manang Bali was responsible for the disposal of the dead and burial was a source of much of his income and riches. 'Legend say, must bury on hill rising from river. Burial ground in right place now. Must not be moved.'

'Dr Adam say burial unclean. People not buried deep enough and many without a box to put them in. This Dr Adam say spoil water when it runs next to burial ground. Pigs and dogs no fenced so they come to burial ground and eat dead. When we eat pigs and drink water it cause sickness.'

'If woman die bleeding when giving child, she cannot have coffin,' the Manang Bali answered. 'If warrior die he must be buried close to water to ease his journey to Sebayan.'

'But when you bury him with all that food in the ground, the animals dig it up!'

'How can he travel to Sebayan without food? Besides, Dr Adam, in Sebayan he no longer has trouble so is better to get there,' Bintang said.

'If chief die,' Pirak added, 'he must be burned and given to Fire Spirit. Dr Adam no understand we must bury depending on how someone die.'

Moving the cemetery site now became another utterly useless pursuit. Kelno was being swamped under the weight of mysticism and taboos. He persisted.

'Dr Adam say, last time he come he brought seeds and vines of okra to plant in field near sago forest. Bintang promise to plant okra because is good for us to eat and make us strong.'

'We learn,' Pirak said, 'in omen from birds that fields by sago forest are cursed.'

'Just how did you come to that?'

'Very difficult to read bird omens,' Pirak said, 'take many years learning. Way bird fly, way bird sing, way bird cry, way two birds fly together. Birds give such bad omen we slaughter pig in ceremony and read markings on pig's liver. Everything say fields are cursed.'

'Dr Adam say we have only half the farm land we need. We must make use of all of it. Okra will drive out evil spirits from the fields. Okra is sacred food,' Mudich translated, as Kelno tried to use their own taboos to gain his end. But the frustration wore on.

'Dr Adam buy four water buffalo from Chinese. Why you no go to town of Sarebas and bring back?'

'Buffalo sacred omen, like moth and blue bird.'

'But you not bring them to eat but only to work with in field.'

'Curse to make sacred omen labor.'

After another hour of it, Adam was exhausted. He begged to be excused from the feast and the cockfight and tersely bid them farewell. Pirak, the Manang Bali, was now filled with kindness, having won all his arguments. Dr Adam would not return till after the monsoon. As he climbed into his boat and curtly ordered the boatmen to cast off, the Ulus on shore waved a half-hearted farewell. When the boat turned the bend, Bintang looked to Mudich and asked, 'Why does Dr Adam come here if he hate us so much?'

Chapter Nine

The closeness of the British compound at Fort Bobang imposed friendships on persons who would have spent a lifetime avoiding each other. Angela was particularly adaptable to the narrow social circle. Adam was not.

He had a particular dislike for L. Clifton-Meek, the Commissioner of Agriculture for the Second Division. Clifton-Meek's office adjoined his clinic and their homes were only separated by that of the commissioner, Jack Lambert.

The Empire was a haven that saved the mediocre from obscurity. Lionel Clifton-Meek was a prime example of the shoe clerk, the railroad ticket seller, the humbled assistant tailor who had wiggled his way into a niche in His Majesty's far-flung interests. It was a small hole to crawl into indeed, but once staked out it was his and his alone. Clifton-Meek carefully guarded against either taking on responsibility, or making decisions, or outside intrusions. He clothed himself in a blanket of paper work to expand a belief in his own importance. In this safe place he could wait it out and end up with a nice pension for loyal service to the crown.

If L. Clifton-Meek personified a low echelon of civil servants, his drab, turkey-necked wife, Mercy, even more vividly portrayed what was hated by the black and yellow people they ruled.

In England, the Clifton-Meeks would have lived a gray life in a brick row house in a gray town or in London in a walk-up cold water flat, where her only qualification to augment her husband's insufficient income would be to hire herself out as a maid.

But the Empire did much for the lowly of England. In Sarawak they had stature. In the Second Division there was no other agricultural commissioner. Clifton-Meek had much to say about the rice fields, and the rubber plantations, and spent much of his time frustrating the Sarawak-Orient Company by the endless chain of command. A bone in the throat of progress.

Mercy Meek had at her beck and call two Malayan houseboys, who slept on the veranda and chased after her with an umbrella to shade her milky freckled skin from the sun. And she had a pure Chinese cook. The artificial snobbery of their low ancestry caused them to hyphenate their name as a further gesture of self-importance. And to top it all, Mercy attempted to bring the God of the Episcopalians to these heathens. On Sunday, the compound vibrated with her playing of the organ and pounding the fear of Jesus into them to a response of listlessly mumbled prayers.

Commissioner Lambert was another sort. Like Adam's superior, MacAlister, Lambert was an old hand in these parts, a good administrator who calmly listened to the complaints of the native chiefs, did little about them, and saw that everyone was well supplied with British flags and portraits of the King for their long houses. Basically, Lambert and Kelno left each other alone.

But that time had to come when L. Clifton-Meek had been buggered about once too often by that certain foreign medical officer and filed an indignant report.

Before Lambert let the report go into channels, he thought a meeting ought to take place between parties. It commenced in the commissioner's boiling peeling office under a tired overhead fan, which did little to bring comfort. L. Clifton-Meek's pinched white face quivered as he clung to the books of governing regulations while Lambert thumbed through the thick report.

Lambert mopped his wet jaw. It was a strange place for a man to perspire from, Adam thought. 'It appears, Dr Kelno, that we have a misunderstanding of sorts. I rather it not go beyond this desk if we can all reach an agreement.'

Clifton-Meek arched his back as Adam glared at him with contempt.

'Have you familiarized yourself with Clifton-Meek's complaint?'

'I read it this morning.'

'Not really a serious matter.'

'I consider it quite serious,' Clifton-Meek said in a voice that trembled with fear.

'What I mean,' Lambert soothed, 'is that there is nothing here that we chaps can't bandy about a bit and simply overcome.'

'That depends on Dr Kelno.'

'Let's take a look here,' Lambert said. 'First, there's the matter of the okra fields proposed for the Ulus on the lower Lemanak.'

'What about the okra fields?' Adam asked.

'According to this, it seems you recommended the planting of okra fields at the fifteen long houses under Chief Bintang, and you brought seeds and pods to them for that purpose.'

'Guilty as charged,' Adam said.

L. Clifton-Meek smirked and rattled his skinny fingers on Lambert's desk. 'Okra is a malvaceous shrub, a planted crop that falls quite clearly under the agricultural commissioner. It has nothing to do with health or medicine,' he bureaucrated.

'Do you believe that okra as an augment to their present diet would be good for their health or bad for their health?' Adam asked.

'I shall not be entrapped with your word games, Doctor. Land usage is clearly in my department, sir, clearly. Right here on page seven hundred and two of the regulations,' and he read the long rule as Jack Lambert stifled a smile. Clifton-Meek temporarily closed the book filled with handy markers. 'I am, sir, making a survey for the Sarawak-Orient Company for proper land use in the Second Division for the possibility of rubber plantations.'

'In the first place,' Adam said, 'the Ulus can't eat rubber. In the second place I don't know how you can make a survey if you haven't once traveled the Lemanak River.'

'I have maps and other methods.'

'Is it your recommendation then that okra fields should not be planted?' Adam asked.

'Yes, Lionel,' Lambert interjected, 'just what do you propose?'

'I am only saying,' he retorted, with voice rising, 'the book clearly defines the duties of both our offices. If the medical officer just pops about taking matters into his own hands chaos will result.'

'May I say candidly that if you were to take a trip down the Lemanak, as I have proposed to you on numerous occasions, common sense would show you there is no land available for rubber plantations. What you would know is that there is universal malnutrition due to insufficient farm land. And as for the rest of your ridiculous report only an ass would protest my purchase of water buffalos and recommending new fishing methods.'

'The regulations clearly state that the agricultural officer is the sole judge in these matters,' Clifton-Meek screamed with veins popping in his neck and his ruddy cheeks becoming crimson.

'Gentlemen, gentlemen,' Lambert said, 'we are all officers of the crown here.'

'The crime I seem to have committed,' Adam Kelno said, 'is to try to better the lives of my patients and see them live longer. Why don't you take your report, Clifton-Meek, and shit all over it.'

Clifton-Meek sprung up. 'I demand this report be sent to the capital, Mr Lambert. It is a pity we have to put up with certain foreign elements who do not understand the meaning of orderly administration. Good day, sir.'

A disgusted silence followed Clifton-Meek's departure.

'Never mind, don't say it,' Lambert said filling a glass with water from his carafe.

'I will make a collection of native omens, taboos, gods, spirits, rituals, and rules of His Majesty's Foreign Office regulations, and I'll call it *Handbook for Idiots*. The Meeks shall inherit the Empire.'

'For some strange reason we've managed to muddle through for almost four centuries,' Lambert said.

'Down the river they fish with spears, hunt with blow-guns, and plow their fields with sticks. Once you get an idea through their savage skulls there is always a Lionel Clifton-Meek to bury it in his paper heap.'

'Well now, Kelno, you've only been out here awhile. You ought to know things go slowly. No use of all this tugging and hauling. Besides, most of the Ibans are nice chaps once you get on to the idea they have their own way of doing things.'

'Savages, damned savages.'

'Do you really think they're savages?'

'Well, what else is there to think?'

'That's rather strange coming from you, Kelno.'

'What do you mean, Lambert?'

'We don't pry into a man's past here but you were a prisoner in the Jadwiga Concentration Camp. What I mean to say is, having gone through all that in Poland, done by an allegedly civilized people, it is rather difficult to really say just who are the savages in this world.'

Chapter Ten

For the most part, Adam Kelno remained aloof of the small, stifling, repetitious, and dull clique of British civil servants at Fort Bobang.

His one meaningful friendship was with Ian Campbell, a craggy Scotsman who supervised a cooperative of small rubber plantations with headquarters at Fort Bobang to oversee the warehousing and shipping operation. Campbell was an unpretentious man, yet steeped in the classics and literature nourished during long, lonely seasons. He was a drinking man, a chess-playing man, a man with terse words and no nonesense for the pale colonials and of wisdom of the jungle and the natives.

A widower, once married to a French plantation owner's daughter, he was left with four small children who were cared for by a Chinese couple. He, himself, was cared for by a striking Eurasian girl in her late teens.

Campbell personally tutored his children with studies beyond their years inflicted with the zeal of a Baptist missionary. His own friendship with Kelno came into being when his children enrolled in the informal classes Angela taught the children of Fort Bobang.

His youngest son was Terrence, a year older than Stephan Kelno, who in short order formed a friendship that was destined to span their lifetimes.

Both Stephan and Terrence made remarkable adaptations to this remote place and both seemed capable of overcoming the disadvantages of their removal from civilization. The boys were like brothers, together most of the time and dreaming aloud of places beyond the sea.

And during those periods when Adam Kelno skidded into a tropical depression, it was always Ian Campbell whom Angela called upon to bring her husband around.

The monsoon season came. The rivers raged to impassability. And with it, MacAlister's prophecy of doom unfolded. In that second year, Angela had a third miscarriage and they had to go about the business of seeing to it that she could not become pregnant again.

Wilted by the heat and turned soggy by the rain and caged in Fort Bobang Adam Kelno took to heavy drinking. His nights were filled with a kind of madness, the recurring dreams of the concentration camp. And that nightmare he had known since boyhood. It always took the form of a large animal, a bear or a gorilla or an unidentifiable monster chasing him, entrapping him, and then crushing him. The spear or weapon he carried or his own strength was totally impotent in stopping the attack. As he was powerless to move, breathing became more and more difficult and always on the brink of death by suffocation he awakened sweating, heart pounding, gasping and at times crying out in terror. And the parade of the dead at the Jadwiga Concentration Camp and the blood of the surgery never stopped.

The relentless rain showed no pity.

Each morning he took longer to lift his head from the pillow from the effects of alcohol and quaking after another night of horror.

A lizard flitted across the floor. Adam picked at his food listlessly. He was in the usual bleary-eyed state of this time of evening and his face showed a six day growth of stubble.

'Please eat, Adam.'

He grunted an indistinguishable answer.

Angela dismissed the servants with a nod of her head. Stephan Kelno was still a child, but he knew the reek of liquor from his father's breath and turned his cheek as Adam kissed him when he left the table.

Adam blinked and narrowed his eyes to get them into focus. Angela, poor Angela, sat in sallow sorrow. There were gray hairs in her head now. He had put them there with his own paint brush of misery.

'I really think you ought to shave and bathe and make an effort to come over to the Lamberts' and welcome the new missionaries,' she said.

'Lord God, will you stop trying to pawn off your only begotten son on these cannibals? Missionaries. Do you really think Jesus comes to places like this? Jesus avoids places like this ... concentration camps ... British prisons. Jesus knows how to stay out of trouble. Tell the missionaries ... I hope the head-hunters get them.'

'Adam.'

'Go sing your hymns with Mercy Meek. What a friend we have in Jeeeeesus. Hail Mary. Mother of God. Keep your nose out of Sarawak.'

Angela pushed back from the table angrily.

'Get me a drink first. No lectures. Just a drink. Even the goddam British gin will do. Aha, says the temperate and long suffering wife, the one thing you don't need is another drink.'

'Adam!'

'Subject of the next lecture. My husband hasn't made love to me for over a month. My husband is impotent.'

'Adam, listen to me. There is talk going around of dismissing you.'

'Where'd you hear that?'

'Clifton-Meek was very happy to slap me with that news,' she said. 'When I heard it I wrote to MacAlister in Kuching. They are gravely concerned.'

'Hurray. I'm sick of cannibals and Englishmen.'

'Where do you think you can go after this?'

'So long as I have these,' he said thrusting his hands before her face, 'I'll find a place.'

'They aren't as steady as they used to be.'

'Where's my damned drink?'

'All right, Adam, you might as well hear the rest of it. I've reached the saturation point. If they sack you here ... if you don't pull yourself together, Stephan and I will not go on with you.'

He stared.

'We've taken all of this silence and we've not complained about Sarawak. Adam, the one thing you've never had to question is my loyalty, and I'll stay here forever if need be. But I shall not go on living with a drunk who has completely given up on life.'

'You mean that, don't you.'

'Yes, I do.' She turned and left for the Lamberts'.

Adam Kelno grunted and held his face in his hands. The sheets of rain plunged the place into darkness until the servants bathed it in swaying lamplight. He continued to sit to force rationality back to his fuzzed brain, then staggered to his feet and shuffled to a mirror. 'You stupid bastard,' he said to himself.

Adam went to Stephan's room. The boy looked from his bed half asleep and apprehensive.

Oh my God, he thought. What have I done? He is my life, this child.

When Angela returned she found Adam asleep in a chair in Stephan's room with the boy asleep in his lap. A storybook, worn from rereading, had fallen to the floor. Angela smiled. Adam's face was clean-shaven. He awakened to her kiss and silently and gently put Stephan in his bed. He placed the mosquito netting around him and put his arm about his wife and led her to the bedroom.

Ian Campbell returned from an extended stay in Singapore at a sorely needed time. He gave himself to his friend to bring him through a soggy brained monsoon rot. It came over long chess games, with children scrambling underfoot. After all, Adam came to realize, Campbell had done it as a widower with four children. And he found the iron.

'It's never so bad, Adam, that it's worth turning one of your children into a drunk or leading them to a life of darkness. After all, man, they didn't bargain for this place.'

Adam Kelno decided he owed Ian Campbell very much and the way to pay it came through young Terrence. Often as not Terrence Campbell's curious eyes peered over the window sill of the dispensary, mouth agape.

'Come on in, Terry. Don't stand there like a Lampur monkey.'

The boy would ease into the room and watch for hours as Dr Adam, the magic Dr Adam, made people well. As Terry's reward, Dr Adam would ask him to fetch something or assist in some small way. And he dreamed of being a doctor.

When Dr Adam was in a good mood, and Terry knew them all, he would ask a never-ending stream of questions about medicine. More than once Adam wished it were his own son, Stephan. But Stephan was outside doing something with a hammer and nails ... a raft, a tree house.

'God works in strange ways,' Adam thought, accepting but not accepting.

One thing was obvious and that was if Terrence Campbell had half a chance, he would be a doctor.

Chapter Eleven

The monsoon season ended. Adam Kelno had returned to life.

A small surgery was installed with a capability of minor operations. MacAlister came from Kuching to attend the dedication and remained for several days. What he saw in the operating theater was a revelation. With Angela assisting, Adam performed a number of operations. MacAlister witnessed a complete change in Kelno with the surgeon's knife in his hands. Extraordinary skill, exquisite movements, command and concentration.

A short time thereafter the police radio received a request from the capital at Kuching to have Dr Kelno come to perform an emergency surgery. A light plane was dispatched to Fort Bobang for him. It soon became fashionable for the British colony in Kuching to have Adam Kelno as their surgeon instead of traveling to Singapore.

As soon as the river was passable, Adam headed up the Lemanak. This time his son, Stephan, traveled with him. He came upon the Ulu long houses to find that disaster had struck during the monsoon season in the form of raging cholera.

Bintang was in mortal grief over the death of his two eldest sons. Pirak had used water from sacred jars, magic oil, specially prepared pepper, and ordered gongs and drums beaten for days to drive away the evil spirits. But it came. Diarrhea followed by unbearable cramps and vomiting, dehydration, and the sunken eyes and fever and the leg pains and the apathetic wait for death. As the epidemic mounted, Bintang and those who were not stricken fled to the hills and left the sick to die.

The twenty families of the tribe who had taken Dr Adam's medicine lived in six different long houses, and none of them fell to the sickness. Out of his own great sorrow, Bintang began to change his attitude. Although he still disliked the terse, cold doctor he now had to respect his medicine. Bintang called his Turahs together and with the disaster still fresh in their minds, they agreed to make changes.

The cemetery, a chief cause of contamination, was moved. It was a brazen step. Then, the long debated okra fields were planted and bullocks brought to plow the fields. The buffalo were able to turn the earth much deeper than their own crude hand plows and the crops of yams and vegetables became larger and finer in taste. Dr Adam brought a fishing expert from Kuching who was able to replace the spear with netting methods. The chickens and pigs were fenced and the place to make human refuse was moved away from each long house. Much new medicine was given through Dr Adam's needle.

And as the year wore on, Bintang noticed a change in Dr Adam himself. In one way he was like the Ulu in his love for his child. With the young son and Terrence Campbell traveling with him, the doctor seemed much more kind. And on the second trip, Dr Adam Kelno brought his wife, who also knew much of medicine and did much to take away the shyness of many of the women.

On the fourth and final trip to the Ulus before the monsoon, Dr Adam's boat turned the bend to Bintang's long house and tied ashore just before nightfall. Something seemed strange. For the first time there was an absence of the greetings of gongs and a gathering of the villagers. Mudich, the translator, alone awaited him.

'Quick, Dr Adam. Bintang's little son very sick. Crocodile bite.'

They raced the path to the long house, climbed the notched steps, and as they reached the veranda he could hear low, rhythmic chanting. Adam shoved his way through the crowd to where the child lay groaning on the floor. The leg wound was covered with wet herbs and sacred healing stones. Pirak had chanted himself into a trance waving a pole topped with beads and feathers over the child.

Adam knelt and abruptly uncovered the wound. Fortunately he had been bitten in the fleshy part of the thigh. Some of the flesh had been torn away, the teeth marks went deep. Pulse, weak but steady. He flashed a light into the child's eyes. No serious hemorrhaging but the wound was dirty and débridement and drainage were needed along with surgery on a severed muscle. Temperature ... very hot, a hundred and four degrees.

'How long has he been lying there?'

Mudich could not answer properly because the Ulus had no sense of hourly time. Adam fished through his bag and prepared a penicillin shot. 'Have him removed to my hut, immediately.'

Suddenly Pirak emerged from his communion with the spirits. As Dr Adam gave the boy an injection he screamed in anger.

'Get him the hell out of here,' Adam snapped.

'He say you are breaking the magic spell.'

'I hope so. He's twice as sick as he need be.'

The Manang Bali picked up his magic potions, magic stones, tusks, roots, herbs, ginger, pepper and he rattled it over the child yelling that he was not finished with his treatment.

Adam snatched the bag and flung it over the veranda.

Pirak, who had been already disgraced by the cholera epidemic and with his power in the village slipping, realized he had to make a bold stand. He grabbed Adam's bag off the floor and flung it away.

Everyone backed away as Adam came to his feet and hovered over the old fakir. He controlled the impulse to strangle Pirak. 'Tell Bintang,' he said in an uneven voice, 'the boy is becoming very sick. Bintang has already lost two of his sons. This child will not live unless he is given to me immediately.'

Pirak jumped up and down and screamed. 'He is breaking my spell. He will bring back evil spirits!'

'Tell Bintang that Pirak is a fraud. Tell him that now. I want him ordered away from this child.'

'I cannot tell that,' Mudich said. 'The chief cannot throw out his own magician.'

'This child's life is in the balance.'

Pirak argued with Bintang heatedly. The chief looked from one to the other in confusion. Centuries of his society and culture weighed on him, and he was afraid of either decision. The Turahs would never understand such a thing as casting out his Manang. But the child. He will die, Dr Adam say. Ulus have uncommon love for their children. When his own two sons died of the fever he adopted two little Chinese girls as his own for the Chinamen often gave away the unwanted females.

'Bintang say, Manang must heal son in the way of our people.'

Pirak thrust out his chest arrogantly and beat it with his fist and strutted as someone returned his bag of sticks and stones to him.

Adam Kelno turned and walked off.

Adam sat in naked futility under the waterfall below the river. He could hear the gongs and chanting from the long house. On the bank, Mudich and his boatmen kept guard for crocodiles and cobras. Poor Dr Adam, Mudich thought. He will never understand.

He dragged himself, with weighted weariness, to a small separate hut that housed his clinic, and his own private room, which held a low palleted bed over the matted floor. He uncorked a bottle of gin and went at it until the sound of gongs and drums faded under the beat of evening rain, and then he stretched on his pallet and groaned to semi-sleep.

'Dr Adam! Dr Adam! Wake! Wake!' Mudich said.

With years of medical training he came awake instantly. Mudich stood over his pallet with a torch.

'Come,' he said urgently.

Adam was on his feet, buttoning his shirt and tucking it into his trousers. In the next room Bintang stood with the child in his arms.

'Save my son,' Bintang cried.

Adam took the boy and laid him on a crude examination table. The fever raged. It's bad, Adam thought, it's very bad. 'Hold the torch closer.'

As he set the thermometer into the child's rectum the boy went into a convulsion.

'How long has he been doing this. Before or after the sun?'

'When sun fall boy jerk around crazy.'

That would mean three or more hours. He withdrew the thermometer. One hundred and nine degrees. The child frothed and writhed. Brain damage! Irreparable brain damage! Even if he could pull the child through he would be an imbecile.

The little olive-skinned man looked up to the doctor with begging eyes. How to explain that the chief's son would be a hopeless idiot?

'Tell Bintang there is very little hope. He must wait outside. Mudich, set the torch in the holder and wait outside also. I will work alone.'

There was no choice but to let the child go off to sleep.

Adam Kelno was back in Jadwiga Concentration Camp. The surgery ... Barrack V. He leaned down close to the child and was compelled to untie the string that held in place a tiny cloth covering the boy's genitals.

IF THESE OPERATIONS ARE NECESSARY, I WILL DO THEM. DO YOU THINK I ENJOY IT?

Adam fondled the tiny pair of testicles, kneaded them in his fingers, ran his hand up the scrotum.

IF THEY MUST COME OFF FOR THE LIFE OF THE PATIENT.

He backed away suddenly and went into a violent trembling, looking somewhat mad, as the boy went into another agonized spasm.

An hour later, Adam emerged from the clinic and faced the anxious father and a dozen waiting tribesmen.

'He went to sleep peacefully.'

When a primitive, as Bintang, emits the sounds of grief it is the cry of a wounded animal. He screamed and threw himself on the ground and beat upon himself in a tantrum of exquisite torment. And he wailed his hurt until exhaustion overcame him and found him face down in the mud bleeding from self-inflicted fury. Only then was Adam able to render him unconscious.

Chapter Twelve

The police radio advised Kuching that the flying weather was marginal so MacAlister came to Fort Bobang by boat. He tied up to the main pier amid a small forest of dugouts, where Chinese and Malayans and Muruts and Ibans jabbered in a multitude of tongues in furious barter. Along the shore, women beat their wash clean and others drew water, carrying it in cans hanging from ox-like yokes.

MacAlister jumped ashore and walked up the dock past the main corrugated tin warehouse, where his nostril was pelted with the odor of slabs of freshly pressed rubber, pepper, and sacks of bat dung collected from the caves by the ingenious Chinese and sold as fertilizer.

The old Asian hand marched stiffly up the dirt road, past the Chinese shops and thatched huts of the Malays and into the British compound. MacAlister grumbled through a gargantuan mustache, as he slowed for his umbrella-bearing servant, who raced to keep the sun from his master's head. Knee-length stockings were met by long khaki shorts, and his cane popped in cadence to the crisp step.

Adam stood up from the chess game to greet him. MacAlister studied the board, then looked to Adam's opponent, his seven-year-old son, who was giving his father a trimming. The boy shook MacAlister's hand and Adam shooed him off.

'The lad plays quite a game.'

Adam could scarcely conceal his pride in Stephan, who at this early age could read and speak English, Polish, and a smattering of Chinese and Malay.

After a time they settled on the screened veranda with the ever constant green view of the flowing rivers of Borneo. Their drinks came and soon the new sounds and smells of dusk invaded along with the blessed relief from the heat. Out on the lawn, Stephan played with Terrence Campbell.

'Cheers,' said MacAlister.

'Well, Dr MacAlister, what's the occasion?' Adam asked with his usual abruptness.

He laughed vaguely. 'Well, Kelno, seems that you've made quite a success in Kuching. Governor's wife's tonsils, Commissioner of Native Affairs' hernia, to say nothing of our leading Chinese citizen's gallstones.'

Adam waited through the trivia. 'Well now, why am I in Bobang, eh?'

'Yes, why?'

'To come right out with it, Sir Edgar,' he said in reference to the governor, 'and I have charted out an entirely new medical facility for the future of Sarawak. We want to move some of the newer men into meaningful positions as quickly as we are able to put the old-timers out to pasture. We'd like you to transfer to Kuching and take over as chief surgeon of the hospital. I think you'll agree it's becoming quite a good facility.'

Adam drank slowly these days. He took it all in deliberately.

'Traditionally,' MacAlister continued, 'whoever is the chief surgeon is automatically assistant chief medical officer of Sarawak. I say, Kelno, you don't seem too pleased by all of this.'

'It sounds very political, and I'm not one much for administrative work.'

'Don't be so modest. You were the C.M.O. at the Polish army hospital at Tunbridge Wells.'

'I never got used to filling out reports and playing politics.'

'What about Jadwiga?'

Adam paled a bit.

'We're not pushing you up past a dozen men in the dark. Nor are we bringing up a past you want to forget, but your responsibilities were for hundreds of thousands of people there. Sir Edgar and I think you're the best man.'

'It has taken me five years to get the trust of the Ulus,' Adam said. 'With Bintang and his Turahs I have been able to get many projects started and just now we are able to draw comparative results. I have become quite caught up in the problem of malnutrition. A surgeon you can get in Kuching, and the British will never be short of administrators, but I feel that eventually something important may come to light out of my work. You see, Dr MacAlister, in Jadwiga we had to depend entirely on what the Germans provided us to support life. Here, no matter how bad the land is and no matter how primitive the society, one can always better one's self, and we are coming close to proving it.'

'Ummmm, I see. I suppose you've considered the fact that Mrs Kelno would be more comfortable in Kuching. She could pop over to Singapore a few more times a year.'

'I must say, in all candor, that Angela is as excited about my work as I am.'

'And the boy? His education?'

'Angela teaches him daily. I will put him against any boy his age in Kuching.

'Then you are quite definite about turning this down.'

'Yes.'

'Shall we let our hair down,' MacAlister said.

'Of course.'

'How much of all this is your fear of leaving the jungle?'

Adam set his drink down and sighed deeply, as MacAlister found him at his source.

'Kuching is not the middle of London. No one is going to find you there.'

'The Jews are everywhere. Every one of them is a potential enemy.'

'Are you going to keep yourself locked up in the jungle for the rest of your life?'

'I don't wish to talk about it anymore.' Adam Kelno answered with tiny beads of perspiration breaking out all over his face.

Chapter Thirteen

Stephan Kelno was the apple of his father's eye and an unusually gifted boy. Perhaps no single thing impressed the natives more than the presence of Dr Adam's son on the river trips.

Adam stood on the wharf, steeped in sorrow as the ferry to Kuching pulled away, and Angela and his son waved to him until they were out of sight. From Kuching they would take a steamer to Singapore and then on to Australia, where Stephan would begin his formal education in a boarding school.

Adam was filled with more than the usual parental fear that something might happen to his child. For the first time in years he prayed. He prayed for the boy's safety.

To fill the terrible void, the relationship with young Terrence broadened. From an early age Terry spoke in medical terms and assisted in minor surgery. There could be no doubt that he would make an extraordinary doctor and to make this possible became Adam's goal. Ian Campbell was for it, though he doubted that a boy from the jungle could compete in the outside world.

Kelno turned his enormous energy to a series of new programs. Adam asked Bintang and the other Turahs of the tribe to send a promising boy or girl in his teens from each long house to Fort Bobang. This took a bit of convincing, for the elders, who had always lived communally, did not wish to give up any manpower. Ultimately Adam was able to convince them that with special training they would be of more value.

He started with fifteen youngsters who built a miniature long house. The first programs were kept very simple. The reading of time, basic first aid, and sanitation programs for each long house. Out of the first group two of the boys were sent to the Batu Lintang Training School in Kuching for more sophisticated schooling.

Within the year Angela was teaching them how to read and write English, as well as some nursing. Even L. Clifton-Meek got caught up in it and opened an experimental plot of land just beyond the compound. At the end of the third year there was a major breakthrough, when one of the boys returned from the Batu Lintang School qualified to operate a radio. For the first time in their thousand year existence, the Ulus were able to speak to and hear from the outside world. During the monsoon season, the radio became a godsend to diagnose and treat a variety of ills.

Terrence Campbell turned out to be the hidden jewel in the program. His ability to communicate with the Ulu youngsters made things happen that awed everyone in the British compound. As more sophisticated textbooks arrived, Terrence devoured them. Adam was now more determined than ever to qualify Terry for a top English college. Perhaps some of Kelno's zeal lay in the realization that his own son would never choose medicine. But there it was, Kelno the mentor and idol and Terry the determined and brilliant student.

Mass inoculation of Bintang's people reduced age old scourges. Bintang's long houses were cleaner, the earth yielded more, and there was a little more time to live with a little less pain. Soon, other chieftains and Turahs petitioned Dr Adam to send children to Fort Bobang and the center grew to forty students.

The budget meetings in Kuching were always a hassle, but MacAlister generally gave Kelno what he wanted. It was no secret that the Sultan of Brunei wanted Dr Adam as his personal physician and offered a lavish new hospital. After two years, he got his helicopter, which increased his movement capability a hundredfold. The Ibans made up a song about the wingless bird and the doctor who came from the sky.

All of this was but a grain of sand. Adam knew that given all the resources he could command and all the money he could spend, there was little that would really change, but each small step forward renewed the determination to continue.

The years passed by and the work continued. But what Adam Kelno really lived for was the return of Stephan on the summer holidays. To no one's surprise the boy was skipping ahead in his classes. Although he fared well in Australia, Fort Bobang was his home, where he could take those wonderful trips on the Lemanak with his father.

And then Adam received news that distressed him more than he believed possible. MacAlister was retiring and moving to England. There had never been either intimacy or affection between the men, and he wondered why it bothered him so.

The Kelnos went to Kuching, where a farewell dinner was given for MacAlister and Sir Edgar Bates, the governor, who was departing for England to attend the coronation of the new queen. Sir Edgar would also remain in England and a new governor assigned to Sarawak.

Even in places so remote, the British knew how to conduct their affairs with flourish and fanfare. The ballroom was white with colonial uniforms and colored with sashes and medals.

There were a multitude of toasts filled with true and mock sentiment. Things were changing quickly these days. The sun was setting on that Empire where the sun was never supposed to set. In Asia, and Africa, and America it fell like a house of dominoes. The Malayans in Sarawak had picked up the cadence of the freedom wind.

As the evening reached its zenith, Adam turned to his wife and took her hand. 'I have a surprise for you,' he said. 'We leave in the morning for Singapore, and we will fly to Australia to visit Stephan and perhaps a short vacation in New Zealand.'

The long night of Adam Kelno was coming to an end.

Chapter Fourteen

The new governor was a persuasive fellow and convinced Adam to take the appointment as chief medical officer of the Second Division. With freedom in the air there was an urgent attempt to leap forward. The training of civil servants and upgrading the medical and educational facility took priority. Development of forests and mines by Sarawak-Orient ran parallel to an infusion of new teachers, nurses, airfields, and ports.

In the Second Division Adam was able to remain in Fort Bobang but inherited over a thousand persons, mostly Ibans with a smattering of Chinese and Malayans in the population centers. Adam had four doctors and a dozen nurses and assistants and of course Terrence Campbell, with primitive aide stations at the long houses. They were badly understaffed to cope with the range of diseases and problems, but he still had a higher ratio than the other Division Medical officers, who could only claim one doctor to every thirty-five thousand people.

His long suit remained the utilization of the land. There simply was not enough grazing land or farm land, so the threat of famine always lurked. Even as taboos were being broken he was unable to penetrate the ones forbidding the eating of deer and goats. It was the Iban belief that these animals were reincarnations of dead ancestors. Conversely he was unable to stop them from eating rats.

In searching United Nations bulletins and other works on the subject, Kelno became entranced by similar work in the new state of Israel. Although they were entirely different in make-up, Israel and Sarawak shared the fate of land shortage and acute deficiencies of beef and protein.

Israel had filled the protein gap with crops requiring very little land. Intense chicken hatcheries worked on a twenty-four hour basis. This idea was not suitable for the Ibans. The buildings required electricity to light them so the hens would lay around the clock. Also, the chicken itself was a disease prone fowl requiring a more advanced mentality to raise properly.

It was the second idea that caught Kelno's fancy, the artificial fish ponds. Israel had a consulate in Burma, her first diplomatic exchange in the Far East, and a number of Israeli agricultural experts were sent to establish experimental farms. He was sorely tempted to go to Burma and study the fish farms, but his fear of being recognized by a Jew overruled it.

He gathered the available literature and near Fort Bobang had his students build a half dozen ponds supplied with water from natural sources with simple canals to feed them and outlet valves for overflow. Each pond was stocked with a different variety of fish and cultured with self-perpetuating algae and plankton.

A half dozen years of trial and error were required to determine the most reliable and hardiest crop. A variety of Asian carp did the job along with imported New Zealand lobster, which flourished in fresh water.

And then came the years of persuasion before fish ponds began to pop up near the fields of the Ulus on the Lemanak.

My Dear Kelno [wrote MacAlister]

Not much is happening in Budleigh-Salterton. I am so pleased we have stayed in correspondence. It is difficult to believe you have been in Fort Bobang over a decade.

I have read your paper on the fish ponds, and your new experiment in grinding whole trash fish from the ocean as a protein supplement. May I say right off that I consider this one of the most dynamic possibilities to do something about the most pressing problem in Sarawak. I'm glad now I didn't convince you to come to Kuching to practice at the hospital.

I fully agree that your paper should be read to the British Academy. However, I cannot go along with your idea obscuring the authorship to that of an unnamed 'research team.' The paper should, and must, have your name on it.

Pursuant to this, I have traveled to London on numerous occasions and working quietly with old friends in Scotland Yard and the Foreign Office we have delved discreetly into the matter of your past unpleasantness with the Polish Communists.

We have been able to extend our inquiries to Poland itself through our diplomats in Warsaw. The results are all quite positive. All the Poles who were in the embassy in London are long since gone, and since you now have British citizenship there is no request for extradition on war crime charges of any kind.

Furthermore, I have spoken to Count Anatol Czerny, a charming chap, and it is also his opinion that it is all water over the dam and you have nothing to fear.

I am pleased to hear that Stephan is doing so well 'down under.' Count Czerny assures me also that Terrence Campbell with his superior grades in special examinations and the fact you applied for entry several years ago will be admitted to Magdalen College. I think it is the most beautiful in Oxford, dating all the way back to the fifteenth century.

Dear Kelno, please look favorably on my request to read the paper in your name before the academy. My kindest regards to your charming wife. In friendship,

Yours sincerely,

J. J. MACALISTER, M.D.

Adam reached the decision to allow MacAlister to read his paper without too much searching. He had traveled on numerous occasions to Singapore, New Zealand, and Australia without incident. His nightmares had all but faded. It was his love of Stephan that cast the deciding vote. He wanted to have his boy proud of him, and that desire outweighed his fears. He owed that much to Angela, too. And so the paper was read under the authorship of Dr Adam Kelno.

These were the days of the new enlightenment, when it became fashionable for white men to ponder about the unproductive fields and life of squalor of black and yellow men and mass death by starvation. A conscience stirred far too late with far too little to save more than half of the world that went hungry. Adam Kelno's paper created a ripple.

As a pure scientist he had to resort to a method believed by many to be extremely cruel. Half the Ulu long houses received his medicine, fish ponds, sanitation programs, and new crops and farming methods. The other half went without these things in order to furnish the comparative statistics. The higher death rate, lower longevity, and level of physical development and vitality dramatized the impact of his program.

The use of human guinea pigs was something the scientists did not like but understood. A secondary part of the paper that concerned the breaking down of ancient taboos particularly proved interesting to those who had struggled in the colonies.

The paper was widely published and acclaimed and became a standard reference for those teams of doctors, scientists, and agricultural experts who were wrestling with hunger throughout the world.

The best of it all was that no adverse reaction was heard anywhere to Adam Kelno's name.

Eighteen months after the paper, 'Artificial Fish Ponds, and Their Effect on the Diet and Health of Primitive Peoples: Use of Ground Whole Trash Fish as a Protein Supplement: Comparative Diet and Vaccine Charts,' an internationally manned UNESCO team arrived in Sarawak and made to Fort Bobang for a firsthand look at Kelno's work. A month later a report was filed that 'United Nations funds and personel should be committed to Fort Bobang to join the study.'

Adam now looked forward to Singapore as a place for joyous reunions with Stephan. This was to be an occasion among occasions. Stephan had been accepted at Harvard and would soon be traveling to America to study architecture.

'I have news, son,' Adam said, unable to constrain himself. 'Mother and I have talked things over. Fifteen years in the jungle is quite enough. We are going to return to England.'

'Father, I'm speechless! It's marvelous, just marvelous. Strange how it all works. Terry in England with you. Me in America.'

'One doctor, one architect from Fort Bobang. Not so bad,' Adam said with just a tinge of sadness. 'The United Nations people really have taken things over at Bobang. In a manner of speaking, my work is done. The medical facility of Sarawak has more than doubled and a lot is going on. I'm pleased to say that when Sarawak becomes part of the Malayan State, Sir Abdel Haji Mohamed, the prime minister apparent, wants me to remain.'

'They're no fools.'

Stephan knew it was his father's dream that they be together and he didn't want to dampen the moment but inside him he felt he had to do his stint in some faraway place.

The Kelnos traveled from Singapore to Kuching in the highest spirits. The capital was something out of Somerset Maugham. Lady Grayson, the governor's wife, sent the Kelnos an invitation to join them at a formal garden party in honor of the Queen's birthday.

As they arrived at the governor's mansion, Lord Grayson met them and escorted them to the lighted garden into an array of the top government officials in their whites and the Malayans and Chinese, who would soon be administering the state. As they entered a hush fell over the lawn and everyone stared at Adam.

The governor nodded and the native orchestra played a ceremonial fanfare.

'What's going on, Lord Grayson?' Adam asked.

He smiled. 'Ladies and gentlemen, refill your glasses. Last night I was advised by the Colonial Office that the Queen's Birthday List has been published in London. Among those chosen for honor to the Empire, Dr Adam Kelno has been awarded the Order of Knight's Bachelor.'

'Oh Adam, Adam.'

'Ladies and gentlemen. A toast. To Sir Adam Kelno.'

'Here, here!'

Chapter Fifteen

Oxford–1964

Beyond the limits of greater London, England and Wales are divided into several legal circuits and numerous times each year, the judges leave London to dispense justice in the assize towns.

The circuit system was founded after the Norman invasion in the eleventh century, when the kings began the custom of sending their justices into the countryside.

Henry II, the first great legalist and reformer, formalized the assize system in the twelfth century and the procession of rulers continued to refine it.

Such a system is possible because England accepts London as the seat of the royal power with one set of laws for the entire country. In America, for example, there are fifty separate sets of state laws, and a man from Louisiana would hardly want to be tried by a judge from Utah.

Several times each year, the counties are visited to dispense justice in the name of the Queen, where the judges try the most difficult and major legal issues.

Anthony Gilray, who was knighted and named a judge fifteen years earlier in the Queen's Bench Division, arrived in Oxford on assize.

Gilray had a commission in the form of a letter from the Queen, which bore the great seal, and he traveled to Oxford with his marshal, his clerk, his cook, and his valet. It was a time for pomp and ceremony. On the first day in Oxford, Gilray and a fellow judge attended an Assize Service at the cathedral, entering the church behind the under-sheriff of the county, the high sheriff's chaplain, the high sheriff in military uniform, the judge's clerks in morning dress of tails, and then the judges attired in full bottomed wigs and ermine-lined scarlet capes.

Here, they prayed for guidance in the administration of justice.

The courtroom. The ceremony continues.

Everyone rises and the commission is opened. The sheriff, chaplain, and undersheriff are on Gilray's right and his clerk on his left. Before him sits the traditional tricorne hat and the clerk, a portly and distinguished-appearing man, reads the commission naming 'beloved and faithful counselors, lord keeper of our privy seal and the lord chief justice of England, most dear cousin counselors, most noble knights' in their full and lengthy titles.

The clerk bows to the judge, who places the tricorne hat on his head for a moment, and the reading continues that all who have grievances can now be heard.

'God save the Queen,' and the court is in session.

In the rear of the court an eager young premedical student, Terrence Campbell, poised his pencil. The first case concerned a medical malpractice suit and would be used in his paper, 'Medicine and the Law.'

Outside the courtroom there was the milling of spectators, barristers, journalists, jurors, all adding to the excitement of the opening of court.

Across the street, Dr Mark Tesslar stopped for a moment on his way and watched the scene and the line of pompous old, highly polished, flag-bedecked ceremonial automobiles lined up before the courthouse.

Tesslar was now a citizen of England and a permanent member of the Radcliffe Medical Research Center at Oxford. He was curiously drawn over the street and into the courtroom. For a moment he stood at the rear as Anthony Gilray nodded to the wigged black-robed barristers to commence.

Tesslar observed the eager row of students, who always were present at such cases, then turned and limped from the building.

Chapter Sixteen

Angela Kelno, who was born and raised in London, was the most anxious about the return and the most shocked. No sudden arctic blast ever chilled more deeply.

AT FIRST, EVERYTHING SEEMED IN ORDER WHEN WE LANDED IN SOUTHAMPTON. I THINK I CRIED DURING THE ENTIRE DRIVE UP TO LONDON. ON EVERY MILE OF THE WAY I REMEMBERED SOMETHING AND MY TENSION GREW. AT LAST WE CAME TO LONDON. MY FIRST IMPRESSION WAS THAT LITTLE HAD CHANGED IN FIFTEEN YEARS.

OH, THERE WERE A FEW NEW SKYSCRAPERS HERE AND THERE AND A NEW WIDE DUAL CARRIAGEWAY INTO LONDON AND SOME ULTRAMODERN BUILDINGS, PARTICULARLY WHERE CENTRAL LONDON HAD BEEN BOMBED OUT. BUT THE OLD

WAS THERE. THE PALACE, THE CATHEDRALS, PICCADILLY, MARBLE ARCH, AND BOND STREET. NONE OF THAT HAD CHANGED.

WHEN I FIRST LAID EYES ON THE YOUNG PEOPLE I WAS UNABLE TO RELATE. AS THOUGH THIS WAS NOT LONDON AT ALL. STRANGE PEOPLE FROM A WORLD I NEVER KNEW TRANSPLANTED HERE. SOME FRENZIED KIND OF UPHEAVAL HAD TAKEN PLACE. YOU KNOW, YOU RECOGNIZE IT QUICKLY IN ENGLAND. THINGS HAD BEEN SO STEADY BEFORE.

MIND YOU, I'VE BEEN A NURSE FOR THIRTY YEARS AND I DON'T SHOCK EASILY. THIS THING ABOUT NUDITY IN THE STREETS. IN SARAWAK NUDITY WENT WITH THE HEAT AND THE COLOR OF THE NATIVES. IT WAS RATHER SILLY TO EQUATE IT WITH THE LILY-WHITE PALENESS OF ENGLISH GIRLS IN CHILLY, STAID LONDON.

AND THE COSTUMES. IN SARAWAK THEY WERE BASED ON TRADITION AND CLIMATE BUT HERE THEY MADE NO SENSE WHATSOEVER. THE HIGH LEATHER BOOTS COULD ONLY REMIND ONE OF WHIP WIELDING SADISTS IN THE SEVENTEENTH CENTURY PARIS BROTHELS. THE WHITE THIGHS TURNED BLUE AND GOOSE FLESHY IN THE BITING COLD SO THEY COULD SPORT HEMLINES AT THEIR BUTTOCKS. WHAT WE ARE BREEDING IN THIS GENERATION OF ICY BACKSIDES IS A FUTURE HISTORY OF ENGLISH HEMORRHOIDS. MOST RIDICULOUS ARE THE CHEAP IMITATION FURS THAT DON'T EVEN COVER THEIR BOTTOMS. WITH THEIR SKINNY WHITE LEGS POKING OUT OF THE GHASTLY PINK AND LAVENDER BUNDLES. THEY LOOK LIKE SOME SORT OF MARTIAN EGG ABOUT TO HATCH.

IN SARAWAK, THE MOST PRIMITIVE IBAN COMBED HIS HAIR NEATLY AND KNOTTED IT. THE DELIBERATE ATTEMPT AT SLOPPINESS AND ANTI-BEAUTY APPEARS TO BE SOME SORT OF PROTEST AGAINST THE OLDER GENERATION. YET, IN THEIR MANIA TO PROCLAIM THEIR INDIVIDUALITY AND BREAK WITH THE PAST THEY ALL NOW LOOK AS THOUGH THEY HAD BEEN CAST FROM THE SAME MOULD. BOYS LOOK LIKE GIRLS AND GIRLS LOOK EXCEEDINGLY DRAB. RATHER AN OBVIOUS ATTEMPT TO LOOK UGLY BECAUSE THEY FEEL UGLY AND A WITHDRAWAL SO THEY WILL NOT BE IDENTIFIED BY SEX. HAVE EVERYTHING ONE BIG NEUTER.

THE FRANTIC DRESS OF THE MEN IN BELL BOTTOMS AND LACES AND JUNK JEWELRY AND VELVET ALL APPEALS LIKE A CALL FOR HELP.

ADAM TELLS ME THAT WHAT IS HAPPENING IN HIS CLINIC INDICATES A TOTAL COLLAPSE OF OLD MORALS. THEY HAVE MISTAKEN SEXUAL FREEDOM FOR THE ABILITY TO GIVE AND RECEIVE LOVE. AND MOST SAD OF ALL IS THE BREAKING UP OF THE FAMILY UNIT. ADAM TELLS ME THE NUMBER OF PREGNANT GIRLS IN THEIR TEENS IS UP FIVE OR SIX HUNDRED PERCENT AND THE STATISTICS ON BARBITURATE AND DRUG USERS ARE FRIGHTENING. AGAIN, THIS SEEMS TO INDICATE AN OVERWHELMING URGE OF THESE YOUNG PEOPLE TO WITHDRAW INTO A FANTASY WORLD, LIKE THE IBANS DID, IN TIMES OF STRESS.

I COULDN'T BELIEVE THE MUSIC. ADAM TELLS ME THERE ARE MANY CASES OF PERMANENT HEARING DAMAGE. THE GARBLED POETRY AND DOUBLE MEANING OF FILTHY LYRICS ARE FAR LESS COHERENT THAN THE IBAN SINGERS. THE MONOTONE AND ELECTRIC DEVICES ARE A FURTHER ATTEMPT TO DROWN OUT REALITY. THE DANCING AS THOUGH ONE WERE WATCHING PATIENTS IN A LUNATIC ASYLUM.

IS THIS REALLY LONDON?

ALL THAT I WAS RAISED BY IS BEING RIDICULED AND IT SEEMS THAT NOTHING IS BEING DONE TO REPLACE OLD IDEAS WITH NEW ONES. THE WORST PART OF IT IS THE YOUNG PEOPLE ARE NOT HAPPY. THEY HAVE ABSTRACT THOUGHTS ABOUT LOVING, MANKIND, AND ENDING WAR, BUT THEY SEEM TO WANT THE PRICE OF LIFE WITHOUT WORKING. THEY RIDICULE US, BUT WE SUPPORT THEM. THEY HAVE POOR LITTLE LOYALTY TO ONE ANOTHER AND ALTHOUGH SEX IS PRACTICED IN

UNIVERSAL LOTS THEY DON'T UNDERSTAND THE TENDERNESS OF AN ENDURING RELATIONSHIP.

COULD ALL OF THIS HAPPEN IN ONLY FIFTEEN YEARS? THE DISMANTLING OF HUNDREDS OF YEARS OF CIVILIZATION AND TRADITION. WHY DID IT HAPPEN? FOR STEPHAN'S AND FOR TERRY'S SAKE, ONE MUST START TO LOOK AROUND FOR ANSWERS.

LONDON, IN MANY WAYS, WAS LIKE WHEN I FIRST WENT TO SARAWAK. IT IS A JUNGLE FILLED WITH STRANGE NOISES AND CUSTOMS. ONLY, THEY ARE NOT AS HAPPY AS THE IBANS. THERE IS NO HUMOUR TO IT ALL, ONLY DESPAIR.

Chapter Seventeen

It was expected that Adam Kelno, having been knighted, would have capitalized on the situation to build himself an exclusive practice in the West End. Instead, he opened a small clinic as a National Health Doctor in a working class section of the Borough of Southwark, close to the Elephant and Castle in the brick row houses near the Thames where most of his patients were warehousemen, longshoremen, and the admixture of immigrants flooding in from India and blacks from Jamaica and the West Indies.

It was as though Adam Kelno did not believe his release from Sarawak and wished to continue his anonymity by living in modest seclusion close to his clinic.

Angela and her cousin walked themselves foot weary in that magic quadrangle bounded by Oxford and Regent and Bond Streets and Piccadilly now swarmed with hundreds of thousands of Christmas shoppers in the gargantuan department stores and the ultra little shops.

Although she had been back in England for more than a year the biting wet penetrating December cold bothered her. The hunt for a taxi was futile. Orderly lines waited with British patience outside the stores and at the bus stops.

Down into the tube.

The underground crossed beneath the Thames to Elephant and Castle and she made home by foot, bogged under a small hill of packages.

Oh, the wonderful weariness, the wonderful tempo of Christmas back in England. All those puddings, and pies, and sauces, and songs, and lights.

Mrs Corkory, the housekeeper, unloaded her arms. 'Doctor is in his study, ma'am.'

'Has Terrence arrived?'

'No, ma'am. He phoned down from Oxford to say he was taking a later train and wouldn't be arriving until past seven or so.'

She poked her head in Adam's study, where he was in the familiar posture of scratching away at lengthy reports.

'Hello, dear, I'm home.'

'Hello, darling. Did you buy out London?'

'Almost. I'll help you with the reports later.'

'I think this paper work for the health service is worse than the Colonial Office.'

'Maybe you'll use a full time secretary. We really can afford one, Adam. And a dictation machine.'

Adam shrugged. 'I'm not used to such luxuries.'

She thumbed through his letters. There were three requests for speeches. One was from the Union of African Medical Students and another from Cambridge. He had scribbled a note on each reading, 'decline with the usual regrets.'

Angela was against it. It was as though Adam were trying to downgrade his small measure of fame. Perhaps he had had his fill of blacks and browns. Then why did he choose Southwark to practice, when half the London Poles would have doted over a knighted Polish doctor. Well, that was Adam. In all their years of marriage she had come to accept it though the lack of personal ambition annoyed her, for his sake. But no pushy wife, she.

'Well we're ready for the invasion from Oxford,' Angela said. 'By the way, dear, did Terrence say how many friends he would be bringing?'

'Probably the usual contingent of homesick Australians, Malayans, and Chinese. I'll be the epitome of Polish gallantry.' They exchanged a small kiss and he returned to his paper work, then threw the pen down. 'By God you're right. I'm going to get a secretary and a voice machine.'

Angela answered the phone ring. 'It's Mr Kelly. He says his wife's pains are coming every nine minutes regularly.'

Adam was up quickly and out of his lounging jacket. 'This is her sixth so she'll be right on time. Have him bring her over to the clinic and call the midwife.'

It was almost midnight before Mrs Kelly delivered and was situated overnight in the clinic. Angela had dozed in the parlor. Adam kissed her softly, and she automatically arose and went to the kitchen to heat water for tea.

'How did it go?'

'Little boy. They're naming him Adam.'

'Isn't that nice. Well we have four infant Adams after you this year. In future years everyone will wonder why every male in Southwark was named Adam.'

'Did Terrence get in?'

'Yes.'

'Sounds rather quiet for five boys.'

'He came in alone. He's up in your study waiting for you. I'll bring the tea up.'

Terrence seemed stiff as they embraced.

'Where are all your friends?'

'They'll be down in a day. May I speak to you about something first?'

'You'll never make a politician. I've been able to read that grim expression since you were born.'

'Sir,' Terrence spoke haltingly. 'Well, you know how it's been with us. Because of you I was a doctor at heart since I can remember. And I know how good you've been to me. My education and how close we are.'

'What's wrong?'

'Well, sir, my father mentioned some little things about you being in prison and up for deportation once, but I never thought ... it never occurred to me ...'

'What?'

'It never entered my mind that you might have ever done anything wrong.'

Angela came in with a tray of tea. She poured in silence. Terrence looked at the floor and licked his lips as Adam stared ahead, hands tight on the arms of his chair.

'I've told him you've suffered enough,' she said, 'and not to pry into things we want to forget.'

'He has just as much right to know everything as Stephan does.'

'I haven't done the prying. Someone else has. This book here, *The Holocaust* by Abraham Cady. Have you ever heard of it?'

'It's quite well known in America. I haven't read it myself,' Adam said.

'Well, the damned thing's just been published in England. I'm afraid I have to show this to you. He handed the book to Dr Kelno. A marker was in page 167. Adam held it under a lamp and read.

'Of all the concentration camps none was more infamous than Jadwiga. It was here that SS Dr Colonel Adolph Voss established an experimental center for the purpose of creating methods of mass sterilization, with the use of human guinea pigs, and SS Dr Colonel Otto Flensberg and his assistant carried on equally horrendous studies on prisoners. In the notorious Barrack V a secret surgery was run by Dr Kelno, who carried out fifteen thousand or more experimental operations without the use of anesthetic.'

Outside a dozen carolers pressed close to the window and with frosty breath sang out.

'We wish you a merry Christmas,
We wish you a merry Christmas,
We wish you a merry Christmas,
And a happy new year.'

Chapter Eighteen

Adam closed the book and placed it on his desk. 'Well, do you think I did that, Terrence Campbell?'

'Of course not, Doctor. I feel like a bloody bastard about all this. God knows I don't want to hurt you but it's published and hundreds of thousands if not millions of people are going to read it.'

'Maybe I felt so strongly about our relationship I never felt the need to explain all of it to you. I suppose I was wrong.' Adam went to the bookcase across the room, unlocked a bottom cupboard drawer, and took out three large cardboard boxes filled with volumes of papers, files, press clippings, letters. 'I think it's time you know everything.'

Adam started from the beginning.

'I think it is impossible to explain to someone exactly what a concentration camp is like or for them to comprehend such a thing could really exist. I still think of it in gray. We never saw a tree or flower for four years and I don't remember the sun. I dream of it. I see a stadium with hundreds of rows and each row filled with lifeless faces, dull eyes, shaved heads and striped uniforms. And beyond the last row the silhouettes of the crematorium ovens, and I can smell the smoke of human flesh. There was never enough food or medicine. I looked from my clinic day and night to an endless line of prisoners dragging themselves to me.'

'Doctor, I just don't know what to say.'

Adam recounted the conspiracy against him, the torment of Brixton Prison, of not seeing his own son Stephan for the first two years of his life, the flight to Sarawak, the nightmares, the drunken stupors, all of it. Tears fell freely down both their cheeks as he continued in monotone until the first light of day cast a gray pall into the room and the first sounds of movement of the city could be heard. The wet tires sung off the pavement and they were silent and motionless.

Terry shook his head. 'I don't understand it. I just don't understand it. Why would the Jews hate you so much?'

'You are naïve, Terry. Before the war there were several million Jews in Poland. We had only gained our own liberation at the end of the First World War. The Jews were always strangers in our midst, always attempting to overthrow us again. They were the soul of the Communist Party and the ones guilty of giving Poland back to Russia. From the beginning it was always a life and death struggle.'

'But why?'

He shrugged. 'In my village all of us owed money to the Jew. Do you know how poor I was when I got to Warsaw? For my first two years my room was a large closet, and my bed was of rags. I had to lock myself in the bathroom in order to have a place to study. I waited and waited to gain admittance to the university but there was no room because the Jews lied about themselves to find ways around the quota system. You think a quota system is wrong. If there hadn't been one they would have bought every seat in every classroom. They are cunning beyond imagination. The Jewish professors and teachers tried to control every facet of university life. Always pushing their way in. I joined the Nationalist Students Movement, proudly, because it was a way to combat them. And afterwards, it was always a Jewish doctor getting the prime positions. Well, my father drank himself to death and my mother worked her way to an early grave paying off the Jewish moneylender. All the way to the end, I stood for my Polish nationalism and because of it I have been driven to hell.'

The boy looked at his mentor. Terry was disgusted with himself. He could see Adam Kelno tenderly calming a frightened Ulu child and reassuring the mother. Dear Lord, it wasn't possible for Dr Kelno to use medicine wrongly.

The Holocaust lay on the desk. A thick gray-covered volume with the lettering of the title and the author's name in red portraying devouring flames.

'No doubt the author is a Jew,' Adam said.

'Yes.'

'Well, no matter. I've been mentioned in other books by them.'

'But this is different. It has hardly been published and already a half a dozen people have asked me about it. It's only a matter of time until some journalist digs it up. With you knighted it will make a hell of a story.'

Angela appeared in a dowdy bathrobe.

'What am I to do,' he said, 'flee to some jungle again?'

'No. Stand and fight. Stop the sale of this book and show the world that the author is a liar.'

'You're young and very innocent, Terry.'

'Along with my father you're everything to me, Dr Kelno. Did you spend fifteen years in Sarawak just for the privilege of carrying this mark to your graves?'

'Do you have any idea of what this involves?'

'I must ask you, Doctor, is there any truth to this at all?'

'How dare you!' Angela cried. 'How dare you say that!'

'I don't believe it either. Can I help you fight it?'

'Are you quite ready for the scandal and the barrage of professional liars they'll parade into the courts? Are you quite certain the honorable thing to do is not to hold our silence with dignity?' Angela said.

Terrence shook his head and walked from the room to hold back the tears.

Much beer and gin were consumed by Terry's mates and many bawdy songs were sung and many of the world's consuming issues were argued with a righteous wrath reserved for the young.

Terry had a key to Dr Kelno's clinic a few blocks from the house, and after hours his chums dispensed of other frustrations by love-making with numerous young ladies on the examination table and the overnight cots amid the smell of medical disinfectants. A minor discomfort.

Christmas came and turkeys and geese were devoured and each guest opened a modest but well-chosen and humorous gift. Dr Kelno opened a number of worthless but sentimental offerings from his patients.

It all seemed Christmasy enough and the visitors were unable to detect the underlying tension. They returned to Oxford filled with the cheer.

Terry and Adam said good-by with reserve. The train pulled out. Angela slipped her arm through her husband's as they left the Victorian loftiness of Paddington Station.

A week passed, then two and three. The listlessness of the student was matched by the listlessness and short temper of Adam Kelno.

It was the longest period of time the two had ever been out of communication.

And he was filled with the memory of the dugout struggling up the Lemanak with Stephan at the tiller and Terry on the bow chatting to the boatman in the Iban language. How warmly the Ulus greeted the boys. It was during the summer holiday, when Stephan was eleven years old, Bintang presented them with costumes and made them a member of the tribe, and they danced with the chief wearing ceremonial feathers and 'painted' tattoo marks.

Terry's bright eyes watched over the surgical mask as Adam operated. Adam always glanced at him. When the boy was there he always performed a better operation.

The hard days of clinic at the long houses would be over and they would all go to the stream and bathe or sit under a waterfall and they slept near each other, never fearing the sounds of the jungle.

All the rest of it flooded his thoughts day and night until he could no longer bear it. It wasn't only Terrence who filled his thoughts. What would happen when Stephan learned of this in America?

Sir Adam Kelno walked the narrow Chancery Lane, that artery of British law flanked by the Law Society on one side and Sweet and Maxwell, the legal publishers and booksellers, on the other side. The window of Ede and Ravenscort, Ltd., tailor of the profession, held its usual grim display of academic and black barrister's robes, unchanged in style since time remembered and garnished with a variety of gray barrister's wigs.

He stopped at 32B Chancery Lane. It was a narrow four story building, one of the few survivors of the great fires centuries earlier. A warped and misshapen Jacobean relic.

Kelno glanced at the registry. The second and third floor held the law offices of Hobbins, Newton, and Smiddy. He entered and disappeared up the creaking stairs.

BOOK TWO

The Defendants

Chapter One

The author of *The Holocaust* was an American writer named Abraham Cady, one-time journalist, one-time flyer, one-time ballplayer.

At the turn of the century the Zionist movement spread like a forest fire over the Jewish Pale of Settlement in Czarist Russia. Bent under universal suppression and pogroms of centuries standing, the groundswell to leave Russia found direction in the resurrection of the ancient homeland. The little Jewish village of Prodno sponsored the Cadyzynski brothers, Morris and Hyman, to go to Palestine as pioneers.

While working in the swamps of Upper Galilee on land redemption, Morris Cadyzynski fell prey to recurrent attacks of malaria and dysentery until he was taken to the hospital in Jaffa. He was advised to leave Palestine as one of those unable to adapt to the severe conditions. His elder brother, Hyman, remained.

It was usual in those days that a relative in America take on the responsibility of getting as many of the family over from the old country as possible. Uncle Abraham Cadyzynski, after whom the author was later named, had a small Jewish bakery on Church Street in the ghetto in Norfolk, Virginia.

Morris had his name shortened to Cady by a perplexed official trying to separate over a hundred 'skis' who immigrated on the same boatload.

Uncle Abraham had two daughters, whose eventual husbands were not interested in the bakery, so it was passed on to Morris when the old man died.

The Jewish community was tiny and close knit, hanging together unable to shake off all the ghetto mentality. Morris met Molly Segal, also an immigrant in the Zionist movement, and they were married in the year of 1909.

Out of deference to his father, the Rabbi of Prodno, they were married in synagogue. The party afterward at the Workman's Circle Hall was in the Yiddish tradition of an endless parade of food, dancing the hora and '*mazel tovfs*' until the middle of the night.

Neither of them were religious, but they were never able to break most of the old country ties of conversing and reading in Yiddish and keeping a mostly kosher kitchen.

Ben was the first born in 1912 and then Sophie came two years later as Europe was going up in flames. During the First World War business prospered. With Norfolk as a major troop and supply shipping point to France, the government gave Morris's bakery a contract to augment overburdened facilities. The output of the bakery tripled and quadrupled but in doing so it lost most of its Jewish identity. The bread and cakes had come from old family recipes and now they had to conform to government specifications. After the war Morris got some of the old flavor back. He was so popular all over Norfolk that he began to ship out grocery stores, some in all gentile neighborhoods.

Abraham Cady was born in 1920. Although it was a prosperous family it was difficult to tear away from the little row house with the white porch on Holt Street in which all the children were born.

The Jewish section started in the one hundred block of Church Street at St Mary's Church and ran for seven blocks to where the Booker T. Pharmacy started the Negro ghetto. The streets were lined with little shops out of the old country and the children were to remember the smells and sounds of it all their lives. Heated discussion in Yiddish where the two newspapers, the *Freiheit* and New York *Vorwärts* vied for opinion. There was the marvelous odor of leather from Cousin Herschel's shoe repair shop and the pungent aroma of the cellar of the 'pickle' man, where you could have a choice of sixty different kinds of pickles and pickled onions from briny old vats. They cost a penny each, two cents for an extra.

In the back yard behind Finkelstein's Prime and Fancy Kosher meats the kids liked to watch the *shochet* kill chickens for a nickel each to conform to religious requirements.

There was endless barter at the vegetable stalls and at Max Lipshitz's Super Stupendous Clothing Mart; Max himself, measuring tape around his neck, pulled potential customers off the street and just a little ways down Sol's Pawn Shop held a junk yard of tragedy, mostly from colored customers.

Much of what Morris Cady earned went either to the families in the old country or to Palestine. Aside from the black Essex parked before the house there was little to testify to their nominal wealth. Morris did not play the stock market so when the crash came he had enough cash to buy out a couple of sinking bakeries at thirty cents on the dollar.

Despite their simplicity, their affluence caught up with them and after a year of discussion they bought a big shingled ten room house on an acre of land at Gosnold and New Hampshire Streets with a view to the estuary. A few Jewish families, upper-middle class merchants and doctors, had penetrated Colonial Place but further down the line around Colley Street and Thirty-first. The Cadys had moved into an all gentile neighborhood.

Not that the Cadys were black, but they weren't exactly white. Ben and Abe were 'the Jew boys.' The Hebes, Yids, Sheenies, Kikes. Much of this was changed at the big circle at Pennsylvania and Delaware, where they played ball near the pumping station. Ben Cady was handy with his dukes and a definite risk to provoke or attack. After Ben established an understanding to live by with the neighborhood kids they all discovered the never ending delights that came from the oven of Molly's kitchen.

Abe had to go through it all again in J. E. B. Stuart Grammar School, filled with youngsters from the nearby Turney Boy's Home, consisting mainly of problem children from broken families. All they seemed to want to do was fight. Abe had to defend some unknown honor until his brother Ben taught him 'all the dirty Jew tricks' to acquit himself.

Fists gave way to a different kind of anti-Semitism at Blair Junior High but by the time Abe was a teen-ager he had a running commentary with the unpleasant aspects of his birth.

It was Ben who brought them honor by becoming a three letter athlete at Maury High by bombing baseballs out of sight in the spring, sharpshooting baskets and plunging for hard yardage in the fall and winter.

After a time the neighbors pointed with certain curious pride to the Jewish family. They were good Jews. They knew their place. But the strangeness of entering a gentile home never exactly wore off.

What Abe Cady remembered the most about his father was his devotion to the family in the old country. His restlessness to get them all out of Poland. Morris brought a half dozen cousins to America and paid passage for another half dozen to Palestine. But try as he might, he could never induce his father, the Rabbi of Prodno, and his two younger brothers to leave. One was a doctor and the other a successful merchant, who were to remain in Poland until the tragic end.

Sophie, the daughter, was plain. She married a plain guy with a promising sales route in Baltimore, where most of the Cadyzynski family had settled. It was nice to travel to Baltimore for family reunions. One couldn't complain. America had been good. They were reasonably successful and always close in a pinch despite the usual family squabbles and feuds.

It was Ben who gave Morris and Molly the heartaches. They were proud enough of their athlete hero son. Such glory he had brought them, they could not deny. There was a school cheer for Ben even after he graduated. BASH EM, BAM EM, BEN, BEN, BEN!

Ben Cady was a child of the thirties. He never saw a coloured person without feeling pain for him. Sensitive to the suffering of the depression, despising the ignorance of the South, he leaned more and more to the clever and fanatic voices that promised liberation of the toiling masses. It made more sense to him than anything in the world. The Earl Browders and Mother Bloors and James Fords who came down from the North and dared preach their gospel in mixed meetings with the blacks in tiny black halls of black town.

'So look, son,' Morris said to Ben, 'you don't want to be a baker and that's fine by me. I don't want my sons to be bakers. We can hire a foreman, we can hire bookkeepers so there should always be income from the business. Don't do me favors. Don't be a baker. Ben, look already, nine colleges, including the University of West Virginia, are on their knees begging humbly to give you an athletic scholarship.'

Ben Cady had black eyes and black brows and black hair, and when not bursting from his intensity on the athletic field it burst from his being in a manner that no one could fail to understand.

'I want to screw around for a few years, Dad. You know, just look things over. Maybe sign on a ship.'

'You want to be a bum.'

Abe turned off the Jack Benny radio show because they were starting to talk loud in the next room. He stood in the door, gangly. He looked about half the size of Ben.

'Abe, go do your homework.'

'It's July, Pop. I don't have any homework.'

'So you've got to come in and take Ben's side and gang up on me.'

At this point Morris Cady went through the story of his youth in Poland and his struggle in Palestine and his continued struggle for the family. All of this lead up to his wife, Molly, the finest woman God ever created and then came the children.

About Sophie, what's to complain? A plain girl with a plain boy. Only three years married and two gorgeous children. Such *nachas* I get from the grandchildren. Maybe her husband Jack is a putz but he's a good provider, and he treats Sophie like she's pure gold.

Abe, look at the grades he gets in school. Nobody in the entire family denies Abe is a genius. Someday he will be a great American Jewish writer.

'Ben,' Morris bargains, 'Ben, let's put *tochis afn tisch.* You got through school through one method, brute force. So, you don't want to be a baker. Honkey dorey with me. But with fifteen colleges, including the University of West Virginia, humbly begging your presence for God's sake get yourself a degree. I'm asking too much that you should educate yourself?'

Ben's face radiated blackness.

'How do you think your mother and I feel when you go to that *goyim* airfield and do those crazy things in an airplane? Spelling out names in the sky with smoke. That's what we struggled to raise you for? Let me tell you, Ben, you should see the look on your mother's face waiting for your footsteps to come on the porch. Your mother dies every minute you're up there in the sky. Some consideration. She cooks the meal, and she says to me, Morris, I know this food will never be eaten by Ben. Look at me, son, when I'm talking to you.'

Both Abe and Ben have their heads hung and wring their hands.

'What's bothering you, son?'

Ben looked up slowly. 'Poverty,' he said, 'fascism, inequality.'

'You think I didn't hear all that Commie crap in Poland. You're a Jew, Ben, and in the end the Communists will betray you. I know from firsthand what kind of butchers they are in Russia.'

'Pop, stop picking on me.'

'Not until you educate yourself. All right, son, it's fashionable for young people to go into the colored section and dance with *schwartzes.* First you dance with them, then you bring them home to your mother.'

Morris held his hand up for silence before Ben could answer.

'Look at this business. Flying. Becoming a Commie, fraternizing with *schwartzes.* Ben, I don't have a prejudiced bone in my body. I'm a Jew from the old country. Don't you know I know how these black people suffer. Who, after all, are the most liberal thinkers and the most decent to the colored people? The Jews are. And if something goes wrong, if the blacks explode . . . who do you think they'll turn on . . . us.'

'Are you finished, Pop?'

'Deaf ears,' Morris opined. 'I'm talking already to the wall.'

Chapter Two

WE DIDN'T LEARN ABOUT MY BROTHER BEN GETTING KILLED BY A TELEGRAM OR ANYTHING LIKE THAT. WE GOT A LETTER FROM ONE OF HIS BUDDIES IN THE LACALLE SQUADRON, A GROUP OF AMERICAN VOLUNTEERS FLYING FOR LOYALIST SPAIN. SOME WERE MERCENARIES AND SOME, LIKE BEN, WERE TRUE ANTI-FASCISTS. IT WAS A RAG-TAG GANG. ANYHOW, IT SEEMED KIND OF STRANGE THAT THE LETTER WAS FILLED MORE WITH TALK ABOUT THE CAUSE FOR WHICH BEN DIED AND THE FACT THAT THE FACIST FLYERS WERE COWARDS.

BEN WAS FLYING A RUSSIAN CHATOS BIPLANE. IT WAS OUTDATED AND THEY WERE ALWAYS OUTNUMBERED BY THE SWARMS OF GERMAN HEINKELS AND ITALIAN FIATS. ON THIS PARTICULAR MISSION BEN HAD DOWNED A JUNKER BOMBER, WHEN THEY GOT INTO A DOGFIGHT. THREE AMERICANS WERE JUMPED BY THIRTY-FIVE HEINKELS, THE LETTER SAID.

BEN'S DEATH WAS LATER CONFIRMED BY A GUY WHO CAME TO VISIT US IN NORFOLK, WHO HAD BEEN A VOLUNTEER IN THE LINCOLN BATTALION OF THE INTERNATIONAL BRIGADE. HE HAD BEEN WOUNDED AND LOST AN ARM, AND WAS SENT BACK TO THE STATES AS A RECRUITER.

ALL THE RELATIVES CAME DOWN FROM BALTIMORE WHEN THEY HEARD BEN HAD BEEN KILLED AND ALL THE OLD FRIENDS CAME FROM CHURCH STREET. THE HOUSE WAS FILLED DAY AND NIGHT.

THERE WERE OTHER PEOPLE TOO. SOME OF BEN'S TEACHERS AND COACHES AND CLASSMATES AND NEIGHBORS, SOME OF WHOM HAD NEVER SAID HELLO OR SET FOOT IN OUR HOUSE BEFORE. EVEN TWO MINISTERS, A BAPTIST PREACHER, AND A CATHOLIC PRIEST CAME TO VISIT MOMMA AND POPPA. POPPA ALWAYS GAVE DONATIONS TO ALL THE CHURCHES IN THE NAME OF THE BAKERY.

FOR THE FIRST TWO WEEKS MOMMA NEVER STOPPED COOKING. SHE KEPT SAYING OVER AND OVER THAT THE COMPANY SHOULDN'T GO HUNGRY. BUT WE ALL KNEW SHE WAS WORKING TO BURN UP THE NERVOUS ENERGY AND KEEP BUSY SO SHE COULDN'T THINK ABOUT BEN.

AND THEN SHE CAME APART AND HAD TO BE PUT UNDER SEDATION. SHE AND POPPA WENT AWAY FOR A LONG REST TO SOPHIE'S IN BALTIMORE AND LATER TO THE CATSKILLS AND MIAMI. BUT EACH TIME THEY CAME BACK TO NORFOLK IT WAS LIKE THEY HAD COME HOME TO A MORTUARY. MOMMA AND POPPA WOULD GO TO BEN'S ROOM AND SIT BY THE HOUR LOOKING AT HIS SCHOOL PICTURES AND TROPHIES AND READ AND REREAD HIS LETTERS.

I DON'T THINK THEY WERE EVER THE SAME AFTER BEN DIED. IT SEEMED THEY STARTED GROWING OLD THE DAY THEY HEARD THE NEWS. FUNNY, UP TILL THEN I NEVER THOUGHT OF MY PARENTS GROWING OLD.

SOME COMMUNIST FRIENDS OF BEN'S CAME TO OUR HOUSE AND TOLD MOMMA AND POPPA THAT BEN'S DEATH SHOULD NOT BE IN VAIN. THEY PERSUADED THEM TO ATTEND A RALLY FOR LOYALIST SPAIN IN WASHINGTON. I WENT UP WITH THEM. BEN WAS EXTOLLED AND THEY GLORIFIED MOMMA AND POPPA FOR GIVING A SON

TO THE CAUSE OF ANTI-FASCISM. WE ALL REALIZED THEY WERE JUST USING US AND WE NEVER ATTENDED ANOTHER OF THOSE MEETINGS.

I GUESS MY BROTHER BEN WAS THE MOST IMPORTANT PERSON IN MY LIFE.

I REMEMBER SO MANY THINGS ABOUT HIM.

HALE'S UNDERTAKING PARLOR HAD THIS BIG BOAT THAT HELD MAYBE FORTY OR FIFTY PEOPLE. YOU COULD RENT IT FROM THEM FOR $15.00 A DAY AND GET UP A BIG PARTY AND CRUISE UP THE CHESAPEAKE. EVEN THOUGH I WAS THE KID BROTHER HE ALWAYS INCLUDED ME. I HAD MY FIRST DRINK OF WHISKY ON ONE OF THE SCHOOL PARTIES. I GOT SICKER THAN HELL.

ON THE BACK END OF OUR LOT WE HAD A GARAGE AND OVER THAT, A LITTLE APARTMENT. THE PEOPLE WHO OWNED THE HOUSE BEFORE US HAD A COLORED COUPLE LIVING IN IT. BUT MOMMA LIKED TO DO HER OWN HOUSEWORK AND ONLY HAD A CLEANING LADY ONCE A WEEK, SO WE USED THE APARTMENT AS A KIND OF HIDEAWAY.

WHEN BEN WAS FLYING HE'D PLAY SEMI-PRO FOOTBALL ON SUNDAYS AT THE OLD LEAGUE PARK FOR THE NORFOLK CLANCY'S. MAN, I'LL NEVER FORGET THE DAY HE MADE TWO TOUCHDOWNS AGAINST RED GRANGE'S VISITING ALL-STARS AND CUT GRANGE DOWN ON THREE OR FOUR OPEN FIELD TACKLES. BEN WAS REALLY SOMETHING. MOST OF THE KIDS DID THEIR NECKING ON MAYFLOWER DRIVE ALONG THE LAFAYETTE RIVER, BUT WE HAD THE APARTMENT AND WE SURE HAD SOME GREAT PARTIES.

THE YARD BY THE GARAGE WAS PRETTY BIG AND WE'D FUNGO FLIES AND GROUNDERS TO EACH OTHER. USING THE SIDE OF THE GARAGE AS A BACKSTOP BEN TAUGHT ME HOW TO PITCH. HE PAINTED A TARGET OF A BATTER ON THE WALL AND MADE ME THROW AT IT UNTIL MY ARM NEARLY FELL OFF. HE WAS REALLY PATIENT.

HE'D PUT HIS HAND ON MY SHOULDER AND TALK BASEBALL TO ME. WHEN BEN TOUCHED ME IT WAS LIKE BEING TOUCHED BY GOD.

'LOOK, ABE,' BEN WOULD SAY, 'YOU'RE NOT GOING TO DAZZLE ANYBODY WITH YOUR SPEED OR BLOW THEM OUT OF THE BOX. SO YOU HAVE TO PITCH WITH YOUR JEWISH HEAD.' I WAS TAUGHT A VARIETY OF SLOW CURVES AND CHANGE-UPS AND A SLIDER. IN THOSE DAYS A SLIDER WAS CALLED A SCREWBALL. WELL, BEN TAUGHT ME TO BE A REAL JUNK PITCHER WITH JUST ENOUGH MUSTARD ON THE FAST BALL TO KEEP THE BATTER HONEST. I WAS NEVER AN OVERPOWERING TYPE PITCHER, BUT BEN TAUGHT ME ENOUGH TO BE FIRST STRING FOR MAURY HIGH AND GET A SCHOLARSHIP TO THE UNIVERSITY OF NORTH CAROLINA. OFTEN WE'D PLAY TILL DARK, THEN KEEP GOING UNDER THE STREET LIGHTS.

THERE WAS A DIRT AIRFIELD WHERE GRANBY STREET CURVED AROUND THE BEND NEAR THE CEMETERY AT DEAD MAN'S CORNER ON THE WAY TO THE BEACH AT OCEAN VIEW. THE WHOLE AREA WAS IN TRUCK FARMS, AND YOU HAD TO MAKE YOUR APPROACHES RIGHT OVER THE TOMBSTONES. IT'S ALL PART OF THE NAVAL AIR BASE NOW BUT ONE OR TWO OF THE OLD BUILDINGS REMAIN. ANYHOW, THERE WAS THIS RICH JEWISH DEPARTMENT STORE OWNER NAMED JAKE GOLDSTEIN, WHO WAS A BIG FAN OF BEN'S AND OWNED A COUPLE OF AIRPLANES, ONE A WACO TAPERWING. IT COULD SHAKE YOUR TEETH OUT BUT COULD YOU EVER DO STUNTS IN IT. BEN STARTED FLYING THE WACO, AND I STARTED HANGING AROUND THE FIELD.

BEN WAS THE ONLY JEWISH PILOT EXCEPT FOR MR GOLDSTEIN BUT EVERYONE RESPECTED HIM. HE WAS A LOT LIKE THEM. YOU KNOW, A BREED APART SO BEING

JEWISH DIDN'T MATTER, AND WE DIDN'T HAVE TO GO THROUGH ALL THOSE FIGHTS AGAIN.

JAKE GOLDSTEIN SPONSORED BEN AT A LOT OF AIR RACES, AND HE'D GO OFF AND BARNSTORM AND STUNT FLY AT FAIRS. WHEN HE WAS GONE I'D RUN ERRANDS FOR THE PILOTS AND CHOCK DOWN PLANES AND THEN I GOT TO TINKERING WITH ENGINES AND ONCE IN A WHILE I'D GET MY REWARD, A PLANE RIDE.

BEN WOULD LET ME TAKE THE STICK AND LIKE EVERYTHING ELSE, HE TAUGHT ME HOW TO FLY. BUT WHEN HE WAS GONE SOME OF THE OTHER GUYS REALLY SHOOK ME UP. I KNOW THEY WERE JUST CLOWNING, BUT THEY'D START LOOPING AND SWAP ROLLING AND WOULDN'T STOP UNTIL I WAS READY TO PASS OUT. I'D STAGGER OUT OF THE COCKPIT AND RUN FOR THE TOILET AND PUKE MY GUTS OUT.

THERE WAS ONE ANTI-SEMITE IN THE CROWD. A GUY BY THE NAME OF STACY. ONCE WHEN BEN WAS GONE HE STUNTED ME UNTIL I FAINTED. SOME OF THE GUYS TOLD BEN ABOUT IT, AND BEN AND I QUIETLY WENT TO WORK. HE TAUGHT ME EVERY TRICK IN THE BOOK.

THEN, ONE DAY BEN SAID, 'HEY, STACY, WHY DON'T YOU GO UP WITH ABE FOR A RIDE. I THINK HE'S ABOUT READY TO SOLO AND MAYBE YOU OUGHT TO CHECK HIM OUT INSTEAD OF ME.' STACY FELL FOR IT. WE GOT INTO THE TWIN COCKPIT WACO, BUT WHAT STACY DIDN'T KNOW WAS THAT HIS SET OF CONTROLS HAD BEEN DISCONNECTED.

BEN GOT EVERYONE OUT TO WATCH. POW! WHAP! ZAM! DID I LET THAT SONOFABITCH HAVE IT. I FLIPPED HER OVER ON HER BACK AND BARREL ROLLED RIGHT OVER THE RUNWAY, THEN ANGLED HER UP SO STEEP SHE POWER STALLED AT THREE G'S RIGHT AT THE HANGAR. I LOOKED BACK. I THOUGHT STACY WOULD SHIT HIS PANTS. ANYHOW, I KEPT IT UP UNTIL HE BEGGED ME TO SET HER DOWN. THEN I LET HIM HAVE A LITTLE MORE, A FEW OUTSIDE LOOPS.

STACY NEVER CAME BACK TO THE AIRSTRIP AGAIN.

I WAS THE YOUNGEST FLYER OF THE GANG AND EVERYTHING WAS GOING FINE UNTIL I HAD TO DO A BELLY LANDING IN A CORNFIELD ONE DAY WHEN THE ENGINE QUIT. I WASN'T SCARED ALL THE WAY IN UNTIL THE PLANE STOPPED DEAD AND NOSED OVER. I GOT SCARED WHEN I CLIMBED OUT AND STARTED CRYING, 'PLEASE DON'T TELL MOMMA AND POPPA.'

I WAS BANGED UP REAL GOOD AND TOLD A WHOPPING LIE ABOUT FALLING OFF THE ROOF OF THE GARAGE, BUT THEY LEARNED THE TRUTH FROM AN INSURANCE ADJUSTER AND INVESTIGATORS.

JESUS, WAS POPPA MAD!

'IF YOU WANT TO BREAK YOUR GOD DAMNED NECK, BEN, THAT'S FINE BY ME, BUT WHEN YOU TAKE A SENSITIVE CHILD LIKE ABE AND MAKE A GANGSTER OUT OF HIM, I'M GOING TO FORBID IT!'

MY POPPA, GOD REST HIS SOUL, HARDLY EVER FORBADE ANYTHING IN HIS LIFE. HIS WAS THE FIRST BAKERY TO UNIONIZE WITHOUT A STRIKE OR BLOODSHED JUST BECAUSE HE WAS A LIBERAL THINKER. THE OTHER BAKERY OWNERS WERE READY TO LYNCH HIM, BUT POPPA DIDN'T SCARE EASILY. AND HE WAS THE FIRST TO HIRE A COLORED BAKER. A LOT OF PEOPLE MIGHT FORGET ABOUT HOW MUCH GUTS IT TOOK TO DO THAT IN THOSE DAYS.

WELL, I DIDN'T FLY FOR A LONG TIME AFTER THAT. NOT UNTIL BEN GOT KILLED IN SPAIN. THEN I HAD TO FLY AND POPPA UNDERSTOOD.

I GUESS WHAT I REMEMBER MOST ABOUT MY BROTHER BEN WERE THOSE QUIET DAYS WE JUST HORSED AROUND. MAYBE WE'D GO TO THE MARSH BEHIND J. E. B. STUART SCHOOL AND CATCH A COUPLE OF FROGS. THERE WOULD ALWAYS BE KIDS FROM THE TURNEY HOME THERE AND WE'D HAVE FROG RACES . . . OR MAYBE WE'D

BOWL A FEW GAMES OF DUCKPINS AT THE OLD BUSH STREET ALLEY. IT WAS THE ONE THING I WAS BETTER AT THAN BEN.

BEST OF ALL WERE THE TIMES AROUND THE CREEK. WE'D GET UP EARLY IN THE MORNING AND TAKE OUR BICYCLES DOWN TO THE DOCKS AND BUY US A WATERMELON FOR A NICKEL. THEY SOLD THEM TO THE KIDS CHEAP BECAUSE THEY HAD SPLIT IN SHIPMENT.

THEN WE'D BIKE TO THE CREEK. I HAD MY DOG IN THE FRONT BASKET AND BEN CARRIED THE WATERMELON IN HIS. WE'D SIT ON THE BANK AND PUT THE WATERMELON IN TO COOL IT AND WHILE IT WAS COOLING WE'D WALK TO A SMALL PIER AND FISH FOR SOFT SHELL CRABS. WE'D TIE A PIECE OF ROTTEN OLD MEAT ON A STRING AND HOLD IT RIGHT ON THE TOP OF THE WATER AND WHEN A CRAB WENT FOR IT, BEN WOULD SWOOP IT UP WITH A NET. THOSE CRABS WERE PRETTY DUMB.

MOMMA DIDN'T KEEP A KOSHER KITCHEN, BUT SHE WOULDN'T LET US BRING CRABS HOME SO WE'D COOK THEM ON THE BANK WITH A PIECE OF CORN OR A POTATO AND WE'D HAVE THE WATERMELON AS DESSERT AND JUST LIE IN THE GRASS AND LOOK AT THE SKY AND TALK THINGS OVER.

WE TALKED A LOT OF BASEBALL. THAT WAS LONG BEFORE BEN STARTED FLYING. BETWEEN US WE KNEW THE BATTING AVERAGE OF EVERY PLAYER IN THE MAJOR LEAGUES. THEY REALLY HAD BALLPLAYERS THEN. JIMMY FOXX AND CARL HUBBELL WERE MY IDOLS. MAYBE BEN WOULD READ A STORY I WAS WRITING.

WELL, WE ALWAYS ATE SO MUCH WE GOT BELLYACHES, AND MOMMA WOULD RAISE HELL BECAUSE WE COULDN'T EAT DINNER.

EVEN WHEN WE GOT OLDER WE'D ALWAYS LIKE TO WANDER DOWN TO THE CREEK TOGETHER. THAT WAS THE FIRST TIME BEN TOLD ME HE WAS GOING TO BE A COMMUNIST.

'IT'S SOMETHING POPPA WILL NEVER UNDERSTAND. HE DID THINGS HIS WAY WHEN HE WAS A KID. HE LEFT HOME TO WORK IN THE SWAMPS IN PALESTINE. WELL, I CAN'T DO THINGS THE WAY HE DID THEM.'

BEN HURT FOR THE COLORED PEOPLE. AND HE FELT COMMUNISM WAS THE ONLY ANSWER. HE USED TO TALK ABOUT THE DAY THEY WOULD HAVE EQUALITY, AND GUYS LIKE JOSH GIBSON AND SATCHEL PAIGE WOULD BE PLAYING IN THE MAJORS AND THERE WOULD BE COLORED SALES PEOPLE AT RICE'S AND SMITH AND WELTON'S DEPARTMENT STORES, AND THEY'D BE ABLE TO EAT IN THE SAME RESTAURANTS AND NOT HAVE TO RIDE ON THE BACK OF THE BUS, AND THEIR KIDS WOULD BE ABLE TO GO TO WHITE SCHOOLS, AND THEY'D BE ABLE TO LIVE IN WHITE NEIGHBORHOODS. IN THE MIDDLE OF THE NINETEEN THIRTIES, BEN'S DREAMS SEEMED PRETTY HARD TO BELIEVE.

I REMEMBER THE LAST TIME I SAW BEN.

HE LEANED OVER MY BED AND TAPPED ME ON THE SHOULDER, THEN HELD HIS FINGERS TO HIS LIPS, AND HE WHISPERED SO AS NOT TO WAKE UP MOMMA AND POPPA.

'I'M GOING AWAY, ABE.'

I WAS HALF ASLEEP AND GROGGY AND DIDN'T UNDERSTAND AT FIRST. I THOUGHT HE WAS GOING ON A FLYING TRIP. 'WHERE YOU GOING?'

'YOU'VE GOT TO KEEP IT A SECRET.'

'SURE.'

'I'M GOING TO SPAIN.'

'TO SPAIN?'

'TO FIGHT FRANCO. I'M GOING TO FLY FOR THE LOYALISTS.'

I GUESS I BEGAN TO CRY. BEN SAT ON THE EDGE OF THE BED AND HUGGED ME. 'REMEMBER SOME OF THE THINGS I TAUGHT YOU AND MAYBE THEY'LL HELP YOU GET ALONG. BUT MAINLY, POPPA IS RIGHT. YOU STICK TO YOUR WRITING.'

'I DON'T WANT YOU TO GO, BEN.'

'I'VE GOT TO, ABE. I'VE GOT TO DO SOMETHING ABOUT ALL THIS.'

STRANGE, ISN'T IT? I WASN'T ABLE TO CRY AFTER BEN'S DEATH. I WANTED TO, BUT I COULDN'T. THAT HAPPENED MUCH LATER, WHEN I DECIDED TO WRITE A BOOK ABOUT MY BROTHER BEN.

I TOOK THE SCHOLARSHIP TO THE UNIVERSITY OF NORTH CAROLINA BECAUSE OF THEIR JOURNALISM COLLEGE, AND THOMAS WOLFE AND ALL THE OTHER WRITERS, REALIZING TWO OF MY AMBITIONS, TO WRITE AND TO PLAY BALL. CHAPEL HILL HAD THE MOST BEAUTIFUL CAMPUS YOU COULD IMAGINE.

I WAS THE ONLY JEWISH BALLPLAYER ON THE FRESHMAN TEAM AND YOU VE GOT TO KNOW SOMEONE WAS ALWAYS TRYING TO STICK A FAST BALL IN MY EAR OR CUT ME IN HALF WITH THEIR SPIKES.

THE TEAM COACH WAS A WASHED-OUT RED NECK, WHO NEVER GOT HIGHER THAN THE B LEAGUES AND EVEN CHAWED HIS TOBACCO LIKE A BUSHER. HE DIDN'T LIKE ME. HE NEVER MADE ANY ANTI-SEMITIC REMARKS TO MY FACE BUT THE WAY HE SAID, 'ABIE,' WAS ENOUGH. I WAS THE BUTT OF ALL THE LOCKER ROOM JOKES AND HEARD THEIR CRUEL REMARKS SUPPOSEDLY OUT OF EARSHOT.

I WAS THE BEST FRESHMAN PITCHER IN THE CONFERENCE, AND WHEN THEY ALL LEARNED I COULD HANDLE MYSELF OFF AND ON THE FIELD, THANKS TO BEN, I STARTED GETTING ALONG. EVEN THAT SONOFABITCH OF A COACH KNEW HE'D BETTER TREAT ME TENDER BECAUSE WITHOUT ME THAT BUNCH OF MACKERELS WOULD BE AT THE BOTTOM OF THE STANDINGS.

THE TEAM HUSTLED FOR ME BUT IT WAS THE OPPOSITION THAT GOT TO ME. YOU SEE, I LOOKED EASY TO HIT, BUT I WASN'T. I PLAYED SOME PRETTY GOOD SEMI-PRO BALL IN NORFOLK AGAINST A LOT OF GUYS WHO HAD ONCE BEEN PROFESSIONAL PLAYERS AND HELL, THESE COLLEGE FRESHMEN WERE A BUNCH OF WILD ASS SWINGERS ALWAYS SHOOTING FOR THE FENCES. THEY CROAKED WITH FRUSTRATION, WHEN THEY COULDN'T HIT MY JUNK AND SOFT STUFF. AFTER I SAW THEM SWING A COUPLE OF TIMES I USUALLY HAD THEM EATING OUT OF MY HAND.

ANYHOW, MY HEAD BECAME THE BIGGEST TARGET IN THE CONFERENCE. IN THE FIRST FOUR GAMES – I WON THEM ALL BY SHUTOUTS – I WAS HIT BY OPPOSING PITCHERS SIX TIMES. FORTUNATELY I CAUGHT THEM ALL IN THE LEGS AND RIBS. BUT NONE OF THEM COULD MAKE ME BACK AWAY AT THE PLATE. I GUESS YOU MIGHT SAY I DARED THEM TO HIT ME.

'ABIE,' OLD RED NECK SAID, 'YOU'RE A RIGHT HANDED PITCHER AND A LEFT HANDED HITTER. WHEN YOU CROWD THE PLATE YOU'RE EXPOSING YOUR PITCHING ARM. I DON'T WANT YOU TO BE NO HERO. DON'T CROWD THE PLATE. YOU'RE BEING PAID TO PITCH, NOT HIT.'

HELL, I KNOW I WAS A BANJO HITTER. LOUD SINGLES AND AN OCCASIONAL DOUBLE, BUT I HUNG IN THERE. I GUESS IT HAD TO HAPPEN. ONE DAY A STRONG BACKED SCATTER-ARMED LEFTY FROM DUKE CAUGHT ME WITH A BLAZER RIGHT ABOVE MY ELBOW AND BUSTED IT.

WHEN I CAME OUT OF THE CAST, I EXERCISED UNTIL I CRIED. THE DAMAGE WASN'T PERMANENT, BUT I COULDN'T REGAIN MY PIN POINT CONTROL. ALL THOSE BALLS I THREW AT THE GARAGE DOOR, ALL THE DAYS OF CATCH WITH BEN WERE DOWN THE DRAIN. THE ATHLETIC DEPARTMENT KINDLY INFORMED ME THAT MY SCHOLARSHIP WASN'T AVAILABLE ANY LONGER.

POPPA WANTED ME TO STAY IN COLLEGE, BUT I WAS GETTING THE FEELING THAT YOU CAN'T LEARN TO WRITE FROM COLLEGE PROFESSORS. ESPECIALLY PROFESSORS WHO DIDN'T KNOW MY BROTHER BEN, OR ANYTHING ABOUT THE THINGS I WANTED TO WRITE. AND MY BASEBALL CAREER WAS OVER, WHICH WAS NO GREAT LOSS.

I QUIT AFTER MY FRESHMAN YEAR AND AFTER NAGGING A LOT OF NEWSPAPERS I WAS HIRED BY THE VIRGINIA PILOT AS THE AVIATION EDITOR AT THIRTY BUCKS A WEEK. AT NIGHT I WROTE FOR THE PULP MAGAZINES LIKE 'DOC SAVAGE' AND 'DIME WESTERN' FOR A PENNY A WORD UNDER THE NAME OF HORACE ABRAHAM.

AND THEN ONE DAY I GOT TIRED OF THE PULPS AND BEGAN TO WORK ON MY NOVEL, THE ONE ABOUT BEN.

Chapter Three

David Shawcross was more than a publisher. He was an editor of near legendary proportions running what was tantamount to a one-man house. He had emerged from the ranks of the English publishing dynasty, starting as errand boy at five shillings a week and working up to editor in chief over a period of two decades.

When he was twenty-one Shawcross headed the popular publication division for the notable sum of thirty shillings a week. In order to exist he deviled on the side synopsizing incoming manuscripts for other publishers.

David Shawcross survived all of this through sheer brilliant editorial talent. He refused to become a company henchman although named to the board.

Shawcross quit at a time of his own choosing and began his own small publishing firm.

Shawcross rarely published more than a dozen books a year but each carried a special merit and it seemed that once a year one of his books dented the best seller lists. Good writers were attracted to the house because of its quality reputation and the desire to have David Shawcross as their editor.

As a small publisher he had to stay afloat through new talent, which not only required sharp instincts but endless digging. Americans were the most popular writers in the world, but he was unable to bid against the large British firms for them. He did it in another way.

By astute analysis he knew that the major American editors ran on a treadmill that gave them little or no time to pursue and develop new talent and, moreover, no American publisher had an adequate system of covering unsolicited manuscripts or nursing along a promising talent.

The senior editors were consumed with manuscripts of their published writers plus a never ending round of sales conferences, making contracts, swimming the sea of cocktail parties, giving lectures, attending the necessary Broadway plays, and entertaining visiting firemen. Junior editors had nearly no power to push a promising manuscript. Furthermore, the pressurized atmosphere of New York generally lead to two or three martinis at lunch and watered down any desire to delve into unpublished manuscripts from unknown authors. David Shawcross commented that publishing was the only business in the world that did nothing to perpetuate itself. Every publisher had a history of allowing eventual best sellers to slip through his hands, mainly through stupidity.

Somewhere in every sludge pile there was a publishable book or a potential author who needed a hand to 'cross the line.' So he made an annual trip to America and dug. In a decade Shawcross discovered a half dozen new American authors including the sensational negro James Morton Linsey, who became a major literary figure.

Abraham Cady's manuscript sat on an agent's desk on a day he was visited by David Shawcross. It had been taken on by the agent on the recommendation of one of his authors, who was a columnist on the *Virginia Pilot*, where Abe worked as aviation editor. The book had been rejected seven times for seven different reasons.

That night at the Algonquin Hotel, Shawcross arranged a half dozen pillows around his back, adjusted the lamp, and laid out an array of tobacco. He perched his specs on his nose and balanced the blue-covered manuscript on his belly. As he turned the pages he dribbled ashes down his front, an absent-minded smoker of cigars, who left a tell-tale calling card of matches, ashes, burn holes, and an occasional flash fire in a wastebasket. At four o'clock in the morning he closed the manuscript of Abraham Cady's *The Brothers*. There were tears in his eyes.

Abe drew a deep breath as he entered the lobby of the Algonquin Hotel, that famed paneled domain of writers and actors. His voice was shaky as he asked for Mr Shawcross's suite.

Abe knocked on the door of 408.

'Please come in.' A plump, ruddy-cheeked tailored Englishman took his raincoat and hung it up. 'Why you're no more than a boy,' he said as he plopped into a high-backed chair with the manuscript spread on the coffee table before him. He thumbed through page after page, dripping a few ashes, brushing them off, then looked at the lad glued to the corner of the sofa and snatched off his glasses with a deliberate gesture.

'There's a million would be writers in this world to every writer,' he said, 'because they're thick-headed and too much in love with their own words to listen. Now, I think what you've got here shows promise but it needs work.'

'I came to listen, Mr Shawcross. I'll try not to be thick-headed but maybe I am, I don't know.'

Shawcross smiled. Cady had his own mind, all right.

'I'll spend a few days working with you. The rest will be up to you.'

'Thank you, sir. I got some time off from the paper in case it was needed.'

'I am going to caution you, young Cady, that I've tried this many times and rarely succeeded. Most writers resent criticism and those who don't mind and seem to understand what I'm driving at lack the ability to comprehend and translate it into publishable material. It's all very, very difficult.'

'You'd better believe I'm going to make it,' Abe said.

'Very well, I've booked a room for you down the hall. Unpack your things and let's have a go at it.'

For Abraham Cady, it was a luxurious experience. David Shawcross showed why he was one of the world's best editors. Not to write through Cady's pen but to get the best out of Cady. Basic storytelling was the key most authors never learn. Get the hero up a tree and cut the limb behind him. Pace. Stopping a chapter at an exquisite instance of suspense. Overwriting, the cardinal curse of all new authors. Underwriting . . . throwing away in two lines a situation that could be milked for several chapters. It is all right to lecture as long as you lecture subtly but never let a speech interfere with the flow of the story.

And the key trick that few novelists know. A novelist must know what his last chapter is going to say and one way or another work toward that last chapter. Too many writers start with a good idea and carry it through the first chapters, then fall apart because they had no idea where the top of the mountain was in the first place.

At the end of three days, Abraham Cady had listened carefully and questioned without anger. Abe returned to Norfolk and began his rewrite. This, Shawcross told him, the rewriting and rewriting separated the authors from the would be authors.

When a young man sets sail on the sea of authorship he is alone with little knowledge of the winds and tides and swells and storms. There are so many questions that can only be answered by persistence. And he went through it again, the awful loneliness, the exhaustion, the rare instances of exhilaration. And his book was done.

'Abe,' Morris called over the phone. 'There's a cablegram for you.'

'Read it, Poppa.'

'O.K. It says, "Manuscript received and read. Well done. I will be pleased to publish it straight away. My regards and congratulations. Signed, David Shawcross."'

The Brothers by Abraham Cady had an excellent reception in England. Old Shawcross had come up with another of his sleepers. It was a simple story, the author was not finely polished, but he struck at the heart. The novel said that because the Western Allies had betrayed Loyalist Spain there would be a great war. The price of diplomatic obscenity would be paid in the blood of millions of English, French, and Americans.

In America *The Brothers* was published by a firm who had originally rejected it (on the grounds it had nothing important to say) and it received an even greater acclaim, for it was published on the eve of World War II.

Chapter Four

FROM THE TIME OF THE SELLOUT AT MUNICH POPPA TRIED EVERYTHING TO GET THE RELATIVES OUT OF POLAND BUT IT WAS IMPOSSIBLE. IN ADDITION TO HIS FATHER AND TWO BROTHERS THERE WERE SOME THIRTY OTHER COUSINS AND AUNTS AND UNCLES. AND THEN GERMANY ATTACKED POLAND. IT WAS A

NIGHTMARE. FOR A SHORT TIME WE BREATHED EASIER, WHEN THE SOVIET UNION TOOK THE EASTERN PART OF POLAND WHICH HELD THE TOWN OF PRODNO. THEN THAT HOPE DIED WHEN GERMANY ATTACKED RUSSIA AND PRODNO FELL INTO GERMAN HANDS.

POPPA'S ATTITUDE ABOUT FASCISM CHANGED. BEN'S DEATH AND THE FEAR FOR HIS FAMILY TURNED HIM INTO A MILITANT. I KNEW IT WOULD BE TERRIBLE FOR THEM WHEN I DECIDED TO GO TO WAR, BUT I COULDN'T WAIT.

IN THE FALL OF 1941 I ENLISTED IN THE ROYAL CANADIAN AIR FORCE IN ORDER TO GET TO ENGLAND AND JOIN THE EAGLE SQUADRON OF AMERICAN VOLUNTEERS. LIKE BEN'S LACALLE SQUADRON IT WAS A HELL BENT GANG, BLAKESLEE, GENTILE, CHESLEY PETERSON, AND A LOT OF OTHERS WHO MADE NAMES AS FIGHTER PILOTS. FUNNY PART OF IT WAS THAT MANY OF THEM HAD WASHED OUT OF THE AMERICAN ARMY AIR CORPS FOR INABILITY TO FLY.

POPPA MADE A SMALL PROTEST ARGUING THAT AMERICA WOULD SOON BE IN THE WAR SO WHY SHOULD I GO OUT SPORTING FOR TROUBLE. MOMMA WAS WORSE. SHE FEARED SHE WOULD END UP LOSING BOTH OF HER SONS. THEY GAVE IN. POPPA CONFIDED THAT HE WAS PROUD AND MOMMA SAID THINGS LIKE, 'TRY TO BE CAREFUL AND DON'T BE A HERO.'

I WAS PRETTY SCARED WHEN I KISSED THEM GOOD-BY AND BOARDED THE TRAIN FOR TORONTO. A FEW MONTHS AFTER I STARTED TRAINING AS A SPITFIRE PILOT, AMERICA WAS ATTACKED AT PEARL HARBOR.

August 19, 1942

Seven thousand Canadians and British Commandos poured ashore at the French beach resort of Dieppe on a reconnaissance raid to test the German coastal defenses.

Engineers moving behind the infantry reached and spiked some large German guns but the operation ran into serious trouble quickly. One flank was hit by a German flotilla and in the center, Canadian tanks were hung up on the sea wall and then the German counterattack turned the raid into a disaster.

Overhead, a blizzard of Spitfires and Messerschmitts raged in a massive dogfight while other allied planes came in low to cover the disaster on the beach. Among them were the American Eagles and their youngest pilot, twenty-two-year-old Abraham Cady flying his fifth mission.

As the planes ran low on fuel and ammunition they streaked back to England to refuel and load and return to the action. Abe came back to Dieppe on his third sortie of the day as the airmen desperately attempted to stall the German counterattack.

Working at treetop level he made pass after pass at a German company crawling out of the woods. With communications largely broken and squadrons scattered all over the sky it became increasingly difficult to warn comrades in trouble. They were all on their own.

Abe swooped down on a bridge and sprayed it clean of the enemy, when a trio of Messerschmitts pounced on him from the cover of a cloud. He peeled off deftly to evade and just as he felt he had slipped away his plane shuddered violently under the impact of a striking of machine gun bullets. The controls jerked his arms half out of their sockets, and he started to spin. Abe muscled her back into control, but she veered crazily like a toy glider in a windstorm.

JESUS H. CHRIST ON A CRUTCH! MY TAIL'S SHOT UP. DITCH HER? HELL NO, NOT OVER WATER. SHAG ASS FOR ENGLAND. LORD, GIVE ME THIRTY MINUTES.

Abe jockeyed his swerving craft a few hundred feet over the Channel racing for England. Fifteen minutes to land, ten ...

'Zenith, Zenith, this is Dog Two Dog on red alert. I'm shot up.'

'Hello, Dog Two Dog. This is Zenith. What are your intentions?'

SONOFABITCH!

A Messerschmitt came up behind Abe. Using every ounce of his strength he pulled the nose of the plane up and into a deliberate stall. The startled German was unable to duplicate the maneuver and passed beneath him. Abe let her dive and pressed the triggers.

'I've got him! I've got him!'

HANG ON. THANK GOD ... COAST OF ENGLAND. CHRIST, I CAN'T HOLD MY ALTITUDE. EASY BABY, EASY, YOU'RE RIPPING MY ARMS OUT.

He veered at the mainland at a sharp angle.

'Hello, Dog Two Dog. This is Drewerry. We see you now. We're advising you to ditch.'

'I can't. I'm too low to jump. I'm going to have to land her.'

'Cleared to land.'

The sirens at Drewerry set off a scramble of activity. Fire wagons and an ambulance and a rescue squad inched up the apron next to the runway as the wounded bird augered in.

'Poor devil, he's really out of control.'

'Hang on there, Yank.'

BOY, I DO NOT LIKE THIS ANGLE. I DO NOT LIKE IT AT ALL. COME ON, SWEETHEART, LINE UP WITH THAT RUNWAY. THAT'S A GOOD GIRL. NOW JUST HOLD IT.

Three hundred, two hundred, cut engine, glide, glide.

'Look at that lad fly!'

COME ON, GROUND, LET ME FEEL YOU. COME ON, GROUND. OH BOY, DOES THAT FEEL ... JESUS! MY FUCKING LANDING GEAR IS BUSTED.

Abe pulled up his landing gear and set her down on her belly. The Spitfire careened off the runway with sparks flying. At the last instant he veered away from a barracks and tore for the woods, then mangled to a halt in the trees. The sirens screamed and bore down on him. Abe shoved the canopy back and crawled out on the wing. Then after a beat of silence a terrible explosion was followed by billowing flames!

Chapter Five

OH MY GOD! I'M DEAD! I KNOW I'M DEAD! GOD! I CAN'T SEE! I CAN'T MOVE! MY HEAD IS BLURRED!

'Help me!' Abe cried.

'Lieutenant Cady,' a woman's voice penetrated the darkness, 'can you hear me?'

'Help me,' he cried, 'where am I? What's happened to me?'

'Lieutenant Cady,' the voice said again. 'If you hear me, please say so.'

'Yes,' he gasped.

'I'm Sister Grace, a nurse, and you're in the RAF Hospital near Bath. You've been badly hurt.'

'I'm blind. Oh God, I'm blind!'

'Will you try to get control of yourself so we can speak?'

'Touch me so I know you're here.'

He forced himself to gain control.

'You've undergone a serious operation,' Sister Grace said, 'and you're all bandaged up. Don't be frightened because you can't see or move. Let me go and get the doctor, and he'll explain everything to you.'

'Please don't go away for long.'

'I'll be right back. You must remain calm now.'

He sucked in air deeply and quivered in fear. His heart raced to urgent footsteps he could hear coming toward him.

'Woke up, have you,' a commanding British voice said. 'I'm Dr Finchly.'

'Tell me, Doctor, tell me if I'm blind.'

'No,' the doctor answered. 'You've had quite a bit of sedation and your mind is apt to be rather fuzzy. Are you able to comprehend?'

'Yes, I'm a little cuckoo, but I understand.'

'Very well, then,' Finchly said, sitting on the edge of the bed. 'You've lost the sight of your right eye, but we're going to be able to save the other one.'

'Are you sure?'

'Yes, we're quite certain of it.'

'What happened?'

'Let me explain it to you in simple terms. Your aircraft exploded shortly after you ran into the woods. You were crawling on the wing at the time and at the instant of explosion your hands went up over your face to protect it.'

'I remember that much.'

'The backs of your hands took most of the shock and were severely burned. Third degree burns. Now, you have four tendons on each hand like rubber bands to each finger. These may be damaged. If the burns don't heal properly we will have to do a skin graft and if the tendons have been damaged we'll do tendon grafts. Do you understand me so far?'

'Yes, sir.'

'In any event we will be able to restore full use of both hands. It may take time, but we're very, very successful with both skin and tendon grafts.'

'What about my eyes,' he whispered.

'With the explosion, some minute fragments hit both your eyes perforating your cornea. The cornea is a thin membrane that covers the eye. Now, each eye is filled with a substance that appears somewhat like egg albumin that keeps it inflated like air in a tire. Your right eye was deeply penetrated, the fluid leaked and the entire eyeball collapsed.'

'As for the other eye, everything was intact except for the perforation of the cornea. We had to replace it with a substitute cornea. The way we did this was to dissect the upper membrane of your eyelid and cover the eye with it, stitching it to the bottom of the lid. The stitches are thinner than a strand of human hair.'

'When can I know if I can see?'

'Well, I promise you, you have vision in your left eye but there are two problems you're going to have to face up to. A fatty embolism can form from the damage to your hands and move up to your eye and destroy further tissue. Secondly, you are suffering from a rather severe concussion from the blast which would put normal vision out of focus. We'll allow you to see for a few minutes each day, when we change bandages and treat your eye and hands.'

'O.K.,' Abe said, 'I'll be good . . . and thanks, Doctor.'

'Quite all right. Your publisher, Mr Shawcross, has been waiting here for almost three days.'

'Sure,' Abe said.

'Well, Abe,' Shawcross said, 'they said you did some fancy flying to get back across the Channel and that was quite a trick getting your landing gear up and avoiding the barrack.'

'Yeah, I'm a hell of a flyer.'

'Is it all right if I smoke, Doctor.'

'Certainly.'

Abe liked the smell of Shawcross's cigar. It reminded him of those days in New York, when they worked day and night on his manuscript.

'My parents know about this?'

'I induced them not to inform your mother and father until you could send word, personally.'

'Thanks. Jesus, I sure bought the farm.'

'Bought a farm?' Dr Finchley asked.

'It's an American phrase. It means he got a bashing about.'

'Yes, rather, I'd say.'

Dear Momma and Poppa:

You shouldn't be alarmed because this letter isn't in my handwriting. The reason I'm not personally writing for a while is that I got into a slight accident and burned my hands a little.

Let me assure you I'm otherwise in good health, in a fine hospital and there is no permanent damage of any kind. Even the food here is good.

I had a little trouble landing my plane and so forth. I probably won't be flying anymore because they're so sticky about perfect health.

There's a nice young lady here who takes my letters and she's happy to let me write to you every few days.

Mainly, you're absolutely not to worry for a minute.

Love to Sophie and everyone.

Your devoted son,
ABE

Chapter Six

PATIENCE.

IF I EVER HEAR THAT WORD AGAIN, I'M GOING TO FLIP MY LID. PATIENCE, THAT'S WHAT THEY TELL ME TWENTY TIMES A DAY. PATIENCE.

I LIE FROZEN ON MY BACK IN TOTAL DARKNESS. WHEN THE EFFECT OF THE DRUGS WEARS OFF THE PAINS IN MY HANDS BECOME EXCRUCIATING. I PLAY GAMES. I PLAY OUT A BASEBALL GAME PITCH BY PITCH. I'M THE RED SOX PITCHER. IN ONE GAME I STRUCK OUT THE WHOLE YANKEE LINE-UP. RIZZUTO, GORDON, DICKEY, KELLER. DIMAGGIO WAS LAST. WE GOT TO THREE AND TWO. HE'S DUG IN TO SAVE THE YANKEE REPUTATION. I GIVE HIM A LOT OF MOTION AND DISH UP A SLOW CURVE. IT TAKES GUTS TO THROW THAT PITCH IN SUCH A SITUATION. DIMAGGIO NEARLY BROKE HIS BACK DIVING AFTER IT. NINE STRAIGHT YANKEES. IT'S A FEAT THAT WILL STAND IN THE RECORD BOOKS FOR YEARS.

I THINK ABOUT THE WOMEN I'VE SLEPT WITH. I'M STILL A KID SO A DOZEN ISN'T BAD. BUT I CAN'T REMEMBER MOST OF THEIR NAMES.

I THINK ABOUT BEN. GOD, I MISS BEN. WHAT A WINNER I AM. I WANTED THREE THINGS IN MY LIFE; TO PLAY BALL, TO FLY, AND TO WRITE. TWO OF THEM ARE GONE FOREVER AND HOW CAN I WRITE, WITH MY PECKER?

ANYHOW, THESE PEOPLE HERE ARE REALLY WONDERFUL. THEY TREAT ME LIKE A PORCELAIN DOLL. EVERYTHING I DO BECOMES AN INVOLVED CHORE. IF SOMEONE LEADS ME TO THE BATHROOM AND SETS ME ON THE POT I CAN DO MY BUSINESS BUT THEN SOMEBODY'S GOT TO WIPE ME. I CAN'T EVEN AIM TO TAKE A LEAK. I'VE GOT TO SIT LIKE A WOMAN. IT'S ABSOLUTELY HUMILIATING.

EVERYDAY THEY LET ME OUT OF MY MUMMY CAGE FOR A FEW MINUTES. MY GOOD EYE IS USUALLY GLUED SHUT. BY THE TIME I GET IT INTO FOCUS THEY'RE WRAPPING ME UP AGAIN. I KEEP TELLING MYSELF IT COULD BE WORSE. EVERYDAY THE EYE IS LESS BLURRED AND I'M STARTING TO GET SOME MOVEMENT IN MY HANDS.

DAVID SHAWCROSS COMES FROM LONDON ONCE OR TWICE A WEEK. HIS WIFE, LORRAINE, NEVER FAILS TO BRING A PACKAGE OF FOOD. SHE'S AS BAD AS MOMMA. I KNOW IT'S COSTING HER VALUABLE RATION COUPONS, AND I TRY TO TELL HER THEY'RE FEEDING ME LIKE ROYALTY.

HOW I WELCOME THE SMELL OF THAT STINKY CIGAR. SHAWCROSS HAS ALL BUT GIVEN UP PUBLISHING TO WORK FOR THE GOVERNMENT TO NEGOTIATE A BOOK EXCHANGE PROGRAM WITH THE RUSSIANS. HIS STORIES OF THE PARANOID BEHAVIOUR AT THE SOVIET EMBASSY ARE A RIOT.

MY BUDDIES VISIT ONCE IN A WHILE BUT IT'S A LONG TRIP FOR THEM, THE EAGLE SQUADRON HAS BEEN TRANSFERRED OUT OF THE RAF INTO THE AMERICAN AIR CORPS. SO, I DON'T KNOW WHAT I AM. I'M NOT MUCH USE TO ANYONE, ANYHOW.

A MONTH PASSES. PATIENCE, THEY TELL ME. JESUS, I HATE THAT WORD. THEY'RE GOING TO START SKIN GRAFTS SOON.

THEN SOMETHING HAPPENED AND THE DAYS DIDN'T SEEM SO LONG OR AGONIZING AFTER THAT. HER NAME IS SAMANTHA LINDSTEAD, AND HER FATHER IS

A SQUIRE WITH AN OLD FAMILY FARM IN THE MINDIP HILLS NOT FAR FROM BATH. SAMANTHA IS TWENTY AND A RED CROSS VOLUNTEER AIDE. AT FIRST SHE CAME IN ON ROUTINE THINGS LIKE TAKING LETTERS AND SPONGING ME OFF. WE GOT TO TALKING A LOT AND PRETTY SOON SHE BROUGHT HER PHONOGRAPH AND SOME RECORDS AND A RADIO SET. SHE'D SPEND A GOOD PART OF THE DAY IN MY ROOM, FEEDING ME, HOLDING MY CIGARETTE, AND SHE READ A LOT TO ME.

CAN A MAN FALL IN LOVE WITH A VOICE?

I NEVER SAW HER. SHE ALWAYS CAME AFTER MY MORNING TREATMENT. ALL I KNEW WAS HER VOICE. I SPENT HALF MY TIME NOW IMAGINING WHAT SHE LOOKED LIKE. SHE INSISTED SHE WAS VERY PLAIN.

ABOUT A WEEK AFTER SHE CAME I WAS ABLE TO TAKE SHORT WALKS WITH HER LEADING ME AROUND THE HOSPITAL GROUNDS. AND THEN, SHE GOT TO TOUCHING ME MORE AND MORE.

'Light me up, Sam,' Abe said.

Samantha sat near the bed and held the cigarette carefully as he puffed. When she snuffed it out, she slipped her hand through the opening of his pajamas and rubbed the tips of her fingers over his chest, barely making contact.

'Sam, I've been thinking. Maybe you'd better not come back to see me, any more.' Her hand drew away from him suddenly. 'I don't like the idea of anyone feeling sorry for me.'

'Do you think that's why I come here?'

'You lie in darkness all day and all night and your mind can play tricks. I'm starting to take things more serious than I ought to. You've been a real wonderful person and shouldn't be a victim of my fantasies.'

'Abe. Don't you know how wonderful it is for me to be with you? Maybe when we see each other you won't care for me, but I don't want to change anything now. And you're not going to get rid of me that easily, and you really aren't in much of a condition to do anything about it.'

Samantha's car passed onto the circular driveway of Linstead Hall. The tires crunched over the gravel and then halted before a small manor house of two centuries ago.

'There's Mommy and Daddy. This is Abe. You can't see too much of him, but his photographs are quite handsome.'

'Welcome to Linstead Hall,' Donald Linstead said.

'Pardon my gloves,' Abe answered, holding up his bandaged hands.

She lead him carefully through a wooded land and then found a soft place in a meadow looking down on the manor and she described the scene to him.

'I can smell cows and horses and smoke and all kinds of flowers. It must be beautiful up here. I can't tell one flower from the other.'

'There's heather and roses and the fires are coming from the peat bogs.'

Oh Abe! she thought. I do love you.

On the third visit to Linstead Hall the family received the happy news that Abe's eye bandages would be removed for a few hours each day.

Samantha seemed edgy during the walk. In the darkness, one can sense things fiercely. The tone of her voice was different, the vibrations were tense.

It had been a long day and Abe was tired. A male nurse came in from the village to bathe and change him. Afterward he stretched out on the bed, grumbling over his entombed hands. Patience. To be able to shave, to be able to blow my nose, to be able to read.

To be able to see Samantha.

He heard the door open and close and could tell by the turn of the knob it was Samantha.

'I hope I didn't awaken you.'

'No.'

The bed sank as she sat beside him. 'It's going to be a great event when they take those bandages off your eyes. I mean your eye. You've been very brave.'

'Like I had a choice. Well, we sure know what humility is.'

Abe could hear the soft sobs she was trying to stifle. He wanted to reach out for her as he had wanted to a hundred times. What did she feel like. Were her breasts large or small. Was her hair soft. Were her lips sensuous.

'What the hell are you crying for?'

'I don't know.' They both knew. In a sad strange way they had experienced something totally unique and it was going to come to an end and neither of them knew if the ending was final or would ignite a new beginning. Samantha was afraid she would be rejected.

She lay beside him as they had done after their walks, and her fingers unbuttoned his shirt, and she laid her cheek on his chest and then her hands and lips became like whispers all about his body.

'I talked to the doctor,' she said. 'He told me it would be all right,' and she reached between his legs. 'Just be still, I'll do everything.'

She undressed him and flung her own clothing off and locked the door.

Oh, fantastic darkness! Every sensation was so vivid, the gentle slaps, the kissing of his feet, the feather soft whip of her hair. Samantha was in a controlled frenzy as he succumbed to her.

And then she cried and told him she had never been so happy, and Abe said he was really a better lover but under the circumstances he was glad some part of him worked. And then the love talk became silly, and they laughed because it was really quite funny.

Chapter Seven

David Shawcross's phone rang angrily. He groped for the bed lamp, yawned his way to a sitting position. 'Good, God,' he mumbled, 'it's three in the morning.'

'Hello!'

'Mr Shawcross?'

'Yes, this is Shawcross.'

'Sergeant Richardson, Military Police attached to the station in Marylebone Lane, sir.'

'Richardson, it's three o'clock in the morning. Get on with it, man.'

'So sorry to disturb you, sir. We've picked up an officer, RAF chap, a Lieutenant Abraham ... C ... A ... D ... Y, Cady.'

'Abe in London?'

'Yes, sir. He was rather intoxicated when we picked him up. Drunk as a lord if you don't mind me saying, sir.'

'Is he all right, Richardson?'

'In a manner of speaking, sir. There was a note pinned to his uniform. Shall I read it?'

'Yes, by all means.'

'"My name is Abraham Cady. If I appear to be drunk, don't be confused. I am having a case of the bends due to tunnel work on a secret project and must be decompressed slowly. Deposit my body to David Shawcross, 77 Cumberland Terrace. NW 8.' Will you accept him, Mr Shawcross? Don't want to press charges on the chap, just out of the hospital and all that.'

'Charges. For what?'

'Well, sir, when we got to him he was swimming in the fountain in Trafalgar Square ... nude.'

'Bring the bugger over, I'll take him.'

'So you were a German U-boat, were you now?' Shawcross taunted.

Abe groaned through one more cup of black coffee. At least the British call it coffee. Ugh!

'Flaunting your up-periscope in the middle of our stately fountain. Really, Abraham.'

'Shawcross, put out the goddam cigar. Can't you see I'm dying.'

'More coffee, dear?' Lorraine asked.

'God no. I mean, no thanks.'

She tinkled a bell for the maid and helped her clear the dishes. 'I've got to be trotting off. The queues are still dreadful and I've got to stock up. Our kiddies are coming down from Manchester tomorrow. She kissed Abe's cheek. 'I do hope you're feeling better, dear.'

When she left, David grumbled. 'I suppose I love my grandchildren as much as the next grandfather but frankly, they're spoiled little bastards. I keep writing Pam and telling her how dangerous it is here in London but damned if she'll listen. Anyhow, I've been thinking seriously about taking Geoff into the business after the war. Now what's all this nonsense about you and this girl, Pinhead, Greenbed ...'

'Linstead. Samantha Linstead.'

'Are you in love with her or what?'

'I don't know. I've never seen her. I've made love to her, but I've never seen her or touched her.'

'Nothing really strange about that. All lovers are blind in one way or another. I've seen her. She's rather attractive, in an outdoorsy sort of way. Sturdy type.'

'She stopped coming to the hospital when they took the bandages off my eyes. She was afraid I wouldn't like her. I was never so damned miserable in my life. I wanted to go beat the manor house door down and claim her, then I got all choked up, too. Suppose she was a real dog? Suppose she got a good look at me in the daylight and got sober? Stupid, isn't it?'

'Very. Well, you'll have to take a look at each other sooner or later. In the meanwhile do you have any company to forget Samantha with?'

'No, I'm out of touch in London.' Abe said. 'The first four calls I made last night, two were married, one pregnant, and on the fourth call a man answered.'

'Well, let's see,' Shawcross said, diving his pudgy fingers into his vest and fishing out an address book. As he thumbed it he grunted in delight a few times. 'Why don't you meet me for lunch at Mirabelle's at two. We ought to be able to come up with something.'

Abraham Cady, sobered and reassembled, turned Curzon Street all filled with the electricity of wartime London and into the plush sanctuary of Mirabelle's. The maître d' was expecting him. Abe stood a moment and looked over the room to Shawcross's traditional table. He had come up with a redhead. Very British looking. Nice body from what he could see. Didn't look too stupid. Seemed nervous. That was par. Everyone gets nervous before meeting a writer and usually disappointed afterward. They expect nothing but gems to flow from the writer's brilliant mind.

'Ah, Abraham,' Shawcross said, struggling out of his seat. Meet Cynthia Greene. Cynthia is a secretary to one of my colleagues in the publishing business and is an admirer of your book.'

Abe took the girl's hand warmly as he always took a woman's hand. It was a bit damp with nerves but otherwise firm. A handshake told so much. He detested the wet limp fish so many women gave. She smiled. The game was on. He sat down.

Nice going, Shawcross, Abe thought.

'Waiter, a little nip of the hair that killed the dog for my friend here.'

'Whisky, over ice,' Abe ordered.

Shawcross commented that ice was barbaric and Abe told about an English girl he knew who drank a pint and a half of Scotch each and every day but would never take ice because she was afraid it would wreck her liver.

Cheers. They sipped and studied the fragile wartime menu. Abe surveyed Miss Greene.

The first thing he liked aside from her general looks and firm handshake was that she was obviously an English lady and kept her mouth shut. All women have volcanoes. Some compulsively erupt from the mouth with unending dribble. Other women kept their volcanoes dormant and exploded them at the right time in the right way. Abe liked quiet women.

The captain handed David Shawcross a note. He adjusted his specs and grumbled. 'I know this sounds like an obvious ploy to get you two alone but the Russians have called me. Uncivilized bastards. Try to muddle through without me. Now, don't you try to steal my writer for your house. He's due for a good book, soon.'

They were alone.

'How long have you known Shawcross?' Abe asked.

'Since he began visiting you in the hospital.'

There was no mistaking that voice. 'Samantha?'

'Yes, Abe.'

'Samantha.'

'Mr Shawcross loves you like a son. He phoned me this morning and told me you cried half the night. I'm sorry I ran. Well, here I am. I know you're terribly disappointed.'

'No . . . no . . . you're just lovely.'

Chapter Eight

From a meadow in the Mindip Hills Abe and Samantha watched wave after wave of airplanes flying toward the Continent. The sky was black with them. Lumbering bombers and swarms of fighters. They passed and their sounds faded and the sky was blue. Abe stared pensively down to Linstead Hall.

Samantha felt a sudden chill. She placed her sweater on her shoulders. The flowers bent to the breeze and her soft red hair danced. She went so well with the countryside. Samantha looked as though she were born riding a horse.

The hospital agreed that he could take a furlough as long as he reported for twice weekly treatments. Dr. Finchly also strongly advised Abe to stay out of London. He needed the peace of Linstead Hall. Heather and horse manure. But the daily flights of planes constantly reminded him that there was a war out there.

'So pensive,' Samantha said.

'The war is passing me by,' he said.

'I know you're restless but when all is said and done perhaps you were never meant to be anything but a writer. I know you've a book churning inside you.'

'My hands. They start to hurt after just a few minutes. I may have to have one more operation, yet.'

'Abe, have you ever thought of me being your hands?'

'I don't know if you can write a book that way ... I just don't know.'

'Why don't we try.'

The thought of it brought Abraham Cady to life. It was very awkward at first and difficult to share a novelist's thoughts. Each day he became better able to organize his mind. He learned to dictate until he was capable of pouring out a torrent of words.

The furlough ended. Abe was discharged from the Air Corps. A farewell bust at the Officer's Club with his old buddies and back to Linstead Hall to write.

Samantha became the silent partner and privileged observer to one of the unique of all human experiences, the writing of a novel. She saw him detach himself from the first world of reality and submerge into the second world of his own creation and wander through it alone. There was no magic. There was no inspiration that people always look for and imagine in the writer. What there was was a relentless plodding requiring a special kind of stamina that makes the profession so limited. Of course there came those moments when things suddenly fell into a natural rhythm and even more rare, that instant of pure flying through creative exhilaration.

But what Samantha witnessed most was the uncertainty, the drain, the emotional downs, the exhaustion. Those times he did not have the strength to eat or undress himself.

David Shawcross stood in the wings, a happy man knowing exactly when to make Abe turn it off with a blast in London. A roaring drunk. A flushing out, and a return to the blank sheet of paper. He told Samantha that Abe had within him the key to greatness on one major premise. He was aware of his weaknesses as a writer as well as his strengths; Shawcross said few writers had the ability of introspection because they were too vain to admit weakness. This was Abraham Cady's power, and he controlled his second novel. He was in his twenties and writing like sixty.

The Jug (a nickname for the P-47 Thunderbolt) was a simple and classical story of men at war. The hero was Major General Vincent Bertelli, a second generation street fighter of Italian-American descent. An officer in the early thirties he rose quickly in the war that had become air oriented. Bertelli was a relentless and apparently heartless driver who was ready to take heavy losses in dangerous raids on the thesis of 'war was war.'

The general's son, Sal, flew as a squadron commander in his father's command. The deep love between them is camouflaged by what appears to be father/son hatred.

General Bertelli orders a raid and places his son's squadron in a suicide position. The news of Sal's death is delivered by Barney, the sole survivor in the squadron.

Bertelli listens without emotion and is spat upon by Barney.

'You're tired,' the general said, 'I'll forget about this.'

Barney turned on his heel. 'Barney!' the general commanded and he halted. Bertelli wanted desperately to show his son's transfer order and tell him he pleaded with Sal to quit. His boy had refused despite everyone knowing he had flown himself into exhaustion.

'Never mind,' General Bertelli said.

And suddenly Barney knew. 'I'm sorry, sir. He just had to go on proving himself, like he had no choice.'

'It's a fucking war,' the general answered, 'people are going to get hurt. Get some rest, Barney. You're going up again in a few hours. Big target. U-boat pens.'

The door closed. General Bertelli opened the top drawer of his desk and swallowed a nitroglycerin tablet for the attack that was coming on. 'Sal,' he said, 'I loved you. Why couldn't I tell you.'

'The end,' Abe's hoarse voice rasped. He stood behind Samantha and watched her type those two beautiful last words.

'Oh, Abe,' she cried, 'it's lovely.'

'I need a belt,' he said.

When she left he took her place at the typewriter and pecked out with stiff fingers, 'Dedicated to Samantha with love, and then the words ... 'will you marry me?'

Chapter Nine

Little by little full use of Abe's hands returned. An eye patch covered his deformity. Abraham Cady was a one-eyed, broken winged eagle, but an eagle, nonetheless. After his discharge and with his book, *The Jug*, selling well, he signed on with United Press in London.

London was a vital place, the heartbeat of the free world building up to burst upon the European Continent aware fully of its own importance and rife with the colors of Allied and Empire troops and those of governments in exile. The smoke of German incendiaries had long died out in the gutted center of London. The nights in the tubes were over but there were still queues, the eternal British queues and sandbags and balloon barrages and blackouts and then the buzz bombs.

Abraham Cady joined a fraternity of those men charged with the mission of telling the story and in these days in London it was a legendary roll call from Quentin Reynolds to Edward R. Murrow on their news beats from the American Embassy to Downing Street to BBC House to the great press artery of Fleet Street.

The Linsteads had traditionally kept a small town house in London in Colchester Mews off Chelsea Square. The mews were once carriage houses and servants quarters behind the stately five story homes bordering London's green squares. After the First World War, when horses faded from the scene, the mews were converted into doll house quarters that were particularly attractive to writers, musicians, actors, and visiting squires.

Abe and Samantha moved into the mews after their wedding at Linstead Hall, and he went searching for a part of the war.

At a time and place that distinguished journalism was commonplace Abe Cady was able to carve a distinctive niche as the flyer's correspondent.

From those first floundering days of the Battle of Britain, all of England became a massive airfield. The British owned the night and the American Eighth Air Force mastered the European skies by day with raids deep into Germany now escorted by swarms of Mustang fighters.

Abe flew with the Halifaxes by night and Flying Fortresses by day, and he wrote of a sort of fairyland war of seemingly harmless puffs of smoke down 'flak alley' and the great swirling ballets of the dogfights. He wrote of the blissful numbness of total exhaustion to the lullaby of five thousand droning engines. And blood. A tail or belly gunner cut in half and men struggling to free him from his prison. Of long streams of smoke and crippled birds struggling in a place out of their element to find the earth again. And sentimental songs around the bars, of silent stares at the empty bunks. Of varnished officers poring over blown-up maps of Germany with a crisp detached vernacular. And the view from the sky as their loads of death rained down on miniature sets that were the cities of Germany.

WE'LL BE OVER BERLIN IN A HALF HOUR. THE ARMADA OUTSIDE HAS BLACKENED THE SKY LIKE A SWARM OF LOCUSTS. WE ARE CLOAKED WITH FIGHTER PLANES OF THE WOLF PACK FLYING RAMROD TO ESCORT THE BOMBERS.

A STARTLED COMMUNICATION. 'LOOK OUT, TONY, MESSERS AT SEVEN O'CLOCK.'

A SHORT, WILD DOGFIGHT BELOW US. A SCARLET-NOSED MUSTANG BELCHES SMOKE AND SPIRALS EARTHWARD WITH A MESSERSCHMITT ON HIS TAIL. OUR KID MUST HAVE BEEN GREEN. THE MESSERS ARE NO MATCH FOR THE MUSTANG. THE KRAUT HAD TO BE GOOD TO HAVE SURVIVED THIS LONG. THE MUSTANG ERUPTS. IT'S DONE. NO PARACHUTE.

LATER I LEARNED HE WAS A SECOND YEAR ENGINEERING STUDENT AT GEORGIA TECH. WHAT WILL IT BE LIKE TOMORROW IN ATLANTA WHEN THE CABLEGRAM ARRIVES AND THE LIVES OF A DOZEN PEOPLE FALL TO A GRIEF-STRICKEN WHISPER. HE WAS THE ONLY MALE HEIR. THE ONE WHO WAS GOING TO CARRY THEIR NAME INTO THE NEXT GENERATION.

THE KRAUTS HAVE BEEN BEATEN OFF. IT COST FOUR MUSTANGS AND TWO BOMBERS. BOMBERS DIE SLOWER. WRITHE IN AGONY, TWIST AND ROLL HEAVILY DESPERATE MEN TUG AT CANOPIES. AND THEN, DISINTEGRATION.

TENSING UP AND ALERT AS WE NEAR BERLIN, ALL EXCEPT THE CO-PILOT ASLEEP TWISTED LIKE A PRETZEL THAT ONLY A YOUNG MAN COULD MANAGE. I'M INVITED TO TAKE THE CONTROLS.

MY HANDS ITCH WITH JOY AS I TAKE THE CONTROLS. THE BOMBS FLOAT DOWN SLOWLY, DESCENDING LIKE A MANTLE OF BLACK SNOW AND THEN GREAT GUSTS OF ORANGE BILLOW FROM THE TORTURED CITY.

I AM SICK AT MY OWN ECSTASY AS OUR BATTERED FLEET LIMPS BACK. WHY DOES MAN PUT HIS GREATEST ENERGY AND TALENT INTO DESTRUCTION?

I AM THE WRITER. I MAKE IT ALL A MORALITY PLAY. WE'RE WHITE UP HERE, LIKE ANGLES. THEY'RE BLACK DOWN THERE LIKE DEVILS. DEVILS, ROAST IN HELL!

AND THEN I WONDER WHO I KILLED TODAY. AN ENGINEER LIKE THE BOY FROM GEORGIA, A MUSICIAN, A DOCTOR, OR A CHILD WHO NEVER EVEN HAD A CHANCE TO ASPIRE. WHAT A WASTE.

Samantha set the receiver down and grunted downheartedly. Her pregnancy had made her ill. She had been queasy all day. She made her way up the narrow stairs to the tiny bedroom where Abe lay in sprawled exhaustion. For a moment she considered ignoring the phone call, but he would be very angry. She tapped his shoulder.

'Abe.'

'Uhhhh.'

'We just got a call from Wing Commander Parsons at Breedsford. They want you there by fourteen hundred.'

I smell it, Abe thought. Ten to one they're going for the ball bearing works outside Hamburg. It will be one hell of a show. The night raids were more vivid in their sharp black and white contrasts. And after their pass, the carpet of red fires on the burning from the target. Abe popped off the bed and read his watch. Time for a shave and a bath.

Samantha appeared piqued and drawn. Her whiteness was even more apparent in London. 'You mustn't be late,' she said, 'I'll draw your bath.'

'You'll be all right, won't you, honey. I mean, about taking you out tonight. This raid must be a big one or Parsons wouldn't call.'

'As a matter of fact, I'm not all right. Decent of you to ask, though.'

'O.K., let's have it,' Abe snapped.

'I'd rather you wouldn't speak to me as if I were on the carpet before the colonel's desk.'

Abe grunted and tied on his robe. 'What's wrong, honey?'

'I've been sick every morning for two weeks, but that's to be expected, I suppose. To escape the confinement of these four walls I get to stand in queues for hours on end or dive into the tube for my life ahead of the buzz bombs. And after living on scraps I'm jolly well homesick for Linstead Hall. I suppose it would be bearable if I saw anything of my husband. You crawl in, write your story and fall flat until the phone rings for the next raid. And those rare evenings you are in London you seem obsessed with shooting the breeze all night with David Shawcross or in some Fleet Street Pub.'

'Finished?'

'Not really. I'm bloody bored and unhappy, but I don't think it means very much to you.'

'Now, just hold on, Samantha. I happen to think we're goddam lucky. With fifty million men and women separated by this war we're plenty lucky to have a few hours together.'

'Perhaps we would be if you weren't on a crusade to make every bombing mission out of England.'

'That's my job.'

'Oh, they all say you love your job. They say you're the best bomber jockey in both air forces.'

'Come off it. They let me take the controls once in a while as a gesture.'

'Not according to Commander Parsons. It's got to be a sign of luck if the old one-eyed eagle leads them in. Steady Abraham, he was know far and wide.'

'My God, Samantha! What in the hell is so hard for you to understand. I hate fascism. I hate Hitler. I hate what the Germans have done to the Jewish people.'

'Abe, you're shouting!' Samantha stiffened, breaking off the assault and quivering and sobbing to blunt male logic. 'It's the loneliness,' she cried.

'Honey, I . . . I don't know what to say. Loneliness is the brother of war and the mother of all writers. He asks his wife to endure it graciously because she will come to know that her ability to endure it can be her greatest gift.'

'I don't understand you, Abe.'

'I know.'

'Well, don't act as if I'm some kind of clod. We have gone through a book together, you know.'

'I didn't have hands so you owned me. Your possession of me was complete. When I had no sight and we made love you were your happiest because your possession was complete then, too. But now I've got my hands and eyes and you don't want to share me or understand what your end of this bargain consists of. It's going to be like this till the end of our lives, Samantha. It will always demand sacrifice and loneliness of both of us.'

'You're great at twisting things to make me look very little.'

'We're just starting out together, honey. Don't make the mistake of standing between me and my writing.'

Samantha returned to Linstead Hall. After all, she was pregnant and life in London wasn't easy. Abe assured her he understood and then he went on with his war.

On D-Day, Ben Cady was born at Linstead Hall. His father, Abraham, wrote at the navigator's desk of a B-24 Liberator sent up from Italy for a saturation raid in conjunction with the invasion.

Chapter Ten

There are no J. Milton Mandelbaums, Abe thought. He's only a fiction from a bad Hollywood novel. He's only trying to act like a J. Milton Mandelbaum.

Mandelbaum, the young producing 'genius' of American Global Studios arrived in London to stir the hearts of man and produce the greatest aviation film of all times based on Abraham Cady's novel, *The Jug*.

He pitched tent in a three bedroom suite at the Savoy; the Oliver Messel Suite wasn't available at the Dorchester because of all the goddam brass and royalty in exile and that crap.

It was stocked to the gunnels with booze and broads and the kinds of things Englishmen had not seen in five years of war.

A 4-F in the draft (ulcers, eye stigmatism, psychosomatic asthma) he conned himself a 'technical war correspondent's' rating and had a Saville Row tailor do him up a half dozen officer's uniforms.

'After all, Abe,' he explained, 'we're all in this thing together.'

Abe suggested that if that was the case it would be good for Milton to fly a few bombing missions for firsthand insight.

'Somebody's got to hold the old fort down here and get the old production rolling,' Milton explained in passing on Abe's kind offer.

Milton always mentioned his own film first, the one which won an Oscar, somehow overlooking the fact it was based on a Hemingway story with the best director and screen writer in Hollywood working on it, and during most of the production he was in the hospital with an ulcer. An assistant (who was fired shortly after the film for disloyalty) had truly done the producing.

There were lengthy dissertations by him on his creative ability, his sincerity, his importance, the women (among them most of the NAME actresses) he had banged, his immaculate taste in all matters, his astute story instinct (if the studio would only get off my back I'd go back to writing. You and me are writers, Abe, we know the importance of the story), his house in Beverly Hills (pool, broads, limo, broads, sports cars, broads, servants, broads), the number of suits he owned, the extravagant gifts (he charged to the studio) his piousness (when I put up a window in the synagogue for my beloved father, I gave the temple an extra five thou), the people he knew by first name, the people who knew him by first name, the way the studio leaned on him for milestone decisions and his high ethical standards and his prowess at gin rummy and, of course, his modesty.

'Abe, we'll make them laugh, cry, die with those boys up there. I got a call into the front office. I'm pitching for Cary [Grant], Clark [Gable], or Spence [er Tracy] for the lead.'

'But, Milt. Maybe Tracy but Grant and Gable aren't my idea of Italian fathers.'

'Cary and Clark don't play anyone's father. You got to know actors, kid. They don't like growing old. Actually I had in mind using Cary for the part of Barney.'

'Cary Grant, a twenty-three-year-old Jewish boy from the slums of New York?'

'We got to update a little. I was thinking of this General Bertelli character. Reads nice in the book, but do we really want to glorify wops when we're at war with them?'

'Bertelli is American born . . .'

'Sure, I know that, you know that. But he's still a wop to the great American Midwest. If we make the Bertellis heroes the boys in the front office in New York will have a hemorrhage. After all they're banking and distributing the flick. There's rules. Don't glorify wops, nigs got to be dumb like animals, krauts have got to be comic, and most of all, don't say you're Jewish on the screen.'

'But Barney is a Jew.'

'Look, Abe, and I say this with all sincerity and thinking back to a similar story line I licked on the Hemingway flick, let's don't get the father-son thing in the way of the action. I draw on my experience to tell you this with honesty. Barney as a Jew won't go.'

'The book is about two Italians and one Jew.'

'Yeah. We got to kick it in the head. It won't play. The public likes . . . Irishmen. What we need is a big tough Irishman with a screwy little sidekick. Frank McHugh type. The way I see, Cary[Grant] or Jim [James Cagney] or Duke [John Wayne] as a hot pilot always beefing with his colonel, a fine character actor like Alan [Hale].

It went like this for several weeks and one day Abe said, 'Milton. Go fuck yourself.'

What Cady did not know was that Mandelbaum was fighting for his life. After a dozen flops, enormous and dubious expenses charged to his productions, a scandal with a sixteen-year-old starlet, the self-proclaimed savior of American Global was on the ropes. *The Jug* was to be his last con job. Cady could write. Mandelbaum couldn't read. In London, there was no button to press to give the script a once-over from a tried and true hack. He had to make it go with Cady, or else.

As Abe started to stomp from the suite, sincere, ethical Milton Mandelbaum said, 'Sit down. We've been going at it hard. Let's talk things over.'

'Who can talk with you in the room? It's greasy crumbs like you who've lied and cheated Hollywood into its state of a low mentality insult. Get yourself another writer.'

J. Milton hissed in a snake's voice, 'Sit down, Abe. We've got a contract, sweetheart, and if you pull a stunt like this you're blackballed for life. What's more you'll never sell another one of your books.'

'But, Milton. You told me that any time I was unhappy and wanted out, just to walk through the door.'

'Now wait a minute, Cady. I had a lot of trouble selling you. The committee knows your brother was a Commie.'

'You son-of-a-bitch.'

He grabbed Mandelbaum by the lapels of his war correspondent's jacket and shook him with such fury his glasses flew off his face. He flung him to the floor, where Milton crawled around like a blind man, found his glasses, doubled over with pain from his ulcer and cried.

'Abie, don't leave me! My enemies at the studio will fry me. We've got eight hundred thou on the line, starting dates, actors, sets, costumes. All my life I've fought for principle, and I get crapped on.'

Abe stayed on the film. Strangely, Mandelbaum let him write what he wished. What he did not know was that Mandelbaum picked up a pair of stumble bums and paid them a few thousand dollars to write behind Abe's back. The pair would remain anonymous, taking Cady's scenes and warping them into Mandelbaum's jibberish.

When Abe left the film, he felt a great sense of relief.

'Every great script, every great film,' J. Milton Mandelbaum said, 'is written with sweat. We got to have a few lover's quarrels. No, Abe, it would be better if you don't come around the set. Your job is done. We'll carry the ball now. Directors get jittery with writers around. They're damned prima donnas. But . . . we got to have them. Frigging actors are dog meat. Those people don't know how to treat a writer with respect, like I do.'

Mercifully, the title of the film was changed to *The Screaming Eagles* and no one really remembered it as based on the Cady novel. Abe quietly had his name removed. The film made money. It was in a time that any dogfight piloted by Flynn or Cagney was box office. And so, flushed with a success and a new lease on life, Mandelbaum returned to resume his honorable career.

Chapter Eleven

I ENDURED THAT MOST AWFUL MOMENT WHEN I RETURNED TO NORFOLK AFTER THE WAR AND REALIZED MOMMA AND POPPA HAD GROWN VERY OLD. THE STEP WAS SLOWER, THEIR GLASSES WERE THICKER, THEIR HAIR WAS GRAYER, AND THERE WERE SPELLS OF ABSENT-MINDEDNESS. ON MANY OCCASIONS MOMMA CALLED ME, 'BEN.'

NORFOLK HAD GROWN SMALL. ABSENCE HAD MADE MY MIND PLAY TRICKS. THE HOUSE THAT I REMEMBERED AS SO LARGE AND AIRY WAS REALLY LITTLE AND MY ROOM WAS TINY. DISTANCES AROUND THE CITY WERE SHORT, PARTICULARLY IN CONTRAST TO THE VASTNESS OF LONDON.

SAMANTHA WAS A FISH OUT OF WATER, AND I WAS GETTING TO FEEL HER ATTEMPTS AT READJUSTMENT IN AMERICA WERE NOT TOTALLY HONEST. NONETHELESS, WE ANTICIPATED STARTING LIFE TOGETHER. NEW CHILD, A FEW THOUSAND DOLLARS IN THE BANK, NEW CAR. SHAWCROSS HAD BROUGHT OUT A BOOK OF MY WARTIME UNITED PRESS COLUMNS, AND THEY WERE BEING RECEIVED BETTER THAN WE ANTICIPATED.

ANYHOW SAMANTHA AND THE BABY AND I WOULD FIND OUR PLACE. THE SOUTH WAS OUT. BEN'S DREAM HAD NOT COME TRUE. THERE WERE FAINT

STIRRINGS. SEVERAL HUNDREDS OF THOUSANDS OF NEGROES WERE HAVING THEIR FIRST CHANCE AT AN EDUCATION THROUGH THE G.I. BILL OF RIGHTS AND THEY'D NEVER GO BACK TO THE WAY THINGS WERE. AT THE END OF WORLD WAR II THE FREEDOM SMELL WAS NOT YET IN THE AIR, BUT I FELT IT WAS GOING TO HAPPEN IN MY LIFETIME AND WHEN IT DID I'D COME TO THE SOUTH AGAIN AND WRITE ABOUT IT.

FROM THE DAY THE WAR ENDED, POPPA AND HIS BROTHER HYMAN IN PALESTINE PUT ON A DESPERATE SEARCH FOR THEIR FATHER, TWO BROTHERS AND OVER TWO DOZEN RELATIVES LAST HEARD FROM IN POLAND SIX YEARS AGO.

BY THE TIME I ARRIVED FROM ENGLAND WITH SAMANTHA AND THE BABY SOME OF THE HORROR STORY HAD ALREADY FILTERED BACK. MY FATHER'S HOME, PRODNO, WAS WALLED OFF AS A GHETTO. LATER, THE JEWS WERE ROUNDED UP AS CATTLE AND SLAUGHTERED IN THE JADWIGA CONCENTRATION CAMP.

AFTER A TIME CONFIRMATION CAME FROM THE HANDFUL OF JEWISH SURVIVORS THAT MADE ALL HOPE DIMINISH. THEY HAD BEEN MURDERED, ALL OF THEM. MY GRANDFATHER, THE RABBI OF PRODNO, WHOM I NEVER KNEW, MY UNCLES AND THIRTY MEMBERS OF THE FAMILY.

ONLY ONE CADYZYNSKI, A COUSIN, SURVIVED BY FIGHTING IN A PARTISAN UNIT. AFTER THE HOLOCAUST HE WAS MADE TO UNDERGO A NIGHTMARISH ODYSSEY IN AN ATTEMPT TO GET TO THE ONLY PLACE IN THE WORLD THAT WOULD TAKE HIM, JEWISH PALESTINE. HE TRIED TO RUN THE BRITISH BLOCKADE IN A TUGBOAT ONLY TO BE TURNED BACK AND INTERNED IN GERMANY. ON THE THIRD TRY, HE MADE IT.

WHEN THE STATE OF ISRAEL WAS DECLARED IN 1948 MY UNCLE HYMAN HAD THREE SONS IN THE WAR. ONE OF THEM WAS KILLED FIGHTING FOR THE OLD CITY OF JERUSALEM.

THE GRIEF OF MY FATHER OVER THE HOLOCAUST WOULD REMAIN WITH HIM TILL THE END OF HIS LIFE.

AFTER SPANNING THE VASTNESS OF AMERICA AND LEARNING MY OWN COUNTRY FOR THE FIRST TIME I FELL IN LOVE WITH SAN FRANCISCO AND THE BAY AREA. MONTEREY, MARIN, ALL OF IT. A WRITER'S MAGNET FROM JACK LONDON TO STEINBECK TO SAROYAN TO MAXWELL ANDERSON. THIS WAS THE PLACE. SAUSALITO, I THOUGHT. UP IN THE HILLS LOOKING DOWN TO THE WATER AND OVER THE BAY TO THE IVORY SAMARKAND OF SAN FRANCISCO.

SAMANTHA WAS ONE WOMAN I COULD READ. SHE SUFFERED A LOT AWAY FROM LINSTEAD HALL.

I THOUGHT I'D BETTER COMPROMISE AND BEGAN LOOKING FOR PROPERTY IN THE CARMEL VALLEY. IT WAS A FAIR BARGAIN. THE VALLEY WAS FILLED WITH WHITE OAKS AND OLD THICK SPANISH RANCH HOUSES THAT STAYED COOL EVEN IN MIDSUMMER. THE COASTLINE PLUNGED DOWN TO A ROARING SEA ALONG BANKS OF WILD FLOWERS AND CYPRESSES TORTURED BY THE WIND. CARMEL WAS ARTSY-CRAFTSY AND THERE WAS A TOUCH OF CLOSENESS WITH STEINBECK IN THE CREAKING FISHING BOATS OF MONTEREY AND THE GLORIOUS AROMAS OF CANNERY ROW. AND ALL OF IT WAS WITHIN REACH OF SAN FRANCISCO. WELL, SAMANTHA . . . WHAT ABOUT IT?

SO, I RATIONALIZED WITH MYSELF. NOBODY MAKES A PERFECT MARRIAGE, RIGHT? WITH ALL HER MOANING I HAPPENED TO LOVE MY WIFE. AND GOD KNOWS, I'D NEVER ENTER THE THOUGHT OF SEPARATING FROM MY SON.

SAMANTHA HAD A POINT. HER ONLY BROTHER HAD BEEN KILLED FIGHTING IN FRANCE. SHE WAS THE HEIR TO LINSTEAD HALL AND AFTER HER, LITTLE BEN. HER PARENTS WERE AGING AND IT WOULD HAVE BEEN TRAGIC TO THINK OF THE TWO HUNDRED YEAR TRADITION OF LINSTEAD HALL COMING TO AN END.

GOT IT? I'M TALKING MYSELF INTO SOMETHING.

GRANTED, I DON'T LIKE HORSES. ALL THEY WANT IS TO BE FED. IN RETURN, THEY ARE UNFAITHFUL, THEY'LL KICK YOU IN THE HEAD, THROW YOU AND MAKE PILES OF HORSE SHIT. BUT ON THE OTHER HAND, I DON'T HAVE TO SLEEP WITH THEM, NOT EVEN IN LINSTEAD HALL. I INTEND TO HAVE A MOTORCYCLE.

THE THOUGHT OF BEN GROWING UP WITHOUT KNOWING THE BEAUTY OF BASEBALL IS A BIT ANNOYING, BUT HE'S GOING TO FRIGGING-A KNOW HOW TO FLY A PLANE BY THE TIME HE'S SIXTEEN. SAMANTHA ISN'T GOING TO WEEP ME OUT OF THAT ONE.

AFTER ALL, WHAT'S SO BAD ABOUT ENGLAND? I'D COME TO LOVE IT ALMOST AS MUCH AS AMERICA. LONDON? ONLY THE GREATEST CITY IN THE WORLD. WHEN YOU GET RIGHT DOWN TO THE NITTY-GRITTY I'VE DONE MOST OF MY WRITING IN ENGLAND AND MY MOST CHERISHED DREAM IS TO WRITE A BOOK ABOUT ISRAEL, SOMEDAY.

I WAVERED A LOT. SOME DAYS I GOT LIVID WITH THE IDEA THAT SAMANTHA HAD THE RIGHT TO TELL AN AUTHOR WHERE HE HAD TO WORK. AND THEN I GOT A CALL FROM MY SISTER SOPHIE THAT MOMMA HAD DIED IN HER SLEEP FROM A STROKE AND WE ALL RUSHED BACK TO NORFOLK.

I CONVINCED POPPA HE SHOULDN'T RATTLE AROUND IN THAT HOUSE ALL BY HIMSELF. SOPHIE OFFERED TO TAKE HIM IN IN BALTIMORE BUT THE OFFER WAS HALF ASSED. I'VE GOT TO SAY SAMANTHA WAS A GOOD DAUGHTER-IN-LAW. SHE INSISTED HE COME BACK WITH US TO ENGLAND. THERE WAS ALL KINDS OF ROOM IN LINSTEAD HALL, AND HE COULD HAVE HIS OWN LITTLE COTTAGE. POPPA WAS ULTRA SENSITIVE ABOUT BEING A BURDEN BUT IT MADE SENSE.

WHEN HE SOLD OUT THE BAKERY DURING THE WAR, HE GOT TAKEN BY A COUPLE OF GONIFFS WHO LET IT RUN INTO THE GROUND AND IT FINALLY WENT INTO BANKRUPTCY. WHAT LITTLE MONEY POPPA HAD WAS GONE. HE HAD GIVEN MOST OF IT AWAY DURING HIS LIFETIME FOR RELATIVES AND THE JEWS IN PALESTINE.

FOR A WHILE EVERYTHING WAS FINE. WE RESETTLED IN ENGLAND, AND I BEGAN WORK ON A NEW NOVEL WHICH WAS GOING TO BE MY BEST. THE LINSTEADS WERE BEAUTIFUL PEOPLE AND POPPA WAS THE GRANDFATHER TO END THEM ALL.

IN 1947 SAMANTHA GAVE US A DAUGHTER. PERSONALLY, I WANTED TO NAME HER AFTER MOMMA, BUT I GOT TO NAME BEN SO I DIDN'T KICK TOO MUCH. VANESSA CADY. NOT BAD.

I NOTICED HALFWAY THROUGH WRITING MY NOVEL THAT POPPA STARTED TURNING RELIGIOUS. IT HAPPENS TO A LOT OF JEWISH PEOPLE WHO GO AWAY FROM THE FAITH. IN THE END, IT SEEMS, THEY ALL WANT TO BE JEWS AGAIN. THE CLOSING OF THE CIRCLE.

WHEN I SUGGESTED HE GO TO ISRAEL HE BROKE DOWN AND CRIED. I NEVER SAW MY FATHER CRY BEFORE, EVEN WHEN BEN AND MOMMA DIED. I ASSURED HIM IT WOULDN'T BE A BURDEN ON ME. MY UNCLE HYMAN HAD A PLACE IN TEL AVIV AND HE WOULD BE WELCOMED WITH OPEN ARMS.

ACTUALLY THINGS WEREN'T GOING WELL AT LINSTEAD HALL. JOE FARMER, I'M NOT. I WAS THINKING OF PUTTING A TORCH TO THE PLACE AND COLLECTING THE INSURANCE BUT YOU HANG ON. TRADITIONS DIE VERY SLOWLY IN ENGLAND. AND MOTHER OF PEARL, AM I HUNG WITH A TRADITION! SO, I BORROW AND PLOW FORWARD ON MY NOVEL. I DON'T FEEL PIOUS ABOUT SENDING MY FATHER TO ISRAEL. HE GAVE TO EVERYONE ALL HIS LIFE, AND HE DESERVED IT. I ARRANGED HIS PASSAGE AND BOUGHT A SMALL FLAT FOR HIM AND SAW THAT HE HAD A LIVABLE INCOME.

LET ME TELL YOU SOMETHING. THE SAME THING THAT WAS KILLING POPPA WAS KILLING ME. IT BURNED MY GUTS, TORE AT MY EYES, RIPPED AT ME DAY AND NIGHT. I WAS SICK AT HEART AT WHAT HAPPENED TO THE JEWS IN POLAND AND GERMANY.

THIS IS WHAT I CRAVED TO WRITE ABOUT. AS SOON AS THE NEW NOVEL WAS DONE, WE'D BE OUT OF THE HOLE AND I'D GO AND LIVE IN ISRAEL AND WRITE ABOUT IT. GOD I WANTED IT. GOD I WANTED IT!

POPPA DIED IN HIS SLEEP JUST AS I FINISHED MY BOOK. MY UNCLE HYMAN WROTE THAT SEEING ISRAEL REBORN ALLOWED HIM TO GO TO HIS REST IN PEACE.

ON MY FATHER'S GRAVE I SWORE I WOULD WRITE A BOOK TO SHAKE THE CONSCIENCE OF THE HUMAN RACE.

AND THEN THE WORST HAPPENED. MY NOVEL, 'THE PARTISANS' WAS PUBLISHED AND LAID AN EGG. ALL THREE AND A HALF YEARS AND SIX HUNDRED AND TWENTY PAGES OF IT BOMBED WITH CRITICS AND READERS ALIKE. ABRAHAM CADY WAS UP THE PROVERBIAL CREEK WITHOUT PADDLE ONE.

Chapter Twelve

IF SAMANTHA HAD AN OUTSTANDING SINGLE QUALITY IT WAS HER ABILITY TO PUT A NEEDLE UP MY BUTT. SHE INSISTED SHE DIDN'T UNDERSTAND WHY 'THE PARTISANS' WAS A FLOP. IT WAS, AFTER ALL, HER VERY FAVORITE OF ALL MY BOOKS.

I'LL TELL YOU WHY SHE LIKED IT. IT WAS A FAILURE AND BROUGHT ME DOWN TO HER LEVEL OF MEDIOCRITY. IT TOOK A LONG TIME, A MORTGAGE OVER MY HEAD AND TWO BEAUTIFUL CHILDREN TO COME RIGHT OUT AND ADMIT IT, BUT SAMANTHA WAS A DULL WOMAN WITH AN INFERIORITY COMPLEX AS DEEP AS THE GRAND CANYON AND AS IMPOSSIBLE TO FILL. SHE WAS INCAPABLE OF LIFTING THE INTELLECTUAL CONTENT OF ANY CONVERSATION OR EVENT, AND SHE WAS FRIGHTENED OUTSIDE THE FAMILIAR ELEMENT OF LINSTEAD HALL.

VERY EARLY IN THE MARRIAGE SHE STOPPED GROWING BUT COULD NOT COME FACE TO FACE WITH HER OWN INEPTNESS, SO THE WAY SHE COULD BECOME BIG WAS TO MAKE ME LITTLE. TEARING ME DOWN WAS AN OBLIQUE WAY OF LIFE.

CONSISTENT WITH HER PERSONALITY, SHE BUILT A HIGH DEFENSIVE WALL ABOUT HERSELF LASHING OUT AT ANYTHING THAT EVEN SMELLED OF CRITICISM. WITHOUT INTROSPECTION SHE WAS INCAPABLE OF ADMITTING MISTAKES OR WRONGDOING.

BUT, YOU KNOW SOMETHING. I LOVED HER. IT WAS A PARADOX THAT SUCH A LIGHTWEIGHT COULD BE THE GREATEST SINGLE EVENT BETWEEN SHEETS OF A BED. AND THAT MAKES UP FOR A LOT.

STRANGE HOW SOME BRAINY BUSINESS WORLD, FEMALE LAWYER TYPES CAN BE SUCH LOUSY LAYS. LIKE STICKING YOUR PECKER IN GROUND GLASS. AND SIMPLE OLD SAMANTHA, THE QUEEN OF THE BALLERS.

SAMANTHA HAD ANOTHER ENDEARING QUALITY, AN UNCANNY ABILITY TO ALWAYS SINK LOWER THAN ME AND NEVER LIFT ME UP. SHE WAS, IN ANY SITUATION, SADDER, SICKER, AND MORE DEPRESSED.

I WAS IN MORTAL PAIN AFTER 'THE PARTISANS' BOMBED. SAMANTHA SIMPLY COULDN'T UNDERSTAND IT. ANYHOW, MY DRUNK STARTED AT AN RAF REUNION IN LONDON AND ENDED THREE DAYS LATER IN A BROTHEL IN SOHO. MY POCKETS WERE CLEANED AND MY CAR IMPOUNDED. BUT FOR THE BENEVOLENCE OF A GOOD NATURED HOOKER I WOULDN'T HAVE HAD TAXI FARE TO GET TO DAVID SHAWCROSS.

BACK AT LINSTEAD HALL THE SILENCE WAS HORRENDOUS. EIGHT DAYS OF TOTAL NIL UNTIL IT ALL HIT THE FAN.

AND THEN STRANGE SALVATION CAME IN THE FORM OF RUDOLPH MAURER, A ONCE REMOVED ROUMANIAN WITH A PICKLE NOSE AND MOLE EYES REPRESENTING A LARGE HOLLYWOOD TALENT AGENCY. LO AND BEHOLD, AMERICAN GLOBAL STUDIOS WANTED TO BUY 'THE PARTISANS', AND THE PRODUCER ASKED IF MY SERVICES WERE AVAILABLE AS THE SCREEN WRITER.

IT DIDN'T TAKE LONG TO TOTE UP THE BOTTOM LINE. I COULD KEEP SAMANTHA'S GODDAM HORSES IN HAY FOR FIVE YEARS.

DAVID SHAWCROSS ARGUED VEHEMENTLY AGAINST MY GOING TO HOLLYWOOD, AND HIS REASONS LATER PROVED RIGHT. BUT FRANKLY, AFTER THE FAILURE OF THE NOVEL I WAS GUN SHY, IN HOCK, AND DAMNED GLAD TO HAVE FOUND AN OUT.

MOMMA ALWAYS USED TO TELL ME, 'ABE, IF YOU HAVEN'T GOT ANYTHING NICE TO SAY, SO KEEP YOUR MOUTH SHUT.' WELL I'M NOT GOING TO SAY MUCH ABOUT MY YEARS IN THAT FUR-LINED MADHOUSE.

I LOVE MOTION PICTURES AND I BELIEVE IN THE MEDIUM. HOLLYWOOD CAN BOAST OF THE GREATEST CONCENTRATION OF TALENT IN THE WORLD ALONG WITH THAT LEGION OF SILKY CON-MEN AND QUASI-MINI-ARTISTS.

BUT THE SUM TOTAL OF ALL OF THEM IS A BLATANT DISRESPECT FOR WRITERS, THE WRITTEN WORD, AND THIS WILL SOME DAY ERODE THE SAND CASTLE AND THEY CAN ALL GO OUT TO DEATH VALLEY AND FRY IN THE AUGUST SUN.

IT IS BITTER FOR ME TODAY TO HAVE THE MEANS OF STRIKING BACK AND HOLD MY SILENCE IN DIGNITY. I BELIEVE THAT THE USE OF THE TYPEWRITER FOR PERSONAL VENGEANCE IS EVIL AND THE WRITER WHO DOES SO REDUCES HIMSELF TO THE LEVEL OF HIS TORMENTORS.

NEVERTHELESS, I'LL NEVER BE UP FOR SAINTHOOD AND I'M ENTITLED TO MY AUTOBIOGRAPHY. IT HAS BEEN WRITTEN ABOUT THOSE YEARS AND TUCKED AWAY. MY MEMORY OF EACH AND EVERY MONSTER IS VIVID. SO LET THEM SWEAT. IN THE END, ABE CADY IS GOING TO HAVE THE LAST WORD.

FOR A DECADE I DIVIDED MY TIME BETWEEN ENGLAND AND HOLLYWOOD.

IN THE MEANWHILE SAMANTHA'S PARENTS PASSED AWAY. I MISS THEM. THEY WERE LOVELY PEOPLE AND SO KIND TO MY FATHER.

I WAS ABLE TO HIRE A GOOD FOREMAN, WHICH KEPT SAMANTHA FROM RUNNING LINSTEAD HALL INTO THE GROUND. COMING OFF TWO STRAIGHT BOX OFFICE SUCCESSES THERE WAS MONEY IN THE BANK AND THE OLD HOMESTEAD WAS IN THE BLACK. I MUST SAY I GOT A VICARIOUS THRILL OUT OF TELLING MY HOLLYWOOD AGENT WHERE HE COULD STICK IT AND IN WHAT MANNER.

I WAS BACK TO WHAT I SHOULD HAVE BEEN DOING . . . WRITING NOVELS. I STARTED THE NEW ONE DETERMINED NOT TO MAKE THE MISTAKES OF 'THE PARTISANS'.

Chapter Thirteen

'I'm coming on home early, love,' David Shawcross said over the phone to his wife in a voice that literally trembled with excitement.

'Is everything all right, David?'

'Right! Right as rain. I've just received Abraham's new manuscript.'

Within the hour, Shawcross unwedged himself from the back seat of his Jaguar and stormed past his chauffeur. Lorraine met him at the door.

'Look!' he said, holding up a cardboard carton. 'By George, it's taken over a decade to get this. There were times I thought he'd never come through. Turn off the bloody phones. No calls, no interruptions.'

'Everything's ready, dear.'

His reading chair was encircled with note pads, sharp pencils, tobacco, liquor, lamp adjusted just so, special glasses. As she unlaced his shoes and replaced them with soft slippers he was already tugging out a voluminous manuscript of over a thousand pages. On the musty treadmill of reading mediocre manuscripts day in, month out, a new Cady book was a king's reward. Lorraine hadn't seen him so happy and excited in years.

THE PLACE by Abraham Cady.

It was not until well after midnight that she found herself dozing in bed, her magazine fallen to the floor. It was uniquely quiet. Not a stir from the connecting study. Usually, when David looked in, he would roar out when something annoyed him, or break into laughter, or give out audible reactions to what he read. Tonight, there was not a peep.

She tied on a robe and approached the study door and knocked softly. No answer. She shoved it open. The leather chair was empty and the manuscript mostly read. David Shawcross stood at the window, hands clasped behind him.

'David?'

He turned. She saw him pale and watery eyed. He walked to his desk slowly, sat with his hands holding his face.

'How bad is it?'

'At first I couldn't believe it. Not of Abraham. I kept saying, he's leading us on. Pretty soon the real Cady will burst out.'

'What's gone wrong?'

'It's a work of slick, pornographic filth for the sake of pornography. Abraham was always a raw writer who gave off heat and swamped you with his passion. He's learned his lessons in California well. He's become polished and glib and plastic. The whole book is dishonest but the tragic part of it is that it will become a smash best seller and grab a fortune from the motion pictures. And the critics will rave ... it's dirty enough.'

'But why? Why on earth?'

'Why do they all eventually do their mattress dance on paper? The money is too bloody tempting. Now that they've succeeded blowing the lid off any moral restraint and anything goes, they masturbate in public under the guise of new freedoms and art. They're all nothing but a gang of mercenary whores. And the bloody critics are just as dishonest. I could just die ...'

He crossed the room wearily and stretched out on the sofa. Lorraine knew there would be no sleep for him tonight. She covered him with a robe. 'Tea or brandy?'

'No, love.'

'Are you going to publish it?'

'Of course. Shawcross Limited announces with great honor the return of that remarkable talent Abraham Cady to the literary scene ...'

'David, Abraham called. He's quite anxious to get your reaction. He came down from Linstead Hall, and he'd like to see you tomorrow.'

'Yes, we might as well get it over with. Call the office in the morning and tell them I'll be working at home.'

'You look haggard,' Abe said; 'that's quite a dose to swallow in one reading. Took me three weekends to knock it off, you know,' he joked. 'Well, Shawcross, what's the verdict?'

He stared across the desk at Cady. He looked and dressed the way he wrote ... polished ... like he had been plucked out of a Saville Row tailor's ass.

'We'll bring it out in the fall,' Shawcross said. 'I called New York and co-ordinated with your American publisher.'

'What's the good word?'

'My personal advice was to go a hundred thousand copies on the first edition in the States. I'm ordering paper for fifty thousand.'

Abe grabbed the desk, sighed deeply, and shook his head. 'Jesus. I didn't think it was that good.'

'It's not. It's that bad.'

'What's that?'

'You told me you wanted to do three things in this world, write, fly, and play baseball. As far as I'm concerned you can't do any of them.'

Abe was on his feet. 'You're sanctimonious. I knew this was going to come up, Shawcross. Your problem, old man, is that you're out of touch with the twentieth century.'

'Abraham. Fly into any kind of rage you wish. Call me any kind of names you'd like but for God's sake don't try to justify this piece of trash.'

'Well, you damned well don't have to publish it!'

'As long as you don't mind being a prostitute, why should you mind if I pander for you.'

Abe's face was violently hued. He shook his fist under Shawcross's nose and shook with desire to smash him, then threw up his hands. 'What the hell, it would be like hitting my father.'

'You've hurt me very deeply. I really haven't been surprised by the writers who have taken this trip, but I never would have believed it of you. If you want to go to another publishing house, all right, I won't hold you. I'll find you an eager young editor who will tell you all the right things, what new boundaries you've opened, how clean and succinct your phrasing is, how magnificently you weave character and plot.'

'Cut . . . cut . . . cut. Maybe I did play it a little close but this kind of thing is all the vogue now. Christ, if I could only get out of Linstead Hall.'

'You're not going to blame this abortion on Samantha.'

'In part. Damned well in part. She says, don't be grim, Abe, the world needs a laugh. That and those goddam horses and the goddam hay they eat. If I'd have had a woman willing to sacrifice I might have risked something else. All right, Shawcross, you've knocked me flat on my ass. I was cautious about writing another one like *The Partisans.*

'I was proud of that book. It cost us both but it seems to have cost you more. Your courage, your anger.'

'Hell, you sound like a goddam literature professor. Starve, writer, starve.'

'You're a frightened man, Abraham, and you're writing scared.'

Abe slumped and hung his head. 'You're right. Ten years in nightmare city. Oh God, what I was going to do with my writing. You're disgusted with me.'

'I can't help but loving my own son,' Shawcross answered. 'I hope there's enough left in you to get disgusted with yourself.'

'I've got to cool down for a few weeks and think about things. I've got to get some sun.'

'Splendid idea.'

'Call Samantha for me, will you. I don't want to get into a hassle with her. She doesn't understand that I've got to dry out by myself, sometimes. Always takes it like I'm trying to run away from her.'

'Aren't you?'

'Maybe. Tell her I've written myself out and just have to break away.'

'Very well. I'm giving a cocktail party tonight at Les Ambassadeurs for a new author. There'll be some interesting women. Do come.'

'See you tonight, Shawcross.'

Chapter Fourteen

Les Ambassadeurs, a posh private dining and gambling club stood on Hamilton Place, Park Lane, in an old converted mansion. The maître d' welcomed correctly over Abraham Cady, a well-known eye patch around London.

'Mr Shawcross's party is in the Hamilton room, Mr Cady.'

'Thanks.'

He breathed deeply and entered. He was greeted by a warm blast of dribble, dribble, dribble. Abe scanned the room like a cyclops searching out a friendly face for palatable conversation, when his eye came to a sudden stop on a chic, poised, raven-haired beauty in her mid-thirties. Will I still love her, Abe wondered, when she opens her mouth and attempts to talk.

'Oh, hello, Abraham.'

'Hi, Shawcross.' Abe nodded in the direction of the woman. 'Who is she?'

'Laura Margarita Alba. Lovely, charming girl. International jet setter. I understand she has quite a collection of jewelry in exchange for her favors. Usually found on the arm of a Greek shipping tycoon or a munitions dealer or someone in that crowd.'

'She here alone?'

'She comes to London from time to time representing clients and sponsors to bid on certain antiques, gems, art, at Christie's and Sotheby's. Frankly, Abe, I think she's a bit pricey for the likes of us. Want to meet her anyhow?'

'Let me consider the possibilities.'

About that time both Shawcross and Cady were whisked off into separate circles of dribble, dribble, dribble. Abe feigned listening and mulled. Then, across the room, she smiled directly to him and nodded.

There were several alternatives of attack, he thought. With a tramp, a bum, a whore, one must always treat them as ladies.

With that great pool in the middle rung, the established actress, the flustered housewife, the oversexed secretary, the ambitious starlet, one had to indulge in a silly game of double entendre, nuances, clever bubbles, promises that were not promises.

But here was an elegant lady. Laura Margarita Alba was that rare courtesan whom men paid dearly to be seen with and who felt it was the best hundred thousand they ever spent. Abe decided to gamble. He oozed out of his trap and moved toward her. She was chatting with some young stud with a lemon rinse, strong posed jaw, penetrating blue eyes, and a velvet and lace suit. She was politely bored and watched Abe coming from the corner of her eye. Abe found out the name of the stud, tapped his shoulder, and told him Shawcross was looking for him.

'Madame Alba,' he said, 'I'm Abraham Cady. I'd like to fuck you.'

'What a lovely idea,' she answered; 'here's the key to my place. Harlequin Suite on the Roof Gardens at the Dorchester.'

Abe stared at the key. 'You're kidding,' he said.

'I did my own reconnaissance before I came. If you hadn't asked me I intended to ask you . . . or would you prefer to go through a few days of games before you make your conquest?'

'You're the end.'

'I admired you when you used to be a writer.'

'Very funny. Did Shawcross put you up to that?'

'No. I read the books, then I saw the movies. I'm leaving in a half hour. Why don't you follow in another half hour. I'll be waiting for you.'

The young lemon-rinsed stud burst back into the scene. 'I say, Shawcross didn't want to see me at all. Rather cheeky of you,' he said indignantly.

Abe turned his back to Madame Alba and faced the stud. He lifted his eye patch revealing an ugly sight. 'Want to make something of it, junior,' he asked.

The stud fled

'Jesus Christ,' Abe said, 'lavender walls, lavender carpet, lavender bedspread.'

'I adore this suite. It goes with my black hair.'

'Before I sweep you off your feet, how about buying me a drink.'

Abe stared at the rug, sipped, then looked to the settee opposite where she was neatly blended in soft flowing lace.

'Mind if I call you Maggie?'

'No, I rather like it.'

'Well, Maggie, no bore in the world like someone with a long, sad story and I've got one. I'm afraid you picked lousy company. Frankly, I ought to be with a hooker in the Soho. I can't afford you.'

'I go down for one of two reasons. Mostly for diamonds as you know. My last sponsor, a French aircraft manufacturer, was very un-French in his jealousy and kept me under virtual lock and key for two years.'

'Here's to all our plush prisons. Why me, Maggie?'

'Of course you must know how attractive you are. Besides, I have a thing about writers. They're all little boys in need of mothering, and you are the saddest little boy I've ever seen.'

'Will you hold me all night and tell me not to be scared and all those words I've longed to hear from my wife?'

'Yes.'

'Christ, the dialogue between us is worse than the book I just wrote.'

'What the critics never seem to learn is that the world runs on a few dozen clichés. We spend our lives repeating ourselves.'

'It's 1962 already,' Abe said. 'I'm forty-two years old. I've got a son eighteen and a daughter fifteen. I'm married almost twenty years to a decent woman who had no business being a writer's wife. You can't put into someone what the Lord didn't give them. She's let me down. I've had numerous affairs and have long since ceased to feel guilt, but I know that we all pay for what we do and someday it's going to come crashing down on me. On the other hand I get almost no satisfaction from my affairs because I'm really not seeking bodies. I'm looking for peace and the conditions to write what I really want to write.

'I was twenty years old when I did my first novel. Yesterday, twenty-two years later I turned in a manuscript that was pure unadulterated crap. What little dignity and self-respect I had I surrendered by writing this book.

'Look at me, Maggie, monogrammed shirt and tailored eye patch. You know, two days ago was Yom Kippur, a Jewish holiday, the Day of Atonement, when we're supposed to meditate about ourselves and our lives. My dad, God rest his soul, passed away on Yom Kippur. I promised him something and I lied. Look at my goddam monogrammed shirt.'

In the morning it was Laura who was pensive and misty-eyed. She poured his coffee. 'There's nothing more exquisite than contemplating an affair,' she said, 'and nothing more sobering than having it, unless you run into Abraham Cady. It's lovely to have a man who knows how to take care of you. You said as much when you looked through me at the cocktail party last night.'

Abe shrugged. 'You've got to establish who's boss.'

'Only one other man was able to treat me that way, my husband. I was very young, just over twenty and Carlos was fifty when we met. I was already playing musical yachts. I thought the marriage would be dull but worth the security. But the bed was a battlefield and he was a master tactician in his kind of warfare. Abe, I have a lovely villa on the Costa del Sol at Marbella and two free weeks. Let me pamper you.'

'I've got a thing about going to Spain,' he said.

'Your brother's been dead almost twenty-five years. Perhaps it might be a good idea to see his grave.'

'One by one I seem to have given up most of my ideals. Even being with a woman like you is wrong. Consort of munitions dealers, widow of a prominent fascist.'

'I know. The underlying hatred is what makes us so exciting. Do you know how I learned about you? From a German actress who was your mistress. What vicarious thrills come from love-hate. Darling, I've said please. We won't even have to leave the villa.'

'All right, let's go.'

'Tomorrow, noon flight to Madrid. I have a car there. We'll drive to Málaga for the night and then on down the coast to Marbella.'

He turned over inside him at the mention of the names on the Spanish land, and he was unaccountably thrilled at the idea of seeing it.

'I have to go,' she said; 'there's an important painting going on auction at Sotheby's after lunch.'

He grabbed her wrist. 'Phone your bid in for someone else to make. I'm taking you back to bed.'

They stared at each other for a long period, neither of them yielding. 'Very well,' she said at last.

Chapter Fifteen

The Villa Alba, outside Marbella, rose from the moody sea as an intricate part of a massive rock on a myriad of levels, cavelets with waterfalls spilling into shimmering pools, and the traditional Spanish white arches and red tiled roofs and floors were enhanced by expansive use of glass and flying wings and jutting patios. It was a violently colored place of great splashes of modern art which were abruptly muted by an ancient tapestry or a wormwood religious statuette.

The villa was set in a baked, terraced land outlined by tall spikes of cypresses that ran to the ragged shores and their long golden stretches. The sands had been trampled under by the hordes of Hannibal and the hordes of bikini clad tourists. A place inundated with lore and Roman walls and the yachts of a fast-paced international set. Of Gothic and Moorish pillage and rape and latter day orgies.

For all the splendor of her home, Abe found an intrinsic sadness about it for nowhere was there to be found a protrait or remembrance of another human being. This was Laura Margarita Alba, strange and lonely as the sea.

Nearby, the swirl of high nothingness was centered at the Marbella Beach Club of Prince Max von Honenhole-Langenberg. In other times Laura made her presence felt there, and she was a most fascinating hostess of a bronzed sun people and rotted old aristocracy whose incredible dribble rarely went beyond who was sleeping with who.

For now she wanted Abe alone. They ravaged each other with a controlled fury born out of physical and spiritual starvation. The long years of emptiness found sudden fulfillment and they squandered it on each other until they had exhausted themselves into spending their time in a magnificent daze. The selfish woman now lavished upon him unselfishly, her will commanded by his.

At times in the middle of the night when both of them were restless they would sit in the shallow end of the pool and watch the machinations of the sea or walk down to the thatched hut in a private cove and talk until dawn. And in the morning they would lay in a half shuttered room in semidarkness with a soft breeze over their bodies as the only intruder. The servants moved around like whispers wondering about this man in the señora's life.

In the middle of the second week mutual thoughts began creeping in of why this shouldn't go on forever though neither of them spoke about this.

The tryst was invaded in the person of Lou Pepper, executive vice-president of International Talent Associates, a monolithic agency representing a lion's share of the creative people in show business.

Lou was a tall, thin man with a sleepy face whose dominating feature was seventy Sy Devore suits, all dark.

'Maggie, meet Lou Pepper, a wart on the ass of humanity.'

'Save the incredibly funny dialogue for your next screenplay. I didn't fly here because you are exactly my favorite person. Well, are you going to offer me a drink?'

'Give him a glass of water. Well, how'd you find me?'

'Most writers have two eyes so nobody recognizes them in public. Everybody knows the eye patch.'

'Let's go out to the patio. You come too, Maggie. I want you to hear all this. Mr Pepper is a very important executive. He doesn't travel thousands of miles to see a mere writer.'

'You see, Señora Alba, Abe and I didn't part on the best of terms, when he stomped out of Hollywood two years ago after being handed the best three picture deal any writer was ever offered.'

'Tell Maggie that you told me that any time I didn't want your services you'd tear up the contract you wrung out of me.'

'Abe has a long memory but even agents have to live.'

'Why?'

'At any rate, I'm still selling your new novel.'

Laura looked from Abe to Lou Pepper, distressed at the harsh language and the hostility between them and angry at the intrusion. Even with Abe, who overtly hated him, Lou Pepper would have to go into an egocentric advertisement of himself before getting into the details. He settled with a drink and droned.

'As soon as Milton Mandelbaum took over as head of American Global Studios he called me in. "Lou," he said, "I'm going to lean on you heavily." Milt is high on you, Abe, always has been. He keeps talking about the wonderful times you had together in London during the war, the bombing missions he flew with you, the whole schmear. I told him a Cady novel is coming. He put ten thousand on the line just to read the book and have first refusal rights. Mind if I take my jacket off.'

Out popped the cuff links. Abe knew it was a big deal because Lou always gave himself away. His armpits went on him. Deals were the way agents got their sex. Lou remained calm. That indicated he was certain of his ground. The begging and crying and breast beating would come later.

'Milt is interested in you as a total person. He wants to see you flourish. He's talking participation in profits.'

'The way that studio keeps books they wouldn't have had a profit if they had produced *Gone with the Wind*.'

'As writer-producer it's a different ball game.'

'But, daddy, I don't want to be a producer.'

'You're sanctimonious, Abe. What the hell did you write that piece of crap for, posterity? You had dollar signs from bedroom scene one through fifty. You want to hear the deal?'

Abe had been cut down, suddenly, cruelly. *The Place* wasn't going to fool anybody. 'What's Mandelbaum got in mind,' he said in almost a whisper.

'Two hundred thousand for *The Place* plus escalation clauses based on sales. Two hundred thousand for your services as a writer and producer and ten percent of the profits. We'll throw a few bones to the publishers to keep it up on the best seller list.'

Abe shoved his hands in his pockets and walked out toward the precipice and looked down where a calm sea merely swelled in and out of the rocks. 'I guess this makes me one of the highest paid hookers in the world,' he mumbled to himself.

Lou Pepper, sensing the kill, swiftened the pace. 'You get a producer's cottage with your own can and bar and privileges in the executive dining room and a parking space in the private lot.'

'I'm moved, sincerely.'

Lou continued to talk at Abe's back. 'Plus first class travel to L.A. and twenty-five hundred a month living expenses. Samantha has agreed to come to L.A. with you.'

Abe whirled around. 'Who in the hell gave you permission to see her. You set me up.'

'You happen to live in England, where should I go, to China?'

Abe laughed sadly, returned to his chair and clapped a hand in a fist over and over. 'Lou Pepper doesn't travel halfway around the world for a piddling forty thousand dollar commission. Who else have you got locked into the deal, male star, female star, director, cameraman, composer . . . all who just happen to be represented by your agency.'

'Don't act like there's anything underhanded. Studios don't like to keep payrolls with big stars. It's up to the agencies to put the package together and lay it in their laps. Mandelbaum was interested in an entire deal he can sell his board.'

'You think your crowd plays rough, Maggie. What Mr Pepper has here is a two million dollar package. That's two hundred thousand dollars in commissions plus pieces of the picture. But, there's a hitch. No star or director will commit to a property without a screenplay . . . that is, unless Lou Pepper can deliver the most commercial writer in the business, namely me. So he knocks down two hundred thousand in commissions, fifty thousand of which will be paid to the International Talent Associates' Geneva office and eventually find its way into a numbered account belonging to J. Milton Mandelbaum.'

'You've got a great imagination, Abe, that's what makes you such a fine writer. Hand a man a half million dollars and he spits on you like you're dirt.'

'Did you give Mandelbaum an option on my next book?'

'Your next three, Abe. I told you, Mandelbaum likes you as a total person. We all want to see you become a rich man. I've got to put in some calls to L.A. and New York. I'll be at the Marbella Club. Torture yourself on your own time. I'll tell you about reporting dates tomorrow.'

Abe paced the patio spitting out epithets, then crumpled. 'He knows I haven't got the guts to blow this deal. If I did, he'd see to it *The Place* never sold to another studio. Anyhow, I'll become the kind of writer Samantha always envisioned.' He filled a half tumbler full of Scotch.

Laura took the glass out of his hand. 'Don't get drunk tonight.'

'I'm busting! Let's drive up the coast.'

'You'll get us killed.'

'Maybe I want to – I'm going alone.'

'No, I'll drive with you. Let me pack a few things for overnight.'

They did not return to the villa until late the next evening after a wild ride in her Porsche along the treacherous twisting sea road to Málaga. There were a dozen messages to call Lou Pepper.

Laura flung open the door to the living room where a haggard David Shawcross waited.

'What the hell is this,' Abe said, 'the General Assembly of the U.N.?'

'I phoned David last night before we left.'

'I must say, Abraham, I've received warmer greetings from German prisoners of war.'

'Maggie tell you the whole story?'

'Yes.'

'Comments?'

'Your behavior is about as much comment as anyone needs. You see, Laura, he loves his family and would go on with his wife forever if she let him pursue the thing that's eating him alive. He's a Jew and he wants to write about Jews. He loathes the contaminated air of the studios. I've seen a lot of writers get caught in that trap. One day, they simply stop writing. Abe smells that day at hand. It's his death warrant and he knows it.'

'What about the alternative, Shawcross. There'll be no movie sale on *The Place*. Lou Pepper will see to that. Samantha will never agree to a book that means two years' research out of England. By the time we finish dividing up with lawyers, I'll be down to zero again. What are we going to do gang, ask Maggie to hock her diamonds?'

'I've spoken to my bank and your American publishers. We'll keep you floating one way or the other.'

'You will?'

'Yes.'

'You think I've got enough stomach left?'

'You write, I'll pay the bills.'

Abe turned away. 'It may be past midnight,' he said. 'I may let you down. I don't know, Shawcross, I just don't know.'

'I always felt you were one Jew who wouldn't be taken to the gas chamber alive.'

The houseboy entered and said Mr Pepper was calling again.

'What are you going to tell him?' Shawcross demanded.

'If you want the truth, I wasn't this scared when I crashed my Spitfire.'

Abe wiped a wet palm, lifted the receiver, and drew a deep breath to stabilize the pounding and trembling.

'Abe, I talked to Milt this morning. He wants to demonstrate his sincerity. Another twenty-five thou on the novel rights.'

Abe was sorely tempted to end it all on a note of profanity. He looked from Shawcross to Laura. 'No dice,' he said softly and hung up.

'I do love you, Abe. Ask me to come with you. Order me not to go away with him.'

'You think I haven't thought about this. We've had a look at paradise. Only a damned fool could believe he could spend his whole life this way. All we can expect is a moment of peace between battles. We've had that. The places I'm going to are hot and sticky. You won't like them after a while. If it means anything, I love you too.'

Chapter Sixteen

SAMANTHA POSSESSED ENOUGH NATIVE FEMALE SHREWDNESS TO MAKE ME MARCH TO HER TUNE FOR TWENTY YEARS. SHE DID NOT HOLD ME BY COMPASSION OR SACRIFICE OR TAKING A PARTNERSHIP IN MY WORK.

I WAS HELD BY BLACKMAIL.

SHE UNDERSTOOD THAT MY GREATEST FEAR WAS THAT OF LONELINESS. LONELINESS HAD DRIVEN ME INTO THE ARMS OF WOMEN I DID NOT CARE FOR OR WISH TO SPEND AN EVENING WITH . . . ONLY TO AVOID BEING ALONE.

SHE ALSO UNDERSTOOD THAT MY GREATEST LOVES WERE MY SON AND MY DAUGHTER, BEN AND VANESSA. SAMANTHA PARLAYED THIS LOVE AND THIS FEAR INTO A CONSTANTLY DANGLING THREAT THAT I WOULD BE LEFT ALONE WITHOUT MY CHILDREN.

IN HER COCKSURENESS SHE ALWAYS BRAGGED THAT I WAS FREE TO GO ANY TIME AND SHE WOULDN'T DEMAND A THING. I WAS FREE TO LEAVE HER JUST AS I WAS FREE TO RID MYSELF OF LOU PEPPER AND MILTON MANDELBAUM.

WHEN I BOTTOMED OUT, WHEN I WAS DEPRESSED AND DISGUSTED WITH THE WAY MY LIFE WAS TURNING, SHE HAD A STANDARD TACTIC OF GETTING ME INTO BED AND MAKING SAVAGE LOVE TO ME. IT WAS A PACIFICATION, LIKE SCRATCHING A DOG'S CHEST. BUT SAMANTHA WAS SOMETHING IN BED AND RARELY FAILED TO BLUNT MY ANGER.

FOR TWO DECADES I PRAYED FOR THE MIRACLE THAT THINGS HAD TO CHANGE AND THAT ONE DAY SHE WOULD TELL ME SHE REALIZED I WAS UNHAPPY AND I SHOULD GO OUT AND FIGHT WINDMILLS AND SHE WOULD STAND BESIDE ME.

WHEN I RETURNED FROM HOLLYWOOD WITH MY BRAINS SCRAMBLED AND PLEADED WITH HER TO LEASE LINSTEAD HALL. PACK UP THE CHILDREN AND COME WITH ME TO FAR OFF LANDS THAT CHALLENGED THE WRITER'S IMAGINATION.

WHO WAS I KIDDING?

THE FEW TIMES SAMANTHA TRAVELED WITH ME SHE WAS MISERABLE ABOUT THE DISCOMFORTS, MY SCHEDULE, THE SOCIAL OBLIGATIONS. SHE SPENT HER DAYS SHOPPING. AT NIGHT I WAS SO WORRIED ABOUT POOR BORED SAMANTHA BEING LEFT AT THE HOTEL WHILE I CONDUCTED INTERVIEWS I WAS UNABLE TO CARRY ON MY WORK PROPERLY. EVERYTHING HAD TO BE PRESENTED TO HER WITH AN APOLOGY.

I WANTED TO WRITE AT LINSTEAD HALL. EVEN THAT PIECE OF CRAP, 'THE PLACE'. BUT SAMANTHA INSISTED MY PRESENCE AT HOME DISRUPTED THE ROUTINE AND TIED HER DOWN. IT WAS ALWAYS TOO PAINFUL FOR HER TO ENTERTAIN MY COLLEAGUES AND BUSINESS ASSOCIATES.

AND NOW I LISTENED TO HER WITH UTTER DISBELIEF. SHE HADN'T LEARNED A THING IN TWENTY YEARS.

'Thank God,' Samantha said, 'for dear friends like Lou Pepper. Your behavior put him in the hospital in London with severe colitis.'

I DIDN'T REALIZE YOU COULD GET COLITIS OF THE MOUTH BUT IN LOU PEPPER'S CASE IT WAS CONSISTENT. HE HAD RETURNED TO LONDON BEFORE ME AND WORKED HER OVER, COMPLETE WITH DISCLOSURES OF LAURA. HE HAD TOLD HER THAT THIS NEW ASSIGNMENT WAS THE MOST IMPORTANT EVENT OF MY LIFE AND SPELLED OUT THE MONEY. IF SHE WAS TO SAVE ME FROM FUTURE LAURA ALBAS I SHOULD NOT GO TO LOS ANGELES ALONE. WHAT HE MEANT, OF COURSE, WAS TO HAVE A BUILT-IN ALLY TO ALWAYS BE READY TO SIT ON MY HEAD IN CASE I GOT OUT OF LINE.

SO, SAMANTHA WAS WILLING TO FORGIVE ME AND MAKE THE SACRIFICE TO COME AND LIVE WITH ME IN A BEVERLY HILLS MANSION. SHE ROUNDED OUT HER ESSAY WITH A DISSERTATION ABOUT HER POOR HEALTH, HOW HARD SHE WORKED, HOW FRUGAL SHE WAS, AND FINALLY, HOW SHE HAD ALWAYS STOOD BY ME AND ENCOURAGED MY WORK.

IT WOULD DO ME NO GOOD TO GO INTO A RAGE. I'VE DONE THAT. I LOOKED AT HER AND REALIZED THAT IT WOULD NEVER CHANGE. SAMANTHA WAS AS SHALLOW AS HER HORSES, AND I NOW ADMITTED THAT I DID NOT BECOME A WRITER BECAUSE OF HER, AND I HAD REMAINED A WRITER DESPITE HER.

'I want a divorce,' I said.

AT FIRST SAMANTHA TRIED TO SOOTHE ME OUT OF IT. I HAD A LONG FLIGHT, I WAS TIRED, ETC., ETC. I PRESSED THE ISSUE. THEN SHE BROUGHT OUT THE FEAR TACTICS. I WOULD BE ALL ALONE. THE CHILDREN WOULD TURN AGAINST ME. MY GUILT WOULD OVERWHELM ME.

WHEN SHE REALIZED I WASN'T GOING TO BUDGE SHE BECAME DESPERATE.

'I'm drowning, Samantha. If I continue on this way of life, I'm done. I have chosen, madam, the alternative of going down fighting.'

AT THIS POINT SAMANTHA, WHO NEVER WANTED ANYTHING, THREATENED TO STRIP ME OF EVERY SHILLING.

'I'm going to make it very easy for you,' I said. 'You can have everything, including the rights to *The Place*, which, I suspect was really inspired by you. I leave here without a nickel. It's yours ... all of it ... everything.'

THEN I HAD TO TELL BEN AND VANESSA WHAT HAD HAPPENED. I TOLD THEM THAT I WOULD START TRAVELING SOON IN EASTERN EUROPE AND IF ALL WENT WELL I'D BE IN ISRAEL FOR THE FOLLOWING SUMMER AND THAT THEY SHOULD COME.

A STRANGE THING HAPPENED. THEY INSISTED ON COMING TO LONDON WITH ME AND SEEING ME OFF.

WHEN I LEFT LINSTEAD HALL, IT WAS SAMANTHA WHO WAS ALONE.

Chapter Seventeen

The odyssey of Abraham Cady began in the Soviet Union, where he was given a canned tour of model factories, new housing, the ballet, museums, children's pioneer homes, and dialectic acrobatics at the writer's union.

In the subways, before loud blaring radios, in the parks, there were clandestine meetings with Jews.

His request to visit Prodno was lost in a bureaucratic maze. He traveled to Kiev to the infamous pits of Babi-Yar, where thirty-five thousand Jews were rounded up and murdered to a chorus of cheering Ukrainians. The large, persecuted Jewish minority of Kiev was more willing to speak to Cady.

His visit was abruptly halted and he was asked to leave Russia.

Starting from Paris with a new passport he traveled to Warsaw, which was intent on selling the point of view that the Poles were blameless in the genocide of the Jews and there now existed under communism a new and liberal attitude.

Abraham made the sorrowful pilgrimage to the Jadwiga Concentration Camp, the place of the murder of nearly all of the Cadyzynski family. It was intact, a national shrine. And the visit was to set off years of nightmares of the gas chamber and crematorium where he viewed it from the viewpoint of the SS murderers as well as the murdered Jews.

He went through the medical barracks where the maniacal experiments in surgery were carried out.

Again, he was talking to too many people and too many were willing to talk to him. He was picked up at the Bristol Hotel in Warsaw in the middle of a meal, detained for three days at the secret police headquarters as a Zionist spy, then ejected from Poland.

It was the same in East Berlin where the prevailing propaganda was that the Eastern Germans had redeemed themselves by turning to communism while the Western Germans remained the true Nazis. On his third trip into East Berlin he was warned not to return.

Next, Abraham Cady took the path of the surviving refugees of the Second World War from Eastern Europe to the main staging center in Vienna. From Vienna to the camps in Italy and France along the sea where the illegal immigration agents purchased leaky, ancient, unfit boats and tried to cross the Mediterranean into Palestine against the British blockade.

He wandered the fabled Island of Cyprus like the resurrected Lazarus had wandered it, for it was here that the British established mass detention camps filled with those refugees turned away from Palestine.

*

He went to Germany and interviewed dozens of former Nazis, none of whom knew the words to the 'Horst Wessel' song, their marching anthem in the Hitler era. Nor did anyone living near Dachau detect any strange smells.

Over the streets of Munich and Frankfurt and Berlin he re-created the 'Night of Crystal,' the dreaded mass assault on German Jewry by the Brown Shirts.

At the end of seven months, Abraham Cady arrived in Israel for a reunion with the few remaining relatives and then, twenty thousand miles of travel within that tiny state. The interviews ran over a thousand backed by three thousand reference photographs. Hundreds of hours were logged in the archives of death. He compiled a mountain of books and documents and he read until his eye nearly collapsed.

And his debt to David Shawcross mounted.

Vanessa and Ben arrived during the first summer. Abe welcomed it because he was wearying of a rather wild Hungarian mistress who stormed out at the infringement of her 'territory.'

At the end of the summer, they announced candidly they were not returning to England.

'Why? What will your mother say?'

'Mom is a bit tired from her devoted service as a mother, she won't mind,' Vanessa said.

'Cut it, Vinny,' Ben said. 'The reason we want to stay is that we've found what you're hoping other people will find through your writing.'

It was pretty hard to argue even though Abe knew his son intended to train to fly for the Israeli Air Force. But the unsaid reason, and he felt it keenly, was that the children didn't want him alone during the writing of the book. All the research had been gathered and consumed and one could feel the tension mount as the actual writing was to begin.

For the next sixteen months Abraham Cady wrote and rewrote and rewrote some two million words.

David Shawcross
77 Cumberland Terrace
London NW8

December 15, 1964

Dear Uncle David:

I have some disturbing news, but fortunately everything is going to turn out well. We found my father on the beach a week ago, collapsed from exhaustion. He is resting in a hospital in Tel Aviv for what is described as a minor heart seizure. All told, we are quite fortunate for this served as a warning.

During the past three months Dad has been writing himself into a frenzy, almost totally detached from the world. He is obsessed with this book and would only quit when his fingers fell off the keys and his mind ceased to function. Often as not he fell asleep over the typewriter.

This has been an experience we shan't forget. Each day, at sunset, we would sojourn to the outside patio and Vanessa would read the day's work, aloud. Dad would listen without interruption, jotting down notes for changes. In a small measure we were able to feel some of the emotional upheaval he was undergoing.

The manuscript is ready except for the last three chapters, which Dad wants to rewrite. I'm sending it, save those three chapters, under separate cover.

My Hebrew is coming along fine. I hope it will be sufficient to begin flight training soon. Vanessa has graduated from the English-speaking gymnasium and may be called into the Army for a year's national service. Technically, she doesn't have to serve, but I don't believe anything will keep her out.

Please don't worry about Dad. He's under good care.

Our affection to Aunt Lorraine.

BEN CADY

NIGHT LETTER
ABRAHAM CADY
KFAR SCHMARYAHU BET
ISRAEL

JANUARY 15, 1964

I HAVE READ YOUR MANUSCRIPT STOP I BELIEVE THAT YOU HAVE ACHIEVED WHAT EVERY WRITER ASPIRES TO AND FEW REALIZE STOP YOU HAVE WRITTEN A BOOK THAT WILL LIVE, NOT ONLY BEYOND YOUR MORTAL TIME ON EARTH, BUT FOR ALL TIMES. YOUR DEVOTED FRIEND, DAVID SHAWCROSS.

Abe had been in Israel for well over a year, but he had avoided the cemetery outside Haifa. With the receipt of Shawcross's cable he felt that he could visit his father, at last.

Chapter Eighteen

'THE HOLOCAUST' WAS PUBLISHED IN THE SUMMER OF 1965. IT HAD TAKEN ME ALL MY LIFE TO BECOME AN OVERNIGHT SUCCESS. NOW THAT I HAD SPILLED MY BLOOD IN WRITING THE BOOK THE VULTURES AND PARASITES SWARMED IN TO GET THEIR CUT. MOST NOTABLE WAS LOU PEPPER, WHO WAS WILLING TO LET BYGONES BE BYGONES.

WHEN I TURNED THE MANUSCRIPT IN EARLIER IN THE YEAR I WAS FILLED WITH AN INSATIABLE DESIRE TO RETURN TO AMERICA. I SETTLED WITH A LONG TERM LEASE IN A LOVELY GLASS AND WOOD CONCOCTION IN THE HILLS OF SAUSALITO WITH A BREATH-STOPPING VIEW OVER THE BAY TO SAN FRANCISCO. THIS DRIVE TO RETURN TO AMERICA HAD GROWN OVER THE YEARS WITH MY DEEPENING CONCERN ABOUT THE THING THAT WAS SHAKING EVERYONE, EVERYWHERE, AND THAT WAS THE ABILITY OR INABILITY OF MAN TO CONTINUE TO EXIST ON PLANET EARTH.

THE BAY AREA WAS THE 'NOW' PLACE WHERE MUCH OF IT ALL WAS HAPPENING AND MUCH OF THE FUTURE FOR OTHER PLACES COULD BE PREDICTED.

IN ORDER TO FALL INTO A STATE OF DEPRESSION THESE DAYS ONE ONLY HAD TO

THINK ABOUT THE MASSIVE DISINTEGRATION OF THE EARTH AND AIR AND WATER AND THE MORAL ROT, THE GREED, AND CORRUPTION AND THAT ENDLESS LIST OF HUMAN FAILURES THAT WE WERE SUDDENLY BEING MADE KEENLY AWARE OF.

MAN THE PREDATOR, THE PLUNDERER, THE DESTROYER WAS COMING FACE TO FACE WITH THE THOUSANDS OF YEARS OF SINS AND CRIMES AND THERE WOULD BE AN ARMAGEDDON IN THIS CENTURY. IT WAS ALL RUSHING TO A TERRIFYING CLIMAX.

IF WE WERE TO CATALOGUE AND MAKE CHARGES OF THE ABUSES OF THE HUMAN RACE, IF WE WERE TO CALCULATE WHAT MAN HAD TAKEN AND WHAT HE OWED, THEN HE WOULD HAVE HAD TO DECLARE BANKRUPTCY.

WE WERE NOW FACED WITH THE FRIGHTENING QUESTION OF WHETHER OR NOT WE WERE COMING TO THE END OF OUR PURPOSE TO EXIST ANY LONGER. THE OLD GODS AND WISDOMS FAILED TO PROVIDE THE ANSWERS. AND A HORRIBLE SENSE OF FUTILITY AND DESPERATION INVADED THE UPCOMING GENERATION.

GREAT AND GRAND WARS WERE NOW A THING OF THE PAST. THERE WERE TWO SUPER POWERS IN THE WORLD, EACH CAPABLE OF RAINING TOTAL DESTRUCTION. THEREFORE, FUTURE WARS WOULD HAVE TO BE FOUGHT IN COMPACT AND LIMITED BOUNDARIES AND UNDER STRINGENT RULES.

NOW THAT A GREAT WAR WAS OUT OF THE QUESTION, MAN SEEMED TO NEED SOMETHING TO REPLACE WAR. THE CRUX OF THE PROBLEM IS THAT THERE EXISTS A BASIC FLAW IN THE HUMAN RACE AND THAT IS MAN'S INEVITABLE DRIVE TOWARD SELF-EXTINCTION.

INSTEAD OF WAR, HE HAS REPLACED WAR WITH THINGS AS DEADLY. HE INTENDS TO DESTROY HIMSELF BY CONTAMINATING THE AIR HE BREATHES, BY BURNING AND RIOTING AND PILLAGING, BY MAKING A SHAMBLES OF THE INSTITUTIONS AND RULES OF SANITY, BY MINDLESS EXTERMINATION OF BREEDS OF ANIMALS AND THE GIFTS OF THE SOIL AND THE SEA, BY POISONING HIMSELF INTO A SLOW LETHARGIC DEATH THROUGH DRUGS AND DOPE.

THE FORMAL AND DECLARED WARS HAVE GIVEN WAY TO A WAR DIRECTED AGAINST HIMSELF AND HIS FELLOW MAN THAT IS DOING THE JOB FASTER THAN IT WAS EVER DONE ON A BATTLEFIELD.

YOUNG PEOPLE HAVE BRUSHED ASIDE AND TRAMPLED DOWN MANY OLD MORES AND ETHICAL CODES. IN MANY CASES IT WAS OVERDUE THAT OUR SOCIETY BE STRIPPED OF HYPOCRISY AND RACISM AND FALSE SEXUAL VALUES. BUT IN THEIR RAMPAGE TO RING OUT THE OLD, THE YOUNG HAVE ALSO BROUGHT DOWN THE GREAT VALUES AND WISDOMS AND FAILED TO REPLACE THEM.

WHAT CAN I DO ABOUT THIS AS A WRITER? VERY LITTLE, I FEAR. AMONG OTHER THINGS I HAVE WATCHED A KIND OF INSANITY PERVERT LITERATURE AND ART AND MUSIC TO WIN FALSE PRAISE BY FALSE PROPHETS. WE HAVE IN MUCH OF IT THE SYMBOLS OF DESPAIR AND CONFUSION. LOOK AT A DANCE FLOOR. HEAR THE LOVELY MUSIC.

WELL, MY THING IS TO WRITE. ALL I CAN HOPE TO DO IS PUT A SINGLE FINGER IN A DAM WITH A MILLION LEAKS.

I FELT THAT IF I COULD CREATE A SINGLE FICTITIOUS AMERICAN CITY AND WRITE ITS HISTORY AND OF ITS PEOPLE FROM EVERY POSSIBLE ASPECT FROM ITS BEGINNINGS TO ITS RISE TO THE DECLINE IT COULD BE MY MOST VALUABLE CONTRIBUTION. WHAT I WANTED TO ACHIEVE IN FICTION WAS TO ISOLATE AND EXAMINE A COMPLETE ENTITY AND THROUGH LOOKING AT ONE TOTAL SEGMENT GAIN SOME INSIGHT INTO THE OTHER THOUSAND SEGMENTS.

ALL OF THIS WILL TAKE THREE OR FOUR YEARS TO RESEARCH AND EVOLVE INTO A NOVEL. VANESSA WILL BE FINISHED WITH HER MILITARY SERVICE IN ISRAEL SOON

AND WILL JOIN ME IN SAUSALITO AND TAKE HER COLLEGE IN BERKELEY, WHICH HAS BECOME A RICH SOURCE OF MY OWN RESEARCH, INCIDENTALLY.

BEN? BEN IS SEGEN MISHNE/LIEUTENANT CADY OF THE ISRAELI AIR FORCE. I'M PROUD. I'M FRIGHTENED. BUT I BELIEVE THAT WITH THE TRAINING HE'S GOTTEN HE'LL BE THE BEST AVIATOR OF THE THREE OF US.

IT IS A COMFORT THAT IN FINDING ISRAEL THE CHILDREN HAVE A PURE AND UNCLUTTERED GOAL IN LIFE, THE SURVIVAL OF OUR PEOPLE.

AFTER ALL, THE ONLY THING THAT IS GOING TO SAVE MANKIND IS IF ENOUGH PEOPLE LIVE THEIR LIVES FOR SOMETHING OR SOMEONE OTHER THAN THEMSELVES.

I AM A SOUGHT AFTER SPEAKER THESE DAYS. I GOT INVITED TO A WRITER'S SEMINAR AND FOR THREE DAYS I GOT QUESTIONS.

'SURE, ANYBODY CAN BE A WRITER. I'LL PUT YOU IN THE BUSINESS. HERE'S A SHEET OF PAPER.'

'HOW? APPLY THE SEAT OF THE PANTS TO THE SEAT OF THE CHAIR.'

OR

'I'M A WRITER TOO, BUT I DIDN'T GET AS LUCKY AS YOU, MR CADY.'

IT CAME MY TIME TO SPEAK AT THE BANQUET. I STUDIED THE TENSE, EAGER FACES AS I APPROACHED THE ROSTRUM. 'WHO HERE WANTS TO BE A WRITER?' I ASKED. EVERYONE IN THE ROOM RAISED HIS HAND. 'WHY THE HELL AREN'T YOU HOME WRITING?' I SAID, AND LEFT THE STAGE. THAT ENDED MY CAREER IN WRITERS' SEMINARS.

HOWEVER, THE JEWS DISCOVERED ME. JEWISH CHARITY WAS ALWAYS A WAY OF LIFE WITH MY FATHER AND MY FAMILY. TAKING CARE OF OUR OWN HAS BEEN OUR KEY TO SURVIVAL. IT IS THE ESSENCE OF ISRAEL. I REMEMBER IN THE BEGINNING IN THE JEWISH SHOPS ON CHURCH STREET IN NORFOLK THERE WAS ALWAYS A 'PUSHKE' – A LITTLE COLLECTION CAN FOR SOMETHING IN PALESTINE.

WELL, LET ME TELL YOU, JEWS NEVER RUN OUT OF CAUSES FOR WHICH TO RAISE MONEY AND IN 1965 I SPOKE FOR ONE HUNDRED AND SIXTEEN OF THEM. THE WHOLE SPEAKING SCENE IS A BAD ONE. I DON'T LIKE IT FROM THE WELCOMING COMMITTEE AT THE AIRPORT TO THE TV INTERVIEWS TO THE INTIMATE DINNERS WITH THE BIG DONORS AND I'M SO TERRIFIED WHEN I APPROACH THE ROSTRUM I HAVE TO BE LOADED WITH BOOZE AND TRANQUILIZERS. ANYHOW, SINCE 'THE HOLOCAUST' I'M THE HOT NUMBER THESE DAYS, AND IT'S VERY HARD FOR ME TO SAY NO TO THESE PEOPLE.

Abe's secretary, Millie, let in Sidney Chernoff, who represented Einstein University, which was the second fully accredited Jewish educational facility in Chicago.

'Mr Cady phoned that he would be a few minutes late. Would you like to wait in his office?'

So, this was where he worked! Chernoff gloried and drank it in. The aging leather chair, the battered typewriter, the desk filled with trinkets, photographs of his two children in Israeli uniform. It was food for a week's conversation! There was a floor to ceiling corked wall. MARK TWAIN CITY, CALIFORNIA. Pinned to the wall were sheets of dates and statistics and names of characters and family groups and the educational, political, industrial, and cultural make-up of the city.

Imagine! A city born out of a man's mind.

A long table opposite held stacks of books and documents and photographs covering every possible facet of urban life. Reports on the influx of minorities, riots and floods, strikes, police and fire methods.

Sidney Chernoff's trek through the inner sanctum was abruptly halted by the loud sound of an approaching motorcycle. He looked out of the window down to the driveway where some roughneck gunned the bike, switched it off, and dismounted. My God! It was Abraham Cady!

Chernoff tried to be nonchalant as the booted, leather-jacketed Cady introduced himself, plopped into the seat behind his desk and propped his feet up and ordered a Bloody Mary from Millie.

'That's quite an interesting piece of machinery,' Chernoff said, trying to say *SOMETHING* cool about the bike.

'Harley C. H. Sportster 900,' Abe said, 'that mother takes off like a striped ass ape.'

'Yes, it appears very powerful.'

'I've got to bust loose and clear my head now and then. I've been riding with the narcotics squad for over two months. It's an ugly scene. We found two kids, age twelve and fourteen, dead from an overdose of heroin last night.'

'That's ghastly.'

'Only trouble with a bike is that it doesn't fly. The CAB is giving me a lot of static about a private pilot's license. The eye, you know.'

Abe's Bloody Mary and Chernoff's tea arrived.

Chernoff sipped and nodded in approval with large puckered lips. He oiled his way into the subject of his visit, speaking in the deep melodious voice of the practiced super intellectual. Cady had an idiosyncrasy with the motorcycle, but he was a great novelist who understood the lofty language of a fellow cultured creature. Chernoff sprinkled his presentation with Hebrew phrases, wisdoms of the Talmud, and quotes from personal conversations he had had with other great men. He explained why a man of the stature of Abraham Cady should identify with Einstein University, the second major Jewish institute in the country. There were a number of chairs in the arts and letters that Abe could raise funds for. In turn, Abraham Cady would receive great spiritual reward in knowing he was advancing the cause of Jewish education and intellectualism.

Abe dropped his feet from the desk with a thud. 'I'll be glad to appear for Einstein,' he said.

Sidney Chernoff could not conceal his unabashed joy! Cady was not the monster he had been painted. A Jew is a Jew and if he is appealed to correctly his Jewishness will shine through.

'I have one small condition,' Abe said.

'Of course.'

'The money I raise is to be used for the sole purpose of recruiting a major football team, hiring a big name coach, and working toward a schedule against the top teams in the country.'

Chernoff was puzzled. 'But Einstein had a fine program of inter-mural sports.'

'It's like this, Mr Chernoff. We've got enough scholars, learned men, doctors, scientists, essayists, lawyers, mathematicians, musicians, and fund raisers to stock every under-developed country in the world, including Texas. The way I see it is like this. The Jews have engaged in conversation for two thousand years without notable success in matters of human dignity. A few thousand of our people in Israel went out and kicked the piss out of somebody and that is where our respect comes from. I want Einstein University to put eleven big buck Jews on the field against Notre Dame. I want Jews who can knock other people down, face mask, pile on, get penalties for unnecessary roughness. I want a Jew who can throw a ball fifty yards to another Jew who can catch it with three monsters hanging on his back.'

After a long siege of research at the longshoreman's hall, debating with the scholars on civic upheaval, looking for action in the ghetto of Fillmore Street, hobnobbing at the Pacific Union Club, riding with the police on emergency calls, freaking with the beatniks, marching with and against campus rebels at Cal . . . Abe would find respite sailing his boat over the bay to San Francisco and going out with the fishing fleet. A few days in rough water, bending his back on a salmon run, letting the beard grow, leaking over the rail, drinking with the Italians, all flushed him for another run at his work.

He was at sea for four lovely days on the *Maria Bella II* in the chilled buffeting January wind and waves. He was sad as she chugged through the Golden Gate into the arms of the great bay.

Dominick, the skipper of *Maria Bella II*, handed Abe a sack of crabs.

'If my mother saw these crabs she'd turn over in her grave.'

'Hey, Abe,' Dominick yelled, 'when you going to write something about me?'

'I already have. It's a one page book called the *Complete Encyclopedia of Italian War Heroes*.'

'Very funny, Jew writer. You're lucky you only got one eye.'

'I've got two. I wear an eye patch because I'm yellow.'

Maria Bella II wobbled in the swells, veered right before Alcatraz, and eased toward Fisherman's Wharf and the magic alabaster city that rose up behind it.

Dom's father was on the pier as they tied up. 'Hey, Abie, you secretary, she call up. She say for you to call her rightaway.'

'Millie, Abe. What's up?'

'A cable arrived from Shawcross in London two days ago. I didn't know whether to radio out to the boat or not.'

'Read it.'

'Libel proceedings launched against *The Holocaust* naming author, publisher, and printer by Sir Adam Kelno former inmate doctor in Jadwiga Concentration Camp over reference to him on page 167 stop Kelno involved in extradition case in London nineteen years ago and freed and later knighted by British government stop Send us all your sources of information immediately stop He is demanding all books on sale be withdrawn stop Unless you can support allegations we are in extremely serious trouble. And it's signed, David Shawcross.'

BOOK THREE

Brief to Counsel

Preface

Greater London encompasses the city of London and thirty-two boroughs, among which are the former city of Westminster, and the former Royal Borough of Kensington, and such other famous areas as Chelsea, Harrow, Hammersmith, Lambeth, and the picturesquely named Tower Hamlets.

THE CITY of London is a tiny fiefdom of one square mile running along the Thames Embankment from about Waterloo Bridge to Tower Bridge. The City is autonomous and each year with great pomp renews its status by payment to the crown of six horseshoes, sixty-one horseshoe nails, a hatchet, and a billhook. Within its seven hundred acres, the Lord Mayor is sovereign only to the crown and when the king or queen enters its boundaries, they must pause for official permission and welcome of the Lord Mayor.

The numerous wigged and gowned ceremonies clash with a twinge of humor with the miniskirted young ladies of the financial district.

In ancient times the various guilds of fishmongers, ironmongers, grocers, vintners, and the like, selected London's officials, who wore robes and carried maces and scepters and swords of state denoting their positions.

The boundaries of The City are marked, the most prominent being the statue of the griffin where the Strand becomes Fleet Street before the Royal Courts. Tradition called for a father to take his son to the boundary and whack him on the backside so he could always remember the limitations of his traveling, a ceremony called 'beating the bounds.'

Within its magic mile, The City holds Fleet Street, the newspaper center of the world, the Old Lady of Threadneedle Street, as the Bank of England is known, Lloyd's, Petticoat Lane, the Tower of London, St Paul's Cathedral, Old Bailey, blackly renowned as the world's most famous criminal court, the great fish markets, all under the protection of ceremonial pikemen and in day to day life by six foot bobbies with distinctive marking on their hats to distinguish them from other London bobbies.

There is yet another great institution in The City, the Royal Courts of Justice and three of the four Inns of Court. As The City is autonomous from greater London, so are the Inns of Court autonomous from The City.

The Inns of Court came into existence centuries ago when the Knights Templar, holy brothers in arms, were given a habitation in 1099 to 'carrie on their vows of chastity and poverty' intermixed with some bloody doings. They were abolished by order of the Pope in 1312 but the Templars survive today through the Masonic Fraternity whose Freemasons cherish the distinction of the degree of Knight Templar.

With the demise of the Templars the lawyers drifted into The Temple in the 1200s. Lawyers as well as doctors in those days were priests and the law was canon in nature.

The Magna Carta and King Henry III ended much canon law and after a time converted to common law. The Inns were then to take permanent possession of legal education and the legal world.

There is an ancient verse that sums up the Inns.

Gray's Inn for walks,
Lincoln's Inn for a wall,
The Inner Temple for a garden,
The Middle Temple for a hall.

Middle Temple Hall is staggering in heraldry. It was here that the first performance of Shakespeare's Twelfth Night was held. The serving table below the dais is made of timber from Sir Francis Drake's *Golden Hind* and Elizabeth and her admirals were its patrons. Under its sign of the Holy Lamb Oliver Goldsmith and Dr Johnson and Blackstone practiced and Chaucer resided and wrote the *Canterbury Tales*. No less than five members of the Middle Temple signed the American Declaration of Independence. In its gardens the thirty year War of the Roses commenced.

Yet it is the hall that remains the overpowering and magnificent mark of Middle Temple. A hundred feet in length it soars fifty feet with a timbered carved roof of Elizabethan hammered beams. In the year of 1574, some time before the Spanish Armada, a magnificent hand-carved wooden screen was erected to span the forty-five foot girth of the hall. Rows of ponderous tables run the length of the hall toward the dais flanked by a wainscoted wall holding the coats of arms of Treasurers and Readers. At the dais the Benchers or Elders of the Temple preside over somber dinners and wild revelry. Over the side and end walls are fourteen stained glass windows with coats of arms of the Lord Chancellors from Middle Temple. Royal patrons painted by Hogarth and Van Dyke stared down on it all.

Crossing a narrow lane one leaves Middle Temple and enters Inner Temple, whose best-known landmark is the Knights Templar Church dedicated in 1185. It miraculously escaped the periodic fires which leveled The City during the Middle Ages but was gutted in the Blitz. Now, brilliantly restored, it is one of England's few round churches, modeled after the Holy Sepulcher in Jerusalem with floors covered with thirteenth century marble effigies of knights and an arcade of grotesque stone heads representing souls in hell. Near them were the cells where paupers, debtors, and other sinners starved to death watching the knights in their holy prayer. Christopher Wren beautified it with a rectangular nave.

Much of the Inner Temple had been destroyed and rebuilt because of fire and war, but it is her names that make her glory permanent. Charles Lamb and William Makepeace Thackeray and Boswell and Charles Dickens. And rich are the names of its buildings and lanes of Hare Court and Figtree Court and Ram Alley and King's Bench Walk with its immensity of lawn flowing down to the Thames.

Both segments of the Temple, Middle and Inner, are cut off from the outside world and the bustle of Fleet Street and the Victoria Embankment by Christopher Wren gates and walls.

On the rear side of the Law Courts, between High Holborn and Carey Street, stands Lincoln's Inn on a site once occupied by the Friars on what is now known as Chancery Lane. When the archbishop of Canterbury changed their name to Blackfriars, their houses were chartered to Henry de Lacy, Earl of Lincoln in 1285. Heart of the pastoral fields of Lincoln's Inn is Old Hall, erected in 1489, and it is still intact and used as a lecture room. This is the Inn of William Pitt and Disraeli and Cromwell and the martyr Thomas More, who was among its nine prime ministers and twenty Lord Chancellors.

Across High Holborn, a street named for a path burned by the great fire, and just beyond the reach of The City, lies the quadrangle of the fourth Inn, Gray's. This is the place of Sir Francis Bacon. Gray's is mostly inactive today as a base for practicing barristers, with most of its offices leased to solicitors.

The Four Inns are part and parcel of English history and greatness. They form the Law University and in addition to their own particular individuality they have enormous libraries, conduct moots or mock trials, are recipients of royal patronage, are filled with students, and hold the formal dinners where new barristers are called to the bar.

While the world swirls around them they continue to live in a quasi-monastic serenity, gowned in their distinctive robes and traditionally going to war together in a single Inns of Court Regiment.

In each building, a Queen's Counsel or senior barrister 'leads' the juniors in a set of chambers. Often two barristers from the same chamber argue from opposite sides of the courtroom.

Some say this is a private debating society and that these two thousand barristers are too privileged and that the thousands upon thousands of examples of common law are too archaic and intricate.

Yet, here is law for law's sake. The barrister argues the case for a set fee and is not allowed to take a portion of a client's judgment. He may not be sued for what he says in court. On the other hand he is not permitted to sue a client for fees.

Within the Inns corruption is unknown.

The barrister is judged by a man who has been chosen from the ranks of Queen's counsels in a no nonsense courtroom.

A new student taken into a chamber to study is fearfully admonished that he is in the home of the Knights Templar, in the midst of kings and queens, statesmen and judges and philosophers and writers. He is to be governed by the Benchers or elders and receives the wisdom of the Reader or chief lecturer.

A young man or many older people possessing a standard diploma and a few hundred pounds may enter an Inn and be taken by a master in chambers.

Many a brilliant barrister in the courtroom is impatient in drafting his pleadings and here a new pupil can worm his way into his master's good graces. Doing research and drafting immaculate, painstaking, technically perfect pleadings can endear the pupil to the master.

The pupil makes as little an ass of himself as possible. He reads his master's papers, looks up points of law for him, accompanies him to court, and works hard and late.

The pupil learns to have every point of law at his master's finger tips. He develops the skill of taking fast and accurate notes in court and anticipating the master's questions.

This goes on for a year or so. There is study, attendance at a number of required dinners at the Inn, and the arguing of a moot or mock trial.

A few things fall the student's way. Some overly busy junior in the chambers may need a hand to 'devil' or prepare his work or even argue a minor case in the county.

Each set of chambers, numbering from two to twenty barristers, is managed by a clerk, an all important man who can speed the pupil on his career or keep him moldering. He deals on the barristers' behalf with the solicitor's offices, assigns cases, sets the fees, and works for a portion of them.

Having deviled, argued minor cases, and shown diligence, the clerk will begin to throw a few things to the bright young man.

To advance his progress the student writes for law journals and puts his name in with the legal aid people.

After the call to the bar and assignment to a decent set of chambers the new junior is with ten or so other juniors and led by an eminent Q.C. Good juniors are in demand. In five years he may be able to afford a larger room in chambers. One day, after a particularly brilliant showing the Q.C. rewards the junior with a red bag to carry his gown, wig, and books in.

After fifteen or so years as a junior the crown may appoint the junior to be a Queen's Counsel. The robe made of 'stuff' is discarded and the Q.C. 'takes silk.'

As a Q.C. one merely has to argue the case with all the preparation being done by the juniors.

At the age of fifty or more a prominent Q.C. may be appointed to the bench as a judge and automatically knighted. It is the pinnacle of the legal career.

On the other hand, he may remain a junior barrister until his dying day.

Chapter One

October 1945

Parliament Square was inundated with the clang of great bells to ring in a new legal year with ancient majestic pageantry.

The war was over and England had survived with the empire intact. Englishmen were going about the business of cleaning up the rubbish in the center of London where the Hun had left his mark and soon all of that would be in the past. There would be the return to order and tradition as it had been before. There was talk of brave new worlds but this kind of talk followed every war, it seemed. No dynamic changes would be in store for England. They liked things tidy without the dramatic upheavals of the Latins and Levantines. Yes, the new era would be exactly like the old one.

If one doubted that, they had only to be there on this day and they would understand what England was all about. Within the walls of Westminster

Abbey, the Lord Chancellor, resplendent in black and gold robes, led the judges of England and the barristers in a sacred service. As they worshiped in pursuit of divine guidance in dispensation of the law, their Roman Catholic counterparts conducted a Red Mass in their cathedral.

The great doors of the abbey swung open. The procession is begun. It is led by the mace bearer, a tall thin grim chap, and then the bearer of the great seal. Each is attired in knee britches, buckled shoes, and a cascade of lace embroidery.

Behind them, Lord Ramsey, the Lord Chancellor, wearied by the burden of office. The train bearer follows the Lord Chancellor's stately pace as they cross the great way toward the House of Lords.

There then followed a flamboyantly cloaked array of the Lord Chancellor's judges: The scarlet-robed Lord Chief Justice whose ermined collar bore the heavy golden chain of the House of Lancaster. Thence the Master of the Rolls, the traditional deputy of the Lord Chancellor and head of the Chancery Courts, and the others in order of their rank, all dressed in britches, buckled shoes, full-bottomed wigs. Now the President of the Probate, Divorce, and Admiralty Division and the Lords Justices of Appeal in cumbersome black and gold and the flaming-robed Justices of the High Court.

A long line of the senior barristers, the King's Counsel, in black silk gowns and great wigs born of the Queen Anne era. Lastly came the junior barristers.

They are received in the Royal Gallery in the House of Lords after crossing from the east end of the abbey.

In this time of talk of dramatic change one hears that the law is archaic, living in a private sanctuary of its practitioners, in shocking need of reform, and choking on its own ancient rituals. One hears that common law is filled with symbols of other times. Yet, nearing its thousandth year of use it would be difficult to argue that any other system devised by man surpasses it and it would be equally difficult to contend that it doesn't fulfill the modern needs of justice with surety and dispatch.

The soul of English law is the Lord Chancellor and in this time it is Cyril Ramsey who has reached the epitome of his profession and taken an office which seems far too demanding for a single man. His head wears three crowns.

The Lord Chancellor is one of the few men in the world who holds positions in all branches of government. As the ranking judge of England, Lord Ramsey is the leader of the entire legal structure. He recommends the judges and appoints the junior barristers to the exalted inner realm of King's Counsel.

He is the Speaker of the House of Lords and presides over that body, sitting on the ancient Woolsack, symbol of his office in Parliament.

He is the chief legal adviser to the Crown.

He is a member of the cabinet.

In Parliament he helps in the passage of the laws. As an adviser and cabinet member he helps execute them. As a judge, he enforces them.

He is imprisoned in the grandeur of an apartment in the Parliament looking out on the Thames. From here he heads over a hundred committees for legal reform, for trustee of public funds, for overseeing legal education, for obtaining legal aid, for patronage of hospitals and colleges and law societies and charities. As though this were not enough Lord Ramsey and all the Lord Chancellors before him are bound and tied with constant ceremonial demands. For all of this he receives the annual salary of some thirty-five thousand dollars.

Yet , as traditional 'keeper of the King's conscience' he is inheritor of an era of greatness bowing neither to tension or tragedy, nor showing public exuberance. Dignity, that is the keynote. The keeper of tradition.

Yes, the average Londoner who saw all of this on this day could scarcely believe that any dynamic changes were in the making.

The new legal year was formally under way. Ramsey greeted all of his judges and all of his barristers, whom he knew from long personal and professional association. He was approached by Anthony Gilray, King's Counsel.

Ramsey had on his desk the nomination of Gilray to judgeship in the High Court. He thought it would be a good appointment. Gilray was as sound as the pound sterling. Ten years earlier, one of Ramsey's first duties as Lord Chancellor had been to promote Gilray from junior to K.C. 'Takes silk' they called it when one became a King's Counsel. Gilray had been far above average in his parade of court hearings. When his appointment as judge went through in an automatic manner, Gilray would be knighted as all of England's high judges are and he would be sworn in to a seat in King's Bench Division of the High Court.

'Lord Ramsey,' Anthony Gilray said, holding out a thin hand.

'Hello, Tony, good to have you back from the Army.'

'Good to be back.'

'How does it look to you?'

'Oh, about the same. England never changes.'

Chapter Two

January 1966

Mr Bullock, the managing clerk of Hobbins, Newton, and Smiddy, contacted Mr Rudd, the clerk of Sir Robert Highsmith, Q.C., and arranged a consultation in chambers at 4 Essex Court, Middle Temple.

In the years that had passed, Robert Highsmith had risen in stature to one of the greatest libel lawyers in England and because of his continued work with political prisoners had attained knighthood.

Despite his status, he doted on impoverished furnishings in a room with peeling walls, a broken down overstuffed sofa, threadbare carpet, and a portable electric heater to augment the inadequate gas burner. The one item of elegance, as in most barristers' chambers, was the desk, a great leather-topped Victorian partner's desk.

However, parked in his space below was a new Rolls Royce.

Sir Robert Highsmith and Sir Adam Kelno penetrated the barrier of years with searching looks of remembrance. Sir Robert was grayer, heavier, and not quite so disheveled. A copy of *The Holocaust* lay on the desk. 'There seems to be very little question but that you've been libeled. Offhand one would think it would be impossible for them to defend. However, we must take into consideration that the offending passage occupies one paragraph of a seven hundred page book. Would the general public identify you, a knighted English citizen, as the same person mentioned in passing as a doctor of unidentified nationality in Jadwiga?'

'Perhaps not,' Adam answered, 'but my son recognized me, as well as my ward.'

'In seeking damages the sting of the libel will weigh heavily and may be exceedingly nominal.'

'The damage is inside ... here ...' Adam said, pointing to his heart.

'What I am saying is that we may be opening up a Pandora's Box. If, mind you, the other people decide to fight, are we certain that we will come out of this untainted. Are our hands completely clean?'

'No one should know that better than you,' Adam answered. 'I think these words were deliberately put into the book as part of the same plot to harass me to my death. At least now, I have a chance to fight back, not in a mock court in Poland, but under British justice.'

'Isn't it rather unlikely they are going to fight this?' Richard Smiddy asked.

'If we make our demands too heavy, they may be forced to fight. It depends on what Sir Adam is really seeking.'

'Seeking? Aside from the hell of Jadwiga I am in Brixton Prison and in exile in Sarawak for seventeen years. I am there because of them. I have done no wrong. What do you think I should be seeking?'

'Very well,' Sir Robert said, 'but I'm going to have to take the position of tempering your passion with the reality of the situation. Do you understand that?'

'Yes.'

'I'm sorry you have to go through it all again, Sir Adam. Let's hope they'll be sensible.'

In the anteroom, Smiddy made mention to Mr Rudd to contact his clerk, Mr Bullock, to set the fees. Smiddy and Adam Kelno walked from the Temple and stopped before the onrush of black taxis and red double decked buses racing up and down the Strand past the statue of the griffin marking the Temple Bar. Over the street the ominous gray stone of the Law Court seemed to glare at them.

'Mark my words, Sir Adam, it will never get into that court.'

Abraham Cady &
Shawcross Publishers, Ltd
& Humble, Ltd Printers
c/o David Shawcross
25 Gracechurch Street EC 3

Hobbins, Newton & Smiddy
Solicitors
32 Chancery Lane
London WC 2

Sirs:

Since our initial communication we have been instructed by our client, Sir Adam Kelno, M.D., to inquire:

1. If you are prepared to make a statement of apology in open court.

2. What proposals you have to make to indemnify Sir Adam Kelno for expenses incurred in this matter.

3. What are you prepared to do in removing all copies of *The Holocaust* from all bookstores and ensuring that no mention of Dr Kelno is made in any future editions.

4. What proposals you have to make by way of damages for the grievous injury done his honorable name.

In that these charges against Sir Adam Kelno are totally without foundation it is impossible to imagine a graver libel upon a professional man in his position.

Since our client requires a statement in open court it is mandatory to issue a writ and we would like to ask you to give us the name of your solicitors who will accept service.

Yours faithfully,

HOBBINS, NEWTON, AND SMIDDY

Chapter Three

In Sausalito, Abraham Cady scrutinized his voluminous notes, then wrote to archives, individuals, and historical societies in Vienna, Warsaw, New York, Munich, and Israel for information. The name Kelno had meant little or nothing to him in the context of the massive book.

In London, the small conference room of Shawcross Publishers was converted into a sort of war room. First, Shawcross dug up all the history of the extradition proceedings against Kelno.

His first major discovery was that Dr Mark Tesslar was still alive and on the permanent staff of the Radcliffe Medical Center in Oxford. The years had neither diminished nor blunted his feeling. Looking beyond Tesslar's accusations, he felt they were basically truthful and this spurred him to widen his own investigation.

Shawcross turned most of the publishing operation over to his son-in-law, Geoffrey Dodd, and his daughter, Pam. Their son, Cecil, was just beginning in the business. Shawcross took young Cecil as his own personal staff on the investigation.

The starting point was the war crimes indictment of SS Colonel Dr Adolph Voss, chief medical officer of the prisoners of Jadwiga Concentration Camp. Unfortunately, Voss never came to trial, he committed suicide in prison. None the less the prosecutor in Hamburg had a list of two hundred prospective witnesses.

The indictment and the prospective witness list were almost twenty years old. Many on the list had died, others had moved or disappeared. Yet Shawcross took a crack at everyone in a correspondence carried out in ten languages. Huge charts blanketed the wall of the conference room plotting the progress and answers to every inquiry.

A smattering of information drifted to London. Most of it was discouraging and shed no light. No one seemed to be willing to state they could identify Adam Kelno and they were even more positive on the point that the surgery in Barrack V was a total secret.

Inquiries to Poland went unanswered. The Polish Embassy in London was evasive. Shawcross concluded that a policy was yet to be set by the Poles in the matter. Cautious bureaucrats from the embassies of the Eastern European countries drown the inquiries in red tape. After all, Abraham Cady was a known anti-Communist writer.

Four months passed. The wall charts were dead-ending the majority of inquiries. Only a few threads, the meagerest clues from Israel, kept the project from collapsing.

And then came a staggering body blow.

Archibald Charles III of Charles, Ltd, the monolithic printing combine, puffed away in his immaculately paneled office in The City, contemplating this nasty piece of business.

The Charles empire had four great printing plants in the British Islands, a forest for paper pulp in Finland, and a conglomerate of partnerships all over the Continent.

The actual business flowing from David Shawcross amounted to a fraction of a single percentile. None the less, Shawcross occupied a special place. It was the same kind of special place he held in the publishing world as a great editor and literary master. Archibald's father had been a close chum of Shawcross and heard on more than one occasion that this was the kind of man a publisher ought to be.

While the business relationship was unimportant in terms of the Charles dynasty, the personal comradery carried over when young Archibald took over as managing director and later, chairman of the board. Shawcross could count on his printers to fill his paper orders and shove a pet book ahead of the largest publishers.

No doubt but that young Charles was a credit. The stockholders were pleased at the steady rise in earnings. He thought in modern terms of mergers and conglomerates more like an American than an Englishman.

'I have Mr Shawcross on the phone,' his secretary said.

'Hello, David, Archie here.'

'How are you?'

'Good. Mind if I pop over this afternoon?'

'Fine.'

Coming out of his magnificent skyscraper to the drab rooms of Shawcross's on Gracechurch Street was a singular act of respect. He was pin-striped and bowlered because that's what the stockholders expected.

He arrived at Shawcross's, was led down the corridor past stuffy little cubicles of the editors and secretaries to the 'war room.' Archibald studied the walls papered with charts. 'Phased out' was encircled in red lettering. Blue stars marked some sort of progress.

'Good Lord, what do you have here?'

'I'm looking for a needle in a haystack. Contrary to public belief, if you look long enough you'll find the needle.'

'Are you intending to publish books anymore?'

'Geoff and Pam are running things out there. We'll have an autumn list of some kind. Tea?'

'Thank you.'

Shawcross erupted a cigar as the tea arrived.

'It's the Kelno affair,' Charles said. 'As you know I've assigned one of my best people full time to analyze everything you've sent over. You've had numerous meetings with old Pearson about this.'

'Yes. Very decent chap.'

'We've put everything in the hands of our solicitors and have had consultations in chambers with Israel Meyer. I think you'll go along with me when I say he's one of the best barristers practicing. Moreover, we picked Meyer because he is a Jew and would be extremely sympathetic to your point of view. At any rate I called a special board meeting to reach a decision.'

'Well, I don't see what decision there is,' Shawcross said. 'Every day we learn another fragment about Kelno. There can be no decision when there is no choice.'

'We have a very marked difference of opinion, David. We're pulling out of the case.'

'What!'

'We sent our solicitor over to see the Smiddy people. They're willing to settle now for under a thousand pounds and an apology in open court. I suggest you do the same.'

'Archie, I don't know what to say. You can't be serious.'

'Dead serious.'

'But don't you see that picking us off one by one means they'll demolish Abraham?'

'My dear David, you and I are innocent victims of a fool writer who didn't get his facts straight. Why should you be responsible because Cady has libeled a distinguished British doctor?'

The chair screeched on the bare wooden floor as David pushed away from the conference table and walked to the charts. 'See this, Archie. Just in the past few days. A statement from a man who was castrated.'

'Now, David, I'm not going into a debate with you. We've done the proper thing. Pearson, our solicitors, our barrister, and my board have studied all the information and have a unanimous decision.'

'Is that your personal feeling also, Archie?'

'I am the head of a public company.'

'In that event, Archie, you have a public duty.'

'Rot. All stockholders are the same. I've restrained myself while you've turned your house into a detective agency. I have not lifted a finger and said that you've got us into this. And I say again, get out of it.'

Shawcross whipped the cigar out of his teeth. 'Apologize to a ruddy bastard who cut the nuts off healthy men! Never, sir! Too bad you don't read some of the words that come from your presses.'

Archibald Charles opened the door. 'Will we be seeing you and Lorraine for dinner and theater tomorrow?'

No answer.

'Come now. We're not going to let this stand in the way of our friendship, are we?'

Chapter Four

For several weeks there had been a cooling in the relationship between Shawcross and his daughter Pam and her husband, Geoffrey Dodd. It was obvious they thought he was spending too much time on the Kelno affair. Shawcross felt it would be a good idea to have them down to the beach house at Ramsgate in Kent for the weekend and mend things up.

The autumn list of new books was very thin and there wasn't much in prospect for the spring. During these lean periods in the past Shawcross had the uncanny knack of coming up with a dark horse and would make the best seller list. But these days every moment went into the volumes of correspondence, the translations, and the attempt to crack the doors at the Communist embassies. There would be no recurrence of the annual Shawcross miracle.

The whole Kelno affair had come at a poor time for Shawcross. He was getting along in years and wanted to spend more and more time at Ramsgate just editing and working with new writers.

Geoff and Pam were doing a good job and now with their son, Cecil, in the firm the family continuation looked secure.

Geoff and Shawcross walked beneath the chalk cliffs as they had done on many occasions for a decade, tossing about company business, paper orders, personnel, layouts, bindings, contracts, printing schedules, the Frankfurt Book Fair, the new list.

Shawcross poked his walking stick in the sand. 'I'm still reeling from this shock from Archie.'

'Perhaps it's an omen, David,' Geoff said.

David looked concerned. He had always taken Geoffrey Dodd so much for granted and expected unqualified loyalty.

'Let's have at it. What's on your mind, Geoff?'

'We haven't had a big winner since, well, *The Holocaust*. Abraham is a year away from starting a new novel, another year to write it and six months for us to get it ready. Usually when we'd get into a situation like this, you'd shake the tree and come up with something.'

Shawcross grumbled and flipped his cigar into the breakers. 'I know what you're going to say, merger. Well, who do we talk merger to? The sanitary napkin manufacturer, the soup company, or the oil tycoon who thinks his idiot son should be a publisher.'

'It would be a case of beefing up the present ten books to thirty books a year and giving us the reserve to bid on the Micheners and Irving Wallaces.'

'I'd always hoped we'd be able to keep things in the family, but I suppose it's not very realistic, is it?'

'The point is,' Geoff said, 'no one will talk merger or partnership so long as we have this lawsuit hanging over our heads.'

'I am not going to abandon Abraham so long as he remains in this case.'

'Then I've got to tell you something, quite candidly. Lambert-Phillips has offered me a directorship.'

'Those cheeky bastards daring to raid me.'

'I had my hand in the courtship.'

'I . . . I see.'

'It's the position of managing editor, seat on the board, stock options. Almost a thousand more than I'm making. Quite frankly I was astonished.'

'You shouldn't be. You're a good man, Geoff. And what about Cecil?'

'He would want to come with me.'

David tried to conceal a convulsing sensation. All of a sudden a lovely little world he had built with dedication and integrity was splitting apart. 'Pam, of course, goes along with all this?'

'Not exactly. She's for us taking a partner and keeping on with Shawcross. But you've got to make up your mind about this business with Kelno. I've got to tell you why I talked this over with Lambert-Phillips. It's not the money really. It's because David Shawcross has a pair of shoes so large, no one can fill them properly. Sure, I'm a good managing editor but God almighty, David, you've run a one man show that neither Cecil nor I could cope with in today's world.'

They reached the beach house.

'Thanks for the chat, Geoff. I'll think about it.'

The ash on David's cigar was four inches long. The galleys were balanced on his stomach, but he had stared aimlessly for an hour without reading them.

Lorraine sat on the edge of the bed and removed his cigar and fed him his pills.

'Pam told me today when you and Geoff took your stroll,' she said. 'What do you think we ought to do, love?'

'Difficult to say. We'll have to make a decision fairly soon. Abraham will be on his way to London next week.'

Chapter Five

The room Abraham Cady loved most in the world was David Shawcross's library and its smell of the plush leather of the rich maroon and green and blue bindings of an incredible collection of first editions. Almost every important writer of the twentieth century was represented. Abe was most proud that *The Holocaust* was the most prominently displayed as the greatest single volume ever published by Shawcross.

In a moment, Shawcross's solicitor, Allen Lewin, arrived. He was fine, as solicitors went, Abe thought, and completely loyal to Shawcross.

'Before we get into our business,' Lewin said, 'I'd like to clear up one point. What are your recollections now of the offending paragraph. How did it get into your book?'

Abe smiled. 'When I give a newspaper interview to a journalist he may end up writing three or four hundred words about me. There's always a dozen errors. In a seven hundred page book of over four hundred thousand words, I made one. I'll admit, it was a dilly. This same information had been published about Kelno before. He was on the list of wanted war criminals. After researching as I did and particularly reading the records of the war crimes trials of doctors I think anyone was willing to believe anything about any of them. What I read about Kelno, in sources that had been totally reliable till then, was completely in keeping with other facts of German atrocities. This doesn't excuse me, of course.'

'Abraham is the most thorough and accurate writer in fiction today,' Shawcross said. 'This mistake could have happened to anyone.'

'I wish it had happened to someone else,' Lewin said, 'preferably from another house.' He unsnapped his briefcase and they ordered whisky all around.

'You and Mr Shawcross have been in close communication so you know our independent findings pretty well coincide. As for the situation inside the house, Geoff and Cecil are planning to leave unless there is a merger or a partnership and this is impossible until the case is settled.'

'I didn't realize that,' Abe said.

'We have to familiarize you with the fiscal situation of Shawcross Limited so you'll understand how we are coming to our decision.'

'Sorry to have to give you all this rubbish, Abe,' Shawcross said, 'but matters are too grave.'

'Shoot.'

'The current and projected new lists and the cash flow will make money. Mr Shawcross, as you may know, is not an extremely wealthy man. His credit has been good with the banks and printers because of a distinguished personal reputation. The actual assets of the company lie in his back list and three outstanding series. The greatest asset for a merger is Mr Shawcross's image.

'His personal fortune,' Lewin continued, 'as I said is not enormous. All of this goes on the line in a major lawsuit of this nature.

'I'm a Jew, Mr Cady. I approached this with all the moral overtones. We have spent months at it and now we have to take a cold-blooded look at the risk and our possibilities. We have a number of vague statements of people operated on in Jadwiga, but no one except Dr Tesslar who claims to be an eyewitness. I've had three barristers go over Tesslar's statement. They all feel he would be an extremely vulnerable witness, particularly in the hands of such an examiner as Sir Robert Highsmith. Then we got into questions of whether or not any others will actually come to London, and if they do their value is questionable. In a British courtroom we don't have much of a chance ... if any.

'And there are other factors,' Lewin said. 'Kelno has a large reputation. The cost factors in fighting such a case are staggering. Technically, Mr Shawcross is held harmless of libel by your contract with him. However, if he remains as a codefendant and there is a judgment against you, Kelno will go after Shawcross first because his money is in England. Any sizable judgment could well force Mr Shawcross into dire straits.

'At the present moment, Richard Smiddy is ready to adopt a reasonable attitude. Just getting Mr Shawcross out of this with a damage settlement plus calling in thirty thousand copies of *The Holocaust* is going to take a heavy toll.

But at least he'll then be able to take in a partner. My own intuition tells me that Kelno wants personal exoneration more than money and in the end will settle reasonably with you. If you are stubborn and lose in England he'll go after some twenty foreign publishers to whom you have a great responsibility.'

'You're suggesting settlement for me?'

'Yes.'

'All right,' Abe said, 'I'd like to hire you as my solicitor.'

Lewin smiled and nodded.

'Now that you're my solicitor, you're fired,' he said and left the library.

Chapter Six

I WANT MY MOTORCYCLE. I WANT THE WIND TO TEAR THROUGH ME AT A HUNDRED MILES AN HOUR. I WANT MY KIDS. BEN IS NERVELESS. THAT'S WHAT MAKES HIM SUCH A GOOD FLYER. BEN KEEPS ME CALM AND VANESSA IS SOFT. EVEN THE ISRAELI ARMY DIDN'T HARDEN HER.

I LOVE LONDON. EVEN NOW I FEEL WARM HERE. I HAVE A MEMORY OF EVERY STREET IN THE MAYFAIR.

IN MY NEXT LIFE I'M GOING TO BE AN ENGLISHMAN. NO, A TOUGH POET PLAYWRIGHT FROM WALES. I'LL CLAW INTO LONDON, THEN INTO THE WEST END THEATERS. I'LL HAVE A MAD FLAT IN CHELSEA AND BE RENOWNED FOR CRAZY BRAWLING PARTIES IN WHICH I RECITE MY POETRY AND OUTDRINK ANY MAN IN THE ROOM.

WELL, THAT'S MY REINCARNATION ORDER, LORD. AS FOR THIS LIFE, I'M ABRAHAM CADY, WRITING JEW. LOOK AT ME CAREFULLY, GOD. I DRINK TOO MUCH. I COMMITTED ADULTERY TEN MILLION TIMES. I FORNICATE WITH OTHER MEN'S WIVES. NOW SERIOUSLY, GOD, DO I LOOK LIKE JESUS'S BROTHER TO YOU? SO WHY ARE YOU TRYING TO NAIL ME UP ON ONE OF YOUR GODDAM CROSSES?

WHY ME?

I'VE PLAYED BALL WITH MY PROFESSION. DID YOU SEE THE CONTRACT I GAVE UP TO WRITE THIS GODDAM BOOK? SO NOW THAT I HAVE A FEW DOLLARS IN THE BANK IS IT FAIR THAT I GET BUSTED?

GOD, I WISH THE KIDS WERE HERE. I WISH I WAS A WELSHMAN.

'All right,' Abe said, 'I give up. Where am I?'

'In my flat,' a woman answered.

'Soho or Chelsea?'

'Neither. West one, Berkeley Square.'

'I'm impressed.'

Abe had worked his way upright and slipped on his eye patch, then got the good one into focus. The bedroom was a display of wealth and taste. The woman . . . forty-five, handsome, pampered, preserved. Thick brown hair and large brown eyes.

'Anything go on between us? I mean, don't take it personally, but I lose my memory when I get too drunk.'

'You didn't do much of anything.'

'Where'd you find me?'

'The Bengal Club. Tucked away in a corner, stiff. It was the first time in my life I've seen a man sitting up straight and looking directly at me and completely unconscious. So I said to my companion, who is the funny man with the one red eye and my companion said, why it's the famous writer, Abraham Cady, and well, one just doesn't leave Abraham Cady sitting upright and unconscious with his one red eye shining like a stop light.'

'God, you're amusing.'

'As a matter of fact, some mutual friends told me to look after you.'

'What friends?' Abe asked suspiciously.

'Our friends at Two Palace Green.'

At the mention of the address of the embassy of Israel, Abe became serious. In his travels he always knew where to reach a 'friend' and 'friends' knew how to contact him. Often the meetings were indirect.

'Who are you?' Abe asked.

'Sarah Wydman.'

'Lady Sarah Wydman?'

'Yes.'

'Widow of Lord Wydman, London branch of Friends of the Hebrew University, Friends of Technion, Friends of the Weizmann Institute?'

She nodded.

'I'd like to meet you again, under happier circumstances.'

Her smile was lovely and warm. 'What can your tummy hold?'

'Orange juice. Gallons of it.'

'You'll find an assortment of things in the guest bathroom.'

'All prepared for me.'

'Never can tell when you'll run into a distressed writer.'

Abe pulled himself together. The guest bathroom was extremely well equipped, especially for a lover. A guy wouldn't have to pack a thing. Razor, after shave lotion, new toothbrush, Alka-Seltzer, talcum, terry cloth robe, slippers, and a deodorant. He showered his way back to life.

Lady Wydman set down the *Times*, letting her glasses fall to her bosom, where they were held by a thin gold chain, and poured the first of Abe's orange juice.

'What's up, Lady Sarah?'

'Sarah will do. There is a prevailing feeling among our friends that Kelno is guilty of some pretty nasty goings on at Jadwiga. They asked me if I would look into the matter. I'm quite active in the Jewish Community.'

'Well, Sarah, I've got a problem.'

'Yes, I know. Does the name Jacob Alexander mean anything to you?'

'Only that he's a prominent Jewish solicitor here in London.'

'He's quite involved with Jewish affairs. There's a great deal of interest in keeping you in this case.'

'Why? The Jews are looking for a new martyr.'

'There seems to be some interesting new evidence.'

Lady Wydman's Bentley passed along Lincoln's Inn Fields, one of the largest squares in Europe. Near the center gazebo nurses from the Royal College of Surgeons played netball during the noon hour and doctors got in a quick set of doubles on the grass courts. At the wall at Searle Street there were posts marking the place where a turnstile once stood to keep the cattle from grazing on Holborn.

They passed into Lincoln's Inn through the New Gateway and just beyond the Great Hall the magnificent gardens and walkways unfolded.

Much of Lincoln's Inn was leased to solicitors. Solicitors had offices. Barristers had chambers. The law offices of Alexander, Bernstein, and Friedman occupied the basement, ground level, and first floor of 8 Park Square. A top-hatted assistant porter waved Lady Wydman's Bentley into a reserved parking space and Abe followed her into a maze of cubbyholes, creaking floors, endless stacks of papers, walls of books, hidden nooks and stairs that made up the quaint OFFICES of Alexander, Bernstein, and Friedman, Commissioners of Oaths.

Alexander's secretary, a miniskirted young lady named Sheila Lamb, who had taken a lifelong ribbing for that name, entered the tiny waiting room inundated with back copies of *Punch*.

'Follow me, please,' she said.

Jacob Alexander arose from behind his desk, a tall slender man with bushy gray hair who could have been someone's conception of a Biblical prophet. He greeted Cady warmly and spoke in the deep tones of a trained rabbi.

Sheila Lamb closed the door behind her as she left.

'We have spoken among ourselves at great length,' Alexander said. 'It would be unthinkable to apologize to Adam Kelno in open court. It could be taken in the same context as apologizing to the Nazis for our outrage over the extermination camps.'

'I'm well aware of the issues,' Abe said, 'also our chances.' He went on to recite Lewin's disastrous predictions and that Shawcross was probably out of it.

'Unfortunately, Mr Cady, you are an international symbol to Jew and non-Jew alike. The man who wrote *The Holocaust* must assume responsibilities he cannot divest himself of.'

'What kind of support am I going to get?'

Alexander shrugged. 'Maybe yes, maybe no.'

'I still can't foot the bill.'

'Neither can we,' Alexander said. 'But once we engage the action, I believe you'll find support.'

'And if a decision goes against us?'

'There's always bankruptcy.'

'I hear that word too often. I think you're asking too much. I am not positive in my own mind that Kelno is guilty.'

'And if I convinced you Kelno is guilty.'

Abe was shaken. Through it all he had hoped for a loophole to get out with some sense of honor. But, if he were shown cold evidence there was hardly a way he could back off. Lady Wydman and Alexander looked at him and both of them searched. Is this the man who wrote *The Holocaust*? Was his courage merely paper courage?

'I guess,' Abe said, 'anybody can be a hero as long as it doesn't cost him anything. I'd better have a look at what you've got.'

Alexander pressed the buzzer and Sheila Lamb responded. 'Mr Cady and I will be flying to Paris. Put us on a flight around six o'clock and book two singles at the Meurice. Call the I.F.J.O. representative in Paris, Mr Edelman, and give him our arrival time and get him to contact Pieter Van Damm and tell him we will be in tonight.'

'Yes, sir.'

'Pieter Van Damm,' Abe whispered.

'That's right,' Alexander answered, 'Pieter Van Damm.'

Chapter Seven

Pieter Van Damm greeted them warmly in the foyer of his sumptuous apartment on Boulevard Maurice Barres. Along with Cady and Alexander there was Samuel Edelman, French representative of the I.F.J.O.

'I'm honored,' Abe said, grasping the hand of the world-famed violinist.

'The honor is mine,' Van Damm answered.

The maid took their coats and hats. 'My wife and children are in the country. Come, come.'

An enormous study held a gallery of presidents and kings photographed with the man whom many believed to be the world's greatest violinist. A French walnut antique Pleyel grand piano was carelessly stacked with sheets of music near his practice stand. Van Damm showed off a pair of Amati Violins with the childish pride of one who obviously enjoyed his renown.

They grouped about on a sofa and chairs in an alcove looking down to the Bois de Boulogne, settling in with cognac and whisky.

'L'Chiam,' Van Damm said.

'L'Chiam,' they responded.

Van Damm set his drink down. 'I suppose I should start from the beginning. I was twenty-four when the war broke out, married, with a child and a first violinist with the Hague Symphony. My name at that time was Menno Donker. You know the story of how we were forced into hiding. Roundups began by the Germans in the summer of 1942 and then, the large scale deportations in the winter and spring of 1943.'

Van Damm halted a moment, pained with memory. 'I was deported in the winter of 1942 in an unheated cattle car. My child froze to death on the way and my wife was taken for gassing at the selection shed when we arrived at Jadwiga.'

Abe bit his lip and clenched his jaw to hold back tears. No matter how many times he heard the story it tore at his soul.

'You told it all so well for all of us in your novel,' Van Damm continued. 'I was sent to work in the medical compound. Adam Kelno was the chief of the prisoner/doctors, and I was assigned more or less as a clerk/orderly. I kept records, ordered medicine, scrubbed floors, whatever.'

'So you had a day to day relationship of sorts with Kelno?'

'Yes. In the summer of 1943 I was approached by a Czech prisoner by the name of Egon Sobotnik. He was a member of the underground and solicited my help in forging death certificates, smuggling medicine, and things of that nature. I agreed, of course. Sobotnik's official job was to keep the surgical records so I learned of the experiments being carried on in Barrack V. Between us we kept a diary on Barrack V and smuggled it out of the camp in bits and pieces.'

'Were you ever in Barrack V, yourself?'

'Only to be operated on. Kelno got wind of my activities and I was transferred to Barrack III, which held the raw material for the experiments. At first I was to look after six younger Dutch boys who had their testicles irradiated by prolonged exposure to X ray. It was part of an experiment to sterilize all the Jews. You wrote about that. We were on the upper floor of the barrack and the women below. It seems they had X-rayed a number of young women also.

'In the evening of November 10, 1943,' Van Damm's voice shook, 'fourteen of us were taken from Barrack III to Barrack V. Eight men, six women. I was the first to go. You see, Mr Cady, I am a eunuch. Adam Kelno removed both of my testicles.'

Abe felt as though he were going to vomit. He stood up quickly and turned his back to the others. Van Damm stirred his cognac and gazed at its color and took a small sip.

'You were healthy when he did this?' Alexander asked.

'Yes.'

'Was Dr Mark Tesslar in the operating room?'

'As I said, I was the first one and Tesslar was not there then. I learned later that there was so much commotion they sent for him to keep the victims calm. Tesslar took care of the men afterward. Without him I don't think I would have lived. A woman doctor, a Maria Viskova, took care of the girls on the floor below. And also, there was a French woman doctor who came from time to time, mostly with the girls.'

'We are in contact with both of them,' Alexander said.

Van Damm told the rest of his story in monotone. After the liberation he made his way back to Holland to learn that all of his family had been exterminated.

He drifted to Paris, sorely in need of medical attention, and was pulled together by a saintly doctor. At first he wanted to study for the rabbinate, but his mutilation and the results of it were so obvious it was not possible.

Menno Donker hovered close to insanity. He was made to take up the violin again as therapy. With the help of a constant and devoted physician he was able to receive shots and hormones to give him a semblance of masculinity; a little beard, a deeper voice. With the physician always in attendance he was able to play. The rare poignancy that marked his music was born from the pits of tragedy. In a short time, the public found his genius. It was a small miracle in itself that a eunuch could have such lust and vigor required of a great virtuoso.

After the war he met the daughter of a prominent Dutch Jewish family of Orthodox learning. They fell in love in a sort of a way that seemed lost in today's world. It was a spiritual and religious union. For a long time he was able to conceal his secret and then came that awful moment when he had to tell her.

It made no difference. She wanted to take the vows with him, regardless. After a bitter struggle with his conscience he went to her parents and as religious Jews, they agreed and made a secret marriage contract knowing the union could never be consummated physically.

It is said that there is no more devoted or happier couple alive than the Van Damms. Twice they left on sabbaticals of a year's duration and each time they returned with an adopted child. Insofar as the world and the children themselves knew, the Van Damms were their natural parents.

Alexander and Edelman wept openly as Pieter Van Damm finished his story. Abraham Cady, now returned to being the practiced journalist, sat granite-faced.

'And you changed your name to Van Damm when you began your concert career.'

'Yes. It was a family name.'

'What became of Sobotnik, the diary you smuggled out, the surgical records?'

'Disappeared. Egon Sobotnik was alive when Jadwiga was liberated, but he simply disappeared.'

'We will turn over heaven and earth to find him,' Alexander said.

'What you have just told us,' Abe said, 'will bring another tragedy to yourself, your wife, and your children. It may bring great harm to your career.'

'I think I understand the consequences.'

'And you are willing to say all of this in a courtroom.'

'I'm a Jew. I know my duty.'

'When Kelno did this to you, did he have any consideration for you at all?'

'He was brutal.'

Abraham Cady was not the kind of man to live protectively, yet he felt both doomed and ashamed of having wanted to pull out. The strain plus the sorrow swept him.

'Do you have any further questions?' Alexander asked.

'No,' Abe whispered, 'no.'

Chapter Eight

Immediately upon his return from Paris a meeting with Shawcross and the solicitors was arranged. It was a nightmare. Haggling went on for hours.

Even with the evidence of Van Damm, Lewin was reluctant to let Shawcross enter the case. Jacob Alexander argued, in return, that Shawcross had made a great deal of profit from *The Holocaust* and other Cady books and should bear a part of the burden, if only a fraction.

A dozen side conferences were called.

'You've whittled them down enough,' Shawcross said. 'Abe is willing to take the full brunt of any judgment against us. I don't think we can ask more.'

'He may sign a contract to that effect but suppose he decides not to honor it?'

'Come to your senses. Geoff Dodd's resignation is sitting on your desk.'

They convened in the cluttered conference room. Shawcross rejected Sheila Lamb's offer of tea. His unlit cigar hung limply as he avoided Abe's searching stare.

'I've been advised to pull out,' Shawcross said.

'What, no lecture about integrity? You're very good at giving those,' Abe said in rising anger.

Alexander grabbed Abe. 'Excuse us for a moment, gentlemen,' he said, and moved out into the hallway where they had conferred a dozen times during the day. Abe sagged against the wall.

'Oh, Jesus,' he moaned.

Alexander's firm hand was on his shoulder as they stood in silence for several moments. 'You've done your best,' Alexander said. 'I have been wearing two hats, the Jewish hat and the hat of a friend. I must speak to you now as a brother. We have no chance with Shawcross out.'

'I keep thinking about my trip to Jadwiga,' Abe said. 'I saw the room where they were operated on. I saw the claw marks gouged out of concrete walls in the gas chamber in that last desperate second of life. Who in the hell has a choice? I keep thinking over and over it was Ben and Vanessa. I wake up and hear her screaming on the operating table. Where do I go from here, Alexander? A clay hero? My boy flies for Israel. What am I going to tell him? All over the world the kids are pointing a finger at us and demanding to know who stands for humanity. Well, at least I have more choice than Pieter Van Damm had. I will not apologize to Adam Kelno.'

Mr Josephson, managing clerk of Alexander, Bernstein, and Friedman for nearly two decades, sat opposite his grim master.

'Cady is going to have a go at it alone,' Alexander said.

'Bit chancy,' the wise old figure answered.

'Yes, a bit. I'm thinking about our lead counsel. Thomas Bannister. He stood for extradition against Kelno two decades ago.'

Josephson shook his head. 'Tom Bannister is the best in England,' he agreed, 'but who can put the bell around the cat's neck. He's so deep in politics he hasn't done much in court in the past few years. On the other hand, Bannister would like the smell of this case.'

'Those were my thoughts. Give old Wilcox a call,' Alexander said in reference to Bannister's clerk.

'I can't promise results.'

'Well, have at it, anyhow.'

Josephson turned at the door. 'Is Abraham Cady daft?'

'The Americans would call it, ballsy.'

Wilcox was a shrewd barrister's clerk of forty years' standing, beginning as a messenger boy and working his way through menial jobs in The Temple from third assistant clerk on up.

For thirty-five years he had been in chambers in the Paper Buildings, Inner Temple, entering almost the same day as the young junior Thomas Bannister. Over the decades he had grown up with his master, helping him achieve a near unmatched eminence at the bar, take silk as a Q.C., growing in the political field, being named a cabinet minister, and now groomed as a possible future prime minister of Britain. In chambers with seven thriving juniors, at a fee of $2\frac{1}{2}$ per cent Wilcox was among the wealthier clerks in Inner Temple.

Thomas Bannister's name was synonymous with impeccable integrity even in a place where integrity was commonplace. A confirmed bachelor, he lived in an apartment in Inner Temple.

After having served successfully as a minister, he was in line to be the party's next leader. Bannister's name was spoken more and more often.

The two foxes, Wilcox and Josephson, fenced about in traditional protocol.

'Well, what have you got, Mr Josephson?'

'Big one, indeed.'

Which brought on lovely thoughts of his commission. Wilcox continued to play it terribly cool.

'We are solicitors for Abraham Cady, defendant against Sir Adam Kelno.'

'That is a juicy morsel, all right. Didn't think he would defend that. Well, which of my gentlemen do you have in mind?'

'Thomas Bannister.'

'Come now, you can't be serious.'

'Extremely serious.'

'I could do right well by you with Devon. Brightest junior I've seen in the last twenty years.'

'We want Bannister. Any barrister is obliged to fight any case so long as his fees are met.'

'Don't be unreasonable,' Wilcox said. 'I've never barred anyone from your offices or any other solicitor. This could affect Bannister's whole career.'

'I'm afraid I have to say that I understand.'

Chapter Nine

'Nightcap, Tom?'

'I'd love it.'

The chauffeur held the door open. Lady Wydman emerged followed by Thomas Bannister. 'Morgan, wait for Mr Bannister and take him back to The Temple.'

'Oh, please let him go. I'd love to walk about a bit and take a taxi back. I don't get much chance to walk around London, these days.'

'As you wish.'

'Good night, ma'am, Mr Bannister. When will you be needing me?'

'Not till noon. I have a fitting at Dior.'

She handed Bannister a cognac. He warmed and paced the floor characteristically. 'Cheers.'

'Cheers.'

'Lovely evening, Sarah. I can't remember when I've enjoyed one more. I'm a cad for neglecting you and forcing you to ask me out but the work load has been extremely heavy.'

'I certainly understand, Tom.'

'Lucky for me I can't turn you down.'

'I hope not,' she said.

Bannister sat and let his legs stretch. 'Now that you've wined and dined me, I would like to know what particular thing you're going to ask of me that I can't turn you down for.'

'It's the libel suit between Sir Adam Kelno and Abraham Cady. I'm certain you know why I would be interested. Jacob Alexander is representing Cady.'

Bannister's usual deadpan betrayed him. 'Didn't I see Josephson in my chambers a few days ago?'

'Yes. We're having trouble getting to you these days. I think the party wants to put you in plastic and deep freeze you until the elections.'

'I've raised hell about this with them before. I wonder what kind of prime minister they think I'll make by ducking controversies.'

'Will you look into it, then?'

'Of course.'

'One thing, Tom, if you decide to take the case they're going to be hard-pressed. It's the kind of thing a single man ought not to be asked to fight. Rather something that a great corporation or a government would undertake.'

Bannister smiled. His smiles were small and infrequent and, therefore, twice as meaningful. 'You are heavy in this. Tell me, Sarah, what kind of a chap is this Abraham Cady?'

'Manners of a dock worker in a boardinghouse, idealistic as a naive child, bellows like a bull, drinks like a fish, and tender as a lamb. He's no English gentleman.'

'Yes, writers can be like that. Strange breed.'

One could not escape the feeling he was entering a holy place when he climbed the ancient stone steps of the Paper Buildings toward the chambers of Thomas Bannister.

His room was a bit more dandy than that of his fellow barristers. Richly and tastefully furnished save the gaudy portable electric heaters on the floor.

Bannister and Cady, two trained professionals, sized each other up as Alexander observed tensely.

'Well,' Thomas Bannister said, 'Kelno did it all right. We're not going to let him get away with it, are we?'

There was visible relief.

'We are all aware of how enormous and difficult the task ahead is going to be. Most of the burden in the next year will fall on you, Alexander.'

'It shall receive my full energies and we are not without allies.'

'Gentlemen,' Abe said, 'I believe I have the finest representation possible. I have no intention of telling you how to conduct this case. But, there is one condition. Under no circumstances is Pieter Van Damm to testify. I know this places an added weight on us, but I think I'd rather lose. It's my first and only order.'

Alexander and Bannister looked at each other and mulled it along. Their admiration was confused by taking their strongest legal point from them. Yet, it's all on principle, isn't it, Bannister thought. I rather like this Cady chap. 'We shall do our best,' Bannister said.

'Must you really leave tomorrow?' Lady Wydman asked Abe.

'I want to see Ben in Israel. Vanessa is coming home with me. I've got to get to work.'

'I'm going to miss you like the devil,' she said.

'Me too.'

'Can I make a tiny scene?'

'You're a girl. It's your prerogative.'

'You know I adore you, but I'm too damned proud to be just another item in your collection, and I know I would be very silly, and fall in love with you, and be a jealous sow throwing temper tantrums bargaining for a commitment, and do all those bloody stupid things women do that I detest. I know I can't handle you and it really aggravates me.'

'That's very good for my morale,' he said, taking both her hands. 'I've got a problem, Sarah. I'm not capable of giving all the love I have to a woman, only to my children. And I'm not capable of receiving the kind of love a woman like you has. I can't commit, even in a game. What we have here between you and me are two chiefs and no Indians.'

'Abe.'

'Yes.'

'You'll need me when you come back for the trial. I'll keep you warm.'

'O.K.'

She flung her arms about him. 'Oh, I'm lying. I'm crazy about you, you bastard.'

He held her very gently. 'The first time I saw you I knew there was something very special about you. You are a lady. A gentleman leaves a lady with her dignity.'

'Have my bill prepared. I'll be leaving for the airport in an hour or so.'

'Yes, Mr Cady. It's been a pleasure to have you with us. Oh, sir, some of the staff brought copies of your book. Would you mind terribly signing them, sir?'

'Sure. Send them up to my room and stick a piece of paper with their name in each book.'

'Thank you, Mr Cady. There's a gentleman waiting for you in the bar.'

Abe took a seat opposite Shawcross slowly and ordered a scotch with ice.

'I changed my mind,' Shawcross said.

'Why?' Abe asked.

'Don't know really. Pieter Van Damm hasn't left my thoughts. Well, Abe, I mean fair play is fair play. It's the only proper thing to do. Damn it all, I am an Englishman.'

'L'Chiam.'

'Cheers. You give Ben and Vanessa my love, will you, and when you get back to Sausalito don't worry yourself about Kelno, get cracking on that novel of yours as soon as you can.'

'Shut up for a minute, will you.' Abe pondered. 'Shawcross, you're what the Lord had in mind when he made publishers.'

'Very kind of you to say. You know I told Geoff and Pam and Cecil I was going to go it with you. They withdrew their resignations. They're standing by me.'

'It doesn't surprise me. They're decent people. Before this is all over with a lot of men and women are going to have to show what they're made of.'

Chapter Ten

February 1966

Sir Adam Kelno's paper was studiously received and deeply respected by the Royal College of Surgeons in Edinburgh. Not an inspired speaker or fully in command of English, he was, nonetheless, an eminent authority on malnutrition, administration of mass medicine, and human durability under duress.

Although his personal practice continued modestly in Southwark among working class patients, he wrote and lectured at length in his specialty.

Speaking at the facility in Edinburgh always came as an added pleasure and he scheduled those lectures so he could combine the trip with a motor holiday.

Once cleared of the population center, the wildness and emptiness of the central lowlands fled by the window. Angela turned up the heater and poured some hot tea from the thermos. Adam could drive all day in the morbidity of Scotland with total enjoyment of the respite from the long hours in London.

They slowed for a thatched roof barren village, where black Angus cluttered the main street and a pair of husky Scots on horseback herded them toward the pasture.

The smell of dung penetrated into the car.

For a moment Adam was in Poland in his own village. It was not like this. His village had been flatter and greener and poorer and even more primitive. But all countryside and all peasants and all their villages stirred a sting of memory.

A third horseman clip-clopped in front of the car, bringing him to a complete halt. There was a boy of perhaps twelve on the horse and a pair of dogs raced at the ankles of the cows.

SO THERE I AM AND THAT BEAST OF A MAN OVER THE ROAD WOULD BE MY FATHER. OH, THAT POOR BOY. WHAT CHANCE DOES HE HAVE IN THIS PLACE? WHAT CHANCE DID I HAVE? AND MY FATHER WITH A MIND AS BLEAK AS THE ROCKS IN THE LONELY FIELDS.

SPUR YOUR HORSE, LAD! SPUR IT AND GALLOP OFF. RUN TO THE CITY AND SAVE YOURSELF.

I HATE YOU, FATHER!

Adam shifted into low gear and inched his way behind the cattle.

I HIDE IN THE HAY. MY FATHER STOMPS INTO THE BARN AND ROARS MY NAME. HE KICKS THE HAY AWAY AND JERKS ME TO MY FEET. I CAN SMELL THE STINK OF ALCOHOL AND GARLIC FROM HIM. HE KICKS ME TO MY KNEES AND BEATS ME UNTIL HE MUST STOP AND WHEEZE TO CATCH HIS BREATH.

HE SITS ACROSS THE TABLE FROM ME REEKING WITH HIS ODORS AND REELING. THE BORSCHT AND MEAT SLITHER DOWN HIS CAKED BEARD AS HE STUFFS HIS MOUTH LIKE AN ANIMAL. HE BELCHES AND LICKS HIS FINGERS AND COMPLAINS THAT HE OWES THE VILLAGE JEW MONEY. EVERYONE IN THE VILLAGE OWES MONEY TO THE JEW.

HE GRABS ME, SHAKES ME, AND LAUGHS AT MY FEAR. WHY DOESN'T HE BEAT MY

BROTHERS AND SISTERS? WHY ONLY ME? BECAUSE MY MOTHER LOVES ME THE MOST, THAT'S WHY.

THROUGH THE CRACKS IN THE WALL THAT SEPARATE OUR ROOMS I SEE HIM STANDING NAKED. HIS PENIS IS ENORMOUS AND BLACK AND UGLY AND FILLED WITH VEINS. IT GLISTENS FROM WHAT CAME OUT OF MY MOTHER. HE SCRATCHES IT AND PLAYS WITH HIS HUGE HANGING TESTICLES.

I HATE HIS PENIS AND TESTICLES! IT MAKES MY MOTHER CRY WHEN HE DOES IT TO HER. HE GRUNTS LIKE A PIG WHEN HE IS ON HER.

IF I HAD MY WAY I'D TAKE A ROCK AND SMASH HIS TESTICLES. I'D CUT THEM OFF WITH A KNIFE.

I WANT TO SLEEP CUDDLED WITH MY MOTHER. LIKE SHE USED TO DO BEFORE I GREW TOO OLD. HER BREASTS WERE LARGE AND WARM AND I COULD BURY MY FACE IN THEM AND TOUCH THEM WITH MY FINGERS. SHE DOESN'T MIND BECAUSE I AM STILL LITTLE. I RUN AND HIDE IN HER SKIRTS AND SHE LIFTS ME TO HER AND HOLDS ME AGAINST HER BREASTS.

THEN HE WILL FIND ME AND PULL ME AWAY FROM HER AND SHAKE ME AND BEAT ME. I AM ALWAYS FILLED WITH BRUISES.

I MUST RUN TO THE CITY, WHERE HE CAN NEVER FIND ME AGAIN.

THE SNOW COVERS THE GROUND AND I STAND BY MY MOTHER'S GRAVE. HE KILLED HER, AS THOUGH WITH HIS OWN HANDS.

HE IS OLD NOW AND UNABLE TO BEAT ME AND HIS FILTHY ORGANS NO LONGER FUNCTION.

'Adam! Adam!'

'What? Eh ... eh ...'

'Adam!'

'What?'

'You are speeding. You're driving almost a hundred miles an hour.'

'Oh, sorry. My mind must have wandered.'

The clinic was filled, as usual, but Terrence Campbell was down from Oxford for a few days so things were right. Terry would begin his medical training in Guy's Hospital in the fall. It would be so wonderful to have him always close at hand. The boy worked with him through the day giving shots, doing lab work, taking tests, consulting his guardian on diagnosis. He was a born physician.

The last of the patients were gone and they retired to his office.

'What do you make of this,' Adam said, putting an X ray to the light.

Terry studied it. 'Shadows. A spot. T.B.?'

'I'm suspicious of cancer.'

Terry looked at the name on the envelope. 'That poor woman has five children.'

'Cancer has no conscience,' Dr Kelno answered.

'I know, but what will happen to the children? They'll have to go to an orphanage.'

'I have been wanting to talk to you about this sort of thing. It is the one part of medicine where you show a marked weakness. In order to be a good physician you must build an intellectual reservoir that will enable you to stand the sight of a dead friend. The physician who gets emotionally involved with his patients cannot exist long.'

Terry shook his head that he understood but continued to stare at the X ray.

'Well, on the other hand, she may not have cancer and if she does it may not be terminal. There's something else I want to show you.' He opened his desk drawer and handed Terry a legal document with a check attached to it, in the amount of nine hundred pounds.

'What is it?'

'An apology from the printers to be read in open court. What is more, the solicitor for Shawcross has been in touch with Richard Smiddy to negotiate a settlement. I understand that Cady was in London and left rather frantically.'

'Thank God it will soon be over,' Terry said.

'I'm glad you helped make me do it, you and Stephan. I'm going after Cady. I will take him to task in every country where his filthy book was published. The Americans in particular will pay dearly.'

'Doctor,' Terry said softly, 'when you went into this, you did it for a lofty purpose. It's beginning to sound as though you are bent on vengeance.'

'Well, what of it?'

'To seek revenge for the sake of revenge is an evil in itself.'

'Don't quote to me from the Oxford philosophers. What do you think this Cady deserves for what he has done?'

'If he concedes his mistake and wishes to purge himself you have to adapt a charitable attitude. You can't hound him to death.'

'The same kind of charity I received in Jadwiga, in Brixton. The same kind of hounding. No more, no less. They're the ones who say an eye for an eye.'

'But don't you see that if you adopt this attitude, you put yourself in a position of behaving like ... well, a Nazi.'

'I thought you would be proud of this,' Adam said, closing the drawer.

'I am, Doctor, but don't destroy yourself seeking revenge. I don't think Stephan would want that either.'

Sir Robert Highsmith snipped away at the myriad of rose stalks, leaving only the healthiest to grow later in the summer. He puttered with a particular detachment in his garden in Richmond Surrey.

'Darling, tea is ready,' Cynthia said.

He tugged off his gloves and made to the conservatory of his small manor, which had been the gatehouse of a royal estate two centuries earlier.

'Roses should be lovely this year,' he mumbled.

'Robert,' his wife said, 'you've been rather far away all weekend.'

'Kelno affair. Strange happenings.'

'Oh? I thought it was almost over with.'

'So did I. Suddenly old Shawcross did a complete turn about when it appeared he was on the verge of an apology in open court. The Cady chap has come to London and is going to fight the case. Shawcross has joined him. The most puzzling thing of all is that Tom Bannister has taken the case.'

'Tom? Isn't that rather risky of him.'

'Chancy, indeed.'

'Do you suppose Sir Adam has told you everything?'

'It would leave one to wonder, wouldn't it?'

Chapter Eleven

Jerusalem – April 1966

Dr Leiberman responded to a ring of the bell in his flat on David Marcus Street.

'I am Shimshon Aroni,' the man before him said.

'I was expecting you'd find me,' Dr Leiberman answered.

Aroni, the famed Nazi hunter, followed the doctor into his study. His sixty-eight years were deceptive. Aroni was keen and active behind a hard wrinkled face. By contrast Franz Leiberman was soft and fatherly.

'I have read the stories you have planted in the newspapers and magazines. Who did you find?'

'Moshe Bar Tov at Kibbutz Ein Gev. He gave me the names of the others. All told, four men, two women, whom you have treated over the years. You know what is going on in London. I have come to you because of your relationship with these people. It would be easier to convince them to testify if their doctor cooperated.'

'I won't cooperate. They've suffered enough.'

'Suffered? If you're a Jew you suffer. You never stop suffering. What about you and your family, Dr Leiberman. How many did you lose?'

'My dear, Aroni. What do you want? To put them on display like animals. To speak in a public courtroom about their mutilations. The women in particular will never be well. With careful treatment, the devotion of their families, they are able to carry on what appears to be a normal existence. But what has happened to them is buried in a dark room. They risk a dangerous traumatic shock if they have to bring it all up again.'

'It will be brought up again. We will never allow this to be forgotten. We will throw it up for the world to look at at every opportunity.'

'You are hardened by years of hunting war criminals. I think you are a professional vengeance seeker.'

'Perhaps I went mad,' Aroni said, 'when my wife and children were torn from my arms at the selection center at Auschwitz. What has to be done, has to be done. Do I see them separately or do you cooperate?'

Franz Leiberman knew Aroni was a relentless tracker. He would never let go. One by one he would drain and shame each of them into testifying. At least if they met together as a group, they could give each other courage.

Alexander, Berstein & Friedman
Solicitors
8 Park Square
Lincoln's Inn
London WC 2

April 30, 1966

Shalom Alexander:

I report progress. I have met with six victims whose names and preliminary statements are attached. I have convinced them they have no choice but to come to London. Franz Leiberman will travel with them. He will be a calming influence.

Through discussions I have learned the name of two other victims, one Ida Peretz nee Cardozo, who lives in Trieste. I leave to see her tomorrow.

Also, one Hans Hasse of Haarlemmerweg 126 in Amsterdam. I suggest you supply this information to the I.F.J.O. in The Hague.

I will continue to report as events warrant.

Yours,
ARONI

Warsaw Zakopane Poland, May 1966

Nathan Goldmark had aged seedily. When his position as an investigator for the secret police in the matter of war crimes ceased to exist he wormed his way into the hierarchy of the Jewish Section of the Polish Communist Party.

Most of Poland's Jews had been exterminated by the Nazis. Most of the survivors fled. A minute minority of a few thousand chose to remain for reasons of old age and fear of the hardships in beginning a new life. A few stayed as idealistic Communists.

Writers such as Abraham Cady took the view that the extermination camps would not have been possible in a civilized Western country that did not agree in spirit with what the Nazis were doing. There were no extermination camps in Norway or Denmark or Holland or France or Belgium despite their occupation nor in Finland or Italy despite the fact they were German allies. Poland, however, with its centuries' tradition of anti-Semitism was a practical place for the Auschwitzs and Treblinkas and Jadwigas.

In order to live down this reputation Poland later went through the motions of keeping a Jewish community in the country as a showpiece to the world that things had changed under communism. Intact were a few synagogues, a small Jewish press, and a national theater kept as superficial and pitiful remnants of the once great community of three and a half million.

Using Nazi methods of forcing the Jews to do it to themselves, a separate Jewish branch of the Communist Party was invoked upon them with the mission of keeping and controlling some kind of Jewish population. They tried vainly to flog life into the theater and press with Communist slogans.

Nathan Goldmark, a crafty politician whose sole ethics were survival and servitude, was put to good use as a tool of the regime.

His train had climbed into the Carpathian Mountains where the last snows of winter were retreating into the glacier fields. Zakopane, in addition to being a winter resort, was Poland's most important center for tuberculars.

He had come to keep an appointment with Dr Maria Viskova, chief medical officer of a workers' sanitarium and of the rarest breed, a Jewish Polish Communist out of belief. As a national heroine she had chosen to work away from Warsaw and the Nathan Goldmarks, whom she despised.

Her appearance, of one who has known enormous tragedy, had been softened by the years and translated into compassion. In her fifties, Maria Viskova was a silvered and handsome woman. She closed her office door behind her. A late spring storm of half rain, half heavy wet snow was falling.

Nathan Goldmark unbundled and crouched over her desk, hiding his bitten nails and tugging at the collar over the skin rash on his neck.

'I am in Zakopane to speak to you on the Kelno matter,' he said. 'It has been brought to our attention you have been contacted by certain Western elements.'

'Yes, by a firm of solicitors in London.'

'You know our position about international Zionism.'

'Goldmark. Don't waste my time or the time of my patients with this nonsense.'

'Please Comrade Doctor. I have traveled a long way. Twenty years ago you made a statement against Kelno. The committee feels your position is no longer valid.'

'Why? You were eager enough to extradite him to Poland for trial. You yourself took my statement. What changed your mind? Kelno has never answered for what he did.'

'The matter became invalid when the Hungarian, Eli Janos, failed to recognize Kelno in a police line-up.'

'You know as well as I do, Goldmark, that Dr Konstanty Lotaki was also doing these operations with Kelno and that in all likelihood it was Lotaki who castrated Janos.'

'Pure speculation. Besides, Lotaki has purged himself of guilt and totally rehabilitated himself as a dedicated Communist.'

'It is nothing short of criminal that Lotaki has never been brought to justice. What is all this about, Goldmark? The guilty have suddenly become innocent. Twenty years or a hundrd years do not absolve them of their crimes. And what of Mark Tesslar, who saw Kelno at his work?'

'The committee feels that the word of Tesslar cannot be relied upon.'

'Why? Because he defected? Does that make him a liar?'

'Comrade Doctor,' Goldmark argued, 'I can only convey the recommendations of the committee. In the days we were trying to extradite Adam Kelno the British were attempting to discredit the legitimate Communist government of Poland. Today we look to the West for cooperation. The committee feels that it is best not to stir up old hatreds. After all, Kelno has been knighted. For Poland to cooperate in this trial could be considered as an affront to the British...'

Goldmark chewed at his fingernails under the heat of the glare of Maria Viskova.

'There is another matter and it is that of Abraham Cady, a Zionist provocator and an enemy of the Polish people.'

'Have you read *The Holocaust*, Goldmark?'

'I don't wish to comment on that.'

'Don't worry, I won't report you to the committee.'

'It is filled with slanders, lies, provocations, and Zionist propaganda.'

The snow fell more heavily. Goldmark, the master at avoiding eyes, was all but shattered. He decided to walk to the window and comment on the weather. The courage of Maria Viskova was well known. Her dedication as a Communist was above question. One might think, for the good of the party, she would yield on the issue and save them embarrassment. How would he be able to report her attitude back to Warsaw? The thought occurred to him that the secret police should enter the matter and silence her. But then, the Zionists would get wind of it and create an international scandal.

'I intend to go to London at the time of the trial, Goldmark. What are your intentions?'

'It is a question for the committee,' he answered.

Paris Rambouillet – June 1966

The home of Dr Susanne Parmentier a few miles south of Paris was neat, quaint, and with a touch of elegance, as Jacob Alexander had envisioned it. He and Samuel Edelman, the French I.F.J.O. representative, were led by a bent old servant to the drawing room after which he fetched Madame Parmentier from the garden.

She was quite aged, in her mid or late seventies, but there was a Gallic twinkle in her eye. She seated them in a room of high taste most prominently adorned with silver framed photographs of her late husband, their children, and grandchildren.

Alexander excused himself for his fractured French accent.

'When I received the letter from Maria Viskova stating she had given you my name I had very mixed thoughts on the matter. As you can see I am quite old and decrepit and not altogether well. I am not so certain I can be of much help, but Maria said to see you and so, here we are.'

'We've studied your situation as an inmate of Jadwiga and we definitely feel the importance of your testimony,' Alexander said.

She shrugged and gestured heavily with her hands and arms as she spoke. 'I only knew of Kelno's activities secondhanded. I cannot swear to it through personal observation.'

'But you are close to Mark Tesslar.'

'We are like brother and sister.'

'Strange, he never gave your name.'

'He was only honoring my wishes. Until I received Maria Viskova's letter I saw no reason to bring up the past.'

'Let me ask you a direct question,' Alexander said.

'I will try not to give you an evasive French answer.'

'The case may largely depend on Tesslar's testimony. What is your opinion of his reliability? As a practicing psychiatrist, Dr Parmentier, I'd like a view detached from your personal friendship with him.'

'To speak to you in lay terms, Mr Alexander, I would say something happened to him that day in November when he witnessed Kelno's surgery. The impact of the trauma may have caused him to cloud his judgment.'

'It is a gamble we must make, as you know. What about Kelno's charges that Tesslar was an abortionist before the war and later in the concentration camps?'

'A fantasy of Adam Kelno. Anyone who knows Mark Tesslar knows he is a humanitarian. He left Poland to finish his medical studies in Switzerland because of anti-Semitism. Both Maria Viskova and I will swear he never performed an abortion for the Nazis.'

'Will you come to London?'

'I have meditated for many hours. I have conferred with my pastor at great length and prayed for divine guidance. As a Christian, I have no choice but to testify.'

The sparkle left her eyes and she was weary. She plodded to a spray of flowers, nipped a pair of tea roses, and placed one in each of their boutonniere buttonholes.

'There is a woman in Antwerp who was operated upon on that day. After the war I gave her psychiatric care for several years. She is a person of great character. Her scar will never heal, but I know she would never forgive me if I did not take you to see her.'

Chapter Twelve

Millie brought in the morning mail. Abe thumbed through the envelopes and smiled. There was a letter from Vanessa. He would save that for last.

He opened a letter from his French publisher, who moaned prolifically but enclosed a check for two thousand dollars to help defend the libel suit.

All of his publishers had now been accounted for. The first to come through with five thousand dollars had been his German publisher, a militant anti-Nazi who had been sentenced to death for his implication in the plot to kill Hitler and who cheated the gallows as a result of a bomb raid on Berlin, which allowed him to escape prison.

They all contributed something, except the Swedes. The smaller publishers beat their chests the loudest.

At last he opened Vanessa's envelope.

Kibbutz Sede Boker
July 25, 1966

10 Morningside Lane
Sausalito

Dear Daddy:

You have been reading between the lines since you left Israel last winter. Yossi and I have fallen deeply in love. The summer in the desert has been hot and oppressive, yet it has failed to dampen our spirits or our feeling for one another.

I don't know why this should make me feel sad except that taking on the commitment to him means ending a part of my past life. Yossi has another year to go in the Army and four years at the university. It is going to be a long pull and I don't feel I ought to burden him with a marriage.

I dread having to write my next words for they say that I won't be coming to America. With things getting worse again on the borders, I am reluctant to leave Israel even for a visit. The exception, of course, is to be with you in London during the trial.

Having shared with you the writing of *The Holocaust* I know what you will have to go through on an even more difficult new novel, and I feel as though I have let you down.

Ben asked me to write in his behalf as he will be on special maneuvers for a fortnight. He's quite the Israeli officer, grown a large moustache, and is filled with sabra bluster and confidence. Ben's not serious about any girl in particular but all of them in general. Rather like his father in that respect.

He will also try to arrange leave in order to be in London so let us know when the trial is due.

Yossi has never been out of Israel. I hope he can also join us.

Daddy, I hope I haven't hurt you too much.

Your loving daughter.

VANESSA

August 3, 1966

My dearest Vinny:

I'd lie if I said I wasn't disappointed, but I agree with your decision one thousand percent. The one thing we have never gone for is a daughter with a daddy hang-up. It's at this time of life I feel some guilt about all the months and years I've had to spend away in my work, but I think we've made it up during our times together and certainly in our relationship.

The closer I come to starting the book the more I realize the less I know. I'm not *young* enough to know everything. Only college kids are young enough to have all the answers and they seem very very intolerant.

It amuses me that this massive anti-establishment of today will be the establishment of tomorrow. In a few years the red hots will have to cool off and take over. Despite a number of innovations they will basically fall in love, marry, have children, struggle to raise their families, and search for a moment of peace. Very same bag I had.

But what is going to happen when *they* inherit the establishment? Will they be as tolerant of beats, junkies, rebels, rioters, and God knows what's coming up in the future. Well, I think they'd better start getting a little more tolerant of us old bastards who may have a little light to shed.

What I really wish is that they had a hero who wasn't an anti-hero. Something to live and strive for rather than the 'divine' mission of leveling everything to the ground. Something in this world like what you and Ben have found.

It appears that we won't come to trial until spring. I hang on every news broadcast gravely concerned over what appears to be an inevitable second round with the Arabs. Well, it's the price of our Jewishness, yours in Israel . . . mine waiting for me in London. Will they ever let us alone?

My love to everyone. Tell your Yossi I wrote him to be sure to attend to his homework.

DAD

Chapter Thirteen

Mary Bates slipped a miniskirt over her panty hose, then zipped up a pair of knee-length boots. Terrence Campbell propped up in bed on an elbow. He loved watching Mary dress, especially when she sat before the mirror without her bra, combing out her long blond hair. Miniskirts were crazy, he thought. They went about with freezing bottoms but if they wanted to show it, Terry would look.

Mary came over and sat on the edge of the bed. He opened the covers to invite her in. 'Love,' she said, 'I can't.'

'Quickie.'

'You are naughty. Up now. You'll be late for your first class.'

'One little taste.'

She threw the covers back and bit his bare behind gently.

'Jesus Christ, it's cold,' Terry cried.

'Look at his poor little shriveled up thingie.'

'Wake him up.'

'Tonight.'

She spun off the bed before he could grab her and made to the tiny sink and stove on the opposite side of the room. It was only one room and a sort of bath, but Mary had managed to doll it up with odds and ends and clever sewing. Anyhow, it was theirs. After a year of Terry coming down from Oxford and making love in parked cars, on living room couches, and in cheap hotels at last they had some privacy.

The room was in a turning off the Old Kent Road, within walking distance of Guy's Hospital and Medical College, where Terry had begun his studies.

Terry shivered at the breakfast table. Mary was a lousy cook. It would be nice if Mary and Mrs Kelno would become friends and she would learn to cook.

'We have a bloody uncivilized country,' Terry grumbled. 'Here in the middle of the twentieth century in an advanced Western nation you'd think the bloody flats would have hot water and central heating.'

'We'll have it someday,' she said.

Young love can overlook a lot of discomforts and they were strong for each other after more than a year.

'I'll be going straight from school to the Kelnos,' he said. It was a weekly ritual he looked forward to. A hearty augment to their thin diet. 'Will you be coming from work?'

'Can't come tonight, Terry. I talked to my sister yesterday and we made a date to take in a flick.'

Terry pouted. His toast was like a board. He broke it, smeared it in the egg yolks, and crunched it. 'This will make three weeks in a row you haven't been to the Kelnos.'

'Terry, let's don't get into an argument now.' Then she sighed and took his hand. 'Love, we've been all over it a thousand times. My family has disowned me. Sir Adam doesn't like me or our living together.'

'He's going to damned well respect you, Mary. I've written my father about you. Hell, he and mother had two children together before they were married and God knows they loved each other. Now, you just call your sister and break your date.'

'We haven't got a phone.'

'Call her from work.'

'Terry. What Sir Adam is really afraid of is that I *will* marry you. I'm just a plain little shop girl, really not good enough.'

'Rubbish.'

Or was it, Terry thought. A lot of their friends had the same arrangement. Students at Guy's. Their girls supporting them. When he graduated from Oxford and came to London they decided they weren't going to yield to the hypocrites, and they'd live together. The families of the girls invariably wanted marriage. Marriage meant respectability. An outdated notion of respectability.

The parents of the boys felt their sons could do better. After all, what kind of a girl would just leave her home and live with a student in a walk-up room? Not the kind they would want him to marry.

And all of the girls, despite their declarations of independence, really wanted marriage. So, in defying tradition they actually sought it.

Mary wanted to marry Terrence Campbell more than anything in life. There really wasn't much novel about it at all.

Dinner was late. Sir Adam Kelno attended a cocktail party in his honor. In the past six weeks there had been as many luncheons, dinners, and parties. The old Polish community of London was suddenly alive with a cause and even though they were permanently settled in England, they would continue to dream.

The libel case was a matter of Polish honor. His supporters were liberally sprinkled with high-standing British sympathizers. Adam silently gloried in this hero's role.

'I do hope,' Angela said, 'Mary knows she is welcome here.'

'I suggest you give her a call and tell her that,' Terry said.

'And teach her how to cook,' Adam said. 'You look like a scarecrow.'

'All medical students look like malnutrition victims,' Terry said. 'Remember?'

After dinner, things calmed. Adam had lectured at Guy's and was vitally interested in every aspect of Terry's studies. For the first year student it was mostly a concentration of chemistry, physics, and biology. Nothing really meaty for him yet.

Adam attempted not to bring up the subject of Mary Bates but instead made a general attack on the younger generation.

'Who,' he asked Terry, 'has to clean up the mess from overdoses of LSD and attempted abortions and venereal disease? I do. I have a clinic full of them. There is no morality left.'

'I have to get home now.'

'I don't understand Stephan, either. I don't understand any of you.'

Chapter Fourteen

One of the prime movers of the British legal machinery is the Master system. Masters are a kind of assistant judges or referees. The Master has been a barrister ten years or more before his appointment and sets the mode and preparation of a trial. They sit in chambers in the Royal Court of Justice doing away with much of the legal boondoggle that lawyers use to plague courts in other parts of the world.

The Master will make rulings on the number of witnesses permitted, the approximate time a case should be scheduled, the pre-questioning of witnesses, rulings on amendments to complaints and pleadings, and issuance of orders to produce documents.

In certain instances the Master will try a case.

His rulings are quick and concise, accurate to the application of the law, and rarely overruled later in court.

The Masters Chambers border a large room called the 'Bear Garden' where solicitors gather to make an appearance. They come in pin stripes, young hopefuls, tired old shabby ones, long haired, short haired.

The Master is seated behind a counter-like affair, calling opposing solicitors before him every several minutes. He scans their briefs.

'Well, what is it you want?'

The solicitors argue. Often an astute Master will say, 'Some things are so clear they shouldn't be argued.'

At that point the solicitors retreat to the Bear Garden having been subtly warned that one side is wasting his client's money and the court's time. An agreement may be made on the spot and a lawsuit stopped dead.

Before a lawsuit appears in court, the Master will have clearly set down the rules of verbal combat.

For an important trial such as the Kelno versus Cady affair, Master Bartholomew will take up the matter in his private chambers in deference to the appearances of barristers of the eminence of Thomas Bannister and Sir Robert Highsmith. In the chambers of Master Bartholomew came the first probings concerning the admissibility of certain witnesses and documents.

In the winter of 1966–67 formality was chucked. Tom Bannister's chambers and apartment were often too busy with political callers. Alexander's office in Lincoln's Inn was an impossible place of nooks and crannies unable to accommodate the mass of data flowing back from all over the world. There was a unanimous feeling that Shawcross's fabled library should become the command center. In an unusual move they gathered every several days to fine-comb the correspondence, discuss strategy, and make the decisions.

The first bridge was the selection of a junior barrister. Traditionally the solicitor selected a junior but because of Bannister's eminence they casually waited for him to drop a name. That name was Brendon O'Conner; a flamboyant, brilliant, sentimental idealist. O'Conner and Bannister represented different styles of advocacy but the junior was an incredibly tireless worker and the soundness of his appointment became apparent very early.

Libel was one of six non-criminal categories in which either party could call for trial by jury. It was extremely rare in civil matters. The jury or not the jury has baffled lawyers since the inception of law. They could be astute or extremely dull or compromise poorly in the pressure of the jury room debates. Again, they yielded to Bannister, who said that twelve Englishmen could not be fooled, and the Junior applied to the Master for a jury. The application was automatically granted.

The list of potential witnesses grew. In the hands of Bannister and O'Conner a weak case could be turned into a strong case. The flaw, obvious to the astute observer, was only a single eyewitness, Dr Mark Tesslar, who was highly vulnerable.

Pieter Van Damm held a mighty answer, but they remained under rigid instructions by Cady that he was not to testify.

There was a long shot that could bail them out, if Egon Sobotnik, the medical clerk at Jadwiga, were still alive, and if he could be found, and if he could be convinced to testify. If, if, if, if, if. All trails to find Sobotnik went cold. Even the dogged hunter Aroni, who was now putting his full time on the project, was unable to piece the clues together.

In his brief to counsel, Jacob Alexander prepared a massive document containing the statements of witnesses and all other relevant material.

The brief began with the year 1939 when Poland was attacked by Germany, then backtracked to a few slim facts on Kelno's prewar life. He was followed into Jadwiga Concentration Camp as a prisoner/doctor.

The document continued that in the middle of the war two Nazis, SS Dr Colonel Adolph Voss and SS Dr Colonel Otto Flensberg, induced Himmler to allow them to establish an experimental center in Jadwiga with the use of human guinea pigs. Voss's main experiments were directed to finding a method of mass sterilization of Jews and others whom the Germans deemed 'unworthy of normal life.' Such sterilized persons could be used as a labor force for the Third Reich with controlled breeding to keep the slave ranks filled. All others would be exterminated.

The brief cited some fifty books and war crimes trials for reference. Voss had committed suicide before his trial and Flensberg had escaped to an African country where he now resides and practices. A number of minor doctors and orderlies including Flensberg's assistant stood trial. Half of them were hanged and the others sentenced to prison.

Assisting Voss in his experiments were named three prisoner/doctors, Adam Kelno, Konstanty Lotaki, and a Jew, Boris Dimshits.

The brief contained an exhaustive study of the medical experiments, the facility, the doctors who refused to cooperate.

When all the material had been gone over and all the discussions weighed and the various defenses studied, a plea of 'Justification' was entered to the effect that what was said in *The Holocaust* was substantially true. The plea stated an admission that the defendants were the writer and publisher of the book. They further stated they could not support the figure of fifteen thousand experiments without anesthetic. They contended that the number was unimportant in that many experiments were carried out and carried out in a brutal manner and therefore the plaintiff had not been seriously libeled.

In the first week of April 1967 Abraham Cady arrived in London. Vanessa was there to greet him. Her fiancé, Yossi, and Ben would come from Israel shortly.

Samantha had remarried a squire type, Reggie Brooke, who was good with horses and hay, and accounts. The years had mellowed her bitterness toward Abe. When she knew he was coming she offered the flat in Colchester Mews for his stay.

The Crown Office of the Supreme Court informed the Sheriff of London to summon seventy-five persons from the Jurors Book.

The undersheriff selected a panel by a random lottery and the prospective jurors were informed and the list of their names made public for inspection.

The challenging of a jury in England is rare because a prima facie evidence must be produced against the juror. A lot of days and weeks of unnecessary courtroom haggling are thus avoided by the acceptance of the jury without challenge.

In Israel four frightened men and two women and their doctor continued to justify the coming trip.

In Warsaw, Dr Maria Viskova picked up her visa.

In Rambouillet, in Brussels, in Trieste, in Sausalito, in Amsterdam ... doubts raged, nightmares recurred. It would all take place soon. The whole thing would be relived.

The time of trial was drawing near with neither side showing an inclination to negotiate a settlement. The case that would 'never go to court' was close at hand and each party wondered how much the other really knew.

The Cady camp was engaged in a huge and urgent manhunt for the long disappeared, Egon Sobotnik, the medical clerk of Jadwiga.

In Oxford, Dr Mark Tesslar drew back from the microscope and set his glasses straight. His hand did not even tremble, which was rather remarkable for a man who had just seen the evidence of his own cancer.

'I'm sorry, Mark,' his colleague said.

'I guess we'll have to do an exploratory. The sooner the better.'

Tesslar shrugged. 'After two massive coronaries, I really don't think I'm going to escape this one. I want you to do the operation, Oscar. I'm not in great pain as yet whether the cancer is terminal or not. You are to keep me alive somehow, until I give my testimony. Afterward, we'll discuss what is necessary.'

BOOK FOUR

The Trial

Chapter One

THE HIGH COURT OF JUSTICE | April 16, 1967
QUEEN'S BENCH DIVISION | QUEEN'S BENCH COURT NO. 7
Before Mr Justice Gilray
Sir Adam Kelno, M.D., vs. Abraham Cady and others.

Jesus, Solomon, and King Alfred rated status over the front entrance of the Royal Courts of Justice, which fronted five hundred feet where the Strand becomes Fleet Street at Temple Bar. These three were joined by twenty-four lesser bishops and scholars.

Moses brought up the rear entrance on Carey Street, a block away.

The bell tower, which soared a hundred and sixty feet over Bell Yard, looked down on an enormity that could be described as neo-Gothic, neo-monastic, and neo-Victorian. A seemingly aimless scramble of spires, towers, oriel windows, cone-shaped steepled buttresses, Norman ornamental moldings, and ribs all in bulky gray stone blackened under years of soot.

On both sides of the entry stood the barrister's robing room. To the left, cameras are checked in. At the entrance to the mosaic-paved great hall is posted the Daily Cause List. The hall, two hundred and fifty feet in length, soars eighty feet in height and all of it is properly garnished with statues of the renowned. Running the lengths of a stone vaulted ceiling is a series of perpendicular trancery windows bearing stained glass coats of arms of all the Lord Chancellors of England.

The office of the Tipstaff stands on a balcony at the far end of the great hall. Once an official who carried a tipped staff to denote his office, today he maintains order within the court as a sergeant at arms.

All of this cumbersome building stands on six acres of ground flanked by St Dunstan's in the West and St Clement Danes, churches of old and stately stature.

The court stands as a giant planet of law with its satellites, the surrounding Inns and Chancery Lane.

The first law court was in Westminster Hall, dating from the thirteenth century, the trial place where Charles I and the martyr Thomas More found mock justice, and from whose bowels thundered history from the installation of Cromwell to the condemnation of Guy Fawkes and Essex. It is here that the royal, the noble, and the eminent lay in state before burial in the abbey over the way. Westminster Hall became outdated and inconveniently located to the proximity of the Inns of Court and so the Royal Courts came into existence in the mid-Victorian times.

Thomas Bannister and Brendon O'Conner, already wigged and gowned, crossed the Strand past a busy knot of assembled journalists, into the court and up the stairs to the consultation room opposite QB VII where Jacob Alexander, Mr Josephson, and Sheila Lamb had already assembled.

Now Sir Robert Highsmith and his junior, Chester Dicks, in bowler, pin stripes and carrying umbrellas and red and blue bags of stuff gowns and silk gowns, made off to the robing room.

Sir Adam Kelno arrived with his wife and Terrence Campbell pushing into the building abruptly. In his hand he clutched a cable from his son.

'There's Cady and Shawcross.'

'Mr Cady, would you say a few words on ...'

'Sorry, fellows. Strict orders. No comment.'

'Who's the girl?'

'I think that's Cady's daughter.'

Samantha and Reggie Brooke arrived unnoticed.

Ushers, court reporters, associates, journalists, spectators buzzed around QB VII in a cold stone hallway as the hour approached.

A narrow polished hallway separates the row of judges' chambers from the rear of their courtrooms. Justice Gilray adjusted his wig and the ermine collar on his scarlet robe. Gilray, a hawk-faced man, was long trained to appear emotionless and seemingly bored, a judge's role he enjoyed. Many judges and barristers sought membership in the Garrick Club, where they could hobnob with theatrical people for they in turn used the courtroom as their own special stage. This was particularly true of libel lawyers, many of whom were frustrated actors.

The courtroom filled slowly through a twin entry of green draped alcoves. Dead ahead was the Queen's Bench on a raised dais looking down on austere wooden benches and tables for the associate, the solicitors, barristers, the press, jury, and spectators. It was all heavily paneled in oak, topped with a series of leaded cathedral windows high up on the balcony level. A pair of chandeliers with bell-shaped shades hovered from a stone ceiling and the monotony of the wood was broken here and there by a wrought iron rail, a row of lawbooks, a relentless clock.

Cady and Shawcross took their places behind Brendon O'Conner in the first row of the spectator's benches. David nudged Abe and nodded down their row to where Angela Kelno and a handsome boy, Terrence Campbell, were seated.

Abe smiled to Samantha and Vanessa, who moved up behind them with Lorraine Shawcross and Geoffrey, Pam, and Cecil Dodd. Then he looked down to the solicitor's table, where Adam Kelno sat with unwavering calm. Abe had interviewed thousands of people and was shrewd in finding a betrayal of that calm as Adam looked around for his wife and son.

Suddenly Kelno and Cady were staring at each other across the room. The first exchange was hostile and then they probed and pondered. Abe continued to feel anger, but Kelno had a sudden puzzled expression of 'What are we doing here?'

Their attention was diverted by the jury filing in. Eight men, four women. They seemed totally nondescript. Twelve commonplace Englishmen and women to be found on any street.

A last flurry of whispers between barristers and solicitors and a shuffling for papers.

'Silence!'

Everyone arose as the Honorable Mr Justice Anthony Gilray entered from a door behind the Queen's Bench. The entire court bowed to him as he took his seat in a deep, high-backed leather chair.

Sir Robert Highsmith bounced to his feet and informally chatted with the judge in reckoning it would be a long trial.

Thomas Bannister arose. Of average build and good English looks, the power generated from within him. His voice was soft and seemingly monotone until one began to find its rhythm. He agreed that the trial would be lengthy.

Gilray swung his chair toward the jury box and advised them in the matter of serving under undue hardship. No reply. 'I should like to ask if any of you lost relatives in a concentration camp?'

Both Bannister and O'Connor came to their feet. Bannister turned and looked over his shoulder to his junior to advise him he had the matter in hand. 'If his Lordship establishes this kind of condition for the jury then we will have to establish opposite conditions, namely any peculiar sympathy in behalf of physicians, knights, former Polish nationalists ... all kinds of conditions.'

'I meant,' the judge answered, 'I would not wish anyone who has lost a relative in a concentration camp to have to undergo undue suffering because of the revelations of this trial.'

'In that case, I have no objection to the question.'

It was asked without reply from the jury and they were sworn in.

The clock ticked audibly between rows of lawbooks on the left wall as Sir Robert Highsmith unfolded his notes on the rostrum on his table and stretched his back with his hands on hips. He studied the jury for a long moment and cleared his throat several times. In an English court the barrister is obliged to remain standing behind the rostrum which limits his physical gestures and mobility. Unable to parade all over the courtroom he must be a quick thinking orator whose elocution is clear and in a manner easily grasped.

'My Lord, members of the jury,' Highsmith began, 'this is an action for damages for libel. A libel, I suggest, as damning as ever came before an English court. We are going to be asked to take ourselves out of the comforts of London in 1967, for what we are concerned with is a nightmare of a Nazi concentration camp that existed over two decades ago against a background of the most incredible hell ever created by man.'

He held up a copy of *The Holocaust* and with deliberate slowness opened it to page 167. Another beat in time passed as he looked directly at every man and woman of the jury individually. He read, pausing carefully, ' "Of all the concentration camps none was more infamous than Jadwiga. It was here that SS Dr Colonel Adolph Voss established an experimental center for the purpose of creating methods of mass sterilization, with the use of human guinea pigs, and SS Dr Colonel Otto Flensberg and his assistant carried on equally horrendous studies on prisoners. In the notorious Barrack V a secret surgery was run by Dr Kelno, who carried out fifteen thousand or more experimental operations without the use of anesthetic." Ladies and gentlemen of the jury, let me repeat this passage ... "fifteen thousand or more experimental operations without the use of anesthetic." '

He slammed the book shut and let it drop from the rostrum to the table with a thud and stared at the ceiling.

'What!' he shouted, 'could be a more horrendous and defamatory and dastardly an insult,' he said, rolling his r's mightily and bouncing off his toes and jabbing at the air like a boxer. 'What greater libel to a physician whose reputation goes far beyond the confines of his clinic. I should like at this time to read the words we have set out in the Plaintiff's Statement of Claim. I suggest, therefore, you be given this bundle of pleadings.'

'Do you have any objection, Mr Bannister?' the judge asked.

'Just what do you intend giving the jury?'

'Pleadings,' Highsmith answered, 'an agreed bundle of pleadings.'

Thomas Bannister took a bundle and handed it back to O'Conner, who thumbed through it, then whispered a few words. 'We are satisfied with reservation. There have been a number of interlocutory proceedings and addendums and there may be other relevant things.'

Each of the jury was given a bundle. Mr Justice Gilray asked them not to read it on their own. It was the first in what was to be a number of confusing steps in their legal education.

'In a libel action, the plaintiff has to prove three things. First, did the defendants publish those words. Well they don't deny that. Secondly, did the words refer to my client? They're not contesting that either. And finally, were the words defamatory. We would have to prove that except the defendant admits they are defamatory. Technically, my case is over with, and I could say go on and prove your case. But I intend to call forward Sir Adam Kelno and let you judge the character of this man and therefore the extent to which he has been libeled.'

Highsmith became cynical. 'Oh well, the defense says, that figure of fifteen thousand is not really accurate and by the way we know he didn't really operate without anesthetics. Well, they say, maybe several hundred or several dozen. You see, they really don't know. You will appreciate, of course, that Sir Adam Kelno was not a German, not a Nazi, but a Polish prisoner. An ally who was subjected to all sorts of terror saved only by the fact he was a skilled physician, and he used that skill to help his fellow creatures. He was an ally whose personal courage saved thousands ... Yes, I will use the number of thousands in clear voice, thousands from disease and death. The fact is, Sir Adam Kelno did perform or assist in some twenty thousand operations, but they were proper, necessary operations, and moreover risked his own life as a member of the underground.'

Sir Robert Highsmith went into Kelno's escape to England, his knighthood, and his distinguished work.

'This man has come here to clear his name. The printers of this book,' he said, snatching it up and holding it high, 'recognized what they had done and had the sense to apologize in open court and you might think that Abraham Cady and David Shawcross would have done the same instead of forcing us to travel this bitter road. You are a British jury and it is your charge to determine the severity of what has been done in an admitted libel to this innocent man.'

Chapter Two

'Sir Adam Kelno.'

He arose from the solicitor's table and gave the tiniest smile to Angela and Terry and walked up to the witness box, which stood to the left of the Queen's Bench and directly over the filled press rows.

'On which Bible do you wish to be sworn?'

'I am a Roman Catholic.'

'The Douay Bible, please.'

The judge turned to Kelno. 'I presume you will be in the witness box for quite a period. I suggest that the usher bring you a chair.'

'Thank you, my Lord.'

Sir Robert Highsmith established through Kelno a history from the graduation from medical school, the coming of the war, the joining of the underground, the arrest by the Gestapo, the fearful inquisition and the imprisonment in Jadwiga Concentration Camp in the summer of 1940.

'We were registered, bathed, shaven clean all over, and issued striped uniforms.'

'What sort of work did you do when you first arrived?'

'General labor.'

'Did the Germans realize you were a doctor?'

'Perhaps, perhaps not. In the confusion of thousands of slave labor arriving, my records may have been overlooked. In the beginning I was afraid to say I was a doctor because of the German policy of destroying educated and professional Poles.'

'But you changed your mind later?'

'Yes. I saw the suffering, and I felt I could help. I could not go on hiding my profession.'

'You yourself were a victim of the early conditions, were you not?'

'I came down with typhus from the lice. I was extremely sick for several months. When I recovered I made application for transfer to the medical compound and was admitted.'

'In addition to typhus, did you suffer otherwise?'

'Yes, personal indignities.'

'Once, twice?'

'On dozens of occasions. We were punished for real or imagined infractions. The corporal in charge ran us from place to place. We were not allowed to walk. For standard punishment we were made to squat and duck walk hundreds of meters and if we fell behind we were beaten. There was also a serious outbreak of dysentery which I contracted. That was actually when I revealed I was a doctor. The Germans could not handle the epidemic.

'And after the epidemic subsided?'

'I was allowed to organize a surgical out patient clinic in a couple of the medical barracks. I treated things that could be done simply such as boils, abscesses, minor injuries.'

'Now, we are speaking of late in 1940. Would you describe the general condition of the medical facility?'

'Bad. We were short on all supplies and even had to use paper bandages.'

'Were there any other qualified prisoner surgeons working with you?'

'Not at first. I had some assistants. The hospital facility was soon overrun with hematoma cases.'

'Would you explain that?'

'Severe bruising, particularly in the buttocks, causing excess bleeding in the tissues. They became septic or infected. Sometimes they contained a pint of pus. This affected the muscles so that the patient could not walk, sit, or lie down. So, I performed surgery to alleviate the suffering by an incision, a draining, and a gradual healing.'

'What was the cause of these hematoma cases?'

'Beatings by the Germans.'

'Dr Kelno, did you do any amputations in this early period?'

'Yes, mostly of small limbs such as fingers and toes due to frostbite or having been broken beyond healing by German beatings.'

Highsmith took off his glasses and leaned hard toward the witness box. 'Dr Kelno,' he said in a rising voice, 'did you ever operate when it wasn't necessary?'

'Never. Not then or later. Never.'

'Now then, during this time from the end of 1940 into 1942, how were you treated?'

'I was beaten on numerous occasions.'

'And what was the effect of those beatings?'

'Enormous bruises, some the size of a soccer ball. The pain was excruciating. I ran a temperature and my legs swelled until I developed varicose veins and formed phlebolith stones, which were removed after the war.'

'When did things take a turn at Jadwiga?'

'In the middle of 1941 when the Germans attacked Russia. Jadwiga was a major camp of slave labor which manufactured many things essential to the German war effort. They realized they were losing too many days of work by their brutal treatment of prisoners so they decided to develop reasonably proper medical facilities.'

'Can you recall a particular event that triggered the building of proper facilities?'

'In midwinter of 1941 a cold wave struck and we had thousands of cases of pneumonia, frostbite, and shock from exposure on our hands. We had little to treat them with, only water to drink. They were stretched out on the barrack floors side by side with barely room to walk between them and they died by the hundreds. Dead people cannot work in factories so the Germans changed their minds.'

'I'm curious, Dr Kelno, if the Germans kept count of the dead?'

'The Germans have a phobia about keeping meticulous records. During the epidemic they kept count by numerous daily roll calls that began at five-thirty in the morning. The living had to carry the dead outside. Everyone had to be accounted for.'

'I see, we'll get back to that later. So after the epidemic in the winter of 1941 you were allowed to build a proper facility.'

'More or less. We did not have enough materials so at night when the compound was clear of SS we went out on raiding parties. Later more supplies became available but never enough. However, it was made more bearable as other doctors were assigned to me. I was able to set up a fairly decent surgery in Barrack XX. The German doctors sent to work with prisoners were inferior and slowly the prisoner/doctors began taking over.'

'And what of your own personal position in all this?'

'For two years I was the chief surgeon and then in August of 1943 I was made titular supervisor of the entire medical facility.'

'Titular?'

'Yes, SS Dr Colonel Adolph Voss was the true superior and any other SS doctors had command of my activities.'

'Did Voss come in to see you often?'

'He was mostly in Barrack I through V. I stayed away as much as possible.'

'Why?'

'He was carrying on experiments.'

Sir Robert slowed and changed the volume and pace of his voice to denote a question. 'Were any records kept of your operations and treatments?'

'I insisted on accurate records. I felt it important so that there could never be doubts of my behavior later.'

'In what manner were these records kept?'

'In a surgical register.'

'One volume?'

'Several volumes were filled.'

'Listing every treatment or operation?'

'Yes.'

'And signed by you?'

'Yes.'

'Who kept this register?'

'A medical clerk. A Czech. I forgot his name.'

Abe passed a note to Shawcross. I FEEL LIKE STANDING UP AND YELLING 'SOBOTNIK' AND SEE IF HE REMEMBERS.

'Do you know what became of the registers?'

'I have no idea. Most of the camp was in chaos when the Russians arrived. I wish to God we had the registers here now because it would prove my innocence.'

Sir Robert was struck silent. The judge turned slowly to Kelno. 'Sir Adam,' Gilray said, 'with reference to proof of your innocence. You are the plaintiff in this case, not the defendant.'

'I meant . . . clear my name.'

'Continue, Sir Robert,' the judge said.

Highsmith jumped in quickly to erase the effect of Sir Adam's bumble. 'Now, all this time you were still a prisoner under German supervision.'

'Yes. Always a prisoner. The SS had orderlies to watch our every move.'

'Can you tell us the particular significance of Jadwiga West?'

'It was the extermination facility.'

'And you know that for a fact?'

'It was common knowledge. History has since proved it. I never personally saw Jadwiga West, but I was first informed by the underground.'

'And these German orderlies under Dr Voss, did they have any other duties than to spy on you?'

'They selected from my patients . . . victims for the gas chamber at Jadwiga West.'

A hush descended on the courtroom. And again, all that was heard was the clock. Englishmen had only heard of this in abstract. Here before them, Sir Adam Kelno, the color of white paste, had drawn the curtain and was playing on a stage of memory and horror.

'Would you like a recess?' the judge asked.

'No,' Adam answered. 'Not a day passes in my life that I do not remember.'

Sir Robert sighed, clutched the lapels of his robe, and lowered his voice so the jury had to strain to catch his words. 'In which manner were these people selected?'

'Sometimes the German would just point a finger at people as he passed through the ward. Those who looked the least able to survive.'

'How many?'

'It depended on how many were shipped to Jadwiga West from the outside. They filled the gas chamber quotas from the hospital. A hundred a day. Some days, two or three hundred. When thousands of Hungarians were shipped in they left us alone for a time.'

'How far was Jadwiga West located from your compound?'

'Three miles. We could see it. And ... we could smell it.'

Abraham Cady was thrown back to his own visit to Jadwiga and it was all vivid again. For an instant he looked to Adam Kelno with remorse. How in the name of God could any man stand up against what was going on?

'What did you personally do about the German selections?'

'Well, when they made a selection they painted a number on the victim's chest. We found that it could be easily washed off. We would replace them with patients who had died during the night. Since the Germans did not personally handle the bodies we were able to get away with it for a time.'

'How many people were you able to save by this method?'

'Ten to twenty out of every hundred.'

'For how long?'

'Many months.'

'Would it be fair to say you saved several thousand people in this manner?'

'We were too busy saving lives to count.'

'And did you use other methods to trick the Germans?'

'When they suspected we were sending corpses to Jadwiga West, they made up lists of names so we switched names. Many people alive today carried the name of a dead person for years in the camp. We studied their plans through the underground and often knew in advance when selections were going to be made. I would clear out the hospital wards as much as possible by sending people back to work or hiding them.'

'When you did this, did you take into consideration the national or religious origin of these prisoners?'

'Lives were lives. We saved those we felt had the best chance of survival.'

Highsmith let all of this sink in for a moment turning to Chester Dicks, his junior, and fetching needed information. He turned back to the rostrum.

'Dr Kelno. Did you ever give your own blood?'

'Yes, on numerous occasions. There were certain intellectuals, scholars, musicians, writers, we were determined to keep alive and at times we donated our own blood.'

'Would you tell the court what your own personal accommodations were like?'

'I shared a barrack with about sixty male staff.'

'And your bed?'

'A straw mattress stuffed inside with heavy paper. We had a sheet, a pillow, and a blanket.'

'And where did you take your meals?'

'At a small kitchen in one end of the same room.'

'What type of sanitation facility did you have?'

'One toilet, four sinks, and a shower.'

'And what kind of clothing did you wear?'

'A sort of striped denim.'

'With distinctive markings?'

'All prisoners had a triangle sewn over their left breast pocket. Mine was red denoting I was a political prisoner and there was a "P" superimposed to denote I was Polish.'

'Now, in addition to the extermination facilities at Jadwiga West, were there any other kinds of killings?'

'In addition to the SS, German criminal prisoners and German Communists were put in charge of the others and were often as brutal as the SS. Anyone they wished to eliminate they simply beat to death, then hanged the victim with his own belt and registered the death as a suicide. The SS knew these brutes were doing their work so they turned their backs.'

'Were there any other killings, official or otherwise?'

'I mentioned earlier that in the medical compound Barrack I to V was the experimental center. Between Barrack II and III there was a wall made of concrete. When the Jadwiga West facilities were overworked, a firing squad would execute dozens to hundreds.'

'Were there any other methods?'

'By a phenol injection in the heart. It caused death in seconds.'

'You saw the results of this?'

'Yes.'

'Were you ever ordered to give a phenol injection?'

'Yes, by an SS Dr Sigmund Rudolf, assistant to Colonel Flensberg. He told me to administer injections of glucose to several patients, but I smelled carbolic and I refused. The patients became alarmed and SS guards beat them to submission and they were tied to chairs, and he gave them a dosage of about 100 cc. They died almost instantly.'

'As a result, were you punished?'

'Yes, Sigmund Rudolf denounced me as a coward and my teeth were smashed.'

'Let us go back for a moment, Dr Kelno, to the experimental Barracks I to V. I believe it's been established that Colonel Voss and his assistant, Sigmund Rudolf, were the two primary doctors. Would you tell my Lord and the jury of your relationship with these two?'

'I had very little to do with Flensberg. Voss was experimenting on sterilization. One of the methods was through heavy exposure to X ray of the female ovaries and the male testicles. He had working with him a Jewish doctor, a Boris Dimshits. Dimshits must have known too much for he was sent to the gas chamber. Shortly afterwards Voss summoned me and another Polish doctor, Konstanty Lotaki, and informed us we would be called upon to operate from time to time in Barrack V.'

At last, the door to Barrack V was opening with its awesome secrets. Bannister and O'Conner made swift notes of every word. Gilray concentrated to cover an obvious strange emotion sweeping through him.

'Continue please, Sir Adam.'

'I asked Voss what kind of operations and he answered that I was to remove dead organs.'

'What was your reaction to all of this?'

'Lotaki and I were very upset. Voss made it clear that we would meet the same fate as Dr Dimshits if we did not cooperate.'

'You would be sent to the gas chamber for refusal?'

'Yes.'

'Having earlier refused to inject phenol, did it occur to you to refuse?'

'This was an entirely different matter. Voss said that SS orderlies would perform the operations if we refused. We decided to discuss it with all the other prisoner/doctors. We all concluded together that it would mean certain death to all of Voss's victims and as skilled surgeons it was mandatory that Lotaki and I save these people.'

'You say you spoke to *all* the other prisoner/doctors?'

'All except Mark Tesslar. There was his personal hatred of me from the time we were students in Warsaw. Later at Jadwiga he worked with Voss in the experiments.'

'Just a moment,' Thomas Bannister said, rising.

Adam Kelno sprung off his chair, gripped the rail, and shouted. 'I will not be silenced! It is Tesslar and his lies who drove me from Poland! It is all a conspiracy of the Communists to hound me to my grave!'

'Obviously,' Thomas Bannister said coolly, 'this situation calls for an objection; however, I don't think I'll make one at the present time.'

'Well, if you're not going to ask me to make a ruling,' Gilray said, 'then I won't make one. It seems that emotions are running rather high. I believe this will be a good time to recess for the day.'

Chapter Three

It was almost midnight when Terry arrived at the Kelno home. 'Where have you been?' Angela asked.

'Walking, just walking.'

'Have you eaten?'

'I'm not hungry. Is Dr Kelno still awake?'

'Yes, he's in his study.'

Adam Kelno was in a fixed, waxen position. He did not hear the knock or see the boy enter.

'Doctor –'

Adam looked up slowly, then turned away.

'Doctor, I've been walking. I mean, I've been thinking about what I heard today or trying to understand it. I guess none of us really knew what that place was like. It's rather different than reading about it. I just didn't know.'

'A little hard for your stomach, Terry? What you heard today may be the only nice parts of it.'

'Oh God, Doctor.' He slumped down and put his head in his hands. 'If I had only realized what I was doing. I'm so damned ashamed of myself.'

'You ought to be. Maybe it's too much for you to hear. Maybe you shouldn't come into the court again.'

'Stop it, please. I feel like the most loathsome kind of bastard. Funny how someone like me who has been given every advantage gets so caught up in his own problems, his own world, his own selfishness, that he loses sight of other people's needs or feelings or suffering.'

'All young people are selfish,' Adam said, 'but your generation takes the prize.'

'Doctor, are you ever going to forgive me?'

'Forgive you? Well, you really didn't bring the Germans to Poland.'

'I'll make it up to you someday.'

'Just do your studies and become a good doctor. That's all your father wants. It's all the making up I want.'

'I had a long talk with Mary today after court. We reached an understanding. I'd like to live here at home during the trial.'

'Of course. I'm glad, Terrence. Mary?'

'I don't know. It would not be good to add to the tension by having her here. We'll just have to see how we feel afterwards.'

Angela entered. 'Come on both of you, you've got to have something to eat.'

Terrence held the door open. As Adam passed he touched the doctor's shoulder, then went into his arms and cried as he hadn't cried since he was a little boy.

Lady Sarah Wydman's plane landed at Heathrow Airport at two in the morning. The weary customs official yawned at her ten pieces of luggage and waved her through.

Morgan, the chauffeur, helped a porter load his cart as Jacob Alexander bussed her on the cheek. 'Jacob, you didn't have to come out here this time of the morning.'

'How was your flight?'

'Routine.'

The Bentley pulled away followed by a taxi carrying the excess baggage. They cleared the tunnel and cloverleaf and sped down the dual carriageway for London.

'How is it going?'

'Well, the opening round goes to Sir Robert, of course. Was your trip successful?'

'Yes. Any word about Sobotnik?'

'Not a trace of him. Aroni doesn't give us much hope, either.'

'Then Abe is simply going to have to allow Pieter Van Damm to testify.'

'We can't budge Abraham on that. I came to meet you tonight because I have to unload on someone, Sarah. I'm worried about Mark Tesslar. We went up to Oxford to take a new statement and we've discovered he is a very sick man. He's only recently recovered from a severe heart attack. At any rate, we've taken a gamble on this Lotaki chap, the one who did some of the operations with Kelno. He's in Lublin, Poland, surgeon at a hospital. Lotaki is a fair-haired Communist now, who has never had any action taken against him. We are going on the theory that if he helps us in London it may help him in Poland so on that basis he may come to testify.'

'On the other hand he may decide to testify for Kelno as the easier alternative of keeping his name clear.'

'We are aware of that risk, but we have to make some desperation moves.'

They pressed on into London to Berkeley Square.

'Jacob, I won't be in condition to show up in court tomorrow. Be a dear and tell Abe I'll phone him after court.'

'Sarah?'

'Yes?'

'Why won't you let me tell him about the money you've contributed and raised?'

'No. You see, he's taken so much on himself I want him to feel he has unseen friends behind him all over the world. Anyhow, he has a thing about Jewish fund raisers.'

Chapter Four

'Before I continue with my examination, my Lord, Sir Adam would like to address the court.'

'I wish to apologize for my outburst yesterday, my Lord,' he said shakily.

'These things are apt to happen now and again,' Mr Justice Gilray said. 'I am certain that Mr Smiddy and Sir Robert advised you on the severity of this sort of thing in a British courtroom. With all due respect to our friends in America, we shall not permit an English courtroom to be turned into a circus. The court accepts your apology and admonishes you that any repitition will be dealt with severely.'

'Thank you, my Lord.'

'You may continue your examination, Sir Robert.'

Sir Robert popped off the balls of his toes, rubbed his hands together, and otherwise warmed himself up. 'Yesterday at recess, Sir Adam, you testified that after Colonel Voss informed you and Dr Lotaki that you would be operating to remove dead organs, you said you spoke to all the other prisoner/doctors save Dr Tesslar. Is that correct?'

'Yes.'

'Precisely, what kind of an opinion, or decision, or understanding was reached?'

'We had the example of Dr Dimshits being sent to the gas chamber, and we had no reason to believe Voss was fooling when he threatened to send us, too. We had his threat that the patients would be mutilated by unskilled SS orderlies. We decided to save as many lives as possible and at the same time try to induce Voss to cut down on his experiments.'

'Yes. And then you were summoned to Barrack V with Dr Lotaki from time to time to perform the removal of dead testicles and ovaries.'

'Yes.'

'How many times would you say this happened?'

'Eight or ten times. Surely under a dozen. I don't know about Dr Lotaki. More than likely the same.'

'Did you also assist him?'

'On occasion.'

'Approximately how many operations were performed on each of these eight or ten visits you made to Barrack V?'

'Oh, one or two.'

'But not a dozen?'

'No, of course not.'

'Or hundreds?'

'No.'

'And did you succeed in getting these experiments stopped?'

'Not entirely, but we continued to make our reluctance known so that Voss carried on only enough experiments to justify continuation of the center to Belin.'

'Did Tesslar ever come into Barrack V while you were performing surgery?'

'No, never.'

'Never, never once? Never once did he see you operate?'

'Mark Tesslar never saw me operate.'

Highsmith mumbled long under his breath to give the jury time to digest the point. 'Never once,' he repeated to himself and played with the papers on the rostrum.

'So then, with the full understanding of your colleagues you performed at very most two dozen of these necessary operations in the course of twenty thousand other operations.'

'Yes. We only removed organs destroyed by X ray. If we didn't remove them we feared they could cause tumor and cancer. In every single case I insisted the operation be entered into the surgical register.'

'Unfortunately,' Sir Robert said, 'the register is lost forever. We shan't go into that. Will you tell my Lord and the jury the manner in which these operations were performed?'

'Well, the victims were in a wretched emotional state so I took exceptional care to comfort them and advise them that what I was doing was for their own good. I was going to save their lives. I used the best of my surgical skill and the best anesthetics available.'

'On the matter of anesthetics. This of course you know is part of the defamatory statement by the defendant that you did not use anesthetics.'

'That is entirely false.'

'Would you explain what kind of anesthetics were administered and how it was done?'

'Yes. For operations below the navel I felt a spinal preferable to an inhalant.'

'Did you also have that opinion in Warsaw, London, and Sarawak?'

'Yes, very much so. A spinal relaxes the muscles much better and usually causes less bleeding.'

'Did you have someone administer these spinals in Jadwiga?'

'I did them myself because of the shortage of trained people. First I gave a pre-injection of morphia to deaden the general area and then the spinal.'

'Does this cause the patient severe pain?'

'No, only a prick when done by a specialist.'

'Where did you give this anesthetic?'

'In the operating room.'

'Now, what about post-operative care?'

'I told Voss that I must treat these patients until they made a full recovery and he agreed.'

'And you continued to visit them.'

'Yes, daily.'

'Do you recall any complications?'

'Only the normal post-operative conditions plus the poor facilities of Jadwiga. It was somewhat worse in these cases because of the trauma of losing a sex gland, but they were so happy to be alive I was warmly greeted and found them cheerful.'

'But they all survived, did they not?'

'No one died of these few necessary operations.'

'Because of your care and skill and post-operative attention.'

Thomas Bannister came up slowly. 'Aren't you leading your witness, Sir Robert?'

'I apologize to my learned friend. Let me rephrase the question. Did you do anything else special for these twenty or so patients?'

'I brought them extra rations.'

'Let us move on to another area for a moment. Dr Kelno, were you a member of the underground?'

'Yes, I was in the Nationalist underground, not the Communist underground. I am a Polish Nationalist.'

'Then there were two undergrounds.'

'Yes. From the moment we entered Jadwiga the Nationalists organized. We arranged escapes. We kept contact with the Nationalist underground in Warsaw and all over Poland. We worked into key positions such as the hospital, the radio factory, in clerical positions to get more rations and medicine. We manufactured our own radio.'

'Was there cooperation with the Communist underground?'

'We knew the Communists planned to take over Poland after the war and many times they turned in our members to the SS. We had to be very careful of them. Tesslar was in the Communist underground.'

'What other accomplishments did your underground achieve?'

'We improved conditions with more rations and medicine and the building of more sanitation facilities. Mainly, twenty thousand prisoners worked in factories outside the camp and the underground on the outside smuggled things to them which they brought back into the camp. In this manner we got vaccine which stopped another typhus epidemic.'

'Would you say this saved many lives?'

'Yes.'

'Thousands?'

'I cannot estimate.'

'By the way, Sir Adam. You mentioned a radio for contact to the outside. Where was it hidden?'

'In my surgery in Barrack XX.'

'Hummmmm,' Highsmith mulled. 'What were your hours in Jadwiga?' he continued.

'Twenty-four hours a day, seven days a week. After regular out patients hours set by the SS we continued to work in surgery and the wards. I took a few hours sleep here and there.'

Abraham watched the jury as Sir Robert and Adam Kelno piled a mountain of heroism, courage, and sacrifice before them. He looked to O'Connor, who was all business, to Bannister, who was totally relaxed and fixed on the witness. Below, Jacob Alexander's secretary, Sheila Lamb, wrote feverishly. At the associates table, the shorthand writers changed periodically. The London *Times* law reporters, both of whom were barristers, were accorded a special place in the courtroom removed from the overcrowded press rows. These were jammed with more and more foreign journalists arriving on the scene.

'We have gone through the administering of anesthetic by you in the operating room,' he repeated to ensure the point. 'Now did you in any way pride yourself in performing operations quickly?'

'No. But in Jadwiga there was so much surgery I trained myself to work fast but never so fast that it endangered a patient.'

'Did you wash your hands before every operation?'

'Of course.'

'And saw to it your patients were properly scrubbed.'

'My God, of course.'

'In the case of an ovariectomy, those performed on orders of Voss, what surgical methods did you adhere to?'

'Well, after the spinal took effect, the patient is taken off a trolley and strapped to the operating table.'

'Strapped? Forcibly?'

'For the patient's own safety.'

'Would you strap someone down for the same operation today in London?'

'Yes. It is standard procedure.'

'Continue, please, Dr Kelno.'

'Well, the operating table may be tilted.'

'How much? As much as thirty degrees?'

'I don't think so. When performing an operation in the lower region such as the pelvis if you tilt the table, the intestines roll back by themselves to give the surgeon an area to operate free from the loops of the intestines. I would make an abdominal incision, insert the forceps to lift the uterus, place a forceps between the tube and the ovary and cut the ovary off.'

'What do you do with the removed ovary?'

'Well, I can't keep it in my hand. It is usually put on a dish or some sort of receptacle held by an assistant. When the ovary is removed it leaves a pedicle or stump. This stump is covered to prevent it from hemorrhaging.'

'The stump or pedicle is *always* covered?'

'Yes, always.'

'How long does such an operation take?'

'Under normal conditions, between fifteen and twenty minutes.'

'And all of this is done with sterile instruments?'

'Naturally.'

'And you are wearing rubber gloves.'

'I prefer to wear sterile cotton gloves over the rubber gloves to prevent slipping. It is an optional matter of the individual surgeon.'

'Would you tell my Lord and the jury if the patient, who is semiconscious and without feeling, is able to observe all this?'

'No. We place a screen made of sterilized sheet so the patient is unable to observe.'

'What on earth do you do that for?'

'To prevent the patient from coughing or spitting into an open wound.'

'So then, the patient cannot see or feel. Would the patient be in a state of extreme distress?'

'Well, Sir Robert, no one is happy to be on an operating table, but they are not in what you would term, "extreme distress" at all.'

'And even though these operations were conducted in the Jadwiga Concentration Camp, would you be satisfied that normal surgical procedures were used.'

'It was more difficult there in many ways but it was proper surgery.'

After the luncheon adjournment, Sir Robert Highsmith took Sir Adam Kelno through his earliest meeting with Mark Tesslar as medical students in Warsaw.

They met again in Jadwiga, where Kelno claimed Tesslar continued to operate on SS prostitutes and later collaborated with the Germans on the experiments.

'Did Dr Tesslar treat any patients or look after them in the general medical compound?'

'He lived in Barrack III in private quarters.'

'Private quarters you say. Not like yourself sharing with sixty others.'

'In Barrack III many of the victims of the experiments were kept. Tesslar may have looked after them. I do not know. I avoided him and when we met I made such meetings brief.'

'Did you ever brag to him about doing thousands of experimental operations without anesthetic?'

'No. I am proud of my record as a surgeon and may have mentioned the thousands of operations performed in Jadwiga.'

'Proper operations.'

'Yes, proper. But my words have been distorted. I warned Tesslar about his own activities and told him he would have to answer for his crimes. It was like signing my own death warrant for when I returned to Warsaw he was already there and to cover his crimes, he brought charges against me and I had to flee.'

'Sir Adam,' the judge interrupted. 'I would like to offer a bit of advice. Try to answer Sir Robert's questions and not volunteer any other information.'

'Yes, my Lord.'

'How long did you remain in Jadwiga?'

'Until early in 1944.'

'Would you tell my Lord and the jury under what circumstances you left the concentration camp?'

'Voss left Jadwiga to take over a private clinic of the wives of high German naval officers in Rostock near the Baltic and he took me with him.'

'As a prisoner?'

'As a prisoner. I was referred to as Voss's dog.'

'How long were you in Rostock?'

'Until January of 1945 when Voss evacuated into the center of Germany. I was not taken with him. There was confusion among the Germans. I stayed in the area to treat many slaves and prisoners now roaming free. In April the Russian Army arrived. At first many of us were put into compounds for lack of papers, then I was released and made my way back to Warsaw. I arrived on

Easter Sunday of 1945 and immediately heard the rumors of charges against me. The Nationalist underground was still in existence so I was given false papers to work as a laborer in a cleanup gang. I fled to Italy to join the Free Polish Forces as soon as I could.'

'What happened then?'

'There was an investigation to clear me. I came to England and served in the Polish Hospital in Tunbridge Wells. I remained until 1946.'

'What happened then?'

'I was arrested and put into Brixton Prison while the Polish Communists tried to extradite me.'

'How long did you remain in prison?' Sir Robert said, with a voice growing acid over the British treatment of his client.

'Two years.'

'And after two years in Brixton following nearly five years in Jadwiga Concentration Camp what happened?'

'The British government apologized and I joined the Colonial Service. I went to Sarawak in Borneo in 1949 and remained for fifteen years.'

'What were the conditions like in Sarawak?'

'Primitive and difficult.'

'Well, why did you choose that place?'

'Out of fear.'

'Then your testimony is that you have spent twenty-two years of your life either as a prisoner or in exile for crimes you did not commit.'

'That is correct.'

'What rank did you attain in the Colonial Service?'

'That of senior medical officer. I rejected higher positions because of my work with malnutrition and lifting the living standards of the natives.'

'Did you write papers on this subject?'

'Yes.'

'How were they received?'

'I was eventually knighted.'

'Hmmmmmmm . . . yes . . .' Sir Robert glared at the jury almost in defiance. 'After which you returned to England.'

'Yes.'

'I'm curious, Sir Adam. Now, as a knighted British doctor, why you chose to practice in a relatively obscure clinic in Southwark?'

'I can only eat two chickens a day. I do not practice medicine for money or social standing. In my clinic I can serve the greatest number of needy people.'

'Sir Adam. Did you then or do you now suffer ill health from your years in Jadwiga, Brixton, and Sarawak?'

'Yes, I have lost almost all my teeth from beatings by the Gestapo and SS. I suffer from varicose veins, a hernia, stomach disorders from excessive recurrences of dysentery. I have neurological symptoms of anxiety and high blood pressure. I have insomnia and a bad heart.'

'How old are you?'

'I am sixty-two.'

'No further questions,' Sir Robert Highsmith said.

Chapter Five

Samantha backed into the door of the Colchester Mews with both arms filled with groceries in bags marked Harrods. A polite cabbie brought in the rest.

Abe was stretched out on the couch, a pile of newspapers strewn on the floor near him.

HERO OR MONSTER – *Evening News*

DILEMMA OF JADWIGA DOCTOR – *Herald*

HELL CAMP DOCTOR TESTIFIES – *Daily Worker*

SIR ADAM KELNO CONTINUES – *Times*

I HAD NO CHOICE – *Mail*

Mirror, *Standard*, *Telegraph*, *Birmingham Post*, *Sketch*, all careful to report accurately the events without editorial comment. Unlike some countries, the British press must be exceedingly careful not to try a man in the newspapers and magazines before he comes to court. In such cases when a newspaper becomes an accuser or prejudger, turning public sentiment, the paper can be named as a defendant to the action. It keeps journalism honest.

Abe yawned himself to his feet.

'Pay the driver, Abe,' Samantha said.

'Three bob on the meter, sir.'

Abe handed him a ten shilling note and told him to keep the change. He liked London cabbies. They were polite. The cabbie liked Americans. They tipped well.

'What's all this, Christmas?'

'The cupboard was bare and knowing you, you'd starve first. Did Ben get in all right?'

'Yes. He's out on King's Road probably hustling for a broad.'

Samantha set the bags down on the kitchen counter and began to empty them. 'Well, how come old Dad isn't out there with him?'

'I'm aging, Sam. I can't handle this young stuff anymore.'

'Why, Abe. Vinny's young man is up at Linstead Hall. I don't see what she sees in him. Very argumentative sort.'

'Just a normal Israeli sabra. Most of them are defensively aggressive from too many years living with their backs to the sea.'

'Abe, I heard a lot of talk after court today. People are ... are ...'

'Wondering?'

'Yes.'

'There's two sides to this story.'

'Scotch?'

'That would be nice.'

'Dreadful, dreadful business,' she said, wrestling with an old model ice cube tray. 'There's a lot of sympathy for Kelno.'

'Yeah, I know.'

'Are you going to be able to overcome it?'

'I didn't come to London to visit the Queen.'

The phone rang. Samantha answered. 'It's for you . . . a woman.'

'Hello.'

'Hello, darling,' Lady Sarah Wydman beamed.

'Hi, good to hear you. Alexander said you got in very late last night.'

'Sorry not to be there at the beginning, but I simply got overbooked with theater in New York. Dreary season. When do I get to see you?'

'Like tonight.'

'We can do one of the little restaurants in Chelsea or come to my place,' she said.

'I'd better stick close to the phone.'

'Good. I'll pick up something at Oakshottes and make dinner for you at the mews.'

'I didn't know you could cook.'

'You don't know a lot of things. Seven-thirtyish?'

'Deal.'

Abe hung up. Samantha was pouting openly as she handed him his drink. 'Who was that?'

'Friend. Friend of the cause.'

'How friendly?'

'Lady Sarah Wydman. She's very big in the Jewish community.'

'Everyone has heard of Lady Sarah and her charitable works. Will you be making love to her here?'

He decided to play her silly game. 'The mews is too small, what with Ben in the next bedroom. I like to ball where I can yell and scream and run around bare-assed.'

Samantha turned crimson and bit her lip.

'Come on, Sam, we've been divorced for years. You can't still be jealous.'

'Oh, I'm just a silly. I mean, Abe, no one has been quite like you. After all we did conceive Ben right here. I always have the memory, when I come down from Linstead Hall, about us. Do you ever get a twinge about me?'

'Truth?'

'I don't know if I want the truth or not.'

'Truthfully, yes. Sam, we lived together for two decades.'

'I got quite excited when I knew you would be in London for a long stay. When Reggie and I offered you the mews I knew I'd come to London and ask you to make love to me.'

'Christ, Sam, we can't do that.'

'Old chums like us? What's so terribly wrong?'

'Reggie.'

'He suspects it anyhow and he'd never be convinced we didn't. Reggie is a dear sweet stout type. As long as we don't throw it in his face, he wouldn't dare bring it up.'

'I've stopped sleeping with other men's wives.'

'Really, since when, darling?'

'Since I found out you can't fool the old man upstairs. You've got to pay off. Sam, please don't put me in the position of rejecting you.'

He handed her a handkerchief and she dabbed her tears. 'Of course, you're right,' she said. 'Frankly, I don't know who I like better, the old Abe or the new one.'

Lady Sarah, dressed in slacks and mink coat, arrived in her Bentley followed by Morgan carrying a sack of groceries.

She was a cordon bleu chef.

Abe turned tired very suddenly. He lay his head in her lap and she rubbed the back of his neck and his temples with a lovely practiced skill, then she slipped down beside him. Sarah was nearing the line when a woman was suddenly no longer attractive, but she knew how to make the best of what she had. He decided she had not yet crossed the line.

'Christ, I'm tired.'

'You really will be by the weekend. Let's go to Paris.'

'I can't. The witnesses will be arriving from Israel. I should be on hand.'

'Paris.'

'I may not be able to resist,' he grunted.

'Don't worry, love. Things will go better when Tom Bannister gets started.'

'Funny, I haven't taken my mind off Kelno. Poor bastard. What he's lived through.'

'It doesn't justify what he did, Abe.'

'I know. But I keep asking myself if I would have done any differently if I had been in Jadwiga.'

Angela was awakened by a gagging noise. She could see the beam of light from the opened bathroom door and rushed to it. Adam was on his knees vomiting into the toilet. When he was finished she helped him to his feet and he fell against the wall gasping. She cleaned the mess and put him down and applied a cold towel to his clammy forehead and neck.

Then, she medicated him and held his hand until the spasm was gone. The scent of disinfectant flowed in from the bathroom.

'I am afraid of Bannister,' Adam said. 'For two days he has sat there never taking his eyes off me.'

'You're in an English court. He can't bully you. Sir Robert will watch his every move.'

'Yes, I suppose you're right.'

'Shhhh ... shhhh ... shhhh ...'

Chapter Six

Abe entered the now familiar courtroom and for an awkward moment found himself standing next to Angela Kelno and Terrence Campbell. They exchanged hard looks. 'Excuse me,' Abe said, and slipped down the row next to Sarah Wydman and Shawcross.

'The plane will be in from Tel Aviv after the weekend, but Alexander said we were not to go out and meet them. We'll see them in mid-week,' Shawcross said.

Bannister and a very weary Brendon O'Conner filed in with Alexander and

Sheila Lamb from the consultation room at the same moment the jury made its appearance. Two of the women and one of the men carried cushions to alleviate the discomfort of the long sit on hard wood.

'Silence!' the usher said.

Gilray entered and the ritual rise and bow was made.

A preliminary announcement was made from the bench. Sir Adam Kelno had received a number of threatening phone calls and Gilray issued a stern warning that it would not be tolerated. Then he told Thomas Bannister to proceed.

Bannister unfolded his legs as Adam Kelno returned to the witness box, seated himself, and set his hands on the rail, thankful his tranquilizer was taking effect. Bannister played with the 'fee bag' on his robe.

'Dr Kelno,' he said in a voice softly contrasting Highsmith's. The entire tone of the room lowered. 'I appreciate the fact that English is not your mother tongue. Please ask me to repeat or rephrase any question you do not follow.'

Adam nodded and slowly sipped from the water glass to moisten his parched throat.

'What is the ordinary medical meaning of the term casus explorativus?'

'Ordinarily it is an operation performed in order to assist in a diagnosis, for example, to see the extent of a cancer.'

'Is that how you would describe the removal of a testicle or ovary?'

'Yes.'

'Sin referring to the left and dex to the right.'

'Yes,' he answered, remembering his instructions to keep his replies brief and not volunteer information.

'Would it not be correct to add that some kind of operation would be performed of this nature as the result of an X-rayed gland.'

'Yes.'

'For example, as part of Voss's experiments.'

'No,' he said sharply. 'I did not experiment.'

'Did you castrate?'

'A castration is done to a healthy man. I never performed a castration.'

'Weren't healthy men and women forced to be X-rayed?'

'Not by me.'

'Isn't it the usual practice to obtain the consent of a patient before you operate?'

'Not in a concentration camp.'

'From time to time weren't there German court orders to castrate a homosexual or other undesirables?'

'I recall no such incidents.'

HE'S FISHING, Chester Dicks wrote to Highsmith, who nodded to Kelno that he was doing fine. Adam became relaxed by the softness of Bannister's voice and the seemingly aimless line of questions.

'Had there been such cases, you would have certainly asked to see the court order.'

'I cannot speculate about something that did not happen.'

'But you would have refused to operate on a healthy man.'

'I never did.'

'Dr Kelno, did any other prisoner/doctors ever leave Jadwiga Concentration Camp to work in private German hospitals.'

'Dr Konstanty Lotaki.'

'Did he also perform operations in Barrack V in connection with Voss's experiments.'

'He did what he was ordered.'

'Was he ordered to remove testicles and ovaries?'

'Yes.'

'And he did that and he also left Jadwiga to work in a private German hospital.'

The first brief flush of comfort began to fade from Adam Kelno along with any ideas of an easy time with Bannister. I must be very alert, he thought, think out my answers with great care.

'Now, when you got to Rostock to work in the private clinic, you no longer wore prison clothing.'

'I don't think high ranking German naval officers would like their wives to be treated by a man in concentration camp stripes. Yes, I was given a suit of clothing.'

'Perhaps, they wouldn't like being treated by a prisoner,' Bannister said.

'I don't know what they liked and didn't like. I was still a prisoner.'

'But a rather special prisoner with special privileges. I am suggesting that you cooperated with Voss to work your passage.'

'What?'

'Would you try again, Mr Bannister,' the judge interjected. 'He does not understand the term.'

'Yes, my Lord. In the beginning you started as a laborer and took beatings and abuse.'

'Yes.'

'Then you became an orderly of sorts.'

'Yes.'

'Then a physician for prisoners.'

'Yes.'

'Then you were placed in charge of a very large medical complex.'

'In a manner of speaking. Under German control.'

'And finally, you became a doctor for German officers' wives.'

'Yes.'

'I suggest that you and Dr Lotaki the only two prisoner/doctors ever released from Jadwiga were released for their cooperation with SS Colonel Dr Adolph Voss.'

'No!'

Bannister stood motionless except for the repeating gesture of rolling his fee bag. He dropped the modulation of his voice even lower. 'Who wanted these operations performed?'

'Voss.'

'You knew full well he was experimenting on sterilization.'

'Yes.'

'By X ray.'

'Yes.'

'In fact, Dr Kelno, wasn't the removal of a testicle or ovary the second stage of the same experiment?'

'I am confused.'

'I'll try to clarify matters. Let's go through it step by step. These people were all Jews.'

'I believe so. Maybe a gypsy. Mostly Jews.'

'Young Jews.'

'They were young.'

'Exactly when were they brought into Barrack V for surgery?'

'Well, they were all kept in Barrack III as material for the experiments. They were X-rayed in Barrack V and sent back for a month, then returned for the operation.'

'Aren't you omitting a step?'

'I don't recall.'

'I suggest that prior to their being X-rayed they were brought to Barrack V and had a piece of wood shoved up their rectums in order to induce an ejaculation and this sperm was analyzed to see if they were potent.'

'I knew nothing about that.'

'Were they shaved before the operation?'

'Yes, they were prepared in a normal way.'

'Did they protest?'

'Of course they were unhappy. I spoke to them and told them it was necessary to save their lives.'

'You testified, I believe, that you were removing dead glands.'

'Yes.'

'How did you know they were dead?'

'It was quite easy to assume by the large radiation burns.'

'And you testified that you were afraid the irradiation could develop into cancer.'

'Yes.'

'So you operated as a doctor fully convinced that what you were doing was for their welfare.'

'Yes.'

'You never said to any of them, if I don't get yours, the Germans will get mine.'

'I deny these kinds of lies with all my soul.'

'You never said that?'

'No, never.'

'On occasion, you testified to assisting Dr Lotaki.'

'Maybe a dozen times.'

'Did you ever overhear him say that?'

'No.'

'You have stated a preference for spinal anesthetic.'

'Under the conditions and for this type of operation.'

'And you testified that you gave a pre-injection of morphia.'

'Yes.'

'Even with morphia, isn't a spinal injection rather painful?'

'Not if given by a skilled surgeon.'

'Why the pre-injection of morphia?'

'To induce a feeling of peace and a state of semiconsciousness.'

'And this was all done by you in the operating room?'

'Yes.'

'Even though there is a screen between the patient's vision and the area of the operation, I suggest he can see it all from the reflection lamp overhead.'

'Reflection is very distorted as a mirror.'

'So then, you saw no reason to put the patient completely under.'

'I have so many operations of all kinds to do in a single day I must use the quickest and safest method.'

'What was the actual state of these patients?'

'Drowsy and semiconscious.'

'I suggest, Dr Kelno, they were quite awake because no morphia had been given.'

'I say I gave them morphia.'

'Yes. Well now, was Voss present at these operations?'

'Yes.'

'And he told you what he was doing. You were aware he was experimenting to sterilize healthy, potent men.'

'I knew.'

'And of course he was conducting those experiments because at that time no one really knew whether X ray could or could not sterilize a sexual gland.'

Kelno gripped the rail and balked as Bannister's trap became obvious. He looked to his counsel quickly but they did not rise.

'Well?' Bannister pressed ever so softly.

'As a physician and surgeon I knew some of the harmful effects of X ray.'

'I suggest that no one really knew about this. I suggest no work had ever been done in this field.'

'Voss may have consulted with a radiologist.'

'I suggest not. I suggest that no radiologist can tell what dosage of radiation will sterilize a potent man because no such work has been done in that field.'

'Any medical man knows radiation is harmful.'

'If this were known, then why was Voss carrying on his experiments?'

'Ask Voss.'

'He's dead but you, Dr Kelno, were closely associated with him when he was doing this. I suggest that Voss wanted to know how much radiation was needed to sterilize a healthy man because he didn't know and no one else knew, and I suggest he told you what he was doing, and I suggest you didn't know either. Now, Dr Kelno, what was done with the removed testicles?'

'I don't know.'

'Weren't they, in fact, taken to a laboratory to ascertain if they were potent or not.'

'Perhaps.'

'I suggest that the removal of such testicles was the second step in the experiment.'

'No.'

'But when these men were X-rayed, the experiment wasn't over, was it?'

'I operated to save lives.'

'Concern for cancer? Who did the X ray?'

'A German medical orderly by name of Kremmer.'

'Was he quite skilled?'

'He was not very skilled and that is why I feared cancer.'

'I see. Not too skilled. He was hanged for what he did, was he not?'

'I am going to object to that,' Sir Robert said, bouncing up.

'Objection sustained.'

'What became of Corporal Kremmer?' Bannister pressed.

'I object, my Lord. My learned friend is clearly trying to implicate Sir Adam as a willing accomplice. He was not a Nazi and he did not volunteer in this work.'

'The nature of my question, my Lord, is completely in order. I am suggesting that these operations were part and parcel of the experiments and therefore experimental surgery. Others were hanged for their participation in these experiments and I suggest Dr Kelno need not have performed these operations and did so in order to work his passage.'

Gilray pondered. 'Well, we all know by this time that SS Corporal Kremmer was hanged. I ask the jury to receive this information with the gravest reservation. You may continue, Mr Bannister.'

Sir Robert slipped to his seat slowly as Bannister thanked the judge.

'Now then, you saw these two dozen or so people in your operating room and observed the results of heavy exposure to radiation.'

'Yes.'

'And you testified that Corporal Kremmer was not too skilled and you were fearful of the effects of the X ray. Is that your testimony?'

'It is.'

'Now, Dr Kelno, let us say that Corporal Kremmer did not do the X ray but the most skilled radiologist did it. Wouldn't there be danger to the partner testicle and ovary?'

'I don't believe I understand.'

'Very well, let us clarify again. The male testicles adjoin each other in separate compartments but under a fraction of an inch apart. Is that correct?'

'Yes.'

'And the female ovaries are probably five to seven inches apart.'

'Yes.'

'In the case of a testicle exposed to an extremely heavy dosage of irradiation by a semiskilled technician I suggest that the partner testicle would also be damaged. You testified they were badly burned and that was your concern.'

'Yes.'

'Well, if you feared cancer, why didn't you remove both testicles? Wasn't it in the interest of the patient to amputate both testicles?'

'I don't know. I mean, Voss told me what to do.'

'I suggest, Dr Kelno, you first thought of this so-called cancer danger when you were being detained in Brixton Prison awaiting extradition to Poland.'

'That's not true.'

'I suggest you had no interest whatsoever in the welfare of the patients, or you would not have left in a cancerous testicle or ovary. I suggest you made it all up later.'

'I didn't.'

'Then why didn't you remove everything damaged?'

'Because Voss was standing over me.'

'Isn't it a fact that Voss told you and Dr Lotaki on several occasions that if you did these operations for him you would be taken away from Jadwiga.'

'Of course not.'

'I suggest it is improper and dangerous to operate on a person suffering from severe irradiation burns. What about that?'

'In London, perhaps, but not in Jadwiga.'

'Without morphia?'

'I tell you I administered morphia.'

'When did you first meet Dr Mark Tesslar?' Bannister said, switching the subject suddenly.

The mention of Tesslar caused a physical flushing and crawling of flesh over

Kelno and his palms became wet. One shorthand writer relieved the other. The clock ticked.

'I think this may be an appropriate time for a recess,' the judge said.

Adam Kelno left the witness stand with the first tarnish stain. He would never again take Thomas Bannister lightly.

Chapter Seven

A routine was forming. Sir Adam Kelno was able to skip across the river to take lunch at home while his counsel dashed off to a ready booth in a private club.

The Three Tuns Tavern on Chancery Lane at the alleyway of Chichester Rents had a small upstairs private room where Abe and Shawcross retired with whomever had joined them in court. The bill of fare at the Three Tuns consisted of the usual London Pub selection of cold cuts, cold salad and Scotch egg, a concoction of egg, meat and breadcrumbs. After teaching the bartender how to make a dry, cold martini things were not so bad as they may have been. On the floor below, the bar was two and three deep with young solicitors, legal secretaries, students, and businessmen, all of whom knew Abraham Cady was upstairs but too British in their manners to annoy him.

And so it went each day. Court convened at ten-thirty in the morning until a one o'clock recess and in the afternoon from two until four-thirty.

After the first taste of Bannister, Adam Kelno felt that with all the insinuation he had not scored heavily and the others too felt that no real damage had been done.

'Now, Dr Kelno,' Bannister continued after the recess, with a cadence in his voice becoming easier to follow. In the beginning it sounded dull but one could gather the rhythm of it and intonations within intonations. 'You told us before the recess you met Dr Tesslar as a student.'

'Yes.'

'How many people lived in Poland before the war?'

'Over thirty million.'

'And how many Jews?'

'About three and a half million.'

'Some of whom had been in Poland for generations ... centuries.'

'Yes.'

'Was there a student's association for medical trainees at the University of Warsaw?'

'Yes.'

'As a matter of fact, because of the anti-Semitic views of the Polish officers clique, the aristocracy, intelligentsia, and the upper class, no Jewish students were allowed to be members of the association.'

'The Jews formed their own association.'

'I suggest that is because they were barred from the other one.'

'It may be.'

'Isn't it also a fact that the Jewish students were placed in separate parts of the rear of the class and otherwise segregated socially, as students and as fellow Poles. And isn't it a fact that the student's association had Jewish days and activated riots against Jewish shops and otherwise indulged in their persecution?'

'These were conditions I did not make.'

'But Poland did. Poland was anti-Semitic in nature, substance, and action, was it not?'

'There was anti-Semitism in Poland.'

'And you joined in it actively as a student?'

'I had to join the association. I was not responsible for its actions.'

'I suggest you were extremely active. Now, after the German invasion of Poland, you knew, of course, of the ghettoes in Warsaw and all over Poland.'

'I was already an inmate in Jadwiga, but I heard.'

Highsmith relaxed and jotted a note to Richard Smiddy. THIS LINE OF QUESTIONING WILL GET HIM NOWHERE. HE MAY HAVE EMPTIED HIS GUN.

'Jadwiga,' Bannister said, 'could accurately be described as an indescribable hell.'

'No hell could be worse.'

'And millions were tortured and murdered. You knew that because you saw some of it firsthand and because the underground gave you information.'

'Yes, we knew what was going on.'

'How many labor camps surrounded Jadwiga?'

'About fifty, holding up to a half million slave laborers for armament factories, a chemical factory, many other kinds of war plants.'

'Mostly Jews were used in this forced labor?'

'Yes.'

'From everywhere in occupied Europe.'

'Yes.'

What in the name of God is he getting at, Kelno wondered. Is he trying to build sympathy for me?

'You knew that the arrivals went to a selection shed and those over forty and all children were sent directly to the gas chambers of Jadwiga West.'

'Yes.'

'Thousands? Millions?'

'I have heard many figures. Some say over two million people were put to death in Jadwiga West.'

'And others were tattooed and wore various types of badges sewn on their clothing to divide them into various classes.'

'We were all prisoners. I don't understand what classes.'

'Well, what kind of different badges were there?'

'There were Jews, gypsies, German criminals, Communists, resistance fighters. Some Russian prisoners of war. I have testified to my own badge, a badge by nationality.'

'Do you remember another badge worn by Kapos?'

'Yes.'

'Would you tell my Lord and the jury who the Kapos were.'

'They were prisoners who watched over other prisoners.'

'Very tough?'

'Yes.'

'And for their cooperation with the SS they were quite privileged?'

'Yes . . . but the Jews even had Kapos.'

'I suggest there were extremely few Jewish Kapos in proportion to the number of Jewish prisoners. Would you agree to that?'

'Yes.'

'Most of the Kapos were Polish, were they not?'

Adam balked for a moment, tempted to argue. The point had been slow in coming but it was quite clear. 'Yes,' he answered.

'Inside the main stammlager of Jadwiga some twenty thousand prisoners built the camp itself and manned the crematoriums of Jadwiga West. Later the number of prisoners increased to forty thousand.'

'I will trust your figures.'

'And those Jews arriving would carry their few valuables and family heirlooms. Some gold rings and diamonds and so forth among their little bits of luggage.'

'Yes.'

'And when they were sent to the gas chambers naked, their belongings were systematically looted. You knew all that?'

'Yes, it was horrible.'

'And you knew the hair was used to stuff mattresses in Germany and to seal submarine periscopes and that gold teeth were pulled from corpses and before the corpses were burned their stomachs were cut open to see if they had swallowed any valuables. You knew that.'

'Yes.'

Abe felt queasy. He covered his face with his hands wishing this kind of questioning were over with. Terrence Campbell was also chalky and the entire room stunned to silence even though it was a story they had heard before.

'At first there were German doctors but later on the prisoners took over. How many personnel did you have?'

'A total of five hundred. Sixty or seventy of these were medical doctors.'

'How many of them were Jews?'

'Perhaps a dozen.'

'But with lower ranking. Orderlies, scrubbers, that sort of thing.'

'If they were qualified physicians, I used them as such.'

'But the Germans didn't, is that not so?'

'No, the Germans didn't.'

'And their number was completely out of proportion to the number of inmates.'

'I used qualified doctors as doctors.'

'You didn't answer my question, Dr Kelno.'

'Yes, the number of Jewish doctors was small by proportion.'

'And you know of some of the other things Voss and Flensberg were doing. Cancer experiments of the cervix, induction of sterilization through injection of caustic fluid into the Fallopian tubes. Other experiments to find the mental breaking point of victims.'

'I don't know exactly. I only went to Barrack V to operate and to Barrack III to see the patients afterward.'

'Well, did you discuss this matter with a French woman doctor. A Dr Susanne Parmentier?'

'I recall no such person.'

'A French Protestant prisoner/doctor. A psychiatrist by the name of Parmentier.'

'My Lord,' Sir Robert Highsmith interrupted with a tone of sarcasm. 'We have all been educated as to the bestiality of Jadwiga. My learned friend is certainly trying to establish that Sir Adam was the blame for the gas chambers and other brutalities of the Germans. I cannot see the relevancy.'

'Yes, get on with it,' the judge said. 'What are you driving at, Mr Bannister.'

'I suggest that even within the horror of Jadwiga Concentration Camp there were rankings of the prisoners and certain prisoners looked upon themselves as superior. There was a definite caste system and privileges given to those who did the Germans' work.'

'I see,' the judge said.

Highsmith slipped back, extremely wary of Bannister's oblique way of getting at it.

'Now then,' Bannister continued, 'I hold here in my hand a copy of a document, prepared by your counsel, Sir Adam, called Statement of Claim. I have true copies, which I should like to give to his Lordship and the jury.'

Highsmith examined it, nodded his approval, and the associate handed copies to the judge, the jury, and one to Sir Adam.

'You state in your claim that you were an associate of SS Colonel Dr Adolph Voss and SS Colonel Dr Otto Flensberg.'

'By associate I meant –'

'Yes, exactly what did you mean by associate?'

'You are distorting a perfectly natural word. They were doctors and...'

'And you considered yourself as their associate. Now, of course you read this Statement of Claim carefully. Your solicitors did go over it with you line by line.'

'The word associate is a slip, an error.'

'But you knew what they were doing, you testified to that, and you know about the indictments against them after the war and you say in your own Statement of Claim they were your associates.' Bannister held another document up as Adam looked to the clock in hopes of a recess to organize himself. After a period of silence, Bannister spoke. 'I have here a part of the indictment against Voss. Will my learned colleague accept this as a true copy?'

Highsmith looked at it and shrugged. 'We have strayed afield. This indictment is again this horrendous business of trying to link together a prisoner with a Nazi war criminal.'

'One moment please,' Bannister said, and turned to O'Connor, who was shuffling through the stacks of papers on his table. He handed one to Bannister. 'Here is the affidavit, which you swore to, Dr Kelno. You swore before a Commissioner for Oaths and you state the following, paragraphs one and two list the documents relating to your case. You're holding it in your hand. Is that your signature, Dr Kelno?'

'I am confused.'

'Let us clarify it then. When you brought this action you disclosed a number of documents on your own behalf. Among the documents you disclosed was the indictment of Voss. You did it.'

'If my solicitors thought it necessary...'

'When you brought this document forth to support your case you thought it to be genuine, did you not?'

'I suppose so.'

'Now then, I shall read to the jury a portion of the indictment of Voss.'

The judge looked to Highsmith, who glanced at the indictment of Voss. 'No objection, my Lord,' he said between his teeth.

'"Headquarters of the Fuehrer, August 1942, Secret Reich matters, single copy. On July 7, 1942, a conference was held at Jadwiga Concentration Camp between Drs Adolph Voss and Otto Flensberg and Reichfuehrer SS Heinrich Himmler on the matter of sterilization of the Jewish race. It was agreed upon that a variety of experiments would be performed on healthy, potent Jews and Jewesses." Now, Dr Kelno, the second letter in your disclosure of documents is from Voss to Himmler in which Voss states he must carry out his radiation program on a minimum of a thousand persons to get conclusive results. Dr Kelno, you have testified that between yourself and Dr Lotaki you operated or assisted in perhaps two dozen such operations. What happened to the minimum of nine hundred and seventy-six other persons in Voss's letter?'

'I don't know.'

'What was the purpose of entering these letters in evidence?'

'Only to show I was a victim. The Germans did it, not me.'

'I am suggesting that in fact there were many more hundreds of these operations not accounted for.'

'Maybe the Jew, Dimshits, did most of them and that is why he was sent to the gas chamber. Maybe it was Tesslar.'

'You knew when you brought this action it would be your word against Dr Tesslar's because the surgical record had disappeared.'

'I must rise,' Sir Robert said, 'and take the greatest exception. You cannot elude to a register that is not in existence. Mr Bannister has asked Sir Adam how many operations he performed and Sir Adam has answered.'

'Mr Bannister,' the judge said. 'May I call your attention to the fact that from time to time editorial comments creep into your questions.'

'I am sorry, my Lord. Speed in the mass sterilization program was also essential to the German purpose. Could it be possible these operations were performed before Dr Voss to demonstrate just how quickly they could be done?'

'I did not operate with such speed as to harm a patient.'

'Weren't you, in fact, proud of the speed with which you could remove Jewish testicles, and didn't you want to demonstrate it to Voss.'

'My Lord,' Sir Robert said, 'this objection is obvious. My client has testified he did not use undue speed.'

'I must admonish you again,' Gilray said. He turned to the jury with his first display of judicial authority. 'Dr Kelno is being distressed through innuendo. I will advise you thoroughly at the proper time as to what is relevant and what is not.'

Bannister did not blink an eye. 'Do you recall a Dr Sandor?'

'Sandor was a Jewish Communist.'

'No, as a matter of fact, Dr Sandor is a Roman Catholic and not a member of any Communist Party. He was one of your doctors. Do you recall him?'

'Somewhat.'

'And do you recall a conversation in which you said to Sandor, "I've got twenty pair of Jewish eggs for scrambling today."'

'I never said that. Sandor was a member of the Communist underground who will swear anything against me.'

'I think it may be a good time to explain to my Lord and the jury about these two undergrounds inside Jadwiga. You referred to your underground as a Nationalist underground, did you not?'

'Yes.'

'Composed of what sort of people?'

'Anti-Germans from every country in occupied Europe.'

'I suggest that is not true. I suggest that ninety-five percent of your underground was made up of Poles and that no one held any position of authority who was not a former Polish officer. Is that not the case?'

'I do not recall.'

'Can you recall any Czech or Dutchman or Yugoslav who had any position of authority in your Nationalist underground?'

'No.'

'But you can certainly recall Polish officers.'

'Some.'

'Yes, some who are in this courtroom as spectors and prospective witnesses. I suggest, Dr Kelno, that the Nationalist underground was the same pre-war anti-Semitic Polish officers' clique inside Jadwiga.'

Kelno did not answer.

'You have testified to a Communist underground. Is this not the same as the international underground?'

'Yes, composed of Communists and Jews.'

'And non-Communists and non-Jews who outnumbered the Polish officers' clique by fifty to one and whose ranks and officials represented every occupied country in equal proportion. Is that not so?'

'They were dominated by Jews and Communists.'

'Is one of the causes for hemorrhaging in the post-operative period the speed with which a surgeon operates?' Bannister said with his now patented change of subjects.

Kelno drank from the water glass and mopped his forehead. 'If a surgeon is qualified, speed can often reduce the possibility of shock.'

'Let us come to the time in mid 1943 when Dr Mark Tesslar arrived at Jadwiga. You were no longer a laborer taking beatings from the Germans, but a doctor with a great deal of authority.'

'Under German direction.'

'But you made decisions completely on your own. For example, who could be admitted to the hospital.'

'I was always under a great deal of moral pressure.'

'But by the time Dr Tesslar arrived you had a rapport with the Germans. You were trusted by them.'

'In a left handed way, yes.'

'And what was your rapport with Dr Tesslar?'

'I learned Tesslar was a Communist. Voss sent for him from another concentration camp. One can draw his own conclusions. I was polite on occasions we met but as you would say in England, I gave him a wide berth. I stayed clear of him.'

'I suggest there were numerous conversations between yourself and Tesslar because you really had no fear of him and he was trying desperately to get more food and medicine for post-operative victims he was taking care of. I suggest that you mentioned to him that you had performed some twenty thousand operations with uncommon speed.'

'You may suggest until your head falls off,' Adam snapped.

'I intend to. Now then, Dr Tesslar has made a statement that on one occasion in November of 1943 you performed fourteen operations at one session. Eight males, seven of them Dutch, were either castrated or had a testicle removed. Six females had ovaries removed by you on the same occasion. There was so much commotion that the SS sent a medical clerk, an Egon Sobotnik, for Dr Tesslar to come over to Barrack V and keep the patients calm while you operated.'

'It is a blatant lie. Dr Tesslar never came into Barrack V while I operated.'

'And Dr Tesslar has stated that you did not give the spinals and that they were not given in the operating theater and that no pre-injection of morphia was given.'

'It is a lie.'

'Now then, let us consider the ovariectomies in Dr Tesslar's statement. Forget for the moment what he has said and let us go through an ordinary operation of this sort. You make an incision in the abdominal wall. Is that correct?'

'Yes, after the patient has been scrubbed and given morphia and a spinal by me.'

'Even those who had serious irradiation burns.'

'I had no choice.'

'You put in the forceps, lifted up the uterus and put a forceps between the ovary and the Fallopian tube, and then snipped off the ovary and placed it in a bowl.'

'More or less.'

'I suggest, Dr Kelno, when this had been done you did not stitch up the ovaries, uterus, and veins properly.'

'It is not true.'

'Are the raw stumps called pedicles?'

'Yes.'

'Isn't it proper to cover these pedicles by using the peritoneal flaps?'

'You are a good lawyer, Mr Bannister, but not much of a surgeon.'

Bannister ignored the ripple of laughter. 'Then kindly educate me.'

'There is no peritoneum to cover the stump. The only way to keep it down is with a cross-stitch from the infundibulo-pelvic ligament. You cover the stump in that way to prevent inflammation and adhesions and excessive bleeding.'

'And you always did that?'

'Naturally.'

'Dr Tesslar recalls that on six ovariectomies he witnessed by you, you didn't do that.'

'It is nonsense. Tesslar was never there. And even if he was in the operating room it is almost impossible to see my work unless he had X-ray eyes. With a theater staff assisting me, with Voss and Germans present, and with a screen at the patient's head, where Tesslar claims he sat, it would be impossible for him to observe.'

'But if he sat to the side and there were no screen?'

'It is all very hypothetical.'

'Then it is your testimony that Dr Tesslar didn't warn you the patients would hemorrhage or get peritonitis?'

'It is not so.'

'And Dr Tesslar did not argue with you about not washing your hands between operations?'

'No.'

'Or using the same instruments without sterilization?'

'I am a proud and competent surgeon, Mr Bannister. I resent the insinuations.'

'Did you keep notes to advise you whether to take out the left or right testicle or the left or right ovary?'

'No.'

'Isn't it true that doctors have amputated the wrong finger or toe or whatever because they didn't check their notes?'

'This was Jadwiga, not Guy's.'

'How did you know where to operate?'

'Corporal Kremmer, who did the X ray, was in the room. He told me left or right.'

'Kremmer? Corporal Kremmer. The semiskilled radiologist told you?'

'He did the X rays.'

'And if Dr Tesslar was not there then he could not have pleaded with you about the irradiation burns or the fact that no general anesthetic was given.'

'I have repeated. I used morphia and a spinal, which I administered myself. I operated quickly as it was safer to prevent pneumonia, heart collapse, and God knows what. How many times do I have to repeat it?'

'Until everything is quite clear.' Bannister paused, studied the weariness of his witness. There is a natural breaking point beyond which the judge and jury are apt to gain sympathy for him. There is also a time that the clock says one must work to the climax of his examination.

'So all these things said by Mark Tesslar are invention.'

'They are lies.'

'Men and women screaming. In frightful pain.'

'Lies.'

'And handling patients in a rough and ready manner on the operating table.'

'I am proud of my record as a surgeon.'

'Why do you think Dr Tesslar has told all these lies against you?'

'Because of our early clashes.'

'You have stated that on occasion when you practiced medicine in Warsaw you sent a member of your family to Tesslar for an abortion without Tesslar's knowledge. I ask you now to identify the member of your family who had an abortion performed by him.'

Kelno looked around for help. Control yourself, he said, control yourself. 'I refuse.'

'I suggest no such abortions were ever performed. I suggest Dr Tesslar had to leave Poland to finish his medical training because of the anti-Semitic activities of your association, and I suggest Dr Tesslar never performed abortions or experiments for the SS in Jadwiga.'

'Tesslar said these lies against me to save himself,' Kelno cried. 'When I returned to Warsaw he was in the Communist secret police with orders to hound me because I am a Polish Nationalist who cries for the loss of his beloved country. The lies were proved as lies eighteen years ago when the British government refused to extradite me.'

'I suggest,' Bannister said in utter calm to contrast Jelno's rising outburst, 'that when you returned to Poland and learned that Tesslar and several other doctors had survived, you fled and subsequently invented a total fiction against him.'

'No.'

'And you never struck a patient on the operating table and called her a damned Jewess?'

'No, it is my word against Tesslar's.'

'As a matter of fact,' Bannister said, 'it has nothing to do with Tesslar's word. It is the word of the woman you struck who is alive and at this moment on her way to London.'

Chapter Eight

Saturday evening was spent in the Paris countryside with Cady's French publisher, and Sunday Abe and Lady Sarah called upon Pieter Van Damm for a lovely dinner with Madame Erica Van Damm and the two children, both students of the Sorbonne.

The daughter, a homely quiet sort, went off to her room. Anton Van Damm excused himself for a date after promising to come to London to meet Ben and Vanessa.

'The trial does not go too well,' Pieter said.

'The jury seems to show no emotion. We have word from Poland that Dr Lotaki will not testify for us and so far, no sign of Egon Sobotnik.'

'Time is growing short,' Pieter said. He nodded to his wife and on cue Erica asked Lady Sarah to have a look around the apartment so the two men were alone. 'Abraham, I have told my children everything.'

'I suspected so tonight. It must have been very difficult.'

'Strange. Not as hard as I thought. You put into your children all the love and wisdom you are able to yet you fear that in a crisis they have lost it. Well, they didn't. They wept, particularly for their mother. My son, Anton, was ashamed he did not know earlier so he could have helped me through difficult periods. And Erica explained to them that we have even greater compensations in our relationship than a sexual life.'

Abe pondered. 'I don't want you to think about testifying,' he said. 'I know it's on your mind.'

'I read your books, Cady. With us, we are able to rise to heights that normal couples cannot attain. Now, there are four of us who feel that strongly.'

'I can't let you do it. After all, the loss of human dignity is one of the things this case is all about.'

Anton Van Damm was waiting in the lobby of the Meurice when Abe and Lady Sarah returned. She whisked off in the open cage elevator, and they made into the bar.

'I know why you're here,' Abe said.

'It's on Father's conscience day and night. If it means losing the case, of having Kelno paid off, Father would suffer more than if he took the stand.'

'Anton, when I went into this I had some ideas about revenge. Well, I've changed that notion. Adam Kelno as a single person is not important. What some people do to other people is important. From this aspect, as Jews we must tell this story over and over. We must continue to protest our demise until we are allowed to live in peace.'

'You're looking for a victory in heaven, Mr Cady. I want one on earth.'

Abe smiled and rumpled the boy's hair. 'I've got a son and a daughter about your age. I've never won an argument with them yet.'

'May I have your attention, please,' the loud-speaker of Heathrow Airport announced, 'El Al from Tel Aviv has just landed.'

As the door from customs opened, Sheila Lamb led the surge toward an uncertain little knot of passengers. Dr Leiberman introduced himself and the two women and four men. The Israeli witnesses.

'How good of you to come,' Sheila said, embracing them each. Jacob Alexander looked on in awe as the girl who had worked for him for five years in abstract suddenly felt the need to take charge to put everyone at ease. They had been numbers in a file but now they were here, the mutilated of Jadwiga.

Sheila passed out small bouquets of flowers and led everyone to a waiting line of cars.

'Abraham Cady was not able to come to meet you and sends his regrets. His face is well known and if he were here it might interfere with your anonymity. However, he is quite anxious to know you all and has asked you to dinner tomorrow evening.'

In a few moments they all seemed more certain and divided up into the cars. 'If they aren't too tired,' Sheila said to Dr Leiberman, 'I think a little spin around London might be nice so they can get the feeling of our city.'

After Kelno's testimony, Dr Harold Boland, a prominent anesthesiologist, testified on behalf of Sir Adam Kelno that the spinal was a simple and reasonable method.

He was an old-timer who had given hundreds of spinals with and without pre-injection of morphia and supported in essence what Sir Adam had testified.

Brendon O'Connor cross-examined him only briefly.

'Then, a spinal blockage, when properly injected, is a relatively simple piece of business?'

'Yes, in the hands of a physician with the experience of Sir Adam.'

'Provided,' O'Connor said, 'one has the full consent and cooperation of the patient. Would you care, Dr Boland, to speculate if the patient were physically restrained against his will, screaming, kicking, biting for his freedom. Could not the spinal under those circumstances become quite painful?'

'I have never administered one under such circumstances.'

'If the needle slipped because of violent movement of the patient.'

'Then it could be painful.'

A parade of witnesses followed. First, the elder of the Polish community in London, Count Czerny, who recounted Sir Adam's successful fight against extradition. Then former Colonel Gajnow who conducted the initial investigation of Kelno in Italy, then Dr August Novak, who had been the executive surgeon of the Polish Hospital in Tunbridge Wells, then three former Polish officers who were prisoners in Jadwiga and members of the Nationalist underground, and then four patients whom Kelno had saved in Jadwiga with particular skill.

O'Connor cross-examined each briefly.

'Are you Jewish?' he asked.

The answer was a uniform, 'no.'

But more interesting, 'When Dr Kelno took out your appendix do you remember a sheet before your face?'

'I remember nothing. I was put to sleep.'

'Not injected in the spine?'

'No, I was put to sleep.'

J. J. MacAlister came up from Budleigh-Salterton. He had difficulty in speaking because of a stroke, but his recounting of Kelno's years in Sarawak were most effective as a former colonial officer speaking the jargon of the jury.

Then another former inmate was called to the witness box.

'Sir Robert,' the judge said, 'to what point is your next witness addressed?'

'The same point, my Lord.'

'I can understand,' Anthony Gilray said, 'that you wish to impress on the jury that Dr Kelno was a kind man. No one is suggesting he wasn't kind to certain patients.'

'I do not wish to seem impertinent, my Lord, but I have two more witnesses to this point.'

'Well,' the judge persisted, 'no one contests that Dr Kelno was considerate of Polish men and women. What is suggested is that when it came to Jews, it was an entirely different matter.'

'My Lord, I must confess I have a witness who has just arrived from out of the country, and I shall agree that he will be my final witness if his Lordship would call an early recess today.'

'Well, I don't think the jury is going to object to an early adjournment.'

Cady, Shawcross, and his people rushed across the hall to the consultation room. In a moment Josephson came with the confirmation and they were shaken. Konstanty Lotaki had arrived from Warsaw to testify for Adam Kelno.

'We shall continue to do our best,' Bannister said.

Chapter Nine

The word spread like a brush fire that Konstanty Lotaki had arrived in London to testify for Kelno. It was a severe blow for Cady.

'I call to the stand as our last witness, Dr Konstanty Lotaki.'

The associate led him up the three steps into the box and a Polish interpreter stood beside him. The jury was particularly alert at the sight of the new arrival and the press section spilled over into extra tables. The oath was issued to the interpreter.

Bannister arose. 'My Lord, since this witness will be testifying through an interpreter and since we have our own Polish interpreter, I should like to request that my learned friend's interpreter transmit all questions and answers loudly and clearly so that we are in a position to challenge if necessary.'

'Do you understand that?' Gilray asked.

The interpreter nodded.

'Would you ask Dr Lotaki what his religious beliefs are and how he wishes to be sworn in?'

There was an exchange of conversation. 'He has no religious beliefs. He is a Communist.'

'Very well,' Gilray said, 'you may affirm the witness.'

The heavy-set pumpkin-faced man spoke low key, as though he were in a trance. He gave his name and his address in Lublin, where he was a chief surgeon of a government hospital.

He had been arrested on false charges in 1942 by the Gestapo and learned later the Germans used this method of pressing doctors into concentration camp service. He arrived at Jadwiga and was assigned to Kelno's section. It was the first time they had ever met. He worked with Kelno in a general way, having his own surgery, dispensary, and hospital wards.

'Did Dr Kelno run a proper establishment?'

'Under the circumstances, no one could have done better.'

'And he treated his patients well and with personal kindness?'

'Exceptionally.'

'Did he discriminate against Jewish patients?'

'I never saw it.'

'Now, when did you first come into contact with SS Dr Adolph Voss?'

'From the first day.'

'Do you recall a particular time when Voss ordered you down to his office and told you that you would be doing operations in Barrack V?'

'I will never forget it.'

'Would you tell my Lord and the jury about that.'

'We all know about Voss's experiments. I was summoned in summer of 1943 after Dr Dimshits had been sent to the gas chamber. Until then Dimshits had been his surgeon.'

'Did you go with Dr Kelno?'

'We were called separately.'

'Please continue.'

'Voss told me we were to remove testicles and ovaries of persons he was experimenting on. I told him I didn't want to take part in this, and he said he would have an SS orderly perform the operations, and I would meet the same fate as Dimshits.'

There was a break down in the translation and a member of the Polish press volunteered a half dozen words.

'Just a moment,' Anthony Gilray said. 'I am delighted to have members of the international press in my court, but I do rather they not take part in the proceedings.'

'Sorry, my Lord,' the reporter apologized.

'Mr Interpreter, if you encounter any difficulty, kindly advise the court. You may continue, Sir Robert.'

'As a result of this meeting with Voss, what did you do?'

'I was distressed and looked to Dr Kelno as my superior. We decided to call a meeting of all the doctors except Dr Tesslar, and we decided it would be in the interest of the patients if we operated.'

'And you did.'

'Yes.'

'How often?'

'I think fifteen to twenty operations.'

'Proper operations.'

'With more than usual care.'

'And you had occasion to observe Dr Kelno and on other occasions he assisted you. Was there ever, I repeat, ever on any occasion any abuse of the patients?'

'No, never.'

'Never?'

'Never.'

'Dr Lotaki. In your learned opinion, is there danger to a patient in leaving in an organ that had been X-rayed?'

'I am not a qualified radiologist. I have no opinion. My concern is that the patients should not be operated on by less skilled people.'

'What kind of anesthetic was administered on these occasions?'

'Larocaine by spinal blockage after a preliminary injection of morphia to comfort the patient.'

'Could you tell us who else was in the operating room?'

'A surgical team, someone to look after the instruments. Dr Kelno and I assisted each other and Voss was present always with one or two other Germans.

'Did you ever personally meet Dr Mark Tesslar?'

'Yes, several times.'

'What was the general discussion about his activities?'

'In a concentration camp there are rumors about everything. I stayed clear of this business. I am a doctor.'

'Then you were not a member of the underground, either the so-called international underground or the Nationalist underground.'

'No.'

'So you had no malice toward Dr Tesslar and he had none toward you?'

'That is right.'

'Did Dr Tesslar ever attend any operations in Barrack V in which you either performed or assisted?'

'No, never.'

'And were any of these operations done with undue speed or in a haphazard manner?'

'No. They were done by standard procedures with almost no pain to the patient.'

'Now then, you were removed from Jadwiga Concentration Camp in 1944, is that correct?'

'I was taken out by Dr Flensberg to a private clinic near Munich. He had me do surgery.'

'Were you paid?'

'Flensberg took all the fees.'

'But life was better than in Jadwiga.'

'Anything was better than Jadwiga.'

'You were dressed, fed decently, free to move about?'

'We had better clothing and food, but I was always under guard.'

'And at the end of the war you made your way back to Poland?'

'I have lived and worked there since.'

'Essentially, in Jadwiga you and Dr Kelno performed the same kind of work for Dr Voss. Did you know that Dr Kelno was wanted as a war criminal?'

'Yes, I heard.'

'But you were not involved in the Nationalist underground so no charges were brought against you.'

'I did nothing wrong.'

'Now then, Dr Lotaki, what is your present political conviction.'

'After what I saw in Jadwiga I have become a determined anti-fascist. I feel the best way to combat fascism is through the Communist party.'

'No further questions.'

Thomas Bannister adjusted his robe carefully, took his set stance, and studied Lotaki with a long period of deliberate silence. Abe passed a note to O'Connor, ARE WE IN TROUBLE?

YES, the return reply came.

'Do you agree, Dr Lotaki, that before Hitler Germany was among the most civilized and cultured countries of the world?'

'Sterilized countries?'

A relief of laughter.

'You shall not laugh at any witness in my court,' Gilray said. 'Now, Mr Bannister, as to this line of questioning ... you know your job and I'm not advising you ... never mind, continue. Explain the question again, Mr Interpreter.'

'I agree that Germany was civilized before Hitler.'

'And if someone would have told you what this civilized country was going to do in the next decade you would have refused to believe that.'

'Yes.'

'Mass murders, experiments on human guinea pigs, forceful removal of sex organs for the eventual purpose of mass sterilization. You wouldn't have believed that before Hitler, would you?'

'No.'

'And would you say that any doctor having taken the Hippocratic oath would not have taken part in these experiments?'

'I am going to intervene,' Gilray said. 'One of the problems of this case is that of voluntary acts as against involuntary acts in its context with human morality.'

'My Lord,' Thomas Bannister said with his voice rising for the first time. 'When I use the words "taken part in" I mean any surgeon who has removed sex organs. I mean that Dr Lotaki knew what Voss was doing and why he was ordered to cut off testicles and hoick out ovaries.'

'I did it under duress.'

'Let me clarify this,' Gilray said. 'We are in the Royal Courts of Justice and this case is being dealt with according to the common law of England. Now then, is it your contention, Mr Bannister, that you are putting a case before the jury on the grounds that an operation performed under duress still amounts to justification against libel?'

'That is my case, my Lord,' Bannister snapped back, 'that no doctor, prisoner or otherwise, had any right to perform such operations!'

A gasp floated over the room. 'Well then, we know where we stand, don't we?'

'Now, Dr Lotaki,' Bannister said. 'Did you really believe Voss would have used an inexperienced SS orderly to perform these operations?'

'I had no reason to doubt it.'

'Voss went to Himmler for permission to conduct these experiments. If these testicles and ovaries were not properly removed they were then useless to the experiment. How in the name of God could anyone believe this nonsense about an SS orderly?'

'Voss was not sane,' Lotaki sputtered. 'All of it was quite mad.'

'But he was bluffing. He had to submit reports to Berlin, and he had to have qualified surgeons.'

'So he would have sent me to the gas chamber like Dimshits and found another surgeon.'

'Dr Lotaki, will you be so kind as to describe Dr Dimshits to my Lord and the jury.'

'He was a Jew, older, perhaps seventy or more.'

'And living in a concentration camp aged him further?'

'Yes.'

'What of his physical appearance?'

'Very old.'

'And feeble and failing?'

'I . . . I . . . I can't say.'

'No longer able to function as a surgeon . . . no longer of use to the Germans.'

'I . . . can't . . . say . . . he knew too much.'

'But you and Kelno knew the same things and you didn't go to the gas chamber. You went to private clinics. I suggest that Dr Dimshits went to the gas chamber because he was old and useless. I suggest that is the real reason, no other. Now then, Dr Kelno has testified that he is a victim of a Communist plot. You are a Communist. Would you comment on that?'

'I am in London to tell the truth,' Lotaki cried out, shaken. 'What makes you think a Communist cannot tell the truth or testify for a non-Communist?'

'Have you heard of Berthold Richter, the high East German Communist?'

'Yes.'

'Are you aware that he and hundreds of Nazis are now in the Communist regime who were former concentration camp officials?'

'Now just a moment,' Gilray said, turning to the jury, 'I am certain Mr Bannister is correct in his last statement but it doesn't mean that it is evidence unless it is offered as evidence.'

'What I am suggesting, my Lord, is that the Communists have a very convenient way to rehabilitate former Nazis and SS who are useful to them. No matter how black their past, if they throw themselves on the altar of Communism, and if they are of use to the regime, their past is forgotten.'

'You certainly are not suggesting Dr Lotaki was a Nazi?'

'I suggest that Dr Lotaki is a genius at the art of survival, and he has not only worked his passage once, but twice, Dr Lotaki, you say you went to Dr Kelno as your superior and discussed the operations. What would you have done if Dr Kelno had refused?'

'I . . . also would have refused.'

'No further questions.'

Chapter Ten

Abe sat in the darkness. A car stopped before the mews, the door was unlocked.

'Dad?'

Ben felt around for the light switch and flicked it on. His father was across the room, legs stretched out straight, a stiff glass of whisky balanced on his chest.

'You drunk, Dad?'

'No.'

'Tipsy?'

'No.'

'Everyone's been gathered at Mr Shawcross's for almost an hour. They're all waiting for you. Mrs Shawcross has put on a beautiful spread, and they have a pianist playing for everyone ... and ... well, Lady Wydman sent me here to get you.'

Abe set the glass aside, pulled himself up, and hung his head. Ben had seen his father like this before, many times. In Israel he'd come into his father's bedroom, which also served as his office, after a long day of writing. His father would be wrung out, sometimes in tears about a character in the book, sometimes, so tired he was unable to lace his shoes. He looked like that now, only worse.

'I can't face them,' Abe said.

'You've got to, Dad. From the minute you meet them, you'll forget about their mutilation. They're a lively bunch, and they laugh and carry on and they want so badly to see you. The other man arrived from Holland this morning as well as the women from Belgium and Trieste. They're all here now.'

'What the hell do they want to see me for? For bringing them to London and putting them on display like freaks in a side show.'

'You know why they're here. And don't forget, you're their hero.'

'Hero, my ass.'

'You're a hero to Vanessa and Yossi and me, too.'

'Sure.'

'Don't you think we know why you're doing this?'

'Sure, we've done you a damned great service. Accept the gift of my generation to your generation. Concentration camps and gas chambers and the rape of human dignity. Now, accept our gift, you kids, and get in there and be civilized.'

'How about the gift of courage.'

'Courage. You mean fear of not going through with it and trying to live with yourself afterwards. That's not courage.'

'No one's in London because they're cowards. Now come along, I'll put your shoes on.'

Ben knelt before his father and laced his shoes up. Abe reached out and patted his son's head. 'What kind of a goddam air force would let you run around with a mustache like that. I wish to hell you'd shave it off.'

From the moment he arrived he was happy that Ben had made him come.

Sheila Lamb continued to take the awkwardness out of the situation by whisking him to the six men and four women she had adopted as her wards. They were there with him, Ben and Vanessa to help his slipshod Hebrew and Yossi was there adoring his daughter. The presence of the three young Israelis put a certain kind of courage into them all. There were no handshakes. There were embraces and kisses and they were all brothers and sisters.

David Shawcross presented each of them signed sets of Abraham Cady's collected works and the air was that of soldiers on the eve of battle. Abe became himself with Dr Leiberman and joked about the fact he had only one eye and that made them all even closer.

Abe and Leiberman moved off by themselves. 'I was called in by your solicitor,' Dr Leiberman said. 'He felt that because most of this testimony will be in Hebrew it would be better if I acted as the translator.'

'What about your medical testimony?' Abe asked.

'They feel, and I agree, that the medical testimony will be more effective coming from an English doctor.'

'They were reluctant at first,' Abe said. 'You know how doctors are about testifying against each other, but a number of good people came forth.'

It had been an evening of unexpected pleasantness, but a sudden weariness struck them all and, with it, an awkwardness. Everyone began looking toward Abraham Cady.

'I'm not drunk enough to give a speech,' he said.

And then without signal they were standing before him, looking at their non-hero, who in turn looked at the floor. Then he looked up. David Shawcross, his cigar stopped, and Lady Sarah, much like a saint. And soft Vanessa still much an English lady and Ben and Yossi, the young lions of Israel. And the victims...

'Our side of this case begins tomorrow,' Abe said, now finding strength to address those ten particular people. 'I know and you know the terrible ordeal before you. But we are here because we can never let the world forget what they did to us. When you are in the witness box remember, all of you, the pyramids of bones and ashes of the Jewish people. And remember when you speak, you are speaking for six million who can no longer speak ... remember that.'

They came to him one at a time, shook his hand and kissed his cheek and filed from the room. And then there was only Ben and Vanessa beside him.

'God,' Abe said, 'give them strength.'

Chapter Eleven

'You may proceed, Mr Bannister.'

Thomas Bannister turned his attention to the eight men and four women who had undergone their task as jurymen without visible emotion. Some were still wearing their 'one suit.' And nearly all of them filed into court with some sort of cushion.

Bannister played with his notes until the room hushed. 'I'm sure the members of the jury have suspected that there are two sides to this case. A great deal of what my learned friend, Sir Robert Highsmith, has said to you is entirely true. We do not dispute that the defendants are the author and publisher of the book or that the passage is defamatory and we agree that the person in the book is Dr Adam Kelno, the plaintiff.'

The press box was now so overfull, the front row of the three row balcony above was fixed with writing clipboards for those who had no room downstairs. Anthony Gilray, who had taken volumes of notes, continued burning out pencils.

'My Lord will address you on all questions of law. But, there are really only two issues. We say in our defense that the gist of the paragraph is true and the plaintiff is saying two things. He says the gist is untrue and because of that he is entitled to very large damages. Now our position is that because of what Dr Kelno did, his reputation really hasn't been damaged, and even though he has been libeled he should not be awarded anything but the lowest coin in the realm, a halfpenny.

'A libel does not depend on what the author meant but how people who read it understood it. We assume that most of the people who read it never heard of Dr Kelno or associated it with a Dr Kelno practicing in Southwark. Certainly, many people did know it was the same Dr Kelno. What did this mean to them?

'Now, I agree with my learned friend that Dr Kelno was a prisoner in an undescribable hell and under German domination. Quite easy for us in jolly, comfortable England to criticize what people did then, but when you consider this case, you must certainly bear in mind how you might have acted under similar circumstances.

'Jadwiga. How did something like this ever happen? Where in the world are the most civilized, advanced, and cultured countries? It would show no disrespect to the United States or our own Commonwealth to say, "the Christian countries of Western Europe were the flower of our civilization, the highest place to which man has come." And if you would have said, "Do you think it possible that within a few years one of these countries would drive millions of old people naked into gas chambers?" Well, everyone would have said, "No, it's not possible. Come now, be serious. The Kaiser and all that militarism have gone. Germany has an ordinary Western democratic government. We cannot conceive of why anyone would want to do anything like that. It would bring the loathing of the world on them." If it were peacetime and they did it, they'd soon be at war with those trying to stop it. And even in wartime, what could they possibly hope to gain with this kind of conduct?'

Thomas Bannister repeated his single gesture of rolling his fee bags and his voice now modulated with the subtlety of Bach counterpoint.

'You'd never get people to do it,' he continued. 'The German Army is made up of people from offices and factories and shops. They have children of their own. They would never get people with families to drive children into gas chambers. And . . . if it had been suggested on top of all this that human guinea pigs would have their sexual organs removed in front of their eyes while they were conscious as part of experiments in mass sterilization, again we should have said, should we not . . . "it's not possible" and furthermore, we should have said, "this kind of thing has to be done by doctors and you could never find any doctor who would do it."

'Well, we would have been wrong because it did happen, all of it, and there was a doctor, an anti-Semitic Polish doctor who did it. And off the evidence it's clear that he had a dominating position and a dominating personality. You heard Dr Lotaki say that if Dr Kelno had refused, he would have too.

'We would have been wrong to think this could not have happened because there was a cause to support and justify what happened. That monstrous cause is anti-Semitism. Those among us who have no religion would rely on their intellect. But all of us, religious or not, have a concept of right and wrong.

'But once you allow yourself to think that there are some people, because of their race, their color, or religion, who are really not human beings you have established a justification for imposing every sort of humiliation on them.

'This ploy becomes quite useful to a national leader who needs a universal scapegoat, someone to blame when anything goes wrong. And then you can whip the masses into a frenzy, put them in a state of mind that such people are animals ... well, we slaughter animals just the way it was done at Jadwiga. Wasn't Jadwiga West the logical end of this particular road?

'We should have been wrong,' Bannister went on with an oration that mesmerized every man and woman who heard it, 'because if you had ordered British troops to drive children and old people into gas chambers, none of whom had done anything wrong except they were the children of their parents, can you imagine British troops doing anything but mutiny against such orders?

'Well, as a matter of fact there were some Germans, soldiers, officers, priests, doctors, and ordinary civilians who refused to obey these orders and said, "I am not going to do this because I would not like to live and have this on my conscience. I'm not going to push them into gas chambers, and then say later I was under orders and justify it by saying that they were going to be pushed in by someone anyhow, and I can't stop it and other people will push them more cruelly. Therefore, it's in their best interest that I shove them in gently." You see, the trouble was, not enough of these people refused.

'So there are three views, are there not, which may be taken by people reading this paragraph in this book.

'If we consider the case of the SS camp guard whom we hanged after the war. That SS guard would say in his defense. "Look here, I was conscripted and found myself in the SS, in a concentration camp and not realizing what was going on." But, of course he learned what was going on and if he was a British soldier, he would have staged a mutiny. I am not suggesting these SS guards should have gone free after the war, but if we put ourselves in their place, conscripts in Hitler's army, perhaps hanging was a bit severe.

'Now, there is a second view. There should have been those who would have risked and taken severe punishment and even death by refusing because this is what we owe future generations. We must say to the future, if this thing happens again you cannot make the excuse that you feared punishment for there comes a moment in the human experience when one's life itself no longer makes sense when it is directed to the mutilation and murder of his fellow man.

'And the final view that this was not a German at all but an ally in whose hands were placed the lives of fellow allies.

'We know, of course, there were risks and punishments for prisoner/doctors. We have also learned, have we not, that the prisoners ran the medical facility and that one in particular, Dr Adam Kelno, was held in high esteem by the Germans and he himself considered himself their associate. We cannot be made to believe that a German medical officer would have cut his own throat by disposing of the one most useful to him. And we know that the orders to remove this most valued doctor to a private clinic came from Himmler himself.

'The defense says that the gist of the paragraph was true and the plaintiff is only entitled to contemptuous damages of a halfpenny for if the paragraph had read so and so had committed twenty murders when in fact he only committed two, then how much real damage is done to the murderer's reputation.

'The paragraph was wrong to state that over fifteen thousand experiments were carried out by surgery. It was also wrong to state it was done without anesthetic. We admit that.

'It is for you, however, to decide what kind of operations were performed, how they were performed in the case of Jews, and how much Dr Kelno's character is worth.'

Chapter Twelve

Because of the immediate and close relationship Sheila Lamb had established with the victims, she was questioned closely to determine a possible order of testimony. He needed a woman first so that the men would be charged to courage and he needed the one with authority, bearing, and common sense, who would not break on the stand. Sheila reckoned that Yolan Shoret, although the quietest of the lot, was the strongest.

Yolan Shoret, smallish and trimly attired, appeared much in control of herself as she sat and waited with Sheila and Dr Leiberman in the second consultation room.

In the courtroom, Mr Justice Gilray turned to the press. 'I cannot give directions to the press,' he said. 'All I can say is that I, as one of Her Majesty's Judges, would be appalled, simply appalled, if any of the witnesses who had undergone these terrible operations were identified or photographed.'

Sir Robert Highsmith winced at the words, TERRIBLE OPERATIONS. Bannister had certainly set up something in the judge's mind and perhaps in everyone else's.

'I have expressed my view and I am satisfied with the discretion of the press from my past knowledge.'

'My Lord,' O'Conner said, 'my instructing solicitors have just passed me a note saying that all representatives of the press have signed a pledge not to publish names or photographs.'

'That is what I expected. Thank you, gentlemen.'

'My witness will testify in Hebrew,' Bannister said.

There was a knock on the consultation room door. Dr Leiberman and Sheila Lamb led Yolan Shoret over the hallway. Sheila squeezed her hand as she moved away to the solicitor's table to begin her notes. A hundred pairs of eyes turned to the door. Adam Kelno stared without emotion, as she and Dr Leiberman mounted the steps into the witness box. Her dignity plunged the room into a hush as they were sworn in on the Old Testament and the judge offered them seats. She preferred to stand.

Gilray issued a few instructions to Dr Leiberman on his translations. He nodded and said he spoke fluent Hebrew and English and that German was his mother tongue. He would have no trouble, as he had known Mrs Shoret for several years.

'What is your name?' Thomas Bannister asked.

'Yolan Shoret.'

She gave her address in Jerusalem, her maiden name of Lovino, and her birthplace as Trieste in 1927. Bannister watched her closely.

'When were you sent to Jadwiga?'

'In the spring of 1943.'

'And were you tattooed with a number?'

'Yes.'

'Do you recall that number?'

She unbuttoned her sleeve and slowly rolled it back to her elbow and a blow fell on the courtroom. She held out her arm with a blue tattoo. Someone in the rear of the court cried aloud and the jury showed its first reaction. 'Seven zero four three two and a triangle to denote a Jew.'

'You may roll your sleeve down,' the judge whispered.

The number was covered.

'Mrs Shoret,' Bannister continued. 'Do you have any children?'

'None of my own. My husband and I adopted two.'

'What did you do in Jadwiga?'

'For four months I worked in a factory. We made parts for field radios.'

'Very hard work?'

'Yes, sixteen hours a day.'

'Did you have enough to eat?'

'No, my weight fell to ninety pounds.'

'Were you beaten?'

'Yes, by Kapos.'

'And what was your barrack like?'

'It was like a normal concentration camp barrack. We were stacked up in layers of six. Some three to four hundred to a barrack with a single stove in the center, a sink, two toilets and two showers. We ate from tin plates in the barracks.'

'After four months what happened?'

'The Germans came looking for twins. They found my sister and me and the Cardozo sisters with whom we grew up in Trieste and who were deported with us. We were taken by truck into the main camp to Barrack III of the medical compound.'

'Did you know what Barrack III was all about?'

'We soon found out.'

'What did you find out?'

'It held men and women who were used in experiments.'

'Who told you that?'

'We were put with another set of twins, the Blanc-Imber sisters of Belgium, who had been X-rayed and operated on. It did not take long to learn from everyone why we were there.'

'Would you describe Barrack III to my Lord and the jury?'

'The women were kept on the ground floor and the men on the upper floor.

All windows facing Barrack II were boarded because there was an execution wall outside, but we could hear everything. The opposite windows were kept shut most of the time so we were always in darkness except for a few small light bulbs. The far end of the barrack was caged off and held about forty girls who were being experimented on by Dr Flensberg. Most of them had been driven insane so they were mumbling and screaming all the time. Many of the other girls like the Blanc-Imber sisters were recovering from operations of Voss's experiments.'

'Did you have knowledge of any prostitutes or women receiving abortions?'

'No.'

'Did you know a Dr Mark Tesslar?'

'Yes, he was with the men upstairs and from time to time helped treat us.'

'But so far as you knew, he did not operate on any women?'

'I never heard of it.'

'Who watched you in Barrack III?'

'Four women Kapos, Polish women armed with truncheons, who had a small room for themselves, and a woman doctor named Gabriela Radnicki, who had a little cell at the end of the barrack.'

'A prisoner?'

'Yes.'

'Jewish?'

'No, a Roman Catholic.'

'Did she treat you badly?'

'Quite contrary. She was very sympathetic. She worked very hard to save those who had been operated on, and she went alone into the cage holding the insane. She would calm them when they became hysterical.'

'What became of Dr Radnicki?'

'She committed suicide. She left a note saying she could no longer bear to watch the agony and not be able to alleviate the suffering. We all felt we had lost our mother.'

Angela felt Terrence's hand grip hers so tightly she almost cried out. Adam continued to stare up at the witness box almost removed from what was being said.

'Was Dr Radnicki replaced?'

'Yes, by Dr Maria Viskova.'

'And how did she treat you?'

'Also like a mother.'

'How long were you kept in Barrack III?'

'A few weeks.'

'Tell us what happened then.'

'SS guards came and got us, the three sets of twins. We were taken to Barrack V to a room with an X-ray machine. An SS orderly spoke to us in German, which we did not understand clearly. Two other orderlies took off our clothing and one at a time a plate was fastened to our abdomen and our back. He took my number from my arm and recorded it and I was X-rayed for five to ten minutes.'

'What was the result of that?'

'A dark-colored spot formed on my abdomen and I vomited very much afterwards.'

'All of you?'

'Yes.'

'Was the spot painful at all?'

'Yes, and it soon formed pus.'

'Then what happened?'

'We remained in Barrack III a few weeks to a month. Time was hard to keep track of. But I remember it growing colder so it must have been towards November. The SS came for us, the three sets of twins, and several men were brought down from upstairs and we were all marched over to Barrack V again and put into a sort of waiting room. I remember we were very embarrassed because we were undressed ...'

'In one room?'

'There was a curtain separating us but soon we were all mixed together in confusion.'

'Naked?'

'Yes.'

'How old were you, Mrs Shoret?'

'Sixteen.'

'From a religious family?'

'Yes.'

'With little experience with life?'

'With no experience. Until then I had not been seen naked by a man, or seen a man's organ.'

'And your heads were shaved.'

'Yes, because of the lice and typhus.'

'And there you were all mixed together. Were you mortified?'

'We were being degraded like animals and we were terrified.'

'And then?'

'Orderlies held us down on some wooden tables and shaved our intimate parts.'

'And then?'

'Two men shoved me on a stool and held my head down between my legs and another man put a needle into my spine. I screamed for pain.'

'Screamed for pain? A moment please. Are you quite certain you weren't already in the operating room?'

'I am quite certain I was in the waiting room.'

'Do you know what an injection is? A small injection?'

'I have had many.'

'Well, didn't you have a small injection prior to the spinal?'

'No, only the one.'

'Go on.'

'In several minutes my lower body went dead. I was thrown on a wagon and rolled out of the room. All around the men and women were screaming and struggling and more guards arrived with clubs and were beating them.'

'And you were the first taken out of the room?'

'No, I am sure a man was first. I was rolled into the surgery and strapped on the table. I remember the lamp over my head.'

'You were totally conscious?'

'Yes. Three men with masks stood over me. One wore the uniform of an SS officer. Suddenly, the door burst open and another man came in and began to argue with the surgeons. I could not understand too much of it because they were speaking mostly in Polish, but I knew the new man was protesting the treatment. At last he came to my side and sat near me and stroked my forehead and spoke to me in French, which I understood better.'

'What did this person say to you?'

'Courage, my little dove, the pain will soon pass. Courage, I will take care of you.'

'Do you know who this person was?'

'Yes.'

'Who?'

'Dr Mark Tesslar.'

Chapter Thirteen

Sima Halevy was a striking contrast to her twin sister, Yolan Shoret. She appeared many years older, ill, and without the vigor or command of her sister. She spoke listlessly as she read her tattoo number to the court and told them she also lived in Jerusalem with two adopted children, orphaned immigrants from Morocco. She repeated the scene of the waiting room and the operation and the presence of Dr Tesslar.

'What happened after the operation?'

'I was carried by stretcher back to Barrack III.'

'And what was your condition?'

'I was very sick for a long time. Two months, maybe longer.'

'Were you in pain?'

'In pain that I feel to this day.'

'What about the extreme pain?'

'For a week we all just lay in bed and cried.'

'Who looked after you?'

'Dr Maria Viskova and often Dr Tesslar would come from upstairs to see us. There was another doctor who came often, a French woman. I do not remember her name. She was very kind.'

'Did any other doctor come to see you?'

'I vaguely recall one time when I was running a high fever that Dr Tesslar and Dr Viskova were arguing with a male doctor about more food and medicine. Only that once, and I am not so sure who it was.'

'Do you know what was wrong with you?'

'The wound had opened. We had only paper bandages. The smell from us was so horrible no one could stand near us.'

'But after a time you recovered and returned to work in the factory?'

'No, I never recovered. My sister was sent back to the factory, but I was unable to. Maria Viskova pretended to keep me as her assistant so they would not send me to the gas chamber. I stayed with her until I was strong enough to do very light work in a book binding barrack which repaired old books to send to the German soldiers. It was a place where we were not treated too harshly.'

'Mrs Halevy, would you tell us the circumstances of your marriage?'

She relayed the story of a sweetheart in Trieste when she was fourteen and he was seventeen. Before her sixteenth birthday she was deported and lost track of him completely. After the war in the staging and relocation centers in Vienna and elsewhere it was customary for the survivors passing through to leave notes on a bulletin board in hopes that a friend or relative might find it. By some sort of miracle her note was found by her sweetheart, who had managed to survive Auschwitz and Dachau. After a two year search he found her in Palestine and they were married.

'What effect has this operation had on your life till now?'

'I am a vegetable. I spend most of my time in bed.'

Sir Robert Highsmith stood before his rostrum with a page of notes of the discrepancies between the testimony of the two sisters. There was no question that Bannister had made inroads and these victims were making a telling effect. Nonetheless, they had not been able conclusively to pin the operations on Dr Kelno and he himself believed it was not Kelno. He realized the girls had sympathy. He had to handle them carefully.

'Madame Halevy,' he said in a manner that contrasted the flair of his earlier examinations. 'My learned friend has suggested that it was Dr Kelno who performed the operations you and your sister described. But you don't know that to be a fact, do you?'

'No.'

'When did you first hear of Dr Kelno?'

'When we were brought from the factory to Barrack III.'

'And you remained there for some time after your operation?'

'Yes.'

'But you never saw him or at least you could not identify him?'

'No.'

'And you know that the gentleman sitting between us is Dr Kelno.'

'Yes.'

'And you still cannot identify him.'

'They were wearing masks in the surgery, but I don't know this man.'

'How do you know you were taken to Barrack V for your operation?'

'I don't understand.'

'Did you see a sign that read Barrack V over an entry?'

'No, I don't believe so.'

'Could it have been Barrack I?'

'It's possible.'

'Are you aware that Dr Flensberg and his assistant were carrying out experiments in Block I and had their own surgeons?'

'I did not know that.'

'I suggest it is all in his indictment as a war criminal. I also suggest that you only recently recalled that you went to Barrack V. Is that not so, Madame Halevy?'

She looked in confusion to Dr Lieberman.

'Please answer the question,' the judge said.

'I spoke to lawyers here.'

'In fact you are not able to identify anyone at all, Voss, Flensberg, Lotaki, or Kelno.'

'No, I cannot.'

'In fact, it might have been a Dr Boris Dimshits who performed the operation.'

'I do not know.'

'But you do know that Dr Kelno has testified that he visited his patients after the operation. If this testimony were true then you would be able to identify him.'

'I was very sick.'

'Dr Kelno also testified that he gave the spinal and anesthetic himself in the operating room.'

'I am not certain I was in the operating room then.'

'Then it might not have been Dr Kelno.'

'Yes.'

'Do you see your sister quite often in Jerusalem?'

'Yes,'

'And you've talked about all of this, particularly since you were contacted for testimony in this case.'

'Yes.'

The robes slipped off Sir Robert's shoulders as he was driving with excitement despite his desire to keep restrained.

'Now both you and your sister are vague and contradictory on a number of points and particularly the dates and time lapses. There is questionable testimony on whether you were taken in by stretcher or wagon ... whether Dr Tesslar sat on your right or your left or at your head ... whether the table was tilted ... whether or not you could actually see a reflection in the overhead lamp ... who was in the room ... how many weeks you spent waiting in Block III after your irradiation ... what people were saying in Polish and German ... you have testified you were quite drowsy and your sister testified she was awake ... you are not absolutely certain your injection was given in the waiting room.'

Highsmith dropped the paper to the table and leaned forward holding the rostrum with both hands and cautioning himself not to raise his voice.

'I suggest, Madame Halevy, you were quite young and all of this happened a long time ago.'

She listened closely as Dr Leiberman told her everything back in Hebrew. She nodded and said something back.

'What is her answer?' the judge asked.

'Mrs Halevy said that Sir Robert is probably correct about her discrepancies on many points but there is one thing that no woman can forget and that is the day she knows she is unable to bear her own child.'

Chapter Fourteen

Hemlines were up in Czechoslovakia. Prague openly displayed her Western heart as well as her Western-oriented thighs. It was the most liberal Communist country, seeing its most liberal days. Flocks of tourists moved in and out from the West in buses and by rail and airline.

Even the landing of an El Al Israel jet created little stir. After all, the affection of the Czechs for their Jewish population and the State of Israel was well established. From the days of Jan Masaryk at the end of the war there was a sincere mourning for the seventy-seven thousand Czech Jews murdered at Teresienstadt and the other extermination camps and it was Masaryk himself who defied the British and allowed Czechoslovakia to be a staging and transit point for the survivors of the holocaust attempting to run the blockade to Palestine.

This El Al flight would have drawn scant attention except that one of the passengers was Shimshon Aroni, whose arrival triggered the usual speculations at police headquarters.

'Jalta Hotel,' he said to the driver of an Opel taxi.

They turned into a swarm of vehicles, trolleys, and buses on Wenceslaus Square and checked in at the reception desk. It was four o'clock. Two hours should get things moving, he thought.

A small single room, the smallest. His life had been lived in small single rooms hunting escaped Nazis. Prague had remained the only decent city among the Communist countries but since the murder of Katzenbach, it too took on a sick smell.

His battered bag was opened and its contents put away in minutes. Two million air miles. Two million miles of hunting and hounding. Two million miles of vengeance.

He walked over to the square on a now familiar pilgrimage, first to the U Fleku Beer Garden. Israeli beer was not so good. In fact, it was rather bad. When Aroni traveled before retirement he had a chance to taste good beer, but lately he had the scant satisfaction of the local product at home. U Fleku, an enormous drinking hall, had the best beer in the world Pilsener to Bohemia.

He gloried in three glasses and studied the crowd and the girls and their short skirts. Czech and Hungarian women were the best. In Spain and Mexico bulls were bred for their courage. In Hungary and Czechoslovakia women were bred for love-making. Subtle, frantic, imaginative, irrational tempers, magnificent sweetness. What a bore it all has been, Aroni thought. He had been too busy hunting Nazis for serious love-making and now he was getting too old, almost seventy, but not that old. No use of dreaming. His trip to Prague precluded a romance.

He mentally converted the Czech koruna into Israeli pounds, paid his bill, and continued on to the Charles Bridge that spanned the Vltava River with its great stone railings adorned every few feet by the statue of a grim saint.

Aroni's step slowed as he walked toward Starometski – the Old Town – for here were the memories, the pitiful remains of a thousand years of Jewish life in Central Europe. The Staronova Synagogue, the oldest in Europe, dating back to 1268, and the Klaus cemetery, with thirteen thousand broken and crooked tombstones going back to before the time of Columbus.

Aroni had seen the old graveyards in Poland, in Russia, in Roumania, largely unkept and vandalized. At least here was a parcel of sacred ground.

Graveyards. The death place of most Jews was the unmarked mountains of nameless bones of the extermination camps.

The Jewish State Museum held a few relics of fifteen hundred villages profaned during the Nazi occupation and the Pinkas Synagogue carried a grizzly memorial.

Read the names again, Aroni. Read them again and again ... Terzin,

Belzec, Auschwitz, Gliwce, Majdanek, Sobibor, Bergen-Belsen, Izbica, Gross-Rosen, Treblinka, Lodz, Dachau, Babi-Yar, Buchenwald, Stutthof, Rosenburg, Piaski, Ravensbruck, Rassiku, Mauthausen, Dora, Neuengamme, Chelmno, Sachsenhausen, Nonowice, Riga, Trostinec, and all the other places his people were murdered.

Seventy-seven thousand names of the dead on a synagogue wall and the words, PEOPLE BE VIGILANT.

Aroni returned to the hotel at six o'clock. As he calculated, Jiri Linka waited in the lobby. They shook hands and made to the bar. DINER'S CLUB WELCOME, the sign of peace and progress proclaimed.

Jiri Linka was a cop, a Jewish cop. He looked like a cartoon of an iron curtain policeman. Aroni ordered a Pilsener and Linka a shot of slivovitz.

'How long since you've been to Prague, Aroni?'

'Almost four years.'

'Things have changed, eh?'

They conversed in Czech, one of Aroni's ten languages. 'How long will your comrades in Moscow permit you such happiness?'

'Nonsense. We are a progressive Soviet country.'

Aroni grunted through rivulets of wrinkles. 'I stood at the Charles Bridge today and looked into the river . . . Katzenbach.'

Linka turned quiet as Aroni made reference to an American member of the Jewish Joint Distribution Committee whose mission it was to liberate Jews. He was found dead, floating in the river.

'First they'll get the Jews,' Aroni said, 'and then the Czechs. You are seeing too many good things from the West. I predict you'll have the Russian Army in Prague within a year.'

Linka giggled. 'I thought you retired. I thought maybe you came this time to go to the spas and take a mud bath.'

'I am working for a private party. I want to see Branik.'

Linka puckered his lips and shrugged at mention of the head of the secret police. Aroni was one of the best men in the business and never sought out things foolishly. In all the years he had come to Czechoslovakia he had been content to work through channels.

'I want to see Branik tonight.'

'I think he is out of the country.'

'Then I leave tomorrow. I have no time for a run around.'

'Maybe you'd like to talk to someone else?'

'Branik. I'll be waiting in my room.' He left.

Linka drummed his fingers on the table, finished his drink, snatched his hat, and hurried out to the square. He hopped in his small Skoda Octavia and raced toward headquarters.

Chapter Fifteen

The first of the male victims, Moshe Bar Tov, was called over from the consultation room. He entered the court with an air of defiance and appearing somewhat awkward in a good suit. He gave a small wave to Abraham Cady and David Shawcross, then glared down hostilely at Adam Kelno, who declined to meet his eye. Kelno appeared tired, quite for the first time.

Moshe Bar Tov had been the first to respond to Aroni's search, and it was he who brought the others in and was their obvious leader.

'Before we swear in this witness,' Anthony Gilray said, turning to the press, 'I must express concern and distress over a report that came in from a Jerusalem newspaper describing one of the witnesses as a woman in her early forties with two adopted children, slightly set and formerly from Trieste. Now people in Jerusalem, and I understand they are following this trial closely, are apt to identify this lady. I reiterate that there should be a refraining from any kind of description of any sort.'

The offending journalist, an Israeli, busied himself with notes and did not look up.

'Dr Leiberman, you are still under oath and will continue to be for any other witnesses in Hebrew.'

Brendon O'Conner conducted the examination as Tom Bannister studied it all from a marbelized pose.

'Your name, sir.'

'Moshe Bar Tov.'

'And your address?'

'Kibbutz Ein Gev in the Galilee of Israel.'

'That is a collective settlement, a large farm.'

'Yes, many hundred families.'

'Did you change your name at any time, sir?'

'Yes, my former name was Herman Paar.'

'And before the war you were from Holland?'

'Yes, Rotterdam.'

'And you were deported by the Germans?'

'Early in 1943 with my two sisters, my mother and father. We were transported in cattle cars to Poland. I am the only survivor.'

In contrast to Thomas Bannister, Brendon O'Conner examined impatiently with the voice of a Shakespearean actor. Bar Tov showed steel over the death of his family.

'You were tattooed?'

'Yes.'

'Will you read your number to the jury.'

'One hundred fifteen thousand, four hundred and ninety and a denotation as a Jew.'

'And what happened to you at Jadwiga?'

'I was sent to work with other Dutch Jews in an I. G. Farben factory making shell casings.'

'One moment,' Gilray interrupted. 'I am not defending any particular German manufacturer. On the other hand there is no German manufacturer here to defend himself.'

Dr Leiberman and Bar Tov engaged in a conversation in Hebrew.

'The court would like to know, Dr Leiberman, exactly what is transpiring.'

Dr Leiberman turned red. 'Your Lordship, I'd rather not . . .'

'I shall place it in the form of a request for the time being.'

'Mr Bar Tov says he will gladly send you a copy of the Jadwiga War Crimes Trials in English from the Kibbutz library. He insists he worked in an I. G. Farben factory.'

Anthony Gilray was perplexed and at an unusual loss of words. He fiddled with his pencil and grumbled, then turned to the witness box. 'Well, tell Mr Bar Tov I appreciate his special knowledge of the situation. Also explain to him that he is in an English courtroom, and we do demand complete respect for the rules of this trial. If I interrupt it is certainly not out of any desire to protect the Nazis or the guilty, but to adhere to normal conduct of fair play.'

After this was told, Bar Tov knew he had his victory and nodded to the judge that he would behave.

'Now, Mr Bar Tov, you worked in this, er, particular munitions factory for how long?'

'Until the middle of 1943.'

'How old were you at the time?'

'Seventeen.'

'And what happened?'

'An SS officer came to the factory one day and began choosing certain people, myself and several other Dutch boys of about my age. We were taken into the main camp of Jadwiga and placed into Barrack III of the medical compound. After several weeks the SS came and took us away to Barrack V. There was myself and five other Dutchmen. We were ordered to undress in a waiting room. Then, after a time I was taken into a room with an examination table and told to get on it on all fours.'

'Did you ask why?'

'I knew and I complained.'

'What were you told?'

'I was told I was a Jewish dog and I had better stop barking.'

'In what language?'

'German.'

'By whom?'

'Voss.'

'Who else was in the room?'

'SS guards, Kapos, two others who were either doctors or orderlies.'

'Can you identify any of them other than Voss?'

'No.'

'Then what happened?'

'I tried to jump off the table and was hit a blow on the side of the head. I was still conscious but too hurt to struggle against three or four of them who held me on the table. One of the orderlies held a piece of glass under my penis and the doctor or someone in white shoved a long wooden stick like a broom handle up my rectum forcing me to eject sperm on the glass.'

'Did it hurt?'

'Are you serious?'

'Quite serious. Did it hurt?'

'I screamed for mercy to every god I knew and all the gods I didn't know.'

'What happened after that?'

'I was dragged bodily into another room and while they held me, they put my testicles on a metal plate on a table. Then, an X-ray machine was directed on one of my testicles for from five to ten minutes. Afterward, I was returned to Barrack III.'

'What was the effect of all this?'

'I was very dizzy and I vomited constantly for three days. Then, some black stains appeared on my testicles.'

'How long did you remain in Barrack III?'

'A number of weeks.'

'Do you know for a fact that your friends got the same treatment?'

'Yes and many other men in the barrack.'

'You say you were quite ill. Who took care of you?'

'Dr Tesslar and, because there were so many Dutch in the barrack, a prisoner, a Dutch prisoner assisted. His name, I remember as Menno Donker.'

'How long did you remain in Barrack III before you were removed again?'

'It must have been November.'

'Why do you say that?'

'I recall talk of liquidating the ghettos around Poland and hundreds of thousands being shipped to Jadwiga West. It was so many the extermination facilities couldn't handle them. There were executions by a firing squad going on all the time outside our barrack, shooting and screaming all the time.'

'Would you tell my Lord and the jury about your removal from Barrack III?'

'The SS came for the six of us who had been irradiated together. They also took a Pole, an older man, and Menno Donker.'

'Had Donker been irradiated?'

'No, I thought it strange he should be taken. I remember that.'

'Go on, please.'

'We were marched to Barrack V, the eight of us and six women from the ground floor of the barrack. Then, a scene of madness took place. Everyone was naked and being manhandled and held for injections.'

'How many injections did you have?'

'Only one, in the spine.'

'How was this administered and where?'

'In the waiting room. A huge Kapo locked my arms behind me so I was powerless, a second shoved my head between my legs and the third gave me the needle.'

'Was it painless?'

'I never have to worry about pain from that time on because nothing could ever give me so much pain. I passed out.'

'And when you awakened?'

'I opened my eyes and saw a reflection lamp. I tried to move but my lower body was dead and I was held by straps. A number of men stood over me. The only one I knew was Voss. One of the men in white and wearing a mask held my testicle in a pair of forceps and showed it to Voss. He put it in a bowl, and I remember them reading the number off my arm and writing it on a tag attached to the bowl. I began to cry. That is when I noticed Dr Tesslar at my side trying to comfort me.'

'And you were returned to Barrack III?'

'Yes.'

'What was your condition?'

'All of us were ill from infection. Menno Donker was the most ill because both of his testicles had been removed. I remember one of the boys, Bernard Holst, was taken away that first night. I heard later he died.'

'And after a time, you were released?'

'No. I remained. We were taken back to Barrack V and X-rayed again.'

'Did you have a second operation?'

'No, I was saved by Dr Tesslar. There was a death in the barrack. He paid off the Kapos to fill in a death certificate in my name. I took the name of the dead man and was able to continue with it until we were liberated.'

'Mr Bar Tov, do you have any children?'

'I have four. Two boys and two girls.'

'Adopted?'

'No, they are my own.'

'You'll forgive me for this next question, but it is extremely important and is not meant to make any inference on the nature of your relationship with your wife. Were you examined in Israel to ascertain that you were potent?'

Bar Tov smiled. 'Yes, I'm too potent. I have already enough children.'

Even Gilray joined in a short laugh, then silenced the room with a frown.

'So, even though you were subjected to severe radiation in both testicles, you were not sterilized?'

'That is right.'

'And whoever took out your testicle may well have been removing a healthy and not a dead gland?'

'Yes.'

'No further questions.'

Sir Robert Highsmith arose and contemplated quickly. This was the third victim paraded before the court. Obviously, Bannister was saving some firepower for later. The web of innuendo was being woven around Kelno with the coup to come in the form of Mark Tesslar.

He went into a swaying motion. 'Mr Bar Tov, in fact weren't you sixteen when you arrived at Jadwiga?'

'Sixteen or seventeen ...'

'You testified you were seventeen, but you were sixteen. It was a long time ago, two decades ago. Many things are hard to remember exactly, isn't that so?'

'Some things I forget. Some things I never forget.'

'Yes. And those things which you forgot, you were refreshed on.'

'Refreshed?'

'Did you ever testify or give a statement before?'

'At the end of the war I made a statement in Haifa.'

'And no other statements until you were contacted within the last several months in Israel.'

'That is true.'

'By a lawyer who took a statement in Hebrew?'

'Yes.'

'And when you arrived in London, you sat down with another lawyer and

Dr Leiberman and went over what you had said in Israel?'

'Yes.'

'And on many points you refreshed your recollection of what you stated in Haifa.'

'We cleared up some points.'

'I see. Points about morphia . . . a pre-injection. Did you talk about that?'

'Yes.'

'I suggest that you passed out in the waiting room, not from the pain of the spinal, but you had been put under by morphia in Barrack III and it took effect in Barrack V.'

'I don't remember any other injection.'

'And being unconscious during the operation you recall no brutality, you remembered nothing.'

'I have testified I was unconscious.'

'And of course you are not identifying Dr Kelno as either the surgeon or the man who induced sperm from yourself.'

'I cannot identify him.'

'You saw photographs of Dr Lotaki in the newspaper, I suppose. Can you identify him?'

'No.'

'Now then, Mr Bar Tov, you are quite grateful to Dr Tesslar, are you not?'

'I owe him my life.'

'In a concentration camp people save people's lives. You know that Dr Kelno saved lives, don't you?'

'I heard.'

'And since the liberation, you have remained in contact with Dr Tesslar, have you not?'

'We lost contact.'

'I see. But you have seen him since you've been in London.'

'Yes.'

'When?'

'Four days ago, in Oxford.'

'To have a reunion as old friends.'

'Yes.'

'Dr Tesslar had quite an influence on you.'

'He was like our father.'

'And you were quite young and your memory quite faulty, you could have forgotten some things.'

'Some things I will never forget. Have you ever had a wooden handle shoved up your rectum, Sir Highsmith?'

'Now, just a moment,' Gilray said. 'You will address yourself to the questions.'

'When did you first hear the name of Dr Kelno?'

'I heard it in Barrack III where we were held.'

'Who told you the name?'

'Dr Tesslar.'

'And recently in London you were shown a floor plan of Barrack V.'

'Yes.'

'To get all the rooms straight in your mind.'

'Yes.'

'Because you did not remember exactly what room you were in at what time. I suggest that. And were you shown photographs of Voss?'

'Yes.'

'Now then, what is your job on your kibbutz?'

'I am in charge of marketing and the truck cooperative with other kibbutzium in the area.'

'And before that?'

'I was a tractor driver for many years.'

'It is very hot in your valley. Wasn't it difficult work?'

'It is hot.'

'And you were a soldier in the Army?'

'In two wars.'

'And you still do your military service each year.'

'Yes.'

'So, with four children, your health was not impaired by this operation.'

'God was more fortunate to me than to some others.'

Bannister now launched a massive frontal assault, coming back with three more men, a Dutchman and two Israelis who had been with Bar Tov on that night in November. As the story was hammered home by repetition, there were fewer and fewer differences in the testimony. Each of them insisted that Dr Tesslar was present in the operating room thus building toward the climax of the defense case. The main difference was that they had no natural children of their own as did the more fortunate Bar Tov.

After the third testified, Bannister called still another man forward, a former Dutchman named Edgar Beets, who was now Professor Shalom of Hebrew University.

In this battle of attrition, Highsmith suddenly wearied. He turned the cross-examination of Shalom over to his junior, Chester Dicks.

Professor Shalom proved extremely articulate as the pace slowed for another recounting of the events. As Dicks ended his questioning, Bannister came to his feet.

'Before this witness is withdrawn, I am going to call your attention to the fact that my learned friend has not challenged this witness on several points of the plaintiff's case, most importantly he did not challenge the witness that Dr Tesslar was present. And I call to his Lordship's attention that neither of my learned friends suggested that the testimony of any of these witnesses was untrue.'

'Yes, I see what you mean,' the judge said. 'Well, what is the situation, Mr Dicks?' He leaned forward. 'I think the jury is entitled to know if you think the witnesses have let their imaginations run loose and dreamed all of this, or if they are perfectly honest men and women who cannot be relied on. Now, just what is your case, Mr Dicks?'

'I do not think they can be relied on,' Dicks answered, 'due to the distressing circumstances.'

'You are not suggesting,' Gilray said, 'they are all telling a pack of lies.'

'No, my Lord.'

'It is usual,' Bannister insisted, 'to challenge a witness if you do not accept the witness's evidence. You have not done that on the major issue.'

'I have asked a number of questions about the presence of Dr Tesslar.'

'There's no need to put every point to the witness. Oh, very well, why don't you put it to the witness,' Gilray said, annoyed somewhat with Bannister.

'I suggest that Dr Tesslar was not in the operating room,' Dicks said.
'He was there,' Shalom answered softly.

Chapter Sixteen

A few moments after the Czech national anthem ended the day's telecast at midnight, a phone summons was answered by Aroni.

'You will walk to the top of the square to the National Museum, and you will wait before the statue.'

Although it was now past midnight, there was music and laughter from the café's of the tree-lined Vaclavske Namesti. How long would the laughter last in Czechoslovakia? Aroni was concerned for his own fate. Certainly in police headquarters they had speculated on his mission and Prague had gotten dangerous since the mysterious death of Katzenbach.

A car slowed before him and the back door opened. He found himself sitting next to a silent guard. Jiri Linka was in front with the driver. Wordlessly they crossed the Charles Bridge to a nondescript large house on Karmelitska bearing the plaque: DEPUTY DIRECTOR OF ANTIQUITIES AND ARCHEOLOGICAL STUDIES, which everyone knew in Prague to be the headquarters of the secret police.

The office was sordidly plain with a long table covered in green felt. The wall at the end of the room was sanctified with the usual portrait of Lenin, who could hardly be considered a Czech hero, and portraits of the current heroes, Lenart and Alexander Dubcek. Aroni reckoned the latter pictures would be off the wall before too long.

Branik did not look like a cop. He was slender, outgoing, and debonair.

'Are you still at it, Aroni?'

'Just enough to keep my hand in.'

Branik nodded for everyone except Linka to leave the room and produced a round of drinks.

'First of all,' Aroni said, 'you have my word I am here on a private matter. I am conducting no government business, moving no funds, and contacting no one.'

Branik placed a cigarette in a long holder and lit it with a very non-proletariat gold lighter. He understood that what Aroni was saying was he didn't want to end up in the river like Katzenbach.

'My business concerns the trial in London.'

'What trial?'

'The one on the front page of every Prague newspaper today.'

'Oh, that trial.'

'There is a strong opinion that Kelno may win unless a certain witness is produced.'

'You think this man is in Czechoslovakia?'

'I don't know. It's a last desperation gamble.'

'I promise nothing,' Branik said, 'except that I'll listen.'

'For obvious reasons the Jewish people cannot lose this case. It would be constructed as a justification of many of the Hitler atrocities. For the most part you have always been fair with us ...'

'Save the speech, Aroni, and let me hear the facts.'

'There was a man in his mid-twenties from Bratislava by the name of Egon Sobotnik, a half Jew on his father's side from a large family of twenty or thirty people by that name. Most of them perished. Sobotnik was deported to Jadwiga and served as a medical clerk in charge of surgical records. He knew Kelno intimately, perhaps observed him closer than any other single person. I have gone through the entire Czech Association of Israel and only a few days ago discovered a distant relative, a man named Carmel. His name used to be Sobotnik but as you know a great number of immigrants changed to Hebrew names. May I?' Aroni asked, nodding to the packet of cigarettes.

Branik whipped out his gold lighter and the old man puffed.

'Carmel had kept a correspondence with a second cousin, a woman by the name of Lena Konska, who still lives in Bratislava. According to Carmel, she escaped the Germans by crossing into Hungary and lived underground in Budapest as a Christian. For a time she hid Egon Sobotnik, but the Gestapo found him. I may add, he was a member of the underground in Jadwiga who was making it a point to record what Kelno was doing.'

Smoke began to swell in the room as Linka joined in.

'It was known he survived the camp.'

'And you believe he is in Czechoslovakia?'

'It is only theory but it seems certain he would have headed back to Bratislava and made some contact with his cousin, this Konska woman.'

'Why his disappearance?'

'It is only a question that Sobotnik can answer, if he is still alive.'

'And you want to see this Konska woman?'

'Yes, and if she can shed light and we find Sobotnik, we want to get him to London immediately.'

'This brings up complications,' Branik said. 'We have no official position in this trial but things with the Jews are touchy.'

Aroni looked directly at Branik transmitting a message the secret police chief could not help but receive. 'We need a favor,' he said. 'In this business favors are reciprocal. Someday, you may need one.'

Someday rather soon, Branik thought.

Just before dawn they raced east from Prague and then south into the Slovakian countryside. Linka nudged Aroni, who had dozed. The first light of day fell on the distant square-turreted Bratislava Castle, which hovered over the Danube River at that place where Austria, Hungary, and Czechoslovakia came together and the landlocked Czechs had their only major port.

It was shortly past noon when the car stopped before Mytna 22. The name of Lena Konska was on the door of Apartment No. 4. A woman in her early sixties opened the door curiously. On a single look, Aroni could well imagine her beauty twenty-five years earlier, enough to live on false papers. Yes, the women of Bratislava were a special sort.

Linka introduced himself. She became apprehensive but showed no fear.

'I am Aroni from Israel. We are here to see you on an important matter.'

Chapter Seventeen

'My Lord, our next witness will testify in Italian.

Ida Peretz, a plumpish woman plainly attired, entered the courtroom seemingly as confused as a bull who had suddenly found itself in the bull ring. Sheila Lamb gave a thumbs-up from the solicitor's table, but she did not see. She searched the courtroom as the Italian interpreter was sworn in, then she seemed to relax as she sighted a young man in his late teens in the last row of spectators and she nodded slightly and he nodded back.

She was sworn in on the Old Testament, giving her maiden name as Cardozo from Trieste.

'Would you tell my Lord approximately when you were sent to the Jadwiga Concentration Camp and under what circumstances.'

There was a lengthy and confused conversation between Ida Peretz and her translator.

'Is there a problem?' Anthony Gilray asked.

'My Lord, Madame Peretz's mother tongue is not Italian. Her Italian is mixed with another language so that I don't seem to be able to give a truly accurate translation.'

'Well, is she speaking Yugoslavian?'

'No, my Lord. She is speaking a mixture of things, some kind of Spanish with which I am not familiar.'

A note was passed from the back row of the courtroom to Abraham Cady; he gave it to O'Conner, who discussed it with Bannister, who rose.

'Can you shed some light on this?' Gilray asked.

'It seems, my Lord, that Mrs Peretz speaks Ladino. It is a medieval Spanish tongue similar to what Yiddish is to German, only more vague. It is spoken by certain Jewish colonies along the Mediterranean.'

'Well, can we find a Ladino translator and return this witness later?'

A flurry of notes passed down.

'My client has, from personal research, run into Ladino and says it is a very rare tongue these days and we may not be able to find anyone in London capable of interpretation. However, Mrs Peretz's son is in the courtroom and has spoken the language with his mother all his life and has volunteered.'

'Would this gentleman kindly approach the bench?'

The son of Abraham Cady and the ward of Adam Kelno watched a very Italian looking young man of nineteen or twenty edge his way to the aisle and down into the knot of standing spectators, through them, and to the associate's table beneath the bench. In the balcony above, the son of Pieter Van Damm also watched as the young man bowed to the judge, awkwardly.

'What is your name, young man?'

'Isaac Peretz.'

'How is your English?'

'I am a student at the London College of Economics.'

Gilray turned immediately to the press.

'I am going to request that this conversation is off the record. Obviously this lady could be easily identified. I should like to call a recess to consider the matter. Sir Robert, would you and Mr Bannister come to my chambers along with Mrs Peretz and her son?'

They walked the solemn polished hallway that separated the courtrooms from the chambers to find Anthony Gilray wigless. He had suddenly taken on a nonjudicial appearance of a rather ordinary Englishman. They were seated about his desk and the usher left the chambers.

'If it will please his Lordship,' Sir Robert said, 'we will concede that a fair translation will be given by Madame Peretz's son here.'

'That is not my main concern. First off, there's this business about identification and secondly, the ordeal it imposes on these two people. Young man, do you know fully of your mother's past unpleasantness?'

'I know I am adopted and that she was experimented on in the concentration camp. When she wrote and told me she planned to testify in London, I felt she should too.'

'How old are you?'

'Nineteen.'

'Are you quite sure you can speak of these things about your mother?'

'I must.'

'And you realize, of course, that everyone at the London College of Economics will soon know about this and everyone in Trieste also.'

'My mother is not ashamed and is not that concerned to remain anonymous.'

'I see. Tell me something for my own curiosity. Was your father a man of means? It is rather unusual to have a student here from Trieste.'

'My father was a simple shopkeeper. My parents hoped I would study in England or America and worked very hard for my education.'

The court was called into order as Isaac Peretz was sworn in and stood behind his mother's chair with his hand on her shoulder.

'We are taking into consideration the relationship of the interpreter and the fact he is not a trained translator, and I do hope that Sir Robert will grant us a reasonable latitude.'

'Of course, my Lord.'

Thomas Bannister arose. 'Would you read your mother's tattoo number?'

The boy did not look at his mother's arm but recited from memory.

'My Lord, in that a great deal of Mrs Peretz's testimony is identical to that of Mrs Shoret and Mrs Halevy, I wonder if my learned friend would object if I lead the witness?'

'No objection.'

The story was told again.

'And you are certain of Dr Tesslar's presence?'

'Yes. I remember his hand stroking me as I saw red in the lamp above, like my own blood. Voss spoke in German, "*macht schnell*" he repeated, "quicker, quicker!" He said he wanted the report to Berlin to show how many operations could be performed in a day. I knew some Polish from my grandfather so I understood Dr Tesslar arguing about the instruments not being sterile.'

'And you were fully conscious?'

'Yes.'

The story of how Dr Viskova and Tesslar kept them alive seemed bitterly clear in her mind. 'My twin sister, Emma, and Tina Blanc-Imber were the worst. I will never forget Tina's cries for water. She was in the next bed hemorrhaging badly.'

'What happened to Tina Blanc-Imber?'

'I don't know. She was gone in the morning.'

'Now, if Dr Kelno had made visits to the barrack to examine you, would he have found you cheerful?'

'Cheerful?'

'He testified that he usually found his patients cheerful.'

'My God, we were dying.'

'And you weren't cheerful about that?'

'No, not hardly.'

'When did you and your sister return to work in the arms factory?'

'Several months after the operation.'

'Would you tell us about that?'

'The Kapos and SS in this factory were particularly cruel. Neither Emma nor I had regained our former health. It was all we could do to live to the end of a day. Then, Emma began to pass out at her work bench. I became frantic to save her. I had nothing to bribe the Kapos with, no way I could hide her. I would sit next to her, propping her up and talking to her for hours to keep her head up and her hands moving. It went on for a few weeks and one day she fainted, and I could not get her to regain consciousness. So ... they took her away ... to Jadwiga West and she was gassed.'

Tears fell down Ida Peretz's plump cheeks. The room was hushed, then everything stopped.

'I believe a short recess is in order.'

'My mother would like to continue,' the boy said.

'As you wish.'

'Then, after the war you made your way back to Trieste and married a Yesha Peretz, a shopkeeper?'

'Yes.'

'Madame Peretz, it is extremely painful for me to have to ask the following question but it is most important that we do. Did anything unusual happen to you physically?'

'I found an Italian doctor who took special interest in me and after a year of treatment, my menstrual period began again.'

'And did you become pregnant?'

'Yes.'

'What happened?'

'I had three miscarriages and the doctor thought it best to remove my other ovary.'

'Now, let us get this clear. You were X-rayed in both ovaries, were you not?'

'Yes.'

'At the same time and for the same period of time, five to ten minutes. Is that correct?'

'Yes.'

'Then being able to conceive with an irradiated ovary, one must assume both ovaries were quite alive.'

'My glands were not dead.'

'So, in fact, a healthy ovary was removed from your body.'

'Yes.'

Sir Robert Highsmith smelled the mood of the room. He slipped a note back to Chester Dicks. TAKE THE CROSS-EXAMINATION AND BE EXTREMELY CAREFUL NOT TO INTIMIDATE HER.

Dicks went through the motions ending on the suggestion that Adam Kelno was not the surgeon.

'You and your mother are free to go,' Gilray said. As the woman stood, her son put a strong arm around her waist; everyone in the courtroom arose as they passed.

Chapter Eighteen

As Sir Francis Waddy was sworn in there was a sense of relaxation from the tension. He was a calm crisp fellow, who could speak to them in their own language.

Brendon O'Conner was up. 'Sir Francis, you are a Fellow of the Royal College of Physicians, A Fellow of the Royal College of Surgeons, A Fellow of the Faculty of Radiologists, a Professor of Therapeutic Radiology at the University of London and the Director of Wessex Medical Center, and Director of the Williams Institute of Radiotherapy.'

'I am.'

'And,' peeled off O'Conner vocally, 'you have been knighted for three decades of distinguished work.'

'I have the honor.'

'Now, you have read the testimony in which we have suggested that if a testicle or ovary is subjected to severe radiation by a semiskilled technician then the partner testicle and ovary would most likely be affected.'

'Beyond question, particularly in the case of the testicle.'

'And a surgeon removing the irradiated testicle or ovary would best be serving the interest of his patient to remove both of them.'

'If those were his grounds, but I should say that his grounds are groundless.'

'Now, sir, if an ovary or testicle is submitted to X ray, no matter how intense in the year of 1943 or today, is there any reason whatsoever to think it might develop cancer?'

'None whatsoever,' Sir Francis answered crisply.

The jury became extremely attentive. Sir Adam Kelno's face pinched with a wave of anger.

'None whatsoever,' O'Conner repeated. 'But of course there must be two medical opinions on that, Sir Francis.'

'Certainly not in 1943 or in any medical literature with which I am familiar.'

'So that in 1943 or now, so far as irradiation of a testicle or ovary is concerned, this is absolutely no medical reason whatsoever for the removal of that organ.'

'Absolutely none.'

'No further questions.'

Sir Robert Highsmith unscrambled himself quickly from the onslaught and went into a consultation with Chester Dicks. Dicks dived into a stack of papers as Sir Robert swayed before the rostrum with a hurt smile on his face.

'Sir Francis, let us say we are in Central Europe two decades ago and a competent surgeon has been locked away in a concentration camp for several years without any enlightenment as to medical progress. Suddenly he is confronted with a serious problem of radiation damage. Might he be anxious about that?'

'Oh, I would rather doubt it.'

'Well, I suggest he is not a radiologist and would be gravely concerned.'

'There is a great deal of misapprehension about radiation hazards.'

'In 1940, 1941, 1942, a doctor is locked away and suddenly comes face to face with sterilization experiments.'

'I think not if he is a suitably qualified physician and surgeon. They did teach those chaps about X rays in Poland, you know.'

Highsmith licked his lips and delivered an audible sigh of frustration. The robes slipped off his shoulders as he went into his swaying motion in search of a question.

'Consider again the circumstances if you will, Sir Francis.'

'Oh, it's all pure supposition. There has never been any information to ever suggest that an irradiated organ could ever become malignant.'

'It was all discussed by competent doctors, more than one of them, and they felt there was risk.'

'I read the testimony, Sir Robert. Dr Kelno seems to be the only one worried about cancer.'

'Are you suggesting, sir, that no other doctor in Jadwiga in 1943 could have also entertained notions of danger?'

'I think I'm quite clear on that.'

'Well now, Sir Francis, exactly what are the limits of irradiation damage when practiced by a semiskilled technician?'

'There would be burning of the skin and if the dosage had been serious enough to damage an ovary, it would have first damaged the more sensitive structure of the intestine.'

'Blisters?'

'Yes, burns that could become infected but certainly not be the cause of cancer.'

Chester Dicks' eyes opened wide with discovery. He tapped Highsmith on the shoulder and handed him a pamphlet. Highsmith was relieved. He held it up then read, '*The Hazards to Man of Nuclear and Allied Radiations.* I shall read to you the paragraph entitled, "cancer." This is a publication of the Royal College of Surgeons. Will you accept that?'

'I most certainly will accept it,' Sir Francis answered. 'I wrote it.'

'Yes, I know,' Highsmith said. 'That's what I want to question you about. Because you imply there was a concern for cancer.'

'Actually we are discussing the risk of leukemia in patients treated for ancylostomiasis, something the ordinary surgeon would have no special knowledge of.'

'But you mention in the paragraph headed "cancer" a study among persons exposed to irradiation after the atomic bombing of Hiroshima and that there is an increase in the death rate and an excess of certain types of cancer, particularly cancer of the skin and abdominal organs.'

'If you will go on to read, Sir Robert, we refer to latent cancer which did not show up for nine or ten years.'

'I suggest that in the eyes of a prisoner/doctor faced with unskilled irradiation, the effect of such irradiation could be in doubt.'

'Sounds more like an excuse to me.'

Highsmith knew he'd better drop it. 'No further questions.'

O'Conner arose. 'Sir Francis. The statistics you used in your pamphlet. Where did you get them?'

'From the American Bomb Casualty Commission.'

'To what conclusion?'

'The incidence of leukemia in those exposed to irradiation was less than a third of one percent.'

'And this evidence was not handed down until many years after the war.'

'Yes.'

'Have you read the medical war crimes trials at Nuremberg on the same question?'

'I have.'

'To what conclusion?'

'There was no evidence to prove that irradiation is a possible cause of cancer.'

Chapter Nineteen

Daniel Dubrowski, the withered remains of a once strapping robust man, approached the witness box a portrait of abject tragedy, a thing, a vegetable who had not laughed for twenty years. Time and again Bannister and the judge asked him to speak up as he gave his home as Cleveland in America and his birthplace in Wolkowysk, then in Poland and now a part of the Soviet Union. At the beginning of World War II he was married, had two daughters, and taught Romantic languages in a Jewish gymnasium.

'Did something particular happen to you in 1942?'

'I was transported with my family into the Warsaw Ghetto.'

'And later, you took part in the uprising?'

'Yes, in the spring of 1943 there was a rebellion. Those of us who had survived till then lived deep below the ground in bunkers. The fight against the Germans lasted over a month. In the end, when the ghetto was in flames, I took to the sewers and escaped to the forest and joined a band of Polish underground.'

'What happened?'

'The Poles didn't want any Jews among them. We were betrayed. The Gestapo seized us, and we were transported to Jadwiga.'

'Would you continue and please speak up, sir.'

Daniel Dubrowski lowered his head and sobbed. As the court fell into silence the reporter wrote: THE WITNESS BECAME DISTRESSED. Gilray offered a recess, but Dubrowski listlessly shook his head and gained his composure.

'Would his lordship and my learned friend object if we spared Mr Dubrowski recounting the details of the demise of his wife and daughters?'

'No objection.'

'May I lead the witness?'

'No objection.'

'Is this all correct? You were taken from a munitions factory to Barrack III at the end of the summer of 1943 and subsequently irradiated in Barrack V and had a testicle removed in the same group of operations as the previous witnesses.'

'Yes,' he whispered, 'that is correct.'

'And Dr Tesslar was present at your operation and later during your recovery.'

'Yes.'

'Three months after the removal of your first testicle, you and Moshe Bar Tov, then known as Herman Paar, were irradiated a second time.'

'Yes.'

'We can assume, can we not, from Mr Bar Tov's testimony that he was not sterilized the first time and that Colonel Voss wanted to have a second go at it and perhaps you had not been sterilized either. Was the second X ray of longer duration?'

'About the same time, but I heard them speak of heavier dosage.'

'Would you tell my Lord and the jury what transpired?'

'After our second exposure to the X ray we had no doubt but that it would only be a matter of time until we were operated on again and made into eunuchs. Menno Donker,' he said in reference to Pieter Van Damm, 'had already been entirely castrated so we realized we would not be spared. There was a corpse one morning as there often was, and Dr Tesslar came to me to speak over the matter of buying off the Kapo guards with a false death registration. It meant either Herman Paar or myself. We were the two waiting for second surgery.

'I made the decision that Paar must be spared. He was the youngest and had a chance for life. I already had lived and had a family.'

'And so, Paar assumed the dead man's identity and never was operated on a second time and you were. Did Paar know of this decision?'

Dubrowski shrugged.

'I'm so sorry,' Mr Justice Gilray said, 'the shorthand writer cannot record a gesture.'

'He was only a boy. I did not discuss this with him. It was the only human thing to do.'

'Would you tell us about your second operation?'

'This time four SS guards came for me. I was beaten, tied and gagged, and dragged to Barrack V. They took the gag from my mouth as I almost choked, then they pulled my pants off and bent me over for a needle in the spine. Although I was bound, I continued to struggle. I screamed and fell to the floor.'

'What happened?'

'The needle broke.'

The courtroom held a mass of queasy stomachs. Eyes were turning to Adam Kelno more often now and he was becoming studied at avoiding contact.

'Go on, sir.'

'I writhed on the floor. Then I heard someone over me speaking in Polish. From the build and voice it was the same doctor who had operated on me the first time. He was in his operating gown and had a mask over his face, and he complained he was waiting for his patient. I cried up to him . . .'

'What did he do?'

'He slammed his heel into my face and cursed me in Polish.'

'What did he say?'

'"*Przestan szezekak jak pies itak itak mrzesz.*"'

'What does that mean?'

'Stop barking like a dog. You will die, anyhow.'

'What happened then?'

'I was given another needle and placed on a stretcher. I begged to be spared another operation. I said, '*dlaczego mnie operujecie jeszcze raz prziciez juzescie mnie ras operowali.* Why operate on me again? I have been operated on once." He continued to be rude and brutal to me.'

'In Jadwiga you were used to being spoken to like that by Germans.'

'Always.'

'But you were Polish and this doctor was Polish.'

'Not exactly. I was a Jew.'

'How long had your family been Polish citizens?'

'Almost a thousand years.'

'Did you expect to be spoken to like this by a Polish doctor?'

'It came as no surprise. I know a Polish anti-Semite when I hear one.'

'I am going to ask the jury,' Gilray interjected, 'to put the last sentence out of their heads. Do you want to leave it at that, Mr Bannister?'

'Yes, my Lord. Go on, Mr Dubrowski.'

'Voss entered in SS uniform and I appealed to him. The doctor then spoke to me in German. He said, "*Ruhig.*"'

'Are you fluent in German?'

'In a concentration camp you learn many German words.'

'What did he mean by "*Ruhig?*"'

'Silence.'

'I am going to rise,' Sir Robert said. 'This testimony is a continuation of unproved innuendo that Dr Kelno was the person who performed this operation. This time my learned friend is not even suggesting that Tesslar was present but that the witness thinks it was the same man who operated earlier. The implication goes deeper because of a conversation held in the Polish language. I suggest an extraordinary amount of liberty has been taken in some of the translations. For example, the word *ruhig* is used in the Heine poem, *Lorelei* as gently. Gently flows the Rhine. If he had meant shut up he would have more likely said, *halte maul.*'

'I see your point, Sir Robert. I take note that Dr Leiberman is among the spectators today. Would you kindly approach the bench and bear in mind you are still under oath. German is your mother tongue, is it not, Dr Leiberman?'

'It is.'

'How would you translate, *ruhig*?'

'In this context it is a command to shut up. Any concentration camp survivor will testify to that.'

'What do you do now, Mr Dubrowksi?'

'I have a used clothing store in a Negro neighborhood of Cleveland.'

'But you are still qualified as a teacher of Romantic languages, are you not?'

'I have no desires left. Perhaps ... that is why I submitted to the second operation in place of Paar ... I have been dead since my wife and daughters were taken from me.'

Moshe Bar Tov had been brought into the consultation room and while Dubrowski underwent cross-examination, Dr Leiberman and Abraham Cady left the courtroom and he was told for the first time about the other man's sacrifice.

'Oh my God!' he wailed in anguish. He fell against the wall and pounded his fist on it and wept. In a little while the door opened and Daniel Dubrowski entered. Moshe Bar Tov turned to face him.

'I think we'd better leave them alone,' Abe said.

Chapter Twenty

THEY'RE ALL GONE NOW EXCEPT HELENE PRINZ, THE LADY FROM ANTWERP. DR SUSANNE PARMENTIER IS WITH HER SO SHE'LL BE ALL RIGHT.

THEY'VE GONE BACK TO ISRAEL AND HOLLAND AND TRIESTE. I AM GOING TO MISS THE GENTLE DR LIEBERMAN LIKE HELL.

MOSHE BAR TOV LEFT STILL IN SHOCK OF THE REVELATION OF THE TRIAL. HE INDUCED DANIEL DUBROWSKI TO COME TO HIS KIBBUTZ FOR A WHILE, TO SHOWER HIM WITH LOVE, TO WEEP AWAY HIS GUILT TO THE ONE WHO GAVE HIM HIS MANHOOD.

I FELT SO EMPTY WATCHING THEM LEAVE. A FAREWELL DINNER, TOASTS, LITTLE GIFTS, AND LOTS OF TEARS. WHAT THEY DID HERE TOOK A SPECIAL KIND OF COURAGE I STILL DO NOT COMPREHEND, BUT I DO KNOW THAT BECAUSE OF IT THEY WILL ALWAYS OWN A FLEETING MOMENT IN HISTORY.

SHEILA LAMB TOOK THEIR DEPARTURE THE HARDEST. FROM THE INSTANT THEY ARRIVED SHE TOOK THEM IN WITH DETERMINATION NOT TO LET THEM FALTER OR FEEL UNLOVED.

SHE WAS PRESENT WHEN THE WOMEN WERE EXAMINED. WHEN SHE SAW THEIR SCARS SHE DID NOT LET HERSELF GIVE AN OUTWARD INDICATION OF THE REVULSION SHE FELT.

AT THE FAREWELL DINNER AT LADY SARAH'S, SHEILA SUDDENLY LEFT THE TABLE AND RAN TO THE BATHROOM AND BROKE INTO TEARS. THE WOMEN WENT AFTER HER. SHE LIED TO THEM THAT SHE WAS UPSET BECAUSE HER PERIOD WAS COMING ON. BECAUSE NONE OF THEM HAD PERIODS, IT TURNED INTO A MOMENT OF EXCITEMENT AND THEN, LAUGHTER.

I WASN'T ALLOWED TO GO TO HEATHROW TO SEE THEM OFF. I DON'T KNOW WHY. THE BRITISH MIND THEIR OWN BUSINESS.

BEN AND I WALKED LIKE WHAT SEEMED FOREVER ALONG THE THAMES EMBANKMENT TRYING TO EQUATE ALL OF WHAT WAS HAPPENING. WE CAME UPON THE IMMENSE LAWNS OF THE TEMPLE AND WERE DRAWN UP MIDDLE TEMPLE LANE.

IT WAS ONE IN THE MORNING BUT THE LIGHTS WERE STILL BURNING IN THE CHAMBERS OF THOMAS BANNISTER AND BRENDON O'CONNER. WANT TO KNOW

ABOUT THOSE PEOPLE? O'CONNER HASN'T SPENT AN EVENING WITH HIS FAMILY SINCE TWO WEEKS BEFORE THE TRIAL STARTED. HE TOOK A SMALL ROOM AT A NEARBY HOTEL SO HE COULD WORK AROUND THE CLOCK. OFTEN AS NOT HE SLEPT ON THE COUCH IN HIS CHAMBERS.

EVERY DAY AFTER COURT, SHEILA TRANSCRIBED THE TESTIMONY AND DELIVERED IT TO THE TEMPLE. O'CONNER, ALEXANDER, AND BANNISTER STUDIED IT ALONG WITH THE NEXT DAY'S WORK AND EVERY NIGHT AT ELEVEN O'CLOCK THEY MET AND WORKED UNTIL TWO OR THREE IN THE MORNING. WEEKENDS WERE A BLESSING. THEY GOT TO WORK STRAIGHT THROUGH.

AND SHEILA? WELL, HER DAY STARTED AT SEVEN IN THE MORNING IN A HOTEL WITH THE WITNESSES. SHE'D BREAKFAST WITH THEM, GET THEM TO COURT CALM, DO HER DAY'S WORK IN COURT, TRANSCRIBE THE TESTIMONY, EAT DINNER WITH THEM AND TAKE THEM TO THE THEATER, MUSEUMS, OUR PRIVATE DINNERS, AND ON THE WEEKEND TO THE COUNTRYSIDE. SHE WAS THERE WITH THEM EACH NIGHT COMFORTING THEM, OUT DRINKING WITH THE MEN OR WHATEVER WAS NEEDED OF HER. I WATCHED HER AGE BEFORE MY EYES FROM THE HURT INSIDE HER.

BEN AND I WALKED FROM THE TEMPLE AND STOOD BEFORE THE LAW COURT. I LOVE THE ENGLISH. I COULDN'T BELIEVE THESE PEOPLE WOULD GO AGAINST ME.

LOOK AT THE QUEUES ON OXFORD STREET. NO PUSHING, NO CUTTING LINES. FORTY MILLION PEOPLE JAMMED TOGETHER IN WEATHER SO FOUL IT DRIVES THE SCANDINAVIANS TO MADNESS. AND FROM IT ALL A SYSTEM OF ORDER BASED ON RESPECT OF ONE'S NEIGHBORS AND THE REASONABLE ASPIRATIONS OF LIFE WITH THE ULTIMATE REWARDS OF KNIGHTHOOD.

LOOK AT THE CALM WAY THEY HAVE TAKEN THE NEW GENERATION. IT ALL STARTED HERE IN ENGLAND. MUSTACHED MEN IN PIN STRIPES, BOWLERS, AND UMBRELLAS IN THE QUEUES BEHIND A CHICK WITH HER SKIRT UP TO HER ASS AND IN FRONT OF A BOY WHO LOOKS LIKE A GIRL.

A BOBBY PASSES US BY AND PUTS A FINGER TO HIS CAP TO SALUTE. HE DOESN'T CARRY A GUN. CAN YOU IMAGINE THAT IN CHICAGO?

EVEN THE PROTESTERS ABIDE BY THE RULES. THEY PROTEST WITH REASONABLE NONVIOLENCE. THEY DON'T SMASH GLASS OR BURN OR RIOT. THEY PROTEST ANGRILY, BUT FAIRLY, AND IN TURN THE POLICE DON'T BASH THEM ABOUT.

HELL, NO BRITISH JURY IS GOING TO DO ME IN.

Ben and his father were in the kind of mood to talk the night out when they returned to the mews.

'What about Vanessa and Yossi. That boy going to be able to make her happy?'

'He's an officer in the paratroops,' Ben said. 'He's been confined in Israel all his life with his back to the sea. You know how tough he is. I think this trip has been good for him. It's good for him to see gentle, gracious, and sophisticated people. He tries to pass it off, but London has impressed him deeply. Now that he's seen it, more and more of Vanessa will rub off on him.'

'Hope so. He's a brain all right.' Abe loaded his glass. Ben held his hand over the rim of his, not wanting anymore. 'You're picking up bad habits in Israel, like not drinking.'

Ben laughed. It was a wide, uninhibited laugh. He was full of the devil. Then, he turned serious. 'Vinny and I hate to see you keep on going through life alone.'

Abe shrugged. 'I'm a writer. I'm alone in the middle of a crowded ballroom. That's my bag.'

'Maybe you wouldn't be so alone if you started looking back at women like Lady Sarah the way she looks at you.'

'I don't know, son. I think maybe your uncle Ben and you and I were all molded out of the same kind of cast. None of us can stand most women socially for more than fifteen minutes. They're only good for balling and not too many of them pass the grade at that. Our problem is that we like to be around men. Air bases, locker rooms, bars, fight clubs, where we don't have to listen to female dribble. Then, you find a woman like Sarah Wydman who is about as complete as a woman can be and even that's not enough. She can't be a man and a woman at the same time. But even if she understood this need I don't think any woman deserves to take the crap of being a writer's wife. I busted your mother. If a woman's got anything to give, I drain her. I'm happy that I'm a writer, but I sure wouldn't want my daughter to marry one.'

Abe sighed and turned his eyes away from his son, dreading to bring up what had been tormenting him all day. 'I saw you and Yossi with the military attaché from the Israel embassy.'

'The situation is not good, Dad,' Ben said.

'God damned Russian son of a bitches,' Abe said. 'They're putting them up to it. When in the name of God are we going to have a day of peace?'

'On the plains of heaven,' Ben whispered.

'Ben . . . now you listen to me. Son . . . for Christ sake . . . don't be a hot pilot.'

Chapter Twenty-one

A bleary-eyed Abraham Cady and his bleary-eyed son entered the court. A man's lavatory stood between the two consultation rooms. Abe made to the urinal. He felt someone next to him and looked over his shoulder. It was Adam Kelno.

'Here's one pair of Jewish balls you're not getting,' he said.

'Silence!'

Helene Prinz was small and pertly dressed and moved into the courtroom with more assurance than any of the other women. Although outwardly she was the leader of them, Sheila felt she was extremely high strung and the most apt to break.

Through a French translator she said that she was from Antwerp, gave her birth date in 1922, and read off her tattoo number. It had been done many times but never failed to affect those who saw it.

'You continued to carry your maiden name of Blanc-Imber even though you and your sister Tina were married after the outbreak of the war.'

'Well, we were not really married. You see, the Germans were sending away married couples so both my sister and I took our vows in a secret ceremony by a rabbi but it was never officially registered. Both our husbands perished at Auschwitz. I married Pierre Prinz after the war.'

'Am I given leave to lead the witness?' Bannister asked.

'No objection.'

'You were taken to Barrack III in the spring of 1943 with your sister Tina and subjected to irradiation treatment. Now, so this is quite clear, this was all done some time before the two other sets of twins the Lovino and Cardozo sisters from Trieste arrived at the barrack.'

'That is quite correct. We were irradiated and operated on quite some time before the other twins arrived.'

'At that time a female doctor, a polish woman, Gabriela Radnicki, was in charge. She is the one who committed suicide and was replaced by Maria Viskova?'

'That is correct.'

'Now then, a month or so after you were irradiated you were taken to Barrack V and will you tell us what happened?'

'Dr Boris Dimshits examined us.'

'How did you know it was Dr Dimshits?'

'He introduced himself.'

'Do you recall his appearance?'

'He seemed very old and somewhat feeble and absentminded and I remember his hands were covered with eczema.'

'Yes, continue please.'

'He sent Tina and me back to Barrack III. He said our irradiation wound had not healed sufficiently to undergo an operation.'

'Was anyone else present?'

'Voss.'

'Well, did Voss protest and tell him to operate anyhow?'

'He complained, but he did nothing. After two weeks the black spots faded and we were taken back to Barrack V. Dr Dimshits said he was going to operate on us and promised us he would leave a healthy ovary. I was injected in the arm and it made me very sleepy. Then, I remember being wheeled into an operating room, and I was put to sleep.'

'Do you know what kind of anesthetic you were given?'

'Chloroform.'

'How long were you bedridden after this operation?'

'Many, many weeks. I had complications. Dr Dimshits visited us often but could hardly see in the semi-darkness. He was failing fast.'

'And afterward you heard that he had been sent to the gas chamber?'

'Yes.'

'And Dr Radnicki committed suicide.'

'Yes, in the barrack.'

'And toward the latter part of the year after the Lovino and Cardozo sisters came to Barrack III you were submitted to X ray again.'

'This time Tina and I became frantic.'

She described the scene of bedlam in the waiting room of Barrack V. 'I struggled. Tina and I fought not to be separated, but they held me and injected my spine. I was injected but my body did not become numb. I could still feel everything.'

'It did not take effect?'

'No.'

'And when you were taken into the operating room you were not given anything to put you under, were you?'

'I was terrified. I could feel everything, and I told them that. I was able to sit up and get off the table. Two of them twisted my arms behind me and dragged me back on the table. The doctor hit me in the face several times and across my breast and shouted at the top of his lungs. "*Verlichte Judin ... you damned Jewess.*" I begged him to kill me for I could not stand the pain. Only because of Dr Tesslar was I able to survive.'

'Were you quite ill after the operation?'

'I ran a very high fever and was half out of my mind. I remember through the haze hearing Tina screaming ... and then I heard nothing. I don't know how much time passed until I was able to think clearly. It may have been days. I asked about Tina, then Dr Viskova told me Tina died of a hemorrhage the first night.'

She swayed and her fists pounded on the witness box rail. Suddenly she sprung to her feet and pointed down to Adam Kelno. 'Murderer! Murderer!' A wail of agony shrieked out from her.

Abe pushed down the aisle knocking people out of his way. 'That's enough!' He shoved past the press box and put his arms around her. 'I'm taking her out of here,' he said.

The usher looked to the judge, who gestured to leave them alone, and as Abe half carried her from the courtroom she cried that she had failed him.

Gilray wanted to start a speech admonishing the scene and serving warning, but he was unable to. 'Are you going to wish to cross-examine the witness, Sir Robert?'

'No. The witness is obviously too distressed to carry on.'

'The jury has seen and heard all this,' the judge answered. 'They aren't apt to forget it. Members of the jury,' Gilray said in a drained and tired voice, 'Sir Robert has made the kind of gesture one would expect of an English barrister. When I am summarizing the evidence for you later I will ask you in all sense of fair play to bear in mind that there was no cross-examination of this witness. Shall we stand adjourned?'

Chapter Twenty-two

'I should like to call to the stand, Mr Basil Marwick,' Brendon O'Conner said. Marwick was totally British of the old school in dress and manner. He took the oath on the New Testament. Marwick gave his name and a Wimpole Street address. It was established that he had a long credential as an anesthesiologist, teacher, and author of numerous papers covering a period of twenty-five years.

'Would you explain to my Lord and the jury the two major types of anesthetics?'

'Certainly. There is the general anesthetic in which the patient is rendered unconscious and the local anesthetic to deaden that part of the body being operated on.'

'And a surgeon, of course, makes the choice and he would make it alone if there were no anesthetist for consultation.'

'Yes. Sometimes he may give a combination.'

'What general anesthetics, those to render a patient unconscious, were available in the early forties in Central and Eastern Europe?'

'Ether, ethyl chloride, chloroform, Evipal, nitrous oxide mixed with oxygen, and others.'

'I must rise,' Highsmith said. 'We have heard testimony from two surgeons at Jadwiga that general anesthetic was not usually available.'

'And we dispute that,' O'Conner snapped back.

'I see,' Gilray mused. 'You are suggesting general anesthetic was readily available in Jadwiga.'

'Well, we've heard testimony from Dr Kelno's own witnesses that they were put under,' O'Conner said. 'You heard the testimony of Mrs Prinz that in her first operation by Dr Dimshits she was put under. I suggest that Dr Kelno found no general anesthetic available only when it came to his Jewish patients.'

'Mr O'Conner, I'm going to allow you to continue, but I suggest you are on thin ice. I am advising the members of the jury that until this is entered as evidence, this part of Mr Marwick's testimony is for the purpose of background.'

O'Conner did not bother to thank his Lordship, but plunged ahead restlessly. 'So some of these anesthetics are given for short operations and others for longer operations.'

'Yes, a surgeon's choice.'

'You have told us what general anesthetics were available in that area of Europe in the 1940s. Would you tell us what local anesthetics were available?'

'Procaine, also known as novocaine, most commonly used by dentists. There was, let me see, percaine and pontocaine and decicaine and others.'

'All used as spinals?'

'Yes. By introduction into the spinal cord it would render the adjacent nerve trunks insensitive or deaden them.'

'Just how is this done?'

'Well, it has been my practice to minimize the discomfort. At the site of the injection I would first inject a little local anesthetic with a very fine needle to deaden the immediate area which will take the larger needle necessary to infiltrate the deeper tissues.'

'Speaking again of the 1940s. Was it standard practice in Poland to first inject the patient with a smaller needle before the main injection?'

'Absolutely. In every text I have seen in that time or today.'

'You heard or read the testimony of four female and six male witnesses who were victims of experiments in Jadwiga. Had you been involved at that time, would you have used a preliminary injection of morphia?'

'I may have refused to be involved. I do not know. But in any event the circumstances called for morphia.'

'Much obliged. And would you have used local or general anesthetic for the operations?'

'My Lord,' Highsmith interrupted. 'We are back to the same thing. My client has testified that when he gave a spinal he used a preliminary injection of morphia.'

'Which a number of witnesses have disputed,' O'Conner said.

'There is still no evidence before this court that Dr Kelno performed these operations,' Highsmith argued.

'That's our case,' O'Connor answered. 'Each of our ten witnesses has not been challenged in that Dr Tesslar was in the operating room. You are aware of Dr Tesslar's statement and what he is going to testify to.'

'I am going to give the same ruling,' Gilray said. 'The jury will consider all of this as hypothetical expert testimony as to general background and not evidence. When I instruct you later I'll define what evidence was brought forth on whether or not Dr Kelno performed the operations in question.'

'But would you say,' O'Conner insisted, 'that you would use a general anesthetic?'

'Yes.'

'Not a spinal?'

'No.'

'Well, exactly why would you put them under?'

'For humane reasons.'

'If there were no preliminary injection is a spinal likely to be painful?'

'Acutely painful.'

'How many spinals do you reckon you've given?'

'Between fifteen hundred and two thousand.'

'Is it always easy to find the exact site to inject the larger needle.'

'No, one must take great care about that.'

'Well, would you carry out a spinal if the patient is screaming and struggling?'

'Certainly not.'

'Why?'

'The actual placing of the needle must be done with extreme accuracy. It is inserted between two bones with very little room to maneuver. It must be in midline and angulated to the curvature of the patient's back. One simply cannot do it without the total cooperation of the patient. I'd say it was impossible. You see, any violent movement of the patient could run the risk of breaking the needle.'

'You heard testimony that a needle broke. What would happen then?'

'If it breaks beneath the skin it could be a frightful disaster. It could cause permanent injury if not retrieved successfully. The pain would be unbearable. Of course if the needle breaks outside, you'd pull it out of the skin.'

'You've heard or read testimony that several of these people still feel the pain today.'

'Considering how they said they were treated, I'd rather suspect they do feel it.'

'Do you have with you in court the kind of needles used in 1940?'

Marwick produced a kit and showed the fine needle for the preliminary injection and then the larger one. They were marked as an exhibit and passed to the jury. The maneuver had its effect by the grimaces as the needle was passed from one to the other.

'Now, in the application of a spinal, we are very concerned, are we not, that the anesthetic stay in the lower part of the body?'

'Yes. If it rises and, say, reaches the nipple line it could produce a fall in blood pressure resulting in the brain being deprived of blood and the patient would become dizzy and faint.'

'You heard the testimony of Mr Bar Tov that he passed out. Was it likely because of this?'

'Oh yes.'

'And you heard the other witnesses say they were quite conscious. Does this surprise you?'

'Not from their testimony.'

'Is morphia always given in surgery?'

'Always.'

'Would you expect people premedicated with morphia to stand in a queue and wait for their operation?'

'Of course not.'

'And if they were ill nourished and debilitated by brutal treatment would morphia tend to be more effective?'

'They would be very dazed by it, all right.'

'It would certainly be difficult for them to struggle with morphia.'

'They could, I suppose, but not effectively.'

'No further questions.'

Highsmith arose as the needle left the jury box and was placed on the associate's table. The shorthand writers changed as Adam Kelno seemed fixed on the kit. His hands drew up as though for an instant he had an unstoppable urge to take up the needle. Smiddy tapped his wrist and his attention turned to Marwick.

'Mr Marwick, did you read or hear testimony of Dr Boland given in behalf of Dr Kelno?'

'I did.'

'And in your expert opinion, would you qualify Dr Boland as also distinguished in the field?'

'Yes.'

'You heard him testify that he himself had received two spinals for surgery done on him and both were given without morphia. He also testified that in the question of premedication it made little difference to the comfort of the patient.'

'Yes, that was his testimony.'

'Would you comment?'

'Well, your own client, Dr Kelno, would disagree with Dr Boland, would he not? And I certainly disagree.'

'But you do agree that in England in 1967 there are two different opinions about this from qualified anesthesiologists.'

'Well, he has his views.'

'Different from yours.'

'Yes.'

'Dr Boland goes on to testify that properly given with a sharp needle a spinal causes very little discomfort. What do you say to that?'

'There is a possibility if given under absolutely perfect conditions.'

'In the hands of a skilled surgeon doing it quickly.'

'As a matter of fact, Sir Robert, it must be done slowly. One must feel his way through delicate ground. On occasion it has taken me ten minutes and there are a number of occasions where experts have failed.'

'You were asked a number of hypothetical questions about surgery in Jadwiga. If you were a surgeon at Jadwiga under pressing circumstances and had no anesthetist or someone trained in giving a general, it would make sense to give a spinal, would it not. What I mean is that a surgeon can't do two things at once, can he? He can't operate at the same time he's giving an anesthetic.'

'The way you phrase it.'

'And while he is operating he just can't put ether or chloroform in the hands of an unskilled assistant?'

'You're quite right that he needs a skilled assistant to give a general.'

'A spinal produces good operating conditions for a surgeon, does it not?'

'Yes.'

'Particularly if a surgeon is pressed and harassed.'

'Yes.'

'Where did you practice in 1940 to 1941?'

'Royal Air Force.'

'In England?'

'Yes. As a matter of fact I recall administering anesthetic to one of the defendants after his plane crashed.'

'Conditions weren't like those in Jadwiga, were they?'

'No.'

'But even in England in those years Dr Boland administered spinal anesthetic without pre-morphia. Does that surprise you?'

'No, but it makes me wince.'

'So what we have here is expert testimony of two anesthesiologists which is diametrically opposed. Two differences of opinion, both of which are right.'

As Highsmith seated himself, O'Conner thumbed through a book he had among his papers. He asked the usher to give a copy to Sir Robert and a copy to Mr Marwick.

'Before we go into this work written by Dr Boland,' O'Conner said, 'you heard and read testimony by Dr Kelno that he was short of trained assistants and for that chief reason he made the choice of a spinal and administered it himself.'

'Yes, I heard that.'

'You also heard or read testimony by Dr Lotaki that he assisted Dr Kelno in a number of these operations.'

'Yes.'

'In your opinion, from Dr Lotaki's background, would he be qualified to administer a general to keep a patient unconscious during an operation?'

'Dr Lotaki is fully qualified.'

'Then the excuse that he didn't have a skilled assistant isn't a valid reason.'

For the first time in the trial, Sir Robert Highsmith found himself glaring at Adam Kelno. Was it a bald lie or an oversight in all the testimony, he wondered.

O'Conner opened the book. 'This work of Dr Boland was published in the year of 1942 and entitled, *New Advancements in the Field of Anesthesia.*'

'I find all of this rather strange,' Highsmith said, 'that none of this was put to Dr Boland when he was in the witness box.'

'With respect to my learned friend,' O'Conner said, 'we had no intention of reading all the books ever written by anesthetists in England, and we had no idea Dr Boland was going to be called for the plaintiff. If you said so beforehand, then we would have brought this into court at that time.'

'Well, I don't think it proper to put to Mr Marwick something Dr Boland wrote and cannot answer for himself.'

'You can recall Dr Boland to the stand if you wish, Sir Robert,' the judge said. 'We won't deny you that.'

Highsmith slumped down.

'I call your attention to page two hundred and fifty-four, paragraph three and I read. "Local anesthesia such as a spinal should never," I repeat, "never be applied indiscriminately and without preparing the patient psychologically or it could result in psychic shock and actual insanity has been known to occur." He states further down the page, "in the case of an extremely nervous or frightened patient the choice of a general anesthetic should be given. If, however, the surgeon deems a spinal more suitable then a premedication by morphia of one and a fourth grain would be in order." What I am saying is that in the circumstances we have described you and Dr Boland are not diametrically opposed at all.'

'We are completely of the same mind,' Mr Marwick said.

Chapter Twenty-three

Angela held the curtain back and peeked outside. They were both there, across the street, a plainclothesman from Scotland Yard and a private detective hired by the Polish Association to guard the house. All phone calls were now screened in the central office.

After the first several days of the trial there were threats and obscenities over the phone, followed by vicious letters and personal visits of people venting their hatred of Adam Kelno.

Scotland Yard assured them it would all die down in due course when the trial was done. Angela, who kept the family spirits up, insisted they leave immediately on a world cruise of a year and then relocate in the anonymity of a small town.

The strain had ground Adam down, and he did not protest the plan. It would be only a matter of a few years when Stephan would have an architect's degree. They could think about retirement. He had to abandon the idea of having Terrence Campbell take over his medical practice. But Sir Adam knew in his heart that Terrence wanted to go back to Sarawak, to his own father, and practice missionary medicine.

Although Adam appeared emotionless in court Angela did her sleeping these nights with one eye open, ready to help him from the terror of the recurring nightmares and to calm his fitful sleep.

They all picked at their dinner, disheartened that it was impossible for Stephan to get back to England.

'How much longer do they think it's going to go on, Doctor?' Terry asked.

'Another week or ten days.'

'It will be over soon enough,' Angela said, 'and we're going to get through it much better if we eat.'

'I suppose there's all kinds of talk at Guy's.'

'You know how those things are,' Terry answered.

'What do they say?'

'Quite frankly, I haven't got time to listen if I expect to do my work. Mary and I have split up, and I think it's rather final.'

'Oh, I'm sorry to hear that,' Angela said.

'No you're not. Anyhow, I should like to remain here with you, now that we all know Stephan can't come.'

'Well, you know how happy that makes us,' Angela said.

'What happened between you and Mary?' Adam asked.

'Nothing really,' he lied. 'We just found that being away from each other gave us a lot more freedom.' Terry did not want to add to the burden he had helped create by telling them Mary had some doubts about Dr Kelno and Terry had stormed out in anger.

The doorbell rang. They could hear Mrs Corkory, the housekeeper, speaking to someone in the vestibule. 'Beg pardon,' Mrs Corkory said, 'but Mr Lowry and Mrs Meyrick are here on a matter they feel quite important.'

'Are they ill?'

'No, sir.'

'Very well, show them into the parlor.'

Lowry, a stocky baker, and Mrs Meyrick, the housewife of a warehouseman, came to their feet awkwardly as the Kelnos entered.

'Evening, Doctor,' Mr Lowry said. 'I hope you'll excuse the interruption. Dr Kelno, we've been talking among ourselves.'

'Your patients, that is,' Mrs Meyrick interrupted.

'Well, anyhow, we want you to know we're with you one million percent.'

'That pleases me a great deal.'

'We are highly incensed, we are, at the lies they're trying to pin on you,' Mr Lowry continued, 'and we feel it's all part of a bloody, beg your pardon, all part of a Communist plot.'

'At any rate, Doctor,' Mrs Meyrick said, 'we've written you this letter of our loyalty and support and went about to everyone collecting their signatures, even the little ones. Here, sir.'

Adam took the letter and thanked them again. After they left he opened it and read it: WE THE UNDERSIGNED EXPRESS OUR HIGH ESTEEM TO SIR ADAM KELNO WHO HAS BEEN GRAVELY MALIGNED. HE HAS TREATED US WITH GREAT CONSIDERATION AND NEVER TURNED A SICK PERSON AWAY FROM HIS DOOR. THIS DOCUMENT IS AN INADEQUATE TOKEN OF OUR AFFECTION.

There were three pages of signatures, some barely legible, some printed, some obviously of children.

'That was a lovely gesture,' Angela said. 'Aren't you pleased?'

'Yes,' Adam said, but he read the names over again. Many patients had not signed and the signatures of all his Jewish patients were missing.

Chapter Twenty-four

An instantaneous murmur of anticipation swept the court as Professor Oliver Lightall was called to the stand. Everyone looked attentively as the man whom many considered England's foremost gynecologist ascended to the witness box. He was tailored but disheveled in a studious way. He had made his adamant decision to testify against a great deal of pressure from a segment of his colleagues.

'This testimony, of course shall be in English,' Tom Bannister said. 'Would you give us your name and address?'

'Oliver Leigh Lighthall. I reside and practice at 2 Cavendish Square in London.'

'You are a doctor of medicine, a Fellow of the Royal College of Surgeons, a Fellow of the Royal College of Obstetrics and Gynecology for the University of London, Cambridge and Wales, and for two decades Director of Obstetrics at the University College Hospital.'

'That is all correct.'

'How long have you practiced in your field?'

'Over forty years.'

'Professor Lighthall. If an ovary is irradiated is there any medical benefit whatsoever to remove it by surgery.'

'Absolutely none.'

'Well, isn't an irradiated ovary or testicle often dead?'

'In so far as its physiological function. For example, the ovary is no longer able to produce eggs nor can the testicle produce sperm.'

'Well doesn't this occur also to a woman when she experiences change of life and often to a man who has undergone certain illnesses?'

'Yes, an ovary ceases to function after menopause, and illness can cause the cessation of male sperm.'

'But you don't go about cutting women's ovaries out just because they've undergone the change of life?'

'No, of course not.'

Arrogant bastard, Adam Kelno thought, arrogant English bastard in his snob clinic on Cavendish Square. O'Conner passed a note back to Shawcross and Cady: WATCH FOR LIGHTNING TO STRIKE.

'Were there two schools of thought about removal of an ovary that had ceased to function in 1943?'

'Only one school.'

'Aren't X-rays, in fact, used to cure cancer?'

'Certain types of cancer will respond to X-ray treatment.'

'Heavy dosages.'

'Yes.'

'And the same goes for a cancerous testicle.'

'Yes, they receive X-ray treatment.'

'Professor Lighthall, it has been suggested that in 1943 it was possible that irradiation of testicles and ovaries could produce cancer. What is your view?'

'That's utter nonsense, poppycock, bordering on the hocus-pocus of a tribal medicine man.'

Adam Kelno flinched. Oliver Lighthall had thrown up at him his own struggle with the fakirs of Sarawak. Behind his English calm, Lighthall was obviously incensed and was not holding back.

'Now, if one was conducting an experiment to see if a testicle is still potent would that testicle be of any use if it were removed by an unqualified operator?'

'If the tissue is to be later examined in a laboratory it is essential that it be removed by a capable surgeon.'

'So that a doctor threatening to use an unskilled SS orderly would more than likely be bluffing for he'd defeat his own purposes.'

'Some things are so logical they need not be argued. I have read the testimony and Voss had no intention of allowing an SS orderly to perform these operations.'

Highsmith started to his feet, stopped midway and seated himself again.

'Have you examined the four women who gave testimony in his case?'

'I have.'

The blood rushed from Adam Kelno's face. Highsmith was once again fixed on his client, trying desperately to glue a passive expression to his face.

'If these women had been exposed to irradiation for a period of five to ten minutes, a surgeon would have been able to see evidence of it, burn marks, blisters perhaps, infection.'

'Some of their burns are visible today,' Lighthall answered.

'Twenty-four years later?'

'In the cases I examined the pigmentation of the skin will remain for the rest of their lives.'

'Well now, if a surgeon sees such burns a short time after the irradiation, would he take the view that an ovary should be removed?'

'I should think quite strongly to the contrary. He would run all sorts of grave risks.'

'Now, Professor Lighthall, in carrying out an ovariectomy in England which is done with a spinal, is it usual to strap the patient to the operating table?'

'Most unusual procedure. Well, one might strap the arms only.'

Adam felt as though his chest were going to burst. A severe pain knifed from his chest to his stomach. He fumbled for a pill and took it as anonymously as possible.

'Not common practice?'

'No. The patient is paralyzed by the injection.'

'Could you tell us what surgical procedures are used after the removal of an ovary.'

Lighthall asked for a life-sized plastic model, which he placed on the rail facing the jury. He brushed the hair back that had fallen into his eyes and he pointed his educated finger. 'This is the womb here. These yellow structures the size of a walnut on either side and behind the womb are the ovaries. What a surgeon must do is cut deeply to the stump which is known as the pedicle to the place where the ovarian artery enters the main artery. The surgeon then clamps and ties to prevent the raw stump from bleeding from the main artery.'

He nipped at his water. The judge offered him a seat, but he answered that he preferred to lecture standing.

'The next procedure is called peritonizing. There exists a very thin membrane which covers the inside of the abdomen. We lift this membrane and use it to cover the stump. In other words, use of the membrane called peritoneum to cover this raw stump is done to prevent adhesions and assure that the stump will clot properly.'

Bannister looked to the jury, incredibly attentive. He let Lighthall's words sink in.

'It's extremely important to do this step, then. It is vital that the raw stump be covered by peritoneal flap?'

'Yes, mandatory.'

'What would happen if you didn't?'

'You'd be leaving a raw stump. The clot which forms in the artery is apt to become infected and adhesions are apt to form from the intestine. If the stump is not properly sealed off there would be hemorrhaging and the possibility of a secondary hemorrhage at a later date of seven to ten days.'

He nodded to the associate who removed the model.

'Are you familiar with the testimony of Dr Kelno?'

'I read it with extreme care.'

'When I asked him if it was proper to cover the stump by use of the peritoneal flap as you have just described he said there was no peritoneum.'

'Well, I can't imagine where he learned surgery. I have been practicing gynecology for forty years and in performing over a thousand ovariectomies I have never failed to find the peritoneum.'

'It's there then?'

'Goodness, yes.'

'Dr Kelno further testified that his method of tying off the raw stump was by a single cross-stitch from the so-called infundibulopelvic ligament. What would you say to that?'

'I'd say it's very bizarre, indeed.'

The eyes of everyone were on Adam Kelno, particularly those of Terrence, who sat openmouthed and felt himself becoming numb.

'How long should an ovariectomy take from the incision to the end?'

'The better part of a half an hour.'

'Is there any virtue in doing it in fifteen minutes?'

'Not unless there is a calamity such as an abdominal hemorrhage. Otherwise I would opine that it is bad surgery to operate with such celerity.'

'Would there be any connection between speed and post-operational hemorrhage?'

Lightfall looked to the high ceiling in meditation. 'Well, if one is working to the clock, one cannot do this surgical toilet which I described. One simply cannot tie off the raw stump and control the bleeding when working at such speed.'

Bannister looked at the jury as Oliver Lighthall continued to collect his thoughts. 'Do you have anything further on this, Professor?'

'When I examined those four women I was not in the least surprised to hear that one of them had died the night of the surgery and another failed to recover. It is my opinion,' he said, looking directly down at the solicitor's table at Adam Kelno, 'it was due to improper tying of the stump.'

It was now becoming apparent that Oliver Lighthall's testimony was an answer in fury over what he had seen.

'If in a series of operations the surgeon did not wash his hands or sterilize his instruments between operations, what is apt to occur?'

'I cannot conceive of any surgeon not attending to these basic principles. Since the days of Lister it would be tantamount criminal negligence.'

'Criminal negligence,' Bannister repeated softly, 'and what would be the results of such criminal negligence?'

'Serious infection.'

'And what of the condition of the operating theater itself?'

'Everyone present should be made as germ free as possible, masks, gowns, antiseptics. For example, in this court now our clothing is filled with bacteria. In a surgery it would spread through the air onto the exposed body of the patient.'

'Is one more or less likely to hemorrhage because of the choice of anesthetic?'

'Yes. Spinals are absolutely notorious for the risk of hemorrhage because of the drop of blood pressure and doubly so if the raw stump is not properly attended to.'

'How long should it take for the wound to heal after a normal successful ovariectomy?'

'A week or so.'

'Not weeks or months?'

'No.'

'In fact, if it were taking weeks and the wounds secreted pus and gave off a noxious odor, what would that indicate?'

'Infection at the time of the operation, an improperly performed operation, not enough care to antiseptic and sterilization.'

'What of the needle?'

'Well, let us see. It has been plunged through the tissues of the back. It has gone into the spinal canal and damage could occur to the membranes covering the spinal cord. This could cause permanent damage.'

'And lifelong pain?'

'Yes.'

'Would you tell us your observations in your examination of the four women?'

'My Lord, may I refer to some notes I took?'

'Certainly.'

He patted through his pockets and slipped on his glasses. 'In order of their testimony. The first lady, one of the twins from Israel. Yolan Shoret. She had a very marked deficiency of the scar. There was a gap, a hole if you please, that was covered only by the thickness of her skin between the outermost layer and innermost layer which covered the cavity of her abdomen.'

He looked to the judge and held up his hand. 'For the sake of demonstrating measurement, I'd like to use the width of my finger tips.'

'Does the jury understand that?' the judge asked. They all nodded slightly.

'Mrs Shoret's scar was three finger tips wide and she had a hernia indicating improper healing.'

He fumbled through his notes again. 'Now her sister, Mrs Halevy, had an extremely short incision two finger tips wide or of about an inch in length. A very small incision, indeed. She also showed a deficiency in the middle of her scar where it had not healed and deep pigmented brown from the radiation.'

'The burn still showed.'

'Yes. Now the worst of them was the third lady, Mrs Peretz from Trieste. The lady whose son translated for her. Her wound was covered literally by the thickness of a piece of paper. She had the same marked deficiency of the layers of the abdominal wall, the belly wall, and also a very small scar of two finger tips.'

'Could I interrupt,' Bannister said. 'You said her wound was covered by the thickness of a piece of paper. How thick is the normal abdominal wall?'

'It consists of several layers, namely skin, fat, a fibrous layer, a layer of muscle, and the peritoneal layer. In her case there was no fat, muscle, or fiber. In fact you could put your finger almost to her spine by poking the scar.'

'Like a hole straight through to the back of her body covered by a piece of paper.'

'Yes.'

'And the last lady?'

'Mrs Prinz from Belgium.'

Highsmith was up. 'I believe we have agreed that due to her distress I had no opportunity to cross-examine her.'

'What I ruled, Sir Robert, was that it would be called to the jury's attention. This is not Mrs Prinz's testimony. It is Professor Lighthall's. You may continue, Professor.'

'Mrs Prinz had two scars from two operations. One was a vertical scar quite longer than the other scar, which resembled the scars of the other ladies. This would indicate to me that the vertical scar was that of a different surgeon. The horizontal scar was very brown from irradiation, again had a deep depression and was a short two finger tips. It had obviously not healed properly.'

'Was the long vertical scar the right, or the left?'

'Left.'

'Mrs Prinz testified that her left ovary was removed by Dr Dimshits. What would you say was the general condition?'

'I found no evidence of depression, infection, or irradiation burn. It appeared to be a proper operation.'

'But not the other one?'

'No, it was like the other ladies, more or less.'

'Now, Professor, what in your experiences is the normal length of such an incision?'

'Oh, three to six inches depending on the surgeon and the case.'

'But never an inch or two inches?' Bannister asked.

'Certainly not.'

'How do you compare these scars with ovariectomies you have observed elsewhere?'

'I have practiced surgery here and in Europe and in Africa, the Middle East, Australia, and India as well. I've never seen such scars in all my years. Even the final stitching was abhorrent. All the wounds reopened.'

As Lighthall shoveled the notes back in his pocket a sickening cloud of disbelief had descended on the courtroom. Sir Robert knew he had been damaged and had better neutralize the testimony.

'From your evidence,' Highsmith said, 'you appreciate the difference between the swank comforts of the posh clinics of Wimpole and Wigmore Streets and that of the Jadwiga Concentration Camp?'

'Very much so, indeed.'

'And you are very aware that her Majesty's government has knighted this man for his skill as a physician and a surgeon.'

'I am aware.'

'Skills so obvious that despite different surgical procedures they would make it impossible for Sir Adam Kelno to have performed the surgery you have described.'

'I'd rather think that no proper surgeon would have done it, but obviously someone did.'

'But not Sir Adam Kelno. Now then, you are aware of the hundreds of thousands of persons put to death in Jadwiga with a single quick snuff.'

'Yes.'

'And we are in a hell, not in Cavendish Square, but an abnormal hell where all human life has been totally minimized.'

'Yes.'

'And you would agree, would you not, that if you were a prisoner/doctor working without hours and in life and death struggle that if an SS officer walked into your surgery without a gown and mask there was poor little you could do about that.'

'I must agree.'

'And you know, do you not, Professor Lighthall, that the British medical journals are filled with articles about irradiation hazards in leukemia and to unborn children and of their genetic effects and that irradiated women have produced monsters or congenitally malformed fetuses.'

'Yes.'

'And you know that doctors and radiologists have died from radiation and that in 1940 it was not the skill it is today.'

'I do.'

'Can you not conceive that a doctor torn away from the world and plunged into a nightmarish hell could not have grave apprehension.'

'I would have to concede that.'

'And will you not concede there were many different opinions about the length of incisions and the time it took to perform certain operations?'

'Just a moment now, Sir Robert, I feel a bit stampeded here. Keyhole surgery and undue speed are bad business and Polish doctors recognized it in those days.'

'Would you tell my Lord and the jury if a British doctor is apt to be far more conservative than a Polish doctor?'

'Well, I must testify with pride that we do stress careful painstaking surgery. But I have testified to the examination of Mrs Prinz, who had surgery by two Polish doctors, one done properly and one not.'

Sir Robert bounced off both feet and his robe fell from his shoulders. 'I suggest that there are so many different theories between British and Continental surgeons that you could have a convention for a year and not agree on certain points.'

Oliver Lighthall waited until the fury of the wind of Sir Robert's blast had dissipated. 'Sir Robert,' he answered softly. 'There cannot be two schools of thought about the examination of those women. It was crude, bad surgery. In nonmedical terms I'd describe it as butchery.'

The silence and the glower between the two was like a burning fuse about to lead to explosion.

My God, Gilray thought, here are two eminent Englishmen going at each other like savages. 'I should like to question Professor Lighthall on certain matters of medical ethics,' the judge said quickly, to save the situation. 'Would you mind, Sir Robert?'

'No, my Lord,' he answered, glad to be taken off the spot.

'Mr Bannister?'

'I certainly think Professor Lighthall is qualified, and I think it proper of your Lordship to do so.'

'Thank you,' the judge said. Anthony Gilray dropped his pencil and leaned his face on his hand and weighed his thoughts. 'What we have here, Professor, is the testimony of two doctors who said they would have been put to death or surgery would have been performed by somebody without proper skill. Mr Bannister has strongly contested whether or not such surgery would have ever been performed by an unskilled SS orderly. However, in the circumstances of Jadwiga we may assume that the threat was truly made and might have been carried out, if only as an example to the other doctors who may have been called upon later. We are not at a point in this case where it has been proved that Sir Adam did the operations you described. What I am seeking from you is an ethical concept. In your view, is a surgeon justified in carrying out an operation with questionable legitimate medical purpose against the will of the patient?'

Lighthall once more withdrew into the sanctity of meditation. 'My Lord, it is completely contrary to any medical practice I have known.'

'Well, we're talking about medical practices no one ever heard of. Say a man in an Arab country had been sentenced to have a hand cut off for thievery and you are the only skilled physician about. It's either you or someone will hack it off.'

'In such a case I would say to the chap that I am without choice.'

Adam Kelno nodded and smiled a little.

'Nothing,' Lighthall continued, 'would have made me consider it if the patient did not agree and nothing could force me to commit crude surgery. But I believe, my Lord, as I was about to do it, I would have the strength to turn the knife on myself.'

'Fortunately,' Gilray said, 'this case will be settled on law and not philosophy.'

'My Lord,' Oliver Lighthall said, 'I am going to take difference with you on the matter of medical practice under duress. Granted, Jadwiga was at the bottom of the pit, but physicians have practiced in all sorts of hells, in all sorts of plagues, famines, battlefields, prisons, and all imaginable evil situations. We are still bound by the Hippocratic oath of twenty-four hundred years standing, which binds us to help our patient but never a view to injury or wrongdoing. You see, my Lord, a prisoner has the right to protection from a physician for the oath also states, "and will abstain from every voluntary act of mischief and corruption and further from the seduction of females or males of freemen and slaves."'

Chapter Twenty-five

The room reverberated from the testimony of Oliver Lighthall, who was smothered in the consultation room by Abe and Shawcross and Ben and Vanessa and Geoffrey and Pam and Cecil Dodd. Lighthall was still angry and felt he had not said enough. The press ran to telephones and down Fleet Street.

FAMED PHYSICIAN RECITES HIPPOCRATIC OATH ON WITNESS STAND the headlines would blare.

'Before we adjourn for the weekend,' Anthony Gilray said, 'I should like to know, and I am certain the members of the jury will be much obliged, if you could tell us how many more witnesses you plan to call and of what duration, Mr Bannister.'

'Three, your Lordship, and an outside chance of a fourth. Only one, Dr Tesslar, will be examined at great length.'

'So taking into consideration your closing speeches and my instructions there is a possibility the case can go to the jury by the next weekend.'

'I should think so, my Lord.'

'Thank you. In that event I am going to ask the associate to pass the jury copies of *The Holocaust.* I take it into consideration that this is a book of over seven hundred pages and it is hardly likely that you could read it carefully in two days. However, I do ask you to go through it as thoroughly as you are able so as to have a basic understanding of what the author wrote. I ask you to do that for when I give you my instructions we will bear in mind that the offending portion of the book takes up a single paragraph and this will have to do with the weight or sting of the libel. The court stands in recess until Monday.'

Chapter Twenty-six

The LOT plane from Warsaw bearing Dr Maria Viskova cut its Soviet-built engines. She passed through customs dressed in a severe two piece suit, flat heels, and without make-up. Even so she could not conceal a certain beauty.

'I'm Abraham Cady. My daughter Vanessa and my son Ben.'

'Ben? I knew your uncle Ben in Spain. He was a fine boy. You resemble him, you know.'

'Thanks. He was a great man. How was your flight?'

'Just fine.'

'We have a surprise for you,' Abe said, taking her arm and leading her into the lobby where Jacob Alexander stood with Dr Susanne Parmentier. The two women approached each other, separated by twenty years absence. They took each other's hands and held them and looked into the other's face, then embraced softly and walked arm in arm from the terminal.

The trial entered its third week. The Shawcross-Cady forces showed the wear of a nonstop weekend of preparation for the final push. Even the frigid Thomas Bannister was showing the effects.

As Maria Viskova entered the court, she paused for a moment to stare at Adam Kelno. Kelno turned away and feigned talking to Richard Smiddy. Abe helped Susanne Parmentier to a seat beside him. Jacob Alexander passed up a note. I TALKED TO MARK TESSLAR THIS MORNING. HE SENDS HIS DEEPEST REGRETS THAT HE WAS NOT THERE TO MEET DR VISKOVA'S PLANE, BUT HE IS A BIT UNDER THE WEATHER AND WANTS TO SAVE HIS STRENGTH FOR HIS TESTIMONY. PLEASE HAVE DR PARMENTIER RELAY THIS TO DR VISKOVA.

Maria Viskova's voice and eyes were mellow as she was affirmed through her Polish interpreter. They had decided her English was not quite good enough for direct testimony.

'I am Maria Viskova,' she said in answer to Bannister's question. 'I work and live at the Miner's Sanitorium, Zakopane, Poland. I was born in Krakow in 1910.'

'What happened after you completed your secondary education?'

'I was unable to get into any medical school in Poland. I am a Jewess and the quotas were filled. I studied in France and after I received my degree I moved to Czechoslovakia and practiced in a mountain health resort in the Tatra Mountains, a tubercular sanitorium. It was in the year of 1936.'

'And you met and married a Dr Visksi?'

'Yes, he was also Polish. Our Czech name is Viskova.'

'Dr Viskova. Are you a member of the Communist Party?'

'I am.'

'Would you tell us the circumstances?'

'I joined the International Brigade with my husband to fight for Loyalist Spain against Franco. When the civil war was over we fled to France, where we worked in a sanitarium for respiratory diseases in the town of Cambo on the French-Spanish border in the Pyrenees Mountains.'

'And during the second war, what kind of activities did you engage in?'

'My husband and I established an underground station in Cambo to smuggle out French officers and soldiers so they could join French forces in Africa. We also smuggled arms in from Spain to the resistance, the FFI in France.'

'After two and a half years of this underground activity you were caught and turned over to the Gestapo in the occupied portion of France, is that right?'

'Yes.'

'After the war, did the French government recognize your activities?'

'I was decorated with the Croix de Guerre with star by General de Gaulle. My husband was awarded one posthumously. He had been executed by the Gestapo.'

'And in the late spring of 1943 you were sent to the Jadwiga Concentration Camp. Would you tell us what happened on your arrival?'

'It was discovered, at the selection shed, I was a doctor, so I was assigned to the medical compound to Barrack III. I was met by SS Colonel Voss and Dr Kelno and learned that a Polish woman doctor had just committed suicide, and I was to take her place in charge of the women on the ground floor. I found out shortly what Barrack III was all about. It always held two to three hundred women being experimented on or waiting to be experimented on.'

'Did you come into contact with the other doctors?'

'Yes. A short time after my arrival, Dr Tesslar came to take care of the men on the upper floor. I was quite sick from exposure in an open wagon on the trip to Poland and contracted pneumonia. Dr Tesslar nursed me back to health.'

'So you saw him on a daily basis?'

'Yes, we were extremely close.'

'It has been testified to by Dr Kelno that it was common knowledge that Dr Tesslar not only cooperated with Voss in his experiments but performed abortions on camp prostitutes.'

'It is too ridiculous to comment on. Nothing but a lie.'

'But we do want your comments, Madame Viskova.'

'We worked together day and night for months. He was the greatest humanitarian I have ever known – a man morally incapable of any wrong-doing. Dr Kelno, who made these accusations, has made them only to cover his own foul deeds.'

'I'm afraid your comments are getting rather editorial,' Judge Gilray said.

'Yes, I know. It is difficult to editorialize a saint.'

'It has also been testified to that Dr Tesslar had private quarters in the barrack.'

Maria Viskova smiled and shook her head in disbelief. 'The doctors and Kapos had a space of seven feet by four feet. Enough for a bed, a chair, and a small stand.'

'But no private toilet or showers or dining facilities. Hardly luxurious?'

'It was smaller than any prison cell. They gave it to us so we could write out our reports.'

'Were there any other doctors associated with this particular area of the medical compound?'

'Dr Parmentier, a French woman. She was the only non-Jew around Barrack III. Actually, she lived in the main compound but had access to come to Barrack III to try to help the victims of Dr Flensberg's experiments. Flensberg was driving people insane. Dr Parmentier was a psychiatrist.'

'How would you describe her?'

'She was a saint.'

'Any other doctors?'

'For a short time, Dr Boris Dimshits. A Russian Jew, a prisoner.'

'What did you discover about him?'

'He was doing ovariectomies for Voss. He told me so. He wept about what he was doing to fellow Jews, but he did not have the strength to protest.'

'How would you describe his physical appearance and his mental state?'

'He seemed ancient. His mind began to wander and his hands were covered with eczema. His patients, whom I cared for, were coming back from surgery in progressively worse condition. It was apparent he had become incompetent.'

'On some of his earlier operations, what did you observe?'

'His operations seemed proper. The scars were of a three inch length, and he used care and put the girls to sleep with general anesthetic. Of course there were always complications because of the terrible sanitation and lack of proper medicines and food.'

'So then when Dr Dimshits was no longer able to do his work, Voss sent him to the gas chamber.'

'That is correct.'

'Are you quite certain he wasn't sent to the gas chamber for other reasons?'

'No, Dr Kelno told me that is what Voss told him. Voss told me the same thing later.'

'Because Dimshits was useless, unable to perform, I see. Is Adam Kelno in this courtroom?'

She pointed with a steady finger.

'Were any other doctors sent to the gas chamber?'

'Of course not.'

'Of course not? Weren't tens of thousands of people being murdered in Jadwiga?'

'Not doctors. The Germans were desperate for doctors. Dimshits was the only one ever sent to the gas chamber.'

'I see. Did you ever meet a Dr Lotaki?'

'Very casually.'

'Dr Kelno testified that when Voss informed him he was going to do those operations, he and Dr Lotaki talked it over with the rest of the doctors. What did he say to you?'

'He never spoke to me about it.'

'He didn't? He didn't discuss the ethical concepts, or ask your blessing, or seek your counsel, or get your decision that it was for the best for the patients.'

'No, he ran things in an arrogant manner. He asked advice from no one.'

'Perhaps that was because you weren't free to leave Barrack III. Maybe he made a mistake and forgot about you?'

'I could move freely all around the main medical compound.'

'And you could talk with all the other doctors.'

'Yes.'

'Did any of the other doctors at any time relate to you conversations they had with Dr Kelno in which he sought their advice and consent?'

'I never heard of any such conversation. We all knew that ...'

'What did you know?'

'We all knew the experiments were a sham, an excuse for Voss to stay off the Eastern Front so he would not have to fight the Russians.'

'How did you know that?'

'Voss joked about it. He said so long as he kept reports going to Berlin he wouldn't have to see action and as long as he wormed his way into Himmler's good graces he would eventually get the reward of a private clinic.'

'So Voss himself realized his experiments had no scientific value.'

'He got pleasure from butchering.'

Bannister let his voice rise on this rare occasion ... 'Did Dr Kelno know that Voss's experiments were useless?'

'It is impossible he did not know.'

Bannister played with some papers on the rostrum. 'Now then, what did you notice after Dr Dimshits's death?'

'The quality of the surgery degenerated. We were faced with all sorts of post-operative complications. There were terrible complaints about the pain from the spinals. Dr Tesslar and I called for Dr Kelno to come many, many times. We were ignored.'

'We come now,' Bannister said with melodious and ominous monotone, 'to a certain night in mid-October of 1943 in which you were summoned to Dr Voss's office in Barrack V.'

'I remember,' she whispered, with tears forming in her eyes.

'What took place?'

'I was alone with Voss in his office. He told me that Berlin wanted more information about his experiments and that he was stepping things up. He needed more doctors and he was assigning me to the surgery.'

'What did you answer?'

'I told him I wasn't a surgeon. He told me I would give anesthetic and assist. Dr Kelno and Dr Lotaki were having trouble with unwilling patients.'

'And what was your answer to that?'

'I told him I would not do it.'

'You mean, you refused.'

'Yes.'

'You refused an SS colonel with power to send people to the gas chambers.'

'Yes.'

'What did Voss do about that?'

'He screamed the usual curses and ordered me to report to Barrack V again the next day for operations.'

'What happened then?'

'I returned to my room in Barrack III and thought it over and came to a decision.'

'What was that decision?'

'To commit suicide.'

A dozen gaps pierced an otherwise stunned silence. Adam Kelno wiped the perspiration from his face.

'What was your intention?'

She slowly unbuttoned the top of her blouse, reached in her bosom, and took out a locket. She opened it and withdrew a pill and held it out. 'I had this cyanide tablet. I have kept it till this day to remind me.' She stared at it as she must have a thousand times.

'Are you able to continue, Dr Viskova?' the judge asked.

'Yes, of course. I placed this on a wooden crate which was used as a nightstand beside my cot and took a pad and wrote a note of farewell to Dr Tesslar and Dr Parmentier. My door opened. Dr Parmentier came in and saw the pill.'

'Did she become alarmed?'

'No. She was quite calm. She sat beside me and took the pencil and paper from my hand ... and she stroked my hair, and she said words to me that I have remembered in all the difficult moments of my life.'

'Would you tell my Lord and the jury what she said?'

Tears fell down the cheeks of Maria Viskova and more than a few who heard her. 'She said ... "Maria ... it is not possible that any of us are going to live and get out of this camp. In the end the Germans must kill us because they cannot allow the outside world to know what they are doing." And she said ... "the only thing that is left for us is to behave for the rest of the short time we have left as human beings ... and as physicians." She said ... "we cannot leave these people to suffer alone."'

Thomas Bannister looked at Adam Kelno as he spoke. 'And you did not report to Barrack V the next day to assist in the operations.'

'I did not.'

'What did Voss do about that?'

'Nothing.'

Chapter Twenty-seven

Lena Konska had undergone four days of intense grilling by Aroni and Jiri Linka but it was impossible to find many flaws in her story. She admitted to seeing her cousin, Egon Sobotnik, briefly at the end of the war and at that time he told her he was going to go somewhere far away, he could not bear the ghosts.

Aroni was not easily discouraged. He knew, after all, that Lena Konska had the wit to live illegally for five years. Each day Aroni brought newspapers of the trial and pleas were interspersed with threats.

As they mounted the steps to her flat, Linka wanted to quit. 'We are wasting our time. Even if she knows something, she's too crafty an old witch.'

'So long as Prague finds no new information on Sobotnik we have to keep going at her.'

'Have it your way.'

'Suppose,' Aroni said to Lena Konska, 'we discovered you have lied to us.'

'Are we going over all that again?'

'We know you are clever, clever enough to keep a secret from everyone but God. You'll answer to God for this.'

'What God?' she answered. 'Where was God in the concentration camps? If you ask me,' she said, 'I think that God has gotten a little old for the job.'

'You lost all your family?'

'Yes, the merciful God took them.'

'Well, they would be proud of you now, Madame Konska. They will be extremely proud of you if Adam Kelno wins this case because of information you withheld. The memory of them will anoy you. You can depend on that, Madame Konska. As you grow older their faces will become more vivid. You can't forget. I tried.'

'Aroni, leave me alone.'

'You've been to the Pinkas Synagogue in Prague. You've seen that, haven't you?'

'Stop it.'

'Your husband's name is on the wall of martyrs. I've seen it, Jan Konska. Is that his picture, there? He was a handsome man.'

'Aroni, you act like a Nazi yourself.'

'We've found some neighbors,' Aroni said. 'They remember Egon Sobotnik returning. They remember him living here with you, in this apartment, for six months then suddenly disappearing. You have lied to us.'

'I told you he stayed for a short while. I didn't count the days. He was restless.'

The phone rang. It was police headquarters for Jiri Linka. He listened for a moment, then handed the phone to Aroni as the words were repeated.

Aroni replaced the phone slowly, his wrinkled face distorted, a sort of madness in his expression. 'We have heard from Prague.'

Lena Konska did not betray what was happening within her, but she saw something horribly different about Aroni, the hunter.

'The police have found statements dating back to 1946, three statements in which Egon Sobotnik was implicated with Kelno's surgery. That's when he fled Bratislava, isn't it? All right, Madame Konska, which way do you want it? Do you tell us where he is or do I find him myself? I'll find him, you know.'

'I don't know where he is,' she repeated firmly.

'Have it your way.'

Aroni picked up his hat and nodded to Linka, and they passed through the draped opening to the small foyer off the parlor.

'Just a moment. What will you do to him?'

'He'll be taken care of if you force me to find him.'

She licked her lips. 'To the best of my knowledge his guilt is very small. If you were to suddenly find him ... what kind of a deal would you make?'

'If he testifies, he will leave the courtroom free.'

She looked desperately to Linka. 'You have my word as a Jew,' he said.

'I swore ... I swore ...' her lips quivered. 'He has changed his name to Tukla, Gustuv Tukla. He is one of the directors of the Lenin Factories in Brno.'

Aroni whispered in Linka's ear, and he nodded. 'We are going to have to detain you to remove the temptation of calling him until we make contact.'

Chapter Twenty-eight

'Dr Viskova, do you recall any particular incident about twins in Barrack III?'

'When I arrived there were twins from Belgium, Tina and Helene Blanc-Imber, who had been irradiated and had an ovary removed by Dr Dimshits. Later, two other sets of twins were sent in, the Cordozo and Lovino sisters from Trieste. I remember how terribly I felt because they were so young, the youngest in the barrack. Sometime later they were irradiated again.'

'And they have testified to their sickness afterwards. We now come to a particular night in early November of 1943. Would you tell us what happened?'

'A number of SS guards and Voss himself entered the barrack. Of course there was always alarm. They ordered the Kapos to get the three sets of twins. From upstairs they brought a number of young Dutch boys, an older Polish man and a medical clerk. His name was Menno Donker. They were taken away quite hysterical. Dr Tesslar sat with me. We knew what would be coming back to us. We were grief-stricken.'

'How long did you and Dr Tesslar wait?'

'A half hour.'

'What happened?'

'Egon Sobotnik, a medical clerk and orderly, came with two SS guards and told Dr Tesslar he must come to Barrack V. There was pandemonium, and he had to keep the people quiet. So he rushed out.'

'How long was Dr Tesslar gone?'

'It was just after seven o'clock when he left and a little after eleven when he came back with the victims. They were brought back on stretchers.'

'So, fourteen of them were operated on in a little over four hours. Would that not be about fifteen minutes each if done by a single surgeon?'

'Yes.'

'Did Dr Tesslar say there was more than one surgeon?'

'No, only Adam Kelno.'

'And with one surgeon doing an operation every fifteen minutes there was not time to sterilize instruments or himself between operations. What was it like in Barrack III?'

'A bedlam of screams and blood.'

'You were on the ground floor and Dr Tesslar on the upper floor, is that right?'

'Yes.'

'Did you see each other?'

'Often. We were running up and down with each new crisis. I first came up to assist with one of the men who was going quickly.'

'What happened to this man?'

'He died of shock.'

'And you returned to your own problems.'

'Yes. Dr Parmentier arrived, and thank God she was there to help. We were in serious trouble with the hemorrhaging and almost helpless. We didn't even have enough water to give them. Dr Tesslar tried to get Dr Kelno to come but got no response. They lay bleeding and screaming on wooden beds with straw mattresses. At the caged end of the barracks, the mental patients of Flensberg became hysterical. I saw I could not stop the hemorrhaging of Tina Blanc-Imber so we moved her into the corridor away from the others. At two in the morning she was dead. All night we struggled to get control of the situation. By some miracle, the three of us managed to keep the others alive. At dawn the Germans came to take away Tina and the man. Egon Sobotnik made out death certificates which we signed. Then I heard him receive orders to change the cause of death to "typhus."'

A sob broke out in the balcony and a woman ran from the courtroom.

Bannister spoke so low he could not be heard, and he had to repeat the question. 'Did Dr Kelno ever come to visit these patients?'

'A few times he came to the door of the barrack. Once, he glanced at them briefly.'

'On that occasion, did he find them cheerful?'

'Are you joking?'

'I assure you I am not.'

'They were very sick for months. I was forced to send the Cordozo sisters back to their factory even though I knew Emma could not last. Sima Halevy was the most ill, and I kept her as an assistant so she would not go to the gas chamber.'

'Is there any question in your mind of who did these operations?'

'I object, my Lord,' Highsmith said without passion.

'Objection sustained. Instruct the witness not to answer.'

Her silent answer, her eyes on Adam Kelno were answer enough.

Chapter Twenty-nine

Linka and Aroni raced north along the Austrian border from Slovakia into the rolling fields of Moravia, rich in the barleys and wheats that immortalized Czechoslovakian beer. A detour forced them near the battlefield of Austerlitz, where Napoleon once took on the imperial armies of Russia and Austria in a short blood-soaked encounter costing the lives of thirty-five thousand men. The Battle of the Three Emperors as it was poetically remembered.

Aroni, who slept sitting upright with head nodding and bobbing, suddenly came awake as though an alarm had been set off inside him.

'I don't quite understand how you got such cooperation from Branik,' Linka said.

Aroni yawned, lit a cigarette. 'We speak the same language. Concentration camp language. Branik was almost hanged for his underground activities in Auschwitz.'

Linka shrugged. He still didn't understand it.

They entered Brno, the pride of Czech industry with one of the greatest heavy industrial complexes in the world and an enormous Trade Fair Center covering hundreds of acres which attracted a million annual buyers and visitors throughout the world.

They checked in at the Hotel International, an ultramodern glass and concrete affair that belied the chunky, drab Communist hotels throughout Eastern Europe.

There was a message waiting. GUSTUV TUKLA HAD BEEN TELEPHONED FROM PRAGUE BY MUTUAL FRIENDS AND TOLD TO COOPERATE. HE IS EXPECTING ARONI AT TEN O'CLOCK. BRANIK

Aroni found Gustuv Tukla a polished, urbane man in his late fifties, yet with the rugged face and hands of a professional engineer. His office, which looked out over a yard to the mammoth Lenin Factories, also showed Western affluence. Along the window a table held a model of the Blansko exhibit at the coming International Trade Fair. Tukla settled opposite each other on a pair of couches separated by a coffee table holding a number of catalogues of the Blansko products. A miniskirted secretary brought them thick espresso. Aroni smiled as she bent over and set it down.

'Set me straight,' Aroni said, 'exactly who called you from Prague?'

'Comrade Janacek, the party chairman for the Committee on Heavy Industry. He is my direct superior except for the head directors here.'

'Did Comrade Janacek tell you anything about my business here in Czechoslovakia?'

'Only that you were a very important gentleman from Israel and, frankly, to make a good deal with you.'

'Good. Then we can get down to cases.'

'Confidentailly,' Tukla said, 'I am glad we are going to do business with Israel. It is not said in public but there is a great deal of admiration for your country.'

'We like the Czechs. Especially their arms when they were available.'

'Masaryk, thank God we can now mention his name, was a friend of the Jews. So, perhaps you are interested in our Kaplan Turbines?'

'Actually I'm interested in one of your personnel.'

'As an adviser?'

'In a manner of speaking.'

'Who?'

'I am interested in Egon Sobotnik.'

'Sobotnik? Who is that?'

'If you will roll up your left sleeve and read me your tattoo number, I think we can stop wasting time.'

Aroni then said who he was and Gustuv Tukla turned from a self-assured executive into a mass of confusion. It had all happened so suddenly. The call from Janacek only this morning. Obviously this Aroni was dealing with the hierarchy.

'Who told you? It must have been Lena.'

'She had no choice. We caught her lying. She did it for your own good.'

Tukla spun off the couch sweating, grunting, pacing. 'What's it about?'

'The trial in London. You know about it. The newspaper on your desk is open to the story. You've got to come to London and give testimony.'

Tukla tried to shake the confusion, tried to think. It was so sudden! So sudden!

'Are these Janacek's orders? Who?'

'Comrade Branik is interested in this case.'

The mention of the head of the secret police had its effect. Aroni watched him coldly as he sat again, wiped his face and bit the back of his hand. Aroni set his cup down and walked to the window. 'Are you ready to listen?'

'I'm listening,' Tukla whimpered.

'You are an important party member and your testimony may prove embarrassing to the Czech government. The Russians have long memories when it comes to assisting Zionism. However, your people think you ought to come to London. Fortunately, even some Communists know right from wrong.'

'What are you suggesting?'

'You know,' Aroni answered.

'A defection?'

Aroni stood over him. 'It's a short distance to Vienna. You are a member of the Brno Flying Club. There will be an airplane at the airport large enough to hold your family. With a defection, no one will be able to blame your government.'

Tukla trembled violently. He managed to gulp down a tranquilizer. He blinked, dazed. 'I know their tricks,' he whispered. 'I will take off from the airport and the plane will develop engine trouble. They can't be trusted.'

'I trust them,' Aroni said, 'and I'll be in the plane with you.'

'But what for?' Tukla wailed. 'I have everything. Everything I've worked for will be gone.'

'Well now, Sobotnik ... you don't mind if I call you Sobotnik? A Czech engineer from the Blansko works isn't going to have much trouble finding a highly suitable position in England or America. Frankly, you're lucky to be getting out of the country. You'll have the Russians down your throats inside a year and there will be purges like the Stalin days.'

'And if I refuse to defect?'

'Well, you know how that works. Transfer to a remote power station. Demotion. Your son may suddenly be dropped from the university. Perhaps the Kelno case publicity will entice Comrade Branik to open certain old files ... certain statements made against you at the end of the war.'

Tukla dropped his face in his hands and cried. Aroni hissed close to his ear. 'You remember Menno Donker. He was also a member of the underground. They cut his nuts off for that. Well ... what happened when Kelno found out you were a member of the underground?'

Sobotnik shook his head.

'Kelno made you assist him, didn't he?'

'God!' he cried, 'I only did it a few times. I've paid! I've lived like a frightened rat. I've run. I've lived in fear of every footstep, every knock on the door.'

'Well, we all know your secret now, Sobotnik. Come to London. You will leave the courtroom a free man.'

'Oh my God!'

'What if your son learns this from someone other than his father. He will, you know.'

'Have mercy on me.'

'No. Get your family ready by this evening. I will meet you at your home at six o'clock.'

'I'll kill myself first.'

'No you won't,' Aroni said cruelly. 'You would have done that years ago if you intended to. Don't ask me to feel sorry for you. If you did those things for Kelno, then the very least you can do is do something decent for us. I'll see you at six, ready to go.'

When Aroni had left, Tukla waited until the tranquilizer took effect. He told his secretary to cancel all appointments and phone calls and locked his office. He opened the bottom drawer of his desk and stared long at the pistol, then put it on the top. The drawer had a false bottom so masterfully built the most trained eye could not detect it. His broad fingers tapped on one end and the lid gave way. Tukla slid it out. In the hidden compartment lay a book. A tattered yellowed book. He set it on the desk next to the pistol and stared. The faded lettering on the cover read, MEDICAL REGISTER, JADWIGA CONCENTRATION CAMP – AUGUST 1943 – DECEMBER 1943.

Chapter Thirty

'The next witness will testify in French.'

Dr Susanne Parmentier ascended to the witness box with the aid of a cane but testily refused a chair. Mr Justice Gilray was in a certain glory being fluent in the French language and having been afforded this opportunity to display his mastery to an audience. He greeted her in her native tongue.

She gave her name and address in a strong, clear voice.

'And when were you born?'

'Must I answer that?'

Gilray stifled a smile. 'No objection to passing on that question,' Highsmith said.

'Your father was a Protestant pastor?'

'Yes.'

'Have you ever belonged to any political party?'

'No.'

'Where did you study medicine?'

'In Paris. I was qualified in 1930 as a psychiatrist.'

'Now, Madame Parmentier. What peculiar position did you find yourself in at the time France was occupied?'

'Northern France was occupied by the Germans. My parents lived in Paris. I was working in Southern France in a clinic. I learned that my father was gravely ill and applied for a travel permit to visit him. These permits were difficult to get. It took days of investigation and red tape, and I felt a great sense of urgency. I tried to cross the demarcation line illegally and the Germans caught me and put me in prison in Bourges in late spring of 1942.'

'What happened there?'

'Well, there were hundreds of Jewish prisoners, including children, extremely maltreated. As a doctor I received permission to work in the prison clinic. Finally, things got so bad I asked to speak to the commandant.'

'Was he regular army or SS?'

'Waffen SS.'

'What did you tell him?'

'I told him the treatment of the Jews was a disgrace. They were human beings and French citizens, and I demanded they receive the same treatment and ration as the rest of the prisoners.'

'How did he react to that?'

'He was stunned at first. I was returned to my cell. Two days later I was taken to his office again. Two other Waffen SS officers were seated on either side of his desk. I was made to stand before them and told I was standing trial there and then.'

'What happened as a result of this so-called trial?'

'I was given a badge of cloth to sew on my clothing with the words, "Friend of the Jews," and early in 1943 I was sent to Jadwiga Concentration Camp for my crime.'

'Were you tattooed?'

'Yes, number 44406.'

'And after a time you were sent to the medical compound?'

'In the late spring of 1943.'

'You worked as a subordinate to Dr Kelno?'

'Yes.'

'And did you meet Dr Lotaki?'

'Yes, on occasions, like anyone working together in a large medical facility.'

'You met Voss?'

'Yes.'

'And you became aware of the fact that Dr Lotaki and Dr Kelno were doing surgery in Barrack V for Voss.'

'It was known, certainly. Kelno did not particularly hide the fact.'

'Of course it became known when Dr Kelno and Dr Lotaki called all of you together and discussed the ethical problems of the operations.'

'If there was any such meeting, I did not attend.'

'Did the other doctors ever tell you they were consulted about this?'

'Dr Kelno did not consult with the other doctors. He told them what to do.'

'I see. Do you think you would have known if such a meeting ever took place?'

'Certainly.'

'Dr Kelno has testified that he does not remember you.'

'That is very strange. We were in daily contact for over a year. He certainly recognized me this morning in the corridor of the court. He said to me, "Well, here is the friend of the Jews again. What lies are you going to tell?" '

Smiddy slipped a note to Adam; IS THAT TRUE?

I BECAME ANGRY, he wrote back.

YOU TESTIFIED YOU DIDN'T REMEMBER HER.

WHEN I SAW HER, I SUDDENLY RECALLED.

'Do you know a Dr Mark Tesslar?'

'Intimately.'

'Whom you met in Jadwiga.'

'Yes, after I saw Flensberg's experiments I went almost every day to Barrack III to try to help the victims.'

'Were there prostitutes being kept in Barrack III?'

'No, only people waiting to be experimented on, or those who had been returned from experiments.'

'Were there prostitutes in the medical compound?'

'No, they were locked up in another camp and they had their own medical facility in their own barrack.'

'How do you know that?'

'There were a number of mental disturbances and I was sent for on numerous occasions.'

'Were there doctors in the prostitutes' barrack who performed abortions?'

'No. Any prostitute who became pregnant was sent to the gas chamber automatically.'

'What of the female Kapos?'

'The same. The gas chamber. It was a closed rule in Jadwiga for all females.'

'Certainly not the wives of SS guards or other German personnel?'

'There were extremely few wives. Only the top-ranking SS officers, and their wives were treated in a private German clinic.'

'In other words, Dr Parmentier, it would have been impossible for Dr Tesslar to commit abortions because none were being performed in an organized manner.'

'That is correct.'

'Well, if a prisoner/doctor found a pregnant woman and wanted to save her from the gas chamber, would a secret abortion be performed?'

'It is an extremely rare situation. The men and women were segregated. Of course they always found ways to get together, but we speak of isolated cases. Any doctor would do it to save a woman's life in much the same way it is done today to save a woman's life.'

'Who were the prostitutes kept for?'

'German personnel and high-ranking Kapos.'

'Is it possible that a favorite prostitute could have been kept alive by an SS guard?'

'Hardly. The prostitutes were very drab and very disturbed. They were only performing in order to stay alive. However, they were dispensable. It was easy to get new women at the selection shed and force them into prostitution.'

'So, in any event, to the best of your knowledge Dr Tesslar could not have been and was not involved with abortions in Jadwiga?'

'No. He was occupied day and night in the men's portion of Barrack III.'

'But that is Adam Kelno's testimony.'

'He seems quite confused on a number of things,' Susanne Parmentier answered.

'Now would you tell us about your first meetings with SS Colonel Dr Otto Flensberg?'

'Otto Flensberg was of equal rank to Voss, and he had an assistant, Dr Sigmund Rudolf. Both of them were in Barrack I and Barrack II in the restricted experimental area. I was taken to Otto Flensberg in the summer of 1943. He had learned I was a psychiatrist and told me he was doing important experiments and needed me. I had heard of the kind of things he was doing, and I told him I would not take part in them.'

'What did he say to that?'

'Well, he tried to convince me. He said that Voss was a pseudo-scientist and what he was doing with X-rays was worthless. And that his own assistant was equally useless.'

'What was Captain Sigmund Rudolf doing?'

'Attempting to introduce cancer into the cervix of the womb, trying sterilization by injections of caustic fluids into the Fallopian tubes, and some other rather bizarre blood and sputum experiments.'

'And his own assistant said they were useless.'

'Yes, he gave his assistant Barrack I to play in and get enough reports back to Berlin to keep him off the Russian front.'

'What did he say about his own work?'

'Flensberg considered himself vital. He said he had worked at Dachau during the mid-thirties when it was a prison for German political prisoners. Later he worked on obedience experiments for the SS. He dreamed up all sorts of tests for SS cadets to prove their loyalty and instant obedience. Some of them were gruesome, such as murdering a puppy they had trained, stabbing prisoners on command, that sort of thing.'

And Otto Flensberg was proud of that?'

'Yes, he said it proved to Himmler the absolute obedience of the German people.'

'What did he tell you about coming to Jadwiga?'

'Himmler gave him carte blanche. He even had his assistant assigned to come with him. Flensberg became nonplused when he found that Voss was his superior. There was a definite rivalry and he felt Voss was wasting human material, while his work was important to Germany's being able to occupy Europe for centuries.'

'How?'

'He felt that the obedience of the German people was an accomplished fact. Yet, there were not enough Germans to control an entire continent of hundreds of millions of people. He wanted to find methods to train the conquered peoples to control the general population. In other words immediate obedience to German orders.'

'Like Kapos?'

'I should say, to sterilize people mentally. To turn them into robots.'

A weird fascination gripped the courtroom. The unreality of a mad scientist in a fiction story. But it was not science fiction. It happened. And Otto Flensberg was still alive, escaped to Africa.

'Would you explain to my Lord and the jury what kind of experiments Otto Flensberg was carrying out in Barrack I?'

Highsmith was up. 'I am going to object to this line of questioning. I fail to see to what point all of this is relevant.'

'It is relevant to the point that a German doctor in a concentration camp was carrying out experiments on prisoners and brought in a prisoner/doctor to assist in these experiments.'

'I think it is relevant,' the judge said. 'What was Flensberg doing, Dr Parmentier?'

'He was running a series of obedience experiments in a number of small rooms. Each room had two chairs. The people were separated from each other by a glass window so they could see each other. In front of their chairs was a panel of switches. Each switch threw an increasingly higher voltage, and was marked, and had words like *slight shock* and up to five hundred volts with the words *possible death*.'

'How ghastly,' Gilray uttered.

'There was an operator's booth where Flensberg was stationed which also had a panel of switches.'

'Just what did you witness, Dr Parmentier?'

'Two prisoners were brought in from Barrack III. They were males. Both of them were strapped into the chairs but had freedom of their hands. Flensberg from his booth called down and told prisoner *A* he must give prisoner *B* on the other side of the glass a shock of fifty volts or he, Flensberg, would punish him for not obeying.'

'Did prisoner *A* do as he was told?'

'Not at first.'

'And Flensberg shocked him.'

'Yes. *A* screamed. Flensberg then ordered prisoner *A* again to shock prisoner *B*. Prisoner *A* resisted until he was getting almost two hundred volts and at that point he began to obey the commands and shock prisoner *B* so he would not receive any more himself.'

'So the gist of what was happening was forcing people to inflict punishment on other people or get it themselves.'

'Yes. To obey out of fear.'

'Prisoner *A* started giving prisoner *B* shocks on command of Flensberg. Didn't he see and hear what he was doing to the other fellow?'

'Yes.'

'How much voltage did prisoner *A* apply on orders?'

'He eventually killed prisoner *B*.'

'I see.' Bannister drew a long breath. The jury seemed puzzled as though they were not certain of what they were hearing. 'After showing you this experiment, what did Flensberg do?'

'First I had to be calmed down. I was demanding that the experiments stop. I was forcibly removed to his office by a guard. He told me he really wasn't interested in killing the fellow, but it happened sometimes. He showed me graphs and charts and records. What he was looking for was the breaking point in each individual. That point in which they would become robots to German commands. Beyond that point they tended to go insane. He showed me experiments on which he forced blood relatives to shock one another.'

'I am curious Dr Parmentier,' the judge said, 'did any people resist entirely from hurting their fellow man?'

'Yes, resistance increased between husbands and wives, parents and children. Some would resist until their own death.'

The judge continued to question her. 'Were there cases of say, a father or mother killing his own child?'

'Yes ... that is why ... I am sorry ... no one asked a question of me ...'

'Please go on, Madame,' Gilray said.

'That is why Flensberg began searching for twins. He felt he could perform some sort of ultimate test on them. The girls from Belgium and Trieste were brought to Barrack III for his experiments and then Voss irradiated them. This upset Flensberg considerably. He threatened to protest to Berlin and was pacified, when Voss told him he would recommend to Himmler to give Flensberg a private clinic and Dr Lotaki to do his surgery.'

'How utterly appalling,' Mr Justice Gilray repeated.

'Let us digress for a moment,' Bannister said. 'After you saw this experiment and read the reports what transpired?'

'Flensberg assured me that once the initial surprise settled, I would become fascinated by the work. It was a rare opportunity for a psychiatrist to have human guinea pigs. Then, I was ordered to work for him.'

'And what did you answer to that?'

'I refused.'

'You refused?'

'Certainly I refused.'

'Well, exactly what was said?'

'Flensberg said that Barrack III was, after all, only filled with Jews. I said I knew it was filled with Jews. Then he said to me, "Don't you realize that some people are different?" '

'What did you answer him?'

'I said, "I have noticed the difference in some people starting with you." '

'Well, he must have taken you out and had you shot for that.'

'What?'

'Were you executed? Were you shot or sent to the gas chamber?'
'But of course not. I am here in London. How could I have been shot?'

Chapter Thirty-one

Sir Robert Highsmith was clearly on the spot. During trial times he abandoned his place in Richmond Surrey for his flat on Codogan Square and its proximity to the West End and the Law Courts. Tonight he studied, hard.

No one could question but that Thomas Bannister had built a powerful case on circumstantial evidence and in catching Kelno on some questionable testimony. Yet, Kelno's mistakes were largely that of a layman up against a mental giant, a master of legal gymnastics. Surely the jury, while recognizing Bannister's genius, would more closely identify themselves with Adam Kelno.

At bedrock it all now hinged on Mark Tesslar, the single alleged eyewitness. Throughout all the years and all the trial, Sir Robert Highsmith refused to believe that Adam Kelno was guilty. Kelno's career had been long and distinguished. Certainly, if he had the qualities of a monster, it would have shown up elsewhere along the line. Highsmith was convinced that this was the most terrible sort of vendetta. Two men, in their blind hatred of the other, unable to judge the truth.

He worked over his line of questioning absolutely determined to discredit Mark Tesslar.

Oh, he had moments of doubt, all right, but he was a British barrister, not judge or jury and Adam Kelno was entitled to the best he had.

'I am going to win this case,' he vowed to himself.

'Where the devil is Terry?' Adam said angrily. He took another sharp drink of vodka. 'I'll bet he went to Mary. Did you phone?'

'There is no phone there.'

'He was in court today,' Adam said. 'Why isn't he here now?'

'Perhaps he's at the college library studying late. He's lost a lot of school time due to the trial.'

'I'm going to Mary's,' Adam said.

'No,' Angela said. 'I went after court. Mary hasn't seen him in days. Adam, I know what is bothering you but these barristers are clever at twisting things. It's their profession. But the jury knows the truth the same as your patients do. They've rallied to you. Please don't drink, Terry will be around soon.'

'For God's sake, woman, for once in my life let me get drunk without whining about it. Do I beat you? Do I do evil things?'

'You'll get that nightmare.'

'Maybe not if I drink enough.'

'Adam, listen to me. You have to be strong in that courtroom tomorrow. You have to be strong when Tesslar is on the stand.'

'Hello, Angela ... Hello, Doctor.'

Terry wobbled in and flopped on the sofa. 'As you know,' he said, 'I do not drink like the son of my father. I've always figured that Father Campbell could drink for the two of us.'

'Where the hell have you been!'

'Drinking.'

'Leave the room, Angela,' Adam commanded.

'No,' she answered.

'We won't need a referee, Angela,' Terry slurred. 'This is clearly a doctor and doctor situation.'

She backed away apprehensively but left the door ajar.

'What's on your mind, Terry?'

'Things.'

'What things?'

Terry hung his head and his voice cracked and wavered to a point of almost being unrecognizable. 'The shadow of doubt has descended upon me,' he mumbled. 'Doctor . . . I . . . I don't care what the jury decides. I want to hear from your own lips, between you and me . . . did you do it?'

Adam stormed to his feet consumed with rage. He rose over the boy with both fists coming down on Terry's neck. Terry doubled over making no attempt to defend himself.

'Bastard! I should have beaten you years ago!' His fists smashed down and Terry slid off the couch on all fours. Adam brought his foot up into the boy's ribs. 'I should have beaten you! That's what my father did to me. He beat me like this . . . like this!'

'Adam!' Angela screamed, throwing herself over Terry as a shield

'Oh my God,' he cried in anguish, sinking to his knees. 'Forgive me, Terry . . . forgive me.'

The morning was fraught with rising tension as Highsmith and Bannister bandied about on some legal points. The night before Mark Tesslar arrived from Oxford. There was a quiet dinner with Susanne Parmentier and Maria Viskova after which Abe, Shawcross, Ben, and Vanessa joined them for coffee.

'I know,' Mark Tesslar said, 'what Highsmith intends to do. I will never be broken about the night of November tenth.'

'I don't know if I can put into words how I feel about you,' Abe said. 'I think you are the most noble and courageous man I have ever met.'

'Courage? No. It is just that I am beyond all pain,' Mark Tesslar answered.

For the first part of the morning, Chester Dicks took Susanne Parmentier through a relatively mild cross-examination until the afternoon recess.

Shawcross, Cady, his son and daughter, and Lady Sarah Wydman hit their drinks hard at the Three Tuns Tavern and played with their kidney pies as Josephson went to fetch Mark Tesslar from the hotel.

Adam Kelno was the first back into the courtroom. He was glassy-eyed, under sedation. He stared pleadingly at his wife and Terry in the first row of spectators as the room filled and then jammed to overflowing.

'Silence.'

Anthony Gilray seated himself and after the bows of the assemblage nodded to Thomas Bannister. At that moment Josephson rushed into the room to the solicitor's table and whispered excitedly into Jacob Alexander's ear. Alexander turned crimson, scribbled a note and handed it to Thomas Bannister. Thomas Bannister totally lost his composure, slumping into his chair. Brendon

O'Conner leaned down from the junior's table, snatched up the note, then wobbled to his feet.

'My Lord, our next witness was to have been Dr Mark Tesslar. We have just been informed that Dr Tesslar has dropped dead of a heart attack on the street outside his hotel. May we ask your Lordship for a recess for the day?'

'Tesslar ... dead ...'

'Yes, my Lord.'

Chapter Thirty-two

The flat in Colchester Mews was dimly lit when Vanessa opened the door for Lady Sarah. Abe looked up, half seeing her, half not. All of them were red-eyed from weeping.

'Abe, don't take this on yourself,' Lady Sarah said. 'He's been very sick for a long time.'

'It's not only Dr Tesslar,' Vanessa said, 'the embassy contacted Ben and Yossi this afternoon and ordered them to return to Israel immediately and report to their commands. It's a mobilization.'

'Oh, dear Lord,' she said, standing above Abe and stroking his hair. 'Abe, I know what you must feel but there are decisions that have to be made. Everyone is gathered at my flat.'

He nodded that he understood and arose and put on his jacket.

They were all there at Lady Sarah's sharing communal grief. Thomas Bannister was there, and Brendon O'Conner was there, and Jacob Alexander, Lorraine and David Shawcross, Josephson, Sheila Lamb, and Geoffery, Pam Dodd, and Cecil Dodd. Oliver Lighthall was there also.

And there were four others. Pieter Van Damm and his family. The missing Menno Donker.

Abe embraced Van Damm and they held each other and patted each other for a moment.

'I flew in from Paris the moment I heard the news,' Pieter said, 'I must go on the stand tomorrow.'

Abe went to the center of the room and faced them all. 'Since I have been involved in this case, he said hoarsely, 'I have found myself the chief barker in a carnival of horrors. I've opened old wounds, brought back nightmares, and taken the lives of people into my hands who should have been left in peace. I told myself that their anonymity would be preserved. But here we have a man who is an international figure and it is impossible for the world not to know. You see, when the light went out in my eye a strange thing happened. Strangers in bars would try to pick fights with me. When people know you are a cripple their blood instincts rise to the surface and you are like a wounded animal on the desert with only a matter of time until the jackals and vultures devour you.'

'May I interrupt you,' Bannister said. 'We all certainly know the problems of Mr Van Damm's future privacy. Fortunately British law takes these rare occasions into consideration. We have a procedure called In Camera. In Camera is testimony given in secret in unusual circumstances. We will appeal to have the courtroom cleared.'

'Who will be there?'

'The judge, the jury, his Lordship's assistant, and the legal representation of both sides.'

'And you really think this can remain a secret? I don't. Pieter, you know how cruel the jokes will be. Do you honestly think you'll ever be able to perform again before an audience with three thousand people staring between your legs? Well, the one thing I will not be responsible for is taking the music of Pieter Van Damm from the world.'

'The trouble with you, Cady,' Alexander snapped, 'is that you've become enchanted with the idea of martyrdom. I think you are glorying in becoming the new Christ figure and want to immortalize yourself by getting lynched.'

'You're very tired,' Abe answered, 'you've been working too hard.'

'Gentlemen,' Bannister said, 'we simply can't afford the luxury of a quarrel among ourselves.'

'Here, here,' Shawcross said.

'Mr Cady,' Bannister said, 'you have won the universal respect and admiration of us all. You are a logical man and you must be made aware of the consequences of not permitting Mr Van Damm to testify. Consider for a moment that Adam Kelno has won a large judgment. You would be responsible for the ruination of your closest friend, David Shawcross, and end his distinguished publishing career on a black note. But more important than Shawcross or yourself would be what Kelno's victory would mean in the eyes of the world. It would be an insult to every Jew, those living, those courageous men and women who came forth in this case, and certainly it would be a most abominable affront to those who had been murdered by Hitler. You would be responsible for that too.'

'There is another matter,' Oliver Lighthall said. 'What about future medical ethics. How ghastly it would be for doctors in the future to point back at this case and use it as a justification for the maltreatment of patients.'

'So you see,' Bannister said, 'your stand, no matter how virtuous, is filled with counter-responsibilities even more important.'

Abe studied them all, his worn-out little band of idealists. 'Ladies and gentlemen of the jury,' he said in a voice that literally moaned with sorrow, 'I should like to make a statement by quoting in effect the words of Thomas Bannister, Q.C., when he said that no one in their wildest imaginations would have believed Hitler's Germany before it actually happened. And he said, if the civilized world knew what Hitler intended to do then they would have stopped him. Well, here we are in 1967, and the Arabs vow daily to finish Hitler's work. Certainly the world will not stand for another chapter of this holocaust. There is a right and a wrong. It is right for people to want to survive. It is wrong to want to destroy them. It's quite simple then. But alas, the kingdom of heaven is concerned with righteousness alone. The kingdoms of the earth run on oil. Well now, certainly the world should be appalled by what is happening in Biafra. The stink of genocide is everywhere. Certainly, after Hitler's Germany, the world should step in and stop genocide in Biafra. However, that becomes impractical when one considers England's investments in Nigeria conflict with France's interests in Biafra. And after all, members of the jury, it is only black people killing other black people.

'We should like to think,' Abe said, 'that Thomas Bannister was right, when he said more people, including the German people, should have risked punishment and death by refusing to obey orders. We should like to believe there would have been a protest and we ask why didn't the Germans protest? Well today, young people march in the streets and protest Biafra and Vietnam and the principle of murdering their fellow man through the medium of war. And we say to them . . . why are you protesting so much? Why don't you go out there and kill like your father killed?

'Let us, for the moment, forget we are in jolly, comfortable London. We are in Jadwiga Concentration Camp. SS Colonel Dr Thomas Bannister has summoned me into his office and says, "See here, you have got to agree to the destruction of Pieter Van Damm. Of course it will all be done IN CAMERA. Barrack V was a secret place just like the courtroom will be. After all, we don't do that sort of thing in public." And I quote to you again from Thomas Bannister, Q.C., when he said, "There comes a moment in the human experience when one's life itself no longer makes sense when it is directed to the mutilation and murder of his fellow man." And I submit, members of the jury, I can bring no greater calamity or no more positive form of destruction upon this man than to allow him to take the witness stand. In closing, I say that I respectfully decline to murder Pieter Van Damm.'

Abe turned and started for the door.

'Daddy!' Vanessa cried and clung to him.

'Let me go alone, Vinny,' he said

He reached the street and stopped to catch his breath. 'Abe! Abe!' Lady Sarah called, catching up to him. 'I'll get my car,' she said.

'I don't want a goddam Bentley. I want a goddam Austin taxi.'

'Abe, please let me be with you.'

'Madame, I am en route to Soho where my intentions are to get shit-faced drunk and sleep with a whore.'

'I'll be your whore!' she cried, grabbing him. 'I'll scratch and scream and bite and curse and you'll drool on me and hit me and cry . . . and then I'll hold you.'

'Oh Jesus, God,' he groaned, clinging to her, 'I'm scared. I'm scared.'

Chapter Thirty-three

There was a cruel expression in Adam Kelno's face as he glared from the plaintiff's table to Abraham Cady. Their eyes met. Adam Kelno smiled slightly.

'Silence!'

Mr Justice Gilray seated himself. 'We are all shocked and distressed over the untimely passing of Dr Tesslar, but I'm afraid nothing can be done about that. What are your intentions, Mr Bannister, about placing his statement into evidence?'

'That won't be necessary,' Bannister answered.

Gilray blinked in disbelief. Highsmith, anticipating a long, involved hassle, was taken aback.

Shimshon Aroni slipped next to Abe and passed him a note. I AM ARONI, it read; WE HAVE SOBOTNIK.

'Where do things stand now, Mr Bannister?' the judge asked.

'I have one more witness to call.'

The smile left Adam Kelno's face and his heart raced.

'There are some rather unusual circumstances surrounding this witness, my Lord, and I should like to seek his Lordship's advice on the matter. This witness held an important position in a Communist country and only last night defected with his family. He arrived in London at two in the morning and has asked for and been granted political asylum. We have been searching for over a year for this gentleman but had no idea if he were alive or if he would come forward until he showed up in London.'

'Is his entry into this trial on a completely voluntary basis?'

'I have no idea what induced him to defect, my Lord.'

'What is our problem? If the witness has volunteered there is no question of issuing a subpoena. If he is here against his will, it would be a muddled bit of business because we don't know if he is in the jurisdiction of the British courts even though he has claimed asylum.'

'No, my Lord. The problem is that usually when a defector asks asylum he is taken into seclusion for a long period of time until his rehabilitation. We cannot rule out the possibility of foul play against this witness and therefore he was accompanied to the Law Court by several gentlemen from Scotland Yard.'

'I see. Are they armed?'

'Yes, my Lord. Both the Foreign Office and Scotland Yard share the opinion they should be handy at all times. We are obliged to protect him.'

'It is indeed distressing to think that any foul play could take place in an English courtroom. I don't like closed courts. We practice our law in the open. Are you asking that this witness be heard In Camera?'

'No, my Lord. The fact that we have discussed this matter and everyone knows there are Scotland Yard men present, that in itself should discourage anyone who intended foul play.'

'Well, I don't like armed men in my court, but I'm not going to clear it. I shall yield to the unusual circumstances. Call your witness, Mr Bannister.'

'He will testify in Czech, your Lordship.'

Adam Kelno strained for remembrance for the name Gustuv Tukla. The standing crowd in the rear of the room was separated by a pair of detectives. Between them walked a haggard, frightened man. Outside the courtroom, Scotland Yard detectives sealed off every exit. As the veil of time lifted Adam Kelno gasped and scribbled a desperate note to Smiddy. STOP HIM.

'Impossible,' Smiddy whispered. 'Get hold of yourself.' Smiddy passed a note up to Sir Robert, KELNO IS EXTREMELY DISTRESSED.

Gustuv Tukla's hand trembled as he was affirmed and he took a seat. He looked about in animal desperation as the translator was sworn in.

'Before we continue,' Mr Justice Gilray said, 'it is apparent that this witness is under a great deal of strain. I will tolerate no harassment of this man. Mr Interpreter, kindly inform Mr Tukla he is in England, in Her Majesty's Court, and he will receive no maltreatment. Advise him to be certain he understands every question clearly before he answers.'

Tukla managed a small smile and nodded to the judge. He gave his last address in Brno and his birthplace as Bratislava, where he lived until the war broke out and worked as a civil engineer.

'What was your most recent position?'

'I am one of the directors and production managers of the Lenin Factories, a large factory of many thousand workers in heavy industrial manufacturing.'

Mr Justice Gilray, in an effort to put the witness at ease, discussed with him a number of articles he had read on the Brno Trade Fair and the Czech reputation in this field.

'Were you, at the time of your defection, an official of the Communist Party?' Bannister began.

'I was District Chairman of the Industrial Committee and a member of the National Committee in the same group.'

'That is a rather important post, is it not?'

'Yes.'

'Were you a member of the Communist Party at the outbreak of the war?'

'No. I officially joined the party in 1948, when I went to work in Brno as an engineer.'

'Have you changed your name, sir?'

'Yes.'

'Would you tell us about the circumstances?'

'At the time of the war my name was Egon Sobotnik. I am half-Jewish on my father's side. After liberation I changed my name because I was afraid to be found out.'

'About what?'

'Some things I was made to do in Jadwiga Concentration Camp.'

'Tell us now, if you will, about being sent to Jadwiga Concentration Camp.'

'I fled to Budapest when the Germans occupied Bratislava and lived with false papers. I was picked up by the Hungarian police and returned to Bratislava and sent by the Gestapo to Jadwiga, where I was assigned to the medical compound. This was late in 1942.'

'Who did you report to?'

'Dr Adam Kelno.'

'Is he in this courtroom?'

Sobotnik pointed a shaky finger. The judge repeated that the shorthand writer could not transcribe a gesture. 'That is him.'

'What kind of work were you given to do?'

'Clerical. Keeping records, mostly. Finally I kept the clinical and surgical record books.'

'Were you, at some time, contacted by the underground? By the underground, I refer to the international underground. Do you understand my question?'

'May I have leave, your Lordship,' the interpreter said, 'to explain this to Mr Tukla?'

'Yes, go on.'

They conversed and Tukla nodded and answered. 'Mr Tukla understands. He says there was a small underground group of Polish officers and a larger one that encompassed everyone. He was contacted in the summer of 1943 and told that there was great concern about the medical experiments. At night he and a

Dutch Jew, Menno Donker, copied from the surgical records what operations had taken place in Barrack V and turned it over to a contact.'

'What did your contact do?'

'I don't know but the plan was to smuggle this information to the outside.'

'Risky business.'

'Yes, Menno Donker was discovered.'

'Do you know what happened to Donker?'

'He was castrated.'

'I see. Did it not occur to you as strange that the Germans wanted records kept of this sort of thing?'

'The Germans have a mania for records. At first I am sure they thought they were going to win the war. Later, they felt by taking records and then falsifying them they could justify a great number of deaths.'

'How long did you keep the surgical record?'

'I started in 1942 and kept it until the liberation in 1945. There were six volumes.'

'Now, going back, sir. You said you changed your name and apparently your identity after the war because of things you were forced to do in Jadwiga. Would you tell us about that?'

'At first I only did clerical work. Then, Kelno found out I was a member of the underground. Fortunately, he did not know I was smuggling out records of his operations. I was terrified he would turn me over to the SS. He forced me to do a number of things to help him.'

'Like what?'

'Hold patients still while they were being given spinals. At times I was made to give the spinals.'

'Were you trained at this?'

'I was shown once for a few minutes.'

'What else were you forced to do?'

'Also restrain patients who were having sperm tests.'

'You mean, shoving a wooden handle up their rectums to induce sperm?'

'Yes.'

'Who did that?'

'Dr Kelno and Dr Lotaki.'

'How many times did you see Dr Kelno do that?'

'At least forty or fifty separate occasions. There could be any number of men worked on each time.'

'Were they in pain?'

Tukla lowered his eyes. 'Very much so.'

'And this was done to healthy men prior to being irradiated and then operated on as the beginning of the experiment.'

'My Lord,' Highsmith said. 'Mr Bannister is leading the witness and asking conclusions of him.'

'I'll put it another way,' Bannister said. 'Was Dr Adam Kelno collaborating with the Germans in medical experiments?'

'Yes.'

'And how do you know that?'

'I saw him.'

'Did you see him operate in Barrack V?'

'Yes.'

'Many times?'

'I saw him perform two or three hundred operations in Barrack V, anyhow.'

'On Jews?'

'Once in a while a court order case but ninety-nine percent Jews.'

'Did you observe Dr Kelno in surgery in his regular clinic, in Barrack XX?'

'Yes, on many occasions. Many dozens of times.'

'And you saw him hold clinic. Perform the minor bits of business such as boils and cuts.'

'Yes.'

'Did you observe any significant difference between Dr Kelno's behavior in Barrack V from his behavior in his regular clinic?'

'Yes, he was brutal to the Jews. He often beat them or cursed them.'

'On the operating table?'

'Yes.'

'Now, Mr Tukla. I am going to refer to a particular series of operations performed in the early part of November of 1943. There were eight men who had testicles removed and three sets of twins who had ovariectomies.'

'I remember it quite clearly. It was November 10. It was the night Menno Donker was castrated.'

'Tell us about it please.'

He drank some water, spilling it with trembling. His face became devoid of color. 'I was told to report to Barrack V. There was a small army of Kapos and SS. Around seven o'clock the fourteen victims were brought to the anteroom and we were told to shave them and give them spinals.'

'In the anteroom, not in the operating room.'

'Always in the anteroom. Dr Kelno didn't want to waste time in the surgery.'

'Had these people been given a previous injection?'

'No. Dr. Viskova and Dr Tesslar complained on several occasions that it was only humane to give them morphia.'

'What did Dr Kelno say to that?'

'He said, "We don't waste morphia on pigs." On other occasions it was suggested it would be better to put the people under, put them to sleep as he did in Barrack XX. Dr Kelno said he didn't have time to waste.'

'So injections were always given in the anteroom without morphia and by unskilled or semiskilled people.'

'That is correct.'

'Were these people in pain?'

'Severe pain. That is my guilt . . . that is my guilt . . .' He rocked back and forth biting his lip to stave off the tears.

'Are you quite able to continue, Mr Tukla?'

'I must continue. I have held this in for over twenty years. I must finish with it so I can have peace.' And he sobbed, 'I was a coward. I should have refused like Donker.' He heaved a number of deep sighs and apologized and nodded that he wished to continue.

'Now, sir, you were present in the anteroom of Barrack V on the night of November 10 and you assisted in the preparation of these fourteen people. Please continue.'

'Menno Donker was first. Kelno told me to come into the surgery and keep him quiet.'

'Did you sterilize yourself?'

'No.'

'Who else was present?'

'Dr Lotaki assisted. There were one or two orderlies and two SS guards. Donker cried that he was healthy, then pleaded for Kelno to leave him one testicle.'

'What did Kelno answer to that?'

'He spit on him. In a moment or two there was such mayhem outside Voss ordered me to go to Barrack V to get Mark Tesslar. I returned with him to a scene so macabre I cannot forget it for a single day or a single night. Those young girls having the clothing torn from them, the screams of pain from the injection, the fighting and beating even on the operating table, the blood. Only Mark Tesslar was sane and human.'

'And you were present in the operating theater?'

'Yes, I moved all the victims in and out.'

'Who did the operations?'

'Adam Kelno.'

'All of them?'

'Yes.'

'Did he clean himself between operations?'

'No.'

'Did he sterilize his instruments?'

'No.'

'Was he considerate of his patients?'

'He was like a butcher turned loose with an ax in a slaughterhouse. It was a massacre.'

'How long did this go on?'

'He was doing it very fast, every ten or fifteen minutes. Around midnight I was told to take them back to Barrack III. There were stretchers, and they were on them side by side. The anteroom floor was gory with their blood. We carried them back to the barrack. Tesslar pleaded with me to get Kelno . . . but I fled in horror.'

Adam Kelno wrote a note. I AM LEAVING THE COURTROOM.

SIT STILL! Smiddy wrote back.

'What was your next contact with this situation, Mr Tukla?'

'I was ordered to Barrack V the next morning and told to fill out death certificates for one of the men and one of the women. At first I put "shock" for the reason of death for the man and "hemorrhage" for the woman, but the Germans made me change the cause of death to "typhus".'

'Now, Mr Tukla, all of this has been preying on your mind for a long time.'

'I lived in fear of being named a war criminal.'

'Do you know what became of the six volumes of surgical records?'

'There was a great deal of confusion when the Russians liberated the camp. Many of us fled as soon as the SS retreated. I do not know what became of five volumes. I kept the sixth one.'

'Hidden all these years.'

'Yes.'

'Out of fear of your own involvement?'

'Yes.'

'What period of time does this volume cover?'

'The second half of 1943.'

'My Lord,' Bannister said, 'I should like to offer in evidence at this time, the medical register of Jadwiga Concentration Camp.'

Chapter Thirty-four

A war of words unleashed. This was law that was!

'My Lord,' Sir Robert Highsmith said, 'my learned friend has achieved a certain drama in a last minute attempt to present new evidence. I am going to object most arduously to its introduction as inadmissible.'

'On what grounds?' Mr Justice Gilray asked.

'Well, in the first place I've never seen this document or had a chance to examine it.'

'My Lord,' Bannister said, 'the register came into our hands at three o'clock this morning. During the night we gathered together a volunteer staff of forty people who have sifted through the pages to find relevant information. I have listed here on two pages of paper that information I feel essential. I will gladly supply this and photocopies of those pages of the register from which we will ask questions for my learned friend to study.'

'Then, you're really asking to amend the Particulars in your claim of justification?' the judge asked.

'Exactly, my Lord.'

'And that's what I object to,' Highsmith said.

Richard Smiddy slipped a note to his secretary to fetch Mr Bullock, his managing clerk, and have him round up a staff of people in the event that Bannister prevailed. She darted from the court.

'It has been my experience,' Mr Justice Gilray said, 'that the defense can amend the Particulars during a trial if new evidence is brought forth.'

'I've seen no such application for an amendment,' Highsmith countered.

'I have one here, drawn up on a single page,' Bannister answered.

The usher handed copies to the judge and Chester Dicks and Richard Smiddy, who pored over it as Sir Robert continued the debate.

'Your Lordship and my learned friend will see that our application is on a single page and relates solely to the medical register,' Bannister said.

'Well, what do you say to that?' Gilray asked Highsmith.

'In my practice of law, which covers several decades, I have never seen or known of a case, particularly one which comes close to the length of this trial, where the court has ever allowed an amendment to a Particulars which would change the entire nature of the case.'

Chester Dicks was handing him down lawbooks and Richard Smiddy was handing them up. Highsmith read a half dozen precedents where such applications had been turned down.

'Would you advise the court on this, Mr Bannister?' Gilray asked.

'I certainly don't agree we are changing the nature of this case.'

'Certainly, we are,' Highsmith cracked back. 'Had this document been placed in evidence at the beginning of this trial, the plaintiff would have presented an entirely different kind of case. Here we are, over a month into the trial in its closing moments. Most of the defense witnesses have returned to Europe, Asia, and America. We have no chance to question them. Our chief witness after Dr Kelno is locked away in Poland. We have inquired if Dr Lotaki can be recalled, and he is not going to be given another visa. It is completely unfair to the plaintiff.'

'What about that, Mr Bannister?' the judge asked.

'I intend to confine my questions solely to the register and none of the witnesses for the defense can shed any light so they wouldn't be needed in any event. As for Dr. Lotaki, we would agree to pay for his passage to return to London but it is not our fault if his government will not let him come. Actually, if Sir Robert is going to allow Dr Kelno to return to the stand I can cover what I want to know in an hour, and I will be glad to supply my learned friend in advance the gist of my questions to his client.'

Here was the soul of the barrister's training. The extemporaneous and instantaneous ability to think and orate on one's feet flanked with a catalogue-like memory and quick-working assistants.

'Sir Robert, in the event the medical register is admitted into evidence, are you going to allow Dr Kelno to be questioned?' asked Mr Justice Gilray.

'I cannot reveal at this time what my tactic will be.'

'I see. Have you anything further to add, Mr Bannister?'

'Yes, my Lord. I see nothing unusual or unique about the introduction of the medical register as evidence. It has been in this courtroom in spirit since the outset of this case. I suggest to his Lordship, that no single piece of evidence in all of English history has cried out more strongly to be heard. Here, after all, is the heart of the matter. Here are the answers we have searched for in every corner of the world and in this courtroom. Inadmissible, indeed! If we attempt to silence this medical register in a British courtroom it will cast a shadow over our very system of justice, for in any event, it will not be ultimately silenced. If we silence it here we are saying that we really don't want to know what happened in Jadwiga or the Nazi era. It was all some people's fantasy. And, are we not to consider the brave men and women who gave their lives to leave behind them such documents for the future to know what really happened?'

'In all fairness,' Highsmith interrupted, 'my learned friend is making a closing speech to the jury. He'll have time to do that later.'

'Yes, Mr Bannister. What other grounds do you have to guide the court?'

'The strongest possible grounds. The testimony of the plaintiff, Dr Adam Kelno, on direct examination by his own counsel. I quote to you. Sir Robert asked, "Were any records kept of your operations and treatments?" To which Dr Kelno answered, "I insisted on accurate records. I felt it important that there could never be doubts of my behavior later." A moment later, Dr Kelno said from that witness box, "I wish to God we had the registers here now because it would prove my innocence." And again later on under direct examination he said: "In every single case I insisted the operation be entered into the surgical register." Your Lordship, nothing can be more clear than that. If Dr Kelno made those statements in testimony are we not led to believe that if the register had been found by him that he would have entered it as a document?'

'What do you have to say to that, Sir Robert?' the judge asked.

'Dr Kelno is, after all, a physician and not a lawyer. Not having seen or studied the document I would have done so and advised my client whether to offer it as evidence or not.'

'I suggest,' Bannister returned quickly, 'that as long as it seemed that there were no chance at all the register could be produced, as long as he felt all these volumes were lost forever, Dr Kelno could use it as implied evidence in his behalf. But alas, one of the missing volumes has survived and found its way into this court and now he is singing a different tune.'

'Thank you, gentlemen,' Gilray said.

He studied Bannister's application. Legally the document seemed in good order, the kind an English judge could rule on in a moment.

Yet, for some reason, he continued to stare, his mind not really on it at all. The vast parade was suddenly passing before him.

During the trial, he was to be affected for the rest of his life. He had seen them ... human beings ... mutilated. It was not Kelno's guilt or innocence that seemed the great question. It was what had happened at the hands of one's fellow man. For an instant he was able to cross the line and understand this strange loyalty of Jew to Jew. Those Jews who lived free in England were only there due to some quirk of fate instead of Jadwiga and every Jew knew that genocide could have happened to his own family except for that quirk of fate. Gilray was strongly taken by those two handsome young people, Cady's son and daughter. After all, they were half English.

Yet, as time stood suspended, Gilray was all gentiles who never quite understood Jews. He could befriend them, work with them, but never totally understand them. He was all white men who could never quite understand black men and all black men who could never quite understand whites. He was all normal men who could tolerate or even defend homosexuals ... but never fully understand them.

There is in us all that line that prevents us from fully understanding those who are different.

He looked up from the document into the eyes of the expectant courtroom.

'The application of the defense for an amended Particulars is approved. The medical register of Jadwiga Concentration Camp is hereby entered as evidence and will be marked as defendant's exhibit W. In fairness to the plaintiff, I shall call a recess for two hours in order for them to study this document so they can prepare a proper defense.'

And with that, he left the courtroom.

The blow had fallen! Highsmith remained stunned. The judge had said, TO PREPARE A PROPER 'DEFENSE.' Dr Adam Kelno, the accuser, had become the accused, even in the mind of the court.

Chapter Thirty-five

Sir Adam Kelno was ushered into the consultation room where Robert Highsmith and Chester Dicks and Richard Smiddy and a half dozen assistants pored over the photocopies of the register and copies of Bannister's proposed questions. He was greeted coldly.

'It was a long time ago,' he whispered. 'Something happened to my mind, there. For years afterwards I was in a state of semiamnesia. I have forgotten so many things. Sobotnik kept the register. He may have falsified entries against me. I did not always look what I was signing.'

'Sir Adam,' Highsmith said curtly. 'You are going to have to take the stand.'

'I can't.'

'You have to,' Highsmith answered tersely. 'You have no choice.'

Adam Kelno was not fully able to disguise the sedation. He seemed departed as he sat in the witness box and Anthony Gilray advised him he was still under oath. Photocopies of certain selected pages were handed to him as well as the judge and jury. Bannister asked the associate to hand the medical register to Adam Kelno. He stared at it, still in disbelief.

'Is the volume in evidence before you the medical register of Jadwiga Concentration Camp for the last five months of 1943?'

'I believe so.'

'You'll have to speak up, Sir Adam,' the judge said.

'Yes ... yes ... it is.'

'Will my learned friend agree that photocopies in his possession and supplied to the court and jury are accurate reproductions of various pages of the register?'

'So agreed,' Highsmith said.

'In order to assist the jury, let us open informally to an ordinary sample page to establish the general format of the register. I ask you to open to a double page, fifty and fifty-one. Going from left to right we see eleven different columns. The first column merely lists the number of the operation and on this particular page we see that we are up to eighteen thousand odd cases of surgery. The second column tells the date. Now what is the third column?'

'It is the tattoo number of the patient.'

'Yes, and that is followed by the patient's name, then a diagnosis of the illness. Is that all correct?'

'Yes.'

'We have now completed the first half of the double page and move on to page fifty-one. What is in the left hand column of that page?'

'A brief description of the operation.'

'And the next short column?'

He did not answer. Bannister repeated the question and received only an inaudible mumbling. 'Isn't that column the name of the surgeon and the next one the name of the assistant?'

'It is.'

'And the next column. Tell my Lord and the jury about that.'

'It's ...'

'Well?'

'It's the name of the anesthetist.'

'The anesthetist,' Bannister repeated in one of his rare raises of voice. 'Would you glance briefly either through the photocopies, or the register itself, in reference to the column concerning the anesthetist.'

Sir Adam turned the pages numbly, then looked up watery-eyed.

'Wasn't there always an anesthetist present? On all occasions?'

'Not fully trained in many cases.'

'But wasn't it your testimony that in most cases you didn't have an anesthetist and therefore you had to give it yourself and that was one of the reasons you chose spinal?'

'I did ... but.'

'Will you accept that the register bears out that in one hundred percent of the cases you either had a qualified doctor as your assistant or a doctor acting as the anesthetist?'

'It appears so.'

'So you were not telling the truth when you testified you did not have a qualified anesthetist present?'

'My memory may have failed me on that point.'

Oh God, Abe thought, I should not be feeling delight from all this. Thomas Bannister is now performing articulate legal surgery on him, and I should not feel any glory or vengeance.

'Let us move along to the next column. I see the word, "neurocrine." Would that describe the actual drug used in the spinal?'

'Yes.'

'And the final column is head, "remarks."'

'Yes.'

'Are pages fifty and fifty-one, including the column headings, in your handwriting, and your signature in the column marked "operator"?'

'They are.'

'Now studying the register again, do you see Dr Tesslar listed anywhere as either the surgeon or the assistant?'

'He probably hid it.'

'How? You were his superior. You had a dialogue with Voss and Flensberg, whom you described as your associates. How could he have hidden it?'

'I can't know. He was very crafty.'

'I suggest he performed no surgery of any kind in Jadwiga.'

'It was rumor,' Adam answered, breaking into a sweat.

'Please turn to page sixty-five. Now that seems to be quite a different handwriting except the signature of the operator. Would you explain that?'

'Sometimes a medical clerk filled out everything except the surgeon's signature. It could be Sobotnik who falsified the operations for the Communist underground.'

'But you aren't suggesting you didn't sign it or the signature is a forgery? If you caught him forging your signature later you'd have done something about that, like what you did to Menno Donker.'

'I am going to object,' Highsmith said.

'The register will bear out what was done to Menno Donker,' Bannister said in an unprecedented show of outright anger. 'Well, Dr Kelno?'

'I was very tired at the end of many days and sometimes I did not read carefully what I signed.'

'I see. We have photocopied twenty double pages from the register and each one of these double pages lists some forty operations. In those operations that are marked amputation testis, sin or dex, we refer, do we not, to the amputation of a right or left testicle.'

'Yes.'

'Now, how does that differ from the operation described as castration?'

'One means the removal of a dead or irradiated gland as I testified. The other means ... well ... it means ...'

'What!'

'Castration.'

'The removal of both testicles?'

'Yes.'

'Thank you. I will now ask the associate to hand you a document which was your sworn statement to the Home Office during the extradition proceedings of 1947. It was written by you in Brixton Prison.'

Highsmith bounced up. 'This is out of order, most out of order. In having approved the defendant's amended Particulars it was understood by us all that the questioning would be confined to the medical register.'

'In the first instance,' Bannister said, 'Dr Kelno entered his Home Office statement as part of his own evidence. It was a document he himself brought forth. There now appear to be enormous discrepancies between what he said in 1947, what he testified to earlier in the trial, and what the medical register is saying. If the register is lying, then all he has to do is say so. I believe the jury has every right to know which is the correct testimony.'

'Your objection is overruled, Sir Robert. You may continue, Mr Bannister.'

'Thank you. On page three of your statement to the Home Office you state, "I may have removed a few unhealthy testicles or ovaries, but I was performing surgery all the time and in thousands of cases one is always bound to find this part of the body diseased like any other part of the body." That's what you swore to in 1947 to escape extradition to Poland, is it not?'

'It was very long ago.'

'And a month ago in this courtroom you testified that you may have performed a few dozen and assisted Dr Lotaki on another dozen. Is that what you said here?'

'Yes, I recalled a few more operations after my statement to the Home Office.'

'Well, Dr Kelno, I suggest that if you add up the ovariectomies and testicle amputations you performed that are recorded in this volume of the medical register it will add up to two hundred and seventy-five, and that you assisted in another hundred.'

'I am very confused as to the exact number of operations. You can see for yourself there were almost twenty thousand operations. How can I remember the exact number?'

'Dr Kelno,' Bannister pressed, now softening his tone again, 'you heard Tukla's testimony that there were two more volumes of the surgical register completed before you left Jadwiga. Is that a fact?'

'Yes, perhaps.'

'Now, what do you think these two volumes would bear out if they suddenly showed up? Wouldn't the total show us that closer to a thousand of these operations were performed or assisted by you?'

'Unless I see it with my own eyes, I would not say so.'

'But you agree that you operated or assisted in three hundred and fifty operations borne out in this volume.'

'I think it may be right.'

'And do you now agree you had an anesthetist available and actually you never did give the anesthetic yourself in the operating theater as you previously testified.'

'I am confused on that point.'

'I ask you to turn to page three of your statement to the Home Office, and I quote your words, "I categorically deny I ever performed surgery on a healthy man or woman." Did you say that in 1947?'

'I believe that was my recollection at the time.'

'And did you give the same testimony in this courtroom?'

'I did.'

'Will you open the medical register to page seventy-two and look at the fourth operation from the bottom performed on an Oleg Solinka and tell the court about this.'

'It says . . . gypsy . . . court order . . .'

'And the operation?'

'Castration.'

'Is that your signature as the surgeon?'

'Yes.'

'Now, kindly turn to page two hundred and sixteen about mid-page. We see a Greek name, Populus. Would you read for my Lord and the jury the diagnosis, the operation, and the surgeon?'

'It is another court order case.'

'A castration performed by you because this man was a homosexual?'

'I . . . I . . .'

'Will you kindly now turn to page two hundred and eighteen. At the very top we see a woman's name, apparently a German woman, a Helga Brockmann. What does it say about her?'

Kelno glared at the page.

'Well?' Gilray prodded.

He took a long sip of water.

'Is it correct,' Thomas Bannister said, 'that this woman, a German criminal sentenced to Jadwig, had her ovaries removed by a court order because she was not a registered prostitute, and she was practicing prostitution?'

'I think . . . it could be.'

'Now kindly turn to page three hundred and ten and let me see, twelfth from the top. A Russian name, Borlatsky, Igor Borlatsky.'

Again Adam Kelno stalled.

'I think you'd better answer the question,' Gilray said.

'It is a court order for castration of a mentally incompetent.'

'Was there anything wrong with these people?'

'Well, the prostitute may have had a venereal disease.'

'Do you hoick out a woman's ovaries for that?'

'In some cases.'

'Well tell my Lord and the jury what kind of disease mental incompetent is and how that can be cured by a castration.'

'It was the crazy things the Germans did.'

'What kind of disease is gypsy?'

'The Germans sentenced certain people by court order, "inferior to Germans."'

'Now kindly turn to page twelve, bottom third of the page, a castration performed on an Albert Goldbauer. What is the diagnosis?'

'Court order.'

'For what?'

'Smuggling.'

'What kind of illness was smuggling?'

Adam did not answer again.

'Isn't it true that smuggling was a way of life and that you yourself engaged in it? It was universal in Jadwiga, was it not?'

'It was,' he croaked.

'I suggest there are in this volume twenty court order cases, fifteen males and five females in which castrations and double ovariectomies were performed by you on healthy people. I suggest you were not telling the truth in that witness box when you testified that you never performed a court order surgery. You did not do this, Dr Kelno, to save their lives or because they had dead organs as you justified before, you did it because the Germans told you to do it.'

'I simply did not recall the court order cases earlier. I did so much surgery.

'I suggest you would have never recalled it unless this register showed up. Now, Dr Kelno, in addition to testicle amputation and ovariectomies, for what other type of operations would you prefer to use a spinal?'

Adam closed his eyes a moment and gasped in air. It was now almost as though he were hearing it all in an echo chamber. 'Well?' Bannister repeated.

'An appendectomy, a hernia, a laparotomy, most anything below the belly.'

'You have testified, have you not, that in addition to your personal preference for a spinal, there was little or no general anesthetic available.'

'We had many shortages.'

'I suggest that in the month before November 10, 1943, and the month afterwards you performed nearly a hundred operations, ninety-six to be exact, in the lower body. I suggest that in ninety of these cases you personally chose a general anesthetic and you used a general anesthetic in dozens of other cases of minor surgery such as boils, and I suggest there was plenty of general anesthetic available as well as an anesthetist to administer it.'

'If the register says so.'

'I suggest that you chose spinal injections in only five percent of the lower body operations in the entire register in your own surgery, and you always wrote under "remarks" that you gave a pre-injection of morphia, except in Barrack V.'

Adam began flipping the pages of the register again and looked up and shrugged.

'I suggest,' Bannister continued to assault, 'that you did not tell the truth to the jury when you testified you preferred spinal but developed a certain penchant for it on the Jews in Barrack V, and you did not give pre-morphia because I think you were getting pleasure out of their pain.'

Highsmith was up but sat without speaking.

'Now then, let us clear up one more point before we get to the night of November 10. You will kindly turn to page three of the register and look at the name Eli Janos, who was castrated for smuggling and black marketeering. Do you recall an identification line-up at the Bow Street Magistrate's Court some eighteen years ago.'

'Yes.'

'And an Eli Janos was unable to identify you although he said he saw the surgeon without a mask. Would you read the name of the surgeon?'

'Dr Lotaki.'

'And if it had been you, who was also doing the same thing, you would have been returned to Poland to stand trial as a war criminal. You know that, don't you?'

Adam longed for a recess, but Anthony Gilray would not call one.

'You will kindly open the register to page three hundred and two and tell my Lord and the jury the date.'

'November 10, 1943.'

'Beginning with tattoo number 109834 and the name Menno Donker you will kindly read the number and names of the next fifteen people listed.'

Adam began after a long silence. He read in monotone, '115490 Herman Paar, 114360 Jan Perk, 115789 Hans Hesse, 115231 Hendrik Bloomgarten, 115009 Edgar Beets, 115488 Bernard Holst, 13214 Daniel Dubrowski, 70432 Yolan Shoret, 70433 Sima Halevy, 70544 Ida Peretz, 70543 Emma Peretz, 116804 Helene Blanc-Imber and 116805 ...'

'I did not hear the last name.'

'Tina.'

'Tina Blanc-Imber?'

'Yes.'

'I hand you the names and tattoo numbers of ten of these persons who have testified in this trial. Considering the name changes to Hebrew in some instances, and by marriage, are these not the same people?'

'Yes,' he whispered even before the associate handed him the paper.

'Is there any listing for a pre-injection of morphia?'

'It may have been overlooked.'

'Is there or isn't there?'

'No.'

'Who is listed as the surgeon? Whose signature is on all fourteen operations?'

'Doctor ...' Terry cried from the balcony.

'I suggest the signature reads Adam Kelno.'

Adam looked up for a brief instant as the young man disappeared from the courtroom.

'And in the remarks column, in your handwriting, what is listed after Tina Blanc-Imber and Bernard Holst?'

Adam shook his head.

'It says, "deceased that night" does it not?'

Adam came to his feet. 'Can't you see all of you it's a new plot against me. When Tesslar died they sent Sobotnik after me! They're out to get me! They'll hound me forever!'

'Sir Adam,' Thomas Bannister said softly, 'may I remind you, it was you who brought this action.'

Chapter Thirty-six

Sir Robert Highsmith adjusted his robes and faced the jury, a drawn, hurt man yet unable to go against the core of his being, a British barrister who would fight for his client until his last breath. He went into his familiar swaying motion and thanked the jury for its patience, then reviewed the case hammering away at the enormous discrepancy between what was written in *The Holocaust* and what actually happened in Jadwiga.

'It is a discrepancy of fifteen thousand operations totally experimental in nature and without the use of any anesthetic. Well, that would be the act of a madman. We have come to learn that Sir Adam Kelno was not a madman, but an ordinary man in an insane situation. He is the tragedy of all of us, suddenly trapped in the most horrendous circumstances.

'We keep returning to a thought of how we in England can really re-create in our minds the nightmare of Jadwiga Concentration Camp. We heard of some of the horror, but can we really relate to it? Can we really understand how this would affect the mind of an ordinary man . . . you or I. How would we have stood up in Jadwiga?

'I think about Dr Flensberg's experiments in obedience. How much voltage can a human being take before bending to the will of an evil master? Any of you who have ever received an electric shock is never apt to forget it.

'Let us say, members of the jury, that you are not in the jury box, but at this moment you are strapped in a chair facing the person you have been sitting side by side with this last month. You have before you a set of switches, and I order you to shock your neighbor. How much voltage are you going to bear before you throw the switch on him? Do you think you'll be very brave about all this?

'Think about it, all of you. You people out there. You newsmen, you solicitors, and all of you who read about it in future years. You are in the chair and a shock rips through your body. And another, of higher voltage, and you scream! And another, and you feel the pain in the fillings of your teeth, in your eyes, your testicles, and another, and you go into a convulsion and bleeding comes from your ears and nose and mouth and whatever agony can be related shrieks out for mercy.

'Well, you've had enough for one day. You've been brought to the point of death. But you get the same thing the next day, and the next, and the next until your mind and your body have been reduced to a blithering vegetable.

'Well, that was what Jadwiga Concentration Camp was all about. A mad hellhole in which every semblance of normal human society had been destroyed. And now you, a British jury, must decide how much the ordinary man can bear in those conditions. Where is the breaking point in all of us?

'We have a man whose life and works have been in complete dedication to the alleviation of suffering among his fellow man. If he could not bear the voltage in that insane place, has he not redeemed himself before the world? If this man had felt guilty of wrongdoing would he have come into this court and asked to clear his name? Is he to be damned forever, if he broke in a moment of agony in a snake pit? Is he to be damned in light of a lifetime of service to humanity?

'Adam Kelno deserves no further degradation. Perhaps for an instant in that horrible situation, a lifetime of social conditioning made him feel that some people are inferior to others. But before we condemn him for that, let us think about ourselves. Adam Kelno did his best for the greatest number of people and how many Jewish lives did he save! If he was broken to compromise with an insane German doctor shrieking in his ear, he did so to keep the other thousands alive. I suggest this is the most terrible decision any of us would ever have to make.

'Where were you ladies and gentlemen on the night of November 10, 1943? Think about that, too.

'We know, do we not, that armies obey orders to kill people under some thin guises of national right. And after all, members of the jury, when God commanded of Abraham to sacrifice his own son, he agreed.

'Adam Kelno should be awarded substantial damages and returned in honor, to a world he has honored with his presence.'

Chapter Thirty-seven

Thomas Bannister reconstructed his case over a period of several hours with the same melodic underplayed voice with which he conducted the trial.

'This is the story, as history will record it, of what the Christians did to the Jews in the middle of the twentieth century in Europe. And in all of history we have no blacker chapter. Of course Hitler and Germany are to bear the brunt of what happened, but it would not have happened if hundreds of thousands of others did not cooperate.

'I agree with my learned friend that armies are taught to obey, but one sees a growing evidence of people refusing to obey orders to kill other people. And the story of Abraham and God. Well, we all know the ending to that. God was using a little semantics and didn't take his son at all. But somehow I cannot equate SS Colonel Dr Adolph Voss to playing God anymore than I can envision Adam Kelno as Abraham. The fact is Voss didn't have to make an Otto Flensberg experiment on Dr Kelno. Dr Kelno took a long look at things and did not resist whatsoever. He did what he did without hesitation, without threats, without terror tactics being used on him.

'Well, you heard him testify that he refused to give a fatal injection of phenol to a prisoner. What happened to him for that? How was he punished. He knew full well doctors weren't shot or sent to the gas chamber. He knew that!

'You'd think a man who has done what Adam Kelno did would shut up and consider himself lucky and try to get along with his conscience, if he has one, and not rake it all up again after almost twenty-five years. He did it because he thought he could get away with it. But alas, the medical register showed up and he had to confess to lie after lie.

'Can anyone in this room with a daughter of his own ever forget Tina? Tina Blanc-Imber had a mother and a father and they survived the holocaust, and they learned that their daughter had been murdered as a human guinea pig. It was not a Nazi doctor who killed her, but a Pole, a fellow ally. And had this happened to any of us and we learned later than an English doctor had destroyed our child in a useless, perverted medical experiment by butchery ... well, we would know what to do with him.

'I agree that Jadwiga Concentration Camp was as awful as things had ever come to. Yet, members of the jury, the inhumanity of man to man is as old as man itself. Just because one is in Jadwiga or anyplace else where people are inhumane, that does not give him leave to discard his morality, his religion, his philosophy, or all of those things that make him a decent member of the human race.

'You heard the testimony of some other doctors in Jadwiga Concentration Camp, two of the most noble and courageous women to ever grace an English court. One a Jewess and a Communist and the other a devout Christian. What happened when Voss threatened to throw the switch on Dr Viskova. She refused and prepared to take her own life. And Dr Susanne Parmentier . . . she was in the very same hellhole of Jadwiga too. Will you kindly remember what she told Dr Flensberg.

'And you heard from the bravest of them all. An ordinary man. A teacher of Romantic languages in a little gymnasium in Poland. Daniel Dubrowski, who sacrificed his own manhood so that a younger man might have a chance to know a normal life.

'Members of the jury, there is a moment in the human experience when one's life itself no longer makes sense when it is directed to the mutilation and murder of his fellow man. There is a demarcation line of morality beyond which no man can cross and still claim membership in the human race and this goes for London or Jadwiga.

'The line was crossed and for that there can be no redemption. Anti-Semitism is the scourge of the human race. It is the mark of Cain upon us all.

'Nothing he did before or since can redeem him for what he did there. He has fortified his rights to our compassion. And I suggest he should not be rewarded by a British jury for what he did with anything but our contempt and the lowest coin of the realm.'

Chapter Thirty-eight

'Members of the jury,' Anthony Gilray said, 'we have come to the end of a month's testimony in what has become the longest libel trial in British history. The kind of evidence given here has never been heard by a civil English court and much of it is filled with conflict. Future generations will describe the Jadwiga Concentration Camp as the greatest crime ever committed. But we are not here to act as a war crimes tribunal. We are here trying a civil case according to the common law of England.'

The summing up was an arduous affair, which Anthony dispensed with unusual brilliance, reducing everything into common law and what issues and evidence were relevant and what had to be settled After a day and a half, he turned the burden over to the jury.

Thomas Bannister arose for a final time. 'My Lord, there are two issues to be settled. Would you explain them before the jury retires.'

'Yes. First you will determine if you hold for the plaintiff or the defendants. If you hold for Dr Kelno and agree he has been libeled, then you must determine how much damages you will award him.'

'Thank you, my Lord.'

'Members of the jury,' Gilray said, 'I can do no more. The task is upon you now. Take as long as you like. My staff will do their best to see that you are supplied with whatever you wish in the way of food and light refreshments. Now, there is one final matter. The government of Poland, through its ambassador, has laid claim to the medical register as a document of great historical significance and wishes it returned to that country for proper display in one of their national museums. Her Majesty's government has agreed to do so. The Polish ambassador has given us leave to have the register in the jury room during the deliberations. Kindly treat it with utmost care. Do keep cigarette ashes away from it and do be careful not to have any coffee or tea stains damage it. We should not like future generations of Poles to think a British jury took this document lightly. You may retire now.'

It was noon. Those nameless nondescript Englishmen left the courtroom, and the door to the jury room closed behind them.

Adam Kelno and Abraham Cady had come to the end of their battle.

At one-thirty Sheila Lamb rushed into the consultation room and said the jury was returning. The corridor was jammed with newsmen who had to obey the stringent rules of no interviews or photographs inside the court. One of them was unable to resist. 'Mr Cady,' he said, 'do you think the short time the jury was out is an indication you're going to win?'

'Nobody is going to win this case,' Abe answered, 'we're all losers.'

He and Shawcross shoved their way in and found themselves standing next to Adam Kelno.

Gilray nodded to the associate who approached the jury box.

'Have you agreed upon a verdict?'

'Yes,' the foreman answered.

'And this is the verdict of you all?'

'It is.'

'Do you hold for the Plaintiff, Sir Adam Kelno, or the Defendants, Abraham Cady and David Shawcross?'

'We hold in favor of the plaintiff, Sir Adam Kelno.'

'And have you all agreed on a sum of damages?'

'We have.'

'What is that sum?'

'We award Sir Adam Kelno one halfpenny.'

Chapter Thirty-nine

Angela burst into the office where Adam sat motionless. 'It's Terry,' she said. 'He's returned and he's packing his suitcases.'

Adam rushed out, bouncing off the corridor walls and up the steps. He flung the door open. Terry was closing the suitcase.

'Haven't taken much,' Terry said, 'just enough to get along with.'

'Are you going back to Mary?'

'I'm going away with Mary.'

'Where?'

'I don't know really. I'm leaving London England. Angela will know where I am.'

Adam blocked the door. 'I demand to know where you're going!'

'Out among the lepers,' he screamed. 'If I'm going to be a doctor, let me be like Dr Tesslar!'

'You stay right here, do you hear me ...'

'You lied to me, Doctor.'

'Lied! I did all of this because of you and Stephan.'

'And I thank you for that. Now stand aside.'

'No.'

'What are you going to do? Cut my nuts off?'

'You ... you ... you're like the rest of them. You're out to get me too. They paid you to leave me. It's the same plot!'

'You're a bloody paranoid whipping through life cutting the balls off Jews to get even with your own father. Isn't that right, Sir Adam?'

Adam slapped him across the mouth. 'Jew!' he screamed. He slapped Terry again and again. 'Jew! Jew! Jew! Jew!'

Chapter Forty

Abe opened the door of the mews. Thomas Bannister stood on the outside. He was let in wordlessly and followed Cady into the living room.

'You had an appointment with me,' Bannister said, 'I waited.'

'I know, sorry about it. Whisky?'

'Please, make it neat.'

Bannister took off his coat as Abe poured the whisky. 'Look, I've had my fill of good-bys in the last couple of days. Plain ones, fancy ones, tear-filled ones. Anyhow, I saw my daughter off to Israel.'

'So sorry to miss your daughter. She seems like a lovely girl I should have liked to have known her better. The news from the Middle East is indeed distressing.'

Abe shrugged. 'You learn to live with it. When I was writing *The Holocaust*, Shawcross would get into a dither every time a new crisi came up, and he'd badger me for the manuscript. I told him, don't worry, whenever I finish the book, the Jews will still be in trouble.'

'Must be very taxing.'

'Writing or being a Jew?'

'Actually I meant the writing. Sort of going inside of people and filming their minds for months on end.'

'Something like that. Bannister, I've been avoiding seeing you because you can be damned frightening.'

Bannister smiled. 'Well, I didn't intend to put you in the witness box.'

'Know who I've been thinking about?' Abe said.

'Adam Kelno.'

'How did you know?'

'Because I've been thinking about him too.'

'Highsmith is right, you know,' Abe said. 'There but for the grace of God go all of us. A simple man with his pecker caught in a wringer. What the hell would I have done?'

'I think I know.'

'I'm not so damned sure. The world doesn't have enough Daniel Dubrowskis or Mark Tesslars or Parmentiers or Viskovas or Van Damms. We talk courage and end up acting like piss ants.'

'There are more than you are willing to believe right now.'

'I left somebody out,' Abe said, 'Thomas Bannister. The night you were listing my responsibilities you didn't mention yourself. Wouldn't that have been a pistol, to deny the English people of you as their prime minister.'

'Oh that. Well, one must do what one thinks right.'

'Why? Why did Kelno bring this suit? Sure, I know he has to be a big fish in a little pond. He feels inferior so he has always gotten himself placed into a position where he could be superior to those around him. In Sarawak, in Jadwiga, in a workingman's clinic in London.'

'Kelno? Tragic figure,' Bannister said. 'He's paranoid, of course, and as a parnoid he is incapable of introspection and cannot judge right from wrong.'

'What made him that way?'

'Perhaps the result of some cruelty toward him as a child. Poland handed him anti-Semitism. He had a place to go with his sickness. You know, Cady, surgeons are a strange breed and often as not surgery fulfills their blood lust. So long as Adam Kelno was in civilized places, surgery took care of his needs. But turn a man like this loose in a place where all social order has collapsed and you have a monster on your hands. And then, when he went back to a civilized society again, he became a proper surgeon with absolutely no guilt about what he had done.'

'After what I heard in that courtroom,' Abe said, 'after learning what people can be made to do to people and after the holocaust seeing it still go on and on, I feel that we are wrecking our world beyond our ability to save ourselves. We have polluted our planet, and the creatures who live on it. I swear to God, and we have destroyed each other. I think we've run out of time, and space, and I think it's not a case of *if* it is going to happen, it's only a matter of *when.* And from the way we're behaving, I think God is getting very impatient.'

'Oh, God is patient enough,' Thomas Bannister said. 'You see, we mortals are so pompous that we have deluded ourselves into believing that in all of eternity, and all of the vast universe, that we are the only ones who have undergone the human experience. I've always believed that it's happened before, on this very earth.'

'Here ... how ...?'

'Well, in God's scheme what is a few billion years, here and there. Perhaps there have come and gone a dozen human civilizations in the past billion years that we know nothing about. And after this civilization we are living in destroys itself, it will all start up again in a few hundred million years when the planet has all its messes cleaned up. Then, finally, one of these civilizations, say five billion years from now, will last for eternity because people will treat each other the way they ought to.'

They were interrupted by the phone. Abe's face became very tense. He wrote out an address and said he would come over within the hour. He set the receiver down, puzzled.

'That was Terrence Campbell. He wants to see me.'

'Well, that shouldn't surprise you. You see, if we are going to hang on to this world for a little longer it's going to be up to him and Kelno's son and your son and daughter. Well, I shan't hold you up any longer. How long will you be about?

'I'm leaving for Israel in a few days. Back where I started, as a journalist.'

They shook hands. 'I can't say you've been my most restrained client, but it's been interesting,' Bannister said, unable to find words in one of the rare instances in his life. 'You know what I mean.'

'I know what you mean, Tom.'

'Good luck, Abe.'

ON THE WAY TO SEE TERRENCE I ASKED THE TAXI TO STOP AT THE LAW COURT. WELL, THAT'S NATURAL. TO SAY GOOD-BY TO THE ONE DECENT THING I'VE DONE IN MY LIFE, FIGHT THIS CASE.

I CANNOT SHAKE BANNISTER'S NOTION THAT THERE HAVE BEEN CIVILIZATIONS BEFORE US, AND IT WILL HAPPEN AGAIN. WHEN THIS ONE GOES, I'M GOING TO BE VERY SORRY ABOUT LONDON.

DOWN THE STREET FROM THE LAW COURT IS ST CLEMENT DANES CHURCH. IT'S THE ROYAL AIR FORCE CHURCH, AND I KNEW IT WELL DURING THE WAR. IN FACT, I WROTE SOME COLUMNS ABOUT IT.

ST CLEMENT DANES IS EXACTLY WHAT THOMAS BANNISTER WAS TALKING ABOUT. IT WAS BUILT BY THE DANES IN 871 OR THEREABOUTS WHEN KING ALFRED EXPELLED THEM BEYOND THE CITY WALL AND THEN IT WAS DESTROYED. IT WAS REBUILT BY WILLIAM THE CONQUEROR, AND DESTROYED, AND REBUILT IN THE MIDDLE AGES AND DESTROYED IN THE FIRE OF 1666 AND REBUILT, AND DESTROYED IN 1680 AND REBUILT BY CHRISTOPHER WREN, AND STOOD UNTIL THE GERMAN BOMBERS DESTROYED IT IN THE SECOND WORLD WAR. AND IT WAS REBUILT AGAIN.

WHAT THE HELL'S THAT NURSERY RHYME SAMANTHA USED TO TELL THE CHILDREN?

ORANGES AND LEMONS,
SAY THE BELLS OF ST CLEMENT'S
YOU OWE ME FIVE FARTHINGS
SAY THE BELLS OF ST MARTIN'S
WHEN WILL YOU PAY ME
SAY THE BELLS OF OLD BAILEY
WHEN I GROW RICH
SAY THE BELLS OF SHOREDITCH
WHEN WILL THAT BE
SAY THE BELLS OF STEPNEY
I DO NOT KNOW
SAY THE GREAT BELLS OF BOW
HERE COMES A COPPER TO PUT YOU TO BED
HERE COMES A CHOPPER TO CHOP OFF YOUR HEAD

Tel Aviv, June 6, 1967 (AP) The Israel Defense Ministry announced that its casualties were light in the strike that destroyed the Arab air forces. Most prominent among those killed was Sergen (Captain) Ben Cady, son of the well-known author.